Classic American
CRIME FICTION
OF THE
1920s

The House Without a Key by Earl Derr Biggers
The Benson Murder Case by S. S. Van Dine
The Roman Hat Mystery by Ellery Queen
Red Harvest by Dashiell Hammett
Little Caesar by W. R. Burnett

EDITED WITH NOTES AND A FOREWORD BY

LESLIE S. KLINGER

PEGASUS CRIME

NEW YORK LONDON

To Sir Arthur Conan Doyle,

who kindled my love of mysteries

∽∾

CLASSIC AMERICAN CRIME FICTION OF THE 1920s

Pegasus Books Ltd.
148 W 37th Street, 13th Floor
New York, NY 10018

First Pegasus Books edition October 2018

Interior design by Maria Fernandez

Library of Congress Cataloging-in-Publication Data is available.

ISBN: 978-1-68177-861-7

10 9 8 7 6 5 4 3 2 1

Printed in the United States of America
Distributed by W. W. Norton & Company, Inc.
www.pegasusbooks.us

Contents

Introduction

by Otto Penzler

Like so many fortunate others, my introduction to the world of mystery fiction was Sherlock Holmes.

When I was ten years old and in grammar school, there was a class called "Library" for which teachers would herd their charges to the magical room that was filled with books. For the first half hour, the librarian would talk to us about how to handle books properly and inculcate us with the notion that reading was invaluable in opening doors of knowledge and wonder. For the second half hour, we were allowed to read any book that caught our fancy.

Some now long-forgotten anthology caught my eye and so did the story it contained, thrillingly titled "The Adventure of the Red-Headed League," which was irresistible. I was entranced for that half hour but, just as an explanation was about to reveal what all this encyclopedia copying was about, the class ended. I had to wait a full week until the next class to know what Sherlock Holmes had deduced—a week filled with my own relentless attempts to solve the mystery.

Having majored in English at the University of Michigan, I returned to New York with a desire to read for fun and to not hurt my head anymore, as James Joyce, Ezra Pound, and their ilk had been doing, so, remembering that captivating story, I got a copy of the Holy Grail, a.k.a. *The Complete Sherlock Holmes*, which launched a lifetime of fascination, not to mention a career, with detective, crime, mystery, and suspense fiction. Leslie S. Klinger, my learned colleague, longtime friend, and editor of this omnibus, is also a devoted Sherlockian who produced one of the most important books in the long history of Sherlock Holmes scholarship, *The New Annotated Sherlock Holmes*, for which he won the prestigious Edgar Allan Poe Award from the Mystery Writers of America.

With normal eight-hour workdays (unlike now, when they never end), I had plenty of time to read and dove wholeheartedly into books by the famous names of this wide genre: Edgar Allan Poe, Agatha Christie, Rex Stout, Dorothy L. Sayers, Ellery Queen, S. S. Van Dine, John Dickson Carr, Raymond Chandler, Dashiell Hammett, and eventually many others, some renowned but others little-known.

There are many reasons to read mystery fiction, not least of which is trying to figure out the puzzle before the author (through his detective character) explains it all. Although I loved the puzzle element, I was pathetic at trying to figure it out, always gullibly convinced that the most obvious suspect was indeed the murderer and utterly stupefied when the least likely person turned out to be the culprit.

Puzzles, however, were only part of the joy of becoming immersed in a mystery novel. Authors spent a good deal of time and care in creating interesting detectives, as well as unusual, creepy, lovable, eccentric, loathsome, or intriguing secondary characters who served as sidekicks, police, or suspects.

Additionally, it was not uncommon to learn something. Tidbits of knowledge might come in the form of an unfamiliar background for a story, a lecture by one of the more pedantic characters, or merely a line of dialogue in which an occasional factoid is dropped in passing.

The books featured in this extraordinary omnibus serve as superb examples of why the mystery novel is endlessly pleasing to untold millions of readers. After all, Agatha Christie's books alone have sold more than two billion copies (yes, *billion*), and Sherlock Holmes has been translated into more languages than William Shakespeare.

Charlie Chan was one of the first fictional characters of East Asian descent to be portrayed favorably and as a fully developed entity. It had been common for Chinese figures to be treated as either insignificant servants or workmen with no role in plot development, or as villains, particularly after the Boxer Rebellion at the turn of the nineteenth century. Dr. Fu Manchu is the most famous name of the "Yellow Peril" thriller category, but there were many others in English literature and in American pulp magazines.

On the other hand, Earl Derr Biggers portrayed Chan as the smartest guy in the room and humanized him by giving him a family and allowing him to mention his children—mainly by referring to them with numbers ("number three son") rather than names. The detective also was made more palatable and somewhat less alien to xenophobic readers by being located in Hawaii rather than in China, the secret kingdom, itself. It was in Hawaii, by the way, where Biggers met a real-life Honolulu policeman named Chang Apana, on whom he based his creation.

For an education in arcane subjects, one couldn't beat the show-offy pedantry of S. S. Van Dine's Philo Vance, who thought nothing of injecting mind-numbing monologues on such subjects as art, music, religion, and philosophy into the middle of a murder investigation. The Vance novels were such a rage in the 1920s and '30s that they were national bestsellers, though (like me) the public soon tired of the affectations of the detective, and sales of the later books did not match those of the first half-dozen. If the novels had been published with the helpful and often fascinating annotations made by Klinger in this omnibus, it strikes me as likely that readers would have maintained their devotion to the series. It is possible to accept being talked down to for only so long until trying to comprehend Latin phrases or glossing over references to obscure artists and authors becomes tiresome. The clarity of Klinger's footnotes would certainly have aided in translations and placing people and objects in context, making the reading experience far more user-friendly.

Still, the books enjoyed so much affection and dedication from readers that they inspired a remarkable succession of motion pictures featuring such major actors of the time as William Powell (in four films), Basil Rathbone, Warren William, Paul Lukas, and Edmund Lowe, among others, between 1929 and 1947. There were more films (sixteen) than books (twelve), as Van Dine died before doing the final rewrite of the last volume, *The Winter Murder Case* (1939).

The staggering success of the Vance novels inspired two Brooklyn cousins, Frederic Dannay and Manfred B. Lee, writing under the pseudonym Ellery Queen, to emulate the character when they decided to write a detective novel. Attracted by a $7,500 first prize in a mystery-writing contest sponsored by *McClure's* magazine, they submitted *The Roman Hat Mystery* in 1928 and won, but, just before receiving the award, the magazine went bankrupt and its assets were assumed by *Smart Set*, which gave the prize to a different novel that it thought would have more appeal to female readers. Fortunately, Frederick A. Stokes, a New York publishing house, took the book and launched one of the most important careers in the history of mystery fiction.

In a brilliant commercial move, the authors decided to use the Ellery Queen name for their character as well as their byline, reasoning that readers might be less likely to forget the name of the author when it kept popping up in the book. A further explanation of the origins of the name may be found in one of Klinger's extensive and valuable annotations to *The Roman Hat Mystery*. After closely basing elements of their detective on Vance, making Queen just as erudite and pompous, the authors soon found their own voice and produced novels that were more modern and appealing, most notably in *Calamity Town* (1942), in which Ellery falls in love, solves a complex crime, and explores, in depth, a small town's mores and attitudes.

The books featuring Charlie Chan, Philo Vance, and Ellery Queen are among the best, most popular, and most historically significant novels of traditional detective fiction. Each of the detectives at the core of the book was confronted with a mystery and set out to locate the clues needed to solve it. That element of puzzle-solving was largely the raison d'etre for the novel.

But while puzzle mysteries were the favored reading of the time, something radically different suddenly exploded on the mystery landscape: realism, in the shape of the hard-boiled novel.

The hard-boiled cop or, especially, private detective, was the idealization of the lone individual, representing justice and decency, pitted against virulent gangs, corrupt politicians, or other agencies who violated that sense of goodness with which most readers identify. The best of these crime-fighting tough guys became series characters, taking on one group of thugs after another, always emerging victorious in spite of the hopeless odds they (and, in the era on which this book is focused, these protagonists were almost always male) encountered.

The inventor of this sub-genre of mystery fiction is the largely forgotten Carroll John Daly, whose first story, "Three Gun Terry," featured the first hard-boiled detective. It was published in the May 15, 1923, issue of *Black Mask*, the greatest of the pulp magazines. Furthermore, Daly then wrote two stories about Race Williams, thus creating the first hard-boiled P.I. series.

While Daly was a creative hack writer devoid of literary pretension, aspiration, and ability, his appearance in *Black Mask* was quickly followed by stories by Dashiell Hammett, who brought serious literature to hard-boiled fiction. His first Continental Op story appeared in the October 1, 1923, issue of *Black Mask*, and most of Hammett's finest work appeared in its pages, including the serialization of his first four novels: *Red Harvest*, which ran in four issues between November 1927 and February 1928 before it was published in book form by Alfred A. Knopf in February 1929; *The Dain Curse* (1930); *The Maltese Falcon* (1930); and *The Glass Key* (1931).

Although *The Maltese Falcon* is his most famous novel, as well as a consensus masterpiece, *Red Harvest* has its advocates who describe it as the best of all Hammett's work. In this platonic ideal of the hard-boiled novel, the Continental Op arrives in Personville, a town so corrupt and contaminated with vice that its citizens casually refer to it as Poisonville, with the mission to clean it up. There have been countless imitators of its basic story line, but none have ever matched its power.

Few novels of the American "Golden Age" of mystery fiction (the two decades between the world wars) had the impact on the public that W. R. Burnett's *Little Caesar*. It wasn't the first novel about organized crime but its naturalistic style, with the story told largely in first person by Cesare Bandello, the tough Chicago gangster known as Rico, instantly gripped readers, making it a national bestseller. It also inspired what is generally recognized as the first film to portray the Prohibition era and the lives of the hoodlums who helped define it. The motion picture starred Edward G. Robinson, rocketing him to fame and opening the floodgates for countless cinematic dramatizations of the Chicago underworld.

Little Caesar is an outlier in this collection as it is not a detective novel. Burnett's book belongs in this omnibus because the mystery story encompasses many sub-genres, and it's good to see it made available to readers who mainly know it from its frequent appearances on late night cable showings. For no other book are Klinger's meticulous annotations more valuable than for *Little Caesar*, as so much of Burnett's fiction is based on real-life characters and events. It is a novel that I have long admired for its non-stop action, and a quick look at the first few pages of annotations compelled me to read it again with renewed pleasure.

As an overview of American mystery fiction of the 1920s, this wide-ranging anthology is peerless in providing readers with a bountiful selection of the most loved books of their time, incalculably enhanced by the scholarship of the deftly produced annotations.

Foreword

by Leslie S. Klinger

Crime writing in America did not begin with Edgar Allan Poe. Unexpectedly, it began in a church. In early New England, hangings were the most popular public events, drawing crowds that reportedly numbered well into the thousands. These audiences did not go unnoticed by the region's moral spokesmen, and, recognizing the mass appeal, clergymen typically delivered sermons dealing with the pending executions, spinning stories of the criminals' reprehensible journeys and warning of the temptations that led to their crimes. Not only were these sermons well-attended, many were printed and achieved greater audiences as publications.

Although the first published "execution" sermons appeared as pamphlets, later works included confessions or warnings by the condemned criminals, records of the conversations between the ministers and the convicted, and factual backgrounds for the crimes. More than twenty volumes were published between 1686 and 1726. The most prolific author of these volumes was Cotton Mather. Mather and his fellow preachers recognized that the public craved far more than theological doctrine—there was a ready audience for accounts of criminals and their crimes. As the trade passed beyond the hands of the clergy after 1730, the published histories included three principal types of narratives: tales of criminal conversions, in which stories of repenting sinners wrung the hearts of the reader; gallows accounts, providing accounts of the hangings, usually replete with the histories of the condemned, for those who could not attend in person; and trial transcripts, with detailed records of the testimony of the corroborating witnesses. Though these forms had their antecedents in England, American entrepreneurs made an industry of such publications, usually in the form of "broadsides," cheap (typically, one penny) publications with extensive audiences and limited shelf life.

Historian Daniel Cohen observes that "[a]n inevitable result of that process was a gradual loosening of the link between crime literature and social reality."[1] By the late eighteenth century, the line between fact and fiction—and indeed, the moral message—was blurring, even vanishing. Many of the popular pamphlets of the day dealt with

---

1   *Pillars of Salt, Monuments of Grace: New England Crime Literature and the Origins of American Popular Culture* (New York and Oxford: Oxford University Press, 1993).

alleged miscarriages of justice. But as the nineteenth century began, American sensibilities moved away from the "execution broadsides" and turned to the penny press. This is not to say that the public lost interest in stories of crimes and criminals. In fact, the public wanted *more*, and the extended tales of robbers, murderers, and assorted scoundrels found in the cheap novels of the first half of the nineteenth century were the first signs of the flood of crime fiction that was to seize the attention of American readers.

In England, William Godwin's *Things as They Are; or, The Adventures of Caleb Williams* (1794)—a foundational work for *Frankenstein*, not coincidentally written by Godwin's daughter Mary Shelley—influenced an entire generation of writers, extending the early traditions of the Gothic novel to veer in the direction of crime fiction. Godwin's story of the relentless hunt for the criminal by the victim/accuser and the intensive study of the psychology of pursuer and pursued can be seen as influencing works as disparate as *Les Misérables* (1862) and *Moby Dick* (1851). In America, Godwin was an inspiration to Charles Brockden Brown, whose novels published between 1798 and 1801, including *Wieland* (1798) and *Ormond* (1799), featured sensational violence, intense drama, and complexity. While none of Brown's novels are explicitly "mysteries" and are often dismissed as merely "Gothic," they focus on extraordinary incidents and the passions that drive the protagonists, with less emphasis on the supernatural than was the fashion.

By the 1830s, the "dime novel," or "penny dreadful," as it was known in England, flooded the literary markets. These serials, which cost a shilling, offered a less-expensive alternative to mainstream fictional partworks, such as those by Charles Dickens. By the 1850s the prime audience for serial stories was young male readers. Although many of the stories were reprints or rewrites of Gothic thrillers, some were about famous criminals, such as Sweeney Todd and Spring-Heeled Jack, or had lurid titles like "The boy detective; or, The crimes of London" (1866), "The dance of death; or, The hangman's plot. A thrilling romance of two cities" (1866, written by Brownlow, "Detective," and Tuevoleur, "Sergeant of the French Police"), or a series like "Lives of the most notorious highwaymen, footpads and murderers" (1836–37). Highwaymen were often the lead characters. *Black Bess or the Knight of the Road* (1863), recounting the fictional exploits of real-life highwayman Dick Turpin, ran to 254 episodes.

While crime fiction—albeit in this crude form—was finding an enormous audience, the Industrial Revolution and the growth of the railroads and the cities served by them led to the formation of official forces to combat a perceived tide of criminals. The first modern police force came into existence in 1667, in Paris under King Louis XIV. A French national civilian police force was organized in 1812 and formalized a year later. The first formal British police force was the Bow Street Runners, founded by magistrate Henry Fielding in 1753, though the organization was quite small until Sir Robert Peel championed the Metropolitan Police Act of 1829. In America, where settlement of the wilderness continued long after it ceased to be a significant factor in English civilization and "frontiersmen" were expected to defend their own communities, the first police force was not established until 1838, in the city of Boston. This was followed by New York City in 1845, St. Louis in 1846, and Chicago in 1854, for example.

It is not surprising, then, that stories of the *detection* of crime did not begin until the nineteenth century, with the rise of the professional criminal investigator. As early as 1827, *Richmond: Scenes from the Life of a Bow Street Runner*, a heavily fictionalized tale of the Bow Street Runners, appeared, but it was not popular and can be viewed only as a "false start" for detective fiction. The first successful writer of tales of criminal detection was the Frenchman Eugène Vidocq (1775–1857), a reformed criminal who had been appointed by Napoleon in 1813 to be the first head of the Sûreté Nationale. Vidocq's memoirs (including some that were plainly fiction) were widely read. Tales of his detection and capture of criminals, often involving disguises and wild flights, and later, recounting his previous criminal career, some probably not written by Vidocq himself, capitalized on his reputation as a bold detective.

The first great purveyor of unabashedly fictional stories about a detective was Edgar Allan Poe (1809–1849). Although Poe was primarily interested in tales of horror and fantasy, his stories of an amateur detective, the Chevalier Auguste Dupin, set the standard for a generation to come. The cerebral sleuth first appeared in Poe's short story "Murders in the Rue Morgue" [1841]. In each of the three Dupin stories (the other two are "The Mystery of Marie Rogêt" [1842] and "The Purloined Letter" [1844]), the detective outwits the police and shows them to be ineffective crime-fighters and problem-solvers. After Poe's death, "mysteries" appeared occasionally in magazines in the form of short stories, but the mainstream of American crime fiction was the flood of dime novels, with early popular titles including *The Old Sleuth* and *Butts the Boy Detective*. A supposed memoir, *Detective Sketches [by a New York Detective]*, probably wholly fictional, appeared in 1881 in the format of a dime novel. Ellery Queen estimates that between 1860 and 1928, more than six thousand different detective dime novels were published in the United States.

Poe's popularity was probably greater in Europe than America, at least for most of the nineteenth century, and Europeans led the way in the growth of crime fiction after Poe. Another Frenchman, Emile Gaboriau, created the detective known as Monsieur Lecoq, using Vidocq as his model. First appearing in *L'Affaire Lerouge* (1866), Lecoq was a minor police detective who rose to fame in six cases, appearing between 1866 and 1880. Gaboriau's works were immensely popular (though Sherlock Holmes later described Lecoq as a "miserable bungler" and dismissed Dupin as a "very inferior fellow"). The prolific English author, Fergus Hume, who wrote *The Mystery of a Hansom Cab* (1886), which sold over 500,000 copies worldwide, claimed that Gaboriau's financial success inspired his own work.

In England, criminals and detectives peopled Charles Dickens's tales as well. While not usually considered an author of crime fiction, Dickens created Inspector Bucket, the first important detective in English literature. When Bucket appeared, in *Bleak House* (1852–53), he became the model police officer: honest, diligent, and confident, but a touch dull. Wilkie Collins, author of two of the greatest novels of suspense of the nineteenth century, *The Woman in White* (1860) and *The Moonstone* (1868), contributed a similar character, Sergeant Cuff, who appears in *The Moonstone*. Cuff is known as the finest police detective in England, a man who solves his cases energetically but with no hint of genius. Sadly, after *The Moonstone*, he is not heard from again. In each case, however, the detective is too late to help any of the affected persons.

In 1866–67, *The Dead Letter: An American Romance*, the first crime novel written by an American woman—some call it the first crime novel written by an American—was published. Its author was Metta Victoria Fuller Victor (1831–85), writing under the name Seely Regester. Victor had written dozens of works and would continue to write others, including novels, short stories, dime novels, poetry, and housewives' manuals that included boys' adventures, westerns, juvenile fiction, and humor. She also wrote two other tales under the name Seely Regester, a novel titled *The Figure Eight; or, The Mystery of Meredith Place* (serialized in *The Illuminated Western World*, 1869) and "The Skeleton at the Banquet."[2] All of these featured detectives. In *The Dead Letter*, there is both a police detective, Mr. Burton, and an amateur, Richard Redfield (who is training to be a lawyer). In *The Figure Eight* and "The Skeleton at the Banquet," the detectives are amateurs. *The Dead Letter* was published both as a serial dime novel and in book form, and it was successful enough to be pirated by *Cassell's Magazine* and reprinted in England in 1866–67.

---

2   The story first appeared in the anthology *Stories and Sketches by Our Best Authors* (Boston: Lee and Shepard, 1867).

With the exception of Edgar Allan Poe, Anna Katharine Green (1846–1935) is the best-known American writer of mystery fiction before the twentieth century. Michael Sims credits Green as the first woman to write a "full-fledged" detective novel, discounting Victor's *The Dead Letter* as dependent on the psychic visions of the detective's young daughter, "thus rejecting the underlying rational basis of detection."[3] Green, the daughter of a lawyer, wrote *The Leavenworth Case* (featuring New York police detective Ebenezer Gryce) after college, though it was not published until 1878. It was an instant bestseller and continues to be hailed as an exemplar of the pitfalls of circumstantial evidence. The book's success led to Green writing another twenty-eight mystery novels, countless short stories, and books in other genres. Though Gryce was the lead detective in three novels, it was the character of Amelia Butterworth, a nosy society spinster, that was Green's greatest innovation. Butterworth was undoubtedly the inspiration for Agatha Christie's Miss Marple. Green also can be credited as inspiring the Nancy Drew series of girls' mysteries: Her young society debutante, Violet Strange, appeared in a series of nine stories, solving crimes in order to earn enough money to support a disinherited sister.

It was the appearance of Sherlock Holmes in 1887 and the enormous success of the detective in a series of novels and stories by Arthur Conan Doyle that appeared between 1890 and 1927 that changed the entire course of the stream of crime fiction. With the limited exception of Dupin, previous crime fiction focused mainly on characters investigating their own mysteries (or those of family members or friends) or official police investigators. With the success of the Holmes canon, the private investigator became the central figure, seemingly the more eccentric the better. When Conan Doyle took a break from writing Holmes stories between 1893 and 1901, dozens rushed to fill the vacuum. At one extreme might be placed the American Jacques Futrelle's "The Thinking Machine," a virtually faceless Holmes substitute; at another extreme is the Englishman Arthur Morrison's Martin Hewitt, in many respects the opposite of Holmes. American crime writers were no exception. Though their work had some unique merits, their characters were largely copies of Sherlock Holmes. The more noteworthy include Samuel Hopkins Adams's Average Jones, an "advertising advisor" living in the Cosmic Club and Arthur B. Reeve's Professor Craig Kennedy, a Columbia University chemist once hailed as the "American Sherlock Holmes." Melville Davisson Post's Uncle Abner, a West Virginia backwoodsman, was as unlike Holmes as imaginable![4]

Not to be overlooked is the work of one of the earliest American "Sherlockians," Carolyn Wells (1870–1942), who wrote more than 170 books of crime fiction, parodies, and humorous verse, including sixty-one titles about a detective named Fleming Stone. Wells was an important critic as well: She published the first edition of her *The Technique of the Mystery Story: A Complete Practical Study of the Theory and Structure of the Form with Examlples from the Best Mystery Writers* in 1913 and founded the American series of the "year's best mystery stories" in 1931. A devoted student of crime fiction, she noted—well before Dorothy Sayers would make the same point in the introduction to her monumental 1931 anthology *The Omnibus of Crime*—the classical origins of crime writing, from Herodotus through the Bible, from the *Arabian Nights* to Voltaire's *Zadig*. Wells hailed the "stirring mental exercise" of writers like Gaston Leroux, Jacque Futrelle, Arthur Reeve, Anna Katharine Green, and the Baroness Orczy and was well aware of the

---

3   *The Dead Witness: A Connoisseur's Collection of Victorian Detective Stories,* edited and introduced by Michael Sims (New York: Walker & Company, 2012), p. xxvii.

4   Post also contributed the stories of Randolph Mason, a brilliant but corrupt lawyer, much admired by Willard Wright—see the title page of *The Benson Murder Case,* at page 252.

many contributions of women to the genre, including those of Augusta Groner and Mary Wilkins Freeman. At least one critic believes that her book may well have influenced the early work of both Agatha Christie and the American Mary Roberts Rinehart (1876–1958).[5]

Rinehart's 1908 novel *The Circular Staircase* was the fountainhead of an enormous body of modern American crime fiction.[6] Rinehart acknowledged Anna Katharine Green as her direct ancestor: When selecting a publisher to which to submit *The Circular Staircase*, Rinehart recalled that she merely looked at who had published Green's latest work. Her career spanned fifty years, and thriller-writer Edgar Wallace called her "the queen of us all." She wrote more than fifty books, a half-dozen plays, and hundreds of short stories. Yet she is little remembered today, except as the founder of the "had-I-but-known" school of mysteries. Rinehart did not view herself to be a writer of "detective" stories, and indeed—despite being christened the "American Agatha Christie"—with minor exceptions,[7] she tended not to create larger-than-life characters such as Poirot and Marple. Like many writers of the day, she broke in writing short stories for magazines. *The Circular Staircase* was itself serialized, and this model was followed by Earl Derr Biggers with *The House Without a Key*, and by Dashiell Hammett, discussed below.

While critics may argue over the exact parameters of the "Golden Age" of crime fiction, most place its beginning between 1908 and 1918 and sweep into its early pantheon writers such as Conan Doyle, E. C. Bentley, Agatha Christie, Dorothy Sayers, Freeman Wills Crofts, H. C. Bailey, Margery Allingham, and Josephine Tey—all notably English. All espoused the clue-based mystery, presenting puzzles for the readers to solve. After Anna Katharine Green, and with the sole exception of Mary Roberts Rinehart, no Americans achieved any fame until S. S. Van Dine, discussed below.[8] As crime fiction historian Howard Haycraft, writing in 1942, put it: "[No American author] was doing work to compare with the exciting developments that were taking place in England. The American detective story stood still, exactly where it had been before the War."[9]

---

5   Stephen Knight, *Crime Fiction since 1800: Detection, Death, Diversity*. ([2nd ed.] Basingstoke, Hampshire, England: Palgrave Macmillan, 2010), p. 82.

6   Though not Rinehart's first novel, it was her first published work.

7   Nurse Hilda Adams, "Miss Pinkerton," appeared in five of Rinehart's lesser-known novels, the first two in 1914 and the remaining in 1932, 1942, and 1950, respectively; and Letitia or "Tish" Carberry starred in a long-running series of Rinehart's stories in *The Saturday Evening Post*, collected into six anthologies between 1911 and 1937.

8   Indeed, among the 100 novels that were listed by *Publishers Weekly* as the ten bestselling books for each of the years 1920–29, only five were crime fiction: English writer E. Phillips Oppenheim's *The Great Impersonation* in 1920, two Mary Roberts Rinehart novels, and, in 1928 and 1929, S. S. Van Dine's second and third novels, discussed below. J. K. Van Dover, in *Making the Detective Story American: Biggers, Van Dine and Hammett and the Turning Point of the Genre, 1925–1930* (Jefferson, NC, and London: McFarland & Company, Inc., 2010) [hereinafter "Van Dover"], tabulated "bestsellers" through various criteria for the period 1920–29. Only Rinehart's *The Red Lamp* and *Lost Ecstasy*, Biggers's *The Chinese Parrot*, *Behind That Curtain*, and *The Black Camel*, Agatha Christie's *The Murder of Roger Ackroyd*, Van Dine's *Canary Murder Case*, *Green Murder Case*, and *Bishop Murder Case*, and Dashiell Hammett's *Red Harvest* made Van Dover's compilation. Though critics have praised the English and damned the American writers of the period, few achieved any real commercial success in America. Contrast that with *Publishers Weekly*'s list of the top ten bestselling titles of 2016, of which four were crime fiction.

9   *Murder for Pleasure: The Life and Times of the Detective Story* (London: Peter Davies, 1942) [hereinafter "*Murder for Pleasure*"], p. 163.

Earl Derr Biggers, ca. 1912

Earl Derr Biggers (1884–1933) was the first to buck that tide. A graduate of Harvard University, he would not have seemed a likely candidate to reinvigorate American crime fiction. He began his career as a journalist for the *Boston Traveler*, writing humorous columns and theatrical criticism. In 1913, however, he tried his hand at a mystery novel, *Seven Keys to Baldpate*, which won an immediate following and became an immensely successful stage play, starring George M. Cohan, was filmed seven times, and was adapted for radio and television. Several other of his novels published in the 1910s also had elements of mystery. Biggers also wrote a stream of short stories between 1913 and 1920 for *The Saturday Evening Post*, *The American Magazine*, and *Ladies' Home Journal*, though none were of any particular note.

For decades, the Chinese had been reviled in popular culture, especially in America. As early as 1880, P. W. Dooner wrote a little-known novel titled *Last Days of the Republic*, published in California—a hotbed of anti-Asian sentiment—depicting a United States under Chinese rule. The evil Oriental genius first appeared in Western literature in 1892. Tom Edison Jr.'s *Electric Sea Spider, or, The Wizard of the Submarine World*, a "dime novel" published by the Nugget Library, features Kiang Ho, a Mongolian or Chinese (there is some confusion in the tale) Harvard-educated pirate-warlord. Ho, defeated by young Edison, was succeeded in 1896 by Yue-Laou, an evil Chinese sorcerer-ruler featured in *The Maker of Moons* series by the American writer Robert Chambers.

In 1898, English novelist M. P. Shiel wrote his most popular book, *The Yellow Danger*. The story tells of Dr. Yen How, who is half-Japanese/half-Chinese ("he combined these antagonistic races in one man") and rises to power in China and fosters war with the West. Yen How is described as a physician educated at Heidelberg and was probably loosely based on the Chinese revolutionary Sun Yat Sen (also a physician). Yen How is defeated by the West in the person of Admiral John Hardy, a consumptive who overcomes his frailties to turn back the Yellow Danger.

Sax Rohmer's short story "The Zayat Kiss" appeared in October 1912 in *The Story-Teller*, a popular magazine. It was well-received, and Rohmer wrote nine more stories in the initial series. In 1913, the series was collected in book form as *The Mystery of Dr. Fu Manchu* (published as *The Insidious Dr. Fu Manchu* in America). Fu Manchu appeared in two more series of stories before the end of the Great War, collected as *The Devil Doctor* (1916) (*The Return of Dr. Fu Manchu* in America) and *Si-Fan Mysteries* (1917) (*The Hand of Fu Manchu* in America).

By 1924, anti-Asian sentiments were at their peak when, with overwhelming support, the United States Congress passed, and President Calvin Coolidge signed, the Immigration Act (also known as the Johnson-Reed Act). The new law adopted the concept of national-origin quotas, limiting overall immigration to 150,000 persons per year, restricting immigration to 2 percent of the quantity of those nationals already present in the United States (according to the 1890 census), and completely prohibiting the immigration of those ineligible for U.S. citizenship. This last standard effectively barred half the world's population and lumped Chinese, Japanese, Koreans, Indians, Thais, Indonesians, and others into the category of "Asiatic." Those Asiatics already living in the United States would be barred from citizenship and prevented from bringing other family members into the country.

In 1920, after exhausting himself with work on some very successful stage plays, Biggers traveled to Honolulu. He continued to write a variety of short stories having nothing to do with Hawaii, but he was apparently fascinated by the melting pot that was 1920s Honolulu. He conceived of a mystery set there, and in 1922 he described the work-in-progress to his editor as including "army people, traders, planters. An Americanized Chinese house boy—the star pitcher on the All-China baseball nine—the lawyer for the opium ring—an Admiral of the Fleet . . .—an old Yankee from New Bedford—a champion Hawaiian swimmer—beachcombers—. . . the president of a Japanese bank."[10] There was no mention of a detective. According to Biggers, in the summer of 1924, he stopped by the New York Public Library Reading Room, and while browsing through Hawaiian newspapers, he found an account of the Honolulu police. "In an obscure corner of an inside page, I found an item to the effect that a certain hapless Chinese, being too fond of opium, had been arrested by Sergeants Chang Apana and Lee Fook, of the Honolulu Police. So Sergeant Charlie Chan entered the story of *The House Without a Key*."[11]

Detective Chang Apana, ca. 1930

Biggers was no racial crusader, and he certainly had no intention of creating a Chinese character who would fly in the face of American stereotypes or alter the public view of foreigners. Chan is decidedly different: He is described as a fat man, with the chubby cheeks of a baby; yet he walks with the dainty step of a woman. He has ivory skin, short black hair, and amber slanted eyes. He does not speak pidgin-English (as do several of the Japanese characters in the book); rather, he speaks his own brand of English, replete with aphorisms. In this respect, he is as foreign as Agatha Christie's Hercule Poirot, whose speech is as distinctive as Chan's. Chan also regularly displays his animosity toward the Japanese—a sentiment common in Hawaii in the 1920s and throughout America. In *The House Without a Key*, though he eventually appreciates Chan's talents, the young Bostonian protagonist cannot erase his sense of a marked gulf between Chan and himself. In this, Biggers accurately reflected the realities facing the American people: Notwithstanding harsh policies such as the Immigration Act, the ethnic populations of America were here to stay.

First serialized in *The Saturday Evening Post* between January 24 and March 7, 1925, the adventures of Charlie Chan struck a chord with the *Post*'s readership. Here, at last, was an American crime writer worth reading, even if his tales were of a slightly less-than-American detective. The book publication of *The House Without a Key* occurred later in 1925, and over the next seven years, five more Chan novels appeared (all first serialized in *The Saturday Evening Post*): *The Chinese Parrot* (1926), *Behind the Curtain* (1928), *The Black Camel* (1929), *Charlie Chan Carries On* (1930),

10   Letter to Laurance Chambers, December 18, 1922, Lilly Library (Indiana University).

11   *Harvard College Class of 1907 Twenty-fifth Anniversary Report*, p. 43 (reported in *Charlie Chan*, by Yunte Huang [New York: W. W. Norton & Co., 2010], p. 109).

Earl Derr Biggers on the set of an early Chan film

and *Keeper of the Keys* (1932). The novels were extremely popular and were adapted into films, cartoons, comic strips, and radio programs.[12] The last Chan film was in 1947, and a cartoon series ran in 1972–73.

Howard Haycraft, in his masterful *Murder for Pleasure: The Life and Times of the Detective Story* (1941), summed up the stories of the Chan series: "They are clean, humorous, unpretentious, more than a little romantic, and—it must be confessed—just a shade mechanical and old fashioned by modern plot standards. This absence of any novel or startling departure, in fact, is probably the reason that the first Chan story created no such popular or critical stir as the first Philo Vance case . . . and it was not until two or three of his adventures had appeared that he struck full stride. Once started, however, he has been difficult to stop. . . . Conventional as the narratives often were, Charlie Chan's personal popularity played a part in the Renaissance of the American detective story that can not be ignored."[13]

12 See Charles P. Mitchell's definitive *A Guide to Charlie Chan Films* (Westport, CT, and London: Greenwood Press, 1999) for a list of the fifty-three films and a discussion of Chan on television and radio. See also Appendix, p. 250, for a discussion of the 1926 film of *The House Without a Key*.

13 *Murder for Pleasure*, pp. 178–79.

S. S. Van Dine with William Powell, who played Philo Vance, in a publicity photo for *The Canary Murder Case*, 1931

S. S. Van Dine, late 1920s

By 1930, declared J. K. Van Dover, "Philo Vance was *the* American detective."[14] S. S. Van Dine's books were consistent successes until, after publication of *The Scarab Murder Case* in 1930, the inevitable decline began. Who was this American phenomenon, the subject of twelve novels and seventeen films, yet barely remembered today? Between 1923 and 1924, Willard Huntington Wright (1888–1939), former editor of *The Smart Set* and a well-regarded art critic, became ill and read widely in crime fiction.[15] Determined to make his fortune at fiction but anxious to preserve his "high-brow" reputation,[16] he adopted the pseudonym "S. S. Van Dine" (based, he said, probably facetiously, on an old family name and the convenient initials of a steamship). He conceived of the central figure and three plots, summarized them, and presented them to the acclaimed editor Maxwell Perkins,

---

14   Van Dover, p. 7.

15   Wright also edited *The Great Detective Stories: A Chronological Anthology* (New York: Scribner's, 1927) and provided an extensive and learned introduction.

16   At the height of his fame in 1928, Van Dine wrote an article, "I Used to Be a Highbrow and Look at Me Now," for *The American Magazine* 106 (September 1928), 14 ff., and reprinted in Howard Haycraft's *The Art of the Mystery Story,* in which he made clear both his pride and his regret at his achievements.

Cover, *Scribner's Magazine* (May 1927), depicting Philo Vance (for *The Canary Murder Case*)

whose other authors included Ernest Hemingway, F. Scott Fitzgerald, Thomas Wolfe, and John P. Marquand. Perkins was impressed and immediately bought them for the Scribner's house. The rest was publishing history.

Van Dine had devised his own "rules"[17] for crime fiction and set out to create a detective with a unique style. Some suggest that the character was intended to out-Holmes Holmes, with a deeper erudition and knowledge of useful trivia. A more likely model is Dorothy Sayers's Lord Peter Wimsey, complete with the affected speech of an upper-class Englishman, a pince-nez, a robust collection of wine and modern art, and a butler. In either case, Philo Vance was established as a New York bachelor, with an inherited fortune and the taste to spend it wisely. Accompanied by his attorney, himself "S. S. Van Dine," Vance partnered with New York District Attorney John F.-X. Markham to solve murders—and only murders. The Vance novels are long by the standards of Agatha Christie and are paced slowly, and they include numerous details about the panoply of suspects and the settings.

Vance insists that physical evidence is of much less importance than understanding "the exact psychological nature of the deed." He maintains that understanding the deep-seated urges of seemingly respectable individuals and recognizing their unique psychological signatures is enough to identify a murderer. Vance frequently makes fun of Markham and the police for the logical conclusions they draw from "clues" and circumstantial evidence. Yet despite Van Dine's ignorance of ballistics and other burgeoning forensic sciences and Vance's disdain for police investigations, there are masses of physical evidence in each book; in *The Benson Murder Case*, for example, Vance relies heavily on tracing the path of the murderous bullet to demonstrate the height of the killer as well as astutely reasoning out the killer's hiding place for the murder weapon.

Why did Van Dine succeed—at least, while he succeeded? Certainly no one could like Philo Vance. Ogden Nash famously quipped, "Philo Vance/Needs a kick in the pance," and Van Dine appreciated the joke, incorporating it into a footnote in a later novel. An effete white upper-class snob, living in a Manhattan that seemed devoid of life above 120th Street, Vance moved among the rich and famous, a set well-known to Willard Wright.

---

17   See Appendix to *The Benson Murder Case*, p. 497. The "rules" were first published in 1928, after the success of the first three books.

Undoubtedly Van Dine's skill as a writer, his ability to bring a finely-honed purpose and polished literacy to the genre, played a significant part. Another factor was that despite the fantasy that was Vance's life, there was verisimilitude and a certain realism: The first two novels were based on actual unsolved murders that had stunned and fascinated New Yorkers.[18] Perhaps the American public yearned for an urban experience more familiar than Biggers's Hawaii/California milieu or the undistinguished locales of many of Rinehart's books. Certainly New York featured prominently in all of Van Dine's books and was central to many of the Ellery Queen mysteries as well. Perhaps the public reveled in tales of the upper classes. Until Black Tuesday in 1929, princes of Wall Street and the effervescence of the stock markets, which touched rich and poor alike, entranced the American public. John Loughery observes, "Philo Vance makes no apologies for his privileged lifestyle. In the Jazz Age none was needed, as Willard had rightly concluded. A man who knew how to spend his money, a know-it-all with style, had automatic appeal."[19]

Dashiell Hammett was at a loss to understand Van Dine's success. He wrote a scathing review of *The Benson Murder Case* in the *Saturday Review of Literature* for January 15, 1927: ". . . The murderer's identity becomes obvious quite early in the story. The authorities, no matter how stupid the author chose to make them, would have cleared up the mystery promptly if they had been allowed to follow the most rudimentary police routine. But then what would there have been for the gifted Vance to do? This Philo Vance is in the Sherlock Holmes tradition and his conversational manner is that of a high-school girl who has been studying the foreign words and phrases in the back of her dictionary. He is a bore when he discusses art and philosophy, but when he switches to criminal psychology he is delightful. There is a theory that any one who talks enough on any subject must, if only by chance, finally say something not altogether incorrect. Vance disproves this theory: he manages always, and usually ridiculously, to be wrong. . . ."

Hammett's own time would come in only a few years, but for the time being, in the late 1920s and through the mid-1930s, the European style of puzzle-mystery dominated American crime fiction, and Willard Huntington Wright was the golden child of publishing and the king of American crime writers. Howard Haycraft credited Van Dine with bringing the American detective story to "a new peak of excellence and popularity," but observed that he did so by doing nothing more than mimic the well-established English tradition.[20] In the end, the pretentiousness and lack of humor of the novels would outweigh readers' initial fascination. Vance's erudition became displayed more and more in large and often gratuitous segments that slowed down the tales, and the snob appeal wore thin. By 1939, when Wright died, both he and Vance had worn out their welcome, and except for the long-lived Ellery Queen mysteries, Van Dine–style stories had been largely replaced by the "hard-boiled" realism of Hammett and others.

<hr />

18 See *The Benson Murder Case*, Author's Note, p. 304, for a discussion of the Joseph Elwell case. *The Canary Murder Case* was based loosely on the killing, in 1923, of Dorothy "Dot" King, the "Broadway Butterfly." See John Loughery's definitive *Alias S. S. Van Dine: The Man Who Created Philo Vance* (New York: Charles Scribner's Sons, 1992), p. 175.

19 Loughery, p. 188.

20 *Murder for Pleasure*, p. 169.

Frederic Dannay in 1943   Manfred B. Lee, ca. 1965

The success of the Philo Vance mysteries also inspired two Brooklyn-based cousins, Frederic Dannay (1905–1982) and Manfred B. Lee (1905–1971),[21] to write an obsessively detailed, highly logical puzzle-mystery and submit it to a magazine contest in 1929. They won the contest, but the organizer went out of business. Fortunately for the cousins, a book publisher stepped in, and *The Roman Hat Mystery* was published, launching the extremely long career of the duo known as "Ellery Queen." Thirty-two novels featuring the detective Ellery Queen followed, the last published in 1971. In addition, the cousins wrote dozens of Ellery Queen short stories, four novels under the name Barnaby Ross, and several "stand-alone" novels, while Dannay edited the highly influential *Ellery Queen's Mystery Magazine* (which continues today), a number of anthologies of other writers' work, and several critical and bibliographic works, including the monumental *Queen's Quorum: A History of the Detective-Crime Short Story as Revealed by the 100 Most Important Books Published in This Field Since 1845* (Boston: Little, Brown,

---

21   The two cousins were children of Jewish immigrants; Daniel Nathan adopted the name Frederic Dannay, and Emanuel Lepofsky used the professional name Manfred Bennington Lee. In a stroke of marketing genius, they named the author *and detective* Ellery Queen. For a discussion of the choice of the name, see the essential *Royal Bloodline: Ellery Queen, Author and Detective*, by Francis M. Nevins Jr. (Bowling Green, OH: Bowling Green University Popular Press, 1974), pp. 4–5.

1951). The Ellery Queen novels took the clue-based mystery to its logical end, making each book a game—complete with a pause in the narrative labeled "Challenge to the Readers"—to be won by the truly astute reader or pleasurably "lost" by the reader who failed to out-deduce the detective.

There is no mistaking the initial influence of S. S. Van Dine's writing on the cousins. In his early years, the character of Ellery Queen was, in the words of the editors of the *Detectionary*, "a supercilious aristocrat who condescendingly assisted his long-suffering father, Inspector Richard Queen of the New York Police Department. Young Ellery was a sartorial cliché, dressed in tweeds, wearing pince-nez, and carrying a walking stick."[22] This version of the detective quoted liberally from a wide range of literary sources and affected a bibliophilia that, while not as obnoxious as Vance's art expertise, could often be annoying, when, for example, he laments a rare book sacrificed to use as notepaper or the lost opportunity to acquire a scarce first edition.

Yet Ellery Queen achieved remarkable longevity, while Van Dine did not; and in the long run, Queen's books achieved greater popularity.[23] Howard Haycraft observed that "the authors modestly speak of the 'absolutely logical' fair-play method of deduction, which, indeed, has been the sign-mark of their work from the beginning. But there is more than this. Although the Messrs. 'Queen' frankly and necessarily regard their output as a means of livelihood, they have brought to the detective story a respect and integrity which—combined with their unflagging zest—accounts largely for the high level they have consistently maintained. . . . For the great part, the Queen tales are as adroit a blending of the intellectual and dramatic aspects of the genre, of meticulous plot-work, lively narration, easy, unforced humor, and entertaining personae, as can be found in the modern detective novel." Haycraft also credits Queen with mating the realism of the "Hammett school" with the puzzle-clue mystery: they were less pretentious than Van Dine's books but agreeably livelier, less impactful than Hammett's but also less mannered.[24]

Cover of *Crackajack Funnies*, No. 25 (1940), one of the twenty issues of the series

---

22   *Detectionary: A Biographical Dictionary of the Leading Characters in Detective and Mystery Fiction*. Compiled by Chris Steinbrunner, Charles Shibuk, Otto Penzler, Marvin Lachman, and Francis M. Nevins Jr. (Lock Haven, PA: Hammermill Paper Company, 1972), pp. 193–94.

23   Between 1930 and 1935, when only one of Van Dine's books made Van Dover's compilation of mystery and detection bestsellers (see note 8, above), five of Queen's books are listed. Frank Luther Mott, in *Golden Multitudes: The Story of Best Sellers in the United States* (New York: Bowker, 1947), examined books against a measuring rod of 1 percent of the decade's population. Three of Queen's works measured up between 1926 and 1935; none of Van Dine's did.

24   *Murder for Pleasure*, pp. 174–76.

Van Dover points to other differences that he argues led to Queen's long-term success and Van Dine's ultimate failure. Aestheticism was intrinsic to Vance's character and ultimately off-putting. Ellery's intelligence is not a matter of zealotry but rather ornamental, a matter of pride to his father. Despite his cardboard companion Van Dine, Vance is alone; in contrast, Ellery is part of a warm and affectionate household. More fundamentally, Vance is consistently unpleasant, while Ellery is quite simply likeable—in Van Dover's words, "a nice fellow."[25] Finally, Vance was like a fly in amber—unable to adapt or change as American readers' tastes evolved. Queen, on the other hand, evolved over time, reflecting the decades in which he worked. So long as the American readership craved puzzle-stories, Ellery Queen would have an appreciative audience.

⌘

In some respects, Burnett's compelling *Little Caesar*, discussed below, is the dark side of Dashiell Hammett's first (and perhaps best) novel, *Red Harvest*. First published in February 1929, with a theme and style far removed from the popular works of Biggers, Van Dine, and Queen, Hammett's book became an unlikely bestseller. Set in "Personville," a totally corrupt city called "Poisonville" by those familiar with it, the book is the first novel-length tale of Hammett's unnamed agent of the Continental Detective Agency, called the "Continental Op."

Samuel Dashiell Hammett (1894–1961) was born in Maryland on a farm to an old-line family. He was raised in Philadelphia and Baltimore, but at the age of thirteen, he dropped out of school and began a series of commonplace jobs, culminating in working for the Pinkerton Detective Agency from 1915 to 1921. During the course of this employment, it appears that he was sent to Butte, Montana, to aid in putting down the miners' strikes.[26] In

Dashiell Hammett, ca. 1929

25   Van Dover, p. 58.

26   Hammett's daughter Jo, in *Dashiell Hammett: A Daughter Remembers*, recalls that Hammett "first saw Butte in his twenties when he was working for the Pinkerton's. The agency had been brough in by the mine owners to help in their struggle with the unions and the radical IWW. Their job was to infiltrate and disrupt. What Papa did there as an undercover man, and what he saw done, left a deep and lasting impression on him" (p. 60). However, this is uncorroborated. It is certain that Hammett's wife Josephine Annis Dolan Hammett (known as Jose) grew up in Anaconda and worked in a Butte hospital during the period that Jo states Hammett was there, though they met in California, where she worked as a nurse in a hospital in which Hammett was being treated.

any event, the labor unrest made a distinct impression on Hammett, and he was active in left-wing political causes all his life. After a failed marriage and another broken romance, in 1931, he began a storied thirty-year relationship with the actress-playwright Lillian Hellman.[27] He wrote novels, short stories, essays, reviews, and screenplays and is probably best remembered today for creating the enduring characters of Sam Spade and Nick and Nora Charles.

Hammett had written previously—and frequently—of the Op, in short stories that appeared in *Black Mask* magazine. This venue, a "pulp" magazine not wholly unlike such "lowbrow" outlets as *Weird Tales* and *Argosy* that were flooding the market, was the brainchild of the journalist H. L. Mencken and the dramatist George Jean Nathan. It was conceived by them and launched in 1920 as a means of supporting their more prestigious magazine *The Smart Set*. Initially, it featured a wide range of fiction, including adventure, romance, supernatural, and crime tales. After the magazine was sold by Mencken and Nathan in 1922, it took a more sensational turn, and by the time Joseph Shaw took over as its editor in 1926, it was featuring almost exclusively crime fiction. Shaw had a keen eye for talent and was an enthusiastic backer of Hammett's writing. Between 1923 and 1929, twenty-eight stories of the Op appeared in *Black Mask*, seven of them after Shaw took the editorial chair.

In 1928, Hammett conceived of reshaping four connected stories that had appeared in late 1927 and early 1928 in *Black Mask* under the aggregate title "The Cleansing of Poisonville." He submitted the combined stories to publisher Alfred A. Knopf for consideration and was thrilled when Blanche Knopf wrote to him expressing enthusiasm for the work. She did want some revisions, however, proposing to reduce the number of violent deaths in the story and eliminating completely the character of Lew Yard. Hammett agreed to excise a horrendous bombing from the section originally titled "Dynamite" but successfully argued that removal of Lew Yard and his gang would weaken the book's structure.

The book was published by Knopf in March 1929 to great acclaim. Although some thought the book superficial and pandering, Herbert Asbury, writing in *The Bookman*, called it "the liveliest detective story that has been published in a decade." Walter R. Brooks, in *Outlook and Independent*, remarked: "A thriller that lives up to the blurb on the jacket is unusal enough to command respect. When, in addition, it is written by a man who plainly knows his underworld and can make it come alive for his readers, when the action is exciting and the conversation racy and amusing—well, you'll want to read it." Not everyone was as positivie: "F.M.," writing in the *Boston Evening Transcript*, complained: "If the story has a purpose, it may be to show up the possible rottenness of certain city governments, but it seems more like an attempt to see how deeply the author can make his readers wade in gore and in the slime of the worst criminal life."

Stylistically, the book could not have been more different from works like *The House Without a Key*, *The Roman Hat Mystery*, or *The Benson Murder Case*. It is filled with violence and fast action, and the language of the characters is the language of the streets, including a great deal of jargon unique to the police and criminal underworld, as well as sarcasm and gallows humor. These characteristics are shared by *Little Caesar*. Nobel Prize winner André Gide wrote in 1943, "[I]n *Red Harvest* the dialogues, written in a masterful way, are such as to give pointers to Hemingway or even to Faulkner, and the entire narrative is ordered with skill and an implacable cynicism. In that very special type of thing it is, I really believe, . . . the most remarkable I have read." In *The Simple Art of Murder* (1944), Raymond

---

27   See Joan Mellen's *Hellman and Hammett* (New York: HarperCollins Publishers, 1996).

Chandler said, "Hammett gave murder back to the kind of people that commit it for reasons, not just to provide a corpse; and with the means at hand, not hand-wrought dueling pistols, curare and tropical fish."

Today Hammett is remembered as the founder of the "hard-boiled detective story," but that is inaccurate. In fact, Carroll John Daly's story "The False Burton Combs" appeared in *Black Mask* in December 1922, almost a year before the first Op story. Daly wrote this and many other naturalistic stories about Race Williams, a tough, no-nonsense detective who liked to shoot first and talk later in a difficult situation, and Daly's work was in high demand throughout the 1920s and 1930s. Williams was certainly the inspiration for Mickey Spillane's Mike Hammer in the 1950s. The Op may be seen in part as a rejection of Williams's credo. In "Corkscrew," for example, published in *Black Mask* in September 1925, he states: "The proper place for guns is after talk has failed." Of course, if he can't avoid fighting, he will wade in and fight as needed for survival.[28] Yet the Op is not as far from the puzzle-solving Sherlock Holmes as many credit. In *Red Harvest*, for example, he solves three killings by careful observation and reasoning, not by using his fists to extract confessions.[29]

LeRoy Lad Panek summed up *Red Harvest* as "[s]peeding cars, machine guns, riot guns, automatics, knives, ice picks, bootleg liquor, laudanum, and fast women . . . the detective novel of the twenties."[30] And yet, as is evident from the discussion of the reception of the books of Biggers, Van Dine, and Queen, it is in many respects the polar opposite of the popular works of the day, and its success more a harbinger of things to come than a true measure of the spirit of the times. The play called *Gunplay* that is the scene of *The Roman Hat Mystery* has many similarities to the narrative of *Red Harvest*. While the fictional drama was the hit of the New York season in 192-, however, in fact there was no such play, and for most of the decade, the American public was not particularly interested in reading about the realities of the Prohibition era.

⌘

But the decade of the 1920s was not exclusively the purview of the New York–based puzzle-mystery nor even *detective*-based crime fiction. It was also the era that spawned the American "crime novel." Rather than focus on the process of capture of the criminal or the work of a criminal investigator such as the Continental Op, these works explored the criminal—his or her background and emotional state before the crime, the circumstances of the commission of the crime, and the impact of the crime on the criminal. Early examples of such works are, of course, the Newgate Calendar in England and the execution-sermons of America, but more literary efforts appeared in diluted versions like M. E. Braddon's *Lady Audley's Secret* (1862) and Marie Belloc Lowndes's *The Lodger* (1913), the latter a thinly veiled exploration of the serial killer known as Jack the Ripper. Later American versions included such outstanding novels as James M. Cain's *The Postman Always Rings Twice* (1934) and *Double Indemnity* (1943),

---

28 William F. Nolan, in *Dashiell Hammett: A Casebook*, computed that during the seven years that his escapades were recounted in *Black Mask*, he killed fifteen people and wounded about twelve (pp. 53–54).

29 Although Hammett is viewed as the leader of the generation after Conan Doyle, it should be remembered that twelve Holmes stories—one-fifth of the total Canon—appeared in the 1920s, and Hammett had already published more than sixty stories, reviews, and essays by the time the last Holmes tale appeared, in 1927.

30 *Probable Cause: Crime Fiction in America* (Bowling Green, OH: Bowling Green University Popular Press, 1990), p. 123.

W. R. Burnett with Edward G. Robinson
on the set of *Little Caesar* (ca. 1931)

Dorothy B. Hughes's *In a Lonely Place* (1947), and Jim Thompson's *The Killer Inside Me* (1952). But in the 1920s, W. R. Burnett pioneered the sub-genre with his brilliant *Little Caesar*.

William Riley Burnett (1899–1982) was born and raised in Springfield, Ohio. He developed literary ambitions early, and when he moved to Chicago, in 1927, he already had produced five novels, several plays, and a hundred short stories, none of which had been published. All of that changed with the publication of *Little Caesar*, in 1929. Burnett went on to write and publish thirty-six more novels, including the highly regarded *High Sierra* (1941) and *The Asphalt Jungle* (1949). Equally importantly, he wrote the screenplay for the 1931 film of *Little Caesar*, setting the bar for dozens of gangster films to follow and launching the career of Edward G. Robinson. Burnett wrote, co-wrote, or contributed to dozens of other film and television scripts, including such classics as *Scarface* (1932), *High Sierra* (1941), and *The Asphalt Jungle* (1950), adapting many of his own stories as well as others (for example, *This Gun for Hire* [1942] was an adaptation of Graham Greene's 1936 novel).

In 1957, Burnett wrote an introduction to a new edition of *Little Caesar*, in which he recalled the struggle of adjusting to life in the big city and the inspiration that found him when he met a local gangster. He had set out to write the story of the rise and fall of a criminal without psychology or description; he determined to make it wholly in dialogue, in the jargon of the Italian mob. It was an instant success, selected by the Literary Guild for the month of June 1929, assuring substantial sales. The *Chicago Daily Tribune* called it "a remarkable first book. . . . The people [Burnett] creates are so real that you see them long after you finish the story."[31] "Here, certainly, is a best-seller," wrote the *Hartford Daily Courant*.[32] The *New York Times* said, "This is an unusually good story about Chicago gangsters. . . . The sentences are as hard and abrupt as the bullet shots that clear the way for Rico's rise to gang dominance and his downfall."[33]

31   June 22, 1929, p. 11.

32   June 15, 1929, p. 8E.

33   June 2, 1929, p. 24.

Not only was the subject of *Little Caesar* timely, as Al Capone and Big Bill Thompson ruled Chicago; Burnett was able to adapt a true story about the Sam Cardinelli gang that he found in a newly published work of sociology, *The Gang: A Study of 1,313 Gangs in Chicago*, by Frederick N. Thrasher.[34] By using these bases, Burnett followed in the tradition of earlier American crime writers. Josiah Flynt and Alfred Hodder were reporters whose "Notes from the Underworld" appeared in *McClure's* in 1901. In 1902, Flynt followed up with a series of more factual pieces called "The World of Graft." Lincoln Steffens's *Shame of the Cities* was published in 1904, collecting a series of articles about American political corruption; Hutchens Hapgood's *The Autobiography of a Thief* appeared in 1905, and Melville Davisson Post (of *Uncle Abner* fame) wrote a six-part series of tales of "Extraordinary Cases" for *The Saturday Evening Post* in 1911. James Boyle wrote *Boston Blackie* in 1919, stories about a professional crook in the underworld of San Francisco, described by LeRoy Lad Panek as "drip[ping] with sentiment and sentimentality."[35]

A mug shot of Alphonse Capone in 1931

Yet Burnett's writing achieved a viewpoint that the earlier writers did not. Although the earlier purveyors of crime writing expressed their compassion and interest, they could not help distancing themselves from their subjects, moralizing or sympathizing as appropriate but not *inhabiting* the criminals. Burnett was the first to do so. *Little Caesar* is an unflinching portrait of men and women as they were, told in their own language and devoid of sentimentality. Although Burnett likened Rico to Julius Caesar, the world does not shake at his downfall. *Little Caesar* has all the trappings of a classical tragedy: Rico's strengths are also his weaknesses, the acts of daring that propel him to the top are also his downfall. But, as Panek observes, "*Little Caesar* isn't a tragedy because that's the way things are in the twentieth century."[36]

---

34   See *Little Caesar*, notes 71 and 72.

35   *Probable Cause*, p. 117.

36   Ibid., p. 138.

A Note on the Texts

The texts following are as they appeared in the first printing of the first book publication. The authors' spelling and punctuation have been retained except in a few cases of obvious typographical errors. As discussed in context below, several of these texts were subsequently revised by editors to be more "politically correct." These are presented here in their original form.

L.S.K.

Facsimile first-edition dust jacket for *The House Without a Key*.

THE HOUSE WITHOUT A KEY[1]

BY
EARL DERR BIGGERS

AUTHOR OF

The Agony Column
Seven Keys to Baldpate, etc.

To my Mother and Father

1.   First published in Indianapolis by The Bobbs-Merrill Company in 1925. The publisher (and Biggers) apparently disliked *The Saturday Evening Post* illustrations of the serialized book, reproduced below, and Biggers asked Bobbs-Merrill to produce an illustrated cover rather than use the illustrations. This may have been in part the result of Biggers's realization that Charlie Chan and not John Quincy Winterslip, who is depicted in most of the illustrations, was the real heart of the book. See Barbara Gregorich's *Charlie Chan's Poppa: Earl Derr Biggers*, p. 34.

CHAPTER I

Kona Weather

M iss Minerva Winterslip was a Bostonian in good standing, and long past the romantic age. Yet beauty thrilled her still, even the semibarbaric beauty of a Pacific island. As she walked slowly along the beach she felt the little catch in her throat that sometimes she had known in Symphony Hall, Boston, when her favorite orchestra rose to some new and unexpected height of loveliness.

It was the hour at which she liked Waikiki[2] best, the hour just preceding dinner and the quick tropic darkness. The shadows cast by the tall cocoanut palms lengthened and deepened, the light of the falling sun flamed on Diamond Head[3] and tinted with gold the rollers sweeping in from the coral reef. A few late swimmers, reluctant to depart, dotted those waters whose touch is like the caress of a lover. On the springboard of the nearest float a slim brown girl poised for one delectable instant. What a figure! Miss Minerva, well over fifty herself, felt a mild twinge of envy—youth, youth like an arrow, straight and sure and flying. Like an arrow the slender figure rose, then fell; the perfect dive, silent and clean.

Miss Minerva glanced at the face of the man who walked beside her. But Amos Winterslip was oblivious to beauty; he had made that the first rule of his life. Born in the Islands, he had never known the mainland beyond San Francisco. Yet there could be no doubt about it, he was the New England conscience personified—the New England conscience in a white duck suit.

2. A neighborhood of Honolulu, the capital of the U.S. Territory of Hawaii, fronting on the southern beach. In 1920, Honolulu (and the Island of Oahu) had a population of 123,496. Honolulu, styled as the "cross-roads of the Pacific," is 2,100 miles from San Francisco, 3,400 miles from Yokohama; 4,410 miles from Sydney; and 4,890 miles from Manila.

3. A volcanic tuff cone adjacent to Waikiki and one of the prominent landmarks of Honolulu (and hence the Hawaiian Islands generally).

"Better turn back, Amos," suggested Miss Minerva. "Your dinner's waiting. Thank you so much."

"I'll walk as far as the fence," he said. "When you get tired of Dan and his carryings-on, come to us again. We'll be glad to have you."

"That's kind of you," she answered, in her sharp crisp way. "But I really must go home. Grace is worried about me. Of course, she can't understand. And my conduct *is* scandalous, I admit. I came over to Honolulu for six weeks, and I've been wandering about these islands for ten months."

"As long as that?"

She nodded. "I can't explain it. Every day I make a solemn vow I'll start packing my trunks—to-morrow."

"And to-morrow never comes," said Amos. "You've been taken in by the tropics. Some people are."

"Weak people, I presume you mean," snapped Miss Minerva. "Well, I've never been weak. Ask anybody on Beacon Street."

He smiled wanly. "It's a strain in the Winterslips," he said. "Supposed to be Puritans, but always sort of yearning toward the lazy latitudes."

"I know," answered Miss Minerva, her eyes on that exotic shore line. "It's what sent so many of them adventuring out of Salem harbor. Those who stayed behind felt that the travelers were seeing things no Winterslip should look at. But they envied them just the same—or maybe for that very reason." She nodded. "A sort of gypsy strain. It's what sent your father over here to set up as a whaler, and got you born so far from home. You know you don't belong here, Amos. You should be living in Milton or Roxbury, carrying a little green bag and popping into a Boston office every morning."

"I've often thought it," he admitted. "And who knows—I might have made something of my life—"

They had come to a barbed-wire fence, an unaccustomed barrier on that friendly shore. It extended well down on to the beach; a wave rushed up and lapped the final post, then receded.

Miss Minerva smiled. "Well, this is where Amos leaves off and Dan begins," she said. "I'll watch my chance and run around the end. Lucky you couldn't build it so it moved with the tide."

"You'll find your luggage in your room at Dan's, I guess," Amos told her. "Remember what I said about—" He broke off suddenly.

A stocky, white-clad man had appeared in the garden beyond the barrier, and was moving rapidly toward them. Amos Winterslip stood rigid for a moment, an angry light flaming in his usually dull eyes. "Good-by," he said, and turned.

"Amos!" cried Miss Minerva sharply. He moved on, and she followed. "Amos, what nonsense! How long has it been since you spoke to Dan?"

He paused under an algaroba tree.[4] "Thirty-one years," he said. "Thirtyone years the tenth of last August."

"That's long enough," she told him. "Now, come around that foolish fence of yours, and hold out your hand to him."

"Not me," said Amos. "I guess you don't know Dan, Minerva, and the sort of life he's led. Time and again he's dishonored us all—"

"Why, Dan's regarded as a big man," she protested. "He's respected—"

"And rich," added Amos bitterly. "And I'm poor. Yes, that's the way it often goes in this world. But there's a world to come, and over there I reckon Dan's going to get his."

Hardy soul though she was, Miss Minerva was somewhat frightened by the look of hate on his thin face. She saw the uselessness of further argument. "Good-by, Amos," she said. "I wish I might persuade you to come East some day—" He gave no sign of hearing, but hurried along the white stretch of sand.

When Miss Minerva turned, Dan Winterslip was smiling at her from beyond the fence. "Hello, there," he cried. "Come this side of the wire and enjoy life again. You're mighty welcome."

"How are you, Dan?" She watched her chance with the waves and joined him. He took both her hands in his.

"Glad to see you," he said, and his eyes backed him up. Yes, he did have a way with women. "It's a bit lonely at the old homestead these days. Need a young girl about to brighten things up."

Miss Minerva sniffed. "I've tramped Boston in galoshes too many winters," she reminded him, "to lose my head over talk like that."

"Forget Boston," he urged. "We're all young in Hawaii. Look at me."

She did look at him, wonderingly. He was sixty-three, she knew, but only the mass of wavy white hair overhanging his temples betrayed his age. His face, burned to the deepest bronze

4. *Ceratonia siliqua*, a carob tree with long bean pods, found throughout the Mediterranean and other tropical climes.

5.   *Delonix regia*, with fern-like leaves and flamboyant flowers.

6.   A fig tree that begins as a parasite on another tree, flowering and often strangling the host tree. There are many species, including *Ficus microcarpa*.

7.   Commonly known as sea hibiscus or mahoe, *Hibiscus tiliaceus* is a small tree or evergreen shrub with heart-shaped leaves and petal-shaped blooms.

8.   The Hawaiian race was indeed vanishing. The total population of the Territory in the 1910 Census was 191,909; by 1920, it had grown to 255,912. However, during the same period, the "pure" Hawaiian population shrank from 26,041 to 23,723 (while the "Asiatic-Hawaiian" category grew from 3,734 to 6,955 and the "Caucasian-Hawaiian" category grew from 8,772 to 11,072). The largest population groups were Japanese, at 109,274 followed by Portuguese, at 27,002, Chinese, at 23,507, and Filipino, at 21,031.

by long years of wandering under the Polynesian sun, was without a line or wrinkle. Deep-chested and muscular, he could have passed on the mainland for a man of forty.

"I see my precious brother brought you as far as the dead-line," he remarked as they moved on through the garden. "Sent me his love, I presume?"

"I tried to get him to come round and shake hands," Miss Minerva said.

Dan Winterslip laughed. "Don't deprive poor Amos of his hate for me," he urged. "It's about all he lives for now. Comes over every night and stands under that algaroba tree of his, smoking cigarettes and staring at my house. Know what he's waiting for? He's waiting for the Lord to strike me down for my sins. Well, he's a patient waiter, I'll say that for him."

Miss Minerva did not reply. Dan's great rambling house of many rooms was set in beauty almost too poignant to be borne. She stood, drinking it all in again, the poinciana trees[5] like big crimson umbrellas, the stately golden glow, the gigantic banyans[6] casting purple shadows, her favorite hau tree,[7] seemingly old as time itself, covered with a profusion of yellow blossoms. Loveliest of all were the flowering vines, the bougainvillea burying everything it touched in brick-red splendor. Miss Minerva wondered what her friends who every spring went into sedate ecstasies over the Boston Public Gardens would say if they could see what she saw now. They would be a bit shocked, perhaps, for this was too lurid to be quite respectable. A scarlet background—and a fitting one, no doubt, for Cousin Dan.

They reached the door at the side of the house that led directly into the living-room. Glancing to her right, Miss Minerva caught through the lush foliage glimpses of the iron fence and tall gates that fronted on Kalia Road. Dan opened the door for her, and she stepped inside. Like most apartments of its sort in the Islands, the living-room was walled on but three sides, the fourth was a vast expanse of wire screening. They crossed the polished floor and entered the big hall beyond. Near the front door a Hawaiian woman of uncertain age rose slowly from her chair. She was a huge, high-breasted, dignified specimen of that vanishing race.[8]

"Well, Kamaikui, I'm back," Miss Minerva smiled.

"I make you welcome," the woman said. She was only a servant, but she spoke with the gracious manner of a hostess.

"Same room you had when you first came over, Minerva," Dan Winterslip announced.[9] "Your luggage is there—and a bit of mail that came in on the boat this morning. I didn't trouble to send it up to Amos's. We dine when you're ready."

"I'll not keep you long," she answered, and hurried up the stairs.

Dan Winterslip strolled back to his living-room. He sat down in a rattan chair that had been made especially for him in Hong-Kong, and glanced complacently about at the many evidences of his prosperity. His butler entered, bearing a tray with cocktails.

"Two, Haku?" smiled Winterslip. "The lady is from Boston."[10]

"Yes-s," hissed Haku, and retired soundlessly.

In a moment Miss Minerva came again into the room. She carried a letter in her hand, and she was laughing.

"Dan, this is too absurd," she said.

"What is?"

"I may have told you that they are getting worried about me at home. Because I haven't been able to tear myself away from Honolulu, I mean. Well, they're sending a policeman for me."

"A policeman?" He lifted his bushy eyebrows.

"Yes, it amounts to that. It's not being done openly, of course. Grace writes that John Quincy has six weeks vacation from the banking house, and has decided to make the trip out here. 'It will give you some one to come home with, my dear,' says Grace. Isn't she subtle?"

"John Quincy Winterslip? That would be Grace's son."

Miss Minerva nodded. "You never met him, did you, Dan? Well, you will, shortly. And he certainly won't approve of you."

"Why not?" Dan Winterslip bristled.

"Because he's proper. He's a dear boy, but oh, so proper. This journey is going to be a great cross for him. He'll start disapproving as he passes Albany, and think of the long weary miles of disapproval he'll have to endure after that."

"Oh, I don't know. He's a Winterslip, isn't he?"

"He is. But the gypsy strain missed him completely. He's a Puritan."

"Poor boy." Dan Winterslip moved toward the tray on which stood the amber-colored drinks. "I suppose he'll stop with Roger in San Francisco. Write him there and tell him I want him to make this house his home while he's in Honolulu."

9. Presumably Dan is referring to her first visit, in the 1880s, when she stayed with Dan's father, Jedidiah Winterslip. Kamikui, who has an adult grandson, we will learn, must have been a servant in the house then, as a young woman in her twenties.

10. It's unclear what this remark is intended to convey. It sounds like Dan is criticizing his servant for bringing two drinks per person, when Haku should know that Minerva is from Boston and hence a conservative and relatively abstemious person who will only have one drink.

11. A series of public lectures sponsored by the Lowell Institute of Boston since 1839. Oliver Wendell Holmes wrote of the Institute, "When you have had said every enthusiastic thing that you may, you will not have half-filled the measure of its importance to Boston—New England—the country at large. No nobler or more helpful institution exists in America than Boston's Lowell Institute." In 1925, probably shortly after the events of this book, Alfred North Whitehead gave a widely published series of lectures for the Institute on "Science and the Modern World."

12. An archaic spelling of "papaya," also called pawpaw, the tropical plant *Carica papaya*, the fruit of which is soft and fragrant.

"That's kind of you, Dan."

"Not at all. I like youth around me—even the Puritan brand. Now that you're going to be apprehended and taken back to civilization, you'd better have one of these cocktails."

"Well," said his guest, "I'm about to exhibit what my brother used to call true Harvard indifference."

"What do you mean?" asked Winterslip.

"I don't mind if I do," twinkled Miss Minerva, lifting a cocktail glass.

Dan Winterslip beamed upon her. "You're a good sport, Minerva," he remarked, as he escorted her across the hall.

"When in Rome," she answered, "I make it a point not to do as the Bostonians do. I fear it would prove a rather thorny path to popularity."

"Precisely."

"Besides, I shall be back in Boston soon. Tramping about to art exhibits and Lowell Lectures,[11] and gradually congealing into senility."

But she was not in Boston now, she reflected, as she sat down at the gleaming table in the dining-room. Before her, properly iced, was a generous slice of papaia,[12] golden yellow and inviting. Somewhere beyond the foliage outside the screens, the ocean murmured restlessly. The dinner would be perfect, she knew, the Island beef dry and stringy, perhaps, but the fruits and the salad more than atoning.

"Do you expect Barbara soon?" she inquired presently.

Dan Winterslip's face lighted like the beach at sunrise. "Yes, Barbara has graduated. She'll be along any day now. Nice if she and your perfect nephew should hit on the same boat."

"Nice for John Quincy, at any rate," Miss Minerva replied. "We thought Barbara a lively, charming girl when she visited us in the East."

"She's all of that," he agreed proudly. His daughter was his dearest possession. "I tell you, I've missed her. I've been mighty lonesome."

Miss Minerva gave him a shrewd look. "Yes, I've heard rumors," she remarked, "about how lonesome you've been."

He flushed under his tan. "Amos, I suppose?"

"Oh, not only Amos. A great deal of talk, Dan. Really, at your age—"

"What do you mean, my age? I told you we're all young out here." He ate in silence for a moment. "You're a good sport—I said it and I meant it. You must understand that here in the Islands a man may behave a—a bit differently than he would in the Back Bay."

"At that," she smiled, "all men in the Back Bay are not to be trusted. I'm not presuming to rebuke you, Dan. But—for Barbara's sake—why not select as the object of your devotion a woman you could marry?"

"I could marry this one—if we're talking about the same woman."

"The one I refer to," Miss Minerva replied, "is known, rather widely, as the Widow of Waikiki."

"This place is a hotbed of gossip. Arlene Compton is perfectly respectable."

"A former chorus girl I believe."

"Not precisely. An actress—small parts—before she married Lieutenant Compton."

"And a self-made widow."

"Just what do you mean by that?" he flared. His gray eyes glittered.

"I understand that when her husband's aeroplane crashed on Diamond Head, it was because he preferred it that way. She had driven him to it."

"Lies, all lies!" Dan Winterslip cried. "Pardon me, Minerva, but you mustn't believe all you hear on the beach." He was silent for a moment. "What would you say if I told you I proposed to marry this woman?"

"I'm afraid I'd become rather bromidic," she answered gently, "and remind you that there's no fool like an old fool." He did not speak. "Forgive me, Dan. I'm your first cousin, but a distant relative for all that. It's really none of my business. I wouldn't care—but I like you. And I'm thinking of Barbara—"

He bowed his head. "I know," he said, "Barbara. Well, there's no need to get excited. I haven't said anything to Arlene about marriage. Not yet."

Miss Minerva smiled. "You know, as I get on in years," she remarked, "so many wise old saws begin to strike me as utter nonsense. Particularly that one I just quoted." He looked at her, his eyes friendly again. "This is the best avocado I ever tasted,"

13. "Kona" means leeward, or in the case of Hawaii, the western side of the island. In the winters, cyclones often form from westerly winds; the phrase "Kona weather," therefore, proverbially means windy, cold weather blown in from the west, elevating to heavy rain, hailstorms, and flash floods when severe.

14. Kalākaua (1836-1891), born David La'amea Kamananakapu Mahinulani Naloiaehuokalani Lumialani Kalākaua, was the last king of the Kingdom of Hawaii. His reign was a renaissance of art and culture and celebrated Hawaiian nationalism. Unfortunately, he surrounded himself with corrupt advisors, and Hawaii reached the point of threatened violent overthrow of the government. Fearing assassination, he signed the so-called Bayonet Constitution, essentially ceding total control over the monarch's powers to the legislature. On a trip to the United States—a trip that some believe was a mission to secure annexation by the United States—Kalākaua died. In the partly fictionalized account of his life written by novelist Eugene Burns in 1952, *The Last King of Paradise*, he is reported saying, "Tell my people I tried." It appears that his actual last words were, "Aue, he kanaka au, eia i loko o ke kukonukonu o ka ma'i!" or "Alas, I am a man who is seriously ill." Kalākaua was succeeded by his sister Liliuokalani.

King Kalākaua, ca. 1882

she added. "But tell me, Dan, are you sure the mango is a food? Seems more like a spring tonic to me."

By the time they finished dinner the topic of Arlene Compton was forgotten and Dan had completely regained his good nature. They had coffee on his veranda—or, in Island parlance, lanai—which opened off one end of the living-room. This was of generous size, screened on three sides and stretching far down on to the white beach. Outside the brief tropic dusk dimmed the bright colors of Waikiki.

"No breeze stirring," said Miss Minerva.

"The trades have died," Dan answered. He referred to the beneficent winds which—save at rare, uncomfortable intervals—blow across the Islands out of the cool northeast. "I'm afraid we're in for a stretch of Kona weather."[13]

"I hope not," Miss Minerva said.

"It saps the life right out of me nowadays," he told her, and sank into a chair. "That about being young, Minerva—it's a little bluff I'm fond of."

She smiled gently. "Even youth finds the Kona hard to endure," she comforted. "I remember when I was here before—in the 'eighties. I was only nineteen, but the memory of the sick wind lingers still."

"I missed you then, Minerva."

"Yes. You were off somewhere in the South Seas."

"But I heard about you when I came back. That you were tall and blonde and lovely, and nowhere near so prim as they feared you were going to be. A wonderful figure, they said—but you've got that yet."

She flushed, but smiled still. "Hush, Dan. We don't talk that way where I come from."

"The 'eighties," he sighed. "Hawaii was Hawaii then. Unspoiled, a land of opera bouffe, with old Kalakaua[14] sitting on his golden throne."

"I remember him," Miss Minerva said. "Grand parties at the palace. And the afternoons when he sat with his disreputable friends on the royal lanai, and the Royal Hawaiian Band played at his feet, and he haughtily tossed them royal pennies. It was such a colorful, naive spot then, Dan."

"It's been ruined," he complained sadly. "Too much aping of the mainland. Too much of your damned mechanical civilization—automobiles, phonographs, radios—bah! And yet—and yet, Minerva—away down underneath there are deep dark waters flowing still."

She nodded, and they sat for a moment busy with their memories. Presently Dan Winterslip snapped on a small reading light at his side. "I'll just glance at the evening paper, if you don't mind."[15]

"Oh, do," urged Miss Minerva.

She was glad of a moment without talk. For this, after all, was the time she loved Waikiki best. So brief, this tropic dusk, so quick the coming of the soft alluring night. The carpet of the waters, apple-green by day, crimson and gold at sunset, was a deep purple now. On top of that extinct volcano called Diamond Head a yellow eye was winking, as though to hint there might still be fire beneath. Three miles down, the harbor lights began to twinkle, and out toward the reef the lanterns of Japanese sampans glowed intermittently. Beyond, in the roadstead, loomed the battered hulk of an old brig slowly moving toward the channel entrance. Always, out there, a ship or two, in from the East with a cargo of spice or tea or ivory, or eastward bound with a load of tractor salesmen. Ships of all sorts, the spic and span liner and the rakish tramp, ships from Melbourne and Seattle, New York and Yokohama, Tahiti and Rio, any port on the seven seas. For this was Honolulu, the Crossroads of the Pacific—the glamorous crossroads where, they said, in time all paths crossed again. Miss Minerva sighed.

She was conscious of a quick movement on Dan's part. She turned and looked at him. He had laid the paper on his knee, and was staring straight ahead. That bluff about being young—no good now. For his face was old, old.

"Why, Dan—" she said.

"I—I'm wondering, Minerva," he began slowly. "Tell me again about that nephew of yours."

She was surprised, but hid it. "John Quincy?" she said. "He's just the usual thing, for Boston. Conventional. His whole life has been planned for him, from the cradle to the grave. So far he's walked the line. The inevitable preparatory school, Harvard, the proper clubs, the family banking house—even gone and got himself engaged to the very girl his mother would have picked for him. There have been times when I hoped he might kick over—the war—but no, he came back and got meekly into the old rut."

15.   This was likely the *Honolulu Star-Bulletin*, which had a "3:30 edition."

16.   The word has been changed to "Japanese" in later editions.

17.   The *President Tyler* is a fictitious ship. Although the American Presidents Line did eventually include a *President Tyler*, it was the old *President Hayes*, previously operated by the Dollar Steamship Co., and not recommissioned as the *President Tyler* until 1940. In 1923, around the time of the events related in *The House Without a Key*, only three carriers made regularly scheduled voyages to Honolulu: the Pacific Mail Steamship Company, which departed every two weeks from San Francisco, the Los Angeles Steamship Company, which departed every two weeks from Los Angeles, and the Matson Navigation Company, which operated weekly trips from San Francisco and trips from Seattle to Honolulu every thirty-five days.

18.   "Quickly," according to Lorrin Andrews's *A Dictionary of the Hawaiian Language* (1865) [hereinafter *Andrews*]. Reverend Andrews (1795–1868) arrived as part of a mission but soon distanced himself from the organization, becoming a teacher and later a judge. His dictionary was a monumental work. Although produced at a time when nearly everyone in Hawaii spoke Hawaiian as his or her primary language, it was the first of its kind.

19.   Dan's anxiety was a result of irregular mail service. Not until November 22–23, 1935, did a Pan American Airways Martin M-130 4-engine flying boat, *China Clipper*, fly from Alameda, California, to Pearl Harbor, carrying airmail. It should also be noted that telephone service to the mainland was not available to the public until late 1931. Mail to the mainland was carried by the regularly scheduled ships (see note 17)..

"Then he's reliable—steady?"

Miss Minerva smiled. "Dan, compared with that boy, Gibraltar wobbles occasionally."

"Discreet, I take it?"

"He invented discretion. That's what I'm telling you. I love him—but a little bit of recklessness now and then—However, I'm afraid it's too late now. John Quincy is nearly thirty."

Dan Winterslip was on his feet, his manner that of a man who had made an important decision. Beyond the bamboo curtain that hung in the door leading to the living-room a light appeared. "Haku!" Winterslip called. The Jap[16] servant came swiftly.

"Haku, tell the chauffeur—quick—the big car! I must get to the dock before the *President Tyler* sails for San Francisco.[17] Wikiwiki!"[18]

The servant disappeared into the living-room, and Winterslip followed. Somewhat puzzled, Miss Minerva sat for a moment, then rose and pushed aside the curtain. "Are you sailing, Dan?" she asked.

He was seated at his desk, writing hurriedly. "No, no—just a note—I must get it off on that boat—"[19]

There was an air of suppressed excitement about him. Miss Minerva stepped over the threshold into the living-room. In another moment Haku appeared with an announcement that was unnecessary, for the engine of an automobile was humming in the drive. Dan Winterslip took his hat from Haku. "Make yourself at home, Minerva—I'll be back shortly," he cried, and rushed out.

Some business matter, no doubt. Miss Minerva strolled aimlessly about the big airy room, pausing finally before the portrait of Jedediah Winterslip, the father of Dan and Amos, and her uncle. Dan had had it painted from a photograph after the old man's death; it was the work of an artist whose forte was reputed to be landscapes—oh, it must assuredly have been landscapes, Miss Minerva thought. But even so there was no mistaking the power and personality of this New Englander who had set up in Honolulu as a whaler. The only time she had seen him, in the 'eighties, he had been broken and old, mourning his lost fortune, which had gone with his ships in an Arctic disaster a short time before.

Well, Dan had brought the family back, Miss Minerva reflected. Won again that lost fortune and much more. There were queer rumors about his methods—but so there were about the methods of Bostonians who had never strayed from home. A charming fellow, whatever his past. Miss Minerva sat down at the grand piano and played a few old familiar bars—*The Beautiful Blue Danube*. Her thoughts went back to the 'eighties.

Dan Winterslip was thinking of the 'eighties too as his car sped townward along Kalakaua Avenue. But it was the present that concerned him when they reached the dock and he ran, panting a little, through a dim pier shed toward the gangplank of the *President Tyler*. He had no time to spare, the ship was on the point of sailing. Since it was a through boat from the Orient it left without the ceremonies that attend the departure of a liner plying only between Honolulu and the mainland. Even so, there were cries of "Aloha," some hearty and some tremulous, most of the travelers were bedecked with leis, and a confused little crowd milled about the foot of the plank.

Dan Winterslip pushed his way forward and ran up the sharp incline. As he reached the dock he encountered an old acquaintance, Hepworth, the second officer.

"You're the man I'm looking for," he cried.

"How are you, sir," Hepworth said. "I didn't see your name on the list."

"No, I'm not sailing. I'm here to ask a favor."

"Glad to oblige, Mr. Winterslip."

Winterslip thrust a letter into his hand. "You know my cousin Roger in 'Frisco. Please give him that—him and no one else—as soon after you land as you possibly can. I'm too late for the mail—and I prefer this way anyhow. I'll be mighty grateful."

"Don't mention it—you've been very kind to me and I'll be only too happy—I'm afraid you'll have to go ashore, sir. Just a minute, there—" He took Winterslip's arm and gently urged him back on to the plank. The instant Dan's feet touched the dock, the plank was drawn up behind him.

For a moment he stood, held by the fascination an Islander always feels at sight of a ship outward bound. Then he turned and walked slowly through the pier-shed. Ahead of him he caught a glimpse of a slender lithe figure which he recognized at once as that of Dick Kaohla, the grandson of Kamaikui. He quickened his pace and joined the boy.

"Hello, Dick," he said.

"Hello." The brown face was sullen, unfriendly.

"You haven't been to see me for a long time," Dan Winterslip said. "Everything all right?"

"Sure," replied Kaohla. "Sure it's all right." They reached the street, and the boy turned quickly away. "Good night," he muttered.

Dan Winterslip stood for a moment, thoughtfully looking after him. Then he got into the car. "No hurry now," he remarked to the chauffeur.

When he reappeared in his living-room, Miss Minerva glanced up from the book she was reading. "Were you in time, Dan?" she asked.

"Just made it," he told her.

"Good," she said, rising. "I'll take my book and go up-stairs. Pleasant dreams."

He waited until she reached the door before he spoke. "Ah—Minerva—don't trouble to write your nephew about stopping here."

"No, Dan?" she said, puzzled again.

"No. I've attended to the invitation myself. Good night."

"Oh—good night," she answered, and left him.

Alone in the great room, he paced restlessly back and forth over the polished floor. In a moment he went out on to the lanai, and found the newspaper he had been reading earlier in the evening. He brought it back to the living-room and tried to finish it, but something seemed to trouble him. His eyes kept straying—straying—with a sharp exclamation he tore one corner from the shipping page, savagely ripped the fragment to bits.

Again he got up and wandered about. He had intended paying a call down the beach, but that quiet presence in the room above—Boston in its more tolerant guise but Boston still—gave him pause.

He returned to the lanai. There, under a mosquito netting, was the cot where he preferred to sleep; his dressing-room was near at hand. However, it was too early for bed. He stepped through the door on to the beach. Unmistakable, the soft treacherous breath of the Kona fanned his cheek—the "sick wind" that would pile the breakers high along the coast and blight temporarily this Island paradise. There was no moon, the stars that usually seemed so friendly and so close were now obscured. The black water rolled in like a threat. He stood staring out into the dark—out there to the crossroads where paths always crossed again. If you gave them time—if you only gave them time—

As he turned back, his eyes went to the algaroba tree beyond the wire, and he saw the yellow flare of a match. His brother Amos. He had a sudden friendly feeling for Amos, he wanted to go over and talk to him, talk of the far days when they played together on this beach. No use, he knew. He sighed, and the screen door of the lanai banged behind him—the screen door without a lock in a land where locks are few.

Tired, he sat in the dark to think. His face was turned toward the curtain of bamboo between him and the living-room. On that curtain a shadow appeared, was motionless a second, then vanished. He caught his breath—again the shadow. "Who's there?" he called.

A huge brown arm was thrust through the bamboo. A friendly brown face was framed there.

"Your fruit I put on the table," said Kamaikui. "I go bed now."

"Of course. Go ahead. Good night."

The woman withdrew. Dan Winterslip was furious with himself. What was the matter with him, anyhow? He who had fought his way through unspeakable terrors in the early days—nervous—on edge—

"Getting old," he muttered. "No, by heaven—it's the Kona. That's it. The Kona. I'll be all right when the trades blow again."

When the trades blew again! He wondered. Here at the crossroads one could not be sure.

CHAPTER II

The High Hat

cars came in different configurations, but for someone with the wealth of the Winterslips, John Quincy would presumably have chosen a car with a private or semi-private drawing room. The trip would have been about a day to a day and a half from Boston to Chicago and another three to three and a half days from Chicago to San Francisco, probably via a luxury train like the Twentieth Century Limited or The Westerner (of the New York Central Railroad line) on the run to Chicago and the Pacific Limited or Continental Limited (of the Union Pacific Railroad Company) on the trip from Chicago to San Francisco. By 1926, the Chicago & Northwestern and Southern Pacific Railroads were advertising new trains that cut the time of the Chicago–San Francisco trip to sixty-three hours. John Quincy's "more than six days" either is an exaggeration or he chose some very slow routes.

John Quincy Winterslip walked aboard the ferry at Oakland feeling rather limp and weary. For more than six days he had been marooned on sleepers[20]—his pause at Chicago had been but a flitting from one train to another—and he was fed up. Seeing America first—that was what he had been doing. And what an appalling lot of it there was! He felt that for an eternity he had been staring at endless plains, dotted here and there by unesthetic houses the inmates of which had unquestionably never heard a symphony concert.

Ahead of him ambled a porter, bearing his two suitcases, his golf clubs and his hatbox. One of the man's hands was gone—chewed off, no doubt, in some amiable frontier scuffle. In its place he wore a steel hook. Well, no one could question the value of a steel hook to a man in the porter's profession. But how quaint—and western!

The boy indicated a spot by the rail on the forward deck, and the porter began to unload. Carefully selecting the man's good hand, John Quincy dropped into it a tip so generous as to result in a touching of hook to cap in a weird salute. The object of this attention sank down amid his elaborate trappings, removed the straw hat from his perspiring head, and tried to figure out just what had happened to him.

Three thousand miles from Beacon Street, and two thousand miles still to go! Why, he inquired sourly of his usually pleasant self, had he ever agreed to make this absurd expedition into heathen country? Here it was late June, Boston was at its best. Tennis at Longwood,[21] long mild evenings in a single shell on the Charles, week-ends and golf with Agatha Parker at Magnolia.[22] And if one must travel, there was Paris. He hadn't seen Paris in two years and had been rather planning a quick run over, when his mother had put this preposterous notion into his head.

Preposterous—it was all of that. Traveling five thousand miles just as a gentle hint to Aunt Minerva to return to her calm, well-ordered life behind purple window-panes on Beacon Street. And was there any chance that his strong-minded relative would take the hint? Not one in a thousand. Aunt Minerva was accustomed to do as she pleased—he had an uncomfortable, shocked recollection of one occasion when she had said she would do as she damn well pleased.

John Quincy wished he was back. He wished he was crossing Boston Common to his office on State Street, there to put out a new issue of bonds. He was not yet a member of the firm—that was an honor accorded only to Winterslips who were bald and a little stooped—but his heart was in his work. He put out a bond issue with loving apprehension, waiting for the verdict as a playwright waits behind the scenes on a first night. Would those First Mortgage Sixes go over big, or would they flop at his feet?

The hoarse boom of a ferry whistle recalled John Quincy to his present unbelievable location on the map. The boat began to move. He was dimly conscious of a young person of feminine gender who came and sat at his side. Away from the slip and out into the harbor the ferry carried John Quincy, and he suddenly sat up and took notice, for he was never blind to beauty, no matter where he encountered it.

And he was encountering beauty now. The morning air was keen and dry and bright. Spread out before him was that harbor which is like a tired navigator's dream come true. They passed Goat Island,[23] and he heard the faint echo of a bugle; he saw Tamalpais[24] lifting its proud head toward the sparkling sky, he turned, and there was San Francisco scattered blithely over its many hills.

The ferry plowed on, and John Quincy sat very still. A forest of masts and steam funnels—here was the water front that had supplied the atmosphere for those romantic tales that held him spellbound when he was a boy at school—a quiet young Winterslip

21. The Longwood Cricket Club in Chestnut Hill, Massachusetts, was founded in 1872 and put in a lawn tennis court in 1878. As cricket waned in popularity in the United States, the club's tennis clientele grew, and the first Davis Cup tournament was held at Longwood in 1900.

Longwood Cricket Club, Chester Hills, Massachusetts.

22. The Magnolia Golf Club, in the village of Magnolia, Gloucester, Massachusetts, was a popular summer outing for Boston golfers until it closed in the 1920s.

23. Originally Yerba Buena Island, in the San Francisco Bay between Oakland and San Francisco, it was renamed Goat Island in 1895, only to have its original name restored in 1931. Home to military strongholds through World War II, it is now a tourist site.

24. Mount Tamalpais, in Marin County north of San Francisco, though only 2,576 feet in elevation (after the top was graded for radar installations), is visible from San Francisco and the East Bay.

25.   Port cities in China, Japan, and Korea, so-called because they were made accessible to trade by treaties with the European powers.

whom the gypsy strain had missed. Now he could distinguish a bark from Antwerp, a great liner from the Orient, a five-masted schooner that was reminiscent of those supposedly forgotten stories. Ships from the Treaty Ports,[25] ships from cocoanut islands in southern seas. A picture as intriguing and colorful as a back drop in a theater—but far more real.

Suddenly John Quincy stood up. A puzzled look had come into his calm gray eyes. "I—I don't understand," he murmured.

He was startled by the sound of his own voice. He hadn't intended to speak aloud. In order not to appear too utterly silly, he looked around for some one to whom he might pretend he had addressed that remark. There was no one about—except the young person who was obviously feminine and therefore not to be informally accosted.

John Quincy looked down at her. Spanish or something like that, blue-black hair, dark eyes that were alight now with the amusement she was striving to hide, a delicate oval face tanned a deep brown. He looked again at the harbor—beauty all about the boat, and beauty on it. Much better than traveling on trains!

The girl looked up at John Quincy. She saw a big, broad-shouldered young man with a face as innocent as a child's. A bit of friendliness, she decided instantly, would not be misunderstood.

"I beg your pardon," she said.

"Oh—I—I'm sorry," he stammered. "I didn't mean—I spoke without intending—I said I didn't understand—"

"You didn't understand what?"

"A most amazing thing has happened," he continued. He sat down, and waved his hand toward the harbor. "I've been here before."

She looked perplexed. "Lots of people have," she admitted.

"But—you see—I mean—I've never been here before."

She moved away from him. "Lots of people haven't." She admitted that, too.

John Quincy took a deep breath. What was this discussion he had got into, anyhow? He had a quick impulse to lift his hat gallantly and walk away, letting the whole matter drop. But no, he came of a race that sees things through.

"I'm from Boston," he said.

"Oh," said the girl. That explained everything.

"And what I'm trying to make clear—although of course there's no reason why I should have dragged you into it—"

"None whatever," she smiled. "But go on."

"Until a few days ago I was never west of New York, never in my whole life, you understand. Been about New England a bit, and abroad a few times, but the West—"

"I know. It didn't interest you."

"I wouldn't say that," protested John Quincy with careful politeness. "But there was such a lot of it—exploring it seemed a hopeless undertaking. And then—the family thought I ought to go, you see—so I rode and rode on trains and was—you'll pardon me—a bit bored. Now—I come into this harbor, I look around me, and I get the oddest feeling. I feel that I've been here before."

The girl's face was sympathetic. "Other people have had that experience," she told him. "Choice souls, they are. You've been a long time coming, but you're home at last." She held out a slim brown hand. "Welcome to your city," she said.

John Quincy solemnly shook hands. "Oh, no," he corrected gently. "Boston's my city. I belong there, naturally. But this—this is familiar." He glanced northward at the low hills sheltering the Valley of the Moon, then back at San Francisco. "Yes, I seem to have known my way about here once. Astonishing, isn't it?"

"Perhaps—some of your ancestors—"

"That's true. My grandfather came out here when he was a young man. He went home again—but his brothers stayed. It's the son of one of them I'm going to visit in Honolulu."

"Oh—you're going on to Honolulu?"

"To-morrow morning. Have you ever been there?"

"Ye—es." Her dark eyes were serious. "See—there are the docks—that's where the East begins. The real East. And Telegraph Hill—" she pointed; no one in Boston ever points, but she was so lovely John Quincy overlooked it—"and Russian Hill and the Fairmont[26] on Nob Hill."

26. A famous hotel even in the early 1920s, it was under construction as the 1906 earthquake devastated San Francisco, and the interior was badly damaged; it opened in 1907 and has operated continuously since.

Fairmont Hotel, fifth story, looking down the corridor. "This view is typical of the upper stories and shows the distorted condition of the partitions and the warped surfaces of the floors, caused by the buckled columns in the lower stories. The man in the rear is standing in a depression, or low point, on the floor. The undulations of the floors can perhaps be best understood by following the intersection of the ceiling and the partition at the right-hand upper corner of the corridor. Only concrete floors and metal lath and plaster partitions would remain in position under such conditions." *The San Francisco Earthquake and Fire: A Brief History of the Disaster*, by Abraham Lincoln Artmann Himmelwright (New York: The Roebling Construction Co., 1906), p. 219.

Panoramic view of San Francisco after the 1906 earthquake.

"Life must be full of ups and downs," he ventured lightly. "Tell me about Honolulu. Sort of a wild place, I imagine?"

She laughed. "I'll let you discover for yourself how wild it is," she told him. "Practically all the leading families came originally from your beloved New England. 'Puritans with a touch of sun,' my father calls them. He's clever, my father," she added, in an odd childish tone that was wistful and at the same time challenging.

"I'm sure of it," said John Quincy heartily. They were approaching the Ferry Building and other passengers crowded about them. "I'd help you with that suitcase of yours, but I've got all this truck. If we could find a porter—"

"Don't bother," she answered. "I can manage very well." She was staring down at John Quincy's hat box. "I—I suppose there's a silk hat in there?" she inquired.

"Naturally," replied John Quincy.

She laughed—a rich, deep-throated laugh. John Quincy stiffened slightly. "Oh, forgive me," she cried. "But—a silk hat in Hawaii!"

John Quincy stood erect. The girl had laughed at a Winterslip. He filled his lungs with the air sweeping in from the open spaces, the broad open spaces where men are men. A weird reckless feeling came over him. He stooped, picked up the hat box, and tossed it calmly over the rail. It bobbed indignantly away. The crowd closed in, not wishing to miss any further exhibition of madness.

"That's that," said John Quincy quietly.

"Oh," gasped the girl, "you shouldn't have done it!"

And indeed, he shouldn't. The box was an expensive one, the gift of his admiring mother at Christmas. And the topper inside, worn in the gloaming along the water side of Beacon Street, had been known to add a touch of distinction even to that distinguished scene.

"Why not?" asked John Quincy. "The confounded thing's been a nuisance ever since I left home. And besides—we do look ridiculous at times, don't we? We easterners? A silk hat in the tropics! I might have been mistaken for a missionary." He began to gather up his luggage. "Shan't need a porter any more," he announced gaily. "I say—it was awfully kind of you—letting me talk to you like that."

"It was fun," she told him. "I hope you're going to like us out here. We're so eager to be liked, you know. It's almost pathetic."

"Well," smiled John Quincy, "I've met only one Californian to date. But—"

"Yes?"

"So far, so good!"

"Oh, thank you." She moved away.

"Please—just a moment," called John Quincy. "I hope—I mean, I wish—"

But the crowd surged between them. He saw her dark eyes smiling at him and then, irrevocably as the hat, she drifted from his sight.

"I say, it was awfully kind of you,
letting me talk to you like that."
"It was fun," she told him. "I hope you're going to like us out here."
From *The House Without a Key*, illustration by William Liepse
(*The Saturday Evening Post*, January 24, 1925)

CHAPTER III

Midnight on Russian Hill

27.   The Ferry Building, at the foot of Market Street, was the transportation terminus for San Francisco until the construction of the Bay Bridge and the Golden Gate Bridge in the 1930s. Before those bridges opened, allowing automobiles to travel to San Francisco, persons traveling there arrived by train or ferry from the East Bay.

The San Francisco Ferry Building, ca. 1925

A few moments later John Quincy stepped ashore in San Francisco. He had taken not more than three steps across the floor of the Ferry Building[27] when a dapper Japanese chauffeur pushed through the crowd and singling out the easterner with what seemed uncanny perspicacity, took complete charge of him.

Roger Winterslip, the Jap announced, was too busy to meet ferries, but had sent word that the boy was to go up to the house and after establishing himself comfortably there, join his host for lunch downtown. Gratified to feel solid ground once more beneath his feet, John Quincy followed the chauffeur to the street. San Francisco glittered under the morning sun.

"I always thought this was a foggy town," John Quincy said.

The Jap grinned. "Maybe fog do come, maybe it do not. Just now one time maybe it will not. Please." He held open the car door.

Through bright streets where life appeared to flow with a pleasant rhythm, they bowled along. Beside the curbs stood the colorful carts of the flower venders, unnecessarily painting the lily of existence. Weary traveler though he was, John Quincy took in with every breath a fresh supply of energy. New ambitions stirred within him; bigger, better bond issues than ever before seemed ridiculously easy of attainment.

Roger Winterslip had not been among those lured to suburban life down the peninsula; he resided in bachelor solitude on Nob

Hill. It was an ancient, battered house viewed from without, but within, John Quincy found, were all known comforts. A bent old Chinaman[28] showed him his room and his heart leaped up when he beheld, at last, a veritable bath.

At one o'clock he sought out the office where his relative carried on, with conspicuous success, his business as an engineer and builder. Roger proved a short florid man in his late fifties.

"Hello, son," he cried cordially. "How's Boston?"

"Every one is quite well," said John Quincy. "You're being extremely kind—"

"Nonsense. It's a pleasure to see you. Come along."

He took John Quincy to a famous club for lunch. In the grill he pointed out several well-known writers. The boy was not unduly impressed, for Longfellow, Whittier and Lowell were not among them. Nevertheless it was a pleasant place, the service perfect, the food of an excellence rare on the codfish coast.

"And what," asked Roger presently, "do you think of San Francisco?"

"I like it," John Quincy said simply.

"No? Do you really mean that?" Roger beamed. "Well, it's the sort of place that ought to appeal to a New Englander. It's had a history, brief, but believe me, my boy, one crowded hour of glorious life. It's sophisticated, knowing, subtle. Contrast it with other cities—for instance, take Los Angeles—"

He was off on a favorite topic and he talked well.

"Writers," he said at last, "are for ever comparing cities to women. San Francisco is the woman you don't tell the folks at home an awful lot about. Not that she wasn't perfectly proper—I don't mean that—but her stockings were just a little thinner and her laugh a little gayer—people might misunderstand. Besides, the memory is too precious to talk about. Hello."

A tall, lean, handsome Englishman was crossing the grill on his way out. "Cope! Cope, my dear fellow!" Roger sped after him and dragged him back. "I knew you at once," he was saying, "though it must be more than forty years since I last saw you."[29]

The Britisher dropped into a chair. He smiled a wry smile. "My dear old chap," he said. "Not so literal, if you don't mind."

"Rot!" protested Roger. "What do years matter? This is a young cousin of mine, John Quincy Winterslip, of Boston. Ah—er—just what is your title now?"

28. This too in later editions was changed to "Chinese man." Other changes include alterations of some of the pidgin expressions of various Japanese and Chinese persons, but those have not been noted.

29. We may deduce that Roger last saw Cope *before* Cope met Minerva. Minerva describes herself as "well over fifty," and she first visited Honolulu at the age of nineteen. If she were fifty-nine, making her nineteen forty years ago, she would have thought of herself as "almost sixty." And of course it is likely Cope would have mentioned to Roger "more than 40 years ago" that he had met Roger's cousin.

30. Fanning's Group is the northern portion of a group of islands collectively known as the Line Islands, in the central Pacific Ocean south of Hawaii, and today is referred to more commonly as the Northern Line Islands. The constituents are the tiny Kingman Reef and Palmyra Atoll (no residents), the 10-sq.-km. Teraina (formerly Washington Island), Tabuaeran (Fanning Island), about 33 sq. km., and Kiritimati (formerly Christmas Island), the largest of the group at about 390 sq. km. (less than a tenth the size of Rhode Island). The latter three islands have a current population of about 8,800 people. They were British colonies at the time of *The House Without a Key* but are now part of the Republic of Kiribati, which gained its independence in 1979 and has a total population of about 110,000.

31. Annexed to the British Empire in 1888, Fanning Island had been a cable station before World War I but was shelled and invaded by the Germans during the war. For a long time, it was a regular port of call for ships cruising from Hawaii (though this was to fulfill a legal requirement to stop at a foreign port rather than to take on coal); however, a change of the legal environment badly crippled Tabuaeran's economy, and it is only slowing regaining the volume of visits from cruise ships that had been a significant part of its post-colonial economy.

"Captain. I'm in the Admiralty."

"Really? Captain Arthur Temple Cope, John Quincy." Roger turned to the Englishman. "You were a midshipman, I believe, when we met in Honolulu. I was talking to Dan about you not a year ago—"

An expression of intense dislike crossed the captain's face. "Ah, yes, Dan. Alive and prospering, I presume?"

"Oh, yes," answered Roger.

"Isn't it damnable," remarked Cope, "how the wicked thrive?"

An uncomfortable silence fell. John Quincy was familiar with the frankness of Englishmen, but he was none the less annoyed by this open display of hostility toward his prospective host. After all, Dan's last name was Winterslip.

"Ah—er—have a cigarette," suggested Roger.

"Thank you—have one of mine," said Cope, taking out a silver case. "Virginia tobacco, though they are put up in Piccadilly. No? And you, sir—" He held the case before John Quincy, who refused a bit stiffly.

The captain nonchalantly lighted up. "I beg your pardon—what I said about your cousin," he began. "But really, you know—"

"No matter," said Roger cordially. "Tell me what you're doing here."

"On my way to Hawaii," explained the captain. "Sailing at three to-day on the Australian boat. A bit of a job for the Admiralty. From Honolulu I drop down to the Fanning Group[30]—a little flock of islands that belongs to us," he added with a fine paternal air.

"A possible coaling station," smiled Roger.[31]

"My dear fellow—the precise nature of my mission is, of course, a secret." Captain Cope looked suddenly at John Quincy. "By the way, I once knew a very charming girl from Boston. A relative of yours, no doubt."

"A—a girl," repeated John Quincy, puzzled.

"Minerva Winterslip."

"Why," said John Quincy, amazed, "you mean my Aunt Minerva."

The captain smiled. "She was no one's aunt in those days," he said. "Nothing auntish about her. But that was in Honolulu in the 'eighties—we'd put in there on the old wooden *Reliance*—the poor unlucky ship was limping home crippled from Samoa.[32] Your aunt was visiting at that port—there were dances at the palace, swimming parties—ah, me, to be young again."

"Minerva's in Honolulu now," Roger told him.

"No—really?"

"Yes. She's stopping with Dan."

"With Dan." The captain was silent for a moment. "Her husband—"

"Minerva never married," Roger explained.

"Amazing," said the captain. He blew a ring of smoke toward the paneled ceiling. "The more shame to the men of Boston. My time is hardly my own, but I shall hope to look in on her." He rose. "This was a bit of luck—meeting you again, old chap. I'm due aboard the boat very shortly—you understand, of course." He bowed to them both, and departed.

"Fine fellow," Roger said, staring after him. "Frank and British, but a splendid chap."

"I wasn't especially pleased," John Quincy admitted, "by the way he spoke of Cousin Dan."

Roger laughed. "Better get used to it," he advised. "Dan is not passionately beloved. He's climbed high, you know, and he's trampled down a few on his way up. By the way, he wants you to do an errand for him here in San Francisco."

"Me!" cried John Quincy. "An errand?"

"Yes. You ought to feel flattered. Dan doesn't trust everybody. However, it's something that must wait until dark."

"Until dark," repeated the puzzled young man from Boston.

"Precisely. In the meantime I propose to show you about town."

"But—you're busy. I couldn't think of taking you away—"

Roger laid his hand on John Quincy's shoulder. "My boy, no westerner is ever too busy to show a man from the East about his city. I've been looking forward to this chance for weeks. And since you insist on sailing to-morrow at ten, we must make the most of our time."

Roger proved an adept at making the most of one's time in San Francisco. After an exhilarating afternoon of motoring over the town and the surrounding country, he brought John Quincy back to the house at six, urging him to dress quickly for a dinner of which he apparently had great hopes.

32.   There were three ships named *Reliance* in the Royal Navy, but none fit this description, and none were in service in the 1880s. Cope may be misremembering the name of his ship: in 1889, there was a standoff in Samoa between American, German, and British forces all attempting to seize control of the port. The confrontation ended when a tropical storm sank all of the American and German ships. HMS *Calliope*, the lone British ship, narrowly avoided being damaged by the storm and, after returning to the Samoan port to try to effect rescue operations, sailed to Australia, not to Hawaii. Its captain received honors for what a historian termed "one of the most famous episodes of seamanship in the 19th century." *Calliope* was iron-hulled but was cased with timber, as were the wooden ships—this could be the source of Cope's "wooden" description. And of course the events were at least thirty-five years previous.

HMS *Calliope* in port

33. The Columbia Theatre was at 70 Eddy Street.

The boy's trunk was in his room, and as he put on a dinner coat he looked forward with lively anticipation to a bit of San Francisco night life in Roger's company. When he came down-stairs his host was waiting, a distinguished figure in his dinner clothes, and they set out blithely through the gathering dusk.

"Little place I want you to try," Roger explained as they sat down at a table in a restaurant that was outwardly of no special note. "Afterward we'll look in on that musical show at the Columbia."[33]

The restaurant more than justified Roger's hopes of it. John Quincy began to glow with a warm friendly feeling for all the world, particularly this city by the western gate. He did not think of himself as a stranger here. He wasn't a stranger, anyhow. The sensation he had first experienced in the harbor returned to him. He had been here before, he was treading old familiar ground. In far, forgotten, happy times he had known the life of this city's streets. Strange, but true. He spoke to Roger about it.

Roger smiled. "A Winterslip, after all," he said. "And they told me you were just a sort of—of Puritan survival. My father used to know that sensation you speak of, only he felt it whenever he entered a new town. Might be something in reincarnation, after all."

"Nonsense," said John Quincy.

"Probably. Just the blood of the roaming Winterslips in your veins." He leaned across the table. "How would you like to come to San Francisco to live?"

"Wha-what?" asked John Quincy, startled.

"I'm getting along in years, and I'm all alone. Lots of financial details in my office—take you in there and let you look after them. Make it worth your while."

"No, no, thank you," said John Quincy firmly. "I belong back east. Besides, I could never persuade Agatha to come out here."

"Agatha who?"

"Agatha Parker—the girl I'm engaged to—in a way. Been sort of understood between us for several years. No," he added, "I guess I'd better stay where I belong."

Roger Winterslip looked his disappointment. "Probably had," he admitted. "I fancy no girl with that name would follow you here. Though a girl worth having will follow her man anywhere—but no matter." He studied John Quincy keenly for a moment. "I must have been wrong about you, anyhow."

John Quincy felt a sudden resentment. "Just what do you mean by that?" he inquired.

"In the old days," Roger said, "Winterslips were the stuff of which pioneers are made. They didn't cling to the apron-strings of civilization. They got up some fine morning and nonchalantly strolled off beyond the horizon. They lived—but there, you're of another generation. You can't understand."

"Why can't I?" demanded John Quincy.

"Because the same old rut has evidently been good enough for you. You've never known a thrill. Or have you? Have you ever forgot to go to bed because of some utterly silly reason—because, for example, you were young and the moon was shining on a beach lapped by southern seas? Have you ever lied like a gentleman to protect a woman not worth the trouble? Ever made love to the wrong girl?"

"Of course not," said John Quincy stiffly.

"Ever run for your life through crooked streets in the rowdy quarter of a strange town? Ever fought with a ship's officer—the old-fashioned kind with fists like flying hams? Ever gone out on a man hunt and when you got your quarry cornered, leaped upon him with no weapon but your bare hands? Have you ever—"

"The type of person you describe," John Quincy cut in, "is hardly admirable."

"Probably not," Roger agreed. "And yet—those are incidents from my own past, my boy." He regarded John Quincy sadly. "Yes, I must have been wrong about you. A Puritan survival after all."

John Quincy deigned no reply. There was an odd light in the older man's eyes—was Roger secretly laughing at him? He appeared to be, and the boy resented it.

But he forgot to be resentful at the revue, which proved to be witty and gay, and Roger and he emerged from the theater at eleven the best of friends again. As they stepped into Roger's car, the older man gave the chauffeur an address on Russian Hill.

"Dan's San Francisco house," he explained, as he climbed in after John Quincy. "He comes over about two months each year, and keeps a place here. Got more money than I have."

Dan's San Francisco house? "Oh," said John Quincy, "the errand you mentioned?"

34. *Metrosideros polymorpha*, commonly known as ohia lehua, is a species of flowering evergreen tree commonly found in the Hawaiian Islands.

35. An ambiguously worded message, like "not at home"—they were unlikely to have worked out a cipher in advance.

Roger nodded. "Yes." He snapped on a light in the top of the limousine, and took an envelope from his pocket. "Read this letter. It was delivered to me two days ago by the Second Officer of the *President Tyler*."

John Quincy removed a sheet of note paper from the envelope. The message appeared to be rather hastily scrawled.

"Dear Roger," he read. "You can do me a great service—you and that discreet lad from Boston who is to stop over with you on his way out here. First of all, give John Quincy my regards and tell him that he must make my house his home while he is in the Islands. I'll be delighted to have him.

"About the errand. You have a key to my house on Russian Hill. Go up there—better go at night when the caretaker's not likely to be around. The lights are off, but you'll find candles in the pantry. In the store room on the top floor is an old brown trunk. Locked, probably—smash the lock if it is. In the lower section you'll find a battered strong box made of ohia wood[34] and bound with copper. Initials on it—T. M. B.

"Wrap it up and take it away. It's rather an armful, but you can manage it. Have John Quincy conceal it in his luggage and some dark night when the ship's about half-way over, I want him to take it on deck and quietly drop it overboard. Tell him to be sure nobody sees him. That's all. But send me a guarded cable[35] when you get the box, and tell him to send me a radio when the Pacific has it at last. I'll sleep better then.

"Not a word, Roger. Not a word to any one. You'll understand. Sometimes the dead past needs a bit of help in burying its dead.

"Your Cousin Dan."

Solemnly John Quincy handed the letter back into Roger's keeping. The older man thoughtfully tore it to bits and tossed them through the car window open beside him. "Well," said John Quincy. "Well—" A fitting comment eluded him.

"Simple enough," smiled Roger. "If we can help poor old Dan to sleep better as easily as that, we must do it, eh?"

"I—I suppose so," John Quincy agreed.

They had climbed Russian Hill, and were speeding along a deserted avenue lined by imposing mansions. Roger leaned forward. "Go on to the corner," he said to the chauffeur. "We can walk back," he explained to John Quincy. "Best not to leave the car before the house. Might excite suspicion."

Still John Quincy had no comment to make. They alighted at the corner and walked slowly back along the avenue. In front of a big stone house, Roger paused. He looked carefully in all directions, then ran with surprising speed up the steps. "Come on," he called softly.

John Quincy came. Roger unlocked the door and they stepped into a dark vestibule. Beyond that, darker still, was a huge hall, the dim suggestion of a grand staircase. Here and there an article of furniture, shrouded in white, stood like a ghost, marooned but patient. Roger took out a box of matches.

"Meant to bring a flashlight," he said, "but I clean forgot. Wait here—I'll hunt those candles in the pantry."

He went off into the dark. John Quincy took a few cautious steps. He was about to sit down on a chair—but it was like sitting on the lap of a ghost. He changed his mind, stood in the middle of the floor, waited. Quiet, deathly quiet. The black had swallowed Roger, with not so much as a gurgle.

After what seemed an age, Roger returned, bearing two lighted candles. One each, he explained. John Quincy took his, held it high. The flickering yellow flame accentuated the shadows, was really of small help.

Roger led the way up the grand staircase, then up a narrower flight. At the foot of still another flight, in a stuffy passage on the third floor, he halted.

"Here we are," he said. "This leads to the storage room under the roof. By gad, I'm getting too old for this sort of thing. I meant to bring a chisel to use on that lock. I know where the tools are—I'll be gone only a minute. You go on up and locate the trunk."

"All—all right," answered John Quincy.

Again Roger left him. John Quincy hesitated. Something about a deserted house at midnight to dismay the stoutest heart—but nonsense! He was a grown man. He smiled, and started up the narrow stair. High above his head the yellow light of the candle flickered on the brown rafters of the unfinished store room.

He reached the top of the stairs, and paused. Gloom, gloom everywhere. Odd how floor boards will creak even when no one is moving over them. One was creaking back of him now.

He was about to turn when a hand reached from behind and knocked the candle out of his grasp. It rolled on the floor, extinguished.

This was downright rude! "See here," cried John Quincy, "wh—who are you?"

A bit of moonlight struggled in through a far window, and suddenly between John Quincy and that distant light there loomed the determined figure of a man. Something told the boy he had better get ready, but where he came from one had a moment or two for preparation. He had none here. A fist shot out and found his face, and John Quincy Winterslip of Boston went down amid the rubbish of a San Francisco attic. He heard, for a second, the crash of planets in collision, and then the clatter of large feet on the stairs. After that, he was alone with the debris.

He got up, thoroughly angry, and began brushing off the dinner coat that had been his tailor's pride. Roger arrived. "Who was that?" he demanded breathlessly. "Somebody went down the back stairs to the kitchen. Who was it?"

"How should I know?" inquired John Quincy with pardonable peevishness. "He didn't introduce himself to me." His cheek was stinging; he put his handkerchief to it and noted in the light of Roger's candle that it was red when it came away. "He wore a ring," added John Quincy. "Damned bad taste!"

"Hit you, eh?" inquired Roger.

"I'll say he did."

"Look!" Roger cried. He pointed. "The trunk-lock smashed." He went over to investigate. "And the box is gone. Poor old Dan!"

John Quincy continued to brush himself off. Poor old Dan's plight gave him a vast pain, a pain which had nothing to do with his throbbing jaw. A fine nerve poor old Dan had to ask a complete stranger to offer his face for punishment in a dusty attic at midnight. What was it all about, anyhow?

"Look!" Roger cried. He pointed. "The trunk-lock smashed!" He went over to investigate. "And the box is gone!" From The House Without a Key, illustration by William Liepse (The Saturday Evening Post, January 24, 1925).

Roger continued his search. "No use," he announced. "The box is gone, that's plain. Come on, we'll go down-stairs and look about. There's your candle on the floor."

John Quincy picked up the candle and relighted it from Roger's flame. Silently they went below. The outer door of the kitchen stood open. "Left that way," said Roger. "And see"—he pointed to a window with a broken pane—"that's where he came in."

"How about the police?" suggested John Quincy.

Roger stared at him. "The police? I should say not! Where's your discretion, my boy? This is not a police matter. I'll have a new glass put in that window to-morrow. Come on—we might as well go home. We've failed."

The note of reproof in his voice angered John Quincy anew. They left the extinguished candles on a table in the hall, and returned to the street.

"Well, I'll have to cable Dan," Roger said, as they walked toward the corner. "I'm afraid he'll be terribly upset by this. It won't tend to endear you to him, either."

"I can struggle along," said John Quincy, "without his affection."

"If you could only have held that fellow till I came—"

"Look here," said John Quincy, "I was taken unawares. How could I know that I was going up against the heavyweight champion in that attic? He came at me out of the dark—and I'm not in condition—"

"No offense, my boy," Roger put in.

"I see my mistake," went on John Quincy. "I should have trained for this trip out here. A stiff course in a gymnasium. But don't worry. The next lad that makes a pass at me will find a different target. I'll do a daily three dozen and I'll take boxing lessons. From now on until I get home, I'll be expecting the worst."

Roger laughed. "That's a nasty cut on your cheek," he remarked. "We'd better stop at this drug store and have it dressed."

A solicitous drug clerk ministered to John Quincy with iodine, cotton and court plaster, and he reentered the limousine bearing honorably the scar of battle. The drive to Nob Hill was devoid of light chatter.

Just inside the door of Roger's house, a whirlwind in a gay gown descended upon them. "Barbara!" Roger said. "Where did you come from?"

"Hello, old dear," she cried, kissing him. "I motored up from Burlingame. Spending the night with you—I'm sailing on the *President Tyler* in the morning. Is this John Quincy?"

"Cousin John," smiled Roger. "He deserves a kiss, too. He's had a bad evening."

The girl moved swiftly toward the defenseless John Quincy. Again he was unprepared, and this time it was his other cheek that suffered, though not unpleasantly. "Just by way of welcome," Barbara laughed. She was blonde and slender. John Quincy thought he had never seen so much energy imprisoned in so slight a form. "I hear you're bound for the Islands?" she said.

"To-morrow," John Quincy answered. "On your boat."

"Splendid!" she cried. "When did you get in?"

"John Quincy came this morning," Roger told her.

"And he's had a bad evening?" the girl said. "How lucky I came along. Where are you taking us, Roger?"

John Quincy stared. Taking them? At this hour?

"I'll be getting along up-stairs," he ventured.

"Why, it's just after twelve," said Barbara. "Lots of places open. You dance, don't you? Let me show you San Francisco. Roger's a dear old thing—we'll let him pay the checks."

"Well—I—I—" stammered John Quincy. His cheek was throbbing and he thought longingly of that bed in the room upstairs. What a place, this West!

"Come along!" The girl was humming a gay little tune. All vivacity, all life. Rather pleasant sort at that. John Quincy took up his hat.

Roger's chauffeur had lingered a moment before the house to inspect his engine. When he saw them coming down the steps, he looked as though he rather wished he hadn't. But escape was impossible; he climbed to his place behind the wheel.

"Where to, Barbara?" Roger asked. "Tait's?"[36]

"Not Tait's," she answered. "I've just come from there."

"What! I thought you motored in from Burlingame?"[37]

"So I did—at five. I've traveled a bit since then. How about some chop-suey for this Boston boy?"

Good lord, John Quincy thought. Was there anything in the world he wanted less? No matter. Barbara took him among the Chinese.

Was there anything in the world he wanted less? No matter.
Barbara took him among the Chinese.
From *The House Without a Key*, illustration by William Liepse
(*The Saturday Evening Post*, January 24, 1925).

36. Tait's at the Beach had an office at 760 Market.

37. Burlingame is a suburb of San Francisco located on the San Francisco Peninsula; it was founded in 1908 and now is home to many of the affluent who work in Silicon Valley.

38.   Pete's Grill was at 893 Mission.

He didn't give a hang about the Chinese. Nor the Mexicans, whose restaurants interested the girl next. At the moment, he was unsympathetic toward Italy. And even toward France. But he struggled on the international round, affronting his digestion with queer dishes, and dancing thousands of miles with the slim Barbara in his arms. After scrambled eggs at a place called Pete's Fashion,[38] she consented to call it an evening.

As John Quincy staggered into Roger's house, the great clock in the hall was striking three. The girl was still alert and sparkling. John Quincy hastily concealed a yawn.

"All wrong to come home so early," she cried. "But we'll have a dance or two on the boat. By the way, I've been wanting to ask. What does it mean? The injured cheek?"

"Why—er—I—" John Quincy remarked. Over the girl's shoulder he saw Roger violently shaking his head. "Oh, that," said John Quincy, lightly touching the wound. "That's where the West begins. Good night. I've had a bully time." And at last he got up-stairs.

He stood for a moment at his bedroom window, gazing down at the torchlight procession of the streets through this amazing city. He was a little dazed. That soft warm presence close by his side in the car—pleasant, very pleasant. Remarkable girls out here. Different!

Beyond shone the harbor lights. That other girl—wonderful eyes she had. Just because she had laughed at him, his treasured hat box floated now forlorn on those dark waters. He yawned again. Better be careful. Mustn't be so easily influenced. No telling where it would end.

CHAPTER IV

A Friend of Tim's

It was another of those mornings on which the fog maybe did not come. Roger and his guests were in the limousine again; it seemed to John Quincy that they had left it only a few minutes before. So it must have seemed to the chauffeur too as, sleepy-eyed, he hurried them toward the water-front.

"By the way, John Quincy," Roger said, "you'll want to change your money before you go aboard."

John Quincy gathered his wandering thoughts. "Oh, yes, of course," he answered.

Roger smiled. "Just what sort of money would you like to change it for?" he inquired.

"Why—" began John Quincy. He stopped. "Why, I always thought—"

"Don't pay any attention to Roger," Barbara laughed. "He's spoofing you." She was fresh and blooming, a little matter like three A. M. made no difference to her. "Only about one person out of a thousand in this country knows that Hawaii is a part of the United States,[39] and the fact annoys us deeply over in the Islands. Dear old Roger was trying to get you in wrong with me by enrolling you among the nine hundred and ninety-nine."

"Almost did it, too," chuckled Roger.

39. On July 17, 1893, according to the so-called Blount Report, a report on affairs in Hawaii presented to President Cleveland in 1894, a committee of thirteen men, calling themselves a "Citizens' committee of safety," seized control of the Hawaiian government. The committee, chaired by Sanford B. Dole, included the following: "Mr. C. Bolte is of German origin, but a regularly naturalized citizen of the Hawaiian Islands. Mr. A. Brown is a Scotchman and has never been naturalized. Mr. W. O. Smith is a native of foreign origin and a subject of the Islands. Mr. Henry Waterhouse, originally from Tasmania, is a naturalized citizen of the islands. Mr. Theo. F. Lansing is a citizen of the United States, owing and claiming allegiance thereto. He has never been naturalized in this country. Mr. Ed. Suhr is a German subject. Mr. L. A. Thurston is a native-born subject of the Hawaiian Islands, of foreign origin. Mr. John Emmeluth is an American citizen. Mr. W. E. Castle is a Hawaiian

of foreign parentage. Mr. J. A. McCandless is a citizen of the United States—never having been naturalized here. Six are Hawaiians subjects; five are American citizens; one English, and one German. A majority are foreign subjects." The committee deposed the queen and established itself as the Provisional Government of Hawaii. The Blount Report remarks, "This is the first time American troops were ever landed on these islands at the instance of a committee of safety without notice to the existing government. It is to be observed that they claim to be a citizens' committee of safety and that they are not simply applicants for the protection of the property and lives of American citizens." President Cleveland demanded that the queen be restored. The Provisional Government refused, demanding instead that the United States annex Hawaii.

In July 1894 the Provisional Government called a constitutional convention, establishing the Republic of Hawaii. On August 12, 1898, President McKinley signed the Newland Resolution." approving annexation of Hawaii. The resolution read, in part: "Whereas, the Government of the Republic of Hawaii having, in due form, signified its consent, in the manner provided by its constitution, to cede absolutely and without reserve to the United States of America . . ." A committee was appointed to study the governance of Hawaii, and it was not until 1900 that Congress enacted the Hawaiian Organic Act, providing for the appointment (by the president) of a territorial governor. The first such was Sanford B. Dole; at the time of the events of *The House Without a Key*, Wallace R. Farrington held the post.

President Dole accepting the resolution of annexation of Hawaii from U.S. Minister Harold M. Sewall, August 12, 1898.

"Nonsense," said Barbara. "John Quincy is too intelligent. He's not like that congressman who wrote a letter to 'the American Consul at Honolulu'."[40]

"Did one of them do that?" smiled John Quincy.

"He certainly did. We almost gave up the struggle after that. Then there was the senator who came out on a junket, and began a speech with: 'When I get home to my country—' Some one in the audience shouted: 'You're there now, you big stiff!' It wasn't elegant, of course, but it expressed our feeling perfectly. Oh, we're touchy, John Quincy."

"Don't blame you a bit," he told her. "I'll be very careful what I say."

They had reached the Embarcadero, and the car halted before one of the piers. The chauffeur descended and began to gather up the baggage. Roger and John Quincy took a share of it, and they traversed the pier-shed to the gangplank.

"Get along to your office, Roger," Barbara said.

"No hurry," he answered. "I'll go aboard with you, of course."

Amid the confusion of the deck, a party of girls swept down on Barbara, pretty lively girls of the California brand. John Quincy learned with some regret that they were there only to see Barbara off. A big broad-shouldered man in white pushed his way through the crowd.

"Hello there!" he called to Barbara.

"Hello, Harry," she answered. "You know Roger, don't you? John Quincy, this is an old friend of mine, Harry Jennison."

Mr. Jennison was extremely good-looking, his face was deeply tanned by the Island sun, his hair blond and wavy, his gray eyes amused and cynical. Altogether, he was the type of man women look at twice and never forget; John Quincy felt himself at once supplanted in the eyes of Barbara's friends.

Jennison seized the boy's hand in a firm grip. "Sailing too, Mr. Winterslip?" he inquired. "That's good. Between us we ought to be able to keep this young woman entertained."

The shore call sounded, and the confusion increased. Along the deck came a little old lady, followed by a Chinese woman servant. They walked briskly, and the crowd gave way before them.

40. The story is apocryphal.

*"Between us we ought to be able to keep this young woman entertained,"
Jennison had said. Well, John Quincy reflected, his portion of the
entertainment promised to be small. From The House Without a Key,
illustration by William Liepse (The Saturday Evening Post, January 31, 1925).*

"Hello—this is luck," cried Roger. "Madame Maynard—just a
moment. I want you to meet a cousin of mine from Boston." He
introduced John Quincy. "I give him into your charge. Couldn't
find a better guide, philosopher and friend for him if I combed
the Islands."

The old lady glanced at John Quincy. Her black eyes snapped.
"Another Winterslip, eh?" she said. "Hawaii's all cluttered up
with 'em now. Well, the more the merrier. I know your aunt."

"Stick close to her, John Quincy," Roger admonished.

She shook her head. "I'm a million years old," she protested.
"The boys don't stick so close any more. They like 'em younger.
However, I'll keep my eye on him. My good eye. Well, Roger,
run over some time." And she moved away.

"A grand soul," said Roger, smiling after her. "You'll like her.
Old missionary family, and her word's law over there."

"Who's this Jennison?" asked John Quincy.

"Him?" Roger glanced over to where Mr. Jennison stood,
the center of an admiring feminine group. "Oh, he's Dan's
lawyer. One of the leading citizens of Honolulu, I believe. John
J. Adonis himself, isn't he?" An officer appeared, herding the
reluctant throng toward the gangplank. "I'll have to leave you,
John Quincy. A pleasant journey. When you come through on
your way home, give me a few more days to try to convince you
on my San Francisco offer."

John Quincy laughed. "You've been mighty kind."

"Not at all." Roger shook his hand warmly. "Take care of yourself over there. Hawaii's a little too much like Heaven to be altogether safe. So long, my boy, so long."

He moved away. John Quincy saw him kiss Barbara affectionately and with her friends join the slow procession ashore.

The young man from Boston stepped to the rail. Several hundred voices were calling admonitions, promises, farewells. With that holiday spirit so alien to John Quincy's experience, those ashore were throwing confetti. The streamers grew in number, making a tangle of color, a last frail bond with the land. The gangplank was taken up; clumsily the *President Tyler* began to draw away from the pier. On the topmost deck a band was playing—*Aloha-oe*, the sweetest, most melancholy song of good-by ever written. John Quincy was amazed to feel a lump rising in his throat.

The frail, gay-colored bond was breaking now. A thin veined hand at John Quincy's side waved a handkerchief. He turned to find Mrs. Maynard. There were tears on her cheeks.

"Silly old woman," she said. "Sailed away from this town a hundred and twenty-eight times. Actual count—I keep a diary. Cried every time. What about? I don't know."

The ship was well out in the harbor now. Barbara came along, Jennison trailing her. The girl's eyes were wet.

"An emotional lot, we Islanders," said the old lady. She put her arm about the girl's slim waist. "Here's another one of 'em. Living way off the way we do, any good-by at all—it saddens us." She and Barbara moved on down the deck.

Jennison stopped. His eyes were quite dry. "First trip out?" he inquired.

"Oh, yes," replied John Quincy.

"Hope you'll like us," Jennison said. "Not Massachusetts, of course, but we'll do our best to make you feel at home. It's a way we have with strangers."

"I'm sure I shall have a bully time," John Quincy remarked. But he felt somewhat depressed. Three thousand miles from Beacon Street—and moving on! He waved to some one he fancied might be Roger on the dock, and went to find his stateroom.

He learned that he was to share his cabin with two missionaries.[41] One was a tall, gloomy old man with a lemon-colored face—an honored veteran of the foreign field named Upton. The other was a ruddy-cheeked boy whose martyrdom was still before

41. Why was John Quincy not in a private stateroom? This would have been consistent with his use of "sleepers" for his rail travel. Perhaps he had not booked his voyage ahead of time and simply took whatever was available in order to expedite what he anticipated would be an unpleasant trip.

42.   The *Matsonia*, a liner of the Matson Navigation Company, was launched in 1913 and (with an interlude of military service carrying troops in World War I) continued to carry passengers for Matson until 1937, when she was sold to private interests. The ship was finally scrapped in 1957. Matson used the name for several other ships built after 1925.

SS *Matsonia* with troops, in 1919.

him. John Quincy suggested drawing lots for a choice of berths, but even this mild form of gambling appeared distasteful to those emissaries of the church.

"You boys take the berths," said Upton. "Leave me the couch. I don't sleep well anyhow." His tone was that of one who prefers to suffer.

John Quincy politely objected. After further discussion it was settled that he was to have the upper berth, the old man the lower, and the boy the couch. The Reverend Mr. Upton seemed disappointed. He had played the role of martyr so long he resented seeing any one else in the part.

The Pacific was behaving in a most unfriendly manner, tossing the great ship about as though it were a piece of driftwood. John Quincy decided to dispense with lunch, and spent the afternoon reading in his berth. By evening he felt better, and under the watchful and somewhat disapproving eyes of the missionaries, arrayed himself carefully for dinner.

His name being Winterslip, he had been invited to sit at the captain's table. He found Madame Maynard, serene and twinkling, at the captain's right, Barbara at his left, and Jennison at Barbara's side. It appeared that oddly enough there was an aristocracy of the Islands, and John Quincy, while he thought it quaint there should be such distinctions in an outpost like Hawaii, took his proper place as a matter of course.

Mrs. Maynard chatted brightly of her many trips over this route. Suddenly she turned to Barbara. "How does it happen, my dear," she asked, "that you're not on the college boat?"

"All booked up," Barbara explained.

"Nonsense," said the frank old lady. "*You* could have got on. But then"—she looked meaningly toward Jennison—"I presume this ship was not without its attractions."

The girl flushed slightly and made no reply.

"What," John Quincy inquired, "is the college boat?"

"So many children from Hawaii at school on the mainland," the old lady explained, "that every June around this time they practically fill a ship. We call it the college boat. This year it's the *Matsonia*.[42] She left San Francisco to-day at noon."

"I've got a lot of friends aboard her," Barbara said. "I do wish we could beat her in. Captain, what are the chances?"

"Well, that depends," replied the captain cautiously.

"She isn't due until Tuesday morning," Barbara persisted. "Wouldn't it be a lark if you could land us the night before? As a favor to me, Captain."[43]

"When you look at me like that," smiled the officer, "I can only say that I'll make a supreme effort. I'm just as eager as you to make port on Monday—it would mean I could get off to the Orient that much sooner."

"Then it's settled," Barbara beamed.

"It's settled that we'll try," he said. "Of course, if I speed up there's always the chance I may arrive off Honolulu after sundown, and be compelled to lay by until morning. That would be torture for you."

"I'll risk it," Barbara smiled. "Wouldn't dear old dad be pleased if I should burst upon his vision Monday evening?"

"My dear girl," the captain said gallantly, "any man would be pleased to have you burst upon his vision any time."

There was, John Quincy reflected, much in what the captain said. Up to that moment there had been little of the romantic in his relations with girls; he was accustomed to look upon them merely as tennis or golf opponents or a fourth at bridge. Barbara would demand a different classification. There was an enticing gleam in her blue eyes, a hint of the eternal feminine in everything she did or said, and John Quincy was no wooden man. He was glad that when he left the dinner table, she accompanied him.

They went on deck and stood by the rail. Night had fallen, there was no moon, and it seemed to John Quincy that the Pacific was the blackest, angriest ocean he had ever seen. He stood gazing at it gloomily.

"Homesick, John Quincy?" Barbara asked. One of his hands was resting on the rail. She laid her own upon it.

He nodded. "It's a funny thing. I've been abroad a lot, but I never felt like this. When the ship left port this morning, I nearly wept."

"It's not so very funny," she said gently. "This is an alien world you're entering now. Not Boston, John Quincy, nor any other old, civilized place. Not the kind of place where the mind rules. Out here it's the heart that charts our course. People you're fond of do the wildest, most unreasonable things, simply because their minds are sleeping and their hearts are beating fast. Just—just remember, please, John Quincy."

There was an odd note of wistfulness in her voice. Suddenly at their side appeared the white-clad figure of Harry Jennison.

43.   The *Matsonia* and other Matson line ships sailed weekly from San Francisco to Honolulu, and the voyage took five to six days, depending on weather. In 1927, Matson introduced the *SS Malolo*, the fastest ship on the line, which could post a top speed of 22 knots (about 25 mph) on the 2,400-mile trip. This is still a typical speed for a cruise ship, though the Cunard Line's *Queen Mary 2* boasts speeds in excess of 29 knots.

A passenger list for the SS *Matsonia*, 1925.

"Coming for a stroll, Barbara?" he inquired.

For a moment she did not reply. Then she nodded. "Yes," she said. And called over her shoulder as she went: "Cheer up, John Quincy."

He watched her go, reluctantly. She might have stayed to assuage his loneliness. But there she walked along the dim deck, close to Jennison's side.

After a time, he sought the smoking-room. It was deserted, but on one of the tables lay a copy of the *Boston Transcript*. Delighted, John Quincy pounced upon it, as Robinson Crusoe might have pounced on news from home.

The issue was ten days old, but no matter. He turned at once to the financial pages. There it was, like the face of a well-beloved friend, the record of one day's trading on the Stock Exchange. And up in one corner, the advertisement of his own banking house, offering an issue of preferred stock in a Berkshire cotton mill. He read eagerly, but with an odd detached feeling. He was gone, gone from that world, away out here on a black ocean bound for picture-book islands. Islands where, not so long ago, brown tribes had battled, brown kings ruled. There seemed no link with that world back home, those gay-colored streamers of confetti breaking so readily had been a symbol. He was adrift. What sort of port would claim him in the end?

New York Stock Exchange, ca. 1929.

He threw the paper down. The Reverend Mr. Upton entered the smoking-room.

"I left my newspaper here," he explained. "Ah—did you care to look at it?"

"Thank you, I have," John Quincy told him.

The old man picked it up in a great bony hand. "I always buy a *Transcript* when I get the chance," he said. "It carries me back. You know, I was born in Salem, over seventy years ago."

John Quincy stared at him. "You've been a long time out here?" he asked.

"More than fifty years in the foreign field," answered the old man. "I was one of the first to go to the South Seas. One of the first to carry the torch down there—and a dim torch it was, I'm afraid. Afterward I was transferred to China." John Quincy regarded him with a new interest. "By the way, sir," the missionary continued, "I once met another gentleman named Winterslip. Mr. Daniel Winterslip."

"Really?" said John Quincy. "He's a cousin of mine. I'm to visit him in Honolulu."

"Yes? I heard he had returned to Hawaii, and prospered. I met him just once—in the 'eighties, it was, on a lonely island in the Gilbert group.[44] It was—rather a turning point in his life, and I have never forgotten." John Quincy waited to hear more, but the old missionary moved away. "I'll go and enjoy my *Transcript*," he smiled. "The church news is very competently handled."

John Quincy rose and went aimlessly outside. A dreary scene, the swish of turbulent waters, dim figures aimless as himself, an occasional ship's officer hurrying by. His stateroom opened directly on the deck and he sank into a steamer chair just outside the door.

In the distance he saw his room steward, weaving his way in and out of the cabins under his care. The man was busy with his last duties for the night, refilling water carafes, laying out towels, putting things generally to rights.

"Evening, sir," he said as he entered John Quincy's room. Presently he came and stood in the door, the cabin light at his back. He was a small man with gold-rimmed eye-glasses and a fierce gray pompadour.

"Everything O.K., Mr. Winterslip?" he inquired.

"Yes, Bowker," smiled John Quincy. "Everything's fine."

44. The Gilbert Islands, halfway between Papua New Guinea and Hawaii, are a group of sixteen islands, sometimes known as the Kingsmill Group. The name "Gilbert" was first applied in 1820, and in 1916 they were incorporated into the British colony called the Gilbert and Elice Islands. Today they are all part of the Republic of Kiribati. See note 30. "Kiribati" is the native pronunciation of "Gilbert."

45. One of the finest hotels in Boston, it opened in 1846 on Washington Street. In 1889, *King's Hand-Book of Boston* noted that the Adams House was "one of the finest and best-equipped hotels in the city, of which its dining-rooms and café are . . . conspicuous features." It declined during Prohibition and closed in 1927.

Boston's Adams House in 1906

46. The Arch Inn Café on Summer Street was a regular watering-hole of the Boston press in the early twentieth century.

47. The Tremont Theatre was a playhouse at 179 Tremont Street. It opened in 1889 and was demolished in 1983. "Tim's place" is untraceable.

The Tremont Theatre, Boston, Massachusetts, 1907

"That's good," said Bowker. He switched off the cabin light and stepped out on to the deck. "I aim to take particular care of you, sir. Saw your home town on the sailing list. I'm an old Boston man myself."

"Is that so?" said John Quincy cordially. Evidently the Pacific was a Boston suburb.

"Not born there, I don't mean," the man went on. "But a newspaper man there for ten years. It was just after I left the University."

John Quincy stared through the dark. "Harvard?" he asked.

"Dublin," said the steward. "Yes, sir—" He laughed an embarrassed little laugh. "You might not think it now, but the University of Dublin, Class of 1901. And after that, for ten years, working in Boston on the *Gazette*—reporting, copy desk, managing editor for a time. Maybe I bumped into you there—at the Adams House[45] bar, say, on a night before a football game."

"Quite possible," admitted John Quincy. "One bumped into so many people on such occasions."

"Don't I know it?" Mr. Bowker leaned on the rail, in reminiscent mood. "Great times, sir. Those were the good old days when a newspaper man who wasn't tanked up was a reproach to a grand profession. The *Gazette* was edited mostly from a place called the Arch Inn.[46] We'd bring our copy to the city editor there—he had a regular table—a bit sloppy on top, but his desk. If we had a good story, maybe he'd stand us a cocktail."

John Quincy laughed.

"Happy days," continued the Dublin graduate, with a sigh. "I knew every bartender in Boston well enough to borrow money. Were you ever in that place in the alley back of the Tremont Theater—?"[47]

"Tim's place," suggested John Quincy, recalling an incident of college days.

"Yeah, bo. Now you're talking. I wonder what became of Tim. Say, and there was that place on Boylston—but they're all gone now, of course. An old pal I met in 'Frisco was telling me it would break your heart to see the cobwebs on the mirrors back in Beantown. Gone to the devil, just like my profession. The newspapers go on consolidating, doubling up, combining the best features of both, and an army of good men go on the town. Good men and true, moaning about the vanished days and maybe landing in jobs like this one of mine." He was silent for a moment. "Well, sir, anything I can do for you—as a mutual friend of Tim's—"

"As a friend of Tim's," smiled John Quincy, "I'll not hesitate to mention it."

Sadly Bowker went on down the deck. John Quincy sat lonely again. A couple passed, walking close, talking in low tones. He recognized Jennison and his cousin. "Between us we ought to be able to keep this young woman entertained," Jennison had said. Well, John Quincy reflected, his portion of the entertainment promised to be small.

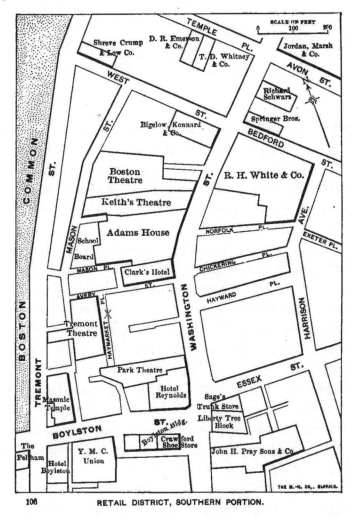

Approximate location of Tim's, behind Tremont Theatre, Boston.

CHAPTER V

The Blood of the Winterslips

The days that followed proved that he was right. He seldom had a moment alone with Barbara; when he did, Jennison seemed always to be hovering near by, and he did not long delay making the group a threesome. At first John Quincy resented this, but gradually he began to feel that it didn't matter.

Nothing appeared to matter any more. A great calm had settled over the waters and over John Quincy's soul. The Pacific was one vast sheet of glass, growing a deeper blue with every passing hour. They seemed to be floating in space in a world where nothing ever happened, nothing could happen. Quiet restful days gave way to long brilliant nights. A little walk, a little talk, and that was life.

Sometimes John Quincy chatted with Madame Maynard on the deck. She who had known the Islands so many years had fascinating tales to tell, tales of the monarchy and the missionaries. The boy liked her immensely, she was a New Englander at heart despite her glamourous lifetime in Hawaii.

Bowker, too, he found excellent company. The steward was that rarity even among college graduates, an educated man; there was no topic upon which he could not discourse at length and brilliantly. In John Quincy's steamer trunk were a number of huge imposing volumes—books he had been meaning to tackle long ago, but it was Bowker who read them, not John Quincy.

As the days slipped by, the blue of the water deepened to ultra-marine, the air grew heavier and warmer. Underfoot throbbed the engines that were doing their best for Barbara and an early landing. The captain was optimistic, he predicted they would make port late Monday afternoon. But Sunday night a fierce sudden storm swept down upon them, and lashed the ship with a wet fury until dawn. When the captain appeared at luncheon Monday noon, worn by a night on the bridge, he shook his head.

"We've lost our bet, Miss Barbara," he said. "I can't possibly arrive off Honolulu before midnight."

Barbara frowned. "But ships sail at any hour," she reminded him. "I don't see why—if we sent radios ahead—"

"No use," he told her. "The Quarantine people keep early hours. No, I'll have to lay by near the channel entrance until official sunrise—about six. We'll get in ahead of the *Matsonia* in the morning. That's the best I can offer you."

"You're a dear, anyhow," Barbara smiled. "That old storm wasn't your fault. We'll drown our sorrow to-night with one last glorious dance—a costume party." She turned to Jennison. "I've got the loveliest fancy dress—Marie Antoinette—I wore it at college. What do you say, Harry?"

"Fine!" Jennison answered. "We can all dig up some sort of costume. Let's go."

Barbara hurried off to spread the news. After dinner that evening she appeared, a blonde vision straight from the French Court, avid for dancing. Jennison had rigged up an impromptu pirate dress, and was a striking figure. Most of the other passengers had donned weird outfits; on the Pacific boats a fancy dress party is warmly welcomed and amusingly carried out.

John Quincy took small part in the gaiety, for he still suffered from New England inhibitions. At a little past eleven he drifted into the main saloon and found Madame Maynard seated there alone.

"Hello," she said. "Come to keep me company? I've sworn not to go to bed until I see the light on Diamond Head."

"I'm with you," John Quincy smiled.

"But you ought to be dancing, boy. And you're not in costume."

"No," admitted John Quincy. He paused, seeking an explanation. "A—a fellow can't make a fool of himself in front of a lot of strangers."

48. Oahu, the third-largest of the Hawaiian islands, is indeed the home of Honolulu, but the city is situated on the southwest corner of the island—San Francisco is far to the north (and east) of the island. Makapuu Point is on the easternmost point of the island.

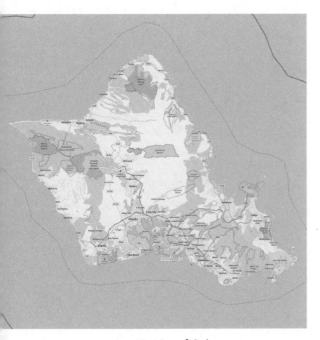

Map of Oahu

49. Rounding the eastern-most point of Oahu, Koko Head is the headland on the southeastern corner of the island—a ship would pass by it to get to Honolulu.

"I understand," nodded the old lady. "It's a fine delicacy, too. But rather rare, particularly out this way."

Barbara entered, flushed and vibrant. "Harry's gone to get me a drink," she panted. She sat down beside Mrs. Maynard. "I've been looking for you, my dear. You know, you haven't read my palm since I was a child. She's simply wonderful—" this to John Quincy. "Can tell you the most amazing things."

Mrs. Maynard vehemently shook her head. "I don't read 'em any more," she said. "Gave it up. As I've grown older, I've come to understand how foolish it is to peer into the future. To-day—that's enough for me. That's all I care to think about."

"Oh, please," the girl pouted.

The old woman took Barbara's slim hand in hers, and studied the palm for a moment. John Quincy thought he saw a shadow cross her face. Again she shook her head.

"*Carpe diem*," she said. "Which my nephew once translated as 'grab the day.' Dance and be happy to-night, and let's not try to look behind the curtain. It doesn't pay, my dear. Take an old woman's word for that."

Harry Jennison appeared in the door. "Oh, here you are," he said. "I've got your drink waiting in the smoking-room."

"I'm coming," the girl said, and went. The old woman stared after her.

"Poor Barbara," she murmured. "Her mother's life was none too happy, either—"

"You saw something in her hand—" John Quincy suggested.

"No matter," the old lady snapped. "There's trouble waiting for us all, if we look far enough ahead. Now, let's go on deck. It's getting on toward midnight."

She led him out to the starboard rail. A solitary light, like a star, gleamed in the distance. Land, land at last. "Diamond Head?" John Quincy asked.

"No," she said. "That's the beacon on Makapuu Point.[48] We shall have to round Koko Head[49] before we sight Honolulu." She stood for a moment by the rail, one frail hand resting upon it. "But that's Oahu," she said gently. "That's home. A sweet land, boy. Too sweet, I often think. I hope you'll like it."

"I'm sure I shall," replied John Quincy gallantly.

"Let's sit down here." They found deck chairs. "Yes, a dear land," she went on. "But we're all sorts, in Hawaii—just as it is the whole world over—honest folks and rascals. From the four corners of the globe men come to us—often because they were no longer welcome at home. We offer them a paradise, and some repay us by becoming good citizens, while others rot away. I often think it will take a lot of stamina to make good in Heaven—and Hawaii is the same."

The tall emaciated figure of the Reverend Mr. Upton appeared before them. He bowed. "Good evening, Madame. You're nearly home."

"Yes," she said. "Glad of it, too."

He turned to John Quincy. "You'll be seeing Dan Winterslip in the morning, young man."

"I expect I shall," John Quincy replied.

"Just ask him if he recalls that day on Apiang Island in the 'eighties. The Reverend Frank Upton."

"Of course," replied John Quincy. "But you haven't told me much about it, you know."

"No, I haven't." The missionary dropped into a chair. "I don't like to reveal any secrets about a man's past," he said. "However, I understand that the story of Dan Winterslip's early life has always been known in Honolulu." He glanced toward Madame Maynard.

"Dan was no saint," she remarked. "We all know that."

He crossed his thin legs. "As a matter of fact, I'm very proud of my meeting with Dan Winterslip," he went on. "I feel that in my humble way I persuaded him to change his course—for the better."

"Humph," said the old lady. She was dubious, evidently.

John Quincy was not altogether pleased at the turn the conversation had taken. He did not care to have the name of a Winterslip thus bandied about. But to his annoyance, the Reverend Mr. Upton was continuing.

"It was in the 'eighties, as I told you," said the missionary. "I had a lonely station on Apiang, in the Gilbert group.[50] One morning a brig anchored just beyond the reef, and a boat came ashore. Of course, I joined the procession of natives down to the beach to meet it. I saw few enough men of my own race.

"There was a ruffianly crew aboard, in charge of a dapper, rather handsome young white man. And I saw, even before they beached her, midway in the boat, a long pine box.

"The white man introduced himself. He said he was First Officer Winterslip, of the brig *Maid of Shiloh*. And when he

50. Apiang (properly, Apaiang or Abaiang) was formerly Charlotte Island and is commonly called Abaiang today. The first contact of the Micronesian natives with Europeans took place in 1606.

51. "Lucilla, Maid of Shiloh" was a popular song written in 1864, and told a tale of the Civil War—there is no record of a ship bearing that name, nor is the name Tom Brade that of a real person. However, there were numerous "callous brutes" working the South Seas trade, some of whom were Americans. The most notorious of the blackbirders was the American-born William Henry "Bully" Hayes, who died in 1877. A great deal has been written about Hayes, by James A. Michener and others. See especially "Bully Hayes, South Sea Buccaneer," "Louis Becke, Adventurer and Writer" in *Rascals in Paradise,* by James A. Michener and A. Grove Day [London: Secker & Warburg 1957]. While it is very difficult to separate the legends from the truth, it appears clear that, in the words of Michener and Day, he was "a cheap swindler, a bully, a minor confidence man, a thief, a ready bigamist."

William Henry "Bully" Hayes, 1863

52. "Blackbirding" was a scourge of the Pacific islands in the 1860s and 1870s. Blackbirders resorted regularly to trickery (sometimes posing as missionaries) and violence to coerce islanders into virtual slavery. The British Navy, though active in the region, was unable to suppress the activity. The conscripts were often taken as far away as Peru to work, though many populated plantations in Fiji, Samoa, and Queensland, Australia.

mentioned the name of the ship, of course I knew at once. Knew her unsavory trade and history. He hurried on to say that their captain had died the day before, and they had brought him ashore to bury him on land. It had been the man's last wish.

"Well." The Reverend Mr. Upton stared at the distant shore line of Oahu. "I looked over at that rough pine box—four Malay sailors were carrying it ashore. 'So Tom Brade's in there,' I said. Young Winterslip nodded. 'He's in there, right enough,' he answered. And I knew I was looking on at the final scene in the career of a famous character of the South Seas, a callous brute who knew no law, a pirate and adventurer, the master of the notorious *Maid of Shiloh.* Tom Brade, the blackbirder."[51]

"Blackbirder?" queried John Quincy.

The missionary smiled. "Ah, yes—you come from Boston. A blackbirder, my boy, is a shipping-master who furnishes contract labor to the plantations at so much a head.[52] It's pretty well wiped out now, but in the 'eighties! A horrible business—the curse of God was on it. Sometimes the laborers came willingly. Sometimes. But mostly they came at the point of a knife or the muzzle of a gun. A bloody, brutal business.

"But there on that bright morning under the palm I consigned to God the soul of a man who had so much to answer for." From *The House Without a Key,* illustration by William Liepse (*The Saturday Evening Post,* January 31, 1925).

"Winterslip and his men went up the beach and began to dig a grave under a cocoanut palm. I followed. I offered to say a prayer.

Winterslip laughed—not much use, he said. But there on that bright morning under the palm I consigned to God the soul of a man who had so much to answer for. Winterslip agreed to come to my house for lunch. He told me that save for a recruiting agent who had remained aboard the brig, he was now the only white man on the ship.

"During lunch, I talked to him. He was so young—I discovered this was his first trip. 'It's no trade for you,' I told him. And after a time, he agreed with me. He said he had two hundred blacks under the hatches that he must deliver to a plantation over in the Kingsmill group, and that after he'd done that, he was through. 'I'll take the *Maid* back to Sydney, Dominie,' he promised, 'and turn her over. Then I'm pau.[53] I'm going home to Honolulu.'"

The Reverend Mr. Upton rose slowly. "I learned later that he kept his word," he finished. "Yes, Dan Winterslip went home, and the South Seas saw him no more. I've always been a little proud of my part in that decision. I've had few rewards. It's not everywhere that the missionaries have prospered in a worldly way—as they did in Hawaii." He glanced at Madame Maynard. "But I've had satisfactions. And one of them arose from that meeting on the shore of Apiang. It's long past my bed hour—I must say good night."

He moved away. John Quincy sat turning this horror over and over in his mind. A Winterslip in the blackbirding business! That was pretty. He wished he was back on Beacon Street.

"Sweet little dig for me," the old lady was muttering indignantly. "That about the missionaries in Hawaii.[54] And he needn't be so cocky. If Dan Winterslip dropped blackbirding, it was only because he'd found something more profitable, I fancy." She stood up suddenly. "At last," she said.

John Quincy rose and stood beside her. Far away a faint yellow eye was winking. For a moment the old lady did not speak.

"Well, that's that," she said finally, in a low voice. "I've seen Diamond Head again. Good night, my boy."

"Good night," John Quincy answered.

He stood alone by the rail. The pace of the *President Tyler* was slowing perceptibly. The moon came from behind a cloud, crept back again. A sort of unholy calm was settling over the hot, airless, deep blue world. The boy felt a strange restlessness in his heart.

53.   *Andrews* translates "pau" as "to be spent; to be finished or completed."

54.   The implication here is that Mrs. Maynard came over as a missionary (or a missionary's wife) and prospered in Hawaii.

55. Bowker refers to American writer and historian James Truslow Adams's *Revolutionary New England, 1691-1776*, first published in 1923. Bowker has borrowed books that John Quincy acquired "long ago," but here, the book cannot be more than twelve to eighteen months old. In light of the "month" references elsewhere, the reference is helpful in confirming that the events of *The House Without a Key* took place in June 1924.

56. Properly *okolehao*, Hawaiian "moonshine," literally means "iron pots," in which the brew was distilled. Its ingredients—as with all "homemade" alcoholic beverages—varied, including rice, the root of the ti plant, sugar cane, and other vegetables. Its alcohol content was as high as 65 percent (130 proof), depending on the maker's tastes.

He ascended to the boat deck, seeking a breath of air. There, in a secluded spot, he came upon Barbara and Jennison—and stopped, shocked. His cousin was in the man's arms, and their bizarre costumes added a weird touch to the scene. They did not see John Quincy, for in their world at that moment there were only two. Their lips were crushed together, fiercely—

John Quincy fled. Good lord! He had kissed a girl or two himself, but it had been nothing like that.

He went to the rail outside his stateroom. Well, what of it? Barbara was nothing to him; a cousin, yes, but one who seemed to belong to an alien race. He had sensed that she was in love with Jennison; this was no surprise. Why did he feel that frustrated pang deep in his heart? He was engaged to Agatha Parker.

He gripped the rail, and sought to see again Agatha's aristocratic face. But it was blurred, indistinct. All Boston was blurred in his memory. The blood of the roaming Winterslips, the blood that led on to blackbirding and hot breathless kisses in the tropic night—was it flowing in his veins too? Oh, lord—he should have stayed at home where he belonged.

Bowker, the steward, came along. "Well, here we are," he said. "We'll anchor in twelve fathoms and wait for the pilot and the doctor in the morning. I heard they'd been having Kona weather out this way, but I imagine this is the tail end of it. There'll be a moon shortly, and by dawn the old trades will be on the job again, God bless them."

John Quincy did not speak. "I've returned all your books, sir," the steward went on, "except that one by Adams on *Revolutionary New England*.[55] It's a mighty interesting work. I intend to finish it to-night, so I can give it to you before you go ashore."

"Oh, that's all right," John Quincy said. He pointed to dim harbor lights in the distance. "Honolulu's over there, I take it."

"Yeah—several miles away. A dead town, sir. They roll up the sidewalks at nine. And let me give you a tip. Keep away from the okolehau."[56]

"The what?" asked John Quincy.

"The okolehau. A drink they sell out here."

"What's it made of?"

"There," said Bowker, "you have the plot for a big mystery story. What *is* it made of? Judging by the smell, of nothing very lovely. A few gulps, and you hit the ceiling of eternity. But oh, boy—when you drop! Keep off it, sir. I'm speaking as one who knows."

"I'll keep off it," John Quincy promised.

Bowker disappeared. John Quincy remained by the rail, that restless feeling growing momentarily. The moon was hidden still, the ship crept along through the muggy darkness. He peered across the black waters toward the strange land that awaited him.

Somewhere over there, Dan Winterslip waited for him too. Dan Winterslip, blood relative of the Boston Winterslips, and ex-blackbirder. For the first time, the boy wished he had struck first in that dark attic in San Francisco, wished he had got that strong box and cast it overboard in the night. Who could say what new scandal, what fresh blot on the honored name of Winterslip, might have been averted had he been quicker with his fists?

As John Quincy turned and entered his cabin, he made a firm resolution. He would linger but briefly at this, his journey's end. A few days to get his breath, perhaps, and then he would set out again for Boston. And Aunt Minerva would go with him, whether she wanted to or not.

CHAPTER VI

Beyond the Bamboo Curtain

57. *Alyxia oliviformis*, the traditional lei plant of Hawaii, with small yellowish flowers and fragrant leaves.

Had John Quincy been able to see his Aunt Minerva at that moment, he would not have been so sure that he could persuade her to fall in with his plans. He would, indeed, have been profoundly shocked at the picture presented by his supposedly staid and dignified relative.

For Miss Minerva was sitting on a grass mat in a fragrant garden in the Hawaiian quarter of Honolulu. Pale golden Chinese lanterns, inscribed with scarlet letters, hung above her head. Her neck was garlanded with ropes of buff ginger blossoms twined with maile.[57] The sleepy, sensuous music of ukulele and steel guitar rose on the midnight air and before her, in a cleared space under the date palms, Hawaiian boys and girls were performing a dance she would not be able to describe in great detail when she got back to Beacon Street.

Miss Minerva was, in her quiet way, very happy. One of the ambitions of her life had been realized, and she was present at a luau, or native Hawaiian feast. Few white people are privileged to attend this intimate ceremony, but Honolulu friends had been invited on this occasion, and had asked her to go with them. At first she had thought she must refuse, for Dan was expecting Barbara and John Quincy on Monday afternoon. When on Monday evening he had informed her that the *President Tyler* would not land its passengers until the next day, she had hastened to the telephone and asked to reconsider her refusal.

Telephone advertisement ca. 1925

And she was glad she had. Before her, on another mat, lay the remnants of a dinner unique in her experience. Dan had called her a good sport, and she had this evening proved him to be correct. Without a qualm she had faced the queer food wrapped in brown bundles, she had tasted everything, poi served in individual calabashes, chicken stewed in cocoanut milk, squid and shrimps, limu, or sea-weed, even raw fish. She would dream to-night!

Now the feasting had given way to the dance. The moonlight was tracing lacy patterns on the lawn, the plaintive wail of the music rose ever louder, the Hawaiian young people, bashful at first in the presence of strangers, were bashful no longer. Miss Minerva closed her eyes and leaned back against the trunk of a tall palm. Even in Hawaiian love songs there is a note of hopeless melancholy; it touched her emotions as no symphony ever could. A curtain was lifted and she was looking into the past, the primitive, barbaric past of these Islands in the days before the white men came.

A long, heart-breaking crescendo, and the music stopped, the swaying bodies of the dancers were momentarily still. It seemed to Miss Minerva's friends an opportune moment to depart. They entered the house and in the stuffy little parlor, took leave of

58. In which sat, among other governmental agencies, the Supreme Court of the Territory of Hawaii and the Hawaii Circuit Court (1st Circuit).

59. Not a surprise—the running time of *Parsifal* by Richard Wagner is 4 hours 5 minutes. Of classical operas, only three have longer times, all by Wagner, with the longest, *Die Meistersinger von Nürnberg*, clocking in at 4 hours 35 minutes.

their brown, smiling host and hostess. The baby whose arrival in the world was the inspiration for the luau awoke for a second and smiled at them too. Outside in the narrow street their car was waiting.

Through silent, deserted Honolulu they motored toward Waikiki. As they passed the Judiciary Building on King Street,[58] the clock in the tower struck the hour of one. She had not been out so late, Miss Minerva reflected, since that night when a visiting company sang *Parsifal* at the Boston Opera House.[59]

The iron gates that guarded the drive at Dan's house were closed. Leaving the car at the curb, Miss Minerva bade her friends good night and started up the walk toward the front door. The evening had thrilled her, and she moved with the long confident stride of youth. Dan's scarlet garden was shrouded in darkness, for the moon, which had been playing an in-and-out game with the fast-moving clouds all evening, was again obscured. Exotic odors assailed her nostrils; she heard all about her the soft intriguing noises of the tropic night. She really should get to bed, she knew, but with a happy truant feeling she turned from the front walk and went to the side of the house for a last look at the breakers.

She stood there under a poinciana tree near the door leading into Dan's living-room. For nearly two weeks the Kona wind had prevailed, but now on her cheek, she thought she felt the first kindly breath of the trades. Very wide awake, she stared out at the dim foaming lines of surf between the shore and the coral reef. Her mind strayed back to the Honolulu she had known in Kalakaua's day, to that era when the Islands were so naive, so colorful—unspoiled. Ruined now, Dan had said, ruined by a damned mechanical civilization. "But away down underneath, Minerva, there are deep dark waters flowing still."

The moon came out, touching with silver the waters at the crossroads, then was lost again under fleecy clouds. With a little sigh that was perhaps for her lost youth and the 'eighties, Miss Minerva pushed open the unlocked door leading into the great living-room, and closed it gently so as not to waken Dan.

An intense darkness engulfed her. But she knew her way across the polished floor and set out confidently, walking on tiptoe. She had gone halfway to the hall door when she stopped, her heart in her mouth. For not five feet away she saw the luminous dial of a watch, and as she stared at it with frightened eyes, it moved.

Not for nothing had Miss Minerva studied restraint through more than fifty years. Many women would have screamed and fainted. Miss Minerva's heart pounded madly, but that was all. Standing very still, she studied that phosphorescent dial. Its movement had been slight, it was now at rest again. A watch worn on some one's wrist. Some one who had been on the point of action, but had now assumed an attitude of cautious waiting.

Well, Miss Minerva grimly asked herself, what was she going to do about it? Should she cry out a sharp: "Who's there?" She was a brave woman, but the foolhardiness of such a course was apparent. She had a vision of that dial flashing nearer, a blow, perhaps strong hands at her throat.

She took a tentative step, and then another. Now, surely, the dial would stir again. But it remained motionless, steady, as though the arm that wore it were rigid at the intruder's side.

Suddenly Miss Minerva realized the situation. The wearer of the watch had forgotten the tell-tale numerals on his wrist, he thought himself hidden in the dark. He was waiting for her to go on through the room. If she made no sound, gave no sign of alarm, she might be safe. Once beyond that bamboo curtain leading into the hall, she could rouse the household.

She was a woman of great will power, but it took all she had to move serenely on her way. She shut her lips tightly and accomplished it, veering a bit from that circle of light that menaced her, looking back at it over her shoulder as she went. After what seemed an eternity the bamboo curtain received her, she was through it, she was on the stairs. But it seemed to her that never again would she be able to look at a watch or a clock and find that the hour was anything save twenty minutes past one!

When she was half-way up the stairs, she recalled that it had been her intention to snap on the lights in the lower hall. She did not turn back, nor did she search for the switch at the head of the stairs. Instead, she went hastily on into her room, and just as though she had been an ordinary woman, she closed her door and dropped down, trembling a little, on a chair.

But she was no ordinary woman, and in two seconds she was up and had reopened her door. Her sudden terror was evaporating; she felt her heart beat in a strong regular rhythm again. Action was required of her now, calm confident action; she was a Winterslip and she was ready.

60. According to *Andrews*, a long, flowing garment.

The servants' quarters were in a wing over the kitchen; she went there at once and knocked on the first door she came to. She knocked once, then again, and finally the head of a very sleepy Jap appeared.

"Haku," said Miss Minerva, "there is some one in the living-room. You must go down and investigate at once."

He stared at her, seeming unable to comprehend.

"We must go down," amended Miss Minerva. "Wikiwiki!"

He disappeared, and Miss Minerva waited impatiently. Where was her nerve, she wondered, why hadn't she seen this through alone? At home, no doubt, she could have managed it, but here there was something strange and terrifying in the very air. The moonlight poured in through a small window beside her, forming a bright square at her feet. Haku reappeared, wearing a gaudy kimono that he often sported on the beach.

Another door opened suddenly, and Miss Minerva started. Bah! What ailed her, anyhow, she wondered. It was only Kamaikui, standing there a massive figure in the dim doorway, a bronze statue clad in a holoku.[60]

"Some one in the living-room," Miss Minerva explained again. "I saw him as I came through."

Kamaikui made no reply, but joined the odd little procession. In the upper hall Haku switched on the lights, both up-stairs and down. At the head of the stairs there was a brief pause—then Miss Minerva took her rightful place at the head of the line. She descended with a firm step, courageous and competent, Boston at its best. After her followed a stolid little Japanese man in a kimono gay with passionate poppies, and a Polynesian woman who wore the fearful Mother Hubbard of the missionaries as though it were a robe of state.

In the lower hall Miss Minerva did not hesitate. She pushed on through the bamboo curtain and her hand—it trembled ever so slightly—found the electric switch and flooded the living-room with light. She heard the crackle of bamboo behind her as her strange companions followed where she led. She stood looking curiously about her.

There was no one in sight, no sign of any disturbance, and it suddenly occurred to Miss Minerva that perhaps she was behaving in a rather silly fashion. After all, she had neither seen nor heard a living thing. The illuminated dial of a watch that moved a little—might it not have been a figment of her imagination? She had experienced a stirring evening. Then, too, she remembered, there had been that small glass of okolehau. A potent concoction!

Kamaikui and Haku were looking at her with the inquiring eyes of little children. Had she roused them for a fool's errand? Her cheeks flushed slightly. Certainly in this big brilliant room, furnished with magnificent native woods and green with many potted ferns, everything seemed proper and in order.

"I—I may have been mistaken," she said in a low voice. "I was quite sure—but there's no sign of anything wrong. Mr. Winterslip has not been resting well of late. If he should be asleep we won't waken him."

She went to the door leading on to the lanai and pushed aside the curtain. Bright moonlight outside revealed most of the veranda's furnishings, and here, too, all seemed well. "Dan," Miss Minerva called softly. "Dan. Are you awake?"

No answer. Miss Minerva was certain now that she was making a mountain out of a molehill. She was about to turn back into the living-room when her eyes, grown more accustomed to the semi-darkness, noted a rather startling fact.

Day and night, over Dan's cot in one corner of the lanai, hung a white mosquito netting. It was not there now.

"Come, Haku," Miss Minerva said. "Turn on the light out here."

Haku came, and the green-shaded lamp glowed under his touch. The little lamp by which Dan had been reading his evening paper that night when he had seemed suddenly so disturbed, and rushed off to send a letter to Roger in San Francisco. Miss Minerva stood recalling that incident, she recalled others, because she was very reluctant to turn toward that cot in the corner. She was conscious of Kamaikui brushing by her, and then she heard a low, half-savage moan of fear and sorrow.

Miss Minerva stepped to the cot. The mosquito netting had been torn down as though in some terrific struggle and there, entangled in the meshes of it, she saw Dan Winterslip. He was lying on his left side, and as she stared down at him, one of the harmless little Island lizards ran up his chest and over his shoulder—and left a crimson trail on his white pajamas.

CHAPTER VII

Enter Charlie Chan

Miss minerva leaned far over, her keen eyes seeking Dan's face. It was turned toward the wall, half buried in the pillow. "Dan," she said brokenly. She put her hand on his cheek. The night air was warm and muggy, but she shivered a little as she drew the hand quickly away. Steady! She must be steady now.

She hurried through the living-room to the hall; the telephone was in a closet under the front stairs. Her fingers were trembling again as she fumbled with the numerals on the dial. She got her number, heard finally an answering voice.

"Amos? Is that you, Amos? This is Minerva. Come over here to Dan's as quickly as you can."

The voice muttered in protest. Miss Minerva cut in on it sharply.

"For God's sake, Amos, forget your silly feud. Your brother is dead."

"Dead?" he repeated dully.

"Murdered, Amos. Will you come now?"

A long silence. What thoughts, Miss Minerva wondered, were passing through the mind of that stern unbending Puritan?

"I'll come," a strange voice said at last. And then, a voice more like that of the Amos she knew: "The police! I'll notify them, and then I'll come right over."

Returning to the hall, Miss Minerva saw that the big front door was closed. Amos would enter that way, she knew, so she went over and opened it. There was, she noted, an imposing lock, but the key had long since been lost and forgotten. Indeed, in all Dan's great house, she could not recall ever having seen a key. In these friendly trusting islands, locked doors were obsolete.

She reentered the living-room. Should she summon a doctor? But no, it was too late, she knew that only too well. And the police—didn't they bring some sort of doctor with them? Suddenly she began to wonder about the police. During all her time in Honolulu she had never given them a thought before. Away off here at the end of the world—did they have policemen? She couldn't remember ever having seen one. Oh, yes—there was that handsome, brown-skinned Hawaiian who stood on a box at the corner of Fort and King Streets, directing traffic with an air that would have become Kamehameha himself.[61] She heard the scrape of a chair being moved on the lanai, and went to the door.

"Nothing is to be touched out here," she said. "Leave it just as it was. You'd better go up-stairs and dress, both of you."

The two frightened servants came into the living-room, and stood there regarding her. They seemed to feel that this terrible affair called for discussion. But what was there to be said? Even in the event of murder, a Winterslip must maintain a certain well-bred aloofness in dealing with servants. Miss Minerva's feeling for them was kindly. She sympathized with their evident grief, but there was, she felt, nothing to discuss.

"After you've dressed," she ordered, "stay within reach. You'll both be wanted."

They went out, Haku in his absurd costume, Kamaikui moaning and muttering in a way that sent shivers up and down Miss Minerva's spine. They left her there alone—with Dan—and she who had always thought herself equal to anything still hesitated about going out on the lanai.

She sat down in a huge chair in the living-room and gazed about her at the trappings of wealth and position that Dan had left for ever now. Poor Dan. Despite all the whispering against him, she had liked him immensely. It is said of many—usually with small reason—that their lives would make an interesting book. It had been said of Dan, and in his case it was true. What a book his life would have made—and how promptly it would have been barred for all time from the shelves of the Boston Public Library! For Dan had lived life to the full, made his own

61. Indeed, there was a police department. County police departments were established in 1905. A. M. Brown served as sheriff of Honolulu, 1905–1906, Curtis P. Iaukea, 1907–1909, William P. Jarrett, 1910-1914, Charles G. Rose, 1915–1923, David K. Trask, 1924–1926, and David L. Desha, from 1927 until the job was abolished in 1931. In 1931, the Honolulu Police Department was formed, and Charles F. Weeber was *appointed* as the Chief of Police by the newly created Police Commission. In 1898, when the model for Charlie Chan, Chang Apana, joined the force, it numbered more than 200 men, with principally Hawaiian officers and white supervisors. For more on Apana, see p. xv, and note 63, as well as the excellent *Charlie Chan: The Untold Story of the Honorable Detective and His Rendezvous with American History* by Yuente Huang (New York: W.W. Norton, 2010).

laws, fought his battles without mercy, prospered and had his way. Dallied often along forbidden paths, they said, but his smile had been so friendly and his voice so full of cheer—always until these last two weeks.

Ever since that night he sent the letter to Roger, he had seemed a different man. There were lines for the first time in his face, a weary apprehensive look in his gray eyes. And how furious he had been when, last Wednesday, he received a cable from Roger. What was in that message, Miss Minerva wondered; what were those few typewritten words that had caused him to fly into such a rage and set him to pacing the floor with tigerish step?

She thought of him as she had seen him last—he had seemed rather pathetic to her then. When the news came that the *President Tyler* could not dock until morning, and that Barbara—

Miss Minerva stopped. For the first time she thought of Barbara. She thought of a sprightly, vivacious girl as yet untouched by sorrow—and of the morning's homecoming. Tears came into her eyes, and it was through a mist she saw the bamboo curtain that led into the hall pushed aside, and the thin white face of Amos framed there.

Amos entered, walking gingerly, for he was treading ground he had sworn his feet should never touch. He paused before Miss Minerva.

"What's this?" he said. "What's all this?"

She nodded toward the lanai, and he went out there. After what seemed a long time, he reappeared. His shoulders drooped wearily and his watery eyes were staring.

"Stabbed through the heart," he muttered. He stood for a moment regarding his father's picture on the wall. "The wages of sin is death," he added, as though to old Jedediah Winterslip.

"Yes, Amos," said Miss Minerva sharply. "I expected we should hear that from you. And there's another one you may have heard—judge not that ye be not judged. Further than that, we'll waste no time moralizing. Dan is dead, and I for one am sorry."

"Sorry!" repeated Amos drearily. "How about me? My brother—my young brother—I taught him to walk on this very beach—"

"Yes." Miss Minerva looked at him keenly. "I wonder. Well, Dan's gone. Some one has killed him. He was one of us—a Winterslip. What are we going to do about it?"

"I've notified the police," said Amos.

"Then why aren't they here? In Boston by this time—but then, I know this isn't Boston. Stabbed, you say. Was there any sign of a weapon?"

"None whatever, that I could see."

"How about that Malay kris[62] on the table out there? The one Dan used as a paper cutter?"

"I didn't notice," Amos replied. "This is a strange house to me, Minerva."

"So it is." Miss Minerva rose and started for the lanai. She was her old competent self again. At that moment a loud knock sounded on the screen door at the front of the house. Presently there were voices in the hall, and Haku ushered three men into the living-room. Though evidently police, they were all in plain clothes. One of them, a tall, angular Yankee with the look of a sailing master about him, stepped forward.

"I'm Hallet," he said. "Captain of Detectives. You're Mr. Amos Winterslip, I believe?"

"I am," Amos answered. He introduced Miss Minerva. Captain Hallet gave her a casual nod; this was man's business and he disliked having a woman involved.

"Dan Winterslip, you said," he remarked, turning back to Amos. "That's a great pity. Where is he?"

Amos indicated the lanai. "Come, Doctor," Hallet said, and went through the curtain, followed by the smaller of the two men.

As they went out, the third man stepped farther into the room, and Miss Minerva gave a little gasp of astonishment as she looked at him. In those warm islands thin men were the rule, but here was a striking exception. He was very fat indeed, yet he walked with the light dainty step of a woman. His cheeks were as chubby as a baby's, his skin ivory tinted, his black hair close-cropped, his amber eyes slanting. As he passed Miss Minerva he bowed with a courtesy encountered all too rarely in a work-a-day world, then moved on after Hallet.

"Amos!" cried Miss Minerva. "That man—why he—"

"Charlie Chan," Amos explained. "I'm glad they brought him. He's the best detective on the force."

62.   A dagger, with hilt and sheath.

A Malay kris and scabard

63. The discovery of gold in California in mid-century led to a wave of Chinese immigration. Only 325 Chinese arrived in 1849, but over 20,000 immigrated in 1852, and by 1870, the Chinese population of the United States was estimated at about 63,000 (with almost 80 percent in California). Forbidden by law from obtaining citizenship (as were all who were "nonwhite"), the Chinese gold miners were taxed heavily but largely resented. By the mid-1860s, the Chinese were incorporated into the workforce of the railroads and pressed into the work on the transcontinental rail project. When that work ended, thousands of Chinese rail workers were unemployed, but many were scooped up by other industries as cheap labor, leading to resentment among white workers. Vigilante violence erupted, and anti-Chinese legislation was widely enacted, including An Act to Discourage the Immigration to this State of Persons Who Cannot Become Citizens Thereof (1855). In 1862, Governor Leland Stanford decried "the presence among us of a degraded and distinct people" and called for legislation against the Chinese.

Nor were these sentiments limited to California. In 1882, Congress passed the Chinese Exclusion Act, suspending the immigration of Chinese laborers for ten years and confirming that the Chinese immigrants were ineligible for citizenship. This law was renewed in 1892 and 1902, and in 1924, in the so-called Johnson-Reed Act (the Immigration Act of 1924), the exclusion was affirmed and expanded to forbid entry into the United States of anyone ineligible for citizenship. The ban on Chinese immigration lasted until 1943.

According to the U.S. Census (which of course did not include Hawaii prior to annexation), Chinese population of the United States

"But—he's a Chinaman!"[63]

"Of course."

Miss Minerva sank into a chair. Ah, yes, they had policemen out here, after all.

In a few moments Hallet came briskly back into the living-room. "Look here," he said. "The doctor tells me Mr. Winterslip has been dead a very short while. I don't want your evidence just yet—but if either of you can give me some idea as to the hour when this thing happened—"

"I can give you a rather definite idea," said Miss Minerva calmly. "It happened just previous to twenty minutes past one. Say about one fifteen."

Hallet stared at her. "You're sure of that?"

"I ought to be. I got the time from the wrist watch of the person who committed the murder."

"What! You saw him!"

"I didn't say that. I said I saw his wrist watch."

Hallet frowned. "I'll get that straight later," he said. "Just now I propose to comb this part of town. Where's the telephone?"

Miss Minerva pointed it out to him, and heard him in earnest conversation with a man at headquarters named Tom. Tom's job, it seemed, was to muster all available men and search Honolulu, particularly the Waikiki district, rounding up any suspicious characters. He was also to have on hand, awaiting his chief's return, the passenger lists of all ships that had made port at Honolulu during the past week.

Hallet returned to the living-room. He took a stand directly in front of Miss Minerva. "Now," he began, "you didn't see the murderer, but you saw his wrist watch. I'm a great believer in taking things in an orderly fashion. You're a stranger here. From Boston, I believe?"

"I am," snapped Miss Minerva.

"Stopping in this house?"

"Precisely."

"Anybody here besides you and Mr. Winterslip?"

Miss Minerva's eyes flashed. "The servants," she said. "And I would like to call your attention to the fact that I am Dan Winterslip's first cousin."

"Oh, sure—no offense. He has a daughter, hasn't he?"

"Miss Barbara is on her way home from college. Her ship will dock in the morning."

"I see. Just you and Winterslip. You're going to be an important witness."

"It will be a novel experience, at any rate," she remarked.

"I dare say. Now, go back—" Miss Minerva glared at him—it was a glare that had frightened guards on the Cambridge subway. He brushed it aside. "You understand that I haven't time for please, Miss Winterslip. Go back and describe last evening in this house."

"I was here only until eight-thirty," she told him, "when I went to a luau with some friends. Previous to that, Mr. Winterslip dined at his usual hour and we chatted for a time on the lanai."

"Did he seem to have anything on his mind?"

"Well, he has appeared a bit upset—"

"Wait a minute!" The captain took out a notebook. "Want to put down some of this. Been upset, has he? For how long?"

"For the past two weeks. Let me think—just two weeks ago to-night—or rather, last night—he and I were sitting on the lanai, and he was reading the evening paper. Something in it seemed to disturb him. He got up, wrote a note to his cousin Roger in San Francisco, and took it down for a friend aboard the *President Tyler* to deliver. From that moment he appeared restless and unhappy."

"Go on. This may be important."

"Last Wednesday morning he received a cable from Roger that infuriated him."

"A cable. What was in it?"

"It was not addressed to me," said Miss Minerva haughtily.

"Well, that's all right. We'll dig it up. Now, about last night. Did he act more upset than ever?"

"He did. But that may have been due to the fact he had hoped his daughter's ship would dock yesterday afternoon, and had learned it could not land its passengers until this morning."

"I see. You said you was only here until eight-thirty?"

"I did not," replied Miss Minerva coldly. "I said I was here only until eight-thirty."

"Same thing."

"Well, hardly."

"I'm not here to talk grammar," Hallet said sharply. "Did anything occur—anything out of the ordinary—before you left?"

peaked in 1890, at over 107,000. It then began to drop steadily, so that by 1920, it shrank to just over 60,000. By the 1930 census, it began to grow again. In contrast, according to the 1920 census, Hawaii had a huge Asian population, with over 40 percent Japanese and almost 10 percent Chinese.

When Chang Apana joined the Honolulu police force in 1898, he was the only Chinese officer, out of a force of over 200; by 1925, however, the presence of a Chinese officer on the force would have been no surprise to a long-time resident of Honolulu. Minerva's dramatic response is that of a mainlander—less than 0.2 percent of the U.S. population in 1920 were Chinese.

"No. Wait a moment. Some one called Mr. Winterslip on the telephone while he was at dinner. I couldn't help overhearing the conversation."

"Good for you!" She glared at him again. "Repeat it."

"I heard Mr. Winterslip say: 'Hello, Egan. What—you're not coming over? Oh, yes you are. I want to see you. I insist on it. Come about eleven. I want to see you.' That was, at least, the import of his remarks."

"Did he seem excited?"

"He raised his voice above the ordinary tone."

"Ah, yes." The captain stared at his notebook. "Must have been Jim Egan, who runs this God-forsaken Reef and Palm Hotel down the beach." He turned to Amos. "Was Egan a friend of your brother?"

"I don't know," said Amos.

"You see, Amos was not a friend of his brother, either," explained Miss Minerva. "There was an old feud between them. Speaking for myself, I never heard Dan mention Egan, and he certainly never came to the house while I was here."

Hallet nodded. "Well, you left at eight-thirty. Now tell us where you went and when you got back. And all about the wrist watch."

Miss Minerva rapidly sketched her evening at the luau. She described her return to Dan's living-room, her adventure in the dark—the luminous dial that waited for her to pass.

"I wish you'd seen more," Hallet complained. "Too many people wear wrist watches."

"Probably not many," said Miss Minerva, "wear a wrist watch like that one."

"Oh. It had some distinguishing mark?"

"It certainly did. The numerals were illuminated, and stood out clearly—with an exception. The figure 2 was very dim—practically obliterated."

He looked at her admiringly. "Well, you certainly had your wits about you."

"That's a habit I formed early in life," replied Miss Minerva. "And old habits are hard to break."

He smiled, and asked her to continue. She told of rousing the two servants and, finally, of the gruesome discovery on the lanai.

"But it was Mr. Amos," Hallet said, "who called the station."

"Yes. I telephoned him at once, and he offered to attend to that."

Hallet turned to Amos. "How long did it take you to reach here, Mr. Winterslip?" he inquired.

"Not more than ten minutes," said Amos.

"You could dress and get here in that time?"

Amos hesitated. "I—I did not need to dress," he explained. "I hadn't gone to bed."

Hallet regarded him with a new interest. "Half past one—and you were still up?"

"I—I don't sleep very well," said Amos. "I'm up till all hours."

"I see. You weren't on friendly terms with your brother? An old quarrel between you?"

"No particular quarrel. I didn't approve of his manner of living, and we went separate ways."

"And stopped speaking to each other, eh?"

"Yes. That was the situation," Amos admitted.

"Humph." For a moment the captain stared at Amos, and Miss Minerva stared at him too. Amos! It flashed through her mind that Amos had been a long time alone out there on the lanai before the arrival of the police.

"Those two servants who came down-stairs with you, Miss Winterslip," Hallet said. "I'll see them now. The others can go over until morning."

Haku and Kamaikui appeared, frightened and wide-eyed. The Jap had nothing to tell, he had been sleeping soundly from nine until the moment Miss Minerva knocked on his door. He swore it. But Kamaikui had something to contribute.

"I come here with fruit." She pointed to a basket on the table. "On lanai out there are talking—Mr. Dan, a man, a woman. Oh, very much angry."

"What time was that?" Hallet asked.

"Ten o'clock I think."

"Did you recognize any voice except your master's?"

Miss Minerva thought the woman hesitated a second. "No. I do not."

"Anything else?"

"Yes. Maybe eleven o'clock. I am sitting close to window up-stairs. More talking on lanai. Mr. Dan and other man. Not so much angry this time."

"At eleven, eh? Do you know Mr. Jim Egan?"

"I have seen him."

"Could you say if it was his voice?"

"I could not say."

"All right. You two can go now." He turned to Miss Minerva and Amos. "We'll see what Charlie has dug up out here," he said, and led the way to the lanai.

The huge Chinese man knelt, a grotesque figure, by a table. He rose laboriously as they entered.

"Find the knife, Charlie?" the captain asked.

Chan shook his head. "No knife are present in neighborhood of crime," he announced.

"On that table," Miss Minerva began, "there was a Malay kris, used as a paper cutter—"

The Chinaman nodded, and lifted the kris from the desk. "Same remains here still," he said, "untouched, unsullied. Person who killed carried individual weapon."

"How about finger-prints?" asked Hallet.

"Considering from recent discovery," Chan replied, "search for finger-prints are hopeless one." He held out a pudgy hand, in the palm of which lay a small pearl button. "Torn from kid's glove," he elucidated. "Aged trick of criminal mind. No fingerprints."

"Is that all you've got?" asked his chief.

"Most sincere endeavors," said Chan, "have revealed not much. However, I might mention this." He took up a leatherbound book from the table. "Here are written names of visitors who have enjoyed hospitality of the house. A guest book is, I believe, the term. You will find that one of the earlier pages has been ruthlessly torn out. When I make discovery the volume are lying open at that locality."

Captain Hallet took the book in his thin hand. "All right, Charlie," he said. "This is your case."

The slant eyes blinked with pleasure. "Most interesting," murmured Chan.

Hallet tapped the note-book in his pocket. "I've got a few facts here for you—we'll run over them later." He stood for a moment, staring about the lanai. "I must say we seem a little shy on clues. A button torn from a glove, a page ripped from a guest book. And a wrist watch with an illuminated dial on which the figure 2 was damaged." Chan's little eyes widened at mention of that. "Not much, Charlie, so far."

"Maybe more to come," suggested the Chinaman. "Who knows it?"

"We'll go along now," Hallet continued. He turned to Miss Minerva and Amos. "I guess you folks would like a little rest. We'll have to trouble you again to-morrow."

Miss Minerva faced the Chinaman. "The person who did this must be apprehended," she said firmly.

He looked at her sleepily. "What is to be, will be," he replied in a high, sing-song voice.

"I know—that's your Confucius," she snapped. "But it's a do-nothing doctrine, and I don't approve of it."

A faint smile flickered over the Chinaman's face. "Do not fear," he said. "The fates are busy, and man may do much to assist. I promise you there will be no do-nothing here." He came closer. "Humbly asking pardon to mention it, I detect in your eyes slight flame of hostility. Quench it, if you will be so kind. Friendly cooperation are essential between us." Despite his girth, he managed a deep bow. "Wishing you good morning," he added, and followed Hallet.[64]

Miss Minerva turned weakly to Amos. "Well, of all things—"

"Don't you worry about Charlie," Amos said. "He has a reputation for getting his man. Now you go to bed. I'll stay here and notify the—the proper people."

"Well, I will lie down for a little while," Miss Minerva said. "I shall have to go early to the dock. Poor Barbara! And there's John Quincy coming too." A grim smile crossed her face. "I'm afraid John Quincy won't approve of this."

She saw from her bedroom window that the night was breaking, the rakish cocoanut palms and the hau tree were wrapped in a gray mist. Changing her dress for a kimono, she lay down under the mosquito netting on the bed. She slept but briefly, however, and presently was at her window again. Day had come, the mist had lifted, and it was a rose and emerald world that sparkled before her tired eyes.

The freshness of that scene revivified her. The trades were blowing now—poor Dan, he had so longed for their return. The night, she saw, had worked its magic on the blossoms of the hau tree, transformed them from yellow to a rich mahogany; through

64. Chan's mode of speech has been incorrectly characterized as "pidgin English" and widely aped in popular culture. That is unfair: Chan (as John Quincy acknowledges later) aspires to a level of articulation not then found in the average Chinese resident of Hawaii. This point was made by Chester A. Doyle, who handled "oriental criminals" for the Hawaii police department, in a letter to the *Honolulu Star-Bulletin* dated December 7, 1935: "No Chinese, unless he was an educated Chinese mandarin of Canton, China, would use the language attributed to the Chinese detective . . ."

the morning they would drop one by one upon the sand. In a distant algaroba a flock of myna birds screamed at the new day. A party of swimmers appeared from a neighboring cottage and plunged gaily into the surf.

A gentle knock sounded on the door, and Kamaikui entered. She placed a small object in Miss Minerva's hand.

Miss Minerva looked down. She saw a quaint old piece of jewelry, a brooch. Against a background of onyx stood the outline of a tree, with emeralds forming the leaves, rubies the fruit, and a frost of diamonds over all.

"What is this, Kamaikui?" she asked.

"Many, many years Mr. Dan have that. One month ago he gives it to a woman down the beach."

Miss Minerva's eyes narrowed. "To the woman they call the Widow of Waikiki?"

"To her, yes."

"How do you happen to have it, Kamaikui?"

"I pick it up from floor of lanai. Before policemen come."

"Very good." Miss Minerva nodded. "Say nothing of this, Kamaikui. I will attend to the matter."

"Yes. Of course." The woman went out.

Miss Minerva sat very still, staring down at that odd bit of jewelry in her hand. It must date back to the 'eighties, at least.

Close above the house sounded the loud whir of an aeroplane. Miss Minerva turned again to the window. A young lieutenant in the air service, in love with a sweet girl on the beach, was accustomed to serenade her thus every morning at dawn. His thoughtfulness was not appreciated by many innocent bystanders, but Miss Minerva's eyes were sympathetic as she watched him sweep exultantly out, far out, over the harbor.

Youth and love, the beginning of life. And on that cot down on the lanai, Dan—and the end.

CHAPTER VIII
Steamer Day

Out in the harbor, by the channel entrance, the *President Tyler* stood motionless as Diamond Head, and from his post near the rail outside his stateroom, John Quincy Winterslip took his first look at Honolulu. He had no feeling of having been here before; this was an alien land. Several miles away he saw the line of piers and unlovely warehouses that marked the water-front; beyond that lay a vast expanse of brilliant green pierced here and there by the top of a modest skyscraper. Back of the city a range of mountains stood on guard, peaks of crystal blue against the azure sky.

A trim little launch from Quarantine chugged importantly up to the big liner's side, and a doctor in a khaki uniform ran briskly up the accommodation ladder to the deck not far from where the boy stood. John Quincy wondered at the man's vitality. He felt like a spent force himself. The air was moist and heavy, the breeze the ship had stirred in moving gone for ever. The flood of energy that had swept over him in San Francisco was but a happy memory now. He leaned wearily on the rail, staring at the bright tropical landscape before him—and not seeing it at all.

He saw instead a quiet, well-furnished Boston office where at this very moment the typewriters were clicking amiably and the stock ticker was busily writing the story of another day. In a few hours—there was a considerable difference of time—the market

65. Twain said many things about Hawaii in a series of twenty-five letters for the *Sacramento Union* written in 1866, some of which he later adapted into chapters of *Roughing It* (1872). Jennison probably had in mind Twain's most oft-quoted description of Hawaii: "The loveliest fleet of islands that lies anchored in any ocean." However, perhaps Twain's most haunting remarks about Hawaii were reminiscences in 1889, more than twenty years after his trip there: "No alien land in all the world has any deep strong charm for me but that one, no other land could so longingly and so beseechingly haunt me, sleeping and waking, through half a lifetime, as that one has done. Other things leave me, but it abides; other things change, but it remains the same. For me the balmy airs are always blowing, its summer seas flashing in the sun; the pulsing of its surf-beat is in my ear; I can see its garlanded crags, its leaping cascades, its plumy palms drowsing by the shore, its remote summits floating like islands above the cloud wrack; I can feel the spirit of its wildland solitudes, I can hear the splash of its brooks; in my nostrils still lives the breath of flowers that perished twenty years ago." From after-dinner remarks on April 8, 1889, published in *Mark Twain Speaking*, Paul Fatout, ed. (Iowa City: Univ. of Iowa Press, 1976), p. 246.

66. In the 1925 *Hawaiian Almanac*, construction of a five-story building was announced. The Aloha Tower, opened in 1926 as the tallest building in Honolulu, was only ten floors. There was, of course, no Van Patten Trust Company.

67. Hawaii was still an exotic destination in 1924. The Immigration Service provided the following statistics regarding 1924 trips: 7,392

would close and the men he knew would be piling into automobiles and heading for the nearest country club. A round of golf, then a calm, perfectly served dinner, and after that a quiet evening with a book. Life running along as it was meant to go, without rude interruption or disturbing incident; life devoid of ohia wood boxes, attic encounters, unwillingly witnessed love scenes, cousins with blackbirding pasts. Suddenly John Quincy remembered, this was the morning when he must look Dan Winterslip in the eye and tell him he had been a bit dilatory with his fists. Oh, well—he straightened resolutely—the sooner that was done, the better.

Harry Jennison came along the deck, smiling and vigorous, clad in spotless white from head to foot. "Here we are," he cried. "On the threshold of paradise!"

"Think so?" said John Quincy.

"Know it," Jennison answered. "Only place in the world, these islands. You remember what Mark Twain said—"[65]

"Ever visited Boston?" John Quincy cut in.

"Once," replied Jennison briefly. "That's Punch Bowl Hill back of the town—and Tantalus beyond. Take you up to the summit some day—wonderful view. See that tallest building?[66] The Van Patten Trust Company—my office is on the top floor. Only drawback about getting home—I'll have to go to work again."

"I don't see how any one can work in this climate," John Quincy said.

"Oh, well, we take it easy. Can't manage the pace of you mainland people. Every now and then some go-getter from the States comes out here and tries to hustle us." He laughed. "He dies of disgust and we bury him in a leisurely way. Been down to breakfast?"

John Quincy accompanied him to the dining saloon. Madame Maynard and Barbara were at the table. The old lady's cheeks were flushed and her eyes sparkled; Barbara, too, was in her gayest mood. The excitement of coming home had made her very happy—or was her happiness all due to that? John Quincy noted her smile of greeting for Jennison, and rather wished he knew less than he did.

"Prepare for a thrill, John Quincy," the girl said. "Landing in Hawaii is like landing nowhere else on the globe.[67] Of course, this is a through boat, and it isn't welcomed as the Matson liners are. But there'll be a crowd waiting for the *Matsonia* this morning, and we'll steal a little of her aloha."

"A little of her what?" inquired John Quincy.

"Aloha—meaning loving welcome.[68] You shall have all my leis, John Quincy. Just to show you how glad Honolulu is you've come at last."

The boy turned to Madame Maynard. "I suppose this is an old story to you?"

"Bless you, my boy," she said. "It's always new. A hundred and twenty-eight times—yet I'm as thrilled as though I were coming home from college." She sighed. "A hundred and twenty-eight times. So many of those who once hung leis about my neck are gone for ever now. They'll not be waiting for me—not on this dock."

"None of that," Barbara chided. "Only happy thoughts this morning. It's steamer day."

Nobody seemed hungry, and breakfast was a sketchy affair. John Quincy returned to his cabin to find Bowker strapping up his luggage.

"I guess you're all ready, sir," said the steward. "I finished that book last night, and you'll find it in your suitcase. We'll be moving on to the dock shortly. All good luck to you—and don't forget about the okolehau."

"It's graven on my memory," smiled John Quincy. "Here—this is for you."

Bowker glanced at the banknote and pocketed it. "You're mighty kind, sir," he remarked feelingly. "That will sort of balance up the dollar each I'll get from those two missionaries when we reach China—if I'm lucky. Of course, it's rather distasteful to me to accept anything. From a friend of Tim's, you know."

"Oh, that's for value received," said John Quincy, and followed Bowker on deck.

"There she is," announced Bowker, pausing by the rail. "Honolulu. The South Seas with a collar on, driving a Ford car. Polynesia with a private still and all the other benefits of the white man's civilization. We'll go out at eight to-night, thank heaven."

"Paradise doesn't appeal to you," suggested John Quincy.

"No. Nor any other of these bright-colored lands my poor old feet must tread. I'm getting fed up, sir." He came closer. "I want

individuals arrived in Hawaii from foreign ports, with 15,002 arriving from the mainland; in comparison, more than 8.94 million visitors arrived in Hawaii in 2016, with 5.6 million coming from the United States alone.

68.   *Andrews* calls it "[a] word expressing different feelings; as, love; affection; gratitude; kindness; pity; compassion; grief; the modern salutation at meeting and parting."

69. In the ninth book of *The Odyssey*, Odysseus and his men are swept by storms onto the island of the lotus-eaters. According to legend, the inhabitants of the island live on the fruit and blossoms of the lotus plant becoming intensely apathetic, and so Odysseus must struggle to induce his crew to leave. There are several species of lotus, and yet none quite match Odysseus's description of appearance and tranquilizing qualities.

to hang my hat somewhere and leave it there. I want to buy a little newspaper in some country town and starve to death on the proceeds of running it. What a happy finish! Well, maybe I can manage it, before long."

"I hope so," said John Quincy.

"I hope so, too," said Bowker. "Here's wishing you a happy time in Honolulu. And one other word of warning—don't linger there."

"I don't intend to," John Quincy assured him.

"That's the talk. It's one of those places—you know—dangerous. Lotus on the menu every day.[69] The first thing you know, you've forgot where you put your trunk. So long, sir."

With a wave of the hand, Tim's friend disappeared down the deck. Amid much confusion, John Quincy took his place in line for the doctor's inspection, passed the careful scrutiny of an immigration official who finally admitted that maybe Boston was in the Union, and was then left to his own devices and his long, long thoughts.

The *President Tyler* was moving slowly toward the shore. Excited figures scurried about her decks, pausing now and then to stare through lifted glasses at the land. John Quincy perceived that early though the hour was, the pier toward which they were heading was alive with people. Barbara came and stood by his side.

"Poor old dad," she said, "he's been struggling along without me for nine months. This will be a big morning in his life. You'll like dad, John Quincy."

"I'm sure I shall," he answered heartily.

"Dad's one of the finest—" Jennison joined them. "Harry, I meant to tell the steward to take my luggage ashore when we land."

"I told him," Jennison said. "I tipped him, too."

"Thanks," the girl replied. "I was so excited, I forgot."

She leaned eagerly over the rail, peering at the dock. Her eyes were shining. "I don't see him yet," she said. They were near enough now to hear the voices of those ashore, gay voices calling flippant greetings. The big ship edged gingerly closer.

"There's Aunt Minerva," cried John Quincy suddenly. That little touch of home in the throng was very pleasant. "Is that your father with her?" He indicated a tall anemic man at Minerva's side.

"I don't see—where—" Barbara began. "Oh—that—why, that's Uncle Amos!"

"Oh, is that Amos?" remarked John Quincy, without interest. But Barbara had gripped his arm, and as he turned he saw a wild alarm in her eyes.

"What do you suppose that means?" she cried. "I don't see dad. I don't see him anywhere."

"Oh, he's in that crowd somewhere—"

"No, no—you don't understand! Uncle Amos! I'm—I'm frightened."

John Quincy didn't gather what it was all about, and there was no time to find out. Jennison was pushing ahead through the crowd, making a path for Barbara, and the boy meekly brought up the rear. They were among the first down the plank. Miss Minerva and Amos were waiting at the foot.

"My dear." Miss Minerva put her arms about the girl and kissed her gently. She turned to John Quincy. "Well, here you are—"

There was something lacking in this welcome. John Quincy sensed it at once.

"Where's dad?" Barbara cried.

"I'll explain in the car—" Miss Minerva began.

"No, now! Now! I must know now!"

The crowd was surging about them, calling happy greetings, the Royal Hawaiian Band was playing a gay tune, carnival was in the air.

"Your father is dead, my dear," said Miss Minerva.

John Quincy saw the girl's slim figure sway gently, but it was Harry Jennison's strong arm that caught her.[70]

For a moment she stood, with Jennison's arm about her. "All right," she said. "I'm ready to go home." And walked like a true Winterslip toward the street.

Amos melted away into the crowd, but Jennison accompanied them to the car. "I'll go out with you," he said to Barbara. She did not seem to hear. The four of them entered the limousine, and in another moment the happy clamor of steamer day was left behind.

No one spoke. The curtains of the car were drawn, but a warm streak of sunlight fell across John Quincy's knees. He was a little dazed. Shocking, this news about Cousin Dan. Must have died suddenly—but no doubt that was how things always happened out

70. Jennison is one "cool customer," in the words of Sir Walter Scott, as we will see.

this way. He glanced at the white stricken face of the girl beside him, and because of her his heart was heavy.

She laid her cold hand on his. "It's not the welcome I promised you, John Quincy," she said softly.

"Why, my dear girl, I don't matter now."

No other word was spoken on the journey, and when they reached Dan's house, Barbara and Miss Minerva went immediately up-stairs. Jennison disappeared through a doorway at the left; evidently he knew his way about. Haku volunteered to show John Quincy his quarters, so he followed the Jap to the second floor.

When his bags were unpacked, John Quincy went down-stairs again. Miss Minerva was waiting for him in the living-room. From beyond the bamboo curtain leading to the lanai came the sound of men's voices, mumbling and indistinct.

"Well," said John Quincy, "how have you been?"

"Never better," his aunt assured him.

"Mother's been rather worried about you. She'd begun to think you were never coming home."

"I've begun to think it myself," Miss Minerva replied.

He stared at her. "Some of those bonds you left with me have matured. I haven't known just what you wanted me to do about them."

"What," inquired Miss Minerva, "is a bond?"

That sort of wild reckless talk never did make a hit with John Quincy. "It's about time somebody came out here and brought you to your senses," he remarked.

"Think so?" said his aunt.

A sound up-stairs recalled John Quincy to the situation. "This was rather sudden—Cousin Dan's death?" he inquired.

"Amazingly so."

"Well, it seems to me that it would be rather an intrusion—our staying on here now. We ought to go home in a few days. I'd better see about reservations—"

"You needn't trouble," snapped Miss Minerva. "I'll not stir from here until I see the person who did this brought to justice."

"The person who did what?" asked John Quincy.

"The person who murdered Cousin Dan," said Miss Minerva.

John Quincy's jaw dropped. His face registered a wide variety of emotions. "Good lord!" he gasped.

"Oh, you needn't be so shocked," said his aunt. "The Winterslip family will still go on."

"Well, I'm not surprised," remarked John Quincy, "when I stop to think. The things I've learned about Cousin Dan. It's a wonder to me—"

"That will do," said Miss Minerva. "You're talking like Amos, and that's no compliment. You didn't know Dan. I did—and I liked him. I'm going to stay here and do all I can to help run down the murderer. And so are you."

"Pardon me. I am not."

"Don't contradict. I intend you shall take an active part in the investigation. The police are rather informal in a small place like this. They'll welcome your help."

"My help! I'm no detective. What's happened to you, anyhow? Why should you want me to go round hobnobbing with policemen—"

"For the simple reason that if we're not careful some rather unpleasant scandal may come out of this. If you're on the ground you may be able to avert needless publicity. For Barbara's sake."

"No, thank you," said John Quincy. "I'm leaving for Boston in three days, and so are you. Pack your trunks."

Miss Minerva laughed. "I've heard your father talk like that," she told him. "But I never knew him to gain anything by it in the end. Come out on the lanai and I'll introduce you to a few policemen."

John Quincy received this invitation with the contemptuous silence he thought it deserved. But while he was lavishing on it his best contempt, the bamboo curtain parted and the policemen came to him. Jennison was with them.

"Good morning, Captain Hallet," said Miss Minerva brightly. "May I present my nephew, Mr. John Quincy Winterslip of Boston."

"I'm very anxious to meet Mr. John Quincy Winterslip," the captain replied.

"How do you do," said John Quincy. His heart sank. They'd drag him into this affair if they could.

"And this, John Quincy," went on Miss Minerva, "is Mr. Charles Chan, of the Honolulu detective force."

John Quincy had thought himself prepared for anything, but—"Mr.—Mr. Chan," he gasped.

71.   Indeed, a "guarded cable"—see note 35.

"Mere words," said Chan, "can not express my unlimitable delight in meeting a representative of the ancient civilization of Boston."

Harry Jennison spoke. "This is an appalling business, Miss Winterslip," he said. "As perhaps you know, I was your cousin's lawyer. I was also his friend. Therefore I hope you won't think I am intruding if I show a keen interest in what is going forward here."

"Not at all," Miss Minerva assured him. "We shall need all the help we can get."

Captain Hallet had taken a paper from his pocket. He faced John Quincy.

"Young man," he began, "I said I wanted to meet you. Last night Miss Winterslip told me of a cablegram received by the dead man about a week ago, which she said angered him greatly. I happen to have a copy of that message, turned over to me by the cable people. I'll read it to you:

> "John Quincy sailing on *President Tyler* stop owing to unfortunate accident he leaves here with empty hands. Signed, Roger Winterslip."[71]

"Yes?" said John Quincy haughtily.

"Explain that, if you will."

John Quincy stiffened. "The matter was strictly private," he said. "A family affair."

Captain Hallet glared at him. "You're mistaken," he replied. "Nothing that concerns Mr. Dan Winterslip is private now. Tell me what that cable meant, and be quick about it. I'm busy this morning."

John Quincy glared back. The man didn't seem to realize to whom he was talking. "I've already said—" he began.

"John Quincy," snapped Miss Minerva. "Do as you're told!"

Oh, well, if she wanted family secrets aired in public! Reluctantly John Quincy explained about Dan Winterslip's letter, and the misadventure in the attic of Dan's San Francisco house.

"An ohia wood box bound with copper," repeated the captain. "Initials on it, T.M.B. Got that, Charlie?"

"It is written in the book," said Chan.

"Any idea what was in that box?" asked Hallet.

"Not the slightest," John Quincy told him.

Hallet turned to Miss Minerva. "You knew nothing about this?" She assured him she did not. "Well," he continued, "one thing more and we'll go along. We've been making a thorough search of the premises by daylight—without much success, I'm sorry to say. However, by the cement walk just outside that door"—he pointed to the screen door leading from the living-room into the garden—"Charlie made a discovery."

Chan stepped forward, holding a small white object in the palm of his hand.

"One-half cigarette, incompletely consumed," he announced. "Very recent, not weather stained. It are of the brand denominated Corsican, assembled in London and smoked habitually by Englishmen."

Hallet again addressed Miss Minerva. "Did Dan Winterslip smoke cigarettes?"

"He did not," she replied. "Cigars and a pipe, but never cigarettes."

"You were the only other person living here."

"I haven't acquired the cigarette habit," snapped Miss Minerva. "Though undoubtedly it's not too late yet."

"The servants, perhaps?" went on Hallet.

"Some of the servants may smoke cigarettes, but hardly of this quality. I take it these are not on sale in Honolulu?"

"They're not," said the captain. "But Charlie tells me they're put up in air-tight tins and shipped to Englishmen the world over. Well, stow that away, Charlie." The Chinaman tenderly placed the half cigarette, incompletely consumed, in his pocketbook. "I'm going on down the beach now to have a little talk with Mr. Jim Egan," the captain added.

"I'll go with you," Jennison offered. "I may be able to supply a link or two there."

"Sure, come along," Hallet replied cordially.

"Captain Hallet," put in Miss Minerva, "it is my wish that some member of the family keep in touch with what you are doing, in order that we may give you all the aid we can. My nephew would like to accompany you—"

"Pardon me," said John Quincy coldly, "you're quite wrong. I have no intention of joining the police force."

"Well, just as you say," remarked Hallet. He turned to Miss Minerva. "I'm relying on you, at any rate. You've got a good mind. Anybody can see that."

"Thank you," she said.

"As good as a man's," he added.

"Oh, now you've spoiled it. Good morning."

The three men went through the screen door into the bright sunshine of the garden. John Quincy was aware that he was not in high favor with his aunt.

"I'll go up and change," he said uncomfortably. "We'll talk things over later—"

He went into the hall. At the foot of the stairs he paused.

From above came a low, heart-breaking moan of anguish. Barbara. Poor Barbara, who had been so happy less than an hour ago.

John Quincy felt his head go hot, the blood pound in his temples. How dare any one strike down a Winterslip! How dare any one inflict this grief on his Cousin Barbara! He clenched his fists and stood for a moment, feeling that he, too, could kill.

Action—he must have action! He rushed through the living-room, past the astonished Miss Minerva. In the drive stood a car, the three men were already in it.

"Wait a minute," called John Quincy. "I'm going with you."

"Hop in," said Captain Hallet.

The car rolled down the drive and out on to the hot asphalt of Kalia Road. John Quincy sat erect, his eyes flashing, by the side of a huge grinning Chinaman.

CHAPTER IX

At the Reef and Palm

They reached Kalakaua Avenue and swerving sharply to the right, Captain Hallet stepped on the gas. Since the car was without a top, John Quincy was getting an unrestricted view of this land that lay at his journey's end. As a small boy squirming about on the hard pew in the First Unitarian Church, he had heard much of Heaven, and his youthful imagination had pictured it as something like this. A warm, rather languid country freshly painted in the gaudiest colors available.

Creamy white clouds wrapped the tops of the distant mountains, and their slopes were bright with tropical foliage. John Quincy heard near at hand the low monotone of breakers lapping the shore. Occasionally he caught a glimpse of apple-green water and a dazzling white stretch of sand. "Oh, Waikiki! Oh, scene of peace—" What was the rest of that poem his Aunt Minerva had quoted in her last letter—the one in which she had announced that she was staying on indefinitely. "And looking down from tum-tum[72] skies, the angels smile on Waikiki." Sentimental, but sentiment was one of Hawaii's chief exports. One had only to look at the place to understand and forgive.

John Quincy had not delayed for a hat, and the sun was beating down fiercely on his brown head. Charlie Chan glanced at him.

"Humbly begging pardon," the Chinaman remarked, "would say it is unadvisable to venture forth without headgear. Especially since you are a malihini."

72. The phrase "tum-tum" here is a placeholder—John Quincy cannot remember the word but remembers the rhythm of the line. In fact, the missing word is "sunset," and the two lines of poetry quoted by Minerva are the conclusion of the poem "Waikiki" by Rollin Mallory Daggett, first published in 1882. Daggett served in Congress for a single term from 1879 to 1881. He became the United States Minister Resident to the Kingdom of Hawaii in 1882 and remained in that post until 1885. Daggett edited *The Legends and Myths of Hawaii* by King Kalākaua, first published in 1888.

73.   According to *Andrews*, "kamaaina" is a word compounded of "kama" (child) and "aina" (land), meaning "a child of the land" or native "born in any place and continuing to live in that place." Chan is exaggerating—he is not native-born, but a long-time resident.

"A what?"

"The term carries no offense. Malihini—stranger, newcomer."

"Oh." John Quincy looked at him curiously. "Are you a malihini?"

"Not in the least," grinned Chan. "I am kamaaina—old-timer.[73] Pursuing the truth further, I have been twenty-five years in the Islands."

They passed a huge hotel, and presently John Quincy saw Diamond Head standing an impressive guardian at the far end of that lovely curving beach. A little farther along the captain drew up to the curb and the four men alighted. On the other side of a dilapidated fence was a garden that might have been Eden at its best.

Entering past a gate that hung sorrowfully on one hinge they walked up a dirt path and in a moment a ramshackle old building came into view. They were approaching it on an angle, and John Quincy saw that the greater part of it extended out over the water. The tottering structure was of two stories, with double-decked balconies on both sides and the rear. It had rather an air about it; once, no doubt, it had been worthy to stand in this setting. Flowering vines clambered over it in a friendly endeavor to hide its imperfections from the world.

"Some day," announced Charlie Chan solemnly, "those rafters underneath will disintegrate and the Reef and Palm Hotel will descend into the sea with a most horrid gurgle."

As they drew nearer, it seemed to John Quincy that the China-man's prophecy might come true at any moment. They paused at the foot of a crumbling stair that led to the front door, and as they did so a man emerged hurriedly from the Reef and Palm. His once white clothes were yellowed, his face lined, his eyes tired and disillusioned. But about him, as about the hotel, hung the suggestion of a distinguished past.

"Mr. Egan," said Captain Hallet promptly.

"Oh—how are you?" the man replied, with an accent that recalled to John Quincy's mind his meeting with Captain Arthur Temple Cope.

"We want to talk to you," announced Hallet brusquely.

A shadow crossed Egan's face. "I'm frightfully sorry," he said, "but I have a most important engagement, and I'm late as it is. Some other time—"

"Now!" cut in Hallet. The word shot through the morning like a rocket. He started up the steps.

"Impossible," said Egan. He did not raise his voice. "Nothing on earth could keep me from the dock this morning—"

The captain of detectives seized his arm. "Come inside!" he ordered.

Egan's face flushed. "Take your hand off me, damn you! By what right—"

"You watch your step, Egan," advised Hallet angrily. "You know why I'm here."

"I do not."

Hallet stared into the man's face. "Dan Winterslip was murdered last night," he said.

Jim Egan removed his hat, and looked helplessly out toward Kalakaua Avenue. "So I read in the morning paper,"[74] he replied. "What has his death to do with me?"

"You were the last person to see him alive," Hallet answered. "Now quit bluffing and come inside."

Egan cast one final baffled glance at the street, where a trolley bound for the city three miles away was rattling swiftly by. Then he bowed his head and led the way into the hotel.

They entered a huge, poorly furnished public room, deserted save for a woman tourist writing postcards at a table, and a shabby Japanese clerk lolling behind the desk. "This way," Egan said, and they followed him past the desk and into a small private office. Here all was confusion, dusty piles of magazines and newspapers were everywhere, battered old ledgers lay upon the floor. On the wall hung a portrait of Queen Victoria; many pictures cut from the London illustrated weeklies were tacked up haphazardly. Jennison spread a newspaper carefully over the window-sill and sat down there. Egan cleared chairs for Hallet, Chan and John Quincy, and himself took his place before an ancient rolltop desk.

"If you will be brief, Captain," he suggested, "I might still have time—" He glanced at a clock above the desk.

"Forget that," advised Hallet sharply. His manner was considerably different from that he employed in the house of a leading citizen like Dan Winterslip. "Let's get to business." He turned to Chan. "Got your book, Charlie?"

"Preparations are complete," replied Chan, his pencil poised.

74. Likely the *Honolulu Advertiser*, the leading morning newspaper of the islands.

"All right." Hallet drew his chair closer to the desk. "Now Egan, you come through and come clean. I know that last night about seven-thirty you called up Dan Winterslip and tried to slide out of an appointment you had made with him. I know that he refused to let you off, and insisted on seeing you at eleven. About that time, you went to his house. You and he had a rather excited talk. At one-twenty-five Winterslip was found dead. Murdered, Egan! Now give me your end of it."

Jim Egan ran his fingers through his curly, close-cropped hair—straw-colored once, but now mostly gray. "That's all quite true," he said. "Do—do you mind if I smoke?" He took out a silver case and removed a cigarette. His hand trembled slightly as he applied the match. "I did make an appointment with Winterslip for last night," he continued. "During the course of the day I—I changed my mind. When I called up to tell him so, he insisted on seeing me. He urged me to come at eleven, and I went."

"Who let you in?" Hallet asked.

"Winterslip was waiting in the garden when I came. We went inside—"

Hallet glanced at the cigarette in Egan's hand. "By the door leading directly into the living-room?" he asked.

"No," said Egan. "By the big door at the front of the house. Winterslip took me out on his lanai, and we had a bit of a chat regarding the—the business that had brought me. About half an hour later, I came away. When I left, Winterslip was alive and well—in good spirits, too. Smiling, as a matter of fact."

"By what door did you leave?"

"The front door—the one I'd entered by."

"I see." Hallet looked at him thoughtfully for a moment. "You went back later, perhaps."

"I did not," said Egan promptly. "I came directly here and went to bed."

"Who saw you?"

"No one. My clerk goes off duty at eleven. The hotel is open, but there is no one in charge. My patronage is—not large."

"You came here at eleven-thirty and went to bed," Hallet said. "But no one saw you. Tell me, were you well acquainted with Dan Winterslip?"

Egan shook his head. "In the twenty-three years I've been in Honolulu, I had never spoken to him until I called him on the telephone yesterday morning."

"Humph." Hallet leaned back in his chair and spoke in a more amiable tone. "As a younger man, I believe you traveled a lot?"

"I drifted about a bit," Egan admitted. "I was just eighteen when I left England—"

"At your family's suggestion," smiled the captain.

"What's that to you?" Egan flared.

"Where did you go?"

"Australia. I ranched it for a time—and later I worked in Melbourne."

"What doing?" persisted Hallet.

"In—in a bank."

"A bank, eh? And then—"

"The South Seas. Just—wandering about—I was restless—"

"Beach-combing, eh?"

Egan flushed. "I may have been on my uppers at times, but damn it—"

"Wait a minute," Hallet cut in. "What I want to know is—those years you were drifting about—did you by any chance run into Dan Winterslip?"

"I—I might have."

"What sort of an answer is that! Yes or no?"

"Well, as a matter of fact, I did," Egan admitted. "Just once—in Melbourne. But it was a quite unimportant meeting. So unimportant Winterslip had completely forgotten it."

"But you hadn't. And yesterday morning, after twenty-three years' silence between you, you called him on the telephone. On rather sudden business."

"I did."

Hallet came closer. "All right, Egan. We've reached the important part of your story. What was that business?"

A tense silence fell in the little office as they awaited Egan's answer. The Englishman looked Hallet calmly in the eye. "I can't tell you that," he said.

Hallet's face reddened. "Oh, yes, you can. And you're going to."

"Never," answered Egan, without raising his voice.

The captain glared at him. "You don't seem to realize your position."

"I realize it perfectly."

"If you and I were alone—"

"I won't tell you under any circumstances, Hallet."

"Maybe you'll tell the prosecutor—"

"Look here," cried Egan wearily. "Why must I say it over and over? I'll tell nobody my business with Winterslip. Nobody, understand?" He crushed the half-smoked cigarette savagely down on to a tray at his side.

John Quincy saw Hallet nod to Chan. He saw the Chinaman's pudgy little hand go out and seize the remnant of cigarette. A happy grin spread over the Oriental's fat face. He handed the stub to his chief.

"Corsican brand!" he cried triumphantly.

"Ah, yes," said Hallet. "This your usual smoke?"

A startled look crossed Egan's tired face. "No, it's not," he said.

"It's a make that's not on sale in the Islands, I believe?"

"No, I fancy it isn't."

Captain Hallet held out his hand. "Give me your cigarette case, Egan." The Englishman passed it over, and Hallet opened it. "Humph," he said. "You've managed to get hold of a few, haven't you?"

"Yes. They were—given me."

"Is that so? Who gave them to you?"

Egan considered. "I'm afraid I can't tell you that, either," he said.

Hallet's eyes glittered angrily. "Let me give you a few facts," he began. "You called on Dan Winterslip last night, you entered and left by the front door, and you didn't go back. Yet just outside the door leading directly into the living-room, we have found a partly smoked cigarette of this unusual brand. Now will you tell me who gave you these Corsicans?"

"No," said Egan, "I won't."

Hallet slipped the silver cigarette case into his pocket, and stood up. "Very well," he remarked. "I've wasted all the time I intend to here. The district court prosecutor will want to talk to you—"

"Of course," agreed Egan, "I'll come and see him—this afternoon—"

Hallet glared at him. "Quit kidding yourself and get your hat!"

Egan rose too. "Look here," he cried, "I don't like your manner. It's true there are certain matters in connection with

Winterslip that I can't discuss, and that's unfortunate. But surely you don't think I killed the man. What motive would I have—"

Jennison rose quickly from his seat on the window-ledge and stepped forward. "Hallet," he said, "there's something I ought to tell you. Two or three years ago Dan Winterslip and I were walking along King Street, and we passed Mr. Egan here. Winterslip nodded toward him. 'I'm afraid of that man, Harry,' he said. I waited to hear more, but he didn't go on, and he wasn't the sort of client one would prompt. 'I'm afraid of that man, Harry.' Just that, and nothing further."

"It's enough," remarked Hallet grimly. "Egan, you're going with me."

Egan's eyes flashed. "Of course," he cried bitterly. "Of course I'm going with you. You're all against me, the whole town is against me, I've been sneered at and belittled for twenty years. Because I was poor. An outcast, my daughter humiliated, not good enough to associate with these New England blue-bloods—these thin-lipped Puritans with a touch of sun—"

At sound of that familiar phrase, John Quincy sat up. Where, where—oh, yes, on the Oakland ferry—

"Never mind that," Hallet was saying. "I'll give you one last chance. Will you tell me what I want to know?"

"I will not," cried Egan.

"All right. Then come along."

"Am I under arrest?" asked Egan.

"I didn't say that," replied Hallet, suddenly cautious. "The investigation is young yet. You are withholding much needed information, and I believe that after you've spent a few hours at the station, you'll change your mind and talk. In fact, I'm sure of it. I haven't any warrant, but your position will be a lot more dignified if you come willingly without one."

Egan considered a moment. "I fancy you're right," he said. "I have certain orders to give the servants, if you don't mind—"

Hallet nodded. "Make it snappy. Charlie will go with you."

Egan and the Chinaman disappeared. The captain, John Quincy and Jennison went out and sat down in the public room. Five minutes passed, ten, fifteen—

Jennison glanced at his watch. "See here, Hallet," he said. "The man's making a monkey of you—"

Hallet reddened, and stood up. At that instant Egan and Chan came down the big open stairway at one side of the room. Hallet went up to the Englishman.

"Say, Egan—what are you doing? Playing for time?"

Egan smiled. "That's precisely what I'm doing," he replied. "My daughter's coming in this morning on the *Matsonia*—the boat ought to be at the dock now. She's been at school on the mainland, and I haven't seen her for nine months. You've done me out of the pleasure of meeting her, but in a few minutes—"

"Nothing doing," cried Hallet. "Now you get your hat. I'm pau."

Egan hesitated a moment, then slowly took his battered old straw hat from the desk. The five men walked through the blooming garden toward Hallet's car. As they emerged into the street, a taxi drew up to the curb. Egan ran forward, and the girl John Quincy had last seen at the gateway to San Francisco leaped out into the Englishman's arms.

"Dad—where were you?" she cried.

"Cary, darling," he said. "I was so frightfully sorry—I meant to be at the dock but I was detained. How are you, my dear?"

"I'm fine, dad—but—where are you going?" She looked at Hallet; John Quincy remained discreetly in the background.

"I've—I've a little business in the city, my dear," Egan said. "I'll be home presently, I fancy. If—if I shouldn't be, I leave you in charge."

"Why, dad—"

"Don't worry," he added pleadingly. "That's all I can say now, Cary. Don't worry, my dear." He turned to Hallet. "Shall we go, Captain?"

The two policemen, Jennison and Egan entered the car. John Quincy stepped forward. The girl's big perplexed eyes met his.

"You?" she cried.

"Coming, Mr. Winterslip?" inquired Hallet.

John Quincy smiled at the girl. "You were quite right," he said. "I haven't needed that hat."

She looked up at him. "But you're not wearing any at all. That's hardly wise—"

"Mr. Winterslip!" barked Hallet.

John Quincy turned. "Oh, pardon me, Captain," he said. "I forgot to mention it, but I'm leaving you here. Good-by."

Hallet grunted and started his car. While the girl paid for her taxi out of a tiny purse, John Quincy picked up her suitcase.

"This time," he said, "I insist on carrying it." They stepped through the gateway into the garden that might have been Eden on one of its better days. "You didn't tell me we might meet in Honolulu," the boy remarked.

They stepped through the gateway into the garden that might have been on one of its loveliest days. "You didn't tell me we might meet in Honolulu," the boy remarked. From *The House Without a Key*, illustration by William Liepse (*The Saturday Evening Post*, February 7, 1925).

"I wasn't sure we would." She glanced at the shabby old hotel. "You see, I'm not exactly a social favorite out here." John Quincy could think of no reply, and they mounted the crumbling steps. The public room was quite deserted. "And why *have* we met?" the girl continued. "I'm fearfully puzzled. What was dad's business with those men? One of them was Captain Hallet—a policeman—"

John Quincy frowned. "I'm not so sure your father wants you to know."

"But I've got to know, that's obvious. Please tell me."

John Quincy relinquished the suit-case, and brought forward a chair. The girl sat down.

75. As stated at note 8, above, the Portuguese were the second-largest population of Hawaii, according to the 1920 Census.

"It's this way," he began. "My Cousin Dan was murdered in the night."

Her eyes were tragic. "Oh—poor Barbara!" she cried. That's right, he mustn't forget Barbara. "But dad—oh, go on please—"

"Your father visited Cousin Dan last night at eleven, and he refuses to say why. There are other things he refuses to tell."

She looked up at him, her eyes filled with sudden tears. "I was so happy on the boat," she said. "I knew it couldn't last."

He sat down. "Nonsense. Everything will come out all right. Your father is probably shielding some one—"

She nodded. "Of course. But if he's made up his mind not to talk, he just simply won't talk. He's odd that way. They may keep him down there, and I shall be all alone—"

"Not quite alone," John Quincy told her.

"No, no," she said. "I've warned you. We're not the sort the best people care to know—"

"The more fools they," cut in the boy. "I'm John Quincy Winterslip, of Boston. And you—"

"Carlota Maria Egan," she answered. "You see, my mother was half Portuguese.[75] The other half was Scotch-Irish—my father's English. This is the melting pot out here, you know." She was silent for a moment. "My mother was very beautiful," she added wistfully. "So they tell me—I never knew."

John Quincy was touched. "I thought how beautiful she must have been," he said gently. "That day I met you on the ferry."

The girl dabbed at her eyes with an absurd little handkerchief, and stood up. "Well," she remarked, "this is just another thing that has to be faced. Another call for courage—I must meet it." She smiled. "The lady manager of the Reef and Palm. Can I show you a room?"

"I say, it'll be a rather stiff job, won't it?" John Quincy rose too.

"Oh, I shan't mind. I've helped dad before. Only one thing troubles me—bills and all that. I've no head for arithmetic."

"That's all right—I have," replied John Quincy. He stopped. Wasn't he getting in a little deep?

"How wonderful," the girl said.

"Why, not at all," John Quincy protested. "It's my line, at home." Home! Yes, he had a home, he recalled. "Bonds and interest and all that sort of thing. I'll drop in later in the day to see how you're getting on." He moved away in a mild panic. "I'd better be going now," he added.

"Of course." She followed him to the door. "You're altogether too kind. Shall you be in Honolulu long?"

"That depends," John Quincy said. "I've made up my mind to one thing. I shan't stir from here until this mystery about Cousin Dan is solved. And I'm going to do everything in my power to help in solving it."

"I'm sure you're very clever, too," she told him.

He shook his head. "I wouldn't say that. But I intend to make the effort of my life. I've got a lot of incentives for seeing this affair through." Something else trembled on his tongue. Better not say it. Oh, lord, he was saying it. "You're one of them," he added, and clattered down the stairs.

"Do be careful," called the girl. "Those steps are even worse than they were when I left. Just another thing to be repaired—some day—when our ship comes in."

He left her smiling wistfully in the doorway and hurrying through the garden, stepped out on Kalakaua Avenue. The blazing sun beat down on his defenseless head. Gorgeous trees flaunted scarlet banners along his path, tall cocoanut palms swayed above him at the touch of the friendly trades, not far away rainbow-tinted waters lapped a snowy beach. A sweet land—all of that.

Did he wish that Agatha Parker were there to see it with him? Pursuing the truth further, as Charlie Chan would put it, he did not.

CHAPTER X

A Newspaper Ripped in Anger

76. *Andrews* defines the word as "[a] diffi-culty; a hindrance; a perilous situation; extreme danger, as in distress."

77. The *Boston Evening Transcript* was a daily afternoon newspaper published in Boston from 1830 to 1941. Had Minerva talked to editors? Or perhaps she simply meant that while she had talked to *Transcript* reporters in the past, it had been on the telephone.

When John Quincy got back to the living-room he found Miss Minerva pacing up and down with the light of battle in her eyes. He selected a large, com-fortablelooking chair and sank into it.

"Anything the matter?" he inquired. "You seem disturbed."

"I've just been having a lot of pilikia,"[76] she announced.

"What's that—another native drink?" he said with interest. "Could I have some too?"

"Pilikia means trouble," she translated. "Several reporters have been here, and you'd hardly credit the questions they asked."

"About Cousin Dan, eh?" John Quincy nodded. "I can imagine."

"However, they got nothing out of me. I took good care of that."

"Go easy," advised John Quincy. "A fellow back home who had a divorce case in his family was telling me that if you're not polite to the newspaper boys they just plain break your heart."

"Don't worry," said Miss Minerva. "I was diplomatic, of course. I think I handled them rather well, under the circumstances. They were the first reporters I'd ever met—though I've had the pleasure of talking with gentlemen from the *Transcript*.[77] What happened at the Reef and Palm Hotel?"

John Quincy told her—in part.

"Well, I shouldn't be surprised if Egan turned out to be guilty," she commented. "I've made a few inquiries about him this morning, and he doesn't appear to amount to much. A sort of glorified beach-comber."

"Nonsense," objected John Quincy. "Egan's a gentleman. Just because he doesn't happen to have prospered is no reason for condemning him without a hearing."

"He's had a hearing," snapped Miss Minerva. "And it seems he's been mixed up in something he's not precisely proud of. There, I've gone and ended a sentence with a preposition. Probably all this has upset me more than I realize."

John Quincy smiled. "Cousin Dan," he reminded her, "was also mixed up in a few affairs he could hardly have looked back on with pride. No, Aunt Minerva, I feel Hallet is on the wrong trail there. It's just as Egan's daughter said—"

She glanced at him quickly. "Oh—so Egan has a daughter?"

"Yes, and a mighty attractive girl. It's a confounded shame to put this thing on her."

"Humph," said Miss Minerva.

John Quincy glanced at his watch. "Good lord—it's only ten o'clock!" A great calm had settled over the house, there was no sound save the soft lapping of waves on the beach outside. "What, in heaven's name, do you do out here?"

"Oh, you'll become accustomed to it shortly," Miss Minerva answered. "At first, you just sit and think. After a time, you just sit."

"Sounds fascinating," said John Quincy sarcastically.

"That's the odd part of it," his aunt replied, "it is. One of the things you think about, at first, is going home. When you stop thinking, that naturally slips your mind."

"We gathered that," John Quincy told her.

"You'll meet a man on the beach," said Miss Minerva, "who stopped over between boats to have his laundry done. That was twenty years ago, and he's still here."

"Probably they haven't finished his laundry," suggested John Quincy, yawning openly. "Ho, hum. I'm going up to my room to change, and after that I believe I'll write a few letters." He rose with an effort and went to the door. "How's Barbara?" he asked.

Miss Minerva shook her head. "Dan was all the poor child had," she said. "She's taken it rather hard. You won't see her for some time, and when you do—the least said about all this, the better."

"Dan was all the poor child had," she said. "She's taken it rather hard."
From *The House Without a Key*, illustration by William Liepse
(*The Saturday Evening Post*, February 7, 1925)

"Why, naturally," agreed John Quincy, and went up-stairs.

After he had bathed and put on his whitest, thinnest clothes, he explored the desk that stood near his bed and found it well supplied with note paper. Languidly laying out a sheet, he began to write.

"DEAR AGATHA: Here I am in Honolulu and outside my window I can hear the lazy swish of waters lapping the famous beach of—"

Lazy, indeed. John Quincy had a feeling for words. He stopped and stared at an agile little cloud flitting swiftly through the sky—got up from his chair to watch it disappear over Diamond

Head. On his way back to the desk he had to pass the bed. What inviting beds they had out here! He lifted the mosquito netting and dropped down for a moment—

Haku hammered on the door at one o'clock, and that was how John Quincy happened to be present at lunch. His aunt was already at the table when he staggered in.

"Cheer up," she smiled. "You'll become acclimated soon. Of course, even then you'll want your nap just after lunch every day."

"I will not," he answered, but there was no conviction in his tone.

"Barbara asked me to tell you how sorry she is not to be with you. She's a sweet girl, John Quincy."

"She's all of that. Give her my love, won't you?"

"Your love?" His aunt looked at him. "Do you mean that? Barbara's only a second cousin—"

He laughed. "Don't waste your time match-making, Aunt Minerva. Some one has already spoken for Barbara."

"Really? Who?"

"Jennison. He seems like a fine fellow, too."

"Handsome, at any rate," Miss Minerva admitted. They ate in silence for a time. "The coroner and his friends were here this morning," said Miss Minerva presently.

"That so?" replied John Quincy. "Any verdict?"

"Not yet. I believe they're to settle on that later. By the way, I'm going downtown immediately after lunch to do some shopping for Barbara. Care to come along?"

"No, thanks," John Quincy said. "I must go up-stairs and finish my letters."

But when he left the luncheon table, he decided the letters could wait. He took a heavy volume with a South Sea title from Dan's library, and went out on to the lanai. Presently Miss Minerva appeared, smartly dressed in white linen.

"I'll return as soon as I'm pau," she announced.

"What is this pau?" John Quincy inquired.

"Pau means finished—through."

"Good lord," John Quincy said. "Aren't there enough words in the English language for you?"

"Oh, I don't know," she answered, "a little Hawaiian sprinkled in makes a pleasant change. And when one reaches my age, John Quincy, one is eager for a change. Good-by."

78. By the mid-1920s, the bathing costumes *were* alluring—far more so than the Puritanical outfits of the nineteenth century. Although (short) bathing-skirts had been fashionable in the previous decade, the suits of the 1920s were not that different from one-piece suits featured in the distant future of the 2010s. However, the height of women's bathing suits above the knee was strictly regulated on many mainland beaches.

A mainland police officer checking the length of a bathing suit.

A beach party in the mid-1920s.

79. And sure enough, June 16 was a Monday in 1924 (and also in 1919, but that long predates the publication of Adams's book—see note 55). The two leading Hawaiian newspapers were the *Honolulu Advertiser* (a morning newspaper) and the *Honolulu Star-Bulletin* (afternoon—the

She left him to his book and the somnolent atmosphere of Dan's lanai. Sometimes he read, colorful tales of other islands farther south. Sometimes he sat and thought. Sometimes he just sat. The blazing afternoon wore on; presently the beach beyond Dan's garden was gay with bathers, sunburned men and girls, pretty girls in brief and alluring costumes.[78] Their cries as they dared the surf were exultant, happy. John Quincy was keen to try these notable waters, but it didn't seem quite the thing—not just yet, with Dan Winterslip lying in that room up-stairs.

Miss Minerva reappeared about five, flushed and—though she well knew it was not the thing for one of her standing in the Back Bay—perspiring. She carried an evening paper in her hand.

"Any news?" inquired John Quincy.

She sat down. "Nothing but the coroner's verdict. The usual thing—person or persons unknown. But as I was reading the paper in the car, I had a sudden inspiration."

"Good for you. What was it?"

Haku appeared at the door leading to the living-room. "You ring, miss?" he said.

"I did. Haku, what becomes of the old newspapers in this house?"

"Take and put in a closet beside kitchen," the man told her.

"See if you can find me—no, never mind. I'll look myself."

She followed Haku into the living-room. In a few minutes she returned alone, a newspaper in her hand.

"I have it," she announced triumphantly. "The evening paper of Monday, June sixteenth[79]—the one Dan was reading the night he wrote that letter to Roger. And look, John Quincy—one corner has been torn from the shipping page!"

"Might have been accidental," suggested John Quincy languidly.

"Nonsense!" she said sharply. "It's a clue, that's what it is. The item that disturbed Dan was on that missing corner of the page."

"Might have been, at that," he admitted. "What are you going to do—"

"You're the one that's going to do it," she cut in. "Pull yourself together and go into town. It's two hours until dinner. Give this paper to Captain Hallet—or better still, to Charlie Chan. I am impressed by Mr. Chan's intelligence."

John Quincy laughed. "Damned clever, these Chinese!" he quoted.[80] "You don't mean to say you've fallen for that bunk. They seem clever because they're so different."

"We'll see about that. The chauffeur's gone on an errand for Barbara, but there's a roadster in the garage—"

"Trolley's good enough for me," said John Quincy. "Here, give me the paper."

She explained to him how he was to reach the city, and he got his hat and went. Presently he was on a trolley-car surrounded by representatives of a dozen different races. The melting pot of the Pacific, Carlota Egan had called Honolulu, and the appellation seemed to be correct. John Quincy began to feel a fresh energy, a new interest in life.

The trolley swept over the low swampy land between Waikiki and Honolulu, past rice fields where quaint figures toiled patiently in water to their knees, past taro patches, and finally turned on to King Street. Every few moments it paused to take aboard immigrants, Japs, Chinamen, Hawaiians, Portuguese, Philippinos, Koreans, all colors and all creeds. On it went. John Quincy saw great houses set in blooming groves, a Japanese theater flaunting weird posters not far from a Ford service station, then a huge building he recognized as the palace of the monarchy. Finally it entered a district of modern office buildings.

Mr. Kipling was wrong, the boy reflected, East and West could meet.[81] They had.

This impression was confirmed when he left the car at Fort Street and for a moment walked about, a stranger in a strange land. A dusky policeman was directing traffic on the corner, officers of the United States army and navy in spotless duck strolled by, and on the shady side of the street Chinese girls, slim and immaculate in freshly laundered trousers and jackets, were window shopping in the cool of the evening.

"I'm looking for the police station," John Quincy informed a big American with a friendly face.

"Get back on to King Street," the man said. "Go to your right until you come to Bethel, then turn makai—"

"Turn what?"

The man smiled. "A malihini, I take it. Makai means toward the sea. The other direction is mauka—toward the mountains. The police station is at the foot of Bethel, in Kalakaua Hale."

"evening" paper to which Minerva undoubtedly refers).

80.   A common racist catchphrase, it became the title of a popular song in 1924.

A 1920s Ford Model T roadster

81.   The most famous stanza of Rudyard Kipling's much-anthologized "The Ballad of East and West" (1889) is:

"Oh, East is East, and West is West, and never the twain shall meet,
"Till Earth and Sky stand presently at God's great Judgment seat;
"But there is neither East nor West, Border, nor Breed, nor Birth,
"When two strong men stand face to face, though they come from the ends of the earth!"

82. A substantial downtown hotel, on Bishop Street between King Street and Hotel Street.

Advertisement for the Alexander Young Hotel.

83. The establishment is not listed in Polk-Husted Directory Co.'s *Directory of the City of Honolulu and Territory of Hawaii* for 1924.

John Quincy thanked him and went on his way. He passed the post-office and was amazed to see that all the lock boxes opened on the street. After a time, he reached the station. A sergeant lounging behind the desk told him that Charlie Chan was at dinner. He suggested the Alexander Young Hotel[82] or possibly the All American Restaurant[83] on King Street.

The hotel sounded easiest, so John Quincy went there first. In the dim lobby a Chinese house boy wandered aimlessly about with broom and dust pan, a few guests were writing the inevitable post-cards, a Chinese clerk was on duty at the desk. But there was no sign of Chan, either in the lobby or in the dining-room at the left. As John Quincy turned from an inspection of the latter, the elevator door opened and a Britisher in mufti came hurriedly forth. He was followed by a Cockney servant carrying luggage.

"Captain Cope," called John Quincy.

The captain paused. "Hello," he said. "Oh—Mr. Winterslip—how are you?" He turned to the servant. "Buy me an evening paper and an armful of the less offensive-looking magazines." The man hurried off, and Cope again addressed John Quincy. "Delighted to see you, but I'm in a frightful rush. Off to the Fanning Islands in twenty minutes."

"When did you get in?" inquired John Quincy. Not that he really cared.

"Yesterday at noon," said Captain Cope. "Been on the wing ever since. I trust you are enjoying your stop here—but I was forgetting. Fearful news about Dan Winterslip."

"Yes," said John Quincy coolly. Judging by the conversation in that San Francisco club, the blow had not been a severe one for Captain Cope. The servant returned.

"Sorry to run," continued the captain. "But I must be off. The service is a stern taskmaster. My regards to your aunt. Best of luck, my boy."

He disappeared through the wide door, followed by his man. John Quincy reached the street in time to see him rolling off in a big car toward the docks.

Noting the cable office near by, the boy entered and sent two messages, one to his mother and the other to Agatha Parker. He addressed them to Boston, Mass. U.S.A., and was accorded a withering look by the young woman in charge as she crossed out the last three letters. There were only two words in each message, but he returned to the street with the comfortable feeling that his correspondence was now attended to for some time to come.

A few moments later he encountered the All American Restaurant and going inside, found himself the only American in the place.[84] Charlie Chan was seated alone at a table, and as John Quincy approached, he rose and bowed.

"A very great honor," said the Chinaman. "Is it possible that I can prevail upon you to accept some of this terrible provision?"

"No, thanks," answered John Quincy. "I'm to dine later at the house. I'll sit down for a moment, if I may."

"Quite overwhelmed," bobbed Charlie. He resumed his seat and scowled at something on the plate before him. "Waiter," he said. "Be kind enough to summon the proprietor of this establishment."

The proprietor, a suave little Jap, came gliding. He bowed from the waist.

"Is it that you serve here insanitary food?" inquired Chan.

"Please deign to state your complaint," said the Jap.

"This piece of pie are covered with finger-marks," rebuked Chan. "The sight is most disgusting. Kindly remove it and bring me a more hygienic sector."

The Jap picked up the offending pastry and carried it away.

"Japanese," remarked Chan, spreading his hands in an eloquent gesture.[85] "Is it proper for me to infer that you come on business connected with the homicide?"

John Quincy smiled. "I do," he said. He took the newspaper from his pocket, pointed out the date and the missing corner. "My aunt felt it might be important," he explained.

"The woman has a brain," said Chan. "I will procure an unmutilated specimen of this issue and compare. The import may be vast."

"You know," remarked John Quincy, "I'd like to work with you on this case, if you'll let me."

"I have only delight," Chan answered. "You arrive from Boston, a city most cultivated, where much more English words are put to employment than are accustomed here. I thrill when you speak. Greatest privilege for me, I would say."

"Have you formed any theory about the crime?" John Quincy asked.

Chan shook his head. "Too early now."

"You have no finger-prints to go on, you said."

84. John Quincy didn't take his rebuke at the post office to heart, apparently, nor did he recall the stories about the congressman or the senator; of course, everyone in the place is *American*, including Chan. John Quincy means he's the only *white* person in the restaurant.

85. Japanese expansion in the Pacific region, the influx of Japanese nationals into Hawaii, and the fear that Japan would attempt to make Hawaii its own was clearly an important factor in the annexation of Hawaii by the United States. In addition, China and Japan had a fractious relationship for centuries. In 1915, Japan made demands on the Chinese government that it was forced to accept, ceding rights formerly controlled by the Germans, and this humiliation ultimately led to the Mukden incident in 1931, leading to the Japanese invasion of Manchuria, and the outbreak of war between the nations in 1937. Chan's disparagement of the Japanese cuisine is in character, then, with these simmering hostilities.

Chan shrugged his shoulders. "Does not matter. Finger-prints and other mechanics good in books, in real life not so much so. My experience tell me to think deep about human people. Human passions. Back of murder, what, always? Hate, revenge, need to make silent the slain one. Greed for money, maybe. Study human people at all times."

"Sounds reasonable," admitted John Quincy.

"Mostly so," Chan averred. "Enumerate with me the clues we must consider. A guest book devoid of one page. A glove button. A message on the cable. Story of Egan, partly told. Fragment of Corsican cigarette. This newspaper ripped maybe in anger. Watch on living wrist, numeral 2 undistinct."

"Quite a little collection," commented John Quincy.

"Most interesting," admitted the Chinaman. "One by one, we explore. Some cause us to arrive at nowhere. One, maybe two, will not be so unkind. I am believer in Scotland Yard method—follow only essential clue. But it are not the method here. I must follow all, entire."

"The essential clue," repeated John Quincy.

"Sure." Chan scowled at the waiter, for his more hygienic sector had not appeared. "Too early to say here. But I have fondness for the guest book with page omitted. Watch also claims my attention. Odd enough, when we enumerate clues this morning, we pass over watch. Foolish. Very good-looking clue. One large fault, we do not possess it. However, my eyes are sharp to apprehend it."

"I understand," John Quincy said, "that you've been rather successful as a detective."

Chan grinned broadly. "You are educated, maybe you know," he said. "Chinese most psychic people in the world. Sensitives, like film in camera. A look, a laugh, a gesture perhaps. Something go click."

John Quincy was aware of a sudden disturbance at the door of the All American Restaurant. Bowker, the steward, gloriously drunk, was making a noisy entrance. He plunged into the room, followed by a dark, anxious-looking youth.

Embarrassed, John Quincy turned away his face, but to no avail. Bowker was bearing down upon him, waving his arms.

"Well, well, well, well!" he bellowed. "My o' college chum. See you through the window." He leaned heavily on the table. "How you been, o' fellow?"

"I'm all right, thanks," John Quincy said.

The dark young man came up. He was, from his dress, a shore acquaintance of Bowker's. "Look here, Ted," he said. "You've got to be getting along—"

"Jush a minute," cried Bowker. "I want y' to meet Mr. Quincy from Boston. One best fellows God ever made. Mushual friend o' Tim's—you've heard me speak of Tim—"

"Yes—come along," urged the dark young man.

"Not yet. Gotta buy shish boy a lil' drink. What you having, Quincy, o' man?"

"Not a thing," smiled John Quincy. "You warned me against these Island drinks yourself."

"Who—me?" Bowker was hurt. "You're wrong that time, o' man. Don' like to conter—conterdict, but it mush have been somebody else. Not me. Never said a word—"

The young man took his arm. "Come on—you're due on the ship—"

Bowker wrenched away. "Don' paw me," he cried. "Keep your hands off. I'm my own mashter, ain't I? I can speak to an o' friend, can't I? Now, Quincy, o' man—what's yours?"

"I'm sorry," said John Quincy. "Some other time."

Bowker's companion took his arm in a firmer grasp. "You can't buy anything here," he said. "This is a restaurant. You come with me—I know a place—"

"Awright," agreed Bowker. "Now you're talking. Quincy, o' man, you come along—"

"Some other time," John Quincy repeated.

Bowker assumed a look of offended dignity. "Jush as you say," he replied. "Some other time. In Boston, hey? At Tim's place. Only Tim's place is gone." A great grief assailed him. "Tim's gone—dropped out—as though the earth swallowed him up—"

"Yes, yes," said the young man soothingly. "That's too bad. But you come with me."

Submitting at last, Bowker permitted his companion to pilot him to the street. John Quincy looked across at Chan.

"My steward on the *President Tyler*," he explained. "The worse for wear, isn't he?"

The waiter set a fresh piece of pie before the Chinaman.

"Ah," remarked Chan, "this has a more perfect appearance." He tasted it. "Appearance," he added with a grimace, "are a hellish liar. If you are quite ready to depart—"

86. The *Atlantic Monthly*, a "magazine of literature, art, and politics," was founded in 1857 and, until 2005, was published in Boston.

In the street Chan halted. "Excuse abrupt departure," he said. "Most honored to work with you. The results will be fascinating, I am sure. For now, good evening."

John Quincy was alone again in that strange town. A sudden homesickness engulfed him. Walking along, he came to a news-cart that was as well supplied with literature as his club reading room. A brisk young man in a cap was in charge.

"Have you the latest *Atlantic*?"[86] inquired John Quincy.

The young man put a dark brown periodical into his hand. "No," said John Quincy. "This is the June issue. I've seen it."

"July ain't in. I'll save you one, if you say so."

"I wish you would," John Quincy replied. "The name is Winterslip."

He went on to the corner, regretting that July wasn't in. A copy of the *Atlantic* would have been a sort of link with home, a reminder that Boston still stood. And he felt the need of a link, a reminder.

A trolley-car marked "Waikiki" was approaching. John Quincy hailed it and hopped aboard. Three giggling Japanese girls in bright kimonos drew in their tiny sandaled feet and he slipped past them to a seat.

CHAPTER XI

The Tree of Jewels

Two hours later, John Quincy rose from the table where he and his aunt had dined together.

"Just to show you how quick I am to learn a new language," he remarked, "I'm quite pau. Now I'm going makai to sit on the lanai, there to forget the pilikia of the day."

Miss Minerva smiled and rose too. "I expect Amos shortly," she said as they crossed the hall. "A family conference seemed advisable, so I've asked him to come over."

"Strange you had to send for him," said John Quincy, lighting a cigarette.

"Not at all," she answered. She explained about the long feud between the brothers.

"Didn't think old Amos had that much fire in him," commented John Quincy, as they found chairs on the lanai. "A rather anemic specimen, judging by the look I had at him this morning. But then, the Winterslips always were good haters."

For a moment they sat in silence. Outside the darkness was deepening rapidly, the tropic darkness that had brought tragedy the night before. John Quincy pointed to a small lizard on the screen.

"Pleasant little beast," he said.

"Oh, they're quite harmless," Miss Minerva told him. "And they eat the mosquitos."

"They do, eh?" The boy slapped his ankle savagely. "Well, there's no accounting for tastes."

Amos arrived presently, looking unusually pale in the half-light. "You asked me to come over, Minerva," he said, as he sat down gingerly on one of Dan Winterslip's Hong-Kong chairs.

"I did. Smoke if you like." Amos lighted a cigarette, which seemed oddly out of place between his thin lips. "I'm sure," Miss Minerva continued, "that we are all determined to bring to justice the person who did this ghastly thing."

"Naturally," said Amos.

"The only drawback," she went on, "is that in the course of the investigation some rather unpleasant facts about Dan's past are likely to be revealed."

"They're bound to be," remarked Amos coldly.

"For Barbara's sake," Miss Minerva said, "I'm intent on seeing that nothing is revealed that is not absolutely essential to the discovery of the murderer. For that reason, I haven't taken the police completely into my confidence."

"What!" cried Amos.

John Quincy stood up. "Now look here, Aunt Minerva—"

"Sit down," snapped his aunt. "Amos, to go back to a talk we had at your house when I was there, Dan was somewhat involved with this woman down the beach. Arlene Compton, I believe she calls herself."

Amos nodded. "Yes, and a worthless lot she is. But Dan wouldn't see it, though I understand his friends pointed it out to him. He talked of marrying her."

"You knew a good deal about Dan, even if you never spoke to him," Miss Minerva went on. "Just what was his status with this woman at the time of his murder—only last night, but it seems ages ago."

"I can't quite tell you that," Amos replied. "I do know that for the past month a malihini named Leatherbee—the black sheep of a good family in Philadelphia, they tell me—has been hanging around the Compton woman, and that Dan resented his presence."

"Humph." Miss Minerva handed to Amos an odd old brooch, a tree of jewels against an onyx background. "Ever see that before, Amos?"

He took it, and nodded. "It's part of a little collection of jewelry Dan brought back from the South Seas in the 'eighties. There were earrings and a bracelet, too. He acted rather queerly about those trinkets—never let Barbara's mother or any one else wear them. But he must have got over that idea recently. For I saw this only a few weeks ago."

"Where?" asked Miss Minerva.

"Our office has the renting of the cottage down the beach occupied at present by the Compton woman. She came in not long ago to pay her rent, and she was wearing this brooch." He looked suddenly at Miss Minerva. "Where did you get it?" he demanded.

"Kamaikui gave it to me early this morning," Miss Minerva explained. "She picked it up from the floor of the lanai before the police came."

John Quincy leaped to his feet. "You're all wrong, Aunt Minerva," he cried. "You can't do this sort of thing. You ask the help of the police, and you aren't on the level with them. I'm ashamed of you—"

"Please wait a moment," said his aunt.

"Wait nothing!" he answered. "Give me that brooch. I'm going to turn it over to Chan at once. I couldn't look him in the eye if I didn't."

"We'll turn it over to Chan," said Miss Minerva calmly, "if it seems important. But there is no reason in the world why we should not investigate a bit ourselves before we do so. The woman may have a perfectly logical explanation—"

"Rot!" interrupted John Quincy. "The trouble with you is, you think you're Sherlock Holmes."

"What is your opinion, Amos?" inquired Miss Minerva.

"I'm inclined to agree with John Quincy," Amos said. "You are hardly fair to Captain Hallet. And as for keeping anything dark on account of Barbara—or on anybody's account—that won't be possible, I'm afraid. No getting round it, Minerva, Dan's indiscretions are going to be dragged into the open at last."

She caught the note of satisfaction in his tone, and was nettled by it. "Perhaps. At the same time, it isn't going to do any harm for some member of the family to have a talk with this woman before we consult the police. If she should have a perfectly sincere and genuine explanation—"

"Oh, yes," cut in John Quincy. "She wouldn't have any other kind."

"It won't be so much what she says," persisted Miss Minerva. "It will be the manner in which she says it. Any intelligent person can see through deceit and falsehood. The only question is, which of us is the intelligent person best fitted to examine her."

"Count me out," said Amos promptly.

"John Quincy?"

The boy considered. He had asked for the privilege of working with Chan, and here, perhaps, was an opportunity to win the Chinaman's respect. But this sounded rather like a woman who would be too much for him.

"No, thanks," he said.

"Very good," replied Miss Minerva, rising. "I'll go myself."

"Oh, no," cried John Quincy, shocked.

"Why not? If none of the men in the family are up to it. As a matter of fact, I welcome the opportunity—"

Amos shook his head. "She'll twist you round her little finger," he predicted.

Miss Minerva smiled grimly. "I should like to see her do it. Will you wait here?"

John Quincy went over and took the brooch from Amos's hand. "Sit down, Aunt Minerva," he said. "I'll see this woman. But I warn you that immediately afterward I shall send for Chan."

"That," his aunt told him, "will be decided at another conference. I'm not so sure, John Quincy, that you are the proper person to go. After all, what experience have you had with women of this type?"

John Quincy was offended. He was a man, and he felt that he could meet and outwit a woman of any type. He said as much.

Amos described the woman's house as a small cottage several hundred yards down the beach, and directed the boy how to get there. John Quincy set out.

Night had fallen over the Island when he reached Kalia Road, a bright silvery night, for the Kona weather was over and the moon traveled a cloudless sky. The scent of plumeria and ginger stole out to him through hedges of flaming hibiscus; the trade winds, blowing across a thousand miles of warm water, still managed a cool touch on his cheek. As he approached what he judged must be the neighborhood of the woman's house, a flock of Indian myna birds in a spreading algaroba screamed loudly, their harsh voices the only note of discord in that peaceful scene.

He had some difficulty locating the cottage, which was almost completely hidden under masses of flowering alamander, its blossoms pale yellow in the moonlight. Before the door, a dark fragrant spot under a heavily laden trellis, he paused uncertainly. A rather delicate errand, this was. But he summoned his courage and knocked.

Only the myna birds replied. John Quincy stood there, growing momentarily more hostile to the Widow of Waikiki. Some huge coarse creature, no doubt, a man's woman, a good fellow at a party—that kind. Then the door opened and the boy got a shock. For the figure outlined against the light was young and slender, and the face, dimly seen, suggested fragile loveliness.

"Is this Mrs. Compton?" he inquired.

"Yeah—I'm Mrs. Compton. What do you want?" John Quincy was sorry she had spoken. For she was, obviously, one of those beauties so prevalent nowadays, the sort whom speech betrays. Her voice recalled the myna birds.

"My name is John Quincy Winterslip." He saw her start. "May I speak with you for a moment?"

"Sure you can. Come in." She led the way along a low narrow passage into a tiny living-room. A pasty-faced young man with stooped shoulders stood by a table, fondling a cocktail shaker.

"Steve," said the woman, "this is Mr. Winterslip. Mr. Leatherbee."

Mr. Leatherbee grunted. "Just in time for a little snifter," he remarked.

"No, thanks," John Quincy said. He saw Mrs. Compton take a smoking cigarette from an ash tray, start to convey it to her lips, then, evidently thinking better of it, crush it on the tray.

"Well," said Mr. Leatherbee, "your poison's ready, Arlene." He proffered a glass.

She shook her head, slightly annoyed. "No."

"No?" Mr. Leatherbee grinned. "The more for little Stevie." He lifted a glass. "Here's looking at you, Mr. Winterslip."

"Say, I guess you're Dan's cousin from Boston," Mrs. Compton remarked. "He was telling me about you." She lowered her voice. "I've been meaning to get over to your place all day. But it was such a shock—it knocked me flat."

"I understand," John Quincy replied. He glanced at Mr. Leatherbee, who seemed not to have heard of prohibition. "My business with you, Mrs. Compton, is private."

Leatherbee stiffened belligerently. But the woman said: "That's all right. Steve was just going."

Steve hesitated a moment, then went. His hostess accompanied him. John Quincy heard the low monotone of their voices in the distance. There was a combined odor of gin and cheap perfume in the air; the boy wondered what his mother would say if she could see him now. A door slammed, and the woman returned.

"Well?" she said. John Quincy perceived that her eyes were hard and knowing, like her voice. He waited for her to sit down, then took a chair facing her.

"You knew my Cousin Dan rather intimately," he suggested.

"I was engaged to him," she answered. John Quincy glanced at her left hand. "He hadn't come across—I mean, he hadn't given me a ring, but it was—you know—understood between us."

"Then his death is a good deal of a blow to you?"

She managed a baby stare, full of pathos. "I'll say it is. Mr. Winterslip was kind to me—he believed in me and trusted me. A lone woman way out here don't get any too much char—kindness."

"When did you see Mr. Winterslip last?"

"Three or four days ago—last Friday evening, I guess it was."

John Quincy frowned. "Wasn't that rather a long stretch?"

She nodded. "I'll tell you the truth. We had a little—misunderstanding. Just a lover's quarrel, you know. Dan sort of objected to Steve hanging around. Not that he'd any reason to—Steve's nothing to me—just a weak kid I used to know when I was trouping. I was on the stage—maybe you heard that."

"Yes," said John Quincy. "You hadn't seen Mr. Winterslip since last Friday. You didn't go to his house last evening?"

"I should say not. I got my reputation to think of—you've no idea how people talk in a place like this—"

John Quincy laid the brooch down upon the table. It sparkled in the lamplight—a reading lamp, though the atmosphere was not in the least literary. The baby stare was startled now. "You recognize that, don't you?" he asked.

"Why—yes—it's—I—"

"Just stick to the truth," said John Quincy, not unkindly. "It's an old piece of jewelry that Mr. Winterslip gave you, I believe."

"Well—"

"You've been seen wearing it, you know."

"Yes, he did give it to me," she admitted. "The only present I ever got from him. I guess from the look of it Mrs. Noah wore it on the Ark. Kinda pretty, though."

"You didn't visit Mr. Winterslip last night," persisted John Quincy. "Yet, strangely enough, this brooch was found on the floor not far from his dead body."

She drew in her breath sharply. "Say—what are you? A cop?" she asked.

"Hardly," John Quincy smiled. "I am here simply to save you, if possible, from the hands of the—er—the cops. If you have any real explanation of this matter, it may not be necessary to call it to the attention of the police."

"Oh!" She smiled. "Say, that's decent of you. Now I will tell you the truth. That about not seeing Dan Winterslip since Friday was bunk. I saw him last night."

"Ah—you did? Where?"

"Right here. Mr. Winterslip gave me that thing about a month ago. Two weeks ago he came to me in a sort of excited way and said he must have it back. It was the only thing he ever give me and I liked it and those emeralds are valuable—so—well, I stalled a while. I said I was having a new clasp put on it. He kept asking for it, and last night he showed up here and said he just had to have it. Said he'd buy me anything in the stores in place of it. I must say he was pretty het up. So I finally turned it over to him and he took it and went away."

"What time was that?"

"About nine-thirty. He was happy and pleasant and he said I could go to a jewelry store this morning and take my pick of the stock." She looked pleadingly at John Quincy. "That's the last I ever saw of him. It's the truth, so help me."

"I wonder," mused John Quincy.

She moved nearer. "Say, you're a nice kid," she said. "The kind I used to meet in Boston when we played there. The kind that's got some consideration for a woman. You ain't going to drag me into this. Think what it would mean—to me."

John Quincy did not speak. He saw there were tears in her eyes. "You've probably heard things about me," she went on, "but they ain't true. You don't know what I been up against out here. An unprotected woman don't have much chance anywhere, but on this beach, where men come drifting in from all over the world—I been friendly, that's my only trouble. I was homesick—oh, God, wasn't I homesick! I was having a good time back there, and then I fell for Bill Compton and came out here with him, and

87. Forty-Second Street in Manhattan is the prime neighborhood of Broadway and indelibly associated with New York theater. Shows planning to open on Broadway often had trial runs ("tryouts") outside New York, in towns like New Haven, Connecticut, although the practice has declined as production costs have risen.

sometimes in the night I'd wake up and remember Broadway was five thousand miles away, and I'd cry so hard I'd wake him. And that made him sore—"

She paused. John Quincy was impressed by the note of true nostalgia in her voice. He was, suddenly, rather sorry for her.

"Then Bill's plane crashed on Diamond Head," she continued, "and I was all alone. And these black sheep along the beach, they knew I was alone—and broke. And I was homesick for Forty-second Street,[87] for the old boarding-house and the old gang and the Automat and the chewing-gum sign, and try-outs at New Haven. So I gave a few parties just to forget, and people began to talk."

"You might have gone back," John Quincy suggested.

"I know—why didn't I? I been intending to, right along, but every day out here is just like any other day, and somehow you don't get round to picking one out—I been drifting—but honest to God if you keep me out of this I'll go home on the first boat. I'll get me a job, and—and—If you'll only keep me out of it. You got a chance now to wreck my life—it's all up to you—but I know you ain't going to—"

She seized John Quincy's hand in both of hers, and gazed at him pleadingly through her tears. It was the most uncomfortable moment of his life. He looked wildly about the little room, so different from any in the house on Beacon Street. He pulled his hand away.

"I'll—I'll see," he said, rising hastily. "I'll think it over."

"But I can't sleep to-night if I don't know," she told him.

"I'll have to think it over," he repeated. He turned toward the table in time to see the woman's slim hand reach out and seize the bit of jewelry. "I'll take the brooch," he added.

She looked up at him. Suddenly John Quincy knew that she had been acting, that his emotions had been falsely played upon, and he felt again that hot rush of blood to the head, that quick surge of anger, he had experienced in Dan Winterslip's hall. Aunt Minerva had predicted he couldn't handle a woman of this type. Well, he'd show her—he'd show the world. "Give me that brooch," he said coldly.

"It's mine," answered the woman stubbornly.

John Quincy wasted no words; he seized the woman's wrist. She screamed. A door opened behind them.

"What's going on here?" inquired Mr. Leatherbee.

"Oh, I thought you'd left us," said John Quincy.

"Steve! Don't let him have it," cried the woman. Steve moved militantly nearer, but there was a trace of caution in his attitude.

John Quincy laughed. "You stay where you are, Steve," he advised. "Or I'll smash that sallow face of yours." Strange talk for a Winterslip. "Your friend here is trying to hang on to an important bit of evidence in the murder up the beach, and with the utmost reluctance I am forced to use strong-arm methods." The brooch dropped to the floor, he stooped and picked it up. "Well, I guess that's about all," he added. "I'm sorry if you've been homesick, Mrs. Compton, but speaking as a Bostonian, I don't believe Broadway is as glamourous as you picture it. Distance has lent enchantment. Good night."

He let himself out, and found his way to Kalakaua Avenue. He had settled one thing to his own satisfaction; Chan must know about the brooch, and at once. Mrs. Compton's story might be true or not, it certainly needed further investigation by some responsible person.

John Quincy had approached the cottage by way of Kalia Road; he was planning to return to Dan's house along the better lighted avenue. Having reached that broad expanse of asphalt, however, he realized that the Reef and Palm Hotel was near at hand. There was his promise to Carlota Egan—he had said he would look in on her again to-day. As for Chan, he could telephone the Chinaman from the hotel. He turned in the direction of the Reef and Palm.

Stumbling through the dark garden, he saw finally the gaunt old hulk of the hotel. Lights of low candle power burned at infrequent intervals on the double-decked veranda. In the huge lobby a few rather shabby-looking guests took their ease. Behind the desk stood—nobody but the Japanese clerk.

John Quincy was directed to a telephone booth, and his keen Bostonian mind required Nipponese aid in mastering the dial system favored by the Honolulu telephone company. At length he got the police station. Chan was out, but the answering voice promised that he would be told to get in touch with Mr. Winterslip immediately on his return.

"How much do I owe you?" inquired John Quincy of the clerk.

"Not a penny," said a voice, and he turned to find Carlota Egan at his elbow. He smiled. This was more like it.

"But I say—you know—I've used your telephone—"

"It's free," she said. "Too many things are free out here. That's why we don't get rich. It was so kind of you to come again."

"Not at all," he protested. He looked about the room. "Your father—"

She glanced at the clerk, and led the way out to the lanai at the side. They went to the far end of it, where they could see the light on Diamond Head, and the silvery waters of the Pacific sweeping in to disappear at last beneath the old Reef and Palm.

"I'm afraid poor dad's having a bad time of it," she said, and her voice broke slightly. "I haven't been able to see him. They're holding him down there—as a witness, I believe. There was some talk of bail, but I didn't listen. We haven't any money—at least, I didn't think we had."

"You didn't think—" he began, puzzled.

She produced a small bit of paper, and put it in his hand. "I want to ask your advice. I've been cleaning up dad's office, and just before you came I ran across that in his desk."

John Quincy stared down at the little pink slip she had given him. By the light of one of the small lamps he saw that it was a check for five thousand dollars, made out to "Bearer" and signed by Dan Winterslip. The date was that of the day before.

"I say, that looks important, doesn't it?" John Quincy said. He handed it back to her, and thought a moment. "By gad—it is important. It seems to me it's pretty conclusive evidence of your father's innocence. If he had that, his business with Cousin Dan must have come to a successful end, and it isn't likely he would—er—do away with the man who signed it and complicate the cashing of it."

The girl's eyes shone. "Just the way I reasoned. But I don't know what to do with it."

"Your father has engaged a lawyer, of course."

"Yes, but a rather poor one. The only kind we can afford. Should I turn this over to him?"

"No—wait a minute. Any chance of seeing your father soon?"

"Yes. It's been arranged I'm to visit him in the morning."

John Quincy nodded. "Better talk with him before you do anything," he advised. He had a sudden recollection of Egan's face when he refused to explain his business with Dan Winterslip. "Take this check with you and ask your father what he wants done with it. Point out to him that it's vital evidence in his favor."

"Yes, I guess that's the best plan," the girl agreed. "Will—will you sit down a moment?"

"Well." John Quincy recalled Miss Minerva waiting impatiently for news. "Just a moment. I want to know how you're getting on. Any big arithmetical problems come up yet?"

She shook her head. "Not yet. It really isn't so bad, the work. We haven't many guests, you know. I could be quite happy—if it weren't for poor dad." She sighed. "Ever since I can remember," she added, "my happiness has had an if in it."

She sighed. "Ever since I can remember," she added, "my happiness has had an if and it." From The House Without a Key, illustration by William Liepse (The Saturday Evening Post, February 14, 1925)

He led her on to speak about herself, there in the calm night by that romantic beach. Through her talk flashed little pictures of her motherless childhood on this exotic shore, of a wearing fight against poverty and her father's bitter struggle to send her to school on the mainland, to give her what he considered her proper place in the world. Here was a girl far different from any he had met on Beacon Street, and John Quincy found pleasure in her talk.

Finally he forced himself to leave. As they walked along the balcony they encountered one of the guests, a meek little man with stooped shoulders. Even at that late hour he wore a bathing suit.

"Any luck, Mr. Saladine?" the girl inquired.

"Luck ith againth me," he lisped, and passed hastily on.

Carlota Egan laughed softly. "Oh, I really shouldn't," she repented at once. "The poor man."

"What's his trouble?" asked John Quincy.

"He's a tourist—a business man," she said. "Des Moines, or some place like that. And he's had the most appalling accident. He's lost his teeth."

"His teeth!" repeated John Quincy.

"Yes. Like so many things in this world, they were false. He got into a battle with a roller out by the second raft, and they disappeared. Since then he spends all his time out there, peering down into the water by day, and diving down and feeling about by night. One of the tragic figures of history," she added.

John Quincy laughed.

"That's the most tragic part of it," the girl continued. "He's the joke of the beach. But he goes on hunting, so serious. Of course, it is serious for him."

They passed through the public room to the front door. Mr. Saladine's tragedy slipped at once from John Quincy's mind.

"Good night," he said. "Don't forget about the check, when you see your father to-morrow. I'll look in on you during the day."

"It was so good of you to come," she said. Her hand was in his. "It has helped me along—tremendously."

"Don't you worry. Happy days are not far off. Happy days without an if. Hold the thought!"

"I'll hold it," she promised.

"We'll both hold it." It came to him that he was also holding her hand. He dropped it hastily. "Good night," he repeated, and fled through the garden.

In the living-room of Dan's house he was surprised to find Miss Minerva and Charlie Chan sitting together, solemnly staring at each other. Chan rose hurriedly at his entrance.

"Hello," said John Quincy. "I see you have a caller."

"Where in the world have you been?" snapped Miss Minerva. Evidently entertaining a Chinaman had got a bit on her nerves.

"Well—I—" John Quincy hesitated.

"Speak out," said Miss Minerva. "Mr. Chan knows everything."

"Most flattering," grinned Chan. "Some things are not entirely well known to me. But about your call on Widow of Waikiki I learn soon after door receives you."

"The devil you did," said John Quincy.

"Simple enough," Chan went on. "Study human people, as I relate to you. Compton lady was friend to Mr. Dan Winterslip. Mr. Leatherbee rival friend. Enter jealous feelings. Since morning both of these people are under watchful regard of Honolulu police. Into the scene, you walk. I am notified and fly to beach."

"Ah—does he also know—" began John Quincy.

"About the brooch?" finished Miss Minerva. "Yes—I've confessed everything. And he's been kind enough to forgive me."

"But not nice thing to do," added Chan. "Humbly begging pardon to mention it. All cards should repose on table when police are called upon."

"Yes," said Miss Minerva, "he forgave me, but I have been gently chided. I have been made to feel, as he puts it, most naughty."

"So sorry," bowed Chan.

"Well, as a matter of fact," said John Quincy, "I was going to tell Mr. Chan the whole story at once." He turned to the Chinaman. "I've already tried to reach you by telephone at the station. When I left the woman's cottage—"

"Police affairs forbid utmost courtesy," interrupted Chan. "I cut in to remark from the beginning, if you will please do so."

"Oh, yes," smiled John Quincy. "Well, the woman herself let me in, and showed me into her little living-room. When I got there this fellow Leatherbee was mixing cocktails by the table—"

Haku appeared at the door. "Mr. Charlie Chan wanted by telephone," he announced.

Chan apologized and hastened out.

"I intend to tell everything," John Quincy warned his aunt.

"I shan't interfere," she answered. "That slant-eyed Chinaman has been sitting here looking at me more in sorrow than in anger for the better part of an hour, and I've made up my mind to one thing. I shall have no more secrets from the police."

88. The RMS *Niagara* was a real ship owned by the Union Steam Ship Company. Launched in 1912, it initially carried mail, freight, and passengers between Australia and Vancouver. In 1940, carrying a large, secret consignment of gold being shipped from England to the United States, it was struck by a mine.

Chan reentered the room. "As I was saying," John Quincy began, "this fellow Leatherbee was standing by the table, and—"

"Most sorry," said Chan, "but the remainder of that interesting recital is to be told at the station-house."

"At the station-house!" cried John Quincy.

"Precisely the fact. I am presuming you do me the great honor to come with me to that spot. The man Leatherbee is apprehended aboard boat *Niagara* on verge of sailing to Australia.[88] Woman are also apprehended in act of tearful farewell. Both now relax at police station."

"I thought so," said John Quincy.

"One more amazing fact comes into light," added Chan. "In pocket of Leatherbee is the page ruthlessly extracted from guest book. Kindly procure your hat. Outside I have waiting for me one Ford automobile."

A 1928 Ford Model A

CHAPTER XII

Tom Brade the Blackbirder

—◦◦◦◦—

I n Hallet's room at headquarters they found the Captain of Detectives seated grimly behind his desk staring at two reluctant visitors. One of the visitors, Mr. Stephen Leatherbee, stared back with a look of sullen defiance. Mrs. Arlene Compton, late of Broadway and the Automat, was dabbing at her eyes with a tiny handkerchief. John Quincy perceived that she had carelessly allowed tears to play havoc with her makeup.

In Hallet's room at headquarters they found the captain of detectives seated grimly behind his desk staring at two reluctant visitors. From *The House Without a Key*, illustration by William Liepse (*The Saturday Evening Post*, February 14, 1925)

"Hello, Charlie," said Hallet. "Mr. Winterslip, I'm glad you came along. As you may have heard, we've just pulled this young

89.   Adams Sherman Hill was a professor of rhetoric at Harvard University. His book *Principles of Rhetoric and Their Application* (1893) was widely taught.

man off the *Niagara*. He seemed inclined to leave us. We found this in his pocket."

He put into the Chinaman's hand a time-yellowed page obviously from Dan Winterslip's guest book. John Quincy and Chan bent over it together. The inscription was written in an old-fashioned hand, and the ink was fading fast. It ran:

"In Hawaii all things are perfect, none more so than the hospitality I have enjoyed in this house.—Joseph E. Gleason, 124 Little Bourke Street, Melbourne, Victoria."

John Quincy turned away, shocked. No wonder that page had been ripped out! Evidently Mr. Gleason had not enjoyed the privilege of studying A. S. Hill's book on the principles of rhetoric.[89] How could one thing be more perfect than another?

"Before I take a statement from these people," Hallet was saying, "what's all this about a brooch?"

John Quincy laid the piece of jewelry on the captain's desk. He explained that it had been given Mrs. Compton by Dan Winterslip, and told of its being discovered on the floor of the lanai.

"When was it found?" demanded the captain, glaring his disapproval.

"Most regrettable misunderstanding," put in Chan hastily. "Now completely wiped out. The littlest said, sooner repairs are made. Mr. Winterslip has already to-night examined this woman—"

"Oh, he has, has he!" Hallet turned angrily on John Quincy. "Just who is conducting this case?"

"Well," began John Quincy uncomfortably, "it seemed best to the family—"

"Damn the family!" Hallet exploded. "This affair is in my hands—"

"Please," broke in Chan soothingly. "Waste of time to winnow that out. Already I have boldness to offer suitable rebukes."

"Well, you talked with the woman, then," said Hallet. "What did you get out of her?"

"Say, listen," put in Mrs. Compton. "I want to take back anything I told this bright-eyed boy."

"Lied to him, eh?" said Hallet.

"Why not? What right did he have to question me?" Her voice became wheedling. "I wouldn't lie to a cop," she added.

"You bet your life you wouldn't," Hallet remarked. "Not if you know what's good for you. However, I want to hear what you told this amateur detective. Sometimes lies are significant. Go on, Winterslip."

John Quincy was deeply annoyed. What was this mix-up he had let himself in for, anyhow? He had a notion to rise, and with a cold bow, leave the room. Something told him, however, that he couldn't get away with it.

Very much on his dignity, he repeated the woman's story to him. Winterslip had come to her cottage the night before to make a final appeal for the brooch. On his promise to replace it with something else, she had given it up. He had taken it and left her at nine-thirty.

"That was the last she saw of him," finished John Quincy.

Hallet smiled grimly. "So she told you, at any rate. But she admits she was lying. If you'd had the sense to leave this sort of thing to the proper people—" He wheeled on the woman. "You were lying, weren't you?"

She nodded nonchalantly. "In a way. Dan did leave my cottage at nine-thirty—or a little later. But I went with him—to his house. Oh, it was perfectly proper. Steve went along."

"Oh, yes—Steve." Hallet glanced at Mr. Leatherbee, who did not appear quite the ideal chaperon. "Now, young woman, go back to the beginning. Nothing but the truth."

"So help me," said Mrs. Compton. She attempted a devastating smile. "I wouldn't lie to you, Captain—you know I wouldn't. I realize you're a big man out here, and—"

"Give me your story," cut in Hallet coldly.

"Sure. Dan dropped into my place for a chat last night about nine, and he found Mr. Leatherbee there. He was jealous as sin, Dan was—honest to God, I don't know why. Me and Steve are just pals—eh, Steve?"

"Pals, that's all," said Steve.

"But anyhow, Dan flew off the handle, and we had one grand blowup. I tried to explain Steve was just stopping over on his way to Australia, and Dan wants to know what's detaining him. So Steve tells about how he lost all his money at bridge on the boat coming out here. 'Will you move on,' says Dan, 'if I pay your passage?' And Steve answers he will, like a shot. Am I getting this straight, Steve?"

"Absolutely," approved Mr. Leatherbee. "It's just as she says, Captain. Winterslip offered to give—loan me passage money. It was only a loan. And I agreed to sail on the *Niagara* to-night. He said he had a little cash in his safe at the house, and invited Arlene and me to go back with him—"

"Which we did," said Arlene. "Dan opened the safe and took out a roll of bills. He peeled off three hundred dollars. You didn't often see him in that frame of mind—but as I was saying, he give the money to Steve. Then Steve begins to beef a little—yes, you did, Steve—and wants to know what he's going to do in Australia. Says he don't know a soul down there and he'll just plain starve. Dan was sore at first, then he laughs a nasty little laugh and goes over and tears that there page out of the guest book and gives it to Steve. 'Look him up and tell him you're a friend of mine,' he says. 'Maybe he'll give you a job. The name is Gleason. I've disliked him for twenty years, though he don't know that!'"

"A dirty dig at me," Leatherbee explained. "I took the loan and this Gleason's address and we started to go. Winterslip said he wanted to talk to Arlene, so I came away alone. That was about ten o'clock."

"Where did you go?" Hallet asked.

"I went back to my hotel downtown. I had to pack."

"Back to your hotel, eh? Can you prove it?"

Leatherbee considered. "I don't know. The boy at the desk may remember when I came in, though I didn't stop there for my key—I had it with me. Anyhow, I didn't see Winterslip after that. I just went ahead with my preparations to sail on the *Niagara*, and I must say you've got your nerve—"

"Never mind that!" Hallet turned to the woman. "And after Leatherbee left—what happened then?"

"Well, Dan started in on that brooch again," she said. "It made me sore, too—I never did like a tightwad. Besides, my nerves was all on edge. I'm funny that way, rows get me all upset. I like everybody pleasant around me. He went on arguing, so finally I ripped off the brooch and threw it at him, and it rolled away under the table somewhere. Then he said he was sorry, and that was when he offered to replace it with something more up-to-date. The best money could buy—that was what he promised. Pretty soon we was friends again—just as good friends as ever when I came away, about ten-fifteen. His last words was that we'd look round the jewelry stores this morning. I ask you, Captain, is it reasonable to think I'd have anything to do with murdering a man who was in a buying mood like that?"

Hallet laughed. "So you left him at ten-fifteen—and went home alone?"

"I did. And when I saw him last he was alive and well—I'll swear to that on a stack of Bibles as high as the Times Building.[90] Gee, don't I wish I was safe on Broadway to-night!"

Hallet thought for a moment. "Well, we'll look into all this. You can both go—I'm not going to hold you at present. But I expect you both to remain in Honolulu until this affair is cleared up, and I advise you not to try any funny business. You've seen to-night what chance you've got to get away."

"Oh, that's all right." The woman stood, looking her relief. "We've got no reason to beat it, have we, Steve?"

"None in the world," agreed Steve. His facetious manner returned. "Speaking for myself," he added, "innocent is my middle name."

"Good night, all," said Mrs. Compton, and they went out.

Hallet sat staring at the brooch. "A pretty straight story," he remarked, looking at Chan.

"Nice and neat," grinned the Chinaman.

"If true." Hallet shrugged his shoulders. "Well, for the present, I'm willing to believe it." He turned to John Quincy. "Now, Mr. Winterslip," he said severely, "I want it understood that any other evidence your family digs up—"

"Oh, that's all right," interrupted the boy. "We'll turn it over at once. I've already given to Chan the newspaper my cousin was reading that night he wrote the letter to Roger Winterslip."

Chan took the paper from his pocket. "Such a busy evening," he explained, "the journal was obscure in my mind. Thanks for the recollection." He called to his chief's attention the mutilated corner.

"Look into that," said Hallet.

"Before sleeping," promised Chan. "Mr. Winterslip, we pursue similar paths. The honor of your company in my humble vehicle would pleasure me deeply." Once in the car on the deserted street, the Chinaman spoke again. "The page ripped from guest book, the brooch lying silent on floor. Both are now followed into presence of immovable stone wall. We sway about, looking for other path."

"Then you think those two were telling the truth?" John Quincy asked.

90. We cannot determine how long Mrs. Compton has been away from Manhattan, but it is likely that she is referring to the eighteen-story building located at 229 West 43rd Street, built in 1912 and the home of the *New York Times* from 1913 to 2007.

"As to that, I do not venture to remark," Chan replied.

"How about those psychic powers?" inquired John Quincy.

Chan smiled. "Psychic powers somewhat drowsy just now," he admitted. "Need prodding into wakefulness."

"Look here," said John Quincy, "there's no need for you to take me out to Waikiki. Just drop me on King Street, and I'll get a trolley."

"Making humble suggestion," Chan replied, "is it not possible you will accompany me to newspaper rooms, where we set out on different path?"

John Quincy looked at his watch; it was ten minutes past eleven. "I'll be glad to, Charlie," he said.

Chan beamed with pleasure. "Greatly honored by your friendly manner," he remarked. He turned into a side street. "Newspaper of this nature burst out at evening, very quiet now. Somebody may loiter in rooms, if we have happy luck."

They had just that, for the building of the evening journal was open, and in the city room an elderly man with a green shade over his eyes hammered on a typewriter.

"Hello, Charlie," he said cordially.

"Hello, Pete. Mr. Winterslip of Boston, I have all the honor to present this Pete Mayberry. For many years he explore water-front ferreting for whatever news are hiding there."

The elderly man rose and removed his eyeshade, revealing a pleasant twinkle. He was evidently interested to meet a Winterslip.

"We pursue," continued Chan, "one copy of paper marked June sixteen, present year. If you have no inclination for objecting."

Mayberry laughed. "Go to it, Charlie. You know where the files are."

Chan bowed and disappeared. "Your first appearance out here, Mr. Winterslip?" inquired the newspaper man.

John Quincy nodded. "I've only just got here," he said, "but I can see it's a rather intriguing place."

"You've said it," smiled Mayberry. "Forty-six years ago I came out from Portsmouth, New Hampshire, to visit relatives. I've been in the newspaper game here ever since—most of the time on the water-front. There's a life-work for you!"

"You must have seen some changes," remarked John Quincy inanely.

Mayberry nodded. "For the worse. I knew Honolulu in the glam-ourous days of its isolation, and I've watched it fade into an eighth carbon copy of Babbittville, U.S.A.[91] The water-front's just a water-front now—but once, my boy! Once it oozed romance at every pore."

Chan returned, carrying a paper. "Much to be thankful for," he said to Mayberry. "Your kindness are quite overwhelming—"

"Anything doing?" asked Mayberry eagerly.

Chan shook his head. "Presently speaking, no. Our motions just now must be blackly clouded in secrecy."

"Well," said the reporter, "when it comes time to roll them clouds away, don't forget me."

"Impossibility," protested Chan. "Good night."

They left Mayberry bending over his typewriter, and at Chan's suggestion went to the All American Restaurant, where the Chinaman ordered two cups of "your inspeakable coffee." While they waited to be served, he spread out on the table his complete copy of the newspaper, and laying the torn page on its counterpart, carefully removed the upper right-hand corner.

"The missing fragment," he explained. For a time he studied it thoughtfully, and finally shook his head. "I apprehend nothing to startle," he admitted. He handed it across the table. "If you will condescend greatly—"

John Quincy took the bit of newspaper. On one side was the advertisement of a Japanese dealer in shirtings who wrote his own publicity. Any one might carry off, he said, six yards for the price of five. And in case the buyer cried loudly in amaze, how can do, it was a matter he was happy to exprain.[92] John Quincy laughed aloud.

"Ah," said Chan, "you are by rights mirthful. Kikuchi, purveyor of shirting cloth, seize on grand English language and make it into idiotic[93] jumble. On that side are nothing to detain us. But humbly hinting you reverse the fragment—"

John Quincy reversed it. The other side was a part of the shipping page. He read it carefully, news of sailings and arrivals, there would be places for five passengers to the Orient on the *Shinyo Maru*,[94] leaving Wednesday, the *Wilhelmina* was six hundred and forty miles east of Makupuu Point, the brig *Mary Jane* from the Treaty Ports—

John Quincy started, and caught his breath. A small item in tiny print had met his eye.

"Among the passengers who will arrive here on the *Sonoma*[95] from Australia a week from Saturday are: Mr. and Mrs. Thomas Macan Brade, of Calcutta—"

91. Mayberry is referring to Sinclair Lewis's 1922 *Babbitt*, a novel satirizing the vacuity of middle-class life and mid-sized industrial cities like the fictional Zenith in which the novel is set. The novel was highly influential, and the word "Babbitt" became part of the language, meaning "a person and especially a business or professional man who conforms unthinkingly to prevailing middle-class standards" (*Merriam-Webster Unabridged Dictionary*).

92. This sentence has been excised in later, less racist editions.

93. Charlie's anti-Japanese "idiotic" is omitted in later editions, replaced with "a."

94. At this time, the *Shinyo Maru* was a steamer engaged in trade. Its claim to notoriety came in 1944. The Japanese Empire, in order to transfer Allied prisoners from prisons in the Philippines and elsewhere, impressed cargo ships into service as prisoner transports, and dire conditions on these ships led to their being called "Hell Ships." The *Shinyo Maru* was part of a convoy of Japanese ships attacked by an American submarine. In the attack, 668 Allied servicemen-prisoners, almost all of whom were Americans, were killed; about eighty prisoners survived.

The *Wilhelmina* was another ship of the Matson Navigation Company plying the West Coast–Hawaii runs until 1917, when she was pressed into service as a transport for the U. S. Navy. After the war, she returned to service in the Pacific.

95. The SS *Sonoma* was a ship of the Matson line, sailing the California–Australia route.

John Quincy sat staring at the unwashed window of the All American Restaurant. His mind went back to the deck of the *President Tyler*, to a lean old missionary telling a tale of a bright morning on Apiang, a grave under a palm tree. "Mr. and Mrs. Thomas Macan Brade, of Calcutta." He heard again the missionary's high-pitched voice. "A callous brute, a pirate and adventurer. Tom Brade, the blackbirder."

But Brade had been buried in a long pine box on Apiang. Even at the Crossroads of the Pacific, his path and that of Dan Winterslip could hardly have crossed again.

The waiter brought the coffee. Chan said nothing, watching John Quincy closely. Finally the Chinaman spoke: "You have much to tell me."

John Quincy looked around quickly, he had forgotten Chan's presence.

His dilemma was acute. Must he here in this soiled restaurant in a far town reveal to a Chinaman that ancient blot on the Winterslip name? What would Aunt Minerva say? Well, only a short time ago she had remarked that she was resolved to have no more secrets from the police. However, there was family pride—

John Quincy's eye fell on the Japanese waiter. What were those lines from *The Mikado*? "But family pride must be denied and mortified and set aside."

The boy smiled. "Yes, Charlie," he admitted, "I have much to tell you." And over the inspeakable coffee of the All American Restaurant he repeated to the detective the story the Reverend Frank Upton had told on the *President Tyler*.

Chan beamed. "Now," he cried, "we arrive in the neighborhood of something! Brade the blackbirder, master *Maid of Shiloh* boat, on which Mr. Dan Winterslip are first officer—"

"But Brade was buried on Apiang," protested John Quincy.

"Yes, indeed. And who saw him, pardon me? Was it then an unsealed box? Oh, no!" Chan's eyes were dancing. "Please recollect something more. The strong box of ohia wood. Initials on it are T.M.B. Mysteries yet, but we move, we advance!"

"I guess we do," admitted John Quincy.

"This much we grasp," Chan continued. "Dan Winterslip repose for quiet hour on lanai, in peaceful reading. This news assault his eye. He now leaps up, paces about, flees to dock to send letter requesting, please, the ohia wood box must be buried deep in Pacific. Why?"

Fumbling in his pocket, Chan took out a sheaf of papers, evidently lists of steamer arrivals. "On Saturday just gone by, the *Sonoma* make this port. Among passengers—yes—yes—Thomas Macan Brade and honorable wife, Calcutta. It is here inscribed they arrive to stay, not being present when *Sonoma* persist on journey. On the night of Monday, Mr. Dan Winterslip are foully slain."

"Which makes Mr. Brade an important person to locate," said John Quincy.

"How very true. But the hurry are not intense. No boats sailing now. Before sleeping, I will investigate down-town hotels, Waikiki to-morrow. Where are you, Mr. Brade?" Chan seized the check. "No—pardon me—the honor of paying for this poi-sontasting beverage must be mine."

Out in the street, he indicated an approaching trolley. "It bears imprint of your destination," he pointed out. "You will require sleep. We meet to-morrow. Congratulations on most fruitful evening."

Once more John Quincy was on a Waikiki car. Weary but thrilled, he took out his pipe and filling it, lighted up. What a day! He seemed to have lived a lifetime since he landed that very morning. He perceived that his smoke was blowing in the face of a tired little Japanese woman beside him. "Pardon me," he remarked, and knocking the pipe against the side rail, put it in his pocket. The woman stared at him in meek startled wonder; no one had ever asked her pardon before.

On the seat behind John Quincy a group of Hawaiian boys with yellow leis about their necks twanged on steel guitars and sang a plaintive love song. The trolley rattled on through the fragrant night; above the clatter of the wheels the music rose with a sweet intensity. John Quincy leaned back and closed his eyes.

A clock struck the hour of midnight. Another day—Wednesday—it flashed through his mind that to-day his firm in Boston would offer that preferred stock for the shoe people in Lynn. Would the issue be oversubscribed? No matter.

Here he was, out in the middle of the Pacific on a trolley-car. Behind him brown-skinned boys were singing a melancholy love song of long ago, and the moon was shining on crimson poinciana trees. And somewhere on this tiny island a man named Thomas Macan Brade slept under a mosquito netting. Or lay awake, perhaps, thinking of Dan Winterslip.

CHAPTER XIII

The Luggage in Room Nineteen

J ohn Quincy emerged from sleep the next morning with a
great effort, and dragged his watch from under the pillow.
Eight-thirty! Good lord, he was due at the office at nine! A
quick bath and shave, a brief pause at the breakfast table, a run
past the Public Gardens and the Common and down to School
Street—

He sat up in bed. Why was he imprisoned under mosquito
netting? What was the meaning of the little lizard that sported
idly outside the cloth? Oh, yes—Honolulu. He was in Hawaii,
and he'd never reach his office by nine. It was five thousand miles
away.

The low murmur of breakers on the beach confirmed him in
this discovery and stepping to his window, he gazed out at the
calm sparkling morning. Yes, he was in Honolulu entangled in a
murder mystery, consorting with Chinese detectives and Waikiki
Widows, following clues. The new day held interesting promise.
He must hurry to find what it would bring forth.

Haku informed him that his aunt and Barbara had already
breakfasted, and set before him a reddish sort of cantaloupe
which was, he explained in answer to the boy's question, a papaia.
When he had eaten, John Quincy went out on the lanai. Barbara
stood there, staring at the beach. A new Barbara, with the old
vivacity, the old joy of living, submerged; a pale girl with sorrow
in her eyes.

John Quincy put his arm about her shoulder; she was a Winterslip and the family was the family. Again he felt in his heart that flare of anger against the "person or persons unknown" who had brought this grief upon her. The guilty must pay—Egan or whoever, Brade or Leatherbee or the chorus girl. Pay and pay dearly—he was resolved on that.

"My dear girl," he began. "What can I say to you—"

"You've said it all, without speaking," she answered. "See, John Quincy, this is my beach. When I was only five I swam alone to that first float. He—he was so proud of me."

"It's a lovely spot, Barbara," he told her.

"I knew you'd think so. One of these days we'll swim together out to the reef, and I'll teach you to ride a surf-board. I want your visit to be a happy one."

He shook his head. "It can't be that," he said, "because of you. But because of you, I'm mighty glad I came."

She pressed his hand. "I'm going out to sit by the water. Will you come?"

The bamboo curtain parted, and Miss Minerva joined them. "Well, John Quincy," she said sharply, "this is a pretty hour for you to appear. If you're going to rescue me from lotus land, you'll have to be immune yourself."

He smiled. "Just getting acclimated," he explained. "I'll follow you in a moment, Barbara," he added, and held open the door for her.

"I waited up," Miss Minerva began, when the girl had gone, "until eleven-thirty. But I'd had very little sleep the night before, and that was my limit. I make no secret of it—I'm very curious to know what happened at the police station."

He repeated to her the story told by Mrs. Compton and Leatherbee. "I wish I'd been present," she said. "A pretty woman can fool all the men in Christendom. Lies, probably."

"Maybe," admitted John Quincy. "But wait a minute. Later on, Chan and I followed up your newspaper clue. And it led us to a startling discovery."

"Of course it did," she beamed. "What was it?"

"Well," he said, "first of all, I met a missionary on the boat." He told her the Reverend Frank Upton's tale of that morning on Apiang, and added the news that a man named Thomas Macan Brade was now in Honolulu.

96. The original *Boston Herald* was founded in 1846. In 1917, the owner purchased the *Boston Journal* and merged the newspapers, so that by 1924, they had become the *Boston Herald and Boston Journal* (though the newspaper was likely operating under the original name at the time when Minerva "once" wrote letters about homicides).

She was silent for a time. "So Dan was a blackbirder," she remarked at last. "How charming! Such a pleasant man, too. But then, I learned that lesson early in life—the brighter the smile, the darker the past. All this will make delightful reading in the Boston papers, John Quincy."

"Oh, they'll never get it," her nephew said.

"Don't deceive yourself. Newspapers will go to the ends of the earth for a good murder. I once wrote letters to all the editors in Boston urging them to print no more details about homicides. It hadn't the slightest effect—though I did get an acknowledgment of my favor from the *Herald*."[96]

John Quincy glanced at his watch. "Perhaps I should go down to the station. Anything in the morning paper?"

"A very hazy interview with Captain Hallet. The police have unearthed important clues, and promise early results. You know—the sort of thing they always give out just after a murder."

The boy looked at her keenly. "Ah," he said, "then you read newspaper accounts of the kind you tried to suppress?"

"Certainly I do," snapped his aunt. "There's little enough excitement in my life. But I gladly gave up my port wine because I felt intoxicants were bad for the lower classes, and—"

Haku interrupted with the news that John Quincy was wanted on the telephone. When the boy returned to the lanai there was a brisk air of business about him.

"That was Charlie," he announced. "The day's work is about to get under way. They've located Mr. and Mrs. Brade at the Reef and Palm Hotel, and I'm to meet Charlie there in fifteen minutes."

"The Reef and Palm," repeated Miss Minerva. "You see, it keeps coming back to Egan. I'd wager a set of Browning against a modern novel that he's the man who did it."

"You'd lose your Browning, and then where would you be when the lecture season started?" laughed John Quincy. "I never knew you to be so stupid before." His face became serious. "By the way, will you explain to Barbara that I can't join her, after all?"

Miss Minerva nodded. "Go along," she said. "I envy you all this. First time in my life I ever wished I were a man."

John Quincy approached the Reef and Palm by way of the beach. The scene was one of bright serenity. A few languid tourists lolled upon the sand; others, more ambitious, were making picture post-card history out where the surf began. A great white steamer puffed blackly into port. Standing in water up to their necks, a group of Hawaiian women paused in their search for luncheon delicacies to enjoy a moment's gossip.

John Quincy passed Arlene Compton's cottage and entered the grounds of the Reef and Palm. On the beach not far from the hotel, an elderly Englishwoman sat on a camp stool with an easel and canvas before her. She was seeking to capture something of that exotic scene—vainly seeking, for John Quincy, glancing over her shoulder, perceived that her work was terrible. She turned and looked at him, a weary look of protest against his intrusion, and he was sorry she had caught him in the act of smiling at her inept canvas.

Chan had not yet arrived at the hotel, and the clerk informed John Quincy that Miss Carlota had gone to the city. For that interview with her father, no doubt. He hoped that the evidence of the check would bring about Egan's release. It seemed to him that the man was being held on a rather flimsy pretext, anyhow.

He sat down on the lanai at the side, where he could see both the path that led in from the street and the restless waters of the Pacific. On the beach near by a man in a purple bathing suit reclined dejectedly, and John Quincy smiled in recollection. Mr. Saladine, alone with his tragedy, peering out at the waters that had robbed him—waiting, no doubt, for the tide to yield up its loot.

Some fifteen or twenty minutes passed, and then John Quincy heard voices in the garden. He saw that Hallet and Chan were coming up the walk and went to meet them at the front door.

"Splendid morning," said Chan. "Nice day to set out on new path leading unevitably to important discovery."

John Quincy accompanied them to the desk. The Japanese clerk regarded them with sullen unfriendliness; he had not forgotten the events of the day before. Information had to be dragged from him bit by bit. Yes, there was a Mr. and Mrs. Brade stopping there. They arrived last Saturday, on the steamship *Sonoma*. Mr. Brade was not about at the moment. Mrs. Brade was on the beach painting pretty pictures.

"Good," said Hallet, "I'll have a look around their room before I question them. Take us there."

The Jap hesitated. "Boy!" he called. It was only a bluff; the Reef and Palm had no bell-boys. Finally, with an air of injured dignity, he led the way down a long corridor on the same floor as the office and unlocked the door of nineteen, the last room on the right. Hallet strode in and went to the window.

"Here—wait a minute," he called to the clerk. He pointed to the elderly woman painting on the beach. "That Mrs. Brade?"

"Yess," hissed the Jap.

"All right—go along." The clerk went out. "Mr. Winterslip, I'll ask you to sit here in the window and keep an eye on the lady. If she starts to come in, let me know." He stared eagerly about the poorly furnished bedroom. "Now, Mr. Brade, I wonder what you've got?"

John Quincy took the post assigned him, feeling decidedly uncomfortable. This didn't seem quite honorable to him. However, he probably wouldn't be called upon to do any searching himself, and if policemen were forced to do disagreeable things—well, they should have thought of that before they became policemen. Not that either Hallet or Chan appeared to be embarrassed by the task before them.

There was a great deal of luggage in the room—English luggage, which is usually large and impressive. John Quincy noted a trunk, two enormous bags, and a smaller case. All were plastered with labels of the *Sonoma*, and beneath were the worn fragments of earlier labels, telling a broken story of other ships and far hotels.

Hallet and Chan were old hands at this game; they went through Brade's trunk rapidly and thoroughly, but without finding anything of note. The captain turned his attention to the small traveling case. With every evidence of delight he drew forth a packet of letters, and sat down with them at a table. John Quincy was shocked. Reading other people's mail was, in his eyes, something that simply wasn't done.

It was done by Hallet, however. In a moment the captain spoke. "Seems to have been in the British civil service in Calcutta, but he's resigned," he announced to Chan. "Here's a letter from his superior in London referring to Brade's thirty-six years on the job, and saying he's sorry to lose him." Hallet took up another letter, his face brightened as he read. "Say—this is more like it!" He handed the typewritten page to Chan. The Chinaman looked at it, and his eyes sparkled. "Most interesting," he cried, and turned it over to John Quincy.

The boy hesitated. The standards of a lifetime are not easily abandoned. But the others had read it first, so he put aside his scruples. The letter was several months old, and was addressed to Brade in Calcutta.

> "Dear Sir: In reply to your inquiry of the sixth instant, would say that Mr. Daniel Winterslip is alive and is a resident of this city. His address is 3947 Kalia Road, Waikiki, Honolulu, T.H."[97]

The signature was that of the British consul at Honolulu. John Quincy returned the epistle to Hallet, who put it in his pocket. At that instant Chan, who had been exploring one of the larger bags, emitted a little grunt of satisfaction.

"What is it, Charlie?" Hallet asked.

The Chinaman set out on the table before his chief a small tin box, and removed the lid. It was filled with cigarettes. "Corsican brand," he announced cheerfully.

"Good," said Hallet. "It begins to look as though Mr. Thomas Macan Brade would have a lot to explain."

They continued their researches, while John Quincy sat silent by the window. Presently Carlota Egan appeared outside. She walked slowly to a chair on the lanai, and sat down. For a moment she stared at the breakers, then she began to weep.

John Quincy turned uncomfortably away. It came to him that here in this so-called paradise sorrow was altogether too rampant. The only girls he knew were given to frequent tears, and not without reason.

"If you'll excuse me—" he said. Hallet and Chan, searching avidly, made no reply, and climbing over the sill, he stepped on to the lanai. The girl looked up as he approached.

"Oh," she said, "I thought I was alone."

"You'd like to be, perhaps," he answered. "But it might help if you told me what has happened. Did you speak to your father about that check?"

She nodded. "Yes, I showed it to him. And what do you think he did? He snatched it out of my hand and tore it into a hundred pieces. He gave me the pieces to—to throw away. And he said I was never to mention it to a soul."

"I don't understand that," frowned John Quincy.

97. "T.H." stood for "Territory of Hawaii."

"Neither do I. He was simply furious—not like himself at all. And when I told him you knew about it, he lost his temper again."

"But you can rely on me. I shan't tell any one."

"I know that. But of course father wasn't so sure of you as—as I am. Poor dad—he's having a horrible time of it. They don't give him a moment's rest—keep after him constantly—trying to make him tell. But all the policemen in the world couldn't—Oh, poor old dad!"

She was weeping again, and John Quincy felt toward her as he had felt toward Barbara. He wanted to put his arm about her, just by way of comfort and cheer. But alas, Carlota Maria Egan was not a Winterslip.

"Now, now," he said, "that won't do a bit of good."

She looked at him through her tears. "Won't it? I—I don't know. It seems to help a little. But"—she dried her eyes—"I really haven't time for it now. I must go in and see about lunch."

She rose, and John Quincy walked with her along the balcony. "I wouldn't worry if I were you," he said. "The police are on an entirely new trail this morning."

"Really?" she answered eagerly.

"Yes. There's a man named Brade stopping at your hotel. You know him, I suppose?"

She shook her head. "No, I don't."

"What! Why, he's a guest here."

"He was. But he isn't here now."

"Wait a minute!" John Quincy laid his hand on her arm, and they stopped. "This is interesting. Brade's gone, you say?"

"Yes. I understand from the clerk that Mr. and Mrs. Brade arrived here last Saturday. But early Tuesday morning, before my boat got in, Mr. Brade disappeared and he hasn't been seen since."

"Mr. Brade gets better all the time," John Quincy said. "Hallet and Chan are in his room now, and they've unearthed some rather intriguing facts. You'd better go in and tell Hallet what you've just told me."

They entered the lobby by a side door. As they did so, a slim young Hawaiian boy was coming in through the big door at the front. Something in his manner caught the attention of John Quincy, and he stopped. At that instant a purple bathing suit slipped by him, and Mr. Saladine also approached the desk.

Carlota Egan went on down the corridor toward room nineteen, but John Quincy remained in the lobby.

The Hawaiian boy moved rather diffidently toward the clerk. "Excuse me, please," he said. "I come to see Mr. Brade. Mr. Thomas Brade."

"Mr. Brade not here," replied the Jap.

"Then I will wait till he comes."

The clerk frowned. "No good. Mr. Brade not in Honolulu now."

"Not in Honolulu!" The Hawaiian seemed startled by the news.

"Mrs. Brade outside on the beach," continued the Jap.

"Oh, then Mr. Brade returns," said the boy with evident relief. "I call again."

He turned away, moving rapidly now. The clerk addressed Mr. Saladine, who was hovering near the cigar case. "Yes, sir, please?"

"Thigarettes," said the bereft Mr. Saladine.

The Jap evidently knew the brand desired, and handed over a box.

"Juth put it on my bill," said Saladine. He stood for a moment staring after the Hawaiian, who was disappearing through the front door. As he swung round his eyes encountered those of John Quincy. He looked quickly away and hurried out.

The two policemen and the girl entered from the corridor. "Well, Mr. Winterslip," said Hallet, "the bird has flown."

"So I understand," John Quincy answered.

"But we'll find him," continued Hallet. "I'll go over these islands with a drag-net. First of all, I want a talk with his wife." He turned to Carlota Egan. "Get her in here," he ordered. The girl looked at him. "Please," he added.

She motioned to the clerk, who went out the door.

"By the way," remarked John Quincy, "some one was just here asking for Brade."

"What's that!" Hallet was interested.

"A young Hawaiian, about twenty, I should say. Tall and slim. If you go to the door, you may catch a glimpse of him."

Hallet hurried over and glanced out into the garden. In a second he returned. "Humph," he said. "I know him. Did he say he'd come again?"

"He did."

Hallet considered. "I've changed my mind," he announced. "I won't question Mrs. Brade, after all. For the present, I don't want her to know we're looking for her husband. I'll trust you to fix that up with your clerk," he added to the girl. She nodded. "Lucky we left things as we found them in nineteen," he went on. "Unless she misses that letter and the cigarettes, which isn't likely, we're all right. Now, Miss Egan, we three will go into your father's office there behind the desk, and leave the door open. When Mrs. Brade comes in, I want you to question her about her husband's absence. Get all you can out of her. I'll be listening."

"I understand," the girl said.

Hallet, Chan and John Quincy went into Jim Egan's sanctum. "You found nothing else in the room?" the latter inquired of the Chinaman.

Chan shook his head. "Even so, fates are in smiling mood. What we have now are plentiful."

"Sh!" warned Hallet.

"Mrs. Brade, a young man was just here inquiring for your husband." It was Carlota Egan's voice.

"Really?" The accent was unmistakably British.

"He wanted to know where he could find him. We couldn't say."

"No—of course not."

"Your husband has left town, Mrs. Brade?"

"Yes. I fancy he has."

"You know when he will return, perhaps?"

"I really couldn't say. Is the mail in?"

"Not yet. We expect it about one."

"Thank you so much."

"Go to the door," Hallet directed John Quincy.

"She's gone to her room," announced the boy.

The three of them emerged from Egan's office.

"Oh, Captain?" said the girl. "I'm afraid I wasn't very successful."

"That's all right," replied Hallet. "I didn't think you would be." The clerk was again at his post behind the desk. Hallet turned to him. "Look here," he said. "I understand some one was here a minute ago asking for Brade. It was Dick Kaohla, wasn't it?"

"Yess," answered the Jap.

"Had he been here before to see Brade?"

"Yess. Sunday night. Mr. Brade and him have long talk on the beach."

Hallet nodded grimly. "Come on, Charlie," he said. "We've got our work cut out for us. Wherever Brade is, we must find him."

John Quincy stepped forward. "Pardon me, Captain," he remarked. "But if you don't mind—just who is Dick Kaohla?"

Hallet hesitated. "Kaohla's father—he's dead now—was a sort of confidential servant to Dan Winterslip. The boy's just plain no good. And oh, yes—he's the grandson of that woman who's over at your place now. Kamaikui—is that her name?"

CHAPTER XIV

What Kaohla Carried

Several days slipped by so rapidly John Quincy scarcely noted their passing. Dan Winterslip was sleeping now under the royal palms of the lovely island where he had been born. Sun and moon shone brightly in turn on his last dwelling place, but those who sought the person he had encountered that Monday night on his lanai were still groping in the dark.

Hallet had kept his word, he was combing the Islands for Brade. But Brade was nowhere. Ships paused at the crossroads and sailed again; the name of Thomas Macan Brade was on no sailing list. Through far settlements that were called villages but were nothing save clusters of Japanese huts, in lonely coves where the surf moaned dismally, over pineapple and sugar plantations, the emissaries of Hallet pursued their quest. Their efforts came to nothing.

John Quincy drifted idly with the days. He knew now the glamour of Waikiki waters; he had felt their warm embrace. Every afternoon he experimented with a board in the malihini surf, and he was eager for the moment when he could dare the big rollers farther out. Boston seemed like a tale that is told, State Street and Beacon memories of another more active existence now abandoned. No longer was he at a loss to understand his aunt's reluctance to depart these friendly shores.

Early Friday afternoon Miss Minerva found him reading a book on the lanai. Something in the nonchalance of his manner irritated her. She had always been for action, and the urge was on her even in Hawaii.

"Have you seen Mr. Chan lately?" she inquired.

"Talked with him this morning. They're doing their best to find Brade."

"Humph," sniffed Miss Minerva. "Their best is none too good. I'd like to have a few Boston detectives on this case."

"Oh, give them time," yawned John Quincy.

"They've had three days," she snapped. "Time enough. Brade never left this island of Oahu, that's certain. And when you consider that you can drive across it in a motor in two hours, and around it in about six, Mr. Hallet's brilliance does not impress. I'll have to end by solving this thing myself."

John Quincy laughed. "Yes, maybe you will."

"Well, I've given them the two best clues they have. If they'd keep their eyes open the way I do—"

"Charlie's eyes are open," protested John Quincy.

"Think so? They look pretty sleepy to me."

Barbara appeared on the lanai, dressed for a drive. Her eyes were somewhat happier; a bit of color had come back to her cheeks. "What are you reading, John Quincy?" she asked.

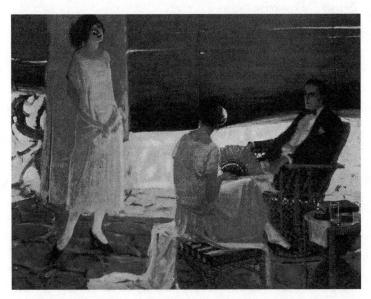

Barbara appeared on the lanai, dressed for a drive. Her eyes were
somewhat happier, a bit of color had come back to her cheeks.
From *The House Without a Key*, illustration by William Liepse
(*The Saturday Evening Post*, February 21, 1925)

He held up the book. "*The City by the Golden Gate*,"[98] he told her.

"Oh, really? If you're interested, I believe dad had quite a library on San Francisco. I remember there was a history of the stock exchange—he wanted me to read it, but I couldn't."

"You missed a good one," John Quincy informed her. "I finished it this morning. I've read five other books on San Francisco since I came."

His aunt stared at him. "What for?" she asked.

"Well—" He hesitated. "I've taken sort of a fancy to the town. I don't know—sometimes I think I'd rather like to live there."

Miss Minerva smiled grimly. "And they sent you out to take me back to Boston," she remarked.

"Boston's all right," said her nephew hastily. "It's Winterslip headquarters—but its hold has never been strong enough to prevent an occasional Winterslip from hitting the trail. You know, when I came into San Francisco harbor, I had the oddest feeling." He told them about it. "And the more I saw of the city, the better I liked it. There's a snap and sparkle in the air, and the people seem to know how to get the most out of life."

Barbara smiled on him approvingly. "Follow that impulse, John Quincy," she advised.

"Maybe I will. All this reminds me—I must write a letter." He rose and left the lanai.

"Does he really intend to desert Boston?" Barbara asked.

Miss Minerva shook her head. "Just a moment's madness," she explained. "I'm glad he's going through it—he'll be more human in the future. But as for leaving Boston! John Quincy! As well expect Bunker Hill Monument to emigrate to England."

In his room up-stairs, however, John Quincy's madness was persisting. He had never completed that letter to Agatha Parker, but he now plunged into his task with enthusiasm. San Francisco was his topic, and he wrote well. He pictured the city in words that glowed with life, and he wondered—just a suggestion—how she'd like to live there.

Agatha was now, he recalled, on a ranch in Wyoming—her first encounter with the West—and that was providential. She had felt for herself the lure of the wide open spaces. Well, the farther you went the wider and opener they got. In California life was all color and light. Just a suggestion, of course.

As he sealed the flap of the envelope, he seemed to glimpse Agatha's thin patrician face, and his heart sank. Her gray eyes were cool, so different from Barbara's, so very different from those of Carlota Maria Egan.

On Saturday afternoon John Quincy had an engagement to play golf with Harry Jennison. He drove up Nuuanu Valley in Barbara's roadster—for Dan Winterslip's will had been read and everything he possessed was Barbara's now. In that sheltered spot a brisk rain was falling, as is usually the case, though the sun was shining brightly. John Quincy had grown accustomed to this phenomenon; "liquid sunshine" the people of Hawaii call such rain, and pay no attention to it. Half a dozen different rainbows added to the beauty of the Country Club links.

Jennison was waiting on the veranda, a striking figure in white. He appeared genuinely glad to see his guest, and they set out on a round of golf that John Quincy would long remember. Never before had he played amid such beauty. The low hills stood on guard, their slopes bright with tropical colors—the yellow of kukui trees, the gray of ferns, the emerald of ohia and banana trees, here and there a splotch of brickred earth. The course was a green velvet carpet beneath their feet, the showers came and went. Jennison was a proficient driver, but the boy was his superior on approaches, and at the end of the match John Quincy was four up. They putted through a rainbow and returned to the locker room.

In the roadster going home, Jennison brought up the subject of Dan Winterslip's murder. John Quincy was interested to get the reaction of a lawyer to the evidence.

"I've kept more or less in touch with the case," Jennison said. "Egan is still my choice."

Somehow, John Quincy resented this. A picture of Carlota Egan's lovely but unhappy face flashed through his mind. "How about Leatherbee and the Compton woman?" he asked.

"Well, of course, I wasn't present when they told their story," Jennison replied. "But Hallet claims it sounded perfectly plausible. And it doesn't seem likely that if he'd had anything to do with the murder, Leatherbee would have been fool enough to keep that page from the guest book."

"There's Brade, too," John Quincy suggested.

"Yes—Brade complicates things. But when they run him down—if they do—I imagine the result will be nil."

"You know that Kamaikui's grandson is mixed up somehow with Brade?"

"So I understand. It's a matter that wants looking into. But mark my words, when all these trails are followed to the end, everything will come back to Jim Egan."

"What have you against Egan?" inquired John Quincy, swerving to avoid another car.

"I have nothing against Egan," Jennison replied. "But I can't forget the look on Dan Winterslip's face that day he told me he was afraid of the man. Then there is the stub of the Corsican cigarette. Most important of all, Egan's silence regarding his business with Winterslip. Men who are facing a charge of murder, my boy, talk, and talk fast. Unless it so happens that what they have to say would further incriminate them."

They drove on in silence into the heart of the city. "Hallet tells me you're doing a little detective work yourself," smiled Jennison.

"I've tried, but I'm a duffer," John Quincy admitted. "Just at present my efforts consist of a still hunt for that watch Aunt Minerva saw on the murderer's wrist. Whenever I see a wrist watch I get as close to it as I can, and stare. But as most of my sleuthing is done in the day time, it isn't so easy to determine whether the numeral two is bright or dim."

"Persistence," urged Jennison. "That's the secret of a good detective. Stick to the job and you may succeed yet."

The lawyer was to dine with the family at Waikiki. John Quincy set him down at his office, where he had a few letters to sign, and then drove him out to the beach. Barbara was gowned in white; she was slim and wistful and beautiful, and considering the events of the immediate past, the dinner was a cheerful one.

They had coffee on the lanai. Presently Jennison rose and stood by Barbara's chair. "We've something to tell you," he announced. He looked down at the girl. "Is that right, my dear?"

Barbara nodded.

"Your cousin and I"—the lawyer turned to the two from Boston—"have been fond of each other for a long time. We shall be married very quietly in a week or so—"

"Oh, Harry—not a week," said Barbara.

"Well, as you wish. But very soon."

"Yes, very soon," she repeated.

"And leave Honolulu for a time," Jennison continued. "Naturally, Barbara feels she can not stay here for the present—so many memories—you both understand. She has authorized me to put this house up for sale—"

"But, Harry," Barbara protested, "you make me sound so inhospitable. Telling my guests that the house is for sale and I am leaving—"

"Nonsense, my dear," said Aunt Minerva. "John Quincy and I understand, quite. I sympathize with your desire to get away." She rose.

"I'm sorry," said Jennison. "I did sound a little abrupt. But I'm naturally eager to take care of her now."

"Of course," John Quincy agreed.

Miss Minerva bent over and kissed the girl. "If your mother were here, dear child," she said, "she couldn't wish for your happiness any more keenly than I do." Barbara reached up impulsively and put her arms about the older woman.

John Quincy shook Jennison's hand. "You're mighty lucky."

"I think so," Jennison answered.

The boy went over to Barbara. "All—all good wishes," he said. She nodded, but did not reply. He saw there were tears in her eyes.

Presently Miss Minerva withdrew to the living-room, and John Quincy, feeling like a fifth wheel, made haste to leave the two together. He went out on the beach. The pale moon rode high amid the golden stars; romance whispered through the cocoanut palms. He thought of the scene he had witnessed that breathless night on the *President Tyler*—only two in the world, love quick and overwhelming—well, this was the setting for it. Here on this beach they had walked two and two since the beginning of time, whispering the same vows, making the same promises, whatever their color and creed. Suddenly the boy felt lonely.

Barbara was a Winterslip, and not for him. Why then did he feel again that frustrated pang in his heart? She had chosen and her choice was fitting; what affair was it of his?

He found himself moving slowly toward the Reef and Palm Hotel. For a chat with Carlota Egan? But why should he want to talk with this girl, whose outlook was so different from that of the world he knew? The girls at home were on a level with the

99.   This is inconsistent with John Quincy's earlier comment about women.

men in brains[99]—often, indeed, they were superior, seemed to be looking down from a great height. They discussed that article in the latest *Atlantic*, Shaw's grim philosophy, the new Sargent at the Art Gallery. Wasn't that the sort of talk he should be seeking here? Or was it? Under these palms on this romantic beach, with the moon riding high over Diamond Head?

Carlota Egan was seated behind the desk in the deserted lobby of the Reef and Palm, a worried frown on her face.

"You've come at the psychological moment," she cried, and smiled. "I'm having the most awful struggle."

"Arithmetic?" John Quincy inquired.

"Compound fractions, it seems to me. I'm making out the Brades' bill."

He came round the desk and stood at her side. "Let me help you."

"It's so fearfully involved." She looked up at him, and he wished they could do their sums on the beach. "Mr. Brade has been away since Tuesday morning, and we don't charge for any absence of more than three days. So that comes out of it. Maybe you can figure it—I can't."

"Charge him anyhow," suggested John Quincy.

"I'd like to—that would simplify everything. But it's not dad's way."

John Quincy took up a pencil. "What rate are they paying?" he inquired. She told him, and he began to figure. It wasn't a simple matter, even for a bond expert. John Quincy frowned too.

Some one entered the front door of the Reef and Palm. Looking up, John Quincy beheld the Hawaiian boy, Dick Kaohla. He carried a bulky object, wrapped in newspapers.

"Mr. Brade here now?" he asked.

Carlota Egan shook her head. "No, he hasn't returned."

"I will wait," said the boy.

"But we don't know where he is, or when he will come back," the girl protested.

"He will be here soon," the Hawaiian replied. "I wait on the lanai." He went out the side door, still carrying his clumsy burden. John Quincy and the girl stared at each other.

"'We move, we advance!'" John Quincy quoted in a low voice. "Brade will be here soon! Would you mind going out on the lanai and telling me where Kaohla is now?"

Quickly the girl complied. She returned in a few seconds. "He's taken a chair at the far end."

"Out of earshot?"

"Quite. You want the telephone—"

But John Quincy was already in the booth. Charlie Chan's voice came back over the wire.

"Most warm congratulations. You are number one detective yourself. Should my self-starter not indulge in stubborn spasm, I will make immediate connection with you."

John Quincy returned to the desk, smiling. "Charlie's flying to us in his Ford. Begins to look as though we were getting somewhere now. But about this bill. Mrs. Brade's board and room I make sixteen dollars. The charge against Mr. Brade—one week's board and room minus four days' board—totals nine dollars and sixty-two cents."

"How can I ever thank you?" said the girl.

"By telling me again about your childhood on this beach." A shadow crossed her face. "Oh, I'm sorry I've made you unhappy."

"Oh, no—you couldn't." She shook her head. "I've never been—so very happy. Always an 'if' in it, as I told you before. That morning on the ferry I think I was nearest to real happiness. I seemed to have escaped from life for a moment."

"I remember how you laughed at my hat."

"Oh—I hope you've forgiven me."

"Nonsense. I'm mighty glad I was able to make you laugh like that." Her great eyes stared into the future, and John Quincy pitied her. He had known others like her, others who loved their fathers, built high hopes for them, then saw them drift into a baffled old age. One of the girl's slender, tanned hands lay on the desk, John Quincy put his own upon it. "Don't be unhappy," he urged. "It's such a wonderful night. The moon—you're a what-you-may-call-it—a kamaaina, I know, but I'll bet you never saw the moon looking so well before. It's like a thousand-dollar gold piece, pale but negotiable. Shall we go out and spend it?"

Gently she drew her hand away. "There were seven bottles of charged water sent to the room. Thirty-five cents each—"

"What? Oh, the Brades' bill. Yes, that means two forty-five more. I'd like to mention the stars too. Isn't it odd how close the stars seem in the tropics—"

"I'm mighty glad I was able to make you laugh like that."
Her great eyes stared into the future and John Quincy pitied her.
From *The House Without a Key*, illustration by William Liepse
(*The Saturday Evening Post*, February 21, 1925)

She smiled. "We mustn't forget the trunks and bags. Three dollars for bringing them up from the dock."

"Say—that's rather steep. Well, it goes down on the record. Have I ever told you that all this natural beauty out here has left its imprint on your face? In the midst of so much loveliness, one couldn't be anything but—"

"Mrs. Brade had three trays to the room. That's seventy-five cents more."

"Extravagant lady! Brade will be sorry he came back, for more reasons than one. Well, I've got that. Anything else?"

"Just the laundry. Ninety-seven cents."

"Fair enough. Adding it all up, I get thirty-two dollars and sixty-nine cents. Let's call it an even thirty-three."

She laughed. "Oh, no. We can't do that."

Mrs. Brade came slowly into the lobby from the lanai. She paused at the desk. "Has there been a message?" she inquired.

"No, Mrs. Brade," the girl answered. She handed over the slip of paper. "Your bill."

"Ah, yes. Mr. Brade will attend to this the moment he returns."

"You expect him soon?"

"I really can't say." The Englishwoman moved on into the corridor leading to nineteen.

"Full of information, as usual," smiled John Quincy. "Why, here's Charlie now."

Chan came briskly to the desk, followed by another policeman, also in plain clothes.

"Automobile act noble," he announced, "having fondly feeling for night air." He nodded toward his companion. "Introducing Mr. Spencer. Now, what are the situation? Humbly hinting you speak fast."

John Quincy told him Kaohla was waiting on the lanai, and mentioned the unwieldy package carried by the boy. Chan nodded.

"Events are turning over rapidly," he said. He addressed the girl. "Please kindly relate to this Kaohla that Brade has arrived and would wish to encounter him here." She hesitated. "No, no," added Chan hastily, "I forget nice heathen delicacy. It is not pretty I should ask a lady to scatter false lies from ruby lips. I humbly demand forgiveness. Content yourself with a veiled pretext bringing him here."

The girl smiled and went out. "Mr. Spencer," said Chan, "I make bold to suggest you interrogate this Hawaiian. My reckless wanderings among words of unlimitable English language often fail to penetrate sort of skulls plentiful round here."

Spencer nodded and went to the side door, standing where he would not be seen by any one entering there. In a moment Kaohla appeared, followed by the girl. The Hawaiian came in quickly but seeing Chan, stopped, and a frightened look crossed his face. Spencer startled him further by seizing his arm.

"Come over here," said the detective. "We want to talk to you." He led the boy to a far corner of the room. Chan and John Quincy followed. "Sit down—here, I'll take that." He removed the heavy package from under the boy's arm. For a moment the Hawaiian seemed about to protest, but evidently he thought better of it. Spencer placed the package on a table and stood over Kaohla.

"Want to see Brade, eh?" he began in a threatening tone.

"Yes."

"What for?"

"Business is private."

"Well, I'm telling you to come across. You're in bad. Better change your mind and talk."

"No."

"All right. We'll see about that. What have you got in that package?" The boy's eyes went to the table, but he made no answer.

Chan took out a pocket knife. "Simple matter to discover," he said. He cut the rough twine, unwound several layers of newspapers. John Quincy pressed close, he felt that something important was about to be divulged.

The last layer of paper came off. "Hot dog!" cried Chan. He turned quickly to John Quincy. "Oh, I am so sorry—I pick up atrocious phrase like that from my cousin Mr. Willie Chan, Captain of All Chinese baseball team—"

But John Quincy did not hear, his eyes were glued to the object that lay on the table. An ohia wood box, bound with copper—the initials T.M.B.

"We will unlatch it," said Chan. He made an examination. "No, locked most strongly. We will crash into it at police station, where you and I and this silent Hawaiian will now hasten. Mr. Spencer, you will remain on spot here. Should Brade appear, you know your duty."

"I do," said Spencer.

"Mr. Kaohla, do me the honor to accompany," continued Chan. "At police headquarters much talk will be extracted out of you."

They turned toward the door. As they did so, Carlota Egan came up. "May I speak to you a moment?" she said to John Quincy.

"Surely." He walked with her to the desk.

"I went to the lanai just now," she whispered breathlessly. "Some one was crouching outside the window near where you were talking. I went closer and it was—Mr. Saladine!"

"Aha," said John Quincy. "Mr. Saladine had better drop that sort of thing, or he'll get himself in trouble."

"Should we tell Chan?"

"Not yet. You and I will do a little investigating ourselves first. Chan has other things to think about. And we don't want any of our guests to leave unless it's absolutely necessary."

"We certainly don't," she smiled. "I'm glad you've got the interests of the house at heart."

"That's just where I've got them—" John Quincy began, but Chan cut in.

"Humbly begging pardon," he said, "we must speed. Captain Hallet will have high delight to encounter this Kaohla, to say nothing of ohia wood box."

In the doorway, Kaohla crowded close to John Quincy, and the latter was startled by the look of hate he saw in the boy's stormy eyes. "You did this," muttered the Hawaiian. "I don't forget."

CHAPTER XV
The Man from India

They clattered along Kalakaua Avenue in Chan's car. John Quincy sat alone on the rear seat; at the detective's request he held the ohia wood box on his knees.

He rested his hands upon it. Once it had eluded him, but he had it now. His mind went back to that night in the attic two thousand miles away, the shadow against the moonlit window, the sting of a jewel cutting across his cheek. Roger's heartfelt cry of "Poor old Dan!" Did they hold at last, in this ohia wood box, the answer to the mystery of Dan's death?

Hallet was waiting in his room. With him was a keeneyed, efficient looking man evidently in his late thirties.

"Hello, boys," said the captain. "Mr. Winterslip, meet Mr. Greene, our district court prosecutor."

Greene shook hands cordially. "I've been wanting to meet you, sir," he said. "I know your city rather well. Spent three years at your Harvard Law School."

"Really?" replied John Quincy with enthusiasm.

"Yes. I went there after I got through at New Haven. I'm a Yale man, you know."

"Oh," remarked John Quincy, without any enthusiasm at all. But Greene seemed a pleasant fellow, despite his choice of college.

Chan had set the box on the table before Hallet, and was explaining how they had come upon it. The captain's thin face had brightened perceptibly. He inspected the treasure. "Locked, eh?" he remarked. "You got the key, Kaohla?"

The Hawaiian shook his head sullenly. "No."

"Watch your step, boy," warned Hallet. "Go over him, Charlie."

Chan went over him, rapidly and thoroughly. He found a key ring, but none of the keys fitted the lock on the box. He also brought to light a fat roll of bills.

"Where'd you get all that money, Dick?" Hallet inquired.

"I got it," glowered the boy.

But Hallet was more interested in the box. He tapped it lovingly. "This is important, Mr. Greene. We may find the solution of our puzzle in here." He took a small chisel from his desk, and after a brief struggle, pried open the lid.

John Quincy, Chan and the prosecutor pressed close, their eyes staring eagerly as the captain lifted the lid. The box was empty.

"Filled with nothing," murmured Chan. "Another dream go smash against stone wall."

The disappointment angered Hallet. He turned on Kaohla. "Now, my lad," he said. "I want to hear from you. You've been in touch with Brade, you talked with him last Sunday night, you've heard he's returning to-night. You've got some deal on with him. Come across and be quick about it."

"Nothing to tell," said the Hawaiian stubbornly.

Hallet leaped to his feet. "Oh, yes you have. And by heaven, you're going to tell it. I'm not any too patient to-night and I warn you if you don't talk and talk quick I'm likely to get rough." He stopped suddenly and turned to Chan. "Charlie, that Inter-Island boat is due from Maui about now. Get down to the dock and watch for Brade. You've got his description?"

"Sure," answered Chan. "Thin pale face, one shoulder descended below other, gray mustaches that droop in saddened mood."

"That's right. Keep a sharp lookout. And leave this lad to us. He won't have any secrets when we get through with him, eh, Mr. Greene?"

The prosecutor, more discreet, merely smiled.

"Mr. Winterslip," said Chan. "The night is delicious. A little stroll to moonly dock—"

"I'm with you," John Quincy replied. He looked back over his shoulder as he went, and reflected that he wouldn't care to be in Kaohla's shoes.

The pier-shed was dimly lighted and a small but diversified group awaited the incoming boat. Chan and John Quincy walked to the far end and there, seated on a packing-case, they found the water-front reporter of the evening paper.

"Hello, Charlie," cried Mr. Mayberry. "What you doing here?"

"Maybe friend arrive on boat," grinned Chan.

"Is that so?" responded Mayberry. "You boys over at the station have certainly become pretty mysterious all of a sudden. What's doing, Charlie?"

"All pronouncements come from captain," advised Chan.

"Yeah, we've heard his pronouncements," sneered Mayberry. "The police have unearthed clues and are working on them. Nothing to report at present. It's sickening. Well, sit down, Charlie. Oh—Mr. Winterslip—good evening. I didn't recognize you at first."

"How are you," said John Quincy. He and Chan also found packing-cases. There was a penetrating odor of sugar in the air. Through a wide opening in the pier-shed they gazed along the water-front and out upon the moonlit harbor. A rather exotic and intriguing scene, John Quincy reflected, and he said as much.

"Think so?" answered Mayberry. "Well, I don't. To me it's just like Seattle or Galveston or any of those stereotyped ports. But you see—I knew it when—"

"I think you mentioned that before," John Quincy smiled.

"I'm likely to mention it at any moment. As far as I'm concerned, the harbor of Honolulu has lost its romance. Once this was the most picturesque water-front in the world, my boy. And now look at the damned thing!" The reporter relighted his pipe. "Charlie can tell you—he remembers. The old ramshackle, low-lying wharves. Old Naval Row with its sailing ships. The wooden-hulled steamers with a mast or two—not too proud to use God's good winds occasionally. The bright little rowboats, the *Aloha*, the *Manu*, the *Emma*. Eh, Chan?"

"All extinct," agreed Chan.

"You wouldn't see a Rotary Club gang like this on a pier in those days," Mayberry continued. "Just Hawaiian stevedores with leis on their hats and ukuleles in their hands. Fishermen with their nets, and maybe a breezy old-time purser—a glad-hander and not a mere machine." He puffed a moment in sad silence. "Those were the days, Mr. Winterslip, the days of Hawaii's isolation, and her charm. The cable and the radio hadn't linked us up with the so-called civilization of the mainland. Every boat that came in we'd scamper over it, hunting a newspaper with the very latest news of the outside world. Remember those steamer days, Charlie, when everybody went down to the wharf in the good old hacks of yesteryear, when the women wore holokus and lauhala hats,[100] and Berger was there with his band,[101] and maybe a prince or two—"

"And the nights," suggested Charlie.

"Yeah, old-timer, I was coming to the nights. The soft nights when the serenaders drifted about the harbor in rowboats, and the lanterns speared long paths on the water—"

He seemed about to weep. John Quincy's mind went back to books he had read in his boyhood.

"And occasionally," he said, "I presume somebody went aboard a ship against his will?"

"I'll say he did," replied Mr. Mayberry, brightening at the thought. "Why, it was only in the 'nineties I was sitting one night on a dock a few yards down, when I saw a scuffle near the landing, and one of my best friends shouted to me: 'Good-by, Pete!' I was up and off in a minute, and I got him away from them—I was younger in those days. He was a good fellow, a sailorman, and he wasn't intending to take the journey that bunch had planned for him. They'd got him into a saloon and drugged him, but he pulled out of it just in time—oh, well, those days are gone for ever now. Just like Galveston or Seattle. Yes, sir, this harbor of Honolulu has lost its romance."

The little Inter-Island boat was drawing up to the pier, and they watched it come. As the gangplank went down, Chan rose.

"Who you expecting, Charlie?" asked Mayberry.

"We grope about," said Chan. "Maybe on this boat are Mr. Brade."

"Brade!" Mayberry leaped to his feet.

"Not so sure," warned Chan. "Only a matter we suppose. If correct, humbly suggest you follow to the station. You might capture news."

John Quincy and Chan moved up to the gangplank as the passengers descended. There were not many aboard. A few Island business men, a scattering of tourists, a party of Japanese in western clothes, ceremoniously received by friends ashore—a

100. A lauhala is a pandanus leaf, a palm species—so, a woven-palm hat.

101. Henry Berger (1844–1929) was a Berlin-born composer who served as royal bandmaster of the Kingdom of Hawaii from 1872 to 1915.

The Royal Hawaiian Band, 1889.

Lawrence D'Orsay, the "Earl of Pawtucket."

quaint little group all bowing from the waist. John Quincy was watching them with interest when Chan touched his arm.

A tall stooped Englishman was coming down the plank. Thomas Macan Brade would have been easily spotted in any crowd. His mustache was patterned after that of the Earl of Pawtucket,[102] and to make identification even simpler, he wore a white pith helmet. Pith helmets are not necessary under the kindly skies of Hawaii; this was evidently a relic of Indian days.

Chan stepped forward. "Mr. Brade?"

The man had a tired look in his eyes. He started nervously. "Y—yes," he hesitated.

"I am Detective-Sergeant Chan. Honolulu police. You will do me the great honor to accompany me to the station, if you please."

Brade stared at him, then shook his head. "It's quite impossible," he said.

"Pardon me, please," answered Chan. "It are unevitable."

"I—I have just returned from a journey," protested the man. "My wife may be worried regarding me. I must have a talk with her, and after that—"

"Regret," purred Chan, "are scorching me. But duty remains duty. Chief's words are law. Humbly suggest we squander valuable time."

"Am I to understand that I'm under arrest?" flared Brade.

"The idea is preposterous," Chan assured him. "But the captain waits eager for statement from you. You will walk this way, I am sure. A moment's pardon. I introduce my fine friend, Mr. John Quincy Winterslip, of Boston."

At mention of the name, Brade turned and regarded John Quincy with deep interest. "Very good," he said. "I'll go with you."

They went out to the street, Brade carrying a small hand-bag. The flurry of arrival was dying fast. Honolulu would shortly return to its accustomed evening calm.

When they reached the police station, Hallet and the prosecutor seemed in high good humor. Kaohla sat in a corner, hopeless and defeated; John Quincy saw at a glance that the boy's secret was his no longer.

"Introducing Mr. Brade," said Chan.

"Ah," cried Hallet, "we're glad to see you, Mr. Brade. We'd been getting pretty worried about you."

"Really, sir," said Brade, "I am completely at a loss—"

"Sit down," ordered Hallet. The man sank into a chair. He too had a hopeless, defeated air. No one can appear more humble and beaten than a British civil servant, and this man had known thirty-six years of baking under the Indian sun, looked down on by the military, respected by none. Not only his mustache but his whole figure drooped "in saddened mood."[103] Yet now and then, John Quincy noted, he flashed into life, a moment of self-assertion and defiance.

"Where have you been, Mr. Brade?" Hallet inquired.

"I have visited one of the other islands. Maui."

"You went last Tuesday morning?"

"Yes. On the same steamer that brought me back."

"Your name was not on the sailing list," Hallet said.

"No. I went under another name. I had—reasons."

"Indeed?"

The flash of life. "Just why am I here, sir?" He turned to the prosecutor. "Perhaps you will tell me that?"

Greene nodded toward the detective. "Captain Hallet will enlighten you," he said.

"You bet I will," Hallet announced. "As perhaps you know, Mr. Brade, Mr. Dan Winterslip has been murdered."

Brade's washed-out eyes turned to John Quincy. "Yes," he said. "I read about it in a Hilo newspaper."[104]

"You didn't know it when you left last Tuesday morning?" Hallet asked.

"I did not. I sailed without seeing a paper here."

"Ah, yes. When did you see Mr. Dan Winterslip last?"

"I never saw him."

"What! Be careful, sir."

"I never saw Dan Winterslip in my life."

"All right. Where were you last Tuesday morning at twenty minutes past one?"

"I was asleep in my room at the Reef and Palm Hotel. I'd retired at nine-thirty, as I had to rise early in order to board my boat. My wife can verify that."

"A wife's testimony, Mr. Brade, is not of great value—"

Brade leaped to his feet. "Look here, sir! Do you mean to insinuate—"

"Take it easy," said Hallet smoothly. "I have a few matters to call to your attention, Mr. Brade. Mr. Dan Winterslip was

103. It is impossible to name a single source for the quoted phrase; it appears often in popular poetry and prose—for instance, the ode "The Legend of Count Manfred of Alba," by Robert Bigsby (1844). A volume of Bigsby's prose and poetry was part of the Longfellow Collection in the Harvard College Library and may have been known to John Quincy.

104. This was likely the *Hilo Tribune-Herald*, the largest newspaper in Hilo, formed in 1923 when several older papers were merged.

murdered at one-twenty or thereabouts last Tuesday morning. We happen to know that in his youth he served as first officer aboard the *Maid of Shiloh*, a blackbirder. The master of that vessel had the same name as yourself. An investigation of your room at the Reef and Palm—"

"How dare you!" cried Brade. "By what right—"

"I am hunting the murderer of Dan Winterslip," broke in Hallet coolly. "And I follow the trail wherever it leads. In your room I found a letter from the British Consul here addressed to you, and informing you that Winterslip was alive and in Honolulu. I also found this tin of Corsican cigarettes. Just outside the living-room door of Winterslip's house, we picked up the stub of a Corsican cigarette. It's a brand not on sale in Honolulu."

Brade had dropped back into his chair, and was staring in a dazed way at the tin box in Hallet's hand. Hallet indicated the Hawaiian boy in the corner. "Ever see this lad before, Mr. Brade?" Brade nodded.

"You had a talk with him last Sunday night on the beach?"

"Yes."

"The boy's told us all about it. He read in the paper that you were coming to Honolulu. His father was a confidential servant in Dan Winterslip's employ and he himself was brought up in the Winterslip household. He could make a pretty good guess at your business with Winterslip, and he figured you'd be pleased to lay hands on this ohia wood box. In his boyhood he'd seen it in a trunk in the attic of Winterslip's San Francisco house. He went down to the *President Tyler* and arranged with a friend aboard that boat, the quartermaster, to break into the house and steal the box. When he saw you last Sunday night he told you he'd have the box as soon as the *President Tyler* got in, and he arranged to sell it to you for a good sum. Am I right so far, Mr. Brade?"

"You are quite right," said Brade.

"The initials on the box are T.M.B." Hallet persisted. "They are your initials, are they not?"

"They happen to be," said Brade. "But they were also the initials of my father. My father died aboard ship in the South Seas many years ago, and that box was stolen from his cabin after his death. It was stolen by the first officer of the *Maid of Shiloh*—by Mr. Dan Winterslip."

105. At least £2 million in today's values.

For a moment no one spoke. A cold shiver ran down the spine of John Quincy Winterslip and a hot flush suffused his cheek. Why, oh, why, had he strayed so far from home? In Boston he traveled in a rut, perhaps, but ruts were safe, secure. There no one had ever brought a charge such as this against a Winterslip, no whisper of scandal had ever sullied the name. But here Winterslips had run amuck, and there was no telling what would next be dragged into the light.

"I think, Mr. Brade," said the prosecutor slowly, "you had better make a full statement."

Brade nodded. "I intend to do so. My case against Winterslip is not complete and I should have preferred to remain silent for a time. But under the circumstances, of course I must speak out. I'll smoke, if you don't mind." He took a cigarette from his case and lighted it. "I'm a bit puzzled just how to begin. My father disappeared from England in the 'seventies, leaving my mother and me to shift for ourselves. For a time we heard nothing of him, then letters began to arrive from various points in Australia and the South Seas. Letters with money in them, money we badly needed. I have since learned that he had gone into the blackbirding trade; it is nothing to be proud of, God knows, but I like to recall in his favor that he did not entirely abandon his wife and boy.

"In the 'eighties we got word of his death. He died aboard the *Maid of Shiloh* and was buried on the island of Apiang in the Gilbert Group—buried by Dan Winterslip, his first officer. We accepted the fact of his death, the fact of no more letters with remittances, and took up our struggle again. Six months later we received, from a friend of my father in Sydney, a brother captain, a most amazing letter.

"This letter said that, to the writer's certain knowledge, my father had carried a great deal of money in his cabin on the *Maid of Shiloh*. He had done no business with banks, instead he had had this strong box made of ohia wood. The man who wrote us said that he had seen the inside of it, and that it contained jewelry and a large quantity of gold. My father had also shown him several bags of green hide, containing gold coins from many countries. He estimated that there must have been close to twenty thousand pounds, in all.[105] Dan Winterslip, the letter said, had brought the *Maid of Shiloh* back to Sydney and turned over to the proper authorities my father's clothing and personal effects, and a scant ten pounds in money. He had made no mention of anything further. He and the only other white man aboard the *Maid*, an Irishman named Hagin, had left at once for Hawaii. My father's friend suggested that we start an immediate investigation.

"Well, gentlemen"—Brade looked about the circle of interested faces—"what could we do? We were in pitiful circumstances, my mother and I. We had no money to employ lawyers, to fight a case thousands of miles away. We did make a few inquiries through a relative in Sydney, but nothing came of them. There was talk for a time, but the talk died out, and the matter was dropped. But I—I have never forgotten.

"Dan Winterslip returned here, and prospered. He built on the foundation of the money he found in my father's cabin a fortune that inspired the admiration of Honolulu. And while he prospered, we were close to starvation. My mother died, but I carried on. For years it has been my dream to make him pay. I have not been particularly successful, but I have saved, scrimped. I have the money now to fight this case.

"Four months ago I resigned my post in India and set out for Honolulu. I stopped over in Sydney—my father's friend is dead, but I have his letter. I have the depositions of others who knew about that money—about the ohia wood box. I came on here, ready to face Dan Winterslip at last. But I never faced him. As you know, gentlemen"—Brade's hand trembled slightly as he put down his cigarette—"some one robbed me of that privilege. Some unknown hand removed from my path the man I have hated for more than forty years."

"You arrived last Saturday—a week ago," said Hallet, after a pause. "On Sunday evening Kaohla here called on you. He offered you the strong box?"

"He did," Brade replied. "He'd had a cable from his friend, and expected to have the box by Tuesday. I promised him five thousand dollars for it—a sum I intended Winterslip should pay. Kaohla also told me that Hagin was living on a ranch in a remote part of the Island of Maui. That explains my journey there—I took another name, as I didn't want Winterslip to follow my movements. I had no doubt he was watching me."

"You didn't tell Kaohla you were going, either?"

"No, I didn't think it advisable to take him completely into my confidence. I found Hagin, but could get nothing out of him.

Evidently Winterslip had bought his silence long ago. I realized the box was of great importance to me, and I cabled Kaohla to bring it to me immediately on my return. It was then that the news of Winterslip's death came through. It was a deep disappointment, but it will not deter me." He turned to John Quincy. "Winterslip's heirs must pay. I am determined they shall make my old age secure."

John Quincy's face flushed again. A spirit of rebellion, of family pride outraged, stirred within him. "We'll see about that, Mr. Brade," he said. "You have unearthed the box, but so far as any proof about valuables—money—"

"One moment," cut in Greene, the prosecutor. "Mr. Brade, have you a description of any article of value taken from your father?"

Brade nodded. "Yes. In my father's last letter to us—I was looking through it only the other day—he spoke of a brooch he had picked up in Sydney. A tree of emeralds, rubies and diamonds against an onyx background. He said he was sending it to my mother—but it never came."

The prosecutor looked at John Quincy. John Quincy looked away. "I'm not one of Dan Winterslip's heirs, Mr. Brade," he explained. "As a matter of fact, he was a rather distant relative of mine. I can't presume to speak for his daughter, but I'm reasonably sure that when she knows your story, this matter can be settled out of court. You'll wait, of course?"

"I'll wait," agreed Brade. "And now, Captain—"

Hallet raised his hand. "Just a minute. You didn't call on Winterslip? You didn't go near his house?"

"I did not," said Brade.

"Yet just outside the door of his living-room we found, as I told you, the stub of a Corsican cigarette. It's a matter still to be cleared up."

Brade considered briefly. "I don't want to get any one into trouble," he said. "But the man is nothing to me, and I must clear my own name. In the course of a chat with the proprietor of the Reef and Palm Hotel, I offered him a cigarette. He was delighted when he recognized the brand—said it had been years since he'd seen one. So I gave him a handful, and he filled his case—"

"You're speaking of Jim Egan," suggested Hallet delightedly.

"Of Mr. James Egan, yes," Brade replied.

"That's all I want to know," said Hallet. "Well, Mr. Greene—"

The prosecutor addressed Brade. "For the present, we can't permit you to leave Honolulu," he said. "But you are free to go to your hotel. This box will remain here until we can settle its final disposition."

"Naturally." Brade rose.

John Quincy faced him. "I'll call on you very soon," he promised.

"What? Oh, yes—yes, of course." The man stared nervously about him. "If you'll pardon me, gentlemen, I must run—I really must—"

He went out. The prosecutor looked at his watch. "Well, that's that. I'll have a conference with you in the morning, Hallet. My wife's waiting for me at the Country Club. Good night, Mr. Winterslip." He saw the look on John Quincy's face, and smiled. "Don't take those revelations about your cousin too seriously. The 'eighties are ancient history, you know."

As Greene disappeared, Hallet turned to John Quincy. "What about this Kaohla?" he inquired. "It will be a pretty complicated job to prosecute him and his house-breaking friend on the *President Tyler*, but it can be done—"

A uniformed policeman appeared at the door, summoning Chan outside.

"Oh, no," said John Quincy. "Let the boy go. We don't want any publicity about this. I'll ask you, Captain, to keep Brade's story out of the papers."

"I'll try," Hallet replied. He turned to the Hawaiian. "Come here!" The boy rose. "You heard what this gentleman said. You ought to be sent up for this, but we've got more important things to attend to now. Run along—beat it—"

Chan came in just in time to hear the last. At his heels followed a sly little Jap and a young Chinese boy. The latter was attired in the extreme of college-cut clothes; he was an American and he emphasized the fact.

"Only one moment," Chan cried. "New and interesting fact emerge into light. Gentlemen, my Cousin Willie Chan, captain All Chinese baseball team and demon backstopper of the Pacific!"

"Pleased to meetchu," said Willie Chan.

"Also Okamoto, who have auto stand on Kalakaua Avenue, not far from Winterslip household—"

"I know Okamoto," said Hallet. "He sells okolehau on the side."

"No, indeed," protested the Jap. "Auto stand, that is what."

"Willie do small investigating to help out crowded hours," went on Chan. "He have dug up strange event out of this Okamoto here. On early morning of Tuesday, July first, Okamoto is roused from slumber by fierce knocks on door of room. He go to door—"

"Let him tell it," suggested Hallet. "What time was this?"

"Two of the morning," said the Jap. "Knocks were as described. I rouse and look at watch, run to door. Mr. Dick Kaohla here is waiting. Demand I drive him to home over in Iwilei district. I done so."

"All right," said Hallet. "Anything else? No? Charlie—take them out and thank them—that's your specialty." He waited until the Orientals had left the room, then turned fiercely on Kaohla. "Well, here you are back in the limelight," he cried. "Now, come across. What were you doing out near Winterslip's house the night of the murder?"

"Nothing," said the Hawaiian.

"Nothing! A little late to be up doing nothing, wasn't it? Look here, my boy, I'm beginning to get you. For years Dan Winterslip gave you money, supported you, until he finally decided you were no good. So he stopped the funds and you and he had a big row. Now, didn't you?"

"Yes," admitted Dick Kaohla.

"On Sunday night Brade offered you five thousand for the box. You thought it wasn't enough. The idea struck you that maybe Dan Winterslip would pay more. You were a little afraid of him, but you screwed up your courage and went to his house—"

"No, no," the boy cried. "I did not go there."

"I say you did. You'd made up your mind to doublecross Brade. You and Dan Winterslip had another big scrap, you drew a knife—"

"Lies, all lies," the boy shouted, terrified.

"Don't tell me I lie! You killed Winterslip and I'll get it out of you! I got the other and I'll get this." Hallet rose threateningly from his chair.

Chan suddenly reentered the room, and handed Hallet a note. "Arrive this moment by special messenger," he explained.

Hallet ripped open the envelope and read. His expression altered. He turned disgustedly to Kaohla. "Beat it!" he scowled.

The boy fled gratefully. John Quincy and Chan looked wonderingly at the captain. Hallet sat down at his desk. "It all comes back to Egan," he said. "I've known it from the first."

"Wait a minute," cried John Quincy. "What about that boy?"

Hallet crumpled the letter in his hand. "Kaohla? Oh, he's out of it now."

"Why?"

"That's all I can tell you. He's out of it."

"That's not enough," John Quincy said. "I demand to know—"

Hallet glared at him. "You know all you're going to," he answered angrily. "I say Kaohla's out, and that settles it. Egan killed Winterslip, and before I get through with him—"

"Permit me to say," interrupted John Quincy, "that you have the most trusting nature I ever met. Everybody's story goes with you. The Compton woman and that rat Leatherbee come in here and spin a yarn, and you bow them out. And Brade! What about Brade! In bed at onetwenty last Tuesday morning, eh? Who says so? He does. Who can prove it? His wife can. What was to prevent his stepping out on the balcony of the Reef and Palm and walking along the beach to my cousin's house? Answer me that!"

Hallet shook his head. "It's Egan. That cigarette—"

"Yes—that cigarette. Has it occurred to you that Brade may have given him those cigarettes purposely—"

"Egan did it," cut in Hallet stubbornly. "All I need now is his story; I'll get it. I have ways and means—"

"I congratulate you on your magnificent stupidity," cried John Quincy. "Good night, sir."

He walked along Bethel Street, Chan at his side.

"You are partly consumed by anger," said the Chinaman. "Humbly suggest you cool. Calm heads needed."

"But what was in that note? Why wouldn't he tell us?"

"In good time, we know. Captain honest man. Be patient."

"But we're all at sea again," protested John Quincy. "Who killed Cousin Dan? We get nowhere."

"So very true," agreed Chan. "More clues lead us into presence of immovable stone wall. We sway about, seeking still other path."

"I'll say we do," answered John Quincy. "There comes my car. Good night!"

Not until the trolley was halfway to Waikiki did he remember Mr. Saladine. Saladine crouching outside that window at the Reef and Palm. What did that mean? But Saladine was a comic figure, a lisping searcher after bridgework in the limpid waters of Waikiki. Even so, perhaps his humble activities should be investigated.

CHAPTER XVI

The Return of Captain Cope

After breakfast on Sunday morning, John Quincy followed Miss Minerva to the lanai. It was a neat world that lay outside the screen, for Dan Winterslip's yard boy had been busy until a late hour the night before, sweeping the lawn with the same loving thoroughness a housewife might display on a precious Oriental rug.

Barbara had not come down to breakfast, and John Quincy had seized the opportunity to tell his aunt of Brade's return, and repeat the man's story of Dan Winterslip's theft on board the *Maid of Shiloh*. Now he lighted a cigarette and sat staring seriously out at the distant water.

"Cheer up," said Miss Minerva. "You look like a judge. I presume you're thinking of poor Dan."

"I am."

"Forgive and forget. None of us ever suspected Dan of being a saint."

"A saint! Far from it! He was just a plain—"

"Never mind," put in his aunt sharply. "Remember, John Quincy, man is a creature of environment. And the temptation must have been great. Picture Dan on that ship in these easy-going latitudes, wealth at his feet and not a soul in sight to claim it. Ill-gotten wealth, at that. Even you—"

"Even I," said John Quincy sternly, "would have recalled I am a Winterslip. I never dreamed I'd live to hear you offering apologies for that sort of conduct."

She laughed. "You know what they say about white women who go to the tropics. They lose first their complexion, then their teeth, and finally their moral sense." She hesitated. "I've had to visit the dentist a good deal of late," she added.

John Quincy was shocked. "My advice to you is to hurry home," he said.

"When are you going?"

"Oh, soon—soon."

"That's what we all say. Returning to Boston, I suppose?"

"Of course."

"How about San Francisco?"

"Oh, that's off. I did suggest it to Agatha, but I'm certain she won't hear of it. And I'm beginning to think she'd be quite right." His aunt rose. "You'd better go to church," said John Quincy severely.

"That's just where I am going," she smiled. "By the way, Amos is coming to dinner to-night, and he'd best hear the Brade story from us, rather than in some garbled form. Barbara must hear it too. If it proves to be true, the family ought to do something for Mr. Brade."

"Oh, the family will do something for him, all right," John Quincy remarked. "Whether it wants to or not."

"Well, I'll let you tell Barbara about him," Miss Minerva promised.

"Thank you so much," replied her nephew sarcastically.

"Not at all. Are you coming to church?"

"No," he said. "I don't need it the way you do."

She left him there to face a lazy uneventful day. By five in the afternoon Waikiki was alive with its usual Sunday crowd—not the unsavory holiday throng seen on a mainland beach, but a scattering of good-looking people whose tanned straight bodies would have delighted the heart of a physical culture enthusiast. John Quincy summoned sufficient energy to don a bathing suit and plunge in.

There was something soothing in the warm touch of the water, and he was becoming more at home there every day. With long powerful strokes he drew away from the malihini breakers to dare the great rollers beyond. Surf-board riders flashed by him; now and then he had to alter his course to avoid an outrigger canoe.

106. Trace.

107. If John Quincy was more familiar with the Midwest, this might have been a tip-off that Saladine was an imposter—all midwesterners know that the town is pronounced "Dee Moyn," presenting no difficulty to a lisping speaker.

On the farthest float of all he saw Carlota Egan. She sat there, a slender lovely figure vibrant with life, and awaited his coming. As he climbed up beside her and looked into her eyes he was—perhaps from his exertion in the water—a little breathless.

"I rather hoped I'd find you," he panted.

"Did you?" She smiled faintly. "I hoped it too. You see, I need a lot of cheering up."

"On a perfect day like this!"

"I'd pinned such hopes on Mr. Brade," she explained. "Perhaps you know he's back—and from what I can gather, his return hasn't meant a thing so far as dad's concerned. Not a thing."

"Well, I'm afraid it hasn't," John Quincy admitted. "But we mustn't get discouraged. As Chan puts it, we sway about, seeking a new path. You and I have a bit of swaying to do. How about Mr. Saladine?"

"I've been thinking about Mr. Saladine. But I can't get excited about him, somehow. He's so ridiculous."

"We mustn't pass him up on that account," admonished John Quincy. "I caught a glimpse of his purple bathing suit on the first float. Come on—we'll just casually drop in on him. I'll race you there."

She smiled again, and leaped to her feet. For a second she stood poised, then dived in a way that John Quincy could never hope to emulate. He slipped off in pursuit, and though he put forth every effort, she reached Saladine's side five seconds before he did.

"Hello, Mr. Saladine," she said. "This is Mr. Winterslip, of Boston."

"Ah, yeth," responded Mr. Saladine, gloomily. "Mr. Winterthlip." He regarded the young man with interest.

"Any luck, sir?" inquired John Quincy sympathetically.

"Oh—you heard about my accthident?"

"I did, sir, and I'm sorry."

"I am, too," said Mr. Saladine feelingly. "Not a thrath[106] of them tho far. And I muth go home in a few deth."

"I believe Miss Egan said you lived in Des Moines?"

"Yeth. Deth—Deth—I can't they it."[107]

"In business there?" inquired John Quincy nonchalantly.

"Yeth. Wholethale grothery buthineth," answered Mr. Saladine, slowly but not very successfully.

John Quincy turned away to hide a smile. "Shall we go along?" he said to the girl. "Good luck to you, sir." He dove off, and as they swam toward the shore, he reflected that they were on a false trail there—a trail as spurious as the teeth. That little business man was too conventional a figure to have any connection with the murder of Dan Winterslip. He kept these thoughts to himself, however.

Halfway to the beach, they encountered an enormous figure floating languidly on the water. Just beyond the great stomach John Quincy perceived the serene face of Charlie Chan.

"Hello, Charlie," he cried. "It's a small ocean, after all! Got your Ford with you?"

Chan righted himself and grinned. "Little pleasant recreation," he explained. "Forget detective worries out here floating idle like leaf on stream."

"Please float ashore," suggested John Quincy. "I have something to tell you."

"Only too happy," agreed Chan.

He followed them in and they sat, an odd trio, on the white sand. John Quincy told the detective about Saladine's activities outside the window the night before, and repeated the conversation he had just had with the middle westerner. "Of course, the man seems almost too foolish to mean anything," he added.

Chan shook his head. "Begging most humble pardon," he said, "that are wrong attitude completely. Detective business made up of unsignificant trifles. One after other our clues go burst in our countenance. Wise to pursue matter of Mr. Saladine."

"What do you suggest?" John Quincy asked.

"To-night I visit city for night work to drive off my piled tasks," Chan replied. "After evening meal, suggest you join with me at cable office. We despatch message to postmaster of this Des Moines, inquiring what are present locality of Mr. Saladine, expert in wholeselling provisions. Your name will be signed to message, much better than police meddling."

"All right," John Quincy agreed, "I'll meet you there at eight-thirty."

Carlota Egan rose. "I must get back to the Reef and Palm. You've no idea all I have to do—"

John Quincy stood beside her. "If I can help, you know—"

"I know," she smiled. "I'm thinking of making you assistant manager. They'd be so proud of you—in Boston."

108. George Gordon, Lord Byron, "She Walks in Beauty" (1813).

She moved off toward the water for her homeward swim, and John Quincy dropped down beside Chan. The Chinaman's little amber eyes followed the girl. "Endeavoring to make English language my slave," he said, "I pursue poetry. Who were the great poet who said—'She walks in beauty like the night?'"[108]

"Why, that was—er—who was it?" remarked John Quincy helpfully.

"Name is slippery," went on Chan. "But no matter. Lines pop into brain whenever I see this Miss Egan. Beauty like the night, Hawaiian night maybe, lovely as purest jade. Most especially on this beach. Spot of heartbreaking charm, this beach."

"Surely is," agreed John Quincy, amused at Chan's obviously sentimental mood.

"Here on gleaming sand I first regard my future wife," continued Chan. "Slender as the bamboo is slender, beautiful as blossom of the plum—"

"Your wife," repeated John Quincy. The idea was a new one.

"Yes, indeed." Chan rose. "Recalls I must hasten home where she attends the children who are now, by actual count, nine in number." He looked down at John Quincy thoughtfully. "Are you well-fitted with the armor of preparation?" he said. "Consider. Some night the moon has splendor in this neighborhood, the cocoapalms bow lowly and turn away their heads so they do not see. And the white man kisses without intending to do so."

"Oh, don't worry about me," John Quincy laughed. "I'm from Boston, and immune."

"Immune," repeated Chan. "Ah, yes, I grasp meaning. In my home I have idol brought from China with insides of solid stone. He would think he is—immune. But even so I would not entrust him on this beach. As my cousin Willie Chan say with vulgarity, see you later."

John Quincy sat for a time on the sand, then rose and strolled toward home. His path lay close to the lanai of Arlene Compton's cottage, and he was surprised to hear his name called from behind the screen. He stepped to the door and looked in. The woman was sitting there alone.

"Come in a minute, Mr. Winterslip," she said.

John Quincy hesitated. He did not care to make any social calls on this lady, but he did not have it in him to be rude. He went inside and sat down gingerly, poised for flight. "Got to hurry back for dinner," he explained.

"Dinner? You'll want a cocktail."

"No, thanks. I'm—I'm on the wagon."

"You'll find it hard to stick out here," she said a little bitterly. "I won't keep you long. I just want to know—are those boneheads down at the station getting anywhere, or ain't they?"

"The police," smiled John Quincy. "They seem to be making progress. But it's slow. It's very slow."

"I'll tell the world it's slow. And I got to stick here till they pin it on somebody. Pleasant outlook, ain't it?"

"Is Mr. Leatherbee still with you?" inquired John Quincy.

"What do you mean is he still with me?" she flared.

"Pardon me. Is he still in town?"

"Of course he's in town. They won't let him go, either. But I ain't worrying about him. I got troubles of my own. I want to go home." She nodded toward a newspaper on the table. "I just got hold of an old *Variety* and seen about a show opening in Atlantic City. A lot of the gang is in it, working like dogs, rehearsing night and day, worrying themselves sick over how long the thing will last. Gee, don't I envy them. I was near to bawling when you came along."

"You'll get back all right," comforted John Quincy.

"Say—if I ever do! I'll stop everybody I meet on Broadway and promise never to leave 'em again." John Quincy rose. "You tell that guy Hallet to get a move on," she urged.

"I'll tell him," he agreed.

"And drop in to see me now and then," she added wistfully. "Us easterners ought to stick together out here."

"That's right, we should," John Quincy answered. "Good-by."

As he walked along the beach, he thought of her with pity. The story she and Leatherbee had told might be entirely false; even so, she was a human and appealing figure and her homesickness touched his heart.

Later that evening when John Quincy came down-stairs faultlessly attired for dinner, he encountered Amos Winterslip in the living-room. Cousin Amos's lean face was whiter than ever; his manner listless. He had been robbed of his hate; his evenings beneath the algaroba tree had lost their savor; life was devoid of spice.

Dinner was not a particularly jolly affair. Barbara seemed intent on knowing now the details of the search the police were conducting, and it fell to John Quincy to enlighten her. Reluctantly he came at last to the story of Brade. She listened in silence. After dinner she and John Quincy went out into the garden and sat on a bench under the hau tree, facing the water.

"I'm terribly sorry I had to tell you that about Brade," John Quincy said gently. "But it seemed necessary."

"Of course," she agreed. "Poor dad! He was weak—weak—"

"Forgive and forget," John Quincy suggested. "Man is a creature of environment." He wondered dimly where he had heard that before. "Your father was not entirely to blame—"

"You're terribly kind, John Quincy," she told him.

"No—but I mean it," he protested. "Just picture the scene to yourself. That lonely ocean, wealth at his feet for the taking, no one to see or know."

She shook her head. "Oh, but it was wrong, wrong. Poor Mr. Brade. I must make things right with him as nearly as I can. I shall ask Harry to talk with him to-morrow—"

"Just a suggestion," interposed John Quincy. "Whatever you agree to do for Brade must not be done until the man who killed your father is found."

She stared at him. "What! You don't think that Brade—"

"I don't know. Nobody knows. Brade is unable to prove where he was early last Tuesday morning."

They sat silent for a moment; then the girl suddenly collapsed and buried her face in her hands. Her slim shoulders trembled convulsively and John Quincy, deeply sympathetic, moved closer. He put his arm about her. The moonlight shone on her bright hair, the trades whispered in the hau tree, the breakers murmured on the beach. She lifted her face, and he kissed her. A cousinly kiss he had meant it to be, but somehow it wasn't—it was a kiss he would never have been up to on Beacon Street.

"Miss Minerva said I'd find you here," remarked a voice behind them.

John Quincy leaped to his feet and found himself staring into the cynical eyes of Harry Jennison. Even though you are the girl's cousin, it is a bit embarrassing to have a man find you kissing his fiancée. Particularly if the kiss wasn't at all cousinly—John Quincy wondered if Jennison had noticed that.

"Come in—I mean, sit down," stammered John Quincy. "I was just going."

"Good-by," said Jennison coldly.

John Quincy went hastily through the living-room, where Miss Minerva sat with Amos. "Got an appointment downtown," he explained, and picking up his hat in the hall, fled into the night.

He had intended taking the roadster, but to reach the garage he would have to pass that bench under the hau tree. Oh, well, the colorful atmosphere of a trolley was more interesting, anyhow.

In the cable office on the ground floor of the Alexander Young Hotel, Chan was waiting, and they sent off their inquiry to the postmaster at Des Moines, signing John Quincy's name and address. That attended to, they returned to the street. In the park across the way an unseen group of young men strummed steel guitars and sang in soft haunting voices; it was the only sign of life in Honolulu.

"Kindly deign to enter hotel lobby with me," suggested Chan. "It is my custom to regard names in register from time to time."

At the cigar stand just inside the door, the boy paused to light his pipe, while Chan went on to the desk. As John Quincy turned he saw a man seated alone in the lobby, a handsome, distinguished man who wore immaculate evening clothes that bore the stamp of Bond Street. An old acquaintance, Captain Arthur Temple Cope.

At sight of John Quincy, Cope leaped to his feet and came forward. "Hello, I'm glad to see you," he cried, with a cordiality that had not been evident at former meetings. "Come over and sit down."

John Quincy followed him. "Aren't you back rather soon?" he inquired.

"Sooner than I expected," Cope rejoined. "Not sorry, either."

"Then you didn't care for your little flock of islands?"

"My boy, you should visit there. Thirty-five white men, two hundred and fifty natives, and a cable station. Jolly place of an evening, what?"

Chan came up, and John Quincy presented him. Captain Cope was the perfect host. "Sit down, both of you," he urged. "Have a cigarette." He extended a silver case.

"Thanks, I'll stick to the pipe," John Quincy said. Chan gravely accepted a cigarette and lighted it.

"Tell me, my boy," Cope said when they were seated, "is there anything new on the Winterslip murder? Haven't run down the guilty man, by any chance."

"No, not yet," John Quincy replied.

"That's a great pity. I—er—understand the police are holding a chap named Egan?"

"Yes—Jim Egan, of the Reef and Palm Hotel."

"Just what evidence have they against Egan, Mr. Winterslip?"

John Quincy was suddenly aware of Chan looking at him in a peculiar way. "Oh, they've dug up several things," he answered vaguely.

"Mr. Chan, you are a member of the police force," Captain Cope went on. "Perhaps you can tell me?"

Chan's little eyes narrowed. "Such matters are not yet presented to public," he replied.

"Ah, yes, naturally." Captain Cope's tone suggested disappointment.

"You have interest in this murder, I think?" Chan said.

"Why, yes—every one out this way is puzzling about it, I fancy. The thing has so many angles."

"Is it possible that you were an acquaintance with Mr. Dan Winterslip?" the detective persisted.

"I—I knew him slightly. But that was many years ago."

Chan stood. "Humbly begging pardon to be so abrupt," he said. He turned to John Quincy. "The moment of our appointment is eminent—"

"Of course," agreed John Quincy. "See you again, Captain." Perplexed, he followed Chan to the street. "What appointment—" he began, and stopped. Chan was carefully extinguishing the light of the cigarette against the stone facade of the hotel. That done, he dropped the stub into his pocket.

"You will see," he promised. "First we visit police station. As we journey, kindly relate all known facts concerning this Captain Cope."

John Quincy told of his first meeting with Cope in the San Francisco club, and repeated the conversation as he recalled it.

"Evidence of warm dislike for Dan Winterslip were not to be concealed?" inquired Chan.

"Oh, quite plain, Charlie. He certainly had no love for Cousin Dan. But what—"

"Immediately he was leaving for Hawaii—pardon the interrupt. Does it happily chance you know his date of arrival here?"

"I do. I saw him in the Alexander Young Hotel last Tuesday evening when I was looking for you. He was rushing off to the Fanning Islands, and he told me he had got in the previous day at noon—"

"Monday noon to put it lucidly."

"Yes—Monday noon. But Charlie—what are you trying to get at?"

"Groping about," Chan smiled. "Seeking to seize truth in my hot hands."

They walked on in silence to the station, where Chan led the way into the deserted room of Captain Hallet. He went directly to the safe and opened it. From a drawer he removed several small objects, which he carried over to the captain's table.

"Property Mr. Jim Egan," he announced, and laid a case of tarnished silver before John Quincy. "Open it—what do you find now? Corsican cigarettes." He set down another exhibit. "Tin box found in room of Mr. Brade. Open that, also. You find more Corsican cigarettes."

He removed an envelope from his pocket and taking out a charred stub, laid that too on the table. "Fragment found by walk outside door of Dan Winterslip's mansion," he elucidated. "Also Corsican brand."

Frowning deeply, he removed a second charred stub from his pocket and laid it some distance from the other exhibits. "Cigarette offered just now with winning air of hospitality by Captain Arthur Temple Cope. Lean close and perceive. More Corsican brand!"

"Good lord!" John Quincy cried.

"Can it be you are familiar with these Corsicans?" inquired Chan.

"Not at all."

"I am more happily located. This afternoon before the swim I pause at public library for listless reading. In Australian newspaper I encounter advertising talk of Corsican cigarette. It are assembled in two distinct fashions, one, labeled on tin 222, holds Turkish tobacco. Note 222 on tin of Brade. Other labeled 444 made up from Virginia weeds. Is it that you are clever to know difference between Turkish and Virginia tobacco?"

"Well, I think so—" began John Quincy.

"Same with me, but thinking are not enough now. The moment are serious. We will interrogate expert opinion. Honor me by a journey to smoking emporium."

He took a cigarette from Brade's tin, put it in an envelope and wrote something on the outside, then did the same with one from Egan's case. The two stubs were similarly classified.

They went in silence to the street. John Quincy, amazed by this new turn of events, told himself the idea was absurd. But Chan's face was grave, his eyes awake and eager.

John Quincy was vastly more amazed when they emerged from the tobacco shop after a brisk interview with the young man in charge. Chan was jubilant now.

"Again we advance! You hear what he tells us. Cigarette from Brade's tin and little brother from Egan's case are of identical contents, both being of Turkish tobacco. Stub found near walk are of Virginia stuff. So also are remnant received by me from the cordial hand of Captain Arthur Temple Cope!"

"It's beyond me," replied John Quincy. "By gad—that lets Egan out. Great news for Carlota. I'll hurry to the Reef and Palm and tell her—"

"Oh, no, no," protested Chan. "Please to let that happy moment wait. For the present, indulge only in silence. Before asking Captain Cope for statement we spy over his every move. Much may be revealed by the unsuspecting. I go to station to make arrangements—"

"But the man's a gentleman," John Quincy cried. "A captain in the British Admiralty. What you suggest is impossible."

Chan shook his head. "Impossible in Rear Bay at Boston," he said, "but here at moonly crossroads of Pacific, not so much so. Twenty-five years of my life are consumed in Hawaii, and I have many times been witness when the impossible roused itself and occurred."

CHAPTER XVII

Night Life in Honolulu

Monday brought no new developments, and John Quincy spent a restless day. Several times he called Chan at the police station, but the detective was always out.

Honolulu, according to the evening paper, was agog. This was not, as John Quincy learned to his surprise, a reference to the Winterslip case. An American fleet had just left the harbor of San Pedro[109] bound for Hawaii. This was the annual cruise of the graduating class at Annapolis; the war-ships were overflowing with future captains and admirals. They would linger at the port of Honolulu for several days and a gay round of social events impended—dinners, dances, moonlight swimming parties.

John Quincy had not seen Barbara all day; the girl had not appeared at breakfast and had lunched with a friend down the beach. They met at dinner, however, and it seemed to him that she looked more tired and wan than ever. She spoke about the coming of the war-ships.

"It's always such a happy time," she said wistfully. "The town simply blooms with handsome boys in uniform. I don't like to have you miss all the parties, John Quincy. You're not seeing Honolulu at its best."

"Why—that's all right," John Quincy assured her.

She shook her head. "Not with me. You know, we're not such slaves to convention out here. If I should get you a few invitations—what do you think, Cousin Minerva?"

109. San Pedro is still the major port of the City of Los Angeles.

"I'm an old woman," said Miss Minerva. "According to the standards of your generation, I suppose it would be quite the thing. But it's not the sort of conduct I can view approvingly. Now, in my day—"

"Don't you worry, Barbara," John Quincy broke in. "Parties mean nothing to me. Speaking of old women, I'm an old man myself—thirty my next birthday. Just my pipe and slippers by the fire—or the electric fan—that's all I ask of life now."

She smiled and dropped the matter. After dinner, she followed John Quincy to the lanai. "I want you to do something for me," she began.

"Anything you say."

"Have a talk with Mr. Brade, and tell me what he wants."

"Why, I thought that Jennison—" said John Quincy.

"No, I didn't ask him to do it," she replied. For a long moment she was silent. "I ought to tell you—I'm not going to marry Mr. Jennison, after all."

A shiver of apprehension ran down John Quincy's spine. Good lord—that kiss! Had she misunderstood? And he hadn't meant a thing by it. Just a cousinly salute—at least, that was what it had started out to be. Barbara was a sweet girl, yes, but a relative, a Winterslip, and relatives shouldn't marry, no matter how distant the connection. Then, too, there was Agatha. He was bound to Agatha by all the ties of honor. What had he got himself into, anyhow?

"I'm awfully sorry to hear that," he said. "I'm afraid I'm to blame—"

"Oh, no," she protested.

"But surely Mr. Jennison understood. He knows we're related, and that what he saw last night meant—nothing." He was rather proud of himself. Pretty neat the way he'd got that over.

"If you don't mind," Barbara said, "I'd rather not talk about it any more. Harry and I will not be married—not at present, at any rate. And if you'll see Mr. Brade for me—"

"I certainly will," John Quincy promised. "I'll see him at once." He was glad to get away, for the moon was rising on that "spot of heart-breaking charm."

A fellow ought to be more careful, he reflected as he walked along the beach. Fit upon himself the armor of preparation, as Chan had said. Strange impulses came to one here in this far tropic land; to yield to them was weak. Complications would follow, as the night the day. Here was one now, Barbara and Jennison estranged, and the cause was clear. Well, he was certainly going to watch his step hereafter.

On the far end of the Reef and Palm's first floor balcony, Brade and his wife sat together in the dusk. John Quincy went up to them.

"May I speak with you, Mr. Brade?" he said.

The man looked up out of a deep reverie. "Ah, yes—of course—"

"I'm John Quincy Winterslip. We've met before."

"Oh, surely, surely sir." Brade rose and shook hands. "My dear—" he turned to his wife, but with one burning glance at John Quincy, the woman had fled. The boy tingled—in Boston a Winterslip was never snubbed. Well, Dan Winterslip had arranged it otherwise in Hawaii.

"Sit down, sir," said Brade, somewhat embarrassed by his wife's action. "I've been expecting some one of your name."

"Naturally. Will you have a cigarette, sir." John Quincy proffered his case, and when the cigarettes were lighted, seated himself at the man's side. "I'm here, of course, in regard to that story you told Saturday night."

"Story?" flashed Brade.

John Quincy smiled. "Don't misunderstand me. I'm not questioning the truth of it. But I do want to say this, Mr. Brade—you must be aware that you will have considerable difficulty establishing your claim in a court of law. The 'eighties are a long time back."

"What you say may be true," Brade agreed. "I'm relying more on the fact that a trial would result in some rather unpleasant publicity for the Winterslip family."

"Precisely," nodded John Quincy. "I am here at the request of Miss Barbara Winterslip, who is Dan Winterslip's sole heir. She's a very fine girl, sir—"

"I don't question that," cut in Brade impatiently.

"And if your demands are not unreasonable—" John Quincy paused, and leaned closer. "Just what do you want, Mr. Brade?"

Brade stroked those gray mustaches that drooped "in saddened mood." "No money," he said, "can make good the wrong Dan Winterslip did. But I'm an old man, and it would be something to

110. The exchange rate was one pound for U.S. $4.42 in 1924; Brade's request was barely little more than return of the original stolen money.

feel financially secure for the rest of my life. I'm not inclined to be grasping—particularly since Dan Winterslip has passed beyond my reach. There were twenty thousand pounds involved. I'll say nothing about interest for more than forty years. A settlement of one hundred thousand dollars would be acceptable."[110]

John Quincy considered. "I can't speak definitely for my cousin," he said, "but to me that sounds fair enough. I have no doubt Barbara will agree to give you that sum"—he saw the man's tired old eyes brighten in the semi-darkness—"the moment the murderer of Dan Winterslip is found," he added quickly.

"What's that you say?" Brade leaped to his feet.

"I say she'll very likely pay you when this mystery is cleared up. Surely you don't expect her to do so before that time?" John Quincy rose too.

"I certainly do!" Brade cried. "Why, look here, this thing may drag on indefinitely. I want England again—the Strand, Piccadilly—it's twenty-five years since I saw London. Wait! Damn it, why should I wait! What's this murder to me—by gad, sir—" He came close, erect, flaming, the son of Tom Brade, the blackbirder, now. "Do you mean to insinuate that I—"

John Quincy faced him calmly. "I know you can't prove where you were early last Tuesday morning," he said evenly. "I don't say that incriminates you, but I shall certainly advise my cousin to wait. I'd not care to see her in the position of having rewarded the man who killed her father."

"I'll fight," cried Brade. "I'll take it to the courts—"

"Go ahead," John Quincy said. "But it will cost you every penny you've saved, and you may lose in the end. Good night, sir."

"Good night!" Brade answered, standing as his father might have stood on the *Maid of Shiloh*'s deck.

John Quincy had gone half-way down the balcony when he heard quick footsteps behind him. He turned. It was Brade, Brade the civil servant, the man who had labored thirty-six years in the oven of India, a beaten, helpless figure.

"You've got me," he said, laying a hand on John Quincy's arm. "I can't fight. I'm too tired, too old—I've worked too hard. I'll take whatever your cousin wants to give me—when she's ready to give it."

"That's a wise decision, sir," John Quincy answered. A sudden feeling of pity gripped his heart. He felt toward Brade as he had felt toward that other exile, Arlene Compton. "I hope you see London very soon," he added, and held out his hand.

Brade took it. "Thank you, my boy. You're a gentleman, even if your name is Winterslip."

Which, John Quincy reflected as he entered the lobby of the Reef and Palm, was a compliment not without its flaw.

He didn't worry over that long, however, for Carlota Egan was behind the desk. She looked up and smiled, and it occurred to John Quincy that her eyes were happier than he had seen them since that day on the Oakland ferry.

"Hello," he said. "Got a job for a good bookkeeper?"

She shook her head. "Not with business the way it is now. I was just figuring my pay-roll. You know, we've no undertow at Waikiki, but all my life I've had to worry about the overhead."

He laughed. "You talk like a brother Kiwanian.[111] By the way, has anything happened? You seem considerably cheered."

"I am," she replied. "I went to see poor dad this morning in that horrible place—and when I left some one else was going in to visit him. A stranger."

"A stranger?"

"Yes—and the handsomest thing you ever saw—tall, gray, capable-looking. He had such a friendly air, too—I felt better the moment I saw him."

"Who was he?" John Quincy inquired, with sudden interest.

"I'd never seen him before, but one of the men told me he was Captain Cope, of the British Admiralty."

"Why should Captain Cope want to see your father?"

"I haven't a notion. Do you know him?"

"Yes—I've met him," John Quincy told her.

"Don't you think he's wonderful-looking?" Her dark eyes glowed.

"Oh, he's all right," replied John Quincy without enthusiasm. "You know, I can't help feeling that things are looking up for you."

"I feel that too," she said.

"What do you say we celebrate?" he suggested. "Go out among 'em and get a little taste of night life. I'm a bit fed up on the police station. What do people do here in the evening? The movies?"

"Just at present," the girl told him, "everybody visits Punahou to see the nightblooming cereus. It's the season now, you know."

111. Founded in 1915, Kiwanis was an organization of business and professional men. Although its original motto was "We Trade," by 1920, it was changed to "We Build," and later to "Serving the Children of the World." Although conceived as a networking organization fostering business, delegates voted to change the mission to service. John Quincy is joking about the "Babbitt"-like stereotype.

112. Now Punahou School, at 1601 Punahou Street, it was founded in 1841. According to the school's website, it "was originally designed to provide a quality education for the children of Congregational missionaries, allowing them to stay in Hawai'i with their families, instead of being sent away to school. The first class had 15 students." http://www.punahou.edu /about/history/index.aspx Its illustrious alumni include Sun Yat-Sen, Buster Crabbe, and Barack Obama.

"Sounds like a big evening," John Quincy laughed. "Go and look at the flowers. Well, I'm for it. Will you come?"

"Of course." She gave a few directions to the clerk, then joined him by the door. "I can run down and get the roadster," he offered.

"Oh, no," she smiled. "I'm sure I'll never own a motorcar, and it might make me discontented to ride in one. The trolley's my carriage—and it's lots of fun. One meets so many interesting people."

On the stone walls surrounding the campus of Oahu College,[112] the strange flower that blooms only on a summer night was heaped in snowy splendor. John Quincy had been a bit lukewarm regarding the expedition when they set out, but he saw his error now. For here was beauty, breath-taking and rare. Before the walls paraded a throng of sight-seers; they joined the procession. The girl was a charming companion, her spirits had revived and she chatted vivaciously. Not about Shaw and the art galleries, true enough, but bright human talk that John Quincy liked to hear.

He persuaded her to go to the city for a maidenly ice-cream soda, and it was ten o'clock when they returned to the beach. They left the trolley at a stop some distance down the avenue from the Reef and Palm, and strolled slowly toward the hotel. The sidewalk was lined to their right by dense foliage, almost impenetrable. The night was calm; the street lamps shone brightly; the paved street gleamed white in the moonlight. John Quincy was talking of Boston.

"I think you'd like it there. It's old and settled, but—"

From the foliage beside them came the flash of a pistol, and John Quincy heard a bullet sing close to his head. Another flash, another bullet. The girl gave a startled little cry.

John Quincy circled round her and plunged into the bushes. Angry branches stung his cheek. He stopped; he couldn't leave the girl alone. He returned to her side.

"What did that mean?" he asked, amazed. He stared in wonder at the peaceful scene before him.

"I—I don't know." She took his arm. "Come—hurry!"

"Don't be afraid," he said reassuringly.

"Not for myself," she answered.

They went on to the hotel, greatly puzzled. But when they entered the lobby, they had something else to think about. Captain Arthur Temple Cope was standing by the desk, and he came at once to meet them.

John Quincy circled round her and plunged into the bushes. Angry branches stung his cheek. He stopped; he couldn't leave the girl alone. He returned to her side. From *The House Without a Key*, illustration by William Liepse (*The Saturday Evening Post*, February 28, 1925)

"This is Miss Egan, I believe. Ah, Winterslip, how are you?" He turned again to the girl, "I've taken a room here, if you don't mind."

"Why, not at all," she gasped.

"I talked with your father this morning. I didn't know about his trouble until I had boarded a ship for the Fanning Islands. I came back as quickly as I could."

"You came back—" She stared at him.

"Yes. I came back to help him."

"That's very kind of you," the girl said. "But I'm afraid I don't understand—"

"Oh, no, you don't understand. Naturally." The captain smiled down at her. "You see, Jim's my young brother. You're my niece, and your name is Carlota Maria Cope. I fancy I've persuaded old Jim to own up to us at last."

The girl's dark eyes were wide. "I—I think you're a very nice uncle," she said at last.

"Do you really?" The captain bowed. "I aim to be," he added.

John Quincy stepped forward. "Pardon me," he said. "I'm afraid I'm intruding. Good night, Captain."

"Good night, my boy," Cope answered.

The girl went with John Quincy to the balcony. "I—I don't know what to make of it," she said.

"Things are coming rather fast," John Quincy admitted. He remembered the Corsican cigarette. "I wouldn't trust him too far," he admonished.

"But he's so wonderful—"

"Oh, he's all right, probably. But looks are often deceptive. I'll go along now and let you talk with him."

She laid one slim tanned hand on his white-clad arm. "Do be careful!"

"Oh, I'm all right," he told her.

"But some one shot at you."

"Yes, and a very poor aim he had, too. Don't worry about me." She was very close, her eyes glowing in the dark. "You said you weren't afraid for yourself," he added. "Did you mean—"

"I meant—I was afraid—for you."

The moon, of course, was shining. The cocoapalms turned their heads away at the suggestion of the trades. The warm waters of Waikiki murmured near by. John Quincy Winterslip, from Boston and immune, drew the girl to him and kissed her. Not a cousinly kiss, either—but why should it have been? She wasn't his cousin.

"Thank you, my dear," he said. He seemed to be floating dizzily in space. It came to him that he might reach out and pluck her a handful of stars.

It came to him a second later that, despite his firm resolve, he had done it again. Kissed another girl.

Three—that made three with whom he was sort of entangled.

"Good night," he said huskily, and leaping over the rail, fled hastily through the garden.

Three girls now—but he hadn't a single regret. He was living at last. As he hurried through the dark along the beach, his heart was light. Once he fancied he was being followed, but he gave it little thought. What of it?

On the bureau in his room he found an envelope with his name typewritten on the outside. The note within was typewritten too. He read:

"You are too busy out here. Hawaii can manage her affairs without the interference of a malihini. Boats sail almost daily. If you are still here forty-eight hours after you get this—look out! To-night's shots were fired into the air. The aim will quickly improve!"

Delighted, John Quincy tossed the note aside.

Threatening him, eh? His activities as a detective were bearing fruit. He recalled the glowering face of Kaohla when he said: "You did this. I don't forget." And a remark of Dan Winterslip's his aunt had quoted: "Civilized—yes. But far underneath there are deep dark waters flowing still."

Boats were sailing almost daily, were they? Well, let them sail. He would be on one some day—but not until he had brought Dan Winterslip's murderer to justice.

Life had a new glamour now. Look out? He'd be looking—and enjoying it, too. He smiled happily to himself as he took off his coat. This was better than selling bonds in Boston.

CHAPTER XVIII

A Cable from the Mainland

John Quincy awoke at nine the following morning and slipped from under his mosquito netting eager to face the responsibilities of a new day. On the floor near his bureau lay the letter designed to speed the parting guest. He picked it up and read it again with manifest enjoyment.

When he reached the dining-room Haku informed him that Miss Minerva and Barbara had breakfasted early and gone to the city on a shopping tour.

"Look here, Haku," the boy said. "A letter came for me late last night?"

"Yess," admitted Haku.

"Who delivered it?"

"Can not say. It were found on floor of hall close by big front door."

"Who found it?"

"Kamaikui."

"Oh, yes—Kamaikui."

"I tell her to put in your sleeping room."

"Did Kamaikui see the person who brought it?"

"Nobody see him. Nobody on place."

"All right," John Quincy said.

He spent a leisurely hour on the lanai with his pipe and the morning paper. At about half past ten he got out the roadster and drove to the police station.

Hallet and Chan, he was told, were in a conference with the prosecutor. He sat down to wait, and in a few moments word came for him to join them. Entering Greene's office, he saw the three men seated gloomily about the prosecutor's desk.

"Well, I guess I'm some detective," he announced.

Greene looked up quickly. "Found anything new?"

"Not precisely," John Quincy admitted. "But last night when I was walking along Kalakaua Avenue with a young woman, somebody took a couple of wild shots at me from the bushes. And when I got home I found this letter waiting."

He handed the epistle to Hallet, who read it with evident disgust, then passed it on to the prosecutor. "That doesn't get us anywhere," the captain said.

"It may get me somewhere, if I'm not careful," John Quincy replied. "However, I'm rather proud of it. Sort of goes to show that my detective work is hitting home."

"Maybe," answered Hallet, carelessly.

Greene laid the letter on his desk. "My advice to you," he said, "is to carry a gun. That's unofficial, of course."

"Nonsense, I'm not afraid," John Quincy told him. "I've got a pretty good idea who sent this thing."

"You have?" Greene said.

"Yes. He's a friend of Captain Hallet's. Dick Kaohla."

"What do you mean he's a friend of mine?" flared Hallet.

"Well, you certainly treated him pretty tenderly the other night."

"I knew what I was doing," said Hallet grouchily.

"I hope you did. But if he puts a bullet in me some lovely evening, I'm going to be pretty annoyed with you."

"Oh, you're in no danger," Hallet answered. "Only a coward writes anonymous letters."

"Yes, and only a coward shoots from ambush. But that isn't saying he can't take a good aim."

Hallet picked up the letter. "I'll keep this. It may prove to be evidence."

"Surely," agreed John Quincy. "And you haven't got any too much evidence, as I see it."

"Is that so?" growled Hallet. "We've made a rather important discovery about that Corsican cigarette."

"Oh, I'm not saying Charlie isn't good," smiled John Quincy. "I was with him when he worked that out."

A uniformed man appeared at the door. "Egan and his daughter and Captain Cope," he announced to Greene. "Want to see them now, sir?"

"Send them in," ordered the prosecutor.

"I'd like to stay, if you don't mind," John Quincy suggested.

"Oh, by all means," Greene answered. "We couldn't get along without you."

The policeman brought Egan to the door, and the proprietor of the Reef and Palm came into the room. His face was haggard and pale; his long siege with the authorities had begun to tell. But a stubborn light still flamed in his eyes. After him came Carlota Egan, fresh and beautiful, and with a new air of confidence about her. Captain Cope followed, tall, haughty, a man of evident power and determination.

"This is the prosecutor, I believe?" he said. "Ah, Mr. Winterslip, I find you everywhere I go."

"You don't mind my staying?" inquired John Quincy.

"Not in the least, my boy. Our business here will take but a moment." He turned to Greene. "Just as a preliminary," he continued, "I am Captain Arthur Temple Cope of the British Admiralty, and this gentleman"—he nodded toward the proprietor of the Reef and Palm—"is my brother."

"Really?" said Greene. "His name is Egan, as I understand it."

"His name is James Egan Cope," the captain replied. "He dropped the Cope many years ago for reasons that do not concern us now. I am here simply to say, sir, that you are holding my brother on the flimsiest pretext I have ever encountered in the course of my rather extensive travels. If necessary, I propose to engage the best lawyer in Honolulu and have him free by night. But I'm giving you this last chance to release him and avoid a somewhat painful expose of the sort of nonsense you go in for."

John Quincy glanced at Carlota Egan. Her eyes were shining but not on him. They were on her uncle.

Greene flushed slightly. "A good bluff, Captain, is always worth trying," he said.

"Oh, then you admit you've been bluffing," said Cope quickly.

"I was referring to your attitude, sir," Greene replied.

"Oh, I see," Cope said. "I'll sit down, if you don't mind. As I understand it, you have two things against old Jim here. One is that he visited Dan Winterslip on the night of the murder, and now refuses to divulge the nature of that call. The other is the stub of a Corsican cigarette which was found by the walk outside the door of Winterslip's living-room."

Greene shook his head. "Only the first," he responded. "The Corsican cigarette is no longer evidence against Egan." He leaned suddenly across his desk. "It is, my dear Captain Cope, evidence against you."

Cope met his look unflinchingly. "Really?" he remarked.

John Quincy noted a flash of startled bewilderment in Carlota Egan's eyes.

"That's what I said," Greene continued. "I'm very glad you dropped in this morning, sir. I've been wanting to talk to you. I've been told that you were heard to express a strong dislike for Dan Winterslip."

"I may have. I certainly felt it."

"Why?"

"As a midshipman on a British war-ship, I was familiar with Australian gossip in the 'eighties. Mr. Dan Winterslip had an unsavory reputation. It was rumored on good authority that he rifled the sea chest of his dead captain on the *Maid of Shiloh*. Perhaps we're a bit squeamish, but that is the sort of thing we sailors can not forgive. There were other quaint deeds in connection with his blackbirding activities. Yes, my dear sir, I heartily disliked Dan Winterslip, and if I haven't said so before, I say it now."

"You arrived in Honolulu a week ago yesterday," Greene continued. "At noon—Monday noon. You left the following day. Did you, by any chance, call on Dan Winterslip during that period?"

"I did not."

"Ah, yes. I may tell you, sir, that the Corsican cigarettes found in Egan's case were of Turkish tobacco. The stub found near the scene of Dan Winterslip's murder was of Virginia tobacco. So also, my dear Captain Cope, was the Corsican cigarette you gave our man Charlie Chan in the lobby of the Alexander Young Hotel last Sunday night."

Cope looked at Chan, and smiled. "Always the detective, eh?" he said.

"Never mind that!" Greene cried. "I'm asking for an explanation."

"The explanation is very simple," Cope replied. "I was about to give it to you when you launched into this silly cross-examination.

The Corsican cigarette found by Dan Winterslip's door was, naturally, of Virginia tobacco. I never smoke any other kind."

"What!"

"There can be no question about it, sir. I dropped that cigarette there myself."

"But you just told me you didn't call on Dan Winterslip."

"That was true. I didn't. I called on Miss Minerva Winterslip, of Boston, who is a guest in the house. As a matter of fact, I had tea with her last Monday at five o'clock. You may verify that by telephoning the lady."

Greene glanced at Hallet, who glanced at the telephone, then turned angrily to John Quincy. "Why the devil didn't she tell me that?" he demanded.

John Quincy smiled. "I don't know, sir. Possibly because she never thought of Captain Cope in connection with the murder."

"She'd hardly be likely to," Cope said. "Miss Winterslip and I had tea in the living-room, then went out and sat on a bench in the garden, chatting over old times. When I returned to the house I was smoking a cigarette. I dropped it just outside the living-room door. Whether Miss Winterslip noted my action or not, I don't know. She probably didn't, it isn't the sort of thing one remembers. You may call her on the telephone if you wish, sir."

Again Greene looked at Hallet, who shook his head. "I'll talk with her later," announced the Captain of Detectives. Evidently Miss Minerva had an unpleasant interview ahead.

"At any rate," Cope continued to the prosecutor, "you had yourself disposed of the cigarette as evidence against old Jim. That leaves only the fact of his silence—"

"His silence, yes," Greene cut in, "and the fact that Winterslip had been heard to express a fear of Jim Egan."

Cope frowned. "Had he, really?" He considered a moment. "Well, what of it? Winterslip had good reason to fear a great many honest men. No, my dear sir, you have nothing save my brother's silence against him, and that is not enough. I demand—"

Greene raised his hand. "Just a minute. I said you were bluffing, and I still think so. Any other assumption would be an insult to your intelligence. Surely you know enough about the law to understand that your brother's refusal to tell me his business with Winterslip, added to the fact that he was presumably the last person to see Winterslip alive, is sufficient excuse for holding him. I can hold him on those grounds, I am holding him, and, my dear Captain, I shall continue to hold him until hell freezes over."

"Very good," said Cope, rising. "I shall engage a capable lawyer—"

"That is, of course, your privilege," snapped Greene. "Good morning."

Cope hesitated. He turned to Egan. "It means more publicity, Jim," he said. "Delay, too. More unhappiness for Carlota here. And since everything you did was done for her—"

"How did you know that?" asked Egan quickly.

"I've guessed it. I can put two and two together, Jim. Carlota was to return with me for a bit of schooling in England. You said you had the money, but you hadn't. That was your pride again, Jim. It's got you into a lifetime of trouble. You cast about for the funds, and you remembered Winterslip. I'm beginning to see it all now. You had something on Dan Winterslip, and you went to his house that night to—er—"

"To blackmail him," suggested Greene.

"It wasn't a pretty thing to do, Jim," Cope went on. "But you weren't doing it for yourself. Carlota and I know you would have died first. You did it for your girl, and we both forgive you." He turned to Carlota. "Don't we, my dear?"

The girl's eyes were wet. She rose and kissed her father. "Dear old dad," she said.

"Come on, Jim," pleaded Captain Cope. "Forget your pride for once. Speak up, and we'll take you home with us. I'm sure the prosecutor will keep the thing from the newspapers—"

"We've promised him that a thousand times," Greene said.

Egan lifted his head. "I don't care anything about the newspapers," he explained. "It's you, Arthur—you and Cary—I didn't want you two to know. But since you've guessed, and Cary knows too—I may as well tell everything."

John Quincy stood up. "Mr. Egan," he said. "I'll leave the room, if you wish."

"Sit down, my boy," Egan replied. "Cary's told me of your kindness to her. Besides, you saw the check—"

"What check was that?" cried Hallet. He leaped to his feet and stood over John Quincy.

"I was honor bound not to tell," explained the boy gently.

"You don't say so!" Hallet bellowed. "You're a fine pair, you and that aunt of yours—"

"One minute, Hallet," cut in Greene. "Now, Egan, or Cope, or whatever your name happens to be—I'm waiting to hear from you."

Egan nodded. "Back in the 'eighties I was teller in a bank in Melbourne, Australia," he said. "One day a young man came to my window—Williams or some such name he called himself. He had a green hide bag full of gold pieces—Mexican, Spanish and English coins, some of them crusted with dirt—and he wanted to exchange them for bank-notes. I made the exchange for him. He appeared several times with similar bags, and the transaction was repeated. I thought little of it at the time, though the fact that he tried to give me a large tip did rather rouse my suspicion.

"A year later, when I had left the bank and gone to Sydney, I heard rumors of what Dan Winterslip had done on the *Maid of Shiloh*. It occurred to me that Williams and Winterslip were probably the same man. But no one seemed to be prosecuting the case, the general feeling was that it was blood money anyhow, that Tom Brade had not come by it honestly himself. So I said nothing.

"Twelve years later I came to Hawaii, and Dan Winterslip was pointed out to me. He was Williams, right enough. And he knew me, too. But I'm not a blackmailer—I've been in some tight places, Arthur, but I've always played fair—so I let the matter drop. For more than twenty years nothing happened.

"Then, a few months ago, my family located me at last, and Arthur here wrote me that he was coming to Honolulu and would look me up. I'd always felt that I'd not done the right thing by my girl—that she was not taking the place in the world to which she was entitled. I wanted her to visit my old mother and get a bit of English training. I wrote to Arthur and it was arranged. But I couldn't let her go as a charity child—I couldn't admit I'd failed and was unable to do anything for her—I said I'd pay her way. And I—I didn't have a cent.

"And then Brade came. It seemed providential. I might have sold my information to him, but when I talked with him I found he had very little money, and I felt that Winterslip would beat him in the end. No, Winterslip was my man—Winterslip with his rotten wealth. I don't know just what happened—I was quite mad, I fancy—the world owed me that, I figured, just for my girl, not for me. I called Winterslip up and made an appointment for that Monday night.

"But somehow—the standards of a lifetime—it's difficult to change. The moment I had called him, I regretted it. I tried to slip out of it—I told myself there must be some other way—perhaps I could sell the Reef and Palm—anyhow, I called him again and said I wasn't coming. But he insisted, and I went.

"I didn't have to tell him what I wanted. He knew. He had a check ready for me—a check for five thousand dollars. It was Cary's happiness, her chance. I took it, and came away—but I was ashamed. I'm not trying to excuse my action; however, I don't believe I would ever have cashed it. When Cary found it in my desk and brought it to me, I tore it up. That's all." He turned his tired eyes toward his daughter. "I did it for you, Cary, but I didn't want you to know." She went over and put her arm about his shoulder, and stood smiling down at him through her tears.

"If you'd told us that in the first place," said Greene, "you could have saved everybody a lot of trouble, yourself included."

Cope stood up. "Well, Mr. Prosecutor, there you are. You're not going to hold him now?"

Greene rose briskly. "No. I'll arrange for his release at once." He and Egan went out together, then Hallet and Cope. John Quincy held out his hand to Carlota Egan—for by that name he thought of her still.

"I'm mighty glad for you," he said.

"You'll come and see me soon?" she asked. "You'll find a very different girl. More like the one you met on the Oakland ferry."

"She was very charming," John Quincy replied. "But then, she was bound to be—she had your eyes." He suddenly remembered Agatha Parker. "However, you've got your father now," he added. "You won't need me."

She looked up at him and smiled. "I wonder," she said, and went out.

John Quincy turned to Chan. "Well, that's that," he remarked. "Where are we now?"

"Speaking personally for myself," grinned Chan, "I am static in same place as usual. Never did have fondly feeling for Egan theory."

"But Hallet did," John Quincy answered. "A black morning for him."

In the small anteroom they encountered the Captain of Detectives. He appeared disgruntled.

"We were just remarking," said John Quincy pleasantly, "that there goes your little old Egan theory. What have you left?"

"Oh, I've got plenty," growled Hallet.

"Yes, you have. One by one your clues have gone up in smoke. The page from the guest book, the brooch, the torn newspaper, the ohia wood box, and now Egan and the Corsican cigarette."

"Oh, Egan isn't out of it. We may not be able to hold him, but I'm not forgetting Mr. Egan."

"Nonsense," smiled John Quincy. "I asked what you had left. A little button from a glove—useless. The glove was destroyed long ago. A wrist watch with an illuminated dial and a damaged numeral two—"

Chan's amber eyes narrowed. "Essential clue," he murmured. "Remember how I said it."

Hallet banged his fist on a table. "That's it—the wrist watch! If the person who wore it knows any one saw it, it's probably where we'll never find it now. But we've kept it pretty dark—perhaps he doesn't know. That's our only chance." He turned to Chan. "I've combed these islands once hunting that watch," he cried, "now I'm going to start all over again. The jewelry stores, the pawn shops, every nook and corner. You go out, Charlie, and start the ball rolling."

Chan moved with alacrity despite his weight. "I will give it one powerful push," he promised, and disappeared.

"Well, good luck," said John Ouincy, moving on.

Hallet grunted. "You tell that aunt of yours I'm pretty sore," he remarked. He was not in the mood for elegance of diction.

John Quincy's opportunity to deliver the message did not come at lunch, for Miss Minerva remained with Barbara in the city. After dinner that evening he led his aunt out to sit on the bench under the hau tree.

"By the way," he said, "Captain Hallet is very much annoyed with you."

"I'm very much annoyed with Captain Hallet," she replied, "so that makes us even. What's his particular grievance now?"

"He believes you knew all the time the name of the man who dropped that Corsican cigarette."

She was silent for a moment. "Not all the time," she said at length. "What has happened?"

John Quincy sketched briefly the events of the morning at the police station. When he had finished he looked at her inquiringly.

"In the first excitement I didn't remember, or I should have spoken," she explained. "It was several days before the thing came to me. I saw it clearly then—Arthur—Captain Cope—tossing that cigarette aside as we reentered the house. But I said nothing about it."

"Why?"

"Well, I thought it would be a good test for the police. Let them discover it for themselves."

"That's a pretty weak explanation," remarked John Quincy severely. "You've been responsible for a lot of wasted time."

"It—it wasn't my only reason," said Miss Minerva softly.

"Oh—I'm glad to hear that. Go on."

"Somehow, I couldn't bring myself to link up that call of Captain Cope's with—a murder mystery."

Another silence. And suddenly—he was never dense—John Quincy understood.

"He told me you were very beautiful in the 'eighties," said the boy gently. "The captain, I mean. When I met him in that San Francisco club."

Miss Minerva laid her own hand on the boy's. When she spoke her voice, which he had always thought firm and sharp, trembled a little. "On this beach in my girlhood," she said, "happiness was within my grasp. I had only to reach out and take it. But somehow—Boston—Boston held me back. I let my happiness slip away."

"Not too late yet," suggested John Quincy.

She shook her head. "So he tried to tell me that Monday afternoon. But there was something in his tone—I may be in Hawaii, but I'm not quite mad. Youth, John Quincy, youth doesn't return, whatever they may say out here." She pressed his hand, and stood. "If your chance comes, dear boy," she added, "don't be such a fool."

She moved hastily away through the garden, and John Quincy looked after her with a new affection in his eyes.

Presently he saw the yellow glare of a match beyond the wire. Amos again, still loitering under his algaroba tree. John Quincy rose and strolled over to him.

"Hello, Cousin Amos," he said. "When are you going to take down this fence?"

"Oh, I'll get round to it some time," Amos answered. "By the way, I wanted to ask you. Any new developments?"

"Several," John Quincy told him. "But nothing that gets us anywhere. So far as I can see, the case has blown up completely."

"Well, I've been thinking it over," Amos said. "Maybe that would be the best outcome, after all. Suppose they do discover who did for Dan—it may only reveal a new scandal, worse than any of the others."

"I'll take a chance on that," replied John Quincy. "For my part, I intend to see this thing through—"

Haku came briskly through the garden. "Cable message for Mr. John Quincy Winterslip. Boy say collect. Requests money."

John Quincy followed quickly to the front door. A bored small boy awaited him. He paid the sum due and tore open the cable. It was signed by the postmaster at Des Moines, and it read:

"No one named Saladine ever heard of here."

John Quincy dashed to the telephone. Some one on duty at the station informed him that Chan had gone home, and gave him an address on Punchbowl Hill. He got out the roadster, and in five minutes more was speeding toward the city.

CHAPTER XIX
"Good-by, Pete!"

Charlie Chan lived in a bungalow that clung precariously to the side of Punchbowl Hill. Pausing a moment at the Chinaman's gate, John Quincy looked down on Honolulu, one great gorgeous garden set in an amphitheater of mountains. A beautiful picture, but he had no time for beauty now. He hurried up the brief walk that lay in the shadow of the palm trees.

A Chinese woman—a servant, she seemed—ushered him into Chan's dimly-lighted living-room. The detective was seated at a table playing chess; he rose with dignity when he saw his visitor. In this, his hour of ease, he wore a long loose robe of dark purple silk, which fitted closely at the neck and had wide sleeves. Beneath it showed wide trousers of the same material, and on his feet were shoes of silk, with thick felt soles. He was all Oriental now, suave and ingratiating but remote, and for the first time John Quincy was really conscious of the great gulf across which he and Chan shook hands.

"You do my lowly house immense honor," Charlie said. "This proud moment are made still more proud by opportunity to introduce my eldest son." He motioned for his opponent at chess to step forward, a slim sallow boy with amber eyes—Chan himself before he put on weight. "Mr. John Quincy Winterslip, of Boston, kindly condescend to notice Henry Chan. When you appear I am giving him lesson at chess so he may play in such manner as not to tarnish honored name."

113. Are we to believe that in this temple of Chinese beauty, the Chans had hung a scroll on the wall that read "HAPPY NEW YEAR 1924!" or something similar *in English*? If it was in Chinese, how did John Quincy know what it said?

The boy bowed low; evidently he was one member of the younger generation who had a deep respect for his elders. John Quincy also bowed. "Your father is my very good friend," he said. "And from now on, you are too."

Chan beamed with pleasure. "Condescend to sit on this atrocious chair. Is it possible you bring news?"

"It certainly is," smiled John Quincy. He handed over the message from the postmaster at Des Moines.

"Most interesting," said Chan. "Do I hear impressive chug of rich automobile engine in street?"

"Yes, I came in the car," John Quincy replied.

"Good. We will hasten at once to home of Captain Hallet, not far away. I beg of you to pardon my disappearance while I don more appropriate costume."

Left alone with the boy, John Quincy sought a topic of conversation. "Play baseball?" he asked.

The boy's eyes glowed. "Not very good, but I hope to improve. My cousin Willie Chan is great expert at that game. He has promised to teach me."

John Quincy glanced about the room. On the back wall hung a scroll with felicitations, the gift of some friend of the family at New Year's.[113] Opposite him, on another wall, was a single picture, painted on silk, representing a bird on an apple bough. Charmed by its simplicity, he went over to examine it. "That's beautiful," he said.

"Quoting old Chinese saying, a picture is a voiceless poem," replied the boy.

Beneath the picture stood a square table, flanked by straight, low-backed armchairs. On other elaborately carved teakwood stands distributed about the room were blue and white vases, porcelain wine jars, dwarfed trees. Pale golden lanterns hung from the ceiling; a soft-toned rug lay on the floor. John Quincy felt again the gulf between himself and Charlie Chan.

But when the detective returned, he wore the conventional garb of Los Angeles or Detroit, and the gulf did not seem so wide. They went out together and entering the roadster, drove to Hallet's house on Iolani Avenue.

The captain lolled in pajamas on his lanai. He greeted his callers with interest.

"You boys are out late," he said. "Something doing?"

"Certainly is," replied John Quincy, taking a proffered chair. "There's a man named Saladine—"

At mention of the name, Hallet looked at him keenly. John Quincy went on to tell what he knew of Saladine, his alleged place of residence, his business, the tragedy of the lost teeth.

"Some time ago we got on to the fact that every time Kaohla figured in the investigation, Saladine was interested. He managed to be at the desk of the Reef and Palm the day Kaohla inquired for Brade. On the night Kaohla was questioned by your men, Miss Egan saw Mr. Saladine crouching outside the window. So Charlie and I thought it a good scheme to send a cable of inquiry to the postmaster at Des Moines, where Saladine claimed to be in the wholesale grocery business." He handed an envelope to Hallet. "That answer arrived to-night," he added.

An odd smile had appeared on Hallet's usually solemn face. He took the cable and read it, then slowly tore it into bits.

"Forget it, boys," he said calmly.

"Wha—what!" gasped John Quincy.

"I said forget it. I like your enterprise, but you're on the wrong trail there."

John Quincy was greatly annoyed. "I demand an explanation," he cried.

"I can't give it to you," Hallet answered. "You'll have to take my word for it."

"I've taken your word for a good many things," said John Quincy hotly. "This begins to look rather suspicious to me. Are you trying to shield somebody?"

Hallet rose and laid his hand on John Quincy's shoulder. "I've had a hard day," he remarked, "and I'm not going to get angry with you. I'm not trying to shield anybody. I'm as anxious as you are to discover who killed Dan Winterslip. More anxious, perhaps."

"Yet when we bring you evidence you tear it up—"

"Bring me the right evidence," said Hallet. "Bring me that wrist watch. I can promise you action then."

John Quincy was impressed by the sincerity in his tone. But he was sadly puzzled, too. "All right," he said, "that's that. I'm sorry if we've troubled you with this trivial matter—"

"Don't talk like that," Hallet broke in. "I'm glad of your help. But as far as Mr. Saladine is concerned—" he looked at Chan— "let him alone."

Chan bowed. "You are undisputable chief," he replied.

They went back to Punchbowl Hill in the roadster, both rather dejected. As Chan alighted at his gate, John Quincy spoke: "Well, I'm pau. Saladine was my last hope."

The Chinaman stared for a moment at the moonlit Pacific that lay beyond the water-front lamps. "Stone wall surround us," he said dreamily. "But we circle about, seeking loophole. Moment of discovery will come."

"I wish I thought so," replied John Quincy.

Chan smiled. "Patience are a very lovely virtue," he remarked. "Seem that way to me. But maybe that are my Oriental mind. Your race, I perceive, regard patience with ever-swelling disfavor."

It was with swelling disfavor that John Quincy regarded it as he drove back to Waikiki. Yet he had great need of patience in the days immediately following. For nothing happened.

The forty-eight-hour period given him to leave Hawaii expired, but the writer of that threatening letter failed to come forward and relieve the tedium. Thursday arrived, a calm day like the others; Thursday night, peaceful and serene.

On Friday afternoon Agatha Parker broke the monotony by a cable sent from the Wyoming ranch.

"You must be quite mad. I find the West crude and impossible."

John Quincy smiled; he could picture her as she wrote it, proud, haughty, unyielding. She must have been popular with the man who transmitted the message. Or was he, too, an exile from the East?

And perhaps the girl was right. Perhaps he was mad, after all. He sat on Dan Winterslip's lanai, trying to think things out. Boston, the office, the art gallery, the theaters. The Common on a winter's day, with the air bracing and full of life. The thrill of a new issue of bonds, like the thrill of a theatrical first night—would it get over big or flop at his feet? Tennis at Longwood, long evenings on the Charles, golf with people of his own kind at Magnolia. Tea out of exquisite cups in dim old drawing-rooms. Wasn't he mad to think of giving up all that? But what had Miss Minerva said? "If your chance ever comes—"

The problem was a big one, and big problems were annoying out here where the lotus grew. He yawned, and went aimlessly down-town. Drifting into the public library, he saw Charlie Chan hunched over a table that held an enormous volume. John

Quincy went closer. The book was made up of back numbers of the Honolulu morning paper, and it was open at a time-yellowed sporting page.

"Hello, Chan. What are you up to?"

Chan gave him a smile of greeting. "Hello. Little bit of careless reading while I gallop about seeking loophole."

He closed the big volume casually. "You seem in the best of health."

"Oh, I'm all right."

"No more fierce shots out of bushes?"

"Not a trigger pulled. I imagine that was a big bluff—nothing more."

"What do you say—bluff?"

"I mean the fellow's a coward, after all."

Chan shook his head solemnly. "Pardon humble suggestion—do not lose carefulness. Hot heads plenty in hot climate."

"I'll look before I leap," John Quincy promised. "But I'm afraid I interrupted you."

"Ridiculous thought," protested Chan.

"I'll go along. Let me know if anything breaks."

"Most certainly. Up to present, everything are intact."

John Quincy paused at the door of the reference room. Charlie Chan had promptly opened the big book, and was again bending over it with every show of interest.

Returning to Waikiki, John Quincy faced a dull evening. Barbara had gone to the island of Kauai for a visit with old friends of the family. He had not been sorry when she went, for he didn't feel quite at ease in her presence. The estrangement between the girl and Jennison continued; the lawyer had not been at the dock to see her off. Yes, John Quincy had parted from her gladly, but her absence cast a pall of loneliness over the house on Kalia Road.

After dinner, he sat with his pipe on the lanai. Down the beach at the Reef and Palm pleasant company was available—but he hesitated. He had seen Carlota Egan several times by day, on the beach or in the water. She was very happy now, though somewhat appalled at thought of her approaching visit to England. They'd had several talks about that—daylight talks. John Quincy was a bit afraid to entrust himself—as Chan had said in speaking of his stone idol—of an evening. After all, there was Agatha, there was Boston. There was Barbara, too. Being entangled with three girls at once was a rather wearing experience. He rose, and went down-town to the movies.

On Saturday morning he was awakened early by the whir of aeroplanes above the house. The American fleet was in the offing, and the little brothers of the air service hastened out to hover overhead in friendly welcome. That day a spirit of carnival prevailed in Honolulu, flags floated from every masthead, and the streets bloomed, as Barbara had predicted, with handsome boys in spotless uniforms. They were everywhere, swarming in the souvenir stores, besieging the soda fountains, sky-larking on the trolley-cars. Evening brought a great ball at the beach hotel, and John Quincy, out for a walk, saw that every spic and span uniform moved toward Waikiki, accompanied by a fair young thing who was only too happy to serve as sweetheart in that particular port.

John Quincy felt, suddenly, rather out of things. Each pretty girl he saw recalled Carlota Egan. He turned his wandering footsteps toward the Reef and Palm, and oddly enough, his pace quickened at once.

The proprietor himself was behind the desk, his eyes calm and untroubled now.

"Good evening, Mr. Egan—or should I say Mr. Cope," remarked John Quincy.

"Oh, we'll stick to the Egan, I guess," the man replied. "Sort of got out of the hang of the other. Mr. Winterslip, I'm happy to see you. Cary will be down in a moment."

John Quincy gazed about the big public room. It was a scene of confusion, spattered ladders, buckets of paint, rolls of new wallpaper. "What's going on?" he inquired.

"Freshening things up a bit," Egan answered. "You know, we're in society now." He laughed. "Yes, sir, the old Reef and Palm has been standing here a long time without so much as a glance from the better element of Honolulu. But now they know I'm related to the British Admiralty, they've suddenly discovered it's a quaint and interesting place. They're dropping in for tea. Just fancy. But that's Honolulu."

"That's Boston, too," John Quincy assured him.

"Yes—and precisely the sort of thing I ran away from England to escape, a good many years ago. I'd tell them all to go to the devil—but there's Cary. Somehow, women feel differently about those things. It will warm her heart a bit to have these dowagers smile upon her. And they're smiling—you know, they've even dug up the fact that my Cousin George has been knighted for making a particularly efficient brand of soap." He grimaced. "It's nothing I'd have mentioned myself—a family skeleton, as I see it. But society has odd standards. And I mustn't be hard on poor old George. As Arthur says, making soap is good clean fun."

"Is your brother still with you?"

"No. He's gone back to finish his job in the Fanning Group. When he returns, I'm sending Cary to England for a long stop. Yes, that's right—*I'm* sending her," he added quickly. "I'm paying for these repairs, too. You see, I've been able to add a second mortgage to the one already on the poor tottering Reef and Palm. That's another outcome of my new-found connection with the British Admiralty and the silly old soap business. Here's Cary now."

John Quincy turned. And he was glad he had, for he would not willingly have missed the picture of Carlota on the stairs. Carlota in an evening gown of some shimmering material, her dark hair dressed in a new and amazingly effective way, her white shoulders gleaming,[114] her eyes happy at last. As she came quickly toward him he caught his breath, never had he seen her look so beautiful. She must have heard his voice in the office, he reflected, and with surprising speed arrayed herself thus to greet him. He was deeply grateful as he took her hand.

"Stranger," she rebuked. "We thought you'd deserted us."

"I'd never do that," he answered. "But I've been rather busy—"

A step sounded behind him. He turned, and there stood one of those ubiquitous navy boys, a tall, blond Adonis who held his cap in his hand and smiled in a devastating way.

"Hello, Johnnie," Carlota said. "Mr. Winterslip, of Boston, this is Lieutenant Booth, of Richmond, Virginia."

"How are you," nodded the boy, without removing his eyes from the girl's face. Just one of the guests, this Winterslip, no account at all—such was obviously the lieutenant's idea. "All ready, Cary? The car's outside."

"I'm frightfully sorry, Mr. Winterslip," said the girl, "but we're off to the dance. This week-end belongs to the navy, you know. You'll come again, won't you?"

"Of course," John Quincy replied. "Don't let me keep you."

She smiled at him and fled with Johnnie at her side. Looking after them, John Quincy felt his heart sink to his boots, an

114. This must be an idealized description: If Carlota's hands were tanned (as mentioned earlier), her shoulders would have been, too. Women's bathing suit styles, shown here as of 1920, left the shoulders bare.

Women's bathing beauty contest, 1920.

115. The Moana Hotel was the first hotel built in Waikiki, opening in 1901. By 1924, it was operated by a company owned by hotelier Alexander Young; when the company failed in the Depression, the Matson Navigation Company took it over.

unaccountable sensation of age and helplessness. Youth, youth was going through that door, and he was left behind.

"A great pity she had to run," said Egan in a kindly voice.

"Why, that's all right," John Quincy assured him. "Old friend of the family, this Lieutenant Booth?"

"Not at all. Just a lad Cary met at parties in San Francisco. Won't you sit down and have a smoke with me?"

"Some other time, thanks," John Quincy said wearily. "I must hurry back to the house."

He wanted to escape, to get out into the calm lovely night, the night that was ruined for him now. He walked along the beach, savagely kicking his toes into the white sand. "Johnnie!" She had called him Johnnie. And the way she had looked at him, too! Again John Quincy felt that sharp pang in his heart. Foolish, foolish; better go back to Boston and forget. Peaceful old Boston, that was where he belonged. He was an old man out here—thirty, nearly. Better go away and leave these children to love and the moonlit beach.

Miss Minerva had gone in the big car to call on friends, and the house was quiet as the tomb. John Quincy wandered aimlessly about the rooms, gloomy and bereft. Down at the Moana[115] an Hawaiian orchestra was playing and Lieutenant Booth, of Richmond, was holding Carlota close in the intimate manner affected these days by the young. Bah! If he hadn't been ordered to leave Hawaii, by gad, he'd go to-morrow.

The telephone rang. None of the servants appeared to answer it, so John Quincy went himself.

"Charlie Chan speaking," said a voice. "That is you, Mr. Winterslip? Good. Big events will come to pass very quick. Meet me drug and grocery emporium of Liu Yin, number 927 River Street, soon as you can do so. You savvy locality?"

"I'll find it," cried John Quincy, delighted.

"By bank of stream. I will await. Good-by."

Action—action at last! John Quincy's heart beat fast. Action was what he wanted to-night. As usually happens in a crisis, there was no automobile available; the roadster was at a garage undergoing repairs, and the other car was in use. He hastened over to Kalakaua Avenue intending to rent a machine, but a trolley approaching at the moment altered his plans and he swung aboard.

Never had a trolley moved at so reluctant a pace. When they reached the corner of Fort Street in the center of the city, he left it and proceeded on foot. The hour was still fairly early, but the scene was one of somnolent calm. A couple of tourists drifted aimlessly by. About the bright doorway of a shooting gallery loitered a group of soldiers from the fort, with a sprinkling of enlisted navy men. John Quincy hurried on down King Street, past Chinese noodle cafés and pawn shops, and turned presently off into River Street.

On his left was the river, on his right an array of shabby stores. He paused at the door of number 927, the establishment of Liu Yin. Inside, seated behind a screen that revealed only their heads, a number of Chinese were engrossed in a friendly little game. John Quincy opened the door; a bell tinkled, and he stepped into an odor of must and decay. Curious sights met his quick eye: dried roots and herbs, jars of sea-horse skeletons, dejected ducks flattened out and varnished to tempt the palate, gobbets of pork. An old Chinaman rose and came forward.

"I'm looking for Mr. Charlie Chan," said John Quincy.

The old man nodded and led the way to a red curtain across the rear of the shop. He lifted it, and indicated that John Quincy was to pass. The boy did so, and came into a bare room furnished with a cot, a table on which an oil lamp burned dimly behind a smoky chimney, and a couple of chairs. A man who had been sitting on one of the chairs rose suddenly—a huge red-haired man with the smell of the sea about him.

"Hello," he said.

"Is Mr. Chan here?" John Quincy inquired.

"Not yet. He'll be along in a minute. What say to a drink while we're waiting. Hey, Liu, a couple glasses that rotten rice wine!"

The Chinaman withdrew. "Sit down," said the man. John Quincy obeyed; the sailor sat too. One of his eyelids drooped wickedly; he rested his hands on the table—enormous hairy hands. "Charlie'll be here pretty quick," he said. "Then I got a little story to tell the two of you."

"Yes?" John Quincy replied. He glanced about the little vile-smelling room. There was a door, a closed door, at the back. He looked again at the red-haired man. He wondered how he was going to get out of there.

For he knew now that Charlie Chan had not called him on the telephone. It came to him belatedly that the voice was never

Charlie's. "You savvy locality?" the voice had said. A clumsy attempt at Chan's style, but Chan was a student of English; he dragged his words painfully from the poets; he was careful to use nothing that savored of "pidgin." No, the detective had not telephoned; he was no doubt at home now bending over his chess-board, and here was John Quincy shut up in a little room on the fringe of the River District with a husky sailorman who leered at him knowingly.

The old Chinaman returned with two small glasses into which the liquor had already been poured. He set them on the table. The red-haired man lifted one of them. "Your health, sir," he said.

John Quincy took up the other glass and raised it to his lips. There was a suspicious eagerness in the sailor's one good eye. John Quincy put the glass back on the table. "I'm sorry," he said. "I don't want a drink, thank you."

The great face with its stubble of red beard leaned close to his. "Y' mean you won't drink with me?" said the red-haired man belligerently.

"That's just what I mean," John Quincy answered. Might as well get it over with, he felt; anything was better than this suspense. He stood up. "I'll be going along," he announced.

He took a step toward the red curtain. The sailor, evidently a fellow of few words, rose and got in his way. John Quincy, himself feeling the futility of talk, said nothing, but struck the man in the face. The sailor struck back with efficiency and promptness. In another second the room was full of battle, and John Quincy saw red everywhere, red curtain, red hair, red lamp flame, great red hairy hands cunningly seeking his face. What was it Roger had said? "Ever fought with a ship's officer—the old-fashioned kind with fists like flying hams?" No, he hadn't up to then, but that sweet experience was his now, and it came to John Quincy pleasantly that he was doing rather well at his new trade.

This was better than the attic; here he was prepared and had a chance. Time and again he got his hands on the red curtain, only to be dragged back and subjected to a new attack. The sailor was seeking to knock him out, and though many of his blows went home, that happy result—from the standpoint of the red-haired man—was unaccountably delayed. John Quincy had a similar aim in life; they lunged noisily about the room, while the surprising Orientals in the front of the shop continued their quiet game.

John Quincy saw red everywhere—red curtain, red hair, red lamp flame, great red hairy hands cunningly seeking his face. From The House Without a Key, *illustration by William Liepse* (The Saturday Evening Post, *February 28, 1925*)

116. The football stadium of Harvard University, built in 1903.

117. Futurism was an art movement following Cubism, emphasizing speed and technology; its art featured cars, airplanes, and the industrialized city.

John Quincy felt himself growing weary; his breath came painfully; he realized that his adversary had not yet begun to fight. Standing with his back to the table in an idle moment while the red-haired man made plans for the future, the boy hit on a plan of his own. He overturned the table; the lamp crashed down; darkness fell over the world. In the final glimmer of light he saw the big man coming for him and dropping to his knees he tackled in the approved manner of Soldiers' Field, Cambridge, Massachusetts.[116] Culture prevailed; the sailor went on his head with a resounding thump; John Quincy let go of him and sought the nearest exit. It happened to be the door at the rear, and it was unlocked.

He passed hurriedly through a cluttered back yard and climbing a fence, found himself in the neighborhood known as the River District. There in crazy alleys that have no names, no sidewalks, no beginning and no end, five races live together in the dark. Some houses were above the walk level, some below, all were out of alignment. John Quincy felt he had wandered into a futurist drawing.[117] As he paused he heard the whine and clatter of Chinese music, the clicking of a typewriter, the rasp of a cheap phonograph playing American jazz, the distant scream of an auto horn, a child wailing Japanese lamentations. Footsteps in the yard beyond the fence roused him, and he fled.

118. The back seats of the automobile, usually covered.

He must get out of this mystic maze of mean alleys, and at once. Odd painted faces loomed in the dusk; pasty-white faces with just a suggestion of queer costumes beneath. A babel of tongues, queer eyes that glittered, once a lean hand on his arm. A group of moon-faced Chinese children under a lamp who scattered at his approach. And when he paused again, out of breath, the patter of many feet, bare feet, sandaled feet, the clatter of wooden clogs, the squeak of cheap shoes made in his own Massachusetts. Then suddenly the thump of large feet such as might belong to a husky sailor. He moved on.

Presently he came into the comparative quiet of River Street, and realized that he had traveled in a circle, for there was Liu Yin's shop again. As he hurried on toward King Street, he saw, over his shoulder, that the red-haired man still followed. A big touring car, with curtains drawn, waited by the curb. John Quincy leaped in beside the driver.

"Get out of here, quick!" he panted.

A sleepy Japanese face looked at him through the gloom. "Busy now."

"I don't care if you are—" began John Quincy, and glanced down at one of the man's arms resting on the wheel. His heart stood still. In the dusk he saw a wrist watch with an illuminated dial, and the numeral two was very dim.

Even as he looked, strong hands seized him by the collar and dragged him into the dark tonneau.[118] At the same instant, the red-haired man arrived.

"Got him, Mike? Say, that's luck!" He leaped into the rear of the car. Quick able work went forward, John Quincy's hands were bound behind his back, a viletasting gag was put in his mouth. "Damned if this bird didn't land me one in the eye," said the red-haired man. "I'll pay him for it when we get aboard. Hey you—Pier 78. Show us some speed!"

The car leaped forward. John Quincy lay on the dusty floor, bound and helpless. To the docks? But he wasn't thinking of that, he was thinking of the watch on the driver's wrist.

A brief run, and they halted in the shadow of a pier-shed. John Quincy was lifted and propelled none too gently from the car. His cheek was jammed against one of the buttons holding the side curtain, and he had sufficient presence of mind to catch the gag on it and loosen it. As they left the car he tried to get a glimpse of its license plate, but he was able to ascertain only the first two figures—33—before it sped away.[119]

His two huge chaperons hurried him along the dock. Some distance off he saw a little group of men, three in white uniforms, one in a darker garb. The latter was smoking a pipe. John Quincy's heart leaped. He maneuvered the loosened gag with his teeth, so that it dropped about his collar. "Good-by, Pete!" he shouted at the top of his lungs, and launched at once into a terrific struggle to break away from his startled captors.

There was a moment's delay, and then the clatter of feet along the dock. A stocky boy in a white uniform began an enthusiastic debate with Mike, and the other two were prompt to claim the attention of the red-haired man. Pete Mayberry was at John Quincy's back, cutting the rope on his wrists.

"Well, I'll be damned, Mr. Winterslip," he cried.

"Same here," laughed John Quincy. "Shanghaied in another minute but for you." He leaped forward to join the battle, but the red-haired man and his friend had already succumbed to youth and superior forces, and were in full retreat. John Quincy followed joyously along the dock, and planted his fist back of his old adversary's ear. The sailor staggered, but regained his balance and went on.

John Quincy returned to his rescuers. "The last blow is the sweetest," he remarked.

"I can place those guys," said Mayberry. "They're off that tramp steamer that's been lying out in the harbor the past week. An opium runner, I'll gamble on it. You go to the police station right away—"

"Yes," said John Quincy, "I must. But I want to thank you, Mr. Mayberry. And"—he turned to the white uniforms—"you fellows too."

The stocky lad was picking up his cap. "Why, that's all right," he said. "A real pleasure, if you ask me. But look here, old timer," he added, addressing Mayberry, "how about your Honolulu water-front and its lost romance? You go tell that to the marines."

As John Quincy hurried away Pete Mayberry was busily explaining that the thing was unheard of—not in twenty years—maybe more than that—his voice died in the distance.

Hallet was in his room, and John Quincy detailed his evening's adventure. The captain was incredulous, but when the boy came to the wrist watch on the driver of the car, he sat up and took notice.

119. John Quincy did not know this, but all license plates issued by Honolulu County were in the form of x-xxxx; so either the number was 3-3xxx or this car had a plate issued by Maui County, which used the sequence 3x-xxxx.

Hawaii license plate from 1922; later years were similar, with "Hawaii" and the year at the bottom.

"Now you're talking," he cried. "I'll start the force after that car to-night. First two figures 33, you say. I'll send somebody aboard that tramp, too. They can't get away with stuff like that around here."

"Oh, never mind them," said John Quincy magnanimously. "Concentrate on the watch."

Back in the quiet town he walked with his head up, his heart full of the joy of battle. And while he thought of it, he stepped into the cable office. The message he sent was addressed to Agatha Parker on that Wyoming ranch. "San Francisco or nothing," was all it said.

As he walked down the deserted street on his way to the corner to wait for his trolley, he heard quick footsteps on his trail again. Who now? He was sore and weary, a bit fed up on fighting for one evening. He quickened his pace. The steps quickened too. He went even faster. So did his pursuer. Oh, well, might as well stop and face him.

John Quincy turned. A young man rushed up, a lean young man in a cap.

"Mr. Winterslip, ain't it?" He thrust a dark brown object into John Quincy's hand. "Your July *Atlantic*, sir. Came in on the *Maui* this morning."

"Oh," said John Quincy limply. "Well, I'll take it. My aunt might like to look at it. Keep the change."

"Thank you, sir," said the newsman, touching his cap.

John Quincy rode out to Waikiki on the last seat of the car. His face was swollen and cut, every muscle ached. Under his arm, clasped tightly, he held the July *Atlantic*. But he didn't so much as look at the table of contents. "We move, we advance," he told himself exultantly. For he had seen the watch with the illuminated dial—the dial on which the numeral two was very dim.

CHAPTER XX

The Story of Lau Ho

Early Sunday morning John Quincy was awakened by a sharp knock on his door. Rising sleepily and donning dressing-gown and slippers, he opened it to admit his Aunt Minerva. She had a worried air.

"Are you all right, John Quincy?" she inquired.

"Surely. That is, I would be if I hadn't been dragged out of bed a full hour before I intended to get up."

"I'm sorry, but I had to have a look at you." She took a newspaper from under her arm and handed it to him. "What's all this?"

An eight-column head on the first page caught even John Quincy's sleepy eye. "Boston Man has Strange Adventure on Water-Front." Smaller heads announced that Mr. John Quincy Winterslip had been rescued from an unwelcome trip to China, "in the nick of time" by three midshipmen from the *Oregon*. Poor Pete Mayberry! He had been the real hero of the affair, but his own paper would not come out again until Monday evening, and rivals had beaten him to the story.

John Quincy yawned. "All true, my dear," he said. "I was on the verge of leaving you when the navy saved me. Life, you perceive, has become a musical comedy."

"But why should any one want to shanghai you?" cried Miss Minerva.

"Ah, I hoped you'd ask me that. It happens that your nephew has a brain. His keen analytical work as a detective is getting some one's goat. He admitted as much in a letter he sent me the night he took a few shots at my head."

"Some one shot at you!" gasped Miss Minerva.

"I'll say so. You rather fancy yourself as a sleuth, but is anybody taking aim at you from behind bushes? Answer me that."

Miss Minerva sat down weakly on a chair. "You're going home on the next boat," she announced.

He laughed. "About two weeks ago I made that suggestion to you. And what was your reply? Ah, my dear, the tables are turned. I'm not going home on the next boat. I may never go home. This gay, care-free, sudden country begins to appeal to me. Let me read about myself."

He returned to the paper. "The clock was turned back thirty years on the Honolulu water-front last night," began the somewhat imaginative account. It closed with the news that the tramp steamer *Mary S. Allison* had left port before the police could board her. Evidently she'd had steam up and papers ready, and was only awaiting the return of the red-haired man and his victim. John Quincy handed the newspaper back to his aunt.

"Too bad," he remarked. "They slipped through Hallet's fingers."

"Of course they did," she snapped. "Everybody does. I'd like a talk with Captain Hallet. If I could only tell him what I think of him, I'd feel better."

"Save that paper," John Quincy said. "I want to send it to mother."

She stared at him. "Are you mad? Poor Grace—she'd have a nervous breakdown. I only hope she doesn't hear of this until you're back in Boston safe and sound."

"Oh, yes—Boston," laughed John Quincy. "Quaint old town, they tell me. I must visit there some day. Now if you'll leave me a minute, I'll prepare to join you at breakfast and relate the story of my adventurous life."

"Very well," agreed Miss Minerva, rising. She paused at the door. "A little witch-hazel might help your face."

"The scars of honorable battle," said her nephew. "Why remove them?"

"Honorable fiddlesticks," Miss Minerva answered. "After all, the Back Bay has its good points." But in the hall outside she smiled a delighted little smile.

When John Quincy and his aunt were leaving the dining-room after breakfast Kamaikui, stiff and dignified in a freshly-laundered holoku, approached the boy.

"So very happy to see you safe this morning," she announced.

"Why, thank you, Kamaikui," he answered. He wondered. Was Kaohla responsible for his troubles, and if so, did this huge silent woman know of her grandson's activities?

"Poor thing," Miss Minerva said as they entered the living-room. "She's been quite downcast since Dan went. I'm sorry for her. I've always liked her."

"Naturally," smiled John Quincy. "There's a bond between you."

"What's that?"

"Two vanishing races, yours and hers. The Boston Brahman and the pure Hawaiian."

Later in the morning Carlota Egan telephoned him, greatly excited. She had just seen the Sunday paper.

"All true," he admitted. "While you were dancing your heart out, I was struggling to sidestep a Cook's tour of the Orient."

"I shouldn't have had a happy moment if I'd known."

"Then I'm glad you didn't. Big party, I suppose?"

"Yes. You know, I've been terribly worried about you ever since that night on the avenue. I want to talk with you. Will you come to see me?"

"Will I? I'm on my way already."

He hung up the receiver and hastened down the beach. Carlota was sitting on the white sand not far from the Reef and Palm, all in white herself. A serious wide-eyed Carlota quite different from the gay girl who had been hurrying to a party the night before.

John Quincy dropped down beside her, and for a time they talked of the dance and of his adventure. Suddenly she turned to him.

"I have no right to ask it, I know, but—I want you to do something for me."

"It will make me very happy—anything you ask."

"Go back to Boston."

"What! Not that. I was wrong—that wouldn't make me happy."

John Quincy dropped down beside her. Suddenly she turned to him.
"I have no right to ask, I know; but I want you to do something for me."
From *The House Without a Key*, illustration by William Liepse
(*The Saturday Evening Post*, March 7, 1925)

"Yes, it would. You don't think so now, perhaps. You're dazzled by the sun out here, but this isn't your kind of place. We're not your kind of people. You think you like us, but you'd soon forget. Back among your own sort—the sort who are interested in the things that interest you. Please go."

"It would be retreating under fire," he objected.

"But you proved your courage, last night. I'm afraid for you. Some one out here has a terrible grudge against you. I'd never forgive Hawaii if—if anything happened to you."

"That's sweet of you." He moved closer. But—confound it—there was Agatha. Bound to Agatha by all the ties of honor. He edged away again. "I'll think about it," he agreed.

"I'm leaving Honolulu too, you know," she reminded him.

"I know. You'll have a wonderful time in England."

She shook her head. "Oh, I dread the whole idea. Dad's heart is set on it, and I shall go to please him. But I shan't enjoy it. I'm not up to England."

"Nonsense."

"No, I'm not. I'm unsophisticated—crude, really—just a girl of the Islands."

"But you wouldn't care to stay here all your life?"

"No, indeed. It's a beautiful spot—to loll about in. But I've too much northern blood to be satisfied with that. One of these days I want dad to sell and we'll go to the mainland. I could get some sort of work—"

"Any particular place on the mainland?"

"Well, I haven't been about much, of course. But all the time I was at school I kept thinking I'd rather live in San Francisco than anywhere else in the world—"

"Good," John Quincy cried. "That's my choice too. You remember that morning on the ferry, how you held out your hand to me and said: 'Welcome to your city—'"

"But you corrected me at once. You said you belonged in Boston."

"I see my error now."

She shook her head. "A moment's madness, but you'll recover. You're an easterner, and you could never be happy anywhere else."

"Oh, yes, I could," he assured her. "I'm a Winterslip, a wandering Winterslip. Any old place we hang our hats—" This time he did lean rather close. "I could be happy anywhere—" he began. He wanted to add "with you." But Agatha's slim patrician hand was on his shoulder. "Anywhere," he repeated, with a different inflection. A gong sounded from the Reef and Palm.

Carlota rose. "That's lunch." John Quincy stood too. "It's beside the point—where you go," she went on. "I asked you to do something for me."

"I know. If you'd asked anything else in the world, I'd be up to my neck in it now. But what you suggest would take a bit of doing. To leave Hawaii—and say good-by to you—"

"I meant to be very firm about it," she broke in.

"But I must have a little time to consider. Will you wait?"

She smiled up at him. "You're so much wiser than I am," she said. "Yes—I'll wait."

He went slowly along the beach. Unsophisticated, yes—and charming. "You're so much wiser than I am." Where on the mainland could one encounter a girl nowadays who'd say that? He had quite forgotten that she smiled when she said it.

In the afternoon, John Quincy visited the police station. Hallet was in his room in rather a grouchy mood. Chan was out somewhere hunting the watch. No, they hadn't found it yet.

John Quincy was mildly reproving. "Well, you saw it, didn't you?" growled Hallet. "Why in Sam Hill didn't you grab it?"

"Because they tied my hands," John Quincy reminded him. "I've narrowed the search down for you to the taxi drivers of Honolulu."

"Hundreds of them, my boy."

"More than that, I've given you the first two numbers on the license plate of the car. If you're any good at all, you ought to be able to land that watch now."

"Oh, we'll land it," Hallet said. "Give us time."

Time was just what John Quincy had to give them. Monday came and went. Miss Minerva was bitterly sarcastic.

"Patience are a very lovely virtue," John Quincy told her. "I got that from Charlie."

"At any rate," she snapped, "it are a virtue very much needed with Captain Hallet in charge."

In another direction, too, John Quincy was called upon to exercise patience. Agatha Parker was unaccountably silent regarding that short peremptory cable he had sent on his big night in town. Was she offended? The Parkers were notoriously not a family who accepted dictation. But in such a vital matter as this, a girl should be willing to listen to reason.

Late Tuesday afternoon Chan telephoned from the station-house—unquestionably Chan this time. Would John Quincy do him the great honor to join him for an early dinner at the Alexander Young café?

"Something doing, Charlie?" cried the boy eagerly.

"Maybe it might be," answered Chan, "and maybe also not. At six o'clock in hotel lobby, if you will so far condescend."

"I'll be there," John Quincy promised, and he was.

He greeted Chan with anxious, inquiring eyes, but the Chinaman was suave and entirely non-committal. He led John Quincy to the dining-room and carefully selected a table by a front window.

"Do me the great favor to recline," he suggested.

John Quincy reclined. "Charlie, don't keep me in suspense," he pleaded.

Chan smiled. "Let us not shade the feast with gloomy murder talk," he replied. "This are social meeting. Is it that you are in the mood to dry up plate of soup?"

"Why, yes, of course," John Quincy answered. Politeness, he saw, dictated that he hide his curiosity.

"Two of the soup," ordered Chan of a white-jacketed waiter. A car drew up to the door of the Alexander Young. Chan half rose, staring at it keenly. He dropped back to his seat. "It is my high delight to entertain you thus humbly before you are restored to Boston. Converse at some length of Boston. I feel interested."

"Really?" smiled the boy.

"Undubitably. Gentleman I meet once say Boston are like China. The future of both, he say, lies in graveyards where repose useless bodies of honored guests on high. I am fogged as to meaning."

"He meant both places live in the past," John Quincy explained. "And he was right, in a way. Boston, like China, boasts a glorious history. But that's not saying the Boston of to-day isn't progressive. Why, do you know—"

He talked eloquently of his native city. Chan listened, rapt.

"Always," he sighed, when John Quincy finished, "I have unlimited yearning for travel." He paused to watch another car draw up before the hotel. "But it are unavailable. I am policeman on small remuneration. In my youth, rambling on evening hillside or by moonly ocean, I dream of more lofty position. Not so now. But that other American citizen, my eldest son, he are dreaming too. Maybe for him dreams eventuate. Perhaps he become second Baby Ruth, home run emperor, applause of thousands making him deaf. Who knows it?"

The dinner passed, unshaded by gloomy talk, and they went outside. Chan proffered a cigar of which he spoke in the most belittling fashion. He suggested that they stand for a time before the hotel door.

"Waiting for somebody?" inquired John Quincy, unable longer to dissemble.

"Precisely the fact. Barely dare to mention it, however. Great disappointment may drive up here any minute now."

An open car stopped before the hotel entrance. John Quincy's eyes sought the license plate, and he got an immediate thrill. The first two figures were 33.

A party of tourists, a man and two women, alighted. The doorman ran forward and busied himself with luggage. Chan casually strolled across the walk, and as the Japanese driver shifted his gears preparatory to driving away, put a restraining hand on the car door.

"One moment, please." The Jap turned, fright in his eyes. "You are Okuda, from auto stand across way?"

"Yess," hissed the driver.

"You are now returned from exploring island with party of tourists? You leave this spot early Sunday morning?"

"Yess."

"Is it possible that you wear wrist watch, please?"

"Yess."

"Deign to reveal face of same."

The Jap hesitated. Chan leaned far over into the car and thrust aside the man's coat sleeve. He came back, a pleased light in his eyes, and held open the rear door. "Kindly embark into tonneau, Mr. Winterslip." Obediently John Quincy got in. Chan took his place by the driver's side. "The police station, if you will be so kind." The car leaped forward.

The essential clue! They had it at last. John Quincy's heart beat fast there in the rear of the car where, only a few nights before, he had been bound and gagged.

Captain Hallet's grim face relaxed into happy lines when he met them at the door of his room. "You got him, eh? Good work." He glanced at the prisoner's wrist. "Rip that watch off him, Charlie."

Charlie obeyed. He examined the watch for a moment, then handed it to his chief.

"Inexpensive time-piece of noted brand," he announced. "Numeral two faint and far away. One other fact emerge into light. This Jap have small wrist. Yet worn place on strap convey impression of being worn by man with wrist of vastly larger circumference."

Hallet nodded. "Yes, that's right. Some other man has owned this watch. He had a big wrist—but most men in Honolulu have, you know. Sit down, Okuda. I want to hear from you. You understand what it means to lie to me?"

"I do not lie, sir."

"No, you bet your sweet life you don't. First, tell me who engaged your car last Saturday night."

"Saturday night?"

"That's what I said!"

"Ah, yes. Two sailors from ship. Engage for evening paying large cash at once. I drive to shop on River Street, wait long time. Then off we go to dock with extra passenger in back."

"Know the names of those sailors?"

"Could not say."

"What ship were they from?"

"How can I know? Not told."

"All right I'm coming to the important thing. Understand? The truth—that's what I want! Where did you get this watch?"

Chan and John Quincy leaned forward eagerly. "I buy him," said the Jap.

"You bought him? Where?"

"At jewel store of Chinese Lau Ho on Maunakea Street."

Hallet turned to Chan. "Know the place, Charlie?"

Chan nodded. "Yes, indeed."

"Open now?"

"Open until hour of ten, maybe more."

"Good," said Hallet. "Come along, Okuda. You can drive us there."

Lau Ho, a little wizened Chinaman, sat back of his work bench with a microscope screwed into one dim old eye. The four men who entered his tiny store filled it to overflowing, but he gave them barely a glance.

"Come on, Ho—wake up," Hallet cried. "I want to talk to you."

With the utmost deliberation the Chinaman descended from his stool and approached the counter. He regarded Hallet with a hostile eye. The captain laid the wrist watch on top of a showcase in which reposed many trays of jade.

"Ever see that before?" he inquired.

Lau Ho regarded it casually. Slowly he raised his eyes. "Maybe so. Can not say," he replied in a high squeaky voice.

Hallet reddened. "Nonsense. You had it here in the store, and you sold it to this Jap. Now, didn't you?"

Lau Ho dreamily regarded the taxi driver. "Maybe so. Can not say."

"Damn it!" cried Hallet. "You know who I am?"

"Policeman, maybe."

"Policeman maybe yes! And I want you to tell me about this watch. Now wake up and come across or by the Lord Harry—"

Chan laid a deferential hand on his chief's arm. "Humbly suggest I attempt this," he said.

Hallet nodded. "All right, he's your meat, Charlie." He drew back.

Chan bowed with a great show of politeness. He launched into a long story in Chinese. Lau Ho looked at him with slight interest. Presently he squeaked a brief reply. Chan resumed his flow of talk. Occasionally he paused, and Lau Ho spoke. In a few moments Chan turned beaming.

"Story are now completely extracted like aching tooth," he said. "Wrist watch was brought to Lau Ho on Thursday, same week as murder. Offered him on sale by young man darkly colored with small knife scar marring cheek. Lau Ho buy and repair watch, interior works being in injured state. Saturday morning he sell at seemly profit to Japanese, presumably this Okuda here but Lau Ho will not swear. Saturday night dark young man appear much overwhelmed with excitement and demand watch again, please. Lau Ho say it is sold to Japanese. Which Japanese? Lau Ho is not aware of name, and can not describe, all Japanese faces being uninteresting outlook for him. Dark young man curse and fly. Appear frequently demanding any news, but Lau Ho is unable to oblige. Such are story of this jewel merchant here."

They went out on the street. Hallet scowled at the Jap. "All right—run along. I'll keep the watch."[120]

"Very thankful," said the taxi driver, and leaped into his car.

Hallet turned to Chan. "A dark young man with a scar?" he queried.

"Clear enough to me," Chan answered. "Same are the Spaniard Jose Cabrera, careless man about town with reputation not so savory. Mr. Winterslip, is it that you have forgotten him?"

John Quincy started. "Me? Did I ever see him?"

"Recall," said Chan. "It are the night following murder. You and I linger in All American Restaurant engaged in debate regarding hygiene of pie. Door open, admitting Bowker, steward on *President Tyler*, joyously full of okolehau. With him are dark young man—this Jose Cabrera himself."

"Oh, I remember now," John Quincy answered.

"Well, the Spaniard's easy to pick up," said Hallet. "I'll have him inside an hour—"

"One moment, please," interposed Chan. "To-morrow morning at nine o'clock the *President Tyler* return from Orient. No gambler myself but will wager incredible sum Spaniard waits on dock for Mr. Bowker. If you present no fierce objection, I have a yearning to arrest him at that very moment."

"Why, of course," agreed Hallet. He looked keenly at Charlie Chan. "Charlie, you old rascal, you've got the scent at last."

"Who—me?" grinned Chan. "With your gracious permission I would alter the picture. Stone walls are crumbling now like dust. Through many loopholes light stream in like rosy streaks of dawn."

CHAPTER XXI

The Stone Walls Crumble

The stone walls were crumbling and the light streaming through—but only for Chan. John Quincy was still groping in the dark, and his reflections were a little bitter as he returned to the house at Waikiki. Chan and he had worked together, but now that they approached the crisis of their efforts, the detective evidently preferred to push on alone, leaving his fellow-worker to follow if he could. Well, so be it—but John Quincy's pride was touched.

He had suddenly a keen desire to show Chan that he could not be left behind like that. If only he could, by some inspirational flash of deductive reasoning, arrive at the solution of the mystery simultaneously with the detective. For the honor of Boston and the Winterslips.

Frowning deeply, he considered all the old discarded clues again. The people who had been under suspicion and then dropped—Egan, the Compton woman, Brade, Kaohla, Leatherbee, Saladine, Cope. He even considered several the investigation had not touched. Presently he came to Bowker. What did Bowker's reappearance mean?

For the first time in two weeks he thought of the little man with the fierce pompadour and the gold-rimmed eye-glasses. Bowker with his sorrowful talk of vanished bar-rooms and lost friends behind the bar. How was the steward on the *President Tyler* connected with the murder of Dan Winterslip? He had not done it himself, that was obvious, but in some way he was linked up with the crime. John Quincy spent a long and painful period seeking to join Bowker up with one or another of the suspects. It couldn't be done.

All through that Tuesday evening the boy puzzled, so silent and distrait that Miss Minerva finally gave him up and retired to her room with a book. He awoke on Wednesday morning with the problem no nearer solution.

Barbara was due to arrive at ten o'clock from Kauai, and taking the small car, John Quincy went down-town to meet her. Pausing at the bank to cash a check, he encountered his old shipmate on the *President Tyler*, the sprightly Madame Maynard.

"I really shouldn't speak to you," she said. "You never come to see me."

"I know," he answered. "But I've been so very busy."

"So I hear. Running round with policemen and their victims. I have no doubt you'll go back to Boston and report we're all criminals and cutthroats out here."

"Oh, hardly that."

"Yes, you will. You're getting a very biased view of Honolulu. Why not stoop to associate with a respectable person now and then?"

"I'd enjoy it—if they're all like you."

"Like me? They're much more intelligent and charming than I am. Some of them are dropping in at my house to-night for an informal little party. A bit of a chat, and then a moonlight swim. Won't you come too?"

"I want to, of course," John Quincy replied. "But there's Cousin Dan—"

Her eyes flashed. "I'll say it, even if he was your relative. Ten minutes of mourning for Cousin Dan is ample. I'll be looking for you."

John Quincy laughed. "I'll come."

"Do," she answered. "And bring your Aunt Minerva. Tell her I said she might as well be dead as hog-tied by convention."

John Quincy went out to the corner of Fort and King Streets, near which he had parked the car. As he was about to climb into it, he paused. A familiar figure was jauntily crossing the street. The figure of Bowker, the steward, and with him was Willie Chan, demon backstopper of the Pacific.

121. "Fusel oil" (technically "fusel alcohols") is a mixture of alcohols produced as a by-product of alcoholic fermentation with the yeast *Saccharomyces cerevisiae*. The word "fusel" comes from the German, meaning "bad liquor."

"Hello, Bowker," John Quincy called.

Mr. Bowker came blithely to join him. "Well, well, well. My old friend Mr. Winterslip. Shake hands with William Chan, the local Ty Cobb."

"Mr. Chan and I have met before," John Quincy told him.

"Know all the celebrities, eh? That's good. Well, we missed you on the *President Tyler.*"

Bowker was evidently quite sober. "Just got in, I take it," John Quincy remarked.

"A few minutes ago. How about joining us?" He came closer and lowered his voice. "This intelligent young man tells me he knows a taxi-stand out near the beach where one may obtain a superior brand of fusel oil[121] with a very pretty label on the bottle."

"Sorry," John Quincy answered. "My cousin's coming in shortly on an Inter-Island boat, and I'm elected to meet her."

"I'm sorry, too," said the graduate of Dublin University. "If my strength holds out I'm aiming to stage quite a little party, and I'd like to have you in on it. Yes, a rather large affair—in memory of Tim, and as a last long lingering farewell to the seven seas."

"What? You're pau?"

"Pau it is. When I sail out of here to-night at nine on the old *P. T.* I'm through for ever. You don't happen to know a good country newspaper that can be bought for—well, say ten grand."

"This is rather sudden, isn't it?" John Quincy inquired.

"This is sudden country out here, sir. Well, we must roll along. Sorry you can't join us. If the going's not too rough and I can find a nice smooth table top, I intend to turn down an empty glass. For poor old Tim. So long, sir—and happy days."

He nodded to Willie Chan, and they went on down the street. John Quincy stood staring after them, a puzzled expression on his face.

Barbara seemed paler and thinner than ever, but she announced that her visit had been an enjoyable one, and on the ride to the beach appeared to be making a distinct effort to be gay and sprightly. When they reached the house, John Quincy repeated to his aunt Mrs. Maynard's invitation.

"Better come along," he urged.

"Perhaps I will," she answered. "I'll see."

The day passed quietly, and it was not until evening that the monotony was broken. Leaving the dining-room with his aunt and Barbara, John Quincy was handed a cablegram. He hastily opened it. It had been sent from Boston; evidently Agatha Parker, overwhelmed by the crude impossibility of the West, had fled home again, and John Quincy's brief "San Francisco or nothing" had followed her there. Hence the delay.

The cablegram said simply: "Nothing. Agatha." John Quincy crushed it in his hand; he tried to suffer a little, but it was no use. He was a mighty happy man. The end of a romance—no. There had never been any nonsense of that kind between them—just an affectionate regard too slight to stand the strain of parting. Agatha was younger than he, she would marry some nice proper boy who had no desire to roam. And John Quincy Winterslip would read of her wedding—in the San Francisco papers.

He found Miss Minerva alone in the living-room. "It's none of my business," she said, "but I'm wondering what was in your cablegram."

"Nothing," he answered truthfully.

"All the same, you were very pleased to get it."

He nodded. "Yes. I imagine nobody was ever so happy over nothing before."

"Good heavens," she cried. "Have you given up grammar, too?"

"I'm thinking of it. How about going down the beach with me?"

She shook her head. "Some one is coming to look at the house—a leading lawyer, I believe he is. He's thinking of buying, and I feel I should be here to show him about. Barbara appears so listless and disinterested. Tell Sally Maynard I may drop in later."

At a quarter to eight, John Quincy took his bathing suit and wandered down Kalia Road. It was another of those nights; a bright moon was riding high; from a bungalow buried under purple alamander came the soft croon of Hawaiian music. Through the hedges of flaming hibiscus he caught again the exquisite odors of this exotic island.

Mrs. Maynard's big house was a particularly unlovely type of New England architecture, but a hundred flowering vines did much to conceal that fact. John Quincy found his hostess enthroned in her great airy drawing-room, surrounded by a handsome laughing group of the best people. Pleasant people, too; as she introduced him he began to wonder if he hadn't been missing a great deal of congenial companionship.

"I dragged him here against his will," the old lady explained. "I felt I owed it to Hawaii. He's been associating with the riff-raff long enough."

They insisted that he take an enormous chair, pressed cigarettes upon him, showered him with hospitable attentions. As he sat down and the chatter was resumed, he reflected that here was as civilized a company as Boston itself could offer. And why not? Most of these families came originally from New England, and had kept in their exile the old ideals of culture and caste.

"It might interest Beacon Street to know," Mrs. Maynard said, "that long before the days of 'forty-nine the people of California were sending their children over here to be educated in the missionary schools. And importing their wheat from here, too."

"Go on, tell him the other one, Aunt Sally," laughed a pretty girl in blue. "That about the first printing press in San Francisco being brought over from Honolulu."

Madame Maynard shrugged her shoulders. "Oh, what's the use? We're so far away, New England will never get us straight."

John Quincy looked up to see Carlota Egan in the doorway. A moment later Lieutenant Booth, of Richmond, appeared at her side. It occurred to the young man from Boston that the fleet was rather overdoing its stop at Honolulu.

Mrs. Maynard rose to greet the girl. "Come in, my dear. You know most of these people." She turned to the others. "This is Miss Egan, a neighbor of mine on the beach."

It was amusing to note that most of these people knew Carlota too. John Quincy smiled—the British Admiralty and the soap business. It must have been rather an ordeal for the girl, but she saw it through with a sweet graciousness that led John Quincy to reflect that she would be at home in England—if she went there.

Carlota sat down on a sofa, and while Lieutenant Booth was busily arranging a cushion at her back, John Quincy dropped down beside her. The sofa was, fortunately, too small for three.

"I rather expected to see you," he said in a low voice. "I was brought here to meet the best people of Honolulu, and the way I see it, you're the best of all."

She smiled at him, and again the chatter of small talk filled the room. Presently the voice of a tall young man with glasses rose above the general hubbub.

"They got a cable from Joe Clark out at the Country Club this afternoon," he announced.

The din ceased, and every one listened with interest. "Clark's our professional," explained the young man to John Quincy. "He went over a month ago to play in the British Open."

"Did he win?" asked the girl in blue.

"He was put out by Hagen[122] in the semi-finals," the young man said. "But he had the distinction of driving the longest ball ever seen on the St. Andrews course."

"Why shouldn't he?" asked an older man. "He's got the strongest wrists I ever saw on anybody!"

John Quincy sat up, suddenly interested. "How do you account for that?" he asked.

The older man smiled. "We've all got pretty big wrists out here," he answered. "Surf-boarding—that's what does it. Joe Clark was a champion at one time—body-surfing and boardsurfing too. He used to disappear for hours in the rollers out by the reef. The result was a marvelous wrist development. I've seen him drive a golf ball three hundred and eighty yards. Yes, sir, I'll bet he made those Englishmen sit up and take notice."

While John Quincy was thinking this over, some one suggested that it was time for the swim, and confusion reigned. A Chinese servant led the way to the dressing-rooms, which opened off the lanai, and the young people trouped joyously after him.

"I'll be waiting for you on the beach," John Quincy said to Carlota Egan.

"I came with Johnnie, you know," she reminded him.

"I know all about it," he answered. "But it was the week-end you promised to the navy. People who try to stretch their week-end through the following Wednesday night deserve all they get."

She laughed. "I'll look for you," she agreed.

He donned his bathing suit hastily in a room filled with flying clothes and great waving brown arms. Lieutenant Booth, he noted with satisfaction, was proceeding at a leisurely pace. Hurrying through a door that opened directly on the beach, he waited under a nearby hau tree. Presently Carlota came, slender and fragile-looking in the moonlight.

"Ah, here you are," John Quincy cried. "The farthest float."

"The farthest float it is," she answered.

122. Walter Hagen (1892–1969) was the first great American professional golfer, winning eleven professional major tournaments. Hagen (who won the British Open in 1922) was the winner, by one stroke, of the British Open held on June 26–27, 1924. There is no record of a golfer named "Clark" participating in the tournament.

They dashed into the warm silvery water and swam gaily off. Five minutes later they sat on the float together. The light on Diamond Head was winking; the lanterns of sampans twinkled out beyond the reef; the shore line of Honolulu was outlined by a procession of blinking stars controlled by dynamos. In the bright heavens hung a lunar rainbow, one colorful end in the Pacific and the other tumbling into the foliage ashore.

A gorgeous setting in which to be young and in love, and free to speak at last. John Quincy moved closer to the girl's side.

"Great night, isn't it?" he said.

"Wonderful," she answered softly.

"Cary, I want to tell you something, and that's why I brought you out here away from the others—"

"Somehow," she interrupted, "it doesn't seem quite fair to Johnnie."

"Never mind him. Has it ever occurred to you that my name's Johnnie, too."

She laughed. "Oh, but it couldn't be."

"What do you mean?"

"I mean, I simply couldn't call you that. You're too dignified and—and remote. John Quincy—I believe I could call you John Quincy—"

"Well, make up your mind. You'll have to call me something, because I'm going to be hanging round pretty constantly in the future. Yes, my dear, I'll probably turn out to be about the least remote person in the world. That is, if I can make you see the future the way I see it. Cary dearest—"

A gurgle sounded behind them, and they turned around. Lieutenant Booth was climbing on to the raft. "Swam the last fifty yards under water to surprise you," he sputtered.

"Well, you succeeded," said John Quincy without enthusiasm.

The lieutenant sat down with the manner of one booked to remain indefinitely. "I'll tell the world it's some night," he offered.

"Speaking of the world, when do you fellows leave Honolulu?" asked John Quincy.

"I don't know. To-morrow, I guess. Me, I don't care if we never go. Hawaii's not so easy to leave. Is it, Cary?"

She shook her head. "Hardest place I know of, Johnnie. I shall have to be sailing presently, and I know what a wrench it will be.

Perhaps I'll follow the example of Waioli the swimmer, and leave the boat when it passes Waikiki."

They lolled for a moment in silence. Suddenly John Quincy sat up. "What was that you said?" he asked.

"About Waioli? Didn't I ever tell you? He was one of our best swimmers, and for years they tried to get him to go to the mainland to take part in athletic meets, like Duke Kahanamoku.[123] But he was a sentimentalist—he couldn't bring himself to leave Hawaii. Finally they persuaded him, and one sunny morning he sailed on the *Matsonia*, with a very sad face. When the ship was opposite Waikiki he slipped overboard and swam ashore. And that was that. He never got on a ship again. You see—"

John Quincy was on his feet. "What time was it when we left the beach?" he asked in a low tense voice.

"About eight-thirty," said Booth.

John Quincy talked very fast. "That means I've got just thirty minutes to get ashore, dress, and reach the dock before the *President Tyler* sails. I'm sorry to go, but it's vital—vital. Cary, I'd started to tell you something. I don't know when I'll get back, but I must see you when I do, either at Mrs. Maynard's or the hotel. Will you wait up for me?"

She was startled by the seriousness of his tone. "Yes, I'll be waiting," she told him.

"That's great." He hesitated a moment; it is a risky business to leave the girl you love on a float in the moonlight with a handsome naval officer. But it had to be done. "I'm off," he said, and dove.

When he came up he heard the lieutenant's voice. "Say, old man, that dive was all wrong. You let me show you—"

"Go to the devil," muttered John Quincy wetly, and swam with long powerful strokes toward the shore. Mad with haste, he plunged into the dressing-room, donned his clothes, then dashed out again. No time for apologies to his hostess. He ran along the beach to the Winterslip house. Haku was dozing in the hall.

"Wikiwiki," shouted John Quincy. "Tell the chauffeur to get the roadster into the drive and start the engine. Wake up! Travel! Where's Miss Barbara?"

"Last seen on beach—" began the startled Haku.

On the bench under the hau tree he found Barbara sitting alone. He stood panting before her.

"My dear," he said. "I know at last who killed your father—"

123. Waioli appears to be a fictional person, unlike Duke Kahanamoku (1890–1968), certainly the most famous swimmer ever produced by Hawaii. A Native Hawaiian, Kahanamoku was a five-time Olympic medalist in swimming and a great popularizer of the sport of surfing.

She was on her feet. "You do?"

"Yes—shall I tell you?"

"No," she said. "No—I can't bear to hear. It's too horrible."

"Then you've suspected?"

"Yes—just suspicion—a feeling—intuition. I couldn't believe it—I didn't want to believe it. I went away to get it out of my mind. It's all too terrible—"

He put his hand on her shoulder. "Poor Barbara. Don't you worry. You won't appear in this in any way. I'll keep you out of it."

"What—what has happened?"

"Can't stop now. Tell you later." He ran toward the drive. Miss Minerva appeared from the house. "Haven't time to talk," he cried, leaping into the roadster.

"But John Quincy—a curious thing has happened—that lawyer who was here to look at the house—he said that Dan, just a week before he died, spoke to him about a new will—"

"That's good! That's evidence!" John Quincy cried.

"But why a new will? Surely Barbara was all he had—"

"Listen to me," cut in John Quincy. "You've delayed me already. Get the big car and go to the station—tell that to Hallet. Tell him too that I'm on the *President Tyler* and to send Chan there at once."

He stepped on the gas. By the clock in the automobile he had just seventeen minutes, to reach the dock before the *President Tyler* would sail. He shot like a madman through the brilliant Hawaiian night. Kalakaua Avenue, smooth and deserted, proved a glorious speedway. It took him just eight minutes to travel the three miles to the dock. A bit of traffic and an angry policeman in the center of the city caused the delay.

A scattering of people in the dim pier-shed waited for the imminent sailing of the liner. John Quincy dashed through them and up the gangplank. The second officer, Hepworth, stood at the top.

"Hello, Mr. Winterslip," he said. "You sailing?"

"No. But let me aboard!"

"I'm sorry. We're about to draw in the plank."

"No, no—you mustn't. This is life and death. Hold off just a few minutes. There's a steward named Bowker—I must find him at once. Life and death, I tell you."

Hepworth stood aside. "Oh, well, in that case. But please hurry, sir—"

"I will." John Quincy passed him on the run. He was on his way to the cabins presided over by Bowker when a tall figure caught his eye. A man in a long green ulster and a battered green hat—a hat John Quincy had last seen on the links of the Oahu Country Club.

The tall figure moved on up a stairway to the top-most deck. John Quincy followed. He saw the ulster disappear into one of the de luxe cabins. Still he followed, and pushed open the cabin door. The man in the ulster was back to, but he swung round suddenly.

"Ah, Mr. Jennison," John Quincy cried. "Were you thinking of sailing on this boat?"

For an instant Jennison stared at him. "I was," he said quietly.

"Forget it," John Quincy answered. "You're going ashore with me."

"Really? What is your authority?"

"No authority whatever," said the boy grimly. "I'm taking you, that's all."

Jennison smiled, but there was a gleam of hate behind it. And in John Quincy's heart, usually so gentle and civilized, there was hate too as he faced this man. He thought of Dan Winterslip, dead on his cot. He thought of Jennison walking down the gangplank with them that morning they landed, Jennison putting his arm about poor Barbara when she faltered under the blow. He thought of the shots fired at him from the bush, of the red-haired man battering him in that red room. Well, he must fight again. No way out of it. The siren of the *President Tyler* sounded a sharp warning.

"You get out of here," said Jennison through his teeth. "I'll go with you to the gangplank—"

He stopped, as the disadvantages of that plan came home to him. His right hand went swiftly to his pocket. Inspired, John Quincy seized a filled water bottle and hurled it at the man's head. Jennison dodged; the bottle crashed through one of the windows. The clatter of glass rang through the night, but no one appeared. John Quincy saw Jennison leap toward him, something gleaming in his hand. Stepping aside, he threw himself on the man's back and forced him to his knees. He seized the wrist of Jennison's right hand, which held the automatic, in a firm grip. They kept that posture for a moment, and then Jennison began slowly to rise to his feet. The hand that held the pistol began to tear away.

John Quincy shut his teeth and sought to maintain his grip. But he was up against a more powerful antagonist than the red-haired sailor, he was outclassed, and the realization of it crept over him with a sickening force.

Jennison was on his feet now, the right hand nearly free. Another moment—what then, John Quincy wondered? This man had no intention of letting him go ashore; he had changed that plan the moment he put it into words. A muffled shot, and later in the night when the ship was well out on the Pacific—John Quincy thought of Boston, his mother. He thought of Carlota waiting his return. He summoned his strength for one last desperate effort to renew his grip.

Another moment—What then? John Quincy wondered.
From *The House Without a Key*, illustration by William Liepse
(*The Saturday Evening Post*, March 7, 1925)

A serene, ivory-colored face appeared suddenly at the broken window. An arm with a weapon was extended through the jagged opening.

"Relinquish the firearms, Mr. Jennison," commanded Charlie Chan, "or I am forced to make fatal insertion in vital organ belonging to you."

Jennison's pistol dropped to the floor, and John Quincy staggered back against the berth. At that instant the door opened and Hallet, followed by the detective, Spencer, came in.

"Hello, Winterslip, what are you doing here?" the captain said. He thrust a paper into one of the pockets of the green ulster. "Come along, Jennison," he said. "We want you."

Limply John Quincy followed them from the stateroom. Outside they were joined by Chan. At the top of the gangplank Hallet paused. "We'll wait a minute for Hepworth," he said.

John Quincy put his hand on Chan's shoulder. "Charlie, how can I ever thank you? You saved my life."

Chan bowed. "My own pleasure is not to be worded. I have saved a life here and there, but never before one that had beginning in cultured city of Boston. Always a happy item on the golden scroll of memory."

Hepworth came up. "It's all right," he said. "The captain has agreed to delay our sailing one hour. I'll go to the station with you."

On the way down the gangplank, Chan turned to John Quincy. "Speaking heartily for myself, I congratulate your bravery. It is clear you leaped upon this Jennison with vigorous and triumphant mood of heart. But he would have pushed you down. He would have conquered. And why? The answer is, such powerful wrists."

"A great surf-boarder, eh?" John Quincy said.

Chan looked at him keenly. "You are no person's fool. Ten years ago this Harry Jennison are champion swimmer in all Hawaii. I extract that news from ancient sporting pages of Honolulu journal. But he have not been in the water much here lately. Pursuing the truth further, not since the night he killed Dan Winterslip."

CHAPTER XXII

The Light Streams Through

THEY moved on through the pier-shed to the street, where Hepworth, Jennison and the three policemen got into Hallet's car. The captain turned to John Quincy.

"You coming, Mr. Winterslip?" he inquired.

"I've got my own car," the boy explained. "I'll follow you in that."

The roadster was not performing at its best, and he reached the station house a good five minutes after the policemen. He noted Dan Winterslip's big limousine parked in the street outside.

In Hallet's room he found the captain and Chan closeted with a third man. It took a second glance at the latter to identify him as Mr. Saladine, for the little man of the lost teeth now appeared a great deal younger than John Quincy had thought him.

"Ah, Mr. Winterslip," remarked Hallet. He turned to Saladine. "Say, Larry, you've got me into a heap of trouble with this boy. He accused me of trying to shield you. I wish you'd loosen up for him."

Saladine smiled. "Why, I don't mind. My job out here is about finished. Of course, Mr. Winterslip will keep what I tell him under his hat?"

"Naturally," replied John Quincy. He noticed that the man spoke with no trace of a lisp. "I perceive you've found your teeth," he added.

"Oh, yes—I found them in my trunk, where I put them the day I arrived at Waikiki," answered Saladine. "When my teeth were knocked out twenty years ago in a football game, I was broken-hearted, but the loss has been a great help to me in my work. A man hunting his bridge work in the water is a figure of ridicule and mirth. No one ever thinks of connecting him with serious affairs. He can prowl about a beach to his heart's content. Mr. Winterslip, I am a special agent of the Treasury Department sent out here to break up the opium ring. My name, of course, is not Saladine."

"Oh," said John Quincy, "I understand at last."

"I'm glad you do," remarked Hallet. "I don't know whether you're familiar with the way our opium smugglers work. The dope is brought in from the Orient on tramp steamers—the *Mary S. Allison*, for example. When they arrive off Waikiki they knock together a few small rafts and load 'em with tins of the stuff. A fleet of little boats, supposedly out there for the fishing, pick up these rafts and bring the dope ashore. It's taken down-town and hidden on ships bound for 'Frisco—usually those that ply only between here and the mainland, because they're not so closely watched at the other end. But it just happened that the quartermaster of the *President Tyler* is one of their go-betweens. We searched his cabin this evening and found it packed with the stuff."

"The quartermaster of the *President Tyler*," repeated John Quincy. "That's Dick Kaohla's friend."

"Yeah—I'm coming to Dick. He's been in charge of the pick-up fleet here. He was out on that business the night of the murder. Saladine saw him and told me all about it in that note, which was my reason for letting the boy go."

"I owe you an apology," John Quincy said.

"Oh, that's all right." Hallet was in great good humor. "Larry here has got some of the higher-ups, too. For instance, he's discovered that Jennison is the lawyer for the ring, defending any of them who are caught and brought before the commissioner. The fact has no bearing on Dan Winterslip's murder—unless Winterslip knew about it, and that was one of the reasons he didn't want Jennison to marry his girl."

Saladine stood up. "I'll turn the quartermaster over to you," he said. "In view of this other charge, you can of course have Jennison too. That's all for me. I'll go along."

"See you to-morrow, Larry," Hallet answered. Saladine went out, and the captain turned to John Quincy. "Well, my boy, this is our big night. I don't know what you were doing in Jennison's cabin, but if you'd picked him for the murderer, I'll say you're good."

"That's just what I'd done," John Quincy told him. "By the way, have you seen my aunt? She's got hold of a rather interesting bit of information—"

"I've seen her," Hallet said. "She's with the prosecutor now, telling it to him. By the way, Greene's waiting for us. Come along."

They went into the prosecutor's office. Greene was alert and eager, a stenographer was at his elbow, and Miss Minerva sat near his desk.

"Hello, Mr. Winterslip," he said. "What do you think of our police force now? Pretty good, eh, pretty good. Sit down, won't you?" He glanced through some papers on his desk while John Quincy, Hallet and Chan found chairs. "I don't mind telling you, this thing has knocked me all in a heap. Harry Jennison and I are old friends; I had lunch with him at the club only yesterday. I'm going to proceed a little differently than I would with an ordinary criminal."

John Quincy half rose from his chair. "Don't get excited," Greene smiled. "Jennison will get all that's coming to him, friendship or no friendship. What I mean is that if I can save the territory the expense of a long trial by dragging a confession out of him at once, I intend to do it. He's coming in here in a moment, and I propose to reveal my whole hand to him, from start to finish. That may seem foolish, but it isn't. For I hold aces, all aces, and he'll know it as quickly as any one."

The door opened. Spencer ushered Jennison into the room, and then withdrew. The accused man stood there, proud, haughty, defiant, a viking of the tropics, a blond giant at bay but unafraid.

"Hello, Jennison," Greene said. "I'm mighty sorry about this—"

"You ought to be," Jennison replied. "You're making an awful fool of yourself. What is this damned nonsense, anyhow—"

"Sit down," said the prosecutor sharply. He indicated a chair on the opposite side of the desk. He had already turned the shade on his desk lamp so the light would shine full in the face of any one sitting there. "That lamp bother you, Harry?" he asked.

"Why should it?" Jennison demanded.

"Good," smiled Greene. "I believe Captain Hallet served you with a warrant on the boat. Have you looked at it, by any chance?"

"I have."

The prosecutor leaned across the desk. "Murder, Jennison!"

Jennison's expression did not change. "Damned nonsense, as I told you. Why should I murder any one?"

"Ah, the motive," Greene replied. "You're quite right, we should begin with that. Do you wish to be represented here by counsel?"

Jennison shook his head. "I guess I'm lawyer enough to puncture this silly business," he replied.

"Very well." Greene turned to his stenographer. "Get this." The man nodded, and the prosecutor addressed Miss Minerva. "Miss Winterslip, we'll start with you."

Miss Minerva leaned forward. "Mr. Dan Winterslip's house on the beach has, as I told you, been offered for sale by his daughter. After dinner this evening a gentleman came to look at it—a prominent lawyer named Hailey. As we went over the house, Mr. Hailey mentioned that he had met Dan Winterslip on the street a week before his death, and that my cousin had spoken to him about coming in shortly to draw up a new will. He did not say what the provisions of the will were to be, nor did he ever carry out his intention."

"Ah yes," said Greene. "But Mr. Jennison here was your cousin's lawyer?"

"He was."

"If he wanted to draw a new will, he wouldn't ordinarily have gone to a stranger for that purpose."

"Not ordinarily. Unless he had some good reason."

"Precisely. Unless, for instance, the will had some connection with Harry Jennison."

"I object," Jennison cried. "This is mere conjecture."

"So it is," Greene answered. "But we're not in court. We can conjecture if we like. Suppose, Miss Winterslip, the will was concerned with Jennison in some way. What do you imagine the connection to have been?"

"I don't have to imagine," replied Miss Minerva. "I know."

"Ah, that's good. You know. Go on."

"Before I came down here to-night, I had a talk with my niece. She admitted that her father knew she and Jennison were in love, and that he had bitterly opposed the match. He had even gone so far as to say he would disinherit her if she went through with it."

"Then the new will Dan Winterslip intended to make would probably have been to the effect that in the event his daughter married Jennison, she was not to inherit a penny of his money?"

"There isn't any doubt of it," said Miss Minerva firmly.

"You asked for a motive, Jennison," Greene said. "That's motive enough for me. Everybody knows you're money mad. You wanted to marry Winterslip's daughter, the richest girl in the Islands. He said you couldn't have her—not with the money too. But you're not the sort to make a penniless marriage. You were determined to get both Barbara Winterslip and her father's property. Only one person stood in your way—Dan Winterslip. And that's how you happened to be on his lanai that Monday night—"

"Wait a minute," Jennison protested. "I wasn't on his lanai. I was on board the *President Tyler*, and everybody knows that ship didn't land its passengers until nine the following morning—"

"I'm coming to that," Greene told him. "Just now—by the way, what time is it?"

Jennison took from his pocket a watch on the end of a slender chain. "It's a quarter past nine."

"Ah, yes. Is that the watch you usually carry?"

"It is."

"Ever wear a wrist watch?"

Jennison hesitated. "Occasionally."

"Only occasionally." The prosecutor rose and came round his desk. "Let me see your left wrist, please."

Jennison held out his arm. It was tanned a deep brown, but on the wrist was etched in white the outline of a watch and its encircling strap.

Greene smiled. "Yes, you have worn a wrist watch—and you've worn it pretty constantly, from the look of things." He took a small object from his pocket and held it in front of Jennison. "This watch, perhaps?" Jennison regarded it stonily. "Ever see it before?" Greene asked. "No? Well, suppose we try it on, anyhow." He put the watch in position and fastened it. "I can't help noting, Harry," he continued, "that it fits rather neatly over that white outline on your wrist And the prong of the buckle falls naturally into the most worn of the holes on the strap."

"What of that?" asked Jennison.

"Oh, coincidence, probably. You have abnormally large wrists, however. Surf-boarding, swimming, eh? But that's something else I'll speak of later." He turned to Miss Minerva. "Will you please come over here, Miss Winterslip."

She came, and as she reached his side, the prosecutor suddenly bent over and switched off the light on his desk. Save for a faint glimmer through a transom, the room was in darkness. Miss Minerva was conscious of dim huddled figures, a circle of white faces, a tense silence. The prosecutor was lifting something slowly toward her startled eyes. A watch, worn on a human wrist—a watch with an illuminated dial on which the figure two was almost obliterated.

"Look at that and tell me," came the prosecutor's voice. "You have seen it before?"

"I have," she answered firmly.

"Where?"

"In the dark in Dan Winterslip's living-room just after midnight the thirtieth of June."

Greene flashed on the light. "Thank you, Miss Winterslip." He retired behind his desk and pressed a button. "You identify it by some distinguishing mark, I presume?"

"I do. The numeral two, which is pretty well obscured."

Spencer appeared at the door. "Send the Spaniard in," Greene ordered. "That is all for the present, Miss Winterslip."

Cabrera entered, and his eyes were frightened as they looked at Jennison. At a nod from the prosecutor, Chan removed the wrist watch and handed it to the Spaniard.

"You know that watch, Jose?" Greene asked.

"I—I—yes," answered the boy.

"Don't be afraid," Greene urged. "Nobody's going to hurt you. I want you to repeat the story you told me this afternoon. You have no regular job. You're a sort of confidential errand boy for Mr. Jennison here."

"I was."

"Yes—that's all over now. You can speak out. On the morning of Wednesday, July second, you were in Mr. Jennison's office. He gave you this wrist watch and told you to take it out and get it repaired. Something was the matter with it. It wasn't running. You took it to a big jewelry store. What happened?"

"The man said it is very badly hurt. To fix it would cost more than a new watch. I go back and tell Mr. Jennison. He laugh and say it is mine as a gift."

"Precisely." Greene referred to a paper on his desk. "Late in the afternoon of Thursday, July third, you sold the watch. To whom?"

"To Lau Ho, Chinese jeweler in Maunakea Street. On Saturday evening maybe six o'clock Mr. Jennison telephone my home, much excited. Must have watch again, and will pay any price. I speed to Lau Ho's store. Watch is sold once more, now to unknown Japanese. Late at night I see Mr. Jennison and he curse me with anger. Get the watch, he says. I have been hunting, but I could not find it."

Greene turned to Jennison. "You were a little careless with that watch, Harry. But no doubt you figured you were pretty safe—you had your alibi. Then, too, when Hallet detailed the clues to you on Winterslip's lanai the morning after the crime, he forgot to mention that some one had seen the watch. It was one of those happy accidents that are all we have to count on in this work. By Saturday night you realized your danger—just how you discovered it I don't know—"

"I do," John Quincy interrupted.

"What! What's that?" said Greene.

"On Saturday afternoon," John Quincy told him, "I played golf with Mr. Jennison. On our way back to town, we talked over the clues in this case, and I happened to mention the wrist watch. I can see now it was the first he had heard of it. He was to dine with us at the beach, but he asked to be put down at his office to sign a few letters. I waited below. It must have been then that he called up this young man in an effort to locate the watch."

"Great stuff," said Greene enthusiastically. "That finishes the watch, Jennison. I'm surprised you wore it, but you probably knew that it would be vital to you to keep track of the time, and you figured, rightly, that it would not be immediately affected by the salt water—"

"What the devil are you talking about?" demanded Jennison.

Again Greene pressed a button on his desk. Spencer appeared at once. "Take this Spaniard," the prosecutor directed, "and bring in Hepworth and the quartermaster." He turned again to Jennison. "I'll show you what I'm talking about in just a minute. On the night of June thirtieth you were a passenger on the *President Tyler*, which was lying by until dawn out near the channel entrance?"

"I was."

"No passengers were landed from that ship until the following morning?"

"That's a matter of record."

"Very well." The second officer of the *President Tyler* came in, followed by a big hulking sailorman John Quincy recognized as the quartermaster of that vessel. He was interested to note a ring on the man's right hand, and his mind went back to that encounter in the San Francisco attic.

"Mr. Hepworth," the prosecutor began, "on the night of June thirtieth your ship reached this port too late to dock. You anchored off Waikiki. On such an occasion, who is on deck—say, from midnight on?"

"The second officer," Hepworth told him. "In this case, myself. Also the quartermaster."

"The accommodation ladder is let down the night before?"

"Usually, yes. It was let down that night."

"Who is stationed near it?"

"The quartermaster."

"Ah, yes. You were in charge then on the night of June thirtieth. Did you notice anything unusual on that occasion?"

Hepworth nodded. "I did. The quartermaster appeared to be under the influence of liquor. At three o'clock I found him dozing near the accommodation ladder. I roused him. When I came back from checking up the anchor bearings before turning in at dawn—about four-thirty—he was dead to the world. I put him in his cabin, and the following morning I of course reported him."

"You noticed nothing else out of the ordinary?"

"Nothing, sir," Hepworth replied.

"Thank you very much. Now, you—" Greene turned to the quartermaster. "You were drunk on duty the night of June thirtieth. Where did you get the booze?" The man hesitated. "Before you say anything, let me give you a bit of advice. The truth, my man. You're in pretty bad already. I'm not making any promises, but if you talk straight here it may help you in that other matter. If you lie, it will go that much harder with you."

"I ain't going to lie," promised the quartermaster.

"All right. Where did you get your liquor?"

The man nodded toward Jennison. "He gave it to me."

"He did, eh? Tell me all about it."

"I met him on deck just after midnight—we was still moving. I knew him before—him and me—"

"In the opium game, both of you. I understand that. You met him on deck—"

"I did, and he says, you're on watch to-night, eh, and I says I am. So he slips me a little bottle an' says, this will help you pass the time. I ain't a drinking man, so help me I ain't, an' I took just a nip, but there was something in that whiskey, I'll swear to it. My head was all funny like, an' the next I knew I was waked up in my cabin with the bad news I was wanted above."

"What became of that bottle?"

"I dropped it overboard on my way to see the captain. I didn't want nobody to find it."

"Did you see anything the night of June thirtieth? Anything peculiar?"

"I seen plenty, sir—but it was that drink. Nothing you would want to hear about."

"All right." The prosecutor turned to Jennison. "Well, Harry—you drugged him, didn't you? Why? Because you were going ashore, eh? Because you knew he'd be on duty at that ladder when you returned, and you didn't want him to see you. So you dropped something into that whiskey—"

"Guess work," cut in Jennison, still unruffled. "I used to have some respect for you as a lawyer, but it's all gone now. If this is the best you can offer—"

"But it isn't," said Greene pleasantly. Again he pushed the button. "I've something much better, Harry, if you'll only wait." He turned to Hepworth. "There's a steward on your ship named Bowker," he began, and John Quincy thought that Jennison stiffened. "How has he been behaving lately?"

"Well, he got pretty drunk in Hong-kong," Hepworth answered. "But that, of course, was the money."

"What money?"

"It's this way. The last time we sailed out of Honolulu harbor for the Orient, over two weeks ago, I was in the purser's office. It was just as we were passing Diamond Head. Bowker came in, and he had a big fat envelope that he wanted to deposit in the purser's safe. He said it contained a lot of money. The purser wouldn't be responsible for it without seeing it, so Bowker slit the envelope—and there were ten one hundred dollar bills. The purser made another package of it and put it in the safe. He told me Bowker took out a couple of the bills when we reached Hong-kong."

"Where would a man like Bowker get all that money?"

"I can't imagine. He said he'd put over a business deal in Honolulu but—well, we knew Bowker."

The door opened. Evidently Spencer guessed who was wanted this time, for he pushed Bowker into the room. The steward of the *President Tyler* was bedraggled and bleary.

"Hello, Bowker," said the prosecutor. "Sober now, aren't you?"

"I'll tell the world I am," replied Bowker. "They've walked me to San Francisco and back. Can—can I sit down?"

"Of course," Greene smiled. "This afternoon, while you were still drunk, you told a story to Willie Chan, out at Okamoto's auto stand on Kalakaua Avenue. Later on, early this evening, you repeated it to Captain Hallet and me. I'll have to ask you to go over it again."

Bowker glanced toward Jennison, then quickly looked away. "Always ready to oblige," he answered.

"You're a steward on the *President Tyler*," Greene continued. "On your last trip over here from the mainland Mr. Jennison occupied one of your rooms—number 97. He was alone in it, I believe?"

"All alone. He paid extra for the privilege, I hear. Always traveled that way."

"Room 97 was on the main deck, not far from the accommodation ladder?"

"Yes, that's right."

"Tell us what happened after you anchored off Waikiki the night of June thirtieth."

Bowker adjusted his gold-rimmed glasses with the gesture of a man about to make an after-dinner speech. "Well, I was up pretty late that night. Mr. Winterslip here had loaned me some books—there was one I was particularly interested in. I wanted to finish it so I could give it to him to take ashore in the morning. It was nearly two o'clock when I finally got through it, and I was feeling stuffy, so I went on deck for a breath of air."

"You stopped not far from the accommodation ladder?"

"Yes sir, I did."

"Did you notice the quartermaster?"

"Yes—he was sound asleep in a deck chair. I went over and leaned on the rail, the ladder was just beneath me. I'd been standing there a few minutes when suddenly somebody came up out of the water and put his hands on the lowest rung. I drew back quickly and stood in a shadow.

"Well, pretty soon this man comes creeping up the ladder to the deck. He was barefooted, and all in black—black pants and shirt. I watched him. He went over and bent above the quartermaster, then started toward me down the deck. He was walking on tiptoe, but even then I didn't get wise to the fact anything was wrong.

"I stepped out of the shadow. 'Fine night for a swim, Mr. Jennison,' I said. And I saw at once that I'd made a social error. He gave one jump in my direction and his hands closed on my throat. I thought my time had come."

"He was wet, wasn't he?" Greene asked.

"Dripping. He left a trail of water on the deck."

"Did you notice a watch on his wrist?"

"Yes, but you can bet I didn't make any study of it. I had other things to think about just then. I managed to sort of ooze out of his grip, and I told him to cut it out or I'd yell. 'Look here,' he says, 'you and I can talk business, I guess. Come into my cabin.'

"But I wasn't wanting any tête-à-tête with him in any cabin, I said I'd see him in the morning, and after I'd promised to say nothing to anybody, he let me go. I went to bed, pretty much puzzled.

"The next morning, when I went into his cabin, there he was all fresh and rosy and smiling. If I'd had so much as a whiff of booze the night before, I'd have thought I never saw what I did. I went in there thinking I might get a hundred dollars out of the affair, but the minute he spoke I began to smell important money. He said no one must know about his swim the night before. How much did I want? Well, I held my breath and said ten thousand dollars. And I nearly dropped dead when he answered I could have it."

Bowker turned to John Quincy. "I don't know what you'll think of me. I don't know what Tim would think. I'm not a crook by nature. But I was fed up and choking over that steward job. I wanted a little newspaper of my own, and up to that minute

I couldn't see myself getting it. And you must remember that I didn't know then what was in the air—murder. Later, when I did find out, I was scared to breathe. I didn't know what they could do to me." He turned to Greene. "That's all fixed," he said.

"I've promised you immunity," the prosecutor answered. "I'll keep my word. Go on—you agreed to accept the ten thousand?"

"I did. I went to his office at twelve. One of the conditions was that I could stay on the *President Tyler* until she got back to San Francisco, and after that I was never to show my face out this way again. It suited me. Mr. Jennison introduced me to this Cabrera, who was to chaperon me the rest of that day. I'll say he did. When I went aboard the ship, he handed me a thousand dollars in an envelope.

"When I came back this time, I was to spend the day with Cabrera and get the other nine grand when I sailed. This morning when we tied up I saw the Spaniard on the dock, but by the time I'd landed he had disappeared. I met this Willie Chan and we had a large day. This fusel oil they sell out here loosened my tongue, but I'm not sorry. Of course, the rosy dream has faded, and it's my flat feet on the deck from now to the end of time. But the shore isn't so much any more, with all the bar-rooms under cover, and this sea life keeps a man out in the open air. As I say, I'm not sorry I talked. I can look any man in the eye again and tell him to go to—" He glanced at Miss Minerva. "Madam, I will not name the precise locality."

Greene stood. "Well, Jennison, there's my case. I've tipped it all off to you, but I wanted you to see for yourself how air-tight it is. There are two courses open to you—you can let this go to trial with a plea of not guilty. A long humiliating ordeal for you. Or you can confess here and now and throw yourself on the mercy of the court. If you're the sensible man I think you are, that's what you'll do."

Jennison did not answer, did not even look at the prosecutor. "It was a very neat idea," Greene went on. "I'll grant you that. Only one thing puzzles me—did it come as the inspiration of the moment or did you plan it all out in advance? You've been over to the mainland rather often of late—were you waiting your chance? Anyhow, it came, didn't it—it came at last. And for a swimmer like you, child's play. You didn't need that ladder when you left the vessel—perhaps you went overboard while the *President Tyler* was still moving. A quick silent dive, a little way under water in case any one was watching from the deck, and then a long but easy swim ashore. And there you were, on the beach at Waikiki. Not far away Dan Winterslip was asleep on his lanai, with not so much as a locked door between you. Dan Winterslip, who stood between you and what you wanted. A little struggle—a quick thrust of your knife. Come on, Jennison, don't be a fool. It's the best way out for you now. A full confession."

Jennison leaped to his feet, his eyes flashing. "I'll see you in hell first!" he cried.

"Very well—if you feel that way about it—" Greene turned his back upon him and began a low-toned conversation with Hallet. Jennison and Charlie Chan were together on one side of the desk. Chan took out a pencil and accidentally dropped it on the floor. He stooped to pick it up.

John Quincy saw that the butt of a pistol carried in Chan's hip pocket protruded from under his coat. He saw Jennison spring forward and snatch the gun. With a cry John Quincy moved nearer, but Greene seized his arm and held him. Charlie Chan seemed unaccountably oblivious to what was going on.

Jennison put the muzzle of the pistol to his forehead and pulled the trigger. A sharp click—and that was all. The pistol fell from his hand.

"That's it!" cried Greene triumphantly. "That's my confession, and not a word spoken. I've witnesses, Jennison—they all saw you—you couldn't stand the disgrace a man in your position—you tried to kill yourself. With an empty gun." He went over and patted Chan on the shoulder. "A great idea, Charlie," he said. "Chan thought of it," he added to Jennison. "The Oriental mind, Harry. Rather subtle, isn't it?"

But Jennison had dropped back into his chair and buried his face in his hands.

"I'm sorry," said Greene gently. "But we've got you. Maybe you'll talk now."

Jennison looked up slowly. The defiance was gone from his face; it was lined and old.

"Maybe I will," he said hoarsely.

CHAPTER XXIII

Moonlight at the Crossroads

They filed out, leaving Jennison with Greene and the stenographer. In the anteroom Chan approached John Quincy.

"You go home decked in the shining garments of success," he said. "One thought are tantalizing me. At simultaneous moment you arrive at same conclusion we do. To reach there you must have leaped across considerable cavity."

John Quincy laughed. "I'll say I did. It came to me to-night. First, some one mentioned a golf professional with big wrists who drove a long ball. I had a quick flash of Jennison on the links here, and his terrific drives. Big wrists, they told me, meant that a man was proficient in the water. Then some one else—a young woman—spoke of a champion swimmer who left a ship off Waikiki. That was the first time the idea of such a thing had occurred to me. I was pretty warm then, and I felt Bowker was the man who could verify my suspicion. When I rushed aboard the *President Tyler* to find him, I saw Jennison about to sail and that confirmed my theory. I went after him."

"A brave performance," commented Chan.

"But as you can see, Charlie, I didn't have an iota of real evidence. Just guesswork. You were the one who furnished the proof."

"Proof are essential in this business," Chan replied.

"I'm tantalized too, Charlie. I remember you in the library. You were on the crack long before I was. How come?"

Chan grinned. "Seated at our ease in All American Restaurant that first night, you will recall I spoke of Chinese people as sensitive, like camera film. A look, a laugh, a gesture, something go click. Bowker enters and hovering above, says with alcoholic accent, 'I'm my own mashter, ain't I?' In my mind, the click. He is not own master. I follow to dock, behold when Spaniard present envelope. But for days I am fogged. I can only learn Cabrera and Jennison are very close. Clues continue to burst in our countenance. The occasion remains suspensive. At the Library I read of Jennison the fine swimmer. After that, the watch, and triumph."

Miss Minerva moved on toward the door. "May I have great honor to accompany you to car?" asked Chan.

Outside, John Quincy directed the chauffeur to return alone to Waikiki with the limousine. "You're riding out with me," he told his aunt. "I want to talk with you."

She turned to Charlie Chan. "I congratulate you. You've got brains, and they count."

He bowed low. "From you that compliment glows rosy red. At this moment of parting, my heart droops. My final wish—the snowy chilling days of winter and the scorching windless days of summer—may they all be the springtime for you."

"You're very kind," she said softly.

John Quincy took his hand. "It's been great fun knowing you, Charlie," he remarked.

"You will go again to the mainland," Chan said. "The angry ocean rolling between us. Still I shall carry the memory of your friendship like a flower in my heart." John Quincy climbed into the car. "And the parting may not be eternal," Chan added cheerfully. "The joy of travel may yet be mine. I shall look forward to the day when I may call upon you in your home and shake a healthy hand."

John Quincy started the car and slipping away, they left Charlie Chan standing like a great Buddha on the curb.

"Poor Barbara," said Miss Minerva presently. "I dread to face her with this news. But then, it's not altogether news at that. She told me she'd been conscious of something wrong between her and Jennison ever since they landed. She didn't think he killed her father, but she believed he was involved in it somehow. She is planning to settle with Brade to-morrow and leave the next day, probably for ever. I've persuaded her to come to Boston for a long visit. You'll see her there."

John Quincy shook his head. "No, I shan't. But thanks for reminding me. I must go to the cable office at once."

When he emerged from the office and again entered the car, he was smiling happily.

"In San Francisco," he explained, "Roger accused me of being a Puritan survival. He ran over a little list of adventures he said had never happened to me. Well, most of them have happened now, and I cabled to tell him so. I also said I'd take that job with him."

Miss Minerva frowned. "Think it over carefully," she warned. "San Francisco isn't Boston. The cultural standard is, I fancy, much lower. You'll be lonely there—"

"Oh, no, I shan't. Some one will be there with me. At least, I hope she will."

"Agatha?"

"No, not Agatha. The cultural standard was too low for her. She's broken our engagement."

"Barbara, then?"

"Not Barbara, either."

"But I have sometimes thought—"

"You thought Barbara sent Jennison packing because of me. Jennison thought so too—it's all clear now. That was why he tried to frighten me into leaving Honolulu, and set his opium running friends on me when I wouldn't go. But Barbara is not in love with me. We understand now why she broke her engagement."

"Neither Agatha nor Barbara," repeated Miss Minerva. "Then who—"

"You haven't met her yet, but that happy privilege will be yours before you sleep. The sweetest girl in the Islands—or in the world. The daughter of Jim Egan, whom you have been heard to refer to as a glorified beach-comber."

Again Miss Minerva frowned. "It's a great risk, John Quincy. She hasn't our background—"

"No, and that's a pleasant change. She's the niece of your old friend—you knew that?"

"I did," answered Miss Minerva softly.

"Your dear friend of the 'eighties. What was it you said to me? If your chance ever comes—"

"I hope you will be very happy," his aunt said. "When you write it to your mother, be sure and mention Captain Cope of the British Admiralty. Poor Grace! That will be all she'll have to cling to—after the wreck."

"What wreck?"

"The wreck of all her hopes for you."

"Nonsense. Mother will understand. She knows I'm a roaming Winterslip, and when we roam, we roam."

They found Madame Maynard seated in her living-room with a few of her more elderly guests. From the beach came the sound of youthful revelry.

"Well my boy," the old woman cried, "it appears you couldn't stay away from your policemen friends one single evening, after all. I give you up."

John Quincy laughed. "I'm pau now. By the way, Carlota Egan—is she—"

"They're all out there somewhere," the hostess said. "They came in for a bit of supper—by the way, there are sandwiches in the dining-room and—"

"Not just now," said John Quincy. "Thank you so much. I'll see you again, of course—"

He dashed out on the sand. A group of young people under the hau tree informed him that Carlota Egan was on the farthest float. Alone? Well, no—that naval lieutenant—

He was, he reflected as he hurried on toward the water, a bit fed up with the navy. That was hardly the attitude he should have taken, considering all the navy had done for him. But it was human. And John Quincy was human at last.

For an instant he stood at the water's edge. His bathing suit was in the dressing-room, but he never gave it a thought. He kicked off his shoes, tossed aside his coat, and plunged into the breakers. The blood of the wandering Winterslips was racing through his veins; hot blood that tropical waters had ever been powerless to cool.

Sure enough, Carlota Egan and Lieutenant Booth were together on the float. John Quincy climbed up beside them.

"Well, I'm back," he announced.

"I'll tell the world you're back," said the lieutenant. "And all wet, too."

They sat there. Across a thousand miles of warm water the trade winds came to fan their cheeks. Just above the horizon hung the Southern Cross; the Island lights trembled along the shore;

the yellow eye on Diamond Head was winking. A gorgeous setting. Only one thing was wrong with it. It seemed rather crowded.

John Quincy had an inspiration. "Just as I hit the water," he remarked, "I thought I heard you say something about my dive. Didn't you like it?"

"It was rotten," replied the lieutenant amiably.

"You offered to show me what was wrong with it, I believe?"

"Sure. If you want me to."

"By all means," said John Quincy. "Learn one thing every day. That's my motto."

Lieutenant Booth went to the end of the springboard. "In the first place, always keep your ankles close together—like this."

"I've got you," answered John Quincy.

"And hold your arms tight against your ears."

"The tighter the better, as far as I'm concerned."

"Then double up like a jackknife," continued the instructor. He doubled up like a jackknife and rose into the air.

At the same instant John Quincy seized the girl's hands. "Listen to me. I can't wait another second. I want to tell you that I love you—"

"You're mad," she cried.

"Mad about you. Ever since that day on the ferry—"

"But your people?"

"What about my people? It's just you and I—we'll live in San Francisco—that is, if you love me—"

"Well, I—"

"In heaven's name, be quick. That human submarine is floating around here under us. You love me, don't you? You'll marry me?"

"Yes."

He took her in his arms and kissed her. Only the wandering Winterslips could kiss like that. The stay-at-homes had always secretly begrudged them the accomplishment.

The girl broke away at last, breathless. "Johnnie!" she cried.

A sputter beside them, and Lieutenant Booth climbed on to the float, moist and panting. "Wha's that?" he gurgled.

"She was speaking to me," cried John Quincy triumphantly.

The House Without a Key *on Film*

Between 1926 and 1981, Charlie Chan appeared in fifty-three films, all explored in detail in Charles P. Mitchell's definitive *A Guide to Charlie Chan Films* (Westport, CT, and London: Greenwood Press, 1999). The first, *The House Without a Key*, was made by Pathé and released as a ten-chapter serial in November 1926; it has subsequently been lost. Mitchell provides the following information about the film:

"The basic plot [of the novel] was considerably altered, and concentrated on a chest that contained evidence of a twenty year old crime committed by one of a pair of rival brothers. The struggle for possession of this enigmatic chest made up the main action of the plot throughout the serial. The lead performer was screen veteran Walter Miller, former leading man for D. W. Griffith.

"The very first screen Chan was played by a Japanese actor named George Kuwa, who had appeared in bit parts in many productions such as the Rudolph Valentino film *Moran of the Lady Letty* (1922). His participation in the story was reduced to a minor, background character. Kuwa played Charlie as clean-shaven, wearing a dark business suit and an occasional white hat. Chan received eleventh billing in the original cast list."

The chapter titles were:

1. The Spite Fence
2. The Mystery Box

3. The Missing Numeral
4. Suspicion
5. The Death Buoy
6. Sinister Shadows
7. The Mystery Man
8. The Spotted Menace
9. The Wrist Watch
10. The Culprit

A summary of each chapter may be found in Jim Stringham's "Charlie Chan's Number One Movie," which first appeared in *Cliffhangers* 21 (May 1995) and is reprinted here: http://charliechanfamily.tripod.com/id90.html.

THE BENSON MURDER CASE

A PHILO VANCE STORY

D. D. 10

NAME BENSON, Alvin H.

(Surname First)

ADDRESS 87 West 48th St.

CLASSIFICATION NUMBER	PRECINCT NUMBER	COMPLAINT NUMBER	DATE REPORTED
B-266	9	8427	June 14

REMARKS Murder: Shot through head with

45 Colt automatic. Body discovered

7 a.m. by Anna Platz.

IN CHARGE Homicide Bureau and District Attorney.

NEW YORK POLICE DEPARTMENT   INDEX OF HOMICIDES

S.S. VAN DINE

Facsimile first-edition dust jacket for *The Benson Murder Case*

THE BENSON MURDER CASE[1]

A Philo Vance Story

BY

S. S. VAN DINE

"Mr. Mason," he said, "I wish to thank you for my life."

"Sir," said Mason. "I had no interest in your life. The adjustment

of your problem was the only thing of interest to me."

—*Randolph Mason: Corrector of Destinies*[2]

1.   First published in October 1926.

2.   The correct title is *The Corrector of Destinies: Being Tales of Randolph Mason, as Related
by his Private Secretary Courtlandt Parks,* by
Melville Davisson Post (1908). The collection
of stories is a followup to Post's *The Strange
Adventures of Randolph Mason* (1896).

Contents

Publisher's Note

I t gives us considerable pleasure to be able to offer to the public the "inside" record of those of former District Attorney Markham's criminal cases in which Mr. Philo Vance figured so effectively. The true inwardness of these famous cases has never before been revealed; for Mr. S. S. Van Dine, Mr. Vance's lawyer and almost constant companion, being the only person who possessed a complete record of the facts, has only recently been permitted to make them public.

After inspecting Mr. Van Dine's voluminous notes, we decided to publish "The Benson Murder Case" as the first of the series—not because it was the most interesting and startling, nor yet the most complicated and dramatic from the fictional point of view, but because, coming first chronologically, it explains how Mr. Philo Vance happened to become involved in criminal matters, and also because it possesses certain features that reveal very clearly Mr. Vance's unique analytic methods of crime detection.

Introductory

If you will refer to the municipal statistics of the City of New York, you will find that the number of unsolved major crimes during the four years that John F.-X. Markham was District Attorney, was far smaller than under any of his predecessors' administrations. Markham projected the District Attorney's office into all manner of criminal investigations; and, as a result, many abstruse crimes on which the Police had hopelessly gone aground, were eventually disposed of.

But although he was personally credited with the many important indictments and subsequent convictions that he secured, the truth is that he was only an instrument in many of his most famous cases. The man who actually solved them and supplied the evidence for their prosecution, was in no way connected with the city's administration, and never once came into the public eye.

At that time I happened to be both legal advisor and personal friend of this other man; and it was thus that the strange and amazing facts of the situation became known to me. But not until recently have I been at liberty to make them public. Even now I am not permitted to divulge the man's name, and, for that reason, I have chosen, arbitrarily, to refer to him throughout these *ex-officio* reports as Philo Vance.

It is, of course, possible that some of his acquaintances may, through my revelations, be able to guess his identity; and if such should prove the case, I beg of them to guard that knowledge; for though he has now gone to Italy to live, and has given me permission to record the exploits of which he was the unique central character, he has very emphatically imposed his anonymity upon me; and I should not like to feel that, through any lack of discretion or delicacy, I have been the cause of his secret becoming generally known.

The present chronicle has to do with Vance's solution of the notorious Benson murder which, due to the unexpectedness of the crime, the prominence of the persons involved, and the startling evidence adduced, was invested with an interest rarely surpassed in the annals of New York's criminal history.

This sensational case was the first of many in which Vance figured as a kind of *amicus curiæ* in Markham's investigations.

S. S. VAN DINE.
New York.

Characters of the Book

Philo Vance

John F.-X. Markham
    District Attorney of New York County.

Alvin H. Benson
    Well known Wall Street broker and man-about-town,
    who was mysteriously murdered in his home.

Major Anthony Benson
    Brother of the murdered man.

Mrs. Anna Platz
    Housekeeper for Alvin Benson.

Muriel St. Clair
    A young singer.

Captain Philip Leacock
    Miss St. Clair's fiancé.

Leander Pfyfe
    Intimate friend of Alvin Benson's.

Mrs. Paula Banning
    A friend of Leander Pfyfe's.

Elsie Hoffman
    Secretary of the firm of Benson and Benson.

Colonel Bigsby Ostrander
    A retired army officer.

William H. Moriarty
    An alderman, Borough of the Bronx.

Jack Prisco
    Elevator-boy at the Chatham Arms.

George G. Stitt
    Of the firm of Stitt and McCoy, Public Accountants.

Maurice Dinwiddie
    Assistant District Attorney.

Chief Inspector O'Brien
    Of the Police Department of New York City.
William M. Moran
    Commanding Officer of the Detective Bureau.
Ernest Heath
    Sergeant of the Homicide Bureau.
Burke
    Detective of the Homicide Bureau.
Snitkin
    Detective of the Homicide Bureau.
Emery
    Detective of the Homicide Bureau.
Ben Hanlon
    Commanding Officer of Detectives assigned to District
    Attorney's office.
Phelps
    Detective assigned to District Attorney's office.
Tracy
    Detective assigned to District Attorney's office.
Springer
    Detective assigned to District Attorney's office.
Higginbotham
    Detective assigned to District Attorney's office.
Captain Carl Hagedorn
    Fire-arms expert.
Dr. Doremus
    Medical Examiner.
Francis Swacker
    Secretary to the District Attorney.
Currie
    Vance's valet.

CHAPTER I

Philo Vance at Home

(Friday, June 14;[3] 8.30 a.m.)

I t happened that, on the morning of the momentous June the fourteenth when the discovery of the murdered body of Alvin H. Benson created a sensation which, to this day, has not entirely died away, I had breakfasted with Philo Vance in his apartment. It was not unusual for me to share Vance's luncheons and dinners, but to have breakfast with him was something of an occasion. He was a late riser, and it was his habit to remain *incommunicado* until his midday meal.

The reason for this early meeting was a matter of business—or, rather, of æsthetics. On the afternoon of the previous day Vance had attended a preview of Vollard's[4] collection of Cézanne water-colors at the Kessler Galleries,[5] and having seen several pictures he particularly wanted, he had invited me to an early breakfast to give me instructions regarding their purchase.

A word concerning my relationship with Vance is necessary to clarify my rôle of narrator in this chronicle. The legal tradition is deeply imbedded in my family, and when my preparatory-school days were over, I was sent, almost as a matter of course, to Harvard to study law. It was there I met Vance, a reserved, cynical and caustic freshman who was the bane of his professors and the fear of his fellowclassmen. Why he should have chosen me, of all the students at the University, for his extra-scholastic association,

3.   June 14 was a Friday in 1918 and not again until 1929. As will be seen, there is other evidence supporting a 1918 date.

4.   Ambroise Vollard (1866–1939) was an important French art dealer and collector who championed the Impressionist Paul Cézanne as well as Pierre-Auguste Renoir, Pablo Picasso, André Derain, Georges Rouault, Paul Gauguin, Vincent van Gogh, and other contemporary French artists at the beginning of the twentieth century.

Ambroise Vollard, 1910.

5.   These appear to be fictional.

I have never been able to understand fully. My own liking for Vance was simply explained: he fascinated and interested me, and supplied me with a novel kind of intellectual diversion. In his liking for me, however, no such basis of appeal was present. I was (and am now) a commonplace fellow, possessed of a conservative and rather conventional mind. But, at least, my mentality was not rigid, and the ponderosity of the legal procedure did not impress me greatly—which is why, no doubt, I had little taste for my inherited profession—; and it is possible that these traits found certain affinities in Vance's unconscious mind. There is, to be sure, the less consoling explanation that I appealed to Vance as a kind of foil, or anchorage, and that he sensed in my nature a complementary antithesis to his own. But whatever the explanation, we were much together; and, as the years went by, that association ripened into an inseparable friendship.

Upon graduation I entered my father's law firm—Van Dine and Davis—and after five years of dull apprenticeship I was taken into the firm as the junior partner. At present I am the second Van Dine of Van Dine, Davis and Van Dine, with offices at 120 Broadway. At about the time my name first appeared on the letterheads of the firm, Vance returned from Europe, where he had been living during my legal novitiate, and, an aunt of his having died and made him her principal beneficiary, I was called upon to discharge the technical obligations involved in putting him in possession of his inherited property.

This work was the beginning of a new and somewhat unusual relationship between us. Vance had a strong distaste for any kind of business transaction, and in time I became the custodian of all his monetary interests and his agent at large. I found that his affairs were various enough to occupy as much of my time as I cared to give to legal matters, and as Vance was able to indulge the luxury of having a personal legal factotum, so to speak, I permanently closed my desk at the office, and devoted myself exclusively to his needs and whims.

If, up to the time when Vance summoned me to discuss the purchase of the Cézannes, I had harbored any secret or repressed regrets for having deprived the firm of Van Dine, Davis and Van Dine of my modest legal talents, they were permanently banished on that eventful morning; for, beginning with the notorious Benson murder, and extending over a period of nearly four years, it was my privilege to be a spectator of what I believe was the most amazing series of criminal cases that ever passed before the eyes of a young lawyer. Indeed, the grim dramas I witnessed during that period constitute one of the most astonishing secret documents in the police history of this country.

Of these dramas Vance was the central character. By an analytical and interpretative process which, as far as I know, has never before been applied to criminal activities, he succeeded in solving many of the important crimes on which both the police and the District Attorney's office had hopelessly fallen down.

Due to my peculiar relations with Vance it happened that not only did I participate in all the cases with which he was connected, but I was also present at most of the informal discussions concerning them which took place between him and the District Attorney; and, being of methodical temperament, I kept a fairly complete record of them.[6] In addition, I noted down (as accurately as memory permitted) Vance's unique psychological methods of determining guilt, as he explained them from time to time. It is fortunate that I performed this gratuitous labor of accumulation and transcription, for now that circumstances have unexpectedly rendered possible my making the cases public, I am able to present them in full detail and with all their various sidelights and succeeding steps—a task that would be impossible were it not for my numerous clippings and *adversaria*.[7]

Fortunately, too, the first case to draw Vance into its ramifications was that of Alvin Benson's murder. Not only did it prove one of the most famous of New York's *causes célèbres*, but it gave Vance an excellent opportunity of displaying his rare talents of deductive reasoning, and, by its nature and magnitude, aroused his interest in a branch of activity which heretofore had been alien to his temperamental promptings and habitual predilections.

The case intruded upon Vance's life suddenly and unexpectedly, although he himself had, by a casual request made to the District Attorney over a month before, been the involuntary agent of this destruction of his normal routine. The thing, in fact, burst upon us before we had quite finished our breakfast on that mid-June morning, and put an end temporarily to all business connected with the purchase of the Cézanne paintings. When, later in the day, I visited the Kessler Galleries, two of the water-colors that Vance had particularly desired had been sold; and I am convinced

6. John Loughery, in his monumental *Alias S. S. Van Dine: The Man Who Created Philo Vance* (New York: Charles Scribner's Sons, 1992), notes that "Van Dine is a noncharacter, a mute observer and recorder of events who is not allowed to speak—not once—in his own voice in the dialogue of the stories. Unlike, Watson, Hastings, Polton, Archie Goodwin, or any other narrator of comparable importance before or after him Van Dine—a lawyer and a prosaic soul—hasn't been given a trace of a personality himself. He is unmercifully silenced" (p. 177).

7. Originally, a book of accounts—credits and debits—but colloquially, a book of comments or notes.

8.   This appears to be a fictional investment.

that, despite his success in the unravelling of the Benson murder mystery and his saving of at least one innocent person from arrest, he has never to this day felt entirely compensated for the loss of those two little sketches on which he had set his heart.

As I was ushered into the living-room that morning by Currie, a rare old English servant who acted as Vance's butler, valet, major-domo and, on occasions, specialty cook, Vance was sitting in a large armchair, attired in a surah silk dressing-gown and grey suède slippers, with Vollard's book on Cézanne open across his knees.

"Forgive my not rising, Van," he greeted me casually. "I have the whole weight of the modern evolution in art resting on my legs. Furthermore, this plebeian early rising fatigues me, y' know."

He riffled the pages of the volume, pausing here and there at a reproduction.

"This chap Vollard," he remarked at length, "has been rather liberal with our art-fearing country. He has sent a really goodish collection of his Cézannes here. I viewed 'em yesterday with the proper reverence and, I might add, unconcern, for Kessler was watching me; and I've marked the ones I want you to buy for me as soon as the Gallery opens this morning."

He handed me a small catalogue he had been using as a book-mark.

"A beastly assignment, I know," he added, with an indolent smile. "These delicate little smudges with all their blank paper will prob'bly be meaningless to your legal mind—they're so unlike a neatly-typed brief, don't y' know. And you'll no doubt think some of 'em are hung upside-down,—one of 'em is, in fact, and even Kessler doesn't know it. But don't fret, Van old dear. They're very beautiful and valuable little knickknacks, and rather inexpensive when one considers what they'll be bringing in a few years. Really an excellent investment for some money-loving soul, y' know—inf'nitely better than that Lawyer's Equity Stock[8] over which you grew so eloquent at the time of my dear Aunt Agatha's death."*

Vance's one passion (if a purely intellectual enthusiasm may be called a passion) was art—not art in its narrow, personal aspects, but in its broader, more universal significance. And art was not only his dominating interest, but his chief diversion. He was something of an authority on Japanese and Chinese prints; he knew tapestries and ceramics; and once I heard him give an impromptu *causerie*[9] to a few guests on Tanagra figurines,[10] which, had it been transcribed, would have made a most delightful and instructive monograph.

Vance had sufficient means to indulge his instinct for collecting, and possessed a fine assortment of pictures and *objets d'art*. His collection was heterogeneous only in its superficial characteristics: every piece he owned embodied some principle of form or line that related it to all the others. One who knew art could feel the unity and consistency in all the items with which he surrounded himself, however widely separated they were in point of time or *métier*[11] or surface appeal. Vance, I have always felt, was one of those rare human beings, a collector with a definite philosophic point of view.

His apartment in East Thirty-eighth Street—actually the two top floors of an old mansion, beautifully remodelled and in part rebuilt to secure spacious rooms and lofty ceilings—was filled, but not crowded, with rare specimens of oriental and occidental, ancient and modern, art. His paintings ranged from the Italian primitives to Cézanne and Matisse; and among his collection of original drawings were works as widely separated as those of Michelangelo and Picasso. Vance's Chinese prints constituted one of the finest private collections in this country. They included beautiful examples of the work of Ririomin, Rianchu, Jinkomin, Kakei and Mokkei.[12]

"The Chinese," Vance once said to me, "are the truly great artists of the East. They were the men whose work expressed most intensely a broad philosophic spirit. By contrast the Japanese were superficial. It's a long step between the little more than decorative *souci* of a Hokusai[13] and the profoundly thoughtful and conscious artistry of a Ririomin. Even when Chinese art degenerated under the Manchus, we find in it a deep philosophic quality—a spiritual *sensibilité*, so to speak. And in the modern copies of copies—what is called the *bunjinga* style[14]—we still have pictures of profound meaning."

Vance's catholicity of taste in art was remarkable. His collection was as varied as that of a museum. It embraced a blackfigured amphora by Amasis,[15] a proto-Corinthian vase in the Ægean style, Koubatcha and Rhodian plates,[16] Athenian pottery, a sixteenth-century Italian holy-water stoup of rock crystal, pewter of the Tudor period (several pieces bearing the double-rose

9.   An informal talk or article, usually on a literary subject.

10.   In the 1860s, local farmers in Boetiz began to report Greek terra-cotta figurines that they discovered in the fields, principally around the town of Tanagra. These figures, from the late fourth century B.C.E., caught the eye of art collectors and became very popular. Basil Hallward, the painter of the eponymous *Picture of Dorian Gray* (by Oscar Wilde, 1891), has Tanagra figurines in his studio.

11.   An area of expertise or specialty.

12.   These were all real Chinese painters of the twelfth and thirteenth centuries C.E.

13.   Hokousai was a modern Japanese painter (1760–1849), influenced profoundly by the Chinese painters who preceded him.

14.   The *bunjinga* style was that of the Japanese painters who considered themselves literati or intellectuals while emulating and admiring traditional Chinese culture. The style flourished during the late *Edo* period, in the late eighteenth and nineteenth centuries.

15.   A Greek artist active around 550 B.C.E.—the works were signed "Made by Amasis."

16.   From the sixteenth century C.E., typically in red, white, and blue enamels.

17. An emblem of the Tudor kings Henry VII and Henry VIII, combining of the symbols of the Yorks and the Lancesters.

18. Vallfogna is one of several place-names in Catalonia, not a specific artist.

19. The Ming Dynasty spanned 1368 C.E. to 1644.

20. A city in lower Egypt, close to the location of Bubastis.

21. A Theban statuette of a young woman, acquired by the Louvre in 1825.

22. Two of the four sons of the Egyptian god Horus.

23. Arezzo was an important Etruscan city, and its pottery flourished from the fourth century B.C.E. through the first century C.E.

24. A depiction of dancers who performed at the Karneia, a festival important throughout the Doric world and especially to the Spartans.

25. The word is figurative here: "Embayed" means a bay enclosed by ice or other obstacles.

26. The phrase is attributed to Louis Antoine de Bourbon, Duke of Enghien (1772–1804), who was executed for allegedly aiding Britain and betraying France. The phrase means "It's worse than a crime, it's a blunder/mistake."

27. Juvenal was a Roman poet of the late first-second century C.E. known for his *Satires*.

hall-mark),[17] a bronze plaque by Cellini, a triptych of Limoges enamel, a Spanish retable of an altar-piece by Vallfogona,[18] several Etruscan bronzes, an Indian Greco Buddhist, a statuette of the Goddess Kuan Yin from the Ming Dynasty,[19] a number of very fine Renaissance woodcuts, and several specimens of Byzantine, Carolingian and early French ivory carvings.

His Egyptian treasures included a gold jug from Zakazik,[20] a statuette of the Lady Nai (as lovely as the one in the Louvre),[21] two beautifully carved steles of the First Theban Age, various small sculptures comprising rare representations of Hapi and Amset,[22] and several Arrentine[23] bowls carved with Kalathiskos dancers.[24] On top of one of his embayed[25] Jacobean book cases in the library, where most of his modern paintings and drawings were hung, was a fascinating group of African sculpture—ceremonial masks and statuette-fetishes from French Guinea, the Sudan, Nigeria, the Ivory Coast, and the Congo.

A definite purpose has animated me in speaking at such length about Vance's art instinct, for, in order to understand fully the melodramatic adventures which began for him on that June morning, one must have a general idea of the man's *penchants* and inner promptings. His interest in art was an important—one might almost say the dominant—factor in his personality. I have never met a man quite like him—a man so apparently diversified, and yet so fundamentally consistent.

Vance was what many would call a dilettante. But the designation does him injustice. He was a man of unusual culture and brilliance. An aristocrat by birth and instinct, he held himself severely aloof from the common world of men. In his manner there was an indefinable contempt for inferiority of all kinds. The great majority of those with whom he came in contact regarded him as a snob. Yet there was in his condescension and disdain no trace of spuriousness. His snobbishness was intellectual as well as social. He detested stupidity even more, I believe, than he did vulgarity or bad taste. I have heard him on several occasions quote Fouché's famous line: *C'est plus qu'un crime; c'est une faute.*[26] And he meant it literally.

Vance was frankly a cynic, but he was rarely bitter: his was a flippant, Juvenalian[27] cynicism. Perhaps he may best be described as a bored and supercilious, but highly conscious and penetrating, spectator of life. He was keenly interested in all human reactions;

but it was the interest of the scientist, not the humanitarian. Withal he was a man of rare personal charm. Even people who found it difficult to admire him, found it equally difficult not to like him. His somewhat quixotic mannerisms and his slightly English accent and inflection—a heritage of his post-graduate days at Oxford—impressed those who did not know him well, as affectations. But the truth is, there was very little of the *poseur* about him.

He was unusually good-looking, although his mouth was ascetic and cruel, like the mouths on some of the Medici portraits;* moreover, there was a slightly derisive hauteur in the lift of his eyebrows. Despite the aquiline severity of his lineaments his face was highly sensitive. His forehead was full and sloping—it was the artist's, rather than the scholar's, brow. His cold grey eyes were widely spaced. His nose was straight and slender, and his chin narrow but prominent, with an unusually deep cleft. When I saw John Barrymore recently in *Hamlet*[28] I was somehow reminded of Vance; and once before, in a scene of *Cæsar and Cleopatra* played by ForbesRobertson,[29] I received a similar impression.[†]

Vance was slightly under six feet, graceful, and giving the impression of sinewy strength and nervous endurance. He was an expert fencer, and had been the Captain of the University's fencing team. He was mildly fond of outdoor sports, and had a knack of doings things well without any extensive practice. His golf handicap was only three; and one season he had played on our championship polo team against England. Nevertheless, he had a positive antipathy to walking, and would not go a hundred yards on foot if there was any possible means of riding.

In his dress he was always fashionable—scrupulously correct to the smallest detail—yet unobtrusive. He spent considerable time at his clubs: his favorite was the Stuyvesant,[30] because, as he explained to me, its membership was drawn largely from the political and commercial ranks, and he was never drawn into a discussion which required any mental effort. He went occasionally to the more modern operas, and was a regular subscriber to the symphony concerts and chamber-music recitals.

Incidentally, he was one of the most unerring poker players I have ever seen. I mention this fact not merely because it was unusual and significant that a man of Vance's type should have

* [Author's note:] I am thinking particularly of Bronzino's portraits of Pietro de' Medici and Cosimo de' Medici, in the National Gallery, and of Vasari's medallion portrait of Lorenzo de' Medici in the Vecchio Palazzo, Florence.

28. John Barrymore, born John Sidney Blyth (1882–1942), was the scion of the great Drew and Barrymore acting clans; his 1922 *Hamlet* was a milestone in American theater.

29. Johnston Forbes-Robertson (1853–1937) was one of the foremost British actors of the era, also known for his *Hamlet* (preceding Barrymore).

† [Author's note:] Once when Vance was suffering from sinusitis, he had an X–ray photograph of his head made; and the accompanying chart described him as a "marked dolichocephalic" and a "disharmonious Nordic." It also contained the following data:—cephalic index 75; nose, leptorhine, with an index of 48; facial angle, 85°; vertical index, 72; upper facial index, 54; interpupillary width, 67; chin, masognathous, with an index of 103; sella turcica, abnormally large.

30. No such club is listed in the 1922–23 R. L. Polk & Co.'s *Trow's General Directory of the City of New York*.

"Culture," Vance said to me shortly after I had met him, "is polyglot; and the knowledge of many tongues is essential to an understanding of the world's intellectual and æsthetic achievements. Especially are the Greek and Latin classics vitiated by translation." I quote the remark here because his omnivorous reading in languages other than English, coupled with his amazingly retentive memory, had a tendency to affect his own speech. And while it may appear to some that his speech was at times pedantic, I have tried, throughout these chronicles to quote him literally, in the hope of presenting a portrait of the man as he was.

preferred so democratic a game to bridge or chess, for instance, but because his knowledge of the science of human psychology involved in poker had an intimate bearing on the chronicles I am about to set down.

Vance's knowledge of psychology was indeed uncanny. He was gifted with an instinctively accurate judgment of people, and his study and reading had co-ordinated and rationalized this gift to an amazing extent. He was well grounded in the academic principles of psychology, and all his courses at college had either centered about this subject or been subordinated to it. While I was confining myself to a restricted area of torts and contracts, constitutional and common law, equity, evidence and pleading, Vance was reconnoitring the whole field of cultural endeavor. He had courses in the history of religions, the Greek classics, biology, civics and political economy, philosophy, anthropology, literature, theoretical and experimental psychology, and ancient and modern languages.* But it was, I think, his courses under Münsterberg and William James that interested him the most.

Vance's mind was basically philosophical—that is, philosophical in the more general sense. Being singularly free from the conventional sentimentalities and current superstitions, he could look beneath the surface of human acts into actuating impulses and motives. Moreover, he was resolute both in his avoidance of any attitude that savored of credulousness, and in his adherence to cold, logical exactness in his mental processes.

"Until we can approach all human problems," he once remarked, "with the clinical aloofness and cynical contempt of a doctor examining a guineapig strapped to a board, we have little chance of getting at the truth."

Vance led an active, but by no means animated, social life—a concession to various family ties. But he was not a social animal.—I can not remember ever having met a man with so undeveloped a gregarious instinct,—and when he went forth into the social world it was generally under compulsion. In fact, one of his "duty" affairs had occupied him on the night before that memorable June breakfast; otherwise, we would have consulted about the Cézannes the evening before; and Vance groused a good deal about it while Currie was serving our strawberries and eggs *Bénédictine*. Later on I was to give profound thanks to the God of Coincidence that the blocks had been arranged in just that pattern; for had Vance been slumbering peacefully at nine o'clock when the District Attorney called, I would probably have missed four of the most interesting and exciting years of my life; and many of New York's shrewdest and most desperate criminals might still be at large.

Vance and I had just settled back in our chairs for our second cup of coffee and a cigarette when Currie, answering an impetuous ringing of the front-door bell, ushered the District Attorney into the living-room.

"By all that's holy!" he exclaimed, raising his hands in mock astonishment. "New York's leading *flâneur* and art connoisseur is up and about!"

"And I am suffused with blushes at the disgrace of it," Vance replied.

It was evident, however, that the District Attorney was not in a jovial mood. His face suddenly sobered.

"Vance, a serious thing has brought me here. I'm in a great hurry, and merely dropped by to keep my promise. . . . The fact is, Alvin Benson has been murdered."

Vance lifted his eyebrows languidly.

"Really, now," he drawled. "How messy! But he no doubt deserved it. In any event, that's no reason why you should repine. Take a chair and have a cup of Currie's incomp'rable coffee." And before the other could protest, he rose and pushed a bell-button.

Markham hesitated a second or two.

"Oh, well. A couple of minutes won't make any difference. But only a gulp." And he sank into a chair facing us.

CHAPTER II

At the Scene of the Crime

31. Edward Swann, who served as New York County District Attorney from 1916 to 1921, the apparent era of the story, was a Democrat handpicked by Tammany Hall. No independent served as District Attorney after 1909 until the election of Thomas Dewey in 1938. Therefore, John F.-X. Markham must be regarded as fictional, though he may well have been based on William T. Jerome, who was the New York County District Attorney from 1902 to 1909. Jerome had been elected by a coalition of anti-Tammany Democrats, Republicans, and the so-called Citizens Union. He was forty-three when first elected and was a crusader against political corruption and crime. Jerome's uncle Leonard Jerome was the father of Jennie Jerome, who married Lord Randolph Churchill, the maternal grandfather of Winston Churchill.

32. Tammany Hall was the name given to the Democratic political cartel that dominated New York politics from 1854 to 1934. Originally the Tammany Society, at its inception,

(Friday, June 14; 9 a.m.)

John F.-X. Markham, as you remember, had been elected District Attorney of New York County on the Independent Reform Ticket[31] during one of the city's periodical reactions against Tammany Hall.[32] He served his four years, and would probably have been elected to a second term had not the ticket been hopelessly split by the political juggling of his opponents. He was an indefatigable worker, and projected the District Attorney's office into all manner of criminal and civil investigations. Being utterly incorruptible, he not only aroused the fervid admiration of his constituents, but produced an almost unprecedented sense of security in those who had opposed him on partisan lines.

He had been in office only a few months when one of the newspapers referred to him as the Watch Dog; and the sobriquet clung to him until the end of his administration. Indeed, his record as a successful prosecutor during the four years of his incumbency was such a remarkable one that even to-day it is not infrequently referred to in legal and political discussions.

Markham was a tall, strongly-built man in the middle forties, with a cleanshaven, somewhat youthful face which belied his uniformly grey hair. He was not handsome according to conventional standards, but he had an unmistakable air of distinction, and was possessed of an amount of social culture rarely found in our latter-day political office-holders. Withal he was a man of brusque and vindictive temperament; but his brusqueness was an incrustation on a solid foundation of good-breeding, not—as is usually the case—the roughness of substructure showing through an inadequately superimposed crust of gentility.

When his nature was relieved of the stress of duty and care, he was the most gracious of men. But early in my acquaintance with him I had seen his attitude of cordiality suddenly displaced by one of grim authority. It was as if a new personality—hard, indomitable, symbolic of eternal justice—had in that moment been born in Markham's body. I was to witness this transformation many times before our association ended. In fact, this very morning, as he sat opposite to me in Vance's living-room, there was more than a hint of it in the aggressive sternness of his expression; and I knew that he was deeply troubled over Alvin Benson's murder.

He swallowed his coffee rapidly, and was setting down the cup, when Vance, who had been watching him with quizzical amusement, remarked:

"I say; why this sad preoccupation over the passing of one Benson? You weren't, by any chance, the murderer, what?"

Markham ignored Vance's levity.

"I'm on my way to Benson's. Do you care to come along? You asked for the experience, and I dropped in to keep my promise."

I then recalled that several weeks before at the Stuyvesant Club, when the subject of the prevalent homicides in New York was being discussed, Vance had expressed a desire to accompany the District Attorney on one of his investigations; and that Markham had promised to take him on his next important case. Vance's interest in the psychology of human behavior had prompted the desire, and his friendship with Markham, which had been of long standing, had made the request possible.

"You remember everything, don't you?" Vance replied lazily. "An admirable gift, even if an uncomfortable one." He glanced at the clock on the mantel: it lacked a few minutes of nine. "But what an indecent hour! Suppose someone should see me."

Markham moved forward impatiently in his chair.

"Well, if you think the gratification of your curiosity would compensate you for the disgrace of being seen in public at nine o'clock in the morning, you'll have to hurry. I certainly won't

it was part of a network of clubs for "pure Americans." The name is supposedly drawn from the name of Tamanend, a leader of the Lenape (also known as the Delaware Indians) who occupied the Northeast. By 1798, Aaron Burr began to convert it to a body intended to oppose Alexander Hamilton's Society of the Cincinnatis, a political organization, and the New York chapter was instrumental in delivering the electoral votes of the State of New York in 1800 to the Democratic-Republicans, defeating John Adams's presidential relection bid and electing Thomas Jefferson as president and Aaron Burr as vice president.

The whiskered one: "He thinks he has me buried."

A Bob Satterfield cartoon from 1904, showing a reformer who thinks he has buried Tammany Hall.

33. Robert Hichens (1864–1950) wrote *The Green Carnation* (1894), which was first published anonymously. A roman à clef about the notorious affair between Oscar Wilde and "Bosie," Lord Alfred Douglas, it was thought to have been written by Wilde, who denied authorship. Hichens, himself a homosexual, had spent much time in the company of Wilde and Douglas and was eventually revealed as the author. The scenes described in the book and even the dialogue closely mirrored the facts of the relationship between Douglas and Wilde as revealed in the latter's trial.

take you in dressing-gown and bed-room slippers. And I most certainly won't wait over five minutes for you to get dressed."

"Why the haste, old dear?" Vance asked, yawning. "The chap's dead, don't y' know; he can't possibly run away."

"Come, get a move on, you orchid," the other urged. "This affair is no joke. It's damned serious; and from the looks of it, it's going to cause an ungodly scandal.—What are you going to do?"

"Do? I shall humbly follow the great avenger of the common people," returned Vance, rising and making an obsequious bow.

He rang for Currie, and ordered his clothes brought to him.

"I'm attending a levee which Mr. Markham is holding over a corpse, and I want something rather spiffy. Is it warm enough for a silk suit? . . . And a lavender tie, by all means."

"I trust you won't also wear your green carnation," grumbled Markham.

"Tut! Tut!" Vance chided him. "You've been reading Mr. Hichens.[33] Such heresy in a district attorney! Anyway, you know full well I never wear *boutonnières*. The decoration has fallen into disrepute. The only remaining devotees of the practice are roués and saxophone players. . . . But tell me about the departed Benson."

Vance was now dressing, with Currie's assistance, at a rate of speed I had rarely seen him display in such matters. Beneath his bantering pose I recognized the true eagerness of the man for a new experience and one that promised such dramatic possibilities for his alert and observing mind.

"You knew Alvin Benson casually, I believe," the District Attorney said. "Well, early this morning his housekeeper 'phoned the local precinct station that she had found him shot through the head, fully dressed and sitting in his favorite chair in his living-room. The message, of course, was put through at once to the Telegraph Bureau at Headquarters, and my assistant on duty notified me immediately. I was tempted to let the case follow the regular police routine. But half an hour later Major Benson, Alvin's brother, 'phoned me and asked me, as a special favor, to take charge. I've known the Major for twenty years, and I couldn't very well refuse. So I took a hurried breakfast and started for Benson's house. He lived in West Forty-eighth Street; and as I passed your corner I remembered your request, and dropped by to see if you cared to go along."

"Most consid'rate," murmured Vance, adjusting his four-in-hand before a small polychrome mirror by the door. Then he turned to me. "Come, Van. We'll all gaze upon the defunct Benson. I'm sure some of Markham's sleuths will unearth the fact that I detested the bounder and accuse me of the crime; and I'll feel safer, don't y' know, with legal talent at hand. . . . No objections—eh, what, Markham?"

"Certainly not," the other agreed readily, although I felt that he would rather not have had me along. But I was too deeply interested in the affair to offer any ceremonious objections, and I followed Vance and Markham downstairs.

As we settled back in the waiting taxicab and started up Madison Avenue, I marvelled a little, as I had often done before, at the strange friendship of these two dissimilar men beside me—Markham forthright, conventional, a trifle austere, and over-serious in his dealings with life; and Vance casual, mercurial, debonair, and whimsically cynical in the face of the grimmest realities. And yet this temperamental diversity seemed, in some wise, the very cornerstone of their friendship: it was as if each saw in the other some unattainable field of experience and sensation that had been denied himself. Markham represented to Vance the solid and immutable realism of life, whereas Vance symbolized for Markham the care-free, exotic, gypsy spirit of intellectual adventure. Their intimacy, in fact, was even greater than showed on the surface; and despite Markham's exaggerated deprecations of the other's attitudes and opinions, I believe he respected Vance's intelligence more profoundly than that of any other man he knew.

As we rode up town that morning Markham appeared pre-occupied and gloomy. No word had been spoken since we left the apartment; but as we turned west into Forty-eighth Street[34] Vance asked:

"What is the social etiquette of these early-morning murder functions, aside from removing one's hat in the presence of the body?"

"You keep your hat on," growled Markham.

"My word! Like a synagogue, what? Most int'restin'! Perhaps one takes off one's shoes so as not to confuse the footprints."

"No," Markham told him. "The guests remain fully clothed—in which the function differs from the ordinary evening affairs of your smart set."

34.   Today, traffic on 48th Street runs west to east. However, this change did not occur until 1927, when the majority of the streets south of 110th were made one-way, with the even numbers running west to east and the odd numbers east to west. As early as 1915, Manhattan was experimenting with one-way streets to ease the traffic, but prior to 1927, only streets as high as 43rd Street had been converted.

35. The Epworth League was a Christian youth organization associated with the United Methodist Church; after 1939, it became known as the United Methodist Youth Fellowship, and it continues to flourish today. Its workings were explained in detail in Dan B. Brummett's *Epworth League Methods* (1906), updated in 1914 to *The Efficient Epworthian*. The pledge for members included the following: "I will abstain from all those forms of worldly amusement which can not be taken in the name of the Lord Jesus . . ."

36. The Régie, as it was known (formally the Sociéte de la Régie Cointéresée des Tabacs de l'Empire Ottoman), was a monopoly granted control of the production of tobacco in Turkey. The cigarettes were sold around the world. Many brands were available with rose petals wrapped around the tips, to avoid abrading the lips of smokers (especially women smokers).

"My *dear* Markham!"—Vance's tone was one of melancholy reproof—"The horrified moralist in your nature is at work again. That remark of yours was pos'tively Epworth Leaguish."[35]

Markham was too abstracted to follow up Vance's badinage.

"There are one or two things," he said soberly, "that I think I'd better warn you about. From the looks of it, this case is going to cause considerable noise, and there'll be a lot of jealousy and battling for honors. I won't be fallen upon and caressed affectionately by the police for coming in at this stage of the game; so be careful not to rub their bristles the wrong way. My assistant, who's there now, tells me he thinks the Inspector has put Heath in charge. Heath's a sergeant in the Homicide Bureau, and is undoubtedly convinced at the present moment that I'm taking hold in order to get the publicity."

"Aren't you his technical superior?" asked Vance.

"Of course; and that makes the situation just so much more delicate. . . . I wish to God the Major hadn't called me up."

"*Eheu!*" sighed Vance. "The world is full of Heaths. Beastly nuisances."

"Don't misunderstand me," Markham hastened to assure him. "Heath is a good man—in fact, as good a man as we've got. The mere fact that he was assigned to the case shows how seriously the affair is regarded at Headquarters. There'll be no unpleasantness about my taking charge, you understand; but I want the atmosphere to be as halcyon as possible. Heath'll resent my bringing along you two chaps as spectators, anyway; so I beg of you, Vance, emulate the modest violet."

"I prefer the blushing rose, if you don't mind," Vance protested. "However, I'll instantly give the hypersensitive Heath one of my choicest *Régie* cigarettes with the rose-petal tips."[36]

"If you do," smiled Markham, "he'll probably arrest you as a suspicious character."

We had drawn up abruptly in front of an old brownstone residence on the upper side of Forty-eighth Street, near Sixth Avenue. It was a house of the better class, built on a twenty-five-foot lot in a day when permanency and beauty were still matters of consideration among the city's architects. The design was conventional, to accord with the other houses in the block, but a touch of luxury and individuality was to be seen in its decorative copings and in the stone carvings about the entrance and above the windows.

There was a shallow paved areaway between the street line and the front elevation of the house; but this was enclosed in a high iron railing, and the only entrance was by way of the front door, which was about six feet above the street level at the top of a flight of ten broad stone stairs. Between the entrance and the right-hand wall were two spacious windows covered with heavy iron *grilles*.

A considerable crowd of morbid onlookers had gathered in front of the house; and on the steps lounged several alert-looking young men whom I took to be newspaper reporters. The door of our taxicab was opened by a uniformed patrolman who saluted Markham with exaggerated respect and ostentatiously cleared a passage for us through the gaping throng of idlers. Another uniformed patrolman stood in the little vestibule, and on recognizing Markham, held the outer door open for us and saluted with great dignity.

"*Ave, Cæsar, te salutamus,*"[37] whispered Vance, grinning.

"Be quiet," Markham grumbled. "I've got troubles enough without your garbled quotations."

As we passed through the massive carved-oak front door into the main hallway, we were met by Assistant District Attorney Dinwiddie, a serious, swarthy young man with a prematurely lined face, whose appearance gave one the impression that most of the woes of humanity were resting upon his shoulders.

"Good morning, Chief," he greeted Markham, with eager relief. "I'm damned glad you've got here. This case'll rip things wide open. Cut-and-dried murder, and not a lead."

Markham nodded gloomily, and looked past him into the living-room.

"Who's here?" he asked.

"The whole works, from the Chief Inspector down," Dinwiddie told him, with a hopeless shrug, as if the fact boded ill for all concerned.

At that moment a tall, massive, middle-aged man with a pink complexion and a closely-cropped white moustache, appeared in the doorway of the living-room. On seeing Markham he came forward stiffly with outstretched hand. I recognized him at once as Chief Inspector O'Brien, who was in command of the entire Police Department. Dignified greetings were exchanged between him and Markham, and then Vance and I were introduced to him. Inspector O'Brien gave us each a curt, silent nod, and turned

37.   Vance paraphrases the title of a painting of Roman gladiators, *Ave Caesar Morituri te Salutant*, by Jean-Léon Gérôme (1859). The name is based on a quotation from Suetonius: "Hail, Caesar, we who are about to die salute you."

38.   Inlaid with brass, tortoiseshell, or other decorative materials.

39.   America did not officially join in the Great War until 1917; while U.S. troops were in France as early as June 26, 1917, the great mass of American forces joined the conflict in the summer of 1918, fighting until the November armistice. If by June 1918 (if that is the date of these events) Van Dine had spent two years in France, he must have served as a volunteer, one of many who joined the French, British, or Canadian forces prior to the official U.S. declaration of war.

40.   Dashiell Hammett, in his review of *The Benson Murder Case* in the January 15, 1927, issue of the *Saturday Review of Literature*, writes, "That his position should have been so slightly disturbed by the impact of such a bullet at such a range is preposterous, but the phenomenon hasn't anything to do with the plot, so don't, as I did, waste time trying to figure it out."

back to the living-room, with Markham, Dinwiddie, Vance and myself following.

The room, which was entered by a wide double door about ten feet down the hall, was a spacious one, almost square, and with high ceilings. Two windows gave on the street; and on the extreme right of the north wall, opposite to the front of the house, was another window opening on a paved court. To the left of this window were the sliding doors leading into the dining-room at the rear.

The room presented an appearance of garish opulence. About the walls hung several elaborately framed paintings of race-horses and a number of mounted hunting trophies. A highly-colored oriental rug covered nearly the entire floor. In the middle of the east wall, facing the door, was an ornate fireplace and carved marble mantel. Placed diagonally in the corner on the right stood a walnut upright piano with copper trimmings. Then there was a mahogany bookcase with glass doors and figured curtains, a sprawling tapestried davenport, a squat Venetian tabouret with inlaid mother of pearl, a teak-wood stand containing a large brass samovar, and a buhl-topped[38] center table nearly six feet long. At the side of the table nearest the hallway, with its back to the front windows, stood a large wicker lounge chair with a high, fan-shaped back.

In this chair reposed the body of Alvin Benson.

Though I had served two years at the front in the World War and had seen death in many terrible guises, I could not repress a strong sense of revulsion at the sight of this murdered man.[39] In France death had seemed an inevitable part of my daily routine, but here all the organisms of environment were opposed to the idea of fatal violence. The bright June sunshine was pouring into the room, and through the open windows came the continuous din of the city's noises, which, for all their cacophony, are associated with peace and security and the orderly social processes of life.

Benson's body was reclining in the chair in an attitude so natural that one almost expected him to turn to us and ask why we were intruding upon his privacy. His head was resting against the chair's back. His right leg was crossed over his left in a position of comfortable relaxation. His right arm was resting easily on the center-table, and his left arm lay along the chair's arm.[40]

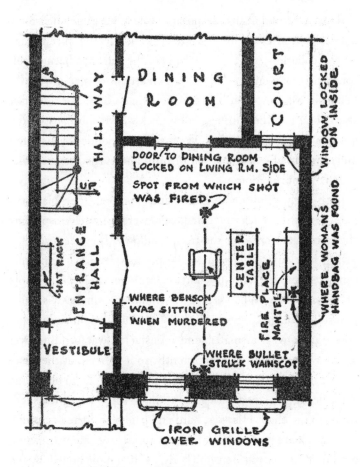

Diagram of Alvin Benson's House,
from *The Benson Murder Case*, artist unknown.

*   [Author's note:] The book was O. Henry's *Strictly Business*, and the place at which it was being held open was, curiously enough, the story entitled "A Municipal Report."

[Editor's note: The book was first published in 1910. Ironically, the story concerns the killing of one Major Caswell.]

But that which most strikingly gave his attitude its appearance of naturalness, was a small book which he held in his right hand with his thumb still marking the place where he had evidently been reading.*

He had been shot through the forehead from in front; and the small circular bullet mark was now almost black as a result of the coagulation of the blood. A large dark spot on the rug at the rear of the chair indicated the extent of the hemorrhage caused by the grinding passage of the bullet through his brain. Had it not been for these grisly indications one might have thought that he had merely paused momentarily in his reading to lean back and rest.

41.   A short decorative drapery, hung on a mantelpiece or over a doorway.

He was attired in an old smoking-jacket and red felt bed-room slippers, but still wore his dress trousers and evening shirt, though he was collarless, and the neck band of the shirt had been unbuttoned as if for comfort. He was not an attractive man physically, being almost completely bald and more than a little stout. His face was flabby, and the puffiness of his neck was doubly conspicuous without its confining collar. With a slight shudder of distaste I ended my brief contemplation of him, and turned to the other occupants of the room.

Two burly fellows with large hands and feet, their black felt hats pushed far back on their heads, were minutely inspecting the iron grill-work over the front windows. They seemed to be giving particular attention to the points where the bars were cemented into the masonry; and one of them had just taken hold of a *grille* with both hands and was shaking it, simian-wise, as if to test its strength. Another man, of medium height and dapper appearance, with a small blond moustache, was bending over in front of the grate looking intently, so it seemed, at the dusty gas-logs. On the far side of the table a thickset man in blue serge and a derby hat, stood with arms a-kimbo scrutinizing the silent figure in the chair. His eyes, hard and pale blue, were narrowed, and his square prognathous jaw was rigidly set. He was gazing with rapt intensity at Benson's body, as though he hoped, by the sheer power of concentration, to probe the secret of the murder.

Another man, of unusual mien, was standing before the rear window, with a jeweller's magnifying glass in his eye, inspecting a small object held in the palm of his hand. From pictures I had seen of him I knew he was Captain Carl Hagedorn, the most famous fire-arms expert in America. He was a large, cumbersome, broad-shouldered man of about fifty; and his black shiny clothes were several sizes too large for him. His coat hitched up behind, and in front hung half way down to his knees; and his trousers were baggy and lay over his ankles in grotesquely comic folds. His head was round and abnormally large, and his ears seemed sunken into his skull. His mouth was entirely hidden by a scraggly, grey-shot moustache, all the hairs of which grew downwards, forming a kind of lambrequin[41] to his lips. Captain Hagedorn had been connected with the New York Police Department for thirty years, and though his appearance and manner were ridiculed at Headquarters, he was profoundly respected. His word on any point pertaining to fire-arms and gunshot wounds was accepted as final by Headquarters men.

In the rear of the room, near the dining-room door, stood two other men talking earnestly together. One was Inspector William M. Moran, Commanding Officer of the Detective Bureau; the other, Sergeant Ernest Heath of the Homicide Bureau, of whom Markham had already spoken to us.

As we entered the room in the wake of Chief Inspector O'Brien everyone ceased his occupation for a moment and looked at the District Attorney in a spirit of uneasy, but respectful, recognition. Only Captain Hagedorn, after a cursory squint at Markham, returned to the inspection of the tiny object in his hand, with an abstracted unconcern which brought a faint smile to Vance's lips.

Inspector Moran and Sergeant Heath came forward with stolid dignity; and after the ceremony of hand-shaking (which I later observed to be a kind of religious rite among the police and the members of the District Attorney's staff), Markham introduced Vance and me, and briefly explained our presence. The Inspector bowed pleasantly to indicate his acceptance of the intrusion, but I noticed that Heath ignored Markham's explanation, and proceeded to treat us as if we were non-existent.

Inspector Moran was a man of different quality from the others in the room. He was about sixty, with white hair and a brown moustache, and was immaculately dressed. He looked more like a successful Wall Street broker of the better class than a police official.*

"I've assigned Sergeant Heath to the case, Mr. Markham," he explained in a low, well-modulated voice. "It looks as though we were in for a bit of trouble before it's finished. Even the Chief Inspector thought it warranted his lending the moral support of his presence to the preliminary rounds. He has been here since eight o'clock."

Inspector O'Brien had left us immediately upon entering the room, and now stood between the front windows, watching the proceedings with a grave, indecipherable face.

"Well, I think I'll be going," Moran added. "They had me out of bed at seven-thirty, and I haven't had any breakfast yet. I won't be needed anyway now that you're here. . . . Good-morning." And again he shook hands.

*   [Author's note:] Inspector Moran (as I learned later) had once been the president of a large up state bank that had failed during the panic of 1907, and during the Gaynor Administration had been seriously considered for the post of Police Commissioner.

[Editor's note: William Jay Gaynor served as the Mayor of New York from 1910 to 1913. George V. McLaughlin, the New York City Police Commissioner from 1926 to 1927, was a well-regarded police official who fought corruption on the force. McLaughlin had served as state superintendent of banks in 1920.]

William J. Gaynor, after being shot in 1913. He died shortly thereafter.

When he had gone Markham turned to the Assistant District Attorney.

"Look after these two gentlemen, will you, Dinwiddie? They're babes in the wood, and want to see how these affairs work. Explain things to them while I have a little confab with Sergeant Heath."

Dinwiddie accepted the assignment eagerly. I think he was glad of the opportunity to have someone to talk to by way of venting his pent-up excitement.

As the three of us turned rather instinctively toward the body of the murdered man—he was, after all, the hub of this tragic drama—I heard Heath say in a sullen voice:

"I suppose you'll take charge now, Mr. Markham."

Dinwiddie and Vance were talking together, and I watched Markham with interest after what he had told us of the rivalry between the Police Department and the District Attorney's office.

Markham looked at Heath with a slow gracious smile, and shook his head.

"No, Sergeant," he replied. "I'm here to work with you, and I want that relationship understood from the outset. In fact, I wouldn't be here now if Major Benson hadn't 'phoned me and asked me to lend a hand. And I particularly want my name kept out of it. It's pretty generally known—and if it isn't, it will be—that the Major is an old friend of mine; so, it will be better all round if my connection with the case is kept quiet."

Heath murmured something I did not catch, but I could see that he had, in large measure, been placated. He, in common with all other men who were acquainted with Markham, knew his word was good; and he personally liked the District Attorney.

"If there's any credit coming from this affair," Markham went on, "the Police Department is to get it; therefore I think it best for you to see the reporters. . . . And, by the way," he added good-naturedly, "if there's any blame coming, you fellows will have to bear that, too."

"Fair enough," assented Heath.

"And now, Sergeant, let's get to work," said Markham.

CHAPTER III

A Lady's Hand-bag

(Friday, June 14; 9.30 a.m.)

The District Attorney and Heath walked up to the body, and stood regarding it.

"You see," Heath explained; "he was shot directly from the front. A pretty powerful shot, too; for the bullet passed through the head and struck the woodwork over there by the window." He pointed to a place on the wainscot a short distance from the floor near the drapery of the window nearest the hallway. "We found the expelled shell, and Captain Hagedorn's got the bullet."

He turned to the fire-arms expert.

"How about it, Captain? Anything special?"

Hagedorn raised his head slowly, and gave Heath a myopic frown. Then after a few awkward movements, he answered with unhurried precision:

"A forty-five army bullet—Colt automatic."

"Any idea how close to Benson the gun was held?" asked Markham.

"Yes, sir, I have," Hagedorn replied, in his ponderous monotone. "Between five and six feet—probably."

Heath snorted.

"'Probably'," he repeated to Markham with good natured contempt. "You can bank on it if the Captain says so. . . . You see, sir, nothing smaller than a forty-four or forty-five will stop a man,[42]

42. Dashiell Hammett declares, in his review of *The Benson Murder Case*, that this is an expression of idiocy. This has been borne out by extensive study: *Handgun Stopping Power*, by Evan Marshall and Edwin J. Sanow (1992), for example, rates handguns by their "one shot stop percentage," the percentage of one shot stops in actual street shootings as culled from police records. Many .38 specials have percentage ratings in excess of 80 percent, and .357 magnums and larger are closer to 90 percent.

43.   This is an accurate description of a typical wound from a .45 bullet fired from "distant" range. A contact wound typically displays an abrasion pattern as well as swelling from the gases emitted from the gun barrel. An "intermediate"-range shot results in powder burns. A "distant"-range shot is clean, free of powder burns. The size of the exit wound has little to do with the distance from the gun; rather, it is a function of the size of the bullet and the solidity of the tissue through which it passes. Here, because the bullet passed through the skull, a smaller exit wound would occur than if the bullet passed through soft tissue. Nonetheless, the exit wound is almost always larger than the entry wound. Note that here the exit wound is described as "ragged." See http://library.med.utah.edu/WebPath/TUTO RIAL/GUNS/GUN014.html. The fact that the bullet exited through the base of the skull indicates that either Benson's head was bent over (because he was reading) and he did not look up, or the shooter was shooting down at an angle, because of the shooter's height.

and these steel-capped army bullets go through a human skull like it was cheese. But in order to carry straight to the woodwork the gun had to be held pretty close; and as there aren't any powder marks on the face, it's a safe bet to take the Captain's figures as to distance."

At this point we heard the front door open and close, and Dr. Doremus, the Chief Medical Examiner, accompanied by his assistant, bustled in. He shook hands with Markham and Inspector O'Brien, and gave Heath a friendly salutation.

"Sorry I couldn't get here sooner," he apologized.

He was a nervous man with a heavily seamed face and the manner of a real-estate salesman.

"What have we got here?" he asked, in the same breath, making a wry face at the body in the chair.

"You tell us, Doc," retorted Heath.

Dr. Doremus approached the murdered man with a callous indifference indicative of a long process of hardening. He first inspected the face closely,—he was, I imagine, looking for powder marks. Then he glanced at the bullet hole in the forehead and at the ragged wound in the back of the head.[43] Next he moved the dead man's arm, bent the fingers, and pushed the head a little to the side. Having satisfied himself as to the state of *rigor mortis*, he turned to Heath.

"Can we get him on the settee there?"

Heath looked at Markham inquiringly.

"All through, sir?"

Markham nodded, and Heath beckoned to the two men at the front windows and ordered the body placed on the davenport. It retained its sitting posture, due to the hardening of the muscles after death, until the doctor and his assistant straightened out the limbs. The body was then undressed, and Dr. Doremus examined it carefully for other wounds. He paid particular attention to the arms; and he opened both hands wide and scrutinized the palms. At length he straightened up and wiped his hands on a large colored silk handkerchief.

"Shot through the left frontal," he announced. "Direct angle of fire. Bullet passed completely through the skull. Exit wound in the left occipital region—base of skull,—you found the bullet, didn't you? He was awake when shot, and death was immediate—probably never knew what hit him. . . . He's been dead about—well, I should judge, eight hours; maybe longer."

"How about twelve-thirty for the exact time?" asked Heath.

The doctor looked at his watch.

"Fits O. K. . . . Anything else?"

No one answered, and after a slight pause the Chief Inspector spoke.

"We'd like a post-mortem report to-day, doctor."

"That'll be all right," Dr. Doremus answered, snapping shut his medical case and handing it to his assistant. "But get the body to the Mortuary as soon as you can."

After a brief hand-shaking ceremony, he went out hurriedly.

Heath turned to the detective who had been standing by the table when we entered.

"Burke, you 'phone Headquarters to call for the body—and tell 'em to get a move on. Then go back to the office and wait for me."

Burke saluted and disappeared.

Heath then addressed one of the two men who had been inspecting the *grilles* of the front windows.

"How about that ironwork, Snitkin?"

"No chance, Sergeant," was the answer. "Strong as a jail—both of 'em. Nobody never got in through those windows."

"Very good," Heath told him. "Now you two fellows chase along with Burke."

When they had gone the dapper man in the blue serge suit and derby, whose sphere of activity had seemed to be the fireplace, laid two cigarette butts on the table.

"I found these under the gaslogs, Sergeant," he explained unenthusiastically. "Not much; but there's nothing else laying around."

"All right, Emery." Heath gave the butts a disgruntled look. "You needn't wait, either. I'll see you at the office later."

Hagedorn came ponderously forward.

"I guess I'll be getting along, too," he rumbled. "But I'm going to keep this bullet a while. It's got some peculiar rifling marks on it. You don't want it specially, do you, Sergeant?"

Heath smiled tolerantly.

"What'll I do with it, Captain? You keep it. But don't you dare lose it."

"I won't lose it," Hagedorn assured him, with stodgy serious-ness; and, without so much as a glance at either the District Attorney or the Chief Inspector, he waddled from the room with a slightly rolling movement which suggested that of some huge amphibious mammal.

Vance, who was standing beside me near the door, turned and followed Hagedorn into the hall. The two stood talking in low tones for several minutes. Vance appeared to be asking questions, and although I was not close enough to hear their conversation, I caught several words and phrases—"trajectory," "muzzle velocity," "angle of fire," "impetus," "impact," "deflection," and the like—and wondered what on earth had prompted this strange interrogation.

As Vance was thanking Hagedorn for his information Inspector O'Brien entered the hall.

"Learning fast?" he asked, smiling patronizingly at Vance. Then, without waiting for a reply: "Come along, Captain; I'll drive you down town."

Markham heard him.

"Have you got room for Dinwiddie, too, Inspector?"

"Plenty, Mr. Markham."

The three of them went out.

Vance and I were now left alone in the room with Heath and the District Attorney, and, as if by common impulse, we all settled ourselves in chairs, Vance taking one near the dining-room door directly facing the chair in which Benson had been murdered.

I had been keenly interested in Vance's manner and actions from the moment of his arrival at the house. When he had first entered the room he had adjusted his monocle carefully—an act which, despite his air of passivity, I recognized as an indication of interest. When his mind was alert and he wished to take on external impressions quickly, he invariably brought out his monocle. He could see adequately enough without it, and his use of it, I had observed, was largely the result of an intellectual dictate. The added clarity of vision it gave him seemed subtly to affect his clarity of mind.*

At first he had looked over the room incuriously and watched the proceedings with bored apathy; but during Heath's brief questioning of his subordinates, an expression of cynical amusement had appeared on his face. Following a few general queries to Assistant District Attorney Dinwiddie, he had sauntered, with apparent aimlessness, about the room, looking at the various articles and occasionally shifting his gaze back and forth between different pieces of furniture. At length he had stooped down and inspected the mark made by the bullet on the wainscot; and once he had gone to the door and looked up and down the hall.

The only thing that had seemed to hold his attention to any extent was the body itself. He had stood before it for several minutes, studying its position, and had even bent over the out-stretched arm on the table as if to see just how the dead man's hand was holding the book. The crossed position of the legs, however, had attracted him most, and he had stood studying them for a considerable time. Finally, he had returned his monocle to his waistcoat pocket, and joined Dinwiddie and me near the door, where he had stood, watching Heath and the other detectives with lazy indifference, until the departure of Captain Hagedorn.

The four of us had no more than taken seats when the patrolman stationed in the vestibule appeared at the door.

"There's a man from the local precinct station here, sir," he announced, "who wants to see the officer in charge. Shall I send him in?"

Heath nodded curtly, and a moment later a large red-faced Irishman, in civilian clothes, stood before us. He saluted Heath, but on recognizing the District Attorney, made Markham the recipient of his report.

"I'm Officer McLaughlin, sir—West Forty-seventh Street station," he informed us; "and I was on duty on this beat last night. Around midnight, I guess it was, there was a big grey Cadillac standing in front of this house—I noticed it particular, because it had a lot of fishing-tackle sticking out the back, and all of its lights were on. When I heard of the crime this morning I reported the car to the station sergeant, and he sent me around to tell you about it."

"Excellent," Markham commented; and then, with a nod, referred the matter to Heath.

"May be something in it," the latter admitted dubiously. "How long would you say the car was here, officer?"

"A good half hour anyway. It was here before twelve, and when I come back at twelve-thirty or thereabouts it was still here. But the next time I come by, it was gone."

"You saw nothing else? Nobody in the car, or anyone hanging around who might have been the owner?"

44. Of course, Sherlock Holmes was an expert on tobacco. In *The Sign of Four* and again in "The Boscombe Valley Mystery," Holmes mentions his monograph on the subject; its title is revealed in the latter to be "Upon the Distinction Between the Ashes of the Various Tobaccos: An Enumeration of 140 Forms of Cigar, Cigarette, and Pipe Tobacco, with Coloured Plates Illustrating the Difference in the Ash."

45. The Ptolemaic dynasty ruled Egypt from 305 B.C.E. to 30 B.C.E. "Scarabs" were amulets in the form of scarab beetles, decorated with cartouches (hieroglyphic images). By the time of the Ptolemaic dynasty, they were generally affixed to mummies rather than worn as jewelry.

Scarab, probably fourteenth-century B.C.E., bearing an image of Amenhotep III.

"No, sir, I did not."

Several other questions of a similar nature were asked him; but nothing more could be learned, and he was dismissed.

"Anyway," remarked Heath, "the car story will be good stuff to hand the reporters."

Vance had sat through the questioning of McLaughlin with drowsy inattention,—I doubt if he even heard more than the first few words of the officer's report,—and now, with a stifled yawn, he rose and, sauntering to the center-table, picked up one of the cigarette butts that had been found in the fireplace. After rolling it between his thumb and forefinger and scrutinizing the tip, he ripped the paper open with his thumb-nail, and held the exposed tobacco to his nose.

Heath, who had been watching him gloweringly, leaned suddenly forward in his chair.

"What are you doing there?" he demanded, in a tone of surly truculence.

Vance lifted his eyes in decorous astonishment.

"Merely smelling of the tobacco," he replied, with condescending unconcern. "It's rather mild, y' know, but delicately blended."

The muscles in Heath's cheeks worked angrily. "Well, you'd better put it down, sir," he advised. Then he looked Vance up and down. "Tobacco expert?" he asked, with ill disguised sarcasm.[44]

"Oh, dear no." Vance's voice was dulcet. "My specialty is scarab-cartouches of the Ptolemaic dynasties."[45]

Markham interposed diplomatically.

"You really shouldn't touch anything around here, Vance, at this stage of the game. You never know what'll turn out to be important. Those cigarette stubs may quite possibly be significant evidence."

"Evidence?" repeated Vance sweetly. "My word! You don't say, really! Most amusin'!"

Markham was plainly annoyed; and Heath was boiling inwardly, but made no further comment: he even forced a mirthless smile. He evidently felt that he had been a little too abrupt with this friend of the District Attorney's, however much the friend might have deserved being reprimanded.

Heath, however, was no sycophant in the presence of his superiors. He knew his worth and lived up to it with his whole energy, discharging the tasks to which he was assigned with a dogged indifference to his own political well-being. This stubbornness of spirit, and the solidity of character it implied, were respected and valued by the men over him.

He was a large, powerful man, but agile and graceful in his movements, like a highly trained boxer. He had hard, blue eyes, remarkably bright and penetrating, a small nose, a broad oval chin, and a stern straight mouth with lips that appeared always compressed. His hair, which, though he was well along in his forties, was without a trace of greyness, was cropped about the edges, and stood upright in a short bristly pompadour. His voice had an aggressive resonance, but he rarely blustered. In many ways he accorded with the conventional notion of what a detective is like. But there was something more to the man's personality, an added capability and strength, as it were; and as I sat watching him that morning, I felt myself unconsciously admiring him, despite his very obvious limitations.

"What's the exact situation, Sergeant?" Markham asked. "Dinwiddie gave me only the barest facts."

Heath cleared his throat.

"We got the word a little before seven. Benson's housekeeper, a Mrs. Platz, called up the local station and reported that she'd found him dead, and asked that somebody be sent over at once. The message, of course, was relayed to Headquarters. I wasn't there at the time, but Burke and Emery were on duty, and after notifying Inspector Moran, they came on up here. Several of the men from the local station were already on the job doing the usual nosing about. When the Inspector had got here and looked the situation over, he telephoned me to hurry along. When I arrived the local men had gone, and three more men from the Homicide Bureau had joined Burke and Emery. The Inspector also 'phoned Captain Hagedorn—he thought the case big enough to call him in on it at once—and the Captain had just got here when you arrived. Mr. Dinwiddie had come in right after the Inspector, and 'phoned you at once. Chief Inspector O'Brien came along a little ahead of me. I questioned the Platz woman right off; and my men were looking the place over when you showed up."

"Where's this Mrs. Platz now?" asked Markham.

"Upstairs being watched by one of the local men. She lives in the house."

"Why did you mention the specific hour of twelve-thirty to the doctor?"

"Platz told me she heard a report at that time, which I thought might have been the shot. I guess now it *was* the shot—it checks up with a number of things."

"I think we'd better have another talk with Mrs. Platz," Markham suggested. "But first: did you find anything suggestive in the room here—anything to go on?"

Heath hesitated almost imperceptibly; then he drew from his coat pocket a woman's hand-bag and a pair of long white kid gloves, and tossed them on the table in front of the District Attorney.

"Only these," he said. "One of the local men found them on the end of the mantel over there."

After a casual inspection of the gloves, Markham opened the hand-bag and turned its contents out onto the table. I came forward and looked on, but Vance remained in his chair, placidly smoking a cigarette.

The hand-bag was of fine gold mesh with a catch set with small sapphires. It was unusually small, and obviously designed only for evening wear. The objects which it had held, and which Markham was now inspecting, consisted of a flat watered-silk cigarette-case, a small gold phial of Roger and Gallet's *Fleurs d'Amour* perfume,[46] a *cloisonné* vanity-compact, a short delicate cigarette-holder of inlaid amber, a gold-cased lip-stick, a small embroidered French-linen handkerchief with "M. St.C." monogrammed in the corner, and a Yale latch-key.

"This ought to give us a good lead," said Markham, indicating the handkerchief. "I suppose you went over the articles carefully, Sergeant."

Heath nodded.

"Yes; and I imagine the bag belongs to the woman Benson was out with last night. The housekeeper told me he had an appointment and went out to dinner in his dress clothes. She didn't hear Benson when he came back, though. Anyway, we ought to be able to run down Miss 'M. St.C.' without much trouble."

Markham had taken up the cigarette-case again, and as he held it upside down a little shower of loose dried tobacco fell onto the table.

Heath stood up suddenly.

"Maybe those cigarettes came out of that case," he suggested. He picked up the intact butt and looked at it. "It's a lady's cigarette, all right. It looks as though it might have been smoked in a holder, too."

"I beg to differ with you, Sergeant," drawled Vance. "You'll forgive me, I'm sure. But there's a bit of lip rouge on the end of the cigarette. It's hard to see, on account of the gold tip."

Heath looked at Vance sharply; he was too much surprised to be resentful. After a closer inspection of the cigarette, he turned again to Vance.

"Perhaps you could also tell us from these tobacco grains, if the cigarettes came from this case," he suggested, with gruff irony.

"One never knows, does one?" Vance replied, indolently rising.

Picking up the case, he pressed it wide open, and tapped it on the table. Then he looked into it closely, and a humorous smile twitched the corners of his mouth. Putting his forefinger deep into the case, he drew out a small cigarette which had evidently been wedged flat along the bottom of the pocket.

"My olfact'ry gifts won't be necess'ry now," he said. "It is apparent even to the naked eye that the cigarettes are, to speak loosely, identical—eh what, Sergeant?"

Heath grinned good-naturedly.

"That's one on us, Mr. Markham." And he carefully put the cigarette and the stub in an envelope, which he marked and pocketed.

"You now see, Vance," observed Markham, "the importance of those cigarette butts."

"Can't say that I do," responded the other. "Of what possible value is a cigarette butt? You can't smoke it, y' know."

"It's evidence, my dear fellow," explained Markham patiently. "One knows that the owner of this bag returned with Benson last night, and remained long enough to smoke two cigarettes."

Vance lifted his eyebrows in mock amazement.

"One does, does one? Fancy that, now."

"It only remains to locate her," interjected Heath.

"She's a rather decided brunette, at any rate—if that fact will facilitate your quest any," said Vance easily; "though why you should desire to annoy the lady, I can't for the life of me imagine—really I can't, don't y' know."

"Why do you say she's a brunette?" asked Markham.

"Well, if she isn't," Vance told him, sinking listlessly back in his chair, "then she should consult a cosmetician as to the proper way to make up. I see she uses 'Rachel' powder and Guerlain's dark lip-stick. And it simply isn't done among blondes, old dear."

"I defer, of course, to your expert opinion," smiled Markham. Then, to Heath: "I guess we'll have to look for a brunette, Sergeant."

"It's all right with me," agreed Heath jocularly. By this time, I think, he had entirely forgiven Vance for destroying the cigarette butt.

CHAPTER IV

The Housekeeper's Story

(Friday, June 14; 11 a.m.)

Now," suggested Markham, "suppose we take a look over the house. I imagine you've done that pretty thoroughly already, Sergeant, but I'd like to see the layout. Anyway, I don't want to question the housekeeper until the body has been removed."

Heath rose.

"Very good, sir. I'd like another look myself."

The four of us went into the hall and walked down the passageway to the rear of the house. At the extreme end, on the left, was a door leading downstairs to the basement; but it was locked and bolted.

"The basement is only used for storage now," Heath explained; "and the door which opens from it into the street areaway is boarded up. The Platz woman sleeps upstairs—Benson lived here alone, and there's plenty of spare room in the house—; and the kitchen is on this floor."

He opened a door on the opposite side of the passageway, and we stepped into a small modern kitchen. Its two high windows, which gave into the paved rear yard at a height of about eight feet from the ground, were securely guarded with iron bars, and, in addition, the sashes were closed and locked. Passing through a swinging door we entered the dining-room which was directly behind the living-room. The two windows here looked upon a small stone court—really no more than a deep airwell between Benson's house and the adjoining one—; and these also were iron-barred and locked.

We now re-entered the hallway and stood for a moment at the foot of the stairs leading above.

"You can see, Mr. Markham," Heath pointed out, "that whoever shot Benson must have gotten in by the front door. There's no other way he could have entered. Living alone, I guess Benson was a little touchy on the subject of burglars. The only window that wasn't barred was the rear one in the living-room; and that was shut and locked. Anyway, it only leads into the inside court. The front windows of the living-room have that ironwork over them; so they couldn't have been used even to shoot through, for Benson was shot from the opposite direction. . . . It's pretty clear the gunman got in the front door."

"Looks that way," said Markham.

"And pardon me for saying so," remarked Vance, "but Benson let him in."

"Yes?" retorted Heath unenthusiastically. "Well, we'll find all that out later, I hope."

"Oh, doubtless," Vance drily agreed.

We ascended the stairs, and entered Benson's bed-room which was directly over the living-room. It was severely but well furnished, and in excellent order. The bed was made, showing it had not been slept in that night; and the window shades were drawn. Benson's dinner-jacket and white piqué waistcoat were hanging over a chair. A winged collar and a black bow-tie were on the bed, where they had evidently been thrown when Benson had taken them off on returning home. A pair of low evening shoes were standing by the bench at the foot of the bed. In a glass of water on the night-table was a platinum plate of four false teeth; and a toupee of beautiful workmanship was lying on the chiffonier.

This last item aroused Vance's special interest. He walked up to it and regarded it closely.

"Most int'restin'," he commented. "Our departed friend seems to have worn false hair; did you know that, Markham?"

"I always suspected it," was the indifferent answer.

Heath, who had remained standing on the threshold, seemed a little impatient.

"There's only one other room on this floor," he said, leading the way down the hall. "It's also a bed-room—for guests, so the housekeeper explained."

Markham and I looked in through the door, but Vance remained lounging against the balustrade at the head of the stairs. He was manifestly uninterested in Alvin Benson's domestic arrangements; and when Markham and Heath and I went up to the third floor, he sauntered down into the main hallway. When at length we descended from our tour of inspection he was casually looking over the titles in Benson's bookcase.

We had just reached the foot of the stairs when the front door opened and two men with a stretcher entered. The ambulance from the Department of Welfare had arrived to take the corpse to the Morgue; and the brutal, business-like way in which Benson's body was covered up, lifted onto the stretcher, carried out and shoved into the wagon, made me shudder. Vance, on the other hand; after the merest fleeting glance at the two men, paid no attention to them. He had found a volume with a beautiful Humphrey-Milford binding, and was absorbed in its Roger Payne tooling and powdering.[47]

"I think an interview with Mrs. Platz is indicated now," said Markham; and Heath went to the foot of the stairs and gave a loud, brisk order.

Presently a grey-haired, middle-aged woman entered the living-room accompanied by a plain-clothes man smoking a large cigar. Mrs. Platz was of the simple, old-fashioned, motherly type, with a calm, benevolent countenance. She impressed me as highly capable, and as a woman given little to hysteria—an impression strengthened by her attitude of passive resignation. She seemed, however, to possess that taciturn shrewdness that is so often found among the ignorant.

"Sit down, Mrs. Platz," Markham greeted her kindly. "I'm the District Attorney, and there are some questions I want to ask you."

She took a straight chair by the door and waited, gazing nervously from one to the other of us. Markham's gentle, persuasive voice, though, appeared to encourage her; and her answers became more and more fluent.

The main facts that transpired from a quarter-of-an-hour's examination may be summed up as follows:

47. Properly "Humphrey Milford"—Milford was the publisher of Oxford University Press from 1913 to 1945 and supervised many beautiful editions of classic literature. Roger Payne (1739–1797) was a noted English bookbinder, and Milford may have published a replica of a book bound by Payne.

Mrs. Platz had been Benson's housekeeper for four years and was the only servant employed. She lived in the house, and her room was on the third, or top, floor in the rear.

On the afternoon of the preceding day Benson had returned from his office at an unusually early hour—around four o'clock—announcing to Mrs. Platz that he would not be home for dinner that evening. He had remained in the living-room, with the hall door closed, until half past six, and had then gone upstairs to dress.

He had left the house about seven o'clock, but had not said where he was going. He had remarked casually that he would return in fairly good season, but had told Mrs. Platz she need not wait up for him—which was her custom whenever he intended bringing guests home. This was the last she had seen him alive. She had not heard him when he returned that night.

She had retired about half past ten, and, because of the heat, had left the door ajar. She had been awakened some time later by a loud detonation. It had startled her, and she had turned on the light by her bed, noting that it was just half past twelve by the small alarm-clock she used for rising. It was, in fact, the early hour which had reassured her. Benson, whenever he went out for the evening, rarely returned home before two; and this fact, coupled with the stillness of the house, had made her conclude that the noise which had aroused her had been merely the backfiring of an automobile in Forty-ninth Street. Consequently, she had dismissed the matter from her mind, and gone back to sleep.

At seven o'clock the next morning she came downstairs as usual to begin her day's duties, and, on her way to the front door to bring in the milk and cream, had discovered Benson's body. All the shades in the living-room were down.

At first she thought Benson had fallen asleep in his chair, but when she saw the bullet hole and noticed that the electric lights had been switched off, she knew he was dead. She had gone at once to the telephone in the hall and, asking the operator for the Police Station, had reported the murder. She had then remembered Benson's brother, Major Anthony Benson, and had telephoned him also. He had arrived at the house almost simultaneously with the detectives from the West Forty-seventh Street station. He had questioned her a little, talked with the plain-clothes men, and gone away before the men from Headquarters arrived.

"And now, Mrs. Platz," said Markham, glancing at the notes he had been making, "one or two more questions, and we won't trouble you further. . . . Have you noticed anything in Mr. Benson's actions lately that might lead you to suspect that he was worried—or, let us say, in fear of anything happening to him?"

"No, sir," the woman answered readily. "It looked like he was in special good-humor for the last week or so."

"I notice that most of the windows on this floor are barred. Was he particularly afraid of burglars, or of people breaking in?"

"Well—not exactly," was the hesitant reply. "But he did use to say as how the police were no good—begging your pardon, sir—and how a man in this city had to look out for himself if he didn't want to get held up."

Markham turned to Heath with a chuckle.

"You might make a special note of that for your files, Sergeant." Then to Mrs. Platz: "Do you know of anyone who had a grudge against Mr. Benson?"

"Not a soul, sir," the housekeeper answered emphatically. "He was a queer man in many ways, but everybody seemed to like him. He was all the time going to parties or giving parties. I just can't see why anybody'd want to kill him."

Markham looked over his notes again.

"I don't think there's anything else for the present. . . . How about it, Sergeant? Anything further you want to ask?"

Heath pondered a moment.

"No, I can't think of anything more just now. . . . But you, Mrs. Platz," he added, turning a cold glance on the woman, "will stay here in this house till you're given permission to leave. We'll want to question you later. But you're not to talk to anyone else—understand? Two of my men will be here for a while yet."

Vance, during the interview, had been jotting down something on the fly-leaf of a small pocket address-book, and as Heath

48. This was a standard model 6-shot .38-caliber revolver made by Smith & Wesson at the time, available with mother-of-pearl handles.

A pearl-handled Smith & Wesson revolver.

was speaking, he tore out the page and handed it to Markham. Markham glanced at it frowningly and pursed his lips. Then after a few moments' hesitation, he addressed himself again to the housekeeper.

"You mentioned, Mrs. Platz, that Mr. Benson was liked by everyone. Did you yourself like him?"

The woman shifted her eyes to her lap.

"Well, sir," she replied reluctantly, "I was only working for him, and I haven't got any complaint about the way he treated me."

Despite her words, she gave the impression that she either disliked Benson extremely or greatly disapproved of him. Markham, however, did not push the point.

"And by the way, Mrs. Platz," he said next, "did Mr. Benson keep any fire-arms about the house? For instance, do you know if he owned a revolver?"

For the first time during the interview, the woman appeared agitated, even frightened.

"Yes, sir, I—think he did," she admitted, in an unsteady voice.

"Where did he keep it?"

The woman glanced up apprehensively, and rolled her eyes slightly as if weighing the advisability of speaking frankly. Then she replied in a low voice:

"In that hidden drawer there in the center-table. You—you use that little brass button to open it with."

Heath jumped up, and pressed the button she had indicated. A tiny, shallow drawer shot out; and in it lay a Smith and Wesson thirty-eight revolver with an inlaid pearl handle.[48] He picked it up, broke the carriage, and looked at the head of the cylinder.

"Full," he announced laconically.

An expression of tremendous relief spread over the woman's features, and she sighed audibly.

Markham had risen and was looking at the revolver over Heath's shoulder.

"You'd better take charge of it, Sergeant," he said; "though I don't see exactly how it fits in with the case."

He resumed his seat, and glancing at the notation Vance had given him, turned again to the housekeeper.

"One more question, Mrs. Platz. You said Mr. Benson came home early and spent his time before dinner in this room. Did he have any callers during that time?"

I was watching the woman closely, and it seemed to me that she quickly compressed her lips. At any rate, she sat up a little straighter in her chair before answering.

"There wasn't no one, as far as I know."

"But surely you would have known if the bell rang," insisted Markham. "You would have answered the door, wouldn't you?"

"There wasn't no one," she repeated, with a trace of sullenness.

"And last night: did the door-bell ring at all after you had retired?"

"No, sir."

"You would have heard it, even if you'd been asleep?"

"Yes, sir. There's a bell just outside my door, the same as in the kitchen. It rings in both places. Mr. Benson had it fixed that way."

Markham thanked her and dismissed her. When she had gone, he looked at Vance questioningly.

"What idea did you have in your mind when you handed me those questions?"

"I might have been a bit presumptuous, y' know," said Vance; "but when the lady was extolling the deceased's popularity, I rather felt she was overdoing it a bit. There was an unconscious implication of antithesis in her eulogy, which suggested to me that she herself was not ardently enamored of the gentleman."

"And what put the notion of fire-arms into your mind?"

"That query," explained Vance, "was a corollary of your own questions about barred windows and Benson's fear of burglars. If he was in a funk about house-breakers or enemies, he'd be likely to have weapons at hand—eh, what?"

"Well, anyway, Mr. Vance," put in Heath, "your curiosity unearthed a nice little revolver that's probably never been used."

"By the bye, Sergeant," returned Vance, ignoring the other's good-humored sarcasm, "just what do you make of that nice little revolver?"

"Well, now," Heath replied, with ponderous facetiousness, "I deduct that Mr. Benson kept a pearl-handled Smith and Wesson in a secret drawer of his center-table."

"You don't say—really!" exclaimed Vance in mock admiration. "Pos'tively illuminatin'!"

Markham broke up this raillery.

"Why did you want to know about visitors, Vance? There obviously hadn't been anyone here."

"Oh, just a whim of mine. I was assailed by an impulsive yearning to hear what La Platz would say."

Heath was studying Vance curiously. His first impressions of the man were being dispelled, and he had begun to suspect that beneath the other's casual and debonair exterior there was something of a more solid nature than he had at first imagined. He was not altogether satisfied with Vance's explanations to Markham, and seemed to be endeavoring to penetrate to his real reasons for supplementing the District Attorney's interrogation of the housekeeper. Heath was astute, and he had the worldly man's ability to read people; but Vance, being different from the men with whom he usually came in contact, was an enigma to him.

At length he relinquished his scrutiny, and drew up his chair to the table with a spirited air.

"And now, Mr. Markham," he said crisply, "we'd better outline our activities so as not to duplicate our efforts. The sooner I get my men started, the better."

Markham assented readily.

"The investigation is entirely up to you, Sergeant. I'm here to help wherever I'm needed."

"That's very kind of you, sir," Heath returned. "But it looks to me as though there'd be enough work for all parties. . . . Suppose I get to work on running down the owner of the hand-bag, and send some men out scouting among Benson's night-life cronies,—I can pick up some names from the housekeeper, and they'll be a good starting point. And I'll get after that Cadillac, too. . . . Then we ought to look into his lady friends—I guess he had enough of 'em."

"I may get something out of the Major along that line," supplied Markham. "He'll tell me anything I want to know. And I can also look into Benson's business associates through the same channel."

"I was going to suggest that you could do that better than I could," Heath rejoined. "We ought to run into something pretty quick that'll give us a line to go on. And I've got an idea that when we locate the lady he took to dinner last night and brought back here, we'll know a lot more than we do now."

"Or a lot less," murmured Vance.

Heath looked up quickly, and grunted with an air of massive petulance.

"Let me tell you something, Mr. Vance," he said, "—since I understand you want to learn something about these affairs: when anything goes seriously wrong in this world, it's pretty safe to look for a woman in the case."

"Ah, yes," smiled Vance. "*Cherchez la femme*—an aged notion. Even the Romans labored under the superstition,—they expressed it with *Dux femina facti*."[49]

"However they expressed it," retorted Heath, "they had the right idea. And don't let 'em tell you different."

Again Markham diplomatically intervened.

"That point will be settled very soon, I hope. . . . And now, Sergeant, if you've nothing else to suggest, I'll be getting along. I told Major Benson I'd see him at lunch time; and I may have some news for you by to-night."

"Right," assented Heath. "I'm going to stick around here a while and see if there's anything I overlooked. I'll arrange for a guard outside and also for a man inside to keep an eye on the Platz woman. Then I'll see the reporters and let them in on the disappearing Cadillac and Mr. Vance's mysterious revolver in the secret drawer. I guess that ought to hold 'em. If I find out anything, I'll 'phone you."

When he had shaken hands with the District Attorney, he turned to Vance.

"Good-bye, sir," he said pleasantly, much to my surprise, and to Markham's too, I imagine. "I hope you learned something this morning."

"You'd be pos'tively dumfounded, Sergeant, at all I did learn," Vance answered carelessly.

Again I noted the look of shrewd scrutiny in Heath's eyes; but in a second it was gone.

"Well, I'm glad of that," was his perfunctory reply.

Markham, Vance and I went out, and the patrolman on duty hailed a taxicab for us.

"So that's the way our lofty *gendarmerie* approaches the mysterious wherefores of criminal enterprise—eh?" mused Vance, as we started on our way across town. "Markham, old dear, how do those robust lads ever succeed in running down a culprit?"

"You have witnessed only the barest preliminaries," Markham explained. "There are certain things that must be done as a matter of routine—*ex abundantia cautelæ*,[50] as we lawyers say."

"But, my word!—such technique!" sighed Vance. "Ah, well, *quantum est in rebus inane!*[51] as we laymen say."

49. Roughly translated as "The woman was the leader of the exploit," the phrase is from Virgil's *Aeneid*, Book I, Line 364.

50. "Out of an abundance of caution."

51. "Ah, how much futility in the world!" (said to be from to the satires of Persius and quoted by many other writers, including Voltaire).

"You don't think much of Heath's capacity, I know,"—Markham's voice was patient—"but he's a clever man, and one that it's very easy to underestimate."

"I dare say," murmured Vance. "Anyway, I'm deuced grateful to you, and all that, for letting me behold the solemn proceedings. I've been vastly amused, even if not uplifted. Your official Æsculapius rather appealed to me, y' know—such a brisk, unemotional chap, and utterly unimpressed with the corpse. He really should have taken up crime in a serious way, instead of studying medicine."

Markham lapsed into gloomy silence, and sat looking out of the window in troubled meditation until we reached Vance's house.

"I don't like the looks of things," he remarked, as we drew up to the curb. "I have a curious feeling about this case."

Vance regarded him a moment from the corner of his eye.

"See here, Markham," he said with unwonted seriousness; "haven't you any idea who shot Benson?"

Markham forced a faint smile.

"I wish I had. Crimes of wilful murder are not so easily solved. And this case strikes me as a particularly complex one."

"Fancy, now!" said Vance, as he stepped out of the machine. "And I thought it extr'ordin'rily simple."

CHAPTER V

Gathering Information

(Saturday, June 15; forenoon.)

You will remember the sensation caused by Alvin Benson's murder. It was one of those crimes that appeal irresistibly to the popular imagination. Mystery is the basis of all romance, and about the Benson case there hung an impenetrable aura of mystery. It was many days before any definite light was shed on the circumstances surrounding the shooting; but numerous *ignes fatui*[52] arose to beguile the public's imagination, and wild speculations were heard on all sides.

Alvin Benson, while not a romantic figure in any respect, had been well-known; and his personality had been a colorful and spectacular one. He had been a member of New York's wealthy bohemian social set—an avid sportsman, a rash gambler, and professional man-about-town; and his life, led on the borderland of the demimonde, had contained many high-lights. His exploits in the night clubs and cabarets had long supplied the subject-matter for exaggerated stories and comments in the various local papers and magazines which batten on Broadway's scandalmongers.[53]

Benson and his brother, Anthony, had, at the time of the former's sudden death, been running a brokerage office at 21 Wall Street, under the name of Benson and Benson. Both were regarded by the other brokers of the Street as shrewd business men, though perhaps a shade unethical when gauged by the constitution and by-laws of the New York Stock Exchange. They

52. Literally, "foolish lights," referring to the intermittent lights seen in marshlands known as "will-o'-the-wisp," used here figuratively.

53. Such magazines included *Town Topics: A Journal of Society*, for which Willard Wright (S. S. Van Dine) had written. The magazines had an interesting method of extortion. An innocuous article about Mr. X would appear (naming names) next to a "blind" article about his scandalous activities, thus protecting the magazine from overt blackmail. Such articles could be suppressed by the subject's purchasing "advertising" in the magazine.

Town Topics (February 1919)

54. As will be seen, Benson's service must have taken place in mid-1917, and at the time of the murder, he was only recently returned to New York.

* [Author's note:] Even the famous Elwell case, which came several years later and bore certain points of similarity to the Benson case, created no greater sensation, despite the fact that Elwell was more widely known than Benson, and the persons involved were more prominent socially. Indeed, the Benson case was referred to several times in descriptions of the Elwell case; and one anti-administration paper regretted editorially that John F.-X. Markham was no longer District Attorney of New York.

[Editor's note: On June 11, 1920, J. B. Elwell was murdered in his locked house. The case has never been solved. The Elwell case is thought to be one of the inspirations for *The Benson Murder Case*. There are many similarities between the two (see in particular Chapter 4 of J. K. Van Dover's *Making the Detective Story American*). Van Dine's reference to it is a joke. See Foreword, p. xix. This author's note is an important clue to dating the events of this case—"several years later" confirms that the events could not possibly have occurred in the mid-1920s, after the Elwell case, as various references to the "war" seem to suggest.]

55. Clairvoyants—psychics—are people with the ability to obtain information through visions or supernatural powers. In the 1920s, belief in mediums such as Mina Crandon ("Margery"), whose abilities were investigated by the Society for Psychical Research and *Scientific American*, was widespread, and the Spiritualist movement had many prominent adherents, including its international

were markedly contrasted as to temperament and taste, and saw little of each other outside the office. Alvin Benson devoted his entire leisure to pleasure-seeking and was a regular patron of the city's leading cafés; whereas Anthony Benson, who was the older and had served as a major in the late war,[54] followed a sedate and conventional existence, spending most of his evenings quietly at his clubs. Both, however, were popular in their respective circles, and between them they had built up a large clientele.

The glamour of the financial district had much to do with the manner in which the crime was handled by the newspapers. Moreover, the murder had been committed at a time when the metropolitan press was experiencing a temporary lull in sensationalism; and the story was spread over the front pages of the papers with a prodigality rarely encountered in such cases.[*] Eminent detectives throughout the country were interviewed by enterprising reporters. Histories of famous unsolved murder cases were revived; and clairvoyants[55] and astrologers were engaged by the Sunday editors to solve the mystery by various metaphysical devices. Photographs and detailed diagrams were the daily accompaniments of these journalistic outpourings.

In all the news stories the grey Cadillac and the pearl-handled Smith and Wesson were featured. There were pictures of Cadillac cars, "touched up" and reconstructed to accord with Patrolman McLaughlin's description, some of them even showing the fishing-tackle protruding from the tonneau. A photograph of Benson's center-table had been taken, with the secret drawer enlarged and reproduced in an "inset". One Sunday magazine went so far as to hire an expert cabinet-maker to write a dissertation on secret compartments in furniture.

The Benson case from the outset had proved a trying and difficult one from the police standpoint. Within an hour of the time that Vance and I had left the scene of the crime a systematic investigation had been launched by the men of the Homicide Bureau in charge of Sergeant Heath. Benson's house was again gone over thoroughly, and all his private correspondence read; but nothing was brought forth that could throw any light on the tragedy. No weapon was found aside from Benson's own Smith and Wesson; and though all the window *grilles* were again inspected, they were found to be secure, indicating that the murderer had either let himself in with a key, or else been admitted by Benson. Heath, by the way, was unwilling to admit this latter possibility despite Mrs. Platz's positive assertion that no other person besides herself and Benson had a key.

Because of the absence of any definite clue, other than the hand-bag and the gloves, the only proceeding possible was the interrogating of Benson's friends and associates in the hope of uncovering some fact which would furnish a trail. It was by this process also that Heath hoped to establish the identity of the owner of the hand-bag. A special effort was therefore made to ascertain where Benson had spent the evening; but though many of his acquaintances were questioned, and the cafés where he habitually dined were visited, no one could at once be found who had seen him that night; nor, as far as it was possible to learn, had he mentioned to anyone his plans for the evening. Furthermore, no general information of a helpful nature came to light immediately, although the police pushed their inquiry with the utmost thoroughness. Benson apparently had no enemies; he had not quarreled seriously with anyone; and his affairs were reported in their usual orderly shape.

Major Anthony Benson was naturally the principal person looked to for information, because of his intimate knowledge of his brother's affairs; and it was in this connection that the District Attorney's office did its chief functioning at the beginning of the case. Markham had lunched with Major Benson the day the crime was discovered, and though the latter had shown a willingness to co-operate—even to the detriment of his brother's character—his suggestions were of little value. He explained to Markham that, though he knew most of his brother's associates, he could not name anyone who would have any reason for committing such a crime, or anyone who, in his opinion, would be able to help in leading the police to the guilty person. He admitted frankly, however, that there was a side to his brother's life with which he was unacquainted, and regretted that he was unable to suggest any specific way of ascertaining the hidden facts. But he intimated that his brother's relations with women were of a somewhat unconventional nature; and he ventured the opinion that there was a bare possibility of a motive being found in that direction.

Pursuant of the few indefinite and unsatisfactory suggestions of Major Benson, Markham had immediately put to work two good men from the Detective Division assigned to the District

spokesperson Sir Arthur Conan Doyle. The popularity of the "scientific" religion was fed in part by the large number of deaths resulting from World War I; families were eager to be in touch with lost loved ones. Clairvoyants often offered their services to official investigators, a practice that continues today. For example, the television drama *Medium* (2005–2011) was based on the real psychic named Allison Dubois and her relationship with the Phoenix police department.

Attorney's office, with instructions to confine their investigations to Benson's women acquaintances so as not to appear in any way to be encroaching upon the activities of the Central Office men. Also, as a result of Vance's apparent interest in the housekeeper at the time of the interrogation, he had sent a man to look into the woman's antecedents and relationships.

Mrs. Platz, it was learned, had been born in a small Pennsylvania town, of German parents both of whom were dead; and had been a widow for over sixteen years. Before coming to Benson, she had been with one family for twelve years, and had left the position only because her mistress had given up housekeeping and moved into a hotel. Her former employer, when questioned, said she thought there had been a daughter, but had never seen the child, and knew nothing of it. In these facts there was nothing to take hold of, and Markham had merely filed the report as a matter of form.

Heath had instigated a city-wide search for the grey Cadillac, although he had little faith in its direct connection with the crime; and in this the newspapers helped considerably by the extensive advertising given the car. One curious fact developed that fired the police with the hope that the Cadillac might indeed hold some clue to the mystery. A street-cleaner, having read or heard about the fishing-tackle in the machine, reported the finding of two jointed fishing-rods, in good condition, at the side of one of the drives in Central Park near Columbus Circle. The question was: were these rods part of the equipment Patrolman McLaughlin had seen in the Cadillac? The owner of the car might conceivably have thrown them away in his flight; but, on the other hand, they might have been lost by someone else while driving through the park. No further information was forthcoming, and on the morning of the day following the discovery of the crime the case, so far as any definite progress toward a solution was concerned, had taken no perceptible forward step.

That morning Vance had sent Currie out to buy him every available newspaper; and he had spent over an hour perusing the various accounts of the crime. It was unusual for him to glance at a newspaper, even casually, and I could not refrain from expressing my amazement at his sudden interest in a subject so entirely outside his normal routine.

"No, Van old dear," he explained languidly, "I am not becoming sentimental or even human, as that word is erroneously used to-day. I can not say with Terence, '*Homo sum, humani nihil a me alienum puto*',[56] because I regard most things that are called human as decidedly alien to myself. But, y' know, this little flurry in crime has proved rather int'restin', or, as the magazine writers say, intriguing—beastly word! . . . Van, you really should read this precious interview with Sergeant Heath. He takes an entire column to say 'I know nothing'. A priceless lad! I'm becoming pos'tively fond of him."

"It may be," I suggested, "that Heath is keeping his true knowledge from the papers, as a bit of tactical diplomacy."

"No," Vance returned, with a sad wag of the head; "no man has so little vanity that he would delib'rately reveal himself to the world as a creature with no per'ceptible powers of human reasoning—as he does in all these morning journals—for the mere sake of bringing one murderer to justice. That would be martyrdom gone mad."

"Markham, at any rate, may know or suspect something that hasn't been revealed," I said.

Vance pondered a moment.

"That's not impossible," he admitted. "He has kept himself modestly in the background in all this journalistic palaver. Suppose we look into the matter more thoroughly—eh, what?"

Going to the telephone he called the District Attorney's office, and I heard him make an appointment with Markham for lunch at the Stuyvesant Club.

"What about that Nadelmann statuette at Stieglitz's,"[57] I asked, remembering the reason for my presence at Vance's that morning.

"I ain't[*] in the mood for Greek simplifications to-day," he answered, turning again to his newspapers.

To say that I was surprised at his attitude is to express it mildly. In all my association with him I had never known him to forgo his enthusiasm for art in favor of any other divertisement; and heretofore anything pertaining to the law and its operations had failed to interest him. I realized, therefore, that something of an unusual nature was at work in his brain, and I refrained from further comment.

Markham was a little late for the appointment at the Club, and Vance and I were already at our favorite corner table when he arrived.

56. Usually translated as "I am human, and I think that nothing of that which is human is alien to me." From Terence's play *Heauton Timorumenos*, written in the second century B.C.E.

57. Elie Nadelman (1882–1946) was a Polish sculptor (and later prominent collector). Nadelman lived in Paris from 1904 to 1914, where he became associated with the avant-garde artists. At the outbreak of the war in 1914, he moved to New York, where he lived for the rest of his life. His early work was classical in style, though he later adopted Cubist ideas. Photographer's Alfred Stieglitz's "291" gallery, at 291 Fifth Avenue, which flourished from 1905 to 1917, exhibited Nadelman's sculptures in 1915. After closing the gallery in 1917, Stieglitz began his relationship with Georgia O'Keefe. She moved to New York, and, essentially, she and Stieglitz were together until his death in 1946. It may well be that he retained some of Nadelman's work after the closing of 291 and showed it privately to collectors.

* [Author's note:] Vance, who had lived many years in England, frequently said "ain't"—a contraction which is regarded there more leniently than in this country. He also pronounced *ate* as if it were spelled *et*; and I can not remember his ever using the word "stomach" or "bug", both of which are under the social ban in England.

"Well, my good Lycurgus," Vance greeted him, "aside from the fact that several new and significant clues have been unearthed and that the public may expect important developments in the very near future, and all that sort of tosh, how are things really going?"

Markham smiled.

"I see you have been reading the newspapers. What do you think of the accounts?"

"Typical, no doubt," replied Vance. "They carefully and painstakingly omit nothing but the essentials."

"Indeed?" Markham's tone was jocular. "And what, may I ask, do you regard as the essentials of the case?"

"In my foolish amateur way," said Vance, "I looked upon dear Alvin's toupee as a rather conspicuous essential, don't y' know."

"Benson, at any rate, regarded it in that light, I imagine. . . . Anything else?"

"Well, there was the collar and the tie on the chiffonier."

"And," added Markham chaffingly, "don't overlook the false teeth in the tumbler."

"You're pos'tively coruscatin'!" Vance exclaimed. "Yes, they, too, were an essential of the situation. And I'll warrant the incomp'rable Heath didn't even notice them. But the other Aristotles present were equally sketchy in their observations."

"You weren't particularly impressed by the investigation yesterday, I take it," said Markham.

"On the contrary," Vance assured him. "I was impressed to the point of stupefaction. The whole proceedings constituted a masterpiece of absurdity. Everything relevant was sublimely ignored. There were at least a dozen *points de départ*,[58] all leading in the same direction, but not one of them apparently was even noticed by any of the officiating *pourparleurs*.[59] Everybody was too busy at such silly occupations as looking for cigarette-ends and inspecting the ironwork at the windows.—Those *grilles*, by the way, were rather attractive—Florentine design."

Markham was both amused and ruffled.

"One's pretty safe with the police, Vance," he said. "They get there eventually."

"I simply adore your trusting nature," murmured Vance. "But confide in me: what do you know regarding Benson's murderer?"

Markham hesitated.

"This is, of course, in confidence," he said at length; "but this morning, right after you 'phoned, one of the men I had put to work on the amatory end of Benson's life, reported that he had found the woman who left her hand-bag and gloves at the house that night,—the initials on the handkerchief gave him the clue. And he dug up some interesting facts about her. As I suspected, she was Benson's dinner companion that evening. She's an actress—musical comedy, I believe. Muriel St. Clair by name."

"Most unfortunate," breathed Vance. "I was hoping, y' know, your myrmidons wouldn't discover the lady. I haven't the pleasure of her acquaintance, or I'd send her a note of commiseration. . . . Now, I presume, you'll play the *juge d'instruction*[60] and chivvy her most horribly, what?"

"I shall certainly question her, if that's what you mean."

Markham's manner was preoccupied, and during the rest of the lunch we spoke but little.

As we sat in the Club's lounge-room later having our smoke, Major Benson, who had been standing dejectedly at a window close by, caught sight of Markham and came over to us. He was a full-faced man of about fifty, with grave kindly features and a sturdy, erect body.

He greeted Vance and me with a casual bow, and turned at once to the District Attorney.

"Markham, I've been thinking things over constantly since our lunch yesterday," he said, "and there's one other suggestion I think I might make. There's a man named Leander Pfyfe who was very close to Alvin; and it's possible he could give you some helpful information. His name didn't occur to me yesterday, for he doesn't live in the city; he's on Long Island somewhere—Port Washington,[61] I think.—It's just an idea. The truth is, I can't seem to figure out anything that makes sense in this terrible affair."

He drew a quick, resolute breath, as if to check some involuntary sign of emotion. It was evident that the man, for all his habitual passivity of nature, was deeply moved.

"That's a good suggestion, Major," Markham said, making a notation on the back of a letter. "I'll get after it immediately."

Vance, who, during this brief interchange, had been gazing unconcernedly out of the window, turned and addressed himself to the Major.

60. A magistrate who interrogates the witnesses.

61. A small hamlet in the northwest corner of Hampstead County.

"How about Colonel Ostrander? I've seen him several times in the company of your brother."

Major Benson made a slight gesture of deprecation.

"Only an acquaintance. He'd be of no value."

Then he turned to Markham.

"I don't imagine it's time even to hope that you've run across anything."

Markham took his cigar from his mouth, and turning it about in his fingers, contemplated it thoughtfully.

"I wouldn't say that," he remarked, after a moment. "I've managed to find out whom your brother dined with Thursday night; and I know that this person returned home with him shortly after midnight." He paused as if deliberating the wisdom of saying more. Then: "The fact is, I don't need a great deal more evidence than I've got already to go before the Grand Jury and ask for an indictment."

A look of surprised admiration flashed in the Major's sombre face.

"Thank God for that, Markham!" he said. Then, setting his heavy jaw, he placed his hand on the District Attorney's shoulder. "Go the limit—for my sake!" he urged. "If you want me for anything, I'll be here at the Club till late."

With this he turned and walked from the room.

"It seems a bit cold-blooded to bother the Major with questions so soon after his brother's death," commented Markham. "Still, the world has got to go on."

Vance stifled a yawn.

"Why—in Heaven's name?" he murmured listlessly.

CHAPTER VI

Vance Offers an Opinion

(Saturday, June 15; 2 p.m.)

We sat for a while smoking in silence, Vance gazing lazily out into Madison Square, Markham frowning deeply at the faded oil portrait of old Peter Stuyvesant that hung over the fireplace.

Presently Vance turned and contemplated the District Attorney with a faintly sardonic smile.

"I say, Markham," he drawled; "it has always been a source of amazement to me how easily you investigators of crime are misled by what you call clues. You find a footprint, or a parked automobile, or a monogrammed handkerchief, and then dash off on a wild chase with your eternal *Ecce signum*![62] 'Pon my word, it's as if you chaps were all under the spell of shillin' shockers. Won't you ever learn that crimes can't be solved by deductions based merely on material clues and circumst'ntial evidence?"[63]

I think Markham was as much surprised as I at this sudden criticism; yet we both knew Vance well enough to realize that, despite his placid and almost flippant tone, there was a serious purpose behind his words.

"Would you advocate ignoring all the tangible evidence of a crime?" asked Markham, a bit patronizingly.

"Most emphatically," Vance declared calmly. "It's not only worthless but dangerous. . . . The great trouble with you chaps,

62. "Here is the sign (proof)!"

63. "Circumstantial evidence is a very tricky thing," said Sherlock Holmes, in "The Boscombe Valley Mystery." "It may seem to point very straight to one thing, but if you shift your own point of view a little, you may find it pointing in an equally uncompromising manner to something entirely different." And yet, he quoted with approval from Thoreau: "Circumstantial evidence is occasionally very convincing, as when you find a trout in the milk."

64. Vance is undoubtedly right about the kind of stories that appear in mystery fiction and crimes perpetrated by the "better" class of criminals, including those who studied the tales of Sherlock Holmes and the vast outpouring of mystery fiction after the success of Holmes. Fortunately for law enforcement, however, most criminals are not drawn from the class of mystery readers, and crime-scene evidence has been an essential tool of law enforcement for the great majority of crimes.

d' ye see, is that you approach every crime with a fixed and unshakable assumption that the criminal is either half-witted or a colossal bungler. I say, has it never by any chance occurred to you that if a detective could see a clue, the criminal would also have seen it, and would either have concealed it or disguised it, if he had not wanted it found? And have you never paused to consider that anyone clever enough to plan and execute a successful crime these days, is, *ipso facto*, clever enough to manufacture whatever clues suit his purpose? Your detective seems wholly unwilling to admit that the surface appearance of a crime may be delib'rately deceptive, or that the clues may have been planted for the def'nite purpose of misleading him."[64]

"I'm afraid," Markham pointed out, with an air of indulgent irony, "that we'd convict very few criminals if we were to ignore all indicatory evidence, cogent circumstances and irresistible inferences. . . . As a rule, you know, crimes are not witnessed by outsiders."

"That's your fundamental error, don't y' know," Vance observed impassively. "Every crime is witnessed by outsiders, just as is every work of art. The fact that no one sees the criminal, or the artist, actu'lly at work, is wholly incons'quential. The modern investigator of crime would doubtless refuse to believe that Rubens painted the *Descent from the Cross* in the Cathedral at Antwerp if there was sufficient circumst'ntial evidence to indicate that he had been away on diplomatic business, for instance, at the time it was painted. And yet, my dear fellow, such a conclusion would be prepost'rous. Even if the inf'rences to the contr'ry were so irresistible as to be legally overpowering, the picture itself would prove conclusively that Rubens did paint it. Why? For the simple reason, d' ye see, that no one but Rubens could have painted it. It bears the indelible imprint of his personality and genius—and his alone."

"I'm not an æsthetician," Markham reminded him, a trifle testily. "I'm merely a practical lawyer, and when it comes to determining the authorship of a crime, I prefer tangible evidence to metaphysical hypotheses."

"Your pref'rence, my dear fellow," Vance returned blandly, "will inev'tably involve you in all manner of embarrassing errors."

He slowly lit another cigarette, and blew a wreath of smoke toward the ceiling.

"Consider, for example, your conclusions in the present murder case," he went on, in his emotionless drawl. "You are laboring under the grave misconception that you know the person who prob'bly killed the unspeakable Benson. You admitted as much to the Major; and you told him you had nearly enough evidence to ask for an indictment. No doubt, you do possess a number of what the learned Solons of to-day regard as convincing clues. But the truth is, don't y' know, you haven't your eye on the guilty person at all. You're about to bedevil some poor girl who had nothing whatever to do with the crime."

Markham swung about sharply.

"So!" he retorted. "I'm about to bedevil an innocent person, eh? Since my assistants and I are the only ones who happen to know what evidence we hold against her, perhaps you will explain by what occult process you acquired your knowledge of this person's innocence."

"It's quite simple, y' know," Vance replied, with a quizzical twitch of the lips. "You haven't your eye on the murderer for the reason that the person who committed this particular crime was sufficiently shrewd and perspicacious to see to it that no evidence which you or the police were likely to find, would even remotely indicate his guilt."

He had spoken with the easy assurance of one who enunciates an obvious fact—a fact which permits of no argument.

Markham gave a disdainful laugh.

"No law-breaker," he asserted oracularly, "is shrewd enough to see all contingencies. Even the most trivial event has so many intimately related and serrated points of contact with other events which precede and follow, that it is a known fact that every criminal—however long and carefully he may plan—leaves some loose end to his preparations, which in the end betrays him."

"A known fact?" Vance repeated. "No, my dear fellow—merely a conventional superstition, based on the childish idea of an implacable, avenging Nemesis. I can see how this esoteric notion of the inev'tability of divine punishment would appeal to the popular imagination, like fortune-telling and Ouija boards, don't y' know; but—my word!—it desolates me to think that you, old chap, would give credence to such mystical moonshine."

"Don't let it spoil your entire day," said Markham acridly.

"Regard the unsolved, or successful, crimes that are taking place every day," Vance continued, disregarding the other's irony,

"—crimes which completely baffle the best detectives in the business, what? The fact is, the only crimes that are ever solved are those planned by stupid people. That's why, whenever a man of even mod'rate sagacity decides to commit a crime, he accomplishes it with but little diff'culty, and fortified with the pos'tive assurance of his immunity to discovery."

"Undetected crimes," scornfully submitted Markham, "result, in the main, from official bad luck—not from superior criminal cleverness."

"Bad luck"—Vance's voice was almost dulcet—"is merely a defensive and self-consoling synonym for inefficiency. A man with ingenuity and brains is not harassed by bad luck. . . . No, Markham old dear; unsolved crimes are simply crimes which have been intelligently planned and executed. And, d' ye see, it happens that the Benson murder falls into that categ'ry. Therefore, when, after a few hours' investigation, you say you're pretty sure who committed it, you must pardon me if I take issue with you."

He paused and took a few meditative puffs on his cigarette.

"The factitious and casuistic methods of deduction you chaps pursue are apt to lead almost anywhere. In proof of which assertion I point triumphantly to the unfortunate young lady whose liberty you are now plotting to take away."

Markham, who had been hiding his resentment behind a smile of tolerant contempt, now turned on Vance and fairly glowered.

"It so happens—and I'm speaking *ex cathedra*[65]—" he proclaimed defiantly, "that I come pretty near having the goods on your 'unfortunate young lady'."

Vance was unmoved.

"And yet, y' know," he observed drily, "no woman could possibly have done it."

I could see that Markham was furious. When he spoke he almost spluttered.

"A woman couldn't have done it, eh—no matter what the evidence?"

"Quite so," Vance rejoined placidly: "not if she herself swore to it and produced a tome of what you scions of the law term, rather pompously, incontrovertible evidence."

"Ah!" There was no mistaking the sarcasm of Markham's tone. "I am to understand then that you even regard confessions as valueless?"

"Yes, my dear Justinian," the other responded, with an air of complacency; "I would have you understand precisely that. Indeed, they are worse than valueless—they're downright misleading. The fact that occasionally they may prove to be correct—like woman's prepost'rously overrated intuition—renders them just so much more unreliable."

Markham grunted disdainfully.

"Why should any person confess something to his detriment unless he felt that the truth had been found out, or was likely to be found out?"

"'Pon my word, Markham, you astound me! Permit me to murmur, *privatissime et gratis,*[66] into your innocent ear that there are many other presumable motives for confessing. A confession may be the result of fear, or duress, or expediency, or mother-love, or chivalry, or what the psycho-analysts call the inferiority complex, or delusions, or a mistaken sense of duty, or a perverted egotism, or sheer vanity, or any other of a hundred causes. Confessions are the most treach'rous and unreliable of all forms of evidence; and even the silly and unscientific law repudiates them in murder cases unless substantiated by other evidence."[67]

"You are eloquent; you wring me," said Markham. "But if the law threw out all confessions and ignored all material clues, as you appear to advise, then society might as well close down all its courts and scrap all its jails."

"A typical *non sequitur* of legal logic," Vance replied.

"But how would you convict the guilty, may I ask?"

"There is one infallible method of determining human guilt and responsibility," Vance explained; "but as yet the police are as blissfully unaware of its possibilities as they are ignorant of its operations. The truth can be learned only by an analysis of the psychological factors of a crime, and an application of them to the individual. The only real clues are psychological—not material. Your truly profound art expert, for instance, does not judge and authenticate pictures by an inspection of the underpainting and a chemical analysis of the pigments, but by studying the creative personality revealed in the picture's conception and execution. He asks himself: Does this work of art embody the qualities of form and technique and mental attitude that made up the genius—namely, the personality—of Rubens, or Michelangelo,

66.   That is, privately and freely.

67.   False confessions are discussed in *Anatomy of Innocence: Testimonies of the Wrongfully Convicted*, edited by Laura Caldwell and this editor (New York: Liveright Publishing Corp./W. W. Norton, 2017). Vance's statement about the requirement of substantiation is the law in some states but not all.

or Veronese, or Titian, or Tintoretto, or whoever may be the artist to whom the work has been tentatively credited."

"My mind is, I fear," Markham confessed, "still sufficiently primitive to be impressed by vulgar facts; and in the present instance—unfortunately for your most original and artistic analogy—I possess quite an array of such facts, all of which indicate that a certain young woman is the—shall we say?—creator of the criminal *opus* entitled *The Murder of Alvin Benson.*"

Vance shrugged his shoulders almost imperceptibly.

"Would you mind telling me—in confidence, of course—what these facts are?"

"Certainly not," Markham acceded. "*Imprimis:*[68] the lady was in the house at the time the shot was fired."

Vance affected incredibility.

"Eh—my word! She was actu'lly there? Most extr'ordin'ry!"

"The evidence of her presence is unassailable," pursued Markham. "As you know, the gloves she wore at dinner, and the hand-bag she carried with her, were both found on the mantel in Benson's living-room."

"Oh!" murmured Vance, with a faintly deprecating smile. "It was not the lady, then, but her gloves and bag which were present,—a minute and unimportant distinction, no doubt, from the legal point of view. . . . Still," he added, "I deplore the inability of my layman's untutored mind to accept the two conditions as identical. My trousers are at the dry-cleaners; therefore, I am at the dry-cleaners, what?"

Markham turned on him with considerable warmth.

"Does it mean nothing in the way of evidence, even to your layman's mind, that a woman's intimate and necessary articles, which she has carried throughout the evening, are found in her escort's quarters the following morning?"

"In admitting that it does not," Vance acknowledged quietly, "I no doubt expose a legal perception lamentably inefficient."

"But since the lady certainly wouldn't have carried these particular objects during the afternoon, and since she couldn't have called at the house that evening during Benson's absence without the housekeeper knowing it, how, may one ask, did these articles happen to be there the next morning if she herself did not take them there late that night?"

"'Pon my word, I haven't the slightest notion," Vance rejoined. "The lady herself could doubtless appease your curiosity. But there are any number of possible explanations, y' know. Our departed Chesterfield might have brought them home in his coat pocket,—women are eternally handing men all manner of gewgaws and bundles to carry for 'em, with the cooing request: 'Can you put this in your pocket for me?' . . . Then again, there is the possibility that the real murderer secured them in some way, and placed them on the mantel delib'rately to mislead the *polizei*. Women, don't y' know, never put their belongings in such neat, out-of-the-way places as mantels and hat-racks. They invariably throw them down on your fav'rite chair or your center-table."

"And, I suppose," Markham interjected, "Benson also brought the lady's cigarette butts home in his pocket?"

"Stranger things have happened," returned Vance equably; "though I sha'n't accuse him of it in this instance. . . . The cigarette butts may, y' know, be evidence of a previous *conversazione*."

"Even your despised Heath," Markham informed him, "had sufficient intelligence to ascertain from the housekeeper that she sweeps out the grate every morning."

Vance sighed admiringly.

"You're *so* thorough, aren't you? . . . But, I say, that can't be, by any chance, your only evidence against the lady?"

"By no means," Markham assured him. "But, despite your superior distrust, it's good corroboratory evidence nevertheless."

"I dare say," Vance agreed, "—seeing with what frequency innocent persons are condemned in our courts. . . . But tell me more."

Markham proceeded with an air of quiet selfassurance.

"My man learned, first, that Benson dined alone with this woman at the Marseilles, a little bohemian restaurant in West Fortieth Street;[69] secondly, that they quarrelled; and thirdly, that they departed at midnight, entering a taxicab together. . . . Now, the murder was committed at twelve-thirty; but since the lady lives on Riverside Drive, in the Eighties, Benson couldn't possibly have accompanied her home—which obviously he would have done had he not taken her to his own house—and returned by the time the shot was fired. But we have further proof pointing to her being at Benson's. My man learned, at the woman's apartment-house, that actually she did not get home until shortly after one.

69.   The restaurant is not listed in the 1922–23 *Trow's* *General Directory of the City of New York* but may have closed after 1918.

Moreover, she was without her gloves and hand-bag, and had to be let in to her rooms with a pass-key, because, as she explained, she had lost hers. As you remember, we found the key in her bag. And—to clinch the whole matter—the smoked cigarettes in the grate corresponded to the one you found in her case."

Markham paused to relight his cigar.

"So much for that particular evening," he resumed. "As soon as I learned the woman's identity this morning, I put two more men to work on her private life. Just as I was leaving the office this noon the men 'phoned in their reports. They had learned that the woman has a fiancé, a chap named Leacock, who was a captain in the army, and who would be likely to own just such a gun as Benson was killed with. Furthermore, this Captain Leacock lunched with the woman the day of the murder and also called on her at her apartment the morning after."

Markham leaned slightly forward, and his next words were emphasized by the tapping of his fingers on the arm of the chair.

"As you see, we have the motive, the opportunity, and the means. . . . Perhaps you will tell me now that I possess no incriminating evidence."

"My dear Markham," Vance affirmed calmly, "you haven't brought out a single point which could not easily be explained away by any bright school-boy." He shook his head lugubriously. "And on such evidence people are deprived of their life and liberty! 'Pon my word, you alarm me. I tremble for my personal safety."

Markham was nettled.

"Would you be so good as to point out, from your dizzy pinnacle of sapience, the errors in my reasoning?"

"As far as I can see," returned Vance evenly, "your particularization concerning the lady is innocent of reasoning. You've simply taken several unaffined facts, and jumped to a false conclusion. I happen to know the conclusion is false because all the psychological indications of the crime contradict it—that is to say, the only real evidence in the case points unmistakably in another direction."

He made a gesture of emphasis, and his tone assumed an unwonted gravity.

"And if you arrest any woman for killing Alvin Benson, you will simply be adding another crime—a crime of delib'rate and unpardonable stupidity—to the one already committed. And between shooting a bounder like Benson and ruining an innocent woman's reputation, I'm inclined to regard the latter as the more reprehensible."

I could see a flash of resentment leap into Markham's eyes; but he did not take offense. Remember: these two men were close friends; and, for all their divergency of nature, they understood and respected each other. Their frankness—severe and even mordant at times—was, indeed, a result of that respect.

There was a moment's silence; then Markham forced a smile.

"You fill me with misgivings," he averred mockingly; but, despite the lightness of his tone, I felt that he was half in earnest. "However, I hadn't exactly planned to arrest the lady just yet."

"You reveal commendable restraint," Vance complimented him. "But I'm sure you've already arranged to ballyrag[70] the lady and perhaps trick her into one or two of those contradictions so dear to every lawyer's heart,—just as if any nervous or high-strung person could help indulging in apparent contradictions while being cross-questioned as a suspect in a crime they had nothing to do with. . . . To 'put 'em on the grill'—a most accurate designation. So reminiscent of burning people at the stake, what?"

"Well, I'm most certainly going to question her," replied Markham firmly, glancing at his watch. "And one of my men is escorting her to the office in half an hour; so I must break up this most delightful and edifying chat."

"You really expect to learn something incriminating by interrogating her?" asked Vance. "Y' know, I'd jolly well like to witness your humiliation. But I presume your heckling of suspects is a part of the legal arcana."

Markham had risen and turned toward the door, but at Vance's words he paused and appeared to deliberate.

"I can't see any particular objection to your being present," he said, "if you really care to come."

I think he had an idea that the humiliation of which the other had spoken would prove to be Vance's own; and soon we were in a taxicab headed for the Criminal Courts Building.[71]

70. A variant of "bullyrag," meaning to harass or intimidate someone.

71. The Manhattan Criminal Courts Building was built in 1892 and in 1902 was connected by the "Bridge of Sighs" above Franklin Street to the new City Prison; the latter replaced the structure known as The Tombs, originally built in 1888, but the old name persisted (it is referenced below by Van Dine). The Criminal Courts Building was not replaced until 1938, when construction on the new building began.

The Tombs, 1907.

CHAPTER VII

Reports and an Interview

72. The "ancient" building was twenty-two years old.

(Saturday, June 15; 3 p.m.)

We entered the ancient building,[72] with its discolored marble pillars and balustrades and its old-fashioned iron scroll-work, by the Franklin Street door, and went directly to the District Attorney's office on the fourth floor. The office, like the building, breathed an air of former days. Its high ceilings, its massive golden-oak woodwork, its elaborate low-hung chandelier of bronze and china, its dingy bay walls of painted plaster, and its four high narrow windows to the south—all bespoke a departed era in architecture and decoration.

On the floor was a large velvet carpet-rug of dingy brown; and the windows were hung with velour draperies of the same color. Several large comfortable chairs stood about the walls and before the long oak table in front of the District Attorney's desk. This desk, directly under the windows and facing the room, was broad and flat, with carved uprights and two rows of drawers extending to the floor. To the right of the high-backed swivel desk-chair, was another table of carved oak. There were also several filing cabinets in the room, and a large safe. In the center of the east wall a leather-covered door, decorated with large brass nail-heads, led into a long narrow room, between the office and the waiting-room, where the District Attorney's secretary and several clerks had their desks. Opposite to this door was another one opening into the District Attorney's inner sanctum; and still another door, facing the windows, gave on the main corridor.

Vance glanced over the room casually.

"So this is the matrix of municipal justice—eh, what?" He walked to one of the windows and looked out upon the grey circular tower of the Tombs opposite. "And there, I take it, are the oubliettes where the victims of our law are incarc'rated so as to reduce the competition of criminal activity among the remaining citizenry. A most distressin' sight, Markham."

The District Attorney had sat down at his desk and was glancing at several notations on his blotter.

"There are a couple of my men waiting to see me," he remarked, without looking up; "so, if you'll be good enough to take a chair over here, I'll proceed with my humble efforts to undermine society still further."

He pressed a button under the edge of his desk, and an alert young man with thick-lensed glasses appeared at the door.

"Swacker, tell Phelps to come in," Markham ordered. "And also tell Springer, if he's back from lunch, that I want to see him in a few minutes."

The secretary disappeared, and a moment later a tall, hawk-faced man, with stoop-shoulders and an awkward, angular gait, entered.

"What news?" asked Markham.

"Well, Chief," the detective replied in a low grating voice, "I just found out something I thought you could use right away. After I reported this noon, I ambled around to this Captain Leacock's house, thinking I might learn something from the house-boys, and ran into the Captain coming out. I tailed along; and he went straight up to the lady's house on the Drive, and stayed there over an hour. Then he went back home, looking worried."

Markham considered a moment.

"It may mean nothing at all, but I'm glad to know it anyway. St. Clair'll be here in a few minutes, and I'll find out what she has to say.—There's nothing else for to-day. . . . Tell Swacker to send Tracy in."

Tracy was the antithesis of Phelps. He was short, a trifle stout, and exuded an atmosphere of studied suavity. His face was rotund and genial; he wore a *pince-nez*; and his clothes were modish and fitted him well.

73. That is, the Metropolitan Opera Company, formed in 1883 and based in Manhattan—one of the premier opera companies in the world.

74. The Criterion Theatre, at 1514 Broadway, opened in 1895 as the Olympic Theatre. It ran into financial difficulties and became a cinema in 1914 but by 1916 had returned to legitimate theater. The complex included smaller venues in addition to the main stage (which featured the play *Happiness* in the winter of 1917), and it is likely that Miss St. Clair performed in either the Concert Hall or the Roof Garden.

"Good-morning, Chief," he greeted Markham in a quiet, ingratiating tone. "I understand the St. Clair woman is to call here this afternoon, and there are a few things I've found out that may assist in your questioning."

He opened a small note-book and adjusted his *pince-nez*.

"I thought I might learn something from her singing teacher, an Italian formerly connected with the Metropolitan,[73] but now running a sort of choral society of his own. He trains aspiring *prima donnas* in their rôles with a chorus and settings, and Miss St. Clair is one of his pet students. He talked to me, without any trouble; and it seems he knew Benson well. Benson attended several of St. Clair's rehearsals, and sometimes called for her in a taxicab. Rinaldo—that's the man's name—thinks he had a bad crush on the girl. Last winter, when she sang at the Criterion[74] in a small part, Rinaldo was back stage coaching, and Benson sent her enough hot-house flowers to fill the star's dressing-room and have some left over. I tried to find out if Benson was playing the 'angel' for her, but Rinaldo either didn't know or pretended he didn't." Tracy closed his note-book and looked up. "That any good to you, Chief?"

"First-rate," Markham told him. "Keep at work along that line, and let me hear from you again about this time Monday."

Tracy bowed, and as he went out the secretary again appeared at the door.

"Springer's here now, sir," he said. "Shall I send him in?"

Springer proved to be a type of detective quite different from either Phelps or Tracy. He was older, and had the gloomy capable air of a hard-working bookkeeper in a bank. There was no initiative in his bearing, but one felt that he could discharge a delicate task with extreme competency.

Markham took from his pocket the envelope on which he had noted the name given him by Major Benson.

"Springer, there's a man down on Long Island that I want to interview as soon as possible. It's in connection with the Benson case, and I wish you'd locate him and get him up here as soon as possible. If you can find him in the telephone book you needn't go down personally. His name is Leander Pfyfe, and he lives, I think, at Port Washington."

Markham jotted down the name on a card and handed it to the detective.

"This is Saturday, so if he comes to town to-morrow, have him ask for me at the Stuyvesant Club. I'll be there in the afternoon."

When Springer had gone, Markham again rang for his secretary and gave instructions that the moment Miss St. Clair arrived she was to be shown in.

"Sergeant Heath is here," Swacker informed him, "and wants to see you if you're not too busy."

Markham glanced at the clock over the door.

"I guess I'll have time. Send him in."

Heath was surprised to see Vance and me in the District Attorney's office, but after greeting Markham with the customary handshake, he turned to Vance with a good-natured smile.

"Still acquiring knowledge, Mr. Vance?"

"Can't say that I am, Sergeant," returned Vance lightly. "But I'm learning a number of most int'restin' errors. . . . How goes the sleuthin'?"

Heath's face became suddenly serious.

"That's what I'm here to tell the Chief about." He addressed himself to Markham. "This case is a jaw-breaker, sir. My men and myself have talked to a dozen of Benson's cronies, and we can't worm a single fact of any value out of 'em. They either don't know anything, or they're giving a swell imitation of a lot of clams. They all appear to be greatly shocked—bowled over, floored, flabbergasted—by the news of the shooting. And have they got any idea as to why or how it happened? They'll tell the world they haven't. You know the line of talk: Who'd want to shoot good old Al? Nobody could've done it but a burglar who didn't know good old Al. If he'd known good old Al, even the burglar wouldn't have done it. . . . Hell! I felt like killing off a few of those birds myself so they could go and join their good old Al."

"Any news of the car?" asked Markham.

Heath grunted his disgust.

"Not a word. And that's funny, too, seeing all the advertising it got. Those fishing-rods are the only thing we've got. . . . The Inspector, by the way, sent me the post-mortem report this morning; but it didn't tell us anything we didn't know. Translated into human language, it said Benson died from a shot in the head, with all his organs sound. It's a wonder, though, they didn't discover that he'd been poisoned with a Mexican bean or

75. Annibale Carracci (1560–1609) and his brothers were important Italian painters who, along with Carravaggio, were hailed as bringing about a "renaissance" of the talent of previous painters such as Rembrandt and Michelangelo and created the Baroque style.

Self-portrait of Annibale Carracci, ca. 1600.

bit by an African snake, or something, so's to make the case a little more intrikkit than it already is."

"Cheer up, Sergeant," Markham exhorted him. "I've had a little better luck. Tracy ran down the owner of the hand-bag and found out she'd been to dinner with Benson that night. He and Phelps also learned a few other supplementary facts that fit in well; and I'm expecting the lady here at any minute. I'm going to find out what she has to say for herself."

An expression of resentment came into Heath's eyes as the District Attorney was speaking, but he erased it at once and began asking questions. Markham gave him every detail, and also informed him of Leander Pfyfe.

"I'll let you know immediately how the interview comes out," he concluded.

As the door closed on Heath Vance looked up at Markham with a sly smile.

"Not exactly one of Nietzche's *Übermenschen*—eh, what? I fear the subtleties of this complex world bemuse him a bit, y' know. . . . And he's so disappointin'. I felt pos'tively elated when the bustling lad with the thick glasses announced his presence. I thought surely he wanted to tell you he had jailed at least six of Benson's murderers."

"Your hopes run too high, I fear," commented Markham.

"And yet, that's the usual procedure—if the headlines in our great moral dailies are to be credited. I always thought that the moment a crime was committed the police began arresting people promiscuously—to maintain the excitement, don't y' know. Another illusion gone! . . . Sad, sad," he murmured. "I sha'n't forgive our Heath: he has betrayed my faith in him."

At this point Markham's secretary came to the door and announced the arrival of Miss St. Clair.

I think we were all taken a little aback at the spectacle presented by this young woman as she came slowly into the room with a firm graceful step, and with her head held slightly to one side in an attitude of supercilious inquiry. She was small and strikingly pretty, although "pretty" is not exactly the word with which to describe her. She possessed that faintly exotic beauty that we find in the portraits of the Carracci,[75] who sweetened the severity of Leonardo and made it at once intimate and decadent. Her eyes were dark and widely spaced; her nose was delicate and straight, and her forehead broad. Her full sensuous lips were almost sculpturesque in their linear precision, and her mouth wore an enigmatic smile, or hint of a smile. Her rounded firm chin was a bit heavy when examined apart from the other features, but not in the *ensemble*. There was poise and a certain strength of character in her bearing; but one sensed the potentialities of powerful emotions beneath her exterior calm. Her clothes harmonized with her personality: they were quiet and apparently in the conventional style, but a touch of color and originality here and there conferred on them a fascinating distinction.

Markham rose and, bowing with formal courtesy, indicated a comfortable upholstered chair directly in front of his desk. With a barely perceptible nod, she glanced at the chair, and then seated herself in a straight armless chair standing next to it.

"You won't mind, I'm sure," she said, "if I choose my own chair for the inquisition."

Her voice was low and resonant—the speaking voice of the highly trained singer. She smiled as she spoke, but it was not a cordial smile: it was cold and distant, yet somehow indicative of levity.

"Miss St. Clair," began Markham, in a tone of polite severity, "the murder of Mr. Alvin Benson has intimately involved yourself. Before taking any definite steps, I have invited you here to ask you a few questions. I can, therefore, advise you quite honestly that frankness will best serve your interests."

He paused, and the woman looked at him with an ironically questioning gaze.

"Am I supposed to thank you for your generous advice?"

Markham's scowl deepened as he glanced down at a typewritten page on his desk.

"You are probably aware that your gloves and hand-bag were found in Mr. Benson's house the morning after he was shot."

"I can understand how you might have traced the hand-bag to me," she said; "but how did you arrive at the conclusion that the gloves were mine?"

Markham looked up sharply.

"Do you mean to say the gloves are not yours?"

"Oh, no." She gave him another wintry smile. "I merely wondered how you knew they belonged to me, since you couldn't have known either my taste in gloves or the size I wore."

76.　Hailed (in a 1905 advertisement in the *Los Angeles Times*) as the finest gloves produced. They were of French manufacture.

An advertisement for Trefousse gloves.

"They're your gloves, then?"

"If they are Tréfousse,[76] size five-and-three-quarters, of white kid and elbow length, they are certainly mine. And I'd so like to have them back, if you don't mind."

"I'm sorry," said Markham; "but it is necessary that I keep them for the present."

She dismissed the matter with a slight shrug of the shoulders.

"Do you mind if I smoke?" she asked.

Markham instantly opened a drawer of his desk, and took out a box of Benson and Hedges cigarettes.

"I have my own, thank you," she informed him. "But I would so appreciate my holder. I've missed it horribly."

Markham hesitated. He was manifestly annoyed by the woman's attitude.

"I'll be glad to lend it to you," he compromised; and reaching into another drawer of his desk, he laid the holder on the table before her.

"Now, Miss St. Clair," he said, resuming his gravity of manner, "will you tell me how these personal articles of yours happened to be in Mr. Benson's living-room?"

"No, Mr. Markham, I will not," she answered.

"Do you realize the serious construction your refusal places upon the circumstances?"

"I really hadn't given it much thought." Her tone was indifferent.

"It would be well if you did," Markham advised her. "Your position is not an enviable one; and the presence of your belongings in Mr. Benson's room is, by no means, the only thing that connects you directly with the crime."

The woman raised her eyes inquiringly, and again the enigmatic smile appeared at the corners of her mouth.

"Perhaps you have sufficient evidence to accuse me of the murder?"

Markham ignored this question.

"You were well acquainted with Mr. Benson, I believe?"

"The finding of my hand-bag and gloves in his apartment might lead one to assume as much, mightn't it?" she parried.

"He was, in fact, much interested in you?" persisted Markham.

She made a *moue*, and sighed.

"Alas, yes! Too much for my peace of mind. . . . Have I been brought here to discuss the attentions this gentleman paid me?"

Again Markham ignored her query.

"Where were you, Miss St. Clair, between the time you left the Marseilles at midnight and the time you arrived home—which, I understand, was after one o'clock?"

"You are simply wonderful!" she exclaimed. "You seem to know everything. . . . Well, I can only say that during that time I was on my way home."

"Did it take you an hour to go from Fortieth Street to Eighty-first and Riverside Drive?"

"Just about, I should say,—a few minutes more or less, perhaps."

"How do you account for that?" Markham was becoming impatient.

"I can't account for it," she said, "except by the passage of time. Time does fly, doesn't it, Mr. Markham?"

"By your attitude you are only working detriment to yourself," Markham warned her, with a show of irritation. "Can you not see the seriousness of your position? You are known to have dined with Mr. Benson, to have left the restaurant at midnight, and to have arrived at your own apartment after one o'clock. At twelve-thirty, Mr. Benson was shot; and your personal articles were found in the same room the morning after."

"It looks terribly suspicious, I know," she admitted, with whimsical seriousness. "And I'll tell you this, Mr. Markham: if my thoughts could have killed Mr. Benson, he would have died long ago. I know I shouldn't speak ill of the dead—there's a saying about it beginning '*de mortuis*,' isn't there?[77]—but the truth is, I had reason to dislike Mr. Benson exceedingly."

"Then why did you go to dinner with him?"

"I've asked myself the same question a dozen times since," she confessed dolefully. "We women are such impulsive creatures—always doing things we shouldn't. . . . But I know what you're thinking:—if I had intended to shoot him, that would have been a natural preliminary. Isn't that what's in your mind? I suppose all murderesses do go to dinner with their victims first."

While she spoke she opened her vanity-case and looked at her reflection in its mirror. She daintily adjusted several imaginary stray ends of her abundant dark-brown hair, and touched her arched eyebrows gently with her little finger as if to rectify some infinitesimal disturbance in their pencilled contour. Then she tilted her head, regarded herself appraisingly, and returned her

77. *De mortuis nihil nisi bonum*, "speak nothing but good of the dead," is a saying attributed to Chilon of Sparta (approximately 600 B.C.E.).

gaze to the District Attorney only as she came to the end of her speech. Her actions had perfectly conveyed to her listeners the impression that the subject of the conversation was, in her scheme of things, of secondary importance to her personal appearance. No words could have expressed her indifference so convincingly as had her little pantomime.

Markham was becoming exasperated. A different type of district attorney would no doubt have attempted to use the pressure of his office to force her into a more amenable frame of mind. But Markham shrank instinctively from the bludgeoning, threatening methods of the ordinary Public Prosecutor, especially in his dealings with women. In the present case, however, had it not been for Vance's strictures at the Club, he would no doubt have taken a more aggressive stand. But it was evident he was laboring under a burden of uncertainty superinduced by Vance's words and augmented by the evasive deportment of the woman herself.

After a moment's silence he asked grimly:

"You did considerable speculating through the firm of Benson and Benson, did you not?"

A faint ring of musical laughter greeted this question.

"I see that the dear Major has been telling tales. . . . Yes, I've been gambling most extravagantly. And I had no business to do it. I'm afraid I'm avaricious."

"And is it not true that you've lost heavily of late—that, in fact, Mr. Alvin Benson called upon you for additional margin and finally sold out your securities?"

"I wish to Heaven it were not true," she lamented, with a look of simulated tragedy. Then: "Am I supposed to have done away with Mr. Benson out of sordid revenge, or as an act of just retribution?" She smiled archly and waited expectantly, as if her question had been part of a guessing game.

Markham's eyes hardened as he coldly enunciated his next words.

"Is it not a fact that Captain Philip Leacock owned just such a pistol as Mr. Benson was killed with—a forty-five army Colt automatic?"

At the mention of her fiancé's name she stiffened perceptibly and caught her breath. The part she had been playing fell from her, and a faint flush suffused her cheeks and extended to her forehead. But almost immediately she had reassumed her rôle of playful indifference.

"I never inquired into the make or calibre of Captain Leacock's fire-arms," she returned carelessly.

"And is it not a fact," pursued Markham's imperturbable voice, "that Captain Leacock lent you his pistol when he called at your apartment on the morning before the murder?"

"It's most ungallant of you, Mr. Markham," she reprimanded him coyly, "to inquire into the personal relations of an engaged couple; for I am betrothed to Captain Leacock—though you probably know it already."

Markham stood up, controlling himself with effort.

"Am I to understand that you refuse to answer any of my questions, or to endeavor to extricate yourself from the very serious position you are in?"

She appeared to consider.

"Yes," she said slowly, "I haven't anything I care especially to say just now."

Markham leaned over and rested both hands on the desk.

"Do you realize the possible consequences of your attitude?" he asked ominously. "The facts I know regarding your connection with the case, coupled with your refusal to offer a single extenuating explanation, give me more grounds than I actually need to order your being held."

I was watching her closely as he spoke, and it seemed to me that her eyelids drooped involuntarily the merest fraction of an inch. But she gave no other indication of being affected by the pronouncement, and merely looked at the District Attorney with an air of defiant amusement.

Markham, with a sudden contraction of the jaw, turned and reached toward a bell-button beneath the edge of his desk. But, in doing so, his glance fell upon Vance; and he paused indecisively. The look he had encountered on the other's face was one of reproachful amazement: not only did it express complete surprise at his apparent decision, but it stated, more eloquently than words could have done, that he was about to commit an act of irreparable folly.

There were several moments of tense silence in the room. Then calmly and unhurriedly Miss St. Clair opened her vanity-case and powdered her nose. When she had finished, she turned a serene gaze upon the District Attorney.

"Well, do you want to arrest me now?" she asked.

Markham regarded her for a moment, deliberating. Instead of answering at once, he went to the window and stood for a full minute looking down upon the Bridge of Sighs which connects the Criminal Courts Building with the Tombs.

"No, I think not to-day," he said slowly.

He stood a while longer in absorbed contemplation; then, as if shaking off his mood of irresolution, he swung about and confronted the woman.

"I'm not going to arrest you—yet," he reiterated, a bit harshly. "But I'm going to order you to remain in New York for the present. And if you attempt to leave, you *will* be arrested. I hope that is clear."

He pressed a button, and his secretary entered.

"Swacker, please escort Miss St. Clair downstairs, and call a taxicab for her. . . . Then you can go home yourself."

She rose and gave Markham a little nod.

"You were very kind to lend me my cigarette-holder," she said pleasantly, laying it on his desk.

Without another word, she walked calmly from the room.

The door had no more than closed behind her when Markham pressed another button. In a few moments the door leading into the outer corridor opened, and a white-haired, middle-aged man appeared.

"Ben," ordered Markham hurriedly, "have that woman that Swacker's taking downstairs followed. Keep her under surveillance, and don't let her get lost. She's not to leave the city—understand? It's the St. Clair woman Tracy dug up."

When the man had gone, Markham turned and stood glowering at Vance.

"What do you think of your innocent young lady now?" he asked, with an air of belligerent triumph.

"Nice gel—eh, what?" replied Vance blandly. "Extr'ordin'ry control. And she's about to marry a professional milit'ry man! Ah, well. *De gustibus* . . . Y' know, I was afraid for a moment you were actu'lly going to send for the manacles. And if you had, Markham old dear, you'd have regretted it to your dying day."

Markham studied him for a few seconds. He knew there was something more than a mere whim beneath Vance's certitude of manner; and it was this knowledge that had stayed his hand when he was about to have the woman placed in custody.

"Her attitude was certainly not conducive to one's belief in her innocence," Markham objected. "She played her part damned cleverly, though. But it was just the part a shrewd woman, knowing herself guilty, would have played."

"I say, didn't it occur to you," asked Vance, "that perhaps she didn't care a farthing whether you thought her guilty or not?—that, in fact, she was a bit disappointed when you let her go?"

"That's hardly the way I read the situation," returned Markham. "Whether guilty or innocent, a person doesn't ordinarily invite arrest."

"By the bye," asked Vance, "where was the fortunate swain during the hour of Alvin's passing?"

"Do you think we didn't check up on that point?" Markham spoke with disdain. "Captain Leacock was at his own apartment that night from eight o'clock on."

"Was he, really?" airily retorted Vance. "A most model young fella!"

Again Markham looked at him sharply.

"I'd like to know what weird theory has been struggling in your brain to-day," he mused. "Now that I've let the lady go temporarily—which is what you obviously wanted me to do—, and have stultified my own better judgment in so doing, why not tell me frankly what you've got up your sleeve?"

"'Up my sleeve?' Such an inelegant metaphor! One would think I was a prestidig'tator, what?"

Whenever Vance answered in this fashion it was a sign that he wished to avoid making a direct reply; and Markham dropped the matter.

"Anyway," he submitted, "you didn't have the pleasure of witnessing my humiliation, as you prophesied."

Vance looked up in simulated surprise.

"Didn't I, now?" Then he added sorrowfully: "Life is so full of disappointments, y' know."

CHAPTER VIII

Vance Accepts a Challenge

(Saturday, June 15; 4 p.m.)

After Markham had telephoned Heath the details of the interview, we returned to the Stuyvesant Club. Ordinarily the District Attorney's office shuts down at one o'clock on Saturdays; but to-day the hour had been extended because of the importance attaching to Miss St. Clair's visit. Markham had lapsed into an introspective silence which lasted until we were again seated in the alcove of the Club's lounge-room. Then he spoke irritably.

"Damn it! I shouldn't have let her go. . . . I still have a feeling she's guilty."

Vance assumed an air of gushing credulousness.

"Oh, really? I dare say you're so psychic. Been that way all your life, no doubt. And haven't you had lots and lots of dreams that came true? I'm sure you've often had a 'phone call from someone you were thinking about at the moment. A delectable gift. Do you read palms, also? . . . Why not have the lady's horoscope cast?"

"I have no evidence as yet," Markham retorted, "that your belief in her innocence is founded on anything more substantial than your impressions."

"Ah, but it is," averred Vance. "I *know* she's innocent. Furthermore, I know that no woman could possibly have fired the shot."

"Don't get the erroneous idea in your head that a woman couldn't have manipulated a forty-five army Colt."

"Oh, that?" Vance dismissed the notion with a shrug. "The material indications of the crime don't enter into my calculations, y' know,—I leave 'em entirely to you lawyers and the lads with the bulging deltoids. I have other, and surer, ways of reaching conclusions. That's why I told you that if you arrested any woman for shooting Benson you'd be blundering most shamefully."

Markham grunted indignantly.

"And yet you seem to have repudiated all processes of deduction whereby the truth may be arrived at. Have you, by any chance, entirely renounced your faith in the operations of the human mind?"

"Ah, there speaks the voice of God's great common people!" exclaimed Vance. "Your mind is so typical, Markham. It works on the principle that what you don't know isn't knowledge, and that, since you don't understand a thing, there is no explanation. A comfortable point of view. It relieves one from all care and uncertainty. Don't you find the world a very sweet and wonderful place?"

Markham adopted an attitude of affable forbearance.

"You spoke at lunch time, I believe, of one infallible method of detecting crime. Would you care to divulge this profound and priceless secret to a mere district attorney?"

Vance bowed with exaggerated courtesy.[*]

"Delighted, I'm sure," he returned. "I referred to the science of individual character and the psychology of human nature. We all do things, d' ye see, in a certain individual way, according to our temp'raments. Every human act—no matter how large or how small—is a direct expression of a man's personality, and bears the inev'table impress of his nature. Thus, a musician, by looking at a sheet of music, is able to tell at once whether it was composed, for example, by Beethoven, or Schubert, or Debussy, or Chopin. And an artist, by looking at a canvas, knows immediately whether it is a Corot, a Harpignies, a Rembrandt, or a Franz Hals. And just as no two faces are exactly alike, so no two natures are exactly alike: the combination of ingredients which go to make up our personalities, varies in each individual. That is why, when twenty artists, let us say, sit down to paint the same subject, each one conceives and executes it in a different manner. The result in each

[*] [Author's note:] The following conversation in which Vance explains his psychological methods of criminal analysis, is, of course, set down from memory. However, a proof of this passage was sent to him with a request that he revise and alter it in whatever manner he chose; so that, as it now stands, it describes Vance's theory in practically his own words.

78. Sherlock Holmes, in *The Valley of Fear* (1915), said of a crime that he deduced had been planned by his archnemesis Professor James Moriarty: "You can tell an old master by the sweep of his brush. I can tell a Moriarty when I see one."

case is a distinct and unmistakable expression of the personality of the painter who did it. . . . It's really rather simple, don't y' know."

"Your theory, doubtless, would be comprehensible to an artist," said Markham, in a tone of indulgent irony. "But its metaphysical refinements are, I admit, considerably beyond the grasp of a vulgar worldling like myself."

"'The mind inclined to what is false rejects the nobler course,'" murmured Vance, with a sigh.

"There is," argued Markham, "a slight difference between art and crime."

"Psychologically, old chap, there's none," Vance amended evenly. "Crimes possess all the basic factors of a work of art—approach, conception, technique, imagination, attack, method, and organization. Moreover, crimes vary fully as much in their manner, their aspects, and their general nature, as do works of art. Indeed, a carefully planned crime is just as direct an expression of the individual as is a painting, for instance. And therein lies the one great possibility of detection. Just as an expert æsthetician can analyze a picture and tell you who painted it, or the personality and temp'rament of the person who painted it, so can the expert psychologist analyze a crime and tell you who committed it—that is, if he happens to be acquainted with the person—, or else can describe to you, with almost mathematical surety, the criminal's nature and character. . . .[78] And that, my dear Markham, is the only sure and inev'table means of determining human guilt. All others are mere guess-work, unscientific, uncertain, and—perilous."

Throughout this explanation Vance's manner had been almost casual; yet the very serenity and assurance of his attitude conferred upon his words a curious sense of authority. Markham had listened with interest, though it could be seen that he did not regard Vance's theorizing seriously.

"Your system ignores motive altogether," he objected.

"Naturally," Vance replied, "—since it's an irrelevant factor in most crimes. Every one of us, my dear chap, has just as good a motive for killing at least a score of men, as the motives which actuate ninety-nine crimes out of a hundred. And, when anyone is murdered, there are dozens of innocent people who had just as strong a motive for doing it as had the actual murderer. Really, y' know, the fact that a man has a motive is no evidence whatever that he's guilty,—such motives are too universal a possession of the human race. Suspecting a man of murder because he has a motive is like suspecting a man of running away with another man's wife because he has two legs. The reason that some people kill and others don't, is a matter of temp'rament—of individual psychology. It all comes back to that. . . . And another thing: when a person does possess a real motive—something tremendous and overpowering—he's pretty apt to keep it to himself, to hide it and guard it carefully—eh, what? He may even have disguised the motive through years of preparation; or the motive may have been born within five minutes of the crime through the unexpected discovery of facts a decade old. . . . So, d' ye see, the absence of any apparent motive in a crime might be regarded as more incriminating than the presence of one."

"You are going to have some difficulty in eliminating the idea of *cui bono* from the consideration of crime."

"I dare say," agreed Vance. "The idea of *cui bono* is just silly enough to be impregnable. And yet, many persons would be benefited by almost anyone's death. Kill Sumner,[79] and, on that theory, you could arrest the entire membership of the Authors' League."

"Opportunity, at any rate," persisted Markham, "is an insuperable factor in crime,—and by opportunity, I mean that affinity of circumstances and conditions which make a particular crime possible, feasible and convenient for a particular person."

"Another irrelevant factor," asserted Vance. "Think of the opportunities we have every day to murder people we dislike! Only the other night I had ten insuff'rable bores to dinner in my apartment—a social devoir.[80] But I refrained—with consid'rable effort, I admit—from putting arsenic in the Pontet Canet.[81] The Borgias and I, y' see, merely belong in different psychological categ'ries. On the other hand, had I been resolved to do murder, I would—like those resourceful *cinquecento* patricians—have created my own opportunity. . . . And there's the rub:—one can either make an opportunity or disguise the fact that he had it, with false alibis and various other tricks. You remember the case of the murderer who called the police to break into his victim's house before the latter had been killed, saying he suspected foul play, and who then preceded the policemen indoors and stabbed the man as they were trailing up the stairs."[*]

79. A reference to John S. Sumner, successor in 1915 to Anthony Comstock, founder of the New York Society for the Succession of Vice and a leading advocate of censorship. Sumner served as the society's head for thirty-five years. In 1917, he pressured Theodore Dreiser's publisher to withdraw publication of the latter's novel *The Genius*; H. L. Mencken, then head of the Authors League of America, attempted to rally its members to cry out against the censorship. In 1923, the society lobbied unsuccessfully for revision of the New York obscenity laws. After the defeat of the legislation in 1925, the society continued its efforts (eventually changing its name to the Society to Maintain Public Decency) but its influence faded, and it dissolved after Sumner's death in 1950.

80. Obligation or duty.

81. One of the great Bordeaux wines.

* [Author's note:] I don't know what case Vance was referring to; but there are several instances of this device on record, and writers of detective fiction have often used it. The latest instance is to be found in G. K. Chesterton's *The Innocence of Father Brown*, in the story entitled "The Wrong Shape."

82. In Israel Zangwill's 1891 *The Big Bow Mystery*, one of the first "locked-room" mysteries, the murder is committed by (spoiler alert!) the detective who entered the room to discover the body!

83. Cesare Lombroso, the Italian physician and criminologist, made the first use of a scientific instrument to test veracity. He modified an existing instrument called a hydrosphygmograph to measure crime suspects' blood pressure and pulse rate during interrogation to detect changes. In 1914, another Italian, psychologist Vittorio Benussi, discovered that by using a pneumograph—a device that recorded a subject's breathing patterns—he could detect respiratory disturbances that indicate an emotional change indicative of great stress or deception. Only a few years before the Benson murder case, in 1915, Dr. William Marston, an American attorney and psychologist renowned for (among other things) later creating the comic book character Wonder Woman, used a standard blood pressure cuff and a stethoscope to test discontinuous systolic blood pressure indicating lying during questioning. In 1918, however, "psychological machines" were at best "int'restin' toys" with no real evidentiary value.

84. The Presbyterian minister, speaker, and columnist Frank Crane (1861–1928) wrote a series of popular volumes of *Four Minute Essays*, published in 1919. These consisted of homilies of populist politics and positive thinking.

"Well, what of actual proximity, or presence,—the proof of a person being on the scene of the crime at the time it was committed?"

"Again misleading," Vance declared. "An innocent person's presence is too often used as a shield by the real murderer who is actu'lly absent. A clever criminal can commit a crime from a distance through an agency that is present. Also, a clever criminal can arrange an alibi and then go to the scene of the crime disguised and unrecognized.[82] There are far too many convincing ways of being present when one is believed to be absent—and *vice versa*. . . . But we can never part from our individualities and our natures. And that is why all crime inev'tably comes back to human psychology—the one fixed, undisguisable basis of deduction."

"It's a wonder to me," said Markham, "in view of your theories, that you don't advocate dismissing nine-tenths of the police force and installing a gross or two of those psychological machines so popular with the Sunday Supplement editor."[83]

Vance smoked a minute meditatively.

"I've read about 'em. Int'restin' toys. They can no doubt indicate a certain augmented emotional stress when the patient transfers his attention from the pious platitudes of Dr. Frank Crane[84] to a problem in spherical trigonometry. But if an innocent person were harnessed up to the various tubes, galvanometers, electromagnets, glass plates, and brass knobs of one of these apparatuses, and then quizzed about some recent crime, your indicat'ry needle would cavort about like a Russian dancer as a result of sheer nervous panic on the patient's part."

Markham smiled patronizingly.

"And I suppose the needle would remain static with a guilty person in contact?"

"Oh, on the contr'ry." Vance's tone was unruffled. "The needle would bob up and down just the same—but not *because* he was guilty. If he was stupid, for instance, the needle would jump as a result of his resentment at a seemingly newfangled third-degree torture. And if he was intelligent, the needle would jump because of his suppressed mirth at the puerility of the legal mind for indulging in such nonsense."

"You move me deeply," said Markham. "My head is spinning like a turbine. But there are those of us poor worldlings who believe that criminality is a defect of the brain."

"So it is," Vance readily agreed. "But unfortunately the entire human race possesses the defect. The virtuous ones haven't, so to speak, the courage of their defects. . . . However, if you were referring to a criminal type, then, alas! we must part company. It was Lombroso, that darling of the yellow journals, who invented the idea of the congenital criminal. Real scientists like DuBois, Karl Pearson and Goring have shot his idiotic theories full of holes."*

"I am floored by your erudition," declared Markham, as he signalled to a passing attendant and ordered another cigar. "I console myself, however, with the fact that, as a rule, murder will leak out."

Vance smoked his cigarette in silence, looking thoughtfully out through the window up at the hazy June sky.

"Markham," he said at length, "the number of fantastic ideas extant about criminals is pos'tively amazing. How a sane person can subscribe to that ancient hallucination that 'murder will out' is beyond me. It rarely 'outs', old dear. And, if it did 'out', why a Homicide Bureau? Why all this whirlin'-dervish activity by the police whenever a body is found? . . . The poets are to blame for this bit of lunacy. Chaucer probably started it with his 'Mordre wol out', and Shakespeare helped it along by attributing to murder a miraculous organ that speaks in lieu of a tongue. It was some poet, too, no doubt, who conceived the fancy that carcasses bleed at the sight of the murderer. . . . Would you, as the great Protector of the Faithful, dare tell the police to wait calmly in their offices, or clubs, or favorite beauty-parlors—or wherever policemen do their waiting—until a murder 'outs'? Poor dear!—if you did, they'd ask the Governor for your detention as *particeps criminis*, or apply for a *de lunatico inquirendo*."†

Markham grunted good-naturedly. He was busy cutting and lighting his cigar.

"I believe you chaps have another hallucination about crime," continued Vance, "—namely, that the criminal always returns to the scene of the crime. This weird notion is even explained on some recondite and misty psychological ground. But, I assure you, psychology teaches no such prepost'rous doctrine. If ever a murderer returned to the body of his victim for any reason other than to rectify some blunder he had made, then he is a subject for

*   [Author's note:] It was Pearson and Goring who, about twenty years ago, made an extensive investigation and tabulation of professional criminals in England, the results of which showed (1) that criminal careers began mostly between the ages of 16 and 21; (2) that over ninety per cent of criminals were mentally normal; and (3) that more criminals had criminal older brothers than criminal fathers.

[Editor's note: English criminologist Charles Goring's *The English Convict* (1913) challenged Lombroso's findings of significant physiological differences between criminals and non-criminals. Karl Pearson was an English mathematician who used statistical analysis on populations, disputing Lombroso's conclusions. W. E. B. Dubois, the great American sociologist and (later) civil rights leader disputed that race was a determining factor in a predisposition toward criminality, though he argued that the social consequences of racial discrimination bred crime.]

†   [Author's note:] Sir Basil Thomson, K.C.B., former Assistant Commissioner of Metropolitan Police, London, writing in *The Saturday Evening Post* several years after this conversation, said: "Take, for example, the proverb that murder will out, which is employed whenever one out of many thousands of undiscovered murderers is caught through a chance coincidence that captures the popular imagination. It is because murder will not out that the pleasant shock of surprise when it does out calls for a proverb to enshrine the phenomenon. The poisoner who is brought to justice has almost invariably proved to have killed other victims without exciting suspicion until he has grown careless."

85. Broadmoor was an infamous asylum in Berkshire, England; Bloomingdale was the name of a New York insane asylum that in 1889 changed its name to the Payne Whitney Psychiatric Clinic; and departed from its home in Morningside Heights moving to White Plains, New York.

*   [Author's note:] In "Popular Fallacies About Crime" (*The Saturday Evening Post*: April 21, 1923, p. 8) Sir Basil Thomson also upheld this point of view.

Broadmoor—or Bloomingdale. . . .[85] How easy it would be for the police if this fanciful notion were true! They'd merely have to sit down at the scene of a crime, play bezique or Mah Jongg until the murderer returned, and then escort him to the *bastille*, what? The true psychological instinct in anyone having committed a punishable act, is to get as far away from the scene of it as the limits of this world will permit."*

"In the present case, at any rate," Markham reminded him, "we are neither waiting inactively for the murder to out, nor sitting in Benson's living-room trusting to the voluntary return of the criminal."

"Either course would achieve success as quickly as the one you are now pursuing," Vance said.

"Not being gifted with your singular insight," retorted Markham, "I can only follow the inadequate processes of human reasoning."

"No doubt," Vance agreed commiseratingly. "And the results of your activities thus far force me to the conclusion that a man with a handful of legalistic logic can successfully withstand the most obst'nate and heroic assaults of ordin'ry commonsense."

Markham was piqued.

"Still harping on the St. Clair woman's innocence, eh? However, in view of the complete absence of any tangible evidence pointing elsewhere, you must admit I have no choice of courses."

"I admit nothing of the kind," Vance told him; "for, I assure you, there is an abundance of evidence pointing elsewhere. You simply failed to see it."

"You think so!" Vance's nonchalant cocksureness had at last overthrown Markham's equanimity. "Very well, old man; I hereby enter an emphatic denial to all your fine theories; and I challenge you to produce a single piece of this evidence which you say exists."

He threw his words out with asperity, and gave a curt, aggressive gesture with his extended fingers, to indicate that, as far as he was concerned, the subject was closed.

Vance, too, I think, was pricked a little.

"Y' know, Markham old dear, I'm no avenger of blood, or vindicator of the honor of society. The rôle would bore me."

Markham smiled loftily, but made no reply.

Vance smoked meditatively for a while. Then, to my amazement, he turned calmly and deliberately to Markham, and said in a quiet, matter-of-fact voice:

"I'm going to accept your challenge. It's a bit alien to my tastes; but the problem, y' know, rather appeals to me: it presents the same diff'culties as the *Concert Champêtre* affair,—a question of disputed authorship, as it were."*

Markham abruptly suspended the motion of lifting his cigar to his lips. He had scarcely intended his challenge literally: it had been uttered more in the nature of a verbal defiance; and he scrutinized Vance a bit uncertainly. Little did he realize that the other's casual acceptance of his unthinking and but half-serious challenge, was to alter the entire criminal history of New York.

"Just how do you intend to proceed?" he asked.

Vance waved his hand carelessly.

"Like Napoleon, *je m'en gage, et puis je vois.*[86] However, I must have your word that you'll give me every possible assistance, and will refrain from all profound legal objections."

Markham pursed his lips. He was frankly perplexed by the unexpected manner in which Vance had met his defiance. But immediately he gave a good-natured laugh, as if, after all, the matter was of no serious consequence.

"Very well," he assented. "You have my word. . . . And now what?"

After a moment Vance lit a fresh cigarette, and rose languidly.

"First," he announced, "I shall determine the exact height of the guilty person. Such a fact will, no doubt, come under the head of indicat'ry evidence—eh, what?"

Markham stared at him incredulously.

"How, in Heaven's name, are you going to do that?"

"By those primitive deductive methods to which you so touchingly pin your faith," he answered easily. "But come; let us repair to the scene of the crime."

He moved toward the door, Markham reluctantly following in a state of perplexed irritation.

"But you know the body was removed," the latter protested; "and the place by now has no doubt been straightened up."

"Thank Heaven for that!" murmured Vance. "I'm not particularly fond of corpses; and untidiness, y' know, annoys me frightfully."

* [Author's note:] For years the famous *Concert Champêtre* in the Louvre was officially attributed to Titian. Vance, however, took it upon himself to convince the Curator, M. Lepelletier, that it was a Giorgione, with the result that the painting is now credited to that artist.

Le Concert Champêtre, by Titian or Gorgione (1509).

86. Generally attributed to Napoleon, it means something like "First you commit yourself, then you figure out what to do."

As we emerged into Madison Avenue, he signalled to the *commissionnaire* for a taxicab, and without a word, urged us into it.

"This is all nonsense," Markham declared ill-naturedly, as we started on our journey up town. "How do you expect to find any clues now? By this time everything has been obliterated."

"Alas, my dear Markham," lamented Vance, in a tone of mock solicitude, "how woefully deficient you are in philosophic theory! If anything, no matter how inf'nitesimal, could really be obliterated, the universe, y' know, would cease to exist,—the cosmic problem would be solved, and the Creator would write Q.E.D. across an empty firmament. Our only chance of going on with this illusion we call Life, d' ye see, lies in the fact that consciousness is like an inf'nite decimal point. Did you, as a child, ever try to complete the decimal, one-third, by filling a whole sheet of paper with the numeral three? You always had the fraction, one-third, left, don't y' know. If you could have eliminated the smallest one-third, after having set down ten thousand threes, the problem would have ended. So with life, my dear fellow. It's only because we can't erase or obliterate anything that we go on existing."

He made a movement with his fingers, putting a sort of tangible period to his remarks, and looked dreamily out of the window up at the fiery film of sky.

Markham had settled back into his corner, and was chewing morosely at his cigar. I could see he was fairly simmering with impotent anger at having let himself be goaded into issuing his challenge. But there was no retreating now. As he told me afterward, he was fully convinced he had been dragged forth out of a comfortable chair, on a patent and ridiculous fool's errand.

CHAPTER IX

The Height of the Murderer

(Saturday, June 15; 5 p.m.)

When we arrived at Benson's house a patrolman leaning somnolently against the iron paling of the areaway came suddenly to attention and saluted. He eyed Vance and me hopefully, regarding us no doubt as suspects being taken to the scene of the crime for questioning by the District Attorney. We were admitted by one of the men from the Homicide Bureau who had been in the house on the morning of the investigation.

Markham greeted him with a nod.

"Everything going all right?"

"Sure," the man replied good-naturedly. "The old lady's as meek as a cat—and a swell cook."

"We want to be alone for a while, Sniffin," said Markham, as we passed into the living-room.

"The gastronome's name is Snitkin—not Sniffin," Vance corrected him, when the door had closed on us.

"Wonderful memory," muttered Markham churlishly.

"A failing of mine," said Vance. "I suppose you are one of those rare persons who never forget a face but just can't recall names, what?"

But Markham was in no mood to be twitted.

---

87. Shakespeare, *Henry IV*, Part I, Act V, Scene 1.

88. Iago makes this remark in Shakespeare's *Othello*, Act II, Scene 3.

"Now that you've dragged me here, what are you going to do?" He waved his hand depreciatingly, and sank into a chair with an air of contemptuous abdication.

The living-room looked much the same as when we saw it last, except that it had been put neatly in order. The shades were up, and the late afternoon light was flooding in profusely. The ornateness of the room's furnishings seemed intensified by the glare.

Vance glanced about him and gave a shudder.

"I'm half inclined to turn back," he drawled. "It's a clear case of justifiable homicide by an outraged interior decorator."

"My dear æsthete," Markham urged impatiently, "be good enough to bury your artistic prejudices, and to proceed with your problem. . . . Of course," he added, with a malicious smile, "if you fear the result, you may still withdraw, and thereby preserve your charming theories in their present virgin state."

"And permit you to send an innocent maiden to the chair!" exclaimed Vance, in mock indignation. "Fie, fie! *La politesse* alone forbids my withdrawal. May I never have to lament, with Prince Henry, that 'to my shame I have a truant been to chivalry'."[87]

Markham set his jaw, and gave Vance a ferocious look.

"I'm beginning to think that, after all, there is something in your theory that every man has some motive for murdering another."

"Well," replied Vance cheerfully, "now that you have begun to come round to my way of thinking, do you mind if I send Mr. Snitkin on an errand?"

Markham sighed audibly and shrugged his shoulders.

"I'll smoke during the *opéra bouffe*, if it won't interfere with your performance."

Vance went to the door and called Snitkin.

"I say, would you mind going to Mrs. Platz and borrowing a long tape-measure and a ball of string. . . . The District Attorney wants them," he added, giving Markham a sycophantic bow.

"I can't hope that you're going to hang yourself, can I?" asked Markham.

Vance gazed at him reprovingly.

"Permit me," he said sweetly, "to commend *Othello* to your attention:

'How poor are they that have not patience!
What wound did ever heal but by degrees?'[88]

Or—to descend from a poet to a platitudinarian—let me present for your consid'ration a pentameter from Longfellow: 'All things come round to him who will but wait.' Untrue, of course, but consolin'. Milton said it much better in his 'They also serve—'. But Cervantes said it best: 'Patience and shuffle the cards.' Sound advice, Markham—and advice expressed rakishly, as all good advice should be. . . . To be sure, patience is a sort of last resort—a practice to adopt when there's nothing else to do. Still, like virtue, it occasionally rewards the practitioner; although I'll admit that, as a rule, it is—again like virtue—bootless. That is to say, it is its own reward. It has, however, been swathed in many verbal robes. It is 'sorrow's slave,' and the 'sov'reign o'er transmuted ills,' as well as 'all the passion of great hearts.' Rousseau wrote, *La patience est amère mais son fruit est doux.*[89] But perhaps your legal taste runs to Latin. *Superanda omnis fortuna ferendo est,*[90] quoth Virgil. And Horace also spoke on the subject. *Durum!* said he, *sed levius fit patientia—*"[91]

"Why the hell doesn't Snitkin come?" growled Markham.

Almost as he spoke the door opened, and the detective handed Vance the tape-measure and string.

"And now, Markham, for your reward!"

Bending over the rug Vance moved the large wicker chair into the exact position it had occupied when Benson had been shot. The position was easily determined, for the impressions of the chair's castors on the deep nap of the rug were plainly visible. He then ran the string through the bullet-hole in the back of the chair, and directed me to hold one end of it against the place where the bullet had struck the wainscot. Next he took up the tape-measure and extending the string through the hole, measured a distance of five feet and six inches along it, starting at the point which corresponded to the location of Benson's forehead as he sat in the chair. Tying a knot in the string to indicate the measurement, he drew the string taut, so that it extended in a straight line from the mark on the wainscot, through the hole in the back of the chair, to a point five feet and six inches in front of where Benson's head had rested.

"This knot in the string," he explained, "now represents the exact location of the muzzle of the gun that ended Benson's career. You see the reasoning—eh, what? Having two points in the bullet's course—namely, the hole in the chair and the mark on the wainscot—, and also knowing the approximate vertical line of explosion, which was between five and six feet from the

89. "Patience is bitter but its fruit is sweet."

90. Usually translated as "Every misfortune is to be subdued by patience."

91. The full saying is *Durum! Sed levius fit patientia quicquid corrigere est nefas* ("It is hard! But that which we are not permitted to correct is made lighter by patience").

gentleman's skull, it was merely necess'ry to extend the straight line of the bullet's course to the vertical line of explosion in order to ascertain the exact point at which the shot was fired."

"Theoretically very pretty," commented Markham; "though why you should go to so much trouble to ascertain this point in space I can't imagine. . . . Not that it matters, for you have overlooked the possibility of the bullet's deflection."

"Forgive me for contradicting you," smiled Vance; "but yesterday morning I questioned Captain Hagedorn at some length, and learned that there had been no deflection of the bullet. Hagedorn had inspected the wound before we arrived; and he was really pos'tive on that point. In the first place, the bullet struck the frontal bone at such an angle as to make deflection practically impossible even had the pistol been of smaller calibre. And in the second place, the pistol with which Benson was shot was of so large a bore—a point-forty-five—and the muzzle velocity was so great, that the bullet would have taken a straight course even had it been held at a greater distance from the gentleman's brow."

"And how," asked Markham, "did Hagedorn know what the muzzle velocity was?"

"I was inquis'tive on that point myself," answered Vance; "and he explained that the size and character of the bullet and the expelled shell told him the whole tale. That's how he knew the gun was an army Colt automatic—I believe he called it a U. S. Government Colt—and not the ordinary Colt automatic. The weight of the bullets of these two pistols is slightly different: the ordinary Colt bullet weighs 200 grains, whereas the army Colt bullet weighs 230 grains. Hagedorn, having a hypersensitive tactile sense, was able, I presume, to distinguish the difference at once, though I didn't go into his physiological gifts with him,—my reticent nature, you understand. . . . However, he could tell it was a forty-five army Colt automatic bullet; and knowing this, he knew that the muzzle velocity was 809 feet, and that the striking energy was 329—which gives a six-inch penetration in white pine at a distance of twenty-five yards. . . . An amazin' creature, this Hagedorn. Imagine having one's head full of such entrancing information! The old mysteries of why a man should take up the bass-fiddle as a life work and where all the pins go, are babes' conundrums compared with the one of why a human being should devote his years to the idiosyncrasies of bullets."

"The subject is not exactly an enthralling one," said Markham wearily; "so, for the sake of argument, let us admit that you have now found the precise point of the gun's explosion. Where do we go from there?"

"While I hold the string on a straight line," directed Vance, "be good enough to measure the exact distance from the floor to the knot. Then my secret will be known."

"This game doesn't enthrall me, either," Markham protested. "I'd much prefer 'London Bridge'."

Nevertheless he made the measurement.

"Four feet, eight and a half inches," he announced indifferently.

Vance laid a cigarette on the rug at a point directly beneath the knot.

"We now know the exact height at which the pistol was held when it was fired. . . . You grasp the process by which this conclusion was reached, I'm sure."

"It seems rather obvious," answered Markham.

Vance again went to the door and called Snitkin.

"The District Attorney desires the loan of your gun for a moment," he said. "He wishes to make a test."

Snitkin stepped up to Markham and held out his pistol wonderingly.

"The safety's on, sir: shall I shift it?"

Markham was about to refuse the weapon when Vance interposed.

"That's quite all right. Mr. Markham doesn't intend to fire it—I hope."

When the man had gone Vance seated himself in the wicker chair, and placed his head in juxtaposition with the bullet-hole.

"Now, Markham," he requested, "will you please stand on the spot where the murderer stood, holding the gun directly above that cigarette on the floor, and aim delib'rately at my left temple. . . . Take care," he cautioned, with an engaging smile, "not to pull the trigger, or you will never learn who killed Benson."

Reluctantly Markham complied. As he stood taking aim, Vance asked me to measure the height of the gun's muzzle from the floor.

The distance was four feet and nine inches.

"Quite so," he said, rising. "Y' see, Markham, you are five feet, eleven inches tall; therefore the person who shot Benson was very nearly your own height—certainly not under five feet, ten. . . . That, too, is rather obvious, what?"

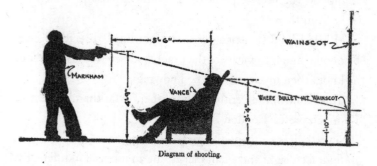

Diagram of shooting.

Vance's analysis of the shooting,
from *The Benson Murder Case*, artist unknown.

His demonstration had been simple and clear. Markham was frankly impressed; his manner had become serious. He regarded Vance for a moment with a meditative frown; then he said:

"That's all very well; but the person who fired the shot might have held the pistol relatively higher than I did."

"Not tenable," returned Vance. "I've done too much shooting myself not to know that when an expert takes delib'rate aim with a pistol at a small target, he does it with a stiff arm and with a slightly raised shoulder, so as to bring the sight on a straight line between his eye and the object at which he aims. The height at which one holds a revolver, under such conditions, pretty accurately determines his own height."

"Your argument is based on the assumption that the person who killed Benson was an expert taking deliberate aim at a small target?"

"Not an assumption, but a fact," declared Vance. "Consider: had the person not been an expert shot, he would not—at a distance of five or six feet—have selected the forehead, but a larger target—namely, the breast. And having selected the forehead, he most certainly took delib'rate aim, what? Furthermore, had he not been an expert shot, and had he pointed the gun at the breast without taking delib'rate aim, he would, in all prob'bility, have fired more than one shot."

Markham pondered.

"I'll grant that, on the face of it, your theory sounds plausible," he conceded at length. "On the other hand, the guilty man could have been almost any height over five feet, ten; for certainly a man may crouch as much as he likes and still take deliberate aim."

"True," agreed Vance. "But don't overlook the fact that the murderer's position, in this instance, was a perfectly natural one. Otherwise, Benson's attention would have been attracted, and he would not have been taken unawares. That he was shot unawares was indicated by his attitude. Of course, the assassin might have stooped a little without causing Benson to look up. . . . Let us say, therefore, that the guilty person's height is somewhere between five feet, ten, and six feet, two. Does that appeal to you?"

Markham was silent.

"The delightful Miss St. Clair, y' know," remarked Vance, with a japish smile, "can't possibly be over five feet, five or six."

Markham grunted, and continued to smoke abstractedly.

"This Captain Leacock, I take it," said Vance, "is over six feet—eh, what?"

Markham's eyes narrowed.

"What makes you think so?"

"You just told me, don't y' know."

"I told you!"

"Not in so many words," Vance pointed out. "But after I had shown you the approximate height of the murderer, and it didn't correspond at all to that of the young lady you suspected, I knew your active mind was busy looking around for another possibility. And, as the lady's *inamorato* was the only other possibility on your horizon, I concluded that you were permitting your thoughts to play about the Captain. Had he, therefore, been the stipulated height, you would have said nothing; but when you argued that the murderer might have stooped to fire the shot, I decided that the Captain was inord'nately tall. . . . Thus, in the pregnant silence that emanated from you, old dear, your spirit held sweet communion with mine, and told me that the gentleman was a six-footer no less."

"I see that you include mind-reading among your gifts," said Markham. "I now await an exhibition of slate-writing."[92]

His tone was irritable, but his irritation was that of a man reluctant to admit the alteration of his beliefs. He felt himself yielding to Vance's guiding rein, but he still held stubbornly to the course of his own previous convictions.

"Surely you don't question my demonstration of the guilty person's height?" asked Vance mellifluously.

92. "Slate-writing"—the appearance of words on blank slates, purportedly written by a supernatural hand—was a common effect performed by mediums in séances.

"Not altogether," Markham replied. "It seems colorable enough. . . . But why, I wonder, didn't Hagedorn work the thing out, if it was so simple?"

"Anaxagoras said that those who have occasion for a lamp, supply it with oil. A profound remark, Markham—one of those seemingly simple quips that contain a great truth. A lamp without oil, y' know, is useless. The police always have plenty of lamps—every variety, in fact—but no oil, as it were. That's why they never find anyone unless it's broad daylight."

Markham's mind was now busy in another direction, and he rose and began to pace the floor.

"Until now I hadn't thought of Captain Leacock as the actual agent of the crime."

"Why hadn't you thought of him? Was it because one of your sleuths told you he was at home like a good boy that night?"

"I suppose so." Markham continued pacing thoughtfully. Then suddenly he swung about. "That wasn't it, either. It was the amount of damning circumstantial evidence against the St. Clair woman. . . . And, Vance, despite your demonstration here to-day, you haven't explained away any of the evidence against her.—Where was she between twelve and one? Why did she go with Benson to dinner? How did her hand-bag get here? And what about those burned cigarettes of hers in the grate?—they're the obstacle, those cigarette butts; and I can't admit that your demonstration wholly convinces me—despite the fact that it *is* convincing—as long as I've got the evidence of those cigarettes to contend with, for that evidence is also convincing."

"My word!" sighed Vance. "You're in a pos'tively ghastly predic'ment. However, maybe I can cast illumination on those disquietin' cigarette butts."

Once more he went to the door, and summoning Snitkin, returned the pistol.

"The District Attorney thanks you," he said. "And will you be good enough to fetch Mrs. Platz. We wish to chat with her."

Turning back to the room, he smiled amiably at Markham.

"I desire to do all the conversing with the lady this time, if you don't mind. There are potentialities in Mrs. Platz which you entirely overlooked when you questioned her yesterday."

Markham was interested, though sceptical.

"You have the floor," he said.

CHAPTER X

Eliminating a Suspect

(Saturday, June 15; 5.30 p.m.)

When the housekeeper entered she appeared even more composed than when Markham had first questioned her. There was something at once sullen and indomitable in her manner, and she looked at me with a slightly challenging expression. Markham merely nodded to her, but Vance stood up and indicated a low tufted Morris chair near the fireplace, facing the front windows. She sat down on the edge of it, resting her elbows on its broad arms.

"I have some questions to ask you, Mrs. Platz," Vance began, fixing her sharply with his gaze; "and it will be best for everyone if you tell the whole truth. You understand me—eh, what?"

The easy-going, half-whimsical manner he had taken with Markham had disappeared. He stood before the woman, stern and implacable.

At his words she lifted her head. Her face was blank, but her mouth was set stubbornly, and a smouldering look in her eyes told of a suppressed anxiety.

Vance waited a moment and then went on, enunciating each word with distinctness.

"At what time, on the day Mr. Benson was killed, did the lady call here?"

The woman's gaze did not falter, but the pupils of her eyes dilated.

"There was nobody here."

"Oh, yes, there was, Mrs. Platz." Vance's tone was assured. "What time did she call?"

"Nobody was here, I tell you," she persisted.

Vance lit a cigarette with interminable deliberation, his eyes resting steadily on hers. He smoked placidly until her gaze dropped. Then he stepped nearer to her, and said firmly:

"If you tell the truth no harm will come to you. But if you refuse any information you will find yourself in trouble. The withholding of evidence is a crime, y' know, and the law will show you no mercy."

He made a sly grimace at Markham, who was watching the proceedings with interest.

The woman now began to show signs of agitation. She drew in her elbows, and her breathing quickened.

"In God's name, I swear it!—there wasn't anybody here." A slight hoarseness gave evidence of her emotion.

"Let us not invoke the Deity," suggested Vance carelessly. "What time was the lady here?"

She set her lips stubbornly, and for a whole minute there was silence in the room. Vance smoked quietly, but Markham held his cigar motionless between his thumb and forefinger in an attitude of expectancy.

Again Vance's impassive voice demanded: "What time was she here?"

The woman clinched her hands with a spasmodic gesture, and thrust her head forward.

"I tell you—I swear it—"

Vance made a peremptory movement of his hand, and smiled coldly.

"It's no go," he told her. "You're acting stupidly. We're here to get the truth—and you're going to tell us."

"I've told you the truth."

"Is it going to be necess'ry for the District Attorney here to order you placed in custody?"

"I've told you the truth," she repeated.

Vance crushed out his cigarette decisively in an ash-receiver on the table.

"Right-o, Mrs. Platz. Since you refuse to tell me about the young woman who was here that afternoon, I'm going to tell you about her."

His manner was easy and cynical, and the woman watched him suspiciously.

"Late in the afternoon of the day your employer was shot, the door-bell rang. Perhaps you had been informed by Mr. Benson that he was expecting a caller, what? Anyhow, you answered the door and admitted a charming young lady. You showed her into this room . . . and—what do you think, my dear Madam!—she took that very chair on which you are resting so uncomfortably."

He paused, and smiled tantalizingly.

"Then," he continued, "you served tea to the young lady and Mr. Benson. After a bit she departed, and Mr. Benson went upstairs to dress for dinner. . . . Y' see, Mrs. Platz, I happen to know."

He lit another cigarette.

"Did you notice the young lady particularly? If not, I'll describe her to you. She was rather short—*petite* is the word. She had dark hair and dark eyes, and she was dressed quietly."

A change had come over the woman. Her eyes stared; her cheeks were now grey; and her breathing had become audible.

"Now, Mrs. Platz," demanded Vance sharply, "what have you to say?"

She drew a deep breath.

"There wasn't anybody here," she said doggedly. There was something almost admirable in her obstinacy.

Vance considered a moment. Markham was about to speak, but evidently thought better of it, and sat watching the woman fixedly.

"Your attitude is understandable," Vance observed finally. "The young lady, of course, was well known to you, and you had a personal reason for not wanting it known she was here."

At these words she sat up straight, a look of terror in her face.

"I never saw her before!" she cried; then stopped abruptly.

"Ah!" Vance gave her an amused leer. "You had never seen the young lady before—eh, what? . . . That's quite possible. But it's immaterial. She's a nice girl, though, I'm sure—even if she did have a dish of tea with your employer alone in his home."

"Did she tell you she was here?" The woman's voice was listless. The reaction to her tense obduracy had left her apathetic.

"Not exactly," Vance replied. "But it wasn't necess'ry: I knew without her informing me. . . . Just when did she arrive, Mrs. Platz?"

"About a half-hour after Mr. Benson got here from the office." She had at last given over all denials and evasions. "But he didn't expect her—that is, he didn't say anything to me about her coming; and he didn't order tea until after she came."

Markham thrust himself forward.

"Why didn't you tell me she'd been here, when I asked you yesterday morning?"

The woman cast an uneasy glance about the room.

"I rather fancy," Vance intervened pleasantly, "that Mrs. Platz was afraid you might unjustly suspect the young lady."

She grasped eagerly at his words.

"Yes, sir—that was all. I was afraid you might think she—did it. And she was such a quiet, sweet-looking girl. . . . That was the only reason, sir."

"Quite so," agreed Vance consolingly. "But tell me: did it not shock you to see such a quiet, sweet-looking young lady smoking cigarettes?"

Her apprehension gave way to astonishment.

"Why—yes, sir, it did. . . . But she wasn't a bad girl—I could tell that. And most girls smoke nowadays. They don't think anything of it, like they used to."

"You're quite right," Vance assured her. "Still, young ladies really shouldn't throw their cigarettes in tiled, gas-log fireplaces, should they, now?"

The woman regarded him uncertainly; she suspected him of jesting.

"Did she do that?" She leaned over and looked into the fireplace. "I didn't see any cigarettes there this morning."

"No, you wouldn't have," Vance informed her. "One of the District Attorney's sleuths, d' ye see, cleaned it all up nicely for you yesterday."

She shot Markham a questioning glance. She was not sure whether Vance's remark was to be taken seriously; but his casualness of manner and pleasantness of voice tended to put her at ease.

"Now that we understand each other, Mrs. Platz," he was saying, "was there anything else you particularly noticed when the young lady was here? You will be doing her a good service by telling us, because both the District Attorney and I happen to know she is innocent."

She gave Vance a long shrewd look, as if appraising his sincerity. Evidently the results of her scrutiny were favorable, for her answer left no doubt as to her complete frankness.

"I don't know if it'll help, but when I came in with the toast Mr. Benson looked like he was arguing with her. She seemed worried about something that was going to happen, and asked him not to hold her to some promise she'd made. I was only in the room a minute, and I didn't hear much. But just as I was going out, he laughed and said it was only a bluff, and that nothing was going to happen."

She stopped, and waited anxiously. She seemed to fear that her revelation might, after all, prove injurious rather than helpful to the girl.

"Was that all?" Vance's tone indicated that the matter was of no consequence.

The woman demurred.

"That was all I heard; but . . . there was a small blue box of jewellery sitting on the table."

"My word!—a box of jewellery! Do you know whose it was?"

"No, sir, I don't. The lady hadn't brought it, and I never saw it in the house before."

"How did you know it was jewellery?"

"When Mr. Benson went upstairs to dress, I came in to clear the tea things away, and it was still sitting on the table."

Vance smiled.

"And you played Pandora and took a peep—eh, what? Most natural,—I'd have done it myself."

He stepped back, and bowed politely.

"That will be all, Mrs. Platz. . . . And you needn't worry about the young lady. Nothing is going to happen to her."

When she had left us, Markham leaned forward and shook his cigar at Vance.

"Why didn't you tell me you had information about the case unknown to me?"

"My dear chap!" Vance lifted his eyebrows in protestation. "To what do you refer specifically?"

"How did you know this St. Clair woman had been here in the afternoon?"

"I didn't; but I surmised it. There were cigarette butts of hers in the grate; and, as I knew she hadn't been here on the night Benson was shot, I thought it rather likely she had been here earlier in the day. And since Benson didn't arrive from his office until four, I whispered into my ear that she had called sometime

93. "In esse" means "in actuality"—"in posse" means "in possibility." That is, according to Vance, psychological deductions do not reveal what *actually* happened, only what *possibly* (or likely) happened.

between four and the hour of his departure for dinner. . . . An element'ry syllogism, what?"

"How did you know she wasn't here that night?"

"The psychological aspects of the crime left me in no doubt. As I told you, no woman committed it,—my metaphysical hypotheses again; but never mind. . . . Furthermore, yesterday morning I stood on the spot where the murderer stood, and sighted with my eye along the line of fire, using Benson's head and the mark on the wainscot as my points of coinc'dence. It was evident to me then, even without measurements, that the guilty person was rather tall."

"Very well. . . . But how did you know she left here that afternoon before Benson did?" persisted Markham.

"How else could she have changed into an evening gown? Really, y' know, ladies don't go about *décolletées* in the afternoon."

"You assume, then, that Benson himself brought her gloves and hand-bag back here that night?"

"Someone did,—and it certainly wasn't Miss St. Clair."

"All right," conceded Markham. "And what about this Morris chair?—how did you know she sat in it?"

"What other chair could she have sat in, and still thrown her cigarettes into the fireplace? Women are notoriously poor shots, even if they were given to hurling their cigarette stubs across the room."

"That deduction is simple enough," admitted Markham. "But suppose you tell me how you knew she had tea here unless you were privy to some information on the point?"

"It pos'tively shames me to explain it. But the humiliating truth is that I inferred the fact from the condition of yon samovar. I noted yesterday that it had been used, and had not been emptied or wiped off."

Markham nodded with contemptuous elation.

"You seem to have sunk to the despised legal level of material clues."

"That's why I'm blushing so furiously. . . . However, psychological deductions alone do not determine facts *in esse*, but only *in posse*.[93] Other conditions must, of course, be considered. In the present instance the indications of the samovar served merely as the basis for an assumption, or guess, with which to draw out the housekeeper."

"Well, I won't deny that you succeeded," said Markham. "I'd like to know, though, what you had in mind when you accused the woman of a personal interest in the girl. That remark certainly indicated some pre-knowledge of the situation."

Vance's face became serious.

"Markham, I give you my word," he said earnestly, "I had nothing in mind. I made the accusation, thinking it was false, merely to trap her into a denial. And she fell into the trap. But—deuce take it!—I seemed to hit some nail squarely on the head, what? I can't for the life of me imagine why she was frightened.—But it really doesn't matter."

"Perhaps not," agreed Markham, but his tone was dubious. "What do you make of the box of jewellery and the disagreement between Benson and the girl?"

"Nothing yet. They don't fit in, do they?"

He was silent a moment. Then he spoke with unusual seriousness.

"Markham, take my advice and don't bother with these side-issues. I'm telling you the girl had no part in the murder. Let her alone,—you'll be happier in your old age if you do."

Markham sat scowling, his eyes in space.

"I'm convinced that you *think* you know something."

"*Cogito, ergo sum,*" murmured Vance. "Y' know, the naturalistic philosophy of Descartes has always rather appealed to me. It was a departure from universal doubt and a seeking for positive knowledge in self-consciousness. Spinoza in his pantheism, and Berkeley in his idealism, quite misunderstood the significance of their precursor's favorite enthymeme.[94] Even Descartes' errors were brilliant. His method of reasoning, for all its scientific inaccuracies, gave new signif'cation to the symbols of the analyst. The mind, after all, if it is to function effectively, must combine the mathematical precision of a natural science with such pure speculations as astronomy. For instance, Descartes' doctrine of Vortices—"

"Oh, be quiet," growled Markham. "I'm not insisting that you reveal your precious information. So why burden me with a dissertation on seventeenth-century philosophy?"

"Anyhow, you'll admit, won't you," asked Vance lightly, "that, in elim'nating those disturbing cigarette butts, so to speak, I've elim'nated Miss St. Clair as a suspect?"

Markham did not answer at once. There was no doubt that the developments of the past hour had made a decided impression upon him. He did not underestimate Vance, despite his persistent opposition; and he knew that, for all his flippancy,

94.   An argument or syllogism in which one premise is not expressed.

95.   "There are sparrows in the vines," the beginning of a popular song, recorded to great success by Dranem in 1931.

Vance was fundamentally serious. Furthermore, Markham had a finely developed sense of justice. He was not narrow, even though obstinate at times; and I have never known him to close his mind to the possibilities of truth, however opposed to his own interests. It did not, therefore, surprise me in the least when, at last, he looked up with a gracious smile of surrender.

"You've made your point," he said; "and I accept it with proper humility. I'm most grateful to you."

Vance walked indifferently to the window and looked out.

"I am happy to learn that you are capable of accepting such evidence as the human mind could not possibly deny."

I had always noticed, in the relationship of these two men, that whenever either made a remark that bordered on generosity, the other answered in a manner which ended all outward show of sentiment. It was as if they wished to keep this more intimate side of their mutual regard hidden from the world.

Markham therefore ignored Vance's thrust.

"Have you perhaps any enlightening suggestions, other than negative ones, to offer as to Benson's murderer?" he asked.

"Rather!" said Vance. "No end of suggestions."

"Could you spare me a good one?" Markham imitated the other's playful tone.

Vance appeared to reflect.

"Well, I should advise that, as a beginning, you look for a rather tall man, cool-headed, familiar with fire-arms, a good shot, and fairly well known to the deceased—a man who was aware that Benson was going to dinner with Miss St. Clair, or who had reason to suspect the fact."

Markham looked narrowly at Vance for several moments.

"I think I understand. . . . Not a bad theory, either. You know, I'm going to suggest immediately to Heath that he investigate more thoroughly Captain Leacock's activities on the night of the murder."

"Oh, by all means," said Vance carelessly, going to the piano.

Markham watched him with an expression of puzzled interrogation. He was about to speak when Vance began playing a rollicking French café song which opens, I believe, with

"*Ils sont dans les vignes les moineaux.*"[95]

CHAPTER XI

A Motive and a Threat

(Sunday, June 16; afternoon.)

The following day, which was Sunday, we lunched with Markham at the Stuyvesant Club. Vance had suggested the appointment the evening before; for, as he explained to me, he wished to be present in case Leander Pfyfe should arrive from Long Island.

"It amuses me tremendously," he had said, "the way human beings delib'rately complicate the most ordin'ry issues. They have a downright horror of anything simple and direct. The whole modern commercial system is nothing but a colossal mechanism for doing things in the most involved and roundabout way. If one makes a ten-cent purchase at a department store nowadays, a complete history of the transaction is written out in triplicate, checked by a dozen floor-walkers and clerks, signed and countersigned, entered into innum'rable ledgers with various colored inks, and then elab'rately secreted in steel filing-cabinets. And not content with all this superfluous *chinoiserie*, our business men have created a large and expensive army of efficiency experts whose sole duty it is to complicate and befuddle this system still further. . . . It's the same with everything else in modern life. Regard that insup'rable mania called golf. It consists merely of knocking a ball into a hole with a stick. But the devotees of this pastime have developed a unique and distinctive livery in which to play it. They concentrate for twenty years on the correct angulation of their feet and the proper method of entwining their fingers about the stick. Moreover, in order to discuss the pseudo-intr'cacies of this idiotic sport, they've invented an outlandish vocabulary which is unintelligible even to an English scholar."

He pointed disgustedly at a pile of Sunday newspapers.

"Then here's this Benson murder—a simple and incons'quential affair. Yet the entire machinery of the law is going at high pressure and blowing off jets of steam all over the community, when the matter could be settled quietly in five minutes with a bit of intelligent thinking."

At lunch, however, he did not refer to the crime; and, as if by tacit agreement, the subject was avoided. Markham had merely mentioned casually to us as we went into the dining-room that he was expecting Heath a little later.

The sergeant was waiting for us when we retired to the lounge-room for our smoke, and by his expression it was evident he was not pleased with the way things were going.

"I told you, Mr. Markham," he said, when he had drawn up our chairs, "that this case was going to be a tough one. . . . Could you get any kind of a lead from the St. Clair woman?"

Markham shook his head.

"She's out of it." And he recounted briefly the happenings at Benson's house the preceding afternoon.

"Well, if you're satisfied," was Heath's somewhat dubious comment, "that's good enough for me. But what about this Captain Leacock?"

"That's what I asked you here to talk about," Markham told him. "There's no direct evidence against him, but there are several suspicious circumstances that tend to connect him with the murder. He seems to meet the specifications as to height; and we mustn't overlook the fact that Benson was shot with just such a gun as Leacock would be likely to possess. He was engaged to the girl, and a motive might be found in Benson's attentions to her."

"And ever since the big scrap," supplemented Heath, "these army boys don't think anything of shooting people. They got used to blood on the other side."

"The only hitch," resumed Markham, "is that Phelps, who had the job of checking up on the Captain, reported to me that he was home that night from eight o'clock on. Of course, there may be a loop-hole somewhere, and I was going to suggest that you have one of your men go into the matter thoroughly and see just what the situation is. Phelps got his information from one of the hall-boys; and I think it might be well to get hold of the boy again and apply a little pressure. If it was found that Leacock was not at home at twelve-thirty that night, we might have the lead you've been looking for."

"I'll attend to it myself," said Heath. "I'll go round there to-night, and if this boy knows anything, he'll spill it before I'm through with him."

We had talked but a few minutes longer when a uniformed attendant bowed deferentially at the District Attorney's elbow and announced that Mr. Pfyfe was calling.

Markham requested that his visitor be shown into the loungeroom, and then added to Heath: "You'd better remain, and hear what he has to say."

Leander Pfyfe was an immaculate and exquisite personage. He approached us with a mincing gate of self-approbation. His legs, which were very long and thin, with knees that seemed to bend slightly inward, supported a short bulging torso; and his chest curved outward in a generous arc, like that of a pouter-pigeon. His face was rotund, and his jowls hung in two loops over a collar too tight for comfort. His blond sparse hair was brushed back sleekly; and the ends of his narrow, silken moustache were waxed into needle-points. He was dressed in light-grey summer flannels, and wore a pale turquoise-green silk shirt, a vivid foulard tie, and grey suède Oxfords. A strong odor of oriental perfume was given off by the carefully arranged batiste handkerchief in his breast pocket.

He greeted Markham with viscid urbanity, and acknowledged his introduction to us with a patronizing bow. After posing himself in a chair the attendant placed for him, he began polishing a gold-rimmed eye-glass which he wore on a ribbon, and fixed Markham with a melancholy gaze.

"A very sad occasion, this," he sighed.

"Realizing your friendship for Mr. Benson," said Markham, "I deplore the necessity of appealing to you at this time. It was very good of you, by the way, to come to the city to-day."

Pfyfe made a mildly deprecating movement with his carefully manicured fingers. He was, he explained with an air of ineffable self-complacency, only too glad to discommode himself to give aid

96.   In Virgil's *Aeneid*, Achates—*fidus Achates* (faithful Achates)—was the close friend of the hero Aeneas.

to servants of the public. A distressing necessity, to be sure; but his manner conveyed unmistakably that he knew and recognized the obligations attaching to the dictum of *noblesse oblige*, and was prepared to meet them.

He looked at Markham with a self-congratulatory air, and his eyebrows queried: "What can I do for you?" though his lips did not move.

"I understand from Major Anthony Benson," Markham said, "that you were very close to his brother, and therefore might be able to tell us something of his personal affairs, or private social relationships, that would indicate a line of investigation."

Pfyfe gazed sadly at the floor.

"Ah, yes. Alvin and I were very close,—we were, in fact, the most intimate of friends. You can not imagine how broken up I was at hearing of the dear fellow's tragic end." He gave the impression that here was a modern instance of Æneas and Achates.[96] "And I was deeply grieved at not being able to come at once to New York to put myself at the service of those that needed me."

"I'm sure it would have been a comfort to his other friends," remarked Vance, with cool politeness. "But in the circumst'nces you will be forgiven."

Pfyfe blinked regretfully.

"Ah, but I shall never forgive myself—though I cannot hold myself altogether blameworthy. Only the day before the tragedy I had started on a trip to the Catskills. I had even asked dear Alvin to go along; but he was too busy." Pfyfe shook his head as if lamenting the incomprehensible irony of life. "How much better—ah, how infinitely much better—if only—"

"You were gone a very short time," commented Markham, interrupting what promised to be a homily on perverse providence.

"True," Pfyfe indulgently admitted. "But I met with a most unfortunate accident." He polished his eye-glass a moment. "My car broke down, and I was necessitated to return."

"What road did you take?" asked Heath.

Pfyfe delicately adjusted his eye-glass, and regarded the Sergeant with an intimation of boredom.

"My advice, Mr.—ah—Sneed—"

"Heath," the other corrected him surlily.

"Ah, yes—Heath. . . . My advice, Mr. Heath, is, that if you are contemplating a motor trip to the Catskills, you apply to the

Automobile Club of America for a road-map. My choice of itinerary might very possibly not suit you."

He turned back to the District Attorney with an air that implied he preferred talking to an equal.

"Tell me, Mr. Pfyfe," Markham asked; "did Mr. Benson have any enemies?"

The other appeared to think the matter over.

"No-o. Not one, I should say, who would actually have killed him as a result of animosity."

"You imply nevertheless that he had enemies. Could you not tell us a little more?"

Pfyfe passed his hand gracefully over the tips of his golden moustache, and then permitted his index-finger to linger on his cheek in an attitude of meditative indecision.

"Your request, Mr. Markham,"—he spoke with pained reluctance—"brings up a matter which I hesitate to discuss. But perhaps it is best that I confide in you—as one gentleman to another. Alvin, in common with many other admirable fellows, had a—what shall I say?—a weakness—let me put it that way—for the fair sex."

He looked at Markham, seeking approbation for his extreme tact in stating an indelicate truth.

"You understand," he continued, in answer to the other's sympathetic nod, "Alvin was not a man who possessed the personal characteristics that women hold attractive." (I somehow got the impression that Pfyfe considered himself as differing radically from Benson in this respect.) "Alvin was aware of his physical deficiency, and the result was,—I trust you will understand my hesitancy in mentioning this distressing fact,—but the result was that Alvin used certain—ah—methods in his dealings with women, which you and I could never bring ourselves to adopt. Indeed—though it pains me to say it—he often took unfair advantage of women. He used underhand methods, as it were."

He paused, apparently shocked by this heinous imperfection of his friend, and by the necessity of his own seemingly disloyal revelation.

"Was it one of these women whom Benson had dealt with unfairly, that you had in mind?" asked Markham.

"No—not the woman herself," Pfyfe replied; "but a man who was interested in her. In fact, this man threatened Alvin's life. You will appreciate my reluctance in telling you this; but my excuse is that the threat was made quite openly. There were several others besides myself who heard it."

"That, of course, relieves you from any technical breach of confidence," Markham observed.

Pfyfe acknowledged the other's understanding with a slight bow.

"It happened at a little party of which I was the unfortunate host," he confessed modestly.

"Who was the man?" Markham's tone was polite but firm.

"You will comprehend my reticence. . . ." Pfyfe began. Then, with an air of righteous frankness, he leaned forward. "It might prove unfair to Alvin to withhold the gentleman's name. . . . He was Captain Philip Leacock."

He allowed himself the emotional outlet of a sigh.

"I trust you won't ask me for the lady's name."

"It won't be necessary," Markham assured him. "But I'd appreciate your telling us a little more of the episode."

Pfyfe complied with an expression of patient resignation.

"Alvin was considerably taken with the lady in question, and showed her many attentions which were, I am forced to admit, unwelcome. Captain Leacock resented these attentions; and at the little affair to which I had invited him and Alvin, some unpleasant and, I must say, unrefined words passed between them. I fear the wine had been flowing too freely, for Alvin was always punctilious—he was a man, indeed, skilled in the niceties of social intercourse; and the Captain, in an outburst of temper, told Alvin that, unless he left the lady strictly alone in the future, he would pay with his life. The Captain even went so far as to draw a revolver half-way out of his pocket."

"Was it a revolver, or an automatic pistol?" asked Heath.

Pfyfe gave the District Attorney a faint smile of annoyance, without deigning even to glance at the Sergeant.

"I misspoke myself; forgive me. It was not a revolver. It was, I believe, an automatic army pistol—though, you understand, I didn't see it in its entirety."

"You say there were others who witnessed the altercation?"

"Several of my guests were standing about," Pfyfe explained; "but, on my word, I couldn't name them. The fact is, I attached little importance to the threat—indeed, it had entirely slipped my memory until I read the account of poor Alvin's death.

Then I thought at once of the unfortunate incident, and said to myself: Why not tell the District Attorney . . . ?"

"Thoughts that breathe and words that burn,"[97] murmured Vance, who had been sitting through the interview in oppressive boredom.

Pfyfe once more adjusted his eye-glass, and gave Vance a withering look.

"I beg your pardon, sir?"

Vance smiled disarmingly.

"Merely a quotation from Gray. Poetry appeals to me in certain moods, don't y' know. . . . Do you, by any chance, know Colonel Ostrander?"

Pfyfe looked at him coldly, but only a vacuous countenance met his gaze.

"I am acquainted with the gentleman," he replied haughtily.

"Was Colonel Ostrander present at this delightful little social affair of yours?" Vance's tone was artlessly innocent.

"Now that you mention it, I believe he was," admitted Pfyfe, and lifted his eyebrows inquisitively.

But Vance was again staring disinterestedly out of the window.

Markham, annoyed at the interruption, attempted to re-establish the conversation on a more amiable and practical basis. But Pfyfe, though loquacious, had little more information to give. He insisted constantly on bringing the talk back to Captain Leacock, and, despite his eloquent protestations, it was obvious he attached more importance to the threat than he chose to admit. Markham questioned him for fully an hour, but could learn nothing else of a suggestive nature.

When Pfyfe rose to go Vance turned from his contemplation of the outside world and, bowing affably, let his eyes rest on the other with ingenuous good-nature.

"Now that you are in New York, Mr. Pfyfe, and were so unfortunate as to be unable to arrive earlier, I assume that you will remain until after the investigation."

Pfyfe's studied and habitual calm gave way to a look of oily astonishment.

"I hadn't contemplated doing so."

"It would be most desirable—if you could arrange it," urged Markham; though I am sure he had no intention of making the request until Vance suggested it.

97. "Poetry is thoughts that breathe and words that burn"—from Thomas Gray's "The Progress of Poesy" (1754).

98. A well-known residential hotel whose denizens included Babe Ruth, Theodore Dreiser, Enrico Caruso, Stravinsky, and Toscanini; it was converted to condominiums in the 1990s.

The Ansonia Hotel, in the 1920s.

99. Another comment on "poesy," this one from Shakespeare's *Love's Labours Lost*, Act IV, Scene 2.

Pfyfe hesitated, and then made an elegant gesture of resignation.

"Certainly I shall remain. When you have further need of my services, you will find me at the Ansonia."[98]

He spoke with exalted condescension, and magnanimously conferred upon Markham a parting smile. But the smile did not spring from within. It appeared to have been adjusted upon his features by the unseen hands of a sculptor; and it affected only the muscles about his mouth.

When he had gone Vance gave Markham a look of suppressed mirth.

"'Elegancy, facility and golden cadence.' . . . [99] But put not your faith in poesy, old dear. Our Ciceronian friend is an unmitigated fashioner of deceptions."

"If you're trying to say that he's a smooth liar," remarked Heath, "I don't agree with you. I think that story about the Captain's threat is straight goods."

"Oh, that! Of course, it's true. . . . And, y' know, Markham, the knightly Mr. Pfyfe was frightfully disappointed when you didn't insist on his revealing Miss St. Clair's name. This Leander, I fear, would never have swum the Hellespont for a lady's sake."

"Whether he's a swimmer or not," said Heath impatiently, "he's given us something to go on."

Markham agreed that Pfyfe's recital had added materially to the case against Leacock.

"I think I'll have the Captain down to my office to-morrow, and question him," he said.

A moment later Major Benson entered the room, and Markham invited him to join us.

"I just saw Pfyfe get into a taxi," he said, when he had sat down. "I suppose you've been asking him about Alvin's affairs. . . . Did he help you any?"

"I hope so, for all our sakes," returned Markham kindly. "By the way, Major, what do you know about a Captain Philip Leacock?"

Major Benson lifted his eyes to Markham's in surprise.

"Didn't you know? Leacock was one of the captains in my regiment,—a first-rate man. He knew Alvin pretty well, I think; but my impression is they didn't hit it off very chummily. . . . Surely you don't connect him with this affair?"

Markham ignored the question.

"Did you happen to attend a party of Pfyfe's the night the Captain threatened your brother?"

"I went, I remember, to one or two of Pfyfe's parties," said the Major. "I don't, as a rule, care for such gatherings, but Alvin convinced me it was a good business policy."

He lifted his head, and frowned fixedly into space, like one searching for an elusive memory.

"However, I don't recall—By George! Yes, I believe I do. . . . But if the instance I am thinking of is what you have in mind, you can dismiss it. We were all a little moist that night."

"Did Captain Leacock draw a gun?" asked Heath.

The Major pursed his lips.

"Now that you mention it, I think he did make some motion of the kind."

"Did you see the gun?" pursued Heath.

"No, I can't say that I did."

Markham put the next question.

"Do you think Captain Leacock capable of the act of murder?"

"Hardly," Major Benson answered with emphasis. "Leacock isn't cold-blooded. The woman over whom the tiff occurred is more capable of such an act than he is."

A short silence followed, broken by Vance.

"What do you know, Major, about this glass of fashion and mould of form, Pfyfe? He appears a rare bird. Has he a history, or is his presence his life's document?"

"Leander Pfyfe," said the Major, "is a typical specimen of the modern young do-nothing,—I say young, though I imagine he's around forty. He was pampered in his upbringing—had everything he wanted, I believe; but he became restless, and followed several different fads till he tired of them. He was two years in South Africa hunting big game, and, I think, wrote a book recounting his adventures. Since then he has done nothing that I know of. He married a wealthy shrew some years ago—for her money, I imagine. But the woman's father controls the purse-strings, and holds him down to a rigid allowance. . . . Pfyfe's a waster and an idler, but Alvin seemed to find some attraction in the man."

The Major's words had been careless in inflection and undeliberated, like those of a man discussing a neutral matter; but all of

100. Jicky is the oldest perfume in continuous existence, first sold in 1899 by Guerlain, and used by both men and women; it is a vanilla and lavender-based scent.

us, I think, received the impression that he had a strong personal dislike for Pfyfe.

"Not a ravishing personality, what?" remarked Vance. "And he uses far too much *Jicky*."[100]

"Still," supplied Heath, with a puzzled frown, "a fellow's got to have a lot of nerve to shoot big game. . . . And, speaking of nerve, I've been thinking that the guy who shot your brother, Major, was a mighty cool-headed proposition. He did it from the front when his man was wide awake, and with a servant upstairs. That takes nerve."

"Sergeant, you're pos'tively brilliant!" exclaimed Vance.

CHAPTER XII

The Owner of a Colt-.45

(Monday, June 17; forenoon.)

Though Vance and I arrived at the District Attorney's office the following morning a little after nine, the Captain had been waiting twenty minutes; and Markham directed Swacker to send him in at once.

Captain Philip Leacock was a typical army officer, very tall—fully six feet, two inches,—clean-shaven, straight and slender. His face was grave and immobile; and he stood before the District Attorney in the erect, earnest attitude of a soldier awaiting orders from his superior officer.

"Take a seat, Captain," said Markham, with a formal bow. "I have asked you here, as you probably know, to put a few questions to you concerning Mr. Alvin Benson. There are several points regarding your relationship with him, which I want you to explain."

"Am I suspected of complicity in the crime?" Leacock spoke with a slight Southern accent.

"That remains to be seen," Markham told him coldly. "It is to determine that point that I wish to question you."

The other sat rigidly in his chair and waited.

Markham fixed him with a direct gaze.

"You recently made a threat on Mr. Alvin Benson's life, I believe."

The big "push," the large numbers of U.S. forces arriving on the Western Front occured in summer 1918. Thus, Markham's use of the past tense ("the kind that you fellow carried.") implies that he is speaking well after 1918—a blow to the theory that the murder took place in 1918.

Leacock started, and his fingers tightened over his knees. But before he could answer, Markham continued: "I can tell you the occasion on which the threat was made,—it was at a party given by Mr. Leander Pfyfe."

Leacock hesitated; then thrust forward his jaw.

"Very well, sir; I admit I made the threat. Benson was a cad—he deserved shooting. . . . That night he had become more obnoxious than usual. He'd been drinking too much—and so had I, I reckon."

He gave a twisted smile, and looked nervously past the District Attorney out of the window.

"But I didn't shoot him, sir. I didn't even know he'd been shot until I read the paper next day."

"He was shot with an army Colt—the kind you fellows carried in the war," said Markham, keeping his eyes on the man.[101]

"I know it," Leacock replied. "The papers said so."

"You have such a gun, haven't you, Captain?"

Again the other hesitated.

"No, sir." His voice was barely audible.

"What became of it?"

The man glanced at Markham, and then quickly shifted his eyes.

"I—I lost it . . . in France."

Markham smiled faintly.

"Then how do you account for the fact that Mr. Pfyfe saw the gun the night you made the threat?"

"Saw the gun?" He looked blankly at the District Attorney.

"Yes, saw it, and recognized it as an army gun," persisted Markham, in a level voice. "Also, Major Benson saw you make a motion as if to draw a gun."

Leacock drew a deep breath, and set his mouth doggedly.

"I tell you, sir, I haven't a gun. . . . I lost it in France."

"Perhaps you didn't lose it, Captain. Perhaps you lent it to someone."

"I didn't, sir!" the words burst from his lips.

"Think a minute, Captain. . . . Didn't you lend it to someone?"

"No—I did not!"

"You paid a visit—yesterday—to Riverside Drive. . . . Perhaps you took it there with you."

Vance had been listening closely.

"Oh—deuced clever!" he now murmured in my ear.

Captain Leacock moved uneasily. His face, even with its deep coat of tan, seemed to pale, and he sought to avoid the implacable gaze of his questioner by concentrating his attention upon some object on the table. When he spoke his voice, heretofore truculent, was colored by anxiety.

"I didn't have it with me. . . . And I didn't lend it to anyone."

Markham sat leaning forward over the desk, his chin on his hand, like a minatory graven image.

"It may be you lent it to someone prior to that morning."

"Prior to. . . ?" Leacock looked up quickly and paused, as if analyzing the other's remark.

Markham took advantage of his perplexity.

"Have you lent your gun to anyone since you returned from France?"

"No, I've never lent it—" he began, but suddenly halted and flushed. Then he added hastily. "How could I lend it? I just told you, sir—"

"Never mind that!" Markham cut in. "So you had a gun, did you, Captain? . . . Have you still got it?"

Leacock opened his lips to speak, but closed them again tightly.

Markham relaxed, and leaned back in his chair.

"You were aware, of course, that Benson had been annoying Miss St. Clair with his attentions?"

At the mention of the girl's name the Captain's body became rigid; his face turned a dull red, and he glared menacingly at the District Attorney. At the end of a slow, deep inhalation he spoke through clenched teeth.

"Suppose we leave Miss St. Clair out of this." He looked as though he might spring at Markham.

"Unfortunately, we can't." Markham's words were sympathetic but firm. "Too many facts connect her with the case. Her handbag, for instance, was found in Benson's living room the morning after the murder."

"That's a lie, sir!"

Markham ignored the insult.

"Miss St. Clair herself admits the circumstance." He held up his hand, as the other was about to answer. "Don't misinterpret my mentioning the fact. I am not accusing Miss St. Clair of having anything to do with the affair. I'm merely endeavoring to get some light on your own connection with it."

The Captain studied Markham with an expression that clearly indicated he doubted these assurances. Finally he set his mouth, and announced with determination:

"I haven't anything more to say on the subject, sir."

"You knew, didn't you," continued Markham, "that Miss St. Clair dined with Benson at the Marseilles on the night he was shot?"

"What of it?" retorted Leacock sullenly.

"And you knew, didn't you, that they left the restaurant at midnight, and that Miss St. Clair did not reach home until after one?"

A strange look came into the man's eyes. The ligaments of his neck tightened, and he took a deep, resolute breath. But he neither glanced at the District Attorney nor spoke.

"You know, of course," pursued Markham's monotonous voice, "that Benson was shot at half past twelve?"

He waited; and for a whole minute there was silence in the room.

"You have nothing more to say, Captain?" he asked at length; "—no further explanations to give me?"

Leacock did not answer. He sat gazing imperturbably ahead of him; and it was evident he had sealed his lips for the time being.

Markham rose.

"In that case, let us consider the interview at an end."

The moment Captain Leacock had gone, Markham rang for one of his clerks.

"Tell Ben to have that man followed. Find out where he goes and what he does. I want a report at the Stuyvesant Club to-night."

When we were alone Vance gave Markham a look of half-bantering admiration.

"Ingenious—not to say artful. . . . But, y' know, your questions about the lady were shocking bad form."

"No doubt," Markham agreed. "But it looks now as if we were on the right track. Leacock didn't create an impression of unassailable innocence."

"Didn't he?" asked Vance. "Just what were the signs of his assailable guilt?"

"You saw him turn white when I questioned him about the weapon. His nerves were on edge,—he was genuinely frightened."

Vance sighed.

"What a perfect ready-made set of notions you have, Markham! Don't you know that an innocent man, when he comes under suspicion, is apt to be more nervous than a guilty one, who, to begin with, had enough nerve to commit the crime, and, secondly, realizes that any show of nervousness is regarded as guilt by you lawyer chaps? 'My strength is as the strength of ten because my heart is pure' is a mere Sunday-school pleasantry. Touch almost any innocent man on the shoulder and say 'You're arrested', and his pupils will dilate, he'll break out in a cold sweat, the blood will rush from his face, and he'll have tremors and dyspnœa. If he's a *hystérique*, or a cardiac neurotic, he'll probably collapse completely. It's the guilty person who, when thus accosted, lifts his eyebrows in bored surprise and says, 'You don't mean it, really,—here have a cigar'."

"The hardened criminal may act as you say," Markham conceded; "but an honest man who's innocent doesn't go to pieces, even when accused."

Vance shook his head hopelessly.

"My dear fellow, Crile and Voronoff might have lived in vain for all of you.[102] Manifestations of fear are the result of glandular secretions—nothing more. All they prove is that the person's thyroid is undeveloped or that his adrenals are subnormal. A man accused of a crime, or shown the bloody weapon with which it was committed, will either smile serenely, or scream, or have hysterics, or faint, or appear disint'rested—according to his hormones, and irrespective of his guilt. Your theory, d' ye see, would be quite all right if everyone had the same amount of the various internal secretions. But they haven't. . . . Really, y' know, you shouldn't send a man to the electric chair simply because he's deficient in endocrines. It isn't cricket."

Before Markham could reply Swacker appeared at the door and said Heath had arrived.

The Sergeant, beaming with satisfaction, fairly burst into the room. For once he forgot to shake hands.

"Well, it looks like we'd got hold of something workable. I went to this Captain Leacock's apartment-house last night, and here's the straight of it:—Leacock was at home the night of the thirteenth all right; but shortly after midnight he went out, headed west—get that!—and he didn't return till about quarter of one!"

"What about the hall-boy's original story?" asked Markham.

102. Serge Voronoff (1866–1951) was a French physician of Russian heritage, who was an early proponent of the ingestion of monkey-gland extracts for therapeutic, regenerative purposes. His work was largely discredited at his death. George W. Crile (1864–1943) was a respected physician and founder of the Cleveland Clinic, who did extensive work in glandular research. For an example of public interest in glandular therapies, see "The Adventure of the Creeping Man," by Arthur Conan Doyle (1923), in which Sherlock Holmes deals with a user of lemur-gland extract who experiences a Jekyll-and-Hyde-like result.

Serge Voronoff, 1920.

"That's the best part of it. Leacock had the boy fixed. Gave him money to swear he hadn't left the house that night.—What do you think of that, Mr. Markham? Pretty crude—huh? . . . The kid loosened up when I told him I was thinking of sending him up the river for doing the job himself." Heath laughed unpleasantly. "And he won't spill anything to Leacock, either."

Markham nodded his head slowly.

"What you tell me, Sergeant, bears out certain conclusions I arrived at when I talked to Captain Leacock this morning. Ben put a man on him when he left here, and I'm to get a report to-night. To-morrow may see this thing through. I'll get in touch with you in the morning, and if anything's to be done, you understand, you'll have the handling of it."

When Heath had left us, Markham folded his hands behind his head and leaned back contentedly.

"I think I've got the answer," he said. "The girl dined with Benson and returned to his house afterward. The Captain, suspecting the fact, went out found her there, and shot Benson. That would account not only for her gloves and hand-bag, but for the hour it took her to go from the Marseilles to her home. It would also account for her attitude here Saturday, and for the Captain's lying about the gun. . . . There, I believe, I have my case. The smashing of the Captain's alibi about clinches it."

"Oh, quite," said Vance airily. "'Hope springs exulting on triumphant wing'."

Markham regarded him a moment.

"Have you entirely forsworn human reason as a means of reaching a decision? Here we have an admitted threat, a motive, the time, the place, the opportunity, the conduct, and the criminal agent."

"Those words sound strangely familiar," smiled Vance. "Didn't most of 'em fit the young lady also? . . . And you really haven't got the criminal agent, y' know. But it's no doubt floating about the city somewhere.—A mere detail, however."

"I may not have it in my hand," Markham countered. "But with a good man on watch every minute, Leacock won't find much opportunity of disposing of the weapon."

Vance shrugged indifferently.

"In any event, go easy," he admonished. "My humble opinion is that you've merely unearthed a conspiracy."

"Conspiracy? . . . Good Lord! What kind?"

"A conspiracy of circumst'nces, don't y' know."

"I'm glad, at any rate, it hasn't to do with international politics," returned Markham good-naturedly.

He glanced at the clock.

"You won't mind if I get to work? I've a dozen things to attend to, and a couple of committees to see. . . . Why don't you go across the hall and have a talk with Ben Hanlon, and then come back at twelve-thirty? We'll have lunch together at the Bankers' Club. Ben's our greatest expert on foreign extradition, and has spent most of his life chasing about the world after fugitives from justice. He'll spin you some good yarns."

"How perfectly fascinatin'!" exclaimed Vance, with a yawn.

But instead of taking the suggestion, he walked to the window and lit a cigarette. He stood for a while puffing at it, rolling it between his fingers, and inspecting it critically.

"Y' know, Markham," he observed, "everything's going to pot these days. It's this silly democracy. Even the nobility is degen'rating. These *Régie* cigarettes, now: they've fallen off frightfully. There was a time when no self-respecting potentate would have smoked such inferior tobacco."

Markham smiled.

"What's the favor you want to ask?"

"Favor? What has that to do with the decay of Europe's aristocracy?"

"I've noticed that whenever you want to ask a favor which you consider questionable etiquette, you begin with a denunciation of royalty."

"Observin' fella," commented Vance drily. Then he, too, smiled. "Do you mind if I invite Colonel Ostrander along to lunch?"

Markham gave him a sharp look.

"Bigsby Ostrander, you mean? . . . Is he the mysterious colonel you've been asking people about for the past two days?"

"That's the lad. Pompous ass and that sort of thing. Might prove a bit edifyin', though. He's the papa of Benson's crowd, so to speak; knows all parties. Regular old scandalmonger."

"Have him along, by all means," agreed Markham.

Then he picked up the telephone.

"Now I'm going to tell Ben you're coming over for an hour or so."

CHAPTER XIII

The Grey Cadillac

(Monday, June 17; 12.30 p.m.)

When, at half past twelve, Markham, Vance and I entered the Grill of the Bankers' Club in the Equitable Building, Colonel Ostrander was already at the bar engaged with one of Charlie's prohibition clam-broth-and-Worcestershire-sauce cocktails. Vance had telephoned him immediately upon our leaving the District Attorney's office, requesting him to meet us at the Club; and the Colonel had seemed eager to comply.

"Here is New York's gayest dog," said Vance, introducing him to Markham (I had met him before); "a sybarite and a hedonist. He sleeps till noon, and makes no appointments before tiffin-time. I had to knock him up and threaten him with your official ire to get him down town at this early hour."

"Only too pleased to be of any service," the Colonel assured Markham grandiloquently. "Shocking affair! Gad! I couldn't credit it when I read it in the papers. Fact is, though—I don't mind sayin' it—I've one or two ideas on the subject. Came very near calling you up myself, sir."

When we had taken our seats at the table Vance began interrogating him without preliminaries.

"You know all the people in Benson's set, Colonel. Tell us something about Captain Leacock. What sort of chap is he?"

"Ha! So you have your eye on the gallant Captain?"

Colonel Ostrander pulled importantly at his white moustache. He was a large pink-faced man with bushy eyelashes and small blue eyes; and his manner and bearing were those of a pompous light-opera general.

"Not a bad idea. Might possibly have done it. Hot-headed fellow. He's badly smitten with a Miss St. Clair—fine girl, Muriel. And Benson was smitten, too. If I'd been twenty years younger myself—"

"You're too fascinatin' to the ladies, as it is, Colonel," interrupted Vance. "But tell us about the Captain."

"Ah, yes—the Captain. Comes from Georgia originally. Served in the war—some kind of decoration. He didn't care for Benson—disliked him, in fact. Quick-tempered, single-track-minded sort of person. Jealous, too. You know the type—a product of that tribal etiquette below the Mason and Dixon line. Puts women on a pedestal—not that they shouldn't be put there, God bless 'em! But he'd go to jail for a lady's honor. A shielder of womanhood. Sentimental cuss, full of chivalry; just the kind to blow out a rival's brains:—no questions asked—*pop*—and it's all over. Dangerous chap to monkey with. Benson was a confounded idiot to bother with the girl when he knew she was engaged to Leacock. Playin' with fire. I don't mind sayin' I was tempted to warn him. But it was none of my affair—I had no business interferin'. Bad taste."

"Just how well did Captain Leacock know Benson?" asked Vance. "By that I mean: how intimate were they?"

"Not intimate at all," the Colonel replied.

He made a ponderous gesture of negation, and added:

"I should say not! Formal, in fact. They met each other here and there a good deal, though. Knowing 'em both pretty well, I've often had 'em to little affairs at my humble diggin's."

"You wouldn't say Captain Leacock was a good gambler—level-headed and all that?"

"Gambler—huh!" The Colonel's manner was heavily contemptuous. "Poorest I ever saw. Played poker worse than a woman. Too excitable—couldn't keep his feelin's to himself. Altogether too rash."

Then, after a momentary pause:

"By George! I see what you're aimin' at. . . . And you're dead right. It's rash young puppies just like him that go about shootin' people they don't like."

"The Captain, I take it, is quite different in that regard from your friend, Leander Pfyfe," remarked Vance.

The Colonel appeared to consider.

"Yes and no," he decided. "Pfyfe's a cool gambler—that I'll grant you. He once ran a private gambling place of his own down on Long Island—roulette, monte, baccarat, that sort of thing. And he popped tigers and wild boars in Africa for a while. But Pfyfe's got his sentimental side, and he'd plunge on a pair of deuces with all the betting odds against him. Not a good scientific gambler. Flighty in his impulses, if you understand me. I don't mind admittin', though, that he could shoot a man and forget all about it in five minutes. But he'd need a lot of provocation. . . . He may have had it—you can't tell."

"Pfyfe and Benson were rather intimate, weren't they?"

"Very—very. Always saw 'em together when Pfyfe was in New York. Known each other years. Boon companions, as they called 'em in the old days. Actually lived together before Pfyfe got married. An exacting woman, Pfyfe's wife; makes him toe the mark. But loads of money."

"Speaking of the ladies," said Vance: "what was the situation between Benson and Miss St. Clair?"

"Who can tell?" asked the Colonel sententiously. "Muriel didn't cotton to Benson—that's sure. And yet . . . women are strange creatures—"

"Oh, no end strange," agreed Vance, a trifle wearily. "But really, y' know, I wasn't prying into the lady's personal relations with Benson. I thought you might know her mental attitude concerning him."

"Ah—I see. Would she, in short, have been likely to take desperate measures against him? . . . Egad! That's an idea!"

The Colonel pondered the point.

"Muriel, now, is a girl of strong character. Works hard at her art. She's a singer, and—I don't mind tellin' you—a mighty fine one. She's deep, too—deuced deep. And capable. Not afraid of taking a chance. Independent. I myself wouldn't want to be in her path if she had it in for me. Might stick at nothing."

He nodded his head sagely.

"Women are funny that way. Always surprisin' you. No sense of values. The most peaceful of 'em will shoot a man in cold blood without warnin'—"

He suddenly sat up, and his little blue eyes glistened like china.

"By Gad!" He fairly blurted the ejaculation. "Muriel had dinner alone with Benson the night he was shot—the very night. Saw 'em together myself at the Marseilles."

"You don't say, really!" muttered Vance incuriously. "But I suppose we all must eat. . . . By the bye; how well did you yourself know Benson?"

The Colonel looked startled, but Vance's innocuous expression seemed to reassure him.

"I? My dear fellow! I've known Alvin Benson fifteen years. At least fifteen—maybe longer. Showed him the sights in this old town before the lid was put on. A live town it was then. Wide open. Anything you wanted. Gad—what times we had! Those were the days of the old Haymarket. Never thought of toddlin' home till breakfast—"

Vance again interrupted his irrelevancies.

"How intimate are your relations with Major Benson?"

"The Major? . . . That's another matter. He and I belong to different schools. Dissimilar tastes. We never hit it off. Rarely see each other."

He seemed to think that some explanation was necessary, for before Vance could speak again, he added:

"The Major, you know, was never one of the boys, as we say. Disapproved of gaiety. Didn't mix with our little set. Considered me and Alvin too frivolous. Serious-minded chap."

Vance ate in silence for a while, then asked in an off-hand way:

"Did you do much speculating through Benson and Benson?"

For the first time the Colonel appeared hesitant about answering. He ostentatiously wiped his mouth with his napkin.

"Oh—dabbled a bit," he at length admitted airily. "Not very lucky, though. . . . We all flirted now and then with the Goddess of Chance in Benson's office."

Throughout the lunch Vance kept plying him with questions along these lines; but at the end of an hour he seemed to be no nearer anything definite than when he began. Colonel Ostrander was voluble, but his fluency was vague and disorganized. He talked mainly in parentheses, and insisted on elaborating his answers with rambling opinions, until it was almost impossible to extract what little information his words contained.

Vance, however, did not appear discouraged. He dwelt on Captain Leacock's character, and seemed particularly interested in his personal relationship with Benson. Pfyfe's gambling proclivities also occupied his attention, and he let the Colonel ramble on tiresomely about the man's gambling house on Long Island and his hunting experiences in South Africa. He asked numerous questions about Benson's other friends, but paid scant attention to the answers.

The whole interview impressed me as pointless, and I could not help wondering what Vance hoped to learn. Markham, I was convinced, was equally at sea. He pretended polite interest, and nodded appreciatively during the Colonel's incredibly drawn-out periods; but his eyes wandered occasionally, and several times I saw him give Vance a look of reproachful inquiry. There was no doubt, however, that Colonel Ostrander knew his people.

When we were back in the District Attorney's office, having taken leave of our garrulous guest at the subway entrance, Vance threw himself into one of the easy chairs with an air of satisfaction.

"Most entertainin', what? As an elim'nator of suspects the Colonel has his good points."

"Eliminator!" retorted Markham. "It's a good thing he's not connected with the police: he'd have half the community jailed for shooting Benson."

"He *is* a bit blood-thirsty," Vance admitted. "He's determined to get somebody jailed for the crime."

"According to that old warrior, Benson's coterie was a camorra of gunmen—not forgetting the women. I couldn't help getting the impression, as he talked, that Benson was miraculously lucky not to have been riddled with bullets long ago."

"It's obvious," commented Vance, "that you overlooked the illuminatin' flashes in the Colonel's thunder."

"Were there any?" Markham asked. "At any rate, I can't say that they exactly blinded me by their brilliance."

"And you received no solace from his words?"

"Only those in which he bade me a fond farewell. The parting didn't exactly break my heart. . . . What the old boy said about Leacock, however, might be called a confirmatory opinion. It verified—if verification had been necessary—the case against the Captain."

Vance smiled cynically.

"Oh, to be sure. And what he said about Miss St. Clair would have verified the case against her, too—last Saturday.—Also, what he said about Pfyfe would have verified the case against that Beau Sabreur,[103] if you had happened to suspect him—eh, what?"

Vance had scarcely finished speaking when Swacker came in to say that Emery from the Homicide Bureau had been sent over by Heath, and wished, if possible, to see the District Attorney.

When the man entered I recognized him at once as the detective who had found the cigarette butts in Benson's grate.

With a quick glance at Vance and me, he went directly to Markham.

"We've found the grey Cadillac, sir; and Sergeant Heath thought you might want to know about it right away. It's in a small, one-man garage on Seventy-fourth Street near Amsterdam Avenue, and has been there three days. One of the men from the Sixty-eighth Street station located it and 'phoned in to Headquarters; and I hopped up town at once. It's the right car—fishing-tackle and all, except for the rods; so I guess the ones found in Central Park belonged to the car after all: fell out probably. . . . It seems a fellow drove the car into the garage about noon last Friday, and gave the garage-man twenty dollars to keep his mouth shut. The man's a wop, and says he don't read the papers. Anyway, he came across *pronto* when I put the screws on."

The detective drew out a small notebook.

"I looked up the car's number. . . . It's listed in the name of Leander Pfyfe, 24 Elm Boulevard, Port Washington, Long Island."

Markham received this piece of unexpected information with a perplexed frown. He dismissed Emery almost curtly, and sat tapping thoughtfully on his desk.

Vance watched him with an amused smile.

"It's really not a madhouse, y' know," he observed comfortingly. "I say, don't the Colonel's words bring you any cheer, now that you know Leander was hovering about the neighborhood at the time Benson was translated into the Beyond?"

"Damn your old Colonel!" snapped Markham. "What interests me at present is fitting this new development into the situation."

"It fits beautifully," Vance told him. "It rounds out the mosaic, so to speak. . . . Are you actu'lly disconcerted by learning that Pfyfe was the owner of the mysterious car?"

103. A "handsome swordsman," the nickname applied by Sir Walter Scott to Napoleon's brother-in-law Joachim Murat.

"Not having your gift of clairvoyance, I am, I confess, disturbed by the fact."

Markham lit a cigar—an indication of worry.

"You, of course," he added, with sarcasm, "knew before Emery came here that it was Pfyfe's car."

"I didn't know," Vance corrected him; "but I had a strong suspicion. Pfyfe overdid his distress when he told us of his breakdown in the Catskills. And Heath's question about his itiner'ry annoyed him frightfully. His hauteur was too melodramatic."

"Your *ex post facto* wisdom is most useful!"

Markham smoked a while in silence.

"I think I'll find out about this matter."

He rang for Swacker.

"Call up the Ansonia," he ordered angrily; "locate Leander Pfyfe, and say I want to see him at the Stuyvesant Club at six o'clock. And tell him he's to be there."

"It occurs to me," said Markham, when Swacker had gone, "that this car episode may prove helpful, after all. Pfyfe was evidently in New York that night, and for some reason he didn't want it known. Why, I wonder? He tipped us off about Leacock's threat against Benson, and hinted strongly that we'd better get on the fellow's track. Of course, he may have been sore at Leacock for winning Miss St. Clair away from his friend, and taken this means of wreaking a little revenge on him. On the other hand, if Pfyfe was at Benson's house the night of the murder, he may have some real information. And now that we've found out about the car, I think he'll tell us what he knows."

"He'll tell you something anyway," said Vance. "He's the type of congenital liar that'll tell anybody anything as long as it doesn't involve himself unpleasantly."

"You and the Cumæan Sibyl,[104] I presume, could inform me in advance what he's going to tell me."

"I couldn't say as to the Cumæan Sibyl, don't y' know," Vance returned lightly; "but speaking for myself, I rather fancy he'll tell you that he saw the impetuous Captain at Benson's house that night."

Markham laughed.

"I hope he does. You'll want to be on hand to hear him, I suppose."

"I couldn't bear to miss it."

Vance was already at the door, preparatory to going, when he turned again to Markham.

"I've another slight favor to ask. Get a *dossier* on Pfyfe—there's a good fellow. Send one of your innumerable Dogberrys[105] to Port Washington and have the gentleman's conduct and social habits looked into. Tell your emiss'ry to concentrate on the woman question. . . . I promise you, you sha'n't regret it."

Markham, I could see, was decidedly puzzled by this request, and half inclined to refuse it. But after deliberating a few moments, he smiled, and pressed a button on his desk.

"Anything to humor you," he said. "I'll send a man down at once."

105. Dogberry was the buffoonish constable in Shakespeare's *Much Ado About Nothing*.

A Cadillac with swimmers at the Fleishacker Pool in San Francisco, 1927.

CHAPTER XIV

Links in the Chain

106. Art galleries at Park Avenue and 59th Street, in business from 1887 to 1934.

The Anderson Galleries, ca. 1925.

107. A well-known restaurant, founded in 1880 by Louis Sherry; by 1919, it had moved to the Hotel New Netherland, on 59th Street at Fifth Avenue, where it remained until the hotel was demolished in 1927.

108. Informal attire generally consisting of a tweed jacket and tan breeches, traditionally worn for fox hunting.

(Monday, June 17; 6 p.m.)

Vance and I spent an hour or so that afternoon at the Anderson Galleries[106] looking at some tapestries which were to be auctioned the next day, and afterward had tea at Sherry's.[107] We were at the Stuyvesant Club a little before six. A few minutes later Markham and Pfyfe arrived; and we went at once into one of the conference rooms.

Pfyfe was as elegant and superior as at the first interview. He wore a ratcatcher suit[108] and New-market gaiters of unbleached linen, and was redolent of perfume.

"An unexpected pleasure to see you gentlemen again so soon," he greeted us, like one conferring a blessing.

Markham was far from amiable, and gave him an almost brusque salutation. Vance had merely nodded, and now sat regarding Pfyfe drearily as if seeking to find some excuse for his existence, but utterly unable to do so.

Markham went directly to the point.

"I've found out, Mr. Pfyfe, that you placed your machine in a garage at noon on Friday, and gave the man twenty dollars to say nothing about it."

Pfyfe looked up with a hurt look.

"I've been deeply wronged," he complained sadly. "I gave the man fifty dollars."

"I am glad you admit the fact so readily," returned Markham. "You knew, by the newspapers, of course, that your machine was seen outside Benson's house the night he was shot."

"Why else should I have paid so liberally to have its presence in New York kept secret?" His tone indicated that he was pained at the other's obtuseness.

"In that case, why did you keep it in the city at all?" asked Markham. "You could have driven it back to Long Island."

Pfyfe shook his head sorrowfully, a look of commiseration in his eyes. Then he leaned forward with an air of benign patience:— he would be gentle with this dull-witted District Attorney, like a fond teacher with a backward child, and would strive to lead him out of the tangle of his uncertainties.

"I am a married man, Mr. Markham." He pronounced the fact as if some special virtue attached to it. "I started on my trip for the Catskills Thursday after dinner, intending to stop a day in New York to make my adieus to someone residing here. I arrived quite late—after midnight—and decided to call on Alvin. But when I drove up, the house was dark. So, without even ringing the bell, I walked to Pietro's in Forty-third Street[109] to get a night-cap,—I keep a bit of my own pinch-bottle Haig and Haig there,—but, alas! the place was closed, and I strolled back to my car. . . . To think, that while I was away poor Alvin was shot!"

He stopped and polished his eye-glass.

"The irony of it! . . . I didn't even guess that anything had happened to the dear fellow,—how could I? I drove, all unsuspecting of the tragedy, to a Turkish bath, and remained there the night. The next morning I read of the murder; and in the later editions I saw the mention of my car. It was then I became—shall I say worried? But no. 'Worried' is a misleading word. Let me say, rather, that I became aware of the false position I might be placed in if the car were traced to me. So I drove it to the garage and paid the man to say nothing of its whereabouts, lest its discovery confuse the issue of Alvin's death."

One might have thought, from his tone and the self-righteous way he looked at Markham, that he had bribed the garage-man wholly out of consideration for the District Attorney and the police.

"Why didn't you continue on your trip?" asked Markham. "That would have made the discovery of the car even less likely."

109. No Pietro's is listed in the 1922–23 *Trow's General Directory of the City of New York*. The establishment may have closed sometime after 1918.

Pfyfe adopted an air of compassionate surprise.

"With my dearest friend foully murdered? How could one have the heart to seek diversion at such a sad moment? . . . I returned home, and informed Mrs. Pfyfe that my car had broken down."

"You might have driven home in your car, it seems to me," observed Markham.

Pfyfe offered a look of infinite forbearance for the other's inspection, and took a deep sigh, which conveyed the impression that, though he could not sharpen the world's perceptions, he at least could mourn for its deplorable lack of understanding.

"If I had been in the Catskills away from any source of information, where Mrs. Pfyfe believed me to be, how would I have heard of Alvin's death until, perhaps, days afterward? You see, unfortunately I had not mentioned to Mrs. Pfyfe that I was stopping over in New York. The truth is, Mr. Markham, I had reason for not wishing my wife to know I was in the city. Consequently, if I had driven back at once, she would, I regret to say, have suspected me of breaking my journey. I therefore pursued the course which seemed simplest."

Markham was becoming annoyed at the man's fluent hypocrisy. After a brief silence he asked abruptly:

"Did the presence of your car at Benson's house that night have anything to do with your apparent desire to implicate Captain Leacock in the affair?"

Pfyfe lifted his eyebrows in pained astonishment, and made a gesture of polite protestation.

"My dear sir!" His voice betokened profound resentment of the other's unjust imputation. "If yesterday you detected in my words an undercurrent of suspicion against Captain Leacock, I can account for it only by the fact that I actually saw the Captain in front of Alvin's house when I drove up that night."

Markham shot a curious look at Vance; then said to Pfyfe:

"You are sure you saw Leacock?"

"I saw him quite distinctly. And I would have mentioned the fact yesterday had it not involved the tacit confession of my own presence there."

"What if it had?" demanded Markham. "It was vital information, and I could have used it this morning. You were placing your comfort ahead of the legal demands of justice; and your attitude puts a very questionable aspect on your own alleged conduct that night."

"You are pleased to be severe, sir," said Pfyfe with selfpity. "But having placed myself in a false position, I must accept your criticism."

"Do you realize," Markham went on, "that many a district attorney, if he knew what I now know about your movements, and had been treated the way you've treated me, would arrest you on suspicion?"

"Then I can only say," was the suave response, "that I am most fortunate in my inquisitor."

Markham rose.

"That will be all for to-day, Mr. Pfyfe. But you are to remain in New York until I give you permission to return home. Otherwise, I will have you held as a material witness."

Pfyfe made a shocked gesture in deprecation of such acerbities, and bade us a ceremonious good-afternoon.

When we were alone, Markham looked seriously at Vance.

"Your prophecy was fulfilled, though I didn't dare hope for such luck. Pfyfe's evidence puts the final link in the chain against the Captain."

Vance smoked languidly.

"I'll admit your theory of the crime is most satisfyin'. But alas! the psychological objection remains. Everything fits, with the one exception of the Captain; and he doesn't fit at all. . . . Silly idea, I know. But he has no more business being cast as the murderer of Benson than the bisonic Tetrazzini had being cast as the phthisical *Mimi*."[*]

"In any other circumstances," Markham answered, "I might defer reverently to your charming theories. But with all the circumstantial and presumptive evidence I have against Leacock, it strikes my inferior legal mind as sheer nonsense to say, 'He just couldn't be guilty because his hair is parted in the middle and he tucks his napkin in his collar.' There's too much logic against it."

"I'll grant your logic is irrefutable—as all logic is, no doubt. You've prob'bly convinced many innocent persons by sheer reasoning that they were guilty."

Vance stretched himself wearily.

"What do you say to a light repast on the roof? The unutt'rable Pfyfe has tired me."

In the summer dining-room on the roof of the Stuyvesant Club we found Major Benson sitting alone, and Markham asked him to join us.

[*] [Author's note:] Obviously a reference to Tetrazzini's performance in *La Bohème* at the Manhattan Opera House in 1908.

[Editor's note: Luisa Tetrazzini, an Italian coloratura of great international fame, did indeed perform in a number of operas for Oscar Hammerstein's Manhattan Opera Company in 1908, but there is no record of a production of *La Bohème* by Hammerstein's company; however, his competitor, the Metropolitan Opera Company, produced *La Bohème* in Manhattan in 1908, with Geraldine Farrar in the role of Mimi.]

110. The "other side" can only refer to Europe and World War I. It is highly unlikely that Major Benson served as a major in any army other than the U.S. Army; hence, we must conclude that he served *in World War I* in the U.S. Army and not as a volunteer, as Van Dine himself had done. Benson and his troops (including Leacock) presumably arrived in France in the first landing of U.S. troops, which took place on June 26, 1917. Leacock's three years of service under Benson must have begun in 1914 or 1915, and Benson's troops left France in late 1917 or early 1918 to return home, in time to take part in the events of the Benson case.

"I have good news for you, Major," he said, when we had given our order. "I feel confident I have my man; everything points to him. To-morrow will see the end, I hope."

The Major gave Markham a questioning frown.

"I don't understand exactly. From what you told me the other day, I got the impression there was a woman involved."

Markham smiled awkwardly, and avoided Vance's eyes.

"A lot of water has run under the bridge since then," he said. "The woman I had in mind was eliminated as soon as we began to check up on her. But in the process I was led to the man. There's little doubt of his guilt. I felt pretty sure about it this morning, and just now I learned that he was seen by a credible witness in front of your brother's house within a few minutes of the time the shot was fired."

"Is there any objection to your telling me who it was?" The Major was still frowning.

"None whatever. The whole city will probably know it to-morrow. . . . It was Captain Leacock."

Major Benson stared at him in unbelief.

"Impossible! I simply can't credit it. That boy was with me three years on the other side, and I got to know him pretty well.[110] I can't help feeling there's a mistake somewhere. . . . The police," he added quickly, "have got on the wrong track."

"It's not the police," Markham informed him. "It was my own investigations that turned up the Captain."

The Major did not answer, but his silence bespoke his doubt.

"Y' know," put in Vance, "I feel the same way about the Captain that you do, Major. It rather pleases me to have my impressions verified by one who has known him so long."

"What, then, was Leacock doing in front of the house that night?" urged Markham acidulously.

"He might have been singing carols beneath Benson's window," suggested Vance.

Before Markham could reply he was handed a card by the head-waiter. When he glanced at it, he gave a grunt of satisfaction, and directed that the caller be sent up immediately. Then, turning back to us, he said:

"We may learn something more now. I've been expecting this man Higginbotham. He's the detective that followed Leacock from my office this morning."

Higginbotham was a wiry, pale-faced youth with fishy eyes and a shifty manner. He slouched up to the table and stood hesitantly before the District Attorney.

"Sit down and report, Higginbotham," Markham ordered. "These gentlemen are working with me on the case."

"I picked up the bird while he was waiting for the elevator," the man began, eyeing Markham craftily. "He went to the subway and rode up town to Seventy-ninth and Broadway. He walked through Eightieth to Riverside Drive and went in the apartment-house at No. 94. Didn't give his name to the boy—got right in the elevator. He stayed upstairs a coupla hours, come down at one-twenty, and hopped a taxi. I picked up another one, and followed him. He went down the Drive to Seventy-second, through Central Park, and east on Fifty-ninth. Got out at Avenue A, and walked out on the Queensborough Bridge. About half way to Blackwell's Island he stood leaning over the rail for five or six minutes. Then he took a small package out of his pocket, and dropped it in the river."

"What size was the package?" There was repressed eagerness in Markham's question.

Higginbotham indicated the measurements with his hands.

"How thick was it?"

"Inch or so, maybe."

Markham leaned forward.

"Could it have been a gun—a Colt automatic?"

"Sure, it could. Just about the right size. And it was heavy, too,—I could tell by the way he handled it, and the way it hit the water."

"All right." Markham was pleased. "Anything else?"

"No, sir. After he'd ditched the gun, he went home and stayed. I left him there."

When Higginbotham had gone Markham nodded at Vance with melancholy elation.

"There's your criminal agent. . . . What more would you like?"

"Oh, lots," drawled Vance.

Major Benson looked up, perplexed.

"I don't quite grasp the situation. Why did Leacock have to go to Riverside Drive for his gun?"

"I have reason to think," said Markham, "that he took it to Miss St. Clair the day after the shooting—for safe-keeping probably. He wouldn't have wanted it found in his place."

"Might he not have taken it to Miss St. Clair's before the shooting?"

"I know what you mean," Markham answered. (I, too, recalled the Major's assertion the day before that Miss St. Clair was more capable of shooting his brother than was the Captain.) "I had the same idea myself. But certain evidential facts have eliminated her as a suspect."

"You've undoubtedly satisfied yourself on the point," returned the Major; but his tone was dubious. "However, I can't see Leacock as Alvin's murderer."

He paused, and laid a hand on the District Attorney's arm.

"I don't want to appear presumptuous, or unappreciative of all you've done; but I really wish you'd wait a bit before clapping that boy into prison. The most careful and conscientious of us are liable to error: even facts sometimes lie damnably; and I can't help believing that the facts in this instance have deceived you."

It was plain that Markham was touched by this request of his old friend; but his instinctive fidelity to duty helped him to resist the other's appeal.

"I must act according to my convictions, Major," he said firmly, but with a great kindness.

CHAPTER XV

"Pfyfe—Personal"

(Tuesday, June 18; 9 a.m.)

The next day—the fourth of the investigation—was an important and, in some ways, a momentous one in the solution of the problem posed by Alvin Benson's murder. Nothing of a definite nature came to light, but a new element was injected into the case; and this new element eventually led to the guilty person.

Before we parted from Markham after our dinner with Major Benson, Vance had made the request that he be permitted to call at the District Attorney's office the next morning. Markham, both disconcerted and impressed by his unwonted earnestness, had complied; although, I think, he would rather have made his arrangements for Captain Leacock's arrest without the disturbing influence of the other's protesting presence. It was evident that, after Higginbotham's report, Markham had decided to place the Captain in custody, and to proceed with his preparation of data for the Grand Jury.

Although Vance and I arrived at the office at nine o'clock Markham was already there. As we entered the room, he picked up the telephone receiver, and asked to be put through to Sergeant Heath.

At that moment Vance did an amazing thing. He walked swiftly to the District Attorney's desk and, snatching the receiver out of Markham's hand, clamped it down on the hook. Then he placed the telephone to one side, and laid both hands on the other's shoulders. Markham was too astonished and bewildered to protest; and before he could recover himself, Vance said in a low, firm voice, which was all the more impelling because of its softness:

"I'm not going to let you jail Leacock,—that's what I came here for this morning. You're not going to order his arrest as long as I'm in this office and can prevent it by any means whatever. There's only one way you can accomplish this act of unmitigated folly, and that's by summoning your policemen and having me forcibly ejected. And I advise you to call a goodly number of 'em, because I'll give 'em the battle of their bellicose lives!"

The incredible part of this threat was that Vance meant it literally. And Markham knew he meant it.

"If you do call your henchmen," he went on, "you'll be the laughing stock of the city inside of a week; for, by that time, it'll be known who really did shoot Benson. And I'll be a popular hero and a martyr—God save the mark!—for defying the District Attorney and offering up my sweet freedom on the altar of truth and justice and that sort of thing. . . ."

The telephone rang, and Vance answered it.

"Not wanted," he said, closing off immediately. Then he stepped back and folded his arms.

At the end of a brief silence, Markham spoke, his voice quavering with rage.

"If you don't go at once, Vance, and let me run this office myself, I'll have no choice but to call in those policemen."

Vance smiled. He knew Markham would take no such extreme measures. After all, the issue between these two friends was an intellectual one; and though Vance's actions had placed it for a moment on a physical basis, there was no danger of its so continuing.

Markham's belligerent gaze slowly turned to one of profound perplexity.

"Why are you so damned interested in Leacock?" he asked gruffly. "Why this irrational insistence that he remain at large?"

"You priceless, inexpressible ass!" Vance strove to keep all hint of affection out of his voice. "Do you think I care particularly what happens to a Southern army captain? There are hundreds of Leacocks, all alike—with their square shoulders and square chins, and their knobby clothes, and their totemistic codes of barbaric chivalry. Only a mother could tell 'em apart. . . . I'm int'rested in *you*, old chap. I don't want to see you make a mistake that's going to injure you more than it will Leacock."

Markham's eyes lost their hardness: he understood Vance's motive, and forgave him. But he was still firm in his belief of the Captain's guilt. He remained thoughtful for some time. Then, having apparently arrived at a decision, he rang for Swacker and asked that Phelps be sent for.

"I've a plan that may nail this affair down tight," he said. "And it'll be evidence that not even you, Vance, can gainsay."

Phelps came in, and Markham gave him instructions.

"Go and see Miss St. Clair at once. Get to her some way, and ask her what was in the package Captain Leacock took away from her apartment yesterday and threw in the East River." He briefly summarized Higginbotham's report of the night before. "Demand that she tell you, and intimate that you know it was the gun with which Benson was shot. She'll probably refuse to answer, and will tell you to get out. Then go downstairs and wait developments. If she 'phones, listen in at the switchboard. If she happens to send a note to anyone, intercept it. And if she goes out—which I hardly think likely—follow her and learn what you can. Let me hear from you the minute you get hold of anything."

"I get you, Chief." Phelps seemed pleased with the assignment, and departed with alacrity.

"Are such burglarious and eavesdropping methods considered ethical by your learned profession?" asked Vance. "I can't harmonize such conduct with your other qualities, y' know."

Markham leaned back and gazed up at the chandelier.

"Personal ethics don't enter into it. Or, if they do, they are crowded out by greater and graver considerations—by the higher demands of justice. Society must be protected; and the citizens of this county look to me for their security against the encroachments of criminals and evil-doers. Sometimes, in the pursuance of my duty, it is necessary to adopt courses of conduct that conflict with my personal instincts. I have no right to jeopardize the whole of society because of an assumed ethical obligation to an individual. . . . You understand, of course, that I would not use any information obtained by these unethical methods, unless it pointed to criminal activities on the part of that individual. And in such a case, I would have every right to use it, for the good of the community."

"I dare say you're right," yawned Vance. "But society doesn't int'rest me particularly. And I inf'nitely prefer good manners to righteousness."

As he finished speaking Swacker announced Major Benson, who wanted to see Markham at once.

The Major was accompanied by a pretty young woman of about twenty-two with yellow bobbed hair, dressed daintily and simply in light blue *crêpe de Chine*. But for all her youthful and somewhat frivolous appearance, she possessed a reserve and competency of manner that immediately evoked one's confidence.

Major Benson introduced her as his secretary, and Markham placed a chair for her facing his desk.

"Miss Hoffman has just told me something that I think is vital for you to know," said the Major; "and I brought her directly to you."

He seemed unusually serious, and his eyes held a look of expectancy colored with doubt.

"Tell Mr. Markham exactly what you told me, Miss Hoffman."

The girl raised her head prettily, and related her story in a capable, well-modulated voice.

"About a week ago—I think it was Wednesday—Mr. Pfyfe called on Mr. Alvin Benson in his private office. I was in the next room, where my typewriter is located. There's only a glass partition between the two rooms, and when anyone talks loudly in Mr. Benson's office I can hear them. In about five minutes Mr. Pfyfe and Mr. Benson began to quarrel. I thought it was funny, for they were such good friends; but I didn't pay much attention to it, and went on with my typing. Their voices got very loud, though, and I caught several words. Major Benson asked me this morning what the words were; so I suppose you want to know, too. Well, they kept referring to a note; and once or twice a check was mentioned. Several times I caught the word 'father-in-law', and once Mr. Benson said 'nothing doing'. . . . Then Mr. Benson called me in and told me to get him an envelope marked 'Pfyfe-Personal' out of his private drawer in the safe. I got it for him, but right after that our bookkeeper wanted me for something, so I didn't hear any more. About fifteen minutes later, when Mr. Pfyfe had gone, Mr. Benson called me to put the envelope back. And he told me that if Mr. Pfyfe ever called again, I wasn't, under any circumstances, to let him into the private office unless he himself was there. He also told me that I wasn't to give the envelope to anybody—not even on a written order. . . . And that is all, Mr. Markham."

During her recital I had been as much interested in Vance's actions as in what she had been saying. When first she had entered the room, his casual glance had quickly changed to one of attentive animation and he had studied her closely. When Markham had placed the chair for her, he had risen and reached for a book lying on the table near her; and, in doing so, he had leaned unnecessarily close to her in order to inspect—or so it appeared to me—the side of her head. And during her story he had continued his observation, at times bending slightly to the right or left to better his view of her. Unaccountable as his actions had seemed, I knew that some serious consideration had prompted the scrutiny.

When she finished speaking Major Benson reached in his pocket, and tossed a long manilla envelope on the desk before Markham.

"Here it is," he said. "I got Miss Hoffman to bring it to me the moment she told me her story."

Markham picked it up hesitantly, as if doubtful of his right to inspect its contents.

"You'd better look at it," the Major advised. "That envelope may very possibly have an important bearing on the case."

Markham removed the elastic band, and spread the contents of the envelope before him. They consisted of three items—a cancelled check for $10,000 made out to Leander Pfyfe and signed by Alvin Benson; a note for $10,000 to Alvin Benson signed by Pfyfe, and a brief confession, also signed by Pfyfe, saying the check was a forgery. The check was dated March 20th of the current year. The confession and the note were dated two days later. The note—which was for ninety days—fell due on Friday, June 21st, only three days off.

For fully five minutes Markham studied these documents in silence. Their sudden introduction into the case seemed to mystify him. Nor had any of the perplexity left his face when he finally put them back in the envelope.

He questioned the girl carefully, and had her repeat certain parts of her story. But nothing more could be learned from her; and at length he turned to the Major.

"I'll keep this envelope a while, if you'll let me. I don't see its significance at present, but I'd like to think it over."

111. From George Eliot, *The Spanish Gypsy*, Book III.

112. Possibly a reference to Katinka, the eldest sister of *The Seven Sisters*, a successful 1911 romantic comedy by Edith Ellis and Ferenc Herczeg, filmed in 1915.

113. "Truth from his lips prevailed with double sway, / And fools, who came to scoff, remained to pray," from Oliver Goldsmith's "The Deserted Village" (1770).

When Major Benson and his secretary had gone, Vance rose and extended his legs.

"*À la fin!*" he murmured. "'All things journey: sun and moon, morning, noon, and afternoon, night and all her stars.'[111] *Videlicet*: we begin to make progress."

"What the devil are you driving at?" The new complication of Pfyfe's peccadilloes had left Markham irritable.

"Int'restin' young woman, this Miss Hoffman—eh, what?" Vance rejoined irrelevantly. "Didn't care especially for the deceased Benson. And she fairly detests the aromatic Leander. He has prob'bly told her he was misunderstood by Mrs. Pfyfe, and invited her to dinner."

"Well, she's pretty enough," commented Markham indifferently. "Benson, too, may have made advances—which is why she disliked him."

"Oh, absolutely." Vance mused a moment. "Pretty—yes; but misleadin'. She's an ambitious gel, and capable, too—knows her business. She's no ball of fluff. She has a solid, honest streak in her—a bit of Teutonic blood, I'd say." He paused meditatively. "Y' know, Markham, I have a suspicion you'll hear from little Miss Katinka[112] again."

"Crystal-gazing, eh?" mumbled Markham.

"Oh, dear no!" Vance was looking lazily out of the window. "But I did enter the silence, so to speak, and indulged in a bit of craniological contemplation."

"I thought I noticed you ogling the girl," said Markham. "But since her hair was bobbed and she had her hat on, how could you analyse the bumps?—if that's the phrase you phrenologists use."

"Forget not Goldsmith's preacher," Vance admonished. "Truth from his lips prevailed, and those who came to scoff remained *et cetera*. . . .[113] To begin with, I'm no phrenologist. But I believe in epochal, racial, and heredit'ry variations in skulls. In that respect I'm merely an old-fashioned Darwinian. Every child knows that the skull of the Piltdown man differs from that of the Cromagnard; and even a lawyer could distinguish an Aryan head from a Ural-Altaic head, or a Maylaic from a Negrillo. And, if one is versed at all in the Mendelian theory, heredit'ry cranial similarities can be detected. . . . But all this erudition is beyond you, I fear. Suffice it to say that, despite the young woman's hat and hair, I could see the contour of her head and the bone structure in her face; and I even caught a glimpse of her ear."

"And thereby deduced that we'd hear from her again," added Markham scornfully.

"Indirectly—yes," admitted Vance. Then, after a pause: "I say, in view of Miss Hoffman's revelation, do not Colonel Ostrander's comments of yesterday begin to take on a phosph'rescent aspect?"

"Look here!" said Markham impatiently. "Cut out these circumlocutions, and get to the point."

Vance turned slowly from the window, and regarded him pensively.

"Markham—I put the question academically—doesn't Pfyfe's forged check, with its accompanying confession and its shortly-due note, constitute a rather strong motive for doing away with Benson?"

Markham sat up suddenly.

"You think Pfyfe guilty—is that it?"

"Well, here's the touchin' situation: Pfyfe obviously signed Benson's name to a check, told him about it, and got the surprise of his life when his dear old pal asked him for a ninety-day note to cover the amount, and also for a written confession to hold over him to insure payment. . . . Now consider the subs'quent facts:—First, Pfyfe called on Benson a week ago and had a quarrel in which the check was mentioned,—Damon was prob'bly pleading with Pythias to extend the note, and was vulgarly informed that there was 'nothing doing'. Secondly, Benson was shot two days later, less than a week before the note fell due. Thirdly, Pfyfe was at Benson's house the hour of the shooting, and not only lied to you about his whereabouts, but bribed a garage owner to keep silent about his car. Fourthly, his explanation, when caught, of his unrewarded search for Haig and Haig was, to say the least, a bit thick. And don't forget that the original tale of his lonely quest for nature's solitudes in the Catskills—with his mysterious stop-over in New York to confer a farewell benediction upon some anonymous person—was not all that one could have hoped for in the line of plausibility. Fifthly, he is an impulsive gambler, given to taking chances; and his experiences in South Africa would certainly have familiarized him with fire-arms. Sixthly, he was rather eager to involve Leacock, and did a bit of caddish tale-bearing to that end, even informing you that he saw the Captain on the spot at the fatal moment. Seventhly—but why bore you? Have I not supplied you with all the factors you hold so dear,—what are they now?—motive, time, place, opportunity, conduct? All that's wanting is the criminal agent. But then, the Captain's gun is at the bottom of the East River; so you're not very much better off in his case, what?"

Markham had listened attentively to Vance's summary. He now sat in rapt silence gazing down at the desk.

"How about a little chat with Pfyfe before you make any final move against the Captain?" suggested Vance.

"I think I'll take your advice," answered Markham slowly, after several minutes' reflection. Then he picked up the telephone. "I wonder if he's at his hotel now."

"Oh, he's there," said Vance. "Watchful waitin' and all that."

Pfyfe was in; and Markham requested him to come at once to the office.

"There's another thing I wish you'd do for me," said Vance, when the other had finished telephoning. "The fact is, I'm longing to know what everyone was doing during the hour of Benson's dissolution—that is, between midnight and one a. m. on the night of the thirteenth, or to speak pedantically, the morning of the fourteenth."

Markham looked at him in amazement.

"Seems silly, doesn't it?" Vance went on blithely. "But you put such faith in alibis—though they do prove disappointin' at times, what? There's Leacock, for instance. If that hall-boy had told Heath to toddle along and sell his violets, you couldn't do a blessed thing to the Captain. Which shows, d' ye see, that you're too trustin'. . . . Why not find out where everyone was? Pfyfe and the Captain were at Benson's; and they're about the only ones whose whereabouts you've looked into. Maybe there were others hovering around Alvin that night. There may have been a crush of friends and acquaintances on hand—a regular *soirée*, y' know. . . . Then again, checking up on all these people will supply the desolate Sergeant with something to take his mind off his sorrows."

Markham knew, as well as I, that Vance would not have made a suggestion of this kind unless actuated by some serious motive; and for several moments he studied the other's face intently, as if trying to read his reason for this unexpected request.

"Who, specifically," he asked, "is included in your 'everyone'?" He took up his pencil and held it poised above a sheet of paper.

"No one is to be left out," replied Vance. "Put down Miss St. Clair—Captain Leacock—the Major—Pfyfe—Miss Hoffman—"

"Miss Hoffman!"

"Everyone! . . . Have you Miss Hoffman? Now jot down Colonel Ostrander—"

"Look here!" cut in Markham.

"—and I may have one or two others for you later. But that will do nicely for a beginning."

Before Markham could protest further, Swacker came in to say that Heath was waiting outside.

"What about our friend Leacock, sir?" was the Sergeant's first question.

"I'm holding that up for a day or so," explained Markham. "I want to have another talk with Pfyfe before I do anything definite." And he told Heath about the visit of Major Benson and Miss Hoffman.

Heath inspected the envelope and its enclosures, and then handed them back.

"I don't see anything in that," he said. "It looks to me like a private deal between Benson and this fellow Pfyfe.—Leacock's our man; and the sooner I get him locked up, the better I'll feel."

"That may be to-morrow," Markham encouraged him. "So don't feel downcast over this little delay. . . . You're keeping the Captain under surveillance, aren't you?"

"I'll say so," grinned Heath.

Vance turned to Markham.

"What about that list of names you made out for the Sergeant?" he asked ingenuously. "I understood you to say something about alibis."

Markham hesitated, frowning. Then he handed Heath the paper containing the names Vance had called off to him.

"As a matter of caution, Sergeant," he said morosely, "I wish you'd get me the alibis of all these people on the night of the murder. It may bring something contributory to light. Verify those you already know, such as Pfyfe's; and let me have the reports as soon as you can."

When Heath had gone Markham turned a look of angry exasperation upon Vance.

"Of all the confounded trouble-makers—" he began.

But Vance interrupted him blandly.

"Such ingratitude! If only you knew it, Markham, I'm your tutelary genius, your *deus ex machina*, your fairy godmother."

CHAPTER XVI

Admissions and Suppressions

(Tuesday, June 18; afternoon.)

An hour later Phelps, the operative Markham had sent to 94 Riverside Drive, came in radiating satisfaction.

"I think I've got what you want, Chief." His raucous voice was covertly triumphant. "I went up to the St. Clair woman's apartment and rang the bell. She came to the door herself, and I stepped into the hall and put my questions to her. She sure refused to answer. When I let on I knew the package contained the gun Benson was shot with, she just laughed and jerked the door open. 'Leave this apartment, you vile creature,' she says to me."

He grinned.

"I hurried downstairs, and I hadn't any more than got to the switchboard when her signal flashed. I let the boy get the number, and then I stood him to one side, and listened in. . . . She was talking to Leacock, and her first words were: 'They know you took the pistol from here yesterday and threw it in the river.' That must've knocked him out, for he didn't say anything for a long time. Then he answered, perfectly calm and kinda sweet: 'Don't worry, Muriel; and don't say a word to anybody for the rest of the day. I'll fix everything in the morning.' He made her promise to keep quiet until to-morrow, and then he said good-bye."

Markham sat a while digesting the story.

"What impression did you get from the conversation?"

"If you ask me, Chief," said the detective, "I'd lay ten to one that Leacock's guilty and the girl knows it."

Markham thanked him and let him go.

"This sub-Potomac chivalry," commented Vance, "is a frightful nuisance. . . . But aren't we about due to hold polite converse with the genteel Leander?"

Almost as he spoke the man was announced. He entered the room with his habitual urbanity of manner, but for all his suavity, he could not wholly disguise his uneasiness of mind.

"Sit down, Mr. Pfyfe," directed Markham brusquely. "It seems you have a little more explaining to do."

Taking out the manilla envelope, he laid its contents on the desk where the other could see them.

"Will you be so good as to tell me about these?"

"With the greatest pleasure," said Pfyfe; but his voice had lost its assurance. Some of his poise, too, had deserted him, and as he paused to light a cigarette I detected a slight nervousness in the way he manipulated his gold match-safe.

"I really should have mentioned these before," he confessed, indicating the papers with a delicately inconsequential wave of the hand.

He leaned forward on one elbow, taking a confidential attitude, and as he talked, the cigarette bobbed up and down between his lips.

"It pains me deeply to go into this matter," he began; "but since it is in the interests of truth, I shall not complain. . . . My—ah—domestic arrangements are not all that one could desire. My wife's father has, curiously enough, taken a most unreasonable dislike to me; and it pleases him to deprive me of all but the meagerest financial assistance, although it is really my wife's money that he refuses to give me. A few months ago I made use of certain funds—ten thousand dollars, to be exact—which, I learned later, had not been intended for me. When my father-in-law discovered my error, it was necessary for me to return the full amount to avoid a misunderstanding between Mrs. Pfyfe and myself—a misunderstanding which might have caused my wife great unhappiness. I regret to say, I used Alvin's name on a check. But I explained it to him at once, you understand, offering him the note and this little confession as evidence of my good faith. . . . And that is all, Mr. Markham."

"Was that what your quarrel with him last week was about?"

Pfyfe gave him a look of querulous surprise.

"Ah, you heard of our little *contretemps*? . . . Yes—we had a slight disagreement as to the—shall I say terms of the transaction?"

"Did Benson insist that the note be paid when due?"

"No—not exactly." Pfyfe's manner became unctuous. "I beg of you, sir, not to press me as to my little chat with Alvin. It was, I assure you, quite irrelevant to the present situation. Indeed, it was of a most personal and private nature." He smiled confidingly. "I will admit, however, that I went to Alvin's house the night he was shot, intending to speak to him about the check; but, as you already know, I found the house dark and spent the night in a Turkish bath."

"Pardon me, Mr. Pfyfe,"—it was Vance who spoke—"but did Mr. Benson take your note without security?"

"Of course!" Pfyfe's tone was a rebuke. "Alvin and I, as I have explained, were the closest friends."

"But even a friend, don't y' know," Vance submitted, "might ask for security on such a large amount. How did Benson know that you'd be able to repay him?"

"I can only say that he did know," the other answered, with an air of patient deliberation.

Vance continued to be doubtful.

"Perhaps it was because of the confession you had given him."

Pfyfe rewarded him with a look of beaming approval.

"You grasp the situation perfectly," he said.

Vance withdrew from the conversation, and though Markham questioned Pfyfe for nearly half an hour, nothing further transpired. Pfyfe clung to his story in every detail, and politely refused to go deeper into his quarrel with Benson, insisting that it had no bearing on the case. At last he was permitted to go.

"Not very helpful," Markham observed. "I'm beginning to agree with Heath that we've turned up a mare's-nest in Pfyfe's frenzied financial deal."

"You'll never be anything but your own sweet trusting self, will you?" lamented Vance sadly. "Pfyfe has just given you your first intelligent line of investigation—and you say he's not helpful! . . . Listen to me and *nota bene*. Pfyfe's story about the ten thousand dollars is undoubtedly true: he appropriated the money and forged Benson's name to a check with which to replace it. But I don't for a second believe there was no security in addition to the confession. Benson wasn't the type of man—friend or no friend—who'd hand over that amount without security. He wanted his money back—not somebody in jail. That's why I put my oar in, and asked about the security. Pfyfe, of course, denied it; but when pressed as to how Benson knew he'd pay the note, he retired into a cloud. I had to suggest the confession as the possible explanation; which showed that something else was in his mind—something he didn't care to mention. And the way he jumped at my suggestion bears out my theory."

"Well, what of it?" Markham asked impatiently.

"Oh, for the gift of tears!"[114] moaned Vance. "Don't you see that there's someone in the background—someone connected with the security? It must be so, y' know; otherwise Pfyfe would have told you the entire tale of the quarrel, if only to clear himself from suspicion. Yet, knowing that his position is an awkward one, he refuses to divulge what passed between him and Benson in the office that day. . . . Pfyfe is shielding someone—and he is not the soul of chivalry, y' know. Therefore, I ask: Why?"

He leaned back and gazed at the ceiling.

"I have an idea, amounting to a cerebral cyclone," he added, "that when we put our hands on that security, we'll also put our hands on the murderer."

At this moment the telephone rang, and when Markham answered it a look of startled amusement came into his eyes. He made an appointment with the speaker for half past five that afternoon. Then, hanging up the receiver, he laughed outright at Vance.

"Your auricular researches have been confirmed," he said. "Miss Hoffman just called me confidentially on an outside 'phone to say she has something to add to her story. She's coming here at five-thirty."

Vance was unimpressed by the announcement.

"I rather imagined she'd telephone during her lunch hour."

Again Markham gave him one of his searching scrutinies.

"There's something damned queer going on around here," he observed.

"Oh, quite," returned Vance carelessly. "Queerer than you could possibly imagine."

For fifteen or twenty minutes Markham endeavored to draw him out; but Vance seemed suddenly possessed of an ability to

114. "Oh, for the gift of tears, that I might weep," is a line from a hymn called "The Last Word," by Lady Catherine Howard Petre, included in Orby Shipley's *Annus Sanctus: Hymns of the Church for the Ecclesiastical Year* (1884).

say nothing with the blandest fluency. Markham finally became exasperated.

"I'm rapidly coming to the conclusion," he said, "that either you had a hand in Benson's murder, or you're a phenomenally good guesser."

"There is, y' know, an alternative," rejoined Vance. "It might be that my æsthetic hypotheses and metaphysical deductions—as you call 'em—are working out—eh, what?"

A few minutes before we went to lunch Swacker announced that Tracy had just returned from Long Island with his report.

"Is he the lad you sent to look into Pfyfe's *affaires du cœur*?" Vance asked Markham. "For, if he is, I am all aflutter."

"He's the man. . . . Send him in, Swacker."

Tracy entered smiling silkily, his black note-book in one hand, his *pince-nez* in the other.

"I had no trouble learning about Pfyfe," he said. "He's well known in Port Washington—quite a character, in fact—and it was easy to pick up gossip about him."

He adjusted his glasses carefully, and referred to his note-book.

"He married a Miss Hawthorn in nineteen-ten. She's wealthy, but Pfyfe doesn't benefit much by it, because her father sits on the money-bags—"

"Mr. Tracy, I say," interrupted Vance; "never mind the *née-*Hawthorn and her doting papa,—Mr. Pfyfe himself has confided in us about his sad marriage. Tell us, if you can, about Mr. Pfyfe's extra-nuptial affairs. Are there any other ladies?"

Tracy looked inquiringly at the District Attorney: he was uncertain as to Vance's *locus standi*. Receiving a nod from Markham, he turned a page in his note-book and proceeded.

"I found one other woman in the case. She lives in New York, and often telephones to a drug store near Pfyfe's house, and leaves messages for him. He uses the same 'phone to call her by. He had made some deal with the proprietor, of course; but I was able to obtain her 'phone number. As soon as I came back to the city I got her name and address from Information, and made a few inquiries. . . . She's a Mrs. Paula Banning, a widow, and a little fast, I should say; and she lives in an apartment at 268 West Seventy-fifth Street."

This exhausted Tracy's information; and when he went out, Markham smiled broadly at Vance.

"He didn't supply you with very much fuel."

"My word! I think he did unbelievably well," said Vance. "He unearthed the very information we wanted."

"*We* wanted?" echoed Markham. "I have more important things to think about than Pfyfe's amours."

"And yet, y' know, this particular amour of Pfyfe's is going to solve the problem of Benson's murder," replied Vance; and would say no more.

Markham, who had an accumulation of other work awaiting him and numerous appointments for the afternoon, decided to have his lunch served in the office; so Vance and I took leave of him.

We lunched at the Élysée, dropped in at Knoedler's[115] to see an exhibition of French Pointillism, and then went to Aeolian Hall[116] where a string quartette from San Francisco was giving a programme of Mozart. A little before half past five we were again at the District Attorney's office, which at that hour was deserted except for Markham.

Shortly after our arrival Miss Hoffman came in, and told the rest of her story in direct, business-like fashion.

"I didn't give you all the particulars this morning," she said; "and I wouldn't care to do so now unless you are willing to regard them as confidential, for my telling you might cost me my position."

"I promise you," Markham assured her, "that I will entirely respect your confidence."

She hesitated a moment, and then continued.

"When I told Major Benson this morning about Mr. Pfyfe and his brother, he said at once that I should come with him to your office and tell you also. But on the way over, he suggested that I might omit a part of the story. He didn't exactly tell me not to mention it; but he explained that it had nothing to do with the case and might only confuse you. I followed his suggestion; but after I got back to the office I began thinking it over, and knowing how serious a matter Mr. Benson's death was, I decided to tell you anyway. In case it did have some bearing on the situation, I didn't want to be in the position of having withheld anything from you."

She seemed a little uncertain as to the wisdom of her decision.

"I do hope I haven't been foolish. But the truth is, there was something else besides that envelope, which Mr. Benson asked me to bring him from the safe the day he and Mr. Pfyfe had their

115. M. Knoedler & Co was a well-known art dealership in New York City; founded in 1846, it operated at 556 Fifth Avenue between 1911 and 1925. The dealership closed in 2011 beset by numerous litigations alleging sales of fakes.

116. A concert hall on the third floor of 29–33 West 42nd Street, built for the Aeolian Company (a manufacturer of pianos) in 1912; it closed in 1926.

The Vocalion display room at
the Aeolian Hall, 1916.

quarrel. It was a square heavy package, and, like the envelope, was marked 'Pfyfe-Personal'. And it was over this package that Mr. Benson and Mr. Pfyfe seemed to be quarrelling."

"Was it in the safe this morning when you went to get the envelope for the Major?" asked Vance.

"Oh, no. After Mr. Pfyfe left last week, I put the package back in the safe along with the envelope. But Mr. Benson took it home with him last Thursday—the day he was killed."

Markham was but mildly interested in the recital, and was about to bring the interview to a close when Vance spoke up.

"It was very good of you, Miss Hoffman, to take this trouble to tell us about the package; and now that you are here, there are one or two questions I'd like to ask. . . . How did Mr. Alvin Benson and the Major get along together?"

She looked at Vance with a curious little smile.

"They didn't get along very well," she said. "They were so different. Mr. Alvin Benson was not a very pleasant person, and not very honorable, I'm afraid. You'd never have thought they were brothers. They were constantly disputing about the business; and they were terribly suspicious of each other."

"That's not unnatural," commented Vance, "seeing how incompatible their temp'raments were. . . . By the bye, how did this suspicion show itself?"

"Well, for one thing, they sometimes spied on each other. You see, their offices were adjoining, and they would listen to each other through the door. I did the secretarial work for both of them, and I often saw them listening. Several times they tried to find out things from me about each other."

Vance smiled at her appreciatively.

"Not a pleasant position for you."

"Oh, I didn't mind it," she smiled back. "It amused me."

"When was the last time you caught either one of them listening?" he asked.

The girl quickly became serious.

"The very last day Mr. Alvin Benson was alive I saw the Major standing by the door. Mr. Benson had a caller—a lady—and the Major seemed very much interested. It was in the afternoon. Mr. Benson went home early that day—only about half an hour after the lady had gone. She called at the office again later, but he wasn't there of course, and I told her he had already gone home."

"Do you know who the lady was?" Vance asked her.

"No, I don't," she said. "She didn't give her name."

Vance asked a few other questions, after which we rode up town in the subway with Miss Hoffman, taking leave of her at Twenty-third Street.

Markham was silent and preoccupied during the trip. Nor did Vance make any comment until we were comfortably relaxed in the easy chairs of the Stuyvesant Club's lounge-room. Then, lighting a cigarette lazily, he said:

"You grasp the subtle mental processes leading up to my prophecy about Miss Hoffman's second coming—eh, what, Markham? Y' see, I knew friend Alvin had not paid that forged check without security, and I also knew that the tiff must have been about the security, for Pfyfe was not really worrying about being jailed by his *alter ego*. I rather suspect Pfyfe was trying to get the security back before paying off the note, and was told there was 'nothing doing'. . . . Moreover, Little Goldylocks may be a nice girl and all that; but it isn't in the feminine temp'rament to sit next door to an altercation between two such rakes and not listen attentively. I shouldn't care, y' know, to have to decipher the typing she said she did during the episode. I was quite sure she heard more than she told; and I asked myself: Why this curtailment? The only logical answer was: Because the Major had suggested it. And since the *gnädiges Fräulein* was a forthright Germanic soul, with an inbred streak of selfish and cautious honesty, I ventured the prognostication that as soon as she was out from under the benev'lent jurisdiction of her tutor, she would tell us the rest, in order to save her own skin if the matter should come up later. . . . Not so cryptic when explained, what?"

"That's all very well," conceded Markham petulantly. "But where does it get us?"

"I shouldn't say that the forward movement was entirely imperceptible."

Vance smoked a while impassively.

"You realize, I trust," he said, "that the mysterious package contained the security."

"One might form such a conclusion," agreed Markham. "But the fact doesn't dumbfound me—if that's what you're hoping for."

"And, of course," pursued Vance easily, "your legal mind, trained in the technique of ratiocination, has already identified it as the box of jewels that Mrs. Platz espied on Benson's table that fatal afternoon."

Markham sat up suddenly; then sank back with a shrug.

"Even if it was," he said, "I don't see how that helps us. Unless the Major knew the package had nothing to do with the case, he would not have suggested to his secretary that she omit telling us about it."

"Ah! But if the Major knew that the package was an irrelevant item in the case, then he must also know something about the case—eh, what? Otherwise, he couldn't determine what was, and what was not, irrelevant. . . . I have felt all along that he knew more than he admitted. Don't forget that he put us on the track of Pfyfe, and also that he was quite pos'tive Captain Leacock was innocent."

Markham thought for several minutes.

"I'm beginning to see what you're driving at," he remarked slowly. "Those jewels, after all, may have an important bearing on the case. . . . I think I'll have a chat with the Major about things."

Shortly after dinner at the Club that night Major Benson came into the lounge-room where we had retired for our smoke; and Markham accosted him at once.

"Major, aren't you willing to help me a little more in getting at the truth about your brother's death?" he asked.

The other gazed at him searchingly: the inflection of Markham's voice belied the apparent casualness of the question.

"God knows it's not my wish to put obstacles in your way," he said, carefully weighing each word. "I'd gladly give you any help I could. But there are one or two things I can not tell you at this time. . . . If there was only myself to be considered," he added, "it would be different."

"But you do suspect someone?" Vance put the question.

"In a way—yes. I overheard a conversation in Alvin's office one day, that took on added significance after his death."

"You shouldn't let chivalry stand in the way," urged Markham. "If your suspicion is unfounded, the truth will surely come out."

"But when I don't *know*, I certainly ought not to hazard a guess," affirmed the Major. "I think it best that you solve this problem without me."

Despite Markham's importunities, he would say no more; and shortly afterward he excused himself and went out.

Markham, now profoundly worried, sat smoking restlessly, tapping the arm of his chair with his fingers.

"Well, old bean, a bit involved, what?" commented Vance.

"It's not so damned funny," Markham grumbled. "Everyone seems to know more about the case than the police or the District Attorney's office."

"Which wouldn't be so disconcertin' if they all weren't so deuced reticent," supplemented Vance cheerfully. "And the touchin' part of it is that each of 'em appears to be keeping still in order to shield someone else. Mrs. Platz began it: she lied about Benson's having any callers that afternoon, because she didn't want to involve his tea companion. Miss St. Clair declined point-blank to tell you anything, because she obviously didn't desire to cast suspicion on another. The Captain became voiceless the moment you suggested his affianced bride was entangled. Even Leander refused to extricate himself from a delicate situation lest he implicate another. And now the Major! . . . Most annoyin'.—On the other hand, don't y' know, it's comfortin'—not to say upliftin'—to be dealing exclusively with such noble, self-sacrificin' souls."

"Hell!" Markham put down his cigar and rose. "The case is getting on my nerves. I'm going to sleep on it, and tackle it in the morning."

"That ancient idea of sleeping on a problem is a fallacy," said Vance, as we walked out into Madison Avenue, "—an *apologia*, as it were, for one's not being able to think clearly. Poetic idea, y' know. All poets believe in it—nature's soft nurse, the balm of woe, childhood's mandragora, tired nature's sweet restorer, and that sort of thing. Silly notion. When the brain is keyed up and alive, it works far better than when apathetic from the torpor of sleep. Slumber is an anodyne—not a stimulus."

"Well, you sit up and think," was Markham's surly advice.

"That's what I'm going to do," blithely returned Vance; "but not about the Benson case. I did all the thinking I'm going to do along that line four days ago."

CHAPTER XVII

The Forged Check

(Wednesday, June 19; forenoon.)

We rode down town with Markham the next morning, and though we arrived at his office before nine o'clock, Heath was already there waiting. He appeared worried, and when he spoke his voice held an ill-disguised reproof for the District Attorney.

"What about this Leacock, Mr. Markham?" he asked. "It looks to me like we'd better grab him quick. We've been tailing him right along; and there's something funny going on. Yesterday morning he went to his bank and spent half an hour in the chief cashier's office. After that he visited his lawyer's, and was there over an hour. Then he went back to the bank for another half-hour. He dropped in to the Astor Grill for lunch, but didn't eat anything—sat staring at the table. About two o'clock he called on the realty agents who have the handling of the building he lives in; and after he'd left, we found out he'd offered his apartment for sub-lease beginning to-morrow. Then he paid six calls on friends of his, and went home. After dinner my man rang his apartment bell and asked for Mr. Hoozitz:—Leacock was packing up! . . . It looks to me like a get-away."

Markham frowned. Heath's report clearly troubled him; but before he could answer, Vance spoke.

"Why this perturbation, Sergeant? You're watching the Captain. I'm sure he can't slip from your vigilant clutches."

Markham looked at Vance a moment; then turned to Heath.

"Let it go at that. But if Leacock attempts to leave the city, nab him."

Heath went out sullenly.

"By the bye, Markham," said Vance; "don't make an appointment for half past twelve to-day. You already have one, don't y' know. And with a lady."

Markham put down his pen, and stared.

"What new damned nonsense is this?"

"I made an engagement for you. Called the lady by 'phone this morning. I'm sure I woke the dear up."

Markham spluttered, striving to articulate his angry protest.

Vance held up his hand soothingly.

"And you simply must keep the engagement. Y' see, I told her it was you speaking; and it would be shocking taste not to appear. . . . I promise, you won't regret meeting her," he added. "Things looked so sadly befuddled last night,—I couldn't bear to see you suffering so. Cons'quently, I arranged for you to see Mrs. Paula Banning—Pfyfe's Éloïse,[117] y' know. I'm pos'tive she'll be able to dispel some of this inspissated[118] gloom that's enveloping you."

"See here, Vance!" Markham growled. "I happen to be running this office—" He stopped abruptly, realizing the hopelessness of making headway against the other's blandness. Moreover, I think, the prospect of interviewing Mrs. Paula Banning was not wholly alien to his inclinations. His resentment slowly ebbed, and when he again spoke his voice was almost matter-of-fact.

"Since you've committed me, I'll see her. But I'd rather Pfyfe wasn't in such close communication with her. He's apt to drop in—with preconcerted unexpectedness."

"Funny," murmured Vance. "I thought of that myself. . . . That's why I 'phoned him last night that he could return to Long Island."

"You 'phoned him—!"

"Awf'lly sorry and all that," Vance apologized. "But you'd gone to bed. Sleep was knitting up your ravell'd sleeve of care; and I couldn't bring myself to disturb you. . . . Pfyfe was so grateful, too. Most touchin'. Said his wife also would be grateful. He was pathetically consid'rate about Mrs. Pfyfe. But I fear he'll need all his velvety forensic powers to explain his absence."

117. Vance is facetiously referring to the legendary romance of Heloise and Abelard. Peter Abelard, a twelfth-century theologian, fell in love with his student Heloise, and their romance has been the subject of ballads for centuries.

118. Congealed.

"In what other quarters have you involved me during my absence?" asked Markham acrimoniously.

"That's all," replied Vance, rising and strolling to the window.

He stood looking out, smoking thoughtfully. When he turned back to the room, his bantering air had gone. He sat down facing Markham.

"The Major has practically admitted to us," he said, "that he knows more about this affair than he has told. You naturally can't push the point, in view of his hon'rable attitude in the matter. And yet, he's willing for you to find out what he knows, as long as he doesn't tell you himself,—that was unquestionably the stand he took last night. Now, I believe there's a way you can find out without calling upon him to go against his principles. . . . You recall Miss Hoffman's story of the eavesdropping; and you also recall that he told you he heard a conversation which, in the light of Benson's murder, became significant. It's quite prob'ble, therefore, that the Major's knowledge has to do with something connected with the business of the firm, or at least with one of the firm's clients."

Vance slowly lit another cigarette.

"My suggestion is this: call up the Major, and ask permission to send a man to take a peep at his ledger accounts and his purchase and sales books. Tell him you want to find out about the transactions of one of his clients. Intimate that it's Miss St. Clair—or Pfyfe, if you like. I have a strange mediumistic feeling that, in this way, you'll get on the track of the person he's shielding. And I'm also assailed by the premonition that he'll welcome your interest in his ledger."

The plan did not appeal to Markham as feasible or fraught with possibilities; and it was evident he disliked making such a request of Major Benson. But so determined was Vance, so earnestly did he argue his point, that in the end Markham acquiesced.

"He was quite willing to let me send a man," said Markham, hanging up the receiver. "In fact, he seemed eager to give me every assistance."

"I thought he'd take kindly to the suggestion," said Vance. "Y' see, if you discover for yourself whom he suspects, it relieves him of the onus of having tattled."

Markham rang for Swacker.

"Call up Stitt and tell him I want to see him here before noon—that I have an immediate job for him."

"Stitt," Markham explained to Vance, "is the head of a firm of public accountants over in the New York Life Building. I use him a good deal on work like this."

Shortly before noon Stitt came. He was a prematurely old young man, with a sharp, shrewd face and a perpetual frown. The prospect of working for the District Attorney pleased him.

Markham explained briefly what was wanted, and revealed enough of the case to guide him in his task. The man grasped the situation immediately, and made one or two notes on the back of a dilapidated envelope.

Vance also, during the instructions, had jotted down some notations on a piece of paper.

Markham stood up and took his hat.

"Now, I suppose, I must keep the appointment you made for me," he complained to Vance. Then: "Come, Stitt, I'll take you down with us in the judges' private elevator."

"If you don't mind," interposed Vance, "Mr. Stitt and I will forgo the honor, and mingle with the commoners in the public lift. We'll meet you downstairs."

Taking the accountant by the arm, he led him out through the main waiting-room. It was ten minutes, however, before he joined us.

We took the subway to Seventy-second Street and walked up West End Avenue to Mrs. Paula Banning's address. She lived in a small apartment-house just around the corner in Seventy-fifth Street. As we stood before her door, waiting for an answer to our ring, a strong odor of Chinese incense drifted out to us.

"Ah! That facilitates matters," said Vance, sniffing. "Ladies who burn joss-sticks are invariably sentimental."

Mrs. Banning was a tall, slightly adipose woman of indeterminate age, with strawcolored hair and a pink-and-white complexion. Her face in repose possessed a youthful and vacuous innocence; but the expression was only superficial. Her eyes, a very light blue, were hard; and a slight puffiness about her cheekbones and beneath her chin attested to years of idle and indulgent living. She was not unattractive, however, in a vivid, flamboyant way; and her manner, when she ushered us into her over-furnished and rococo living-room, was one of easy-going good-fellowship.

When we were seated and Markham had apologized for our intrusion, Vance at once assumed the rôle of interviewer. During his opening explanatory remarks he appraised the woman carefully, as if seeking to determine the best means of approaching her for the information he wanted.

After a few minutes of verbal reconnoitring, he asked permission to smoke, and offered Mrs. Banning one of his cigarettes, which she accepted. Then he smiled at her in a spirit of appreciative geniality, and relaxed comfortably in his chair. He conveyed the impression that he was fully prepared to sympathize with anything she might tell him.

"Mr. Pfyfe strove very hard to keep you entirely out of this affair," said Vance; "and we fully appreciate his delicacy in so doing. But certain circumst'nces connected with Mr. Benson's death have inadvertently involved you in the case; and you can best help us and yourself—and particularly Mr. Pfyfe—by telling us what we want to know, and trusting to our discretion and understanding."

He had emphasized Pfyfe's name, giving it a significant intonation; and the woman had glanced down uneasily. Her apprehension was apparent, and when she looked up into Vance's eyes, she was asking herself: How much does he know? as plainly as if she had spoken the words audibly.

"I can't imagine what you want me to tell you," she said, with an effort at astonishment. "You know that Andy was not in New York that night." (Her designating of the elegant and superior Pfyfe as "Andy" sounded almost like *lèse-majesté*.) "He didn't arrive in the city until nearly nine the next morning."

"Didn't you read in the newspapers about the grey Cadillac that was parked in front of Benson's house?" Vance, in putting the question, imitated her own astonishment.

She smiled confidently.

"That wasn't Andy's car. He took the eight o'clock train to New York the next morning. He said it was lucky that he did, seeing that a machine just like his had been at Mr. Benson's the night before."

She had spoken with the sincerity of complete assurance. It was evident that Pfyfe had lied to her on this point.

Vance did not disabuse her; in fact, he gave her to understand that he accepted her explanation, and consequently dismissed the idea of Pfyfe's presence in New York on the night of the murder.

"I had in mind a connection of a somewhat diff'rent nature when I mentioned you and Mr. Pfyfe as having been drawn into the case. I referred to a personal relationship between you and Mr. Benson."

She assumed an attitude of smiling indifference.

"I'm afraid you've made another mistake." She spoke lightly. "Mr. Benson and I were not even friends. Indeed, I scarcely knew him."

There was an overtone of emphasis in her denial—a slight eagerness which, in indicating a conscious desire to be believed, robbed her remark of the complete casualness she had intended.

"Even a business relationship may have its personal side," Vance reminded her; "especially when the intermediary is an intimate friend of both parties to the transaction."

She looked at him quickly; then turned her eyes away.

"I really don't know what you're talking about," she affirmed; and her face for a moment lost its contours of innocence, and became calculating. "You're surely not implying that I had any business dealings with Mr. Benson?"

"Not directly," replied Vance. "But certainly Mr. Pfyfe had business dealings with him; and one of them, I rather imagined, involved you consid'rably."

"Involved me?" She laughed scornfully, but it was a strained laugh.

"It was a somewhat unfortunate transaction, I fear," Vance went on, "—unfortunate in that Mr. Pfyfe was necessitated to deal with Mr. Benson; and doubly unfortunate, y' know, in that he should have had to drag you into it."

His manner was easy and assured, and the woman sensed that no display of scorn or contempt, however well simulated, would make an impression upon him. Therefore, she adopted an attitude of tolerantly incredulous amusement.

"And where did you learn about all this?" she asked playfully.

"Alas! I didn't learn about it," answered Vance, falling in with her manner. "That's the reason, d' ye see, that I indulged in this charming little visit. I was foolish enough to hope that you'd take pity on my ignorance and tell me all about it."

"But I wouldn't think of doing such a thing," she said, "even if this mysterious transaction had really taken place."

"My word!" sighed Vance. "That is disappointin'. . . . Ah, well. I see that I must tell you what little I know about it, and trust to your sympathy to enlighten me further."

Despite the ominous undercurrent of his words, his levity acted like a sedative to her anxiety. She felt that he was friendly, however much he might know about her.

"Am I bringing you news when I tell you that Mr. Pfyfe forged Mr. Benson's name to a check for ten thousand dollars?" he asked.

She hesitated, gauging the possible consequences of her answer.

"No, that isn't news. Andy tells me everything."

"And did you also know that Mr. Benson, when informed of it, was rather put out?—that, in fact, he demanded a note and a signed confession before he would pay the check?"

The woman's eyes flashed angrily.

"Yes, I knew that too.—And after all Andy had done for him! If ever a man deserved shooting, it was Alvin Benson. He was a dog. And he pretended to be Andy's best friend. Just think of it,—refusing to lend Andy the money without a confession! . . . You'd hardly call that a business deal, would you? I'd call it a dirty, contemptible, underhand trick."

She was enraged. Her mask of breeding and good-fellowship had fallen from her; and she poured out vituperation on Benson with no thought of the words she was using. Her speech was devoid of all the ordinary reticencies of intercourse between strangers.

Vance nodded consolingly during her tirade.

"Y' know, I sympathize fully with you." The tone in which he made the remark seemed to establish a closer *rapprochement*.

After a moment he gave her a friendly smile.

"But, after all, one could almost forgive Benson for holding the confession, if he hadn't also demanded security."

"What security?"

Vance was quick to sense the change in her tone. Taking advantage of her rage, he had mentioned the security while the barriers of her pose were down. Her frightened, almost involuntary query told him that the right moment had arrived. Before she could gain her equilibrium or dispel the momentary fear which had assailed her, he said, with suave deliberation:

"The day Mr. Benson was shot he took home with him from the office a small blue box of jewels."

She caught her breath, but otherwise gave no outward sign of emotion.

"Do you think he had stolen them?"

The moment she had uttered the question she realized that it was a mistake in technique. An ordinary man might have been momentarily diverted from the truth by it. But by Vance's smile she recognized that he had accepted it as an admission.

"It was rather fine of you, y' know, to lend Mr. Pfyfe your jewels to cover the note with."

At this she threw her head up. The blood had left her face, and the rouge on her cheeks took on a mottled and unnatural hue.

"You say I lent my jewels to Andy! I swear to you—"

Vance halted her denial with a slight movement of the hand and a *coup d'œil*.[119] She saw that his intention was to save her from the humiliation she might feel later at having made too emphatic and unqualified a statement; and the graciousness of his action, although he was an antagonist, gave her more confidence in him.

She sank back into her chair, and her hands relaxed.

"What makes you think I lent Andy my jewels?"

Her voice was colorless, but Vance understood the question. It was the end of her deceptions. The pause which followed was an amnesty—recognized as such by both. The next spoken words would be the truth.

"Andy had to have them," she said, "or Benson would have put him in jail." One read in her words a strange, self-sacrificing affection for the worthless Pfyfe. "And if Benson hadn't done it, and had merely refused to honor the check, his father-in-law would have done it. . . . Andy is so careless, so unthinking. He does things without weighing the consequences: I am all the time having to hold him down. . . . But this thing has taught him a lesson—I'm sure of it."

I felt that if anything in the world could teach Pfyfe a lesson, it was the blind loyalty of this woman.

"Do you know what he quarrelled about with Mr. Benson in his office last Wednesday?" asked Vance.

"That was all my fault," she explained, with a sigh. "It was getting very near to the time when the note was due, and I knew Andy didn't have all the money. So I asked him to go to Benson and offer him what he had, and see if he couldn't get my jewels back. . . . But he was refused,—I thought he would be."

Vance looked at her for a while sympathetically.

119. A "stroke of the eye," a quick, meaningful glance.

"I don't want to worry you any more than I can help," he said; "but won't you tell me the real cause of your anger against Benson a moment ago?"

She gave him an admiring nod.

"You're right—I had good reason to hate him." Her eyes narrowed unpleasantly. "The day after he had refused to give Andy the jewels, he called me up—it was in the afternoon—and asked me to have breakfast with him at his house the next morning. He said he was home and had the jewels with him; and he told me—hinted, you understand—that maybe—*maybe* I could have them.—That's the kind of beast he was! . . . I telephoned to Port Washington to Andy and told him about it, and he said he'd be in New York the next morning. He got here about nine o'clock, and we read in the paper that Benson had been shot that night."

Vance was silent for a long time. Then he stood up and thanked her.

"You have helped us a great deal. Mr. Markham is a friend of Major Benson's, and, since we have the check and the confession in our possession, I shall ask him to use his influence with the Major to permit us to destroy them—very soon."

CHAPTER XVIII

A Confession

(Wednesday, June 19; 1 p.m.)

When we were again outside Markham asked: "How in Heaven's name did you know she had put up her jewels to help Pfyfe?"

"My charmin' metaphysical deductions, don't y' know," answered Vance. "As I told you, Benson was not the open-handed, big-hearted altruist who would have lent money without security; and certainly the impecunious Pfyfe had no collateral worth ten thousand dollars, or he wouldn't have forged the check. *Ergo*: someone lent him the security. Now, who would be so trustin' as to lend Pfyfe that amount of security except a sentimental woman who was blind to his amazin' defects? Y' know, I was just evil-minded enough to suspect there was a Calypso in the life of this Ulysses[120] when he told us of stopping over in New York to murmur *au revoir* to someone. When a man like Pfyfe fails to specify the sex of a person, it is safe to assume the feminine gender. So I suggested that you send a Paul Pry[121] to Port Washington to peer into his trans-matrimonial activities: I felt certain a *bonne amie* would be found. Then, when the mysterious package, which obviously was the security, seemed to identify itself as the box of jewels seen by the inquisitive housekeeper, I said to myself: 'Ah! Leander's misguided Dulcinea has lent him her gewgaws to save him from the yawning dungeon.' Nor did I overlook the fact

120. Calypso is the beautiful Titan who, in *The Odyssey*, attempts to prevent Ulysses from returning to his wife.

121. E. Cobham Brewer's *Dictionary of Phrase and Fable* (1898) identifies "Paul Pry" as "[a]n idle, meddlesome fellow, who has no occupation of his own, and is always interfering with other folks' business. (*John Poole: Paul Pry, a comedy* [1825].) The original was Thomas Hill."

122. The Charles M. Schwab residence (known as Riverside) was a seventy-five-room mansion built in 1902–1906 at a cost of $6 million, the equivalent of over $165 million today. Schwab lost his fortune in the Depression and died nearly penniless in 1939. He left the home to the City of New York, to be used as the mayoral residence, but Fiorello La Guardia refused it; the building was eventually torn down in 1948, and an apartment building was erected on the site.

Charles M. Schwab house, ca. 1925.

123. Who is "Sir Hubert"? Perhaps Vance is alluding to *Sir Hubert's Marriage* by Gertrude Townshend Meyer, an 1876 novel in which the title character is apparently unfailingly generous despite covering up a secret. The reference is obscure.

that he had been shielding someone in his explanation about the check. Therefore, as soon as the lady's name and address were learned by Tracy, I made the appointment for you. . . ."

We were passing the Gothic-Renaissance Schwab residence[122] which extends from West End Avenue to Riverside Drive at Seventy-third Street; and Vance stopped for a moment to contemplate it.

Markham waited patiently. At length Vance walked on.

" . . . Y' know, the moment I saw Mrs. Banning I knew my conclusions were correct. She was a sentimental soul, and just the sort of professional good sport who would have handed over her jewels to her *amoroso*. Also, she was bereft of gems when we called,—and a woman of her stamp always wears her jewels when she desires to make an impression on strangers. Moreover, she's the kind that would have jewellery even if the larder was empty. It was therefore merely a question of getting her to talk."

"On the whole, you did very well," observed Markham.

Vance gave him a condescending bow.

"Sir Hubert is too generous.[123]—But tell me, didn't my little chat with the lady cast a gleam into your darkened mind?"

"Naturally," said Markham. "I'm not utterly obtuse. She played unconsciously into our hands. She believed Pfyfe did not arrive in New York until the morning after the murder, and therefore told us quite frankly that she had 'phoned him that Benson had the jewels at home. The situation now is: Pfyfe knew they were in Benson's house, and was there himself at about the time the shot was fired. Furthermore, the jewels are gone; and Pfyfe tried to cover up his tracks that night."

Vance sighed hopelessly.

"Markham, there are altogether too many trees for you in this case. You simply can't see the forest, y' know, because of 'em."

"There is the remote possibility that you are so busily engaged in looking at one particular tree that you are unaware of the others."

A shadow passed over Vance's face.

"I wish you were right," he said.

It was nearly half past one, and we dropped into the Fountain Room of the Ansonia Hotel for lunch. Markham was preoccupied throughout the meal, and when we entered the subway later, he looked uneasily at his watch.

"I think I'll go on down to Wall Street and call on the Major a moment before returning to the office. I can't understand his asking Miss Hoffman not to mention the package to me. . . . It might not have contained the jewels, after all."

"Do you imagine for one moment," rejoined Vance, "that Alvin told the Major the truth about the package? It was not a very cred'table transaction, y' know; and the Major most likely would have given him what-for."

Major Benson's explanation bore out Vance's surmise. Markham, in telling him of the interview with Paula Banning, emphasized the jewel episode in the hope that the Major would voluntarily mention the package; for his promise to Miss Hoffman prevented him from admitting that he was aware of the other's knowledge concerning it.

The Major listened with considerable astonishment, his eyes gradually growing angry.

"I'm afraid Alvin deceived me," he said. He looked straight ahead for a moment, his face softening. "And I don't like to think it, now that he's gone. But the truth is, when Miss Hoffman told me this morning about the envelope, she also mentioned a small parcel that had been in Alvin's private safe-drawer; and I asked her to omit any reference to it from her story to you. I knew the parcel contained Mrs. Banning's jewels, but I thought the fact would only confuse matters if brought to your attention. You see, Alvin told me that a judgment had been taken against Mrs. Banning, and that, just before the Supplementary Proceedings, Pfyfe had brought her jewels here and asked him to sequester them temporarily in his safe."

On our way back to the Criminal Courts Building Markham took Vance's arm and smiled.

"Your guessing luck is holding out, I see."

"Rather!" agreed Vance. "It would appear that the late Alvin, like Warren Hastings,[124] resolved to die in the last dyke of prevarication. . . . *Splendide mendax*,[125] what?"

"In any event," replied Markham, "the Major has unconsciously added another link in the chain against Pfyfe."

"You seem to be making a collection of chains," commented Vance drily. "What have you done with the ones you forged about Miss St. Clair and Leacock?"

"I haven't entirely discarded them—if that's what you think," asserted Markham gravely.

124. Warren Hastings (1732–1818), an English statesman, was the first de facto governor-general of India serving from 1772 to 1785. He was accused of crimes and misdemeanors during his time of office, including the execution of a maharajah. Hastings was impeached; his trial lasted for seven years, and he was ultimately acquitted. The charges, prepared by Edmund Burke, accused him of "palpable prevarication."

125. "Nobly untruthful," from Horace's *Odes*, Book III.

When we reached the office Sergeant Heath was awaiting us with a beatific grin.

"It's all over, Mr. Markham," he announced. "This noon, after you'd gone, Leacock came here looking for you. When he found you were out, he 'phoned Headquarters, and they connected him with me. He wanted to see me—very important, he said; so I hurried over. He was sitting in the waiting-room when I came in, and he called me over and said: 'I came to give myself up. I killed Benson.' I got him to dictate a confession to Swacker, and then he signed it. . . . Here it is." He handed Markham a typewritten sheet of paper.

Markham sank wearily into a chair. The strain of the past few days had begun to tell on him. He sighed heavily.

"Thank God! Now our troubles are ended."

Vance looked at him lugubriously, and shook his head.

"I rather fancy, y' know, that your troubles are only beginning," he drawled.

When Markham had glanced through the confession he handed it to Vance, who read it carefully with an expression of growing amusement.

"Y' know," he said, "this document isn't at all legal. Any judge worthy the name would throw it precip'tately out of court. It's far too simple and precise. It doesn't begin with 'greetings'; it doesn't contain a single 'wherefore-be-it' or 'be-it-known' or 'do-here-by'; it says nothing about 'free will' or 'sound mind' or 'disposin' mem'ry'; and the Captain doesn't once refer to himself as 'the party of the first part'. . . . Utterly worthless, Sergeant. If I were you, I'd chuck it."

Heath was feeling too complacently triumphant to be annoyed. He smiled with magnanimous tolerance.

"It strikes you as funny, doesn't it, Mr. Vance?"

"Sergeant, if you knew how inord'nately funny this confession is, you'd pos'tively have hysterics."

Vance then turned to Markham.

"Really, y' know, I shouldn't put too much stock in this. It may, however, prove a valuable lever with which to prise open the truth. In fact, I'm jolly glad the Captain has gone in for imag'native lit'rature. With this entrancin' fable in our possession, I think we can overcome the Major's scruples, and get him to tell us what he knows. Maybe I'm wrong, but it's worth trying."

He stepped to the District Attorney's desk, and leaned over it cajolingly.

"I haven't led you astray yet, old dear; and I'm going to make another suggestion. Call up the Major and ask him to come here at once. Tell him you've secured a confession,—but don't you dare say whose. Imply it's Miss St. Clair's, or Pfyfe's—or Pontius Pilate's. But urge his immediate presence. Tell him you want to discuss it with him before proceeding with the indictment."

"I can't see the necessity of doing that," objected Markham. "I'm pretty sure to see him at the Club to-night, and I can tell him then."

"That wouldn't do at all," insisted Vance. "If the Major can enlighten us on any point, I think Sergeant Heath should be present to hear him."

"I don't need any enlightenment," cut in Heath.

Vance regarded him with admiring surprise.

"What a wonderful man! Even Goethe cried for *mehr Licht*; and here are you in a state of luminous saturation! . . . Astonishin'!"

"See here, Vance," said Markham: "why try to complicate the matter? It strikes me as a waste of time, besides being an imposition, to ask the Major here to discuss Leacock's confession. We don't need his evidence now, anyway."

Despite his gruffness there was a hint of reconsideration in his voice; for though his instinct had been to dismiss the request out of hand, the experiences of the past few days had taught him that Vance's suggestions were not made without an object.

Vance, sensing the other's hesitancy, said:

"My request is based on something more than an idle desire to gaze upon the Major's rubicund features at this moment. I'm telling you, with all the meagre earnestness I possess, that his presence here now would be most helpful."

Markham deliberated, and argued the point at some length. But Vance was so persistent that in the end he was convinced of the advisability of complying.

Heath was patently disgusted, but he sat down quietly, and sought solace in a cigar.

Major Benson arrived with astonishing promptness, and when Markham handed him the confession, he made little attempt to conceal his eagerness. But as he read it his face clouded, and a look of puzzlement came into his eyes.

At length he looked up, frowning.

"I don't quite understand this; and I'll admit I'm greatly surprised. It doesn't seem credible that Leacock shot Alvin. . . . And yet, I may be mistaken, of course."

He laid the confession on Markham's desk with an air of disappointment, and sank into a chair.

"Do *you* feel satisfied?" he asked.

"I don't see any way around it," said Markham. "If he isn't guilty, why should he come forward and confess? God knows, there's plenty of evidence against him. I was ready to arrest him two days ago."

"He's guilty all right," put in Heath. "I've had my eye on him from the first."

Major Benson did not reply at once: he seemed to be framing his next words.

"It might be—that is, there's the bare possibility—that Leacock had an ulterior motive in confessing."

We all, I think, recognized the thought which his words strove to conceal.

"I'll admit," acceded Markham, "that at first I believed Miss St. Clair guilty, and I intimated as much to Leacock. But later I was persuaded that she was not directly involved."

"Does Leacock know this?" the Major asked quickly.

Markham thought a moment.

"No, I can't say that he does. In fact, it's more than likely he still thinks I suspect her."

"Ah!" The Major's exclamation was almost involuntary.

"But what's that got to do with it?" asked Heath irritably. "Do you think he's going to the chair to save her reputation?—Bunk! That sort of thing's all right in the movies, but no man's that crazy in real life."

"I'm not so sure, Sergeant," ventured Vance lazily. "Women are too sane and practical to make such foolish gestures; but men, y' know, have an illim'table capacity for idiocy."

He turned an inquiring gaze on Major Benson.

"Won't you tell us why you think Leacock is playing Sir Galahad?"

But the Major took refuge in generalities, and was disinclined even to follow up his original intimation as to the cause of the Captain's action. Vance questioned him for some time, but was unable to penetrate his reticence.

Heath, becoming restless, finally spoke up.

"You can't argue Leacock's guilt away, Mr. Vance. Look at the facts. He threatened Benson that he'd kill him if he caught him with the girl again. The next time Benson goes out with her, he's found shot. Then Leacock hides his gun at her house, and when things begin to get hot, he takes it away and ditches it in the river. He bribes the hall-boy to alibi him; and he's seen at Benson's house at twelve-thirty that night. When he's questioned he can't explain anything. . . . If that ain't an open-and-shut case, I'm a mock-turtle."

"The circumstances are convincing," admitted Major Benson. "But couldn't they be accounted for on other grounds?"

Heath did not deign to answer the question.

"The way I see it," he continued, "is like this: Leacock gets suspicious along about midnight, takes his gun and goes out. He catches Benson with the girl, goes in, and shoots him like he threatened. They're both mixed up in it, if you ask me; but Leacock did the shooting. And now we got his confession. . . . There isn't a jury in the country that wouldn't convict him."

"*Probi et legales homines*[126]—oh, quite!" murmured Vance.

Swacker appeared at the door.

"The reporters are clamoring for attention," he announced with a wry face.

"Do they know about the confession?" Markham asked Heath.

"Not yet. I haven't told 'em anything so far—that's why they're clamoring, I guess. But I'll give 'em an earful now, if you say the word."

Markham nodded, and Heath started for the door. But Vance quickly planted himself in the way.

"Could you keep this thing quiet till to-morrow, Markham?" he asked.

Markham was annoyed.

"I could if I wanted to—yes. But why should I?"

"For your own sake, if for no other reason. You've got your prize safely locked up. Control your vanity for twenty-four hours. The Major and I both know that Leacock's innocent, and by this time to-morrow the whole country'll know it."

Again an argument ensued; but the outcome, like that of the former argument, was a foregone conclusion. Markham had realized for some time that Vance had reason to be convinced of

126. "Good and lawful men"—the long-standing criterion for those eligible for jury service in England.

something which as yet he was unwilling to divulge. His opposition to Vance's requests were, I had suspected, largely the result of an effort to ascertain this information; and I was positive of it now as he leaned forward and gravely debated the advisability of making public the Captain's confession.

Vance, as heretofore, was careful to reveal nothing; but in the end his sheer determination carried his point; and Markham requested Heath to keep his own council until the next day. The Major, by a slight nod, indicated his approbation of the decision.

"You might tell the newspaper lads, though," suggested Vance, "that you'll have a rippin' sensation for 'em to-morrow."

Heath went out, crestfallen and glowering.

"A rash fella, the Sergeant—so impetuous!"

Vance again picked up the confession, and perused it.

"Now, Markham, I want you to bring your prisoner forth—*habeas corpus* and that sort of thing. Put him in that chair facing the window, give him one of the good cigars you keep for influential politicians, and then listen attentively while I politely chat with him. . . . The Major, I trust, will remain for the interlocut'ry proceedings."

"That request, at least, I'll grant without objections," smiled Markham. "I had already decided to have a talk with Leacock."

He pressed a buzzer, and a brisk, ruddy-faced clerk entered.

"A requisition for Captain Philip Leacock," he ordered.

When it was brought to him he initialed it.

"Take it to Ben, and tell him to hurry."

The clerk disappeared through the door leading to the outer corridor.

Ten minutes later a deputy sheriff from the Tombs entered with the prisoner.

CHAPTER XIX

Vance Cross-examines

(Wednesday, June 19; 3.30 p.m.)

Captain Leacock walked into the room with a hopeless indifference of bearing. His shoulders drooped; his arms hung listlessly. His eyes were haggard like those of a man who had not slept for days. On seeing Major Benson, he straightened a little and, stepping toward him, extended his hand. It was plain that, however much he may have disliked Alvin Benson, he regarded the Major as a friend. But suddenly, realizing the situation, he turned away, embarrassed.

The Major went quickly to him and touched him on the arm.

"It's all right, Leacock," he said softly. "I can't think that you really shot Alvin."

The Captain turned apprehensive eyes upon him.

"Of course, I shot him." His voice was flat. "I told him I was going to."

Vance came forward, and indicated a chair.

"Sit down, Captain. The District Attorney wants to hear your story of the shooting. The law, you understand, does not accept murder confessions without corroborat'ry evidence. And since, in the present case, there are suspicions against others than yourself, we want you to answer some questions in order to substantiate your guilt. Otherwise, it will be necess'ry for us to follow up our suspicions."

Taking a seat facing Leacock, he picked up the confession.

"You say here you were satisfied that Mr. Benson had wronged you, and you went to his house at about half past twelve on the night of the thirteenth. . . . When you speak of his wronging you, do you refer to his attentions to Miss St. Clair?"

Leacock's face betrayed a sulky belligerence.

"It doesn't matter why I shot him.—Can't you leave Miss St. Clair out of it?"

"Certainly," agreed Vance. "I promise you she shall not be brought into it. But we must understand your motive thoroughly."

After a brief silence Leacock said:

"Very well, then. That was what I referred to."

"How did you know Miss St. Clair went to dinner with Mr. Benson that night?"

"I followed them to the Marseilles."

"And then you went home?"

"Yes."

"What made you go to Mr. Benson's house later?"

"I got to thinking about it more and more, until I couldn't stand it any longer. I began to see red, and at last I took my Colt and went out, determined to kill him."

A note of passion had crept into his voice. It seemed unbelievable that he could be lying.

Vance again referred to the confession.

"You dictated: 'I went to 87 West Forty-eighth Street, and entered the house by the front door.' . . . Did you ring the bell? Or was the front door unlatched?"

Leacock was about to answer, but hesitated. Evidently he recalled the newspaper accounts of the housekeeper's testimony in which she asserted positively that the bell had not rung that night.

"What difference does it make?" He was sparring for time.

"We'd like to know—that's all," Vance told him. "But no hurry."

"Well, if it's so important to you: I didn't ring the bell; and the door wasn't unlocked." His hesitancy was gone. "Just as I reached the house, Benson drove up in a taxicab—"

"Just a moment. Did you happen to notice another car standing in front of the house? A grey Cadillac?"

"Why—yes."

"Did you recognize its occupant?"

There was another short silence.

"I'm not sure. I think it was a man named Pfyfe."

"He and Mr. Benson were outside at the same time, then?"

Leacock frowned.

"No—not at the same time. There was nobody there when I arrived. . . . I didn't see Pfyfe until I came out a few minutes later."

"He arrived in his car when you were inside,—is that it?"

"He must have."

"I see. . . . And now to go back a little: Benson drove up in a taxicab. Then what?"

"I went up to him and said I wanted to speak to him. He told me to come inside, and we went in together. He used his latch-key."

"And now, Captain, tell us just what happened after you and Mr. Benson entered the house."

"He laid his hat and stick on the hat-rack, and we walked into the living-room. He sat down by the table, and I stood up and said—what I had to say. Then I drew my gun, and shot him."

Vance was closely watching the man, and Markham was leaning forward tensely.

"How did it happen that he was reading at the time?"

"I believe he did pick up a book while I was talking. . . . Trying to appear indifferent, I reckon."

"Think now: you and Mr. Benson went into the living-room directly from the hall, as soon as you entered the house?"

"Yes."

"Then how do you account for the fact, Captain, that when Mr. Benson was shot he had on his smoking-jacket and slippers?"

Leacock glanced nervously about the room. Before he answered he wet his lips with his tongue.

"Now that I think of it, Benson did go upstairs for a few minutes first. . . . I guess I was too excited," he added desperately, "to recollect everything."

"That's natural," Vance said sympathetically. "But when he came downstairs did you happen to notice anything peculiar about his hair?"

Leacock looked up vaguely.

"His hair? I—don't understand."

"The color of it, I mean. When Mr. Benson sat before you under the tablelamp, didn't you remark some—difference, let us say—in the way his hair looked?"

The man closed his eyes, as if striving to visualize the scene.

"No—I don't remember."

"A minor point," said Vance indifferently. "Did Benson's speech strike you as peculiar when he came downstairs—that is, was there a thickness, or slight impediment of any kind, in his voice?"

Leacock was manifestly puzzled.

"I don't know what you mean," he said. "He seemed to talk the way he always talked."

"And did you happen to see a blue jewel-case on the table?"

"I didn't notice."

Vance smoked a moment thoughtfully.

"When you left the room after shooting Mr. Benson, you turned out the lights, of course?"

When no immediate answer came, Vance volunteered the suggestion:

"You must have done so, for Mr. Pfyfe says the house was dark when he drove up."

Leacock then nodded an affirmative.

"That's right. I couldn't recollect for the moment."

"Now that you remember the fact, just how did you turn them off?"

"I—" he began, and stopped. Then, finally:

"At the switch."

"And where is that switch located, Captain?"

"I can't just recall."

"Think a moment. Surely you can remember."

"By the door leading into the hall, I think."

"Which side of the door?"

"How can I tell?" the man asked piteously. "I was too—nervous. . . . But I think it was on the right-hand side of the door."

"The right-hand side when entering or leaving the room?"

"As you go out."

"That would be where the bookcase stands?"

"Yes."

Vance appeared satisfied.

"Now, there's the question of the gun," he said. "Why did you take it to Miss St. Clair?"

"I was a coward," the man replied. "I was afraid they might find it at my apartment. And I never imagined she would be suspected."

"And when she was suspected, you at once took the gun away and threw it into the East River?"

"Yes."

"I suppose there was one cartridge missing from the magazine, too—which in itself would have been a suspicious circumstance."

"I thought of that. That's why I threw the gun away."

Vance frowned.

"That's strange. There must have been two guns. We dredged the river, y' know, and found a Colt automatic, but the magazine was full. . . . Are you sure, Captain, that it was *your* gun you took from Miss St. Clair's and threw over the bridge?"

I knew no gun had been retrieved from the river, and I wondered what he was driving at. Was he, after all, trying to involve the girl? Markham, too, I could see, was in doubt.

Leacock made no answer for several moments. When he spoke, it was with dogged sullenness.

"There weren't two guns. The one you found was mine. . . . I refilled the magazine myself."

"Ah, that accounts for it." Vance's tone was pleasant and reassuring. "Just one more question, Captain. Why did you come here to-day and confess?"

Leacock thrust his chin out, and for the first time during the cross-examination his eyes became animated.

"Why? It was the only honorable thing to do. You had unjustly suspected an innocent person; and I didn't want anyone else to suffer."

This ended the interview. Markham had no questions to ask; and the deputy sheriff led the Captain out.

When the door had closed on him a curious silence fell over the room. Markham sat smoking furiously, his hands folded behind his head, his eyes fixed on the ceiling. The Major had settled back in his chair, and was gazing at Vance with admiring satisfaction. Vance was watching Markham out of the corner of his eye, a drowsy smile on his lips. The expressions and attitudes of the three men conveyed perfectly their varying individual reactions to the interview—Markham troubled, the Major pleased, Vance cynical.

It was Vance who broke the silence. He spoke easily, almost lazily.

"You see how silly the confession is, what? Our pure and lofty Captain is an incredibly poor Munchausen. No one could lie as badly as he did who hadn't been born into the world that way. It's simply impossible to imitate such stupidity. And he did so want us to think him guilty. Very affectin'. He prob'bly imagined you'd merely stick the confession in his shirt-front and send him to the hangman. You noticed, he hadn't even decided how he got into Benson's house that night. Pfyfe's admitted presence outside almost spoiled his impromptu explanation of having entered *bras dessus bras dessous*[127] with his intended victim. And he didn't recall Benson's semi-négligé attire. When I reminded him of it, he had to contradict himself, and send Benson trotting upstairs to make a rapid change. Luckily, the toupee wasn't mentioned by the newspapers. The Captain couldn't imagine what I meant when I intimated that Benson had dyed his hair when changing his coat and shoes. . . . By the bye, Major, did your brother speak thickly when his false teeth were out?"

"Noticeably so," answered the Major. "If Alvin's plate had been removed that night—as I gathered it had been from your question—Leacock would surely have noticed it."

"There were other things he didn't notice," said Vance: "the jewel-case, for instance, and the location of the electric-light switch."

"He went badly astray on that point," added the Major. "Alvin's house is old-fashioned, and the only switch in the room is a pendant one attached to the chandelier."

"Exactly," said Vance. "However, his worst break was in connection with the gun. He gave his hand away completely there. He said he threw the pistol into the river largely because of the missing cartridge, and when I told him the magazine was full, he explained that he had refilled it, so I wouldn't think it was anyone else's gun that was found. . . . It's plain to see what's the matter. He thinks Miss St. Clair is guilty, and is determined to take the blame."

"That's my impression," said Major Benson.

"And yet," mused Vance, "the Captain's attitude bothers me a little. There's no doubt he had something to do with the crime, else why should he have concealed his pistol the next day in Miss St. Clair's apartment? He's just the kind of silly beggar, d' ye see, who would threaten any man he thought had designs on his fiancée, and then carry out the threat if anything happened. And he has a guilty conscience—that's obvious. But for what?

Certainly not the shooting. The crime was planned; and the Captain never plans. He's the kind that gets an *idée fixe*, girds up his loins, and does the deed in knightly fashion, prepared to take the cons'quences. That sort of chivalry, y' know, is sheer *beau geste*: its acolytes want everyone to know of their valor. And when they go forth to rid the world of a Don Juan, they're always clear-minded. The Captain, for instance, wouldn't have overlooked his Lady Fair's gloves and hand-bag,—he would have taken 'em away. In fact, it's just as certain he would have shot Benson as it is he didn't shoot him. That's the beetle in the amber. It's psychologically possible he would have done it, and psychologically impossible he would have done it the way it was done."

He lit a cigarette and watched the drifting spirals of smoke.

"If it wasn't so fantastic, I'd say he started out to do it, and found it already done. And yet, that's about the size of it. It would account for Pfyfe's seeing him there, and for his secreting the gun at Miss St. Clair's the next day."

The telephone rang: Colonel Ostrander wanted to speak to the District Attorney. Markham, after a short conversation, turned a disgruntled look upon Vance.

"Your blood-thirsty friend wanted to know if I'd arrested anyone yet. He offered to confer more of his invaluable suggestions upon me in case I was still undecided as to who was guilty."

"I heard you thanking him fulsomely for something or other. . . . What did you give him to understand about your mental state?"

"That I was still in the dark."

Markham's answer was accompanied by a sombre, tired smile. It was his way of telling Vance that he had entirely rejected the idea of Captain Leacock's guilt.

The Major went to him and held out his hand.

"I know how you feel," he said. "This sort of thing is discouraging; but it's better that the guilty person should escape altogether than that an innocent man should be made to suffer. . . . Don't work too hard, and don't let these disappointments get to you. You'll soon hit on the right solution, and when you do—" His jaw snapped shut, and he uttered the rest of the sentence between clenched teeth. "—you'll meet with no opposition from me. I'll help you put the thing over."

He gave Markham a grim smile, and took up his hat.

128. Attributed to Lady Morgan (1781–1859), author of *The Wild Irish Girl* (1806).

129. Alvin the Bald.

130. Literally, "born to consume crops"—a more common expression is "born with a silver spoon in his mouth."

"I'm going back to the office now. If you want me at any time, let me know. I may be able to help you—later on."

With a friendly, appreciative bow to Vance, he went out.

Markham sat in silence for several minutes.

"Damn it, Vance!" he said irritably. "This case gets more difficult by the hour. I feel worn out."

"You really shouldn't take it so seriously, old dear," Vance advised lightly. "It doesn't pay y' know, to worry over the *trivia* of existence.

'Nothing's new,
And nothing's true,
And nothing really matters.'[128]

Several million johnnies were killed in the war, and you don't let the fact bedevil your phagocytes or inflame your brain-cells. But when one rotter is mercifully shot in your district, you lie awake nights perspiring over it, what? My word! You're deucedly inconsistent."

"Consistency—" began Markham; but Vance interrupted him.

"Now don't quote Emerson. I inf'nitely prefer Erasmus. Y' know, you ought to read his *Praise of Folly*, it would cheer you no end. That goaty old Dutch professor would never have grieved inconsolably over the destruction of Alvin *Le Chauve*."[129]

"I'm not a *fruges consumere natus*[130] like you," snapped Markham. "I was elected to this office—"

"Oh, quite,—'loved I not honor more' and all that," Vance chimed in. "But don't be so sens'tive. Even if the Captain has succeeded in bungling his way out of jail, you have at least five possibilities left. There's Mrs. Platz . . . and Pfyfe . . . and Colonel Ostrander . . . and Miss Hoffman . . . and Mrs. Banning.—I say! Why don't you arrest 'em all, one at a time, and get 'em to confess? Heath would go crazy with joy."

Markham was in too crestfallen a mood to resent this chaffing. Indeed, Vance's light-heartedness seemed to buoy him up.

"If you want the truth," he said; "that's exactly what I feel like doing. I am restrained merely by my indecision as to which one to arrest first."

"Stout fella!" Then Vance asked: "What are you going to do with the Captain now? It'll break his heart if you release him."

"His heart'll have to break, I'm afraid." Markham reached for the telephone. "I'd better see to the formalities now."

"Just a moment!" Vance put forth a restraining hand. "Don't end his rapturous martyrdom just yet. Let him be happy for another day at least. I've a notion he may be most useful to us, pining away in his lonely cell like the prisoner of Chillon."[131]

Markham put down the telephone without a word. More and more, I had noticed, he was becoming inclined to accept Vance's leadership. This attitude was not merely the result of the hopeless confusion in his mind, though his uncertainty probably influenced him to some extent; but it was due in large measure to the impression Vance had given him of knowing more than he cared to reveal.

"Have you tried to figure out just how Pfyfe and his Turtledove fit into the case?" Vance asked.

"Along with a few thousand other enigmas—yes," was the petulant reply. "But the more I try to reason it out, the more of a mystery the whole thing becomes."

"Loosely put, my dear Markham," criticized Vance. "There are no mysteries originating in human beings, y' know; there are only problems. And any problem originating in one human being can be solved by another human being. It merely requires a knowledge of the human mind, and the application of that knowledge to human acts. Simple, what?"

He glanced at the clock.

"I wonder how your Mr. Stitt is getting along with the Benson and Benson books. I await his report with anticipat'ry excitement."

This was too much for Markham. The wearing-down process of Vance's intimations and veiled innuendoes had at last dissipated his self-control. He bent forward and struck the desk angrily with his hand.

"I'm damned tired of this superior attitude of yours," he complained hotly. "Either you know something or you don't. If you don't know anything, do me the favor of dropping these insinuations of knowledge. If you do know anything, it's up to you to tell me. You've been hinting around in one way or another ever since Benson was shot. If you've got any idea who killed him, I want to know it."

He leaned back, and took out a cigar. Not once did he look up as he carefully clipped the end and lit it. I think he was a little ashamed at having given way to his anger.

131. Chillon is a place, not a jailer; a Genevois monk, François Bonivard, was imprisoned there, and his confinement inspired the 1816 poem "The Prisoner of Chillon," by Lord Byron.

Castle Chillon (*photo by Zacherie Grossen, licensed under CCA-SA 4.0 International*).

132. From Ralph Waldo Emerson's 1863 poem "Voluntaries."

133. "What is your duty? What the day demands"—from Goethe's *Maxims and Reflections* (1833).

134. Although Vance's meaning is not clear, the sentiment expressed following his reference to "Postume" suggests that he probably is referring to a line from Horace's *Odes*: "Eheu fugaces, Postume, Postume/labuntur anni . . ." (loosely meaning "Alas, Postume, the years slip away"). Postume was a friend of Horace.

*   [Author's note:] This quotation from Ecclesiastes reminds me that Vance regularly read the Old Testament. "When I weary of the professional liter'ry man," he once said, "I find stimulation in the majestic prose of the Bible. If the moderns feel that they simply must write, they should be made to spend at least two hours a day with the Biblical historians."

Vance had sat apparently unconcerned during the outburst. At length he stretched his legs, and gave Markham a long contemplative look.

"Y' know, Markham old bean, I don't blame you a bit for your unseemly ebullition. The situation has been most provokin'. But now, I fancy, the time has come to put an end to the comedietta. I really haven't been spoofing, y' know. The fact is, I've some most int'restin' ideas on the subject."

He stood up and yawned.

"It's a beastly hot day, but it must be done—eh, what?

'So nigh is grandeur to our dust,
So near is God to man.
When duty whispers low, *Thou must*,
The youth replies, *I can*.'[132]

I'm the noble youth, don't y'know. And you're the voice of duty—though you didn't exactly whisper, did you? . . . *Was aber ist deine Pflicht?* And Goethe answered: *Die Forderung des Tages*.[133] But—deuce take it!—I wish the demand had come on a cooler day."

He handed Markham his hat.

"Come, *Postume*.[134] To everything there is a season, and a time to every purpose under the heaven.* You are through with the office for to-day,—inform Swacker of the fact, will you?—there's a dear! We attend upon a lady—Miss St. Clair, no less."

Markham realized that Vance's jesting manner was only the masquerade of a very serious purpose. Also, he knew that Vance would tell him what he knew or suspected only in his own way, and that, no matter how circuitous and unreasonable that way might appear, Vance had excellent reasons for following it. Furthermore, since the unmasking of Captain Leacock's purely fictitious confession, he was in a state of mind to follow any suggestion that held the faintest hope of getting at the truth. He therefore rang at once for Swacker, and informed him he was quitting the office for the day.

In ten minutes we were in the subway on our way to 94 Riverside Drive.

CHAPTER XX

A Lady Explains

(Wednesday, June 19; 4.30 p.m.)

The quest for enlightenment upon which we are now embarked," said Vance, as we rode up town, "may prove a bit tedious. But you must exert your will-power, and bear with me. You can't imagine what a ticklish task I have on my hands. And it's not a pleasant one either. I'm a bit too young to be sentimental, and yet, d' ye know, I'm half inclined to let your culprit go."

"Would you mind telling me why we are calling on Miss St. Clair?" asked Markham resignedly.

Vance amiably complied.

"Not at all. Indeed, I deem it best for you to know. There are several points connected with the lady that need eluc'dation. First, there are the gloves and the hand-bag. Nor poppy nor mandragora shall ever medicine thee to that sweet sleep which thou ow'dst yesterday[135] until you have learned about those articles—eh, what?—Then, you recall, Miss Hoffman told us that the Major was lending an ear when a certain lady called upon Benson the day he was shot. I suspect that the visitor was Miss St. Clair; and I am rather curious to know what took place in the office that day, and why she came back later. Also, why did she go to Benson's for tea that afternoon? And what part did the jewels play in the chit-chat?—But there are other items. For example: Why did the

135. Vance misquotes Iago in *The Merchant of Venice*, Act III, Scene 3: "Not poppy, nor mandragora, / For all the drowsy syrups of the world, / Shall ever medicine thee to that sweet sleep / Which thou owedst yesterday."

136. The "verray parfit gentil knyght" (the "very perfect gentle knight") is mentioned in the General Prologue to Chaucer's *Canterbury Tales*.

137. Softness, gentleness.

138. A typographical error consistent in various editions: The correct word is "elenchus," a dialogue consisting of short questions and answers, used by Socrates for his teaching technique.

Captain take his gun to her? What makes him think she shot Benson?—he really believes it, y' know. And why did she think that he was guilty from the first?"

Markham looked skeptical.

"You expect her to tell us all this?"

"My hopes run high," returned Vance. "With her verray parfit gentil knight[136] jailed as a self-confessed murderer, she will have nothing to lose by unburdening her soul. . . . But we must have no blustering. Your police brand of aggressive cross-examination will, I assure you, have no effect upon the lady."

"Just how do you propose to elicit your information?"

"With *morbidezza*,[137] as the painters say. Much more refined and gentlemanly, y' know."

Markham considered a moment.

"I think I'll keep out of it, and leave the Socratic elenctus[138] entirely to you."

"An extr'ordin'rily brilliant suggestion," said Vance.

When we arrived Markham announced over the house-telephone that he had come on a vitally important mission; and we were received by Miss St. Clair without a moment's delay. She was apprehensive, I imagine, concerning the whereabouts of Captain Leacock.

As she sat before us in her little drawing-room overlooking the Hudson, her face was quite pale, and her hands, though tightly clasped, trembled a little. She had lost much of her cold reserve, and there were unmistakable signs of sleepless worry about her eyes.

Vance went directly to the point. His tone was almost flippant in its lightness: it at once relieved the tension of the atmosphere, and gave an air bordering on inconsequentiality to our visit.

"Captain Leacock has, I regret to inform you, very foolishly confessed to the murder of Mr. Benson. But we are not entirely satisfied with his *bona fides*. We are, alas! awash between Scylla and Charybdis. We can not decide whether the Captain is a deep-dyed villain or a *chevalier sans peur et sans reproche*. His story of how he accomplished the dark deed is a bit sketchy: he is vague on certain essential details; and—what's most confusin'—he turned the lights off in Benson's hideous living-room by a switch which pos'tively doesn't exist. Cons'quently, the suspicion has crept into my mind that he has concocted this tale of derring-do in order to shield someone whom he really believes guilty."

He indicated Markham with a slight movement of the head.

"The District Attorney here does not wholly agree with me. But then, d' ye see, the legal mind is incredibly rigid and unreceptive once it has been invaded by a notion. You will remember that, because you were with Mr. Alvin Benson on his last evening on earth, and for other reasons equally irrelevant and trivial, Mr. Markham actu'lly concluded that you had had something to do with the gentleman's death."

He gave Markham a smile of waggish reproach, and went on:

"Since you, Miss St. Clair, are the only person whom Captain Leacock would shield so heroically, and since I, at least, am convinced of your own innocence, will you not clear up for us a few of those points where your orbit crossed that of Mr. Benson? . . . Such information cannot do the Captain or yourself any harm, and it very possibly will help to banish from Mr. Markham's mind his lingering doubts as to the Captain's innocence."

Vance's manner had an assuaging effect upon the woman; but I could see that Markham was boiling inwardly at Vance's animadversions on him, though he refrained from any interruption.

Miss St. Clair stared steadily at Vance for several minutes.

"I don't know why I should trust you, or even believe you," she said evenly; "but now that Captain Leacock has confessed,—I was afraid he was going to, when he last spoke to me,—I see no reason why I should not answer your questions. . . . Do you truly think he is innocent?"

The question was like an involuntary cry: her pent-up emotion had broken through her carapace of calm.

"I truly do," Vance avowed soberly. "Mr. Markham will tell you that before we left his office I pleaded with him to release Captain Leacock. It was with the hope that your explanations would convince him of the wisdom of such a course, that I urged him to come here."

Something in his tone and manner seemed to inspire her confidence.

"What do you wish to ask me?" she asked.

Vance cast another reproachful glance at Markham, who was restraining his outraged feelings only with difficulty; and then turned back to the woman.

"First of all, will you explain how your gloves and hand-bag found their way into Mr. Benson's house? Their presence there has been preying most distressin'ly on the District Attorney's mind."

She turned a direct, frank gaze upon Markham.

"I dined with Mr. Benson at his invitation. Things between us were not pleasant, and when we started for home, my resentment of his attitude increased. At Times Square I ordered the chauffeur to stop—I preferred returning home alone. In my anger and my haste to get away, I must have dropped my gloves and bag. It was not until Mr. Benson had driven off that I realized my loss, and having no money, I walked home. Since my things were found in Mr. Benson's house, he must have taken them there himself."

"Such was my own belief," said Vance. "And—my word!—it's a deucedly long walk out here, what?"

He turned to Markham with a tantalizing smile.

"Really, y' know, Miss St. Clair couldn't have been expected to reach here before one."

Markham, grim and resolute, made no reply.

"And now," pursued Vance, "I should love to know under what circumst'nces the invitation to dinner was extended."

A shadow darkened her face, but her voice remained even.

"I had been losing a lot of money through Mr. Benson's firm, and suddenly my intuition told me that he was purposely seeing to it that I did lose, and that he could, if he desired, help me to recoup." She dropped her eyes. "He had been annoying me with his attentions for some time; and I didn't put any despicable scheme past him. I went to his office, and told him quite plainly what I suspected. He replied that if I'd dine with him that night we could talk it over. I knew what his object was, but I was so desperate I decided to go anyway, hoping I might plead with him."

"And how did you happen to mention to Mr. Benson the exact time your little dinner party would terminate?"

She looked at Vance in astonishment, but answered unhesitatingly.

"He said something about—making a gay night of it; and then I told him—very emphatically—that if I went I would leave him sharply at midnight, as was my invariable rule on all parties. . . . You see," she added, "I study very hard at my singing, and going home at midnight, no matter what the occasion, is one of the sacrifices—or rather, restrictions—I impose on myself."

"Most commendable and most wise!" commented Vance. "Was this fact generally known among your acquaintances?"

"Oh yes. It even resulted in my being nicknamed Cinderella."

"Specifically, did Colonel Ostrander and Mr. Pfyfe know it?"

"Yes."

Vance thought a moment.

"How did you happen to go to tea at Mr. Benson's home the day of the murder, if you were to dine with him that night?"

A flush stained her cheeks.

"There was nothing wrong in that," she declared. "Somehow, after I had left Mr. Benson's office, I revolted against my decision to dine with him, and I went to his house—I had gone back to the office first, but he had left—to make a final appeal, and to beg him to release me from my promise. But he laughed the matter off, and after insisting that I have tea, sent me home in a taxicab to dress for dinner. He called for me about half past seven."

"And when you pleaded with him to release you from your promise you sought to frighten him by recalling Captain Leacock's threat; and he said it was only a bluff."

Again the woman's astonishment was manifest.

"Yes," she murmured.

Vance gave her a soothing smile.

"Colonel Ostrander told me he saw you and Mr. Benson at the Marseilles."

"Yes; and I was terribly ashamed. He knew what Mr. Benson was, and had warned me against him only a few days before."

"I was under the impression the Colonel and Mr. Benson were good friends."

"They were—up to a week ago. But the Colonel lost more money than I did in a stock pool which Mr. Benson engineered recently, and he intimated to me very strongly that Mr. Benson had deliberately misadvised us to his own benefit. He didn't even speak to Mr. Benson that night at the Marseilles."

"What about these rich and precious stones that accompanied your tea with Mr. Benson?"

"Bribes," she answered; and her contemptuous smile was a more eloquent condemnation of Benson than if she had resorted to the bitterest castigation. "The gentleman sought to turn my head with them. I was offered a string of pearls to wear to dinner; but I declined them. And I was told that, if I saw things in the right light—or some such charming phrase—I could have jewels just like them for my very, very own—perhaps even those identical ones, on the twenty-first."

"Of course—the twenty-first," grinned Vance. "Markham, are you listening? On the twenty-first Leander's note falls due, and if it's not paid the jewels are forfeited."

He addressed himself again to Miss St. Clair.

"Did Mr. Benson have the jewels with him at dinner?"

"Oh, no! I think my refusal of the pearls rather discouraged him."

Vance paused, looking at her with ingratiating cordiality.

"Tell us now, please, of the gun episode—in your own words, as the lawyers say, hoping to entangle you later."

But she evidently feared no entanglement.

"The morning after the murder Captain Leacock came here and said he had gone to Mr. Benson's house about half past twelve with the intention of shooting him. But he had seen Mr. Pfyfe outside and, assuming he was calling, had given up the idea and gone home. I feared that Mr. Pfyfe had seen him, and I told him it would be safer to bring his pistol to me and to say, if questioned, that he'd lost it in France. . . . You see, I really thought he had shot Mr. Benson and was—well, lying like a gentleman, to spare my feelings. Then, when he took the pistol from me with the purpose of throwing it away altogether, I was even more certain of it."

She smiled faintly at Markham.

"That was why I refused to answer your questions. I wanted you to think that maybe I had done it, so you'd not suspect Captain Leacock."

"But he wasn't lying at all," said Vance.

"I know now that he wasn't. And I should have known it before. He'd never have brought the pistol to me if he'd been guilty."

A film came over her eyes.

"And—poor boy!—he confessed because he thought that I was guilty."

"That's precisely the harrowin' situation," nodded Vance. "But where did he think you had obtained a weapon?"

"I know many army men—friends of his and of Major Benson's. And last summer at the mountains I did considerable pistol practice for the fun of it. Oh, the idea was reasonable enough."

Vance rose and made a courtly bow.

"You've been most gracious—and most helpful," he said. "Y' see, Mr. Markham had various theories about the murder. The first, I believe, was that you alone were the Madam Borgia. The second was that you and the Captain did the deed together—*à quatre mains*, as it were. The third was that the Captain pulled the trigger *a cappella*. And the legal mind is so exquisitely developed that it can believe in several conflicting theories at the same time. The sad thing about the present case is that Mr. Markham still leans toward the belief that both of you are guilty, individually and collectively. I tried to reason with him before coming here; but I failed. Therefore, I insisted upon his hearing from your own charming lips your story of the affair."

He went up to Markham who sat glaring at him with lips compressed.

"Well, old chap," he remarked pleasantly, "surely you are not going to persist in your obsession that either Miss St. Clair or Captain Leacock is guilty, what? . . . And won't you relent and unshackle the Captain as I begged you to?"

He extended his arms in a theatrical gesture of supplication.

Markham's wrath was at the breaking-point, but he got up deliberately and, going to the woman, held out his hand.

"Miss St. Clair," he said kindly—and again I was impressed by the bigness of the man—, "I wish to assure you that I have dismissed the idea of your guilt, and also Captain Leacock's, from what Mr. Vance terms my incredibly rigid and unreceptive mind. . . . I forgive him, however, because he has saved me from doing you a very grave injustice. And I will see that you have your Captain back as soon as the papers can be signed for his release."

As we walked out onto Riverside Drive, Markham turned savagely on Vance.

"So! *I* was keeping her precious Captain locked up, and *you* were pleading with me to let him go! You know damned well I didn't think either one of them was guilty—you—you lounge lizard!"

Vance sighed.

"Dear me! Don't you want to be of any help at all in this case?" he asked sadly.

"What good did it do you to make an ass of me in front of that woman?" spluttered Markham. "I can't see that you got anywhere, with all your tom-foolery."

"What!" Vance registered utter amazement. "The testimony you've heard to-day is going to help immeasurably in convicting the culprit. Furthermore, we now know about the gloves and hand-bag, and who the lady was that called at Benson's office, and what Miss St. Clair did between twelve and one, and why she dined alone with Alvin, and why she first had tea with him, and how the jewels came to be there, and why the Captain took her his gun and then threw it away, and why he confessed. . . . My word! Doesn't all this knowledge soothe you? It rids the situation of so much débris."

He stopped and lit a cigarette.

"The really important thing the lady told us was that her friends knew she invariably departed at midnight when she went out of an evening. Don't overlook or belittle that point, old dear; it's most pert'nent. I told you long ago that the person who shot Benson knew she was dining with him that night."

"You'll be telling me next you know who killed him," Markham scoffed.

Vance sent a ring of smoke circling upward.

"I've known all along who shot the blighter."

Markham snorted derisively.

"Indeed! And when did this revelation burst upon you?"

"Oh, not more than five minutes after I entered Benson's house that first morning," replied Vance.

"Well, well! Why didn't you confide in me, and avoid all these trying activities?"

"Quite impossible," Vance explained jocularly. "You were not ready to receive my apocryphal knowledge. It was first necess'ry to lead you patiently by the hand out of the various dark forests and morasses into which you insisted upon straying. You're so dev'lishly unimag'native, don't y' know."

A taxicab was passing, and he hailed it.

"Eighty-seven West Forty-eighth Street," he directed.

Then he took Markham's arm confidingly.

"Now for a brief chat with Mrs. Platz. And then—then I shall pour into your ear all my maidenly secrets."

CHAPTER XXI

Sartorial Revelations

(Wednesday, June 19; 5.30 p.m.)

The housekeeper regarded our visit that afternoon with marked uneasiness. Though she was a large powerful woman, her body seemed to have lost some of its strength, and her face showed signs of prolonged anxiety. Snitkin informed us, when we entered, that she had carefully read every newspaper account of the progress of the case, and had questioned him interminably on the subject.

She entered the living-room with scarcely an acknowledgment of our presence, and took the chair Vance placed for her like a woman resigning herself to a dreaded but inevitable ordeal. When Vance looked at her keenly, she gave him a frightened glance and turned her face away, as if, in the second their eyes met, she had read his knowledge of some secret she had been jealously guarding.

Vance began his questioning without prelude or protasis.

"Mrs. Platz, was Mr. Benson very particular about his toupee—that is, did he often receive his friends without having it on?"

The woman appeared relieved.

"Oh, no, sir—never."

"Think back, Mrs. Platz. Has Mr. Benson never, to your knowledge, been in anyone's company without his toupee?"

She was silent for some time, her brows contracted.

"Once I saw him take off his wig and show it to Colonel Ostrander, an elderly gentleman who used to call here very often. But Colonel Ostrander was an old friend of his. He told me they lived together once."

"No one else?"

Again she frowned thoughtfully.

"No," she said, after several minutes.

"What about the tradespeople?"

"He was very particular about them. . . . And strangers, too," she added. "When he used to sit in here in hot weather without his wig, he always pulled the shade on that window." She pointed to the one nearest the hallway. "You can look in it from the steps."

"I'm glad you brought up that point," said Vance. "And anyone standing on the steps could tap on the window or the iron bars, and attract the attention of anyone in this room?"

"Oh, yes, sir—easily. I did it myself once, when I went on an errand and forgot my key."

"It's quite likely, don't you think, that the person who shot Mr. Benson obtained admittance that way?"

"Yes, sir." She grasped eagerly at the suggestion.

"The person would have had to know Mr. Benson pretty well to tap on the window instead of ringing the bell. Don't you agree with me, Mrs. Platz?"

"Yes—sir." Her tone was doubtful: evidently the point was a little beyond her.

"If a stranger had tapped on the window would Mr. Benson have admitted him without his toupee?"

"Oh, no—he wouldn't have let a stranger in."

"You are sure the bell didn't ring that night?"

"Positive, sir." The answer was very emphatic.

"Is there a light on the front steps?"

"No, sir."

"If Mr. Benson had looked out of the window to see who was tapping, could he have recognized the person at night?"

The woman hesitated.

"I don't know—I don't think so."

"Is there any way you can see through the front door who is outside, without opening it?"

"No, sir. Sometimes I wished there was."

"Then, if the person knocked on the window, Mr. Benson must have recognized the voice?"

"It looks that way, sir."

"And you're certain no one could have got in without a key?"

"How could they? The door locks by itself."

"It's the regulation spring-lock, isn't it?"

"Yes, sir."

"Then it must have a catch you can turn off so that the door will open from either side even though it's latched."

"It did have a catch like that," she explained, "but Mr. Benson had it fixed so's it wouldn't work. He said it was too dangerous,—I might go out and leave the house unlocked."

Vance stepped into the hallway, and I heard him opening and shutting the front door.

"You're right, Mrs. Platz," he observed, when he came back. "Now tell me: are you quite sure no one had a key?"

"Yes, sir. No one but me and Mr. Benson had a key."

Vance nodded his acceptance of her statement.

"You said you left your bed-room door open on the night Mr. Benson was shot. . . . Do you generally leave it open?"

"No, I 'most always shut it. But it was terrible close that night."

"Then it was merely an accident you left it open?"

"As you might say."

"If your door had been closed as usual, could you have heard the shot, do you think?"

"If I'd been awake, maybe. Not if I was sleeping, though. They got heavy doors in these old houses, sir."

"And they're beautiful, too," commented Vance.

He looked admiringly at the massive mahogany double door that opened into the hall.

"Y' know, Markham, our so-called civ'lization is nothing more than the persistent destruction of everything that's beautiful and enduring, and the designing of cheap makeshifts. You should read Oswald Spengler's *Untergang des Abendlands*—a most penetratin' document. I wonder some enterprisin' publisher hasn't embalmed it in our native argot.[*] The whole history of this degen'rate era we call modern civ'lization can be seen in our woodwork. Look at that fine old door, for instance, with its bevelled panels and ornamented bolection,[139] and its Ionic pilasters and carved lintel. And then compare it with the flat, flimsy, machinemade,

[*] [Author's note:] The book (or a part of it) has, I believe, been recently translated into English.

[Editor's note: The book, *Decline of the West*, was first published in German in 1918; the English translation was first published in 1926, before publication of *The Benson Murder Case*. This note was clearly added just before publication.]

139. A convex molding separating two panels.

shellacked boards which are turned out by the thousand to-day. *Sic transit. . . .*"

He studied the door for some time; then turned abruptly back to Mrs. Platz, who was eyeing him curiously and with mounting apprehension.

"What did Mr. Benson do with the box of jewels when he went out to dinner?" he asked.

"Nothing, sir," she answered nervously. "He left them on the table there."

"Did you see them after he had gone?"

"Yes; and I was going to put them away. But I decided I'd better not touch them."

"And nobody came to the door, or entered the house, after Mr. Benson left?"

"No, sir."

"You're quite sure?"

"I'm positive, sir."

Vance rose, and began to pace the floor. Suddenly, just as he was passing the woman, he stopped and faced her.

"Was your maiden name Hoffman, Mrs. Platz?"

The thing she had been dreading had come. Her face paled, her eyes opened wide, and her lower lip drooped a little.

Vance stood looking at her, not unkindly. Before she could regain control of herself, he said:

"I had the pleasure of meeting your charmin' daughter recently."

"My daughter. . . ?" the woman managed to stammer.

"Miss Hoffman, y' know—the attractive young lady with the blond hair. Mr. Benson's secret'ry."

The woman sat erect, and spoke through clamped teeth.

"She's not my daughter."

"Now, now, Mrs. Platz!" Vance chided her, as if speaking to a child. "Why this foolish attempt at deception? You remember how worried you were when I accused you of having a personal interest in the lady who was here to tea with Mr. Benson? You were afraid I thought it was Miss Hoffman. . . . But why should you be anxious about her, Mrs. Platz? I'm sure she's a very nice girl. And you really can't blame her for preferring the name of Hoffman to that of Platz. *Platz* means generally a place, though it also means a crash or an explosion; and sometimes a *Platz* is a bun or a yeast-cake. But a *Hoffman* is a courtier—much nicer than being a yeast-cake, what?"

He smiled engagingly, and his manner had a quieting effect upon her.

"It isn't that, sir," she said, looking at him appealingly. "I made her take the name. In this country any girl who's smart can get to be a lady, if she's given a chance. And—"

"I understand perfectly," Vance interposed pleasantly. "Miss Hoffman is clever, and you feared that the fact of your being a housekeeper, if it became known, would stand in the way of her success. So you elim'nated yourself, as it were, for her welfare. I think it was very generous of you. . . . Your daughter lives alone?"

"Yes, sir—in Morningside Heights. But I see her every week." Her voice was barely audible.

"Of course—as often as you can, I'm sure. . . . Did you take the position as Mr. Benson's housekeeper because she was his secret'ry?"

She looked up, a bitter expression in her eyes.

"Yes, sir—I did. She told me the kind of man he was; and he often made her come to the house here in the evenings to do extra work."

"And you wanted to be here to protect her?"

"Yes, sir—that was it."

"Why were you so worried the morning after the murder, when Mr. Markham here asked you if Mr. Benson kept any fire-arms around the house?"

The woman shifted her gaze.

"I—wasn't worried."

"Yes, you were, Mrs. Platz. And I'll tell you why. You were afraid we might think Miss Hoffman shot him."

"Oh, no, sir, I wasn't!" she cried. "My girl wasn't even here that night—I swear it!—she wasn't here. . . ."

She was badly shaken: the nervous tension of a week had snapped, and she looked helplessly about her.

"Come, come, Mrs. Platz," pleaded Vance consolingly. "No one believes for a moment that Miss Hoffman had a hand in Mr. Benson's death."

The woman peered searchingly into his face. At first she was loath to believe him,—it was evident that fear had long been preying on her mind,—and it took him fully a quarter of an hour

140. A Gothic-style structure at 5 East 48th Street, since 1978 the home of the Swedish Seamen's Church, it was built in 1920–21, and thus Vance's remarks render a crushing blow to the 1918 dating of the events. We must ultimately conclude that either (a)(i) the dates given in the chapter headings and (ii) the mention that the Elwell case occurred a few years after the Benson case are fictions or (b) this incident did not occur and was inserted long after the events by Van Dine. In light of the numerous references to the war and the tight time frame in which Major Benson's and Captain Leacock's French service would have had to occur in order to place the events in 1918, it seems more likely that the case actually occurred some time in the early 1920s and—for reasons unknown—other fictional date references were scattered carelessly throughout Van Dine's account of the event.

New York Bible Society Building.

141. Vance paraphrases Alfred, Lord Tennyson's 1842 poem "Lady Clara Vere de Vere":

"Kind hearts are more than coronets, / And simple faith than Norman blood." Lady Vere de Vere became a stereotype of the English nobility.

to convince her that what he had said was true. When, finally, we left the house she was in a comparatively peaceful state of mind.

On our way to the Stuyvesant Club Markham was silent, completely engrossed with his thoughts. It was evident that the new facts educed by the interview with Mrs. Platz troubled him considerably.

Vance sat smoking dreamily, turning his head now and then to inspect the buildings we passed. We drove east through Forty-eighth Street, and when we came abreast of the New York Bible Society House[140] he ordered the chauffeur to stop, and insisted that we admire it.

"Christianity," he remarked, "has almost vindicated itself by its architecture alone. With few exceptions, the only buildings in this city that are not eyesores, are the churches and their allied structures. The American æsthetic credo is: Whatever's big is beautiful. These depressin' gargantuan boxes with rectangular holes in 'em, which are called skyscrapers, are worshipped by Americans simply because they're huge. A box with forty rows of holes is twice as beautiful as a box with twenty rows. Simple formula, what? . . . Look at this little five-story affair across the street. It's inf'nitely lovelier—and more impressive, too—than any skyscraper in the city. . . ."

Vance referred but once to the crime during our ride to the Club, and then only indirectly.

"Kind hearts, y' know, Markham, are more than coronets.[141] I've done a good deed to-day, and I feel pos'tively virtuous. Frau Platz will *schlafen* much better to-night. She has been frightfully upset about little Gretchen. She's a doughty old soul; motherly and all that. And she couldn't bear to think of the future Lady Vere de Vere being suspected. . . . Wonder why she worried so?" And he gave Markham a sly look.

Nothing further was said until after dinner, which we ate in the Roof Garden. We had pushed back our chairs, and sat looking out over the treetops of Madison Square.

"Now, Markham," said Vance, "give over all prejudices, and consider the situation judiciously—as you lawyers euphemistically put it. . . . To begin with, we now know why Mrs. Platz was so worried at your question regarding fire-arms, and why she was upset by my ref'rence to her personal int'rest in Benson's tea-companion. So, those two mysteries are elim'nated. . . ."

"How did you find out about her relation to the girl?" interjected Markham.

"'T was my ogling did it." Vance gave him a reproving look. "You recall that I 'ogled' the young lady at our first meeting,—but I forgive you. . . . And you remember our little discussion about cranial idiosyncrasies? Miss Hoffman, I noticed at once, possessed all the physical formations of Benson's housekeeper. She was brachycephalic;[142] she had over-articulated cheek-bones, an orthognathous[143] jaw, a low flat parietal structure, and a mesorrhinian[144] nose. . . . Then I looked for her ear, for I had noted that Mrs. Platz had the pointed, lobeless, 'satyr' ear—sometimes called the Darwin ear.[145] These ears run in families; and when I saw that Miss Hoffman's were of the same type, even though modified, I was fairly certain of the relationship. But there were other similarities—in pigment, for instance; and in height,—both are tall, y' know. And the central masses of each were very large in comparison with the peripheral masses: the shoulders were narrow and the wrists and ankles small, while the hips were bulky. . . . That Hoffman was Platz's maiden name was only a guess. But it didn't matter."

Vance adjusted himself more comfortably in his chair.

"Now for your judicial considerations. . . . First, let us assume that at a little before half past twelve on the night of the thirteenth the villain came to Benson's house, saw the light in the living-room, tapped on the window, and was instantly admitted. . . . What, would you say, do these assumptions indicate regarding the visitor?"

"Merely that Benson was acquainted with him," returned Markham. "But that doesn't help us any. We can't extend the *sus. per coll.*[146] to everybody the man knew."

"The indications go much further than that, old chap," Vance retorted. "They show unmistakably that Benson's murderer was a most intimate crony, or, at least, a person before whom he didn't care how he looked. The absence of the toupee, as I once suggested to you, was a prime essential of the situation. A toupee, don't y' know, is the sartorial *sine qua non* of every middle-aged Beau Brummel afflicted with baldness. You heard Mrs. Platz on the subject. Do you think for a second that Benson, who hid his hirsute deficiency even from the grocer's boy, would visit with a mere acquaintance thus bereft of his crowning glory? And besides being thus denuded, he was without his full complement

142. A short, broad skull.

143. Neither projecting nor receding, making the face nearly vertical.

144. Medium-width.

145. The so-called satyr ear has an abnormally small upper portion; when the lobe is also underdeveloped, it is called the "devil ear." "Darwin's point" is on the inside of the earlobe. It was first described by Charles Darwin in *The Descent of Man* (where he called it the "Woolnerian tip," after British sculptor Thomas Woolner, who incorporated it in his work) and is cited by Darwin as a vestigial feature proving common ancestry among primates. It is present in about 10 percent of the population.

146. In England, judges were in the practice of writing the adjudicated sentence in the margin of the calendar. When the sentence was capital, the Latin verdict *"suspendatur per collum"* ("hang by the neck"), abbreviated as *sus. per coll.*, was entered.

of teeth. Moreover, he was without collar or tie, and attired in an old smoking-jacket and bed-room slippers! Picture the spectacle, my dear fellow. . . . A man does not look fascinatin' without his collar and with his shirt-band and gold stud exposed. Thus attired he is the equiv'lent of a lady in curl-papers. . . . How many men do you think Benson knew with whom he would have sat down to a *tête-à-tête* in this undress condition?"

"Three or four, perhaps," answered Markham. "But I can't arrest them all."

"I'm sure you would if you could. But it won't be necess'ry."

Vance selected another cigarette from his case, and went on:

"There are other helpful indications, y' know. For instance, the murderer was fairly well acquainted with Benson's domestic arrangements. He must have known that the housekeeper slept a good distance from the living-room and would not be startled by the shot if her door was closed as usual. Also, he must have known there was no one else in the house at that hour. And another thing: don't forget that his voice was perfectly familiar to Benson. If there had been the slightest doubt about it Benson would not have let him in, in view of his natural fear of house-breakers, and with the Captain's threat hanging over him."

"That's a tenable hypothesis. . . . What else?"

"The jewels, Markham—those orators of love. Have you thought of them? They were on the center-table when Benson came home that night; and they were gone in the morning. Wherefore, it seems inev'table that the murderer took 'em—eh, what? . . . And may they not have been one reason for the murderer's coming there that night? If so, who of Benson's most intimate *personæ gratæ* knew of their presence in the house? And who wanted 'em particularly?"

"Exactly, Vance." Markham nodded his head slowly. "You've hit it. I've had an uneasy feeling about Pfyfe right along. I was on the point of ordering his arrest to-day when Heath brought word of Leacock's confession; and then, when that blew up, my suspicions reverted to him. I said nothing this afternoon because I wanted to see where your ideas had led you. What you've been saying checks up perfectly with my own notions. Pfyfe's our man—"

He brought the front legs of his chair down suddenly.

"And now, damn it, you've let him get away from us!"

"Don't fret, old dear," said Vance. "He's safe with Mrs. Pfyfe, I fancy. And anyhow, your friend, Mr. Ben Hanlon, is well versed in retrieving fugitives. . . . Let the harassed Leander alone for the moment. You don't need him to-night—and to-morrow you won't want him."

Markham wheeled about.

"What's that!—I won't want him? . . And why, pray?"

"Well," Vance explained indolently; "he hasn't a congenial and lovable nature, has he? And he's not exactly an object of blindin' beauty. I shouldn't want him around me more than was necess'ry, don't y' know. . . . Incidentally, he's not guilty."

Markham was too nonplussed to be exasperated. He regarded Vance searchingly for a full minute.

"I don't follow you," he said. "If you think Pfyfe's innocent, who, in God's name, do you think is guilty?"

Vance glanced at his watch.

"Come to my house to-morrow for breakfast, and bring those alibis you asked Heath for; and I'll tell you who shot Benson."

Something in his tone impressed Markham. He realized that Vance would not have made so specific a promise unless he was confident of his ability to keep it. He knew Vance too well to ignore, or even minimize, his statement.

"Why not tell me now?" he asked.

"Awf'lly sorry, y' know," apologized Vance; "but I'm going to the Philharmonic's 'special' to-night. They're playing César Franck's D-minor, and Stransky's[147] temp'rament is em'nently suited to its diatonic sentimentalities. . . . You'd better come along, old man. Soothin' to the nerves and all that."

"Not me!" grumbled Markham. "What I need is a brandy-and-soda."

He walked down with us to the taxicab.

"Come at nine to-morrow," said Vance, as we took our seats. "Let the office wait a bit. And don't forget to 'phone Heath for those alibis."

Then, just as we started off, he leaned out of the car.

"And I say, Markham: how tall would you say Mrs. Platz was?"

147. Josef Stránský (1872–1936) conducted the New York Philharmonic from 1911 to 1923. César-Auguste-Jean-Guillaume-Hubert Franck (1822–1890), whose ideas about "cyclic" music had a strong influence on Claude Debussy and Maurice Ravel, is remembered today almost exclusively for his *Symphony in D Minor*.

CHAPTER XXII

Vance Outlines a Theory

(Thursday, June 20; 9 a.m.)

Markham came to Vance's apartment at promptly nine o'clock the next morning. He was in bad humor.

"Now, see here, Vance," he said, as soon as he was seated at the table; "I want to know what was the meaning of your parting words last night."

"Eat your melon, old dear," said Vance. "It comes from northern Brazil, and is very delicious. But don't devitalize its flavor with pepper or salt. An amazin' practice, that,—though not as amazin' as stuffing a melon with ice-cream. The American does the most dumbfoundin' things with ice-cream. He puts it on pie; he puts it in soda-water; he encases it in hard chocolate like a *bon-bon*; he puts it between sweet biscuits and calls the result an ice-cream sandwich; he even uses it instead of whipped cream in a Charlotte Russe. . . ."

"What I want to know—" began Markham; but Vance did not permit him to finish.

"It's surprisin', y' know, the erroneous ideas people have about melons. There are only two species—the muskmelon and the watermelon. All breakfast melons—like cantaloups, citrons, nutmegs, Cassabas, and Honeydews—are varieties of the muskmelon. But people have the notion, d' ye see, that cantaloup is a generic term. Philadelphians call all melons cantaloups; whereas this type of muskmelon was first cultivated in Cantalupo, Italy. . . ."

"Very interesting," said Markham, with only partly disguised impatience. "Did you intend by your remark last night—"

"And after the melon, Currie has prepared a special dish for you. It's my own gustat'ry *chefd'œuvre*—with Currie's collaboration, of course. I've spent months on its conception—composing and organizing it, so to speak. I haven't named it yet,—perhaps you can suggest a fitting appellation. . . . To achieve this dish, one first chops up a hard-boiled egg and mixes it with grated *Port du Salut* cheese, adding a *soupçon* of tarragon. This paste is then enclosed in a *filet* of white perch—like a French pancake. It is tied with silk, rolled in a specially prepared almond batter, and cooked in sweet butter.—That, of course, is the barest outline of its manufacture, with all the truly exquisite details omitted."

"It sounds appetizing." Markham's tone was devoid of enthusiasm. "But I didn't come here for a cooking lesson."

"Y' know, you underestimate the importance of your ventral pleasures," pursued Vance. "Eating is the one infallible guide to a people's intellectual advancement, as well as the inev'table gauge of the individual's temp'rament. The savage cooked and ate like a savage. In the early days of the human race, mankind was cursed with one vast epidemic of indigestion. There's where his devils and demons and ideas of hell came from: they were the nightmares of his dyspepsia. Then, as man began to master the technique of cooking, he became civilized; and when he achieved the highest pinnacles of the culin'ry art, he also achieved the highest pinnacles of cultural and intellectual glory. When the art of the *gourmet* retrogressed, so did man. The tasteless, standardized cookery of America is typical of our decadence. A perfectly blended soup, Markham, is more ennoblin' than Beethoven's C-minor Symphony. . . ."

Markham listened stolidly to Vance's chatter during breakfast. He made several attempts to bring up the subject of the crime, but Vance glibly ignored each essay. It was not until Currie had cleared away the dishes that he referred to the object of Markham's visit.

"Did you bring the alibi reports?" was his first question.

Markham nodded.

"And it took me two hours to find Heath after you'd gone last night."

"Sad," breathed Vance.

He went to the desk, and took a closely written double sheet of foolscap from one of the compartments.

"I wish you'd glance this over, and give me your learned opinion," he said, handing the paper to Markham. "I prepared it last night after the concert."

I later took possession of the document, and filed it with my other notes and papers pertaining to the Benson case. The following is a verbatim copy:

HYPOTHESIS

Mrs. Anna Platz shot and killed Alvin Benson on the night of June 13th.

PLACE

She lived in the house, and admitted being there at the time the shot was fired.

OPPORTUNITY

She was alone in the house with Benson.

All the windows were either barred or locked on the inside. The front door was locked. There was no other means of ingress.

Her presence in the living-room was natural: she might have entered ostensibly to ask Benson a domestic question.

Her standing directly in front of him would not necessarily have caused him to look up. Hence, his reading attitude.

Who else could have come so close to him for the purpose of shooting him, without attracting his attention?

He would not have cared how he appeared before his housekeeper. He had become accustomed to being seen by her without his teeth and toupee and in négligé condition.

Living in the house, she was able to choose a propitious moment for the crime.

TIME

She waited up for him. Despite her denial, he might have told her when he would return.

When he came in alone and changed to his smoking-jacket, she knew he was not expecting any late visitors. She chose a time shortly after his return because it would appear that he had brought someone home with him, and that this other person had killed him.

MEANS

She used Benson's own gun. Benson undoubtedly had more than one; for he would have been more likely to keep a gun in his bed-room than in his living-room; and since a Smith and Wesson was found in the living-room, there probably was another in the bed-room.

Being his housekeeper, she knew of the gun upstairs. After he had gone down to the living-room to read, she secured it, and took it with her, concealed under her apron.

She threw the gun away or hid it after the shooting. She had all night in which to dispose of it.

She was frightened when asked what fire-arms Benson kept about the house, for she was not sure whether or not we knew of the gun in the bed-room.

MOTIVE

She took the position of housekeeper because she feared Benson's conduct toward her daughter. She always listened when her daughter came to his house at night to work.

Recently she discovered that Benson had dishonorable intentions, and believed her daughter to be in imminent danger.

A mother who would sacrifice herself for her daughter's future, as she has done, would not hesitate at killing to save her.

And: there are the jewels. She has them hidden and is keeping them for her daughter. Would Benson have gone out and left them on the table? And if he had put them away, who but she, familiar with the house and having plenty of time, could have found them?

CONDUCT

She lied about St. Clair's coming to tea, explaining later that she knew St. Clair could not have had anything to do with the crime. Was this feminine intuition? No. She could know St. Clair was innocent only because she herself was guilty. She was too motherly to want an innocent person suspected.

She was markedly frightened yesterday when her daughter's name was mentioned, because she feared the discovery of the relationship might reveal her motive for shooting Benson.

She admitted hearing the shot, because, if she had denied it, a test might have proved that a shot in the living-room would have sounded loudly in her room; and this would have aroused suspicion against her. Does a person, when awakened, turn on the lights and determine the exact hour? And if she had heard a report which sounded like a shot being fired in the house, would she not have investigated, or given an alarm?

When first interviewed, she showed plainly she disliked Benson.

Her apprehension has been pronounced each time she has been questioned.

She is the hard-headed, shrewd, determined German type, who could both plan and perform such a crime.

HEIGHT

She is about five feet, ten inches tall—the demonstrated height of the murderer.

Markham read this *précis* through several times,—he was fully fifteen minutes at the task,—and when he had finished he sat silent for ten minutes more. Then he rose and walked up and down the room.

"Not a fancy legal document, that," remarked Vance. "But I think even a Grand Juror could understand it. You, of course, can rearrange and elab'rate it, and bedeck it with innum'rable meaningless phrases and recondite legal idioms."

Markham did not answer at once. He paused by the French windows and looked down into the street. Then he said:

"Yes, I think you've made out a case. . . . Extraordinary! I've wondered from the first what you were getting at; and your questioning of Platz yesterday impressed me as pointless. I'll admit it never occurred to me to suspect her. Benson must have given her good cause."

He turned and came slowly toward us, his head down, his hands behind him.

"I don't like the idea of arresting her. . . . Funny I never thought of her in connection with it."

He stopped in front of Vance.

"And you yourself didn't think of her at first, despite your boast that you knew who did it after you'd been in Benson's house five minutes."

Vance smiled mirthfully, and sprawled in his chair.

Markham became indignant.

"Damn it! You told me the next day that no woman could have done it, no matter what evidence, was adduced, and harangued me about art and psychology and God knows what."

"Quite right," murmured Vance, still smiling. "No woman did it."

"No woman did it!" Markham's gorge was rising rapidly.

"Oh, dear no!"

He pointed to the sheet of paper in Markham's hand.

"That's just a bit of spoofing, don't y' know. . . . Poor old Mrs. Platz!—she's as innocent as a lamb."

Markham threw the paper on the table and sat down. I had never seen him so furious; but he controlled himself admirably.

"Y' see, my dear old bean," explained Vance, in his unemotional drawl, "I had an irresistible longing to demonstrate to you how utterly silly your circumst'ntial and material evidence is. I'm rather proud, y' know, of my case against Mrs. Platz. I'm sure you could convict her on the strength of it. But, like the whole theory of your exalted law, it's wholly specious and erroneous. . . . Circumst'ntial evidence, Markham, is the utt'rest tommyrot imag'nable. Its theory is not unlike that of our presentday democracy. The democratic theory is that if you accumulate enough ignorance at the polls you produce intelligence; and the theory of circumst'ntial evidence is that if you accumulate a sufficient number of weak links you produce a strong chain."

"Did you get me here this morning," demanded Markham coldly, "to give me a dissertation on legal theory?"

"Oh, no," Vance blithely assured him. "But I simply must prepare you for the acceptance of my revelation; for I haven't a scrap of material or circumst'ntial evidence against the guilty man. And yet, Markham, I know he's guilty as well as I know you're sitting in that chair planning how you can torture and kill me without being punished."

"If you have no evidence, how did you arrive at your conclusion?" Markham's tone was vindictive.

"Solely by psychological analysis—by what might be called the science of personal possibilities. A man's psychological nature is as clear a brand to one who can read it as was Hester Prynne's scarlet letter. . . . I never read Hawthorne, by the bye. I can't abide the New England temp'rament."

Markham set his jaw, and gave Vance a look of arctic ferocity.

"You expect me to go into court, I suppose, leading your victim by the arm, and say to the Judge: 'Here's the man that shot Alvin Benson. I have no evidence against him, but I want you to sentence him to death, because my brilliant and sagacious friend, Mr. Philo Vance, the inventor of stuffed perch, says this man has a wicked nature.'"

Vance gave an almost imperceptible shrug.

"I sha'n't wither away with grief if you don't even arrest the guilty man. But I thought it no more than humane to tell you who he was, if only to stop you from chivvying all these innocent people."

"All right—tell me; and let me get on about my business."

I don't believe there was any longer a question in Markham's mind that Vance actually knew who had killed Benson. But it was not until considerably later in the morning that he fully understood why Vance had kept him for days upon tenter-hooks. When, at last, he did understand it, he forgave Vance; but at the moment he was angered to the limit of his control.

"There are one or two things that must be done before I can reveal the gentleman's name," Vance told him. "First, let me have a peep at those alibis."

Markham took from his pocket a sheaf of typewritten pages and passed them over.

Vance adjusted his monocle,[148] and read through them carefully. Then he stepped out of the room; and I heard him telephoning. When he returned he re-read the reports. One in particular he lingered over, as if weighing its possibilities.

"There's a chance, y' know," he murmured at length, gazing indecisively into the fireplace.

He glanced at the report again.

"I see here," he said, "that Colonel Ostrander, accompanied by a Bronx alderman named Moriarty, attended the Midnight Follies at the Piccadilly Theatre in Forty-seventh Street on the night of the thirteenth, arriving there a little before twelve and remaining through the performance, which was over about half past two a.m. . . . Are you acquainted with this particular alderman?"

Markham's eyes lifted sharply to the other's face.

"I've met Mr. Moriarty. What about him?" I thought I detected a note of suppressed excitement in his voice.

"Where do Bronx aldermen loll about in the forenoons?" asked Vance.

"At home, I should say. Or possibly at the Samoset Club. . . . Sometimes they have business at City Hall."

"My word!—such unseemly activity for a politician! . . . Would you mind ascertaining if Mr. Moriarty is at home or at his club. If it's not too much bother, I'd like to have a brief word with him."

Markham gave Vance a penetrating gaze. Then, without a word, he went to the telephone in the den.

"Mr. Moriarty was at home, about to leave for City Hall," he announced, on returning. "I asked him to drop by here on his way down town."

"I do hope he doesn't disappoint us," sighed Vance. "But it's worth trying."

"Are you composing a charade?" asked Markham; but there was neither humor nor good-nature in the question.

"'Pon my word, old man, I'm not trying to confuse the main issue," said Vance. "Exert a little of that simple faith with which

148. What happened to Vance's pince-nez? Or is this a *second* affectation?

you are so gen'rously supplied,—it's more desirable than Norman blood, y' know. I'll give you the guilty man before the morning's over. But, d' ye see, I must make sure that you'll accept him. These alibis are, I trust, going to prove most prof'table in paving the way for my *coup de boutoir*. . . . An alibi—as I recently confided to you—is a tricky and dang'rous thing, and open to grave suspicion. And the absence of an alibi means nothing at all. For instance, I see by these reports that Miss Hoffman has no alibi for the night of the thirteenth. She says she went to a motion-picture theatre and then home. But no one saw her at any time. She was prob'bly at Benson's visiting mama until late. Looks suspicious—eh, what? And yet, even if she was there, her only crime that night was filial affection. . . . On the other hand, there are several alibis here which are, as one says, cast-iron,—silly metaphor: cast-iron's easily broken—, and I happen to know one of 'em is spurious. So be a good fellow and have patience; for it's most necess'ry that these alibis be minutely inspected."

Fifteen minutes later Mr. Moriarty arrived. He was a serious, good-looking, well-dressed youth in his late twenties—not at all my idea of an alderman—, and he spoke clear and precise English with almost no trace of the Bronx accent.

Markham introduced him, and briefly explained why he had been requested to call.

"One of the men from the Homicide Bureau," answered Moriarty, "was asking me about the matter, only yesterday."

"We have the report," said Vance, "but it's a bit too general. Will you tell us exactly what you did that night after you met Colonel Ostrander?"

"The Colonel had invited me to dinner and the Follies. I met him at the Marseilles at ten. We had dinner there, and went to the Piccadilly a little before twelve, where we remained until about two-thirty. I walked to the Colonel's apartment with him, had a drink and a chat, and then took the subway home about three-thirty."

"You told the detective yesterday you sat in a box at the theatre."

"That's correct."

"Did you and the Colonel remain in the box throughout the performance?"

"No. After the first act a friend of mine came to the box, and the Colonel excused himself and went to the wash-room. After the second act, the Colonel and I stepped outside into the alleyway and had a smoke."

"What time, would you say, was the first act over?"

"Twelve-thirty or thereabouts."

"And where is this alley-way situated?" asked Vance. "As I recall, it runs along the side of the theatre to the street."

"You're right."

"And isn't there an 'exit' door very near the boxes, which leads into the alleyway?"

"There is. We used it that night."

"How long was the Colonel gone after the first act?"

"A few minutes—I couldn't say exactly."

"Had he returned when the curtain went up on the second act?"

Moriarty reflected.

"I don't believe he had. I think he came back a few minutes after the act began."

"Ten minutes?"

"I couldn't say. Certainly no more."

"Then, allowing for a ten-minute intermission, the Colonel might have been away twenty minutes?"

"Yes—it's possible."

This ended the interview; and when Moriarty had gone, Vance lay back in his chair and smoked thoughtfully.

"Surprisin' luck!" he commented. "The Piccadilly Theatre, y' know, is practically round the corner from Benson's house. You grasp the possibilities of the situation, what? . . . The Colonel invites an alderman to the Midnight Follies, and gets box seats near an exit giving on an alley. At a little before half past twelve he leaves the box, sneaks out *via* the alley, goes to Benson's, taps and is admitted, shoots his man, and hurries back to the theatre. Twenty minutes would have been ample."

Markham straightened up, but made no comment.

"And now," continued Vance, "let's look at the indicat'ry circumst'nces and the confirmat'ry facts. . . . Miss St. Clair told us the Colonel had lost heavily in a pool of Benson's manipulation, and had accused him of crookedness. He hadn't spoken to Benson for a week; so it's plain there was bad blood between 'em.—He saw Miss St. Clair at the Marseilles with Benson; and, knowing she always went home at midnight, he chose half past twelve as a propitious hour; although originally he may have intended to wait until much later; say, one-thirty or two—before sneaking out of the theatre.—Being an army officer, he would have had a Colt forty-five; and he was probably a good shot.—He was most anxious to have you arrest someone—he didn't seem to care who; and he even 'phoned you to inquire about it.—He was one of the very few persons in the world whom Benson would have admitted, attired as he was. He'd known Benson int'mately for fifteen years, and Mrs. Platz once saw Benson take off his toupee and show it to him.—Moreover, he would have known all about the domestic arrangements of the house: he no doubt had slept there many a time when showing his old pal the wonders of New York's night life. . . . How does all that appeal to you?"

Markham had risen, and was pacing the floor, his eyes almost closed.

"So that was why you were so interested in the Colonel—asking people if they knew him, and inviting him to lunch? . . . What gave you the idea, in the first place, that he was guilty?"

"Guilty!" exclaimed Vance. "That priceless old dunderhead guilty! Really, Markham, the notion's prepost'rous. I'm sure he went to the wash-room that night to comb his eyebrows and arrange his tie. Sitting, as he was, in a box, the gels on the stage could see him, y' know."

Markham halted abruptly. An ugly color crept into his cheeks, and his eyes blazed. But before he could speak Vance went on, with serene indifference to his anger.

"And I played in the most astonishin' luck. Still, he's just the kind of ancient popinjay who'd go to the wash-room and dandify himself,—I rather counted on that, don't y' know. . . . My word! We've made amazin' progress this morning, despite your injured feelings. You now have five different people, any one of whom you can, with a little legal ingenuity, convict of the crime,—in any event, you can get indictments against 'em."

He leaned his head back meditatively.

"First, there's Miss St. Clair. You were quite pos'tive she did the deed, and you told the Major you were all ready to arrest her. My demonstration of the murderer's height could be thrown out on the grounds that it was intelligent and conclusive, and therefore had no place in a court of law. I'm sure the judge would concur.—Secondly, I give you Captain Leacock. I actu'lly had to use physical force to keep you from jailing the chap. You had a beautiful case against him—to say nothing of his delightful confession. And if you met with any diff'culties, he'd help you out: he'd adore having you convict him.—Thirdly, I submit Leander the Lovely. You had a better case against him than against almost any one of the others—a perfect wealth of circumst'ntial evidence—an *embarras de richesse*, in fact. And any jury would delight in convicting him,—I would, myself, if only for the way he dresses.—Fourthly, I point with pride to Mrs. Platz. Another perfect circumst'ntial case, fairly bulging with clues and inf'rences and legal whatnots.—Fifthly, I present the Colonel. I have just rehearsed your case against him; and I could elab'rate it touchin'ly, given a little more time."

He paused, and gave Markham a smile of cynical affability.

"Observe, please, that each member of this quintette meets all the demands of presumptive guilt: each one fulfills the legal requirements as to time, place, opportunity, means, motive, and conduct. The only drawback, d' ye see, is that all five are quite innocent. A most discomposin' fact—but there you are. . . . Now, if all the people against whom there's the slightest suspicion, are innocent, what's to be done? . . . Annoyin', ain't it?"

He picked up the alibi reports.

"There's pos'tively nothing to be done but to go on checking up these alibis."

I could not imagine what goal he was trying to reach by these apparently irrelevant digressions; and Markham, too, was mystified. But neither of us doubted for a moment that there was method in his madness.

"Let's see," he mused. "The Major's is the next in order. What do you say to tackling it? It shouldn't take long: he lives near here; and the entire alibi hinges on the evidence of the night-boy at his apartment-house.—Come!" He got up.

"How do you know the boy is there now?" objected Markham.

"I 'phoned a while ago and found out."

"But this is damned nonsense!"

Vance now had Markham by the arm, playfully urging him toward the door.

"Oh, undoubtedly," he agreed. "But I've often told you, old dear, you take life much too seriously."

Markham, protesting vigorously, held back, and endeavored to disengage his arm from the other's grip. But Vance was determined; and after a somewhat heated dispute, Markham gave in.

"I'm about through with this hocus-pocus," he growled, as we got into a taxicab.

"I'm through already," said Vance.

CHAPTER XXIII

Checking an Alibi

(Thursday, June 20; 10.30 a.m.)

*   [Author's note:] The boy was Jack Prisco, of 621 Kelly Street.

The Chatham Arms, where Major Benson lived, was a small exclusive bachelor apartment-house in Forty-sixth Street, midway between Fifth and Sixth Avenues. The entrance, set in a simple and dignified façade, was flush with the street, and only two steps above the pavement. The front door opened into a narrow hallway with a small reception room, like a *cul-de-sac*, on the left. At the rear could be seen the elevator; and beside it, tucked under a narrow flight of iron stairs which led round the elevator shaft, was a telephone switchboard.

When we arrived two youths in uniform were on duty, one lounging in the door of the elevator, the other seated at the switchboard.

Vance halted Markham near the entrance.

"One of these boys, I was informed over the telephone, was on duty the night of the thirteenth. Find out which one it was, and scare him into submission by your exalted title of District Attorney. Then turn him over to me."

Reluctantly Markham walked down the hallway. After a brief interrogation of the boys, he led one of them into the reception room, and peremptorily explained what he wanted.*

Vance began his questioning with the confident air of one who has no doubt whatever as to another's exact knowledge.

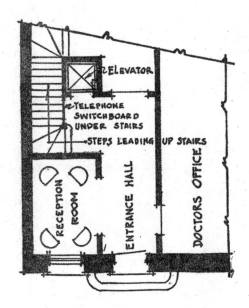

WEST 46TH. STREET

First floor of Chatham Arms Apartment in
West Forty-sixth Street

Diagram of the first floor of Major Benson's apartment-house,
from *The Benson Murder Case*, artist unknown.

"What time did Major Benson get home the night his brother was shot?"

The boy's eyes opened wide.

"He came in about 'leven—right after show time," he answered, with only a momentary hesitation.

(I have set down the rest of the questions and answers in dramatic-dialogue form, for purposes of space economy.)

VANCE: He spoke to you, I suppose?

BOY: Yes, sir. He told me he'd been to the theatre, and said what a rotten show it was—and that he had an awful headache.

VANCE: How do you happen to remember so well what he said a week ago?

BOY: Why, his brother was murdered that night!

VANCE: And the murder caused so much excitement that you naturally recalled everything that happened at the time in connection with Major Benson?

BOY: Sure—he was the murdered guy's brother.

VANCE: When he came in that night did he say anything about the day of the month?

BOY: Nothin' except that he guessed his bad luck in pickin' a bum show was on account of it bein' the thirteenth.

VANCE: Did he say anything else?

BOY (*grinning*): He said he'd make the thirteenth my lucky day, and he gave me all the silver he had in his pocket—nickels and dimes and quarters and one fifty-cent piece.

VANCE: How much altogether?

BOY: Three dollars and forty-five cents.

VANCE: And then he went to his room?

BOY: Yes, sir—I took him up. He lives on the third floor.

VANCE: Did he go out again later?

BOY: No, sir.

VANCE: How do you know?

BOY: I'd 've seen him. I was either answerin' the switchboard or runnin' the elevator all night. He couldn't 've got out without my seein' him.

VANCE: Were you alone on duty?

BOY: After ten o'clock there's never but one boy on.

VANCE: And there's no other way a person could leave the house except by the front door?

BOY: No, sir.

VANCE: When did you next see Major Benson?

BOY (*after thinking a moment*): He rang for some cracked ice, and I took it up.

VANCE: What time?

BOY: Why—I don't know exactly. . . . Yes, I do! It was half past twelve.

VANCE (*smiling faintly*): He asked you the time, perhaps?

BOY: Yes, sir, he did. He asked me to look at his clock in his parlor.

VANCE: How did he happen to do that?

BOY: Well, I took up the ice, and he was in bed; and he asked me to put it in his pitcher in the parlor. When I was doin' it he called to me to look at the clock on the mantel and tell him what time it was. He said his watch had stopped and he wanted to set it.

VANCE: What did he say then?

BOY: Nothin' much. He told me not to ring his bell, no matter who called up. He said he wanted to sleep, and didn't want to be woke up.

VANCE: Was he emphatic about it?

BOY: Well—he meant it, all right.

VANCE: Did he say anything else?

BOY: No. He just said good-night and turned out the light, and I came on downstairs.

VANCE: What light did he turn out?

BOY: The one in his bed-room.

VANCE: Could you see into his bed-room from the parlor?

BOY: No. The bed-room's off the hall.

VANCE: How could you tell the light was turned off then?

BOY: The bed-room door was open, and the light was shinin' into the hall.

VANCE: Did you pass the bed-room door when you went out?

BOY: Sure—you have to.

VANCE: And was the door still open?

BOY: Yes.

VANCE: Is that the only door to the bed-room?

BOY: Yes.

VANCE: Where was Major Benson when you entered the apartment?

BOY: In bed.

VANCE: How do you know?

BOY (*mildly indignant*): I saw him.

VANCE (*after a pause*): You're quite sure he didn't come downstairs again?

BOY: I told you I'd 've seen him if he had.

VANCE: Couldn't he have walked down at some time when you had the elevator upstairs, without your seeing him?

BOY: Sure, he could. But I didn't take the elevator up after I'd took the Major his cracked ice until round two-thirty, when Mr. Montagu came in.

VANCE: You took no one up in the elevator, then, between the time you brought Major Benson the ice and when Mr. Montagu came in at two-thirty?

BOY: Nobody.

VANCE: And you didn't leave the hall here between those hours?

BOY: No. I was sittin' here all the time.

VANCE: Then the last time you saw him was in bed at twelve-thirty?

BOY: Yes—until early in the morning when some dame* 'phoned him and said his brother had been murdered. He came down and went out about ten minutes after.

VANCE (*giving the boy a dollar*): That's all. But don't you open your mouth to anyone about our being here, or you may find yourself in the lock-up—understand? . . . Now, get back to your job.

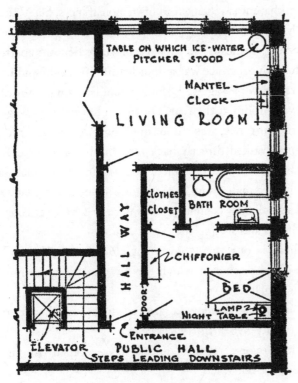

Third floor of Chatham Arms Apartment in West Forty-sixth Street.

Diagram of the third floor of Chatham Arms Apartment, from *The Benson Murder Case*, artist unknown.

149. See note 155, below, for the problems such an approach would cause today.

When the boy had left us, Vance turned a pleading gaze upon Markham.

"Now, old man, for the protection of society, and the higher demands of justice, and the greatest good for the greatest number, and *pro bono publico*, and that sort of thing, you must once more adopt a course of conduct contr'ry to your innate promptings—or whatever the phrase you used. Vulgarly put, I want to snoop through the Major's apartment at once."[149]

"What for?" Markham's tone was one of exclamatory protest. "Have you completely lost your senses? There's no getting round the boy's testimony. I may be weak-minded, but I know when a witness like that is telling the truth."

"Certainly, he's telling the truth," agreed Vance serenely. "That's just why I want to go up.—Come, my Markham. There's no danger of the Major returning *en surprise* at this hour. . . . And"—he smiled cajolingly—"you promised me every assistance, don't y' know."

Markham was vehement in his remonstrances, but Vance was equally vehement in his insistence; and a few minutes later we were trespassing, by means of a pass-key, in Major Benson's apartment.

The only entrance was a door leading from the public hall into a narrow passageway which extended straight ahead into the living-room at the rear. On the right of this passageway, near the entrance, was a door opening into the bed-room.

Vance walked directly back into the living-room. On the right-hand wall was a fireplace and a mantel on which sat an oldfashioned mahogany clock. Near the mantel, in the far corner, stood a small table containing a silver ice-water service consisting of a pitcher and six goblets.

"There is our very convenient clock," said Vance. "And there is the pitcher in which the boy put the ice—imitation Sheffield plate."

Going to the window he glanced down into the paved rear court twenty-five or thirty feet below.

"The Major certainly couldn't have escaped through the window," he remarked.

He turned and stood a moment looking into the passageway.

"The boy could easily have seen the light go out in the bed-room, if the door was open. The reflection on the glazed white wall of the passage would have been quite brilliant."

Then, retracing his steps, he entered the bed-room. It contained a small canopied bed facing the door, and beside it stood a nighttable on which was an electric lamp. Sitting down on the edge of the bed, he looked about him, and turned the lamp on and off by the socketchain. Presently he fixed his eyes on Markham.

"You see how the Major got out without the boy's knowing it—eh, what?"

"By levitation, I suppose," submitted Markham.

"It amounted to that, at any rate," replied Vance. "Deuced ingenious, too. . . . Listen, Markham:—At half past twelve the Major rang for cracked ice. The boy brought it, and when he entered he looked in through the door, which was open, and saw the Major in bed. The Major told him to put the ice in the pitcher in the living-room. The boy walked on down the passage and across the living-room to the table in the corner. The Major then called to him to learn the time by the clock on the mantel. The boy looked: it was half past twelve. The Major replied that he was not to be disturbed again, said good-night, turned off this light on this night-table, jumped out of bed—he was dressed, of course—and stepped quickly out into the public hall before the boy had time to empty the ice and return to the passage. The Major ran down the stairs and was in the street before the elevator descended. The boy, when he passed the bed-room door on his way out, could not have seen whether the Major was still in bed or not, even if he had looked in, for the room was then in darkness.—Clever, what?"

"The thing would have been possible, of course," conceded Markham. "But your specious imaginings fail to account for his return."

"That was the simplest part of the scheme. He prob'bly waited in a doorway across the street for some other tenant to go in. The boy said a Mr. Montagu returned about two-thirty. Then the Major slipped in when he knew the elevator had ascended, and walked up the stairs."

Markham, smiling patiently, said nothing.

"You perceived," continued Vance, "the pains taken by the Major to establish the date and the hour, and to impress them on the boy's mind. Poor show—headache—unlucky day. Why unlucky? The thirteenth, to be sure. But lucky for the boy. A handful of money—all silver. Singular way of tipping, what? But a dollar bill might have been forgotten."

A shadow clouded Markham's face, but his voice was as indulgently impersonal as ever.

"I prefer your case against Mrs. Platz."

"Ah, but I've not finished." Vance stood up. "I have hopes of finding the weapon, don't y' know."

Markham now studied him with amused incredulity.

"That, of course, would be a contributory factor. . . . You really expect to find it?"

"Without the slightest diff'culty," Vance pleasantly assured him.

He went to the chiffonier and began opening the drawers.

"Our absent host didn't leave the pistol at Alvin's house; and he was far too canny to throw it away. Being a major in the late war, he'd be expected to have such a weapon: in fact, several persons may actu'lly have known he possessed one. And if he is innocent—as he fully expects us to assume—why shouldn't it be in its usual place? Its absence, d' ye see, would be more incriminatin' than its presence. Also, there's a most int'restin' psychological factor involved. An innocent person who was afraid of being thought guilty, would have hidden it, or thrown it away—like Captain Leacock, for example. But a guilty man, wishing to create an appearance of innocence, would have put it back exactly where it was before the shooting."

He was still searching through the chiffonier.

"Our only problem, then, is to discover the custom'ry abiding place of the Major's gun. . . . It's not here in the chiffonier," he added, closing the last drawer.

He opened a kit-bag standing at the foot of the bed, and rifled its contents.

"Nor here," he murmured indifferently. "The clothes-closet is the only other likely place."

Going across the room, he opened the closet door. Unhurriedly he switched on the light. There, on the upper shelf, in plain view, lay an army belt with a bulging holster.

Vance lifted it with extreme delicacy and placed it on the bed near the window.

"There you are, old chap," he cheerfully announced, bending over it closely. "Please take particular note that the entire belt and holster—with only the exception of the holster's flap—is thickly coated with dust. The flap is comparatively clean, showing it has been opened recently. . . . Not conclusive, of course; but you're so partial to clues, Markham."

He carefully removed the pistol from the holster.

"Note, also, that the gun itself is innocent of dust. It has been recently cleaned, I surmise."

His next act was to insert a corner of his handkerchief into the barrel. Then, withdrawing it, he held it up.

"You see—eh, what? Even the inside of the barrel is immaculate. . . . And I'll wager all my Cézannes against an LL.B. degree, that there isn't a cartridge missing."

He extracted the magazine, and poured the cartridges onto the night-table, where they lay in a neat row before us. There were seven—the full number for that style of gun.

"Again, Markham, I present you with one of your revered clues. Cartridges that remain in a magazine for a long time become slightly tarnished, for the catch-plate is not air-tight. But a fresh box of cartridges is well sealed, and its contents retain their lustre much longer."

He pointed to the first cartridge that had rolled out of the magazine.

"Observe that this one cartridge—the last to be inserted into the magazine—is a bit brighter than its fellows. The inf'rence is—you're an adept at inf'rences, y' know—that it is a newer cartridge, and was placed in the magazine rather recently."

He looked straight into Markham's eyes.

"It was placed there to take the place of the one which Captain Hagedorn is keeping."

Markham lifted his head jerkily, as if shaking himself out of an encroaching spell of hypnosis. He smiled, but with an effort.

"I still think your case against Mrs. Platz is your masterpiece."

"My picture of the Major is merely blocked in," answered Vance. "The revealin' touches are to come. But first, a brief catechism: . . . How did the Major know that brother Alvin would be home at twelve-thirty on the night of the thirteenth?—He heard Alvin invite Miss St. Clair to dinner—remember Miss Hoffman's story of his eavesdropping?—and he also heard her say she'd unfailingly leave at midnight. When I said yesterday, after we had left Miss St. Clair, that something she told us would help convict the guilty person, I referred to her statement that midnight was her invariable hour of departure. The Major therefore knew Alvin would be home about half past twelve, and he was pretty sure that no one else would be there. In any event, he could have waited for him, what? . . . Could he have secured an immediate audience with his brother *en déshabillé*?—Yes. He tapped on the window: his voice was recognized beyond any shadow of doubt; and he was admitted instanter. Alvin had no sartorial modesties in front of his brother, and would have thought nothing of receiving him without his teeth and toupee. . . . Is the Major the right height?—He is. I purposely stood beside him in your office the other day; and he is almost exactly five feet, ten and a half."

Markham sat staring silently at the disembowelled pistol. Vance had been speaking in a voice quite different from that he had used when constructing his hypothetical cases against the others; and Markham had sensed the change.

"We now come to the jewels," Vance was saying. "I once expressed the belief, you remember, that when we found the security for Pfyfe's note, we would put our hands on the murderer. I thought then the Major had the jewels; and after Miss Hoffman told us of his requesting her not to mention the package, I was sure of it. Alvin took them home on the afternoon of the thirteenth, and the Major undoubtedly knew it. This fact, I imagine, influenced his decision to end Alvin's life that night. He wanted those baubles, Markham."

He rose jauntily and stepped to the door.

"And now, it remains only to find 'em. . . . The murderer took 'em away with him; they couldn't have left the house any other way. Therefore, they're in this apartment. If the Major had taken them to the office, someone might have seen them; and if he had placed them in a safe deposit-box, the clerk at the bank might have remembered the episode. Moreover, the same psychology that applies to the gun, applies to the jewels. The Major has acted throughout on the assumption of his innocence; and, as a matter of fact, the trinkets were safer here than elsewhere. There'd be time enough to dispose of them when the affair blew over. . . . Come with me a moment, Markham. It's painful, I know; and your heart's too weak for an anæsthetic."

Markham followed him down the passageway in a kind of daze. I felt a great sympathy for the man, for now there was no question that he knew Vance was serious in his demonstration of the Major's guilt. Indeed, I have always felt that Markham suspected the true purpose of Vance's request to investigate the Major's alibi, and that his opposition was due as much to his fear of the results as to his impatience with the other's irritating methods. Not that he would have balked ultimately at the truth, despite his long friendship for Major Benson; but he was struggling—as I see it now—with the inevitability of circumstances, hoping against hope that he had read Vance incorrectly, and that, by vigorously contesting each step of the way, he might alter the very shape of destiny itself.

Vance led the way to the living-room, and stood for five minutes inspecting the various pieces of furniture, while Markham remained in the doorway watching him through narrowed lids, his hands crowded deep into his pockets.

"We could, of course, have an expert searcher rake the apartment over inch by inch," observed Vance. "But I don't think it necess'ry. The Major's a bold, cunning soul: witness his wide square forehead, the dominating stare of his globular eyes, the perpendicular spine, and the indrawn abdomen. He's forthright in all his mental operations. Like Poe's Minister D—[150], he would recognize the futility of painstakingly secreting the jewels in some obscure corner. And anyhow, he had no object in secreting them. He merely wished to hide 'em where there'd be no chance of their being seen. This naturally suggests a lock and key, what? There was no such *cache* in the bed-room—which is why I came here."

He walked to a squat rose-wood desk in the corner, and tried all its drawers; but they were unlocked. He next tested the table drawer; but that, too, was unlocked. A small Spanish cabinet by the window proved equally disappointing.

"Markham, I simply must find a locked drawer," he said.

He inspected the room again, and was about to return to the bed-room when his eye fell on a Circassian-walnut humidor half hidden by a pile of magazines on the under-shelf of the center-table. He stopped abruptly, and going quickly to the box, endeavored to lift the top. It was locked.

"Let's see," he mused: "what does the Major smoke? *Romeo y Juliet a Perfeccionados*, I believe—but they're not sufficiently valuable to keep under lock and key."

150. "Minister D—" is the thief who hid the "purloined letter" in plain sight in the eponymous tale by Edgar Allan Poe.

151. Vance here misquotes Shakespeare's *Two Gentlemen of Verona*: "Dumb jewels often in their silent kind. / More than quick words do move a woman's mind," in Act III, Scene 1.

He picked up a strong bronze paper-knife lying on the table, and forced its point into the crevice of the humidor just above the lock.

"You can't do that!" cried Markham; and there was as much pain as reprimand in his voice.

Before he could reach Vance, however, there was a sharp click, and the lid flew open. Inside was a blue-velvet jewel-case.

"Ah! 'Dumb jewels more quick than words,'"[151] said Vance, stepping back.

Markham stood staring into the humidor with an expression of tragic distress. Then slowly he turned and sank heavily into a chair.

"Good God!" he murmured. "I don't know what to believe."

"In that respect," returned Vance, "you're in the same disheartenin' predic'ment as all the philosophers.—But you were ready enough, don't y' know, to believe in the guilt of half a dozen innocent people. Why should you gag at the Major, who actu'lly is guilty?"

His tone was contemptuous, but a curious, inscrutable look in his eyes belied his voice; and I remembered that, although these two men were welded in an indissoluble friendship, I had never heard a word of sentiment, or even sympathy, pass between them.

Markham had leaned forward in an attitude of hopelessness, elbows on knees, his head in his hands.

"But the motive!" he urged. "A man doesn't shoot his brother for a handful of jewels."

"Certainly not," agreed Vance. "The jewels were a mere addendum. There was a vital motive—rest assured. And, I fancy, when you get your report from the expert accountant, all—or at least a goodly part—will be revealed."

"So that was why you wanted his books examined?"

Markham stood up resolutely.

"Come: I'm going to see this thing through."

Vance did not move at once. He was intently studying a small antique candlestick of oriental design on the mantel.

"I say!" he muttered. "That's a dev'lish fine copy!"

CHAPTER XXIV

The Arrest

(Thursday, June 20; noon.)

On leaving the apartment, Markham took with him the pistol and the case of jewels. In the drug store at the corner of Sixth Avenue he telephoned Heath to meet him immediately at the office, and to bring Captain Hagedorn. He also telephoned Stitt, the public accountant, to report as soon as possible.

"You observe, I trust," said Vance, when we were in the taxicab headed for the Criminal Courts Building, "the great advantage of my methods over yours. When one knows at the outset who committed a crime, one isn't misled by appearances. Without that foreknowledge, one is apt to be deceived by a clever alibi, for example. . . . I asked you to secure the alibis because, knowing the Major was guilty, I thought he'd have prepared a good one."

"But why ask for all of them? And why waste time trying to disprove Colonel Ostrander's?"

"What chance would I have had of securing the Major's alibi, if I had not injected his name surreptitiously, as it were, into a list of other names? . . . And had I asked you to check the Major's alibi first, you'd have refused. I chose the Colonel's alibi to start with because it seemed to offer a loophole,—and I was lucky in the choice. I knew that if I could puncture one of the other alibis, you would be more inclined to help me test the Major's."

"But if, as you say, you knew from the first that the Major was guilty, why, in God's name, didn't you tell me, and save me this week of anxiety?"

"Don't be ingenuous, old man," returned Vance. "If I had accused the Major at the beginning, you'd have had me arrested for *scandalum magnatum* and criminal libel. It was only by deceivin' you every minute about the Major's guilt, and drawing a whole school of red herrings across the trail, that I was able to get you to accept the fact even to-day. And yet, not once did I actu'lly lie to you. I was constantly throwing out suggestions, and pointing to significant facts, in the hope that you'd see the light for yourself; but you ignored all my intimations, or else misinterpreted them, with the most irritatin' perversity."

Markham was silent a moment.

"I see what you mean. But why did you keep setting up these straw men and then knocking them over?"

"You were bound, body and soul, to circumst'ntial evidence," Vance pointed out. "It was only by letting you see that it led you nowhere that I was able to foist the Major on you. There was no evidence against him,—he naturally saw to that. No one even regarded him as a possibility: fratricide has been held as inconceivable—a *lusus naturæ*—since the days of Cain. Even with all my finessing you fought every inch of the way, objectin' to this and that, and doing everything imag'nable to thwart my humble efforts. . . . Admit, like a good fellow, that, had it not been for my assiduousness, the Major would never have been suspected."

Markham nodded slowly.

"And yet, there are some things I don't understand even now. Why, for instance, should he have objected so strenuously to my arresting the Captain?"

Vance wagged his head.

"How deuced obvious you are! Never attempt a crime, my Markham,—you'd be instantly apprehended. I say, can't you see how much more impregnable the Major's position would be if he showed no int'rest in your arrests—if, indeed, he appeared actu'lly to protest against your incarc'ration of a victim. Could he, by any other means, have elim'nated so completely all possible suspicion against himself? Moreover, he knew very well that nothing he could say would swerve you from your course. You're so noble, don't y' know."

"But he did give me the impression once or twice that he thought Miss St. Clair was guilty."

"Ah! There you have a shrewd intelligence taking advantage of an opportunity. The Major unquestionably planned the crime so as to cast suspicion on the Captain. Leacock had publicly threatened his brother in connection with Miss St. Clair; and the lady was about to dine alone with Alvin. When, in the morning, Alvin was found shot with an army Colt, who but the Captain would be suspected? The Major knew the Captain lived alone, and that he would have diff'culty in establishing an alibi. Do you now see how cunning he was in recommending Pfyfe as a source of information? He knew that if you interviewed Pfyfe, you'd hear of the threat. And don't ignore the fact that his suggestion of Pfyfe was an apparent after-thought: he wanted to make it appear casual, don't y' know.—Astute devil, what?"

Markham, sunk in gloom, was listening closely.

"Now for the opportunity of which he took advantage," continued Vance. "When you upset his calculations by telling him you knew whom Alvin dined with, and that you had almost enough evidence to ask for an indictment, the idea appealed to him. He knew no charmin' lady could ever be convicted of murder in this most chivalrous city, no matter what the evidence; and he had enough of the sporting instinct in him to prefer that no one should actu'lly be punished for the crime. Cons'quently, he was willing to switch you back to the lady. And he played his hand cleverly, making it appear that he was most reluctant to involve her."

"Was that why, when you wanted me to examine his books and to ask him to the office to discuss the confession, you told me to intimate that I had Miss St. Clair in mind?"

"Exactly!"

"And the person the Major was shielding—"

"Was himself. But he wanted you to think it was Miss St. Clair."

"If you were certain he was guilty, why did you bring Colonel Ostrander into the case?"

"In the hope that he could supply us with faggots for the Major's funeral pyre. I knew he was acquainted intimately with Alvin Benson and his entire *camarilla*; and I knew, too, that he was an egregious quidnunc who might have got wind of some enmity between the Benson boys, and have suspected the truth. And I also wanted to get a line on Pfyfe, by way of elim'nating every remote counter possibility."

"But we already had a line on Pfyfe."

"Oh, I don't mean material clues. I wanted to learn about Pfyfe's nature—his psychology, y' know,—particularly his personality as a gambler. Y' see, it was the crime of a calculating, cold-blooded gambler; and no one but a man of that particular type could possibly have committed it."

Markham apparently was not interested just now in Vance's theories.

"Did you believe the Major," he asked, "when he said his brother had lied to him about the presence of the jewels in the safe?"

"The wily Alvin prob'bly never mentioned 'em to Anthony," rejoined Vance. "An ear at the door during one of Pfyfe's visits was, I fancy, his source of information. . . . And speaking of the Major's eavesdropping, it was that which suggested to me a possible motive for the crime. Your man Stitt, I hope, will clarify that point."

"According to your theory, the crime was rather hastily conceived." Markham's statement was in reality a question.

"The details of its execution were hastily conceived," corrected Vance. "The Major undoubtedly had been contemplating for some time elim'nating his brother. Just how or when he was to do it, he hadn't decided. He may have thought out and rejected a dozen plans. Then, on the thirteenth, came the opportunity: all the conditions adjusted themselves to his purpose. He heard Miss St. Clair's promise to go to dinner; and he therefore knew that Alvin would prob'bly be home alone at twelve-thirty, and that, if he were done away with at that hour, suspicion would fall on Captain Leacock. He saw Alvin take home the jewels—another prov'dential circumst'nce. The propitious moment for which he had been waiting, d' ye see, was at hand. All that remained was to establish an alibi and work out a *modus operandi*. How he did this, I've already eluc'dated."

Markham sat thinking for several minutes. At last he lifted his head.

"You've about convinced me of his guilt," he admitted. "But damn it, man! I've got to prove it; and there's not much actual legal evidence."

Vance gave a slight shrug.

"I'm not int'rested in your stupid courts and your silly rules of evidence. But, since I've convinced you, you can't charge me with not having met your challenge, don't y' know."

"I suppose not," Markham assented gloomily.

Slowly the muscles about his mouth tightened.

"You've done your share, Vance. I'll carry on."

Heath and Captain Hagedorn were waiting when we arrived at the office, and Markham greeted them in his customary reserved, matter-of-fact way. By now he had himself well in hand, and he went about the task before him with the sombre forcefulness that characterized him in the discharge of all his duties.

"I think we at last have the right man, Sergeant," he said. "Sit down, and I'll go over the matter with you in a moment. There are one or two things I want to attend to first."

He handed Major Benson's pistol to the fire-arms expert.

"Look that gun over, Captain, and tell me if there's any way of identifying it as the weapon that killed Benson."

Hagedorn moved ponderously to the window. Laying the pistol on the sill, he took several tools from the pockets of his voluminous coat, and placed them beside the weapon. Then, adjusting a jeweller's magnifying glass to his eye, he began what seemed an interminable series of tinkerings. He opened the plates of the stock, and drawing back the sear, took out the firing-pin. He removed the slide, unscrewed the link, and extracted the recoil spring. I thought he was going to take the weapon entirely apart, but apparently he merely wanted to let light into the barrel; for presently he held the gun to the window and placed his eye at the muzzle. He peered into the barrel for nearly five minutes, moving it slightly back and forth to catch the reflection of the sun on different points of the interior.

At last, without a word, he slowly and painstakingly went through the operation of redintegrating the weapon. Then he lumbered back to his chair, and sat blinking heavily for several moments.

"I'll tell you," he said, thrusting his head forward and gazing at Markham over the tops of his steel-rimmed spectacles. "This, now, may be the right gun. I wouldn't say for sure. But when I saw the bullet the other morning I noticed some peculiar rifling marks on it; and the rifling in this gun here looks to me as though

[Editor's note: This is a dating clue. The helixometer was developed no earlier than 1920 (some sources say 1923) by John H. Fisher of the New York Bureau of Forensic Ballistics.]

A helixometer at work
(Cover of *Popular Science*, August 1931).

it would match up with the marks on the bullet. I'm not certain. I'd like to look at this barrel through my helixometer."*

"But you believe it's the gun?" insisted Markham.

"I couldn't say, but I think so. I might be wrong."

"Very good, Captain. Take it along, and call me the minute you've inspected it thoroughly."

"It's the gun, all right," asserted Heath, when Hagedorn had gone. "I know that bird. He wouldn't 've said as much as he did if he hadn't been sure. . . . Whose gun is it, sir?"

"I'll answer you presently." Markham was still battling against the truth—withholding, even from himself, his pronouncement of the Major's guilt until every loop-hole of doubt should be closed. "I want to hear from Stitt before I say anything. I sent him to look over Benson and Benson's books. He'll be here any moment."

After a wait of a quarter of an hour, during which time Markham attempted to busy himself with other matters, Stitt came in. He said a sombre good-morning to the District Attorney and Heath; then, catching sight of Vance, smiled appreciatively.

"That was a good tip you gave me. You had the dope. If you'd kept Major Benson away longer, I could have done more. While he was there he was watching me every minute."

"I did the best I could," sighed Vance. He turned to Markham: "Y' know, I was wondering all through lunch yesterday how I could remove the Major from his office during Mr. Stitt's investigation; and when we learned of Leacock's confession, it gave me just the excuse I needed. I really didn't want the Major here,—I simply wished to give Mr. Stitt a free hand."

"What did you find out?" Markham asked the accountant.

"Plenty!" was the laconic reply.

He took a sheet of paper from his pocket, and placed it on the desk.

"There's a brief report. . . . I followed Mr. Vance's suggestion, and took a look at the stock record and the cashier's collateral blotter, and traced the transfer receipts. I ignored the journal entries against the ledger, and concentrated on the activities of the firm heads. Major Benson, I found, has been consistently hypothecating securities transferred to him as collateral for marginal trading, and has been speculating steadily in mercantile curb stocks. He has lost heavily—how much, I can't say."

"And Alvin Benson?" asked Vance.

"He was up to the same tricks. But he played in luck. He made a wad on a Columbus Motors pool a few weeks back; and he has been salting the money away in his safe—or, at least, that's what the secretary told me."

"And if Major Benson has possession of the key to that safe," suggested Vance, "then it's lucky for him his brother was shot."

"Lucky?" retorted Stitt. "It'll save him from State prison."

When the accountant had gone, Markham sat like a man of stone, his eyes fixed on the wall opposite. Another straw at which he had grasped in his instinctive denial of the Major's guilt, had been snatched from him.

The telephone rang. Slowly he took up the receiver, and as he listened I saw a look of complete resignation come into his eyes. He leaned back in his chair, like a man exhausted.

"It was Hagedorn," he said. "That was the right gun."

Then he drew himself up, and turned to Heath.

"The owner of that gun, Sergeant, was Major Benson."

The detective whistled softly, and his eyes opened slightly with astonishment. But gradually his face assumed its habitual stolidity of expression.

"Well, it don't surprise me any," he said.

Markham rang for Swacker.

"Get Major Benson on the wire, and tell him—tell him I'm about to make an arrest, and would appreciate his coming here immediately." His deputizing of the telephone call to Swacker was understood by all of us, I think.

Markham then summarized, for Heath's benefit, the case against the Major. When he had finished, he rose and rearranged the chairs at the table in front of his desk.

"When Major Benson comes, Sergeant," he said, "I am going to seat him here." He indicated a chair directly facing his own. "I want you to sit at his right; and you'd better get Phelps—or one of the other men, if he isn't in—to sit at his left. But you're not to make any move until I give the signal. Then you can arrest him."

When Heath had returned with Phelps and they had taken their seats at the table, Vance said:

"I'd advise you, Sergeant, to be on your guard. The minute the Major knows he's in for it, he'll go bald-headed for you."[152]

Heath smiled with heavy contempt.

152. To "go bald-headed" is nineteenth-century American slang for eager impetuousity or great haste.

153. Although Van Dine was finishing this book not long after publication of *The House Without a Key*, the similarities between the scene that follows and the climax of the latter novel are probably purely coincidental. At least, there is no direct evidence that Van Dine had read Biggers's book.

"This isn't the first man I've arrested, Mr. Vance—with many thanks for your advice. And what's more, the Major isn't that kind; he's too nervy."

"Have it your own way," replied Vance indifferently. "But I've warned you. The Major is cool-headed; he'd take big chances, and he could lose his last dollar without turning a hair. But when he is finally cornered, and sees ultimate defeat, all his repressions of a lifetime, having had no safety-valve, will explode physically. When a man lives without passions or emotions or enthusiasms, there's bound to be an outlet some time. Some men explode, and some commit suicide,—the principle is the same: it's a matter of psychological reaction. The Major isn't the self-destructive type,—that's why I say he'll blow up."

Heath snorted.

"We may be short on psychology down here," he rejoined, "but we know human nature pretty well."

Vance stifled a yawn, and carelessly lit a cigarette. I noticed, however, that he pushed his chair back a little from the end of the table where he and I were sitting.

"Well, Chief," rasped Phelps, "I guess your troubles are about over—though I sure did think that fellow Leacock was your man. . . . Who got the dope on this Major Benson?"

"Sergeant Heath and the Homicide Bureau will receive entire credit for the work," said Markham; and added: "I'm sorry, Phelps, but the District Attorney's office, and everyone connected with it, will be kept out of it altogether."

"Oh, well, it's all in a lifetime," observed Phelps philosophically.

We sat in strained silence until the Major arrived.[153] Markham smoked abstractedly. He glanced several times over the sheet of notations left by Stitt, and once he went to the water-cooler for a drink. Vance opened at random a law book before him, and perused with an amused smile a bribery-case decision by a Western judge. Heath and Phelps, habituated to waiting, scarcely moved.

When Major Benson entered Markham greeted him with exaggerated casualness, and busied himself with some papers in a drawer to avoid shaking hands. Heath, however, was almost jovial. He drew out the Major's chair for him, and uttered a ponderous banality about the weather. Vance closed the law book and sat erect with his feet drawn back.

Major Benson was cordially dignified. He gave Markham a swift glance; but if he suspected anything, he showed no outward sign of it.

"Major, I want you to answer a few questions—if you care to." Markham's voice, though low, had in it a resonant quality.

"Anything at all," returned the other easily.

"You own an army pistol, do you not?"

"Yes—a Colt automatic," he replied, with a questioning lift of the eyebrows.

"When did you last clean and refill it?"

Not a muscle of the Major's face moved.

"I don't exactly remember," he said. "I've cleaned it several times. But it hasn't been refilled since I returned from overseas."

"Have you lent it to anyone recently?"

"Not that I recall."

Markham took up Stitt's report, and looked at it a moment.

"How did you hope to satisfy your clients if suddenly called upon for their marginal securities?"

The Major's upper lip lifted contemptuously, exposing his teeth.

"So! That was why—under the guise of friendship—you sent a man to look over my books!" I saw a red blotch of color appear on the back of his neck, and swell upward to his ears.

"It happens that *I* didn't send him there for that purpose." The accusation had cut Markham. "But I did enter your apartment this morning."

"You're a house-breaker, too, are you?" The man's face was now crimson; the veins stood out on his forehead.

"And I found Mrs. Banning's jewels. . . . How did they get there, Major?"

"It's none of your damned business how they got there," he said, his voice as cold and even as ever.

"Why did you tell Miss Hoffman not to mention them to me?"

"That's none of your damned business either."

"Is it any of my business," asked Markham quietly, "that the bullet which killed your brother was fired from your gun?"

The Major looked at him steadily, his mouth a sneer.

"That's the kind of double-crossing you do!—invite me here to arrest me, and then ask me questions to incriminate myself when I'm unaware of your suspicions. A fine dirty sport *you* are!"

Vance leaned forward.

"You fool!" His voice was very low, but it cut like a whip. "Can't you see he's your friend, and is asking you these questions in a last desp'rate hope that you're not guilty?"

The Major swung round on him hotly.

"Keep out of this—you damned sissy!"

"Oh, quite," murmured Vance.

"And as for *you*,"—he pointed a quivering finger at Markham—"I'll make you sweat for this! . . ."

Vituperation and profanity poured from the man. His nostrils were expanded, his eyes blazing. His wrath seemed to surpass all human bounds: he was like a person in an apoplectic fit—contorted, repulsive, insensate.

Markham sat through it patiently, his head resting on his hands, his eyes closed. When, at length, the Major's rage became inarticulate, he looked up and nodded to Heath. It was the signal the detective had been watching for.

But before Heath could make a move, the Major sprang to his feet. With the motion of rising he swung his body swiftly about, and brought his fist against Heath's face with terrific impact. The Sergeant went backward in his chair, and lay on the floor dazed. Phelps leaped forward, crouching; but the Major's knee shot upward and caught him in the lower abdomen. He sank to the floor, where he rolled back and forth groaning.

The Major then turned on Markham. His eyes were glaring like a maniac's, and his lips were drawn back. His nostrils dilated with each stertorous breath. His shoulders were hunched, and his arms hung away from his body, his fingers rigidly flexed. His attitude was the embodiment of a terrific, uncontrolled malignity.

"You're next!" The words, guttural and venomous, were like a snarl.

As he spoke he sprang forward.

Vance, who had sat quietly during the mêlée, looking on with half-closed eyes and smoking indolently, now stepped sharply round the end of the table. His arms shot forward. With one hand he caught the Major's right wrist; with the other he grasped the elbow. Then he seemed to fall back with a swift pivotal motion. The Major's pinioned arm was twisted upward behind his shoulder-blades. There was a cry of pain, and the man suddenly relaxed in Vance's grip.

By this time Heath had recovered. He scrambled quickly to his feet and stepped up. There was the click of handcuffs, and the Major dropped heavily into a chair, where he sat moving his shoulder back and forth painfully.

"It's nothing serious," Vance told him. "The capsular ligament is torn a little. It'll be all right in a few days."

Heath came forward and, without a word, held out his hand to Vance. The action was at once an apology and a tribute. I liked Heath for it.

When he and his prisoner had gone, and Phelps had been assisted into an easy chair, Markham put his hand on Vance's arm.

"Let's get away," he said. "I'm done up."

CHAPTER XXV

Vance Explains His Methods

(Thursday, June 20; 9 p.m.)

That same evening, after a Turkish bath and dinner, Markham, grim and weary, and Vance, bland and debonair, and myself were sitting together in the alcove of the Stuyvesant Club's lounge-room.

We had smoked in silence for half an hour or more, when Vance, as if giving articulation to his thoughts, remarked:

"And it's stubborn, unimag'native chaps like Heath who constitute the human barrage between the criminal and society! . . . Sad, sad."

"We have no Napoleons to-day," Markham observed. "And if we had, they'd probably not be detectives."

"But even should they have yearnings toward that profession," said Vance, "they would be rejected on their physical measurements. As I understand it, your policemen are chosen by their height and weight; they must meet certain requirements as to heft—as though the only crimes they had to cope with were riots and gang feuds. Bulk,—the great American ideal, whether in art, architecture, table d'hôte meals, or detectives. An entrancin' notion."

"At any rate, Heath has a generous nature," said Markham palliatingly. "He has completely forgiven you for everything."

Vance smiled.

"The amount of credit and emulsification he received in the afternoon papers would have mellowed anyone. He should even forgive the Major for hitting him.—A clever blow, that; based on rotary leverage. Heath's constitution must be tough, or he wouldn't have recovered so quickly. . . . And poor Phelps! He'll have a horror of knees the rest of his life."

"You certainly guessed the Major's reaction," said Markham. "I'm almost ready to grant there's something in your psychological flummery, after all. Your æsthetic deductions seemed to put you on the right track."

After a pause he turned and looked inquisitively at Vance.

"Tell me exactly why, at the outset, you were convinced of the Major's guilt?"

Vance settled back in his chair.

"Consider, for a moment, the characteristics—the outstanding features—of the crime. Just before the shot was fired Benson and the murderer undoubtedly had been talking or arguing—the one seated, the other standing. Then Benson had pretended to read: he had said all he had to say. His reading was his gesture of finality; for one doesn't read when conversing with another unless for a purpose. The murderer, seeing the hopelessness of the situation, and having come prepared to meet it heroically, took out a gun, aimed it at Benson's temple, and pulled the trigger. After that, he turned out the lights and went away. . . . Such are the facts, indicated and actual."

He took several puffs on his cigarette.

"Now, let's analyze 'em. . . . As I pointed out to you, the murderer didn't fire at the body, where, though the chances of hitting would have been much greater, the chances of death would have been less. He chose the more diff'cult and hazardous—and, at the same time, the more certain and efficient—course. His technique, so to speak, was bold, direct, and fearless. Only a man with iron nerves and a highly developed gambler's instinct would have done it in just this forthright and audacious fashion. Therefore, all nervous, hot-headed, impulsive, or timid persons were automatically elim'nated as suspects. The neat, business-like aspect of the crime, together with the absence of any material clues that, could possibly have incrim'nated the culprit, indicated unmistakably that it had been premeditated and planned with coolness and precision, by a person of tremendous self-assurance,

154. Inopportune; the wrong choice.

and one used to taking risks. There was nothing subtle or in the least imag'native about the crime. Every feature of it pointed to an aggressive, blunt mind—a mind at once static, determined and intrepid, and accustomed to dealing with facts and situations in a direct, concrete and unequivocal manner. . . . I say, Markham, surely you're a good enough judge of human nature to read the indications, what?"

"I think I get the drift of your reasoning," the other admitted a little doubtfully.

"Very well, then," Vance continued. "Having determined the exact psychological nature of the deed, it only remained to find some int'rested person whose mind and temp'rament were such that, if he undertook a task of this kind in the given circumst'nces, he would inev'tably do it in precisely the manner in which it was done. As it happened, I had known the Major for a long time; and so it was obvious to me, the moment I had looked over the situation that first morning, that he had done it. The crime, in every respect and feature, was a perfect psychological expression of his character and mentality. But even had I not known him personally, I would have been able—since I possessed so clear and accurate a knowledge of the murderer's personality—to pick him out from any number of suspects."

"But suppose another person of the Major's type had done it?" asked Markham.

"We all differ in our natures—however similar two persons may appear at times," Vance explained. "And while, in the present case, it is barely conceivable that another man of the Major's type and temp'rament might have done it, the law of probability must be taken into account. Even supposing there were two men almost identical in personality and instincts in New York, what would be the chance of their both having had a reason to kill Benson? However, despite the remoteness of the possibility, when Pfyfe came into the case, and I learned he was a gambler and a hunter, I took occasion to look into his qualifications. Not knowing him personally, I appealed to Colonel Ostrander for my information; and what he told me put Pfyfe at once *hors de propos*."[154]

"But he had nerve: he was a rash plunger; and he certainly had enough at stake," objected Markham.

"Ah! But between a rash plunger and a bold, level-headed gambler like the Major, there is a great difference—a psychological abyss. In fact, their animating impulses are opposites. The plunger is actuated by fear and hope and desire; the cool-headed gambler is actuated by expediency and belief and judgment. The one is emotional, the other mental. The Major, unlike Pfyfe, is a born gambler, and inf'nitely self-confident. This kind of self-confidence, however, is not the same as recklessness, though superficially the two bear a close resemblance. It is based on an instinctive belief in one's own infallibility and safety. It's the reverse of what the Freudians call the inferiority complex,—a form of egomania, a variety of *folie de grandeur*. The Major possessed it, but it was absent from Pfyfe's composition; and as the crime indicated its possession by the perpetrator, I knew Pfyfe was innocent."

"I begin to grasp the thing in a nebulous sort of way," said Markham after a pause.

"But there were other indications, psychological and otherwise," went on Vance, "—the undress attire of the body, the toupee and teeth upstairs, the inferred familiarity of the murderer with the domestic arrangements, the fact that he had been admitted by Benson himself, and his knowledge that Benson would be at home alone at that time—all pointing to the Major as the guilty person. Another thing: the height of the murderer corresponded to the Major's height. This indication, though, was of minor importance; for had my measurements not tallied with the Major, I would have known that the bullet had been deflected, despite the opinions of all the Captain Hagedorns in the universe."

"Why were you so positive a woman couldn't have done it?"

"To begin with: it wasn't a woman's crime—that is, no woman would have done it in the way it was done. The most mentalized women are emotional when it comes to a fundamental issue like taking a life. That a woman could have coldly planned such a murder and then executed it with such business-like efficiency—aiming a single shot at her victim's temple at a distance of five or six feet—, would be contr'ry, d' ye see, to everything we know of human nature. Again: women don't stand up to argue a point before a seated antagonist. Somehow they seem to feel more secure sitting down. They talk better sitting; whereas men talk better standing. And even had a woman stood before Benson, she could not have taken out a gun and aimed it without his looking up. A man's reaching in his pocket is a natural action;

but a woman has no pockets and no place to hide a gun except her hand-bag. And a man is always on guard when an angry woman opens a hand-bag in front of him,—the very uncertainty of women's natures has made men suspicious of their actions when aroused. . . . But—above all—it was Benson's bald pate and bed-room slippers that made the woman hypothesis untenable."

"You remarked a moment ago," said Markham, "that the murderer went there that night prepared to take heroic measures if necessary. And yet you say he planned the murder."

"True. The two statements don't conflict, y' know. The murder was planned—without doubt. But the Major was willing to give his victim a last chance to save his life. My theory is this: The Major, being in a tight financial hole with State prison looming before him, and knowing that his brother had sufficient funds in the safe to save him, plotted the crime, and went to the house that night prepared to commit it. First, however, he told his brother of his predic'ment and asked for the money; and Alvin prob'bly told him to go to the devil. The Major may even have pleaded a bit in order to avoid killing him; but when the liter'ry Alvin turned to reading, he saw the futility of appealing further, and proceeded with the dire business."

Markham smoked a while.

"Granting all you've said," he remarked at length, "I still don't see how you could know, as you asserted this morning, that the Major had planned the murder so as to throw suspicion deliberately on Captain Leacock."

"Just as a sculptor, who thoroughly understands the principles of form and composition, can accurately supply any missing integral part of a statue," Vance explained, "so can the psychologist who understands the human mind, supply any missing factor in a given human action. I might add, parenthetically, that all this blather about the missing arms of the Aphrodite of Melos—the Milo Venus, y' know—is the utt'rest fiddle-faddle. Any competent artist who knew the laws of æsthetic organization could restore the arms exactly as they were originally. Such restorations are merely a matter of context,—the missing factor, d' ye see, simply has to conform and harmonize with what is already known."

He made one of his rare gestures of delicate emphasis.

"Now, the problem of circumventing suspicion is an important detail in every deliberated crime. And since the general conception of this particular crime was pos'tive, conclusive and concrete, it followed that each one of its component parts would be pos'tive, conclusive and concrete. Therefore, for the Major merely to have arranged things so that he himself should *not* be suspected, would have been too negative a conception to fit consistently with the other psychological aspects of the deed. It would have been too vague, too indirect, too indef'nite. The type of literal mind which conceived this crime would logically have provided a specific and tangible object of suspicion. Cons'quently, when the material evidence began to pile up against the Captain, and the Major waxed vehement in defending him, I knew he had been chosen as the dupe. At first, I admit, I suspected the Major of having selected Miss St. Clair as the victim; but when I learned that the presence of her gloves and hand-bag at Benson's was only an accident, and remembered that the Major had given us Pfyfe as a source of information about the Captain's threat, I realized that her projection into the rôle of murderer was unpremeditated."

A little later Markham rose and stretched himself.

"Well, Vance," he said, "your task is finished. Mine has just begun. And I need sleep."

Before a week had passed, Major Anthony Benson was indicted for the murder of his brother. His trial before Judge Rudolph Hansacker, as you remember, created a nation-wide sensation. The Associated Press sent columns daily to its members; and for weeks the front pages of the country's newspapers were emblazoned with spectacular reports of the proceedings. How the District Attorney's office won the case after a bitter struggle; how, because of the indirect character of the evidence, the verdict was for murder in the second degree; and how, after a retrial in the Court of Appeals, Anthony Benson finally received a sentence of from twenty years to life,—all these facts are a matter of official and public record.

Markham personally did not appear as Public Prosecutor. Having been a life-long friend of the defendant's, his position was an unenviable and difficult one, and no word of criticism was directed against his assignment of the case to Chief Assistant District Attorney Sullivan. Major Benson surrounded himself with an array of counsel such as is rarely seen in our criminal courts. Both Blashfield and Bauer were among the attorneys for the defense—Blashfield fulfilling the duties of the English

155. At the time, objections to admission of the jewels or the gun in evidence would have been viewed as frivolous. Of course, the trial would have gone quite differently today. The Fourth Amendment to the U.S. Constitution, prohibiting unreasonable searches and seizures (interpreted to mean searches without "probable cause," and in most cases, a search warrant issued by a judge), did not apply to state and local law enforcement officials. The decision in *Wolf v. Colorado*, 338 U.S. 25 (1949), changed that: The U.S. Supreme Court held that the Fourth Amendment was part of the liberty protected by the Fourteenth Amendment's due process clause against infringement by *state and local officials*. In 1961, in *Mapp v. Ohio*, 367 U.S. 643, the Supreme Court decreed that, in general, evidence obtained by means of an illegal search and seizure could not be used by the prosecution. Under today's rules, then, the presence of the jewels and murder weapon in Benson's apartment would be inadmissible evidence.

solicitor, and Bauer acting as advocate. They fought with every legal device at their disposal, but the accumulation of evidence against their client overwhelmed them.[155]

After Markham had been convinced of the Major's guilt, he had made a thorough examination of the business affairs of the two brothers, and found the situation even worse than had been indicated by Stitt's first report. The firm's securities had been systematically appropriated for private speculations; but whereas Alvin Benson had succeeded in covering himself and making a large profit, the Major had been almost completely wiped out by his investments. Markham was able to show that the Major's only hope of replacing the diverted securities and saving himself from criminal prosecution lay in Alvin Benson's immediate death. It was also brought out at the trial that the Major, on the very day of the murder, had made emphatic promises which could have been kept only in the event of his gaining access to his brother's safe. Furthermore, these promises had involved specific amounts in the other's possession; and, in one instance, he had put up, on a forty-eight-hour note, a security already pledged—a fact which, in itself, would have exposed his hand, had his brother lived.

Miss Hoffman was a helpful and intelligent witness for the prosecution. Her knowledge of conditions at the Benson and Benson offices went far toward strengthening the case against the Major.

Mrs. Platz also testified to overhearing acrimonious arguments between the brothers. She stated that less than a fortnight before the murder the Major, after an unsuccessful attempt to borrow $50,000 from Alvin, had threatened him, saying: "If I ever have to choose between your skin and mine, it won't be mine that'll suffer."

Theodore Montagu, the man who, according to the story of the elevator boy at the Chatham Arms, had returned at half past two on the night of the murder, testified that, as his taxicab turned in front of the apartment house, the head-lights flashed on a man standing in a tradesmen's entrance across the street, and that the man looked like Major Benson. This evidence would have had little effect had not Pfyfe come forward after the arrest and admitted seeing the Major crossing Sixth Avenue at Forty-sixth Street when he had walked to Pietro's for his drink of Haig and Haig. He explained that he had attached no importance to it at the time, thinking the Major was merely returning home from some Broadway restaurant. He himself had not been seen by the Major.

This testimony, in connection with Mr. Montagu's, annihilated the Major's carefully planned alibi; and though the defense contended stubbornly that both witnesses had been mistaken in their identification, the jury was deeply impressed by the evidence, especially when Assistant District Attorney Sullivan, under Vance's tutoring, painstakingly explained, with diagrams, how the Major could have gone out and returned that night without being seen by the boy.

It was also shown that the jewels could not have been taken from the scene of the crime except by the murderer; and Vance and I were called as witnesses to the finding of them in the Major's apartment. Vance's demonstration of the height of the murderer was shown in court, but, curiously, it carried little weight, as the issue was confused by a mass of elaborate scientific objections. Captain Hagedorn's identification of the pistol was the most difficult obstacle with which the defense had to contend.

The trial lasted three weeks, and much evidence of a scandalous nature was taken, although, at Markham's suggestion, Sullivan did his best to minimize the private affairs of those innocent persons whose lives unfortunately touched upon the episode. Colonel Ostrander, however, has never forgiven Markham for not having had him called as a witness.

During the last week of the trial Miss Muriel St. Clair appeared as *prima donna* in a large Broadway light-opera production which ran successfully for nearly two years. She has since married her chivalrous Captain Leacock, and they appear perfectly happy.[156]

Pfyfe is still married and as elegant as ever. He visits New York regularly, despite the absence of his "dear old Alvin"; and I have occasionally seen him and Mrs. Banning together. Somehow, I shall always like that woman. Pfyfe raised the $10,000—how, I have no idea—and reclaimed her jewels. Their ownership, by the way, was not divulged at the trial, for which I was very glad.

On the evening of the day the verdict was brought in against the Major, Vance and Markham and I were sitting in the Stuyvesant Club. We had dined together, but no word of the events of the past few weeks had passed between us. Presently, however, I saw an ironic smile creep slowly to Vance's lips.

156. J. K. Van Dover suggests that this echoes the fact that the ex-husband of the final female companion of Joseph Elwell (see p. 304, note *) married the "woman in black" who accompanied the companion (p. 107).

"I say, Markham," he drawled; "what a grotesque spectacle the trial was! The real evidence, y' know, wasn't even introduced. Benson was convicted entirely on suppositions, presumptions, implications and inf'rences. . . . God help the innocent Daniel who inadvertently falls into a den of legal lions!"

Markham, to my surprise, nodded gravely.

"Yes," he concurred; "but if Sullivan had tried to get a conviction on your so-called psychological theories, he'd have been adjudged insane."

"Doubtless," sighed Vance. "You illuminati of the law would have little to do if you went about your business intelligently."

"Theoretically," replied Markham at length, "your theories are clear enough; but I'm afraid I've dealt too long with material facts to forsake them for psychology and art. . . . However," he added lightly, "if my legal evidence should fail me in the future, may I call on you for assistance?"

"I'm always at your service, old chap, don't y' know," Vance rejoined. "I rather fancy, though, that it's when your legal evidence is leading you irresistibly to your victim that you'll need me most, what?"

And the remark, though intended merely as a good-natured sally, proved strangely prophetic.

S. S. Van Dine Sets Down
Twenty Rules for Detective Stories[157]

The detective story is a kind of intellectual game. It is more—it is a sporting event. And for the writing of detective stories there are very definite laws—unwritten, perhaps, but none the less binding; and every respectable and self-respecting concoter of literary mysteries lives up to them. Herewith, then, is a sort of Credo, based partly on the practice of all the great writers of stories, and partly on the promptings of the honest author's inner conscience. To wit:

1.   The reader must have equal opportunity with the detective for solving the mystery. All clues must be plainly stated and described.

2.   No willful tricks or deceptions may be played on the reader other than those played legitimately by the criminal on the detective himself.

3.   There must be no love interest in the story. The business in hand is to bring a criminal to the bar of justice, not to bring a lovelorn couple to the hymeneal altar.[158]

4.   The detective himself, or one of the official investigators, should never turn out to be the culprit. This is bald

157. The essay first appeared in the September 1928 issue of *The American Magazine*, pp. 129–31. Longer versions have appeared elsewhere.

158. Compare this to Watson's observation of Sherlock Holmes: "He never spoke of the softer passions, save with a gibe and a sneer. They were admirable things for the observer—excellent for drawing the veil from men's motives and actions. But for the trained reasoner to admit such intrusions into his own delicate and finely adjusted temperament was to introduce a distracting factor which might throw a doubt upon all his mental results. Grit in a sensitive instrument, or a crack in one of his own high-power lenses, would not be more disturbing than a strong emotion in a nature such as his" ("A Scandal in Bohemia").

159. Murder features infrequently in the Sherlock Holmes canon, but all four of the Holmes novels do include murders.

trickery, on a par with offering some one a bright penny for a five-dollar gold piece. It's false pretenses.

5. The culprit must be determined by logical deductions—not by accident or coincidence or unmotivated confession. To solve a criminal problem in this latter fashion is like sending the reader on a deliberate wild-goose chase, and then telling him, after he has failed, that you had the object of his search up your sleeve all the time. Such an author is no better than a practical joker.

6. The detective novel must have a detective in it; and a detective is not a detective unless he detects. His function is to gather clues that will eventually lead to the person who did the dirty work in the first chapter; and if the detective does not reach his conclusions through an analysis of those clues, he has no more solved his problem than the schoolboy who gets his answer out of the back of the arithmetic.

7. There simply must be a corpse in a detective novel, and the deader the corpse the better. No lesser crime than murder will suffice. Three hundred pages is far too much pother for a crime other than murder. After all, the reader's trouble and expenditure of energy must be rewarded.[159]

8. The problem of the crime must be solved by strictly naturalistic means. Such methods for learning the truth as slate-writing, ouija-boards, mind-reading, spiritualistic sèances, crystal-gazing, and the like, are taboo. A reader has a chance when matching his wits with a rationalistic detective, but if he must compete with the world of spirits and go chasing about the fourth dimension of metaphysics, he is defeated *ab initio*.

9. There must be but one detective—that is, but one protagonist of deduction—one *deus ex machina*. To bring the minds of three or four, or sometimes a gang of

detectives to bear on a problem, is not only to disperse the interest and break the direct thread of logic, but to take an unfair advantage of the reader. If there is more than one detective the reader doesn't know who his co-deductor is. It's like making the reader run a race with a relay team.

10. The culprit must turn out to be a person who has played a more or less prominent part in the story—that is, a person with whom the reader is familiar and in whom he takes an interest.

11. Servants must not be chosen by the author as the culprit.[160] This is begging a noble question. It is a too easy solution. The culprit must be a decidedly worth-while person—one that wouldn't ordinarily come under suspicion.

12. There must be but one culprit, no matter how many murders are committed. The culprit may, of course, have a minor helper or co-plotter; but the entire onus must rest on one pair of shoulders: the entire indignation of the reader must be permitted to concentrate on a single black nature.

13. Secret societies, camorras, mafias, *et al.*, have no place in a detective story. Here the author gets into adventure fiction and secret-service romance. A fascinating and truly beautiful murder is irremediably spoiled by any such wholesale culpability. To be sure, the murderer in a detective novel should be given a sporting chance, but it is going too far to grant him a secret society to fall back on. No high-class, self-respecting murderer would want such odds in his jousting-bout with the police.

14. The method of murder, and the means of detecting it, must be rational and scientific. That is to say, pseudo-science and purely imaginative and speculative devices are not to be tolerated in the *roman policier*. Once an author soars into the realm of fantasy, in the Jules Verne

160. The butler "did it" in one of the Holmes stories, "The Musgrave Ritual," but that may be the first instance of the cliché in detective fiction.

161. That is, Professor James Moriarty, the "Napoleon of Crime," need not apply.

manner, he is outside the bounds of detective fiction, cavorting in the uncharted reaches of adventure.

15. The truth of the problem must at all times be apparent—provided the reader is shrewd enough to see it. By this I mean that if the reader, after learning the explanation for the crime, should reread the book, he would see that the solution had, in a sense, been staring him in the face—that all the clues really pointed to the culprit—and that, if he had been as clever as the detective, he could have solved the mystery himself without going on to the final chapter. That the clever reader does often thus solve the problem goes without saying.

16. A detective novel should contain no long descriptive passages, no literary dallying with side-issues, no subtly worked-out character analyses, no "atmospheric" preoccupations. Such matters have no vital place in a record of crime and deduction. They hold up the action, and introduce issues irrelevant to the main purpose, which is to state a problem, analyze it, and bring it to a successful conclusion. To be sure, there must be a sufficient descriptiveness and character delineation to give the novel verisimilitude.

17. A professional criminal must never be shouldered with the guilt of a crime in a detective story. Crimes by house-breakers and bandits are the province of the police department—not of authors and brilliant amateur detectives. A really fascinating crime is one committed by a pillar of a church, or a spinster noted for her charities.[161]

18. A crime in a detective story must never turn out to be an accident or a suicide. To end an odyssey of sleuthing with such an anti-climax is to hoodwink a trusting and kind-hearted reader.

19. The motives for all crimes in detective stories should be personal. International plottings and war politics belong in a different category of fiction—in secret-service

tales, for instance. But a murder story must be kept *gemütlich*, so to speak. It must reflect the reader's everyday experiences, and give him a certain outlet for his own repressed desires and emotions.

20. And (to give my Credo an even score of items) I herewith list a few of the devices which no self-respecting detective-story writer will now avail himself of. They have been employed too often, and are familiar to all true lovers of literary crime. To use them is a confession of the author's ineptitude and lack of originality. (*a*) Determining the identity of the culprit by comparing the butt of a cigarette left at the scene of the crime with the brand smoked by a suspect.[162] (*b*) The bogus spiritualistic sèance to frighten the culprit into giving himself away. (*c*) Forged finger-prints. (*d*) The dummy-figure alibi. (*e*) The dog that does not bark and thereby reveals the fact that the intruder is familiar.[163] (*f*) The final pinning of the crime on a twin, or a relative who looks exactly like the suspected, but innocent, person. (*g*) The hypodermic syringe and the knockout drops. (*h*) The commission of the murder in a locked room after the police have actually broken in. (*i*) The word-association test for guilt. (*j*) The cipher, or code letter, which is eventually unravelled by the sleuth.[164]

162. Of course, Sherlock Holmes pioneered this forensic technique and wrote a monograph on tobacco ash.

163. Van Dine here refers to the incident of the dog in the night-time central to the solution of the "Silver Blaze" mystery by Sherlock Holmes.

164. Another knock on Holmes, who deciphers code in *The Valley of Fear* and "The Dancing Men" (and before Holmes, Poe featured a cipher in "The Gold-Bug").

Facsimile first-edition dust jacket for *The Roman Hat Mystery*.

THE ROMAN HAT MYSTERY[1]

A Problem in Deduction

BY

ELLERY QUEEN

Grateful Acknowledgement is Made to

Professor Alexander Goettler

Chief Toxicologist of the City of New York

For His Friendly Offices

In the Preparation of This Tale

1.　First published in August 1929 in New
York by Frederick A. Stokes.

Contents

Foreword

have been asked by both publisher and author to write a cursory preface to the story of Monte Field's murder.[2] Let me say at once that I am neither a writer nor a criminologist. To make authoritative remarks, therefore, anent the techniques of crime and crime-fiction is obviously beyond my capacity. Nevertheless, I have one legitimate claim to the privilege of introducing this remarkable story, based as it is upon perhaps the most mystifying crime of the past decade . . . If it were not for me, "The Roman Hat Mystery" would never have reached the fiction-reading public. I am responsible for its having been brought to light; and there my pallid connection with it ends.

During the past winter I shook off the dust of New York and went a-traveling in Europe. In the course of a capricious roving about the corners of the Continent (a roving induced by that boredom which comes to every Conrad[3] in quest of his youth)—I found myself one August day in a tiny Italian mountain-village. How I got there, its location and its name do not matter; a promise is a promise, even when it is made by a stockbroker. Dimly I remembered that this toy hamlet perched on the lip of a sierra harbored two old friends whom I had not seen for two years. They had come from the seething sidewalks of New York to bask in the brilliant peace of an Italian countryside—well, perhaps it was as much curiosity about their regrets as anything else, that prompted me to intrude upon their solitude.

2.   Lee and Dannay, great admirers of the Sherlock Holmes Canon, here indulge in an even greater meta-fiction than Doyle. Of course, the Holmes adventures are primarily narrated by John H. Watson, M.D., who is Holmes's flatmate and partner; Watson, over the course of the series of tales, becomes a successful writer of stories, and that success is alluded to—often with irony—by Holmes. Only in one book, *The Case-Book of Sherlock Holmes*, does the reader hear the voice of Arthur Conan Doyle, as he bids farewell to Holmes and Watson, and there Doyle makes no pretense that Holmes and Watson are not fictional. Here, we learn of "J. J. McC.," who served as the go-between twixt Ellery Queen and Frederick A. Stokes. "J. J. McC." appears in this limited role in several of the early Queen novels (and, although he describes himself here as a stockbroker, likely is Judge J. J. McCue, a minor character in the late Queen novel *Face to Face* (1967). Three J. J. McCues are listed in *Trow's General Directory of New York City* for 1922–23, but none are stockbrokers.

3. At the age of sixteen, novelist Joseph Conrad (1857–1924) left his home in Poland and began a career as a seafarer; only in his mid-thirties did he settle down in England, begin writing, and marry. McC. may be referring to a four-month trip Conrad took to Poland in 1918, during which he visiting his childhood home in Krakow. After his return to England, Conrad became a vocal partisan for Polish sovereignty. However, with the exception of that Polish trip, his post-marital travel was limited to sedate vacations.

4. This witty remark—that Ellery's wife is as gracious as the name she bore (that being Queen)—makes little sense when we learn that Queen is a pseudonym. Later in the series, not only does it become apparent that the name Queen is *not* a pseudonym, the wife and child have disappeared without explanation.

5. The name was based on Djuna Barnes (1892–1982), American writer and artist, best remembered for the 1936 lesbian novel *Nightwood*. In 1924, Barnes was living in Paris, where she had already established a reputation as a feminist journalist and writer.

6. One who may be said to have escaped the grace of God—an incorrigible rascal.

My reception at the hands of old Richard Queen, keener and greyer than ever, and of his son Ellery was cordial enough. We had been more than friends in the old days; perhaps, too, the vinous air of Italy was too heady a cure for their dust-choked Manhattan memories. In any case, they seemed profoundly glad to see me. Mrs. Ellery Queen—Ellery was now the husband of a glorious creature and the startled father of an infant who resembled his grandfather to an extraordinary degree—was as gracious as the name she bore.[4] Even Djuna,[5] no longer the scapegrace[6] I had known, greeted me with every sign of nostalgia.

Despite Ellery's desperate efforts to make me forget New York and appreciate the lofty beauties of his local scenery, I had not been in their tiny villa for many days before a devilish notion took possession of me and I began to pester poor Ellery to death. I have something of a reputation for persistence, if no other virtue; so that before I left, Ellery in despair agreed to compromise. He took me into his library, locked the door and attacked an old steel filing-cabinet. After a slow search he managed to bring out what I suspect was under his fingers all the time. It was a faded manuscript bound Ellery-like in blue legal paper.

The argument raged. I wished to leave his beloved Italian shores with the manuscript in my trunk, whereas he insisted that the sheaf of contention remain hidden in the cabinet. Old Richard was wrenched away from his desk, where he was writing a treatise for a German magazine on "American Crime and Methods of Detection," to settle the affair. Mrs. Queen held her husband's arm as he was about to close the incident with a workmanlike fist; Djuna clucked gravely; and even Ellery, Jr., extracted his pudgy hand from his mouth long enough to make a comment in the gurgle-language of his kind.

The upshot of it all was that "The Roman Hat Mystery" went back to the States in my luggage. Not unconditionally, however—Ellery is a peculiar man. I was forced solemnly and by all I held dear to swear that the identities of my friends and of the important characters concerned in the story be veiled by pseudonyms; and that, on pain of instant annihilation, their names be permanently withheld from the reading public.

Consequently "Richard Queen" and "Ellery Queen" are not the true names of those gentlemen. Ellery himself made the selections; and I might add at once that his choices were deliberately contrived to baffle the reader who might endeavor to ferret the truth from some apparent clue of anagram.[7]

"The Roman Hat Mystery" is based on records actually in the police archives of New York City. Ellery and his father, as usual, worked hand-in-hand on the case. During this period in his career Ellery was a detective-story writer of no mean reputation. Adhering to the aphorism that truth is often stranger than fiction, it was his custom to make notes of interesting investigations for possible use in his murder tales. The affair of the Hat so fascinated him that he kept unusually exhaustive notes, at his leisure coördinating the whole into fiction form, intending to publish it. Immediately after, however, he was plunged into another investigation which left him scant opportunity for business; and when this last case was successfully closed, Ellery's father, the Inspector, consummated a lifelong ambition by retiring and moving to Italy, bag and baggage. Ellery, who had in this affair[*] found the lady of his heart, was animated by a painful desire to do something "big" in letters; Italy sounded idyllic to him; he married with his father's blessing and the three of them, accompanied by Djuna, went off to their new European home. The manuscript was utterly forgotten until I rescued it.

On one point, before I close this painfully unhandsome preface, I should like to make myself clear.

I have always found it extremely difficult to explain to strangers the peculiar affinity which bound Richard to Ellery Queen, as I must call them. For one thing, they are persons of by no means uncomplicated natures. Richard Queen, sprucely middle-aged after thirty-two years' service in the city police, earned his Inspector's chevrons not so much through diligence as by an extraordinary grasp of the technique of criminal investigation. It was said, for example, at the time of his brilliant detective efforts during the now-ancient Barnaby Ross murder case,[†8] that "Richard Queen by this feat firmly establishes his fame beside such masters of crime-detection as Tamaka Hiero, Brillon the Frenchman, Kris Oliver, Renaud, and James Redix the Younger."[‡9]

Queen, with his habitual shyness toward newspaper eulogy, was the first to scoff at this extravagant statement; although Ellery maintains that for many years the old man secretly preserved a clipping of the story. However that may he—and I like to think of Richard Queen in terms of human personality, despite the

7.   Dannay's real name was Daniel *Nathan*; Manfred Lee's real name was Emanuel *Lepofsky*. Thus their initials were N and L. "En el queerly" (an anagram of Ellery Queen) is how a British crossword puzzle would describe an anagram of their names. According to a 1979 interview with Dannay in *People* magazine, Ellery was a schoolyard friend, and Queen was chosen because it was euphonious. "'We were so naïve,' laughs Dannay, 'we had absolutely no idea that "queen" had another possible meaning.'"

*   [Author's note:] "The Mimic Murders." This crime in its fiction form has not yet reached the public. J. J. McC.

     [Editor's note: The case has never been published, but it is mentioned in Ellery Queen's *The Dutch Shoe Mystery* (1931) as involving reporter Peter Harper.]

†   [Author's note:] Ellery Queen made his bow as his father's unofficial counsel during this investigation.

8.   The Barnaby Ross murder case refers to one of the mysteries recounted in a series of four novels written by Lee and Dannay under the name of Barnaby Ross: *The Tragedy of X* (1932), *The Tragedy of Y* (1932), *The Tragedy of Z* (1933), and *Drury Lane's Last Case* (1933). The novels feature Drury Lane, a deaf amateur detective who is a retired Shakespearean actor, Inspector Thumm, and Thumm's daughter Patience. Of course, none of these had been published at the time of *The Roman Hat Mystery*, and Ellery does not appear in any of these publications.

‡   [Author's note:] Chicago Press, January 16, 191–.

9.   In Ellery Queen's *The French Powder Mystery* (1930), Tamaka Hiero's *A Thousand Leaves* and *There Is an Under World* by James Redix (the Elder) are quoted; no other mention of any of these authors may be found in any book other than the present volume.

10.   West 87th Street, running between Central Park West and Riverside Drive on the Upper West Side of Manhattan, is a mixed residential/commercial street. Rex Stout's Nero Wolfe, an amateur detective of some note, lived on West 35th Street.

11.   Dannay and Lee here ape the modus operandi of John H. Watson, M.D., who indicates throughout the Sherlock Holmes Canon that there are many stories that he either cannot tell (for privacy reasons) or has not yet chosen to tell. Many of these Holmes cases are listed by name (for example, the affair of the Giant Rat of Sumatra) and have tantalized readers for a century.

efforts of imaginative journalists to make a legend of him—I cannot emphasize too strongly the fact that he was heavily dependent upon his son's wit for success in many of his professional achievements.

This is not a matter of public knowledge. Some mementoes of their careers are still reverently preserved by friends: the small bachelor establishment maintained during their American residence on West 87th Street,[10] and now a semiprivate museum of curios collected during their productive years; the really excellent portrait of father and son, done by Thiraud and hanging in the art gallery of an anonymous millionaire; Richard's precious snuff-box, the Florentine antique which he had picked up at an auction and which he therefore held dearer than rubies, only to succumb to the blandishments of a charming old lady whose name he cleared of slander; Ellery's enormous collection of books on violence, perhaps as complete as any in the world, which he regretfully discarded when the Queens left for Italy; and, of course, the many as yet unpublished documents containing records of cases solved by the Queens and now stored away from prying eyes in the City's police archives.[11]

But the things of the heart—the spiritual bonds between father and son—have until this time remained secret from all except a few favored intimates, among whom I was fortunate enough to be numbered. The old man, perhaps the most famous executive of the Detective Division in the last half century, overshadowing in public renown, it is to be feared, even those gentlemen who sat briefly in the Police Commissioner's suite—the old man, let me repeat, owed a respectable portion of his reputation to his son's genius.

In matters of pure tenacity, when possibilities lay frankly open on every hand, Richard Queen was a peerless investigator. He had a crystal-clear mind for detail; a retentive memory for complexities of motive and plot; a cool viewpoint when the obstacle seemed insuperable. Give him a hundred facts, bungled and torn, out of proportion and sequence, and he had them assembled in short order. He was like a bloodhound who follows the true scent in the clutter of a hopelessly tangled trail.

But the intuitive sense, the gift of imagination, belonged to Ellery Queen, the fiction writer. The two might have been twins possessing abnormally developed faculties of mind, impotent by themselves but vigorous when applied one to the other. Richard Queen, far from resenting the bond which made his success so spectacularly possible—as a less generous nature might have done—took pains to make it plain to his friends. The slender, grey old man whose name was anathema to contemporary lawbreakers, used to utter his "confession," as he called it, with a *naïveté* explicable only on the score of his proud fatherhood.

One word more. Of all the affairs pursued by the two Queens this, which Ellery has titled "The Roman Hat Mystery" for reasons shortly to be made clear, was surely the crowning case of them all. The dilettante of criminology, the thoughtful reader of detective literature, will understand as the tale unfolds why Ellery considers the murder of Monte Field worthy of study. The average murderer's motives and habits are fairly accessible to the criminal specialist. Not so, however, in the case of the Field killer. Here the Queens dealt with a person of delicate perception and extraordinary finesse. In fact, as Richard pointed out shortly after the dénouement, the crime planned was as nearly perfect as human ingenuity could make it. As in so many "perfect crimes," however, a small mischance of fate coupled with Ellery's acute deductive analyses gave the hunting Queens the single clue which led ultimately to the destruction of the plotter.

J. J. McC.
NEW YORK.
March 1, 1929.

Lexicon of Persons Connected with the Investigation

Note: The complete list of individuals, male and female, brought into the story of Monte Field's murder and appended below is given solely for the convenience of the reader. It is intended to simplify rather than mystify. In the course of perusing mysterio-detective literature the reader is, like as not, apt to lose sight of a number of seemingly unimportant characters who eventually prove of primary significance in the solution of the crime. The writer therefore urges a frequent study of this chart during the reader's pilgrimage through the tale, if toward no other end than to ward off the inevitable cry of "Unfair!"—the consolation of those who read and do not reason.

E. Q.

MONTE FIELD, an important personage indeed—the victim.

WILLIAM PUSAK, clerk. Cranially a brachycephalic.

DOYLE, a *gendarme* with brains.

LOUIS PANZER, a Broadway theatre-manager.

JAMES PEALE, the Don Juan of "Gunplay."

EVE ELLIS. The quality of friendship is not strained.

STEPHEN BARRY. One can understand the perturbation of the juvenile lead.

LUCILLE HORTON, the "lady of the streets"—in the play.

HILDA ORANGE, a celebrated English character-actress.

THOMAS VELIE, Detective-Sergeant who knows a thing or two about crime.

HESSE, PIGGOTT, FLINT, JOHNSON, HAGSTROM, RITTER, gentlemen of the Homicide Squad.

DR. SAMUEL PROUTY, Assistant to the Chief Medical Examiner.

MADGE O'CONNELL, usherette on the fatal aisle.

DR. STUTTGARD. There is always a doctor in the audience.

JESS LYNCH, the obliging orangeade-boy.

JOHN CAZZANELLI, *alias* "Parson Johnny," naturally takes a professional interest in "Gunplay."

BENJAMIN MORGAN. What do you make of him?

FRANCES IVES-POPE. Enter the society interest.

STANFORD IVES-POPE, man-about-town.

HARRY NEILSON. He revels in the sweet uses of publicity.

HENRY SAMPSON, for once an intelligent District Attorney.

CHARLES MICHAELS, the fly—or the spider?

MRS. ANGELA RUSSO, a lady of reputation.

TIMOTHY CRONIN, a legal ferret.

ARTHUR STOATES, another.

OSCAR LEWIN, the Charon of the dead man's office.

FRANKLIN IVES-POPE. If wealth meant happiness—

MRS. FRANKLIN IVES-POPE, a maternal hypochondriac.

MRS. PHILLIPS. Middle-aged angels have their uses.

DR. THADDEUS JONES, toxicologist of the City of New York.

EDMUND CREWE, architectural expert attached to the Detective Bureau.

DJUNA, an Admirable Crichton of a new species.

The Problem Is—
Who Killed Monte Field?
Meet the astute gentlemen whose business it is
to discover such things—
MR. RICHARD QUEEN
MR. ELLERY QUEEN

Explanation for the Map of the Roman Theatre

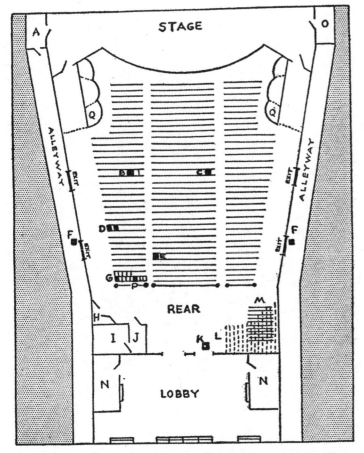

Map of the Roman Theatre
Drawn by Ellery Queen

Map of the Roman Theater by Ellery Queen.

A: Actors' dressing-rooms.

B: Frances Ives-Pope's seat.

C: Benjamin Morgan's seat.

D: Aisle-seats occupied by "Parson Johnny" Cazzanelli and Madge O'Connell

E: Dr. Stuttgard's seat.

F, F: Orangeade boys' stands (only during intermissions).

G: Area in vicinity of crime. Black square represents seat occupied by Monte Field. Three white squares to the right and four white squares directly in front represent vacant seats.

H: Publicity office, occupied by Harry Neilson.

I: Manager Louis Panzer's private office.

J: Anteroom to manager's office.

K: Ticket-taker's box.

L: Only stairway leading to the balcony.

M: Stairway leading downstairs to General Lounge.

N, N: Cashiers' offices.

O: Property Room.

P: William Pusak's seat.

Q, Q: Orchestra boxes.

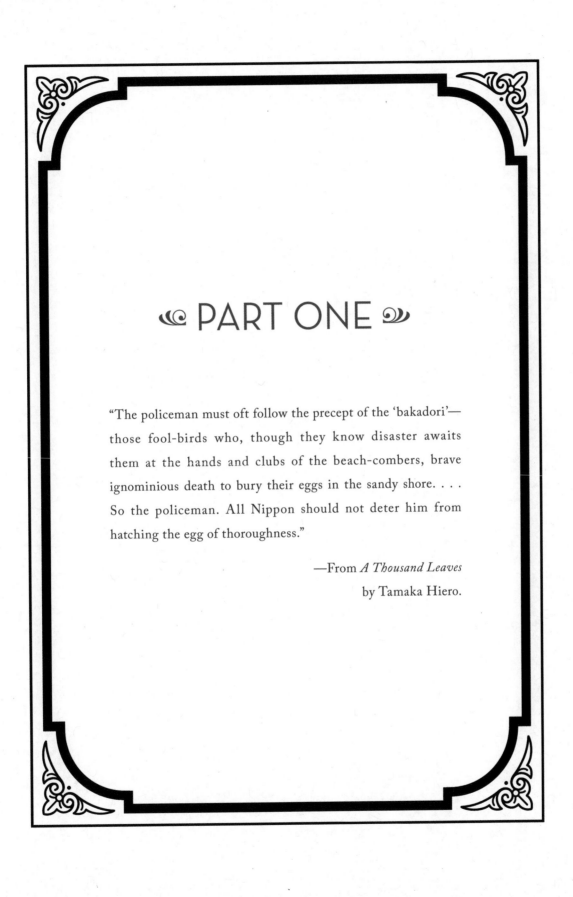

❧ PART ONE ❧

"The policeman must oft follow the precept of the 'bakadori'—those fool-birds who, though they know disaster awaits them at the hands and clubs of the beach-combers, brave ignominious death to bury their eggs in the sandy shore. . . . So the policeman. All Nippon should not deter him from hatching the egg of thoroughness."

—From *A Thousand Leaves*
by Tamaka Hiero.

CHAPTER I

In Which Are Introduced a Theatre-Audience and a Corpse

The dramatic season of 192-[12] began in a disconcerting manner. Eugene O'Neill had neglected to write a new play[13] in time to secure the financial encouragement of the *intelligentzia;* and as for the "low-brows," having attended play after play without enthusiasm, they had deserted the legitimate theatre for the more ingenuous delights of the motion picture palaces.

On the evening of Monday, September 24th, therefore, when a misty rain softened the electric blaze of Broadway's theatrical district, it was viewed morosely by house managers and producers from 37th Street to Columbus Circle.[14] Several plays were then and there given their walking papers by the men higher up, who called upon God and the weather bureau to witness their discomfiture. The penetrating rain kept the play-going public close to its radios and bridge-tables. Broadway was a bleak sight indeed to those few who had the temerity to patrol its empty streets.

The sidewalk fronting the Roman Theatre,[15] on 47th Street west of the "White Way," however, was jammed with a mid-season, fair-weather crowd. The title "Gunplay" flared from a gay marquee. Cashiers dexterously attended the chattering throng lined up at the "To-night's Performance" window. The buff-and-blue doorman, impressive with the dignity of his uniform and the placidity of his years, bowed the evening's top-hatted and befurred customers into the orchestra with an air of satisfaction, as if inclemencies of weather held no terrors for those implicated in "Gunplay's" production.

12.   September 24 was a Monday in 1923. September 23 does not fall on a Monday again in the 1920s until 1928, after publication of this book.

13.   Indeed, one of the prolific American dramatist's plays appeared on Broadway every season from 1917 to 1934, with the sole exception of 1923.

14.   Today, the Great White Way (so named for its early adoption of arc lighting in 1880, one of the first streets in America to be electrically lit) includes only Manhattan playhouses located in the area between the Avenue of the Americas and Ninth Avenue and from West 41st Street to West 53rd Street. Columbus Circle is at 59th St., now slightly farther uptown than the theater district.

15.   There was not in 1923 nor has there ever been a Roman Theatre in Manhattan; and no drama named *Gunplay* ever ran on Broadway. Can the real Roman Theatre be identified?

The name selected as an alias (the Roman) may be a hint, suggesting candidates among contemporary Broadway venues that would include the Coliseum (much too large and located at 181st St.), the Hippodrome (even larger), the Empire (236 West 42nd St.), and the Olympic (small and on East 14th, near 3rd Ave.). The other strong clue is the stated location on 47th St.

The Empire is a candidate with mixed qualifications. Built in 1912, it was hardly "one of Broadway's newest," and it was on 42nd St., not 47th St. (though it was definitely west of Broadway). A seating chart is reproduced here, and, comparing it to Ellery's diagram of the Roman Theatre (p. 515), the Empire appears to be significantly smaller. However, *The Woman on the Jury*, by Bernard K. Burns (a play in which gunshots are heard), was running at the Empire in the autumn of 1923, and the play closed at around the time of the conclusion of *The Roman Hat Mystery*.

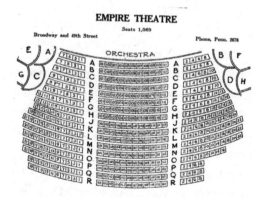

Seating plan of Empire Theatre from *Brooklyn Daily Eagle Almanac 1927*.

Turning to theatres actually located on 47th St., in 1923 there were only two. The Palace was at 1564 Broadway (at 47th St.), on the east side of the White Way. It was devoted to vaudeville. However, the Central Theatre, at 1567 Broadway (at 47th St.), was west of Broadway. Built by the Schuberts in 1918, it also fits the description of "one of Broadway's newest"—only a few of the dozens of Broadway theaters were newer. A seating chart of the Central Theatre is reproduced here. Comparing it to the diagram of the Roman Theatre, it can be seen that the Roman Theatre, while similarly laid out, was larger than the Central Theatre. Furthermore, no play was running at the Central Theatre in September 1923.

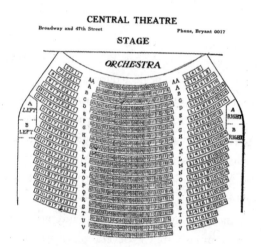

Seating plan of Central Theatre from *Brooklyn Daily Eagle Almanac 1927*.

In short, no candidate meets all of the criteria of location, name, size, and history. Not only did J. J. McC. conceal the name and location of the actual theater, it appears that even the name of the play involved in the case was changed—presumably to protect the cast and crew members from unwanted notoriety.

The Broadway theater scene in the 1920s.

Inside the theatre, one of Broadway's newest, people bustled to their seats visibly apprehensive, since the boisterous quality of the play was public knowledge. In due time the last member of the audience ceased rustling his program; the last latecomer stumbled over his neighbor's feet; the lights dimmed and the curtain rose. A pistol coughed in the silence, a man screamed . . . the play was on.

"Gunplay" was the first drama of the season to utilize the noises customarily associated with the underworld.[16] Automatics, machine guns, raids on night-clubs, the lethal sounds of gang vendettas—the entire stock-in-trade of the romanticized crime society was jammed into three swift acts. It was an exaggerated reflection of the times—a bit raw, a bit nasty and altogether satisfying to the theatrical public. Consequently it played to packed houses in rain and shine. This evening's house was proof of its popularity.

The performance proceeded smoothly. The audience was properly thrilled at the thunderous climax to the first act. The rain having stopped, people strolled out into the side alleys for a breath of air during the first ten-minute intermission. With the rising of the curtain on Act II, the detonations on the stage increased in volume. The second act hurtled to its big moment as explosive dialogue shot across the footlights. A slight commotion at the rear of the theatre went unnoticed, not unnaturally, in the noise and the darkness. No one seemed aware of anything amiss and the play crashed on. Gradually, however, the commotion increased in volume. At this point a few spectators at the rear of the left section squirmed about in their seats, to assert their rights in angry

16.   Gangsters had long been a popular subject of films, even before Prohibition sparked speakeasies, illicit sources of alcohol, and fueled the spread of gangsterism. One of the first gangster films was D. W. Griffith's *The Musketeers of Pig Alley* (1912), about organized crime. Outdoor scenes were shot in gang territory, the Lower East Side of New York, depicting slum tenements, and allegedly some of the cast included actual gang members. Legendary director Raoul Walsh's first feature film was the crime drama *The Regeneration* (1915). Shot in the Bowery on the Lower East Side of New York, it highlighted lawless violence on the streets of New York.

Gangsters had also appeared on the stage, only a year before the opening of *Gunplay*. In William A. Page's *The Bootleggers*, which ran for a month in late 1922 at Broadway's 39th St. Theatre, a battle is waged between gangsters who control the liquor trade on the East Side and the West Side of Manhattan. Before *The Roman Hat Mystery* appeared, two other gangster plays did well on Broadway: William Anthony McGuire's *Twelve Miles Out* (also about bootleggers), which ran for six months at the Playhouse Theatre on West 48th St., beginning on November 16, 1925; and *Broadway*, by Philip Dunning and George Abbott (still more bootleggers), which ran for 603 performances beginning on September 16, 1926, at the Broadhurst Theatre on West 44th St. (the latter was revived unsuccessfully at the Royale Theatre on West 45th St. in 1987, where it ran for only three performances).

whispers. The protest was contagious. In an incredibly short time scores of eyes turned toward that section of the orchestra.

Suddenly a sharp scream tore through the theatre. The audience, excited and fascinated by the swift sequence of events on the stage, craned their necks expectantly in the direction of the cry, eager to witness what they thought was a new sensation of the play.

Without warning the lights of the theatre snapped on, revealing puzzled, fearful, already appreciative faces. At the extreme left, near a closed exit-door, a large policeman stood holding a slight nervous man by the arm. He fended off a group of inquisitive people with a huge hand, shouting in stentorian tones, "Everybody stay right where he is! Don't move! Don't get out of your seat, any of you!"

People laughed.

The smiles were soon wiped away. For the audience began to perceive a curious hesitancy on the part of the actors. Although they continued to recite their lines behind the footlights they were casting puzzled glances out into the orchestra. People, noting this, half-rose from their seats, panicky in the presence of a scented tragedy. The officer's jovian voice continued to thunder, "Keep your seats, I say! Stay where you are!"

The audience suddenly realized that the incident was not play-acting but reality. Women shrieked and clutched their escorts. Bedlam broke loose in the balcony, whose occupants were in no position to see anything below.

The policeman turned savagely to a stocky, foreign-looking man in evening clothes who was standing by, rubbing his hands together.

"I'll have to ask you to close every exit this minute and see that they're kept closed, Mr. Panzer," he growled. "Station an usher at all the doors and tell 'em to hold everybody tryin' to get in or out. Send somebody outside to cover the alleys, too, until help comes from the station. Move fast, Mr. Panzer, before hell pops!"

The swarthy little man hurried away, brushing aside a number of excited people who had disregarded the officer's bellowed admonition and had jumped up to question him.

The bluecoat stood wide-legged at the entrance to the last row of the left section, concealing with his bulk the crumpled figure of a man in full evening dress, lying slumped in a queer attitude on the floor between rows. The policeman looked up, keeping a firm grip on the arm of the cowering man at his side, and shot a quick glance toward the rear of the orchestra.

"Hey, Neilson!" he shouted.

A tall tow-headed man hustled out of a small room near the main entrance and pushed his way through to the officer. He looked sharply down at the inert figure on the floor.

"What's happened here, Doyle?"

"Better ask this feller here," replied the policeman grimly. He shook the arm of the man he was holding. "There's a guy dead, and Mr."—he bent a ferocious glance upon the shrinking little man—"Pusak, W-William Pusak," he stammered—"this Mr. Pusak," continued Doyle, "says he heard him whisper he'd been croaked."

Neilson stared at the dead body, stunned.

The policeman chewed his lip. "I'm in one sweet mess, Harry," he said hoarsely. "The only cop in the place, and a pack of yellin' fools to take care of. . . . I want you to do somethin' for me."

"Say the word. . . . This is one hell of a note!"

Doyle wheeled in a rage to shout to a man who had just risen three rows ahead and was standing on his seat, peering at the proceedings. "Hey you!" he roared. "Get down offa there! Here—get back there, the whole bunch o' you. Back to your seats, now, or I'll pinch the whole nosey mob!"

He turned on Neilson. "Beat it to your desk, Harry, and give headquarters a buzz about the murder," he whispered. "Tell 'em to bring down a gang—make it a big one. Tell 'em it's a theatre—they'll know what to do. And here, Harry—take my whistle and toot your head off outside. I gotta get some help right away."

As Neilson fought his way back through the crowd, Doyle shouted after him: "Better ask 'em to send old man Queen down here, Harry!"

The tow-headed man disappeared into the office. A few moments later a shrill whistle was heard from the sidewalk in front of the theatre.

The swarthy theatre-manager whom Doyle had commanded to place guards at the exits and alleys came scurrying back through the press. His dress shirt was slightly rumpled and he was mopping his forehead with an air of bewilderment. A woman stopped him as he wriggled his way forward. She squeaked,

"Why is this policeman keeping us here, Mr. Panzer? I've a right to leave, I should like you to know! I don't care if an accident *did* happen—I had nothing to do with it—that's your affair-please tell him to stop this silly disciplining of innocent people!"

IN WHICH ARE INTRODUCED A THEATRE-AUDIENCE AND A CORPSE

17.   A "Van Dyke" style of facial hair, named after the Dutch painter Anthony van Dyck (1599–1641), consisted of a moustache and goatee.

Self-portrait of Anthony van Dyck
(van Dyke), after 1633.

The little man stammered, trying to escape. "Now, madam, please. I'm sure the officer knows what he is doing. A man has been killed here—it is a serious matter. Don't you see. . . . As manager of the theatre I must follow his orders. Please be calm—have a little patience. . . ."

He wormed his way out of her grasp and was off before she could protest.

Doyle, his arms waving violently, stood on a seat and bellowed: "I told you to sit down and keep quiet, the pack o' you! I don't care if you're the Mayor himself, you—yeah, you there, in the monocle—stay down or I'll shove you down! Don't you people realize what's happened? Pipe down, I say!" He jumped to the floor, muttering as he wiped the perspiration from his cap-band.

In the turmoil and excitement, with the orchestra boiling like a huge kettle, and necks stretched over the railing of the balcony as the people there strove vainly to discover the cause of the confusion, the abrupt cessation of activity on the stage was forgotten by the audience. The actors had stammered their way through lines rendered meaningless by the drama before the footlights. Now the slow descent of the curtain put an end to the evening's entertainment. The actors, chattering, hurried toward the stage-stairs. Like the audience they peered toward the nucleus of the trouble in bewilderment.

A buxom old lady, in garish clothes—the very fine imported actress billed in the character of Madame Murphy, "keeper of the public house"—her name was Hilda Orange; the slight, graceful figure of "the street waif, Nanette"—Eve Ellis, leading-lady of the piece; the tall robust hero of "Gunplay," James Peale, attired in a rough tweed suit and cap; the juvenile, smart in evening clothes, portraying the society lad who had fallen into the clutches of the "gang"—Stephen Barry; Lucille Horton, whose characterization of the "lady of the streets" had brought down a shower of adjectives from the dramatic critics, who had little enough to rant about that unfortunate season; a vandyked[17] old man whose faultless evening clothes attested to the tailoring genius of M. Le Brun, costumer extraordinary to the entire cast of "Gunplay"; the heavy-set villain, whose stage scowl was dissolved in a foggy docility as he surveyed the frantic auditorium; in fact, the entire personnel of the play, bewigged and powdered, rouged and painted—some wielding towels as they hastily removed their make-up—scampered in a body under the lowering curtain and trooped down the stage-steps into the orchestra, where they elbowed their way up the aisle toward the scene of the commotion.

Another flurry, at the main entrance, caused many people despite Doyle's vigorous orders to rise in their seats for a clearer view. A group of bluecoats were hustling their way inside, their night-sticks ready. Doyle heaved a gargantuan sigh of relief as he saluted the tall man in plainclothes at their head.

"What's up, Doyle?" asked the newcomer, frowning at the pandemonium raging about them. The bluecoats who had entered with him were herding the crowd to the rear of the orchestra, behind the seat-sections. People who had been standing tried to slip back to their seats; they were apprehended and made to join the angry cluster jammed behind the last row.

"Looks like this man's been murdered, Sergeant," said Doyle.

"Uh-huh." The plainclothes man looked incuriously down at the one still figure in the theatre lying at their feet, a black-sleeved arm flung over his face, his legs sprawled gawkily under the seats in the row before.

"What is it—gat?"[18] asked the newcomer of Doyle, his eyes roving.

"No, sir—don't seem to be," said the policeman. "Had a doctor from the audience look him over the very first thing—thinks it's poison."

The Sergeant grunted. "Who's this?" he rapped, indicating the trembling figure of Pusak by Doyle's side.

"Chap who found the body," returned Doyle. "He hasn't moved from the spot since."

"Good enough." The detective turned toward a compact group huddled a few feet behind them and asked, generally: "Who's the manager here?"

Panzer stepped forward.

"I'm Velie, detective-sergeant from headquarters," said the plainclothes man abruptly. "Haven't you done anything to keep this yelling pack of idiots quiet?"

"I've done my best, Sergeant," mumbled the manager, wringing his hands. "But they all seem incensed at the way this officer"—he indicated Doyle apologetically—"has been storming at them. I don't know how I can reasonably expect them to keep sitting in their seats as if nothing had happened."

18.   Slang for a gun, and more specifically a machine gun, the weapon of choice of gangsters in the 1920s. The name derives from the Gatling gun, a rapid-fire, crank-driven weapon with a cylindrical cluster of barrels. Invented by Richard Gatling, it was used by Union forces in the Civil War.

"Well, we'll take care of that," snapped Velie. He gave a rapid order to a uniformed man nearby. "Now"—he turned back to Doyle—"how about the doors, the exits? Done anything yet in that direction?"

"Sure thing, Sergeant," grinned the policeman. "I had Mr. Panzer here station ushers at every door. They've been there all night, anyway. But I just wanted to make sure."

"You were right. Nobody try to get out?"

"I think I can vouch for that, Sergeant," put in Panzer meekly. "The action of the play necessitates having ushers posted near every exit, for atmosphere. This is a crook play, with a good deal of shooting and screaming and that sort of thing going on, and the presence of guards around the doors heightens the general effect of mystery. I can very easily find out for you if . . .'"

"We'll attend to that ourselves," said Velie. "Doyle, who'd you send for?"

"Inspector Queen," answered Doyle. "I had the publicity man, Neilson, 'phone him at headquarters."

Velie allowed a smile to crease his wintry face. "Thought of everything, didn't you? Now how about the body? Has it been touched at all since this fellow found it?"

The cowering man held in Doyle's hard grasp broke out, half-crying. "I—I only found him, officer—honest to God, I—"

"All right, all right," said Velie coldly. "You'll keep, won't you? What are you blubbering about? Well, Doyle?"

"Not a finger was laid on the body since I came over," replied Doyle, with a trace of pride in his voice. "Except, of course, for a Dr. Stuttgard. I got him out of the audience to make sure the man was dead. He was, and nobody else came near."

"You've been busy, haven't you, Doyle? I'll see you won't suffer by it," said Velie. He wheeled on Panzer, who shrank back. "Better trot up to the stage and make an announcement, Mr. Manager. The whole crew of 'em are to stay right where they are until Inspector Queen lets them go home—understand? Tell them it won't do any good to kick—and the more they kick the longer they'll be here. Make it plain, too, that they're to stick to their seats, and any suspicious move on anybody's part is going to make trouble."

"'Yes. Yes. Good Lord, what a catastrophe!" groaned Panzer as he made his way down the aisle toward the stage.

At the same moment a little knot of people pushed open the big door at the rear of the theatre and stepped across the carpet in a body.

CHAPTER II

In Which One Queen Works and Another Queen Watches

There was nothing remarkable in either the physique or the manner of Inspector Richard Queen. He was a small, withered, rather mild-appearing old gentleman. He walked with a little stoop and an air of deliberation that somehow accorded perfectly with his thick grey hair and mustaches, veiled grey eyes and slender hands.

As he crossed the carpet with short, quick steps Inspector Queen was far from impressive to the milling eyes that observed his approach from every side. And yet, so unusual was the gentle dignity of his appearance, so harmless and benevolent the smile that illumined his lined old face, that an audible rustle swept over the auditorium, preceding him in a strangely fitting manner.

In his own men the change was appreciable. Doyle retreated into a corner near the left exits. Detective-Sergeant Velie, poised over the body—sardonic, cold, untouched by the near-hysteria about him—relaxed a trifle, as if he were satisfied to relinquish his place in the sun. The bluecoats guarding the aisles saluted with alacrity. The nervous, muttering, angry audience sank back with an unreasoning relief.

Inspector Queen stepped forward and shook hands with Velie.

"Too bad, Thomas, my boy. I hear you were going home when this happened," he murmured. To Doyle he smiled in a fatherly fashion. Then, in a mild pity, he peered down at the man on the floor. "Thomas," he asked, "are all the exits covered?" Velie nodded.

The old man turned back and let his eyes travel interestedly about the scene. He asked a low-voiced question of Velie, who nodded his head in assent; then he crooked his finger at Doyle.

"Doyle, where are the people who were sitting in these seats?" He pointed to three chairs adjoining the dead man's and four directly to the front of them in the preceding row.

The policeman appeared puzzled. "Didn't see anybody there, Inspector. . . ."

Queen stood silent for a moment, then waved Doyle back with the low remark to Velie, "In a crowded house, too. . . . Remember that." Velie raised his eyebrows gravely. "I'm cold on this whole business," continued the Inspector genially. "All I can see right now are a dead man and a lot of perspiring people making noise. Have Hesse and Piggott direct traffic for a while, eh, son?"

Velie spoke sharply to two of the plainclothes men who had entered the theatre with the Inspector. They wriggled their way toward the rear and the people who had been crowding around found themselves pushed aside. Policemen joined the two detectives. The group of actors and actresses were ordered to move back. A section was roped off behind the central tier of seats and some fifty men and women packed into the small space. Quiet men circulated among them, instructing them to show their tickets and return to their seats one by one. Within five minutes not a member of the audience was left standing. The actors were cautioned to remain within the roped enclosure for the time being.

In the extreme left aisle Inspector Queen reached into his topcoat pocket, carefully extracted a brown carved snuff-box and took a pinch with every evidence of enjoyment.

"That's more like it, Thomas," he chuckled. "You know how fussy I am about noises. . . . Who is the poor chap on the floor—do you know?"

Velie shook his head. "I haven't even touched the body, Inspector," he said. "I got here just a few minutes before you did. A man on the 47th Street beat called me up from his box and reported Doyle's whistle. Doyle seems to have been doing things, sir. . . . His lieutenant reports favorably on his record."

"Ah," said the Inspector, "ah, yes. Doyle. Come here, Doyle."

The policeman stepped forward and saluted.

"Just what," went on the little grey man, leaning comfortably against a seat-back, "just what happened here, Doyle?"

"All I know about it, Inspector," began Doyle, "is that a couple of minutes before the end of the second act this man"—he pointed to Pusak, who stood wretchedly in a corner—"came running up to me where I was standin' in the back, watchin' the show, and he says, 'A man's been murdered, officer! . . . A man's murdered!' He was blubberin' like a baby and I thought he was pie-eyed.[19] But I stepped mighty quick and came over here—the place was dark and there was a lot of shootin' and screamin' on the stage—and I took a look at the feller on the floor. I didn't move him, but I felt his heart and there wasn't anything to feel. To make sure he was croaked I asked for a doctor and a gent by the name of Stuttgard answered my call. . . ."

Inspector Queen stood pertly, his head cocked on a side like a parrot's. "That's excellent," he said. "Excellent, Doyle. I'll question Dr. Stuttgard later. Then what happened?" he went on.

"Then," continued the policeman, "then I got the usherette on this aisle to beat it back to the manager's office for Panzer. Louis Panzer—that's the manager right over there . . ."

Queen regarded Panzer, who was standing a few feet to the rear talking to Neilson, and nodded. "That's Panzer, you say. All right, all right. . . . Ellery! You got my message?"

He darted forward, brushing aside Panzer, who fell back apologetically, and clapped the shoulder of a tall young man who had slipped through the main door and was slowly looking about the scene. The old man passed his aim through the younger man's.

"Haven't inconvenienced you any, son? What bookstore did you haunt to-night? Ellery, I'm mighty glad you're here!"

He dipped into his pocket, again extracted the snuff-box, sniffed deeply—so deeply that he sneezed—and looked up into his son's face.

"As a matter of fact," said Ellery Queen, his eyes restlessly roving, "I can't return the compliment. You just lured me away from a perfect book-lover's paradise. I was at the point of getting the dealer to let me have a priceless Falconer first-edition,[20] intending to borrow the money from you at headquarters. I telephoned—and here I am. A Falconer—Oh, well. To-morrow will do, I suppose."

The Inspector chuckled. "Now if you told me you were picking up an old snuff-box I might be interested. As it is—trot along. Looks as if we have some work to-night."

19. Intoxicated.

20. This likely refers to a work by William Falconer (1732–1769), the Scottish epic poet best remembered for his poem "The Shipwreck." The first edition of the book version of "The Shipwreck" was published in 1762. However, the book seems a bit far afield for a man known for his collection of books on violence, and there is another tantalizing possibility: A rare book dealer recently offered a significant, original manuscript journal, untitled, circa 1880–90s through 1900s, compiled and created by one "Wm. A. Falconer Fort Smith and Fayetteville Ark." According to the dealer's research, this is the work of Judge William A. Falconer, who was born in Charleston, Arkansas, in 1869.

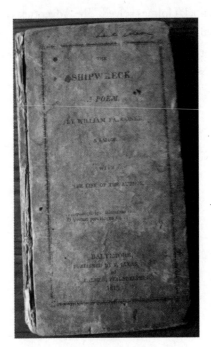

Early edition of *The Shipwreck*,
by W. E. Falconer

There Falconer received his early education, studied law at the University of Arkansas in Fayetteville, then practiced law in Fort Smith,

Arkansas, beginning in 1895. In 1902 Falconer became a Sebastian County judge. Although his published papers focus on the American Civil War, the manuscript offered by the dealer appears to be a compilation of nearly everything written about the notorious Mountain Meadows Massacre, the most famous mass killing of the era and one of the most controversial episodes in the history of the Mormon church. There is no evidence of actual publication of this book, but clearly the true first edition would have been a highlight of Ellery's collection.

21. Eyeglasses without earpieces. They were popular in the nineteenth century and in the twentieth century were a bit of an affectation. Sherlock Holmes solved "The Adventure of the Golden Pince-Nez." Note that pince-nez are mentioned also in *The Benson Murder Case* and *Red Harvest.*

They walked toward the little knot of men on the left, the old man's hand grasping his son's coat-sleeve. Ellery Queen towered six inches above his father's head. There was a square cut to his shoulders and an agreeable swing to his body as he walked. He was dressed in oxford grey and carried a light stick. On his nose perched what seemed an incongruous note in so athletic a man—a rimless pince-nez.[21] But the brow above, the long delicate lines of the face, the bright eyes were those of a man of thought rather than action.

They joined the group at the body. Ellery was greeted respectfully by Velie. He bent over the seat, glanced earnestly at the dead man, and stepped back.

"Go on, Doyle," said the Inspector briskly. "You looked at the body, detained the man who found it, got the manager. . . . Then what?"

"Panzer at my orders closed all the doors at once and saw that no one either came in or went out," answered Doyle. "There was a lot of fuss here with the audience, but nothing else happened."

"Right, right!" said the Inspector, feeling for his snuff-box. "You did a mighty good job. Now—That gentleman there."

He gestured in the direction of the trembling little man in the corner, who stepped forward hesitantly, licked his lips, looked about him with a helpless expression, and then stood silent.

"What's your name?" asked the Inspector, in a kindly tone.

"Pusak—William Pusak," said the man. "I'm a bookkeeper, sir. I was just—"

"One at a time, Pusak. Where were you sitting?"

Pusak pointed eagerly to the sixth seat from the aisle, in the last row. A frightened young girl in the fifth seat sat staring in their direction.

"I see." said the Inspector. "Is that young lady with you?"

"Yes, sir—yes, sir. That's my fiancée, sir. Her name is Esther—Esther Jablow. . . ."

A little to the rear a detective was scribbling in a notebook. Ellery stood behind his father, glancing from one exit to another. He began to draw a diagram on the fly-leaf of a small book he had taken from his topcoat pocket.

The Inspector scrutinized the girl, who immediately averted her eyes. "Now, Pusak, I want you to tell me just what happened."

"I—I didn't do a thing out of the way, sir."

Inspector Queen patted his arm. "Nobody is accusing you of anything, Pusak. All I want is your story of what happened. Take your time—tell it your own way. . . ."

Pusak gave him a curious glance. Then he moistened his lips and began. "Well, I was sitting there in that seat with my—with Miss Jablow—and we were enjoying the show pretty much. The second act was kind of exciting—there was a lot of shooting and yelling on the stage—and then I got up and started to go out the row to the aisle. This aisle—here." He pointed nervously to the spot of carpet on which he was standing. Queen nodded, his face benign.

"I had to push past my—Miss Jablow, and there wasn't any-body except one man between her and the aisle. That's why I went that way. I didn't sort of like to"—he hesitated apologetically—"to bother people going out that way in the middle of the most exciting part . . ."

"That was very decent of you, Pusak," said the Inspector, smiling.

"Yes, sir. So I walked down the row, feeling my way, because it was pretty dark in the theatre, and then I came to—to this man." He shuddered, and continued more rapidly. "He was sitting in a funny way, I thought. His knees were touching the seat in front of him and I couldn't get past. I said, 'I'm sorry,' and tried again, but his knees hadn't moved an inch. I didn't know what to do, sir—I'm not nervy, like some fellows, and I was going to turn around and go back when all of a sudden I felt the man's body slip to the floor—I was still pressed up close to him. Of course, I got kind of scared—it was only natural. . . ."

"I should say," said the Inspector, with concern. "It must have given you quite a turn. Then what happened?"

"Well, sir. . . . Then, before I realized what was happening, he fell clean out of his seat and his head bumped against my legs. I didn't know what to do. I couldn't call for help—I don't know why, but I couldn't somehow—and I just naturally bent over him, thinking he was drunk or sick or something, and meant to lift him up. I hadn't figured on what I'd do after that . . ."

"I know just how you felt, Pusak. Go on."

"Then it happened—the thing I told this policeman about. I'd just got hold of his head when I felt his hand come up and grab mine, just like he was trying awfully hard to get a grip on something, and he moaned. It was so low I could hardly hear it, but sort of horrible. I can't quite describe it exactly. . . ."

"Now, we're getting on," said the Inspector. "And?"

"And then he talked. It wasn't really talking—it was more like a gurgle, as if he was choking. He said a few words that I didn't catch at all, but I realized that this was something different from just being sick or drunk, so I bent even lower and listened hard. I heard him gasp, 'It's murder . . . Been murdered . . .' or something like that. . . ."

"So he said, 'It's murder,' eh?" The Inspector regarded Pusak with severity. "Well, now. That must have given you a shock, Pusak." He snapped suddenly, "Are you certain this man said 'murder'?"

"That's what I heard, sir. I've got good hearing," said Pusak doggedly.

"Well!" Queen relaxed, smiling again. "Of course. I just wanted to make sure. Then what did you do?"

"Then I felt him squirm a little and all of a sudden go limp in my arms. I was afraid he'd died and I don't know how—but next thing I knew I was in the back telling it all to the policeman—this policeman here." He pointed to Doyle, who rocked on his heels impersonally.

"And that's all?"

"Yes, sir. Yes, sir. That's all I know about it," said Pusak, with a sigh of relief.

Queen grasped him by the coat front and barked, "That isn't all, Pusak. You forgot to tell us why you left your seat in the first place!" He glared into the little man's eyes.

Pusak coughed, teetered back and forth a moment, as if uncertain of his next words, then leaned forward and whispered into the Inspector's astonished ear.

"Oh!" Queen's lips twitched in the suspicion of a smile,[22] but he said gravely, "I see, Pusak. Thank you very much for your help. Everything is all right now—you may go back to your seat and leave with the others later on." He waved his hand in a gesture of dismissal. Pusak, with a sickly glance at the dead man on the floor, crept around the rear wall of the last row and reappeared by the girl's side. She immediately engaged him in a whispered but animated conversation.

As the Inspector with a little smile turned to Velie, Ellery made a slight movement of impatience, opened his mouth to speak, appeared to reconsider, and finally moved quietly backwards, disappearing from view.

"Well, Thomas," sighed the Inspector, "let's have a look at this chap."

He bent nimbly over the dead man, on his knees in the space between the last row and the row directly before it. Despite the brilliant sparkle of light from the fixtures overhead, the cramped space near the floor was dark. Velie produced a flashlight and stooped over the Inspector, keeping its bright beam on the corpse, shifting it as the Inspector's hands roved about. Queen silently pointed to an ugly ragged brown stain on the otherwise immaculate shirt-front.

"Blood?" grunted Velie.

The Inspector sniffed the shirt cautiously. "Nothing more dangerous than whisky," he retorted.

He ran his hands swiftly over the body, feeling over the heart and at the neck, where the collar was loosened. He looked up at Velie.

"Looks like a poisoning case, all right, Thomas. Get hold of this Dr. Stuttgard for me, will you? I'd like to have his professional opinion before Prouty gets here."

Velie snapped an order and a moment later a medium-sized man in evening clothes, olive-skinned and wearing a thin black mustache, came up behind a detective.

"Here he is, Inspector," said Velie.

"Ah, yes." Queen looked up from his examination. "How do you do, Doctor? I am informed that you examined the body almost immediately after it was discovered. I see no obvious sign of death—what is your opinion?"

"My examination was necessarily a cursory one," said Dr. Stuttgard carefully, his fingers brushing a phantom speck from his satin lapel. "In the semi-dark and under these conditions I could not at first discern any abnormal sign of death. From the construction of the facial muscles I thought that it was a simple case of heart failure, but on closer examination I noticed that blueness of the face—it's quite clear in this light, isn't it? That combined with the alcoholic odor from the mouth seems to point to some form of alcoholic poisoning. Of one thing I can assure you—this man did not die of a gunshot wound or a stab. I naturally made sure of that at once. I even examined his neck—you see I loosened the collar—to make sure it was not strangulation."

23. Wood alcohol or methanol, used in industry, can cause blindness and is a potent toxin. Bootleggers often acquired industrial alcohol and re-distilled it to remove the methanol. Queen's suspicion was that either wood alcohol was deliberately substituted for grain alcohol or Fields somehow got ahold of a bad batch. However, in 1926, in order to discourage the rising amount of alcohol being consumed, the U.S. government actually ordered the addition of methanol to ethanol. A number of deaths by alcohol poisoning resulted and were publicized by the government. In a public statement, New York City medical examiner Charles V. Norris accused the U.S. government of this heinous action. "The government knows it is not stopping drinking by putting poison in alcohol, yet it continues its poisoning processes, heedless of the fact that people determined to drink are daily absorbing that poison. Knowing this to be true, the U.S. government must be charged with the moral responsibility for the deaths that poisoned liquor causes, although it cannot be held legally responsible." See Deborah Blum's *The Poisoner's Handbook: Murder and the Birth of Forensic Medicine in Jazz Age New York* (New York: Penguin Press, 2010).

24. Inspector Queen was looking for so-called patent fingerprints, those visible with the unaided eye. Such prints usually occur because the surface is highly reflective and retains oils from the skin or the person touching the object had something on his or her fingers (for example, blood). Apparently no prints were immediately visible, notwithstanding the "silver" of the flask; therefore, Queen would have taken the flask back to the crime laboratory for dusting for *latent* (invisible) fingerprints.

"I see." The Inspector smiled, "Thank you very much, Doctor. Oh, by the way," he added, as Dr. Stuttgard with a muttered word turned aside, "do you think this man might have died from the effects of wood alcohol?"[23]

Dr. Stuttgard answered promptly. "Impossible," he said. "It was something much more powerful and quick-acting."

"Could you put a name to the exact poison which killed this man?"

The olive-skinned physician hesitated. Then he said stiffly, "I am very sorry, Inspector; you cannot reasonably expect me to be more precise. Under the circumstances . . ." His voice trailed off, and he backed away.

Queen chuckled as he bent again to his grim task.

The dead man sprawled on the floor was not a pleasant sight. The Inspector gently lifted the clenched hand and stared hard at the contorted face. Then he looked under the seat. There was nothing there. However, a black silk-lined cape hung carelessly over the back of the chair. He emptied all of the pockets of both dress-suit and cape, his hands diving in and out of the clothing. He extracted a few letters and papers from the inside breast pocket, delved into the vest pockets and trouser-pockets, heaping his discoveries in two piles—one containing papers and letters, the other coins, keys, and miscellaneous material. A silver flask initialed "M. F." he found in one of the hip-pockets. He handled the flask gingerly, holding it by the neck, and scanning the gleaming surface as if for fingerprints.[24] Shaking his head, he wrapped the flask with infinite care in a clean handkerchief, and placed it aside.

A ticket stub colored blue and bearing the inscription "LL32 Left," he secreted in his own vest pocket.

Without pausing to examine any of the other objects individually, he ran his hands over the lining of the vest and coat, and made a rapid pass over the trouser-legs. Then, as he fingered the coat-tail pocket, he exclaimed in a low tone, "Well, well, Thomas—here's a pretty find!" as he extracted a woman's evening bag, small, compact and glittering with rhinestones.

He turned it over in his hands reflectively, then snapped it open, glanced through it and took out a number of feminine accessories. In a small compartment, nestling beside a lipstick, he found a tiny card-case. After a moment, he replaced all the contents and put the bag in his own pocket.

The Inspector picked up the papers from the floor and swiftly glanced through them. He frowned as he came to the last one—a letterhead.

"Ever hear of Monte Field, Thomas?" he asked, looking up.

Velie tightened his lips. "I'll say I have. One of the crookedest lawyers in town."

The Inspector looked grave. "Well, Thomas, this is Mr. Monte Field—what's left of him." Velie grunted.

"Where the average police system falls down," came Ellery's voice over his father's shoulder, "is in its ruthless tracking down of gentlemen who dispose of such fungus as Mr. Monte Field."

The Inspector straightened, dusted his knees carefully, took a pinch of snuff, and said, "Ellery, my boy, you'll never make a policeman. I didn't know you knew Field."

"I wasn't exactly on terms of intimacy with the gentleman," said Ellery. "But I remember having met him at the Pantheon Club,[25] and from what I heard at the time I don't wonder somebody has removed him from our midst."

"Let's discuss the demerits of Mr. Field at a more propitious time," said the Inspector gravely. "I happen to know quite a bit about him, and none of it is pleasant."

He wheeled and was about to walk away when Ellery, gazing curiously at the dead body and the seat, drawled, "Has anything been removed, dad—anything at all?"

Inspector Queen turned his head. "And why do you ask that bright question, young man?"

"'Because," returned Ellery, with a grimace, "unless my eyesight fails me, the chap's tophat is not under the seat, on the floor beside him, or anywhere in the general vicinity."

"So you noticed that too, did you, Ellery?" said the Inspector grimly. "It's the first thing I saw when I bent down to examine him—or rather the first thing I didn't see." The Inspector seemed to lose his geniality as he spoke. His brow wrinkled and his grey mustache bristled fiercely. He shrugged his shoulders. "And no hat-check in his clothes, either. Flint!"

A husky young man in plain clothes hurried forward.

"Flint, suppose you exercise those young muscles of yours by getting down on your hands and knees and hunting for a tophat. It ought to be somewhere around here."

In 1923, the D. C. Circuit laid down the standard for admitting scientific evidence: "Just when a scientific principle or discovery crosses the line between the experimental and demonstrable stages is difficult to define. Somewhere in this twilight zone the evidential force of the principle must be recognized, and while courts will go a long way in admitting expert testimony deduced from a well-recognized scientific principle or discovery, the thing from which the deduction is made must be sufficiently established to have gained general acceptance in the particular field to which it belongs" (*Frye v. U.S.*, 293 F. 1030 [1923]). *Frye* involved testimony regarding a polygraph test; fingerprint evidence had long before been accepted. However, recent cases have established that errors do occasionally occur in matching fingerprints.

25. There is no indication of whether the Pantheon Club was a speakeasy—there were hundreds in Manhattan alone in the 1920s—or a gentleman's club, though the lofty-sounding name suggests the latter rather than the former. According to *Trow's General Directory of New York City* for 1922–23, the Pantheon Society had a location at 220 W. 118th St.

26. There is no recognizable author or publisher with the name "Stendhause," and it is unclear what a private edition means here. In the Victorian era, volumes of pornography were often printed in limited editions by subscription and sold only to subscribers—perhaps this is what Ellery is carrying around!

27. Then as now, a fashionable residential neighborhood on the Upper West Side, about two blocks west of Central Park and just a few short blocks from the American Museum of Natural History.

28. In lower Manhattan, just a block from City Hall.

29. As will be seen, Inspector Queen sends the string to a hatter to check the hat size. However, one would expect that the Inspector (or Ellery) would know that hat sizes follow a definite formula: a 21¼-inch head circumference takes a 6¾-size hat (commonly, the smallest); for every additional ⅜ inch of head circumference, the hat size increases by ⅛. So, for example, a 22¾-inch head circumference is four additional ⅜-inch segments larger than 21¼ inches and produces a hat size of 7¼. The formula is Hat size = 6¾ + ((X − 21¼) ÷ 3), where X is the head circumference, rounded to the nearest ⅜ inch.

"Right, Inspector," said Flint cheerfully, and he began a methodical search of the indicated area.

"Velie," said Queen, in a businesslike tone, "suppose you find Ritter and Hesse and—no, those two will do—for me, will you?" Velie walked away.

"Hagstrom!" shouted the Inspector to another detective standing by.

"Yes, Chief."

"Get busy with this stuff"—he pointed to the two small piles of articles he had taken from Field's pockets and which lay on the floor—"and be sure to put them safely away in my own bags."

As Hagstrom knelt by the body, Ellery quietly bent over and opened the coat. He immediately jotted a memorandum on the fly-leaf of the book in which he had drawn a diagram some time before. He muttered to himself, patting the volume, "And it's a Stendhause private edition, too!"[26]

Velie returned with Ritter and Hesse at his heels. The Inspector said sharply, "Ritter, go to this man's apartment. His name is Monte Field, he was an attorney, and he lived at 113 West 75th Street.[27] Stick around until you're relieved. If any one shows up, nab him."

Ritter, touching his hat, mumbled, "Yes, Inspector," and turned away.

"Now Hesse, my lad," continued the Inspector to the other detective, "hurry down to 51 Chambers Street,[28] this man's office, and wait there until you hear from me. Get inside if you can, otherwise park outside the door all night."

"Right, Inspector." Hesse disappeared.

Queen turned about and chuckled as he saw Ellery, broad shoulders bent over, examining the dead man.

"Don't trust your father, eh, Ellery?" the Inspector chided. "What are you snooping for?"

Ellery smiled, straightening up. "I'm merely curious, that's all," he said. "There are certain things about this unsavory corpse that interest me hugely. For example, have you taken the man's head measurement?" He held up a piece of string, which he had slipped from a wrapped book in his coat pocket, and offered it for his father's inspection.[29]

The Inspector took it, scowled and summoned a policeman from the rear of the theatre. He issued a low-voiced order, the string exchanged hands and the policeman departed.

"Inspector."

Queen looked up. Hagstrom stood by his elbow, eyes gleaming.

"I found this pushed way back under Field's seat when I picked up the papers. It was against the back wall."

He held up a dark-green bottle, of the kind used by ginger ale manufacturers. A gaudy label read, "Paley's Extra Dry Ginger Ale." The bottle was half-empty.

"Well, Hagstrom, you've got something up your sleeve. Out with it!" the Inspector said curtly.

"Yes, sir! When I found this bottle under the dead man's seat, I knew that he had probably used it to-night. There was no matinee to-day and the cleaning women go over the place every twenty-four hours. It wouldn't have been there unless this man, or somebody connected with him, had used it and put it there to-night. I thought, 'Maybe this is a clue,' so I dug up the refreshment boy who had this section of the theatre and I asked him to sell me a bottle of ginger ale. He said"—Hagstrom smiled—"he said they don't sell ginger ale in this theatre!"

"You used your head that time, Hagstrom," said the Inspector approvingly. "Get hold of the boy and bring him here."

As Hagstrom left, a stout little man in slightly disarranged evening clothes bustled up, a policeman doggedly holding his arm. The Inspector sighed.

"Are you in charge of this affair, sir?" stormed the little man, drawing himself up to five feet two inches of perspiring flesh.

"I am," said Queen gravely.

"Then I want you to know," burst out the newcomer—"here, you, let go of my arm, do you hear?—I want you to know, sir . . ."

"Detach yourself from the gentleman's arm, officer," said the Inspector, with deepening gravity.

". . . that I consider this entire affair the most vicious outrage! I have been sitting here with my wife and daughter since the interruption to the play for almost an hour, and your officers refuse to allow us even to stand up. It's a damnable outrage, sir! Do you think you can keep this entire audience waiting at your leisure? I've been watching you—don't think I haven't. You've been dawdling around while we sat and suffered. I want you to know, sir—I want you to know!—that unless you permit my party to leave at once, I shall get in touch with my very good friend District Attorney Sampson and lodge a personal complaint against you!"

Inspector Queen gazed distastefully into the empurpled face of the stout little man. He sighed and said with a note of sternness, "My dear man, has it occurred to you that at this moment, while you stand beefing about a little thing like being detained an hour or so, a person who has committed murder may be in this very audience—perhaps sitting next to your wife and daughter? He is just as anxious as you to get away. If you wish to make a complaint to the District Attorney, your very good friend, you may do so after you leave this theatre. Meanwhile, I'll trouble you to return to your seat and be patient until you are permitted to go . . . I hope I make myself clear."

A titter arose from some spectators nearby, who seemed to be enjoying the little man's discomfiture. He flounced away, with the policeman stolidly following. The Inspector, muttering "Jackass!" turned to Velie.

"Take Panzer with you to the box-office and see if you can find complete tickets for these numbers." He bent over the last row and the row before it, scribbling the numbers LL30 Left, LL28 Left, LL2tl Left, KK32 Left, KK30 Left, KK28 Left, and KK26 Left on the back of an old envelope. He handed the memorandum to Velie, who went away.

Ellery, who had been leaning idly against the rear wall of the last row, watching his father, the audience, and occasionally restudying the geography of the theatre, murmured in the Inspector's ear: "I was just reflecting on the unusual fact that with such a popular bit of dramatic trash as 'Gunplay,' seven seats in the direct vicinity of the murdered man's seat should remain empty during the performance."

"When did you begin to wonder, my son?" said Queen, and while Ellery absently tapped the floor with his stick, barked, "Piggott!"

The detective stepped forward.

"Get the usherette who was on this aisle and the outside doorman—that middle-aged fellow on the sidewalk—and bring 'em here."

As Piggott walked off, a disheveled young man appeared by Queen's side, wiping his face with a handkerchief.

"Well, Flint?" asked Queen instantly.

"I've been over this floor like a scrub-woman, Inspector. If you're looking for a hat in this section of the theatre, it's mighty well hidden."

"All right, Flint, stand by."

The detective trudged off. Ellery said slowly, "Didn't really think your young Diogenes[30] would find the tophat, did you, dad?"

The Inspector grunted. He walked down the aisle and proceeded to lean over person after person, questioning each in low tones. All heads turned in his direction as he went from row to row, interrogating the occupants of the two aisle seats successively. As he walked back in Ellery's direction, his face expressionless, the policeman whom he had sent out with the piece of string saluted him.

"What size, officer?" asked the Inspector.

"The clerk in the hat store said it was exactly 7⅛," answered the bluecoat. Inspector Queen nodded, dismissing him. Velie strode up, with Panzer trailing worriedly behind. Ellery leaned forward with an air of keen absorption to catch Velie's words. Queen grew tense, the light of a great interest on his face.

"Well, Thomas," he said, "what did you find in the box-office?"

"Just this, Inspector," reported Velie unemotionally. "The seven tickets for which you gave me the numbers are not in the ticket-rack. They were sold from the box-office window, at what date Mr. Panzer has no way of knowing."

"The tickets might have been turned over to an agency, you know, Velie," remarked Ellery.

"I verified that, Mr. Queen," answered Velie. "Those tickets were not assigned to any agency. There are definite records to prove it."

Inspector Queen stood very still, his grey eyes gleaming. Then he said, "In other words, gentlemen, it would seem that at a drama which has been playing to capacity business ever since its opening, seven tickets in a group were bought—and then the purchasers conveniently forgot to attend the performance!"

30. Diogenes was a Greek philosopher who died about 320 B.C.E. He is said to have wandered the streets of Athens carrying a lantern in daylight, looking for an honest man, and it is this searching aspect of his character to which Ellery refers.

CHAPTER III

In Which a "Parson" Comes to Grief

There was a silence as the four men regarded each other with a dawning conviction. Panzer shuffled his feet and coughed nervously; Velie's face was a study in concentrated thought; Ellery stepped backward and fell into a rapt contemplation of his father's grey-and-blue necktie.

Inspector Queen stood biting his mustache. He shook his shoulders suddenly and turned on Velie.

"Thomas, I'm going to give you a dirty job," he said. "I want you to marshal a half-dozen or so of the uniformed men and set 'em to a personal examination of every soul in this place. All they have to do is get the name and address of each person in the audience. It's quite a job, and it will take time, but I'm afraid it's absolutely necessary. By the way, Thomas, in your scouting around, did you question any of the ushers who take care of the balcony?"

"I got hold of the very man to give me information," said Velie. "He's the lad who stands at the foot of the stairs in the orchestra, directing holders of balcony tickets to the upper ftoor. Chap by the name of Miller."

"A very conscientious boy," interposed Panzer, rubbing his hands.

"Miller is ready to swear that not a person in this theatre either went upstairs from the orchestra or came downstairs from the balcony from the moment the curtain went up on the second act."

"That sort of cuts down your work, Thomas," remarked the Inspector, who had been listening intently. "Have your men go through the orchestra boxes and orchestra only. Remember—I want the name and address of every person here—every single one. And Thomas—"

"Yes, Inspector?" said Velie, turning back.

"While they're at it, have 'em ask these people to show the ticket-stubs belonging to the seats in which they are sitting. Every case of loss of stub should be noted beside the name of the loser; and in cases—it is a bare possibility—where a person holds a stub which does not agree with the seat-number of the chair in which he's sitting, a notation is also to be made. Think you can get all that done, my boy?"

"Sure thing!" Velie grunted as he strode away.

The Inspector smoothed his grey mustache and took a pinch of snuff, inhaling deeply.

"Ellery," he said, "there's something worrying you. Out with it, son!"

"Eh?" Ellery started, blinking his eyes. He removed his pince-nez, and said slowly, "My very revered father, I am beginning to think that—Well! There's little peace in this world for a quiet book-loving man." He sat down on the arm of the dead man's seat, his eyes troubled. Suddenly he smiled. "Take care that you don't repeat the unfortunate error of that ancient butcher who, with his twoscore apprentices, sought high and low for his most treasured knife when all the time it reposed quietly in his mouth."[31]

"You're very informative these days, my son," said the Inspector petulantly. "Flint!"

The detective came forward.

"Flint," said Queen, "you've had one pleasant job to-night and I've another for you. Think your back could stand a little more bending? Seems to me I remember you took a weight-lifting contest in the Police Games when you were pounding a beat."

"Yes, sir," said Flint, grinning broadly. "I guess I can stand the strain."

"Well, then," continued the Inspector, jamming his hands into his pockets, "here's your job. Get a squad of men together—good Lord, I should have brought the Reserves along with me!—and make an exhaustive search of every square foot of the theatre-property, inside and out. You'll be looking for ticket-stubs, do

31. The proverbial tale of the butcher who looked for his knife when he had it in his mouth was first recorded in England in 1639, though it undoubtedly predates that record. The English statesman John Selden (1584–1654) said, "We look after religion as the butcher did after his knife, when he had it in his mouth." However, Ellery's point here is obscure—as will be seen, as of this moment, he had not yet formulated a theory of who committed the crime.

32. Canada Dry manufactured a product called Sparkling Orangeade that was widely distributed in the 1920s. The business, owned by the John J. McLaughlin family, was sold to a public company in 1923. However, Canada Dry also marketed ginger ale and other products, so it is an unlikely candidate for the purveyor in question. Orange Crush® was the orange-flavored soda produced by a California-based company that also achieved success in the 1920s, and, offering no other beverages, it is not unlikely that the distributor would have insisted on orangeade being sold exclusively.

1920s Orange Crush advertisemen.

you understand? Anything resembling half a ticket has to be in my possession when you're through. Search the theatre floor particularly; but don't neglect the rear, the steps leading up to the balcony, the lobby outside, the sidewalk in front of the theatre, the alleyways at both sides, the lounge downstairs, the men's room, the ladies' room—Here, here! That'll never do. Call up the nearest precinct for a matron and have her do that. Thoroughly clear?"

Flint was off with a cheerful nod.

"Now, then." Queen stood rubbing his hands. "Mr. Panzer, would you step this way a minute? Very kind of you, sir. I'm afraid we're making unholy nuisances of ourselves tonight, but it can't be helped. I see the audience is on the verge of rebellion. I'd be obliged if you would trot up to the stage and announce that they will be held here just a little while longer, to have patience, and all that sort of thing. Thank you!"

As Panzer hurried down the center aisle, people clutching at his coat to detain him, Detective Hagstrom, standing a few feet away, caught the Inspector's eye. By his side was a small slim youth of nineteen, chewing gum with vehement motions of his jaw, and obviously quite nervous at the ordeal he was facing. He was clad in a black-and-gold uniform, very ornate and resplendent, and incongruously fitted out with a starched shirt-front and a wing collar and bow tie. A cap resembling the headgear of a bell-boy perched on his blond head. He coughed deprecatingly as the Inspector motioned him forward. "Here is the boy who says they don't sell ginger ale in this theatre," said Hagstrom severely, grasping the lad's arm in a suggestive grip.

"You don't, eh, son?" asked Queen affably. "How is that?"

The boy was plainly in a funk. His eyes rolled alarmingly as they sought the broad face of Doyle. The policeman patted him encouragingly on the shoulder and said to the Inspector, "He's a little scared, sir—but he's a good boy. I've known him since he was a shaver. Grew up on my beat.—Answer the Inspector, Jessie. . . ."

"Well, I—I don't know, sir," stammered the boy, shuffling his feet. "The only drinks we're allowed to sell during the intermissions is orangeade. We got a contract with the ——"—he mentioned the name of a well-known manufacturer of the concoction[32]—"people and they give us a big discount if we sell their stuff and nobody else's. So—"

"I see," said the Inspector. "Are drinks sold only during intermissions?"'

"Yes, sir," answered the boy, more naturally. "As soon as the curtain goes down the doors to the alleys on both sides are opened, and there we are—my partner and me, with our stands set up, and the cups filled ready to serve."

"Oh, so there are two of you, eh?"

"No, sir, three all together. I forgot to tell you—one feller is downstairs in the main lounge, too."

"Ummmm." The Inspector fixed him with a large and kindly eye. "Now, son, if the Roman Theatre sells nothing but orangeade, do you think you could explain how this ginger-ale bottle got here?"

His hand dove down and reappeared brandishing the dark green bottle discovered by Hagstrom. The boy paled and began to bite his lips. His eyes roved from side to side as if they sought a quick avenue of escape. He inserted a large and dirty finger between his neck and collar and coughed.

"Why—why . . ." He had some difficulty in speaking.

Inspector Queen put down the bottle and rested his wiry length against the arm of a seat. He folded his arms sternly. "What's your name?" he demanded.

The boy's color changed from blue-white to a pasty yellow. He furtively eyed Hagstrom, who had with a flourish taken a note-book and pencil from his pocket and was waiting forbiddingly.

The boy moistened his lips. "Lynch—Jess Lynch," he said hoarsely.

"And where is your station between acts, Lynch?" said the Inspector balefully.

"I'm—I'm right here, in the left-side alley, sir," stuttered the boy.

"Ah!" said the Inspector, knitting his brows ferociously. "And were you selling drinks in the left alley to-night, Lynch?"'

"Why, why—yes, sir."

"Then you know something about this ginger-ale bottle."

The boy peered about, saw the stout small form of Louis Panzer on the stage, about to make an announcement, and leaning forward, whispered, "Yes, sir—I do know about that bottle. I—I didn't want to tell before because Mr. Panzer's a strict guy when it comes to breaking rules, and he'd fire me in a minute if he knew what I did. You won't tell, sir?"

33. Ginger ale, orangeade, and tonic water were popular means of covering up the flavor of the poorly-made liquors of the Prohibition era.

The Inspector started, then smiled. "Shoot, son. You've got something on your conscience—might as well get it off." He relaxed and at a flick of a finger Hagstrom unconcernedly walked away.

"This is how it happened, sir," began Jess Lynch eagerly. "I'd set my stand up in the alley here about five minutes before the end of the first act, like we're supposed to. When the girl on this aisle opened the doors after the first act, I began to give the people comin' out a nice refined selling chatter. We all do. A lot of people bought drinks, and I was so busy I didn't have time to notice anything going on around me. In a little while I had a breathing spell, and then a man came up to me and said, 'Let me have a bottle of ginger ale, boy.' I looked up and saw he was a ritzy feller in evening dress, actin' kind of tipsy. He was laughing to himself and he looked pretty happy. I says to myself, 'I bet I know what *he* wants ginger ale for' and sure enough he taps his back pocket and winks.[33] Well—"

"Just a minute, son," interrupted Queen. "Ever see a dead man before?"

"Why—why, no, sir, but I guess I could stand it once," said the boy nervously.

"Fine! Is this the man who asked you for the ginger ale?" The Inspector took the boy by the arm and made him bend over the dead body.

Jess Lynch regarded it with awed fascination. He bobbed his head vigorously.

"Yes, sir. That's the gentleman."

"You're sure of that now, Jess?" The boy nodded. "By the way, is that the outfit he was wearing when he accosted you?"

"Yes, sir."

"Anything missing, Jess?" Ellery, who had been nestling in a dark corner, leaned forward a little.

The boy regarded the Inspector with puzzlement on his face, looking from Queen to the body and back again. He was silent for a full minute, while the Queens hung on his words. Then his face lit up suddenly and he cried, "Why—yes, sir! He was wearin' a hat—a shiny topper—when he spoke to me!"

Inspector Queen looked pleased. "Go on, Jess—Doc Prouty! It's taken you a long time getting here. What held you up?"

A tall lanky man had come striding across the carpet, a black bag in his hand. He was smoking a vicious-looking cigar with no apparent concern for local fire rules, and appeared in something of a hurry.

"You said something there, Inspector," he said, setting down the bag and shaking hands with both Ellery and Queen. "You know we just moved and I haven't got my new phone yet. I had a hard day to-day and I was in bed anyway. They couldn't get hold of me—had to send a man around to my new place. I rushed down here as fast as I could. Where's the casualty?"

He dropped to his knees in the aisle as the Inspector indicated the body on the floor. A policeman was summoned to hold a flashlight as the Assistant Medical Examiner worked.

Queen took Jess Lynch by the arm and walked him off to one side. "What happened after he asked you for the ginger ale, Jess?"

The boy, who had been staring at the proceedings, gulped and continued. "Well, sir, of course I told him that we didn't sell ginger ale, only orangeade. He leaned a little closer, and then I could smell the booze on his breath. He says confidentially, 'There's a half a dollar in it for you if you get me a bottle, kid! But I want it right away!' Well—you know how it is—they don't give tips nowadays. . . . Anyway, I said I couldn't get it that minute but that I'd duck out and buy a bottle for him right after the second act started. He walked away—after tellin' me where he was sitting—I saw him go back into the theatre. As soon as the intermission ended and the usherette closed the doors, I left my stand in the alleyway and hopped across the street to Libby's ice-cream parlor. I—"

"Do you usually leave your stand in the alley, Jess?"

"No, sir. I always hop inside the doors with the stand just before she locks the doors, and then take it downstairs to the lounge. But the man said he wanted the ginger ale right away, so I figured I'd save time by getting the bottle for him first. Then I thought I'd go back into the alley, get my stand, and bring it into the theatre through the front door. Nobody'd say anything . . . Anyway, I left the stand in the alley and ran over to Libby's. I bought a bottle of Paley's ginger ale,[34] sneaked it inside to this man, and he gave me a buck. Pretty nice of him, I thought, seeing as how he'd only promised me four bits."

"You told that very nicely, Jess," said the Inspector with approval. "Now, a few things more. Was he sitting in this seat—was this the seat he told you to come to?"

34.   The manufacturer is untraceable today.

---

35.   Hermes, an Olympian god of the Greeks, was the messenger of the gods—Ellery alludes to Jess's role as the delivery boy.

"Oh, yes, sir. He said LL32 Left, and sure enough that's where I found him."

"Quite right." The Inspector, after a pause, asked casually, "Did you notice if he was alone, Jess?"

"Sure thing, sir," returned the boy in a cheerful tone. "He was sittin' all alone on this end seat. The reason I noticed it was that the show's been packed ever since it opened, and I thought it was queer that there should be so many seats empty around here."

"That's fine, Jess. You'll make a detective yet. . . . You couldn't tell me how many seats were empty, I suppose?"

"Well, sir, it was kind of dark and I wasn't payin' much attention. I guess it was about half a dozen, all told—some next to him in the same row and some right in the row in front."

"Just a moment, Jess." The boy turned, licking his lips in honest fright at the sound of Ellery's low cool voice: "Did you see anything more of that shiny topper when you handed him the bottle of ginger ale?" asked Ellery, tapping the point of his neat shoe with his stick.

"Why, yes—yes, sir!" stammered the boy. "When I gave him the bottle he was holding the hat in his lap, but before I left I saw him stick it underneath his seat."

"Another question, Jess." The boy sighed with relief at the sound of the Inspector's reassuring voice. "About how long, do you reckon, did it take you to deliver the bottle to this man after the second act started?"

Jess Lynch thought gravely for a moment, and then said with finality, "It was just about ten minutes, sir. We got to keep pretty close tabs on the time, and I know it was ten minutes because when I came into the theatre with the bottle it was just the part on the stage when the girl is caught in the gang's hang-out and is being grilled by the villain."

"An observant young Hermes!"[35] murmured Ellery, smiling suddenly. The orangeade boy caught the smile and lost the last vestige of his fear. He smiled back. Ellery crooked his finger and bent forward. "Tell me, Jess. Why did it take you ten minutes to cross the street, buy a bottle of ginger ale and return to the theatre? Ten minutes is a long time, isn't it?"

The boy turned scarlet as he looked appealingly from Ellery to the Inspector. "Well, sir—I guess I stopped to talk for a few minutes with my girl . . ."

"Your girl?" The Inspector's voice was mildly curious.

"Yes, sir. Elinor Libby—her old man owns the ice-cream parlor. She—she wanted me to stay there in the store with her when I went for the ginger ale. I told her I had to deliver it in the theatre, so she said all right but wouldn't I come right back. And I did. We stayed there a couple of minutes and then I remembered the stand in the alley. . . ."

"The stand in the alley?" Ellery's tone was eager. "Quite so, Jess—the stand in the alley. Don't tell me that, by some remarkable whim of fortune, you went back to the alley!"

"Sure I did!" rejoined the boy, in surprise. "I mean—we both did, Elinor and me."

"Elinor and you, eh, Jess?" said Ellery softly. "And how long were you there?"

The Inspector's eyes flashed at Ellery's question. He muttered approvingly to himself and listened intently as the boy answered.

"Well, I wanted to take the stand right away, sir, but Elinor and me—we got to talking there—and Elinor said why not stay in the alley till the next intermission. . . . I figured that was a good idea, I'd wait till a few minutes before 10:05, when the act ends, and I'd duck down for some more orangeade, and then when the doors opened for the second intermission I'd be all ready. So we stayed there, sir. . . . It wasn't wrong, sir. I didn't mean anything wrong."

Ellery straightened and fixed the boy with his eyes. "Jess, I want you to be very careful now. At exactly what time did you and your Elinor get to the alley?"

"Well . . . ," Jess scratched his head. "It was about 9:25 when I gave that man the ginger ale. I went across for Elinor, stayed a few minutes and then came over to the alley. Musta been just about 9:35—just about—when I went back for my orangeade stand."

"Very good. And what time exactly did you leave the alley?"

"It was just ten o'clock, sir. Elinor looked at her wrist watch when I asked her if it was time to go in for my orangeade refills."

"You didn't hear anything going on in the theatre?"

"No, sir. We were too busy talking, I guess. . . . I didn't know anything had happened inside until we walked out of the alley and I met Johnny Chase, one of the ushers, standing there, like he was on guard. He told me there was an accident inside and Mr. Panzer had sent him to stand outside the left alley."

"I see. . . ." Ellery removed his pince-nez in some agitation and flourished it before the boy's nose. "Carefully now, Jess. Did anyone go in or out of the alley all the time you were there with Elinor?"

The boy's answer was immediate and emphatic. "No, sir. Not a soul."

"Right, my lad." The Inspector gave the boy a spanking slap on the back and sent him off grinning. Queen looked around sharply, spied Panzer, who had made his announcement on the stage with ineffectual results, and beckoned with an imperative finger.

"Mr. Panzer," he said abruptly, "I want some information about the time-schedule of the play. . . . At what time does the curtain go up on the second act?"

"The second act begins at 9:15 sharp and ends at 10:05 sharp," said Panzer instantly.

"Was to-night's performance run according to this schedule?"

"Certainly. We must be on the dot because of cues, lights, and so on," responded the manager.

The Inspector muttered some calculations to himself. "That makes it 9:25 the boy saw Field alive," he mused. "He was found dead at . . ."

He swung about and called for Officer Doyle. The man came running.

"Doyle," asked the Inspector, "Doyle, do you remember exactly at what time this fellow Pusak approached you with his story of the murder?"

The policeman scratched his head. "Why, I don't remember exactly, Inspector," he said. "All I do know is that the second act was almost over when it happened."

"Not definite enough, Doyle," said Queen irritably. "Where are the actors now?"

"Got 'em herded right over there back of the center section, sir," said Doyle. "We didn't know what to do with 'em except that."

"Get one of them for me!" snapped the Inspector.

Doyle ran off. Queen beckoned to Detective Piggott, who was standing a few feet to the rear between a man and a woman.

"Got the doorman there, Piggott?" asked Queen. Piggott nodded and a tall, corpulent old man, cap trembling in his hand, uniform shrunken on his flabby body, stumbled forward.

"Are you the man who stands outside the theatre—the regular doorman?" asked the Inspector.

"Yes, sir," the doorman answered, twisting the cap in his hands.

"Very well. Now think hard. Did anyone—anyone, mind you—leave the theatre by the front entrance during the second act?" The Inspector was leaning forward, like a small greyhound.

The man took a moment before replying. Then he said slowly, but with conviction, "No, sir. Nobody went out of the theatre. Nobody, I mean, but the orangeade boy."

"Were you there all the time?" barked the Inspector.

"Yes, sir."

"Now then. Do you remember anybody coming *in* during the second act?"

"We-e-ll. . . . Jessie Lynch, the orangeade boy, came in right after the act started."

"Anybody else?"

There was silence as the old man made a frenzied effort at concentration. After a moment he looked helplessly from one face to another, eyes despairing. Then he mumbled, "I don't remember, sir."

The Inspector regarded him irritably. The old man seemed sincere in his nervous way. He was perspiring and frequently looked sidewise at Panzer, as if he sensed that his defection of memory would cost him his position.

"I'm awfully sorry, sir," the doorman repeated. "Awfully sorry. There might've been some one, but my memory ain't as good as it used to be when I was younger. I—I just can't seem to recall."

Ellery's cool voice cut in on the old man's thick accents:

"How long have you been a doorman?"

The old man's bewildered eyes shifted to this new inquisitor. "Nigh onto ten years, sir. I wasn't always a doorman. Only when I got old and couldn't do nothin' else—"

"I understand," said Ellery kindly. He hesitated a moment, then added inflexibly, "A man who has been a doorman for as many years as you have might forget something about the first act. But people do not often come into a theatre during the second act. Surely if you think hard enough you can answer positively, one way or the other?"

The response came painfully. "I—I don't remember, sir. I could say no one did, but that mightn't be the truth. I just can't answer."

36. As noted above, Lee and Dannay were great fans of Sherlock Holmes—devoted enough to have known that this phrase never appears in the Holmes Canon in this formulation. There are numerous ejaculations of "elementary" and frequent murmurings of "my dear Watson," but Holmes never uttered this infamous formulation. Indeed, it does not even appear in William Gillette's *Sherlock Holmes*, a play that had been staged hundreds of times between 1899, when it was first performed, and 1923 and filmed in 1916, though there are several permutations of the phrase.

"All right." The Inspector put his hand on the old man's shoulder. "Forget it. Perhaps we're asking too much. That's all for the time being." The doorman shuffled away with the pitiful alacrity of old age.

Doyle clumped toward the group, a tall handsome man dressed in rough tweeds in his wake, traces of stage make-up streaking his face.

"This is Mr. Peale, Inspector. He's the leading man of the show," reported Doyle.

Queen smiled at the actor, offering his hand. "Pleased to make your acquaintance, Mr. Peale. Perhaps you can help us out with a little information."

"Glad to be of service, Inspector," replied Peale, in a rich baritone. He glanced at the back of the Medical Examiner, who was busy over the dead man; then looked away with repugnance.

"I suppose you were on the stage at the time the hue-and-cry went up in this unfortunate affair?" pursued the Inspector.

"Oh, yes. In fact, the entire cast was. What is it you would like to know?"

"Could you definitely place the time that you noticed something wrong in the audience?"

"Yes, I can. We had just about ten minutes before the end of the act. It was at the climax of the play, and my rôle demands the discharge of a pistol. I remember we had some discussion during rehearsals of this point in the play, and that is how I can be so sure of the time."

The Inspector nodded. "Thank you very much, Mr. Peale. That's exactly what I wanted to know . . . Incidentally, let me apologize for having kept you people crowded back here in this fashion. We were quite busy and had no time to make other arrangements. You and the rest of the cast are at liberty to go backstage now. Of course, make no effort to leave the theatre until you are notified."

"I understand completely, Inspector. Happy to have been able to help." Peale bowed and retreated to the rear of the theatre.

The Inspector leaned against the nearest seat, absorbed in thought. Ellery, at his side, was absently polishing the lenses of his pince-nez. Father motioned significantly to son.

"Well, Ellery?" Queen asked in a low voice.

"Elementary, my dear Watson,"[36] murmured Ellery. "Our respected victim was last seen alive at 9:25, and he was found dead at approximately 9:55. Problem: What happened between times? Sounds ludicrously simple."

"You don't say?" muttered Queen. "Piggott!"

"Yes, sir."

"Is that the usherette? Let's get some action."

Piggott released the arm of the young woman standing at his side. She was a pert and painted lady with even white teeth and a ghastly smile. She minced forward and regarded the Inspector brazenly.

"Are you the regular usherette on this aisle, Miss—?" asked the Inspector briskly.

"O'Connell, Madge O'Connell. Yes, I am!"

The Inspector took her arm gently. "I'm afraid I'll have to ask you to be as brave as you are impertinent, my dear," he said. "Step over here for a moment." The girl's face was deathly white as they paused at the LL row. "Pardon me a moment, Doc. Mind if we interrupt your work?"

Dr. Prouty looked up with an abstracted scowl. "No, go right ahead, Inspector. I'm nearly through." He stood up and moved aside, biting the cigar between his teeth.

Queen watched the girl's face as she stooped over the dead man's body. She drew her breath in sharply.

"Do you remember ushering this man to his seat to-night, Miss O'Connell?"

The girl hesitated. "Seems like I do. But I was very busy to-night, as usual, and I must have ushered two hundred people all told. So I couldn't say positively."

"Do you recall whether these seats which are empty now"—he indicated the seven vacant chairs—"were unoccupied all during the first and second acts?"

"Well . . . I do seem to remember noticing them that way as I walked up and down the aisle. . . . No, sir. I don't think anybody sat in those seats all night."

"Did anyone walk up or down this aisle during the second act, Miss O'Connell? Think hard, now; it's important that you answer correctly."

The girl hesitated once more, flashing bold eyes at the impassive face of the Inspector. "No—I didn't see anybody walk up or down the aisle." She quickly added, "I couldn't tell you much. I don't know a thing about this business. I'm a hard-working girl, and I—"

"Yes, yes, my dear, we understand that. Now—where do you generally stand when you're not ushering people to their seats?"

The girl pointed to the head of the aisle.

"Were you there all during the second act, Miss O'Connell?" asked the Inspector softly.

The girl moistened her lips before she spoke. "Well—yes, I was. But, honest, I didn't see anything out of way all night."

"Very well." Queen's voice was mild. "That's all." She turned away with quick, light steps.

There was a stir behind the group. Queen wheeled to confront Dr. Prouty, who had risen to his feet and was closing his bag. He was whistling dolefully.

"Well, Doc—I see you're through. What's the verdict?" asked Queen.

"It's short and snappy, Inspector. Man died about two hours ago. Cause of death puzzled me for a while but it's pretty well settled in my mind as poison. The signs all point to some form of alcoholic poisoning—you've probably noticed the sallow blue color of the skin. Did you smell his breath? Sweetest odor of bum booze I ever had the pleasure of inhaling. He must have been drunk as a lord. At the same time, it couldn't have been ordinary alcoholic poisoning—he wouldn't have dropped off so fast. That's all I can tell you right now," He paused, buttoning his coat.

Queen took Field's kerchief-wrapped flask from his pocket and handed it to Dr. Prouty. "This is the dead man's flask, Doc. Suppose you analyze the contents for me. Before you handle it, though, let Jimmy down at the laboratory look it over for finger-prints. And—but wait a minute." The Inspector peered about and picked up the half-empty ginger-ale bottle where it stood in a corner of the carpet. "You can analyze this ginger ale for me, too, Doc," he added.

The Assistant Medical Examiner, after stowing the flask and bottle into his bag, tenderly adjusted the hat on his head.

"'Well, I'll be going, Inspector," he drawled. "I'll have a fuller report for you when I've performed the autopsy. Ought to give you something to work on. Incidentally, the morgue-wagon must be outside—I 'phoned for one on my way down. So long." He yawned and slouched away.

As Dr. Prouty disappeared, two white-garbed orderlies hurried across the carpet, bearing a stretcher between them. At a sign from Queen they lifted the inert body, deposited it on the stretcher, covered it with a blanket and hustled out. The detectives and policemen around the door watched with relief as the grisly burden was borne away—the main work of the evening for them was almost over. The audience—rustling, shifting, coughing, murmuring—twisted about with a renewal of interest as the body was unceremoniously carted off.

Queen had just turned to Ellery with a weary sigh when from the extreme right-hand side of the theatre came an ominous commotion. People everywhere popped out of their seats, staring while policemen shouted for quiet. Queen spoke rapidly to a uniformed officer nearby. Ellery slipped to one side, eyes gleaming. The disturbance came nearer by jerky degrees. Two policemen appeared hauling a struggling figure between them. They dragged their capture to the head of the left aisle and hustled the man to his feet, holding him up by main force.

The man was short and ratlike. He wore cheap store-clothes of a sombre cut. On his head was a black hat of the kind sometimes worn by country dominies.[37] His mouth writhed in an ugly manner; imprecations issued from it venomously. As he caught the eye of the Inspector fixed upon him, however, he ceased struggling and went limp at once.

"Found this man tryin' to sneak out the alley door on the other side of the buildin', Inspector," panted one of the bluecoats, shaking the captive roughly.

The Inspector chuckled, took his brown snuff-box from his pocket, inhaled, sneezed his habitual joyful sneeze, and beamed upon the silent cowering man between the two officers.

"Well, well, Parson," he said genially. "Mighty nice of you to turn up so conveniently!"

37.   Clergymen.

CHAPTER IV

In Which Many Are Called and Two Are Chosen

38. As late as the mid-nineteenth century, there were more than a dozen boat slips on the eastern edge of lower Manhattan. These included Coffee House Slip, at the end of Wall St.; Fly Market Slip, at the bottom of Maiden Lane; Peck's Slip, at the foot of Ferry St.; and Old Slip, at the bottom of William St. Most of the slips were filled in by 1898, but some still remain as malls, parks, and roads. The *Brooklyn Daily Eagle Almanac* for 1927 still lists Old Slip as a Manhattan street.

Some natures, through peculiar weakness, cannot endure the sight of a whining man. Of all the silent, threatening group ringed about the abject figure called "Parson," Ellery alone experienced a sick feeling of disgust at the spectacle the prisoner was making of himself.

At the hidden lash in Queen's words, the Parson drew himself up stiffly, glared into the Inspector's eyes for a split second, then with a resumption of his former tactics began to fight against the sturdy arms which encircled him. He writhed and spat and cursed, finally becoming silent again. He was conserving his breath. The fury of his threshing body communicated itself to his captors; another policeman joined the *mêlée* and helped pin the prisoner to the floor. And suddenly he wilted and shrank like a pricked balloon. A policeman hauled him roughly to his feet, where he stood, eyes downcast, body still, hat clutched in his hand.

Ellery turned his head.

"Come now, Parson," went on the Inspector, just as if the man had been a balky child at rest after a fit of temper, "you know that sort of business doesn't go with me. What happened when you tried it last time at the Old Slip[38] on the riverfront?"

"Answer when you're spoken to!" growled a bluecoat, prodding him in the ribs.

"I don't know nothin' and besides I got nothin' to say," muttered the Parson, shifting from one foot to the other.

"I'm surprised at you, Parson," said Queen gently. "I haven't asked you what you know."

"You got no right to hold an innocent man!" shouted the Parson indignantly. "Ain't I as good as anybody else here? I bought a ticket and I paid for it with real dough, too! Where do you get that stuff—tryin' to keep me from goin' home!"

"So you bought a ticket, did you?" asked the Inspector, rocking on his heels. "Well, well! Suppose you snap out the old stub and let Papa Queen look it over."

The Parson's hand mechanically went to his lower vest pocket, his fingers dipping into it with a quite surprising deftness. His face went blank as he slowly withdrew his hand, empty. He began a search of his other pockets with an appearance of fierce annoyance that made the Inspector smile.

"Hell!" grunted the Parson. "If that ain't the toughest luck. I always hangs onto my ticket-stubs, an' just to-night I have to go and throw it away. Sorry, Inspector!"

"Oh, that's quite all right," said Queen. His face went bleak and hard. "Quit stalling, Cazzanelli! What were you doing in this theatre to-night? What made you decide to duck out so suddenly? Answer me!"

The Parson looked about him. His arms were held very securely by two bluecoats. A number of hard-looking men surrounded him. The prospect of escape did not seem particularly bright. His face underwent another change. It assumed a priestly, outraged innocence. A mist filmed his little eyes, as if he were truly the Christian martyr and these tyrants his pagan inquisitors. The Parson had often employed this trick of personality to good purpose.

"Inspector," he said, "you know you ain't got no right to grill me this way, don't you, Inspector? A man's got a right to his lawyer, ain't he? Sure he's got a right!" And he stopped as if there were nothing more to be said.

The Inspector eyed him curiously. "When did you see Field last?" he asked.

"Field? You don't mean to say—Monte Field? Never heard of him, Inspector," muttered the Parson, rather shakily. "What are you tryin' to put over on me?"

"Not a thing, Parson, not a thing. But as long as you don't care to answer now, suppose we let you cool your heels for a while.

39. G. P. Bonomo was a principal in the Anthracite Silk Throwing Co. of Pennsylvania in 1915. What the Bonomo Silk affair was, however, remains a mystery.

40. A homily oft repeated—for example, it can be found in *Proverbs; or The Manual of Wisdom* (1804).

Perhaps you'll have something to say later . . . Don't forget, Parson, there's still that little matter of the Bonomo Silk[39] robbery to go into." He turned to one of the policemen. "Escort our friend to that anteroom off the manager's office, and keep him company for a while, officer."

Ellery, reflectively watching the Parson being dragged toward the rear of the theatre, was startled to hear his father say, "The Parson isn't too bright, is he? To make a slip like that—!"

"Be thankful for small favors," smiled Ellery. "One error breeds twenty more."[40]

The Inspector turned with a grin to confront Velie, who had just arrived with a sheaf of papers in his hand.

"Ah, Thomas is back," chuckled the Inspector, who seemed in good spirits. "And what have you found, Thomas?"

"Well, Inspector," replied the detective, ruffling the edges of his papers, "it's hard to say. This is half of the list—the other half isn't ready yet. But I think you'll find something interesting here."

He handed Queen a batch of hastily written names and addresses. They were the names which the Inspector had ordered Velie to secure by interrogation of the audience.

Queen, with Ellery at his shoulder, examined the list, studying each name carefully. He was half-way through the sheaf when he stiffened. He squinted at the name which had halted him and looked up at Velie with a puzzled air.

"Morgan," he said thoughtfully. "Benjamin Morgan. Sounds mighty familiar, Thomas. What does it suggest to you?"

Velie smiled frostily. "I thought you'd ask me that, Inspector. Benjamin Morgan was Monte Field's law partner until two years ago!"

Queen nodded. The three men stared into each other's eyes. Then the old man shrugged his shoulders and said briefly. "Have to see some more of Mr. Morgan, I'm afraid."

He turned back to the list with a sigh. Again he studied each name, looking up at intervals reflectively, shaking his head, and going on. Velie, who knew Queen's reputation for memory even more thoroughly than Ellery, watched his superior with respectful eyes.

Finally the Inspector handed the papers back to the detective. "Nothing else there, Thomas," he said. "Unless you caught something that escaped me. Did you?" His tone was grave.

Velie stared at the old man wordlessly, shook his head and started to walk away.

"Just a minute, Thomas," called Queen. "Before you get that second list completed, ask Mr. Morgan to step into Panzer's office, will you? Don't scare him. And by the way, see that he has his ticket-stub before he goes to the office." Velie departed.

The Inspector motioned to Panzer, who was watching a group of policemen being marshaled by detectives for Queen's work. The stout little manager hurried up.

"Mr. Panzer," inquired the Inspector, "at what time do your scrub-women generally start cleaning up?"

"Why, they've been here for quite a while now, Inspector, waiting to get to work. Most theatres are tidied early in the morning, but I've always had my employees come immediately after the evening performance. Just what is on your mind?"

Ellery, who had frowned slightly when the Inspector spoke, brightened at the manager's reply. He began to polish his pince-nez with satisfaction.

"Here's what I want you to do, Mr. Panzer," continued Queen evenly. "Arrange to have your cleaning-women make a particularly thorough search to-night, after everybody is gone. They must pick up and save everything—everything, no matter how seemingly trivial—and they're to watch especially for ticket-stubs. Can you trust these people?"

"Oh, absolutely, Inspector. They've been with the theatre ever since it was built. You may be sure that nothing will be overlooked. What shall I do with the sweepings?"

"Wrap them carefully, address them to me and send them by a trustworthy messenger to headquarters to-morrow morning." The Inspector paused. "I want to impress upon you, Mr. Panzer, the importance of this task. It's much more important than it seems. Do you understand?"

"Certainly, certainly!" Panzer hastened away.

A detective with grizzled hair walked briskly across the carpet, turned down the left aisle and touched his hat to Queen. In his hand was a sheaf of papers resembling the one which Velie had presented.

"Sergeant Velie has asked me to give you this list of names. He says that it's the rest of the names and addresses of the people in the audience, Inspector."

Queen took the papers from the detective's hand with a sudden show of eagerness. Ellery leaned forward. The old man's eyes traveled slowly from name to name as his thin finger moved down each sheet. Near the bottom of the last one he smiled, looked at Ellery triumphantly, and finished the page. He turned and whispered into his son's ear. A light came over Ellery's face as he nodded.

The Inspector turned back to the waiting detective. "Come here, Johnson," he said. Queen spread out the page he had been studying for the man's scrutiny. "I want you to find Velie and have him report to me at once. After you've done that, get hold of this woman"—his finger pointed to a name and a row-and-seat number next to it—"and ask her to step into the manager's office with you. You'll find a man by the name of Morgan there. Stay with both of them until you hear from me. Incidentally, if there's any conversation between them keep your ears open—I want to know what is said. Treat the woman courteously."

"Yes, sir. Velie also asked me to tell you," continued Johnson, "that he has a group of people separated from the rest of the audience—they're the ones who have no ticket-stubs. He'd like to know what you want done with them."

"Do their names appear on both lists, Johnson?" asked Queen, handing him the second sheaf for return to Velie.

"Yes, sir."

"Then tell Velie to let them leave with the others, but not before he makes a special list of their names. It won't be necessary for me to see or speak to them."

Johnson saluted and disappeared.

Queen turned to converse in low tones with Ellery, who seemed to have something on his mind. They were interrupted by the reappearance of Panzer.

"Inspector?" The manager coughed politely.

"Oh, yes, Panzer!" said the Inspector, whirling about. "Everything straight with regard to the cleaning-women?"

"Yes, sir. Is there anything else you would like me to do . . . ? And, Inspector, I hope you will pardon me for asking, but how much longer will the audience have to wait? I have been receiving most disturbing inquiries from many people. I am hoping no trouble comes of this affair." His dark face was glistening with perspiration.

"Oh, don't worry about that, Panzer," said the Inspector casually. "Their wait is almost over. In fact, I am ordering my men to get them out of here in a few minutes. Before they leave, however, they'll have one thing more to complain about," he added with a grim smile.

"Yes, Inspector?"

"Oh, yes," said Queen. "They're going to submit to a search. No doubt they'll protest, and you'll hear threats of lawsuits and personal violence, but don't worry about it. I'm responsible for everything done here to-night, and I'll see that you're kept out of trouble. . . . Now, we'll need a woman-searcher to help our men. We have a police-matron here, but she's busy downstairs. Do you think you could get me a dependable woman—middle-aged preferably—who won't object to a thankless job and will know how to keep her mouth shut?"

The manager pondered for a moment. "I think I can get you the woman you want. She's a Mrs. Phillips, our wardrobe-mistress. She's well on in years and as pleasant as anyone you could get for such a task."

"Just the person," said Queen briskly. "Get her at once and station her at the main exit. Detective-Sergeant Velie will give her the necessary instructions."

Velie had come up in time to hear the last remark. Panzer bustled down the aisle toward the boxes.

"Morgan set?" asked Queen.

"Yes, Inspector."

"Well, then, you have one more job and you'll be through for the night, Thomas. I want you to superintend the departure of the people seated in the orchestra and boxes. Have them leave one by one, and overhaul them as they go out. No one is to leave by any exit except the main door, and just to make sure tell the men at the side exits to keep 'em moving toward the rear." Velie nodded. "Now, about the search. Piggott!" The detective came on the run. "Piggott, you accompany Mr. Queen and Sergeant Velie and help search every man who goes out the main door. There'll be a matron there to search the women. Examine every parcel. Go over their pockets for anything suspicious; collect all the ticket-stubs; and watch especially for *an extra hat*. The hat I want is a silk topper. But if you find any other kind of extra hat, nab the owner and be sure he's nabbed properly. Now, boys, get to work!"

Ellery, who had been lounging against a pillar, straightened up and followed Piggott. As Velie stalked behind, Queen called, "Don't release the people in the balcony until the orchestra is empty. Send somebody up there to keep them quiet."

With his last important instruction given the Inspector turned to Doyle, who was standing guard nearby, and said quietly, "Shoot downstairs to the cloak-room, Doyle, my lad, and keep your eyes open while the people are getting their wraps. When they're all gone, search the place with a fine-comb. If there is anything left in the racks, bring it to me."

Queen leaned back against the pillar which loomed, a marble sentinel, over the seat in which murder had been done. As he stood there, eyes blank, hands clutching his lapels, the broad-shouldered Flint hurried up with a gleam of excitement in his eyes. Inspector Queen regarded him critically.

"Found something, Flint?' he asked, fumbling for his snuff-box.

The detective silently offered him a half-ticket, colored blue, and marked "LL30 Left."

"Well, well!" exclaimed Queen. "Wherever did you find that?"

"Right inside the main door," said Flint. "Looked as if it was dropped just as the owner came into the theatre."

Queen did not answer. With a swooping dip of his fingers he extracted from his vest pocket the blue-colored stub he had found on the dead man's person. He regarded them in silence—two identically colored and marked stubs, one with the inscription LL32 Left, the other LL30 Left.

His eyes narrowed as he studied the innocent-appearing paste-boards. He bent closer, slowly turning the stubs back to back. Then, with a puzzled light in his grey eyes, he turned them front to front. Still unsatisfied, he turned them back to front.

In none of the three positions did the torn edges of the tickets coincide!

CHAPTER V

In Which Inspector Queen Conducts Some Legal Conversations

Queen made his way across the broad red carpet covering the rear of the orchestra, his hat pulled down over his eyes. He was searching the recesses of his pocket for the inevitable snuff-box. The Inspector was evidently engaged in a weighty mental process, for his hand closed tightly upon the two blue ticket-stubs and he grimaced, as if he were not at all satisfied with his thoughts.

Before opening the green-speckled door marked "Manager's Office," he turned to survey the scene behind him. The stir in the audience was businesslike. A great chattering filled the air; policemen and detectives circulated among the rows, giving orders, answering questions, hustling people out of their seats, lining them up in the main aisles to be searched at the huge outer door. The Inspector noticed absently that there was little protest from the audience at the ordeal they were facing. They seemed too tired to resent the indignity of a search. A long queue of half-angry, half-amused women was lined up at one side being examined rapidly, one by one, by a motherly woman dressed in black. Queen glanced briefly at the detectives blocking the door. Piggott with the experience of long practice was making rapid passes over the clothing of the men. Velie, at his side, was studying the reactions of the various people undergoing examination. Occasionally he searched a man himself.[41] Ellery stood a little apart, hands in his capacious topcoat pockets, smoking a

41. One wonders what in fact the police were searching for. We learn later that it was not ticket-stubs. Perhaps weapons? Vials marked poison? At this stage, with the cause of death unknown, what could the police regard as unnoteworthy?

cigarette and seeming to be thinking of nothing more important than the first edition he had missed buying.

Queen sighed, and went in.

The anteroom to the main office was a tiny place, fitted out in bronze and oak. On one of the chairs against the wall, burrowed into the deep leather cushions, sat Parson Johnny, puffing at a cigarette with a show of unconcern. A policeman stood by the chair, one massive hand on the Parson's shoulder.

"Trail along, Parson," said Queen casually, without stopping. The little gangster lounged to his feet, spun his cigarette butt deftly into a shining brass cuspidor, and slouched after the Inspector, the policeman treading on his heels.

Queen opened the door to the main office, glancing quickly about him as he stood on the threshold. Then he stepped aside, allowing the gangster and the bluecoat to precede him. The door banged shut behind them.

Louis Panzer had an unusual taste in office appointments. A clear green light-shade shone brilliantly above a carved desk. Chair and smoking-stands; a skillfully wrought clothes-tree; silk-covered divan—these and other articles were strewn tastefully about the room. Unlike most managers' offices, Panzer's did not exploit photographs of stars, managers, producers and "angels." Several delicate prints, a huge tapestry, and a Constable oil painting hung on the wall.

But Inspector Queen's scrutiny at the moment was not for the artistic quality of Mr. Panzer's private chamber. It was rather for the six people who faced him. Beside Detective Johnson sat a middle-aged man inclining to corpulence, with shrewd eyes and a puzzled frown. He wore faultless evening clothes. In the next chair sat a young girl of considerable beauty, attired in a simple evening gown and wrap. She was looking up at a handsome young man in evening clothes, hat in hand, who was bending over her chair and talking earnestly in an undertone. Beside them were two other women, both leaning forward and listening intently.

The stout man held aloof from the others. At Inspector Queen's entrance he immediately got to his feet with an inquiring look. The little group became silent and turned solemn faces on Queen.

With a deprecating cough Parson Johnny, accompanied by his escort, sidled across the rug and into a corner. He seemed overwhelmed by the splendor of the company in which he found himself. He shuffled his feet and cast a despairing look in the direction of the Inspector.

Queen moved over to the desk and faced the group. At a motion of his hand Johnson came quickly to his side. "Who are the three extra people, Johnson?" he asked in a tone inaudible to the others.

"The old fellow there is Morgan," whispered Johnson, "and the good-looker sitting near him is the woman you told me to get. When I went for her in the orchestra I found the young chap and the other two women with her. The four of 'em were pretty chummy. I gave her your message, and she seemed nervous. But she stood up and came along like a major—only the other three came, too. I didn't know but what you'd like to see 'em, Inspector. . . ."

Queen nodded. "Hear anything?" he asked in the same low tone.

"Not a peep, Inspector. The old chap doesn't seem to know any of these people. The others have just been wondering why you could possibly want *her*."

The Inspector waved Johnson to a corner and addressed the waiting group.

"I've summoned two of you," he said pleasantly, "for a little chat. And since the others are here, too, it will be all right for them to wait. But for the moment I must ask you all to step into the anteroom while I conduct a little business with this gentleman." He inclined his head toward the gangster, who stiffened indignantly.

With a flutter of excited conversation the two men and three women departed, Johnson closing the door behind them.

Queen whirled on Parson Johnny.

"Bring that rat here!" he snapped to the policeman. He sat down in Panzer's chair and drew the tips of his fingers together. The gangster was jerked to his feet and marched across the carpet, to be pushed directly in front of the desk.

"Now, Parson," said Queen menacingly, "I've got you where I want you. We're going to have a nice little talk with nobody to interrupt. Get me?"

The Parson was silent, his eyes liquid with distrust.

"So you won't say anything, eh, Johnny? How long do you think I'll let you get away with that?"

"I told you before—I don't know nothin' and besides I won't say nothin' till I see my lawyer," the gangster said sullenly.

"Your lawyer? Well, Parson, who *is* your lawyer?" asked the Inspector in an innocent tone.

The Parson bit his lip, remaining silent. Queen turned to Johnson.

"Johnson, my boy, you worked on the Babylon stick-up, didn't you?" he asked.

"Sure did, Chief," said the detective.

"That," explained Queen gently, to the gangster, "was when you were sent up for a year. Remember, Parson?"

Still silence.

"And Johnson," continued the Inspector, leaning back in his chair, "refresh my memory. Who was the lawyer defending our friend here?"

"Field. By—" Johnson exclaimed, staring at the Parson.

"Exactly. The gentleman now lying on one of our unfeeling slabs at the morgue. Well, what about it? Cut the comedy! Where do you come off saying you don't know Monte Field? You knew his first name, all right, when I mentioned only his last. Come clean, now!"

The gangster had sagged against the policeman, a furtive despair in his eyes. He moistened his lips and said, "You got me there, Inspector. I—I don't know nothin' about this, though, honest. I ain't seen Field in a month. I didn't—my Gawd, you're not tryin' to tie this croakin' around my neck, are you?"

He stared at Queen in anguish. The policeman jerked him straight.

"Parson, Parson," said Queen, "how you do jump at conclusions. I'm merely looking for a little information. Of course, if you want to confess to the murder I'll call my men in and we can get your story all straight and go home to bed. How about it?"

"No!" shouted the gangster, thrashing out suddenly with his arm. The officer caught it deftly and twisted it behind the squirming back. "Where do you get that stuff? I ain't confessin' nothin'. I don't know nothin'. I didn't see Field to-night an' I didn't even know he was here! Confess . . . I got some mighty influential friends, Inspector—you can't pull that stuff on me, I'll tell you!"

"That's too bad, Johnny," sighed the Inspector. He took a pinch of snuff. "All right, then. You didn't kill Monte Field. What time did you get here to-night, and where's your ticket?" The Parson twisted his hat in his hands. "I wasn't goin' to say nothin' before, Inspector, because I figured you was tryin' to railroad me. I can explain when and how I got here all right. It was about half past eight, and I got in on a pass, that's how. Here's the stub to prove it." He searched carelessly in his coat pocket and produced a perforated blue stub. He handed it to Queen, who glanced at it carefully and put it in his pocket.

"And where," he asked, "and where did you get the pass, Johnny?"

"I—my girl give it to me, Inspector," replied the gangster nervously.

"Ah—the woman enters the case," said Queen jovially. "And what might this young Circe's[42] name be, Johnny?"

"Who?—why, she's—hey, Inspector, don't get her in no trouble, will you?" burst out Parson Johnny. "She's a reg'lar kid, an' she don't know nothin' either. Honest, I—"

"Her name?" snapped Queen.

"Madge O'Connell," whined Johnny. "She's an usher here."

Queen's eyes lit up. A quick glance passed between him and Johnson. The detective left the room.

"So," continued the Inspector, leaning back again comfortably, "so my old friend Parson Johnny doesn't know a thing about Monte Field. Well, well, well! We'll see how your lady-friend's story backs you up." As he talked he looked steadily at the hat in the gangster's hand. It was a cheap black fedora, matching the sombre suit which the man was wearing. "Here, Parson," he said suddenly. "Hand over that hat of yours."

He took the head-piece from the gangster's reluctant hand and examined it. He pulled down the leather band inside, eyed it critically and finally handed it back.

"We forgot something, Parson," he said. "Officer, suppose you frisk Mr. Cazzanelli's person, eh?"

The Parson submitted to the search with an ill grace, but he was quiescent enough. "No gat," said the policeman briefly, and continued. He put his hand into the man's hip-pocket, extracting a fat wallet. "Want this, Inspector?"

Queen took it, counted the money briskly, and handed it back to the policeman, who returned it to the pocket.

"One hundred and twenty-two smackers, Johnny," the old man murmured.[43] "Seems to me I can smell Bonomo silk in

42.   Circe, a minor Greek goddess who was said to have the power—through herbs or magic or innate abilities—to coerce men to her will, is the symbol of the predatory female, taking advantage of and controlling her male partner.

43.   By the standard of wages of an unskilled laborer, this would be almost $6,000 today, a very substantial amount for a known thug to be carrying around.

these bills. However!" He laughed and said to the bluecoat, "No flask?" The policeman shook his head. "Anything under his vest or shirt?" Again a negative. Queen was silent until the search was completed. Parson Johnny relaxed with a sigh.

"Well, Johnny, mighty lucky night this is for you.—Come in!" Queen said at a knock on the door. It opened to disclose the slender girl in usherette's uniform whom he had questioned earlier in the evening. Johnson came in after her and closed the door.

Madge O'Connell stood on the rug and stared with tragic eyes at her lover, who was thoughtfully studying the floor. She flashed a glance at Queen. Then her mouth hardened and she snapped at the gangster. "Well? So they got you after all, you sap! I told you not to try to make a break for it!" She turned her back contemptuously on the Parson and began to ply a powder-puff with vigor.

"Why didn't you tell me before, my girl," said Queen softly, "that you got a pass for your friend John Cazzanelli?"

"I ain't telling everything, Mr. Cop," she answered pertly. "Why should I? Johnny didn't have anything to do with this business."

"We won't discuss that," said the Inspector, toying with his snuff-box. "What I want you to tell me now, Madge, is whether your memory has improved any since I spoke to you."

"What d'ya mean?" she demanded.

"I mean this. You told me that you were at your regular station just before the show started—that you conducted a lot of people to their seats—that you didn't remember whether you ushered Monte Field, the dead man, to his row or not—and that you were standing up at the head of the left aisle all during the performance. *All* during the performance, Madge. Is that correct?"

"Sure it is, Inspector. Who says I wasn't?" The girl was growing excited, but Queen glanced at her fluttering fingers and they became still.

"Aw, cut it out, Madge," snapped the Parson unexpectedly. "Don't make it no worse than it is. Sooner or later he'll find out we were together anyways, and then he'd have something on you. You don't know this bud. Come clean, Madge!"

"So!" said the Inspector, looking pleasantly from the gangster to the girl. "Parson, you're getting sensible in your old age. Did

I hear you say you two were together? When, and why, and for how long?"

Madge O'Connell's face had gone red and white by turns. She favored her lover with a venomous glance, then turned back to Queen.

"I guess I might as well spill it," she said disgustedly, "after this half-wit shows a yellow streak. Here's all I know, Inspector—and Gawd help you if you tell that little mutt of a manager about it!" Queen's eyebrow went up, but he did not interrupt her. "I got the passion for Johnny, all right," she continued defiantly, "because—well, Johnny kind of likes blood-and-thunder stuff, and it was his off-night. So I got him the pass. It was for two—all the passes are—so that the seat next to Johnny was empty all the time. It was an aisle seat on the left—best I could get for that loud-mouthed shrimp! During the first act I was pretty busy and couldn't sit with him. But after the first intermission, when the curtain went up on Act II, things got slack and it was a good chance to sit next to him. Sure, I admit it—I was sittin' next to him nearly the whole act! Why not—don't I deserve a rest once in a while?"

"I see." Queen bent his brows. "You would have saved me a lot of time and trouble, young lady, if you'd told me this before. Didn't you get up at all during the second act?"

"Well, I did a couple of times, I guess," she said guardedly. "But everything was okay, and the manager wasn't around, so I went back."

"Did you notice this man Field as you passed?"

"No—no, sir."

"Did you notice if somebody was sitting next to him?"

"No, sir. I didn't know he was there. Wasn't—wasn't looking that way, I guess."

"I suppose, then," continued Queen coldly, "you don't remember ushering somebody into the last row, next to the last seat, during the second act?"

"No, sir. . . . Aw, I know I shouldn't have done it, maybe, but I didn't see a thing wrong all night." She was growing more nervous at each question. She furtively glanced at the Parson, but he was staring at the floor.

"You're a great help, young lady," said Queen, rising suddenly. "Beat it."

As she turned to go, the gangster with an innocent leer slid across the rug to follow her. Queen made a sign to the policeman. The Parson found himself yanked back to his former position.

"Not so fast, Johnny," said Queen icily. "O'Connell!" The girl turned, trying to appear unconcerned. "For the time being I shan't say anything about this to Mr. Panzer. But I'd advise you to watch your step and learn to keep your mouth clean when you talk to your superiors. Get out now, and if I ever hear of another break on your part God help *you!*"

She started to laugh, wavered and fled from the room. Queen whirled on the policeman. "Put the nippers on him, officer," he snapped, jerking his finger toward the gangster, "and run him down to the station!"

The policeman saluted. There was a flash of steel, a dull click, and the Parson stared stupidly at the handcuffs on his wrists. Before he could open his mouth he was hustled out of the room.

Queen made a disgusted motion of his hand, threw himself into the leather-covered chair, took a pinch of snuff, and said to Johnson in an entirely different tone, "I'll trouble you, Johnson my boy, to ask Mr. Morgan to step in here."

⌀

Benjamin Morgan entered Queen's temporary sanctum with a firm step that did not succeed entirely in concealing a certain bewildered agitation. He said in a cheerful, hearty baritone, "Well, sir, here I am," and sank into a chair with much the same air of satisfaction that a man exhales when he seats himself in his club-room after a hard day. Queen was not taken in. He favored Morgan with a long, earnest stare, which made the paunchy grizzled man squirm.

"My name is Queen, Mr. Morgan," he said in a friendly voice, "Inspector Richard Queen."

"I suspected as much," said Morgan, rising to shake hands. "I think you know who I am, Inspector. I was under your eye more than once in the Criminal Court years ago. There was a case—do you remember it?—I was defending Mary Doolittle when she was being tried for murder. . . ."

"Indeed, yes!" exclaimed the Inspector heartily. "I wondered where I'd seen you before. You got her off, too, if I'm not mistaken. That was a mighty nice piece of work, Morgan—very, very nice. So you're the fellow! Well, well!"

Morgan laughed. "Was pretty nice, at that," he admitted. "But those days are over, I'm afraid, Inspector. You know—I'm not in the criminal end of it any more."

"No?" Queen took a pinch of snuff. "I didn't know that. Anything"—he sneezed—"anything go wrong?" he asked sympathetically.

Morgan was silent. After a moment he crossed his legs and said, "Quite a bit went wrong. May I smoke?" he asked abruptly. On Queen's assent he lit a fat cigar and became absorbed in its curling haze.

Neither man spoke for a long time. Morgan seemed to sense that he was under a rigid inspection, for he crossed and uncrossed his legs repeatedly, avoiding Queen's eyes. The old man appeared to be ruminating, his head sunk on his breast.

The silence became electric, embarrassing. There was not a sound in the room, except the ticking of a floor-clock in a corner. From somewhere in the theatre came a sudden burst of conversation. Voices were raised to a high pitch of indignation or protest. Then even this was cut off.

"Come, now, Inspector. . . ." Morgan coughed. He was enveloped in a thick rolling smoke from his cigar, and his voice was harsh and strained. "What is this—a refined third degree?"

Queen looked up, startled. "Eh? I beg your pardon, Mr. Morgan. My thoughts went wool-gathering, I guess. Been rubbing it in, have I? Dear me! I must be getting old." He rose and took a short turn about the room, his hands clasped loosely behind his back. Morgan's eyes followed him.

"Mr. Morgan"—the Inspector pounced on him with one of his habitual conversational leaps—"do you know why I've asked you to stay and talk to me?"

"Why—I can't say I do, Inspector. I suppose, naturally, that it has to do with the accident here to-night. But what connection it can possibly have with me, I'll confess I don't know." Morgan puffed violently at his weed.

"Perhaps, Mr. Morgan, you will know in a moment," said Queen, leaning back against the desk. "The man murdered here to-night—it wasn't any accident, I can assure you of that—was a certain Monte Field."

The announcement was placid enough but the effect upon Morgan was astounding. He fairly leaped from his chair, eyes popping, hands trembling, breath hoarse and heavy. His cigar dropped to the floor. Queen regarded him with morose eyes.

"Monte—Field!" Morgan's cry was terrible in its intensity. He stared at the Inspector's face. Then he collapsed in the chair, his whole body sagging.

"Pick up your cigar, Mr. Morgan," said Queen. "I shouldn't like to abuse Mr. Panzer's hospitality." The lawyer stooped mechanically and retrieved the cigar.

"My friend," thought Queen to himself, "either you are one of the world's greatest actors or you just got the shock of your life!" He straightened up. "Come now, Mr. Morgan—pull yourself together. Why should the death of Field affect you in this way?"

"But—but, man! Monte Field . . . Oh, my God!" And he threw back his head and laughed—a wild humor that made Queen sit up alertly. The spasm continued, Morgan's body rocking to and fro in hysteria. The Inspector knew the symptoms. He slapped the lawyer in the face, pulling him to his feet by his coat-collar.

"Don't forget yourself, Morgan," commanded Queen. The rough tone had its effect. Morgan stopped laughing, regarded Queen with a blank expression, and dropped heavily into the chair—still shaken, but himself.

"I'm—I'm sorry, Inspector," he muttered, dabbing his face with a handkerchief. "It was—quite a surprise."

"Evidently," said Queen dryly. "You couldn't have acted more surprised if the earth had opened under your feet. Now, Morgan, what's this all about?"

The lawyer continued to wipe the perspiration from his face. He was shaking like a leaf, his jowls red. He gnawed at his lip in indecision.

"All right, Inspector," he said at last. "What do you want to know?"

"That's better," said Queen approvingly. "Suppose you tell me when you last saw Monte Field?"

The lawyer cleared his throat nervously. "Why—why, I haven't seen him for ages," he said in a low voice. "I suppose you know that we were partners once—we had a successful legal practice. Then something happened and we broke up. I—I haven't seen him since."

"And that was how long ago:"

"A little over two years."

"Very good." Queen leaned forward. "I'm anxious to know, too, just why the two of you broke up your partnership."

The lawyer looked down at the rug, fingering his cigar. "I—well, I guess you know Field's reputation as well as I. We didn't agree on ethics, had a little argument and decided to dissolve."

"You parted amicably?"

"Well—under the circumstances, yes."

Queen drummed on the desk. Morgan shifted uneasily. He was evidently still laboring under the effects of his astonishment.

"What time did you get to the theatre to-night, Morgan?" asked the Inspector.

Morgan seemed surprised at the question. "Why—about a quarter after eight," he replied.

"Let me see your ticket-stub, please," said Queen.

The lawyer handed it over after fumbling for it in several pockets. Queen took it, extracted from his own pocket the three stubs he had secreted there, and lowered his hands below the level of the desk. He looked up in a moment, his eyes expressionless as he returned the four bits of pasteboard to his own pocket.

"So you were sitting in M2 Center, were you? Pretty good seat, Morgan," he remarked. "Just what made you come to see 'Gunplay' to-night, anyway?"

"Why, it *is* a rum sort of show, isn't it, Inspector?" Morgan appeared embarrassed. "I don't know that I would ever have thought of coming—I'm not a theatre-going man, you know—except that the Roman management was kind enough to send me a complimentary ticket for this evening's performance."

"Is that a fact?" exclaimed Queen ingenuously. "Quite nice of them, I'd say. When did you receive the ticket?"

"Why, I got the ticket and the letter Saturday morning, Inspector, at my office."

"Oh, you got a letter, too, eh? You don't happen to have it around you, do you?"

"I'm—pretty—sure I—have," grunted Morgan as he began to search his pockets. "Yes! Here it is."

He offered the Inspector a small, rectangular sheet of white paper, deckle-edged and of crushed bond stock. Queen handled it gingerly as he held it up to the light. Through the few typewritten lines on it a watermark was distinctly visible. His lips puckered, and he laid the sheet cautiously on the desk-blotter. As Morgan watched, he opened the top drawer of Panzer's desk and rummaged about until he found a piece of note-paper. It was large, square, and heavily glazed with an ornate theatre-insignia engraved on an upper quarter. Queen put the two pieces of paper side by side, thought a moment, then sighed and picked up the sheet which Morgan had handed him. He read it through slowly.

The Management of the Roman Theatre cordially invites the attendance of Mr. Benjamin Morgan at the Monday evening, September twenty-fourth performance of GUNPLAY. As a leading figure of the New York bar, Mr. Morgan's opinion of the play as a social and legal document is earnestly solicited. This, however, is by no means obligatory; and the Management wishes further to assure Mr. Morgan that the acceptance of its invitation entails no obligation whatsoever.

(Signed) THE ROMAN THEATRE
Per: S.

The "S" was a barely decipherable ink-scrawl.

Queen looked up, smiling. "Mighty nice of the Theatre, Mr. Morgan. I just wonder now—" Still smiling, he signaled to Johnson, who had been sitting in a comer chair, silent spectator to the interview.

"Get Mr. Panzer, the manager, for me, Johnson," said Queen. "And if the publicity man—chap by the name of Bealson, or Pealson, or something—is around, have him step in here, too."

He turned to the lawyer after Johnson left.

"Let me trouble you for your gloves a moment, Mr. Morgan," he said lightly.

With a puzzled stare, Morgan dropped them on the desk in front of Queen, who picked them up curiously. They were of white silk—the conventional gloves for evening-wear. The Inspector pretended to be very busy examining them. He turned them inside out, minutely scrutinized a speck on the tip of one finger, and even went so far as to try them on his own hands, with a jesting remark to Morgan. His examination concluded, he gravely handed the gloves back to the lawyer. "And—oh, yes, Mr. Morgan—that's a mighty spruce-looking tophat you've got there. May I see it a moment?"

Still silently, the lawyer placed his hat on the desk. Queen picked it up with a carefree air, whistling in a slightly flat key, "The Sidewalks of New York."[44] He turned the hat over in his hand. It was a glistening affair of extremely fine quality. The lining was of shimmering white silk, with the name of the maker, "James Chauncey Co.,"[45] stamped in gold. Two initials, "B.M.," were similarly inlaid on the band.

Queen grinned as he placed the hat on his own head. It was a close fit. He doffed it almost immediately and returned it to Morgan.

"Very kind of you to allow me these liberties, Mr. Morgan," he said as he hastily scribbled a note on a pad which he took from his pocket.

The door opened to admit Johnson, Panzer and Harry Neilson. Panzer stepped forward hesitantly and Neilson dropped into an armchair.

"What can we do for you, Inspector?" quavered Panzer, making a valiant attempt to disregard the presence of the grizzled aristocrat slumped in his chair.

"Mr. Panzer," said Queen slowly, "how many kinds of stationery are used in the Roman Theatre?"

The manager's eyes opened wide. "Just one, Inspector. There's a sheet of it on the desk in front of you."

"Ummmm." Queen handed Panzer the slip of paper which he had received from Morgan. "I want you to examine that sheet very carefully, Mr. Panzer. To your knowledge, are there any samples of it in the Roman?"

The manager looked it over with an unfamiliar stare. "No, I don't think so. In fact, I'm sure of it. What's this?" he exclaimed,

44.   A popular song about life in New York City in the 1890s, it was composed in 1894 by Charles B. Lawlor and James W. Blake. Governor Al Smith (of New York) used it as the theme song of his Presidential campaigns in 1920, 1924, and 1928.

45.   There is no trace now of this manufacturer. Popular American top-hat-makers of the day included Rogers Peet, Dunlap & Co., B&K Browning King & Co., the Knox Hat Company (which maintained a large store on 40th St. and Fifth Avenue in Manhattan), and of course Stetson, which made far more than their eponymous cowboy hats.

A 1910 advertisement for the Knox Hat Co., showing President Theodore Roosevelt's hand waving farewell to the Grand Fleet with his Knox hat.

as his eye caught the first few typewritten lines. "Neilson!" he cried, whirling on the publicity man. "What's this—your latest publicity stunt?" He waved the sheet in Neilson's face.

Neilson snatched it from his employer's hand and read it quickly. 'Well, I'll be switched!" he said softly. "If that doesn't beat the non-stop exploitation record!" He reread it, an admiring look on his face. Then, with four pairs of eyes trained accusingly on him, he handed it back to Panzer. "I'm sorry I have to deny any share in this brilliant idea," he drawled. "Why the deuce didn't *I* think of it?" And he retreated to his corner, arms folded on his chest.

The manager turned to Queen in bewilderment. "This is very peculiar, Inspector. To my knowledge the Roman Theatre has never used this stationery, and I can state positively that I never authorized any such publicity stunt. And if Neilson denies a part in it—" He shrugged his shoulders.

Queen placed the paper carefully in his pocket. "That will be all, gentlemen. Thank you." He dismissed the two men with a nod.

He looked appraisingly at the lawyer, whose face was suffused with a fiery color that reached from his neck to the roots of his hair. The Inspector raised his hand and let it drop with a little bang on the desk.

"What do you think of *that*, Mr. Morgan?" he asked simply. Morgan leaped to his feet. "It's a damned frame-up!" he shouted, shaking his fist in Queen's face. "I don't know any more about it than—than *you* do, if you'll pardon a little impertinence! What's more, if you think you can scare me by this hocus-pocus searching of gloves and hats and—and, by God, you haven't examined my underwear yet, Inspector!" He stopped for lack of breath, his face purple.

"But, my dear Morgan," said the Inspector mildly, "why do you upset yourself so? One would think I've been accusing you of Monte Field's murder. Sit down and cool off, man; I asked you a simple question."

Morgan collapsed in his chair. He passed a quivering hand over his forehead and muttered, "Sorry, Inspector. Lost my temper. But of all the rotten deals—" He subsided, mumbling to himself.

Queen sat staring quizzically at him. Morgan was making a great to-do with his handkerchief and cigar. Johnson coughed deprecatingly, looking up at the ceiling. Again a burst of sound penetrated the walls, only to be throttled in mid-air.

Queen's voice cut sharply into the silence. "That's all, Morgan. You may go."

The lawyer lumbered to his feet, opened his mouth as if to speak, clamped his lips together and, clapping his hat on his head, walked out of the room. Johnson innocently lounged forward to help him with the door, on a signal from the Inspector. Both men disappeared.

Queen, left alone in the room, immediately fell into a fierce preoccupation. He took from his pockets the four stubs, the letter Morgan had given him and the woman's rhinestone evening bag which he had found in the dead man's pocket. This last article he opened for the second time that evening and spread its contents on the desk before him. A few calling cards, with the name "Frances Ives-Pope" neatly engraved; two dainty lace handker-chiefs; a vanity case filled with powder, rouge and lipstick; a small change-purse containing twenty dollars in bills and a few coins; and a house-key. Queen fingered these articles thought-fully for a moment, returned them to the handbag and putting bag, stubs and letter back into his pocket once more, rose and looked slowly about. He crossed the room to the clothes-tree, picked up the single hat, a derby, hanging there and examined its interior. The initials "L.P." and the head-size "6¾," seemed to interest him.

He replaced the hat and opened the door.

The four people sitting in the anteroom jumped to their feet with expressions of relief. Queen stood smiling on the threshold, his hands jammed into his coat pockets.

"Here we are at last," he said. "Won't you all please step into the office?"

He politely stood aside to let them pass—the three women and the young man. They trooped in with a flurry of excitement, the women sitting down as the young man busied himself setting chairs for them. Four pairs of eyes gazed earnestly at the old man by the door. He smiled paternally, took one quick glance into the anteroom, closed the door and marched in a stately way to the desk, where he sat down, feeling for his snuff-box.

"Well," he said genially. "I must apologize for having kept you people waiting so long—official business, you know. . . . Now, let's see. Hmmm. Yes. . . . Yes, yes. I must—All right! Now, in the first place, ladies and gentleman, how do we stand?" He turned his mild gaze on the most beautiful of the three women. "I believe, miss, that your name is Frances Ives-Pope, although I haven't had the pleasure of being introduced. Am I correct?"

The girl's eyebrows went up. "That's quite correct, sir," she said in a vibrant musical voice. "Although I don't quite understand how you know my name."

She smiled. It was a magnetic smile, full of charm and a certain strong womanliness that was extremely attractive. A full-bodied creature in the bloom of youth, with great brown eyes and a creamy complexion, she radiated a wholesomeness that the Inspector found refreshing.

He beamed down at her. "Well, Miss Ives-Pope," he chuckled, "I suppose it is mysterious to a layman. And the fact that I am a policeman no doubt heightens the general effect. But it's quite simple. You are by no means an unphotographed young lady—I saw your picture in the paper to-day, as a matter of fact, on the society page."

The girl laughed, a trifle nervously. "So that's how it was!" she said. "I was beginning to be frightened. Just what is it, sir, that you want of me?"

"Business—always business," said the Inspector ruefully. "Just when I'm getting interested in someone, I'm brought bang-up against my profession. . . . Before we conduct our inquisition, may I ask who your friends are?"

An embarrassed coughing arose from the three people on whom Queen bent his eye. Frances said charmingly, "I'm sorry—Inspector, is it? Allow me to introduce Miss Hilda Orange and Miss Eve Ellis, my very dear friends. And this is Mr. Stephen Barry, my fiancé."

Queen glanced at them in some surprise. "If I'm not mistaken—aren't you members of the cast of 'Gunplay'?"

There was a unanimous nodding of heads.

Queen turned to Frances. "I don't want to seem too officious, Miss Ives-Pope, but I want you to explain something. . . . Why are you accompanied by your friends?" he asked with a disarming smile. "I know it sounds impertinent, but I distinctly recall ordering my man to summon you—alone. . . ."

The three thespians rose stiffly. Frances turned from her companions to the Inspector with a pleading look.

"I—please forgive me, Inspector," she said swiftly. "I—I've never been questioned by the police before. I was nervous and—and I asked my fiancé and these two ladies, who are my most intimate friends, to be present during the interview. I didn't realize that I was going against your wishes. . . ."

"I understand," returned Queen, smiling. "I understand completely. But you see—" He made a gesture of finality.

Stephen Barry leaned over the girl's chair. "I'll stay with you, dear, if you give the word." He glared at the Inspector belligerently.

"But, Stephen, dear—" Frances cried helplessly. Queen's face was adamant. "You—you'd better all go. But please wait for me outside. It won't take long, will it, Inspector?" she asked, her eyes unhappy.

Queen shook his head. "Not so very long." His entire attitude had changed. He seemed to be growing truculent. His audience sensed the metamorphosis in him and in an intangible manner grew antagonistic.

Hilda Orange, a large buxom woman of forty, with traces of a handsome youth in her face, now brutally shorn of its make-up in the cold light of the room, leaned over Frances and glared at the Inspector.

"We'll be waiting outside for you, my dear; she said grimly. "And if you feel faint, or something, just screech a little and you'll see what action means." She flounced out of the room. Eve Ellis patted Frances' hand. "Don't worry, Frances," she said in her soft, clear voice. "We're with you." And taking Barry's arm, she followed Hilda Orange. Barry looked back with a mixture of anger and solicitude, shooting a vitriolic glance at Queen as he slammed the door.

Queen was instantly on his feet, his manner brisk and impersonal. He gazed fully into Frances' eyes, his palms pressed against the top surface of the desk. "Now, Miss Frances Ives-Pope," he said curtly, "this is all the business I have to transact with you . . ." He dipped into his pocket and produced with something of the stage-magician's celerity the rhinestone bag. "I want to return your bag."

Frances half-rose to her feet, staring from him to the shimmering purse, the color drained from her face. "Why, that's—that's my evening bag!" she stammered.

"Precisely, Miss Ives-Pope," said Queen. "It was found in the theatre—to-night."

"Of course!" The girl dropped back into her seat with a little nervous laugh. "How stupid of me! And I didn't miss it until just now . . ."

"But, Miss Ives-Pope," the little Inspector continued deliberately, "the finding of your purse is not nearly so important as the place in which it was found." He paused. "You know that there was a man murdered here this evening?"

She stared at him open-mouthed, a wild fear gathering in her eyes. "Yes, I heard so," she breathed.

"Well, your bag, Miss Ives-Pope," continued Queen inexorably, "was found in the murdered man's pocket!"

Terror gleamed in the girl's eyes. Then, with a choked scream, she toppled forward in the chair, her face white and strained.

Queen sprang forward, concern and sympathy instantly apparent on his face. As he reached the limp form, the door burst open and Stephen Barry, coat-tails flying, catapulted into the room. Hilda Orange, Eve Ellis and Johnson, the detective, hurried in behind him.

"What in hell have you done to her, you damned snooper!" the actor cried, shouldering Queen out of the way. He gathered Frances' body tenderly in his arms, pushing aside the wisps of black hair tumbled over her eyes, crooning desperately in her ear. She sighed and looked up in bewilderment as she saw the flushed young face close to hers. "Steve, I—fainted," she murmured, and dropped back in his arms.

"Get some water, somebody," the young man growled, chafing her hands. A tumbler was promptly pushed over his shoulder by Johnson. Barry forced a few drops down Frances' throat and she choked, coming back to consciousness. The two actresses pushed Barry aside and brusquely ordered the men to leave. Queen meekly followed the protesting actor and the detective.

"You're a fine cop, you are!" said Barry scathingly, to the Inspector. "What did you do to her—hit her over the head with the policeman's usual finesse?"

"Now, now, young man," said Queen mildly, "no harsh words, please. The young lady simply received a shock."

They stood in a strained silence until the door opened and the actresses appeared supporting Frances between them. Barry flew to her side. "Are you all right now, dear?" he whispered, pressing her hand.

"Please—Steve—take me—home," she gasped, leaning heavily on his arm.

Inspector Queen stood aside to let them pass. There was a mournful look in his eyes as he watched them walk slowly to the main door and join the short line going out.

CHAPTER VI

In Which the District Attorney Turns Biographer

Inspector Richard Queen was a peculiar man. Small and wiry, thatched with grey and wrinkled in fine lines of experience, he might have been a business executive, a night-watchman, or what he chose. Certainly, in the proper raiment, his quiet figure would mold itself to any disguise.

This ready adaptability was carried out in his manner as well. Few people knew him as he was. To his associates, to his enemies, to the forlorn scraps of humanity whom he turned over to the due processes of the law, he remained ever a source of wonder. He could be theatrical when he chose, or mild, or pompous, or fatherly, or bull-dogging.

But underneath, as someone has said with an over-emphatic sentimentality, the Inspector had "a heart of gold." Inside he was harmless, and keen, and not a little hurt by the cruelties of the world. It was true that to the people who officially came under his eye he was never twice the same. He was constantly whirling into some new facet of personality. He found this to be good business; people never understood him, never knew what he was going to do or say, and consequently they were always a little afraid of him.

Now that he was alone, back in Panzer's office, the door shut tight, his investigations temporarily halted, the true character of the man shone from his face. At this moment it was an old face—old physically, old and wise spiritually. The incident of the girl he had startled into unconsciousness was uppermost in his mind. The memory of her drawn, horrified face made him wince. Frances Ives-Pope seemed to personify everything a man of years could hope for in his own daughter. To see her shrink under the lash pained him. To see her fiancé turn fiercely in her defense made him blush.

Abstemious except for his one mild dissipation, the Inspector reached for his snuff-box with a sigh and sniffed freely. . . .

When there came a peremptory knock on the door, he was the chameleon again—a detective-inspector sitting at a desk and no doubt thinking clever and ponderous thoughts. In truth, he was wishing that Ellery would come back.

At his hearty "Come in!" the door swung open to admit a thin, bright-eyed man dressed in heavy overclothes, a woolen muffler wound about his neck.

"Henry!" exclaimed the Inspector, starting to his feet. "'What the dickens are you doing here? I thought the doctor had ordered you to stay in bed!"

District Attorney Henry Sampson winked as he slumped into an armchair.

"Doctors," he said didactically, "doctors give me a pain in the neck. How are tricks?"

He groaned and felt his throat gingerly. The Inspector sat down again.

"For a grown man, Henry," he said decisively, "you're the most unruly patient I've ever seen. Man alive, you'll catch pneumonia if you don't watch out!"

"Well," grinned the District Attorney, "'I carry a lot of insurance, so I should worry . . . You haven't answered my question."

"Oh, yes," grunted Queen. "Your question. How's tricks, I think you asked? Tricks, my dear Henry, are at present in a state of complete nullity. Does that satisfy you?"

"Kindly be more explicit," said Sampson. "Remember, I'm a sick man and my head is buzzing."

"Henry," said Queen, leaning forward earnestly, "I warn you that we're in the midst of one of the toughest cases this department has ever handled. . . . Is your head buzzing? I'd hate to tell you what's happening in mine!"

Sampson regarded him with a frown. "If it's as you say—and I suppose it is—this comes at a rotten time. Election's not so far off—an unsolved murder handled by the improper parties . . ."

"Well, that's one way of looking at it," remarked Queen, in a low voice. "I wasn't exactly thinking of this affair in terms of votes, Henry. A man's been killed—and at the moment I'll be frank enough to admit that I haven't the slightest idea who did the job or how."

"I accept your well-meant rebuke, Inspector," said Sampson, in a lighter tone. "But if you'd heard what I did a few moments ago—over the telephone . . ."

"One moment, my dear Watson, as Ellery would say," chuckled Queen, with that startling change of temperament so character-istic of him. "I'll bet I know what happened. You were at home, probably in bed. Your telephone rang. A voice began to crab, protest, gurgle, and do all the other things a voice does when its owner is excited. The voice said, 'I won't stand for being cooped up by the police, like a common criminal! I want that man Queen severely reprimanded! He's a menace to personal liberty!' And so on, in words of that general tenor. . . ."

"My dear fellow!" said Sampson, laughing.

"This gentleman, the owner of the protesting voice," con-tinued the Inspector, "is short, rather stout, wears gold-rimmed eyeglasses, has an exceedingly disagreeable feminine voice, displays a really touching concern for his family—one wife and one-daughter—in the presence of possible publicity agents, and always refers to you as his 'very good friend, District Attorney Sampson.' Correct?"

Sampson sat staring at him. Then his keen face creased into a smile.

"Perfectly astounding, my dear Holmes!" he murmured. "Since you know so much about my friend, perhaps it would be child's-play for you to give me his name?"

"Er—but that was the fellow, wasn't it?" said Queen, his face scarlet. "I—Ellery, my boy! I'm glad to see you!"

Ellery had entered the room. He shook hands cordially with Sampson, who greeted him with a pleasure born of long associa-tion, and made a remark about the dangers of a District Attorney's life, briskly setting down on the desk a huge container of coffee and a paper bag pleasantly suggestive of French pastry.

"Well, gentlemen, the great search is finished, over, *kaput*, and the perspiring detectives will now partake of midnight tiffin." He laughed and slapped his father affectionately on the shoulder.

"But, Ellery!" cried Queen delightedly. "This is a welcome surprise! Henry, will you join us in a little celebration?" He filled three paper cups with the steaming coffee.

"I don't know what you're celebrating, but count me in," said Sampson and the three men fell to with enthusiasm.

"What's happened, Ellery?" asked the old man, sipping his coffee contentedly.

"Gods do not eat, neither do they drink," murmured Ellery from behind a cream puff. "I am not omnipotent, and suppose you tell me what happened in your impromptu torture-chamber. . . . I can tell you one thing you don't know, however. Mr. Libby, of Libby's ice-cream parlor, whence came these elegant cakes, confirms Jess Lynch's story about the ginger ale. And Miss Elinor Libby nicely corroborated the alley story."

Queen wiped his lips daintily with a huge handkerchief. "Well, let Prouty make sure about the ginger ale, anyway. As for me, I interviewed several people and now I have nothing to do."

"Thank you," remarked Ellery dryly. "That was a perfect recitation. Have you acquainted the D. A. with the events of this tumultuous evening?"

"Gentlemen," said Sampson, setting down his cup, "here's what I know. About a half-hour ago I was telephoned by 'one of my very good friends'—who happens to wield a little power behind the scenes—and he told me in no uncertain terms that during to-night's performance a man was murdered. Inspector Richard Queen, he said, had descended upon the theatorium like a whirlwind, accompanied by his minor whirlwinds, and had proceeded to make everybody wait over an hour—an inexcusable, totally unwarranted procedure, my friend charged. He further deposed that said Inspector even went so far as to accuse him personally of the crime, and had domineering policemen search him and his wife and daughter before they were allowed to leave the theatre.

"So much for my informant's story—the rest of his conversation, being rather profane, is irrelevant. The only other thing I know is that Velie told me outside who the murdered man was. And *that*, gentlemen, was the most interesting part of the whole story."

"You know almost as much about this case as I do," grunted Queen. "Probably more, because I have an idea you are thoroughly familiar with Field's operation . . . Ellery, what happened outside during the search?"

46. "Bucket-shops" were unregulated stock brokers specializing in day traders, who purchased securities on thin margins and indulged in high volume speculations. In fact most bucket-shops did not even purchase or sell securities for customers; rather, they merely booked the supposed transactions, often made up the supposed trading history, and paid (or failed to pay) their customers out of their own pockets—exactly like a gambling establishment or bookie. There were many such "scandals," so it is impossible without more to identify the *particular* bucket-shop scandal in which Fields was involved.

Ellery crossed his legs comfortably. "As you might have guessed, the search of the audience was entirely without result. Nothing out of the way was found. Not one solitary thing. Nobody looked guilty, and nobody took it upon himself to confess. In other words, it was a complete fiasco."

"Of course, of course," said Queen. "There's somebody almighty clever behind this business. I suppose you didn't even come across the suspicion of an extra hat?"

"That, dad," remarked Ellery, "was what I was decorating the lobby for. No—no hat."

"Are they all through out there?"

"Just finished when I strolled across the street for the refreshments," said Ellery. "There was nothing else to do but allow the angry mob in the gallery to file downstairs and out into the street. Everybody's out now—the galleryites, the employees, the cast. . . . Queer species, actors. All night they play God and then suddenly they find themselves reduced to ordinary street clothes and the ills that flesh is heir to. By the way, Velie also searched the five people who came out of this office. Quite a motor that young lady possesses. Miss Ives-Pope and her party, I gathered. . . . Didn't know but that you might have forgotten them," he chuckled.

"So we're up a tree, eh?" muttered the Inspector. "Here's the story, Henry." And he gave a concise résumé of the evening's events to Sampson, who sat silently throughout, frowning.

"And that," concluded Queen, after describing briefly the scenes enacted in the little office, "is that. Now, Henry, you must have something to tell us about Monte Field. We know that he was a slick article—but that's all we do know."

"That would be putting it mildly," said Sampson savagely. "I can give you almost by rote the story of his life. It looks to me as if you're going to have a difficult time and some incident in his past might give you a clue.

"Field first came under the scrutiny of my office during my predecessor's régime. He was suspected of negotiating a swindle connected with the bucket-shop scandals.[46] Cronin, an assistant D. A. at the time, couldn't get a thing on him. Field had covered his operations well. All we had was the telltale story, which might or might not have been true, of a 'stool-pigeon' who had been kicked out of the mob. Of course, Cronin never let on to Field directly or indirectly that he was under suspicion. The affair blew over and although Cronin was a bulldog, every time he thought he had something he found that he had nothing after all. Oh, no question about it—Field was slick.

"When I came into office, on Cronin's fervent suggestion we began an exhaustive investigation of Field's background. On the q. t.,[47] of course. And this is what we discovered: Monte Field came of a blue-blood New England family—the kind that doesn't brag about its Mayflower descendants. He had private tutoring as a kid, went to a swanky prep school, got through by the skin of his teeth and then was sent to Harvard by his father as a sort of last despairing gesture. He seems to have been a pretty bad egg even as a boy. Nothing criminal, but just wild. On the other hand, he must have had a grain of pride because when the blow-up came he actually shortened his name. The family name was Fielding—and he became Monte Field."

Queen and Ellery nodded, Ellery's eyes introspective, Queen staring steadily at Sampson.

"Field," resumed Sampson, "wasn't a total loss, understand. He had brains. He studied law brilliantly at Harvard. He seemed to have a flair for oratory that was considerably aided by his profound knowledge of legal technology. But just after his graduation, before his family could get even the bit of pleasure out of his scholastic career that should have been theirs, he was mixed up in a dirty deal with a girl. His father cut him off in jig-time. He was through—out—he'd disgraced the family name—you know the sort of thing. . . .

"Well, this friend of ours didn't let grief overwhelm him, evidently. He made the best of being done out of a nice little legacy, and decided to go out and make some money on his own. How he managed to get along during this period we couldn't find out, but the next thing we hear of him is that he has formed a partnership with a fellow by the name of Cohen. One of the smoothest shysters in the business. What a partnership that was! They cleaned up a fortune between them establishing a select clientele chosen from among the biggest crooks in crookdom. Now, you know as well as I just how hard it is to 'get' anything on a bird who knows more about the loopholes of the law than the Supreme Court judges. They got away with everything—it was a golden era for crime. Crooks considered themselves top-notch when Cohen & Field were kind enough to defend them.

47. Slang for "on the *quiet*." Its first print appearance was in 1870, in the broadside ballad "The Man from Poplar."

"And then Mr. Cohen, who was the experienced man of the combination, knowing the ropes, making the 'contacts' with the firm's clients, fixing the fees—and he could do that beautifully in spite of his inability to speak untainted English—Mr. Cohen, I say, met a very sad end one winter night on the North River waterfront. He was found shot through the head, and although it's twelve years since the happy event, the murderer is still unknown. That is—unknown in the legal sense. We had grave suspicions as to his identity. I shouldn't be at all surprised if Mr. Field's demise this evening removed the Cohen case from the register."

"So that's the kind of playboy he was," murmured Ellery. "Even in death his face is most disagreeable. Too bad I had to lose my first-edition on his account."

"Forget it, you bookworm," growled his father, "Go on, Henry."

"Now," said Sampson, taking the last piece of cake from the desk and munching it heartily, "now we come to a bright spot in Mr. Field's life. For after the unfortunate decease of his partner, he seemed to turn over a new leaf. He actually went to work—real legal work—and of course he had the brains to pull it through. For a number of years he worked alone, gradually effacing the bad reputation he had built up in the profession and even gaining a little respect now and then from some of our hoity-toity legal lights.

"This period of apparent good behavior lasted for six years. Then he met Ben Morgan—a solid man with a spotless record and a good reputation, although perhaps lacking the vital spark which makes the great lawyer. Somehow Field persuaded Morgan to join him in partnership. Then things began to hum.

"You'll remember that in that period some highly shady things were happening in New York. We got faint inklings of a gigantic criminal ring, composed of 'fences,' crooks, lawyers, and in some cases politicians. Some smashing big robberies were pulled off; bootlegging got to be a distinct art in the city environs; and a number of daring hold-ups resulting in murder put the department on its toes. But you know that as well as I do. You fellows 'got' some of them; but you never broke the ring, and you never reached the men higher up. And I have every reason to believe that our late friend Mr. Monte Field was the brains behind the whole business.

"See how easy it was for a man of his talents. Under the tutelage of Cohen, his first partner, he had become thoroughly familiar with the underworld moguls. When Cohen outlived his usefulness, he was conveniently bumped off. Then Field—remember, I am working now on speculation chiefly, because the evidence is practically nil—then Field, under the cloak of a respectable legal business, absolutely above-board, quietly built up a far-flung criminal organization. How he accomplished this we have no way of knowing, of course. When he was quite ready to shoot the works, he tied up with a well-known respectable partner, Morgan, and now secure in his legal position, began to engineer most of the big crooked deals pulled off in the last five years or so. . . ."

"Where does Morgan come in?" asked Ellery idly.

"I was coming to that. Morgan, we have every reason to believe, was absolutely innocent of any connection with Field's under-cover operations. He was as straight as a die and in fact had often refused cases in which the defendant was a shady character. Their relations must have become strained when Morgan got a hint of what was going on. Whether this is so or not I don't know—you could easily find out from Morgan himself. Anyway, they broke up. Since the dissolution, Field has operated a little more in the open, but still not a shred of tangible evidence which would count in a court of law."

"Pardon me for interrupting, Henry," said Queen reflectively, "but can't you give me a little more information on their break-up? I'd like to use it as a check on Morgan when I talk to him again."

"Oh, yes!" replied Sampson grimly. "I'm glad you reminded me. Before the last word was written in the dissolving of the partnership, the two men had a terrific blow-up which almost resulted in tragedy. At the Webster Club,[48] where they were lunching, they were heard quarreling violently. The argument increased until it was necessary for the bystanders to interfere. Morgan was beside himself with rage and actually threatened Field's life right then and there. Field, I understand, was quite calm."

"Did any of the witnesses get an inkling of the cause of the quarrel?" asked Queen.

"Unfortunately, no. The thing blew over soon enough; they dissolved quietly, and that was the last anybody ever heard of it. Until, of course, to-night."

48. No Webster Club is listed in *Trow's General Directory of New York City* for 1922–23; however, the Webster *Hotel* was at 40 W. 45th St. in Manhattan, and this may well have been a dining venue there.

There was a pregnant silence when the District Attorney stopped talking. Ellery whistled a few bars of a Schubert air, while Queen frankly took a pinch of snuff with a ferocious vigor.

"I'd say, off-hand," murmured Ellery, looking off into space, "that Mr. Morgan is in deucedly hot water."

His father grunted. Sampson said seriously, "Well, that's your affair, gentlemen. I know what my job is. Now that Field is out of the way, I'm going to have his files and records gone over with a fine-comb. If nothing else, his murder will accomplish eventually, I hope, the complete annihilation of his gang. I'll have a man at his office in the morning."

"One of my men is camping there already," remarked Queen absently. "So you think it's Morgan, do you?" he asked Ellery, with a flash of his eyes.

"I seem to recall making a remark a minute ago," said Ellery calmly, "to the effect that Mr. Morgan is in hot water. I did not commit myself further. I admit that Morgan seems to be the logical man.—Except, gentlemen, for one thing," he added.

"The hat," said Inspector Queen instantly.

"*No,*" said Ellery, "*the other hat.*"

CHAPTER VII

The Queens Take Stock

L et's see where we stand," continued Ellery without pausing. "Let's consider this thing in its most elementary light.

"These, roughly, are the facts: A man of shady character, Monte Field, probable head of a vast criminal organization, with undoubtedly a host of enemies, is found murdered in the Roman Theatre ten minutes before the end of the second act, at precisely 9: 55 o'clock. He is discovered by a man named William Pusak, a clerk of an inferior type of intelligence, who is sitting five seats away in the same row. This man, attempting to leave, pushes his way past the victim who before he dies mutters, 'Murder! Been murdered!' or words to that effect.

"A policeman is called and to make sure the man is dead, secures the services of a doctor in the audience, who definitely pronounces the victim killed by some form of alcoholic poisoning. Subsequently Dr. Prouty, the Assistant Medical Examiner, confirms this statement, adding that there is only one disturbing factor—that a man would not die so soon from lethal alcohol. The question of the cause of death, therefore, we must leave for the moment, since only an autopsy can definitely determine it.

"With a large audience to attend to, the policeman calls for help, officers of the vicinity come in to take charge and subsequently the headquarters men arrive to conduct the immediate investigation. The first important issue that arises is the question of whether the murderer had the opportunity to leave the scene of the crime between the time it was committed and the time it was discovered. Doyle, the policeman who was first on the scene, immediately ordered the manager to station guards at all exits and both alleys.

"When I arrived, I thought of this point the very first thing and conducted a little investigation of my own. I went around to all the exits and questioned the guards. I discovered that there was a guard at every door of the auditorium during the entire second act, with two exceptions which I shall mention shortly. Now, it had been determined from the testimony of the orangeade boy, Jess Lynch, that the victim was alive not only during the intermission between Act I and Act II—when he saw and talked to Field in the alleyway—but that Field was also in apparently good health ten minutes after the raising of the curtain for Act II. This was when the boy delivered a bottle of ginger ale to Field at the seat in which he was later found dead. Inside the theatre, an usher stationed at the foot of the stairs leading to the balcony swore that no one had either gone up or come down during the second act. This eliminates the possibility that the murderer had access to the balcony.

"The two exceptions I noted a moment ago are the two doors on the extreme left aisle, which should have been guarded but were not because the usherette, Madge O'Connell, was sitting in the audience next to her lover. This presented to my mind the possibility that the murderer might have left by one of these two doors, which were conveniently placed for an escape should the murderer have been so inclined. However, even this possibility was eliminated by the statement of the O'Connell girl, whom I hunted up after she was questioned by dad."

"You talked to her on the sly, did you, you scalawag?" roared Queen, glaring at Ellery.

"I certainly did," chuckled Ellery, "and I discovered the one important fact that seems pertinent to this phase of the investigation. O'Connell swore that before she left the doors to sit down next to Parson Johnny she stepped on the inside floor-lock that latches them top and bottom. When the commotion began the girl sprang from the Parson's side and finding the doors locked as she had left them, unlatched them while Doyle was attempting to quiet the audience. Unless she was lying—and I don't think she was—this proves that the murderer did not leave by these doors, since at the time the body was found they were still locked from the inside."

"Well, I'll be switched!" growled Queen. "She didn't tell me a thing about that part of it, drat her! Wait till I get my hands on her, the little snip!"

"Please be logical, *M. le Gardien de la Paix*," [49] laughed Ellery. "The reason she didn't tell you about bolting the doors was that you didn't ask her. She felt that she was in enough of an uncomfortable position already.

"At any rate, that statement of hers would seem to dispose of the two side-doors near the murdered man's seat. I will admit that all sorts of possibilities enter into the problem—for example, Madge O'Connell might have been an accomplice. I mention this only as a possibility, and not even as a theory. At any rate, it seems to me that the murderer would not have run the risk of being seen leaving from side doors. Besides, a departure in so unusual a manner and at so unusual a time would have been all the more noticeable especially since few people leave during a second act. And again—the murderer could have no foreknowledge of the O'Connell girl's dereliction in duty—if she were not an accomplice. As the crime was carefully planned—and we must admit that from all indications it was—the murderer would have discarded the side-doors as a means of escape.

"This probe left, I felt, only one other channel of investigation. That was the main entrance. And here again we received definite testimony from the ticket-taker and the doorman outside to the effect that no one *left* the building during the second act by that route. Except, of course, the harmless orangeade boy.

"All the exits having been guarded or locked, and the alley having been under constant surveillance from 9:35 on by Lynch. Elinor, Johnny Chase—the usher—and after him the police—these being the facts, all my questioning and checking, gentlemen," continued Ellery in a grave tone, "lead to the inevitable conclusion that, from the time the murder was discovered and all the time thereafter while the investigation was going on, *the murderer was in the theatre!*"

A silence followed Ellery's pronouncement. "Incidentally," he added calmly, "it occurred to me when I talked to the ushers to ask if they had seen any one leave his seat after the second act started, and they can't recall anyone changing seats!"

49. *Gardien de la Paix* means literally guardian of the peace, the term is applied to the common French policeman, so Ellery is jestingly calling his father "Mr. Policeman."

Queen idly took another pinch of snuff. "Nice work—and a very pretty piece of reasoning, my son—but nothing, after all, of a startling or conclusive nature. Granted that the murderer was in the theatre all that time—how could we possibly have laid our hands on him?"

"He didn't say you could," put in Sampson, smiling. "Don't be so sensitive, old boy; nobody's going to report you for negligence in the performance of your duty. From all I've heard to-night you handled the affair well."

Queen grunted. "I'll admit I'm a little peeved at myself for not following up that matter of the doors more thoroughly. But even if it were possible for the murderer to have left directly after the crime, I nevertheless would have had to pursue the inquiry as I did, on the chance that he was still in the theatre."

"But dad—of course!" said Ellery seriously. "You had so many things to attend to, while all I had to do was stand around and look Socratic."

"How about the people who have come under the eye of the investigation so far?" asked Sampson curiously.

"Well, what about them?" challenged Ellery. "We certainly can draw no definite conclusions from either their conversation or their actions. We have Parson Johnny, a thug, who was there apparently for no other reason than to enjoy a play giving some interesting sidelights on his own profession. Then there is Madge O'Connell, a very doubtful character about whom we can make no decision at this stage of the game. She might be an accomplice—she might be innocent—she might be merely negligent—she might be almost anything. Then there is William Pusak, who found Field. Did you notice the moronic cast of his head? And Benjamin Morgan—here we strike fallow ground in the realm of probability. But what do we know of his actions to-night? True, his story of the letter and the complimentary ticket sounds queer, since any one could have written the letter, even Morgan himself. And we must always remember the public threat against Field; and also the enmity, reason unknown, which has existed between them for two years. And, lastly, we have Miss Frances Ives-Pope. I'm exceedingly sorry I was absent during that interview. The fact remains—and isn't it an interesting one?—that her evening bag was found in the dead man's pocket. Explain that if you can.

"So you see where we are," Ellery continued ruefully. "All we have managed to derive from this evening's entertainment is a plethora of suspicions and a poverty of facts."

"So far, son," said Queen casually, "you have kept on mighty safe ground. But you've forgotten the important matter of the suspiciously vacant seats. Also the rather startling fact that Field's ticket-stub and the only other stub that could be attributed to the murderer—I refer to the LL30 Left stub found by Flint—that these two stubs do not coincide. That is to say, that the torn edges indicate they were gathered by the ticket-taker at different times!"

"Check," said Ellery. "But let's leave that for the moment and get on to the problem of Field's tophat."

"The hat—well, what do you think of it?" asked Queen curiously.

"Just this. In the first place, we have fairly established the fact that the hat is not missing through accident. The murdered man was seen by Jess Lynch with the hat in his lap ten minutes after Act II began. Since it is now missing, the only reasonable theory that would explain its absence is that the murderer took it away with him. Now—for the moment, let's forget the problem of where the hat is now. The immediate conclusion to draw is that the hat was taken away for one of two reasons: first, that it was in some way incriminating in itself, so that if it were left behind it would point to the murderer's identity. What the nature of this incriminating indication is we cannot even guess at the moment. Second, the hat may have contained something which the murderer wanted. You will say: Why couldn't he take this mysterious object and leave the hat? Probably, if this supposition is true, because he either had not sufficient time to extract it, or else did not know *how* to extract it and therefore took the hat away with him to examine it at his leisure. Do you agree with me so far?"

The District Attorney nodded slowly. Queen sat still, his eyes vaguely troubled.

"Let us for a moment consider what the hat could possibly have contained," resumed Ellery, as he vigorously polished his glasses. "Due to its size, shape and cubic content our field of speculation is not a broad one. What could be hidden in a tophat? The only things that present themselves to my mind are: papers of some sort, jewelry, banknotes, or any other small object of value which could not easily be detected in such a place. Obviously, this problematical object would not be carried merely in the crown of the hat since it would fall out whenever the wearer uncovered his head. We are led to believe therefore that, whatever the object was, it was concealed in the lining of the hat. This immediately narrows our list of possibilities. Solid objects of bulk must be eliminated. A jewel might have been concealed; banknotes or papers might have been concealed. We can, I think, discard the jewel, from what we know of Monte Field. If he was carrying anything of value, it would probably be connected in some way with his profession.

"One point remains to be considered in this preliminary analysis of the missing tophat. And, gentlemen, it may very well become a pivotal consideration before we are through.—It is of paramount importance for us to know whether the murderer knew in advance of his crime that it would be necessary for him to take away Monte Field's tophat. In other words, did the murderer have *foreknowledge* of the hat's significance, whatever it may prove to be? I maintain that the facts prove deductively, as logically as facts *can* prove deductively, that the murderer had no foreknowledge.

"Follow me closely . . . Since Monte Field's tophat is missing, and since no other tophat has been found in its place, it is an undeniable indication that it was essential that it be taken away. You must agree that, as I pointed out before, the murderer is most plausibly the remover of the hat. Now! Regardless of *why* it had to be taken away, we are faced with two alternatives: one, that the murderer knew in advance that it had to be taken away; or two, that he did not know in advance. Let us exhaust the possibilities in the former case. If he knew in advance, it may be surely and logically assumed that he would have brought with him to the theatre a hat to replace Field's, rather than leave an obvious clue by the provocative absence of the murdered man's hat. To bring a replacement hat would have been the safe thing to do. The murderer would have had no difficulty in securing a replacement hat, since knowing its importance in advance, he could certainly have armed himself with a further knowledge of Field's head-size, style of tophat, and other minor details. *But there is no replacement hat.* We have every right to expect a replacement hat in a crime so carefully concocted as this one. There being none, our only conclusion can be that the murderer did not know beforehand the importance of Field's hat; otherwise he would assuredly have taken the intelligent precaution of leaving another hat behind. In this way the police would never know that Field's hat had any significance at all.

"Another point in corroboration. Even if the murderer didn't desire, for some dark reason of his own, to leave a replacement hat, he certainly would have arranged to secure what was in the hat by cutting it out. All he had to do was to provide himself in advance with a sharp instrument—a pocket-knife, for example. The *empty* hat, though cut, would not have presented the problem of disposal that the *missing* hat would. Surely the murderer would have preferred this procedure, had he foreknowledge of the hat's contents. But he did not do even this. This, it seems to me, is strong corroborative evidence that he did not know before he came to the Roman Theatre that he would have to take away a hat or its contents. *Quod erat demonstrandum.*"[50]

The District Attorney gazed at Ellery with puckered lips. Inspector Queen seemed sunk in a lethargy. His hand hovered midway between his snuff-box and his nose.

"Just what's the point, Ellery?" inquired Sampson. "Why is it important for you to know that the murderer had no foreknowledge of the hat's significance?"

Ellery smiled. "Merely this. The crime was committed after the beginning of the second act. I want to be sure in my own mind that the murderer, by not knowing in advance of the hat's significance, could not have used the first intermission in any manner whatsoever as an essential element of his plan. . . . Of course, Field's hat may turn up somewhere on the premises, and its discovery would invalidate all these speculations. But—I don't think it will. . . ."

"That analysis of yours might be elementary, boy, but it sounds quite logical to me," said Sampson approvingly. "You should have been a lawyer."

"You can't beat the Queen brains," chuckled the old man suddenly, his face wreathed in a wide smile. "But I'm going to get busy on another tack that ought to jibe somewhere with this puzzle of the hat. You noticed, Ellery, the name of the clothier sewed into Field's coat?"

"No sooner said than done," grinned Ellery. Producing one of the small volumes which he carried in his topcoat pocket, he opened it and pointed to a notation on the fly-leaf. "Browne Bros.,[51] gentlemen—no less."

50. "Thus, the thing has been demonstrated."

51. Another fictitious vendor.

"That's right; and I'll have Velie down there in the morning to check up," said the Inspector. "You must have realized that Field's clothing is of exceptional quality. That evening-suit cost three hundred dollars,[52] if it cost a penny. And Browne Bros. are the artists to charge such fashionable prices. But there's another point in this connection: every stitch of clothing on the dead man's body had the same manufacturer's mark. That's not uncommon with wealthy men; and Browne's made a specialty of outfitting their customers from head to foot. What more probable to assume—"

"Than that Field bought his hats there, too!" exclaimed Sampson, with an air of discovery.

"Exactly, Tacitus,"[53] said Queen, grinning. "Velie's job is to check up on this clothing business and if possible secure an exact duplicate of the hat Field wore to-night. I'm mighty anxious to look it over."

Sampson rose with a cough. "I suppose I really ought to get back to bed," he said. "The only reason I came down here was to see that you didn't arrest the Mayor. Boy, that friend of mine was sore! I'll never hear the end of it!"

Queen looked up at him with a quizzical smile. "Before you go, Henry, suppose you tell me just where I stand on this thing. I know that I used a pretty high hand to-night, but you must realize how necessary it was. Are you going to put one of your own men on the case?"

Sampson glared at him. "When did you get the idea I wasn't satisfied with your conduct of the investigation, you old canary bird!" he growled. "I've never checked you up yet, and I'm not going to start now. If you can't bring this thing to a successful conclusion, I certainly don't think any of my men can. My dear Q, go ahead and detain half of New York if you think it's necessary. I'll back you up."

"Thanks, Henry," said Queen. "I just wanted to be sure. And now, since you're so nice about it, watch my smoke!"

He ambled across the room into the anteroom, stuck his head past the doorway into the theatre, and shouted, "Mr. Panzer, will you come here a moment?"

He came back smiling grimly to himself, the swarthy theatre-manager close on his heels.

"Mr. Panzer, meet District Attorney Sampson," said Queen. The two men shook hands. "Now, Mr. Panzer, you've got one more job and you can go home and go to sleep. I want this theatre shut down so tight a mouse couldn't get into it!"

Panzer grew pale. Sampson shrugged his shoulders, as if to indicate that he washed his hands of the entire affair. Ellery nodded sagely in approval.

"But—but Inspector, just when we're playing to capacity!" groaned the little manager. "Is it absolutely necessary?"

"So necessary, my dear man," answered the Inspector coolly, "that I'm going to have two men here patrolling the premises all the time."

Panzer wrung his hands, looking furtively at Sampson. But the District Attorney was standing with his back to them, examining a print on the wall.

"This is terrible, Inspector!" wailed Panzer. "I'll never hear the end of it from Gordon Davis, the producer. . . . But of course—if you say so, it will be done."

"Heck, man, don't look so blue," said Queen, more kindly. "You'll be getting so much publicity out of this that when the show reopens you'll have to enlarge the theatre. I don't expect to have the theatre shut down more than a few days, anyway. I'll give the necessary orders to my men outside. After you've transacted your routine business here to-night, just tip off the men I've left and go home. I'll let you know in a few days when you can reopen."

Panzer waggled his head sadly, shook hands all around and left. Sampson immediately whirled on Queen and said, "By the Lord Harry, Q, that's going some! Why do you want the theatre closed? You've milked it dry, haven't you?"

"Well, Henry," said Queen slowly, "the hat hasn't been found. All those people filed out of the theatre and were searched—and each one had just one hat. Doesn't that indicate that the hat we're looking for is still here somewhere? And if it's still here, I'm not giving anybody a chance to come in and take it away. If there's any taking to be done, I'll do it."

Sampson nodded. Ellery was still wearing a worried frown as the three men walked out of the office into the almost deserted orchestra. Here and there a busy figure was stooping over a seat, examining the floor. A few men could be seen darting in and out of the boxes up front. Sergeant Velie stood by the main door, talking in low tones to Piggott and Hagstrom. Detective Flint, superintending a squad of men, was working far to the front of the orchestra. A small group of cleaning-women operated vacuum cleaners tiredly here and there. In one corner, to the rear, a buxom police matron was talking with an elderly woman—the woman Panzer had called Mrs. Phillips.

The three men walked to the main door. While Ellery and Sampson were silently surveying the always depressing scene of an untenanted auditorium, Queen spoke rapidly to Velie, giving orders in an undertone. Finally he turned and said, "Well, gentlemen, that's all for to-night. Let's be going." On the sidewalk a number of policemen had roped off a large space, behind which a straggling crowd of curiosity-seekers was gaping.

"Even at two o'clock in the morning these night-birds patrol Broadway," grunted Sampson. With a wave of the hand he entered his automobile after the Queens politely refused his offer of a "lift." A crowd of businesslike reporters pushed through the lines and surrounded the two Queens.

"Here, here! What's this, gentlemen?" asked the old man, frowning.

"How about the low-down on to-night's job, Inspector?" asked one of them urgently.

"You'll get all the information you want, boys, from Detective-Sergeant Velie—inside." He smiled as they charged in a body through the glass doors.

Ellery and Richard Queen stood silently on the curb, watching the policemen herd back the crowd. Then the old man said with a sudden wave of weariness, "Come on, son, let's walk part of the way home."

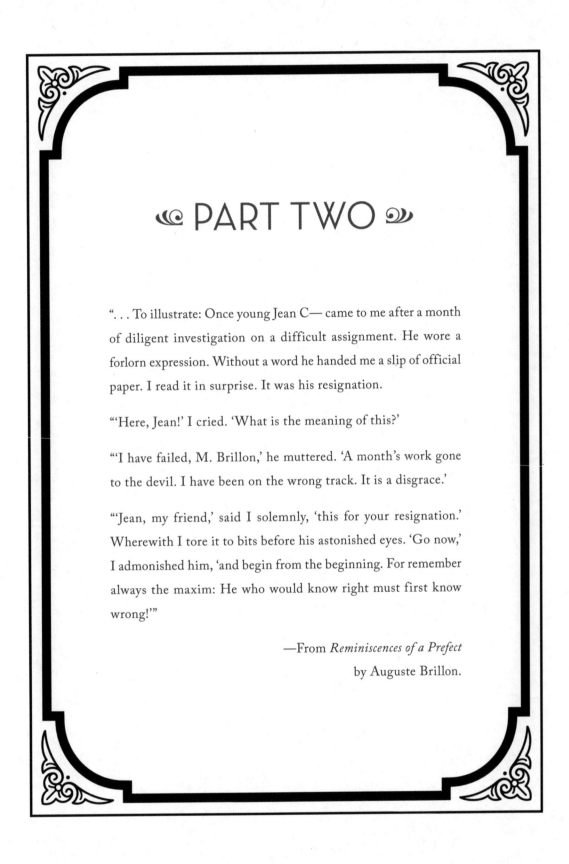

✄ PART TWO ✄

". . . To illustrate: Once young Jean C— came to me after a month of diligent investigation on a difficult assignment. He wore a forlorn expression. Without a word he handed me a slip of official paper. I read it in surprise. It was his resignation.

"'Here, Jean!' I cried. 'What is the meaning of this?'

"'I have failed, M. Brillon,' he muttered. 'A month's work gone to the devil. I have been on the wrong track. It is a disgrace.'

"'Jean, my friend,' said I solemnly, 'this for your resignation.' Wherewith I tore it to bits before his astonished eyes. 'Go now,' I admonished him, 'and begin from the beginning. For remember always the maxim: He who would know right must first know wrong!'"

—From *Reminiscences of a Prefect*
by Auguste Brillon.

CHAPTER VIII

In Which the Queens Meet Mr. Field's Very Best Friend

The Queens' apartment on West 87th Street was a man's domicile from the pipe-rack over the hearth to the shining sabers on the wall. They lived on the top floor of a three-family brownstone house, a relic of late Victorian times. You walked up the heavily-carpeted stairs through seemingly endless halls of dismal rectitude. When you were quite convinced that only mummified souls could inhabit such a dreary place, you came upon the huge oaken door marked, "The Queens"—a motto lettered neatly and framed. Then Djuna grinned at you from behind a crack and you entered a new world.

More than one individual, exalted in his own little niche, had willingly climbed the uninviting staircases to find sanctuary in this haven. More than one card bearing a famous name had been blithely carried by Djuna through the foyer into the living-room.

The foyer was Ellery's inspiration, if the truth were told. It was so small and so narrow that its walls appeared unnaturally towering. With a humorous severity one wall had been completely covered by a tapestry depicting the chase—a most appropriate appurtenance to this medieval chamber. Both Queens detested it heartily, preserving it only because it had been presented to them with regal gratitude by the Duke of—, the impulsive gentleman whose son Richard Queen had saved from a noisome scandal, the details of which have never been made public. Beneath the tapestry stood a heavy mission table, displaying a parchment lamp and a pair of bronze book-ends bounding a three-volume set of the *Arabian Nights' Entertainment*.

Two mission chairs and a small rug completed the foyer. When you walked through this oppressive place, always gloomy and almost always hideous, you were ready for anything except the perfect cheeriness of the large room beyond. This study in contrast was Ellery's private jest, for if it were not for him the old man would long since have thrown the foyer and its furnishings into some dark limbo.

The living-room was lined on three sides with a bristling and leathern-reeking series of bookcases, rising tier upon tier to the high ceiling. On the fourth wall was a huge natural fireplace, with a solid oak beam as a mantel and gleaming iron-work spacing the grate. Above the fireplace were the famous crossed sabers, a gift from the old fencing-master of Nuremberg with whom Richard had lived in his younger days during his studies in Germany. Lamps winked and gleamed all over the great sprawling room; easy-chairs, armchairs, low divans, foot-stools, bright-colored leather cushions, were everywhere. In a word, it was the most comfortable room two intellectual gentlemen of luxurious tastes could devise for their living-quarters. And where such a place might after a time have become stale through sheer variety, the bustling person of Djuna, man-of-work, general factotum, errand boy, valet and mascot prevented such a dénouement.

Djuna had been picked up by Richard Queen during the period of Ellery's studies at college, when the old man was very much alone. This cheerful young man, nineteen years old, an orphan for as long as he could remember, ecstatically unaware of the necessity for a surname—slim and small, nervous and joyous, bubbling over with spirit and yet as quiet as a mouse when the occasion demanded—this Djuna, then, worshipped old Richard in much the same fashion as the ancient Alaskans bowed down to their totem-poles. Between him and Ellery, too, there was a shy kinship which rarely found expression except in the boy's passionate service. He slept in a small room beyond the bedroom used by father and son and, according to Richard's own chuckling expression, "could hear a flea singing to its mate in the middle of the night."

On the morning after the eventful night of Monte Field's murder, Djuna was laying the cloth for breakfast when the telephone bell rang. The boy, accustomed to early morning calls, lifted the receiver:

"This is Inspector Queen's man Djuna talking. Who is calling, please?"

"Oh, it is, is it?" growled a bass voice over the wire. "Well, you son of a gypsy policeman, wake the Inspector for me and be quick about it!"

"Inspector Queen may not be disturbed, sir, unless his man Djuna knows who's calling." Djuna, who knew Sergeant Velie's voice especially well, grinned and stuck his tongue in his cheek.

A slim hand firmly grasped Djuna's neck and propelled him half-way across the room. The Inspector, fully dressed, his nostrils quivering appreciatively with his morning's first ration of snuff, said into the mouthpiece, "Don't mind Djuna, Thomas. What's up? This is Queen talking."

"Oh, that you, Inspector? I wouldn't have buzzed you so early in the morning except that Ritter just phoned from Monte Field's apartment. Got an interesting report," rumbled Velie.

"Well, well!" chuckled the Inspector. "So our friend Ritter's bagged someone, eh? Who is it, Thomas?"

"You guessed it, sir," came Velie's unmoved voice. "He said he's got a lady down there in an embarrassing state of deshabille[54] and if he stays alone with her much longer his wife will divorce him. Orders, sir?"

Queen laughed heartily. "Sure enough, Thomas. Send a couple of men down there right away to chaperon him. I'll be there myself in two shakes of a lamb's tail—which is to say, as soon as I can drag Ellery out of bed."

He hung up, grinning. "Djuna!" he shouted. The boy's head popped out from behind the kitchenette door immediately. "Hurry up with the eggs and coffee, son!" The Inspector turned toward the bedroom to find Ellery, collarless[55] but unmistakably on the road to dress, confronting him with an air of absorption.

"So you're really up?" grumbled the Inspector, easing himself into an armchair. "I thought I'd have to drag you out of bed, you sluggard!"

"You may rest easy," said Ellery absently. "I most certainly am up, and I am going to stay up. And as soon as Djuna replenishes

54. Literally, dressed in a casual or careless manner, but usually connoting an inappropriate exposure of skin.

55. Men's shirts still had collars that were detachable from the shirt body. If necessary, one could change one's collar without changing the shirt.

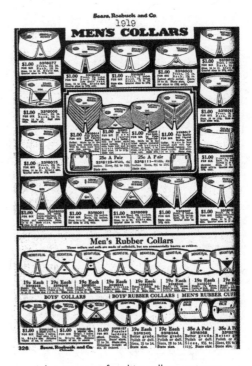

Advertisement for shirt collars, ca. 1925.

the inner man I'll be off and out of your way." He lounged into the bedroom, reappearing a moment later brandishing his collar and tie.

"Here! Where d'ye think you're going, young man?" roared Queen, starting up.

"Down to my book-shop, Inspector darling," replied Ellery judicially. "You don't think I'm going to allow that Falconer first-edition to get away from me? Really—it may still be there, you know."

"Falconer fiddle-sticks," said his father grimly. "You started something and you're going to help finish it. Here—Djuna—where in time is that kid?"

Djuna stepped briskly into the room balancing a tray in one hand and a pitcher of milk in the other. In a twinkling he had the table ready, the coffee bubbling, the toast browned; and father and son hurried through their breakfast without a word. "Now," remarked Ellery, setting down his empty cup, "now that I've finished this Arcadian repast, tell me where the fire is."

"Get your hat and coat on and stop asking pointless questions, son of my grief," growled Queen. In three minutes they were on the sidewalk hailing a taxicab.

The cab drew up before a monumental apartment building. Lounging on the sidewalk, a cigarette drooping from his lips, was Detective Piggott. The Inspector winked and trotted into the lobby. He and Ellery were whisked up to the fourth floor where Detective Hagstrom greeted them, pointing to an apartment door numbered 4-D. Ellery, leaning forward to catch the inscription on the nameplate, was about to turn on his father with an amused expostulation when the door swung open at Queen's imperious ring and the broad flushed face of Ritter peered out at them.

"Morning, Inspector," the detective mumbled, holding the door open. "I'm glad you've come, sir."

Queen and Ellery marched inside. They stood in a small foyer, profusely furnished. Directly in their line of vision was a living-room, and beyond that a closed door. A frilled feminine slipper and a slim ankle were visible at the edge of the door.

The Inspector stepped forward, changed his mind and quickly opening the hall door called to Hagstrom, who was sauntering about outside. The detective ran up.

"Come inside here," said Queen sharply. "Got a job for you."

With Ellery and the two plainclothes men following at his heels, he strode into the living-room.

A woman of mature beauty, a trifle worn, the pastiness of a ruined complexion apparent beneath heavily applied rouge, sprang to her feet. She was dressed in a flowing flimsy *négligee* and her hair was tousled. She nervously crushed a cigarette underfoot.

"Are you the big cheese around here?" she yelled in a strident fury to Queen. He stood stock still and examined her impersonally. "Then what the hell do you mean by sending one o' your flat-foots to keep me locked up all night, hey?"

She jumped forward as if to come to grips with the old man. Ritter lumbered swiftly toward her and squeezed her arm. "Here you," he growled, "shut up until you're spoken to."

She glared at him. Then with a tigerish twist she was out of his grasp and in a chair, panting, wild-eyed.

Arms akimbo, the Inspector stood looking her up and down with unconcealed distaste. Ellery glanced at the woman briefly and had begun to putter about the room, peering at the wall-hangings and Japanese prints, picking up a book from an end-table, poking his head into dark corners.

Queen motioned to Hagstrom. "Take this lady into the next room and keep her company for a while," he said. The detective unceremoniously hustled the woman to her feet.

She tossed her head defiantly and marched into the next room, Hagstrom following.

"Now, Ritter, my boy," sighed the old man, sinking into an easy-chair, "tell me what happened."

Ritter answered stiffly. His eyes were strained, bloodshot. "I followed out your orders last night to the dot. I beat it down here in a police car, left it on the corner because I didn't know but what somebody might be keeping a lookout, and strolled up to this apartment. Everything was quiet—and I hadn't noticed any lights either, because before I went in I beat it down to the court and looked up at the back windows of the apartment. So I gave 'em a nice short ring on the bell and waited.

"No answer," continued Ritter, with a tightening of his big jaw. "I buzzed again—this time longer and louder. This time I got results. I heard the latch on the inside rattle and this woman yodels, 'That you, honey? Where's your key?' Aha—thinks I—Mr. Field's lady-friend! So I shoved my foot in the door and grabbed her before she knew what was what. Well, sir, I got a surprise. Sort of expected," he grinned sheepishly, "sort of expected to find the woman dressed, but all I grabbed was a thin piece o' silk night-gown. I guess I must have blushed. . . ."

"Ah, the opportunities of our good minions of the law!" murmured Ellery, head bent over a small lacquered vase.

"Anyway," continued the detective, "I got my hands on her and she yelped—plenty. Hustled her into the living-room here where she'd put on the light, and took a good look at her. She was scared blue but she was kind of plucky, too, because she began to cuss me and she wanted to know who in hell I was, what I was tryin' to do in a woman's apartment at night, and all that sort of stuff. I flashed my badge. And Inspector, that hefty Sheba—the minute she sees the badge, she shuts up tight like a bluepoint[56] and won't answer a question I ask her!"

"Why was that?" The old man's eyes roved from floor to ceiling as he looked over the appointments of the room.

"Hard to tell, Inspector," said Ritter. "First she seemed scared, but when she saw my badge she bucked up wonderful. And the longer I was here the more brazen she became."

"You didn't tell her about Field, did you?" queried the Inspector, in a sharp, low tone.

Ritter gave his superior a reproachful glance. "Not a peep out o' me, sir," he said. "Well, when I saw it was no go tryin' to get anything out of her—all she'd yell was, 'Wait till Monte gets home, you bozo!'—I took a look at the bedroom. Nobody there, so I shoved her inside, kept the door open and the light on and stayed all night. She climbed into bed after a while and I guess she went to sleep. At about seven this morning she popped out and started to yell all over again. Seemed to think that Field had been grabbed by headquarters. Insisted on having a newspaper. I told her nothin' doin' and then phoned the office. Not another thing happened since."

"I say, dad!" exclaimed Ellery suddenly, from a comer of the room. "What do you think our legal friend reads—you'll never guess. 'How to Tell Character from Handwriting'!"

The Inspector grunted as he rose. "Stop fiddling with those eternal books," he said, "and come along."

He flung open the bedroom door. The woman was sitting cross-legged on the bed, an ornate affair of a bastard French period-style, canopied and draped from ceiling to floor with heavy damask curtains. Hagstrom leaned stolidly against the window.

Queen looked quickly about. He turned to Ritter. "Was that bed mussed up when you came in here last night—did it look as if it had been slept in?" he whispered aside.

Ritter nodded. "All right then, Ritter," said Queen in a genial tone. "Go home and get some rest. You deserve it. And send up Piggott on your way out." The detective touched his hat and departed.

Queen turned on the woman. He walked to the bed and sat down beside her, studying her half-averted face. She lit a cigarette defiantly.

"I am Inspector Queen of the police, my dear," announced the old man mildly. "I warn you that any attempt to keep a stubborn silence or lie to me will only get you into a heap of trouble. But there! Of course you understand."

She jerked away. "I'm not answering any questions, Mr. Inspector, until I know what right you have to ask 'em. I haven't done anything wrong and my slate's clean. You can put that in your pipe and smoke it!"

The Inspector took a pinch of snuff, as if the woman's reference to the vile weed had reminded him of his favorite vice. He said: "That's fair enough," in dulcet tones. "Here you are, a lonely woman suddenly tumbled out of bed in the middle of the night—you *were* in bed, weren't you—?"

"Sure I was," she flashed instantly, then bit her lip.

"—and confronted by a policeman. . . . I don't wonder you were frightened, my dear."

"I was not!" she said shrilly.

"We'll not argue about it," rejoined the old man benevolently. "But certainly you have no objection to telling me your name?"

"I don't know why I should, but I can't see any harm in it," retorted the woman. "My name is Angela Russo—Mrs. Angela Russo—and I'm, well, I'm engaged to Mr. Field."

"I see," said Queen gravely. "Mrs. Angela Russo and you are engaged to Mr. Field. Very good! And what were you doing in these rooms last night, Mrs. Angela Russo?"

"None of your business!" she said coolly. "You'd better let me go now—I haven't done a thing out of the way. You've got no right to jabber at me, old boy!"

Ellery, in a corner peering out of the window, smiled. The Inspector leaned over and took the woman's hand gently.

"My dear Mrs. Russo," he said, "believe me—there is every reason in the world why we should be anxious to know what you were doing here last night. Come now—tell me."

"I won't open my mouth till I know what you've done with Monte!" she cried, shaking off his hand. "If you've got him, why are you pestering me? I don't know anything."

"Mr. Field is in a very safe place at the moment," snapped the Inspector, rising, "I've given you plenty of rope, madam. Monte Field is dead."

"Monte—Field—is—." The woman's lips moved mechanically. She leaped to her feet, clutching the *négligee* to her plump figure, staring at Queen's impassive face.

She laughed shortly and threw herself back on the bed. "Go on—you're taking me for a ride," she jeered.

"I'm not accustomed to joking about death," returned the old man with a little smile. "I assure you that you may take my word for it—Monte Field is dead." She was staring up at him, her lips moving soundlessly. "And what is more, Mrs. Russo, he has been murdered. Perhaps now you'll deign to answer my questions. Where were you at a quarter to ten last night?" he whispered in her ear, his face close to hers.

Mrs. Russo relaxed limply on the bed, a dawning fright in her large eyes. She gaped at the Inspector, found little comfort in his face and with a cry whirled to sob into the rumpled pillow. Queen stepped back and spoke in a low tone to Piggott, who had come into the room a moment before. The woman's heaving sobs subsided suddenly. She sat up, dabbing her face with a lace handkerchief. Her eyes were strangely bright.

"I get you now," she said in a quiet voice. "I was right here in this apartment at a quarter to ten last night."

"Can you prove that, Mrs. Russo?" asked Queen, fingering his snuff-box.

"I can't prove anything and I don't have to," she returned dully. "But if you're looking for an alibi, the doorman downstairs must have seen me come into the building at about nine-thirty."

"We can easily check that up," admitted Queen. "Tell me—why did you come here last night at all?"

"I had an appointment with Monte," she explained lifelessly. "He called me up at my own place yesterday afternoon and we made a date for last night. He told me he'd be out on business until about ten o'clock, and I was to wait here for him. I come up"—she paused and continued brazenly—"I come up quite often like that. We generally have a little 'time' and spend the evening together. Being engaged—you know."

"Ummm. I see, I see." The Inspector cleared his throat in some embarrassment.

"And then, when he didn't come on time—?"

"I thought he might've been detained longer than he'd figured. So I—well, I felt tired and took a little nap."

"Very good," said Queen quickly. "Did he tell you where he was going, or the nature of his business?"

"No."

"I should be greatly obliged to you, Mrs. Russo," said the Inspector carefully, "if you would tell me what Mr. Field's attitude was toward theatre-going."

The woman looked at him curiously. She seemed to be recovering her spirits. "Didn't go very often," she snapped. "Why?"

The Inspector beamed. "Now, that's a question, isn't it?" he asked. He motioned to Hagstrom, who pulled a notebook out of his pocket.

"Could you give me a list of Mr. Field's personal friends?" resumed Queen. "And any business acquaintances you might know of?"

Mrs. Russo put her hands behind her head, coquettishly. "To tell the truth," she said sweetly, "I don't know any. I met Monte about six months ago at a masque ball in the Village. We've kept our engagement sort of quiet, you see. In fact, I've never met his friends at all . . . I don't think," she confided, "I don't think Monte had many friends. And of course I don't know a thing about his business associates."

"What was Field's financial condition, Mrs. Russo?"

"Trust a woman to know those things!" she retorted, completely restored to her flippant manner. "Monte was always a good spender. Never seemed to run out of cash. He's spent five hundred a night on me many a time. That was Monte—a damned good sport. Tough luck for him!—poor darling." She wiped a tear from her eye, sniffling hastily.

"But—his bank account?" pursued the Inspector firmly.

Mrs. Russo smiled. She seemed to possess an inexhaustible fund of shifting emotions. "Never got nosey," she said. "As long as Monte was treating me square it wasn't any of my business. At least," she added, "he wouldn't tell me, so what did I care?"

"Where were you, Mrs. Russo," came Ellery's indifferent tones, "*before* nine-thirty last night?"

She turned in surprise at the new voice. They measured each other carefully, and something like warmth crept into her eyes. "I don't know who you are, mister, but if you want to find out ask the lovers in Central Park. I was taking a little stroll in the Park—all by my lonesome—from about half-past seven until the time I reached here."

"How fortunate!" murmured Ellery. The Inspector hastily went to the door, crooking his finger at the other three men. "We'll leave you now to dress, Mrs. Russo. That will be all for the present." She watched quizzically as they filed out. Queen, last, shut the door after a fatherly glance at her face.

In the living-room the four men proceeded to make a hurried but thorough search. At the Inspector's command Hagstrom and Piggott went through the drawers of a carved desk in one corner of the room. Ellery was interestedly rifling the pages of the book on character through handwriting. Queen prowled restlessly about, poking his head into a clothes closet just inside the room, off the foyer. This was a commodious storage compartment for clothes—assorted topcoats, overcoats, capes and the like hung from a rack. The Inspector rifled the pockets. A few miscellaneous articles—handkerchiefs, keys, old personal letters, wallets—came to light. These he put to one side. A top shelf held several hats. "Ellery—hats," he grunted.

Ellery quickly crossed the room, stuffing into his pocket the book he had been reading. His father pointed out the hats meaningly; together they reached up to examine them. There were four—a discolored Panama, two fedoras, one grey and one brown, and a derby. All bore the imprint of Browne Bros.

The two men turned the hats over in their hands. Both noticed immediately that three of them had no linings—the Panama and the two fedoras. The fourth hat, an excellent derby, Queen examined critically. He felt the lining, turned down the leather sweat-band, then shook his head.

"To tell the truth, Ellery," he said slowly, "I'll be switched if I know why I should expect to find clues in these hats. We know that Field wore a tophat last night and obviously it would be impossible for that hat to be in these rooms. According to our findings the murderer was still in the theatre when we arrived. Ritter was down here by eleven o'clock. The hat therefore *couldn't* have been brought to this place. For that matter, what earthly reason would the murderer have for such an action, even if it were physically possible for him to do it? He must have realized that we would search Field's apartment at once. No, I guess I'm feeling a little off-color, Ellery. There's nothing to be squeezed out of these hats." He threw the derby back onto the shelf disgustedly.

Ellery stood thoughtful and unsmiling. "You're right enough, dad; these hats mean nothing. But I have the strangest feeling. . . . By the way!" He straightened up and took off his pince-nez. "Did it occur to you last night that something else belonging to Field might have been missing besides the hat?"

"I wish they were all as easy to answer as that," said Queen grimly. "Certainly—a walking-stick. But what could I do about that? Working on the premise that Field brought one with him—it would have been simple enough for someone who had entered the theatre without a walking-stick to leave the theatre with Field's. And how could we stop him or identify the stick? So I didn't even bother thinking about it. And if it's still on the Roman premises, Ellery, it will keep—no fear about that."

Ellery chuckled. "I should be able to quote Shelley or Wordsworth at this point," he said, "in proof of my admiration for your mental prowess. But I can't think of a more poetical phrase than 'You've put one over on me.' Because I didn't think of it until just now. But here's the point: there is no cane of any kind in the closet. A man like Field, had he possessed a swanky halberd to go with evening dress, would most certainly have owned other sticks to match other costumes. That fact—unless we find sticks in the bedroom closet, which I doubt, since all the overclothes seem to be here—that fact, therefore, eliminates the possibility that Field had a stick with him last night. *Ergo*—we may forget all about it."

"Good enough, El," returned the Inspector absently. "I hadn't thought of that. Well—let's see how the boys are getting on."

57. This was, after all, during Prohibition.

They walked across the room to where Hagstrom and Piggott were rifling the desk. A small pile of papers and notes had accumulated on the lid.

"Find anything interesting?" asked Queen.

"Not a thing of value that I can see, Inspector," answered Piggott. "Just the usual stuff—some letters, chiefly from this Russo woman, and pretty hot too!—a lot of bills and receipts and things like that. Don't think you'll find anything here."

Queen went through the papers. "No, nothing much," he admitted. "Well, let's get on."

They restored the papers to the desk. Piggott and Hagstrom rapidly searched the room. They tapped furniture, poked beneath cushions, picked up the rug—a thorough, workmanlike job. As Queen and Ellery stood silently watching, the bedroom door opened. Mrs. Russo appeared, saucily appareled in a brown walking-suit and toque. She paused at the door, surveying the scene with wide, innocent eyes. The two detectives proceeded with their search without looking up.

"What are they doing, Inspector?" she inquired in a languid tone. "Looking for pretty-pretties?" But her eyes were keen and interested.

"That was remarkably rapid dressing for a female, Mrs. Russo," said the Inspector admiringly. "Going home?"

Her glance darted at him. "Sure thing," she answered, looking away.

"And you live at—?"

She gave an address on MacDougal Street in Greenwich Village.

"Thank you," said Queen courteously, making a note. She began to walk across the room. "Oh, Mrs. Russo!" She turned. "Before you go—perhaps you could tell us something about Mr. Field's convivial habits. Was he, now, what you would call a heavy drinker?"

She laughed merrily. "Is that all?" she said. "Yes and no. I've seen Monte drink half a night and be sober as a—as a parson. And then I've seen him at other times when he was pickled silly on a couple of tots. It all depended—don't you know?" She laughed again.

"Well, many of us are that way," murmured the Inspector. "I don't want you to abuse any confidences, Mrs. Russo—but perhaps you know the source of his liquor supply?"[57]

She stopped laughing instantly, her face reflecting an innocent indignation. "What do you think I am, anyway?" she demanded. "I don't know, but even if I did I wouldn't tell. There's many a hard-working bootlegger who's head and shoulders above the guys who try to run 'em in, believe me!"

"The way of all flesh, Mrs. Russo," said Queen soothingly. "Nevertheless, my dear," he continued softly, "I'm sure that if I need that information eventually, you will enlighten me. Eh?" There was a silence. "I think that will be all, then, Mrs. Russo. Just stay in town, won't you? We may require your testimony soon."

"Well—so long," she said, tossing her head. She marched out of the room to the foyer.

"Mrs. Russo!" called Queen suddenly, in a sharp tone. She turned with her gloved hand on the front-door knob, the smile dying from her lips. "What's Ben Morgan been doing since he and Field dissolved partnership—do you know?"

Her reply came after a split-second of hesitation. "Who's he?" she asked, her forehead wrinkled into a frown.

Queen stood squarely on the rug. He said sadly, "Never mind. Good day," and turned his back on her. The door slammed. A moment later Hagstrom strolled out, leaving Piggott, Queen and Ellery in the apartment.

The three men, as if inspired by a single thought, ran into the bedroom. It was apparently as they had left it. The bed was disordered and Mrs. Russo's nightgown and *négligee* were lying on the floor. Queen opened the door of the bedroom clothes-closet. "Whew!" said Ellery. "This chap had a quiet taste in clothes, didn't he? Sort of Mulberry Street Beau Brummell."[58] They ransacked the closet with no results. Ellery craned his neck at the shelf above. "No hats—no canes; that settles that!" he murmured with an air of satisfaction. Piggott, who had disappeared into a small kitchen, returned staggering under the burden of a half-empty case of liquor-bottles.

Ellery and his father bent over the case. The Inspector removed a cork gingerly, sniffed the contents, then handed the bottle to Piggott, who followed his superior's example critically.

"Looks and smells okay," said the detective. "But I'd hate to take a chance tasting this stuff—after last night."

"You're perfectly justified in your caution," chuckled Ellery. "But if you should change your mind and decide to invoke the

58. Mulberry Street was the heart of Little Italy. The remark implies that Field was well-dressed in the manner of an Italian gangster.

* [Author's note:] Ellery Queen was here probably paraphrasing the Shakespearian quotation: "O thou invisible spirit of wine, if thou hast no name to be known by, let us call thee devil."

[Editor's note: *Othello*, Act II, Scene 3.]

spirit of Bacchus, Piggott, let me suggest this prayer: O wine, if thou hast no name to be known by, let us call thee Death."*

"I'll have the firewater analyzed," growled Queen. "Scotch and rye mixed, and the labels look like the real thing. But then you never can tell. . . ." Ellery suddenly grasped his father's arm, leaning forward tensely. The three men stiffened.

A barely audible scratching came to their ears, proceeding from the foyer.

"Sounds as if somebody is using a key on the door," whispered Queen. "Duck out, Piggott—jump whoever it is as soon as he gets inside!"

Piggott darted through the livingroom into the foyer. Queen and Ellery waited in the bedroom, concealed from view.

There was utter silence now except for the scraping on the outer door. The newcomer seemed to be having difficulty with the key. Suddenly the rasp of the lock-tumblers falling back was heard and an instant later the door swung open. It slammed shut almost immediately.

A muffled cry, a hoarse bull-like voice, Piggott's half-strangled oath, the frenzied shuffling of feet—and Ellery and his father were speeding across the living-room to the foyer. Piggott was struggling in the arms of a burly, powerful man dressed in black. A suit-case lay on the floor to one side, as if it had been thrown there during the tussle. A newspaper was fluttering through the air, settling on the parquet just as Ellery reached the cursing men.

It took the combined efforts of the three to subdue their visitor. Finally, panting heavily, he lay on the floor, Piggott's arm jammed tightly across his chest.

The Inspector bent down, gazed curiously into the man's red, angry features and said softly, "And who are you, mister?"

CHAPTER IX

In Which the Mysterious Mr. Michaels Appears

The intruder rose awkwardly to his feet. He was a tall, ponderous man with solemn features and blank eyes. There was nothing distinguished in either his appearance or his manner. If anything unusual could be said of him at all, it was that both his appearance and manner were so unremarkable. It seemed as if, whoever he was or whatever his occupation, he had made a deliberate effort to efface all marks of personality.

"Just what's the idea of the strong-arm stuff?" he said in a bass voice. But even his tones were flat and colorless. Queen turned to Piggott. "What happened?" he demanded, with a pretense of severity.

"I stood behind the door, Inspector," gasped Piggott, still winded, "and when this wildcat stepped in I touched him on the arm. He jumped me like a trainload o' tigers, he did. Pushed me in the face—he's got a wallop, Inspector. . . . Tried to get out the door again."

Queen nodded judicially. The newcomer said mildly, "That's a lie, sir. He jumped me and I fought back."

"Here, here!" murmured Queen. "This will never do. . . ."

The door swung open suddenly and Detective Johnson stood on the threshold. He took the Inspector to one side. "Velie sent me down the last minute on the chance you might need me, Inspector. . . . And as I was coming up I saw that chap there.

59.   "Massa's in de Cold Ground" is a minstrel song by Stephen Foster (1826–1864) first published in 1852. The chorus is:

"Down in de cornfield
"Hear dat mournful sound:
"All de darkeys am a weeping—
"Massa's in de cold, cold ground."

Didn't know but what he might be snooping around, so I followed him up." Queen nodded vigorously. "Glad you came—I can use you," he muttered and motioning to the others, he led the way into the living-room.

"Now, my man," he said curtly to the big intruder, "the show is over. Who are you and what are you doing here?"

"My name is Charles Michaels—sir. I am Mr. Monte Field's valet." The Inspector's eyes narrowed. The man's entire demeanor had in some intangible manner changed. His face was blank, as before, and his attitude seemed in no way different. Yet the old man sensed a metamorphosis; he glanced quickly at Ellery and saw a confirmation of his own thought in his son's eyes.

"Is that so?" inquired the Inspector steadily. "Valet, eh? And where are you going at this hour of the morning with that traveling-bag?" He jerked his hand toward the suit-case, a cheap black affair, which Piggott had picked up in the foyer and carried into the living-room. Ellery suddenly strolled away in the direction of the foyer. He bent over to pick up something.

"Sir?" Michaels seemed upset by the question. "That's mine, sir," he confided. "I was just going away this morning on my vacation and I'd arranged with Mr. Field to come here for my salary-check before I left."

The old man's eyes sparkled. He had it! Michaels' expression and general bearing had remained unchanged, but his voice and enunciation were markedly different.

"So you arranged to get your check from Mr. Field this morning?" murmured the Inspector. "That's mighty funny now, come to think of it."

Michaels permitted a fleeting amazement to scud across his features. "Why—why, where is Mr. Field?" he asked,

"'Massa's in de cold, cold ground,'"[59] chuckled Ellery, from the foyer. He stepped back into the living-room, flourishing the newspaper which Michaels had dropped during the fracas with Piggott. "Really, now, old chap, that's a bit thick, you know. Here is the morning paper you brought in with you. And the first thing I see as I pick it up is the nice black headline describing Mr. Field's little accident. Smeared over the entire front-page. And—er, you failed to see the story?"

Michaels stared stonily at Ellery and the paper. But his eyes fell as he mumbled, "I didn't get the opportunity of reading the paper this morning, sir. What has happened to Mr. Field?"

The Inspector snorted. "Field's been killed, Michaels, and you knew it all the time."

"But I didn't, I tell you, sir," objected the valet respectfully.

"Stop lying!" rasped Queen. "Tell us why you're here or you'll get plenty of opportunity to talk behind bars!"

Michaels regarded the old man patiently. "I've told you the truth, sir," he said. "Mr. Field told me yesterday that I was to come here this morning for my check. That's all I know."

"You were to meet him here?"

"Yes, sir."

"Then why did you forget to ring the bell? Used a key as if you didn't expect to find any one here, my man," said Queen.

"The bell?"' The valet opened his eyes wide. "I always use my key, sir. Never disturb Mr. Field if I can help it."

"Why didn't Field give you a check yesterday?" barked the Inspector.

"He didn't have his check-book handy, I think, sir."

Queen's lip curled. "You haven't even a fertile imagination, Michaels. At what time did you last see him yesterday?"

"At about seven o'clock, sir," said Michaels promptly. "I don't live here at the apartment. It's too small and Mr. Field likes—liked privacy. I generally come early in the morning to make breakfast for him and prepare his bath and lay out his clothes. Then when he's gone to the office I clean up a bit and the rest of the day is my own until dinner-time. I return about five, prepare dinner unless I've heard from Mr. Field during the day that he is dining out, and get his dinner or evening clothes ready. Then I am through for the night. . . . Yesterday after I laid out his things he told me about the check."

"Not an especially fatiguing itinerary," murmured Ellery. "And what things did you lay out last evening, Michaels?"

The man faced Ellery respectfully. "There was his underwear, sir, and his socks, his evening shoes, stiff shirt, studs, collar, white tie, full evening dress, cape, hat—"

"Ah, yes—his hat," interrupted Queen. "And what kind of hat was it, Michaels?"

"His regular tophat, sir," answered Michaels. "He had only one, and a very expensive one it was, too," he added warmly. "Browne Bros., I think."

Queen drummed lazily on the arm of his chair. "Tell me, Michaels," he said, "what did you do last night after you left here—that is, after seven o'clock?"

"I went home, sir. I had my bag to pack and I was rather fatigued. I went right to sleep after I'd had a bite to eat—it must have been near nine-thirty when I climbed into bed, sir," he added innocently.

"Where do you live?" Michaels gave a number of East 146th Street, in the Bronx section. "I see. . . . Did Field have any regular visitors here?" went on the Inspector.

Michaels frowned politely. "That's hard for me to say, sir. Mr. Field wasn't what you would call a friendly person. But then I wasn't here evenings, so I can't say who came after I left. But—"

"Yes?"

"There was a lady, sir. . . ." Michaels hesitated primly. "I dislike mentioning names under the circumstances—"

"Her name?" said Queen wearily.

"Well, sir—it isn't sort of right—Russo. Mrs. Angela Russo, her name is," answered Michaels.

"How long did Mr. Field know this Mrs. Russo?"

"Several months, sir. I think he met her at a party in Greenwich Village somewhere."

"I see. And they were engaged, perhaps?"

Michaels seemed embarrassed. "You might call it that, sir, although it was a little less formal. . . ."

Silence. "How long have you been in Monte Field's employ, Michaels?" pursued the Inspector.

"Three years next month."

Queen switched to a new line of questioning. He asked Michaels about Field's addiction to theatre-going, his financial condition and his drinking habits. In these particulars Michaels corroborated Mrs. Russo's statements. Nothing of a fresh nature was disclosed.

"A few moments ago you said you have been working for Field a matter of three years," continued Queen, settling back in his chair. "How did you get the job?"

Michaels did not answer immediately. "I followed up an ad in the papers, sir."

"Quite so. . . . If you have been in Field's service for three years, Michaels, you should know Benjamin Morgan."

Michaels permitted a proper smile to cross his lips. "Certainly I know Mr. Benjamin Morgan," he said heartily. "And a very fine gentleman he is, too, sir. He was Mr. Field's partner, you know, in their law business. But then they separated about two years ago and I haven't seen much of Mr. Morgan since."

"Did you see him often before the split?"

"No, sir," returned the burly valet, in a tone which implied regret. "Mr. Field was not Mr. Morgan's—ah—type, and they didn't mix socially. Oh, I remember seeing Mr. Morgan in this apartment three or four times, but only when it was a matter of most urgent business. Even then I couldn't say much about it since I didn't stay all evening. . . . Of course, he hasn't been here, so far as I know, since they broke up the firm."

Queen smiled for the first time during the conversation. "Thank you for your frankness, Michaels. . . . I'm going to be an old gossip—do you recall any unpleasantness about the time they dissolved?"

"Oh, no, sir!" protested Michaels. "I never heard of a quarrel or anything like that. In fact, Mr. Field told me immediately after the dissolution that he and Mr. Morgan would remain friends—very good friends, he said."

Michaels turned with his politely blank expression at a touch of his arm. He found himself face to face with Ellery. "Yes, sir?" he asked respectfully.

"Michaels, dear man," said Ellery with severity, "I detest raking up old coals, but why haven't you told the Inspector about the time you were in jail?"

As if he had stepped on an exposed live-wire Michaels' body stiffened and grew still. The ruddy color drained out of his face. He stared open-mouthed, aplomb swept away, into Ellery's smiling eyes.

"Why—why—how did you find that out?" gasped the valet, his speech less soft and polished. Queen appraised his son with approval. Piggott and Johnson moved closer to the trembling man.

Ellery lit a cigarette. "I didn't know it at all," he said cheerfully. "That is, not until you told me. It would pay you to cultivate the Delphic oracles, Michaels."[60]

60. The Temple of Apollo at Delphi was headed by the Pythia, known as the Oracle of Delphi. She provided divinely-inspired advice to supplicants in response to questions asked.

Michaels' face was the color of dead ashes. He turned, shaking, toward Queen. "You—you didn't ask me about that, sir," he said weakly. Nevertheless his tone had again become taut and blank. "Besides, a man doesn't like to tell things like that to the police. . . ."

"Where did you do time, Michaels?" asked the Inspector in a kindly voice.

"Elmira Reformatory, sir," muttered Michaels. "It was my first offense—I was up against it, starving, stole some money. . . . I got a short stretch, sir."

Queen rose. "Well, Michaels, of course you understand that you are not exactly a free agent at present. You may go home and look for another job if you want to, but stay at your present lodgings and be ready for a call at any time. . . . Just a moment, before you go." He strode over to the black suit-case and snapped it open. A jumbled mass of clothing—a dark suit, shirts, ties, socks—some clean, some dirty—was revealed. Queen rummaged swiftly through the bag, closed it and handed it to Michaels, who was standing to one side with an expression of sorrowful patience.

"Seems to me you were taking mighty few duds with you, Michaels," remarked Queen, smiling. "It's too bad that you've been done out of your vacation. Well! That's the way life is!" Michaels murmured a low good-by, picked up the bag and departed. A moment later Piggott strolled out of the apartment.

Ellery threw back his head and laughed delightedly. "What a mannerly beggar! Lying in his teeth, Pater! . . . And what did he want here, do you think?"

"He came to get something, of course," mused the Inspector. "And that means there's something here of importance that we have apparently overlooked. . . ."

He grew thoughtful. The telephone bell rang. "Inspector?" Sergeant Velie's voice boomed over the wire.

"I called headquarters but you weren't there, so I guessed you were still at Field's place. . . . I've some interesting news for you from Browne Bros. Do you want me to come up to Field's?"

"No," returned Queen. "We're through here. I'll be at my office just as soon as I've paid a visit to Field's on Chambers Street. I'll be there if anything important comes up in the interim. Where are you now?"

"Fifth Avenue—I've just come out of Browne's."

"Then go back to headquarters and wait for me. And, Thomas—send a uniformed man up here right away."

Queen hung up and turned to Johnson.

"Stay here until a cop shows up—it won't be long," he grunted. "Have him keep a watch in the apartment and arrange for a relief. Then report back to the main office. . . . Come along, Ellery. This is going to be a busy day!"

Ellery's protests were in vain. His father fussily hustled him out of the building and into the street, where the roar of a taxicab's exhaust effectually drowned out his voice.

CHAPTER X

In Which Mr. Field's Tophats Begin to Assume Proportions

It was exactly ten o'clock in the morning when Inspector Queen and his son opened the frosted glass door marked:

MONTE FIELD

ATTORNEY-AT-LAW

The large waiting-room they entered was decorated in just such a fashion as might have been expected from a man of Field's taste in clothes. It was deserted, and with a puzzled glance Inspector Queen pushed through the door, Ellery strolling behind, and went into the General Office. This was a long room filled with desks. It resembled a newspaper "city room" except for its rows of bookcases filled with ponderous legal tomes.

The office was in a state of violent upheaval. Stenographers chattered excitedly in small groups. A number of male clerks whispered in a corner; and in the center of the room stood Detective Hesse, talking earnestly to a lean saturnine man with greyed temples. It was evident that the demise of the lawyer had created something of a stir in his place of business.

At the entrance of the Queens the employees looked at each other in a startled way and began to slip back to their desks. An embarrassed silence fell. Hesse hurried forward. His eyes were red and strained.

"Good morning, Hesse," said the Inspector abruptly, "Where's Field's private office?"

The detective led them across the room to still another door, a large PRIVATE lettered on its panels. The three men went into a small office which was overwhelmingly luxurious.

"This chap went in for atmosphere, didn't he?" Ellery chuckled, sinking into a red-leather armchair.

"Let's have it, Hesse," said the Inspector, following Ellery's suit.

Hesse began to talk rapidly. "Got here last night and found the door locked. No sign of a light inside. I listened pretty closely but couldn't hear a sound, so I took it for granted that there was no one inside and camped in the corridor all night. At about a quarter to nine this morning the office-manager breezed in and I collared him. He was that tall bird I was talking to when you came in. Name's Lewin—Oscar Lewin."

"Office-manager, eh?" remarked the old man, inhaling snuff.

"Yes, Chief. He's either dumb or else he knows how to keep his mouth shut," continued Hesse. "Of course, he'd already seen the morning paper and was upset by the news of Field's murder. I could see he didn't like my questions any too well, either. . . . I didn't get a thing out of him. Not a thing. He said he'd gone straight home last night—it seems Field had left about four o'clock and didn't come back—and he didn't know anything about the murder until he read the papers. We've been sort of sliding along here all morning, waiting for you to come."

"Get Lewin for me."

Hesse returned with the lanky office-manager in his wake. Oscar Lewin was physically unprepossessing. He had shifty black eyes and was abnormally thin. There was something predatory in his beaked nose and bony figure. The Inspector looked him over coldly.

"So you're the office-manager," he remarked. "Well, what do you think of this affair, Lewin?"

"It's terrible—simply terrible," groaned Lewin. "I can't imagine how it happened or why. Good Lord, I was talking to him only four o'clock yesterday afternoon!" He seemed genuinely distressed.

"Did Mr. Field appear strange or worried when you spoke to him?"

61.   Although it is tempting to take this as a reference to one of the great inventions of the 1920s, the National Football League, the New York Giants football team was not founded until 1925, after the events of this story. However, the New York Giants *baseball* team was active in 1923. The New York Gothams were founded in 1883 and changed its name in 1886 to the New York Giants. The team eventually moved to San Francisco in 1958. The Giants played in four straight World Series in the early 1920s, winning in 1921 and 1922 over the Yankees, their arch-rivals, despite the Yankees' young star Babe Ruth. The Giants lost to the Yankees in the World Series in 1923, and this may well have been the subject of Field's jesting—one can well imagine Fields as a Yankee fan, while his office manager supported the Giants.

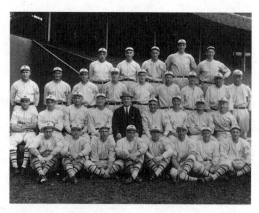

The New York Giants, 1922.

"Not at all, sir," replied Lewin nervously. "In fact, he was in unusually good spirits. Cracked a joke about the Giants[61] and said he was going to see a darned good show last night—'Gunplay.' And now I see by the papers that he was killed there!"

"Oh, he told you about the play, did he?" asked the Inspector. "He didn't happen to remark by any chance that he was going with anybody?"

"No, sir." Lewin shuffled his feet.

"I see." Queen paused. "Lewin, as manager you must have been closer to Field than any other of his employees. Just what do you know about him personally?"

"Not a thing, sir, not a thing," said Lewin hastily. "Mr. Field was not a man with whom an employee could become familiar. Occasionally he said something about himself, but it was always of a general nature and more jesting than serious. To us outside he was always a considerate and generous employer—that's all."

"What exactly was the calibre of the business he conducted, Lewin? You must certainly know something about that."

"Business?" Lewin seemed startled. "Why, it was as fine a practice as any I've encountered in the law profession. I've worked for Field only two years or so, but he had some high-and-mighty clients, Inspector. I can give you a list of them. . . ."

"Do that, and mail it to me," said Queen. "So he had a flourishing and respectable practice, eh? Any personal visitors to your knowledge—especially recently?"

"No. I can't remember ever seeing any one up here except his clients. Of course, he may have known some of them socially . . . Oh, yes! Of course his valet came here at times—tall, brawny fellow by the name of Michaels."

"Michaels? I'll have to remember that name," said the Inspector thoughtfully. He looked up at Lewin. "All right, Lewin. That will be all now. You might dismiss the force for the day. And—just stay around for a while. I expect one of Mr. Sampson's men soon, and undoubtedly he will need your help." Lewin nodded gravely and retired.

The moment the door closed Queen was on his feet. "Where's Field's private washroom, Hesse?" he demanded. The detective pointed to a door in a far corner of the room.

Queen opened it, Ellery crowding close behind. They were peering into a tiny cubicle spaced off in an angle of the wall. It contained a wash-bowl, a medicine chest and a small clothes-closet. Queen looked into the medicine chest first. It held a bottle of iodine, a bottle of peroxide, a tube of shaving-cream, and other shaving articles. "Nothing there," said Ellery. "How about the closet?" The old man pulled the door open curiously. A suit of street-clothes hung there, a half-dozen neckties and a fedora hat. The Inspector carried the hat back into the office and examined it. He handed it to Ellery, who disdainfully returned it at once to its peg in the closet.

"Dang those hats!" exploded the Inspector. There was a knock on the door and Hesse admitted a bland young man.

"Inspector Queen?" inquired the newcomer politely.

"Right," snapped the Inspector, "and if you're a reporter you can say the police will apprehend the murderer of Monte Field within twenty-four hours. Because that's all I'm going to give you right now."

The young man smiled. "Sorry, Inspector, but I'm not a reporter. I'm Arthur Stoates, new man at District Attorney Sampson's office. The Chief couldn't reach me until this morning and I was busy on something else—that's why I'm a little late. Too bad about Field, isn't it?" He grinned as he threw his coat and hat on a chair.

"It's all in the point of view," grumbled Queen. "He's certainly causing a heap of trouble. Just what were Sampson's instructions?"

"Well, I'm not as familiar with Field's career as I might be, naturally, but I'm pinch-hitting for Tim Cronin, who's tied up this morning on something else. I'm to make a start until Tim gets untangled, which will be some time this afternoon. Cronin, you know, was the man after Field a couple of years ago. He's aching to get busy with these files."

"Fair enough. From what Sampson told me about Cronin—if there's anything incriminating in these records and files, he'll ferret it out.—Hesse, take Mr. Stoates outside and introduce him to Lewin.—That's the office-manager, Stoates. Keep your eye on him—he looks like a wily bird. And, Stoates—remember you're looking not for legitimate business and clientele in these records, but for something crooked. . . . See you later."

Stoates gave him a cheery smile and followed Hesse out. Ellery and his father faced each other across the room.

"What's that you've got in your hand?" asked the old man sharply.

"A copy of 'What Handwriting Tells,' which I picked up in this bookcase," replied Ellery lazily. "Why?"

"Come to think of it now, El," declared the Inspector slowly, "there's something fishy about this handwriting business." He shook his head in despair and rose. "Come along, son—there isn't a blamed thing here."

On their way through the main office, now empty except for Hesse, Lewin and Stoates, Queen beckoned to the detective. "Go home, Hesse," he said kindly. "Can't have you coming down with the grippe." Hesse grinned and sped through the door.

In a few minutes Inspector Queen was sitting in his private office at Center Street. Ellery termed it "the star chamber." It was small and cozy and homelike. Ellery draped himself over a chair and began to con the books on handwriting which he had filched from Field's apartment and office. The Inspector pressed a buzzer and the solid figure of Thomas Velie loomed in the doorway.

"Morning, Thomas," said Queen. "What is this remarkable news you have for me from Browne Bros.?"

"I don't know how remarkable it is, Inspector," said Velie coolly, seating himself in one of the straight-backed chairs which lined the wall, "but it sounded like the real thing to me. You told me last night to find out about Field's tophat. Well, I've an exact duplicate of it on my desk. Like to see it?"

"Don't be silly, Thomas," said Queen. "On the run!" Velie departed and was back in a moment carrying a hatbox. He tore the string and uncovered a shining tophat, of such fine quality that Queen blinked. The Inspector picked it up curiously. On the inside was marked the size: 7⅛.

"I spoke to the clerk, an old-timer, down at Browne's. Been waiting on Field for years," resumed Velie. "It seems that Field bought every stitch of his clothing there—for a long time. And it happens that he preferred one clerk. Naturally the old buzzard knows quite a bit about Field's tastes and purchases.

"He says, for one thing, that Field was a fussy dresser. His clothes were always made to order by Browne's special tailoring department. He went in for fancy suits and cuts and the latest in underclothes and neckwear. . . ."

"What about his taste in hats?" interposed Ellery, without looking up from the book he was reading.

"I was coming to that, sir," continued Velie. "This clerk made a particular point of the hat business. For instance, when I questioned him about the tophat, he said: 'Mr. Field was almost a fanatic on the subject. Why, in the last six months he has bought no less than *three* of them!' I caught that up, of course—made him check back with the sales-records. Sure enough, Field bought three silk-toppers in the last half-year!"

Ellery and his father found themselves staring at each other, the same question on their lips.

"Three—" began the old man.

"Now . . . isn't that an extraordinary circumstance?" asked Ellery slowly, reaching for his pince-nez.

"Where in heaven's name are the other two?" continued Queen, in a bewildered manner.

Ellery was silent.

Queen turned impatiently toward Velie. "What else did you find out, Thomas?"

"Nothing much of value, except for this point"—answered Velie—"that Field was an absolute fiend when it came to clothes. So much so that last year he bought fifteen suits and no less than a dozen hats, including the toppers!"

"Hats, hats, hats!" groaned the Inspector. "The man must have been a lunatic. Look here—did you find out whether Field ever bought walking-sticks at Browne's?"

A look of consternation spread over Velie's face. "Why—why, Inspector," he said ruefully, "I guess I slipped up there. I never even thought of asking, and you hadn't told me last night—"

"Heck! We're none of us perfect," growled Queen. "Get that clerk on the wire for me, Thomas."

Velie picked up one of the telephones on the desk and a few moments later handed the instrument to his superior.

"This is Inspector Queen speaking," said the old man rapidly. "I understand that you served Monte Field for a good many years? . . . Well, I want to check up on a little detail. Did Field ever purchase canes or walking sticks from you people? . . . What? Oh, I see. . . . Yes. Now, another thing. Did he ever give special orders about the manufacture of his clothes—extra pockets, or things like that? . . . You don't think so. All right. . . . What? Oh, I see. Thank you very much."

He hung up the receiver and turned about.

"Our lamented friend," he said disgustedly, "seems to have had as great an aversion to sticks as he had a love for hats. This clerk said he tried many times to interest Field in canes, and Field invariably refused to buy. Didn't like 'em, he said. And the clerk just confirmed his own impression about the special pockets—nothing doing. So that leaves us up a blank alley."

"On the contrary," said Ellery coolly, "it does nothing of the kind. It proves fairly conclusively that the *only article of apparel* taken away by the murderer last night was the hat. It seems to me that simplifies matters."

"I must have a moron's intelligence," grunted his father. "It doesn't mean a thing to me."

"By the way, Inspector," put in Velie, scowling, "Jimmy reported about the fingerprints on Field's flask. There are a few, but there's no question, he says, that they're all Field's. Jimmy got a print from the Morgue, of course, to check up."

"Well," said the Inspector, "maybe the flask has nothing to do with the crime at all. We'll have to wait, anyway, for Prouty's report on its contents."

"There's something else, Inspector," added Velie. "That junk—the sweepings of the theatre—that you told Panzer to send over to you this morning came a couple of minutes ago. Want to see it?"

"Sure thing, Thomas," said Queen. "And while you're out bring me the list you made last night containing the names of the people who had no stubs. The seat numbers are attached to each name, aren't they?"

Velie nodded and disappeared. Queen was looking morosely at the top of his son's head when the Sergeant returned with an unwieldy package and a typewritten list.

They spread the contents of the package carefully on the desk. For the most part the collected material consisted of crumpled programs, stray scraps of paper, chiefly from candy-boxes, and many ticket-stubs—those which had not been found by Flint and his searchers. Two women's gloves of different design; a small brown button, probably from a man's coat; the cap of a fountain pen; a woman's handkerchief and a few other scattered articles of the kind usually lost or thrown away in theatres came to light.

"Doesn't look as if there's much here, does it?" commented the Inspector. "Well, at least we'll be able to check up on the ticket-stub business."

Velie heaped the lost stubs in a small pile and began to read off their numbers and letters to Queen, who checked them off on the list Velie had brought him. There were not many of these and the checking-off process was completed in a few moments.

"That all, Thomas?" inquired the Inspector, looking up.

"That's all, Chief."

"Well, there are about fifty people still unaccounted for according to this list. Where's Flint?"

"He's in the building somewhere, Inspector."

Queen picked up his telephone and gave a rapid order. Flint appeared almost at once.

"What did you find last night?" asked Queen abruptly.

"Well, Inspector," answered Flint sheepishly, "we practically dry-cleaned that place. We found quite a bit of stuff, but most of it was programs and things like that, and we left those for the cleaning-women, who were working along with us. But we did pick up a raft of ticket-stubs, especially out in the alleys." He brought forth from his pocket a package of pasteboards neatly bound with a rubber band. Velie took them and continued the process of reading off numbers and letters. When he was finished Queen slapped the typewritten list down on the desk before him.

"No fruit in the loom?"[62] murmured Ellery, looking up from the book.

"Ding it, every one of those people who had no stubs is accounted for!" growled the Inspector. "There isn't a stub or a name left unchecked. . . . Well, there's one thing I can do." He searched through the pile of stubs, referring to the lists, until he found the stub which had belonged to Frances Ives-Pope. He fished from his pocket the four stubs he had collected Monday night and carefully tested the girl's stub with the one for Field's seat. The torn edges did not coincide.

"There's one consolation," the Inspector continued, stuffing the five tickets into his vest pocket, "we haven't found a trace of the six tickets for the seats next to and in front of Field's seat!"

"I didn't think you would," remarked Ellery. He put the book down and regarded his father with unwonted seriousness. "Have you ever stopped to consider, dad, that we don't know definitely why Field was in the theatre last night?"

62.　Fruit of the Loom® is one of the earliest trademarks granted in America, issued in 1871 for fabric. The name was a play on the Biblical expression, "fruit of the womb," meaning children. Despite a bankruptcy in 1999, the company remains one of the largest manufacturers of underwear and casual wear.

1920s Fruit of the Loom advertisement.

Queen knit his grey brows. "That particular problem has been puzzling me, of course. We know from Mrs. Russo and Michaels that Field did not care for the theatre—"

"You can never tell what vagary will seize a man," said Ellery decisively. "Many things might make a non-theatre-going man decide suddenly to go in for that sort of entertainment. The fact remains—he was there. But what I want to know is *why* he was there."

The old man shook his head gravely. "Was it a business appointment? Remember what Mrs. Russo said—that Field had promised to be back at 10 o'clock."

"I fancy the business appointment idea," applauded Ellery. "But consider how many probabilities there are—the Russo woman might be lying and Field said nothing of the sort; or if he did, he might have had no intention of keeping the appointment with her at 10 o'clock."

"I've quite made up my mind, Ellery," said the Inspector, "whatever the probabilities, that he didn't go to the Roman Theatre last night to see the show. He went there with his eyes open—for business."

"I think that's correct, myself" returned Ellery, smiling. "But you can never be too careful in weighing possibilities. Now, if he went on business, he went to meet somebody. Was that somebody the murderer?"

"You ask too many questions, Ellery," said the Inspector.— "Thomas, let's have a look at the other stuff in that package."

Velie carefully handed the Inspector the miscellaneous articles one by one. The gloves, fountain-pen cap, button and handkerchief Queen threw to one side after a quick scrutiny. Nothing remained except the small bits of candy paper and the crumpled programs. The former yielding no clues, Queen took up the programs. And suddenly, in the midst of his examination, he cried delightedly: "See what I've found, boys!"

The three men leaned over his shoulder. Queen held a program in his hand, its wrinkles smoothed out. It showed evidences of having been crushed and thrown away. On one of the inside pages, bordering the usual article on men's wear, was a number of varied marks, some forming letters, some forming numbers, still others forming cabalistic designs such as a person scribbles in moments of idle thought.

"Inspector, it looks as if you've found Field's own program!" exclaimed Flint.

"Yes, sir, it certainly does," said Queen sharply. "Flint, look through the papers we found in the dead man's clothing last night and bring me a letter showing his signature." Flint hurried out.

Ellery was studying the scrawls intently. On the top margin of the paper appeared:

Program with Monty Field's notes.

Flint returned with a letter. The Inspector compared the signatures—they were plainly by the same hand.

"We'll have them checked by Jimmie down in the laboratory," muttered the old man. "But I guess this is pretty authentic. It's Field's program, there can't be any doubt of that. . . . What do you make of it, Thomas?"

Velie grated: "I don't know what those other numbers refer to, but that '50,000' couldn't mean anything but dollars, Chief."

"The old boy must have been figuring his bank account," said Queen. "He loved the sight of his own name, didn't he?"

"That's not quite fair to Field," protested Ellery. "When a man is sitting idle, waiting for something to happen—as he will when he is in a theatre before the performance begins—one of his most natural actions is to scribble his initials or his name on the handiest object. In a theatre the handiest object would be the program. . . . The writing of one's own name is fundamental in psychology. So perhaps Field wasn't as egotistical as this seems to make him."

63. Henry Fielding, English novelist and dramatist (1707–1754), wrote in his play *Don Quixote in England* (1734), "Money is the fruit of evil, as often as the root of it." Scene 6.

"It's a small point," said the Inspector, studying the scrawls with a frown.

"Perhaps," returned Ellery. "But to get back to a more pressing matter.—I don't agree with you when you say the '50,000' probably refers to Field's bank account. When a man jots down his bank balance he will not do it in such round numbers."

'We can prove or disprove that easily enough," retorted the Inspector, picking up a telephone. He asked the police operator to get him the number of Field's office. When he had spoken to Oscar Lewin for some time, he turned back to Ellery with a crestfallen air.

"You were right, El," he said. "Field had an amazingly small personal account. All his accounts balance to less than six thousand dollars. And this despite the fact that he frequently made deposits of ten and fifteen thousand dollars. Lewin himself was surprised. He hadn't known, he said, how Field's personal finances stood until I asked him to look the matter up. . . . I'll bet dollars to doughnuts Field played the stock market or the horses!"

"I'm not particularly overwhelmed by the news," remarked Ellery. "It points to the probable reason for the '50,000' on the program. That number not only represents dollars, but more than that—it indicates a business deal in which the stakes were fifty thousand! Not a bad night's work, if he had come out of it alive."

"How about the other two numbers?" asked Queen.

"I'm going to mull over them a bit," replied Ellery, subsiding in his chair. "I *would* like to know what the business deal was that involved such a large financial consideration," he added, absently polishing his pince-nez.

"Whatever the business deal was," said the Inspector sententiously, "you may be sure, my son, it was an evil one."

"An evil one?" inquired Ellery in a serious tone.

"Money's the root of all evil," retorted the Inspector with a grin.

Ellery's tone did not change. "Not only the root, dad—but the fruit, too."

"Another quotation?" mocked the old man.

"Fielding," said Ellery imperturbably.[63]

CHAPTER XI

In Which the Past Casts a Shadow

The telephone bell tinkled.

"Q? Sampson speaking," came the District Attorney's voice over the wire.

"Good morning, Henry," said Queen. "Where are you and how do you feel this morning?"

"I'm at the office and I feel rotten," returned Sampson, chuckling. "The doctor insists I'll be a corpse if I keep this up and the office insists the City will go under unless I attend to business. So what's a feller to do? . . . I say, Q."

The Inspector winked at Ellery across the table, as if to say, "I know what's coming!"

"Yes, Henry?"

"There's a gentleman in my private office whom I think it would be greatly to your advantage to meet," continued Sampson in a subdued tone. "He wants to see you and I'm afraid you'll have to chuck whatever you're doing and hotfoot it up here. He"—Sampson's voice became a whisper—"he's a man I can't afford to antagonize unnecessarily, Q, old boy."

The Inspector frowned. "I suppose you're referring to Ives-Pope," he said. "Riled, is he, because we questioned the apple of his eye last night?"

"Not exactly," said Sampson. "He's really a decent old chap. Just—er—just be nice to him, Q, won't you?"

"I'll handle him with silk gloves," chuckled the old man. "If it will ease your mind any I'll drag my son along. He generally attends to our social obligations."

"That will be fine," said Sampson gratefully.

The Inspector turned to Ellery as he hung up. "Poor Henry's in something of a mess," he said quizzically, "and I can't say I blame him for trying to please. Sick as a dog and the politicians hopping on him, this Croesus howling in his front office. . . . Come along, son, we're going to meet the celebrated Franklin Ives-Pope!"

Ellery groaned, stretching his arms. "You'll have another sick man on your hands if this continues." Nevertheless he jumped up and clamped his hat on his head. "Let's look over this captain of industry."

Queen grinned at Velie. "Before I forget, Thomas. . . . I want you to do a bit of sleuthing to-day. Your job is to find out why Monte Field, who did a rushing legal business and lived in princely style, had only six thousand dollars in his personal account. It's probably Wall Street and the racetrack but I want you to make sure. You might learn something from the cancelled vouchers—Lewin down at Field's office could help you there . . . And while you're at it—this might be extremely important, Thomas—get a complete line-up on Field's movements all day yesterday."

The two Queens departed for Sampson's headquarters.

The office of the District Attorney was a busy place and even an Inspector of Detectives was treated with scant ceremony in the sacred chambers. Ellery was wroth, and his father smiled, and finally the District Attorney himself came rushing out of his sanctum with a word of displeasure to the clerk who had allowed his friends to cool their heels on a hard bench.

"Watch your throat, young man," warned Queen, as Sampson led the way to his office, muttering maledictions on the head of the offender. "Are you sure I look all right to meet the money-mogul?"

Sampson held the door open. The two Queens on the threshold saw a man, hands clasped behind his back, looking through the window on the uninteresting vista outside. As the District Attorney closed the door the occupant of the room wheeled about with astonishing agility for a man of his weight.

Franklin Ives-Pope was a relic of more virile financial days. He resembled the strong self-assertive type of magnate who like old Cornelius Vanderbilt had dominated Wall Street as much by force of personality as by extent of wealth. Ives-Pope had clear grey eyes, iron-grey hair, a grizzled mustache, a husky body still springy with youth and an air of authority unmistakably masterful. Standing against the light of the dingy window, he was a most impressive figure of a man and Ellery and Queen, stepping forward, realized at once that here was an individual whose intelligence required no patronage.

The financier spoke in a deep pleasant voice even before Sampson, slightly embarrassed, could make the introduction. "I suppose you're Queen, the man-hunter," he said. "I've been anxious to meet you for a long time, Inspector." He offered a large square hand, which Queen took with dignity.

"It would be unnecessary for me to echo that statement, Mr. Ives-Pope," he said, smiling a little. "Once I took a flyer in Wall Street and I think you've got some of my money.—This, sir, is my son Ellery, who is the brains and beauty of the Queen family."

The big man's eyes measured Ellery's bulk appreciatively. He shook hands, saying, "You've got a smart father there, son!"

"Well!" sighed the District Attorney, setting three chairs. "I'm glad that's over. You haven't the slightest idea, Mr. Ives-Pope, how nervous I've been about this meeting. Queen is the devil himself when it comes to the social amenities, and I shouldn't have been surprised if he had clapped his handcuffs on you as you shook hands!"

The tension snapped with the big man's hearty chuckle. The District Attorney came abruptly to the point. "Mr. Ives-Pope is here, Q, to find out for himself just what can be done in the matter of his daughter." Queen nodded. Sampson turned to the financier. "As I told you before, sir, we have every confidence in Inspector Queen—always have had. He generally works without any check or supervision from the District Attorney's office. In view of the circumstances, I thought I should make that clear."

"That's a sane method, Sampson," said Ives-Pope, with approval. "I've always worked on that principle in my own business. Besides, from what I've heard about Inspector Queen, your confidence is well placed."

"Sometimes," said Queen gravely, "I have to do things that go against the grain. I will be frank to say that some things I did last night in the line of duty were extremely disagreeable to me. I suppose, Mr. Ives-Pope, your daughter is upset because of our little talk last night?"

Ives-Pope was silent for a moment. Then he raised his head and met the Inspector's gaze squarely. "Look here, Inspector," he said. "We're both men of the world and men of business. We've had dealings with all sorts of queer people, both of us, and we have, too, solved problems that presented enormous difficulties to others. So I think we can converse frankly. . . . Yes, my daughter Frances is more than a little upset. Incidentally, so is her mother, who is an ill woman at the best of times; and her brother Stanford, my son—but we needn't go into that. . . . Frances told me last night when she got home with—her friends—everything that happened. I know my daughter, Inspector; and I'd stake my fortune that there isn't the slightest connection between her and Field."

"My dear sir," returned the Inspector quietly, "I didn't accuse her of anything. Nobody knows better than I what peculiar things can happen in the course of a criminal investigation; therefore I never let the slightest blind spot escape my notice. All I did was to ask her to identify the bag. When she did so, I told her where it was found. I was waiting, of course, for an explanation. It did not come. . . . You must understand, Mr. Ives-Pope, that when a man is murdered and a woman's bag is found in his pocket it is the duty of the police to discover the owner of the bag and his or her connection with the crime. But of course—I do not have to convince you of that."

The magnate drummed on the arm of his chair. "I see your point of view, Inspector," he said. "It was obviously your duty, and it is still your duty to go to the bottom of the thing. In fact, I want you to make every effort to. My own personal opinion is that she is the victim of circumstances. But I don't want to plead her case. I trust you sufficiently to rely on your judgment after you've thoroughly probed the problem." He paused. "Inspector Queen, how would you like to have me arrange a little interview at my home to-morrow morning? I would not ask you to go to this trouble," he added apologetically, "except that Frances is quite ill, and her mother insists she stay at home. May we expect you?"

"Very good of you, Mr. Ives-Pope," remarked Queen calmly, "We'll be there."

The financier seemed indisposed to end the interview. He shifted heavily in his chair. "I've always been a fair man, Inspector," he said. "I feel somehow that I may be accused of using my position as a means of securing special privileges. That is not so. The shock of your tactics last night made it impossible for Frances to tell her story. At home, among the members of her family, I am sure she will be able to clear up her connection with the affair to your satisfaction." He hesitated for a moment, then continued in a colder tone. "Her fiancé will be there and perhaps his presence will help to calm her." His voice expressed the thought that he personally did not think so. "May we expect you, let us say, at ten-thirty?"

"That will be fine," said Queen, nodding. "I should like to know more definitely, sir, just who will be present."

"I can arrange it as you wish, Inspector," replied Ives-Pope, "but I imagine Mrs. Ives-Pope will want to be there and I know that Mr. Barry will—my future son-in-law," he explained dryly. "Perhaps a few of Frances' friends—theatrical friends. My son Stanford may also grace us with his presence—a very busy young man, you know," he added with a suspicion of bitterness.

The three men shifted embarrassedly. Ives-Pope rose with a sigh and Ellery, Queen and Sampson followed suit. "That's all, I think, Inspector," said the financier in a lighter tone. "Is there anything else I can do?"

"Not a thing."

"Then I'll be getting along." Ives-Pope turned to Ellery and Sampson. "Of course, Sampson, if you can get away, I'd like you to be there. Do you think you can make it?" The District Attorney nodded. "And Mr. Queen"—the big man turned to Ellery—"will you come also? I understand that you have been following the investigation very closely at your father's side. We shall be happy to have you."

"I'll be there," said Ellery softly, and Ives-Pope left the office.

"Well, what do you think, Q?" asked Sampson, fidgeting in his swivel-chair.

"A most interesting man," returned the Inspector. "How fair-minded he is!"

"Oh, yes—yes," said Sampson. "Er—Q, he asked me before you came if you wouldn't go easy on the publicity. Sort of special favor, you know."

"He didn't have the nerve to come out with it to me, eh?" chuckled the Inspector. "He's quite human. . . . Well, Henry, I'll do my best, but if that young woman is implicated seriously, I won't vouch for hands off with the press."

"All right, all right, Q—it's up to you," said Sampson irritably. "Damn this throat of mine!" He took an atomizer from a desk-drawer and sprinkled his throat wryly.

"Didn't Ives-Pope recently donate a hundred thousand dollars to the Chemical Research Foundation?"[64] asked Ellery suddenly, turning to Sampson.

64. While there is no trace of an organization with this name, there were well-established chemical research funds at numerous institutions in and around New York. A gift of $100,000 would have been a newsworthy event for any of them, being the modern equivalent of a gift of more than $21 million, using the "economy cost" method of valuation. (https://measuringworth.com/)

"I seem to remember something of that sort," said Sampson, gargling. "Why?"

Ellery mumbled an inaudible explanation that was lost in Sampson's violent gyrations with the sprayer. Queen, who was regarding his son speculatively, shook his head, consulted his watch and said,

"Well, son, it's time we knocked off for lunch. What do you say—Henry, think you'd like to join us in a bite?"

Sampson grinned with an effort. "I'm full up to my neck with work, but even a District Attorney has to eat," he said. "I'll go on only one condition—that I pay the check. I owe you something, anyway."

As they donned their coats Queen picked up Sampson's telephone.

"Mr. Morgan? . . . Oh, hello, Morgan. I say, do you think you can find a little time this afternoon for a chat? . . . Right. Two-thirty will be fine. Good-by."

"That settles that," said the Inspector comfortably. "Always pays to be polite, Ellery—remember that."

At two-thirty promptly the two Queens were ushered into the quiet law-office of Benjamin Morgan. It was noticeably different from Field's lavish suite—richly furnished but with a more business-like simplicity. A smiling young woman closed the door after them. Morgan greeted them with some reserve. He held out a box of cigars as they sat down.

"No thanks—my snuff will do," said the Inspector genially, while Ellery after being introduced lit a cigarette and blew smoke-rings. Morgan lit a cigar with shaking fingers.

"I suppose you're here to continue that talk of ours last night, Inspector?" said Morgan.

Queen sneezed, replaced his snuff-box, and leaned back in the chair. "Look here, Morgan old man," he said evenly. "You haven't been quite on the up-and-up with me."

"What do you mean?" asked Morgan, coloring.

"You told me last night," said the Inspector reflectively, "you told me last night that you parted amicably with Field two years ago, when you dissolved the firm of Field & Morgan. Did you say that?"

"I did," said Morgan.

"How, then, my dear fellow," asked Queen, "do you explain the little incident of the quarrel at the Webster Club? I certainly would not call a threat against another man's life an 'amicable' way of dissolving a partnership!"

Morgan sat quietly for several minutes while Queen stared patiently at him and Ellery sighed. Then he looked up and began to speak in a passionate undertone.

"I'm sorry, Inspector," he muttered, glancing away. "I might have known that a threat like that would be remembered by somebody. . . . Yes, it's true enough. We had lunch one day in the Webster Club at Field's suggestion. As far as I was concerned, the less I had to do with him socially the better I liked it. But the purpose of the luncheon was to go over some last details of the dissolution, and of course I had no choice. . . . I'm afraid I lost my temper. I did make a threat against his life, but it was—well, it was said in the heat of an angry moment. I forgot the whole thing before the week was over."

The Inspector nodded sagely. "Yes, things do happen like that sometimes. But"—and Morgan licked his lips in despairing anticipation—"a man doesn't threaten another man's life, even if he doesn't mean it, merely over a matter of business detail." He leveled his finger at Morgan's shrinking body. "Come on now, man—out with it. What are you holding back?"

Morgan's entire body had gone flaccid. His lips were ashy as he turned from one Queen to the other, mute appeal in his eyes. But their glances were inexorable and Ellery, who was regarding him much as a vivisectionist regards a guinea-pig, interrupted.

"My dear Morgan," he said coldly, "Field had something on you, and he thought that that was a good time to tell you about it. It's as obvious as the red in your eye."

"You've guessed it in part, Mr. Queen. I've been one of the most unfortunate men God ever created. That devil Field—whoever killed him deserves to be decorated for his service to humanity. He was an octopus—a soulless beast in human form. I can't tell you how happy—yes, happy!—I am that he is dead!"

"Softly there, Morgan," said Queen. "Although I gather our mutual friend was a good deal of a skunk, your remarks might be overheard by a less sympathetic audience. And—?"

"Here's the whole story," mumbled Morgan, his eyes fixed on the desk-blotter. "It's a hard one to tell. . . . When I was a kid at college I got into some trouble with a girl—a waitress in the college restaurant. She was not bad—just weak,[65] and I suppose I was wild in those days. At any rate she had a child—my child. . . . I suppose you know that I come from a strait-laced family. If you

65. "Weak" presumably means she didn't have the strength of character to turn him down when he sought to have sex with her! The double-standard has a long history . . .

don't, you would find out soon enough on investigation. They had great plans for me, they were socially ambitious—to cut it short. I couldn't very well marry the girl and bring her to father's house as my wife. It was a caddish thing to do. . . ."

He paused.

"But it was done, and that's all that matters. I've—I've always loved her. She was sensible enough about the arrangements. . . . I managed to provide for her out of my generous allowance. No one—I'll swear not a soul in this world with the exception of her widowed mother, a fine old lady—knew about the affair. I'll swear to that, I say. And yet—" His fist clenched, but he resumed with a sigh. "Eventually, I married the girl whom my family had selected for me." There was a painful silence as he stopped to clear his throat. "It was a *mariage de convenance*—just that and nothing else. She came from an old aristocratic family, and I had the money. We have lived fairly happily together. . . . Then I met Field. I curse the day I ever consented to go into partnership with him—but my own business was not exactly all it might have been and Field, if nothing else, was an aggressive and clever lawyer."

The Inspector took a pinch of snuff.

"Everything went smoothly at first," continued Morgan in the same low tone. "But by degrees I began to suspect that my partner was not everything he should have been. Queer clients—queer clients indeed—would enter his private office after hours; he would evade my questions about them; things began to look peculiar. Finally I decided my own reputation would suffer if I continued to be linked with the man, and I broached the subject of dissolution. Field objected strenuously, but I was stubborn and after all he could not dominate my desires. We dissolved."

Ellery's fingers tapped an absent tattoo on the handle of his stick.

"Then the affair at the Webster. He insisted we have lunch together for the settlement of the last few details. That wasn't his purpose at all, of course. You can guess, I suppose, his intentions. . . . He came out quite suavely with the overwhelming statement that he knew I was supporting a woman and my illegitimate child. He said that he had some of my letters to prove it, and a number of cancelled vouchers of checks I had sent her. . . . He admitted he had stolen them from me. I hadn't looked at them for years, of course. . . . Then he blandly announced that he meant to make capital out of this evidence!"

"Blackmail!" muttered Ellery, a light creeping into his eyes.

"Yes, blackmail," retorted Morgan bitterly. "Nothing less. He described in very graphic terms what would happen if the story should come out. Oh, Field was a clever crook! I saw the entire structure of social position I had built up—a process which took years—destroyed in an instant. My wife, her family, my own family—and more than that, the circle in which we moved—I shouldn't have been able to lift my head out of the muck. And as for business—well, it doesn't take much to make important clients go elsewhere for their legal work. I was trapped—I knew it and he knew it."

"Just how much did he want, Morgan?" asked Queen.

"Enough! He wanted twenty-five thousand dollars—just to keep quiet. I didn't even have any assurances that the affair would end there. I was caught and caught properly. Because, remember, this was not an affair which had died years before. I was still supporting that poor woman and my son. I am supporting them now. I will—continue to support them." He stared at his fingernails.

"I paid the money," he resumed morosely. "It meant stretching a bit, but I paid it. But the harm was done. I saw red there at the Club, and—but you know what happened."

"And this blackmail has continued all the while, Morgan?" asked the Inspector.

"Yes, sir—for two solid years. The man was insatiable, I tell you! Even to-day I can't completely understand it. He must have been earning tremendous fees in his own practice, and yet he always seemed to be needing money. No small change, either—I have never paid him less than ten thousand dollars at one time!"

Queen and Ellery looked at each other fleetingly. Queen said, "Well, Morgan, it's a pretty kettle of fish. The more I hear about Field the more I dislike putting the irons on the fellow who did away with him. However! In the light of what you've told me, your statement last night that you hadn't seen Field for two years is patently untrue. When *did* you see him last?"

Morgan appeared to be racking his memory. "Oh, it was about two months ago, Inspector," he said at last.

The Inspector shifted in his chair. "I see. . . . I'm sorry you didn't tell me all this last night. You understand, of course, that your story is perfectly safe with the police. And it's mighty vital information. Now then—do you happen to know a woman by the name of Angela Russo?"

Morgan stared. "Why, no, Inspector. I've never heard of her."

Queen was silent for a moment. "Do you know a gentleman called 'Parson Johnny'?"

"I think I can give you some information there, Inspector. I'm certain that during our partnership Field was using the little thug for some shady business of his own. I caught him sneaking up into the office a number of times after hours, and when I asked Field about him, he would sneer and say, 'Oh, that's only Parson Johnny, a friend of mine!' But it was sufficient to establish the man's identity. What their connection was I can't tell you, because I don't know."

"Thanks, Morgan," said the Inspector. "I'm glad you told me that. And now—one last question. Have you ever heard the name Charles Michaels?"

"To be sure I have," responded Morgan grimly. "Michaels was Field's so-called valet—he acted in the capacity of bodyguard and was really a blackguard, or I'm greatly mistaken in my judgment of men. He came to the office once in a while. I can't think of anything else about him, Inspector."

"He knows you, of course?" asked Queen.

"Why—I suppose so," returned Morgan doubtfully. "I never spoke to him, but undoubtedly he saw me during his visits to the office."

"Well, now, that's fine, Morgan," grunted Queen, rising, "This has been a most interesting and informative chat. And—no, I don't think there's anything else. That is, at the moment, just ride along, Morgan, and keep in town—available if we need you for anything. Remember that, won't you?"

"I'm not likely to forget it," said Morgan dully. "And—of course the story I told you—about my son—it won't come out?"

"You needn't have the slightest fear—about that, Morgan," said Queen, and a few moments later he and Ellery were on the sidewalk.

"So it was blackmail, dad," murmured Ellery. "That gives me an idea, do you know?"

"Well, son, I've a few ideas of my own!" chuckled Queen, and in a telepathic silence they walked briskly down the street in the direction of headquarters.

CHAPTER XII

In Which the Queens Invade Society

Wednesday morning found Djuna pouring the coffee before a bemused Inspector and a chattering Ellery. The telephone bell rang. Both Ellery and his father jumped for the instrument.

"Here! What are you doing?" exclaimed Queen. "I'm expecting a call and that's it!"

"Now, now, sir, allow a bibliophile the privilege of using his own telephone," retorted Ellery. "I have a feeling that that's my friend the book-dealer calling me about the elusive Falconer."

"Look here, Ellery, don't start—" While they were chaffing each other good-naturedly across the table, Djuna picked up the telephone.

"The Inspector—the Inspector, did you say? Inspector—" said Djuna, grinning as he held the mouthpiece to his thin chest, "it's for you."

Ellery subsided in his chair while Queen, with an air of triumph, snatched the instrument.

"Yes?"

"Stoates calling from Field's office, Inspector," came a fresh cheery young voice. "I want to put Mr. Cronin on the wire."

The Inspector's brow wrinkled in anticipation. Ellery was listening intently, and even Djuna, with the monkey-like eagerness of his sharp features, had become rooted to his corner, as if he, too, awaited important news. Djuna in this respect resembled his brother anthropoid—there was an alertness, a bright inquisitiveness in his attitude and mien which delighted the Queens eternally.

Finally a high-pitched voice came over the wire. "This is Tim Cronin speaking, Inspector," it said. "How are you? I haven't got round to seeing you for an age."

"I'm getting a little bent and withered, Tim, but otherwise I'm still all there," returned Queen. "What's on your mind? Have you found anything?"

"Now that's the very peculiar part of the whole business, Inspector," came Cronin's excited tones. "As you know, I've been watching this bird Field for years, He's been my pet nightmare for as long as I can remember. The D. A. tells me that he gave you the story night before last, so I needn't go into it. But in all these years of watching and waiting and digging I've never been able to find a solitary piece of evidence against that crook that I could bring into a courtroom. And he was a crook, Inspector—I'd stake my life on that. . . . Anyway, it's the old story here. I really shouldn't have hoped for anything better, knowing Field as I did. And yet—well, I couldn't help praying that somewhere, somehow, he would slip up, and that I'd nail it when I could get my hands on his private records. Inspector—there's nothing doing."

Queen's face reflected a fleeting disappointment, which Ellery interpreted with a sigh, rising as he did so to walk restlessly up and down the room.

"I guess we can't help it, Tim," returned Queen, with an effort at heartiness. "Don't worry—we've other irons in the fire."

"Inspector," said Cronin abruptly, "you've got your hands full. Field was a really slick article. And from the way it looks to me, the genius who could get past his guard and put him away is a really slick article, too. He couldn't be anything else. Incidentally, we're not halfway through with the files and maybe what we've looked over isn't as unpromising as I made it sound. There's plenty here to suggest shady work on Field's part—it's just that there's no direct incriminating evidence. We're hoping that we find something as we go on."

"All right, Tim—keep up the good work," muttered the Inspector. "And let me know how you make out. . . . Is Lewin there?"

"You mean the office-manager?" Cronin's voice lowered. "He's around somewhere. Why?"

"You want to keep your eye peeled," said Queen. "I have a sneaking suspicion he's not as stupid as he sounds. Just don't let him get too familiar with any records lying around. For all we know, he may have been in on Field's little side-line."

"Right, Inspector. Call you sometime later," and the receiver clicked as Cronin hung up.

At ten-thirty Queen and Ellery pushed open the high gate at the entrance to the Ives-Pope residence on Riverside Drive. Ellery was moved to remark that the atmosphere was a perfect invitation to formal morning-dress and that he was going to feel extremely uncomfortable when they were admitted through the stone portals.

In truth, the house which concealed the destinies of the Ives-Popes was in many respects awe-inspiring to men of the modest tastes of the Queens. It was a huge rambling old stone house, set far back from the Drive, hunched on the greensward of a respectable acreage. "Must have cost a pretty penny," grunted the Inspector as his eyes swept the rolling lawns surrounding the building. Gardens and summer-houses; walks and bowered nooks—one would have thought himself miles away from the city which roared by a scant few rods away, behind the high iron palings which circled the mansion. The Ives-Popes were immensely wealthy and brought to this not uncommon possession a lineage stretching back into the dim recesses of American colonization.

The front door was opened by a whiskered patrician whose back seemed composed of steel and whose nose was elevated at a perilous angle toward the ceiling. Ellery lounged in the doorway, surveying this uniformed nobleman with admiration, while Inspector Queen fumbled in his pockets for a card. He was a long time producing one; the stiff-backed flunkey stood graven into stone. Red-faced, the Inspector finally discovered a battered card. He placed it on the extended salver and watched the butler retreat to some cavern of his own.

Ellery chuckled as his father drew himself up at the sight of Franklin Ives-Pope's burly figure emerging from a wide carved doorway.

The financier hurried toward them.

"Inspector! Mr. Queen!" he exclaimed in a cordial tone, "come right in. Have you been waiting long?"

The Inspector mumbled a greeting. They walked through a high-ceilinged shining-floored hall, decorated with austere old furniture.

"You're on the dot, gentlemen," said Ives-Pope, standing aside to allow them to pass into a large room. "Here are some additional members of our little board-meeting. I think you know all of us present."

The Inspector and Ellery looked about. "I know everybody, sir, except that gentleman—I presume he is Mr. Stanford Ives-Pope," said Queen. "I'm afraid my son has still to make the acquaintance of—Mr. Peale, is it?—Mr. Barry—and, of course, Mr. Ives-Pope."

The introductions were made in a strained fashion. "Ah, Q!" murmured District Attorney Sampson, hurrying across the room. "I wouldn't have missed this for the world," he said in a low tone. "First time I've met most of the people who'll be present at the inquisition."

"What is that fellow Peale doing here?" muttered Queen to the District Attorney, while Ellery crossed the room to engage the three young men on the other side in conversation. Ives-Pope had excused himself and disappeared.

"He's a friend of young Ives-Pope, and, of course, he's chummy with Barry there, too," returned the District Attorney. "I gathered from the chit-chat before you came that Stanford, Ives-Pope's son, originally introduced these professional people to his sister Frances. That's how she met Barry and fell in love with him. Peale seems on good terms with the young lady, too."

"I wonder how much Ives-Pope and his aristocratic spouse like the bourgeois company their children keep," said the Inspector, eyeing the small group on the other side of the room with interest.

"You'll find out soon enough," chuckled Sampson. "Just watch the icicles dripping from Mrs. Ives-Pope's eyebrows every time she sees one of these actors. I imagine they're about as welcome as a bunch of Bolsheviks."

Queen put his hands behind his back and stared curiously about the room. It was a library, well stocked with rich and rare books, catalogued carefully and immaculate behind shining glass. A desk dominated the center of the room. It was unpretentious for a millionaire's study, the Inspector noted with approval.

"Incidentally," resumed Sampson, "Eve Ellis, the girl who you said was with Miss Ives-Pope and her fiancé at the Roman Theatre Monday night is here, too. She's upstairs keeping the little heiress company, I imagine. Don't think the old lady likes it much. But they're both charming girls."

"What a pleasant place this must be when the Ives-Popes and the actors get together in private!" grunted Queen.

The four young men strolled towards them. Stanford Ives-Pope was a slender well-manicured young man, fashionably dressed. There were deep pouches under his eyes. He wore a restless air of boredom that Queen was quick to note. Both Peale and Barry, the actors, were attired faultlessly.

"Mr. Queen tells me that you've got a pretty problem on your hands, Inspector," drawled Stanford Ives-Pope.[66] "We're all uncommonly sorry to see poor Sis dragged into it. How in the world did her purse ever get into that chap's pocket? Barry hasn't slept for days over Frances' predicament, I give you my word!"

"My dear young man," said the Inspector, with a twinkle in his eye, "if I knew how Miss Ives-Pope's purse found its way into Monte Field's pocket, I wouldn't be here this morning. That's just one of the things that make this case so infernally interesting."

"The pleasure's all yours, Inspector. But you certainly can't think Frances had the slightest connection with all this?"

Queen smiled. "I can't think anything yet, young man," he protested. "I haven't heard what your sister has to say about it."

"She'll explain all right, Inspector," said Stephen Barry, his handsome face drawn into lines of fatigue. "You needn't worry about that. It's the damnable suspicion that she's open to that makes me angry—the whole thing is ridiculous!"

"I know just how you feel, Mr. Barry," said the Inspector kindly. "And I want to take this opportunity of apologizing for my conduct the other night. I was perhaps a little—harsh."

"I suppose I ought to apologize, too," returned Barry, with a wan smile. "I guess I said a few things I didn't mean in that office. In the heat of the moment—seeing Frances—Miss Ives-Pope go off in a faint—" He paused awkwardly.

Peale, a massive giant, ruddy and wholesome in his morning clothes, put his arm affectionately about Barry's shoulders. "I'm

66. This is an odd comment—clearly "Mr. Queen" (Ellery) never met Stanford Ives-Pope before. Did the latter mean Sampson?

sure the Inspector understood, Steve old boy," he said cheerfully. "Don't take it so much to heart—everything's bound to come out all right."

"You can leave it to Inspector Queen," said Sampson, nudging the Inspector jovially in the ribs. "He's the only bloodhound I've ever met who has a heart under his badge—and if Miss Ives-Pope can clear this thing up to his satisfaction, even to a reasonable extent, that will be the end of it."

"Oh, I don't know," murmured Ellery thoughtfully. "Dad's a great one for surprises. As for Miss Ives-Pope"—he smiled ruefully and bowed to the actor—"Mr. Barry, you're a deucedly lucky fellow."

"You wouldn't think so if you saw the mater," drawled Stanford Ives-Pope. "If I'm not mistaken, here she barges in now."

The men turned toward the door. An enormously stout woman was waddling in. A uniformed nurse supported her carefully under one huge arm, holding a large green bottle in her other hand. The financier followed briskly, by the side of a white-haired youngish looking man, wearing a dark coat and holding a black bag in his hand.

"Catharine, my dear," said Ives-Pope in a low voice to the stout woman as she sank into a great-chair, "these are the gentlemen whom I told you about—Inspector Richard Queen and Mr. Ellery Queen."

The two Queens bowed, receiving a stony glance from the myopic eyes of Mrs. Ives-Pope. "Charmed, I'm sure," she shrilled. "Where's Nurse? Nurse! I feel faint, please."

The uniformed girl hurried to her side, the green bottle ready. Mrs. Ives-Pope closed her eyes and inhaled, sighing with relief. The financier hurriedly introduced the white-haired man, Dr. Vincent Cornish, the family physician. The physician made swift apologies and disappeared behind the butler.

"Great chap, this Cornish," whispered Sampson to Queen. "Not only the most fashionable doctor on the Drive, but a genuine scientist as well." The Inspector elevated· his brows, but said nothing.

"The mater's one reason why I never cared for the medical profession," Stanford Ives-Pope was saying in a loud whisper to Ellery.

"Ah! Frances, my dear!" Ives-Pope hurried forward, followed by Barry, who dashed for the door. Mrs. Ives-Pope's fishy stare enveloped his back with cold disapproval. James Peale coughed embarrassedly and made a mumbled remark to Sampson.

Frances, attired in a filmy morning-gown, her face pale and drawn, entered the room leaning heavily on the arm of Eve Ellis, the actress. Her smile was somewhat forced as she murmured a greeting to the Inspector. Eve Ellis was introduced by Peale and the two girls seated themselves near Mrs. Ives-Pope. The old lady was sitting squarely in her chair, glaring about her like a lioness whose cub has been threatened. Two servants appeared silently and set chairs for the men. At Ives-Pope's urgent request Queen sat down at the big desk. Ellery refused a chair, preferring to lean against a bookcase behind and to the side of the company.

When the conversation had died away the Inspector cleared his throat and turned toward Frances, who after a startled flutter of the eyelids returned his glance steadily.

"First of all, Miss Frances—I hope I may call you that," began Queen in a fatherly tone, "allow me to explain my tactics of Monday night and to apologize for what must have seemed to you a totally unwarranted severity. From what Mr. Ives-Pope has told me, you can explain your actions on the night of the murder of Monte Field. I take it, therefore, that as far as you are concerned our little chat this morning will effectually remove you from the investigation. Before we have that chat, please believe me when I say that Monday night you were to me merely one of a number of suspicious characters. I acted in accordance with my habits in such cases. I see now how, to a woman of your breeding and social position, a grilling by a policeman under such tense circumstances would cause sufficient shock to bring on your present condition."

Frances smiled wearily. "You're forgiven, Inspector," she said in a clear, low voice. "It was my fault for being so foolish. I'm ready to answer any questions you may care to ask me."

"In just a moment, my dear." The Inspector shifted a bit to include the entire silent company in his next remark. "I should like to make one point, ladies and gentlemen," he said gravely. "We are assembled here for a definite purpose, which is to discover a possible connection, and there must be one, between the fact that Miss Ives-Pope's bag was found in the dead man's pocket, and the fact that Miss Ives-Pope apparently was unable to explain this circumstance. Now, whether this morning's work bears fruit or not, I must ask you all to keep whatever is said a profound secret. As District Attorney Sampson knows very well, I do not generally conduct an investigation with such a large audience. But I am making this exception because I believe you are all deeply concerned in the unfortunate young lady who has been drawn into this crime. You cannot, however, expect any consideration at my hands if one word of to-day's conversation reaches outside ears. Do we understand each other?"

"I say, Inspector," protested young Ives-Pope, "that's putting it a bit strong, don't you think? We all of us know the story, anyway."

"Perhaps, Mr. Ives-Pope," retorted the Inspector with a grim smile, "that is the reason I have consented to have all of you here."

There was a little rustle and Mrs. Ives-Pope opened her mouth as if to burst into wrathful speech. A sharp look from her husband made her lips droop together, with the protest unuttered. She transferred her glare to the actress sitting by Frances' side. Eve Ellis blushed. The nurse stood by Mrs. Ives-Pope with the smelling salts, like a setter dog about to point.

"Now, Miss Frances," resumed Queen kindly, "this is where we stand. I examine the body of a dead man named Monte Field, prominent lawyer, who was apparently enjoying an interesting play before he was so unceremoniously done away with, and find, in the rear coat-tail pocket of his full-dress suit, an evening bag. I identify this as yours by a few calling cards and some personal papers inside. I say to myself, 'Aha! A lady enters the problem!'—naturally enough. And I send one of my men to summon you, with the idea of allowing you to explain a most suspicious circumstance. You come—and you faint on being confronted with your property and the news of its place of discovery. At the time, I say to myself, 'This young lady knows something!'—a not unnatural conclusion. Now, in what way can you convince me that you know nothing—and that your fainting was caused only by the shock of the thing? Remember, Miss Frances—I am putting the problem not as Richard Queen but as a policeman looking for the truth."

"My story is not as illuminating, perhaps, as you might like it to be, Inspector," answered Frances quietly, in the deep hush that followed Queen's peroration. "I don't see how it is going to help you at all. But some facts which I think unimportant may be significant to your trained mind. . . . Roughly, this is what happened.

"I came to be in the Roman Theatre Monday night in a natural way. Since my engagement to Mr. Barry, although it has been a very quiet affair"—Mrs. Ives-Pope sniffed; her husband looked steadfastly at a point beyond his daughter's dark hair—"I have often dropped into the theatre, following a habit of meeting my fiancé after the performance. At such times he would either escort me home or take me to some place in the neighborhood for supper. Generally we make arrangements beforehand for these theatre-meetings; but sometimes I drop in unexpectedly if the opportunity presents itself. Monday night was one of those times. . . .

"I got to the Roman a few minutes before the end of the first act, since I have of course seen 'Gunplay' any number of times. I had my regular seat—arranged for me many weeks ago by Mr. Barry through Mr. Panzer—and had no more than settled myself to watch the performance when the curtain came down for the first intermission. I was feeling a little warm; the air was none too good. . . . I went first to the ladies' rest-room downstairs off the general lounge. Then I came up again and went out into the alley through the open door. There was quite a crowd of people there, enjoying the air."

She paused for a moment and Ellery, leaning against the bookcase, sharply surveyed the faces of the little audience. Mrs. Ives-Pope was looking about in her leviathan manner: Ives-Pope was still staring at the wall above Frances' head; Stanford was biting his fingernails; Peale and Barry were both watching Frances with nervous sympathy, looking furtively at Queen as if to gauge the effect of her words upon him; Eve Ellis' hand had stolen forward to clasp Frances' firmly.

The Inspector cleared his throat once more.

"Which alley was it, Miss Frances—the one on the left or the one on the right?" he asked.

"The one on the left, Inspector," she answered promptly. "You know I was sitting in M8 Left, and I suppose it was natural for me to go to the alley on that side."

"Quite so," said Queen smiling. "Go on, please."

"I stepped out into the alley," she resumed, less nervously, "and, not seeing any one I knew, stood close to the brick wall of the theatre, a little behind the open iron door. The freshness of the night air after the rain was delightful. I hadn't been standing there more than two minutes when I felt somebody brush up against me. I naturally moved a little to one side, thinking the person had stumbled. But when he—it was a man—when he did it again, I became a little frightened and started to walk away. He—he grasped my wrist and pulled me back. We were half-way behind the iron door, which was not pushed back completely and I doubt if any one noticed his action."

"I see—I see," murmured the Inspector sympathetically. "It seems an unusual thing for a total stranger to do in a public place."

"It seemed as if he wanted to kiss me, Inspector. He leaned over and whispered, 'Good evening, honey!' and—well, of course, I jumped to that conclusion. I drew back a little and said as coldly as I could, 'Please let me go, or I will call for help.' He just laughed at that and bent closer. The reek of whisky on his breath was overpowering. It made me ill."

She stopped. Eve Ellis patted her hand reassuringly. Peale nudged Barry forcibly as the young man half-rose to his feet in muttered protest. "Miss Frances, I'm going to ask you a peculiar question—it's almost ridiculous when you come to think of it," said the Inspector, leaning back in his chair. "Did the reek on his breath suggest good liquor or bad liquor? . . . There! I knew you'd smile." And the entire company tittered at the whimsical expression on Queen's face.

"Well, Inspector—it's hard to answer that," returned the girl freely. "I'm afraid I'm not on intimate terms with spirits. But from what I can remember, it had the odor of rather fine liquor. Fine liquor—but plenty of it!" she concluded with a grim little toss of her head.

"I would've spotted the vintage in a minute if I'd been there!" muttered Stanford Ives-Pope.

His father's lips tightened, but after a moment they relaxed into the suspicion of a grin. He shook his head warningly at his son.

"Go ahead, Miss Frances," said the Inspector.

"I was terribly frightened," the girl confessed, with a tremor of her red lips. "And feeling nauseated and all—I wrenched away from his outstretched hand and stumbled blindly into the theatre. The next thing I remember is sitting in my seat listening to the warning ring of the backstage bell, announcing the beginning of the second act. I really don't remember how I got there. My heart was in my throat and now I distinctly recall thinking that I would not tell Stephen—Mr. Barry—anything about the incident for fear he would want to look up this man and punish him. Mr. Barry is terribly jealous, you know." She smiled tenderly at her fiancé, who suddenly smiled back at her.

"And that, Inspector, is all I know about what happened Monday night," she resumed. "I know you're going to ask me where my purse comes into it. Well—it doesn't at all, Inspector. Because on my word of honor I can't remember a thing about it!"

Queen shifted in his chair. "And how is that, Miss Frances?"

"Actually, I didn't even know I had lost it until you showed it to me in the manager's office," she answered bravely. "I recall taking it with me when I rose at the end of the first act to go to the rest-room; and also opening it there to use my powder-puff. But whether I left it there or dropped it later, somewhere else, I don't know to this minute."

"Don't you think, Miss Frances," interposed Queen, reaching for his snuff-box and then guiltily dropping it back into his pocket as he met the icy gaze of Mrs. Ives-Pope, "that you might have dropped it in the alley after this man accosted you?"

A look of relief spread over the girl's face, and it became almost animated. "Why, Inspector!" she cried. "That was just what I have thought about it all the time, but it seemed such a lame explanation—and I was so horribly afraid that I might be caught in a sort of—of spider's web. . . . I just couldn't bring myself to tell you that! While I don't actually remember, it seems logical, doesn't it?—that I dropped it when he grasped my wrist and entirely forgot about it afterward."

The Inspector smiled. "On the contrary, my dear," he said, "it is the only explanation which seems to cover the facts. In all probability this man found it there—picked it up—and in a moment of half-drunken amorousness put it into his pocket, probably intending to return it to you later. In this way he would have had another opportunity to meet you. He seems to have been quite smitten by your charms, my dear—and no wonder." And the Inspector bowed a little stiffly while the girl, the color in her face now completely restored, favored him with a dazzling smile.

"Now—a few things more, Miss Frances, and this little inquisition will be over," continued Queen. "Can you describe his physical appearance?"

"Oh, yes!" Frances returned quickly. "He made a rather forcible impression on me, as you can imagine. He was a trifle taller than I—that would make him about five feet eight—and inclined to

The traditional statement made by the officiant after a Bible reading, according to the Book of Common Prayer.

corpulence. His face was bloated and he had deep leaden-colored pouches under his eyes. I've never seen a more dissipated-looking man. He was clean-shaven. There was nothing remarkable about his features except perhaps a prominent nose."

"That would be our friend Mr. Field, all right," remarked the Inspector grimly. "Now—think carefully, Miss Frances. Did you ever meet this man anywhere before—did you recognize him at all?"

The girl responded instantly. "I don't have to think much about that, Inspector. I can answer positively that I never saw the man before in my life!"

The pause which ensued was broken by the cool, even tones of Ellery. All heads turned toward him in a startled manner as he spoke.

"I beg your pardon, Miss Ives-Pope, for interrupting," he said affably. "But I am curious to know whether you noticed how the man who accosted you was dressed."

Frances turned her smile upon Ellery, who blinked quite humanly. "I didn't take particular notice of his clothes, Mr. Queen," she said, displaying white, brilliant teeth. "But I seem to remember his wearing a full-dress suit—his shirt-bosom was a little stained—they were like liquor-stains—and a tophat. From what I recall of his attire, it was rather fastidious and in good taste, except, of course, for the stains on his shirt."

Ellery murmured a fascinated thanks and subsided against the bookcase. With a sharp look at his son, Queen rose to his feet.

"Then that will be all, ladies and gentlemen. I think we may safely consider the incident closed."

There was an instantaneous little burst of approval and everybody rose to press in on Frances, who was radiant with happiness. Barry, Peale and Eve Ellis bore Frances off in triumphal march, while Stanford, with a lugubrious smile, offered his mother a carefully elbowed arm.

"Thus endeth the first lesson,"[67] he announced gravely. "Mater, my arm before you faint!" A protesting Mrs. Ives-Pope departed, leaning ponderously on her son.

Ives-Pope shook Queen's hand vigorously. "Then you think it's all over as far as my girl is concerned?" he asked.

"I think so, Mr. Ives-Pope," answered the Inspector. "Well, sir, thank you for your courtesy. And now we must be going—lots of work to do. Coming, Henry?"

Five minutes later Queen, Ellery and District Attorney Sampson were striding side by side down Riverside Drive toward 72nd Street, earnestly discussing the events of the morning.

"I'm glad that line of investigation is cleared up with no result," said Sampson dreamily. "By the Lord Harry, I admire that girl's pluck, Q!"

"Good child," said the Inspector. "What do you think, Ellery?" he asked suddenly, turning on his son, who was walking along staring at the River.

"Oh, she's charming," Ellery said at once, his abstracted eyes brightening.[68]

"I didn't mean the girl, my son," said his father irritably. "I meant the general aspect of the morning's work."

"Oh, that!" Ellery smiled a little. "Do you mind if I become Æsopian?"

"Yes," groaned his father.

"A lion," said Ellery, "may be beholden to a mouse."[69]

68. There is a faint suggestion in the introduction by J. J. McC. that Ellery met his wife in the course of "this affair." It is unlikely that McC. meant *The Roman Hat Mystery*. Ellery had only the slightest response to Ms. Frances Ives-Pope, and Ellery did not respond at all to Eve Ellis, the only other female of an appropriate age whom he met during the course of this affair.

69. The fable tells of a lion who spares the life of a mouse, only to later be saved by the mouse from entrapment in a net. Who is the mouse here—Ms. Ives-Pope?

CHAPTER XIII

Queen to Queen

70. Paracelsus, whose real name was Theophrastus von Hohenheim (1493 or 1494–1541), was a medieval scholar and physician, regarded as the father of toxicology.

Djuna had just cleared the table of the dinner dishes and was serving coffee to the two Queens at six-thirty that evening when the outer doorbell rang. The little man-of all-work straightened his tie, pulled down his jacket (while the Inspector and Ellery eyed him in twinkling amusement), and marched gravely into the foyer. He was back in a moment bearing a silver tray upon which lay two calling-cards. The Inspector picked them up with beetling brows.

"Such ceremony, Djuna!" he murmured. "Well, well! So 'Doc' Prouty's bringing a visitor. Show 'em in, you imp!"

Djuna marched back and returned with the Chief Assistant Medical Examiner and a tall, thin, emaciated man, entirely bald and wearing a closely clipped beard. Queen and Ellery rose.

"I've been expecting to hear from you, Doc!" Queen grinned, shaking hands with Prouty. "And if I'm not mistaken, here's Professor Jones himself! Welcome to our castle, Doctor." The thin man bowed.

"This is my son and keeper of my conscience, Doctor," Queen added, presenting Ellery. "Ellery—Dr. Thaddeus Jones."

Dr. Jones offered a large limp hand. "So you're the chap Queen and Sampson keep prattling about!" he boomed. "Certainly happy to meet you, sir."

"I've been fairly itching to be introduced to New York City's Paracelsus[70] and eminent Toxicologist," smiled Ellery. "The honor of rattling the City's skeletons is all yours." He shuddered elaborately and indicated some chairs. The four men sat down.

"Join us in some coffee, gentlemen," urged Queen, and shouted to Djuna, whose bright eyes were visible from behind the kitchenette door. "Djuna! You rascal! Coffee for four!" Djuna grinned and disappeared, to pop out a moment later like a jack-in-the-box, bearing four cups of steaming coffee.

Prouty, who resembled the popular conception of Mephistopheles, whipped from his pocket one of his black, dangerous looking cigars and began to puff away furiously.

"This chitter-chatter may be all right for you men of leisure," he said briskly, between puffs, "but I've been working like a beaver all day analyzing the contents of a lady's stomach, and I want to get home for some sleep."

"Hear, hear!" murmured Ellery, "I gather from your soliciting the aid of Professor Jones that you met with some obstruction in your analysis of Mr. Field's corporeal remains. Lay on, Æsculapius!"[71]

"I'll lay on," returned Prouty grimly. "You're right—I met with a violent obstruction. I've had some little experience, if you'll pardon the professional modesty, in examining the innards of deceased ladies and gentlemen, but I'll confess I never saw 'em in such a mess as this chap Field's. Seriously, Jones will attest to the truth of *that*. His æsophagus, for example, and the entire tracheal tract looked as if some one had taken a blow-torch and played it gently over his insides."

"What was it—couldn't have been bichloride of mercury, could it, Doc?"[72] asked Ellery, who prided himself on a complete ignorance of the exact sciences.

"Hardly," growled Prouty. "But let me tell you what happened. I analyzed for every poison on the calendar, and although this one had familiar petroleum components I couldn't place it exactly. Yes, sir—I was stumped good and proper. And to let you in on a secret—the Medical Examiner himself, who thought I was pie-eyed from overwork, made a stab at it with his own fine Italian hand.[73] The net result in his case, my boys, was zero. And the M. E.'s not exactly a novice either when it comes to chemical analysis. So we surrendered the problem to our fountain-head of learning. Let him spout his own story."

Dr. Thaddeus Jones cleared his throat forbiddingly. "Thank you, my friend, for a most dramatic introduction," he said in his

71. According to legend, Æsculapius was a son of Apollo and a god of medicine; his healing staff, the "rod of Æsculapius," is a common symbol of the healing arts.

72. Mercury bichloride was a popular poison of the day, readily available at pharmacies. It was routinely used for topical treatment of syphilis and, in highly diluted form, for tonsillitis. The poisonous aspects were well known: Mercury bichloride was implicated in the 1920 death of silent film star Olive Thomas, wife of leading man Jack Pickford, brother of Mary Pickford, who died from an "accidental" dose of mercury bichloride. The poison also featured in the 1925 death of Madge Oberholtzer, who had been kidnapped, tortured, and raped by the head of Indiana's powerful Ku Klux Klan. After writing a detailed accusation, Oberholtzer took her own life by swallowing mercury bichloride tablets to avoid further torture.

73. In fact, the Chief Medical Examiner of the City of New York from 1918 to 1935 was Charles V. Norris. *The Poisoner's Handbook*, note 23, is largely about Norris's campaign to advance the use of toxicology in criminal investigations.

deep lumbering voice. "Yes, Inspector, the remains were turned over to me, and in all seriousness, I want to say here and now that my discovery was the most startling the Toxicologist's office has made in fifteen years!"

"My, my!" murmured Queen, taking a pinch of snuff. "I'm beginning to respect the mentality of our friend the murderer. So many things point to the unusual lately! And what did you find, Doctor?"

"I took it for granted that Prouty and the Medical Examiner had done the preliminaries very well," began Dr. Jones, crossing his bony knees. "They generally do. And so, before anything else, I analyzed for the obscure poisons. Obscure, that is to say, from the standpoint of the criminal user. To show you how minutely I searched—I even thought of that favorite stand-by of our friends the fiction-writers: *curare*, the South American toxin which makes the grade in four out of five detective stories. But even that sadly abused member of the toxic family disappointed me. . . ."

Ellery leaned back and laughed. "If you're referring in a mildly satirical way to my profession, Dr. Jones, let me inform you that I have never used *curare* in any of my novels."

The toxicologist's eyes twinkled. "So you're one of them, too, eh? Queen, old man," he added dolorously, turning to the Inspector, who was thoughtfully chewing on a piece of French pastry, "allow me to offer you my condolences. . . . At any rate, gentlemen, let me explain that in the case of rare poisons we can generally come to a definite conclusion without much trouble—that is, rare poisons that are in the pharmacopœia. Of course, there are any number of rare poisons of which we have no knowledge whatever—Eastern drugs particularly.

"Well, to make a long story short, I found myself faced with the unpleasant conclusion that I was up a tree." Dr. Jones chuckled in reminiscence. "It wasn't a pleasant conclusion. The poison I analyzed had certain properties which were vaguely familiar, as Prouty has said, and others which didn't jibe at all. I spent most of yesterday evening mulling over my retorts and test-tubes, and late last night I suddenly got the answer."

Ellery and Queen sat up straight and Dr. Prouty relaxed in his chair with a sigh, reaching for a second cup of coffee. The toxicologist uncrossed his legs, his voice booming more terrifyingly than ever.

THE ROMAN HAT MYSTERY

"The poison that killed your victim, Inspector, is known as tetra ethyl lead!"[74]

To a scientist this announcement, in Dr. Jones's profoundest tones, might have carried a dramatic quality. To the Inspector it meant less than nothing. As for Ellery, he murmured, "Sounds like a mythological monster to me!"

Dr. Jones went on, smiling. "So it hasn't impressed you much, eh? But let me tell you a little about tetra ethyl lead. It is almost colorless—to be more exact, it resembles chloroform in physical appearance. Point number one. Point number two—it has an odor—faint, to be sure—but distinctly like that of ether. Point number three—it is fearfully potent. So potent—but let me illustrate just what this devilishly powerful chemical substance will do to living tissue."

By this time the toxicologist had gained the entire attention of his audience.

"I took a healthy rabbit, of the sort we use for experiment, and painted—just painted, mind you—the tender area behind the creature's ear with an undiluted dose of the stuff. Remember, this was not an internal injection. It was merely a painting of the skin. It would have to be absorbed through the dermis before it reached the blood-stream. I watched the rabbit for an hour—and after that I didn't have to watch him any more. He was as dead as any dead rabbit I ever saw."

"That doesn't seem so powerful to me, Doctor," protested the Inspector.

"It doesn't, eh? Well, take my word for it that it's extraordinary. For a mere daubing of whole, healthy skin—I tell you, I was astounded. If the skin had an incision of some sort, or if the poison were administered internally, that would be a different story. You can imagine, therefore, what happened to Field's insides when he *swallowed* the stuff—and he swallowed plenty!"

Ellery's brow was wrinkled in thought. He began to polish the lenses of his pince-nez.

"And that isn't all," resumed Dr. Jones. "As far as I know—and I have been in the service of the city for God knows how many years, and I've not kept uninformed about the progress of my science in other parts of the world, either—as far as I know, tetra ethyl lead has never before been used for criminal purposes!"

74.   Tetraethyl lead (TEL), for much of the twentieth century, was the chief antiknock agent for automotive gasoline. Beginning in the 1970s, as scientists learned that leaded gasoline interfered with catalytic converters, used to reduce smog, it was phased out. From its inception, TEL was recognized as a common source of lead poisoning, but it was not until a spate of deaths occurred in manufacturing plants of General Motors, Standard Oil, and Dupont in 1923–25 that strict safety procedures for the handling of TEL were introduced. The investigation was instigated by the New York City medical examiner Charles Norris and his toxicologist Alexander Gettler, the real "Dr. Thaddeus Jones." See *The Poisoner's Handbook*, note 23. Remaining concerns about the introduction of lead into the atmosphere have led to a nearly-universal ban on the use of leaded fuels in road vehicles, though they are still used in aviation.

The Inspector drew up, startled. "That's saying something, Doctor!" he muttered. "Are you sure?"

"Positive. That's why I'm so keenly interested."

"Just how long would it take for this poison to kill a man, Doctor?" asked Ellery slowly.

Dr. Jones grimaced. "That's something I can't answer definitely, for the very good reason that to my knowledge no human being has ever died of its effects before. But I can make a fairly good guess. I can't conceive of Field having lived more than from fifteen to twenty minutes at the utmost after having taken the poison internally."

The silence that followed was broken by a cough from Queen. "On the other hand, Doctor, this very strangeness of the poison should make it fairly easy to trace. What, would you say, is its commonest source? Where does it come from? How would I go about getting it if I wanted some for a criminal purpose and didn't want to leave a trail?"

A gaunt smile lit up the features of the toxicologist. "The job of tracing this stuff, Inspector," he said fervently, "I'll leave to you. You can have it. Tetra ethyl lead, as far as I've been able to determine—remember, it is almost entirely new to us—occurs most commonly in certain petroleum products, I tinkered around quite a bit before I found the easiest way of making it in quantity. You'll never guess how it's done. It can be extracted from common, ordinary, everyday gasoline!"

The two Queens exclaimed under their breaths. "Gasoline!" cried the Inspector, "Why—how on earth could a man trace that?"

"That's the point," answered the toxicologist. "I could go to the corner gas-station, fill up the tank of my car, run it home, extract some of the gasoline from the tank, go into my laboratory and distill the tetra ethyl lead in remarkably little time with remarkably little effort!"

"Doesn't that imply, Doctor," put in Ellery hopefully, "that the murderer of Field had some laboratory experience—knew something about chemical analysis, and all that sort of rot?"

"No, it doesn't. Any man with a home-brew 'still' in his house could distill that poison without leaving a trace. The beauty of the process is that the tetra ethyl lead in the gasoline has a higher boiling-point than any other of the fluid's constituents. All you have to do is distill everything out up to a certain temperature, and what's left is this poison."

The Inspector took a pinch of snuff with trembling fingers. "All I can say is—I take my hat off to the murderer," he muttered. "Tell me—Doctor—wouldn't a man have to know quite a bit about toxicology to possess such knowledge? How could he ever know this without some special interest—and therefore training—in the subject?"

Dr. Jones snorted. "Inspector, I'm surprised at you. Your question is already answered."

"How? What do you mean?"

"Haven't I just told you how to do it? And if you heard about the poison from a toxicologist, couldn't you make some provided you had the 'still'? You would require no knowledge except the boiling-point of tetra ethyl lead. Get along with you, Queen! You haven't a chance in the world of tracing the murderer through the poison. In all probability he overheard a conversation between two toxicologists, or even between two medical men who had heard about the stuff. The rest was easy. I'm not saying this is so. The man might be a chemist, at that. But I'm concerned only in giving you the possibilities."

"I suppose it was administered in whisky, eh, Doctor?" asked Queen abstractedly.

"No doubt about it," returned the toxicologist. "The stomach showed a large whisky content. Certainly, it would be an easy way for the murderer to slip it over on his victim. With the whisky you get nowadays, most of it smells etherized, anyway. And besides, Field probably had it down before he realized anything was wrong—if he did at all."

"Wouldn't he taste the stuff?" asked Ellery wearily.

"I've never tasted it, young man, so I can't say definitely," answered Dr. Jones, a trifle tartly. "But I doubt whether he would—sufficiently to alarm him, at any rate. Once he had it down it wouldn't make any difference."

Queen turned to Prouty, whose cigar had gone out. He had fallen into a hearty doze. "Say, Doc!"

Prouty opened his eyes sleepily. "Where are my slippers—I can't ever seem to find my slippers, damn it!"

Despite the tension of the moment, there was a spontaneous roar of amusement at the expense of the Assistant Medical

75. W. Francis H. King's *Classical and Foreign Quotations* (1889) explains the Latin motto drawn from Pliny, *Ne supra crepidam sutor judicaret* (literally, "do not judge above the sandal"): "When a cobbler, not content with pointing out defects in a shoe of Apelles' painting, presumed to criticise the drawing of the leg, the artist checked him with the rebuke here quoted. It is often said of those who offer opinions on subjects with which they are not professionally acquainted." Ellery here reminds himself to write *only* what he knows.

Examiner. When he had come to with sufficient thoroughness to understand what he had said, he joined the chuckling group and said, "Just goes to prove that I'd better be going home, Queen. What did you want to know?"

"Tell me," said Queen, still shaking, "what did you get from your analysis of the whisky?"

"Oh!" Prouty sobered instantly. "The whisky in the flask was as fine as any I've ever tested—and I've been doing nothing but testing booze for years now. It was the poison in the liquor on his breath that made me think at first that Field had drunk rotten booze. The Scotch and rye that you sent me in bottles from Field's apartment were also of the very highest quality. Probably the flask's contents came from the same place as the bottled stuff. In fact, I should say that both samples were imported goods. I haven't come across domestic liquor of that calibre ever since the War—that is, except for the pre-War stuff that was stored away. . . . And I suppose Velie communicated my report to you that the ginger ale is okay."

Queen nodded. 'Well, that seems to settle it," he said heavily. "It looks as if we're up against a blank wall on this tetra ethyl lead business. But just to make sure, Doc—work along with the professor here and try to locate a possible leak somewhere in the distribution of the poison. You fellows know more about that than anybody I could put on the case. It's just a stab in the dark and probably nothing will come of it."

"There's no question about it," murmured Ellery. "A novelist should stick to his last."[75]

⌒∞⌒

"I think," remarked Ellery eagerly, after the two doctors had gone, "that I'll amble down to my bookseller for that Falconer." He rose and began a hasty search for his coat.

"Here!" bellowed the Inspector, pulling him down into a chair. "Nothing doing. That blasted book of yours won't run away. I want you to sit here and keep my headache company."

Ellery nestled into the leather cushions with a sigh. "Just when I get to feeling that all investigations into the foibles of the human mind are useless and a waste of time, my worthy sire puts the onus of thought upon me again. Heigh-ho! What's on the menu?"

"I'm not putting any onus on you at all," growled Queen. "And stop using such big words. I'm dizzy enough. What I want you to do is help me go over this confounded mess of a case and see—well, what we can see."

"I might have suspected it," said Ellery. "Where do I start?"

"You don't," grunted his father. "I'm doing the talking to-night and you're going to listen. And you might make a few notes, too.

"Let's begin with Field. I think, in the first place, that we can take it for granted our friend went to the Roman Theatre Monday night not for pleasure but for business. Right?"

"No doubt about it in my mind," said Ellery. "What did Velie report about Field's movements Monday?"

"Field got to his office at 9:30—his usual morning arrival-hour. He worked until noon. He had no personal visitors all day. At twelve o'clock he lunched at the Webster Club alone, and at 1:30 returned to his office. He worked steadily until 4:00—and seems to have gone straight home, as the doorman and elevator-man both testify he arrived at the apartment about 4:30. Velie could get no further data except that Michaels arrived at 5:00 and left at 6:00. Field left at 7:30, dressed as we found him. I have a list of the clients whom he saw during the day, but it doesn't tell much."

"How about the reason for his small bank account?" asked Ellery.

"Just what I figured," returned Queen. "Field has been losing steadily on the stock market—and not chicken feed, either. Velie's just run a little tip to earth which makes Field out as a frequent visitor to the racetrack, where he's also dropped plenty. For a shrewd man, he certainly was an easy-mark for the wiseacres. Anyway, that explains his having so little cash in his personal account. And more than that—it probably also explains more conclusively the item of '50,000' on the program we found. That meant money, and the money it referred to was in some way connected, I'm sure, with the person he was to meet at the theatre.

"Now, I think that we can pretty well conclude that Field knew his murderer rather intimately. For one thing, he accepted a drink obviously without suspicion, or at least question; for another, the meeting seems to have been definitely arranged for purposes of concealment—why, else, if that is not so, was the theatre chosen for the meeting at all?"

"All right. Let me ask you the same question," interposed Ellery, puckering his lips. "Why *should* a theatre be chosen as a meeting-place to transact a secret and undoubtedly nefarious business? Wouldn't a park be more secret? Wouldn't a hotel lobby have its advantages? Answer that."

"Unfortunately, my son," said the Inspector mildly, "Mr. Field could have had no definite knowledge that he was going to be murdered. As far as he was concerned, all he was going to do was to take care of his part of the transaction. As a matter of fact, Field *himself* might have chosen the theatre as the place of meeting. Perhaps he wanted to establish an alibi for something. There's no way of telling yet just what he wanted to do. As for the hotel lobby—certainly he would run a grave risk of being seen. He might have been unwilling, further, to risk himself in such a lonely place as a park. And, lastly, he may have had some particular reason for not wanting to be seen in the company of the second party. Remember—the ticket-stubs we found showed that the other person did not come into the theatre at the same time as Field. But this is all fruitless conjecture—"

Ellery smiled in a thoughtful manner, but said nothing. He was thinking to himself that the old man had not completely satisfied the objection, and that this was a strange thing in a man of Inspector Queen's direct habits of thought. . . .

But Queen was continuing. "Very well. We must always bear in mind the further possibility that the person with whom Field transacted his business was *not* his murderer. Of course, this is merely a possibility. The crime seems to have been too well planned for that. But if this *is* so, then we must look for *two* people in the audience Monday night who were directly connected with Field's death."

"Morgan?" asked Ellery idly.

The Inspector shrugged his shoulders. "Perhaps. Why didn't he tell us about it when we spoke to him yesterday afternoon? He confessed everything else. Well, maybe because he felt that a confession of having paid blackmail to the murdered man, together with the fact that he was found in the theatre, would be too damning a bit of circumstantial evidence."

"Look at it this way," said Ellery. "Here we find a man dead who has written on his program the number '50,000,' obviously referring to dollars. We know from what both Sampson and Cronin have told us about Field that he was a man of unscrupulous and probably criminal character. Further, we know from Morgan that he was also a blackmailer. I think, therefore, we can deduce safely that he went to the Roman Theatre on Monday night to collect or arrange for the payment of $50,000 in blackmail from some person unknown. Right so far?"

"Go ahead," grunted the Inspector noncommittally.

"Very well," continued Ellery. "If we conclude that the person blackmailed that night and the murderer were one and the same, we need look no further for a motive. There's the motive ready made—to choke off the blackmailing Field. *If*, however, we proceed on the assumption that the murderer and the person blackmailed were not the same, but two entirely different individuals, *then* we must still scrabble about looking for a motive for the crime. My personal opinion is that this is unnecessary—that the murderer and the blackmailed person are one. What do you think?"

"I'm inclined to agree with you, Ellery," said the Inspector. "I merely mentioned the other possibility—did not state my own conviction. Let us proceed, for the time being, then, on the assumption that Field's blackmail victim and his murderer were the same. . . ."

"Now—I want to clear up the matter of the missing tickets."

"Ah—the missing tickets," murmured Ellery. "I was wondering what you made of that."

"Don't be funny, now, you rascal," growled Queen. "Here's what I make of it. All in all, we are dealing with eight seats—one in which Field sat, for which we have the stub found on Field's person; one in which the murderer sat, for which we have the stub found by Flint; and finally the six empty seats for which tickets were bought, as established by the box-office report, and for which stubs were not found, torn or whole, anywhere in the theatre or box-office. First of all, it is barely possible that all of those six whole tickets were in the theatre Monday night, and went out of the theatre on somebody's person. Remember, the search of individuals was necessarily not so exhaustive as to include an examination for small things like tickets. This, however, is highly improbable. The best explanation is that either Field or his murderer bought all eight tickets at one time, intending to use two and reserving the other six to insure absolute privacy during the short time that the business was to be transacted. In this case, the most sensible thing to have done was to destroy the tickets as soon as they were bought; which was probably done by either Field or the murderer, according to who made the arrangements. We must, therefore, forget those six tickets—they're gone and we'll never get our hands on them.

"To proceed," continued the Inspector. "We know that Field and his victim entered the theatre separately. This may positively be deduced from the fact that when I put the two stubs back to front, the torn edges did not match. When two people enter together, the tickets are presented together and are invariably torn together. Now—this does not say that they did not come in at practically the same time, because for purposes of safety they may have come in one after the other, as if they did not know each other. However, Madge O'Connell claims no one sat in LL30 during Act I, and the orangeade-boy, Jess Lynch, testified that ten minutes after Act II had started, there was still no one in LL30. This means that the murderer either had not yet entered the theatre, or he had come in before but was sitting in some other part of the orchestra, having a ticket necessarily for another seat."

Ellery shook his head. "I realize that as well as you, son," said the old man testily. 'I'm just following the thought through. I was going to say that it doesn't seem likely the murderer had come into the theatre at the regular time. It's probable that he entered at least ten minutes after the second act started."

"I can give you a proof of that," said Ellery lazily.

The Inspector took a pinch of snuff. "I know—those cabalistic figures on the program. How did they read?

930

815

50,000

"We know what the fifty-thousand represented. The other two figures must have referred not to dollars, but to time. Look at the '815.' The play started at 8:25. In all likelihood Field arrived about 8:15, or if he arrived sooner, he had some cause to refer to his watch at that time. Now, if he had an appointment with some one who, we assume, arrived much later, what more likely than that Field should have idly jotted down on his program—first, the '50,000,' which indicates that he was thinking about the impending transaction, which involved $50,000 in blackmail; then 8:15, the time he was thinking about it; and finally 9:30—the time the blackmail victim was due to arrive! It's the most natural thing in the world for Field to have done this, as it would be for any one who is in the habit of scribbling in idle moments. It's very fortunate for us, because it points to two things: first, to the exact time of the appointment with the murderer—9:30; and, second, it corroborates our conjecture as regards the actual time the murder was committed. At 9:25 Lynch saw Field alive and alone; at 9:30, by Field's written evidence, the murderer was due to arrive, and we take it for granted he did; according to Dr. Jones' statement it would take the poison from fifteen to twenty minutes to kill Field—and in view of Pusak's discovery at 9:55 of the dead body, we may say that the poison was administered about 9:35. If the tetra ethyl lead took at the most twenty minutes—that gives us 9:55. Much before then, of course, the murderer left the scene of the crime. Remember—he could not have known that our friend Mr. Pusak would suddenly desire to rise and leave his seat. The murderer was probably figuring that Field's body would not be discovered until the intermission, at 10:05, which would have been ample time for Field to have died without being able to murmur any message at all. Luckily for our mysterious murderer Field was discovered too late to gasp more than the information that he'd been murdered. If Pusak had walked out five minutes earlier we'd have our elusive friend behind the bars right now."

"Bravo!" murmured Ellery, smiling affectionately. "A perfect recitation. My congratulations."

"Oh, go jump in the bath-tub," growled his father. "At this point I just want to repeat what you brought out Monday night in Panzer's office—the fact that although the murderer quitted the scene of the crime between 9:30 and 9:55, he was present in the theatre all the rest of the evening until we allowed everybody to go home. Your examination of the guards and the O'Connell girl, together with the doorman's evidence, Jess Lynch's presence in the alley, the usher's corroboration of this fact and all the rest of it, takes care of that. . . . He was there, all right.

"This leaves us momentarily up a tree. All we can do now is consider some of the personalities we've bumped into in the course of the investigation," went on the Inspector with a sigh. "First—did Madge O'Connell tell the truth when she said she had seen no one pass up or down the aisle during the second act? And that she had not seen, at any time during the evening at all, the person who we know sat in LL30 from half-past nine until ten or fifteen minutes before the body was discovered?"

"It's a tricky question, dad," remarked Ellery seriously, "because if she *was* lying about these things, we are losing a mine of information. If she was lying—good Lord!—she might be in a position at this moment either to describe, or identify, or possibly name the murderer! However, her nervousness and peculiar attitude might be ascribed to her knowledge that Parson Johnny was in the theatre, with a pack of policemen just aching to get their fingers on him."

"Sounds reasonable to me," grumbled Queen. "Well, what about Parson Johnny? How does he fit into this—or does he fit into it at all? We must always remember that, according to Morgan's statement, Cazzanelli was actively associated with Field. Field had been his lawyer, and perhaps had even bought the Parson's services for this shady business Cronin is nosing around about. If the Parson was not there by accident, was he there through Field or through Madge O'Connell, as she and he both say? I think, my son," he added with a fierce tug at his mustache, "that I'm going to give Parson Johnny a taste of the lash—it won't hurt his thick hide! And that snippy little O'Connell chit—won't do any harm to scare the wits out of her either. . . ."

He took an enormous pinch of snuff, sneezing to the tune of Ellery's sympathetic chuckles.

"And dear old Benjamin Morgan," continued the Inspector, "was he telling the truth about the anonymous letter which so conveniently gave him a mysterious source for his theatre ticket?

"And that most interesting lady, Mrs. Angela Russo . . . Ah, the ladies, bless 'em! They always muddle a man's logic so. What did she say—that she came to Field's apartment at 9:30? Is her alibi perfectly sound? Of course, the doorman at the apartment house confirmed her statement. But it's easy to 'fix' doormen. . . . Does she know more than she had indicated about Field's business—particularly his private business? Was she lying when she said that Field told her he would be back at ten o'clock? Remember, we know that Field had an appointment in the Roman Theatre beginning at 9:30—did he really expect to keep it and be back at his rooms by ten o'clock? By cab it would be a fifteen or twenty-minute drive, through traffic, which would leave only ten minutes for the transaction—possible, of course. Couldn't do it much sooner by subway, either. We mustn't forget, too, that this woman was not in the theatre at any time during the evening."

"You'll have your hands full with that fair flower of Eve," remarked Ellery. "It's so beautifully evident that she's keeping back a story of some sort. Did you notice that brazen defiance? Wasn't mere bravado. She knows something, dad. I would certainly keep my eye on her—sooner or later she'll give herself away."

"Hagstrom will take care of her," said Queen abstractedly. "Now, how about Michaels? He has no supported alibi for Monday evening. But then it might not make any difference. He wasn't in the theatre. . . . There's something fishy about that fellow. Was he really looking for something when he came to Field's apartment Tuesday morning? We've made a thorough search of the premises—is it possible we've overlooked something? It's quite evident that he was lying when he spilled that story about the check, and not knowing that Field was dead. And consider this—he must have realized that he was running into danger in coming to Field's rooms. He'd read about the murder and couldn't have hoped that the police would delay going to the place. So he was taking a desperate chance—for what reason? Answer that one!"

"It might have had something to do with his imprisonment—by George, he looked surprised when I accused him, didn't he?" chuckled Ellery.

"Might at that," returned the Inspector. "By the way, I've heard from Velie about Michaels' term up in Elmira. Thomas reports that it was a hushed-up case—much more serious than the light sentence in the Reformatory indicates. Michaels was suspected of forgery—and it looked mighty black for him. Then Lawyer Field nicely got Mr. Michaels off on an entirely different count—something to do with petty larceny—and nothing was ever heard about the forgery business again. This boy Michaels looks like the real thing—have to step on his heels a bit."

"I have a little idea of my own about Michaels," said Ellery thoughtfully. "But let it go for the present."

Queen seemed not to hear. He stared into the fire roaring in the stone fireplace. "There's Lewin, too," he said. "Seems incredible that a man of Lewin's stamp should have been so confidentially associated with his employer without knowing a good deal more than he professes. Is he keeping something back? If he is, heaven help him—because Cronin will just about pulverize him!"

"I rather like that chap Cronin," sighed Ellery. "How on earth can a fellow be so set on one idea? . . . Has this occurred to you? I wonder if Morgan knows Angela Russo? Despite the fact that both of them deny a mutual acquaintance. Would be deucedly interesting if they did, wouldn't it?"

"My son," groaned Queen, "don't go looking for trouble. We've a peck of it now without going out of our way for more. . . . By jingo!"

There was a comfortable silence as the Inspector sprawled in the light of the leaping flames. Ellery munched contentedly on a succulent piece of pastry. Djuna's bright eyes gleamed from the far corner of the room, where he had stolen noiselessly and squatted on his thin haunches on the floor, listening to the conversation.

Suddenly the old man's eyes met Ellery's in a spasmodic transference of thought.

"The hat . . ." muttered Queen. "We always come back to the hat."

Ellery's glance was troubled. "And not a bad thing to come back to, dad. Hat—hat—hat! Where does it fit in? Just what do we know about it?"

The Inspector shifted in his chair. He crossed his legs, took another pinch of snuff and proceeded with a fresh vigor. "All right. We can't afford to be lazy in the matter of that blamed silk-topper," he said briskly. "What do we know so far? First, that the hat did not leave the theatre. It seems funny, doesn't it? Doesn't seem possible that we would find no trace at all after such a thorough search. . . . Nothing was left in the cloak-room after everybody was gone; nothing was found in the sweepings that might indicate a hat torn to small pieces or bunched; in fact, not a trace, not a thing for us to go on. Therefore, Ellery, the only sensible conclusion we can make at this point is that we haven't looked for the hat in the right place! And further, wherever it is, it's still there, due to our precaution of closing the theatre down since Monday night. Ellery, we've got to go back to-morrow morning and turn that place upside down. I won't sleep until we see light somewhere in this matter."

Ellery was silent. "I'm not at all satisfied with things as you've stated them, dad," he muttered at last. "Hat—hat—there's something wrong somewhere!" He fell silent once more. "No! The hat is the focal point of this investigation—I cannot see any other way out of it. Solve the mystery of Field's hat and you will find the one essential clue that will point to the murderer. I'm so convinced of this that I'll be satisfied we're on the right track only when we're making progress in the explanation of the hat."

The old man nodded his head vigorously. "Ever since yesterday morning, when I had time to think over the hat business, I've felt that we had gone astray somewhere. And here it is Wednesday night—still no light. We've done necessary things—they've led nowhere. . . ." He stared into the fire. "Everything is so badly muddled. I've got all the loose ends at my fingertips, but for some blasted reason I can't seem to make them cohere—fit together—*explain* anything. . . . Undoubtedly, son, what is missing is the story of the top-piece."

The telephone bell rang. The Inspector sprang for the instrument. He listened attentively to a man's unhurried tones, made a brisk comment and finally hung up.

"Who's the latest midnight babbler, O recipient of many confidences?" asked Ellery, grinning.

"That was Edmund Crewe," said Queen. "You remember I asked him yesterday morning to go over the Roman. He spent all of yesterday and to-day at it. And he reports positively that there is no secret hiding-place anywhere on the premises of the theatre. If Eddie Crewe, who is about the last word in architectural matters of this kind, says there's no hiding-place there, you may rest assured it's so."

He jumped to his feet and espied Djuna squatting on his hams in the corner. "Djuna! Get the old bed ready," he roared. Djuna slipped through the room and disappeared with a silent grin. Queen wheeled on Ellery, who had already taken off his coat and was fumbling with his tie.

"The first thing we do to-morrow morning is go down to the Roman Theatre and start all over again!" the old man said decisively. "And let me tell you, son—I'm through fooling around! Somebody'd better watch out!"

Ellery affectionately encircled his father's shoulders with one great arm. "Come on to bed, you old fraud!" he laughed.

⟨⟨ PART THREE ⟩⟩

"A good detective is born, not made. Like all genius, he springs not from a carefully nurtured polizei but from all mankind. The most amazing detective I ever knew was a dirty old witch-doctor who had never been out of the bush. . . . It is the peculiar gift of the truly great detective that he can apply to the inexorable rules of logic three catalyzers: an abnormal observation of events, a knowledge of the human mind and an insight into the human heart.

—From *The Man-Hunter's Manual*
by James Redix (the Younger).

CHAPTER XIV

In Which the Hat Grows

On Thursday, September 27th, the third morning after the events of the crime in the Roman Theatre, Inspector Queen and Ellery rose at an early hour and dressed hastily. They repaired to a makeshift breakfast under the protesting eye of Djuna, who had been pulled bodily from his bed and thrust into the sober habiliments which he affected as majordomo of the Queen menage.

While they were munching at anemic pancakes, the old man asked Djuna to get Louis Panzer on the telephone. In a few moments the Inspector was speaking genially into the mouthpiece. "Good morning, Panzer. Please forgive me for hauling you out of bed at this ungodly time of the morning. . . . There's something important in the wind and we need your help."

Panzer murmured a sleepy reassurance.

"Can you come down to the Roman Theatre right away and open it for us?" went on the old man. "I told you that you wouldn't be shut down very long and now it looks as if you'll be able to cash in on the publicity the affair has been getting. I'm not sure when we can reopen, you understand, but it's barely possible that you'll be able to put your show on to-night. Can I count on you?"

"This is excellent!" Panzer's voice came over the wire in a tremulous eagerness. "Do you want me to come down to the theatre at once? I'll be there in a half-hour—I'm not dressed."

"That will be fine," returned Queen. "Of course, Panzer—no one is to be allowed inside yet. Wait for us on the sidewalk before you use your keys and don't notify any one, either. We'll talk it all over at the theatre . . . Just a moment."

He clamped the mouthpiece against his chest and looked up inquiringly at Ellery, who was gesturing frantically. Ellery formed his lips around the syllables of a name and the old man nodded approvingly. He spoke into the telephone again.

"There's one other thing you can do for me at present, Panzer," he continued. "Can you get hold of that nice old lady, Mrs. Phillips? I'd like to have her meet us at the theatre as soon as she can."

"Certainly, Inspector. If it's at all possible," said Panzer, Queen replaced the receiver on its hook.

"Well, that's that," he remarked, rubbing his hands together and delving into his pocket for the snuff-box. "Ah-h-h! Bless Sir Walter and all those hardy pioneers who championed the cause of the filthy weed!" He sneezed joyously. "One minute, Ellery, then we'll go."

He picked up the telephone once more and called detective headquarters. He gave a few cheery orders, banged the instrument back on the table and hustled Ellery into his coat. Djuna watched them leave with a mournful expression: he had often pleaded with the Inspector to be allowed to accompany the Queens on their sporadic excursions into the byways of New York. The Inspector, who had his own ideas on the subject of rearing adolescents, invariably refused. And Djuna, who regarded his patron much as the Stone-Age man regarded his amulets, accepted the inevitable and hoped for a more auspicious future.

It was a raw, wet day. Ellery and his father turned up their coat-collars as they walked towards Broadway and the subway. Both were extraordinarily taciturn, but the keen anticipatory looks on their faces—so curiously alike and yet so different—portended an exciting and revealing day.

⚬∞⚬

Broadway and its threaded canyons were deserted in the chill wind of the morning as the two men walked briskly down 47th Street towards the Roman Theatre. A drab-coated man lounged on the sidewalk before the closed glass doors of the lobby; another leaned comfortably against the high iron fence which cut off the left alley from the street. The dumpy form of Louis Panzer was visible standing before the central door of the theatre, in conversation with Flint.

Panzer shook hands excitedly. "Well, well!" he cried. "So the ban is to be lifted at last! . . . Exceedingly happy to hear that, Inspector."

"Oh, it isn't exactly lifted, Panzer," smiled the old man. "Have you the keys? Morning, Flint. Rest up any since Monday night?"

Panzer produced a heavy bunch of keys and unlocked the central door of the lobby. The four men filed in. The swarthy manager fumbled with the lock of the inside door and finally managed to swing it open. The dark interior of the orchestra yawned in their faces.

Ellery shivered. "With the possible exceptions of the Metropolitan Opera House and Titus' Tomb, this is the most dismal theatorium I've ever entered. It's a fitting mausoleum for the dear departed. . . ."

The more prosaic Inspector grunted as he pushed his son into the maw of the dark orchestra. "Get along with you! You'll be giving us all the 'willies.'"[76]

Panzer, who had hurried ahead, turned on the main electric switch. The auditorium leaped into more familiar outlines by the light of the big arcs and chandeliers. Ellery's fanciful comparison was not so fantastic as his father had made it appear. The long rows of seats were draped with dirty tarpaulin; murky shadows streaked across the carpets, already dusty; the bare whitewashed wall at the rear of the empty stage made an ugly splotch in the sea of red plush.

"Sorry to see that tarpaulin there," grumbled the Inspector to Panzer. "Because it will have to be rolled up. We're going to conduct a little personal search of the orchestra. Flint, get those two men outside, please. They may as well do something to earn the city's money."

Flint sped away and returned shortly with the two detectives who had been on guard outside the theatre. Under the Inspector's direction they began to haul the huge sheets of rubberized seat-covers to the sides, disclosing rows of cushioned chairs. Ellery, standing to one side near the extreme left aisle, withdrew from his pocket the little book in which he had scribbled notes and drawn a rough map of the theatre on Monday night. He was studying

76. First recorded in 1896 in the sense of nervousness. The origin of the phrase is obscure, perhaps drawn from the itching sensation caused by "woolies," long underwear.

this and biting his underlip. Occasionally he looked up as if to verify the lay-out of the theatre.

Queen bustled back to where Panzer was nervously pacing the rear. "Panzer, we're going to be mighty busy here for a couple of hours and I was too short-sighted to bring extra men with me. I wonder if I may impose upon you. . . . I have something in mind that requires immediate attention—it would take only a small part of your time and it would help me considerably."

"Of course, Inspector!" returned the little manager. "I'm only too glad to be of assistance."

The Inspector coughed. "Please don't feel that I'm using you as an errand-boy or anything like that, old man," he explained apologetically. "But I need these fellows, who are trained in searches of this kind—and at the same time I must have some vital data from a couple of the District Attorney's men who are working downtown on another aspect of the case. Would you mind taking a note for me to one of them—name of Cronin—and bring back the parcel he gives you? I hate to ask you to do this, Panzer," he muttered. "But it's too important to trust to an ordinary messenger, and—ding it all! I'm in a hole."

Panzer smiled in his quick birdlike fashion. "Not another word, Inspector. I'm entirely at your service. I've the materials in my office if you care to write the note now."

The two men retired to Panzer's office. Five minutes later they reëntered the auditorium. Panzer held a sealed envelope in his hand and hurried out into the street. Queen watched him go, then turned with a sigh to Ellery, who had perched himself on the arm of the seat in which Field had been murdered and was still consulting the penciled map.

The Inspector whispered a few words to his son. Ellery smiled and clapped the old man vigorously on the back.

"What do you say we get a move on, son?" said Queen. "I forgot to ask Panzer if he had succeeded in reaching this Mrs. Phillips. I guess he did, though, or he would have said something about it. Where in thunder is she?"

He beckoned to Flint, who was helping the other two detectives in the back-breaking task of removing the tarpaulin.

"I've one of those popular bending-exercises for you this morning, Flint. Go up to the balcony and get busy."

"What am I supposed to be looking for to-day, Inspector?" grinned the broad-shouldered detective. "Because I hope I have better luck than I did Monday night."

"You're looking for a hat—a nice, shiny top-piece such as the swells wear, my boy," announced the Inspector. "But if you should come across anything else, use your lungs!" Flint trotted up the wide marble staircase towards the balcony. Queen looked after him, shaking his head. "I'm afraid the poor lad is doomed to another disappointment," he remarked to Ellery. "But I must make absolutely certain that there's nothing up there—and that the usher Miller who was guarding the balcony staircase Monday night was telling the truth. Come along, lazy-bones . . ."

Ellery shed his topcoat reluctantly and tucked the little book away in his pocket. The Inspector wriggled out of his ulster and preceded his son down the aisle. Working side by side they began to search the orchestra-pit at the extreme end of the auditorium. Finding nothing there, they clambered out into the orchestra again and, Ellery taking the right side and his father the left, began a slow, methodical combing of the theatre-premises. They lifted the seats; probed experimentally into the plush cushions with long needles which the Inspector had produced mysteriously from his breast-pocket; and kneeled to examine every inch of the carpet by the light of electric torches.

The two detectives who had by now completed the task of rolling up the tarpaulin began, on the Inspector's brief command, to work through the boxes, a man to each side of the theatre.

For a long time the four men proceeded in silence, unbroken except for the somewhat labored breathing of Inspector Queen. Ellery was working swiftly and efficiently, the old man more slowly. As they met near the center after completing the search of a row, they would regard each other significantly, shake their heads and continue afresh.

About twenty minutes after Panzer's departure the Inspector and Ellery, absorbed in their examination, were startled by the ringing of a telephone bell. In the silence of the theatre the clear trill of the bell rang out with astonishing sharpness. Father and son looked at each other blankly for an instant, then the old man laughed and plodded up the aisle in the direction of Panzer's office.

He returned shortly, smiling. "It was Panzer," he announced. "Got down to Field's office and found the place closed. No

77.   "Au fai" literally means "to the fact" and usually connotes familiarity or expertise—that is, here, Inspector Queen has done this kind of work before. However, typical of Ellery, this is a somewhat stilted way to express that thought.

wonder—it's only a quarter of nine. But I told him to wait there until Cronin comes. It can't be long now."

Ellery laughed and they set to work again.

Fifteen minutes later, when the two men were almost finished, the front door opened and a small elderly woman dressed in black stood blinking in the brilliant arc-lights. The Inspector sprang forward to meet her.

"You're Mrs. Phillips, aren't you?" he cried warmly. "It's mighty nice of you to come so soon, madam. I think you know Mr. Queen here?"

Ellery came forward, smiling one of his rare smiles and bowing with genuine gallantry. Mrs. Phillips was representative of a lovable old womanhood. She was short and of motherly proportions. Her gleaming white hair and air of kindliness endeared her immediately to Inspector Queen, who had a sentimental weakness for middle-aged ladies of presence.

"I certainly do know Mr. Queen," she said, extending her hand. "He was very nice to an old woman Monday night. . . . And I was so afraid you'd have to wait for me, sir!" she said softly, turning to the Inspector. "Mr. Panzer sent a messenger for me this morning—I haven't a telephone, you see. There was a time, when I was on the stage. . . . I came just as soon as I could."

The Inspector beamed. "For a lady it was remarkably prompt, *remarkably* prompt, Mrs. Phillips!"

"My father kissed the Blarney Stone several centuries ago, Mrs. Phillips," said Ellery gravely. "Don't believe a word ov 'im. . . . I suppose it will be *au fait*[77] if I leave you to tackle the rest of the orchestra, dad? I'd like to have a little chat with Mrs. Phillips. Do you think you're physically able to complete the job alone?"

"Physically able—!" snorted the Inspector. "You plump right down that aisle and go about your business, son. . . . I should appreciate your giving Mr. Queen all the help you can, Mrs. Phillips."

The white-haired lady smiled and Ellery, taking her arm, led her off in the direction of the stage. Inspector Queen, looking after them wistfully, shrugged his shoulders after a moment and turned back to resume the search. A short time later, when he chanced to straighten up, he espied Ellery and Mrs. Phillips seated on the stage conversing earnestly, like two players rehearsing their rôles. Queen proceeded slowly up and down the rows, weaving in and out among the empty seats, shaking his head dolefully as he approached the last few rows still empty-handed. When he looked up again the two chairs on the stage held no occupants. Ellery and the old lady had disappeared.

Queen came at last to LL32 Left—the seat in which Monte Field had died. He made a painstaking examination of the cushions, a light of resignation in his eyes. Muttering to himself he walked slowly across the carpet at the rear of the theatre and entered Panzer's office. A few moments later he reappeared, only to make his way to the cubicle which was used as an office by the publicity man, Harry Neilson. He was in this compartment for some time. He came out and visited the cashiers' offices. Shutting the door behind him when he had finished, he wended his way down the steps on the right of the theatre leading to the general lounge, on the floor below the orchestra. Here he took his time, delving into every corner, every niche in the wall, every waste-container—all of which he found to be empty. He speculatively eyed the large bin standing directly under the water-fountain. He peered into this receptacle and pottered away, finding nothing. Thereupon with a sigh he opened the door on which was gilt-lettered, LADIES' REST ROOM, and went inside. A few moments later he reappeared to push his way through the swinging-doors marked GENTLEMEN.

When his meticulous search of the lower floor was completed he trudged up the steps again. In the orchestra he found Louis Panzer waiting, slightly flushed from his exertions but displaying a triumphant smile. The little manager was carrying a small parcel wrapped in brown paper.

"So you saw Cronin after all, Panzer?" said the Inspector, scurrying forward. "This is mighty nice of you, my boy—I appreciate it more than I can say. Is this the package Cronin gave you?"

"It is. A very nice chap, Cronin. I didn't have to wait long after I telephoned you. He came in with two other men named Stoates and Lewin. He didn't keep me more than ten minutes altogether. I hope it was important, Inspector?" Panzer continued, smiling. "I should like to feel that I've been instrumental in clearing up part of the puzzle."

"Important?" echoed the Inspector, taking the parcel from the manager's hand. "You have no idea how important it is. Some day I'll tell you more about it. . . . Will you excuse me a moment, Panzer?"

78. Not surprisingly, there was no Electra Theatre on 43rd St.—indeed, the only theaters on 43rd St. were Henry Miller's Theatre, the home of the English actor-producer, and George M. Cohan's Theatre, built by Cohan and his partner Sam H. Harris but sold in 1915. Harris also owned the Sam H. Harris Theatre on 42nd St. Could Harris be Gordon Davis? Not a single Gordon Davis is listed in *Trow's General Directory of New York City* for 1922–23.

The little man nodded in a fleeting disappointment as the Inspector grinned, backing off into a dark corner. Panzer shrugged and disappeared into his office.

When he came out, hat and coat left behind, the Inspector was stuffing the parcel into his pocket.

"Did you get what you wanted, sir?" inquired Panzer.

"Oh, yes, yes, indeed!" Queen said, rubbing his hands.

"And now—I see Ellery is still gone—suppose we go into your office for a few minutes and while away the time until he returns."

They went into Panzer's sanctum and sat down. The manager lit a long Turkish cigarette while the Inspector dipped into his snuff-box.

"If I'm not presuming, Inspector," said Panzer casually, crossing his short fat legs and emitting a cloud of smoke, "how are things going?"

Queen shook his head sadly. "Not so well—not so well. We don't seem to be getting anywhere with the main angles of the case. In fact, I don't mind telling you that unless we get on the track of a certain object we face failure. . . . It's pretty hard on me—I've never encountered a more puzzling investigation." He wore a worried frown as he snapped the lid of his snuff-box shut.

"That's too bad, Inspector," Panzer clucked in sympathy. "And I was hoping—Ah, well! We can't put our personal concerns above the demands of justice, I suppose! Just what is it you are seeking, Inspector, if you don't mind telling an outsider?"

Queen brightened. "Not at all. You've done me a good turn this morning and— By jingo, how stupid of me not to think of this before!" Panzer leaned forward eagerly. "How long have you been manager of the Roman Theatre, Panzer?"

The manager raised his eyebrows. "Ever since it was built," he said. "Before that I managed the old Electra on 43rd Street[78]—it is also owned by Gordon Davis," he explained.

"Oh!" The Inspector seemed to reflect deeply. "Then you would know this theatre from top to bottom—you would be as familiar with its construction as the architect, perhaps?"

"I have a rather thorough knowledge of it, yes," confessed Panzer, leaning back.

"That's excellent! Let me give you a little problem, then, Panzer. . . . Suppose you wished to conceal a—let us say, a tophat—somewhere in the building, in such a way that not even an exhaustive search of the premises would bring it to light. What would you do? Where would you hide it?"

Panzer scowled thoughtfully at his cigarette. "A rather unusual question, Inspector," he said at last, "and one which is not easy to answer. I know the plans of the theatre very well; I was consulted about them in a conference with the architect before the theatre was built. And I can positively state that the original blueprints did not provide for such medieval devices as concealed passage-ways, secret closets or anything of that sort. I could enumerate any number of places where a man might hide a comparatively small object like a tophat, but none of them would be proof against a really thorough search."

"I see." The Inspector squinted at his finger-nails in an appearance of disappointment. "So that doesn't help. We've been over the place from top to bottom, as you know, and we can't find a trace of it. . . ."

The door opened and Ellery, a trifle begrimed but wearing a cheerful smile, entered. The Inspector glanced at him in eager curiosity. Panzer rose hesitantly with the evident intention of leaving father and son alone. A flash of intelligence shot between the Queens.

"It's all right, Panzer—don't go," said the Inspector peremptorily. 'We've no secrets from you. Sit down, man!"

Panzer sat down.

"Don't you think, dad," remarked Ellery, perching on the edge of the desk and reaching for his pince-nez, "that this would be an opportune moment to inform Mr. Panzer of to-night's opening? You remember we decided while he was gone that the theatre might be thrown open to the public this evening and a regular performance given . . . ?"

"How could I have forgotten—!" said the Inspector without blinking, although this was the first time he had heard about the mythical decision. "I think we're about ready, Panzer, to lift the ban on the Roman. We find that we can do nothing further here, so there is no reason for depriving you of your patronage any longer. You may run a performance to-night—in fact, we are most anxious to see a show put on, aren't we Ellery?"

"'Anxious' is hardly the word," said Ellery, lighting a cigarette. "I should say we insist upon it."

"Exactly," murmured the Inspector severely. "We insist upon it, Panzer."

The manager had bobbed out of his chair, his face shining. "That's simply splendid, gentlemen!" he cried. "I'll telephone Mr. Davis immediately to let him know the good news. Of course"—his face fell—"it's terribly late to expect any sort of response from the public for to-night's performance. Such short notice . . ."

"You needn't worry about that, Panzer," retorted the Inspector. "I've caused your shut-down and I'll see that the theatre is compensated for it to-night. I'll get the newspaper boys on the wire and ask them to ballyhoo the opening in the next edition. It will mean a lot of unexpected publicity for you and undoubtedly the free advertising, combined with the normal curiosity of the public, will give you a sell-out."

"That's sporting of you, Inspector," said Panzer, rubbing his hands. "Is there anything else I can do for you at the moment?"

"There's one item you've forgotten, dad," interposed Ellery. He turned to the swart little manager. "Will you see that LL32 and LL30 Left are not sold to-night? The Inspector and I would enjoy seeing this evening's performance. We've not really had that pleasure yet, you know. And naturally we wish to preserve a stately incognito, Panzer—dislike the adulation of the crowd and that sort of thing. You'll keep it under cover, of course."

"Anything you say, Mr. Queen. I'll instruct the cashier to put aside those tickets," returned Panzer pleasantly. "And now, Inspector—you said you would telephone the press, I believe—?"

"Certainly." Queen took up the telephone and held pithy conversations with the city editors of a number of metropolitan newspapers. When he had finished Panzer bade them a hurried good-by to get busy with the telephone.

Inspector Queen and his son strolled out into the orchestra, where they found Flint and the two detectives who had been examining the boxes awaiting them.

"You men hang around the theatre on general principles," ordered the Inspector. "Be particularly careful this afternoon. . . . Any of you find anything?"

Flint scowled. "I ought to be digging clams in Canarsie," he said with a disgruntled air. "I fell down on the job Monday night, Inspector, and I'm blamed if I could find a thing for you to-day.

That place upstairs is swept as clean as a hound's tooth. Guess I ought to go back to pounding a beat."

Queen slapped the big detective on the shoulder. "What's the matter with you? Don't be acting like a baby, lad. How on earth could you find anything when there wasn't anything to find? You fellows get something?" he demanded, swinging on the other two men.

They shook their heads in a gloomy negation.

A moment later the Inspector and Ellery climbed into a passing taxicab and settled back for the short drive to headquarters. The old man carefully closed the glass sliding-window separating the driver's seat from the interior of the car.

"Now, my son," he said grimly, turning on Ellery, who was puffing dreamily at a cigarette, "please explain to your old daddy that hocus-pocus in Panzer's office!"

Ellery's lips tightened. He stared out of the window before replying. "Let me start this way," he said. "You have found nothing in your search to-day. Nor have your men. And although I scouted about myself, I was just as unsuccessful. Dad, make up your mind to this one primary point: The hat which Monte Field wore to the performance of 'Gunplay' on Monday night, in which he was seen at the beginning of the second act, and which presumably the murderer took away after the crime was committed, *is not in the Roman Theatre now and has not been there since Monday night*. To proceed." Queen stared at him with grizzled brows. "In all likelihood Field's tophat no longer exists. I would stake my Falconer against your snuff-box that it has fled this life and now enjoys a reincarnation as ashes in the City dumps. That's point number one."

"Go on," commanded the Inspector.

"Point number two is so elementary as to be infantile. Nevertheless, allow me the privilege of insulting the Queen intelligence.... If Field's hat is not in the Roman Theatre now and has not been in the Roman Theatre since Monday night, it must of necessity have been taken *out* of the Roman Theatre sometime during the course of that evening!"

He paused to gaze thoughtfully through the window. A traffic-officer was waving his arms at the juncture of 42nd Street and Broadway.

"We have established therefore," he continued lightly, "the factual basis of a point which has been running us ragged for

79. This is the full form of the abbreviation of "i.e.," that is, "that is."

three days: to wit, did the hat for which we are looking leave the Roman Theatre. . . . To be dialectic—yes, it did. It left the Roman Theatre the night of the murder. Now we approach a greater problem—*how* did it leave and *when*." He puffed at his cigarette and regarded the glowing tip. "We know that no person left the Roman Monday night with two hats or no hat at all. In no case was there anything incongruous in the attire of any person leaving the theatre. That is, a man wearing a full-dress costume did not go out with a fedora. In a similar way, no one wearing a silk-topper was dressed in ordinary street-clothes. Remember, we noticed nothing wrong from this angle in *anyone*. . . . This leads us inevitably, to my staggering mind, to the third fundamental conclusion: that Monte Field's hat left the theatre in the most natural manner in the world: *id est*,[79] by way of some man's head, its owner being garbed in appropriate evening-clothes!"

The Inspector was keenly interested. He thought over Ellery's statement for a moment. Then he said seriously, "That's getting us somewhere, son. But you say a man left the theatre wearing Monte Field's hat—an important and enlightening statement. But please answer this question: What did he do with his own hat, since no one left with two?"

Ellery smiled. "You now have your hand on the heart of our little mystery, dad. But let it hold for the moment. We have a number of other points to mull over. For example, the man who departed wearing Monte Field's hat could have been only one of two things: either he was the actual murderer, or he was an accomplice of the murderer."

"I see what you're driving at," muttered the Inspector. "Go on."

"If he was the murderer, we have definitely established the sex and also the fact that our man was wearing evening-clothes that night—perhaps not a very illuminating point, since there were scores of such men in the theatre. If he was only an accomplice, we must conclude that the murderer was one of two possibilities: either a man dressed in ordinary clothes, whose possession of a tophat as he left would be patently suspicious; or else a woman, who of course could not sport a tophat at all!"

The Inspector sank back into the leather cushions. "Talk about your logic!" he chortled. "My son, I'm almost proud of you—that is, I would be if you weren't so disgustingly conceited. . . . Things standing where they do, therefore, the reason you pulled your little drama in Panzer's office . . ."

His voice lowered as Ellery leaned forward. They continued to converse in inaudible tones until the taxicab drew up before the headquarters building.

No sooner had Inspector Queen, who had proceeded blithely through the somber corridors with Ellery striding at his side, entered his tiny office than Sergeant Velie lumbered to his feet.

"Thought you were lost, Inspector!" he exclaimed. "That Stoates kid was in here not long ago with a suffering look on his face. Said that Cronin was tearing his hair at Field's office—that they still hadn't found a thing in the files of an incriminating nature."

"Go away, go away, Thomas my lad," gurgled the Inspector softly. "I can't bother myself with petty problems like putting a dead man behind bars. Ellery and I—"

The telephone bell rang. Queen sprang forward and snatched the instrument from the desk. As he listened the glow left his thin cheeks and a frown settled once more on his forehead. Ellery watched him with a strange absorption.

"Inspector?" came the hurried voice of a man. "This is Hagstrom reporting. Just got a minute—can't say much. Been tailing Angela Russo all morning and had a tough time. . . . Seems to be wise that I'm following her. . . . A half hour ago she thought she'd given me the slip—she hopped into a cab and beat it downtown. . . . And say, Inspector—just three minutes ago I saw her enter Benjamin Morgan's office!"

Queen barked, "Nail her the instant she comes out!" and slammed the receiver down. He turned slowly to Ellery and Velie and repeated Hagstrom's report. Ellery's face became a study in frowning astonishment. Velie appeared unmistakably pleased.

But the old man's voice was strained as he sat down weakly in his swivel-chair. Finally he groaned, "What do you know about that!"

CHAPTER XV

In Which an Accusation is Made

Detective Hagstrom was a phlegmatic man. He traced his ancestry to the mountains of Norway, where stolidity was a virtue and stoicism the ultimate cult. Nevertheless, as he leaned against a gleaming marble wall on the twentieth floor of the Maddern Building, thirty feet to the side of the bronze-and-glass door marked:

BENJAMIN MORGAN
Attorney-at-Law

his heart beat a trifle faster than usual. He shuffled his feet nervously as his jaw masticated a wad of chewing-tobacco. If the truth were told Detective Hagstrom, a man of varied experience in the service of the police department, had never clamped his hand on the shoulder of a female with intent to arrest. He faced his coming assignment therefore in some trepidation, remembering with appalling clarity the fiery temperament of the lady for whom he was waiting.

His apprehension was well founded. When he had been lounging in the corridor some twenty minutes, and wondering whether his quarry had not slipped away through another exit, Benjamin Morgan's office-door suddenly swung open and the large, curved figure of Mrs. Angela Russo, garbed in a modish tweed ensemble, appeared. An unbecoming snarl distorted her carefully made-up features; she swung her purse menacingly as she strode toward the line of elevators. Hagstrom glanced quickly at his wrist-watch. It was ten minutes to twelve. In a short time the offices would be disgorging their occupants for the lunch hour, and he was most desirous of making his arrest in the quiet of the deserted hall.

Accordingly he straightened up, adjusted his orange-and-blue necktie and stepped with a fair assumption of coolness into full view of the approaching woman. As she caught sight of him she slackened her stride perceptibly. Hagstrom hurried toward her, anticipating flight. But Mrs. Angela Russo was made of sterner stuff. She tossed her head and came on brazenly.

Hagstrom fixed his large red hand on her arm. "I guess you know what I want you for," he said fiercely. "Come along now, and don't make a fuss or I'll put the nippers on you!"

Mrs. Russo shook off his hand. "My, my—aren't you the big rough cop?" she murmured. "Just what do you think you're doing, anyway?"

Hagstrom glared. "None o' your lip, now!" His finger pressed savagely on the "Down" signal for the elevators. "You just shut up and come along!"

She faced him sweetly. "Are you trying to arrest me, by any chance?" she cooed. "Because you know, my big he-man, you've got to have a warrant to do that!"

"Aw, stow it!" he growled. "I'm not arresting you—I'm just inviting you to step down to headquarters for a little gab with Inspector Queen. You coming, or do I have to call the wagon?"

An elevator flashed to a stop. The elevator-man snapped, "Going down!" The woman glanced with momentary uncertainty at the car, peered slyly at Hagstrom and finally stepped into the elevator, the detective's hand firmly clasped on her elbow. They descended in silence under the curious scrutiny of several passengers.

Hagstrom, uneasy but determined, sensing somehow a storm brewing in the breast of the woman who strode so calmly by his side, was taking no chances. He did not relax his grasp until they sat side by side in a taxicab, bound for headquarters. Mrs. Russo's face had gone pasty under her rouge, despite the bold smile curving her lips. She turned suddenly to face her captor, leaning close to his rigidly official body.

"Mr. Cop, darling," she whispered, "do you think you could use a hundred-dollar bill?"

Her hand fumbled suggestively in her purse. Hagstrom lost his temper.

"Bribery, huh?" he sneered. "We'll have to chalk that one up for the Inspector!"

The woman's smile faded. For the rest of the journey she sat looking fixedly at the back of the driver's neck.

It was only when she was being marched, like a soldier on parade, down the dark corridors of the big police structure that her poise returned. And when Hagstrom held open the door of Inspector Queen's office, she passed inside with an airy tilt to her head and a pleasant smile that would have deceived a police matron.

Inspector Queen's office was a cheery affair of sunlight and color. At the moment it resembled a clubroom. Ellery's long legs were stretched comfortably across the thick carpet, his eyes pleasantly absorbed in the contents of a small cheaply bound book entitled "The Complete Guide to Handwriting Analysis." The smoke of a cigarette curled from his slack fingers. Sergeant Velie was sitting stolidly in a chair against the far wall, engrossed in a contemplation of Inspector Queen's snuff-box, which was held lovingly between the thumb and forefinger of the old police official himself. Queen was seated in his comfortable armchair, smiling in hazy introspection at some secret thought.

"Ah! Mrs. Russo! Come in. come in!" exclaimed the Inspector, bouncing to his feet. "Thomas—a chair for Mrs. Russo, if you please." The Sergeant silently placed one of the bare wooden chairs by the side of the Inspector's desk and as silently retreated to his comer. Ellery had not even glanced in the woman's direction. He read on, the same pleasantly abstracted smile on his lips. The old man was bowing with hospitable courtesy to Mrs. Russo.

She looked about at the peaceful scene with bewilderment. She had been prepared for severity, harshness, brutality—the domestic atmosphere of the little office took her completely by surprise. Nevertheless she seated herself and, the instant of hesitation gone, she exhibited the same agreeable smile, the same ladylike demeanor that she had practiced so successfully in the corridors.

Hagstrom was standing inside the doorway, glaring with offended dignity at the profile of the seated woman.

"She tried to slip me a century note," he said indignantly. "Tried to bribe me, Chief!"

Queen's eyebrows instantly rose in shocked surprise. "My dear Mrs. Russo!" he exclaimed in a sorrowful voice. "You really didn't intend to make this excellent officer forget his duty to the city, did you? But of course not! How stupid of me! Hagstrom, certainly you must be mistaken, my dear fellow. A hundred dollars—" He shook his head dolefully sinking back into the leather swivel-chair.

Mrs. Russo smiled. "Isn't it queer how these cops get the wrong impression?" she asked in a lovely voice. "I assure you, Inspector—I was just having a little fun with him. . . ."

"Exactly," said the Inspector, smiling again, as if this statement restored his faith in human nature. "Hagstrom, that'll be all."

The detective, who was staring open-mouthed from his superior to the smiling woman, recovered in time to intercept a wink which passed from Velie to Queen across the woman's head. He went out quickly, muttering to himself.

"Now, Mrs. Russo," began the Inspector, in a businesslike tone, "what can we do for you to-day?"

She stared at him. "Why—why, I thought you wanted to see me. . . ." Her lips tightened. "Cut the comedy, Inspector!" she said shortly. "I'm not paying any social calls on my own hook to this place and you know it. What did you pinch me for?"

The Inspector spread his sensitive fingers deprecatingly, his mouth pursed in protest. "But, my dear lady!" he said. "Certainly you have something to tell me. Because, if you are here—and we cannot evade that evident fact—you are here for a reason. Granted that you did not come exactly of your own free will—still you were brought here because you have something to say to me. Don't you see?"

Mrs. Russo stared fixedly into his eyes. "What the—Hey, look here, Inspector Queen, what are you driving at? What do you think I've got to tell you? I answered everything you asked me Tuesday morning."

"Well!" The old man frowned. "Let us say that you did *not* answer every question Tuesday morning with absolute veracity. For example—do you know Benjamin Morgan?"

She did not flinch. "All right. You take the cake on that one. Your bloodhound caught me coming out of Morgan's office—what of it?" She deliberately opened her purse and began to dab powder on her nose. As she did so she glanced slyly at Ellery from the corner of her eye. He was still engrossed in his book, oblivious to her presence. She turned back to the Inspector with a toss of the head.

Queen was looking at her sadly. "My dear Mrs. Russo, you're not being fair to a poor old man. I wanted merely to point out that you had—shall I say—lied to me the last time I spoke to you. Now that's a very dangerous procedure with police Inspectors, my dear—very dangerous."

"Listen here!" the woman said suddenly. "You're not going to get anywhere with this soft soap, Inspector. I *did* lie to you Tuesday morning. Because, you see, I didn't think you had anyone here who could follow me very long. Well, I took a gambler's chance and I lost. So you found out I was lying, and you want to know what it's all about. I'll tell you—and then maybe again I won't!"

"Oho!" exclaimed Queen softly. "So you feel you're in a safe enough position to dictate terms, eh? But Mrs. Russo—believe me you're putting your very charming neck into a noose!"

"Yeh?" The mask was fairly off now; the woman's face was stripped to its essential character of intrigue. "You got nothing on me and you know it damn well. All right—I did lie to you—what are you going to do about it? I'm admitting it now. And I'll even tell you what I was doing in that guy Morgan's office, if that'll help you any! That's the kind of a square-shooter *I* am, Mr. Inspector!"

"My dear Mrs. Russo," returned the Inspector in a pained voice, a little puffed smile in his cheeks, "we know already what you were doing in Mr. Morgan's office this morning, so you won't be conferring such a great favor on us after all. . . . I'm really surprised that you should be willing to incriminate yourself to that extent, Mrs. Russo. . . . Blackmail is a mighty serious offense!"

The woman grew deathly white. She half rose in the chair, gripping its arms.

"So Morgan squealed after all, the dirty dog!" she snarled. "And I thought he was a wise guy. I'll get him something to squeal about, take it from me!"

"Ah, now you're beginning to talk my language," murmured the Inspector, leaning forward. "And just what is it you know about our friend Morgan?"

"I know this about him—but look here, Inspector, I can give you a red-hot tip. You wouldn't frame a poor lonely woman on a blackmail charge, would you?"

The Inspector's face lengthened. "Now, now, Mrs. Russo!" he said. "Is that a nice thing to say? Certainly I can't make any promises. . . ." He rose, his slender body deadly in its immobility. She shrank back a little. "You will tell me what you have on your mind, Mrs. Russo," he said deliberately, "on the bare chance that I may show my gratitude in the generally accepted fashion. You will please talk—truthfully, do your understand?"

"Oh, I know well enough you're a tough nut, Inspector!" she muttered. "But I guess you're fair, too. . . . What do you want to know?"

"Everything."

"Well, it isn't my funeral," she said, in a more composed voice. There was a pause while Queen examined her curiously. In accusing her of blackmailing Morgan he had made a successful stab in the dark; now a flash of doubt assailed him. She seemed much too sure of herself if all she knew were the details of Morgan's past, as the Inspector had taken for granted from the beginning of the interview. He glanced at Ellery and was apprehensively quick to note that his son's eyes were no longer on the book but riveted on the profile of Mrs. Russo.

"Inspector," said Mrs. Russo, a shrill triumph creeping into her voice, "I know who killed Monte Field!"

"What's that?" Queen jumped out of his seat, a flush suffusing his white features. Ellery had straightened convulsively in his chair, his sharp eyes boring into the woman's face. The book he had been reading slipped out of his fingers and dropped to the floor with a thud.

"I said I know who killed Monte Field," repeated Mrs. Russo, evidently enjoying the sensation she had caused. "It's Benjamin Morgan, and I heard him threaten Monte *the night before he was murdered!*"

"Oh!" said the Inspector, sitting down. Ellery picked up his book and resumed his interrupted study of "The Complete Guide to Handwriting Analysis." Quiet descended once more. Velie, who had been staring at father and son in struggling amazement, seemed at a loss to understand their suddenly changed manner.

Mrs. Russo grew angry. "I suppose you think I'm lying again, but I'm not!" she screamed. "I tell you I heard with my own ears Ben Morgan tell Monte Sunday night that he'd put him away!"

The Inspector was grave, but undisturbed. "I don't doubt your word in the least, Mrs. Russo. Are you sure it was Sunday night?"

"Sure?" she shrilled. "I'll say I'm sure!"

"And where did this happen?"

"Right in Monte Field's own apartment, that's where!" she said bitingly. "I was with Monte all evening Sunday, and as far as I know he wasn't expecting company, because we didn't usually have company when we spent the evening together. . . . Monte himself jumped when the door-bell rang about eleven o'clock and said, 'Who in hell could that be?' We were in the living-room at the time. But he got up and went to the door, and right after that I heard a man's voice outside. I figured Monte wouldn't want me to be seen by anybody, so I went into the bed-room and closed the door, just leaving a crack open. I could hear Monte trying to stall the man off. Anyway, they finally came into the living-room. Through the crack in the door I saw it was this fellow Morgan—I didn't know who he was at the time, but later on I got it during the talk they had. And afterward Monte told me . . ."

She stopped. The Inspector listened imperturbably and Ellery was paying not the slightest attention to her words. She went on desperately.

"For about a half hour they talked till I could have howled. Morgan was sort of cold and set; he didn't get excited till the last. From which I gathered, Monte had asked Morgan not long before for a big wad of dough in return for some papers; and Morgan said he didn't have the money, couldn't raise it. Said he'd decided to drop into Monte's place for one last reckoning. Monte was kind of sarcastic and mean—he could be awfully mean when he wanted to. Morgan kept getting madder and madder, and I could see he was holding his temper in. . . ."

The Inspector interrupted. "Just what was the reason for Field's demand for money?"

"I wish I knew, Inspector," she returned savagely. "But both of 'em were mighty careful not to mention the reason. . . . Anyway, it was something about those papers that Monte wanted Morgan to buy. It wouldn't take much brains to guess that Monte had something on Morgan and was pushing it to the limit."

At the mention of the word "papers" Ellery's interest in Mrs. Russo's story had revived. He had put the book down and begun to listen intently. The Inspector gave him a fleeting glance as he addressed the woman.

"Just how much money was Field demanding, Mrs. Russo?"

"You wouldn't believe me if I told you," she said, laughing disdainfully. "Monte was no piker. All he wanted was—fifty thousand dollars!"

The Inspector seemed unmoved. "Go on."

"So there they were," she continued, "jabbering back and forth, with Monte getting colder and Morgan getting madder. Finally Morgan picked up his hat and yelled, 'I'll be damned, you crook, if I'm going to be milked any more! You can do what you please—I'm through, do you understand? I'm through for good!' He was blue in the face. Monte didn't get up from his chair. He just said, 'You can do as you please, Benjamin my friend, but I give you exactly three days to hand that money over. And no bargaining, remember! Fifty thousand, or—but surely I don't have to remind you of the unpleasant consequences of refusal.' Monte sure was slick," she added admiringly. "Could sling the lingo like a professional.

"Morgan kept fiddling with his hat," she went on, "just as if he didn't know what to do with his hand. Then he exploded with, 'I told you where you get off, Field, and I mean every word of it. Publish those papers, and if it means ruin to me—I'll see to it that it's the last time you'll ever blackmail *anybody*!' He shook his fist under Monte's nose, and looked for a minute as if he was going to do him in then and there. Then all of a sudden he quieted down and without saying another word walked himself out of the apartment."

"And that's the story, Mrs. Russo?"

"Isn't it enough?" she flared. "What are you trying to do—protect that murdering coward? . . . But it isn't all. After Morgan left, Monte said to me, 'Did you hear what my friend said?' I made believe I didn't, but Monte was wise. He took me on his lap and said playfully, 'He'll regret it, Angel . . .' He always called me Angel," she added coyly.

"I see. . . ." the Inspector mused. "And just what did Mr. Morgan say—that you took for a threat against Field's life?"

She stared at him incredulously. "Good gravy, are you dumb, or what?" she cried. "He said, 'I'll see to it's the last time you'll

80. The tale of Hero (a woman) and Leander is one of the more touching love stories of the Greek myths. Hero, a priestess of Aphrodite, lived in a tower, and Leander, having fallen for her, swam across the Hellespont every night to be with her. On a stormy winter night, Leander drowned in the river, and on seeing his body, Hero threw herself off the tower to be with him in death.

ever blackmail *anybody*!' And then when my darling Monte was killed the very next night . . ."

"A very natural conclusion," smiled Queen. "Do I understand that you are preferring charges against Benjamin Morgan?"

"I'm not preferring anything except a little peace, Inspector," she retorted. "I've told you the story—now do what you want with it." She shrugged her shoulders and made as if to rise.

"One moment, Mrs. Russo." The Inspector held up a small and delicate finger. "You referred in your story to some 'papers' that Field was holding over Morgan's head. Did Field at any time during the quarrel between them actually bring out these papers?"

Mrs. Russo looked the old man coolly in the eye. "No, sir, he didn't. And make believe I'm not sorry he didn't, too!"

"A charming attitude of yours, Mrs. Russo. One of these days . . . I hope you understand that your skirts are not entirely—ah—clean in this matter, in a manner of speaking," said the Inspector. "So please consider very carefully before you answer my next question. Where did Monte Field keep his private documents?"

"I don't have to consider, Inspector," she snapped. "I just don't know. If there was any chance of my knowing I would, don't worry."

"Perhaps you made a few personal forays of your own when Field was absent from his apartment?" pursued Queen, smiling.

"Perhaps I did," she answered with a dimpling cheek. "But it didn't do any good. I'd swear they're not in those rooms . . . Well, Inspector, anything else?"

The clear voice of Ellery seemed to startle her. But she coquettishly patted her hair as she turned towards him.

"As far as you know, Mrs. Russo," said Ellery icily, "from long and no doubt intimate association with your gallant Leander[80]—how many different silk tophats did he possess?"

"You're the original cross-word puzzle, aren't you?" she gurgled. "As far as I know, Mr. Man, he had only one. How many does a guy need?"

"You're certain of that, I suppose," said Ellery.

"Sure's you're born, Mr. Queen." She contrived to slip a caress into her voice. Ellery stared at her as one stares at a strange zoölogical specimen. She made a little *moue* and turned about gaily.

"I'm not so popular around here so I'll beat it. . . . You're not going to put me in a nasty cell, are you, Inspector? I can go now, can't I?"

The Inspector bowed. "Oh yes—you may go, Mrs. Russo, under a certain amount of surveillance. . . . But please understand that we may still require your delightful company at some not distant date. Will you remain in town?"

"Charmed, I'm sure!" she laughed and swept out of the room.

Velie snapped to his feet like a soldier and said, "Well, Inspector, I guess that settles it!"

The Inspector sank wearily into his chair. "Are you insinuating, Thomas, like some of Ellery's stupid fiction-sergeants—which you are not—that Mr. Morgan be arrested for the murder of Monte Field?"

"Why—what else?" Velie seemed at a loss.

"We'll wait a while, Thomas," returned the old man heavily.

CHAPTER XVI

In Which the Queens Go to the Theatre

81. The characters of P. G. Wodehouse, the author of numerous British satires, are often nervous, suffering the "willies." See note 76.

82. Handwriting.

Ellery and his father regarded each other across the length of the little office. Velie had resumed his seat with a puzzled frown. He sat quietly for a time in the growing silence, seemed suddenly to make a decision and asking permission left the room.

The Inspector grinned as he fumbled with the lid of his snuff-box.

"Did you get a scare, too, Ellery?"

Ellery, however, was serious. "That woman gives me a case of Wodehouse 'willies,'"[81] he said, shuddering. "Scare is much too mild a word."

"I couldn't for the moment grasp the significance of her attitude," said Inspector Queen. "To think that she *knew*, while we have been fumbling around. . . . It scattered my wits."

"I should say the interview was highly successful," commented Ellery. "Principally because I've been gathering a few interesting facts from this ponderous tome on chirography.[82] But Mrs. Angela Russo does not measure up to my conception of perfect womanhood. . . ."

"If you ask me," chuckled the Inspector, "our beauteous friend has a crush on you. Consider the opportunities, my son—!"

Ellery made a grimace of profound distaste.

"Well!" Queen reached for one of the telephones on the desk. "Do you think we ought to give Benjamin Morgan another chance, Ellery?"

"Hanged if he deserves it," grumbled Ellery. "But I suppose it's the routine thing to do."

"'You forget the papers, son—the papers," retorted the Inspector, a twinkle in his eye.

He spoke to the police operator in pleasant accents and a few moments later the buzzer sounded.

"Good afternoon, Mr. Morgan!" Queen said cheerfully. "And how are you to-day?"

"Inspector Queen?" asked Morgan after a slight hesitation. "Good afternoon to you, sir. How is the case progressing?"'

"That's a fair question, Mr. Morgan," laughed the Inspector. "One, however, which I daren't answer for fear of being accused of incompetency. . . . Mr. Morgan, are you free this evening by any chance?"

Pause. "Why—not free exactly." The lawyer's voice was barely audible. "I am due at home, of course, for dinner, and I believe my wife has arranged a little bridge. Why, Inspector?"

"I was thinking of asking you to dine with my son and me this evening," said the Inspector regretfully. "Could you possibly get away for the dinner-hour?"

A longer pause. "If it's absolutely necessary, Inspector—?"

"I wouldn't put it that way exactly, Mr. Morgan. . . . But I would appreciate your accepting the invitation."

"Oh." Morgan's voice came more resolutely now. "In that case I'm at your command, Inspector. Where shall I meet you?"

"That's fine, that's fine!" said Queen. "How about Carlos,'[83] at six?"

"Very well, Inspector," returned the lawyer quietly and hung up the receiver.

"I can't help feeling sorry for the poor chap," murmured the old man.

Ellery grunted. He was not feeling inclined to sympathize. The taste of Mrs. Angela Russo was still strong in his mouth, and it was not a pleasant taste at all.

⁓∞⸲

Promptly at six o'clock Inspector Queen and Ellery joined Benjamin Morgan in the convivial atmosphere of Carlos' restaurant-foyer. He was sitting dejectedly in a red-leather chair, staring at

83.   Carlos Table D' Hote was at 25 West 24th Street between Broadway and 6th Avenue.

Postcard depicting Carlos Table d'Hote, ca. 1920.

the backs of his hands. His lips drooped sadly, his knees were widely separated in an instinctive attitude of depression.

He made a laudable attempt to smile as the two Queens approached. He rose with a firmness that indicated to his keen hosts a mind determined upon a fixed course of action. The Inspector was at his bubbling best, partly because he felt a genuine liking for the corpulent attorney and partly because it was his business. Ellery, as usual, was noncommittal.

The three men shook hands like old friends.

"Glad to see you're on time, Morgan," said the Inspector, as a stiff headwaiter conducted them to a corner-table. "I really must apologize for taking you away from your dinner at home. There was a time once—" He sighed and they sat down.

"No apology necessary," said Morgan with a wan smile. "I suppose you know that every married man relishes a bachelor dinner at times. . . . Just what is it, Inspector, you wanted to talk to me about?"

The old man raised a warning finger. "No business now, Morgan," he said. "I have an idea Louis has something up his sleeve in the way of solid refreshment—right, Louis?"

The dinner was a culinary delight. The Inspector, who was quite indifferent to the nuances of the art, had left the details of the menu to his son. Ellery was fanatically interested in the delicate subject of foods and their preparation. Consequently the three men dined well. Morgan was at first inclined to taste his food abstractedly, but he became more and more alive to the delightful concoctions placed before him, until finally he forgot his troubles altogether and chatted and laughed with his hosts.

With *cafè au lait* and excellent cigars, which Ellery smoked cautiously, the Inspector diffidently, and Morgan with enjoyment, Queen came to the point.

"Morgan, I'm not going to beat around the bush. I have an idea you know why I asked you here to-night. I'm going to be perfectly honest. I want the true explanation for your silence regarding the events of Sunday night, September the twenty-third—four nights ago."

Morgan had become grave immediately after the Inspector began to speak. He put the cigar on the ash-tray and regarded the old man with an expression of ineffable weariness.

"It was bound to come," he said. "I might have known that you would find out sooner or later. I suppose Mrs. Russo told you out of spite."

"She did," confessed Queen frankly. "As a gentleman I refuse to listen to tales; as a policeman it is my duty. Why have you kept this from me, Morgan?"

Morgan traced a meaningless figure on the cloth with a spoon. "Because—well, because a man is always a fool until he is made to realize the extent of his folly," he said quietly, looking up. "I hoped and prayed—it is a human failing, I suppose—that the incident would remain a secret between a dead man and myself. And to find that that prostitute was hiding in the bedroom—listening to every word I said—it rather took the wind out of my sails."

He gulped down a glass of water, rushing ahead. "The God's honest truth, Inspector, is that I thought I was being drawn into a trap and I couldn't bring myself to furnish contributory evidence. There I found myself in the theatre, not so far away from my worst enemy found murdered. I could not explain my presence except by an apparently silly and unsubstantiated story; and I remembered in a bitter flash that I had actually quarreled with the dead man the night before. It was a tight position, Inspector—take my word for it."

Inspector Queen said nothing. Ellery was leaning far back in his chair, watching Morgan with gloomy eyes. Morgan swallowed hard and went on.

"That's why I didn't say anything. Can you blame a man for keeping quiet when his legal training warns him so decisively of the net of circumstantial evidence he is helping to manufacture?"

Queen was silent for a moment. Then—"We'll let that pass for the moment, Morgan. Why did you go to see Field Sunday night?"

"For a very good reason," answered the lawyer bitterly. "On Thursday, a week ago, Field called me up at my office and told me that he was making a last business venture that entailed his procuring fifty thousand dollars at once. Fifty thousand dollars!" Morgan laughed dryly. "After he had milked me until I was as flabby financially as an old cow. . . . And his 'business venture'—can you imagine what it was? If you knew Field as well as I did, you would find the answer on the race-tracks and the stock-market. . . . Perhaps I'm wrong. Perhaps he was hard pressed for money and was cleaning up his old 'accounts.' At any rate, he wanted the fifty thousand on a brand-new proposition—that he would actually return the original documents to me for that sum! It was the first time he had even suggested such a thing. Every time—before—he had insolently asked blackmail for silence. This time it was a buy-and-sell proposition."

"That's an interesting point, Mr. Morgan," put in Ellery, with a flicker of his eyes. "Did anything in his conversation definitely lead you to suspect that he was 'clearing up old accounts,' as you phrase it?"

"Yes. That is why I said what I did. He gave me the impression that he was hard up, meant to take a little vacation—vacation to him would be a three-year jaunt on the continent, nothing less—and was soliciting all his 'friends.' I never knew that he was in the blackmailing business on a large scale; but this time—!"

Ellery and the Inspector exchanged glances. Morgan forged ahead.

"I told him the truth. That I was in a bad way financially, chiefly through him, and that it would be absolutely impossible for me to raise, the preposterous amount he demanded. He merely laughed—insisted on getting the money. I was most anxious to get the papers back, of course. . . ."

"Had you verified from your cancelled vouchers the fact that some were missing?" asked the Inspector.

"It wasn't necessary, Inspector," grated Morgan. "He actually exhibited the vouchers and letters for my benefit in the Webster Club two years ago—when we had the quarrel. Oh, there is no question about it. He was top man."

"Go on."

"He hung up on me with a thinly veiled threat last Thursday. I had tried desperately during the conversation to make him believe that I would in some way meet his demands, because I knew that he would have no scruples at all about publishing the papers once he realized he had sucked me dry . . ."

"Did you ask him if you could see the documents?" asked Ellery.

"I believe I did—but he laughed at me and said I would see the color of my checks and letters when he saw the color of my money. He was nobody's fool, that crook—he was taking no chances on my doing him in while he brought out the damning evidence. . . . You see how frank I am. I will even admit that at times the thought of violence entered my head. What man could keep from thinking such thoughts under those circumstances? But I never entertained homicidal fancies seriously, gentlemen—for a very good reason." He paused.

"It wouldn't have done you any good," said Ellery softly. "'You didn't know where the documents were!"

"Exactly," returned Morgan with a tremulous smile. "I didn't know. And with those papers liable to come to light at any time—to fall into anybody's hands—what good would Field's death have done me? I would probably have exchanged a bad taskmaster for a worse. . . . On Sunday night, after trying for three terrible days to get together the money he asked for—with no result—I decided to come to a final settlement with him. I went to his apartment and found him in a dressing-gown, much surprised and not at all apprehensive at seeing me. The living-room was upset—I did not know at the time that Mrs. Russo was hiding in the next room."

He re-lit the cigar with shaking fingers.

"We quarreled—or rather I quarreled and he sneered. He would listen to no argument, to no plea. He wanted the fifty thousand or he would send the story around—and the proofs. It sort of got on my nerves after a while. . . . I left before I lost control of myself utterly. And that's all, Inspector, on my word of honor as a gentleman and as an unfortunate victim of circumstances."

He turned his head away. Inspector Queen coughed and threw his cigar into the ash-tray. He fumbled in his pocket for the brown snuff-box, took a pinch, inhaled deeply and leaned back in his chair. Ellery suddenly poured a glass of water for Morgan, who took it and drained it.

"Thank you, Morgan," said Queen. "And since you have been so frank in your story, please be honest and tell me whether you threatened Field's life Sunday night during your quarrel. It is only fair to let you know that Mrs. Russo flatly accused you of Field's murder because of something you said in the heat of the moment."

Morgan grew pale. His brows twitched and his eyes, glazed and worried, stared pitifully at the Inspector.

"She was lying!" he cried hoarsely. Several diners nearby looked around curiously, and Inspector Queen tapped Morgan's arm. He bit his lip and lowered his voice. "I did nothing of the sort,

Inspector. I was honest with you a moment ago when I said that I had thought savagely from time to time of killing Field. It was a crippled, silly, pointless thought. I—I wouldn't have the courage to kill a man. Even at the Webster Club when I lost my temper completely and shouted that threat I didn't mean it. Certainly Sunday night—please believe me rather than that unscrupulous, money-grubbing harlot, Inspector—you must!"

"I merely want you to explain what you said. Because," said the Inspector quietly, "strange as it may seem, I do believe that you made the statement she attributes to you."

"What statement?" Morgan was in a sweat of fear; his eyes started from his head.

"'Publish those papers, and if it means ruin to me—I'll see to it that it's the last time you'll ever blackmail *anybody*!'" replied the Inspector. "Did you say that, Mr. Morgan?"

The lawyer stared incredulously at the Queens, then threw back his head and laughed. "Good heavens!" he gasped, at last. "Is that the 'threat' I made? Why, Inspector, what I meant was that if he published those documents, in the event that I couldn't meet his blackguard demands, that I'd make a clean breast of it to the police and drag him down with me. That's what I meant! And she thought I was threatening his life!" He wiped his eyes hysterically.

Ellery smiled, his finger summoning the waiter. He paid the check and lit a cigarette, looking sidewise at his father, who was regarding Morgan with a mixture of abstraction and sympathy.

"Very well, Mr. Morgan." The Inspector rose, pushed back his chair. "That's all we wanted to know." He stood aside courteously to allow the dazed, still trembling lawyer to precede them toward the cloak-room.

⁓⁓⁓

The sidewalk fronting the Roman Theatre was jammed when the two Queens strolled up 47th Street from Broadway. The crowd was so huge that police lines had been established. Traffic was at a complete standstill along the entire length of the narrow thoroughfare. The electric lights of the marquee blared forth the title "Gunplay" in vigorous dashes of light and in smaller lights the legend, "Starring James Peale and Eve Ellis, Supported by an

All-Star Cast." Women and men wielded frenzied elbows to push through the milling mob; policemen shouted hoarsely, demanding tickets for the evening's performance before they would allow any one to pass through the lines.

The Inspector showed his badge and he and Ellery were hurled with the jostling crowd into the small lobby of the theatre. Beside the box-office, his Latin face wreathed in smiles, stood Manager Panzer, courteous, firm and authoritative, helping to speed the long line of cash customers from the box-office window to the ticket-taker. The venerable doorman, perspiring mightily, was standing to one side, a bewildered expression on his face. The cashiers worked madly. Harry Neilson was huddled in a corner of the lobby, talking earnestly to three young men who were obviously reporters.

Panzer caught sight of the two Queens and hurried forward to greet them. At an imperious gesture from the Inspector he hesitated, then with an understanding nod turned back to the cashier's window. Ellery stood meekly in line and procured two reserved tickets from the box-office. They entered the orchestra in the midst of a pushing throng.

A startled Madge O'Connell fell back as Ellery presented two tickets plainly marked LL32 Left and LL30 Left. The Inspector smiled as she fumbled with the pasteboards and threw him a half-fearful glance. She led them across the thick carpet to the extreme left aisle, silently indicated the last two seats of the last row and fled. The two men sat down, placed their hats in the wire holders below the seats and leaned back comfortably, for all the world like two pleasure-seekers contemplating an evening's gory entertainment.

The auditorium was packed. Droves of people being ushered down the aisles were rapidly consuming the empty seats. Heads twisted expectantly in the direction of the Queens, who became unwittingly the center of a most unwelcome scrutiny.

"Heck!" grumbled the old man. "We should have come in after the curtain went up."

"You're much too sensitive to public acclaim, *mon père*," laughed Ellery. "I don't mind the limelight." He consulted his wrist watch and their glances met significantly. It was exactly 8:25. They wriggled in their seats and settled down.

The lights were blotted out, one by one. The chatter of the audience died in a responsive sympathy. In total darkness the curtain rose on a weirdly dim stage. A shot exploded the silence; a man's gurgling shout raised gasps in the theatre. "Gunplay" was off in its widely publicized and theatrical manner.

Despite the preoccupation of his father, Ellery, relaxed in the chair which three nights before had held the dead body of Monte Field, was able to sit still and enjoy the exceedingly mellow melodrama. The fine rich voice of James Peale, ushered onto the stage by a series of climactic incidents, rang out and thrilled him with its commanding art. Eve Ellis's utter absorption in her rôle was apparent—at the moment she was conversing in low throbbing tones with Stephen Barry, whose handsome face and pleasant voice were evoking admiring comment from a young girl seated directly to the Inspector's right. Hilda Orange was huddled in a comer, dressed flamboyantly as befitted her stage character. The old "character-man" pottered aimlessly about the stage. Ellery leaned toward his father.

"It's a well cast production," he whispered. "Watch that Orange woman!"

The play stuttered and crackled on. With a crashing symphony of words and noise the first act came to an end. The Inspector consulted his watch as the lights snapped on. It was 9:05.

He rose and Ellery followed him lazily. Madge O'Connell, pretending not to notice them, pushed open the heavy iron doors across the aisle and the audience began to file out into the dimly lit alleyway. The two Queens sauntered out among the others.

A uniformed boy standing behind a neat stand covered with paper cups was crying his wares in a subdued, "refined" voice. It was Jess Lynch, the boy who had testified in the matter of Monte Field's request for ginger ale.

Ellery strolled behind the iron door—there was a cramped space between the door and the brick wall. He noticed that the wall of the building flanking the other side of the alley was easily six stories high and unbroken. The Inspector bought an orange-drink from the boy. Jess Lynch recognized him with a start and Inspector Queen greeted the boy pleasantly.

People were standing in small groups, their attitudes betokening a strange interest in their surroundings. The Inspector heard a woman remark, in a fearful, fascinated voice, "They say he was standing right out here Monday night, buying an orange-drink!"

The warning-bell soon clanged inside the theatre, and those who had come outside for a breath of air hurried back into the orchestra. Before he sat down, the Inspector glanced over across the rear of the auditorium to the foot of the staircase leading to the balcony. A stalwart, uniformed young man stood alertly on the first step.

The second act exploded into being. The audience swayed and gasped in the approved fashion while the dramatic fireworks were shot off on the stage. The Queens seemed suddenly to have become absorbed in the action. Father and son leaned forward, bodies taut, eyes intent. Ellery consulted his watch at 9:30—and the two Queens settled back again while the play rumbled on.

At 9:50 exactly they rose, took their hats and coats and slipped out of the LL row into the clear space behind the orchestra. A number of people were standing—at which the Inspector smiled and blessed the power of the press beneath his breath. The white-faced usherette, Madge O'Connell, was leaning stiffly against a pillar, staring unseeingly ahead.

The Queens, espying Manager Panzer in the doorway of his office beaming delightedly at the crowded auditorium, made their way towards him. The Inspector motioned him inside and rapidly stepped into the little anteroom, Ellery close behind. The smile faded from Panzer's face.

"I hope you've had a profitable evening?" he asked nervously.

"Profitable evening? Well—it depends upon what you mean by the word." The old man gestured briefly and led the way through the second door into Panzer's private office.

"Look here, Panzer," he said, pacing up and down in some excitement, "'have you a plan of the orchestra handy which shows each seat, numbered, and all the exits?"

Panzer stared. "I think so. Just a moment." He fumbled in a filing-cabinet, rummaged among some folders and finally brought out a large map of the theatre separated into two sections—one for the orchestra and the other for the balcony.

The Inspector brushed the second away impatiently as he and Ellery bent over the orchestra-plan.* They studied it for a moment. Queen looked up at Panzer, who was shifting from one foot to another on the rug, evidently at a loss to know what would be required of him next.

"May I have this map, Panzer?" asked the Inspector shortly. "I'll return it unbanned in a few days."

* [Author's note:] The plan illustrated in the frontispiece and drawn by Ellery Queen was designed from Manager Panzer's map.—THE EDITOR.

"Certainly, certainly!" said Panzer. "Is there anything else I can do for you now, Inspector? . . . I want to thank you for your consideration m the matter of publicity, sir—Gordon Davis is extremely pleased at the 'house' to-night. He asked me to relay his thanks."

"Not at all—not at all," grumbled the Inspector, folding the map and putting it in his breast-pocket. "It was coming to you—what's right is right. . . . And now, Ellery—If you'll come along. . . . Good night, Panzer. Not a word about this, remember!"

The two Queens slipped out of Panzer's office while he was babbling his reassurances of silence.

They crossed the rear of the orchestra once more, in the direction of the extreme left aisle. The Inspector beckoned curtly to Madge O'Connell.

"Yes," she breathed, her face chalky.

"Just open those doors wide enough to let us through, O'Connell, and forget all about *it* afterward. Understand?" said the Inspector grimly.

She mumbled under her breath as she pushed open one of the big iron doors opposite the LL row. With a last warning shake of the head the Inspector slipped through, Ellery following—and the door came softly back into place again.

∞

At 11 o'clock, as the wide exits were disgorging their first flocks of theatre-goers after the final curtain, Richard and Ellery Queen re-entered the Roman Theatre through the main door.

CHAPTER XVII

In Which More Hats Grow

S it down, Tim—have a cup of coffee?"

Timothy Cronin, a keen-eyed man of medium height thatched plentifully with fire-red hair, seated himself in one of the Queens' comfortable chairs and accepted the Inspector's invitation in some embarrassment.

It was Friday morning and the Inspector and Ellery, garbed romantically in colorful dressing gowns, were in high spirits. They had retired the night before at an uncommonly early hour—for them; they had slept the sleep of the just; now Djuna had a pot of steaming coffee, of a variety which he blended himself, ready on the table; and indubitably all seemed right with the world.

Cronin had stalked into the cheery Queen quarters at an ungodly hour—disheveled, morose and unashamedly cursing. Not even the mild protests of the Inspector were able to stem the tide of profanity which streamed from his lips; and as for Ellery, he listened to the lawyer's language with an air of grave enjoyment, as an amateur harkens to a professional.

Then Cronin awoke to his environment, and blushed, and was invited to sit down, and stared at the unbending back of Djuna as that nimble man-of-affairs busied himself with the light appurtenances of the morning meal.

"I don't suppose you're in a mood to apologize for your shocking language, Tim Cronin, me lad," chided the Inspector, folding his hands Buddha-like over his stomach. "Do I have to inquire the reason for the bad temper?"

"Not much, you don't," growled Cronin, shifting his feet savagely on the rug. "You ought to be able to guess. I'm up against a blank wall in the matter of Field's papers. Blast his black soul!"

"It's blasted, Tim—it's blasted, never fear," said Queen sorrowfully. "Poor Field is probably roasting his toes over a sizzling little coal-fire in Hell just now—and chortling to himself over your profanity. Exactly what is the situation—how do things stand?"

Cronin grasped the cup Djuna had set before him and drained its scalding contents in a gulp. "Stand?" he cried, banging down the cup. "They don't stand—they're nil, nit, not! By Christopher, if I don't get my hands on some documentary evidence soon I'll go batty! Why, Inspector—Stoates and I ransacked that swell office of Field's until I don't think there's a rat in the walls who dares show his head outside a ten-foot hole—and there's nothing. Nothing! Man—it's inconceivable. I'd stake my reputation that somewhere—the Lord alone knows where—Field's papers are hidden, just begging somebody to come along and carry them away."

"You seem possessed of a phobia on the subject of hidden papers, Cronin," remarked Ellery mildly. "One would think we are living in the days of Charles the First. There's no such thing as hidden papers. You merely have to know where to look."

Cronin grinned impertinently. "That's very good of you, Mr. Queen. Suppose you suggest the place Mr. Monte Field selected to hide *his* papers."

Ellery lit a cigarette. "All right. I accept the challenge to combat. . . . You say—and I don't doubt your word in the least—that the documents you suppose to be in existence are not in Field's office. . . . By the way, what makes you so sure that Field kept papers which would incriminate him in this vast clique of gangsters you told us about?"

"He must have," retorted Cronin. "Queer logic, but it works. . . . My information absolutely establishes the fact that Field had correspondence and written plans connecting him with men higher up in gangdom whom we're constantly trying to 'get' and whom we haven't been able to touch so far. You'll have to take my word for it; it's too complicated a story to go into here. But you mark my words, Mr. Queen—Field had papers that he couldn't afford to destroy. Those are the papers I'm looking for."

"Granted," said Ellery in a rhetorical tone. "I merely wished to make certain of the facts. Let me repeat, then, these papers are not in his office. We must therefore look for them farther afield. For example, they might be secreted in a safety-deposit vault."

"But, El," objected the Inspector, who had listened to the interplay between Cronin and Ellery in amusement, "didn't I tell you this morning that Thomas had run that lead to earth? Field did not have a box in a safety-deposit vault. That is established. He had no general delivery or private postoffice box either—under his real name or any other name.

"Thomas has also investigated Field's club affiliations and discovered that the lawyer had no residence, permanent or temporary, besides the flat on 75th Street. Furthermore, in all Thomas' scouting around, he found not the slightest indication of a possible hiding-place. He thought that Field might have left the papers in a parcel or bag in the keeping of a shopkeeper, or something of the sort. But there wasn't a trace. . . . Velie's a good man in these matters, Ellery. You can bet your bottom dollar that hypothesis of yours is false."

"I was making a point for Cronin's benefit," retorted Ellery. He spread his fingers on the table elaborately and winked. "You see, we must narrow the field of search to the point where we can definitely say: 'It must be here.' The office, the safety-deposit vault, the post-office boxes have been ruled out. Yet we know that Field could not afford to keep these documents in a place difficult of access. I cannot vouch for the papers *you're* seeking, Cronin; but it's different with the papers *we're* seeking. No; Field had them somewhere near at hand. . . . And, to go a step further, it's reasonable to assume that he would have kept all his important secret papers in the same hiding-place."

Cronin scratched his head and nodded.

"We shall now apply the elementary precepts, gentlemen." Ellery paused as if to emphasize his next statement. "Since we have narrowed our area of inquiry to the exclusion of all possible hiding-places save one—the papers must be in that one hiding-place. . . . Nothing to that."

"Now that I pause to consider," interpolated the Inspector, his good humor suddenly dissipated into gloom, "perhaps we weren't as careful in that place as we might have been."

"I'm as certain we're on the right track," said Ellery firmly, "as that to-day is Friday and there will be fish suppers in thirty million homes to-night."

Cronin was looking puzzled. "I don't quite get it, Mr. Queen. What do you mean when you say there's only one possible hiding-place left?"

"Field's apartment, Cronin," replied Ellery imperturbably. "The papers are there."

"But I was discussing the case with the D. A. only yesterday," objected Cronin, "and he said you'd already ransacked Field's apartment and found nothing."

"True—true enough," said Ellery. "We searched Field's apartment and found nothing. The trouble was, Cronin, that we didn't look in the right place."

"Well, by ginger, if you know now, let's get a move on!" cried Cronin, springing from his chair.

The Inspector tapped the red-haired man's knee gently and pointed to the seat. "Sit down, Tim," he advised. "Ellery is merely indulging in his favorite game of ratiocination. He doesn't know where the papers are any more than you do. He's guessing. . . . In detective literature," he added with a sad smile, "they call it the 'art of deduction.'"

"I should say," murmured Ellery, emitting a cloud of smoke, "that I am being challenged once more. Nevertheless, although I haven't been back to Field's rooms I intend, with Inspector Queen's kind permission, to return there and find the slippery documents."

"In the matter of these papers—" began the old man, when he was interrupted by the doorbell ringing. Djuna admitted Sergeant Velie, who was accompanied by a small, furtive young man so ill at ease as to be trembling. The Inspector sprang to his feet and intercepted them before they could enter the living-room. Cronin stared as Queen said. "This the fellow, Thomas?" and the big detective answered with grim levity, "Large as life, Inspector."

"Think you could burgle an apartment without being caught, do you?" inquired the Inspector genially, taking the newcomer by the arm. "You're just the man I want."

The furtive young man seemed overcome by a species of terrified palsy. "Say, Inspector, yer not takin' me fer a ride, are ya?" he stammered.

The Inspector smiled reassuringly and led him out into the foyer. They held a whispered and one-sided conversation, with the stranger grunting assents at every second word uttered by the old man. Cronin and Ellery in the living-room caught the flash of a small sheet of paper as it passed from the Inspector's hand into the clutching paw of the young man.

Queen returned, stepping sprily. "All right, Thomas. You take care of the other arrangements and see that our friend here gets into no trouble. . . . Now, gentlemen—"

Velie made his adieu monosyllabically and led the frightened stranger from the apartment.

The Inspector sat down. "Before we go over to Field's rooms, boys," he said thoughtfully, "I want to make certain things plain. In the first place, from what Benjamin Morgan has told us, Field's business was law but his great source of income—blackmail. Did you know that, Tim? Monte Field sucked dozens of prominent men dry, in all likelihood to the tune of hundreds of thousands of dollars. In fact, Tim, we're convinced that the motive behind Field's murder was connected with this phase of his undercover activities. There is no doubt but that he was killed by somebody who was being taken in for huge sums of hush-money and could stand the gaff no longer.

"You know as well as I, Tim, that blackmail depends largely for its ugly life on the possession of incriminating documents by the blackmailer. That's why we're so sure that there are hidden papers about somewhere—and Ellery here maintains that they're in Field's rooms. Well, we'll see. If eventually we find those papers, the documents you've been hunting so long will probably come to light also, as Ellery pointed out a moment ago."

He paused reflectively. "I can't tell you, Tim, how badly I want to get my hands on those confounded documents of Field's. They mean a good deal to me. They'd clear up a lot of questions about which we're still in the dark. . . ."

"Well, then, let's get going!" cried Cronin, leaping from his chair. "Do you realize, Inspector, that I've worked for years on Field's tail for this one purpose? It will be the happiest day of my life. . . . Inspector—come on!"

Neither Ellery nor his father, however, seemed to be in haste. They retired to the bedroom to dress while Cronin fretted in the living-room. If Cronin had not been so preoccupied with his own thoughts he would have noticed that the light spirits which had suffused the Queens when he arrived were now scattered into black gloom. The Inspector particularly seemed out of sorts, irritable and for once slow to push the investigation into an inevitable channel.

Eventually the Queens appeared fully dressed. The three men descended to the street. As they climbed into a taxicab Ellery sighed.

"Afraid you're going to be shown up, son?" muttered the old man, his nose buried in the folds of his topcoat.

"I'm not thinking of that," returned Ellery. "It's something else. . . . The papers will be found, never fear."

"I hope to Christmas you're right!" breathed Cronin fervently, and it was the last word spoken until the taxicab growled to a stop before the lofty apartment-house on 75th Street.

The three men took the elevator to the fourth floor and stepped out into the quiet corridor. The Inspector peered about quickly, then punched the doorbell of the Field apartment. There was no answer, although they could hear the vague rustling of someone behind the door. Suddenly it swished open to reveal a red-faced policeman whose hand hovered uneasily in the region of his hip-pocket.

"Don't be scared, man—we won't bite you!" growled the Inspector, who was completely out of temper for no reason that Cronin, nervous and springy as a racing-colt, could fathom.

The uniformed man saluted. "Didn't know but it might be someone snoopin' around, Inspector," he said feebly.

The three men walked into the foyer, the slim, white hand of the old man pushing the door violently shut.

"Anything been happening around here?" snapped Queen, striding to the entrance to the livingroom and looking inside.

"Not a thing, sir," said the policeman. "I'm on four-hour shifts with Cassidy as relief and once in a while Detective Ritter drops in to see if everything is all right."

"Oh, he does, does he?" The old man turned back. "Anybody try to get into the place?"

"Not while I was here, Inspector—nor Cassidy neither," responded the policeman nervously. "And we've been alternating ever since Tuesday morning. There hasn't been a soul near these rooms except Ritter."

"Park out here in the foyer for the next couple of hours, officer," commanded the Inspector. "Get yourself a chair and take a snooze if you want to—but if anybody should start monkeying with the door tip us off pronto."

The policeman dragged a chair from the living-room into the foyer, sat down with his back against the front door, folded his arms and unashamedly closed his eyes.

The three men took in the scene with gloomy eyes. The foyer was small but crowded with oddments of furniture and decoration. A bookcase filled with unused-appearing volumes; a small table on which perched a "modernistic" lamp and some carved ivory ash-trays; two Empire chairs; a peculiar piece of furniture which seemed half sideboard and half secretary; and a number of cushions and rugs were scattered about. The Inspector stood regarding this melange wryly.

"Here, son—I guess the best way for us to tackle the search is for the three of us to go through everything piece by piece, one checking up on the other. I'm not very hopeful about it. I'll tell you that."

"The gentleman of the Wailing Wall,"[84] groaned Ellery. "Grief is writ and large on his noble visage. You and I, Cronin—we're not such pessimists, are we?"

Cronin growled, "I'd say—less talk and more action, with all the respects in the world for these little family ructions."

Ellery stared at him with admiration. "You're almost insectivorous in your determination, man. More like an army ant than a human being. And poor Field's lying in the morgue, too. . . . *Allons, enfants!*"[85]

They set to work under the nodding head of the policeman. They worked silently for the most part. Ellery's face reflected a calm expectancy; the Inspector's a doleful irritation; Cronin's a savage indomitability. Book after book was extracted from the case and carefully inspected—leaves shaken out—covers examined minutely—backboards pinched and pierced. There were over two hundred books and the thorough search took a long time. Ellery, after a period of activity, seemed inclined to allow his father and Cronin to do the heavier work of inspection while he devoted his attention more and more to the titles of the volumes. At one point he uttered a delighted exclamation and held up to the light a thin, cheaply bound book. Cronin leaped

84. The Wailing Wall, the Western Wall in the old city of Jerusalem, is a place where traditionally Jews have mourned the destruction of the Temple by the Romans.

85. The French national anthem, "Le Marseillaise," begins with the line, "Allons enfants de la Patrie (Arise, children of the fatherland)."

forward immediately, his eyes blazing. The Inspector looked up with a flicker of interest. But Ellery had merely discovered another volume on handwriting analysis.

The old man stared at his son in silent curiosity, his lips puckered thoughtfully. Cronin turned back to the bookcase with a groan. Ellery, however, riffling the pages rapidly cried out again. The two men craned over his shoulder. On the margins of several pages were some penciled notations. The words spelled names: "Henry Jones," "John Smith," George Brown." They were repeated many times on the margins of the page, as if the writer were practicing different styles of penmanship.

"Didn't Field have the most adolescent yen for scribbling?" asked Ellery, staring fascinatedly at the penciled names.

"As usual you have something up your sleeve, my son," remarked the Inspector wearily . . . I see what you mean, but I don't see that it helps us any. Except for—By jinks, that's an idea!"

He bent forward and attacked the search once more, his body vibrant with fresh interest. Ellery, smiling, joined him. Cronin stared uncomprehendingly at both.

"Suppose you let me in on this thing, folks," he said in an aggrieved voice.

The Inspector straightened up. "Ellery's hit on something that, if it's true, is a bit of luck for us and reveals still another sidelight on Field's character. The black-hearted rascal! See here, Tim—if a man's an inveterate blackmailer and you find continual evidence that he has been practicing handwriting from textbooks on the subject, what conclusion would you draw?"

"You mean that he's a forger, too?" frowned Cronin. "I never suspected that in spite of all these years of hounding him."

"Not merely a forger, Cronin," laughed Ellery. "I don't think you will find Monte Field has penned somebody else's name to a check, or anything of that sort. He was too wily a bird to make such a grievous error. What he probably did do was secure original and incriminating documents referring to a certain individual, make copies of them and sell the *copies* back to the owner, retaining the originals for further use!"

"And in that case, Tim," added the Inspector portentously, "if we find this gold mine of papers somewhere about—which I greatly doubt—we'll also find, as like as not, the original or originals of the papers for which Monte Field was murdered!"

The red-haired Assistant District Attorney pulled a long face at his two companions. "Seems like a lot of 'if's'," he said finally, shaking his head.

They resumed the search in growing silence.

Nothing was concealed in the foyer. After an hour of steady, back-breaking work they were forced reluctantly to that conclusion. Not a square inch was left unexamined. The interior of the lamp and of the bookcase; the slender, thin-topped table; the secretary, inside and outside; the cushions; even the walls tapped carefully by the Inspector, who by now was aroused to a high pitch of excitement, suppressed but remarkable in his tight lips and color-touched cheeks.

They attacked the living-room. Their first port-of-call was the big clothes-closet inside the room directly off the foyer. Again the Inspector and Ellery went through the topcoats, overcoats and capes hanging on the rack. Nothing. On the shelf above were the four hats they had examined on Tuesday morning: the old Panama, the derby and the two fedoras. Still nothing. Cronin bumped down on his knees to peer savagely into the darker recesses of the closet, tapping the wall, searching for signs of tampered woodwork. And still nothing. With the aid of a chair the Inspector poked into the corners of the area above the shelf. He climbed down, shaking his head.

"Forget the closet, boys," he muttered. They descended upon the room proper.

The large carved desk which Hagstrom and Piggott had rifled three days before invited their scrutiny. Inside was the pile of papers, canceled bills and letters they had offered for the old man's inspection. Old Queen actually peered through these torn and ragged sheets as if they might conceal messages in invisible ink. He shrugged his shoulders and threw them down.

"Darned if I'm not growing romantic in my old age," he growled. "The influence of a fiction-writing rascal of a son."

He picked up the miscellaneous articles he himself had found on Tuesday in the pockets of the closet coats. Ellery was scowling now; Cronin was beginning to wear a forlorn, philosophical expression; the old man shuffled abstractedly among the keys, old letters, wallet, and then turned away.

"Nothing in the desk," he announced wearily. "I doubt if that clever limb of Satan would have selected anything as obvious as a desk for a hiding-place."

86. Ellery refers to "The Purloined Letter," an 1844 story of Poe's featuring the Chevalier Auguste Dupin, in which the titular purloined letter is found hidden in plain sight.

"He would if he'd read Edgar Allan Poe," murmured Ellery.[86] "Let's get on. Sure there is no secret drawer here?" he asked Cronin. The red head was shaken sadly but emphatically.

They probed and poked about in the furniture, under the carpets and lamps, in book-ends, curtain-rods. With each successive failure the apparent hopelessness of the search was reflected in their faces. When they had finished with the living-room it looked as if it had innocently fallen in the path of a hurricane—a bare and comfortless satisfaction.

"Nothing left but the bedroom, kitchenette and lavatory," said the Inspector to Cronin; and the three men went into the room which Mrs. Angela Russo had occupied Monday night.

Field's bedroom was distinctly feminine in its accoutrements—a characteristic which Ellery ascribed to the influence of the charming Greenwich Villager. Again they scoured the premises, not an inch of space eluding their vigilant eyes and questing hands; and again there seemed nothing to do but admit failure. They took apart the bedding and examined the spring of the bed; they put it together again and attacked the clothes-closet. Every suit was mauled and crushed by their insistent fingers—bathrobes, dressing-gowns, shoes, cravats. Cronin halfheartedly repeated his examination of the walls and moldings. They lifted rugs and picked up chairs; shook out the pages of the telephone book in the bedside telephone-table. The Inspector even lifted the metal disk which fitted around the steam-pipe at the floor, because it was loose and seemed to present possibilities.

From the bedroom they went into the kitchenette. It was so crowded with kitchen furnishings that they could barely move about. A large cabinet was rifled; Cronin's exasperated fingers dipped angrily into the flour- and sugar-bins. The stove, the dish-closet, the pan-closet—even the single marble washtub in a corner—was methodically gone over. On the floor to one side stood the half-empty case of liquor bottles. Cronin cast longing glances in this direction, only to look guiltily away as the Inspector glared at him.

"And now—the bathroom," murmured Ellery. In an ominous silence they trooped into the tiled lavatory. Three minutes later they came out, still silently, and went into the living-room where they disposed themselves in chairs. The Inspector drew out his snuff-box and took a vicious pinch; Cronin and Ellery lit cigarettes.

"I should say, my son," said the Inspector in sepulchral tones after a painful interval broken only by the snores of the policeman in the foyer, "I should say that the deductive method which has brought fame and fortune to Mr. Sherlock Holmes and his legions has gone awry. Mind you, I'm not scolding. . . ." But he slouched into the fastnesses of the chair.

Ellery stroked his smooth jaw with nervous fingers. "I seem to have made something of an ass of myself," he confessed. "And yet those papers are here somewhere. Isn't that a silly notion to have? But logic bears me out. When ten is the whole and two plus three plus four are discarded, only one is left. . . . Pardon me for being old-fashioned. I insist the papers are here."

Cronin grunted and expelled a huge mouthful of smoke.

"Your objection sustained," murmured Ellery, leaning back. "Let's go over the ground again. No, no!" he explained hastily, as Cronin's face lengthened in dismay—"I mean orally . . . Mr. Field's apartment consists of a foyer, a living-room, a kitchenette, a bedroom and a lavatory. We have fruitlessly examined a foyer, a living-room, a kitchenette, a bedroom and a lavatory. Euclid would regretfully force a conclusion here. . . ." He mused. "How have we examined these rooms?" he asked suddenly. "We have gone over the obvious things, pulled the obvious things to pieces. Furniture, lamps, carpets—I repeat, the obvious things. And we have tapped floors, walls and moldings. It would seem that nothing has escaped the search. . . ."

He stopped, his eyes brightening. The Inspector threw off his look of fatigue at once. From experience he was aware that Ellery rarely grew excited over inconsequential things.

"And yet," said Ellery slowly, gazing in fascination at his father's face, "by the Golden Roofs of Seneca,[87] we've overlooked something—actually overlooked something!"

"What!" growled Cronin. "You're kidding."

"Oh, but I'm not," chuckled Ellery, lounging to his feet. "We have examined floors and we have examined walls, but have we examined—ceilings?"

He shot the word forth theatrically while the two men stared at him in amazement.

"Here, what are you driving at, Ellery?" asked his father, frowning.

Ellery briskly crushed his cigarette in an ash-tray. "Just this," he said. "Pure reasoning has it that when you have exhausted

87.   Lucius Annaeus Seneca, a Roman philosopher and dramatist who lived around the time of Jesus, is often cited as the source of the maxim, "Golden roofs break men's rest."

88. Compare Sherlock Holmes on the subject: "How often have I said to you that when you have eliminated the impossible, whatever remains, *however improbable*, must be the truth?" (*The Sign of Four*, 1890). Holmes repeated versions of the maxim in numerous tales.

every possibility but one in a given equation that one, no matter how impossible, no matter how ridiculous it may seem in the postulation—*must be the correct one.* . . .[88] A theorem analogous to the one by which I concluded that the papers were in this apartment."

"But, Mr. Queen, for the love of Pete—ceilings!" exploded Cronin, while the Inspector looked guiltily at the living-room ceiling. Ellery caught the look and laughed, shaking his head.

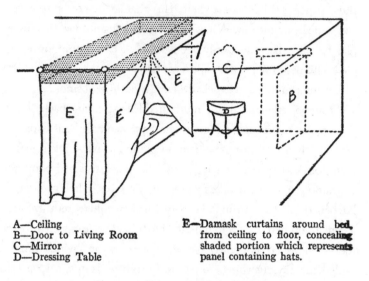

A—Ceiling
B—Door to Living Room
C—Mirror
D—Dressing Table

E—Damask curtains around bed, from ceiling to floor, concealing shaded portion which represents panel containing hats.

Diagram of Monty Field's bedroom.

"I'm not suggesting that we call in a plasterer to maul these lovely middle-class ceilings," he said. "Because I have the answer already. What is it in these rooms somewhere that is on the ceiling?"

"The chandeliers," muttered Cronin doubtfully, gazing upward at the heavily bronzed fixture above their heads.

"By jinks—the canopy over the bed!" shouted the Inspector. He jumped to his feet and ran into the bedroom. Cronin pounded hard after him, Ellery sauntering interestedly behind.

They stopped at the foot of the bed and stared up at the canopy. Unlike the conventional canopies of American style, this florid ornament was not merely a large square of cloth erected on four posts, an integral part of the bed only. The bed was so constructed that the four posts, beginning at the four corners, stretched from floor to ceiling. The heavy maroon-colored damask of the canopy also reached from floor to ceiling, connected at the top by a ringed rod from which the folds of the damask hung gracefully.

"Well, if it's anywhere," grunted the Inspector, dragging one of the damask-covered bedroom chairs to the bed, "it's up there. Here, boys, lend a hand."

He stood on the chair with a fine disregard for the havoc his shoes were wreaking on the silken material. Finding upon stretching his arms above his head that he was still many feet short of touching the ceiling, he stepped down.

"Doesn't look as if you could make it either, Ellery," he muttered. "And Field was no taller than you. There must be a ladder handy somewhere by which Field himself got up here!"

Cronin dashed into the kitchenette at Ellery's nod in that direction. He was back in a moment with a six-foot stepladder. The Inspector, mounting to the highest rung, found that his fingers were still short of touching the rod. Ellery solved the difficulty by ordering his father down and climbing to the top himself. Standing on the ladder he was in a position to explore the top of the canopy.

He grasped the damask firmly and pulled. The entire fabric gave way and fell to the sides, revealing a wooden panel about twelve inches deep—a framework which the hangings had concealed. Ellery's fingers swept swiftly over the wooden relief-work of this panel. Cronin and the Inspector were staring with varying expressions up at him. Finding nothing that at the moment presented a possibility of entrance, Ellery leaned forward and explored the damask directly beneath the floor of the panel.

"Rip it down!" growled the Inspector.

Ellery jerked violently at the material and the entire canopy of damask fell to the bed. The bare unornamented floor of the panel was revealed.

"It's hollow," announced Ellery, rapping his knuckles on the under-side paneling.

"That doesn't help much," said Cronin. "It wouldn't be a solid chunk, anyway. Why don't you try the other side of the bed, Mr. Queen?"

But Ellery, who had drawn back and was again examining the side of the panel, exclaimed triumphantly. He had been seeking a complicated, Machiavellian "secret door"—he found now that the secret door was nothing more subtle than a sliding-panel. It was cleverly concealed—the juncture of sliding and stationary panels was covered by a row of wooden rosettes and clumsy

89. Ellery refers to the Biblical episode recorded in *Daniel* 5, in which this phrase appears, written on the wall by a mysterious hand—the source of the proverbial handwriting on the wall.

90. "Lay on, Macduff" is a phrase from the final scene of Shakespeare's *Macbeth*, often misquoted as "Lead on, Macduff," Act V, Scene 8.

91. "Friends, Romans, countrymen" is the first line of a speech by Marc Antony in Shakespeare's *Julius Caesar*, Act III, Scene 2.

decorations—but it was nothing that a student of mystery lore would have hailed as a triumph of concealment.

"It begins to appear as if I were being vindicated," Ellery chuckled as he peered into the black recesses of the hole he had uncovered. He thrust a long arm into the aperture. The Inspector and Cronin were staring at him with bated breath.

"By all the pagan gods," shouted Ellery suddenly, his lean body quivering with excitement. "Do you remember what I told you, dad? Where would those papers be except in—hats!"

His sleeve coated with dust, he withdrew his arm and the two men below saw in his hand a musty silk tophat!

Cronin executed an intricate jig as Ellery dropped the hat on the bed and dipped his arm once more into the yawning hole. In a moment he had brought out another hat—and another—and still another! There they lay on the bed—two silk hats and two derbies.

"Take this flashlight, son," commanded the Inspector. "See if there's anything else up there."

Ellery took the proffered electric torch and flashed its beam into the aperture. After a moment he clambered down, shaking his head.

"That's all," he announced, dusting his sleeve, "but I should think it would be enough."

The Inspector picked up the four hats and carried them into the living-room, where he deposited them on a sofa. The three men sat down gravely and regarded each other.

"I'm sort of itching to see what's what," said Cronin finally, in a hushed voice.

"I'm rather afraid to look," retorted the Inspector.

"*Mene mene tekel upharsin*,"[89] laughed Ellery. "In this case it might be interpreted as 'the handwriting on the panel.' Examine on, Macduff!"[90]

The Inspector picked up one of the silk hats. It bore on the rich satiny lining the chaste trademark of Browne Bros. Ripping out the lining and finding nothing beneath, he tried to tear out the leather sweat-band. It resisted his mightiest efforts. He borrowed Cronin's pocket-knife and with difficulty slashed away the band. Then he looked up.

"This hat, Romans and countrymen,"[91] he said pleasantly, "contains nothing but the familiar ingredients of hat-wear. Would you care to examine it?"

Cronin uttered a savage cry and snatched it from the Inspector's hand. He literally tore the hat to pieces in his rage.

"Heck!" he said disgustedly, throwing the remnants on the floor. "Explain that to my undeveloped brain, will you, Inspector?"

Queen smiled, taking up the second silk hat and regarding it curiously.

"You're at a disadvantage, Tim," he said. "We know why one of these hats is a blank. Don't we, Ellery?"

"Michaels," murmured Ellery.

"Exactly—Michaels," returned the Inspector.

"Charley Michaels!" exclaimed Cronin. "Field's strong-arm guy, by all that's holy! Where docs he come into this?"

"Can't tell yet. Know anything about him?"

"Nothing except that he hung onto Field's coat-tails pretty closely. He's an ex-jailbird, did you know that?"

"Yes," replied the Inspector dreamily. "We'll have a talk about that phase of Mr. Michaels some other time. . . . But let me explain that hat: Michaels on the evening of the murder laid out, according to his statement, Field's evening clothes, including a silk hat. Michaels swore that as far as he knew Field possessed only *one* topper. Now if we suppose that Field used hats for concealing papers, and was going to the Roman Theatre that night wearing a 'loaded' one he must necessarily have substituted the loaded hat for the empty one which Michaels prepared. Since he was so careful to keep only one silk hat in the closet, he realized that Michaels, should he find a topper, would be suspicious. So, in switching hats, he had to conceal the empty one. What more natural than that he should put it in the place from which he had taken the loaded hat—the panel above the bed?"

"Well, I'll be switched!" exclaimed Cronin.

"Finally," resumed the Inspector, "We can take it as gospel that Field, who was devilishly careful in the matter of his headgear, intended to restore the theatre hat to its hideaway when he got home from the Roman. Then he would have taken out this one which you've just torn up and put it back in the clothes-closet. . . .[92] But let's get on."

He pulled down the leather inner-band of the second silk hat, which also bore the imprint of Browne Bros. "Look at this, will

[92.] There would, of course, have been no reason to do so if the hat Fields wore to the theater was identical to the hat normally kept in the closet. Returning the hat he wore to its hiding-place would have been necessary, however, if it were a different style from that normally kept in the closet (which is certainly possible if it were purchased at a different time than the "closeted" hat), and we learn shortly another reason why the switch would have been made (though this detail was not yet known to the Inspector).

The odds of the first hat seized being the "blank" were only one-in-four, but having the first be empty made for greater drama—perhaps an embellishment of the narrator's?

you!" he exclaimed. The two men bent over and saw on the inner surface of the band, lettered with painful clarity in a purplish ink, the words BENJAMIN MORGAN.[93]

"I've got to pledge you to secrecy, Tim," said the Inspector immediately, turning to the red-haired man. "Never let on that you were a witness to the finding of papers in any way implicating Benjamin Morgan in this affair."

"What do you think I am, Inspector?" growled Cronin. "I'm as dumb as an oyster, believe me!"

"All right, then." Queen felt the lining of the hat. There was a distinct crackle.

"Now," remarked Ellery calmly, "we know for the first time definitely why the murderer *had* to take away the hat Field wore Monday night. In all likelihood the murderer's name was lettered in the same way—that's indelible ink, you know—and the murderer couldn't leave a hat with his own name in it at the scene of the crime."

"By gosh, if you only had that hat, now," cried Cronin, "you'd know who the murderer is!"

"I'm afraid, Tim," replied the Inspector dryly, "that hat is gone forever."

He indicated a row of careful stitches at the base of the inner band, where the lining was attached to the fabric. He ripped these stitches swiftly and inserted his fingers between the lining and the crown. Silently he drew out a sheaf of papers held together by a thin rubber band.

"If I were as nasty as some people think I am," mused Ellery, leaning back, "I might with perfect justice say, 'I told you so.'"

"We know when we're licked, my son—don't rub it in," chortled the Inspector. He snapped off the rubber band, glanced hastily through the papers and with a satisfied grin deposited them in his breast pocket.

"Morgan's, all right," he said briefly, and attacked one of the derbies.

The inner side of the band was marked cryptically with an X. The Inspector found a row of stitches exactly as in the silk hat. The papers he drew out—a thicker bundle than Morgan's—he examined cursorily. Then he handed them to Cronin, whose fingers were trembling.

"A stroke of luck, Tim," he said slowly. "The man you were angling for is dead, but there are a lot of big names in this. I think you'll find yourself a hero one of these days."

Cronin grasped the bundle and feverishly unfolded the papers, one by one. "They're here—they're here!" he shouted. He jumped to his feet, stuffing the sheaf into his pocket.

"I've got to beat it, Inspector," he said rapidly. "There's a load of work to do at last—and besides, what you find in that fourth hat is none of my business. I can't thank you and Mr. Queen enough! So long!"

He dashed from the room, and a moment later the snores of the policeman in the foyer came to an abrupt end. The outer door banged shut.

Ellery and the Inspector looked at each other.

"I don't know what good this stuff is going to do us," grumbled the old man, fumbling with the inner band of the last hat, a derby. "We've found things and deduced things and run rings around our imaginations—well. . . ." He sighed as he held the band up to the light.

It was marked: MISC.

CHAPTER XVIII

Stalemate

At Friday noon, while Inspector Queen, Ellery and Timothy Cronin were deep in their search of Monte Field's rooms, Sergeant Velie, sombre and unmoved as usual, walked slowly up 87th Street from Broadway, mounted the brownstone steps of the house in which the Queens lived and rang the bell. Djuna's cheery voice bade him ascend, which the good Sergeant did with gravity.

"Inspector's not home!" announced Djuna pertly, his slim body completely hidden behind an enormous housewife's apron. Odorous traces of an onion-covered steak pervaded the air.

"Get on with you, you imp!" growled Velie. He took, from his inner breast pocket a bulky envelope sealed, and handed it to Djuna. "Give this to the Inspector when he comes home. Forget, and I'll dip you into the East River."

"You and who else?" breathed Djuna, with a remarkable twitching of his lips. Then he added decorously, "Yes, sir."

"All right, then." Velie deliberately turned about and descended to the street, where his broad back was visible in formidable proportions to the grinning Djuna from the fourth-story window.

When, at a little before six, the two Queens trudged wearily into their rooms, the alert eyes of the Inspector pounced upon the official envelope where it lay on his plate.

He tore off a corner of the envelope and pulled out a number of typewritten sheets on the stationery of the Detective Bureau.

"Well, well!" he muttered to Ellery, who was lazily pulling off his topcoat. "The clans are gathering. . . ."[94]

Sinking into an armchair, his hat forgotten on his head, his coat still buttoned, he set about reading the reports aloud.

The first slip read:

REPORT OF RELEASE

28 September 192-

John Cazzanelli, alias Parson Johnny, alias John the Wop, alias Peter Dominick, released from custody to-day on parole.

Under-cover investigation of J. C.'s complicity in the robbery of the Bonomo Silk Mills (June 2, 192-) not successful. We are searching for "Dinky" Morehouse, police informer, who has disappeared from usual haunts, for further information.

Release effected under advice of District Attorney Sampson. J. C. under surveillance and is available at any time.

T. V.

The second report which the Inspector picked up, laying aside the advices concerning Parson Johnny with a frown, read as follows:

REPORT ON WILLIAM PUSAK

September 28, 192-

Investigation of the history of William Pusak reveals the following:

32 years old; born in Brooklyn, N.Y., of naturalized parents; unmarried; regular habits; socially inclined; has "dates" three or four nights a week; religious. Is book-keeper at Stein & Ranch, clothing merchants, 1076 Broadway. Does not gamble or drink. No evil companions. Only vice seems fondness for girls.

94. The traditional Scottish song "The Gathering of the Clans" begins with the line "The clans are gathering, gathering, gathering . . ."

95.   The prison of the City of New York was known as the Tombs, originally built in 1888, and persons held for arraignment or trial were incarcerated there. See *The Benson Murder Case*, note 71.

Activities since Monday night normal. No letters sent, no money withdrawn from bank, hours fairly regular. No suspicious movements of any kind.

Girl, Esther Jablow; seems Pusak's "steadiest." Has seen E. J. twice since Monday—Tuesday at lunch, Wednesday evening. Went to movies and Chinese restaurant Wednesday evening.

Operative No. 4
(OK'd: T. V.)

The Inspector grunted as he threw the sheet aside. The third report was headed:

REPORT ON MADGE O'CONNELL

To Friday, Sept. 28, '2-

O'Connell, lives at 1436-10th Avenue. Tenement, 4th floor. No lather. Idle after Monday night, due to shutting down of Roman Theatre. Left theatre Monday night at general release of public. Went home, but stopped in drug-store corner 8th Avenue and 48th Street to telephone. Unable to trace call. Overheard reference to Parson Johnny in 'phone conversation. Seemed excited.

Tuesday did not leave house until 1 o'clock. No attempt to get in touch with Parson Johnny at Tombs.[95]

Went around theatre employment agencies looking for usherette position after finding out Roman Theatre was closed indefinitely.

Nothing new Wednesday all day or Thursday. Returned to work at Roman Thursday night after call from manager. No attempt see or communicate with Parson Johnny. No incoming calls, no visitors, no mail. Seemed suspicious—think she is "wise" to tailing.

Operative No. 11
OK'd: T. V.

"Hmph!" muttered the Inspector as he picked up the next sheet of paper. "Let's see what this one says. . . ."

September 28, 192-

F. I.-P. left Roman Theatre Monday night directly after release from Manager's Office by Inspector Queen. Examined with other departing members of audience at main door. Left in company of Eve Ellis, Stephen Barry, Hilda Orange, of the cast. Took taxi to Ives-Pope house on Riverside Drove. Taken out in half-unconscious condition. Three actors left home soon after.

Tuesday she did not leave house. Learned from a gardener she was laid up in bed all day. Learned she received many calls during day.

Did not appear formally until Wednesday morning at interview in house with Inspector Queen. After interview, left house in company of Stephen Barry, Eve Ellis, James Peale, her brother Stanford. Ives-Pope limousine drove party out into Westchester. Outing revived F. Evening stayed at home with Stephen Barry. Bridge-party on.

Thursday went shopping on Fifth Avenue. Met Stephen Barry for luncheon. He took her to Central Park; spent afternoon in open. S. B. escorted her home before five. S. B. stayed to dinner, leaving after dinner for work at Roman Theatre on call from stage manager. F. I.-P. spent evening at home with family.

No report Friday morning. No suspicious actions all week. At no time accosted by strange persons. No communication from or to Benjamin Morgan.

Operative No. 39
OK'd: T. V.

"And that's that," murmured the Inspector. The next report he selected was extremely short.

REPORT ON OSCAR LEWIN
September 28, 192-

Lewin spent all day Tuesday, Wednesday, Thursday and Friday morning at office of Monte Field working with

Messrs. Stoates and Cronin. Three men lunched together on each day.

Lewin married, lives in Bronx, 211 E. 156th Street. Spent every evening at home. No suspicious mail, no suspicious calls. No evil habits. Leads sober, modest life. Has good reputation.

Operative No. 16

Note: Full details of Oscar Lewin's history, habits, etc., available on request through Timothy Cronin, Assistant District Attorney.

T. V.

The Inspector sighed as he deposited the five sheets of paper on his plate, rose, doffed his hat and coat, flung them into Djuna's waiting arms and sat down again. Then he picked up the last report from the contents of the envelope—a larger sheet to which was pinned a small slip marked: MEMORANDUM TO R.Q. This slip read:

Dr. Prouty left the attached report with me this morning for transmission to you. He is sorry he could not report in person, but the Burbridge poison-case is taking all his time.

It was signed with Velie's familiar scrawling initials.

The attached sheet was a hastily typewritten message on the letterhead of the Chief Medical Examiner's office.

Dear Q [the message ran]: Here's the dope on the tetra ethyl lead. Jones and I have been superintending an exhaustive probe of all possible sources of dissemination. No success, and I think you can resign yourself to your fate in this respect. You'll never trace the poison that killed Monte Field. This is the opinion not merely of your humble servant but of the Chief and of Jones. We all agree that the most logical explanation is the gasoline theory. Try to trace *that,* Sherlocko!

A postscript in Dr. Pronty's handwriting ran:

Of course, if anything turns up, I'll let you know imme-diately. Keep sober.

"Fat lot of good *that* is!" mumbled the Inspector, as Ellery without a word attacked the aromatic and tempting meal that the priceless Djuna had prepared. The Inspector dug viciously into the fruit salad. He looked far from happy. He grumbled beneath his breath, cast baleful glances at the sheaf of reports by his plate, peered up at Ellery's tired face and heartily munching jaws and finally threw down his spoon altogether.

"Of all the useless, exasperating, empty bunch of reports I ever saw—!" he growled.

Ellery smiled. "You remember Periander, of course. . . . Eh? You might be polite, sir. . . . Periander of Corinth, who said in a moment of sobriety, 'To industry nothing is impossible!'"[96]

⁓∞⁓

With the fire roaring, Djuna curled up on the floor in a corner, his favorite attitude. Ellery smoked a cigarette and stared comfort-ably into the flames while old Queen crammed his nose venge-fully with the contents of his snuff-box. The two Queens settled down to a serious discussion. To be more exact—Inspector Queen settled down and lent the tone of seriousness to the conversation, since Ellery seemed in a sublimely dreamy mood far removed from the sordid details of crime and punishment.

The old man brought his hand down on the aim of his chair with a sharp slap. "Ellery, did you ever in your born days see a case so positively nerve-racking?"

"On the contrary," commented Ellery, staring with half-closed eyes into the fire. "You are developing a natural case of nerves. You allow little things like apprehending a murderer to upset you unduly. Pardon the hedonistic philosophy. . . . If you will recall, in my story entitled 'The Affair of the Black Widow,' my good sleuths had no difficulty at all in laying their hands on the criminal. And why? Because they kept their heads. Conclusion: Always keep your head. . . . I'm thinking of to-morrow. Glorious vacation!"

"For an educated man, my son," growled the Inspector petu-lantly, "you show a surprising lack of coherence. You say things

96.   Periander was a ruler of Corinth who died in 585 B.C.E. There is no definitive source for the many maxims ascribed to him.

97.   A real place near Jericho, Gehenna was held to be the final resting place of the ungodly or evildoers, as compared to Hades, which was merely a destination of all of the dead.

98.   Hermes, the messenger of the gods and father of Pan, was also the patron of thieves. Pan, on the other hand, was viewed as a god of nature and sexuality. Elllery's remark is opaque.

that mean nothing and mean things when you say nothing. No—I'm all mixed up—"

Ellery burst into laughter. "The Maine woods—the russet—the good Chauvin's cabin by the lake—a rod—air—Oh, Lord, won't to-morrow ever come?"

Inspector Queen regarded his son with a pitiful eagerness. "I—I sort of wish . . . Well, never mind." He sighed. "All I do say, El, is that if my little burglar fails—it's all up with us."

"To the blessed Gehenna[97] with burglars!" cried Ellery. "What has Pan[98] to do with human tribulation? My next book is as good as written, dad."

"Stealing another idea from real life, you rascal!" muttered the old man. "If you're borrowing the Field case for your plot, I'd be extremely interested to read your last few chapters!"

"Poor dad!" chuckled Ellery. "Don't take life so seriously. If you fail, you fail. Monte Field wasn't worth a hill of legumes, anyway."

"That's not the point," said the old man. "I hate to admit defeat. . . . What a queer mess of motives and schemes this case is, Ellery. This is the first time in my entire experience that I have had such a hard nut to crack. It's enough to give a man apoplexy! I know WHO committed the murder—I know WHY the murder was committed—I even know HOW the murder was committed! And where am I? . . ." He paused and savagely took a pinch of snuff. "A million miles from nowhere, *that's* where!" he growled, and subsided.

"Certainly a most unusual situation," murmured Ellery. "Yet—more difficult things have been accomplished. . . . Heigh-ho! I can't wait to bathe myself in that Arcadian stream!"

"And get pneumonia, probably," said the Inspector anxiously. "You promise me now, young man, that you don't do any back-to-Nature stunts out there. I don't want a funeral on my hands—I . . ."

Ellery grew silent suddenly. He looked over at his father. The Inspector seemed strangely old in the flickering light of the fire. An expression of pain humanized the deeply sculptured lines of his face. His hand, brushing back his thick grey hair, looked alarmingly fragile.

Ellery rose, hesitated, colored, then bent swiftly forward and patted his father on the shoulder.

"Brace up, dad," he said in a low voice. "If it weren't for my arrangements with Chauvin . . . Everything will be all right—take my word for it. If there were the slightest way in which I could help you by remaining. . . . But there isn't. It's your job now, dad—and there's no man in the world who can handle it better than you. . . ." The old man stared up at him with a strange affection. Ellery turned abruptly away. "Well," he said lightly, "I'll have to pack now if I expect to make the 7:45 out of Grand Central to-morrow morning."

He disappeared into the bedroom. Djuna, who had been sitting Turkish-wise in his comer, got quickly to his feet and crossed the room to the Inspector's chair. He slipped to the floor, his head resting against the old man's knees. The silence was punctuated by the snapping of wood in the fireplace and the muffled sounds of Ellery moving about in the next room.

Inspector Queen was very tired. His face, worn, thin, white, lined, was like a cameo in the dull red light. His hand caressed Djuna's curly head.

"Djuna, lad," he muttered, "never be a policeman when you grow up."

Djuna twisted his neck and stared gravely at the old man. "I'm going to be just what you are," he announced. . . .

The old man leaped to his feet as the telephone bell rang. He snatched the instrument from its table, his face livid, and said in a choked voice: "Queen speaking. Well?"

After a time he put down the 'phone and trudged across the room toward the bedroom. He leaned against the lintel heavily. Ellery straightened up from his suitcase—and jumped forward.

"Dad!" he cried. "What's the matter?"

The Inspector essayed a feeble smile. "Just—a little—tired, son, I guess," he grunted. "I just heard from our housebreaker . . ."

"And—?"

"He found absolutely nothing."

Ellery gripped his father's arm and led him to the chair by the bed. The old man slumped into it, his eyes ineffably weary. "Ellery, old son," he said, "the last shred of evidence is gone. It's maddening! Not a morsel of physical, tangible evidence that would convict the murderer in court. What have we? A series of perfectly sound deductions—and that's all. A good lawyer would make Swiss cheese out of our case. . . . Well! The last word hasn't been spoken yet," he added with a sudden grimness as he rose from the chair. He pounded Ellery's broad back in returning vigor.

"Get to bed, son," he said. "You've got to get up early to-morrow morning. I'm going to sit up and think."

In Which the Reader's Attention is Respectfully Requested

The current vogue in detective literature is all for the practice of placing the reader in the position of chief sleuth. I have prevailed upon Mr. Ellery Queen to permit at this point in The Roman Hat Mystery the interpolation of a challenge to the reader. . . . "Who killed Monte Field?" "How was the murder accomplished?" . . . Mr. Queen agrees with me that the alert student of mystery tales, now being in possession of all the pertinent facts, should at this stage of the story have reached definite conclusions on the questions propounded. The solution—or enough of it to point unerringly to the guilty character—may be reached by a series of logical deductions and psychological observations. . . . In closing my last personal appearance in the tale let me admonish the reader with a variation of the phrase *Caveat Emptor:* "Let the reader beware!"

J. J. McC.

 PART FOUR

"'The perfect criminal is a superman. He must be meticulous in his techniques: unseen, unseeable, a Lone Wolf. He must have neither friends nor dependents. He must be careful to a fault, quick of brain, hand and foot. . . . But these are nothing. There have been such men. . . . On the other hand, he must be a favored child of Fate—for circumstances over which he cannot have the remotest control must never contrive his downfall. This, I think, is more difficult to achieve. . . . But the last is most difficult of all. *He must never repeat his crime, his weapon or his motive! . . .* In all my two-score years as an official of the American police I have not once encountered the perfect criminal nor investigated the perfect crime."

—From *American Crime and Methods of Detection,*
by Richard Queen.

CHAPTER XIX

In Which Inspector Queen Conducts More Legal Conversations

It was notable, particularly to District Attorney Sampson, that on Saturday evening Inspector Richard Queen was far from being himself. The old man was irritable, snappish and utterly uncongenial. He paced fretfully across the carpet of Manager Louis Panzer's office, biting his lips and muttering beneath his breath. He seemed oblivious to the presence of Sampson, Panzer and a third person who had never been in that theatrical sanctum before and was seated, mouse-like, in one of Panzer's big chairs, his eyes like saucers. This was bright-eyed Djuna, granted the unprecedented privilege of accompanying his grey patron on this latest incursion into the Roman Theatre.

In truth, Queen was singularly depressed. He had many times in his official life been confronted by apparently insoluble problems; he had as many times brought triumph out of failure. The Inspector's strange manner therefore was doubly inexplicable to Sampson, who had been associated with the old man for years and had never seen him so completely unstrung.

The old man's moodiness was not due to the progress of the Field investigation, as Sampson worriedly thought. Wiry little Djuna, sitting open-mouthed in his comer, was the only spectator to the Inspector's mad pacing who could have put his finger on the truth. Djuna, wise by virtue of *gamin* perspicacity, observant by nature, familiar with Queen's temperament through a loving association, knew that his patron's manner was due solely to Ellery's absence from the scene. Ellery had left New York on the 7:45 express that morning, having been gloomily accompanied to the station by his father. At the last moment the younger man had changed his mind, announcing his decision to forego the trip to Maine and abide in New York by his father's side until the case was concluded. The old man would have none of it. With his shrewd insight into Ellery's nature, he realized how keenly his highly strung son had been looking forward to this first vacation in over a year. It was not in his heart, impatient as he was for the constant presence of his son, to deprive him of this long contemplated pleasure trip.

Accordingly, he had swept aside Ellery's proposal and pushed him up the steps of the train, with a parting clap and a wan smile. Ellery's last words, shouted from the platform as the train glided out of the station, were: "I'm not forgetting you, dad. You'll hear from me sooner than you expect!"

Now, torturing the nap of Manager Panzer's rug, the Inspector was feeling the full impact of their separation. His brain was addled, his constitution flabby, his stomach weak, his eyes dim. He felt completely out of tune with the world and its denizens, and he made no attempt to conceal his irritation.

"Should be about time now, Panzer," he growled to the stout little manager. "How long does this infernal audience take to clear out, anyway?"

"In a moment, Inspector, in a moment," replied Panzer. The District Attorney sniffed away the remnants of his cold. Djuna stared in fascination at his god.

A rap on the door twisted their heads about. Tow-headed Harry Neilson, the publicity man, poked his rugged face into the room. "Mind if I join the little party, Inspector?" he inquired cheerfully. "I was in at the birth, and if there's going to be a death—why, I'm aiming to stick around, with your permission!"

The Inspector shot him a dour glance from beneath his shaggy eyebrows. He stood in a Napoleonic attitude, his every hair and muscle bristling with ill-nature. Sampson regarded him in surprise. Inspector Queen was showing an unexpected side to his temper.

"Might's well," he barked. "One more won't hurt. There's an army here as it is."

Neilson reddened slightly and made a move as if to withdraw. The Inspector's eye twinkled with a partial return to good spirits.

"Here—sit down, Neilson," he said, not unkindly. "Mustn't mind an old fogey like me. I'm just frazzled a bit. Might need you to-night at that."

"Glad to be let in on it, Inspector," grinned Neilson. "What's the idea—sort of Spanish Inquisition?"

"Just about." The old man bent his brows. "But—we'll see."

At this moment the door opened and the tall, broad figure of Sergeant Velie stepped quickly into the room. He was carrying a sheet of paper which he handed to the Inspector.

"All present, sir," he said.

"Everybody out?" snapped Queen.

"Yes, sir. I've told the cleaning-women to go down into the lounge and hang around until we're through. Cashiers have gone home, so have the ushers and usherettes. Cast is backstage, I guess, getting dressed."

"'Right. Let's go, gentlemen." The Inspector stalked out of the room followed closely by Djuna, who had not opened his mouth all evening except to emit noiseless gasps of admiration, for no reason that the bemused District Attorney could see. Panzer, Sampson and Neilson also followed, Velie bringing up the rear.

The auditorium was again a vast and deserted place, the empty rows of seats stark and cold. The lights of the theatre had been switched on in full and their cold radiance lit up every corner of the orchestra.

As the five men and Djuna swung toward the extreme left aisle, there was a concerted bobbing of heads from the left section of seats. It was apparent now that a small group of people were awaiting the arrival of the Inspector, who walked heavily down the aisle and took up a position in front of the left boxes, so that all the seated people faced him. Panzer, Neilson and Sampson stood at the head of the aisle with Djuna at one side, a feverish spectator.

The assembled party was placed peculiarly. From the row nearest the Inspector, who stood about half-way down the orchestra, and proceeding towards the rear the only seats occupied were those directly on the left aisle. The end two seats of the dozen rows were filled by a motley aggregation—men and women, old and young. They were the same people who had occupied these chairs on the night of the fatal performance and whom

Inspector Queen had personally examined after the discovery of the body. In the section of eight seats—Monte Field's and the empty ones which had surrounded it—were grouped William Pusak, Esther Jablow, Madge O'Connell, Jess Lynch and Parson Johnny—the Parson furtive-eyed, uneasy and whispering to the usherette behind nicotined fingers.

At the Inspector's sudden gesture all became silent as the grave. Sampson, looking about him at the bright chandeliers and lights, the deserted theatre, the lowered curtain, could not help feeling that the stage was being set for dramatic revelations. He leaned forward interestedly. Panzer and Neilson were quiet and watchful. Djuna kept his eyes fixed on the old man.

"Ladies and gentlemen," Queen announced curtly, staring at the assembled company, "I've brought you here for a definite purpose. I will not keep you any longer than is absolutely necessary, but what is necessary and what is not necessary is entirely up to me. If I find that I do not receive what I consider truthful answers to my questions, everybody will stay here until I am satisfied. I want that thoroughly understood before we proceed."

He paused and glared about. There was a ripple of apprehension, a sudden crackle of conversation which died as quickly as it was born.

"On Monday night," continued the Inspector frostily, "you people attended the performance at this theatre and, with the exception of certain employees and others now seated at the rear, occupied the seats in which you now find yourselves." Sampson grinned as he noticed the stiffening of backs at these words, as if each individual felt his seat grow suddenly warm and uncomfortable beneath him.

"I want you to imagine that this is Monday night. I want you to think back to that night and try to remember everything that happened. By everything I mean any occurrence, no matter how trivial or apparently unimportant, that might have left an impression on your memory. . . ."

As the Inspector warmed to his words, a number of people drifted into the orchestra at the rear. Sampson greeted them in whispers. The little party was composed of Eve Ellis, Hilda Orange, Stephen Barry, James Peale and three or four other members of the cast of "Gunplay." They were dressed in their street-clothes. Peale whispered to Sampson that they had just come from their dressing-rooms and had dropped into the audi-torium on hearing voices.

"Queen's holding a little pow-wow," whispered Sampson in return.

"Do you think the Inspector has any objections to our staying a while and listening?" asked Barry in a low tone, with an appre-hensive glance toward the Inspector, who had stopped and was staring icily in their direction.

"Don't see why—" began Sampson worriedly, when Eve Ellis murmured "Shhh!" and they all became silent.

"*Now*—" said the Inspector venomously, when the flurry had subsided, "this is the situation. Remember, you are now back in Monday evening. The curtain has gone up on the second act and the theatre is dark. There is a lot of noise from the stage and you are intent on the exciting sequences of the play. . . . Did any of you, especially those sitting in the aisle seats, notice anything peculiar, unusual or disturbing around or near you at that time?"

He paused expectantly. There were puzzled, fearful shakings of the head. No one answered.

"Think hard," growled the Inspector. "You remember on Monday night I went down this aisle and questioned all of you in the same vein. Naturally I don't want lies, and I can't rea-sonably expect that you will tell me something startling now when you could remember nothing Monday night. But this is a desperate situation. A man was murdered here and we are frankly up against it. One of the most difficult cases we have ever encountered! In the light of such a condition, when we find ourselves against a blank wall with not the slightest idea where to turn—I am being honest with you as I expect you to be with me—I *must* turn to you as the only members of the audience five nights ago who were in a position to see something important, if anything important occurred. . . . It has been my experience that often, under stress of nervousness and excitement, a man or woman will forget a little detail that returns to memory after a few hours, days, weeks of normalcy. It is my hope that some-thing of the sort has taken place with you. . . ."

As Inspector Queen spoke, the words dropping acidly from his lips, the company lost its nervousness in its fascinated interest. When he paused, people put their heads together and whispered excitedly, shaking their heads at times, arguing in fierce, low tones at others. The Inspector waited in a resigned patience.

"Raise your hands if you have something to tell me. . . ." he said.

A woman's timid white hand fluttered aloft.

"Yes, madam?" commanded Queen, pointing his finger. "Do you recall anything unusual?"

A withered old lady rose embarrassedly to her feet and began to stammer in a squeaking voice. "I don't know whether it's important or not, sir," she said tremulously. "But I do remember some time during the second act a woman, I think it was, walking down the aisle and a few seconds later walking up again."

"Yes? That's interesting, madam," commented the Inspector. "About what time was this—can you recall?"

"I don't remember the time, sir," shrilled the old lady, "but it was about ten minutes or so after the beginning of the act."

"I see. . . . And do you recall anything of her appearance? Was she young or old? What did she wear?"

The old lady looked troubled. "I don't exactly remember, sir," she quavered. "I wasn't paying—"

A high, clear voice interrupted from the rear. Heads twisted about. Madge O'Connell had jumped to her feet.

"You don't have to mess around with that any more, Inspector," she announced coldly. "That lady saw *me* walking down the aisle and back again. That was before I—you know." She winked pertly in the Inspector's direction.

People gasped. The old lady stared with pitiful bewilderment at the usherette, then at the Inspector and finally sat down.

"I'm not surprised," said the Inspector quietly. "Well, anybody else?"

There was no answer. Realizing that the company might feel shy of announcing their thoughts in public Queen started up the aisle, working from row to row, questioning each person separately in tones inaudible to the rest. When he had finished he returned slowly to his original position.

"I see that I must allow you ladies and gentlemen to return to your peaceful firesides. Thank you very much for your help. . . . Dismissed!"

He flung the word at them. They stared at him dazedly, then rose in muttering groups, took up their coats and hats and under

Velie's stern eye began to file out of the theatre. Hilda Orange, standing in the group behind the last row, sighed.

"It's almost embarrassing to see that poor old gentleman's disappointment," she whispered to the others. "Come on, folks, let's be going, too."

The actors and actresses left the theatre among the departing company.

When the last man and woman had disappeared, the Inspector marched back up the aisle and stood gloomily staring at the little group who were left. They seemed to sense the seething fire in the old man and they cowered. But the Inspector, with a characteristic lightning change of front, became human again.

He sat down in one of the seats and folded his arms over the back, surveying Madge O'Connell, Parson Johnny and the others.

"All right, folks," he said in a genial tone. "How about you, Parson? You're a free man, you don't have to worry about silks any more and you can speak up now like any self-respecting citizen. Can you give us any help in this affair?"

"Naw," grunted the little gangster. "I told you all I knew. Ain't got a thing to say."

"I see. . . . You know, Parson, that we're interested in your dealings with Field." The gangster looked up in shocked surprise. "Oh, yes," continued the Inspector. "We want you to tell us sometime about your business with Mr. Field in the past. You'll keep that in mind, won't you? . . . Parson," he said sharply, "who killed Monte Field? Who had it in for him? If you know—out with it!"

"Aw, Inspector," the Parson whined, "you ain't pullin' that stuff on me again, are you? How should I know? Field was one slick guy—he didn't go around welching on his enemies. No, sir! *I* wouldn't know. . . . He was pretty good to me—got me off on a couple of charges," he admitted unblushingly. "But I didn't have no more idea he was here Monday night than—hell, than anything."

The Inspector turned to Madge O'Connell.

"How about you, O'Connell?" he asked softly. "My son, Mr. Queen, tells me that on Monday night you confided in him about closing the exit-doors. You didn't say anything to me about that. What do *you* know?"

The girl returned his stare coolly. "I told you once, Inspector. I haven't a thing to say."

"And you, William Pusak—" Queen turned to the wizened little bookkeeper. "Do you remember anything now that you forgot Monday night?"

Pusak wriggled uncomfortably. "Meant to tell you, Inspector," he mumbled. "And when I read about it in the papers it came back to me . . . As I bent over Mr. Field Monday night I smelled a terrible smell of whisky. I don't remember if I told you that before."

"Thank you," remarked the Inspector dryly, rising. "A very important contribution to our little investigation. You may go, the whole lot of you . . ."

The orangeade-boy, Jess Lynch, looked disappointed. "Don't you want to talk to me, too, sir?" he asked anxiously.

The Inspector smiled despite his abstraction. "Ah, yes. The helpful purveyor of orangeade. . . . And what have you to say, Jess?"

"Well, sir, before this fellow Field came over to my stand to ask for the ginger ale, I happened to notice that he picked up something in the alleyway," said the boy eagerly. "It was shiny, sort of, but I couldn't see it clear enough. He put it in his hip-pocket right away."

He concluded triumphantly, glancing about him as if to invite applause. The Inspector seemed interested enough.

"What was this shiny object like, Jess?" he inquired. "Might it have been a revolver?"

"Revolver? Gosh, I don't think so," said the orangeade boy doubtfully. "It was square, like. . . ."

"Might it have been a woman's purse?" interrupted the Inspector.

The boy's face brightened. "That's it!" he cried. "I'll bet that's what it was. Shined all over, like colored stones."

Queen sighed. "Very good, Lynch," he said. "You go home now like a good boy."

Silently the gangster, the usherette, Pusak and his feminine charge, and the orangeade-boy rose and departed. Velie accompanied them to the outer door.

Sampson waited until they had gone before he took the Inspector to one side.

"What's the matter, Q?" he demanded. "Aren't things going right?"

"Henry, my boy," smiled the Inspector, "we've done as much as mortal brains could. Just a little more time . . . I wish—" He did not say what he wished. He grasped Djuna firmly by the arm and bidding Panzer, Neilson, Velie and the District Attorney a placid good-night, left the theatre.

At the apartment, as the Inspector wielded his key and the door swung open, Djuna pounced on a yellow envelope lying on the floor. It had evidently been stuck through the crack at the bottom of the door. Djuna flourished it in the old man's face.

"It's from Mr. Ellery, I'll bet!" he cried. "I knew he wouldn't forget!" He seemed more extraordinarily like a monkey than ever as he stood grinning, the telegram in his hand.

The Inspector snatched the envelope from Djmm's hand and, not pausing to take off his hat or coat, switched on the lights in the living-room and eagerly extracted the yellow slip of paper.

Djuna had been correct.

ARRIVED SAFELY [it ran] CHAUVIN WILD WITH DELIGHT FISHING PROJECT EXCEPTIONAL stop THINK I HAVE SOLVED YOUR LITTLE PROBLEM stop JOIN DISTINGUISHED COMPANY OF RABELAIS CHAUCER SHAKESPEARE DRYDEN WHO SAID MAKE A VIRTUE OF NECESSITY stop WHY NOT GO INTO BLACKMAILING BUSINESS YOURSELF stop DONT CROWL DJUNA TO DEATH AFFECTIONATELY ELLERY

The Inspector stared down at the harmless yellow slip, a startled comprehension transmuting the harsh lines of his face.

He whirled on Djnna, clapped that young gentleman's cap on his tousled head and pulled his arm purposefully.

"Djuna, old son," he said gleefully, "let's go around the comer and celebrate with a couple of ice-cream sodas!"

CHAPTER XX

In Which Mr. Michaels Writes a Letter

For the first time in a week Inspector Queen was genuinely himself as he strode cheerfully into his tiny office at the headquarters building and shied his coat at a chair.

It was Monday morning. He rubbed his hands, hummed "The Sidewalks of New York," as he plumped down at his desk and briskly ran through his voluminous mail and reports. He spent a half-hour issuing instructions by word of mouth and telephone to subordinates in various offices of the Detective Bureau, studied briefly a number of reports which a stenographer placed before him and finally pressed one of a row of buttons on his desk.

Velie appeared at once.

"Howdy, Thomas," said the Inspector heartily. "How are you this fine Fall morning?"

Velie permitted himself a smile. "Well enough. Inspector," he said. "And you? You seemed a little under the weather Saturday night."

The Inspector chuckled. "Let bygones be bygones, Thomas, my lad. Djuna and I visited the Bronx Zoo yesterday and spent a delightful four hours among our brethren, the animals."

"That imp of yours was in his element, I'll bet," growled Velie, "among the monkeys especially."

"Now, now, Thomas," chided the Inspector. "Don't be mistaken about Djuna. He's a smart little whippersnapper. Going to be a great man some day, mark my words!"

"Djuna?" Velie nodded gravely. "Guess you're right, Inspector. I'd give my right paw for that kid. . . . What's the program to-day, sir?"

"There's a lot on the program to-day, Thomas," Queen said mysteriously. "Did you get hold of Michaels after I telephoned you yesterday morning?"

"Sure thing, Inspector. He's been waiting outside for an hour. Came in early, with Piggott hanging on his heels. Piggott's been tailing him all over creation and he's pretty disgusted."

"Well, I always said a man's a fool to become a policeman," chuckled Queen. "Bring in the lamb."

Velie went out, to reappear a moment later with the tall, portly Michaels. Field's valet was dressed sombrely. He seemed nervous and ill at ease.

"'Now, Thomas, my lad," said the Inspector after he had motioned Michaels to the chair beside his desk, "you go out and lock that door and don't let the Commissioner himself disturb me. Get that?"

Velie repressed a curious glance, grunted and departed. A few moments later a bulky figure was dimly discernible in silhouette through the frosted glass of the door.

At the expiration of a half-hour Velie was summoned by telephone to his superior's office. He unlocked the door. On the desk before the Inspector reposed a cheap square envelope unsealed, a sheet of notepaper partly visible as it lay inside. Michaels was on his feet, pale and trembling, his hat crushed in two beefy hands. Velie's sharp eyes noticed a generous ink stain on the fingers of the man's left hand.

"You are going to take *very* good care of Mr. Michaels, Thomas," said the Inspector genially. "To-day, for instance, I want you to entertain him. I have no doubt you'll find something to do—go to a movie—there's an idea! In any event be friendly with the gentleman until you hear from me. . . . No communication with anybody, Michaels, do you hear?" he added brusquely, turning to the big man. "Just you tag along with Sergeant Velie and play nicely."

"You know I'm on the square, Inspector," mumbled Michaels sullenly. "You don't have to—"

"Just a precaution, Michaels—just an elementary precaution," interrupted the Inspector, smiling. "Have a nice time, boys!"

The two men left. Seated at his desk, Queen tilted his swivel chair, picked up the envelope before him reflectively, took out the slip of cheap white paper and read it over with a little smile.

The note bore neither date nor salutation. The message began abruptly.

"The writer is Chas. Michaels, I think you know me. I have been Monte Field's right-hand man for over two years.

I won't beat around the bush. Last Monday night you killed Field in the Roman Theatre. Monte Field told me Sunday he had an appointment with you at the Theatre. And I am the only one who does know this.

Another thing. I also know *why* you killed him. You put him away to get hold of the papers in Field's hat. But you do not know that the papers you stole from him *are not the originals*. To prove this to you, I am enclosing one sheet from the testimony of Nellie Johnson which was in Field's possession.[99] If the papers you took from Field's hat are still in existence, compare what you have with this one. You will soon see that I am giving you the straight goods. And I have the rest of the originals safely put away where you will never lay hands on them. I might say that the police are looking for them with their tongues hanging out. Wouldn't it be nice if I stepped into Inspector Queen's office with the papers and my little story?

I will give you a chance to buy these papers. You can bring $25,000 in cold cash to the place I describe, and I will hand them over to you. I need money and you need the papers and my silence.

Meet me to-morrow, Tuesday night, at twelve o'clock, at the seventh bench on the right-hand side of the paved path in Central Park which starts at the northwest corner of 59th Street and 5th Avenue. I will be dressed in a grey overcoat and a grey slouch hat. Just say the word Papers to me.

This is the only way you can get the papers. Don't look for me before the appointment. If you are not there, I know what I have to do."

The scrawl, closely and painfully written, was signed: "Charles Michaels."

Inspector Queen sighed, licked the flap of the envelope and sealed it. He stared steadily at the name and address written in the same handwriting on the envelope. Unhurriedly he affixed a stamp on one corner.

He pressed another button. The door opened to admit Detective Ritter.

"Good morning, Inspector."

"Morning, Ritter." The Inspector weighed the envelope reflectively in his hand. "What are you working on now?"

The detective shuffled his feet. "Nothing special, Inspector. I was helping Sergeant Velie up to Saturday, but I haven't had any work yet on the Field case this morning."

"Well, then, I'll give you a nice little job." The Inspector suddenly grinned, holding out the envelope. Ritter took it with a bewildered air. "Here, son, go to the corner of 149th Street and Third Avenue and post this letter in the nearest mail-box!"

Ritter stared, scratched his head, looked at Queen and finally went out, depositing the letter in his pocket.

The Inspector tilted his chair and took a pinch of snuff with every evidence of satisfaction.

CHAPTER XXI

In Which Inspector Queen Makes a Capture—

On Tuesday evening, October second, promptly at 11:30 P.M., a tall man wearing a soft black hat and a black overcoat, the collar pulled up around his face to keep out the raw night-air, sauntered out of the lobby of a small hotel on 53rd Street near Seventh Avenue and proceeded at a sharp pace up Seventh Avenue toward Central Park.

Arrived at 59th Street he turned to the east and made his way along the deserted thoroughfare in the direction of Fifth Avenue. When he reached the Fifth Avenue entrance to Central Park, off the Plaza circle, he stopped in the shadow of one of the big concrete comer posts and leaned back idly. As he lit a cigarette the flare from the match illumined his face. It was that of an elderly man, a trifle lined. A grizzled mustache drooped in a straggling line from his upper lip. Under his hat a grey patch of hair was visible. Then the light from the match flickered out.

He stood quietly against the concrete post, hands jammed into his overcoat pockets, puffing away at his cigarette. An observer would have noticed, had he been keen, that the man's fingers trembled slightly and that his black-shod feet tapped the sidewalk in an unsteady tattoo.

When his cigarette burned down, he threw it away and glanced at a watch on his wrist. The hands stood at 11:50. He swore impatiently and stepped past the portals of the Park entrance.

The light from the overhead arcs bordering the Plaza dimmed as he walked up the stone lane. Hesitating, as if he were undecided as to his course of action, he looked about him, considered for a moment, then crossed over to the first bench and sat down heavily—like a man tired from his day's work and contemplating a restful quarter of an hour in the silence and darkness of the Park.

Slowly his head dropped; slowly his figure grew slack. He seemed to have fallen into a doze.

The minutes ticked away. No one passed the quiet figure of the black-clad man as he sat on his bench. On Fifth Avenue the motors roared past. The shrill whistle of the traffic officer in the Plaza pierced the chill air periodically. A cold wind soughed through the trees. From somewhere in the Stygian recesses of the Park came a girl's clear laugh—soft and far-off, but startlingly distinct. The minutes drowsed on; the man was falling into a deeper sleep.

And yet, just as the bells of the neighborhood churches began to toll the hour of twelve, the figure tensed, waited an instant and then rose determinedly.

Instead of heading toward the entrance he turned and plodded farther up the walk, his eyes bright and inquisitive in the gloomy depths created by his hat-brim and coat-collar. He seemed to be counting the benches as he proceeded in a steady, unhurried gait. Two—three—four—five— He stopped. In the semi-darkness ahead he could barely make out a still grey figure seated on a bench.

The man walked slowly on. Six—seven— He did not pause, but went straight ahead. Eight—nine—ten. . . . Only then did he wheel and retrace his steps. This time his gait was brisker, more definite. He approached the seventh bench rapidly, then stopped short. Suddenly, as if he had made up his mind, he crossed over to the spot where the indistinctly looming figure rested quietly and sat down. The figure grunted and moved over a trifle to give the newcomer more room.

The two men sat in silence. After a time the black-garbed man dipped into the folds of his coat and produced a packet of cigarettes. He lit one and held the match for a moment after the tip of the cigarette glowed red. In the ray of the match-light he covertly examined the quiet man at his side. The brief moment told him little—the occupant of the bench was as well-muffled and concealed as himself. Then the light puffed out and they were in darkness once more.

The black-coated man seemed to come to a decision. He leaned forward, tapped the other man sharply on the knee and said in a low, husky voice the one word:

"Papers."

The second man came to life immediately. He half-shifted his position, scrutinized his companion and grunted as if in satisfaction. He carefully leaned away from the other man on the bench and with his right gloved hand dug into his right overcoat pocket. The first man bent eagerly forward, his eyes bright. The gloved hand of his companion came out of the pocket, holding something tightly.

Then the owner of the hand did a surprising thing. With a fierce bunching of muscles he sprang from the bench and leaped backward, away from the first man. At the same time he leveled his right hand straight at the crouched frozen figure. And a fragmentary gleam of light from an arc-lamp far off revealed the thing he held in his hand—a revolver.

Crying out hoarsely, the first man sprang to his feet with the agility of a cat. His hand plunged with a lightning-like movement into his overcoat pocket. He darted, reckless of the weapon pointed at his heart, straight forward at the tense figure before him.

But things were happening. The peaceful tableau, so suggestive a bare instant before of open spaces and dark country silence, was transformed magically into a scene of intense activity—a writhing, yelling pandemonium. From a cluster of bushes a few feet behind the bench a swiftly moving group of men with drawn guns materialized. At the same time, from the farther side of the walk, a similar group appeared, running toward the pair. And from both ends of the walk—from the entrance about a hundred feet away and from the opposite direction, in the blackness of the Park—came several uniformed policemen, brandishing revolvers. The four groups converged almost as one.

The man who had drawn his gun and leaped from the bench did not await the arrival of reënforcements. As his companion of a moment before plunged his hand into his coat pocket the gunwielder took careful aim and fired. The weapon roared, awakening echoes in the Park. An orange flame streaked into the body of the black-coated man. He lurched forward, clutching his shoulder spasmodically. His knees buckled and he fell to the stone walk. His hand still fumbled in his coat.

But an avalanche of men's bodies kept him from whatever furious purpose was in his mind. Ungentle fingers gripped his arms and pinned them down, so that he could not withdraw his hand from his pocket. They held him in this way, silently, until a crisp voice behind them said, "Careful, boys—watch his hands!"

Inspector Richard Queen wriggled into the hard-breathing group and stood contemplatively above the writhing figure on the pavement.

"Take his hand out, Velie—easy, now! Hold it stiff, and—stiff, man stiff! He'd jab you in a flash!"

Sergeant Thomas Velie, who was straining at the arm, gingerly pulled it from the pocket despite the violent flounderings of the man's body. The hand appeared—empty, muscles loosened at the last moment. Two men promptly fastened it in a vise.

Velie made a movement as if to explore the pocket. The Inspector stopped him with a sharp word and himself bent over the threshing man on the walk.

Carefully, delicately, as if his life depended upon caution, the old man lowered his hand into the pocket and felt about its exterior. He gripped something and just as cautiously withdrew it, holding it up to the light.

It was a hypodermic needle. The light of the arc-lamp made its pale limpid contents sparkle.

Inspector Queen grinned as he knelt by the wounded man's side. He jerked off the black felt hat.

"Disguised and everything." he murmured.

He snatched at the grey mustache, passed his hand rapidly over the man's lined face. A smudge immediately appeared on the skin.

"Well, well!" said the Inspector softly, as the man's feverish eyes glared up at him. "Happy to meet you again, Mr. Stephen Barry, and your good friend, Mr. Tetra Ethyl Lead!"

CHAPTER XXII

—And Explains

Inspector Queen sat at the writing-desk in his living-room scribbling industriously on a long narrow sheet of note-paper headed THE QUEENS.

It was Wednesday morning—a fair Wednesday morning, with the sun streaming into the room through the dormer windows and the cheerful noises of 87th Street faintly audible from the pavements below. The Inspector wore his dressing-gown and slippers. Djuna was busy at the table clearing away the breakfast dishes.

The old man had written:

DEAR SON: As I wired you late last night, the case is finished. We got Stephen Barry very nicely by using Michaels' name and handwriting as bait. I really ought to congratulate myself on the psychological soundness of the plan. Barry was desperate and like so many other criminals thought he could duplicate his crime without being caught.

I hate to tell you how tired I am and how unsatisfying spiritually the job of man-hunter is sometimes. When I think of that poor lovely little girl Frances, having to face the world as the sweetheart of a murderer. . . . Well, El, there's little justice and certainly no mercy in this world. And, of course, I'm more or less responsible for her shame. . . . Yet Ives-Pope himself was quite decent a while ago when he telephoned me on hearing the news. I suppose in one way I did him and Frances a service. We—"

The doorbell rang and Djuna, drying his hands hastily on a kitchen towel, ran to the door. District Attorney Sampson and Timothy Cronin walked in—excited, happy, both talking at once. Queen rose, covering the sheet of paper with a blotter.

"Q, old man!" cried Sampson, extending both hands. "My congratulations! Have you seen the papers this morning?"

"Glory to Columbus!" grinned Cronin, holding up a newspaper on which in screaming head-lines New York was appraised of the capture of Stephen Barry. The Inspector's photograph was displayed prominently and a rhapsodic story captioned "Queen Adds Another Laurel" ran two full columns of type down the sheet.

The Inspector, however, seemed singularly unimpressed. He waved his visitors to chairs, and called for coffee, and began to talk about a projected change in the personnel of one of the city departments as if the Field case interested him not at all.

"Here, here!" growled Sampson. "What's the matter with you? You ought to be throwing out your chest, Q. You act as if you'd pulled a dud rather than succeeded."

"It's not that, Henry," said the Inspector with a sigh. "I just can't seem to be enthusiastic about anything when Ellery isn't by my side. By jingo, I wish he were here instead of in those blamed Maine woods!"

The two men laughed. Djuna served the coffee and for a time the Inspector was too occupied with his pastry to brood. Over his cigarette Cronin remarked: "I for one merely dropped in to pay my respects, Inspector, but I'm curious about some aspects of this case. . . . I don't know much about the investigation as a whole, except what Sampson told me on the way up."

"I'm rather at sea myself, Q," put in the District Attorney. "I imagine you have a story to tell us. Let's have it!"

Inspector Queen smiled sadly. "To save my own face I'll have to relate it as if I did most of the work. As a matter of fact, the only really intelligent work in the whole sordid business was Ellery's. He's a sharp lad, that son of mine."

[Editor's note: What exactly was Morgan guilty of?]

Sampson and Cronin relaxed as the Inspector took some snuff and settled back in his armchair. Djuna folded himself quietly in a corner, ears cocked.

"In going over the Field case," began the Inspector, "I will have to refer at times to Benjamin Morgan, who is really the most innocent victim of all.* I want you to bear in mind, Henry, that whatever I say about Morgan is to go no further, either professionally or socially. I already have Tim's assurance of silence. . . ."

Both men nodded wordlessly. The Inspector continued:

"I needn't explain that most investigations of crime begin with a search for the motive. Many times you can discard suspect after suspect when you know the reason behind the crime. In this case the motive was obscure for a long time. There were certain indications, like Benjamin Morgan's story, but these were inconclusive. Morgan had been blackmailed by Field for years—a part of Field's activities of which you gentlemen were ignorant, despite your knowledge of his other social habits. This seemed to point to blackmail as a possible motive—or rather the choking off of blackmail. But then any number of things could have been the motive—revenge, by some criminal whom Field had been instrumental in 'sending up.' Or by a member of his criminal organization. Field had a host of enemies, and undoubtedly a host of friends who were friends only because Field held the whip-hand. Any one of scores of people—men and women both—might have had a *motive* for killing the lawyer. So that, since we had so many other pressing and immediate things to think about and do that night at the Roman Theatre, we did not bother much with motive. It was always in the background, waiting to be called into service.

"But mark this point. If it was blackmail—as Ellery and I eventually decided, since it seemed the most likely possibility—there were most certainly some papers floating about in Field's possession which would be enlightening, to say the least. We knew that Morgan's papers existed. Cronin insisted that the papers for which *he* was looking were about somewhere. So we had to keep our eyes constantly on the alert for papers—tangible evidence which might or might not make clear the essential circumstances behind the crime.

"At the same time, in the matter of documents, Ellery was piqued by the great number of books on handwriting-analysis he found among Field's effects. We concluded that a man like Field, who had blackmailed once to our knowledge (in the case of Morgan) and many times to our suspicions; and who was keenly interested in the science of handwriting, might have been a forger to boot. If this were true, and it seemed a plausible explanation, then it probably meant that Field made a habit of forging the original blackmail papers. The only reason he could have for doing this, of course, would be to sell the forgeries and keep the originals for further extortion. His association with the underworld undoubtedly helped him master the tricks of the trade. Later, we discovered that this hypothesis was true. And by that time we had definitely established blackmail as the motive of the crime. Remember, though, that this led us nowhere, since any one of our suspects might have been the blackmail victim and we had no way of telling who it was."

The Inspector frowned, settled back into his seat more comfortably.

"But I'm tackling this explanation the wrong way. It just goes to show you how habit will take hold of a man. I'm so accustomed to beginning with motive. . . . However! There is only one important and central circumstance which stands out in the investigation. It was a confounding clue—rather, the lack of a clue. I refer to the missing hat. . . .

"Now the unfortunate thing about the missing hat was that we were so busy pressing the immediate inquiry at the Roman Theatre on Monday night we couldn't grasp the full significance of its absence. Not that we weren't bothered by it from the beginning—far from it. It was one of the first things I noticed when I examined the body. As for Ellery, he caught it as soon as he entered the theatre and bent over the dead man. But what could we do? There were a hundred details to take care of—questions to ask, orders to give, discrepancies and suspicious discoveries to clean up—so that, as I say, we inadvertently missed our great opportunity. If we had analyzed the meaning of the hat's disappearance then and there—we might have clinched the case that very night."

"Well, it hasn't taken so long after all, you growler," laughed Sampson. "This is Wednesday and the murder was a committed a week ago Monday. Only nine days—what are you kicking about?"

The Inspector shrugged. "But it would have made a considerable difference," he said. "If only we had reasoned it out—Well!

When finally we did get round to dissecting the problem of the hat, we asked ourselves first of all: Why was the hat taken? Only two answers seemed to make sense: one, that the hat was incriminating in itself; two, that it contained something which the murderer wanted and for which the crime was committed. As it turned out, both were true. The hat was incriminating in itself because on the underside of the leather sweatband was Stephen Barry's name, printed in indelible ink; and the hat contained something which the murderer very emphatically wanted—the blackmail papers. He thought at the time, of course, that they were the originals.

"This did not get us very far, but it was a starting-point. By the time we left Monday night with the command to shut down the theatre, we had not yet found the missing hat despite a sweeping search. However, we had no way of knowing whether the hat had managed in some mysterious manner to leave the theatre, or whether it was still there though unrevealed by our search. When we returned to the theatre on Thursday morning we settled once and for all the question of the location of Monte Field's pesky topper—that is, negatively. It was *not* in the theatre—that much was certain. And since the theatre had been sealed since Monday night, it follows that the hat must have left that same evening.

"Now everybody who left Monday night left with only one hat. In the light of our second search, therefore, we were compelled to conclude that somebody had walked out that night with Monte Field's hat in his hand or on his head, necessarily leaving his own in the theatre.

"He could not have disposed of the hat outside the theatre except when he left at the time the audience was allowed to leave; for up to that time all exits were guarded or locked, and the left-hand alley was blocked first by Jess Lynch and Elinor Libby, next by John Chase, the usher, and after that by one of my policemen. The right-hand alley, having no exit other than the orchestra doors, which were guarded all night, offered no avenue of disposal.

"To go on with the thought—since Field's hat was a tophat, and since nobody left the theatre dressed in a tophat who was not wearing evening clothes—this we watched for very closely—therefore the man who took away the missing hat *must* have been garbed in full dress. You might say that a man planning such a crime in advance would have come to the theatre without a hat, and therefore would have none to dispose of. But if you will stop to think, you must see that this is highly improbable. He would have been quite conspicuous, especially while entering the theatre, if he went in minus a tophat.[100] It was a possibility, of course, and we kept it in mind; but we reasoned that a man working out such a consummate crime as this would have shied from taking any unnecessary chance of being identified. Also, Ellery had satisfied his own mind that the murderer had no foreknowledge of the Field hat's importance. This made still more improbable the possibility that the murderer arrived without a hat of his own. Having a hat of his own, he might have disposed of it, we thought, during the first intermission—which is to say, before the crime was committed. But Ellery's deductions proving the murderer's lack of foreknowledge made this impossible, since he would not have known at the first intermission of the *necessity* of doing away with his own hat. At any rate, I think we were justified in assuming that our man had to leave his own hat in the theatre and that it must have been a tophat. Does it follow so far?"

"It seems logical enough," admitted Sampson, "though very complicated."

"You have no idea how complicated it was," said the Inspector grimly, "since at the same time we had to bear in mind the other possibilities—such as the man walking out with Field's hat being not the murderer but an accomplice. But let's get on.

"The next question we asked ourselves was this: what *happened* to the tophat which the murderer left behind in the theatre? What did he do with it? Where did he leave it? . . . I can tell you that was a puzzler. We had ransacked the place from top to bottom. True, we found several hats backstage which Mrs. Phillips, the wardrobe-mistress, identified as the personal property of various actors. But none of these was a personally owned tophat. Where then was the tophat which the murderer had left behind in the theatre? Ellery with his usual acumen struck right at the heart of the truth. He said to himself, 'The murderer's tophat must be here. We have not found any tophat whose presence is remarkable or out of the ordinary. Therefore the tophat we are seeking must be one whose presence is *not* out of the ordinary.' Fundamental? Almost ridiculously so. And yet I myself did not think of it.

100. The Inspector is telling the story dramatically, for that is exactly what Barry did! He went into the theatre in plainclothes and changed into evening dress as a *costume*, leaving his street clothes in the theater when he left later that evening. Why didn't the police discover his street clothes in his dressing room and therefore immediately identify him as the culprit?

"What tophats were there whose *presence* was not out of the ordinary—so natural and in so natural a place that they were not even questioned? In the Roman Theatre, where all the costumes were hired from Le Brun, the answer is simply: the rented tophats being used for purposes of the play. Where would such tophats be? Either in the actors' dressing-rooms or in the general wardrobe room backstage. When Ellery had reached this point in his reasoning he took Mrs. Phillips backstage and checked up on every tophat in the actors rooms and the wardrobe room. Every tophat there—and all were accounted for, none being missing—was a property tophat bearing on its lining the Le Brun insignia. Field's hat, which we had proved to be a Browne Bros. topper, was not among the property tophats or anywhere backstage.

"Since no one left the theatre Monday night with more than one tophat, and since Monte Field's hat was unquestionably taken out of the theatre that same night, it was positively established that the murderer's own tophat must have been in the Roman all the time the house was sealed, and was still there at the time of our second search. Now, the only tophats remaining in the theatre were property tophats. It therefore follows that the murderer's own tophat (which he was forced to leave behind because he walked out with Field's) *must* have been one of the property hats backstage, since let me repeat, these were the only tophats of which it could physically have been one.

"In other words—one of these property tophats backstage belonged to the man who left the theatre Monday night in full dress wearing Field's silk topper.

"If this man were the murderer—and he could scarcely be anyone else—then our field of inquiry was narrowed to a considerable degree. He could only have been either a male member of the cast who left the theatre in evening clothes, or somebody closely connected with the theatre and similarly dressed. In the latter case, such a person would have had to have, first, a property tophat to leave behind; second, undisputed access to the wardrobe and dressing rooms; and, third, the opportunity to leave his property tophat in either place.

"Now let us examine the possibilities in the latter case—that the murderer was closely connected with the theatre, yet not an actor." The Inspector paused to sniff deeply of the snuff in his treasured box. "The workmen backstage could be discarded because none of them wore the evening clothes which were necessary in order to take away Field's tophat. The cashiers, ushers, doormen and other minor employees were eliminated for the same reason. Harry Neilson, the publicity man, was also dressed in ordinary street clothes; Panzer, the manager, was attired in full dress, it is true, but I took the trouble to check up his head-size and found it to be 6¾—an unusually small size. It would be virtually impossible for him to have *worn* Field's hat, which was 7⅛. It is true that we left the theatre before he did. On my way out, however, I definitely instructed Thomas Velie to make no exception in Panzer's case, but to search him as the others had been searched. I had examined Panzer's hat merely from a sense of duty while in his office earlier in the evening, and found it to be a derby. Velie subsequently reported that Panzer walked out with this derby on his head and no other hat in his possession. Now—if Panzer had been the man we were looking for, he might have walked out with Field's hat despite its larger size by merely holding it in his hand. But when he left with a derby, that was conclusive that he could not have taken away Field's hat, since the theatre was shut down immediately after his departure and no one—my men on duty saw to that—no one entered the premises until Thursday morning under my own eye. Theoretically it was possible for Panzer, or anyone else in the Roman personnel, to have been the murderer had he been able to secrete Field's tophat in the theatre. But this last hypothesis was dissipated by the report of Edmund Crewe, our official architectural expert, who definitely stated that there was no secret hiding-place anywhere in the Roman Theatre.

"The elimination of Panzer, Neilson and the employees left only the cast as possibilities. How we finally narrowed down the field of inquiry until we got to Barry, let's leave for the moment. The interesting part of this case is really the startling and complex series of deductions which gave us the truth purely through logical reasoning. I say 'us'—I should say Ellery . . ."

"For a police Inspector you are certainly a shrinking violet," chuckled Cronin. "By gee, this is better than a detective-story. I ought to be working now, but since my boss seems to be as interested as I am—keep going, Inspector!"

Queen smiled, forging ahead.

"The fact that the murderer was traced to the cast," he continued, "answers a question which has probably occurred to you and which certainly troubled us in the beginning. We could not at first understand why the theatre should have been chosen as a meeting-place for the transaction of secret business. When you stop to think about it, a theatre presents enormous disadvantages under ordinary circumstances. Extra tickets, to mention only one thing, have to be bought to insure privacy through empty seats in the vicinity. What a silly tangle to get into when other meeting-places are so much more convenient! A theatre is dark most of the time and disturbingly quiet. Any untoward noise or conversation is remarked. The crowds present a constant danger—one of recognition. However, all this is automatically explained when you realize that Barry was a member of the cast. From his standpoint the theatre was ideal—for who would dream of suspecting an actor of murder when the victim is found dead in the orchestra? Of course Field acquiesced, never suspecting what was in Barry's mind and that he was conniving his own death. Even if he were a little suspicious, you must remember that he was accustomed to dealing with dangerous people and probably felt capable of taking care of himself. This may have made him a little overconfident—we have no way, of course, of knowing.

"'Let me get back to Ellery again—my favorite subject,'" continued the Inspector, with one of his recurrent dry chuckles. "Aside from these deductions about the hat—as a matter of fact, before the deductions were completely worked out—Ellery got his first indication of which way the wind blew during the meeting at the Ives-Pope house. It was clear that Field had not accosted Frances Ives-Pope in the alleyway between acts with merely flirtatious intentions. It seemed to Ellery that some connection existed between the two widely separated individuals. Now, this does not mean that Frances had to be aware of the connection. She was positive that she had never heard of or seen Field before. We had no reason to doubt her and every reason to believe her. That possible connection might have been Stephen Barry, provided Stephen Barry and Field knew each other without Frances' knowledge. If, for example, Field had an appointment at the theatre Monday night with the actor and suddenly saw Frances, it was possible that in his half-drunken mood he would venture to approach her, especially since the subject he and Barry had in common concerned her so deeply. As for recognizing her—thousands of people who read the daily papers know every line of her features—she is a much-photographed young society lady. Field certainly would have acquainted himself with her description and appearance out of sheer thoroughness of business method. . . . But to return to the triangle connection—Field, Frances, Barry—which I will go into detail later. You realize that no one else in the cast except Barry, who was engaged to Frances and had been publicly announced as her fiancé, with pictures and all the rest of the journalistic business, could have satisfied so well the question: Why did Field accost Frances?

"The other disturbing factor concerning Frances—the discovery of her bag in Field's clothes—was plausibly explained by her dropping it in the natural excitement of the moment when the drunken lawyer approached her. This was later confirmed by Jess Lynch's testimony to the effect that he saw Field pick up Frances' bag. Poor girl—I feel sorry for her." The Inspector sighed.

"To get back to the hat—you'll notice we always return to that blasted top-piece," resumed Queen, after a pause. "I never knew of a case in which a single factor so dominated every aspect of the investigation. . . . Now mark this: Of the entire cast Barry was *the only one* who left the Roman Theatre Monday night dressed in evening clothes and tophat. As Ellery watched at the main door Monday night while the people were filing out, his mind characteristically registered the fact that the entire cast, except Barry, left the theatre wearing street clothes; in fact, he even mentioned this to Sampson and me in Panzer's office later, although at the time neither of us realized its full significance. . . . Barry was therefore the only member of the cast who could have taken away Field's tophat. Think this over a moment and you will see that, in view of Ellery's hat-deductions, we could now pin the guilt to Barry's shoulders beyond the shadow of a doubt.

"Our next step was to witness the play, which we did the evening of the day on which Ellery made the vital deductions—Thursday. You can see why. We wanted to confirm our conclusion by seeing whether Barry had the *time* during the second act to commit the murder. And, amazingly enough, of all the members of the cast, Barry was the only one who did have the time. He was absent from the stage from 9:20—he opened the business of the act and left almost at once—until 9:50, when he returned to the stage to remain there until the act ended. This was incontrovertible—part of a fixed and unchanging time-schedule. Every other player was either on the stage all the time or else went on and off at extremely short intervals. This means that last Thursday night, more than five days ago—and the whole case took only nine days to consummate—we had solved our mystery. But solving the mystery of the murderer's identity was a far cry from bringing him to justice. You'll see why in a moment.

"The fact that the murderer could not enter until 9:30 or thereabouts explains why the torn edges of LL32 Left and LL30 Left did not coincide. It was necessary for Field and Barry, you see, to come in at different times. Field could not very well enter with Barry or even at a noticeably late hour—the matter of secrecy was too important to Barry, and Field understood, or thought he did, how necessary it was for him to play the secret game.

"When we pinned the guilt on Barry Thursday night, we resolved to question subtly the other members of the cast as well as workmen backstage. We wanted to find out, of course, whether any one had actually seen Barry leave or return. As it happened, no one had. Everybody was busy either acting, redressing, or working backstage. We conducted this little investigation after the performance that night, when Barry had already left the theatre. And it was checkmate, right enough.

"We had already borrowed a seating-plan from Panzer. This map, together with the examination of the alleyway on the left and the dressing-room arrangement backstage—an examination made directly after the second act Thursday night—showed us how the murder was committed."

Sampson stirred. "I've been puzzling my wits about that," he confessed. "After all, Field was no babe-in-the-woods. This Barry must be a wizard, Q. How did he do it?"

"Every riddle is simple when you know the answer," retorted the Inspector. "Barry, whose freedom began at 9:20, immediately returned to his dressing-room, slapped on a quick but thorough facial disguise, donned an evening-cloak and the tophat which was part of his costume—you'll remember he was already dressed in evening-clothes—and slipped out of his room into the alley.

"Of course you can't be expected to know the topography of the theatre. There is a series of tiers in a wing of the building backstage, facing the left alley, which is made up of dressing-rooms.

Barry's room is on the lowest tier, the door opening into the alleyway. There is a flight of iron steps leading down to the pavement.

"It was through this door that he quitted the dressing-room, walking through the dark alley while the side doors of the theatre were shut during Act II. He sneaked out into the street, since there was no guard at the head of the alley at that time—and he knew it—nor had Jess Lynch and his 'girl' arrived, luckily for him; and entered the theatre brazenly through the regular front entrance, as if he were a latecomer. He presented his ticket—LL30 Left—at the door, muffled in his cloak and of course well disguised. As he passed into the theatre he deliberately threw away his ticket-stub. This appeared to him to be a wise move, since he figured that if the ticket-stub were found there, it would point to a member of the audience and directly away from the stage. Also, if his plans fell through and he were later searched carefully, the finding of the stub on his person would be damning evidence. All in all, he thought his move not only misleading but protective."

"But how did he plan to get to the seat without being ushered to it—and therefore seen?" objected Cronin.

"He hadn't planned to evade the usher," returned the Inspector. "Naturally, he had hoped, since the play was well on and the theatre dark, to gain the last row, the nearest to the door, before the usher could approach. However, even if the usher forestalled him and escorted him to the seat he was well disguised and the blackness of the theatre was proof enough against recognition. So that, if things turned out as badly as possible for him, the most that would be remembered was that some man, unknown, barely describable in general contour, arrived during the second act. As it happened he was not accosted, since Madge O'Connell was luckily seated with her lover. He managed to slip into the seat next to Field without being noticed.

"Remember, what I've just told you," went on the Inspector, clearing his dry throat, "is not the result of deduction or investigation. We could have no means of discovering such facts. Barry made his confession last night and cleared up all these points. . . . Knowing the culprit was Barry, of course, we might have reasoned out the entire procedure—it follows simply and is the natural situation if you know the criminal. It wasn't necessary, however.

Does that sound like an alibi for Ellery or myself? Hmph!" The old man barely smiled.

"When he sat down next to Field he had a carefully planned idea of his course of action. Don't forget that he was on a strict time-schedule and could not afford to waste a minute. On the other hand, Field, too, knew that Barry had to get back so he made no unnecessary delays. The truth of the matter, as Barry has told us, is that he expected to have a more difficult time with Field than he actually did have. But Field was sociably amenable to Barry's suggestions and conversation, probably because he was quite drunk and expected to receive a huge sum of money within a short time.

"Barry first requested the papers. When Field cannily asked for the money before he produced the documents, Barry showed him a wallet bulging with apparently genuine bills. It was quite dark in the theatre and Barry did not take the bills apart. Actually they were stage-money. He patted them suggestively and did what Field must have expected: refused to hand over the money until he had checked the documents. Bear in mind that Barry was an accomplished actor and could handle the difficult situation with the confidence imparted to him by his stage training. . . . Field reached under his seat and to Barry's utter astonishment and consternation produced his tophat. Barry says that Field remarked: 'Never thought I'd keep the papers in this, did you? As a matter of fact, I've dedicated this hat to your history quite exclusively. See—it has your name in it.' And with this astounding statement he turned back the band! Barry used his pocket-pencil flashlight and saw his name inked in on the underside of the leather sweat-band.

"Just imagine what went through his mind at this moment. Here he saw what seemed at the moment a ruinous accident to his careful plans. Should Field's hat be examined—and of course it would be—at the time of the discovery of the body, then the name Stephen Barry on the band would be over-whelming evidence. . . . Barry had no time to rip out the band. In the first place he had no knife—unfortunately for him; and in the second place the hat-band was closely and securely stitched to the tough fabric. Working on split-time, he saw at once that the only course open to him was to take the hat away after he killed Field. Since he and Field were of the same general

physique, with Field wearing an average-sized hat, 7⅛, he immediately decided to leave the theatre wearing or carrying Field's
hat. He would deposit his own in the dressing-room, where its
presence was not out of the way, take Field's hat from the theatre
with him and destroy it as soon as he reached his rooms. It also
occurred to him that if the hat were by some chance examined
as he was leaving the theatre, his name printed inside would
certainly ward off suspicion. In all probability it was this fact
that made Barry feel he was running into no particular danger,
even though he had not foreseen the unexpected circumstance."

"Clever rogue," murmured Sampson.

"The quick brain, Henry, the quick brain," said Queen gravely.
"It has run many a man's neck into the noose. . . . As he made
the lightning decision to take the hat, he realized that he could
not leave his own in its place. For one thing, his hat was a snap-
down—an opera hat—but more important, it had the name of
Le Brun, the theatrical costumer, stamped in it. You can see that
this would immediately point to someone in the cast—just the
thing he wished to avoid. He told me also that at the moment,
and for quite some time thereafter, he felt that the most the police
could deduce from the hat's being missing was that it was taken
because it contained something valuable. He could not see how
this investigatory guess would point the finger of suspicion anywhere near him. When I explained to him the series of deductions
Ellery made from the mere fact that the tophat was missing, he
was utterly astounded. . . . You can see, now, that the only really
fundamental weakness of his crime was due not to an oversight
or a mistake on his part, but to an occurrence which he could not
possibly have foreseen. It forced his hand and the entire chain
was started. Had Barry's name not been lettered in Field's hat,
there is no question in my mind but that he would be a free and
unsuspected man to-day. The police records would carry another
unsolved murder on its pages.

"I need not state that this entire train of thought flashed
through his brain in less time than it takes to describe. He saw
what he had to do and his plans adjusted themselves instantly
to the new development. . . . When Field extracted the papers
from the hat, Barry examined them cursorily under the lawyer's
watchful eye. He did this by the same pencil flashlight—a tiny
streak of illumination quite obscured by their shielding bodies.

The papers seemed in good order and complete. But Barry did not spend much time over the papers at the moment. He looked up with a rueful smile and said: 'Seem to be all here, damn you'— very naturally, as if they were enemies under a truce and he was being a good sport. Field interpreted the remark for what it was intended to convey. Barry dipped into his pocket—the light was out now—and, as if he was nervous, took a swig at a pocket-flask of good whisky. Then as if recollecting his manners, he asked Field pleasantly enough if he would not take a drink to bind the bargain. Field, having seen Barry drink from the flask, could have no suspicion of foul play. In fact, he probably never dreamed that Barry would try to do him in. Barry handed him a flask. . . .

"But it wasn't the same flask. Under cover of the darkness he had taken out two flasks—the one he himself used coming from his left hip-pocket, the flask he gave Field coming from his right hip-pocket. In handing it over to Field, he merely switched flasks. It was very simple—and made simpler because of the darkness and the fuddled condition of the lawyer. . . . The ruse of the flask worked. But Barry had taken no chances. He had in his pocket a hypodermic filled with the poison. If Field had refused to drink Barry was prepared to plunge the needle into the lawyer's arm or leg. He possessed a hypodermic needle which a physician had procured for him many years before. Barry had suffered from nervous attacks and could not remain under a doctor's care since he was traveling from place to place with a stock company. The hypodermic was untraceable, therefore, on a cold trail years old; and he was ready if Field refused to drink. So you see—his plan, even in this particular, was fool-proof. . . .

"The flask from which Field drank contained good whisky, all right, but mixed with tetra ethyl lead in a copious dose. The poison's slight ether smell was lost in the reek of the liquor; and Field, drinking, gulped down a huge mouthful before he realized that anything was wrong, if he did at all.

"Mechanically he returned the flask to Barry, who pocketed it and said: 'I guess I'll look over these papers more carefully—there's no reason why I should trust you, Field. . . .' Field, who was feeling extremely disinterested by this time, nodded in a puzzled sort of way and slumped down in his seat. Barry really did examine the papers but he watched Field like a hawk out of the corner of his eye all the time. In about five minutes he saw that

Field was out—out for good. He was not entirely unconscious but well under way; his face was contorted and he was gasping for breath. He seemed unable to make any violent muscular movement or outcry. Of course, he'd utterly forgotten Barry—in his agony—perhaps didn't remain conscious very long. When he groaned those few words to Pusak it was the superhuman effort of a practically dead man. . . .

"Barry now consulted his watch. It was 9:40. He had been with Field only ten minutes. He had to be back on the stage at 9:50. He decided to wait three minutes more—it had taken less time than he had figured—to make sure that Field would not raise a rumpus. At 9:43 exactly, with Field terribly inanimate in his internal agonies, Barry took Field's hat, snapped down his own and slipped it under his cloak, and rose. The way was clear. Hugging the wall, walking down the aisle as carefully and unobstrusively as possible, he gained the rear of the leftside boxes without anyone noticing him. The play was at its highest point of tension. All eyes were riveted on the stage.

"In the rear of the boxes he ripped off the false hair, rapidly adjusted his make-up and passed through the stage-door. The door leads into a narrow passageway which in turn leads into a corridor, branching out to various parts of the backstage area. His dressing-room is a few feet from the entrance to the corridor. He slipped inside, threw his stage hat among his regular effects, dashed the remaining contents of the death-flask into the wash-bowl and cleaned out the flask. He emptied the contents of the hypodermic into the toilet drain and put away the needle, cleaned. If it was found—what of it? He had a perfectly sound excuse for owning it and besides the murder had not been committed by such an instrument at all. . . . He was now ready for his cue, calm, debonair, a little bored. The call came at exactly 9:50, he went on the stage and was there until the hue-and-cry was raised at 9:55 in the orchestra. . . .

"Talk about your complicated plots!" ejaculated Sampson.

"It is not so complicated as it seems at first hearing," returned the Inspector. "Remember that Barry is an exceptionally clever young man and above all an excellent actor. No one *but* an accomplished actor could have carried off such a plan the procedure was simple, after all; his hardest job was to keep to his time-schedule. If he was seen by anyone he was disguised. The only dangerous part of his scheme was the getaway—when he walked down the aisle and went backstage through the box stagedoor. The aisle he took care of by keeping an eye out for the usher while he sat next to Field. He had known beforehand, of course, that the ushers, due to the nature of the play, kept their stations more or less faithfully, but he counted on his disguise and hypodermic to help him through any emergency that might arise. However, Madge O'Connell was lax in her duty and so even this was in his favor. He told me last night, not without a certain pride, that he had prepared for every contingency. . . . As for the stagedoor, he knew from experience that at that period in the play's progress practically every one was on the stage. The technical men were busy at their stations, too. . . . Remember that he planned the crime knowing in advance the exact conditions under which he would have to operate. And if there was an element of danger, of uncertainty—well, it was all a risky business, wasn't it?—he asked me last night, smiling; and I had to admire him for his philosophy if for nothing else."

The Inspector shifted restlessly. "This makes clear, I hope, just how Barry did the job. As for our investigation. . . . With the hat-deductions made and our knowledge of the murderer's identity, we still had no inkling of the exact circumstances behind the crime. If you've been keeping in mind the material evidence which we had collected by Thursday night, you will see that we had nothing at all with which to work. The best thing we could hope for was that somewhere among the papers for which all of us were looking was a clue which would tie up to Barry. Even that would not be enough, but . . . So the next step," said the Inspector, after a sigh, "was the discovery of the papers in Field's neat hiding-place at the top of the bed-canopy in his apartment. This was Ellery's work from start to finish. We had found out that Field had no safety-deposit box, no post-office box, no outside residence, no friendly neighbor or tradesman, and that the documents were not in his office. By a process of elimination Ellery insisted that they must be somewhere in Field's rooms. You know how this search ended—an ingenious bit of pure reasoning on Ellery's part. We found Morgan's papers; we found Cronin's stuff relating to the gang activities—and by the way, Tim, I'm going to be keenly alive to what happens when we start on the big clean-up—and we found finally a wad of miscellaneous papers. Among these were

Michaels' and Barry's. . . . You'll remember, Tim, that Ellery, from the handwriting analysis business, deduced that possibly we would find the originals of Barry's papers—and so we did.

"Michaels' case was interesting. That time he went to Elmira on the 'petty larceny' charge, it was through Field's clever manipulations with the law. But Field had the goods on Michaels and filed the documentary evidence of the man's real guilt away in his favorite hiding-place, in the event that he might wish to use it at some future date. A very saving person, this Field. . . . When Michaels was released from prison Field used him unscrupulously for his dirty work, holding the threat of those papers over the man's head

"Now Michaels had been on the lookout for a long time. He wanted the papers badly, as you may imagine. At every opportunity he searched the apartment for them. And when he didn't find them time after time, he became desperate. I don't doubt that Field, in his devilishly sardonic way, enjoyed the knowledge that Michaels was ransacking the place day after day. . . . On Monday night Michaels did what he said he did—went home and to bed. But early Tuesday morning, when he read the papers and learned that Field had been killed, he realized that the jig was up. He had to make one last search for the papers—if he didn't find them, the police might and he would be in hot water. So he risked running into the police net when he returned to Field's rooms Tuesday morning. The story about the check was nonsense, of course.

"But let's get on to Barry. The original papers we found in the hat marked 'Miscellaneous' told a sordid story. Stephen Barry, to make it short and ugly, has a strain of negroid blood in his veins. He was born in the South of a poor family and there was definite documentary evidence—letters, birth-records and the like—to prove that his blood had the black taint. Now Field, as you know, made it his business to run things like this to earth. In some way he got hold of the papers, how long ago we can't say, but certainly quite a while back. He looked up Barry's status at the time and found him to be a struggling actor, on his uppers more often than he was in funds. He decided to let the fellow alone for the time. If ever Barry came into money or in the limelight, there would be time enough to blackmail him. . . . Field's wildest dreams could not have foreseen Barry's engagement to Frances Ives-Pope, daughter of a multi-millionaire and blue-blood society

101. One might have expected that the shrewd Field, knowing that his victim was impoverished—an actor—would have waited either until the eve of the wedding, when there might have been wedding-gifts of cash, or after the wedding, when the husband might well have had access to the family's wealth, to demand a large payment. Compare "Charles Augustus Milverton," a blackmail case handled by Sherlock Holmes that would have been well known to Lee and Dannay.

102. In some states, the "hypodescent" laws—held constitutional by the U.S. Supreme Court—defined as black anyone with any black ancestry, even the smallest portion. Tennessee adopted such a "one-drop" statute in 1910, followed that same year by Louisiana. Similar laws were enacted in Texas and Arkansas in 1911, in Mississippi in 1917, in North Carolina in 1923, in Virginia in 1924, in Alabama and Georgia in 1927, and in Oklahoma as recently as 1931. During the 1920s, Florida, Indiana, Kentucky, Maryland, Missouri, Nebraska, North Dakota, and Utah amended the fractions of black ancestry required for classification as black to one-sixteenth or one-thirty-second. Thus in the eyes of many, Barry would have been irrevocably classed as a black man, no matter his appearance. Apparently it was unimaginable that a magnate like Ives-Pope would permit "black blood" to marry into his family. The taint of "black blood" mixing with white was one that did not lose its horror until well into the 1960s, when interracial celebrity couples were regularly in the news.

"This is precisely the detached, intellectualized take on race one would expect in a formal deductive puzzle of the time," writes Francis M. Nevins Jr., in *Ellery Queen: The Art of Detection*

girl. I needn't explain what it would have meant to Barry to have the story of his mixed blood become known to the Ives-Popes. Besides—and this is quite important—Barry was in a constant state of impoverishment due to his gambling. What money he earned went into the pockets of the bookmakers at the racetrack and in addition he had contracted enormous debts which he could never have wiped out unless his marriage to Frances went through. So pressing was his need, in fact, that it was he who subtly urged an early marriage. I have been wondering just how he regarded Frances sentimentally. I don't think, in all fairness to him, that he was marrying wholly because of the money involved. He really loves her, I suppose—but then, who wouldn't?"

The old man smiled reminiscently and went on. "Field approached Barry some time ago with the papers—secretly, of course. Barry paid what he could, but it was woefully little and naturally did not satisfy the insatiable blackmailer. He kept putting Field off desperately. But Field himself was getting into hot water because of his own gambling and was 'calling in' his little business deals one by one.[101] Barry, pushed to the wall, realized that unless Field were silenced everything would be lost. He planned the murder. He saw that even if he did manage to raise the $50,000 Field demanded—a palpable impossibility—and even if he did get the original papers, yet Field might still wreck his hopes by merely circulating the story. There was only one thing to do—kill Field. He did it."

"Black blood, eh?" murmured Cronin. "Poor devil."

"You would scarcely guess it from his appearance," remarked Sampson. "He looks as white as you or I."

"Barry isn't anywhere near a full-blooded Negro," protested the Inspector. "He has just a drop in his veins—just a drop, but it would have been more than enough for the Ives-Popes. . . .[102] "To get on. When the papers had been discovered and read—we knew everything. Who—how—why the crime was committed. So we took stock of our evidence to bring about a conviction. You can't hale a man into court on a murder charge without evidence. . . . Well, what do you think we had? Nothing!

"Let me discuss the clues which might have been useful as evidence. The lady's purse—that was out. Valueless, as you know. . . . The source of the poison—a total failure. Incidentally, Barry did procure it exactly as Dr. Jones suggested—Jones, the toxicologist. Barry bought ordinary gasoline and distilled the tetra ethyl lead from it. There was no trace left. . . . Another possible clue—Monte Field's hat. It was gone. . . . The extra tickets for the six vacant seats—we had never seen them and there seemed little chance that we ever would. . . . The only other material evidence—the papers—indicated motive but proved nothing. By this token Morgan might have committed the crime, or any member of Field's criminal organization.[103]

"Our only hope for bringing about a conviction depended upon our scheme to have Barry's apartment burglarized in the hope that either the hat, or the tickets, or some other clue like the poison or the poison-apparatus, would be found. Velie got me a professional housebreaker, and Barry's apartment was rifled Friday night while he was acting his rôle in the theatre. Not a trace of any of these clues came to light. The hat, the tickets, the poison—everything had been destroyed. Obviously, Barry would have done that; we could only make sure.[104]

"In desperation, I called a meeting of a number of the Monday night audience, hoping that I would find someone who remembered seeing Barry that night. Sometimes, you know, people recall events later which they forgot completely in the excitement of a previous quizzing. But this too, as it happened, was a failure. The only thing of value that turned up was the orangeade-boy's testimony about seeing Field pick up an evening bag in the alley. This got us nowhere as far as Barry was concerned, however. And remember that when we questioned the cast Thursday night we got no direct evidence from them.

"So there we were with a beautifully hypothetical statement of facts for a jury, but not a shred of genuine evidence. The case we had to present would have offered no difficulties to a shrewd defending attorney. It was all circumstantial evidence, based chiefly on reasoning. You know as well as I do what a chance such a case would have in court. . . . Then my troubles really began, for Ellery had to leave town.

"I racked my brains—the few I have." Queen scowled at his empty coffee-cup. "Things looked black enough. How could I convict a man without evidence? It was maddening. And then Ellery did me the final service of wiring me a suggestion."

"A suggestion?" asked Cronin.

"A suggestion that I do a little blackmailing myself. . . ."

(Perfect Crime Books, 2013): "not racist but not outraged or even upset by the racism of the society, stoically accepting as unalterable that (in Richard's words to Ellery) 'there's little justice and certainly no mercy in this world,'" (p. 17).

103. In fact, the discovery of the Barry papers in the apartment—the only papers not in duplicate and the only papers belonging to someone who had been at the theater (other than Morgan, whose two sets of papers exonerated him)—was really all that was necessary to identify the murderer. All of the reasoning about hats, etc., added nothing to the solid evidence that Barry had motive and his (copied) papers were missing, meaning that Field had taken them with him to the theater where they had been stolen. The other reasoning is only relevant to the "Reader's Challenge."

104. We must deduce, then, that Barry distilled more tetra ethyl lead after the search—how else would he have been able to fill his syringe before his visit to Central Park?

"Blackmailing yourself?" Sampson stared. "I don't see the point."

"Trust Ellery to make a point that on the surface is obscure," retorted the Inspector. "I saw at once that the only course left open to me was to *manufacture* evidence!"

Both men frowned in puzzlement.

"It's simple enough," said Queen. "Field was killed by an unusual poison. And Field was killed because he was blackmailing Barry. Wasn't it fair for me to assume that if Barry were suddenly blackmailed on the identical score, he would again use poison—and in all likelihood the *same* poison? I don't have to tell you that 'Once a poisoner always a poisoner.' In the case of Barry, if I could only get him to try to use that tetra ethyl lead on somebody else, I'd have him! The poison is almost unknown—but I needn't explain further. You can see that if I caught him with tetra ethyl lead, that would be all the evidence I needed.

"How to accomplish the feat was another matter. . . . The blackmail opportunity fitted the circumstances perfectly. I actually had the original papers pertaining to Barry's parentage and tainted blood. Barry thought these destroyed—he had no reason to suspect that the papers he took from Field were clever forgeries. If I blackmailed him he was in the same boat as before. Consequently he would have to take the same action.

"And so I used our friend Charley Michaels. The only reason I utilized him was that to Barry it would seem logical that Michaels, Field's crony and bully and constant companion, should be in possession of the original papers. I got Michaels to write a letter, dictated by me. The reason I wanted Michael to write it was that possibly Barry, through association with Field, was familiar with the man's handwriting. This may seem a small point but I couldn't take any chances. If I slipped up on my ruse, Barry would see through it at once and I'd never get him again.

"I enclosed a sheet of the original papers in the letter, to show that the new blackmailing threat had teeth. I stated that Field had brought Barry copies—the sheet enclosed proved my statement. Barry had no reason in the world to doubt that Michaels was milking him as his master had done before. The letter was so worded as to be an ultimatum. I set the time and the place and, to make a long story short, the plan worked. . . .

"I guess that's all, gentlemen. Barry came, he had his trusty little hypodermic filled with tetra ethyl lead, also a flask—an exact replica, you see, of the Field crime except for locale. My man—it was Ritter—was instructed to take no chances. As soon as he recognized Barry he covered him and raised the alarm. Luckily we were almost at their elbows behind the bushes. Barry was desperate and would have killed himself and Ritter, too, if he'd had half a chance."

There was a significant silence as the Inspector finished, sighed, leaned forward and took some snuff.

Sampson shifted in his chair. "Listens like a thriller, Q," he said admiringly. "But I'm not clear on a few points. For example, if this tetra ethyl lead is so little known, how on earth did Barry ever find out about it—to the degree of actually making some himself?"

"Oh." The Inspector smiled. "That worried me from the moment Jones described the poison. I was in the dark even after the capture. And yet—it just goes to show how stupid I am—the answer was under my nose all the time. You will remember that at the Ives-Pope place a certain Dr. Cornish was introduced. Now Cornish is a personal friend of the old financier and both of them are interested in medical science. In fact, I recall Ellery's asking at one time: 'Didn't Ives-Pope recently donate $100,000 to the Chemical Research Foundation?' That was true. It was on the occasion of a meeting in the Ives-Pope house one evening several months ago that Barry accidentally found out about tetra ethyl lead. A delegation of scientists had called upon the magnate, introduced by Cornish, to request his financial aid in the Foundation. In the course of the evening, the talk naturally turned to medical gossip and the latest scientific discoveries. Barry admitted that he overheard one of the directors of the Foundation, a famous toxicologist, relate to the group the story of the poison. At this time Barry had no idea that he would put the knowledge to use; when he decided to kill Field, he saw the advantages of the poison and its untraceable source immediately."

"What the deuce was the significance of that message you sent to me by Louis Panzer Thursday morning, Inspector?" inquired Cronin curiously. "Remember? Your note requested that I watch Lewin and Panzer when they met to see if they knew each other. As I reported to you, I asked Lewin later and he denied any acquaintance with Panzer. What was the idea?"

"Panzer," repeated the Inspector softly. "Panzer has always intrigued me, Tim. At the time I sent him to you, remember the hat deductions which absolved him had not yet been made. . . . I sent him to you merely out of a sense of curiosity. I thought that if Lewin recognized him, it might point to a connection between Panzer and Field. My thought was not borne out; it wasn't too hopeful to begin with. Panzer might have been acquainted with Field on the outside without Lewin's knowledge. On the other hand, I didn't particularly want Panzer hanging around the theatre that morning; so the errand did both of us a lot of good."

"Well, I hope you were satisfied with that package of newspapers I sent you in return, as you instructed," grinned Cronin.

"How about the anonymous letter Morgan received? Was that a blind, or what?" demanded Sampson.

"It was a sweet little frame-up," returned Queen grimly. "Barry explained that to me last night. He had heard of Morgan's threat against Field's life. He didn't know, of course, that Field was blackmailing Morgan. But he thought it might plant a strong false trail if he got Morgan to the theatre on a thin story Monday night. If Morgan didn't come, there was nothing lost. If he did— He worked it this way. He chose ordinary cheap notepaper, went down to one of the typewriter agencies and, wearing gloves, typed the letter, signed it with that useless scrawled initial, and mailed the thing from the general post-office. He was careful about fingerprints and certainly the note could never be traced to him. As luck would have it, Morgan swallowed the bait and came. The very ridiculousness of Morgan's story and the obvious falsity of the note, as Barry figured, made Morgan a strong suspect. On the other hand, Providence seems to provide compensations. For the information we got from Morgan about Field's blackmailing activities did Mr. Barry a heap of harm. He couldn't have foreseen that, though."

Sampson nodded. "I can think of only one other thing. How did Barry arrange for the purchase of the tickets—or did he arrange for it at all?"

"He certainly did. Barry convinced Field that as a matter of fairness to himself, the meeting and the transfer of papers should take place in the theatre under a cloak of absolute secrecy. Field was agreeable and was easily persuaded to purchase the eight tickets at the box-office. He himself realized that the six extra tickets were needed to insure privacy. He sent Barry seven and Barry promptly destroyed them all except LL30 Left."

The Inspector rose, smiling tiredly. "Djuna!" he said in a low voice. "Some more coffee."

Sampson stopped the boy with a protesting hand. "Thanks, Q, but I've got to be going. Cronin and I have loads of work on this gang affair. I couldn't rest, though, until I got the whole story from your own lips. . . . Q, old man," he added awkwardly, "I'm really sincere when I say that I think you've done a remarkable piece of work."

"I never heard of anything like it," put in Cronin heartily. "What a riddle, and what a beautiful piece of clear reasoning, from beginning to end!"

"Do you really think so?" asked the Inspector quietly. "I'm so glad, gentlemen. Because all the credit rightfully belongs to Ellery. I'm rather proud of that boy of mine . . ."

∽

When Sampson and Cronin had departed and Djuna had retired to his tiny kitchen to wash the breakfast dishes, the Inspector turned to his writing-desk and took up his fountain-pen. He rapidly read over what he had written to his son. Sighing, he put pen to paper once more.

> Let's forget what I just wrote. More than an hour has passed since then. Sampson and Tim Cronin came up and I had to crystallize our work on the case for their benefit. I never saw such a pair! Kids, both of 'em. Gobbled the story as if it were a fairy-tale. . . . As I talked, I saw with appalling clarity how little I actually did and how much you did. I'm pining for the day when you will pick out some nice girl and be married, and then the whole darned Queen family can pack off to Italy and settle down to a life of peace. . . . Well, El, I've got to dress and go down to headquarters. A lot of routine work has collected since last Monday and my job is just about cut out for me. . . .
>
> When are you coming home? Don't think I want to rush you, but it's so gosh-awful lonesome, son. I— No, I guess I'm selfish as well as tired. Just a doddering old fogey who needs coddling. But you *will* come home soon, won't you? Djuna sends his regards. The rascal is taking my ears off with the dishes in the kitchen.
>
> Your loving
Father

Facsimile first-edition dust jacket for *Red Harvest*.

RED HARVEST[1]

A Thrilling Detective Story

BY

DASHIELL HAMMETT

New York • Alfred A. Knopf • London

1929

To Joseph Thompson Shaw[2]

1.   The original version of what was eventually published as *Red Harvest* first appeared in *Black Mask* magazine in the November 1927, December 1927, January 1928, and February 1928 issues, under the collective title *The Cleansing of Poisonville*. The first installment had that title and contained the material later edited into Chapters I through VII; the second installment, "Crime Wanted—Male or Female," became Chapters VIII through XIII; the third installment, "Dynamite," Chapters XIV through XIX; and the fourth, "The 19th Murder," Chapters XX through XXVII. Hammett suggested several titles for the edited novel, including *The Poisonville Murders, The Seventeenth Murder, Murder Plus, The Willson Matter, The City of Death, The Cleansing of Poisonville, The Black City,* and finally *Red Harvest* (letter to Mrs. Alfred A. Knopf dated March 20, 1928). Knopf published it in February 1929.

Black Mask, December 1927, in which the second installment of the serialized version appeared, under the title "Crime Wanted—Male or Female."

2.   Joseph T. "Cap" Shaw was the editor of *Black Mask* magazine when the story was first published and frequently worked with Hammett.

Contents

CHAPTER I

A Woman in Green and a Man in Gray

first heard Personville called Poisonville by a red-haired mucker[3] named Hickey Dewey in the Big Ship in Butte.[4] He also called his shirt a shoit. I didn't think anything of what he had done to the city's name. Later I heard men who could manage their r's give it the same pronunciation. I still didn't see anything in it but the meaningless sort of humor that used to make richardsnary the thieves' word for dictionary.[5] A few years later I went to Personville and learned better.

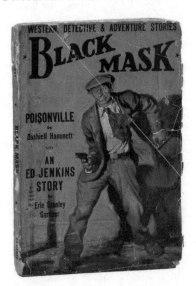

Cover of the November 1927 issue of *Black Mask*,
including the first part of "The Cleansing of Poisonville."

3   Miner's slang for a person who moves unwanted rock ("muck") out of a mine or tunnel.

4   The "Big Ship" was the local nickname for the Florence Hotel in Butte, Montana. Of course, "Personville" is a fictional town, but it bears many similarities to Butte geographically and historically. Broadway—mentioned a few paragraphs below—was a principal street of Butte.

Hammett's daughter Jo, in *Dashiell Hammett: A Daughter Remembers*, recalls that Hammett "first saw Butte in his twenties when he was working for the Pinkerton's. The agency had been brought in by the mine owners to help in their struggle with the unions and the radical I.W.W. Their job was to infiltrate and disrupt. What Papa did there as an undercover man, and what he saw done, left a deep and lasting impression on him," (p. 60). However, this is uncorroborated, and while the knowledge of the hotel's nickname is some evidence that Hammett was familiar with Butte, there is no direct evidence that he lived there. It is

Main street, Butte, Montana, ca. 1920.

certain that Hammett's wife Josephine Annis Dolan Hammett (known as Jose) grew up in Anaconda and worked in a Butte hospital during the period that Jo states Hammett was there, though they met in California where she worked as a nurse in a hospital where Hammett was being treated.

Hirbour Tower, the first "skyscraper" in Butte, Montana, built in 1901.

New Symons block, built in 1918, Butte, Montana.

5   The usage has been traced as far back as 1627: William Hawkins, in his play *Apollo Shroving*, wrote: "Talke not to me of Dick snary, nor Richard-snary; I care not how little I come neare them."

Using one of the phones in the station, I called the *Herald*, asked for Donald Willsson, and told him I had arrived.

"Will you come out to my house at ten this evening?" He had a pleasantly crisp voice. "It's 2101 Mountain Boulevard. Take a Broadway car, get off at Laurel Avenue, and walk two blocks west."

I promised to do that. Then I rode up to the Great Western Hotel, dumped my bags, and went out to look at the city.

Not the fictional Great Western Hotel
but rather the Butte Hotel, ca. 1920s.

The city wasn't pretty. Most of its builders had gone in for gaudiness. Maybe they had been successful at first. Since then the smelters whose brick stacks stuck up tall against a gloomy mountain to the south had yellow-smoked everything into uniform dinginess. The result was an ugly city of forty thousand people, set in an ugly notch between two ugly mountains that had been all dirtied up by mining. Spread over this was a grimy sky that looked as if it had come out of the smelters' stacks.

Anaconda Hill outside Butte in 1930.

The first policeman I saw needed a shave. The second had a couple of buttons off his shabby uniform. The third stood in the center of the city's main intersection—Broadway and Union Street—directing traffic, with a cigar in one corner of his mouth. After that I stopped checking them up.

Butte police officers, ca. 1930.

Not Broadway and Union (no such intersection existed);
Park Street from Main Street in Butte, ca. 1928.

At nine-thirty I caught a Broadway car and followed the directions Donald Willsson had given me. They brought me to a house set in a hedged grassplot on a corner.

The maid who opened the door told me Mr. Willsson was not home. While I was explaining that I had an appointment with him a slender blonde woman of something less than thirty in green crêpe came to the door. When she smiled her blue eyes didn't lose their stoniness. I repeated my explanation to her.

"My husband isn't in now." A barely noticeable accent slurred her s's. "But if he's expecting you he'll probably be home shortly."

She took me upstairs to a room on the Laurel Avenue side of the house, a brown and red room with a lot of books in it. We sat in leather chairs, half facing each other, half facing a burning coal grate, and she set about learning my business with her husband.

"Do you live in Personville?" she asked first.

"No. San Francisco."

6   It was, of course, still the time of Prohibition, when average citizens procured their
liquor from "bootleggers," purveyors (and
occasionally the makers) of illicit alcoholic
beverages.

"But this isn't your first visit?"

"Yes."

"Really? How do you like our city?"

"I haven't seen enough of it to know." That was a lie. I had. "I got in only this afternoon."

Her shiny eyes stopped prying while she said:

"You'll find it a dreary place." She returned to her digging with: "I suppose all mining towns are like this. Are you engaged in mining?"

"Not just now."

She looked at the clock on the mantel and said:

"It's inconsiderate of Donald to bring you out here and then keep you waiting, at this time of night, long after business hours."

I said that was all right.

"Though perhaps it isn't a business matter," she suggested.

I didn't say anything.

She laughed—a short laugh with something sharp in it.

"I'm really not ordinarily so much of a busybody as you probably think," she said gaily. "But you're so excessively secretive that I can't help being curious. You aren't a bootlegger, are you?[6] Donald changes them so often."

I let her get whatever she could out of a grin.

A telephone bell rang downstairs. Mrs. Willsson stretched her green-slippered feet out toward the burning coal and pretended she hadn't heard the bell. I didn't know why she thought that necessary.

She began: "I'm afraid I'll ha—" and stopped to look at the maid in the doorway.

The maid said Mrs. Willsson was wanted at the phone. She excused herself and followed the maid out. She didn't go downstairs, but spoke over an extension within earshot.

I heard: "Mrs. Willsson speaking. . . . Yes. . . . I beg your pardon? . . . Who? . . . Can't you speak a little louder? . . . *What?* . . . Yes. . . . Yes. . . . Who is this? . . . Hello! Hello!"

The telephone hook rattled. Her steps sounded down the hallway—rapid steps.

I set fire to a cigarette and stared at it until I heard her going down the steps. Then I went to a window, lifted an edge of the blind, and looked out at Laurel Avenue, and at the square white garage that stood in the rear of the house on that side.

Presently a slender woman in dark coat and hat came into sight hurrying from house to garage. It was Mrs. Willsson. She drove away in a Buick coupé. I went back to my chair and waited.

A 1920s Ford Model T coupe.

Three-quarters of an hour went by. At five minutes after eleven, automobile brakes screeched outside. Two minutes later Mrs. Willsson came into the room. She had taken off hat and coat. Her face was white, her eyes almost black.

"I'm awfully sorry," she said, her tight-lipped mouth moving jerkily, "but you've had all this waiting for nothing. My husband won't be home tonight."

I said I would get in touch with him at the *Herald* in the morning.

I went away wondering why the green toe of her left slipper was dark and damp with something that could have been blood.

∞

I walked over to Broadway and caught a street car. Three blocks north of my hotel I got off to see what the crowd was doing around a side entrance of the City Hall.

Thirty or forty men and a sprinkling of women stood on the sidewalk looking at a door marked *Police Department*. There were men from mines and smelters still in their working clothes, gaudy boys from pool rooms and dance halls, sleek men with slick pale faces, men with the dull look of respectable husbands, a few just as respectable and dull women, and some ladies of the night.[7]

On the edge of this congregation I stopped beside a square-set man in rumpled gray clothes. His face was grayish too, even

7   This is a strange combination of people for a town "out here in the bushes," as someone later says—clearly a mythic combination of a small Western town and an urban population, notes Sinda Gregory, in *Private Investigations: The Novels of Dashiell Hammett* (p. 32).

8   A deception or false tale. The meaning likely is derived from the "Punch-and-Judy" puppet shows of England that featured tales of a disharmonious married couple who regularly deceived each other. (See Dalzell, Tom and Terry Victor, *The New Partridge Dictionary of Slang and Unconventional English* [London and New York: Routledge, 2006], hereinafter "*New Partridge*", vol. 2, p. 1557.)

9.   "A. B." means "able-bodied."

10   The I.W.W., known disparagingly as the "Wobblies," was an organization founded in 1905 in Chicago ("Chi"), by organizers including William D. "Big Bill" Haywood, Mary "Mother" Jones, and Eugene V. Debs. It had Socialist (or anarchist) aims, depending on the source, describing its aim as "revolutionary industrial unionism" and was associated with radical or Communist organizations throughout its history.

the thick lips, though he wasn't much older than thirty. His face was broad, thick-featured and intelligent. For color he depended on a red Windsor tie that blossomed over his gray flannel shirt.

"What's the rumpus?" I asked him.

He looked at me carefully before he replied, as if he wanted to be sure that the information was going into safe hands. His eyes were gray as his clothes, but not so soft.

"Don Willsson's gone to sit on the right hand of God, if God don't mind looking at bulletholes."

"Who shot him?" I asked.

The gray man scratched the back of his neck and said:

"Somebody with a gun."

I wanted information, not wit. I would have tried my luck with some other member of the crowd if the red tie hadn't interested me. I said:

"I'm a stranger in town. Hang the Punch and Judy[8] on me. That's what strangers are for."

"Donald Willsson, Esquire, publisher of the *Morning* and *Evening Heralds*, was found in Hurricane Street a little while ago, shot very dead by parties unknown," he recited in a rapid singsong. "Does that keep your feelings from being hurt?"

"Thanks." I put out a finger and touched a loose end of his tie. "Mean anything? Or just wearing it?"

"I'm Bill Quint."

"The hell you are!" I exclaimed, trying to place the name. "By God, I'm glad to meet you!"

I dug out my card case and ran through the collection of credentials I had picked up here and there by one means or another. The red card was the one I wanted. It identified me as Henry F. Neill, A. B. seaman,[9] member in good standing of the Industrial Workers of the World.[10] There wasn't a word of truth in it.

I passed this card to Bill Quint. He read it carefully, front and back, returned it to my hand, and looked me over from hat to shoes, not trustfully.

"He's not going to die any more," he said. "Which way you going?"

"Any."

We walked down the street together, turned a corner, aimlessly as far as I knew.

"What brought you in here, if you're a sailor?" he asked casually.

"Where'd you get that idea?"

"There's the card."

"I got another that proves I'm a timber beast," I said. "If you want me to be a miner I'll get one for that tomorrow."

"You won't. I run 'em here."

"Suppose you got a wire from Chi?" I asked.

"Hell with Chi! I run 'em here." He nodded at a restaurant door and asked: "Drink?"

"Only when I can get it."

We went through the restaurant, up a flight of steps, and into a narrow second-story room with a long bar and a row of tables. Bill Quint nodded and said, "Hullo!" to some of the boys and girls at tables and bar, and steered me into one of the green-curtained booths that lined the wall opposite the bar.

We spent the next two hours drinking whiskey and talking.

The gray man didn't think I had any right to the card I had showed him, nor to the other one I had mentioned. He didn't think I was a good wobbly. As chief muckademuck of the I. W. W. in Personville, he considered it his duty to get the low-down on me, and to not let himself be pumped about radical affairs while he was doing it.

That was all right with me. I was interested in Personville affairs. He didn't mind discussing them between casual pokings into my business with the red cards.

What I got out of him amounted to this:

For forty years old Elihu Willsson—father of the man who had been killed this night—had owned Personville, heart, soul, skin and guts. He was president and majority stockholder of the Personville Mining Corporation, ditto of the First National Bank, owner of the *Morning Herald* and *Evening Herald*, the city's only newspapers, and at least part owner of nearly every other enterprise of any importance. Along with these pieces of property he owned a United States senator, a couple of representatives, the governor, the mayor, and most of the state legislature. Elihu Willsson was Personville, and he was almost the whole state.[11]

Back in the war days the I. W. W.—in full bloom then throughout the West[12]—had lined up the Personville Mining Corporation's help. The help hadn't been exactly pampered. They

11 By the 1920s, this was no longer true of the State of Montana. At the turn of the nineteenth century, it may well have been true, as Marcus Daly, who purchased the Anaconda silver mine to organize the Anaconda Copper Mining Company, founded the town of Anaconda, built a railroad between Anaconda (where he built smelters) and Butte to carry ore, and completely dominated the economy and politics of Montana. By the time of *Red Harvest*, however, the Anaconda Copper Mining Company had merged with other companies to become the fourth-largest corporation in the world and was dominated by the Rockefeller interests and Wall Street, not a local "Copper King."

12 The I.W.W. probably reached its peak membership in 1917, when it was estimated at 150,000, but its ranks swelled and waned rapidly, with members often joining during labor unrest and dropping out when the unrest ended. After the mid-1920s, it shrank considerably as a result of a schism in the leadership.

13   The exact date of the events described in *Red Harvest* is impossible to determine. It cannot be earlier than 1922 (see Quint's mention of "Italian history," discussed in note 14, which suggests a lapse of a few years after the events in question) nor later than 1927, when the first installment appeared in *Black Mask*. The presence of a Stutz touring car (see note 16) supports an approximate date of 1925 or 1926.

14   In 1922, workers in Italy mounted a general strike. To put down the strike, the Italian democratic government armed Mussolini and his Fascist cohorts. The strike was broken, but Mussolini seized power and the democracy was overthrown.

15   Later, Reno Starkey accuses Pete of being a "fish-eater" (a Catholic). Therefore, it's unlikely that "Pete the Finn" was actually from Finland, where the Lutheran religion prevails; rather, he was more likely Irish, with a last name like Finnegan. There was a strong Irish community in Butte, lured there in no small part by the presence of Marcus Daly, owner of Anaconda Copper Mining Company (see note 11), who was himself Irish.

used their new strength to demand the things they wanted. Old Elihu gave them what he had to give them, and bided his time.

In 1921 it came.[13] Business was rotten. Old Elihu didn't care whether he shut down for a while or not. He tore up the agreements he had made with his men and began kicking them back into their pre-war circumstances.

Of course the help yelled for help. Bill Quint was sent out from I. W. W. headquarters in Chicago to give them some action. He was against a strike, an open walk-out. He advised the old sabotage racket, staying on the job and gumming things up from the inside. But that wasn't active enough for the Personville crew. They wanted to put themselves on the map, make labor history.

They struck.

The strike lasted eight months. Both sides bled plenty. The wobblies had to do their own bleeding. Old Elihu hired gunmen, strike-breakers, national guardsmen and even parts of the regular army, to do his. When the last skull had been cracked, the last rib kicked in, organized labor in Personville was a used firecracker.

But, said Bill Quint, old Elihu didn't know his Italian history.[14] He won the strike, but he lost his hold on the city and the state. To beat the miners he had to let his hired thugs run wild. When the fight was over he couldn't get rid of them. He had given his city to them and he wasn't strong enough to take it away from them. Personville looked good to them and they took it over. They had won his strike for him and they took the city for their spoils. He couldn't openly break with them. They had too much on him. He was responsible for all they had done during the strike.

Bill Quint and I were both fairly mellow by the time we had got this far. He emptied his glass again, pushed his hair out of his eyes and brought his history up to date:

"The strongest of 'em now is probably Pete the Finn.[15] This stuff we're drinking's his. Then there's Lew Yard. He's got a loan shop down on Parker Street, does a lot of bail bond business, handles most of the burg's hot stuff, so they tell me, and is pretty thick with Noonan, the chief of police. This kid Max Thaler—Whisper—has got a lot of friends too. A little slick dark guy with something wrong with his throat. Can't talk. Gambler. Those three, with Noonan, just about help Elihu run his city—help him more than he wants. But he's got to play with 'em or else—"

"This fellow who was knocked off tonight—Elihu's son—where did he stand?" I asked.

"Where papa put him, and he's where papa put him now."

"You mean the old man had him—?"

"Maybe, but that's not my guess. This Don just came home and began running the papers for the old man. It wasn't like the old devil, even if he was getting close to the grave, to let anybody cop anything from him without hitting back. But he had to be cagey with these guys. He brought the boy and his French wife home from Paris and used him for his monkey—a damned nice fatherly trick. Don starts a reform campaign in the papers. Clear the burg of vice and corruption—which means clear it of Pete and Lew and Whisper, if it goes far enough. Get it? The old man's using the boy to shake 'em loose. I guess they got tired of being shook."

"There seems to be a few things wrong with that guess," I said.

"There's more than a few things wrong with everything in this lousy burg. Had enough of this paint?"

I said I had. We went down to the street. Bill Quint told me he was living in the Miners' Hotel in Forest Street. His way home ran past my hotel, so we walked down together. In front of my hotel a beefy fellow with the look of a plainclothes man stood on the curb and talked to the occupant of a Stutz touring car.[16]

"That's Whisper in the car," Bill Quint told me.

I looked past the beefy man and saw Thaler's profile. It was young, dark and small, with pretty features as regular as if they had been cut by a die.

"He's cute," I said.

"Uh-huh," the gray man agreed, "and so's dynamite."

16   The Stutz Motor Company was founded in 1915 and was headquartered in Indianapolis, Indiana. It went bankrupt in 1935, having produced approximately 35,000 cars. Although best remembered for the high-performance four-cylinder Stutz Bearcat, its powerful eight-cylinder touring car was its principal product after 1925.

1925 Stutz eight-cylinder touring car.

CHAPTER II

The Czar of Poisonville

17 The .32 ACP cartridge was devised during the latter half of the nineteenth century by John Browning, and it was used in the FN M1900 semi-automatic pistol, Colt Model 1903 Pocket Hammerless, Savage Arms Model 1907, Remington Model 51, and many other handguns. These were popular for self-defense and as a military and police sidearm, used extensively in World War I and by law-enforcement departments throughout Europe. By the end of the 1920s, however, it was viewed as underpowered compared with other larger models, and its popularity waned. The cartridge remains in use today principally in "concealed-carry" weapons of private individuals.

Colt Model 1903 Pocket Hammerless pistol.

The Morning Herald gave two pages to Donald Willsson and his death. His picture showed a pleasant intelligent face with curly hair, smiling eyes and mouth, a cleft chin and a striped necktie.

The story of his death was simple. At ten-forty the previous night he had been shot four times in stomach, chest and back, dying immediately. The shooting had taken place in the eleven-hundred block of Hurricane Street. Residents of that block who looked out after hearing the shots saw the dead man lying on the sidewalk. A man and a woman were bending over him. The street was too dark for anyone to see anybody or anything clearly. The man and woman had disappeared before anybody else reached the street. Nobody knew what they looked like. Nobody had seen them go away.

Six shots had been fired at Willsson from a .32 calibre pistol.[17] Two of them had missed him, going into the front wall of a house. Tracing the course of these two bullets, the police had learned that the shooting had been done from a narrow alley across the street. That was all anybody knew.

Editorially the *Morning Herald* gave a summary of the dead man's short career as a civic reformer and expressed a belief that he had been killed by some of the people who didn't want Personville cleaned up. The *Herald* said the chief of police could best show his own lack of complicity by speedily catching and convicting the murderer or murderers. The editorial was blunt and bitter.

I finished it with my second cup of coffee, jumped a Broadway car, dropped off at Laurel Avenue, and turned down toward the dead man's house.

I was half a block from it when something changed my mind and my destination.

A smallish young man in three shades of brown crossed the street ahead of me. His dark profile was pretty. He was Max Thaler, alias Whisper. I reached the corner of Mountain Boulevard in time to catch the flash of his brown-covered rear leg vanishing into the late Donald Willsson's doorway.

I went back to Broadway, found a drug store with a phone booth in it, searched the directory for Elihu Willsson's residence number, called it, told somebody who claimed to be the old man's secretary that I had been brought from San Francisco by Donald Willsson, that I knew something about his death, and that I wanted to see his father.

When I made it emphatic enough I got an invitation to call.

The czar of Poisonville was propped up in bed when his secretary—a noiseless slim sharpeyed man of forty—brought me into the bedroom.

The old man's head was small and almost perfectly round under its close-cut crop of white hair. His ears were too small and plastered too flat to the sides of his head to spoil the spherical effect. His nose also was small, carrying down the curve of his bony forehead. Mouth and chin were straight lines chopping the sphere off. Below them a short thick neck ran down into white pajamas between square meaty shoulders. One of his arms was outside the covers, a short compact arm that ended in a thick-fingered blunt hand. His eyes were round, blue, small and watery. They looked as if they were hiding behind the watery film and under the bushy white brows only until the time came to jump out and grab something. He wasn't the sort of man whose pocket you'd try to pick unless you had a lot of confidence in your fingers.

He ordered me into a bedside chair with a two-inch jerk of his round head, chased the secretary away with another, and asked:

"What's this about my son?"

His voice was harsh. His chest had too much and his mouth too little to do with his words for them to be very clear.

"I'm a Continental Detective Agency operative, San Francisco branch," I told him. "A couple of days ago we got a check from your son and a letter asking that a man be sent here to do some work for him. I'm the man. He told me to come out to his house last night. I did, but he didn't show up. When I got downtown I learned he had been killed."

Elihu Willsson peered suspiciously at me and asked:

"Well, what of it?"

"While I was waiting your daughter-in-law got a phone message, went out, came back with what looked like blood on her shoe, and told me her husband wouldn't be home. He was shot at ten-forty. She went out at ten-twenty, came back at eleven-five."

The old man sat straight up in bed and called young Mrs. Willsson a flock of things. When he ran out of words of that sort he still had some breath left. He used it to shout at me:

"Is she in jail?"

I said I didn't think so.

He didn't like her not being in jail. He was nasty about it. He bawled a lot of things I didn't like, winding up with:

"What the hell are you waiting for?"

He was too old and too sick to be smacked. I laughed and said:

"For evidence."

"Evidence? What do you need? You've—"

"Don't be a chump," I interrupted his bawling. "Why should she kill him?"

"Because she's a French hussy! Because she—"

The secretary's frightened face appeared at the door.

"Get out of here!" the old man roared at it, and the face went.

"She jealous?" I asked before he could go on with his shouting. "And if you don't yell maybe I'll be able to hear you anyway. My deafness is a lot better since I've been eating yeast."

He put a fist on top of each hump his thighs made in the covers and pushed his square chin at me.

"Old as I am and sick as I am," he said very deliberately, "I've a great mind to get up and kick your behind."

I paid no attention to that, repeating:

"Was she jealous?"

"She was," he said, not yelling now, "and domineering, and spoiled, and suspicious, and greedy, and mean, and unscrupulous, and deceitful, and selfish, and damned bad—altogether damned bad!"

"Any reason for her jealousy?"

"I hope so," he said bitterly. "I'd hate to think a son of mine would be faithful to her. Though likely enough he was. He'd do things like that."

"But you don't know any reason why she should have killed him?"

"Don't know any reason?" He was bellowing again. "Haven't I been telling you that—"

"Yeah. But none of that means anything. It's kind of childish."

The old man flung the covers back from his legs and started to get out of bed. Then he thought better of it, raised his red face and roared:

"Stanley!"

The door opened to let the secretary glide in.

"Throw this bastard out!" his master ordered, waving a fist at me.

The secretary turned to me. I shook my head and suggested:

"Better get help."

He frowned. We were about the same age. He was weedy, nearly a head taller than I, but fifty pounds lighter. Some of my hundred and ninety pounds were fat, but not all of them. The secretary fidgeted, smiled apologetically, and went away.

"What I was about to say," I told the old man: "I intended talking to your son's wife this morning. But I saw Max Thaler go into the house, so I postponed my visit."

Elihu Willsson carefully pulled the covers up over his legs again, leaned his head back on the pillows, screwed his eyes up at the ceiling, and said:

"Hm-m-m, so that's the way it is, is it?"

"Mean anything?"

"She killed him," he said certainly. "That's what it means."

Feet made noises in the hall, huskier feet than the secretary's. When they were just outside the door I began a sentence:

"You were using your son to run a—"

"Get out of here!" the old man yelled at those in the doorway. "And keep that door closed." He glowered at me and demanded: "What was I using my son for?"

"To put the knife in Thaler, Yard and the Finn."

"You're a liar."

"I didn't invent the story. It's all over Personville."

"It's a lie. I gave him the papers. He did what he wanted with them."

"You ought to explain that to your playmates. They'd believe you."

"What they believe be damned! What I'm telling you is so."

"What of it? Your son won't come back to life just because he was killed by mistake—if he was."

"That woman killed him."

"Maybe."

"Damn you and your maybes! She did."

"Maybe. But the other angle has got to be looked into too—the political end. You can tell me—"

"I can tell you that that French hussy killed him, and I can tell you that any other damned numbskull notions you've got are way off the lode."[18]

"But they've got to be looked into," I insisted. "And you know the inside of Personville politics better than anyone else I'm likely to find. He was your son. The least you can do is—"

"The least I can do," he bellowed, "is tell you to get to hell back to Frisco, you and your numbskull—"

I got up and said unpleasantly:

"I'm at the Great Western Hotel. Don't bother me unless you want to talk sense for a change."

I went out of the bedroom and down the stairs. The secretary hovered around the bottom step, smiling apologetically.

"A fine old rowdy," I growled.

"A remarkably vital personality," he murmured.

❧

At the office of the *Herald*, I hunted up the murdered man's secretary. She was a small girl of nineteen or twenty with wide chestnut eyes, light brown hair and a pale pretty face. Her name was Lewis.

She said she hadn't known anything about my being called to Personville by her employer.

"But then," she explained, "Mr. Willsson always liked to keep everything to himself as long as he could. It was— I don't think he trusted anybody here, completely."

"Not you?"

She flushed and said:

"No. But of course he had been here such a short while and didn't know any of us very well."

"There must have been more to it than that."

"Well," she bit her lip and made a row of forefinger prints down the polished edge of the dead man's desk, "his father wasn't—wasn't in sympathy with what he was doing. Since his father really owned the papers, I suppose it was natural for Mr. Donald to think some of the employes might be more loyal to Mr. Elihu than to him."

"The old man wasn't in favor of the reform campaign? Why did he stand for it, if the papers were his?"

She bent her head to study the finger prints she had made. Her voice was low.

"It's not easy to understand unless you know—The last time Mr. Elihu was taken sick he sent for Donald—Mr. Donald. Mr. Donald had lived in Europe most of his life, you know. Dr. Pride told Mr. Elihu that he'd have to give up the management of his affairs, so he cabled his son to come home. But when Mr. Donald got here Mr. Elihu couldn't make up his mind to let go of everything. But he wanted Mr. Donald to stay here, so he gave him the newspapers—that is, made him publisher. Mr. Donald liked that. He had been interested in journalism in Paris. When he found out how terrible everything was here—in civic affairs and so on—he started that reform campaign. He didn't know—he had been away since he was a boy—he didn't know—"

"He didn't know his father was in it as deep as anybody else," I helped her along.

She squirmed a little over her examination of the finger prints, didn't contradict me, and went on:

"Mr. Elihu and he had a quarrel. Mr. Elihu told him to stop stirring things up, but he wouldn't stop. Maybe he would have stopped if he had known—all there was to know. But I don't suppose it would ever have occurred to him that his father was really seriously implicated. And his father wouldn't tell him. I suppose it would be hard for a father to tell a son a thing like that. He threatened to take the papers away from Mr. Donald. I don't know whether he intended to or not. But he was taken sick again, and everything went along as it did."

"Donald Willsson didn't confide in you?" I asked.

"No." It was almost a whisper.

"Then you learned all this where?"

19 Two Democrats, Burton K. Wheeler and Thomas J. Walsh, served as the senators for the State of Montana during the relevant years. Wheeler was first elected in 1922 and held office until 1947; Walsh served from 1913 until his death in 1933. Wheeler first made his reputation in the state legislature, where he became known as a friend of labor in disputes with the Anaconda Copper Mining Company, the dominant force in Montana's economy. Walsh, an Irish-Catholic, had a strong liberal reputation and spoke out on women's suffrage and child labor issues. He was nominated as Attorney General of the United States by Franklin Delano Roosevelt in 1933 but died before he could take office.

In the 1899 election, rivals W.G. Conrad, a wealthy banker from Great Falls, and William A. Clark, millionaire banker and mining man from Butte, allegedly paid more than $1 million in bribes to state legislators in hopes of being appointed to serve as a senator. Clark won the appointment, but the Senate refused to allow him to take office; the seat was vacant for two years. This, along with other state corruption scandals, led ultimately to the adoption of the 17th Amendment to the Constitution, providing for the direct election of senators in lieu of appointment.

"I'm trying—trying to help you learn who murdered him," she said earnestly. "You've no right to—"

"You'll help me most just now by telling me where you learned all this," I insisted.

She stared at the desk, chewing her lower lip. I waited. Presently she said:

"My father is Mr. Willsson's secretary."

"Thanks."

"But you mustn't think that we—"

"It's nothing to me," I assured her. "What was Willsson doing in Hurricane Street last night when he had a date with me at his house?"

She said she didn't know. I asked her if she had heard him tell me, over the phone, to come to his house at ten o'clock. She said she had.

"What did he do after that? Try to remember every least thing that was said and done from then until you left at the end of the day."

She leaned back in her chair, shut her eyes and wrinkled her forehead.

"You called up—if it was you he told to come to his house—at about two o'clock. After that Mr. Donald dictated some letters, one to a paper mill, one to Senator Keefer[19] about some changes in post office regulations, and— Oh, yes! He went out for about twenty minutes, a little before three. And before he went he wrote out a check."

"Who for?"

"I don't know, but I saw him writing it."

"Where's his check book? Carry it with him?"

"It's here." She jumped up, went around to the front of his desk, and tried the top drawer. "Locked."

I joined her, straightened out a wire clip, and with that and a blade of my knife fiddled the drawer open.

The girl took out a thin, flat First National Bank check book. The last used stub was marked *$5,000*. Nothing else. No name. No explanation.

"He went out with this check," I said, "and was gone twenty minutes? Long enough to get to the bank and back?"

"It wouldn't have taken him more than five minutes to get there."

"Didn't anything else happen before he wrote out the check? Think. Any messages? Letters? Phone calls?"

"Let's see." She shut her eyes again. "He was dictating some mail and— Oh, how stupid of me! He did have a phone call. He said: 'Yes, I can be there at ten, but I shall have to hurry away.' Then again he said: 'Very well, at ten.' That was all he said except, 'Yes, yes,' several times."

"Talking to a man or a woman?"

"I didn't know."

"Think. There'd be a difference in his voice."

She thought and said:

"Then it was a woman."

"Which of you—you or he—left first in the evening?"

"I did. He— I told you my father is Mr. Elihu's secretary. He and Mr. Donald had an engagement for the early part of the evening—something about the paper's finances. Father came in a little after five. They were going to dinner together, I think."

That was all the Lewis girl could give me. She knew nothing that would explain Willsson's presence in the eleven-hundred block of Hurricane Street, she said. She admitted knowing nothing about Mrs. Willsson.

We frisked the dead man's desk, and dug up nothing in any way informative. I went up against the girls at the switchboard, and learned nothing. I put in an hour's work on messengers, city editors, and the like, and my pumping brought up nothing. The dead man, as his secretary said, had been a good hand at keeping his affairs to himself.

CHAPTER III

Dinah Brand

At the First National Bank I got hold of an assistant cashier named Albury, a nice-looking blond youngster of twenty-five or so.

"I certified the check for Willsson," he said after I had explained what I was up to. "It was drawn to the order of Dinah Brand—$5,000."

"Know who she is?"

"Oh, yes! I know her."

"Mind telling me what you know about her?"

"Not at all. I'd be glad to, but I'm already eight minutes overdue at a meeting with—"

"Can you have dinner with me this evening and give it to me then?"

"That'll be fine," he said.

"Seven o'clock at the Great Western?"

"Righto."

"I'll run along and let you get to your meeting, but tell me, has she an account here?"

"Yes, and she deposited the check this morning. The police have it."

"Yeah? And where does she live?"

"1232 Hurricane Street."

I said: "Well, well!" and, "See you tonight," and went away.

My next stop was in the office of the chief of police, in the City Hall.

Noonan, the chief, was a fat man with twinkling greenish eyes set in a round jovial face. When I told him what I was doing in his city he seemed glad of it. He gave me a hand-shake, a cigar and a chair.

"Now," he said when we were settled, "tell me who turned the trick."

"The secret's safe with me."

"You and me both," he said cheerfully through smoke. "But what do you guess?"

"I'm no good at guessing, especially when I haven't got the facts."

"'Twon't take long to give you all the facts there is," he said. "Willsson got a five-grand check in Dinah Brand's name certified yesterday just before bank closing. Last night he was killed by slugs from a .32 less than a block from her house. People that heard the shooting saw a man and a woman bending over the remains. Bright and early this morning the said Dinah Brand deposits the said check in the said bank. Well?"

"Who is this Dinah Brand?"

The chief dumped the ash off his cigar in the center of his desk, flourished the cigar in his fat hand, and said:

"A soiled dove, as the fellow says, a de luxe hustler, a big-league gold-digger."

"Gone up against her yet?"

"No. There's a couple of slants to be taken care of first. We're keeping an eye on her and waiting. This I've told you is under the hat."[20]

"Yeah. Now listen to this," and I told him what I had seen and heard while waiting in Donald Willsson's house the previous night.

When I had finished the chief bunched his fat mouth, whistled softly, and exclaimed:

"Man, that's an interesting thing you've been telling me! So it was blood on her slipper? And she said her husband wouldn't be home?"

"That's what I took it for," I said to the first question, and, "Yeah," to the second.

"Have you done any talking to her since then?" he asked.

20 From the phrase "keep it under your hat," meaning confidential—thought but not spoken. The earliest use in print appears to be Thackeray's *History of Pendennis* in 1848: "Thus, oh friendly readers, we see how every man in the world has his own private griefs and business . . . You and your wife have pressed the same pillow for forty years and fancy yourselves united. Psha, does she cry out when you have the gout, or do you lie awake when she has the toothache? . . . Ah, sir—a distinct universe walks about under your hat and under mine."

21 A euphemistic expression for "Jesus Christ," in the same vein as "Jeans Rice" and "cheese and rice."

"No. I was up that way this morning, but a young fellow named Thaler went into the house ahead of me, so I put off my visit."

"Grease us twice!"[21] His greenish eyes glittered happily. "Are you telling me the Whisper was there?"

"Yeah."

He threw his cigar on the floor, stood up, planted his fat hands on the desk top, and leaned over them toward me, oozing delight from every pore.

"Man, you've done something," he purred. "Dinah Brand is this Whisper's woman. Let's me and you just go out and kind of talk to the widow."

❦

We climbed out of the chief's car in front of Mrs. Willsson's residence. The chief stopped for a second with one foot on the bottom step to look at the black crêpe hanging over the bell. Then he said, "Well, what's got to be done has got to be done," and we went up the steps.

Mrs. Willsson wasn't anxious to see us, but people usually see the chief of police if he insists. This one did. We were taken upstairs to where Donald Willsson's widow sat in the library. She was in black. Her blue eyes had frost in them.

Noonan and I took turns mumbling condolences and then he began:

"We just wanted to ask you a couple of questions. For instance, like where'd you go last night?"

She looked disagreeably at me, then back to the chief, frowned, and spoke haughtily:

"May I ask why I am being questioned in this manner?"

I wondered how many times I had heard that question, word for word and tone for tone, while the chief, disregarding it, went on amiably:

"And then there was something about one of your shoes being stained. The right one, or maybe the left. Anyways it was one or the other."

A muscle began twitching in her upper lip.

"Was that all?" the chief asked me. Before I could answer he made a clucking noise with his tongue and turned his genial face to the woman again. "I almost forgot. There was a matter of how you knew your husband wouldn't be home."

She got up, unsteadily, holding the back of her chair with one white hand.

"I'm sure you'll excuse—"

"'S all right." The chief made a big-hearted gesture with one beefy paw. "We don't want to bother you. Just where you went, and about the shoe, and how you knew he wasn't coming back. And, come to think of it, there's another—What Thaler wanted here this morning."

Mrs. Willsson sat down again, very rigidly. The chief looked at her. A smile that tried to be tender made funny lines and humps in his fat face. After a little while her shoulders began to relax, her chin went lower, a curve came in her back.

I put a chair facing her and sat on it.

"You'll have to tell us, Mrs. Willsson," I said, making it as sympathetic as I could. "These things have got to be explained."

"Do you think I have anything to hide?" she asked defiantly, sitting up straight and stiff again, turning each word out very precisely, except that the s's were a bit slurred. "I did go out. The stain was blood. I knew my husband was dead. Thaler came to see me about my husband's death. Are your questions answered now?"

"We knew all that," I said. "We're asking you to explain them."

She stood up again, said angrily:

"I dislike your manner. I refuse to submit to—"

Noonan said:

"That's perfectly all right, Mrs. Willsson, only we'll have to ask you to go down to the Hall with us."

She turned her back to him, took a deep breath and threw words at me:

"While we were waiting here for Donald I had a telephone call. It was a man who wouldn't give his name. He said Donald had gone to the home of a woman named Dinah Brand with a check for five thousand dollars. He gave me her address. Then I drove out there and waited down the street in the car until Donald came out.

"While I was waiting there I saw Max Thaler, whom I knew by sight. He went to the woman's house, but didn't go in. He went away. Then Donald came out and walked down the street. He didn't see me. I didn't want him to. I intended to drive home—get here before he came. I had just started the engine when I heard the shots, and I saw Donald fall. I got out of the car and ran over to him. He was dead. I was frantic. Then Thaler came. He said if I were found there they would say I had killed him. He made me run back to the car and drive home."

Tears were in her eyes. Through the water her eyes studied my face, apparently trying to learn how I took the story. I didn't say anything. She asked:

"Is that what you wanted?"

"Practically," Noonan said. He had walked around to one side. "What did Thaler say this afternoon?"

"He urged me to keep quiet." Her voice had become small and flat. "He said either or both of us would be suspected if anyone learned we were there, because Donald had been killed coming from the woman's house after giving her money."

"Where did the shots come from?" the chief asked.

"I don't know. I didn't see anything—except—when I looked up—Donald falling."

"Did Thaler fire them?"

"No," she said quickly. Then her mouth and eyes spread. She put a hand to her breast. "I don't know. I didn't think so, and he said he didn't. I don't know where he was. I don't know why I never thought he might have."

"What do you think now?" Noonan asked.

"He—he may have."

The chief winked at me, an athletic wink in which all his facial muscles took part, and cast a little farther back:

"And you don't know who called you up?"

"He wouldn't tell me his name."

"Didn't recognize his voice?"

"No."

"What kind of voice was it?"

"He talked in an undertone, as if afraid of being overheard. I had difficulty understanding him."

"He whispered?" The chief's mouth hung open as the last sound left it. His greenish eyes sparkled greedily between their pads of fat.

"Yes, a hoarse whisper."

The chief shut his mouth with a click, opened it again to say persuasively:

"You've heard Thaler talk. . . ."

The woman started and stared big-eyed from the chief to me.

"It was he," she cried. "It was he."

Robert Albury, the young assistant cashier of the First National Bank, was sitting in the lobby when I returned to the Great Western Hotel. We went up to my room, had some ice-water brought, used its ice to put chill in Scotch, lemon juice, and grenadine,[22] and then went down to the dining room.

"Now tell me about the lady," I said when we were working on the soup.

"Have you seen her yet?" he asked.

"Not yet."

"But you've heard something about her?"

"Only that she's an expert in her line."

"She is," he agreed. "I suppose you'll see her. You'll be disappointed at first. Then, without being able to say how or when it happened, you'll find you've forgotten your disappointment, and the first thing you know you'll be telling her your life's history, and all your troubles and hopes." He laughed with boyish shyness. "And then you're caught, absolutely caught."

"Thanks for the warning. How'd you come by the information?"

He grinned shamefacedly across his suspended soup spoon and confessed:

"I bought it."

"Then I suppose it cost you plenty. I hear she likes *dinero*."

"She's money-mad, all right, but somehow you don't mind it. She's so thoroughly mercenary, so frankly greedy, that there's nothing disagreeable about it. You'll understand what I mean when you know her."

"Maybe. Mind telling me how you happened to part with her?"

"No, I don't mind. I spent it all, that's how."

"Cold-blooded like that?"

His face flushed a little. He nodded.

"You seem to have taken it well," I said.

"There was nothing else to do." The flush in his pleasant young face deepened and he spoke hesitantly. "It happens I owe her something for it. She—I'm going to tell you this. I want you to

22 Usually sugar is added, to make what is known as a Scotch Daisy.

23   A sign on a public vehicle such as a bus or tram, directing passengers to pay the fare as they board. It was the title of a popular 1928 film comedy (now lost) with Louise Fazenda and Clyde Cook and featured William Demarest and the twenty-three-year-old Myrna Loy.

24   Tuberculosis, that is. The Op later calls Rolff a "lunger," a slang reference to the disease.

see this side of her. I had a little money. After that was gone—You must remember I was young and head over heels. After my money was gone there was the bank's. I had—You don't care whether I had actually done anything or was simply thinking about it. Anyway, she found it out. I never could hide anything from her. And that was the end."

"She broke off with you?"

"Yes, thank God! If it hadn't been for her you might be looking for me now—for embezzlement. I owe her that!" He wrinkled his forehead earnestly. "You won't say anything about this—you know what I mean. But I wanted you to know she has her good side too. You'll hear enough about the other."

"Maybe she has. Or maybe it was just that she didn't think she'd get enough to pay for the risk of being caught in a jam."

He turned this over in his mind and then shook his head.

"That may have had something to do with it, but not all."

"I gathered she was strictly pay-as-you-enter."[23]

"How about Dan Rolff?" he asked.

"Who's he?"

"He's supposed to be her brother, or half-brother, or something of the sort. He isn't. He's a down-and-outer—t. b.[24] He lives with her. She keeps him. She's not in love with him or anything. She simply found him somewhere and took him in."

"Any more?"

"There was that radical chap she used to run around with. It's not likely she got much money out of him."

"What radical chap?"

"He came here back during the strike—Quint is his name."

"So he was on her list?"

"That's supposed to be the reason he stayed here after the strike was over."

"So he's still on her list?"

"No. She told me she was afraid of him. He had threatened to kill her."

"She seems to have had everybody on her string at one time or another," I said.

"Everybody she wanted," he said, and he said it seriously.

"Donald Willsson was the latest?" I asked.

"I don't know," he said. "I had never heard anything about them, had never seen anything. The chief of police had us try to find any checks he may have issued to her before yesterday, but we found nothing. Nobody could remember ever having seen any."

"Who was her last customer, so far as you know?"

"Lately I've seen her around town quite often with a chap named Thaler—he runs a couple of gambling houses here. They call him Whisper. You've probably heard of him."

∞

At eight-thirty I left young Albury and set out for the Miner's Hotel in Forest Street. Half a block from the hotel I met Bill Quint.

"Hello!" I hailed him. "I was on my way down to see you."

He stopped in front of me, looked me up and down, growled: "So you're a gum-shoe."

"That's the bunk," I complained. "I come all the way down here to rope you, and you're smarted up."

"What do you want to know now?" he asked.

"About Donald Willsson. You knew him, didn't you?"

"I knew him."

"Very well?"

"No."

"What did you think of him?"

He pursed his gray lips, by forcing breath between them made a noise like a rag tearing, and said:

"A lousy liberal."

"You know Dinah Brand?" I asked.

"I know her." His neck was shorter and thicker than it had been.

"Think she killed Willsson?"

"Sure. It's a kick in the pants."

"Then you didn't?"

"Hell, yes," he said, "the pair of us together. Got any more questions?"

"Yeah, but I'll save my breath. You'd only lie to me."

I walked back to Broadway, found a taxi, and told the driver to take me to 1232 Hurricane Street.

CHAPTER IV

Hurricane Street

My destination was a gray frame cottage. When I rang the bell the door was opened by a thin man with a tired face that had no color in it except a red spot the size of a half-dollar high on each cheek. This, I thought, is the lunger Dan Rolff.

"I'd like to see Miss Brand," I told him.

"What name shall I tell her?" His voice was a sick man's and an educated man's.

"It wouldn't mean anything to her. I want to see her about Willsson's death."

He looked at me with level tired dark eyes and said:
"Yes?"

"I'm from the San Francisco office of the Continental Detective Agency. We're interested in the murder."

"That's nice of you," he said ironically. "Come in."

I went in, into a ground-floor room where a young woman sat at a table that had a lot of papers on it. Some of the papers were financial service bulletins, stock and bond market forecasts. One was a racing chart.

The room was disorderly, cluttered up. There were too many pieces of furniture in it, and none of them seemed to be in its proper place.

"Dinah," the lunger introduced me, "this gentleman has come from San Francisco on behalf of the Continental Detective Agency to inquire into Mr. Donald Willsson's demise."

The young woman got up, kicked a couple of newspapers out of her way, and came to me with one hand out.

She was an inch or two taller than I, which made her about five feet eight. She had a broad-shouldered, full-breasted, round-hipped body and big muscular legs. The hand she gave me was soft, warm, strong. Her face was the face of a girl of twenty-five already showing signs of wear. Little lines crossed the corners of her big ripe mouth. Fainter lines were beginning to make nets around her thick-lashed eyes. They were large eyes, blue and a bit blood-shot.

Her coarse hair—brown—needed trimming and was parted crookedly. One side of her upper lip had been rouged higher than the other. Her dress was of a particularly unbecoming wine color, and it gaped here and there down one side, where she had neglected to snap the fasteners or they had popped open. There was a run down the front of her left stocking.

This was the Dinah Brand who took her pick of Poisonville's men, according to what I had been told.

"His father sent for you, of course," she said while she moved a pair of lizard-skin slippers and a cup and saucer off a chair to make room for me.

Her voice was soft, lazy.

I told her the truth:

"Donald Willsson sent for me. I was waiting to see him while he was being killed."

"Don't go away, Dan," she called to Rolff.

He came back into the room. She returned to her place at the table. He sat on the opposite side, leaning his thin face on a thin hand, looking at me without interest.

She drew her brows together, making two creases between them, and asked:

"You mean he knew someone meant to kill him?"

"I don't know. He didn't say what he wanted. Maybe just help in the reform campaign."

"But do you—?"

I made a complaint:

"It's no fun being a sleuth when somebody steals your stuff, does all the questioning."

"I like to find out what's going on," she said, a little laugh gurgling down in her throat.

"I'm that way too. For instance, I'd like to know why you made him have the check certified."

Very casually, Dan Rolff shifted in his chair, leaning back, lowering his thin hands out of sight below the table's edge.

"So you found out about that?" Dinah Brand asked. She crossed left leg over right and looked down. Her eyes focused on the run in her stocking. "Honest to God, I'm going to stop wearing them!" she complained. "I'm going barefooted. I paid five bucks for these socks yesterday. Now look at the damned things. Every day—runs, runs, runs!"

"It's no secret," I said. "I mean the check, not the runs. Noonan's got it."

She looked at Rolff, who stopped watching me long enough to nod once.

"If you talked my language," she drawled, looking narrow-eyed at me, "I might be able to give you some help."

"Maybe if I knew what it was."

"Money," she explained, "the more the better. I like it."

I became proverbial:

"Money saved is money earned. I can save you money and grief."

"That doesn't mean anything to me," she said, "though it sounds like it's meant to."

"The police haven't asked you anything about the check?"

She shook her head, no.

I said:

"Noonan's figuring on hanging the rap on you as well as on Whisper."

"Don't scare me," she lisped. "I'm only a child."

"Noonan knows that Thaler knew about the check. He knows that Thaler came here while Willsson was here, but didn't get in. He knows that Thaler was hanging around the neighborhood when Willsson was shot. He knows that Thaler and a woman were seen bending over the dead man."

The girl picked up a pencil from the table and thoughtfully scratched her cheek with it. The pencil made little curly black lines over the rouge.

Rolff's eyes had lost their weariness. They were bright, feverish, fixed on mine. He leaned forward, but kept his hands out of sight below the table.

"Those things," he said, "concern Thaler, not Miss Brand."

"Thaler and Miss Brand aren't strangers," I said. "Willsson brought a five-thousand dollar check here, and was killed leaving. That way, Miss Brand might have had trouble cashing it—if Willsson hadn't been thoughtful enough to get it certified."

"My God!" the girl protested, "if I'd been going to kill him I'd have done it in here where nobody could have seen it, or waited until he got out of sight of the house. What kind of a dumb onion do you take me for?"

"I'm not sure you killed him," I said. "I'm just sure that the fat chief means to hang it on you."

"What are you trying to do?" she asked.

"Learn who killed him. Not who could have or might have, but who did."

"I could give you some help," she said, "but there'd have to be something in it for me."

"Safety," I reminded her, but she shook her head.

"I mean it would have to get me something in a financial way. It'd be worth something to you, and you ought to pay something, even if not a fortune."

"Can't be done." I grinned at her. "Forget the bank roll and go in for charity. Pretend I'm Bill Quint."

Dan Rolff started up from his chair, lips white as the rest of his face. He sat down again when the girl laughed—a lazy, good-natured laugh.

"He thinks I didn't make any profit out of Bill, Dan." She leaned over and put a hand on my knee. "Suppose you knew far enough ahead that a company's employes were going to strike, and when, and then far enough ahead when they were going to call the strike off. Could you take that info and some capital to the stock market and do yourself some good playing with the company's stock? You bet you could!" she wound up triumphantly. "So don't go around thinking that Bill didn't pay his way."

"You've been spoiled," I said.

"What in the name of God's the use of being so tight?" she demanded. "It's not like it had to come out of your pocket. You've got an expense account, haven't you?"

I didn't say anything. She frowned at me, at the run in her stocking, and at Rolff. Then she said to him:

"Maybe he'd loosen up if he had a drink."

The thin man got up and went out of the room.

She pouted at me, prodded my shin with her toe, and said:

"It's not so much the money. It's the principle of the thing. If a girl's got something that's worth something to somebody, she's a boob if she doesn't collect."

I grinned.

"Why don't you be a good guy?" she begged.

Dan Rolff came in with a siphon, a bottle of gin, some lemons, and a bowl of cracked ice. We had a drink apiece. The lunger went away. The girl and I wrangled over the money question while we had more drinks. I kept trying to keep the conversation on Thaler and Willsson. She kept switching it to the money she deserved. It went on that way until the gin bottle was empty. My watch said one-fifteen.

She chewed a piece of lemon peel and said for the thirtieth or fortieth time:

"It won't come out of your pocket. What do you care?"

"It's not the money," I said, "it's the principle of the thing."

She made a face at me and put her glass where she thought the table was. She was eight inches wrong. I don't remember if the glass broke when it hit the floor, or what happened to it. I do remember that I was encouraged by her missing the table.

"Another thing," I opened up a new argumentative line, "I'm not sure I really need whatever you can tell me. If I have to get along without it, I think I can."

"It'll be nice if you can, but don't forget I'm the last person who saw him alive, except whoever killed him."

"Wrong," I said. "His wife saw him come out, walk away, and fall."

"His wife!"

"She was sitting in a coupé down the street."

"How did she know he was here?"

"She says Thaler phoned her that her husband had come here with the check."

"You're trying to kid me," the girl said. "Max couldn't have known it."

"I'm telling you what Mrs. Willsson told Noonan and me."

The girl spit what was left of the lemon peel out on the floor, further disarranged her hair by running her fingers through it, wiped her mouth with the back of her hand, and slapped the table.

"All right, Mr. Knowitall," she said, "I'm going to play with you. You can think it's not going to cost you anything, but I'll get mine before we're through. You think I won't?" she challenged me, peering at me as if I were a block away.

This was no time to revive the money argument, so I said: "I hope you do." I think I said it three or four times, quite earnestly.

"I will. Now listen to me. You're drunk, and I'm drunk, and I'm just exactly drunk enough to tell you anything you want to know. That's the kind of girl I am. If I like a person I'll tell them anything they want to know. Just ask me. Go ahead, ask me."

I did:

"What did Willsson give you five thousand dollars for?"

"For fun." She leaned back to laugh. Then: "Listen. He was hunting for scandal. I had some of it, some affidavits and things that I thought might be good for a piece of change some day. I'm a girl that likes to pick up a little jack when she can. So I had put these things away. When Donald began going after scalps I let him know that I had these things, and that they were for sale. I gave him enough of a peep at them to let him know they were good. And they were good. Then we talked how much. He wasn't as tight as you—nobody ever was—but he was a little bit close. So the bargain hung fire, till yesterday.

"Then I gave him the rush, phoned him and told him I had another customer for the stuff and that if he wanted it he'd have to show up that night with either five thousand smacks in cash or a certified check. That was hooey, but he hadn't been around much, so he fell for it."

"Why ten o'clock?" I asked.

"Why not? That's as good a time as any other. The main thing on a deal like that is to give them a definite time. Now you want to know why it had to be cash or a certified check? All right, I'll tell you. I'll tell you anything you want to know. That's the kind of girl I am. Always was."

She went on that way for five minutes, telling me in detail just which and what sort of a girl she was, and always had been, and why. I yes-yes'd her until I got a chance to cut in with:

"All right, now why did it have to be a certified check?"

She shut one eye, waggled a forefinger at me, and said:

"So he couldn't stop payment. Because he couldn't have used the stuff I sold him. It was good, all right. It was too good. It would have put his old man in jail with the rest of them. It would have nailed Papa Elihu tighter than anyone else."

I laughed with her while I tried to keep my head above the gin I had guzzled.

"Who else would it nail?" I asked.

"The whole damned lot of them." She waved a hand. "Max, Lew Yard, Pete, Noonan, and Elihu Willsson—the whole damned lot of them."

"Did Max Thaler know what you were doing?"

"Of course not—nobody but Donald Willsson."

"Sure of that?"

"Sure I'm sure. You don't think I was going around bragging about it ahead of time, do you?"

"Who do you think knows about it now?"

"I don't care," she said. "It was only a joke on him. He couldn't have used the stuff."

"Do you think the birds whose secrets you sold will see anything funny in it? Noonan's trying to hang the killing on you and Thaler. That means he found the stuff in Donald Willsson's pocket. They all thought old Elihu was using his son to break them, didn't they?"

"Yes, sir," she said, "and I'm one who thinks the same thing."

"You're probably wrong, but that doesn't matter. If Noonan found the things you sold Donald Willsson in his pocket, and learned you had sold them to him, why shouldn't he add that up to mean that you and your friend Thaler had gone over to old Elihu's side?"

"He can see that old Elihu would be hurt as much as anybody else."

"What was this junk you sold him?"

"They built a new City Hall three years ago," she said, "and none of them lost any money on it. If Noonan got the papers he'll pretty soon find out that they tied as much on old Elihu, or more, than on anybody else."

"That doesn't make any difference. He'll take it for granted that the old man had found an out for himself. Take my word for it, sister, Noonan and his friends think you and Thaler and Elihu are double-crossing them."

"I don't give a damn what they think," she said obstinately. "It was only a joke. That's all I meant it for. That's all it was."

"That's good," I growled. "You can go to the gallows with a clear conscience. Have you seen Thaler since the murder?"

"No, but Max didn't kill him, if that's what you think, even if he was around."

"Why?"

"Lots of reasons. First place, Max wouldn't have done it himself. He'd have had somebody else do it, and he'd have been way off with an alibi nobody could shake. Second place, Max carries a .38, and anybody he sent to do the job would have had that much gun or more. What kind of a gunman would use a .32?"[25]

"Then who did it?"

"I've told you all I know," she said. "I've told you too much."

I stood up and said:

"No, you've told me just exactly enough."

"You mean you think you know who killed him?"

"Yeah, though there's a couple of things I'll have to cover before I make the pinch."

"Who? Who?" She stood up, suddenly almost sober, tugging at my lapels. "Tell me who did it."

"Not now."

"Be a good guy."

"Not now."

She let go my lapels, put her hands behind her, and laughed in my face.

"All right. Keep it to yourself—and try to figure out which part of what I told you is the truth."

I said:

"Thanks for the part that is, anyhow, and for the gin. And if Max Thaler means anything to you, you ought to pass him the word that Noonan's trying to rib him."

25 In fact, Al Capone carried a .32, as did other gangsters who appreciated that the weapon was easily concealed.

CHAPTER V

Old Elihu Talks Sense

26   King George IV Old Scotch Whisky, a blend registered by the Distillers Agency Limited in the 1880s, was "guaranteed to contain the finest Highland malts and other Scotch whisky matured in seasoned wood," according to its label. The brand continues to be sold today.

It was close to two-thirty in the morning when I reached the hotel. With my key the night clerk gave me a memorandum that asked me to call Poplar 605. I knew the number. It was Elihu Willsson's.

"When did this come?" I asked the clerk.

"A little after one."

That sounded urgent. I went back to a booth and put in the call. The old man's secretary answered, asking me to come out at once. I promised to hurry, asked the clerk to get me a taxi, and went up to my room for a shot of Scotch.

I would rather have been cold sober, but I wasn't. If the night held more work for me I didn't want to go to it with alcohol dying in me. The snifter revived me a lot. I poured more of the King George[26] into a flask, pocketed it, and went down to the taxi.

Elihu Willsson's house was lighted from top to bottom. The secretary opened the front door before I could get my finger on the button. His thin body was shivering in pale blue pajamas and dark blue bathrobe. His thin face was full of excitement.

"Hurry!" he said. "Mr. Willsson is waiting. And, please, will you try to persuade him to let us have the body removed?"

I promised and followed him up to the old man's bedroom.

Old Elihu was in bed as before, but now a black automatic pistol lay on the covers close to one of his pink hands.

As soon as I appeared he took his head off the pillows, sat upright and barked at me:

"Have you got as much guts as you've got gall?"

His face was an unhealthy dark red. The film was gone from his eyes. They were hard and hot.

I let his question wait while I looked at the corpse on the floor between door and bed.

A short thick-set man in brown lay on his back with dead eyes staring at the ceiling from under the visor of a gray cap. A piece of his jaw had been knocked off. His chin was tilted to show where another bullet had gone through tie and collar to make a hole in his neck. One arm was bent under him. The other hand held a blackjack as big as a milk bottle. There was a lot of blood.

I looked up from this mess to the old man. His grin was vicious and idiotic.

"You're a great talker," he said. "I know that. A two-fisted, you-be-damned man with your words. But have you got anything else? Have you got the guts to match your gall? Or is it just the language you've got?"

There was no use in trying to get along with the old boy. I scowled and reminded him:

"Didn't I tell you not to bother me unless you wanted to talk sense for a change?"

"You did, my lad." There was a foolish sort of triumph in his voice. "And I'll talk you your sense. I want a man to clean this pig-sty of a Poisonville for me, to smoke out the rats, little and big. It's a man's job. Are you a man?"

"What's the use of getting poetic about it?" I growled. "If you've got a fairly honest piece of work to be done in my line, and you want to pay a decent price, maybe I'll take it on. But a lot of foolishness about smoking rats and pig-pens doesn't mean anything to me."

"All right. I want Personville emptied of its crooks and grafters. Is that plain enough language for you?"

"You didn't want it this morning," I said. "Why do you want it now?"

The explanation was profane and lengthy and given to me in a loud and blustering voice. The substance of it was that he had built Personville brick by brick with his own hands and he was going to keep it or wipe it off the side of the hill. Nobody could

27   $475,000 to $625,000 in real wages in today's economy (https:\\measuringworth.com).

threaten him in his own city, no matter who they were. He had let them alone, but when they started telling him, Elihu Willsson, what he had to do and what he couldn't do, he would show them who was who. He brought the speech to an end by pointing at the corpse and boasting:

"That'll show them there's still a sting in the old man."

I wished I were sober. His clowning puzzled me. I couldn't put my finger on the something behind it.

"Your playmates sent him?" I asked, nodding at the dead man.

"I only talked to him with this," he said, patting the automatic on the bed, "but I reckon they did."

"How did it happen?"

"It happened simple enough. I heard the door opening, and I switched on the light, and there he was, and I shot him, and there he is."

"What time?"

"It was about one o'clock."

"And you've let him lie there all this time?"

"That I have." The old man laughed savagely and began blustering again: "Does the sight of a dead man turn your stomach? Or is it his spirit you're afraid of?"

I laughed at him. Now I had it. The old boy was scared stiff. Fright was the something behind his clowning. That was why he blustered, and why he wouldn't let them take the body away. He wanted it there to look at, to keep panic away, visible proof of his ability to defend himself. I knew where I stood.

"You really want the town cleaned up?" I asked.

"I said I did and I do."

"I'd have to have a free hand—no favors to anybody—run the job as I pleased. And I'd have to have a ten-thousand dollar retainer."

"Ten thousand dollars![27] Why in hell should I give that much to a man I don't know from Adam? A man who's done nothing I know of but talk?"

"Be serious. When I say *me*, I mean the Continental. You know them."

"I do. And they know me. And they ought to know I'm good for—"

"That's not the idea. These people you want taken to the cleaners were friends of yours yesterday. Maybe they will be friends again next week. I don't care about that. But I'm not playing politics for you. I'm not hiring out to help you kick them back in line—with the job being called off then. If you want the job done you'll plank down enough money to pay for a complete job. Any that's left over will be returned to you. But you're going to get a complete job or nothing. That's the way it'll have to be. Take it or leave it."

"I'll damned well leave it," he bawled.

He let me get half-way down the stairs before he called me back.

"I'm an old man," he grumbled. "If I was ten years younger—" He glared at me and worked his lips together. "I'll give you your damned check."

"And authority to go through with it in my own way?"

"Yes."

"We'll get it done now. Where's your secretary?"

Willsson pushed a button on his bedside table and the silent secretary appeared from wherever he had been hiding. I told him:

"Mr. Willsson wants to issue a ten-thousand dollar check to the Continental Detective Agency, and he wants to write the Agency—San Francisco branch—a letter authorizing the Agency to use the ten thousand dollars investigating crime and political corruption in Personville. The letter is to state clearly that the Agency is to conduct the investigation as it sees fit."

The secretary looked questioningly at the old man, who frowned and ducked his round white head.

"But first," I told the secretary as he glided toward the door, "you'd better phone the police that we've got a dead burglar here. Then call Mr. Willsson's doctor."

The old man declared he didn't want any damned doctors.

"You're going to have a nice shot in the arm so you can sleep," I promised him, stepping over the corpse to take the black gun from the bed. "I'm going to stay here tonight and we'll spend most of tomorrow sifting Poisonville affairs."

The old man was tired. His voice, when he profanely and somewhat long-windedly told me what he thought of my impudence in deciding what was best for him, barely shook the windows.

I took off the dead man's cap for a better look at his face. It didn't mean anything to me. I put the cap back in place.

When I straightened up the old man asked, moderately:

"Are you getting anywhere in your hunt for Donald's murderer?"

"I think so. Another day ought to see it finished."

"Who?" he asked.

The secretary came in with the letter and the check. I gave them to the old man instead of an answer to his question. He put a shaky signature on each, and I had them folded in my pocket when the police arrived.

⌐∞⌐

The first copper into the room was the chief himself, fat Noonan. He nodded amiably at Willsson, shook hands with me, and looked with twinkling greenish eyes at the dead man.

"Well, well," he said. "It's a good job he did, whoever did it. Yakima Shorty. And will you look at the sap he's toting?" He kicked the blackjack out of the dead man's hand. "Big enough to sink a battleship. You drop him?" he asked me.

"Mr. Willsson."

"Well, that certainly is fine," he congratulated the old man. "You saved a lot of people a lot of troubles, including me. Pack him out, boys," he said to the four men behind him.

The two in uniform picked Yakima Shorty up by legs and arm-pits and went away with him, while one of the others gathered up the blackjack and a flashlight that had been under the body.

"If everybody did that to their prowlers, it would certainly be fine," the chief babbled on. He brought three cigars out of a pocket, threw one over on the bed, stuck one at me, and put the other in his mouth. "I was just wondering where I could get hold of you," he told me as we lighted up. "I got a little job ahead that I thought you'd like to be in on. That's how I happened to be on tap when the rumble[28] came." He put his mouth close to my ear and whispered: "Going to pick up Whisper. Want to go along?"

"Yeah."

"I thought you would. Hello, Doc!"

He shook hands with a man who had just come in, a little plump man with a tired oval face and gray eyes that still had sleep in them.

The doctor went to the bed, where one of Noonan's men was asking Willsson about the shooting. I followed the secretary into the hall and asked him:

"Any men in the house besides you?"

"Yes, the chauffeur, the Chinese cook."

"Let the chauffeur stay in the old man's room tonight. I'm going out with Noonan. I'll get back as soon as I can. I don't think there'll be any more excitement here, but no matter what happens don't leave the old man alone. And don't leave him alone with Noonan or any of Noonan's crew."

The secretary's mouth and eyes popped wide.

"What time did you leave Donald Willsson last night?" I asked.

"You mean night before last, the night he was killed?"

"Yeah."

"At precisely half-past nine."

"You were with him from five o'clock till then?"

"From a quarter after five. We went over some statements and that sort of thing in his office until nearly eight o'clock. Then we went to Bayard's and finished our business over our dinners. He left at half-past nine, saying he had an engagement."

"What else did he say about this engagement?"

"Nothing else."

"Didn't give you any hint of where he was going, who he was going to meet?"

"He merely said he had an engagement."

"And you didn't know anything about it?"

"No. Why? Did you think I did?"

"I thought he might have said something." I switched back to tonight's doings: "What visitors did Willsson have today, not counting the one he shot?"

"You'll have to pardon me," the secretary said, smiling apologetically, "I can't tell you that without Mr. Willsson's permission. I'm sorry."

"Weren't some of the local powers here? Say Lew Yard, or—"

The secretary shook his head, repeating:

"I'm sorry."

"We won't fight over it," I said, giving it up and starting back toward the bedroom door.

The doctor came out, buttoning his overcoat.

"He will sleep now," he said hurriedly. "Someone should stay with him. I shall be in in the morning." He ran downstairs.

I went into the bedroom. The chief and the man who had questioned Willsson were standing by the bed. The chief grinned as if he were glad to see me. The other man scowled. Willsson was lying on his back, staring at the ceiling.

"That's about all there is here," Noonan said. "What say we mosey along?"

I agreed and said, "Good-night," to the old man. He said, "Good-night," without looking at me. The secretary came in with the chauffeur, a tall sunburned young husky.

The chief, the other sleuth—a police lieutenant named McGraw—and I went downstairs and got into the chief's car. McGraw sat beside the driver. The chief and I sat in back.

"We'll make the pinch along about daylight," Noonan explained as we rode. "Whisper's got a joint over on King Street. He generally leaves there along about daylight. We could crash the place, but that'd mean gun-play, and it's just as well to take it easy. We'll pick him up when he leaves."

I wondered if he meant pick him up or pick him off. I asked:

"Got enough on him to make the rap stick?"

"Enough?" He laughed goodnaturedly. "If what the Willsson dame give us ain't enough to stretch him I'm a pickpocket."

I thought of a couple of wisecrack answers to that. I kept them to myself.

CHAPTER VI

Whisper's Joint

Our ride ended under a line of trees in a dark street not far from the center of town. We got out of the car and walked down to the corner.

A burly man in a gray overcoat, with a gray hat pulled down over his eyes, came to meet us.

"Whisper's hep,"[29] the burly man told the chief. "He phoned Donohoe that he's going to stay in his joint. If you think you can pull him out, try it, he says."

Noonan chuckled, scratched an ear, and asked pleasantly:

"How many would you say was in there with him?"

"Fifty, anyhow."

"Aw, now! There wouldn't be that many, not at this time of morning."

"The hell there wouldn't," the burly man snarled. "They been drifting in since midnight."

"Is that so? A leak somewheres. Maybe you oughtn't to have let them in."

"Maybe I oughtn't." The burly man was angry. "But I did what you told me. You said let anybody go in or out that wanted to, but when Whisper showed to—"

"To pinch him," the chief said.

"Well, yes," the burly man agreed, looking savagely at me.

More men joined us and we held a talk-fest. Everybody was in a bad humor except the chief. He seemed to enjoy it all. I didn't know why.

29   Aware (first used in this manner in 1903, according to *New Partridge Dictionary of Slang*).

Whisper's joint was a three-story brick building in the middle of the block, between two two-story buildings. The ground floor of his joint was occupied by a cigar store that served as entrance and cover for the gambling establishment upstairs. Inside, if the burly man's information was to be depended on, Whisper had collected half a hundred friends, loaded for a fight. Outside, Noonan's force was spread around the building, in the street in front, in the alley in back, and on the adjoining roofs.

"Well, boys," the chief said amiably after everybody had had his say, "I don't reckon Whisper wants trouble any more than we do, or he'd have tried to shoot his way out before this, if he's got that many with him, though I don't mind saying I don't think he has—not that many."

The burly man said: "The hell he ain't."

"So if he don't want trouble," Noonan went on, "maybe talking might do some good. You run over, Nick, and see if you can't argue him into being peaceable."

The burly man said: "The hell I will."

"Phone him, then," the chief suggested.

The burly man growled: "That's more like it," and went away.

When he came back he looked completely satisfied.

"He says," he reported, "'Go to hell.'"

"Get the rest of the boys down here," Noonan said cheerfully. "We'll knock it over as soon as it gets light."

The burly Nick and I went around with the chief while he made sure his men were properly placed. I didn't think much of them—a shabby, shifty-eyed crew without enthusiasm for the job ahead of them.

The sky became a faded gray. The chief, Nick, and I stopped in a plumber's doorway diagonally across the street from our target.

Whisper's joint was dark, the upper windows blank, blinds down over cigar store windows and door.

"I hate to start this without giving Whisper a chance," Noonan said. "He's not a bad kid. But there's no use me trying to talk to him. He never did like me much."

He looked at me. I said nothing.

"You wouldn't want to make a stab at it?" he asked.

"Yeah, I'll try it."

"That's fine of you. I'll certainly appreciate it if you will. You just see if you can talk him into coming along without any fuss. You know what to say—for his own good and all that, like it is."

"Yeah," I said and walked across to the cigar store, taking pains to let my hands be seen swinging empty at my sides.

Day was still a little way off. The street was the color of smoke. My feet made a lot of noise on the pavement.

I stopped in front of the door and knocked the glass with a knuckle, not heavily. The green blind down inside the door made a mirror of the glass. In it I saw two men moving up the other side of the street.

No sound came from inside. I knocked harder, then slid my hand down to rattle the knob.

Advice came from indoors:

"Get away from there while you're able."

It was a muffled voice, but not a whisper, so probably not Whisper's.

"I want to talk to Thaler," I said.

"Go talk to the lard-can that sent you."

"I'm not talking for Noonan. Is Thaler where he can hear me?"

A pause. Then the muffled voice said: "Yes."

"I'm the Continental op who tipped Dinah Brand off that Noonan was framing you," I said. "I want five minutes' talk with you. I've got nothing to do with Noonan except to queer his racket. I'm alone. I'll drop my rod in the street if you say so. Let me in."

I waited. It depended on whether the girl had got to him with the story of my interview with her. I waited what seemed a long time.

The muffled voice said:

"When we open, come in quick. And no stunts."

"All set."

The latch clicked. I plunged in with the door.

Across the street a dozen guns emptied themselves. Glass shot from door and windows tinkled around us.

Somebody tripped me. Fear gave me three brains and half a dozen eyes. I was in a tough spot. Noonan had slipped me a pretty dose. These birds couldn't help thinking I was playing his game.

I tumbled down, twisting around to face the door. My gun was in my hand by the time I hit the floor.

30   A 1927 song written by Seymour Simons and Richard A. Whiting, first recorded by Annette Hanshaw.

Across the street, burly Nick had stepped out of a doorway to pump slugs at us with both hands.

I steadied my gun-arm on the floor. Nick's body showed over the front sight. I squeezed the gun. Nick stopped shooting. He crossed his guns on his chest and went down in a pile on the sidewalk.

Hands on my ankles dragged me back. The floor scraped pieces off my chin. The door slammed shut. Some comedian said:

"Uh-huh, people don't like you."

I sat up and shouted through the racket:

"I wasn't in on this."

The shooting dwindled, stopped. Door and window blinds were dotted with gray holes. A husky whisper said in the darkness:

"Tod, you and Slats keep an eye on things down here. The rest of us might as well go upstairs."

We went through a room behind the store, into a passageway, up a flight of carpeted steps, and into a second-story room that held a green table banked for crap-shooting. It was a small room, had no windows, and the lights were on.

There were five of us. Thaler sat down and lit a cigarette, a small dark young man with a face that was pretty in a chorusman way until you took another look at the thin hard mouth. An angular blond kid of no more than twenty in tweeds sprawled on his back on a couch and blew cigarette smoke at the ceiling. Another boy, as blond and as young, but not so angular, was busy straightening his scarlet tie, smoothing his yellow hair. A thin-faced man of thirty with little or no chin under a wide loose mouth wandered up and down the room looking bored and humming *Rosy Cheeks*.[30]

I sat in a chair two or three feet from Thaler's.

"How long is Noonan going to keep this up?" he asked. There was no emotion in his hoarse whispering voice, only a shade of annoyance.

"He's after you this trip," I said. "I think he's going through with it."

The gambler smiled a thin, contemptuous smile.

"He ought to know what a swell chance he's got of hanging a one-legged rap like that on me."

"He's not figuring on proving anything in court," I said.

"No?"

"You're to be knocked off resisting arrest, or trying to make a getaway. He won't need much of a case after that."

"He's getting tough in his old age." The thin lips curved in another smile. He didn't seem to think much of the fat chief's deadliness. "Any time he rubs me out I deserve rubbing. What's he got against you?"

"He's guessed I'm going to make a nuisance of myself."

"Too bad. Dinah told me you were a pretty good guy, except kind of Scotch with the roll."[31]

"I had a nice visit. Will you tell me what you know about Donald Willsson's killing?"

"His wife plugged him."

"You saw her?"

"I saw her the next second—with the gat in her hand."

"That's no good to either of us," I said. "I don't know how far you've got it cooked. Rigged right, you could make it stick in court, maybe, but you'll not get a chance to make your play there. If Noonan takes you at all he'll take you stiff. Give me the straight of it. I only need that to pop the job."

He dropped his cigarette on the floor, mashed it under his foot, and asked:

"You that hot?"

"Give me your slant on it and I'm ready to make the pinch—if I can get out of here."

He lit another cigarette and asked:

"Mrs. Willsson said it was me that phoned her?"

"Yeah—after Noonan had persuaded her. She believes it now—maybe."

"You dropped Big Nick," he said. "I'll take a chance on you. A man phoned me that night. I don't know him, don't know who he was. He said Willsson had gone to Dinah's with a check for five grand. What the hell did I care? But, see, it was funny somebody I didn't know cracked it to me. So I went around. Dan stalled me away from the door. That was all right. But still it was funny as hell that guy phoned me.

"I went up the street and took a plant in a vestibule. I saw Mrs. Willsson's heap standing in the street, but I didn't know then that it was hers or that she was in it. He came out pretty soon and walked down the street. I didn't see the shots. I heard them. Then this woman jumps out of the heap and runs over to him. I

31   Thaler means that the Op is stingy, as is the proverbial Scot.

A hint, warning, or signal—a usage first recorded in print in 1803, according to the *Oxford English Dictionary*.

knew she hadn't done the shooting. I ought to have beat it. But it was all funny as hell, so when I saw the woman was Willsson's wife I went over to them, trying to find out what it was all about. That was a break, see? So I had to make an out for myself, in case something slipped. I strung the woman. That's the whole damned works—on the level."

"Thanks," I said. "That's what I came for. Now the trick is to get out of here without being mowed down."

"No trick at all," Thaler assured me. "We go any time we want to."

"I want to now. If I were you, I'd go too. You've got Noonan pegged as a false-alarm, but why take a chance? Make the sneak and keep under cover till noon, and his frame-up will be a wash-out."

Thaler put his hand in his pants pocket and brought out a fat roll of paper money. He counted off a hundred or two, some fifties, twenties, tens, and held them out to the chinless man, saying:

"Buy us a get-away, Jerry, and you don't have to give anybody any more dough than he's used to."

Jerry took the money, picked up a hat from the table, and strolled out. Half an hour later he returned and gave some of the bills back to Thaler, saying casually:

"We wait in the kitchen till we get the office."[32]

We went down to the kitchen. It was dark there. More men joined us.

Presently something hit the door.

Jerry opened the door and we went down three steps into the back yard. It was almost full daylight. There were ten of us in the party.

"This all?" I asked Thaler.

He nodded.

"Nick said there were fifty of you."

"Fifty of us to stand off that crummy force!" he sneered.

A uniformed copper held the back gate open, muttering nervously:

"Hurry it up, boys, please."

I was willing to hurry, but nobody else paid any attention to him.

We crossed an alley, were beckoned through another gate by a big man in brown, passed through a house, out into the next street, and climbed into a black automobile that stood at the curb.

One of the blond boys drove. He knew what speed was.

I said I wanted to be dropped off somewhere in the neighborhood of the Great Western Hotel. The driver looked at Whisper, who nodded. Five minutes later I got out in front of my hotel.

"See you later," the gambler whispered, and the car slid away.

The last I saw of it was its police department license plate vanishing around a corner.

CHAPTER VII

That's Why I Sewed You Up

It was half-past five. I walked around a few blocks until I came to an unlighted electric sign that said *Hotel Crawford*, climbed a flight of steps to the second-floor office, registered, left a call for ten o'clock, was shown into a shabby room, moved some of the Scotch from my flask to my stomach, and took old Elihu's ten-thousand dollar check and my gun to bed with me.

At ten I dressed, went up to the First National Bank, found young Albury, and asked him to certify Willsson's check for me. He kept me waiting a while. I suppose he phoned the old man's residence to find out if the check was on the up-and-up. Finally he brought it back to me, properly scribbled on.

I sponged an envelope, put the old man's letter and check in it, addressed it to the Agency in San Francisco, stuck a stamp on it, and went out and dropped it in the mail-box on the corner.

Then I returned to the bank and said to the boy:

"Now tell me why you killed him."

He smiled and asked:

"Cock Robin or President Lincoln?"

"You're not going to admit off-hand that you killed Donald Willsson?"

"I don't want to be disagreeable," he said, still smiling, "but I'd rather not."

"That's going to make it bad," I complained. "We can't stand here and argue very long without being interrupted. Who's the stout party with cheaters[33] coming this way?"

The boy's face pinkened. He said:

"Mr. Dritton, the cashier."

"Introduce me."

The boy looked uncomfortable, but he called the cashier's name. Dritton—a large man with a smooth pink face, a fringe of white hair around an otherwise bald pink head, and rimless nose glasses—came over to us.

. The assistant cashier mumbled the introductions. I shook Dritton's hand without losing sight of the boy.

"I was just saying," I addressed Dritton, "that we ought to have a more private place to talk in. He probably won't confess till I've worked on him a while, and I don't want everybody in the bank to hear me yelling at him."

"Confess?" The cashier's tongue showed between his lips.

"Sure." I kept my face, voice and manner bland, mimicking Noonan. "Didn't you know that Albury is the fellow who killed Donald Willsson?"

A polite smile at what he thought an asinine joke started behind the cashier's glasses, and changed to puzzlement when he looked at his assistant. The boy was rouge-red and the grin he was forcing his mouth to wear was a terrible thing.

Dritton cleared his throat and said heartily:

"It's a splendid morning. We've been having splendid weather."

"But isn't there a private room where we can talk?" I insisted.

Dritton jumped nervously and questioned the boy:

"What—what is this?"

Young Albury said something nobody could have understood.

I said: "If there isn't I'll have to take him down to the City Hall."

Dritton caught his glasses as they slid down his nose, jammed them back in place and said:

"Come back here."

We followed him down the length of the lobby, through a gate, and into an office whose door was labeled *President*—old Elihu's office. Nobody was in it.

I motioned Albury into one chair and picked another for myself. The cashier fidgeted with his back against the desk, facing both of us.

33 Glasses, the usage dating to 1908, according to *New Partridge*. As will be seen, Dritton wears a pince-nez.

"Now, sir, will you explain this," he said.

"We'll get around to that," I told him and turned to the boy. "You're an ex-boy-friend of Dinah's who was given the air. You're the only one who knew her intimately who could have known about the certified check in time to phone Mrs. Willsson and Thaler. Willsson was shot with a .32. Banks like that caliber. Maybe the gun you used wasn't a bank gun, but I think it was. Maybe you didn't put it back. Then there'll be one missing. Anyway I'm going to have a gun expert put his microscopes and micrometers on the bullets that killed Willsson and bullets fired from all the bank guns."

The boy looked calmly at me and said nothing. He had himself under control again. That wouldn't do. I had to be nasty. I said:

"You were cuckoo over the girl. You confessed to me that it was only because she wouldn't stand for it that you didn't—"

"Don't—please don't," he gasped. His face was red again.

I made myself sneer at him until his eyes went down. Then I said:

"You talked too much, son. You were too damned anxious to make your life an open book for me. That's a way you amateur criminals have. You've always got to overdo the frank and open business."

He was watching his hands. I let him have the other barrel:

"You know you killed him. You know if you used a bank gun, and if you put it back. If you did you're nailed now, without an out. The gun-sharks will take care of that. If you didn't, I'm going to nail you anyhow. All right. I don't have to tell you whether you've got a chance or not. You know.

"Noonan is framing Whisper Thaler for the job. He can't convict him, but the frame-up is tight enough that if Thaler's killed resisting arrest, the chief will be in the clear. That's what he means to do—kill Thaler. Thaler stood off the police all night in his King Street joint. He's still standing them off—unless they've got to him. The first copper that gets to him—exit Thaler.

"If you figure you've got a chance to beat your rap, and you want to let another man be killed on your account, that's your business. But if you know you haven't got a chance—and you haven't if the gun can be found—for God's sake give Thaler one by clearing him."

"I'd like," Albury's voice was an old man's. He looked up from his hands, saw Dritton, said, "I'd like," again and stopped.

"Where is the gun?" I asked.

"In Harper's cage," the boy said.

I scowled at the cashier and asked him:

"Will you get it?"

He went out as if he were glad to go.

"I didn't mean to kill him," the youngster said. "I don't think I meant to."

I nodded encouragingly, trying to look solemnly sympathetic.

"I don't think I meant to kill him," he repeated, "though I took the gun with me. You were right about my being cuckoo over Dinah—then. It was worse some days than others. The day Willsson brought the check in was one of the bad ones. All I could think about was that I had lost her because I had no more money, and he was taking five thousand dollars to her. It was the check. Can you understand that? I had known that she and Thaler were—you know. If I had learned that Willsson and she were too, without seeing the check, I wouldn't have done anything. I'm sure of it. It was seeing the check—and knowing I'd lost her because my money was gone.

"I watched her house that night and saw him go in. I was afraid of what I might do, because it was one of the bad days, and I had the gun in my pocket. Honestly I didn't want to do anything. I was afraid. I couldn't think of anything but the check, and why I had lost her. I knew Willsson's wife was jealous. Everybody knew that. I thought if I called her up and told her—I don't know exactly what I thought, but I went to a store around the corner and phoned her. Then I phoned Thaler. I wanted them there. If I could have thought of anyone else who had anything to do with either Dinah or Willsson I'd have called them too.

"Then I went back and watched Dinah's house again. Mrs. Willsson came, and then Thaler, and both of them stayed there, watching the house. I was glad of that. With them there I wasn't so afraid of what I might do. After a while Willsson came out and walked down the street. I looked up at Mrs. Willsson's car and at the doorway where I knew Thaler was. Neither of them did anything, and Willsson was walking away. I knew then why I had wanted them there. I had hoped they would do something—and I wouldn't have to. But they didn't, and he was walking away. If one of them had gone over and said something to him, or even followed him, I wouldn't have done anything.

"But they didn't. I remember taking the gun out of my pocket. Everything was blurred in front of my eyes, like I was crying. Maybe I was. I don't remember shooting—I mean I don't remember deliberately aiming and pulling the trigger—but I can remember the sound the shots made, and that I knew the noise was coming from the gun in my hand. I don't remember how Willsson looked, if he fell before I turned and ran up the alley, or not. When I got home I cleaned and reloaded the pistol, and put it back in the paying teller's cage the next morning."

⌒∞⌒

On the way down to the City Hall with the boy and the gun I apologized for the village cut-up stuff I had put in the early part of the shake-down, explaining:

"I had to get under your skin, and that was the best way I knew. The way you'd talked about the girl showed me you were too good an actor to be broken down by straight hammering."

He winced, and said slowly:

"That wasn't acting, altogether. When I was in danger, facing the gallows, she didn't—didn't seem so important to me. I couldn't—I can't now—quite understand—fully—why I did what I did. Do you know what I mean? That somehow makes the whole thing—and me—cheap. I mean, the whole thing from the beginning."

I couldn't find anything to say except something meaningless, like:

"Things happen that way."

In the chief's office we found one of the men who had been on the storming party the night before—a red-faced official named Biddle. He goggled at me with curious gray eyes, but asked no questions about the King Street doings.

Biddle called in a young lawyer named Dart from the prosecuting attorney's office. Albury was repeating his story to Biddle, Dart and a stenographer, when the chief of police, looking as if he had just crawled out of bed, arrived.

"Well, it certainly is fine to see you," Noonan said, pumping my hand up and down while patting my back. "By God! you had a narrow one last night—the rats! I was dead sure they'd got you till we kicked in the doors and found the joint empty. Tell me how those son-of-a-guns got out of there."

"A couple of your men let them out the back door, took them through the house in back, and sent them away in a department car. They took me along so I couldn't tip you off."

"A couple of my men did that?" he asked, with no appearance of surprise. "Well, well! What kind of looking men were they?"

I described them.

"Shore and Riordan," he said. "I might of known it. Now what's all this?" nodding his fat face at Albury.

I told him briefly while the boy went on dictating his statement.

The chief chuckled and said:

"Well, well, I did Whisper an injustice. I'll have to hunt him up and square myself. So you landed the boy? That certainly is fine. Congratulations and thanks." He shook my hand again. "You'll not be leaving our city now, will you?"

"Not just yet."

"That's fine," he assured me.

I went out for breakfast-and-lunch. Then I treated myself to a shave and hair-cut, sent a telegram to the Agency asking to have Dick Foley and Mickey Linehan shipped to Personville, stopped in my room for a change of clothes, and set out for my client's house.

Old Elihu was wrapped in blankets in an armchair at a sunny window. He gave me a stubby hand and thanked me for catching his son's murderer.

I made some more or less appropriate reply. I didn't ask him how he had got the news.

"The check I gave you last night," he said, "is only fair pay for the work you have done."

"Your son's check more than covered that."

"Then call mine a bonus."

"The Continental's got rules against taking bonuses or rewards," I said.

His face began to redden.

"Well, damn it—"

"You haven't forgotten that your check was to cover the cost of investigating crime and corruption in Personville, have you?" I asked.

"That was nonsense," he snorted. "We were excited last night. That's called off."

"Not with me."

He threw a lot of profanity around. Then:

"It's my money and I won't have it wasted on a lot of damn-foolery. If you won't take it for what you've done, give it back to me."

"Stop yelling at me," I said. "I'll give you nothing except a good job of city-cleaning. That's what you bargained for, and that's what you're going to get. You know now that your son was killed by young Albury, and not by your playmates. They know now that Thaler wasn't helping you double-cross them. With your son dead, you've been able to promise them that the newspapers won't dig up any more dirt. All's lovely and peaceful again.

"I told you I expected something like that. That's why I sewed you up. And you are sewed up. The check has been certified, so you can't stop payment. The letter of authority may not be as good as a contract, but you'll have to go into court to prove that it isn't. If you want that much of that kind of publicity, go ahead. I'll see that you get plenty.

"Your fat chief of police tried to assassinate me last night. I don't like that. I'm just mean enough to want to ruin him for it. Now I'm going to have my fun. I've got ten thousand dollars of your money to play with. I'm going to use it opening Poisonville up from Adam's apple to ankles. I'll see that you get my reports as regularly as possible. I hope you enjoy them."

And I went out of the house with his curses sizzling around my head.

CHAPTER VIII

A Tip on Kid Cooper

I spent most of the afternoon writing my three days' reports on the Donald Willsson operation. Then I sat around, burned Fatimas,[34] and thought about the Elihu Willsson operation until dinner time.

I went down to the hotel dining room and had just decided in favor of pounded rump steak with mushrooms when I heard myself being paged.

The boy took me to one of the lobby booths. Dinah Brand's lazy voice came out of the receiver:

"Max wants to see you. Can you drop in tonight?"

"Your place?"

"Yes."

I promised to drop in and returned to the dining room and my meal. When I had finished eating I went up to my room, fifth floor front. I unlocked the door and went in, snapping on the light.

A bullet kissed a hole in the door-frame close to my noodle.[35]

More bullets made more holes in door, door-frame and wall, but by that time I had carried my noodle into a safe corner, one out of line with the window.

Across the street, I knew, was a four-story office building with a roof a little above the level of my window. The roof would be dark. My light was on. There was no percentage in trying to peep out under those conditions.

34　A popular American brand of cigarette manufactured by Liggett & Myers, reportedly blending Turkish and domestic tobacco; it was discontinued around 1980.

Fatima cigarette tin, twenty for 15 cents.

Package of Fatima cigarettes.

35　The head or brain, an English usage dating to 1803, according to *New Partridge*.

I looked around for something to chuck at the light globe, found a Gideon Bible, and chucked it. The bulb popped apart, giving me darkness.

The shooting had stopped.

I crept to the window, kneeling with an eye to one of its lower corners. The roof across the street was dark and too high for me to see beyond its rim. Ten minutes of this one-eyed spying got me nothing except a kink in my neck.

I went to the phone and asked the girl to send the house copper up.

He was a portly, white-mustached man with the round undeveloped forehead of a child. He wore a too-small hat on the back of his head to show the forehead. His name was Keever. He got too excited over the shooting.

The hotel manager came in, a plump man with carefully controlled face, voice and manner. He didn't get excited at all. He took the this-is-unheard-of-but-not-really-serious-of-course attitude of a street fakir whose mechanical dingus flops during a demonstration.

We risked light, getting a new globe, and added up the bulletholes. There were ten of them.

Policemen came, went, and returned to report no luck in picking up whatever trail there might have been. Noonan called up. He talked to the sergeant in charge of the police detail, and then to me.

"I just this minute heard about the shooting," he said. "Now who do you reckon would be after you like that?"

"I couldn't guess," I lied.

"None of them touched you?"

"No."

"Well, that certainly is fine," he said heartily. "And we'll nail that baby, whoever he was, you can bet your life on that. Would you like me to leave a couple of the boys with you, just to see nothing else happens?"

"No, thanks."

"You can have them if you want them," he insisted.

"No, thanks."

He made me promise to call on him the first chance I got, told me the Personville police department was at my disposal, gave me to understand that if anything happened to me his whole life would be ruined, and I finally got rid of him.

The police went away. I had my stuff moved into another room, one into which bullets couldn't be so easily funneled. Then I changed my clothes and set out for Hurricane Street, to keep my date with the whispering gambler.

∞

Dinah Brand opened the door for me. Her big ripe mouth was rouged evenly this evening, but her brown hair still needed trimming, was parted haphazardly, and there were spots down the front of her orange silk dress.

"So you're still alive," she said. "I suppose nothing can be done about it. Come on in."

We went into her cluttered-up living room. Dan Rolff and Max Thaler were playing pinochle there. Rolff nodded to me. Thaler got up to shake hands.

His hoarse whispering voice said:

"I hear you've declared war on Poisonville."

"Don't blame me. I've got a client who wants the place ventilated."

"Wanted, not wants," he corrected me as we sat down. "Why don't you chuck it?"

I made a speech:

"No. I don't like the way Poisonville has treated me. I've got my chance now, and I'm going to even up. I take it you're back in the club again, all brothers together, let bygones be bygones. You want to be let alone. There was a time when I wanted to be let alone. If I had been, maybe now I'd be riding back to San Francisco. But I wasn't. Especially I wasn't let alone by that fat Noonan. He's had two tries at my scalp in two days. That's plenty. Now it's my turn to run him ragged, and that's exactly what I'm going to do. Poisonville is ripe for the harvest. It's a job I like, and I'm going to it."

"While you last," the gambler said.

"Yeah," I agreed. "I was reading in the paper this morning about a fellow choking to death eating a chocolate eclair in bed."

"That may be good," said Dinah Brand, her big body sprawled in an arm-chair, "but it wasn't in this morning's paper."

She lit a cigarette and threw the match out of sight under the Chesterfield. The lunger had gathered up the cards and was shuffling them over and over, purposelessly.

Thaler frowned at me and said:

"Willsson's willing for you to keep the ten grand. Let it go at that."

"I've got a mean disposition. Attempted assassinations make me mad."

"That won't get you anything but a box. I'm for you. You kept Noonan from framing me. That's why I'm telling you, forget it and go back to Frisco."

"I'm for you," I said. "That's why I'm telling you, split with them. They crossed you up once. It'll happen again. Anyway, they're slated for the chutes. Get out while the getting's good."

"I'm sitting too pretty," he said. "And I'm able to take care of myself."

"Maybe. But you know the racket's too good to last. You've had the cream of the pickings. Now it's get-away day."

He shook his little dark head and told me:

"I think you're pretty good, but I'm damned if I think you're good enough to crack this camp. It's too tight. If I thought you could swing it, I'd be with you. You know how I stand with Noonan. But you'll never make it. Chuck it."

"No. I'm in it to the last nickel of Elihu's ten thousand."

"I told you he was too damned pig-headed to listen to reason," Dinah Brand said, yawning. "Isn't there anything to drink in the dump, Dan?"

The lunger got up from the table and went out of the room.

Thaler shrugged, said:

"Have it your way. You're supposed to know what you're doing. Going to the fights tomorrow night?"

I said I thought I would. Dan Rolff came in with gin and trimmings. We had a couple of drinks apiece. We talked about the fights. Nothing more was said about me versus Poisonville. The gambler apparently had washed his hands of me, but he didn't seem to hold my stubbornness against me. He even gave me what seemed to be a straight tip on the fights—telling me any bet on the main event would be good if its maker remembered that Kid Cooper would probably knock Ike Bush out in the sixth round. He seemed to know what he was talking about, and it didn't seem to be news to the others.

I left a little after eleven, returning to the hotel without anything happening.

CHAPTER IX

A Black Knife

woke next morning with an idea in my skull. Personville had only some forty thousand inhabitants. It shouldn't be hard to spread news. Ten o'clock found me out spreading it.

I did my spreading in pool rooms, cigar stores, speakeasies, soft drink joints, and on street corners—wherever I found a man or two loafing. My spreading technique was something like this:

"Got a match? . . . Thanks. . . . Going to the fights tonight? . . . I hear Ike Bush takes a dive in the sixth. . . . It ought to be straight: I got it from Whisper. . . . Yeah, they all are."

People like inside stuff, and anything that had Thaler's name to it was very inside in Personville. The news spread nicely. Half the men I gave it to worked almost as hard as I did spreading it, just to show they knew what was what.

When I started out, seven to four was being offered that Ike Bush would win, and two to three that he would win by a knock-out. By two o'clock none of the joints taking bets were offering anything better than even money, and by half-past three Kid Cooper was a two-to-one favorite.

I made my last stop a lunch counter, where I tossed the news out to a waiter and a couple of customers while eating a hot beef sandwich.

When I went out I found a man waiting by the door for me. He had bowed legs and a long sharp jaw, like a hog's. He nodded and walked down the street beside me, chewing a toothpick and squinting sidewise into my face. At the corner he said:

"I know for a fact that ain't so."

"What?" I asked.

"About Ike Bush flopping. I know for a fact that ain't so."

"Then it oughtn't bother you any. But the wise money's going two to one on Cooper, and he's not that good unless Bush lets him be."

The hog jaw spit out the mangled toothpick and snapped yellow teeth at me.

"He told me his own self that Cooper was a set-up for him, last night, and he wouldn't do nothing like that—not to me."

"Friend of yours?"

"Not exactly, but he knows I— Hey, listen! Did Whisper give you that, on the level?"

"On the level."

He cursed bitterly. "And I put my last thirty-five bucks in the world on that rat on his say-so. Me, that could send him over for—" He broke off and looked down the street.

"Could send him over for what?" I asked.

"Plenty," he said. "Nothing."

I had a suggestion:

"If you've got something on him, maybe we ought to talk it over. I wouldn't mind seeing Bush win, myself. If what you've got is any good, what's the matter with putting it up to him?"

He looked at me, at the sidewalk, fumbled in his vest pocket for another toothpick, put it in his mouth, and mumbled:

"Who are you?"

I gave him a name, something like Hunter or Hunt or Huntington, and asked him his. He said his name was MacSwain, Bob MacSwain, and I could ask anybody in town if it wasn't right.

I said I believed him and asked:

"What do you say? Will we put the squeeze to Bush?"

Little hard lights came into his eyes and died.

"No," he gulped. "I ain't that kind of fellow. I never—"

"You never did anything but let people gyp you. You don't have to go up against him, MacSwain. Give me the dope, and I'll make the play—if it's any good."

He thought that over, licking his lips, letting the toothpick fall down to stick on his coat front.

"You wouldn't let on about me having any part in it?" he asked. "I belong here, and I wouldn't stand a chance if it got out. And you won't turn him up? You'll just use it to make him fight?"

"Right."

He took my hand excitedly and demanded:

"Honest to God?"

"Honest to God."

"His real monacker[36] is Al Kennedy. He was in on the Keystone Trust[37] knockover in Philly two years ago, when Scissors Haggerty's mob croaked two messengers. Al didn't do the killing, but he was in on the caper. He used to scrap around Philly. The rest of them got copped, but he made the sneak. That's why he's sticking out here in the bushes. That's why he won't never let them put his mug in the papers or on any cards. That's why he's a pork-and-beaner[38] when he's as good as the best. See? This Ike Bush is Al Kennedy that the Philly bulls want for the Keystone trick. See? He was in on the—"

"I see. I see," I stopped the merry-go-round. "The next thing is to get to see him. How do we do that?"

"He flops at the Maxwell, on Union Street. I guess maybe he'd be there now, resting up for the mill."

"Resting for what? He doesn't know he's going to fight. We'll give it a try, though."

"We! We! Where do you get that *we* at? You said—you swore you'd keep me covered."

"Yeah," I said, "I remember that now. What does he look like?"

"A black-headed kid, kind of slim, with one tin ear[39] and eyebrows that run straight across. I don't know if you can make him like it."

"Leave that to me. Where'll I find you afterwards?"

"I'll be hanging around Murry's. Mind you don't tip my mitt. You promised."

The Maxwell was one of a dozen hotels along Union Street with narrow front doors between stores, and shabby stairs leading up to second-story offices. The Maxwell's office was simply a wide place in the hall, with a key- and mail-rack behind a wooden counter

36   A variant of "moniker," a nickname or sobriquet, dating from 1851 (*New Partridge*).

37   The Keystone Trust Company was established in 1916 in Harrisburg, Pennsylvania; it was acquired in 1969 by Fulton National Bank.

38   Meaning someone who eats pork-and-beans from a can, an indigent.

39   Not in the musical sense, but rather an ear damaged by boxing, like a "cauliflower" ear. A 1916 newspaper account reported, "About eight out of every ten fist fighters you see nowadays own the 'cauliflower,' or 'tin' ear; an ear so battered and punched by the bludgeonings of five-ounce gloves that it isn't really an ear any more at all, but just a misshapen chunk of cartilage clinging to the side of the head."

that needed paint just as badly. A brass bell and a dirty day-book register were on the counter. Nobody was there.

I had to run back eight pages before I found *Ike Bush, Salt Lake City, 214*, written in the book. The pigeonhole that had that number was empty. I climbed more steps and knocked on a door that had it. Nothing came of that. I tried it two or three times more and then turned back to the stairs.

Somebody was coming up. I stood at the top, waiting for a look at him. There was just light enough to see by.

He was a slim muscular lad in army shirt, blue suit, gray cap. Black eyebrows made a straight line above his eyes.

I said: "Hello."

He nodded without stopping or saying anything.

"Win tonight?" I asked.

"Hope so," he said shortly, passing me.

I let him take four steps toward his room before I told him:

"So do I. I'd hate to have to ship you back to Philly, Al."

He took another step, turned around very slowly, rested a shoulder against the wall, let his eyes get sleepy, and grunted:

"Huh?"

"If you were smacked down in the sixth or any other round by a palooka like Kid Cooper, it'd make me peevish," I said. "Don't do it, Al. You don't want to go back to Philly."

The youngster put his chin down in his neck and came back to me. When he was within arm's reach, he stopped, letting his left side turn a bit to the front. His hands were hanging loose. Mine were in my overcoat pockets.

He said, "Huh?" again.

I said:

"Try to remember that—if Ike Bush doesn't turn in a win tonight, Al Kennedy will be riding east in the morning."

He lifted his left shoulder an inch. I moved the gun around in my pocket, enough. He grumbled:

"Where do you get that stuff about me not winning?"

"Just something I heard. I didn't think there was anything in it, except maybe a ducat back to Philly."

"I oughta bust your jaw, you fat crook."

"Now's the time to do it," I advised him. "If you win tonight you're not likely to see me again. If you lose, you'll see me, but your hands won't be loose."

I found MacSwain in Murry's, a Broadway pool room.

"Did you get to him?" he asked.

"Yeah. It's all fixed—if he doesn't blow town, or say something to his backers, or just pay no attention to me, or—"

MacSwain developed a lot of nervousness.

"You better damn sight be careful," he warned me. "They might try to put you out the way. He—I got to see a fellow down the street," and he deserted me.

⟞⟝

Poisonville's prize fighting was done in a big wooden ex-casino in what had once been an amusement park on the edge of town. When I got there at eight-thirty, most of the population seemed to be on hand, packed tight in close rows of folding chairs on the main floor, packed tighter on benches in two dinky balconies.

Smoke. Stink. Heat. Noise.

My seat was in the third row, ringside. Moving down to it, I discovered Dan Rolff in an aisle seat not far away, with Dinah Brand beside him. She had had her hair trimmed at last, and marcelled, and looked like a lot of money in a big gray fur coat.

"Get down on Cooper?" she asked after we had swapped hellos.

"No. You playing him heavy?"

"Not as heavy as I'd like. We held off, thinking the odds would get better, but they went to hell."

"Everybody in town seems to know Bush is going to dive," I said. "I saw a hundred put on Cooper at four to one a few minutes ago." I leaned past Rolff and put my mouth close to where the gray fur collar hid the girl's ear, whispering: "The dive is off. Better copper your bets[40] while there's time."

Her big bloodshot eyes went wide and dark with anxiety, greed, curiosity, suspicion.

"You mean it?" she asked huskily.

"Yeah."

She chewed her reddened lips, frowned, asked:

"Where'd you get it?"

I wouldn't say. She chewed her mouth some more and asked:

"Is Max on?"

"I haven't seen him. Is he here?"

40   In craps, a bet that the shooter will lose—a bet on the "No Pass" line.

"I suppose so," she said absent-mindedly, a distant look in her eyes. Her lips moved as if she were counting to herself.

I said: "Take it or leave it, but it's a gut."[41]

She leaned forward to look sharply into my eyes, clicked her teeth together, opened her bag, and dragged out a roll of bills the size of a coffee can. Part of the roll she pushed at Rolff.

"Here, Dan, get it down on Bush. You've got an hour anyway to look over the odds."

Rolff took the money and went off on his errand. I took his seat. She put a hand on my forearm and said:

"Christ help you if you've made me drop that dough."

I pretended the idea was ridiculous.

The preliminary bouts got going, four-round affairs between assorted hams. I kept looking for Thaler, but couldn't see him. The girl squirmed beside me, paying little attention to the fighting, dividing her time between asking me where I had got my information and threatening me with hell-fire and damnation if it turned out to be a bust.

The semi-final was on when Rolff came back and gave the girl a handful of tickets. She was straining her eyes over them when I left for my own seat. Without looking up she called to me:

"Wait outside for us when it's over."

Kid Cooper climbed into the ring while I was squeezing through to my seat. He was a ruddy straw-haired solid-built boy with a dented face and too much meat around the top of his lavender trunks. Ike Bush, alias Al Kennedy, came through the ropes in the opposite corner. His body looked better—slim, nicely ridged, snaky—but his face was pale, worried.

They were introduced, went to the center of the ring for the usual instructions, returned to their corners, shed bathrobes, stretched on the ropes, the gong rang, and the scrap was on.

Cooper was a clumsy bum. He had a pair of wide swings that might have hurt when they landed, but anybody with two feet could have kept away from them. Bush had class—nimble legs, a smooth fast left hand, and a right that got away quick. It would have been murder to put Cooper in the ring with the slim boy if he had been trying. But he wasn't. That is, he wasn't trying to win. He was trying not to, and had his hands full doing it.

Cooper waddled flatfooted around the ring, throwing his wide swings at everything from the lights to the corner posts.

His system was simply to turn them loose and let them take their chances. Bush moved in and out, putting a glove on the ruddy boy whenever he wanted to, but not putting anything in the glove.

The customers were booing before the first round was over. The second round was just as sour. I didn't feel so good. Bush didn't seem to have been much influenced by our little conversation. Out of the corner of my eye I could see Dinah Brand trying to catch my attention. She looked hot. I took care not to have my attention caught.

The room-mate act in the ring was continued in the third round to the tune of yelled Throw-em-outs, Why-don't-you-kiss-hims and Make-em-fights from the seats. The pugs' waltz brought them around to the corner nearest me just as the booing broke off for a moment.

I made a megaphone of my hands and bawled:

"Back to Philly, Al."

Bush's back was to me. He wrestled Cooper around, shoving him into the ropes, so he—Bush—faced my way.

From somewhere far back in another part of the house another yelling voice came:

"Back to Philly, Al."

MacSwain, I supposed.

A drunk off to one side lifted his puffy face and bawled the same thing, laughing as if it were a swell joke. Others took up the cry for no reason at all except that it seemed to disturb Bush.

His eyes jerked from side to side under the black bar of his eyebrows.

One of Cooper's wild mitts clouted the slim boy on the side of the jaw.

Ike Bush piled down at the referee's feet.

The referee counted five in two seconds, but the gong cut him off.

I looked over at Dinah Brand and laughed. There wasn't anything else to do. She looked at me and didn't laugh. Her face was sick as Dan Rolff's, but angrier.

Bush's handlers dragged him into his corner and rubbed him up, not working very hard at it. He opened his eyes and watched his feet. The gong was tapped.

Kid Cooper paddled out hitching up his trunks. Bush waited until the bum was in the center of the ring, and then came to him, fast.

Bush's left glove went down, out—practically out of sight in Cooper's belly. Cooper said, "Ugh," and backed away, folding up.

Bush straightened him with a right-hand poke in the mouth, and sank the left again. Cooper said, "Ugh," again and had trouble with his knees.

Bush cuffed him once on each side of the head, cocked his right, carefully pushed Cooper's face into position with a long left, and threw his right hand straight from under his jaw to Cooper's.

Everybody in the house felt the punch.

Cooper hit the floor, bounced, and settled there. It took the referee half a minute to count ten seconds. It would have been just the same if he had taken half an hour. Kid Cooper was out.

When the referee had finally stalled through the count, he raised Bush's hand. Neither of them looked happy.

A high twinkle of light caught my eye. A short silvery streak slanted down from one of the small balconies.

A woman screamed.

The silvery streak ended its flashing slant in the ring, with a sound that was partly a thud, partly a snap.

Ike Bush took his arm out of the referee's hand and pitched down on top of Kid Cooper. A black knife-handle stuck out of the nape of Bush's neck.

CHAPTER X

Crime Wanted—Male or Female

Half an hour later, when I left the building, Dinah Brand was sitting at the wheel of a pale blue little Marmon,[42] talking to Max Thaler, who stood in the road.

The girl's square chin was tilted up. Her big red mouth was brutal around the words it shaped, and the lines crossing its ends were deep, hard.

The gambler looked as unpleasant as she. His pretty face was yellow and tough as oak. When he talked his lips were paper-thin.

It seemed to be a nice family party. I wouldn't have joined it if the girl hadn't seen me and called:

"My God, I thought you were never coming."

I went over to the car. Thaler looked across the hood at me with no friendliness at all.

"Last night I advised you to go back to Frisco." His whisper was harsher than anybody's shout could have been. "Now I'm telling you."

"Thanks just the same," I said as I got in beside the girl.

While she was stirring the engine up he said to her:

"This isn't the first time you've sold me out. It's the last."

She put the car in motion, turned her head back over her shoulder, and sang to him:

"To hell, my love, with you!"

We rode into town rapidly.

"Is Bush dead?" she asked as she twisted the car into Broadway.

42   The Marmon Motor Car Company was an American manufacturer that produced automobiles between 1902 and 1933. The two-seater Speedster was a popular model.

1923 Marmon two-seater Speedster.

43 A tincture of opium, commonly used as a painkiller and anti-diarrhetic. It was widely available throughout the nineteenth century but was regulated in the early twentieth century. It would of course have been prescribed for a "lunger" like Rolff.

"Decidedly. When they turned him over the point of the knife was sticking out in front."

"He ought to have known better than to double-cross them. Let's get something to eat. I'm almost eleven-hundred ahead on the night's doings, so if the boy friend doesn't like it, it's just too bad. How'd you come out?"

"Didn't bet. So your Max doesn't like it?"

"Didn't bet?" she cried. "What kind of an ass are you? Whoever heard of anybody not betting when they had a thing like that sewed up?"

"I wasn't sure it was sewed up. So Max didn't like the way things turned out?"

"You guessed it. He dropped plenty. And then he gets sore with me because I had sense enough to switch over and get in on the win." She stopped the car violently in front of a Chinese restaurant. "The hell with him, the little tin-horn runt!"

Her eyes were shiny because they were wet. She jabbed a handkerchief into them as we got out of the car.

"My God, I'm hungry," she said, dragging me across the sidewalk. "Will you buy me a ton of *chow mein*?"

She didn't eat a ton of it, but she did pretty well, putting away a piled-up dish of her own and half of mine. Then we got back into the Marmon and rode out to her house.

Dan Rolff was in the dining room. A water glass and a brown bottle with no label stood on the table in front of him. He sat straight up in his chair, staring at the bottle. The room smelled of laudanum.[43]

Dinah Brand slid her fur coat off, letting it fall half on a chair and half on the floor, and snapped her fingers at the lunger, saying impatiently:

"Did you collect?"

Without looking up from the bottle, he took a pad of paper money out of his inside coat pocket and dropped it on the table. The girl grabbed it, counted the bills twice, smacked her lips, and stuffed the money in her bag.

She went out to the kitchen and began chopping ice. I sat down and lit a cigarette. Rolff stared at his bottle. He and I never seemed to have much to say to one another. Presently the girl brought in some gin, lemon juice, seltzer and ice.

We drank and she told Rolff:

"Max is sore as hell. He heard you'd been running around putting last-minute money on Bush, and the little monkey thinks I double-crossed him. What did I have to do with it? All I did was what any sensible person would have done—get in on the win. I didn't have any more to do with it than a baby, did I?" she asked me.

"No."

"Of course not. What's the matter with Max is he's afraid the others will think he was in on it too, that Dan was putting his dough down as well as mine. Well, that's his hard luck. He can go climb trees for all I care, the lousy little runt. Another drink would go good."

She poured another for herself and for me. Rolff hadn't touched his first one. He said, still staring at the brown bottle:

"You can hardly expect him to be hilarious about it."

The girl scowled and said disagreeably:

"I can expect anything I want. And he's got no right to talk to me that way. He doesn't own me. Maybe he thinks he does, but I'll show him different." She emptied her glass, banged it on the table, and twisted around in her chair to face me. "Is that on the level about your having ten thousand dollars of Elihu Willsson's money to use cleaning up the city?"

"Yeah."

Her bloodshot eyes glistened hungrily.

"And if I help you will I get some of the ten—?"

"You can't do that, Dinah." Rolff's voice was thick, but gently firm, as if he were talking to a child. "That would be utterly filthy."

The girl turned her face slowly toward him. Her mouth took on the look it had worn while talking to Thaler.

"I am going to do it," she said. "That makes me utterly filthy, does it?"

He didn't say anything, didn't look up from the bottle. Her face got red, hard, cruel. Her voice was soft, cooing:

"It's just too bad that a gentleman of your purity, even if he is a bit consumptive, has to associate with a filthy bum like me."

"That can be remedied," he said slowly, getting up. He was laudanumed to the scalp.

Dinah Brand jumped out of her chair and ran around the table to him. He looked at her with blank dopey eyes. She put her face close to his and demanded:

"So I'm too utterly filthy for you now, am I?"

He said evenly:

"I said to betray your friends to this chap would be utterly filthy, and it would."

She caught one of his thin wrists and twisted it until he was on his knees. Her other hand, open, beat his hollow-cheeked face, half a dozen times on each side, rocking his head from side to side. He could have put his free arm up to protect his face, but didn't.

She let go his wrist, turned her back on him, and reached for gin and seltzer. She was smiling. I didn't like the smile.

He got up, blinking. His wrist was red where she had held it, his face bruised. He steadied himself upright and looked at me with dull eyes.

With no change in the blankness of his face and eyes, he put a hand under his coat, brought out a black automatic pistol, and fired at me.

But he was too shaky for either speed or accuracy. I had time to toss a glass at him. The glass hit his shoulder. His bullet went somewhere overhead.

I jumped before he got the next one out—jumped at him—was close enough to knock the gun down. The second slug went into the floor.

I socked his jaw. He fell away from me and lay where he fell.

I turned around.

Dinah Brand was getting ready to bat me over the head with the seltzer bottle, a heavy glass siphon that would have made pulp of my skull.

"Don't," I yelped.

"You didn't have to bust him like that," she snarled.

"Well, it's done. You'd better get him straightened out."

She put down the siphon and I helped her carry him up to his bedroom. When he began moving his eyes, I left her to finish the work and went down to the dining room again. She joined me there fifteen minutes later.

"He's all right," she said. "But you could have handled him without that."

"Yeah, but I did that for him. Know why he took the shot at me?"

"So I'd have nobody to sell Max out to?"

"No. Because I'd seen you maul him around."

"That doesn't make sense to me," she said. "I was the one who did it."

"He's in love with you, and this isn't the first time you've done it. He acted like he had learned there was no use matching muscle with you. But you can't expect him to enjoy having another man see you slap his face."

"I used to think I knew men," she complained, "but, by God! I don't. They're lunatics, all of them."

"So I poked him to give him back some of his self-respect. You know, treated him as I would a man instead of a down-and-outer who could be slapped around by girls."

"Anything you say," she sighed. "I give up. We ought to have a drink."

We had the drink, and I said:

"You were saying you'd work with me if there was a cut of the Willsson money in it for you. There is."

"How much?"

"Whatever you earn. Whatever what you do is worth."

"That's uncertain."

"So's your help, so far as I know."

"Is it? I can give you the stuff, brother, loads of it, and don't think I can't. I'm a girl who knows her Poisonville." She looked down at her gray-stockinged knees, waved one leg at me, and exclaimed indignantly: "Look at that. Another run. Did you ever see anything to beat it? Honest to God! I'm going barefoot."

"Your legs are too big," I told her. "They put too much strain on the material."

"That'll do out of you. What's your idea of how to go about purifying our village?"

"If I haven't been lied to, Thaler, Pete the Finn, Lew Yard and Noonan are the men who've made Poisonville the sweet-smelling mess it is. Old Elihu comes in for his share of the blame, too, but it's not all his fault, maybe. Besides, he's my client, even if he doesn't want to be, so I'd like to go easy on him.

"The closest I've got to an idea is to dig up any and all the dirty work I can that might implicate the others, and run it out. Maybe I'll advertise—*Crime Wanted—Male or Female*. If they're as crooked as I think they are I shouldn't have a lot of trouble finding a job or two that I can hang on them."

"Is that what you were up to when you uncooked the fight?"

44 It is a mistake, suggests Charles J. Rzepka, in *Detective Fiction*, to view the Op—and the hard-boiled detective in general—as one who rejects induction or the idea of reliable historical reconstruction, the bedrock of traditional mysteries. He may be "stirring things up," in the Op's words, "but in order to succeed," Rzepka observes, "he must first piece together the events that shaped [the] present, just like his British counterparts" (p. 188). By careful observation and induction, the Op solves multiple murders throughout the story, including one of which he suspects himself! As Peter Wolfe points out in *Beams Falling: The Art of Dashiell Hammett*, Hammett plays fair with the reader: "[The] Op has seen and heard no more than the reader has when he names the two murderers" (p. 91).

In Hammett's short story "The Gutting of Couffignal," which first appeared in Black Mask in December 1925, the Op explains: ". . . I like being a detective, like the work. And liking work makes you want to do it as well as you can. Otherwise there'd be no sense to it. . . . I've been getting my fun out of chasing crooks and tackling puzzles, my satisfaction out of catching crooks and solving riddles. It's the only kind of sport I know anything about, and I can't imagine a pleasanter future than twenty-some more years of it."

"That was only an experiment—just to see what would happen."

"So that's the way you scientific detectives work. My God! for a fat, middle-aged, hard-boiled, pig-headed guy, you've got the vaguest way of doing things I ever heard of."

"Plans are all right sometimes," I said. "And sometimes just stirring things up is all right—if you're tough enough to survive, and keep your eyes open so you'll see what you want when it comes to the top."[44]

"That ought to be good for another drink," she said.

CHAPTER XI

The Swell Spoon

We had another drink.

She put her glass down, licked her lips, and said:

"If stirring things up is your system, I've got a swell spoon for you. Did you ever hear of Noonan's brother Tim, the one who committed suicide out at Mock Lake[45] a couple of years ago?"

"No."

"You wouldn't have heard much good. Anyway, he didn't commit suicide. Max killed him."

"Yeah?"

"For God's sake wake up. This I'm giving you is real. Noonan was like a father to Tim. Take the proof to him and he'll be after Max like nobody's business. That's what you want, isn't it?"

"We've got proof?"

"Two people got to Tim before he died, and he told them Max had done it. They're both still in town, though one won't live a lot longer. How's that?"

She looked as if she were telling the truth, though with women, especially blue-eyed women, that doesn't always mean anything.

"Let's listen to the rest of it," I said. "I like details and things."

"You'll get them. You ever been out to Mock Lake? Well, it's our summer resort, thirty miles up the canyon road. It's a dump, but it's cool in summer, so it gets a good play. This was summer

45   A fictional lake, possibly in Deer Lodge County, near Anaconda, and about 30 miles northwest from Butte; alternatively, this could be the nearby Whitetail Reservoir, a "mock lake."

a year ago, the last week-end in August. I was out there with a fellow named Holly. He's back in England now, but you don't care anything about that, because he's got nothing to do with it. He was a funny sort of old woman—used to wear white silk socks turned inside out so the loose threads wouldn't hurt his feet. I got a letter from him last week. It's around here somewhere, but that doesn't make any difference.

"We were up there, and Max was up there with a girl he used to play around with—Myrtle Jennison. She's in the hospital now—City—dying of Bright's disease[46] or something. She was a classy looking kid then, a slender blonde. I always liked her, except that a few drinks made her too noisy. Tim Noonan was crazy about her, but she couldn't see anybody but Max that summer.

"Tim wouldn't let her alone. He was a big good-looking Irishman, but a sap and a cheap crook who only got by because his brother was chief of police. Wherever Myrtle went, he'd pop up sooner or later. She didn't like to say anything to Max about it, not wanting Max to do anything to put him in wrong with Tim's brother, the chief.

"So of course Tim showed up at Mock Lake this Saturday. Myrtle and Max were just by themselves. Holly and I were with a bunch, but I saw Myrtle to talk to and she told me she had got a note from Tim, asking her to meet him for a few minutes that night, in one of the little arbor things on the hotel grounds. He said if she didn't he would kill himself. That was a laugh for us—the big false alarm. I tried to talk Myrtle out of going, but she had just enough booze in her to feel gay and she said she was going to give him an earful.

"We were all dancing in the hotel that night. Max was there for a while, and then I didn't see him any more. Myrtle was dancing with a fellow named Rutgers, a lawyer here in town. After a while she left him and went out one of the side doors. She winked at me when she passed, so I knew she was going down to see Tim. She had just got out when I heard the shot. Nobody else paid any attention to it. I suppose I wouldn't have noticed it either if I hadn't known about Myrtle and Tim.

"I told Holly I wanted to see Myrtle, and went out after her, by myself. I must have been about five minutes behind her in getting out. When I got outside I saw lights down by one of the summer houses, and people. I went down there, and— This talking is thirsty work."

I poured out a couple of hookers of gin. She went into the kitchen for another siphon and more ice. We mixed them up, drank, and she settled down to her tale again:

"There was Tim Noonan, dead, with a hole in his temple and his gun lying beside him. Perhaps a dozen people were standing around, hotel people, visitors, one of Noonan's men, a dick named MacSwain. As soon as Myrtle saw me she took me away from the crowd, back in the shade of some trees.

"'Max killed him,' she said. 'What'll I do?'

"I asked her about it. She told me she had seen the flash of the gun and at first she thought Tim had killed himself after all. She was too far away and it was too dark for her to see anything else. When she ran down to him, he was rolling around, moaning, 'He didn't have to kill me over her. I'd have—' She couldn't make out the rest of it. He was rolling around, bleeding from the hole in his temple.

"Myrtle was afraid Max had done it, but she had to be sure, so she knelt down and tried to pick up Tim's head, asking: 'Who did it, Tim?'

"He was almost gone, but before he passed out he got enough strength to tell her, 'Max!'

"She kept asking me, 'What'll I do?' I asked her if anybody else had heard Tim, and she said the dick had. He came running up while she was trying to lift Tim's head. She didn't think anybody else had been near enough to hear, but the dick had.

"I didn't want Max to get in a jam over killing a mutt like Tim Noonan. Max didn't mean anything to me then, except that I liked him, and I didn't like any of the Noonans. I knew the dick—MacSwain. I used to know his wife. He had been a pretty good guy, straight as ace-deuce-trey-four-five, till he got on the force. Then he went the way of the rest of them. His wife stood as much of it as she could and then left him.

"Knowing this dick, I told Myrtle I thought we could fix things. A little jack would ruin MacSwain's memory, or, if he didn't like that, Max could have him knocked off. She had Tim's note threatening suicide. If the dick would play along, the hole in Tim's head from his own gun and the note would smooth everything over pretty.

"I left Myrtle under the trees and went out to hunt for Max. He wasn't around. There weren't many people there, and I could hear the hotel orchestra still playing dance music. I couldn't find Max, so I went back to Myrtle. She was all worked up over another idea. She didn't want Max to know that she had found out that he had killed Tim. She was afraid of him.

"See what I mean? She was afraid that if she and Max ever broke off he'd put her out of the way if he knew she had enough on him to swing him. I know how she felt. I got the same notion later, and kept just as quiet as she did. So we figured that if it could be fixed up without his knowing about it, so much the better. I didn't want to show in it either.

"Myrtle went back alone to the group around Tim and got hold of MacSwain. She took him off a little way and made the deal with him. She had some dough on her. She gave him two hundred and a diamond ring that had cost a fellow named Boyle a thousand. I thought he'd be back for more later, but he didn't. He shot square with her. With the help of the letter he put over the suicide story.

"Noonan knew there was something fishy about the lay-out, but he could never peg it. I think he suspected Max of having something to do with it. But Max had an air-tight alibi—trust him for that—and I think even Noonan finally counted him out. But Noonan never believed it happened the way it was made to look. He broke MacSwain—kicked him off the force.

"Max and Myrtle slid apart a little while after that. No row or anything—they just slid apart. I don't think she ever felt easy around him again, though so far as I know he never suspected her of knowing anything. She's sick now, as I told you, and hasn't got long to live. I think she'd not so much mind telling the truth if she were asked. MacSwain's still hanging around town. He'd talk if there was something in it for him. Those two have got the stuff on Max—and wouldn't Noonan eat it up! Is that good enough to give your stirring-up a start?"

"Couldn't it have been suicide?" I asked. "With Tim Noonan getting a last-minute bright idea to stick it on Max?"

"That four-flusher shoot himself? Not a chance."

"Could Myrtle have shot him?"

"Noonan didn't overlook that one. But she couldn't have been a third of the distance down the slope when the shot was fired.

Tim had powder-marks on his head, and hadn't been shot and rolled down the slope. Myrtle's out."

"But Max had an alibi?"

"Yes, indeed. He always has. He was in the hotel bar, on the other side of the building, all the time. Four men said so. As I remember it, they said it openly and often, long before anybody asked them. There were other men in the bar who didn't remember whether Max had been there or not, but those four remembered. They'd remember anything Max wanted remembered."

Her eyes got large and then narrowed to black-fringed slits. She leaned toward me, upsetting her glass with an elbow.

"Peak Murry was one of the four. He and Max are on the outs now. Peak might tell it straight now. He's got a pool room on Broadway."

"This MacSwain, does he happen to be named Bob?" I asked. "A bow-legged man with a long jaw like a hog's?"

"Yes. You know him?"

"By sight. What does he do now?"

"A small-time grifter. What do you think of the stack-up?"

"Not bad. Maybe I can use it."

"Then let's talk scratch."

I grinned at the greed in her eyes and said:

"Not just yet, sister. We'll have to see how it works out before we start scattering pennies around."

She called me a damned nickel-nurser and reached for the gin.

"No more for me, thanks," I told her, looking at my watch. "It's getting along toward five a. m. and I've got a busy day ahead."

She decided she was hungry again. That reminded me that I was. It took half an hour or more to get waffles, ham and coffee off the stove. It took some more time to get them into our stomachs and to smoke some cigarettes over extra cups of coffee. It was quite a bit after six when I got ready to leave.

∞

I went back to my hotel and got into a tub of cold water. It braced me a lot, and I needed bracing. At forty I could get along on gin as a substitute for sleep, but not comfortably.

When I had dressed I sat down and composed a document:

Just before he died, Tim Noonan told me he had been shot by Max Thaler. Detective Bob MacSwain heard him tell me. I gave Detective MacSwain $200 and a diamond ring worth $1,000 to keep quiet and make it look like suicide.

With this document in my pocket I went downstairs, had another breakfast that was mostly coffee, and went up to the City Hospital.

Visiting hours were in the afternoon, but by flourishing my Continental Detective Agency credentials and giving everybody to understand that an hour's delay might cause thousands of deaths, or words to that effect, I got to see Myrtle Jennison.

She was in a ward on the third floor, alone. The other four beds were empty. She could have been a girl of twenty-five or a woman of fifty-five. Her face was a bloated spotty mask. Lifeless yellow hair in two stringy braids lay on the pillow beside her.

I waited until the nurse who had brought me up left. Then I held my document out to the invalid and said:

"Will you sign this, please, Miss Jennison?"

She looked at me with ugly eyes that were shaded into no particular dark color by the pads of flesh around them, then at the document, and finally brought a shapeless fat hand from under the covers to take it.

She pretended it took her nearly five minutes to read the forty-two words I had written. She let the document fall down on the covers and asked:

"Where'd you get that?" Her voice was tinny, irritable.

"Dinah Brand sent me to you."

She asked eagerly:

"Has she broken off with Max?"

"Not that I know of," I lied. "I imagine she just wants to have this on hand in case it should come in handy."

"And get her fool throat slit. Give me a pencil."

I gave her my fountain pen and held my notebook under the document, to stiffen it while she scribbled her signature at the bottom, and to have it in my hands as soon as she had finished. While I fanned the paper dry she said:

"If that's what she wants it's all right with me. What do I care what anybody does now? I'm done. Hell with them all!" She sniggered and suddenly threw the bedclothes down to her knees, showing me a horrible swollen body in a coarse white nightgown. "How do you like me? See, I'm done."

I pulled the covers up over her again and said:

"Thanks for this, Miss Jennison."

"That's all right. It's nothing to me any more. Only"—her puffy chin quivered—"it's hell to die ugly as this."

CHAPTER XII

A New Deal

I went out to hunt for MacSwain. Neither city directory nor telephone book told me anything. I did the pool rooms, cigar stores, speakeasies, looking around first, then asking cautious questions. That got me nothing. I walked the streets, looking for bowed legs. That got me nothing. I decided to go back to my hotel, grab a nap, and resume the hunting at night.

In a far corner of the lobby a man stopped hiding behind a newspaper and came out to meet me. He had bowed legs, a hog jaw, and was MacSwain.

I nodded carelessly at him and walked on toward the elevators. He followed me, mumbling:

"Hey, you got a minute?"

"Yeah, just about." I stopped, pretending indifference.

"Let's get out of sight," he said nervously.

I took him up to my room. He straddled a chair and put a match in his mouth. I sat on the side of the bed and waited for him to say something. He chewed his match a while and began:

"I'm going to come clean with you, brother. I'm—"

"You mean you're going to tell me you knew me when you braced me yesterday?" I asked. "And you're going to tell me Bush hadn't told you to bet on him? And you didn't until afterwards? And you knew about his record because you used to be a bull? And you thought if you could get me to put it to him you could clean up a little dough playing him?"

"I'll be damned if I was going to come through with that much," he said, "but since it's been said I'll put a yes to it."

"Did you clean up?"

"I win myself six hundred iron men."[47] He pushed his hat back and scratched his forehead with the chewed end of his match. "And then I lose myself that and my own two hundred and some in a crap game. What do you think of that? I pick up six hundred berries like shooting fish, and have to bum four bits for breakfast."

I said it was a tough break but that was the kind of a world we lived in.

He said, "Uh-huh," put the match back in his mouth, ground it some more, and added, "That's why I thought I'd come to see you. I used to be in the racket myself and—"

"What did Noonan put the skids under you for?"

"Skids? What skids? I quit. I come into a piece of change when the wife got killed in an automobile accident—insurance—and I quit."

"I heard he kicked you out the time his brother shot himself."

"Well, then you heard wrong. It was just after that, but you can ask him if I didn't quit."

"It's not that much to me. Go on telling me why you came to see me."

"I'm busted, flat. I know you're a Continental op, and I got a pretty good hunch what you're up to here. I'm close to a lot that's going on on both sides of things in this burg. There's things I could do for you, being an ex-dick, knowing the ropes both ways."

"You want to stool-pigeon for me?"

He looked me straight in the eye and said evenly:

"There's no sense in a man picking out the worst name he can find for everything."

"I'll give you something to do, MacSwain." I took out Myrtle Jennison's document and passed it to him. "Tell me about that."

He read it through carefully, his lips framing the words, the match wavering up and down in his mouth. He got up, put the paper on the bed beside me, and scowled down at it.

"There's something I'll have to find out about first," he said, very solemnly. "I'll be back in a little while and give you the whole story."

I laughed and told him:

47   Slang for dollars, so-called because of the heavy weight of the dollar coin.

"Don't be silly. You know I'm not going to let you walk out on me."

"I don't know that." He shook his head, still solemn. "Neither do you. All you know is whether you're going to try to stop me."

"The answer's yeah," I said while I considered that he was fairly hard and strong, six or seven years younger than I, and twenty or thirty pounds lighter.

He stood at the foot of the bed and looked at me with solemn eyes. I sat on the side of the bed and looked at him with whatever kind of eyes I had at the time. We did this for nearly three minutes.

I used part of the time measuring the distance between us, figuring out how, by throwing my body back on the bed and turning on my hip, I could get my heels in his face if he jumped me. He was too close for me to pull the gun. I had just finished this mental mapmaking when he spoke:

"That lousy ring wasn't worth no grand. I did swell to get two centuries for it."

"Sit down and tell me about it."

He shook his head again and said:

"First I want to know what you're meaning to do about it."

"Cop[48] Whisper."

"I don't mean that. I mean with me."

"You'll have to go over to the Hall with me."

"I won't."

"Why not? You're only a witness."

"I'm only a witness that Noonan can hang a bribe-taking, or an accomplice after the act rap on, or both. And he'd be tickled simple to have the chance."

This jaw-wagging didn't seem to be leading anywhere. I said:

"That's too bad. But you're going to see him."

"Try and take me."

I sat up straighter and slid my right hand back to my hip.

He grabbed for me. I threw my body back on the bed, did the hip-spin, swung my feet at him. It was a good trick, only it didn't work. In his hurry to get at me he bumped the bed aside just enough to spill me off on the floor.

I landed all sprawled out on my back. I kept dragging at my gun while I tried to roll under the bed.

Missing me, his lunge carried him over the low footboard, over the side of the bed. He came down beside me, on the back of his neck, his body somersaulting over.

I put the muzzle of my gun in his left eye and said:

"You're making a fine pair of clowns of us. Be still while I get up or I'll make an opening in your head for brains to leak in."

I got up, found and pocketed my document, and let him get up.

"Knock the dents out of your hat and put your necktie in front, so you won't disgrace me going through the streets," I ordered after I had run a hand over his clothes and found nothing that felt like a weapon. "You can suit yourself about remembering that this gat is going to be in my overcoat pocket, with a hand on it."

He straightened his hat and tie and said:

"Hey, listen: I'm in this, I guess, and cutting up won't get me nothing. Suppose I be good. Could you forget about the tussle? See—maybe it'd be smoother for me if they thought I come along without being dragged."

"O. K."

"Thanks, brother."

✺

Noonan was out eating. We had to wait half an hour in his outer office. When he came in he greeted me with the usual *How are you? . . . That certainly is fine . . .* and the rest of it. He didn't say anything to MacSwain—simply eyed him sourly.

We went into the chief's private office. He pulled a chair over to his desk for me and then sat in his own, ignoring the ex-dick.

I gave Noonan the sick girl's document.

He gave it one glance, bounced out of his chair, and smashed a fist the size of a cantaloup into MacSwain's face.

The punch carried MacSwain across the room until a wall stopped him. The wall creaked under the strain, and a framed photograph of Noonan and other city dignitaries welcoming somebody in spats dropped down to the floor with the hit man.

The fat chief waddled over, picked up the picture and beat it to splinters on MacSwain's head and shoulders.

Noonan came back to his desk, puffing, smiling, saying cheerfully to me:

"That fellow's a rat if there ever was one."

MacSwain sat up and looked around, bleeding from nose, mouth and head.

Noonan roared at him:

"Come here, you."

MacSwain said, "Yes, chief," scrambled up and ran over to the desk.

Noonan said: "Come through or I'll kill you."

MacSwain said:

"Yes, chief. It was like she said, only that rock wasn't worth no grand. But she give me it and the two hundred to keep my mouth shut, because I got there just when she asks him, 'Who did it, Tim?' and he says, 'Max!' He says it kind of loud and sharp, like he wanted to get it out before he died, because he died right then, almost before he'd got it out. That's the way it was, chief, but the rock wasn't worth no—"

"Damn the rock," Noonan barked. "And stop bleeding on my rug."

MacSwain hunted in his pocket for a dirty handkerchief, mopped his nose and mouth with it, and jabbered on:

"That's the way it was, chief. Everything else was like I said at the time, only I didn't say anything about hearing him say Max done it. I know I hadn't ought to—"

"Shut up," Noonan said, and pressed one of the buttons on his desk.

A uniformed copper came in. The chief jerked a thumb at MacSwain and said:

"Take this baby down cellar and let the wrecking crew work on him before you lock him up."

MacSwain started a desperate plea, "Aw, chief!" but the copper took him away before he could get any farther.

Noonan stuck a cigar at me, tapped the document with another and asked:

"Where's this broad?"

"In the City Hospital, dying. You'll have the 'cuter[49] get a stiff[50] out of her? That one's not so good legally—I framed it for effect. Another thing—I hear that Peak Murry and Whisper aren't playmates any more. Wasn't Murry one of his alibis?"

The chief said, "He was," picked up one of his phones, said, "McGraw," and then: "Get hold of Peak Murry and ask him to drop in. And have Tony Agosti picked up for that knife-throwing."

He put the phone down, stood up, made a lot of cigar smoke, and said through it:

"I haven't always been on the up-and-up with you."

I thought that was putting it mildly, but I didn't say anything while he went on:

"You know your way around. You know what these jobs are. There's this one and that one that's got to be listened to. Just because a man's chief of police doesn't mean he's chief. Maybe you're a lot of trouble to somebody that can be a lot of trouble to me. Don't make any difference if I think you're a right guy. I got to play with them that play with me. See what I mean?"

I wagged my head to show I did.

"That's the way it was," he said. "But no more. This is something else, a new deal. When the old woman kicked off Tim was just a lad. She said to me, 'Take care of him, John,' and I promised I would. And then Whisper murders him on account of that tramp." He reached down and took my hand. "See what I'm getting at? That's a year and a half ago, and you give me my first chance to hang it on him. I'm telling you there's no man in Personville that's got a voice big enough to talk you down. Not after today."

That pleased me and I said so. We purred at each other until a lanky man with an extremely up-turned nose in the middle of a round and freckled face was ushered in. It was Peak Murry.

"We were just wondering about the time when Tim died," the chief said when Murry had been given a chair and a cigar, "where Whisper was. You were out to the Lake that night, weren't you?"

"Yep," Murry said and the end of his nose got sharper.

"With Whisper?"

"I wasn't with him all the time."

"Were you with him at the time of the shooting?"

"Nope."

The chief's greenish eyes got smaller and brighter. He asked softly:

"You know where he was?"

"Nope."

The chief sighed in a thoroughly satisfied way and leaned back in his chair.

"Damn it, Peak," he said, "you told us before that you were with him at the bar."

"Yep, I did," the lanky man admitted. "But that don't mean nothing except that he asked me to and I didn't mind helping out a friend."

"Meaning you don't mind standing a perjury rap?"

"Don't kid me." Murry spit vigorously at the cuspidor. "I didn't say nothing in no court rooms."

"How about Jerry and George Kelly and O'Brien?" the chief asked. "Did they say they were with him just because he asked them to?"

"O'Brien did. I don't know nothing about the others. I was going out of the bar when I run into Whisper, Jerry and Kelly, and went back to have a shot with them. Kelly told me Tim had been knocked off. Then Whisper says, 'It never hurts anybody to have an alibi. We were here all the time, weren't we?' and he looks at O'Brien, who's behind the bar. O'Brien says, 'Sure you was,' and when Whisper looks at me I say the same thing. But I don't know no reasons why I've got to cover him up nowadays."

"And Kelly said Tim had been knocked off? Didn't say he had been found dead?"

"'Knocked off' was the words he used."

The chief said:

"Thanks, Peak. You oughtn't to have done like you did, but what's done is done. How are the kids?"

Murry said they were doing fine, only the baby wasn't as fat as he'd like to have him. Noonan phoned the prosecuting attorney's office and had Dart and a stenographer take Peak's story before he left.

Noonan, Dart and the stenographer set out for the City Hospital to get a complete statement from Myrtle Jennison. I didn't go along. I decided I needed sleep, told the chief I would see him later, and returned to the hotel.

CHAPTER XIII

–$200.10–

had my vest unbuttoned when the telephone bell rang.

It was Dinah Brand, complaining that she had been trying to get me since ten o'clock.

"Have you done anything on what I told you?" she asked.

"I've been looking it over. It seems pretty good. I think maybe I'll crack it this afternoon."

"Don't. Hold it till I see you. Can you come up now?"

I looked at the vacant white bed and said, "Yes," without much enthusiasm.

Another tub of cold water did me so little good that I almost fell asleep in it.

Dan Rolff let me in when I rang the girl's bell. He looked and acted as if nothing out of the ordinary had happened the night before. Dinah Brand came into the hall to help me off with my overcoat. She had on a tan woolen dress with a two-inch rip in one shoulder seam.

She took me into the living room. She sat on the Chesterfield beside me and said:

"I'm going to ask you to do something for me. You like me enough, don't you?"

I admitted that. She counted the knuckles of my left hand with a warm forefinger and explained:

"I want you to not do anything more about what I told you last night. Now wait a minute. Wait till I get through. Dan was right. I oughtn't sell Max out like that. It would be utterly filthy. Besides, it's Noonan you chiefly want, isn't it? Well, if you'll be a nice darling and lay off Max this time, I'll give you enough on Noonan to nail him forever. You'd like that better, wouldn't you? And you like me too much to want to take advantage of me by using information I gave you when I was mad at what Max had said, don't you?"

"What is the dirt on Noonan?" I asked.

She kneaded my biceps and murmured: "You promise?"

"Not yet."

She pouted at me and said:

"I'm off Max for life, on the level. You've got no right to make me turn rat."

"What about Noonan?"

"Promise first."

"No."

She dug fingers into my arm and asked sharply:

"You've already gone to Noonan?"

"Yeah."

She let go my arm, frowned, shrugged, and said gloomily:

"Well, how can I help it?"

I stood up and a voice said:

"Sit down."

It was a hoarse whispering voice—Thaler's.

I turned to see him standing in the dining room doorway, a big gun in one of his little hands. A red-faced man with a scarred cheek stood behind him.

The other doorway—opening to the hall—filled as I sat down. The loose-mouthed chinless man I had heard Whisper call Jerry came a step through it. He had a couple of guns. The more angular one of the blond kids who had been in the King Street joint looked over his shoulder.

Dinah Brand got up from the Chesterfield, put her back to Thaler, and addressed me. Her voice was husky with rage.

"This is none of my doing. He came here by himself, said he was sorry for what he had said, and showed me how we could make a lot of coin by turning Noonan up for you. The whole thing was a plant, but I fell for it. Honest to Christ! He was to wait upstairs while I put it to you. I didn't know anything about the others. I didn't—"

Jerry's casual voice drawled:

"If I shoot a pin[51] from under her, she'll sure sit down, and maybe shut up. O. K.?"

I couldn't see Whisper. The girl was between us. He said:

"Not now. Where's Dan?"

The angular blond youngster said:

"Up on the bathroom floor. I had to sap him."

Dinah Brand turned around to face Thaler. Stocking seams made s's up the ample backs of her legs. She said:

"Max Thaler, you're a lousy little—"

He whispered, very deliberately:

"Shut up and get out of the way."

She surprised me by doing both, and she kept quiet while he spoke to me:

"So you and Noonan are trying to paste his brother's death on me?"

"It doesn't need pasting. It's a natural."

He curved his thin lips at me and said:

"You're as crooked as he is."

I said:

"You know better. I played your side when he tried to frame you. This time he's got you copped to rights."

Dinah Brand flared up again, waving her arms in the center of the room, storming:

"Get out of here, the whole lot of you. Why should I give a God-damn about your troubles? Get out."

The blond kid who had sapped Rolff squeezed past Jerry and came grinning into the room. He caught one of the girl's flourished arms and bent it behind her.

She twisted toward him, socked him in the belly with her other fist. It was a very respectable wallop—man-size. It broke his grip on her arm, sent him back a couple of steps.

The kid gulped a wide mouthful of air, whisked a blackjack from his hip, and stepped in again. His grin was gone.

Jerry laughed what little chin he had out of sight.

Thaler whispered harshly: "Lay off!"

The kid didn't hear him. He was snarling at the girl.

She watched him with a face hard as a silver dollar. She was standing with most of her weight on her left foot. I guessed blondy was going to stop a kick when he closed in.

The kid feinted a grab with his empty left hand, started the blackjack at her face.

Thaler whispered, "Lay off," again, and fired.

The bullet smacked blondy under the right eye, spun him around, and dropped him backwards into Dinah Brand's arms.

This looked like the time, if there was to be any.

In the excitement I had got my hand to my hip. Now I yanked the gun out and snapped a cap at Thaler, trying for his shoulder.

That was wrong. If I had tried for a bulls-eye I would have winged him. Chinless Jerry hadn't laughed himself blind. He beat me to the shot. His shot burnt my wrist, throwing me off the target. But, missing Thaler, my slug crumpled the red-faced man behind him.

Not knowing how badly my wrist was nicked, I switched the gun to my left hand.

Jerry had another try at me. The girl spoiled it by heaving the corpse at him. The dead yellow head banged into his knees. I jumped for him while he was off-balance.

The jump took me out of the path of Thaler's bullet. It also tumbled me and Jerry out into the hall, all tangled up together.

Jerry wasn't tough to handle, but I had to work quick. There was Thaler behind me. I socked Jerry twice, kicked him, butted him at least once, and was hunting for a place to bite when he went limp under me. I poked him again where his chin should have been—just to make sure he wasn't faking—and went away on hands and knees, down the hall a bit, out of line with the door.

I sat on my heels against the wall, held my gun level at Thaler's part of the premises, and waited. I couldn't hear anything for the moment except blood singing in my head.

Dinah Brand stepped out of the door I had tumbled through, looked at Jerry, then at me. She smiled with her tongue between her teeth, beckoned with a jerk of her head, and returned to the living room. I followed her cautiously.

Whisper stood in the center of the floor. His hands were empty and so was his face. Except for his vicious little mouth he looked like something displaying suits in a clothing store window.

Dan Rolff stood behind him, with a gun-muzzle tilted to the little gambler's left kidney. Rolff's face was mostly blood. The blond kid—now dead on the floor between Rolff and me—had sapped him plenty.

I grinned at Thaler and said, "Well, this is nice," before I saw that Rolff had another gun, centered on my chubby middle. That wasn't so nice. But my gun was reasonably level in my hand. I didn't have much worse than an even break.

Rolff said:

"Put down your pistol."

I looked at Dinah, looked puzzled, I suppose. She shrugged and told me:

"It seems to be Dan's party."

"Yeah? Somebody ought to tell him I don't like to play this way."

Rolff repeated: "Put down your pistol."

I said disagreeably:

"I'm damned if I will. I've shed twenty pounds trying to nab this bird, and I can spare twenty more for the same purpose."

Rolff said:

"I'm not interested in what is between you two, and I have no intention of giving either of you—"

Dinah Brand had wandered across the room. When she was behind Rolff, I interrupted his speech by telling her:

"If you upset him now you're sure of making two friends—Noonan and me. You can't trust Thaler any more, so there's no use helping him."

She laughed and said:

"Talk money, darling."

"Dinah!" Rolff protested. He was caught. She was behind him and she was strong enough to handle him. It wasn't likely that he would shoot her, and it wasn't likely that anything else would keep her from doing whatever she decided to do.

"A hundred dollars," I bid.[52]

"My God!" she exclaimed, "I've actually got a cash offer out of you. But not enough."

"Two hundred."

"You're getting reckless. But I still can't hear you."

"Try," I said. "It's worth that to me not to have to shoot Rolff's gun out of his hand, but no more than that."

"You got a good start. Don't weaken. One more bid, anyway."

"Two hundred dollars and ten cents and that's all."

"You big bum," she said, "I won't do it."

"Suit yourself." I made a face at Thaler and cautioned him: "When what happens happens be damned sure you keep still."

52   Hammett, in his essay "From the Memoirs of a Private Detective," wrote, "Once in Seattle the wife of a fugitive swindler offered to sell me a photograph of her husband for $15. I knew where I could get one free, so I didn't buy it."

Dinah cried:

"Wait! Are you really going to start something?"

"I'm going to take Thaler out with me, regardless."

"Two hundred and a dime?"

"Yeah."

"Dinah," Rolff called without turning his face from me, "you won't—"

But she laughed, came close to his back, and wound her strong arms around him, pulling his arms down, pinning them to his sides.

I shoved Thaler out of the way with my right arm, and kept my gun on him while I yanked Rolff's weapons out of his hands. Dinah turned the lunger loose.

He took two steps toward the dining room door, said wearily, "There is no—" and collapsed on the floor.

Dinah ran to him. I pushed Thaler through the hall door, past the still sleeping Jerry, and to the alcove beneath the front stairs, where I had seen a phone.

I called Noonan, told him I had Thaler, and where.

"Mother of God!" he said. "Don't kill him till I get there."

CHAPTER XIV

Max

The news of Whisper's capture spread quickly. When Noonan, the coppers he had brought along, and I took the gambler and the now conscious Jerry into the City Hall there were at least a hundred people standing around watching us.

All of them didn't look pleased. Noonan's coppers—a shabby lot at best—moved around with whitish strained faces. But Noonan was the most triumphant guy west of the Mississippi. Even the bad luck he had trying to third-degree Whisper couldn't spoil his happiness.

Whisper stood up under all they could give him. He would talk to his lawyer, he said, and to nobody else, and he stuck to it. And, as much as Noonan hated the gambler, here was a prisoner he didn't give the works, didn't turn over to the wrecking crew. Whisper had killed the chief's brother, and the chief hated his guts, but Whisper was still too much somebody in Poisonville to be roughed around.

Noonan finally got tired of playing with his prisoner, and sent him up—the prison was on the City Hall's top floor—to be stowed away. I lit another of the chief's cigars and read the detailed statement he had got from the woman in the hospital. There was nothing in it that I hadn't learned from Dinah and MacSwain.

The chief wanted me to come out to his house for dinner, but I lied out of it, pretending that my wrist—now in a bandage—was bothering me. It was really little more than a burn.

While we were talking about it, a pair of plainclothes men brought in the red-faced bird who had stopped the slug I had missed Whisper with. It had broken a rib for him, and he had taken a backdoor sneak while the rest of us were busy. Noonan's men had picked him up in a doctor's office. The chief failed to get any information out of him, and sent him off to the hospital.

I got up and prepared to leave, saying:

"The Brand girl gave me the tip-off on this. That's why I asked you to keep her and Rolff out of it."

The chief took hold of my left hand for the fifth or sixth time in the past couple of hours.

"If you want her taken care of, that's enough for me," he assured me. "But if she had a hand in turning that bastard up, you can tell her for me that any time she wants anything, all she's got to do is name it."

I said I'd tell her that, and went over to my hotel, thinking about that neat white bed. But it was nearly eight o'clock, and my stomach needed attention. I went into the hotel dining room and had that fixed up.

Then a leather chair tempted me into stopping in the lobby while I burnt a cigar. That led to conversation with a traveling railroad auditor from Denver, who knew a man I knew in St. Louis. Then there was a lot of shooting in the street.

We went to the door and decided that the shooting was in the vicinity of the City Hall. I shook the auditor and moved up that way.

I had done two-thirds of the distance when an automobile came down the street toward me, moving fast, leaking gun-fire from the rear.

I backed into an alley entrance and slid my gun loose. The car came abreast. An arc-light brightened two faces in the front of the car. The driver's meant nothing to me. The upper part of the other's was hidden by a pulled-down hat. The lower part was Whisper's.

Across the street was the entrance to another block of my alley, lighted at the far end. Between the light and me, somebody moved just as Whisper's car roared past. The somebody had dodged from behind one shadow that might have been an ash-can to another.

What made me forget Whisper was that the somebody's legs had a bowed look.

A load of coppers buzzed past, throwing lead at the first car.

I skipped across the street, into the section of alley that held a man who might have bowed legs.

If he was my man, it was a fair bet he wasn't armed. I played it that way, moving straight up the slimy middle of the alley, looking into shadows with eyes, ears and nose.

Three-quarters of a block of this, and a shadow broke away from another shadow—a man going pellmell away from me.

"Stop!" I bawled, pounding my feet after him. "Stop, or I'll plug you, MacSwain."

He ran half a dozen strides farther and stopped, turning.

"Oh, it's you," he said, as if it made any difference who took him back to the hoosegow.

"Yeah," I confessed. "What are all you people doing wandering around loose?"

"I don't know nothing about it. Somebody dynamited the floor out of the can. I dropped through the hole with the rest of them. There was some mugs standing off the bulls. I made the back-trotters[53] with one bunch. Then we split, and I was figuring on cutting over and making the hills. I didn't have nothing to do with it. I just went along when she blew open."

"Whisper was pinched this evening," I told him.

"Hell! Then that's it. Noonan had ought to know he'd never keep that guy screwed up—not in this burg."

We were standing still in the alley where MacSwain had stopped running.

"You know what he was pinched for?" I asked.

"Uh-huh, for killing Tim."

"You know who killed Tim?"

"Huh? Sure, he did."

"You did."

"Huh? What's the matter? You simple?"

"There's a gun in my left hand," I warned him.

"But look here—didn't he tell the broad that Whisper done it? What's the matter with you?"

"He didn't say *Whisper*. I've heard women call Thaler *Max*, but I've never heard a man here call him anything but *Whisper*. Tim didn't say *Max*. He said *MacS*—the first part of *MacSwain*—and died before he could finish it. Don't forget about the gun."

"What would I have killed him for? He was after Whisper's—"

53   Although it doesn't appear in any slang dictionary, the phrase presumably means to scramble away, like a fleeing pig.

"I haven't got around to that yet," I admitted, "but let's see: You and your wife had busted up. Tim was a ladies' man, wasn't he? Maybe there's something there. I'll have to look it up. What started me thinking about you was that you never tried to get any more money out of the girl."

"Cut it out," he begged. "You know there ain't any sense to it. What would I have hung around afterwards for? I'd have been out getting an alibi, like Whisper."

"Why? You were a dick then. Close by was the spot for you—to see that everything went right—handle it yourself."

"You know damned well it don't hang together, don't make sense. Cut it out, for God's sake."

"I don't mind how goofy it is," I said. "It's something to put to Noonan when we get back. He's likely all broken up over Whisper's crush-out.[54] This will take his mind off it."

MacSwain got down on his knees in the muddy alley and cried:

"Oh, Christ, no! He'd croak me with his hands."

"Get up and stop yelling," I growled. "Now will you give it to me straight?"

He whined: "He'd croak me with his hands."

"Suit yourself. If you won't talk, I will, to Noonan. If you'll come through to me, I'll do what I can for you."

"What can you do?" he asked hopelessly, and started sniveling again. "How do I know you'll try to do anything?"

I risked a little truth on him:

"You said you had a hunch what I'm up to here in Poisonville. Then you ought to know that it's my play to keep Noonan and Whisper split. Letting Noonan think Whisper killed Tim will keep them split. But if you don't want to play with me, come on, we'll play with Noonan."

"You mean you won't tell him?" he asked eagerly. "You promise?"

"I promise you nothing," I said. "Why should I? I've got you with your pants down. Talk to me or Noonan. And make up your mind quick. I'm not going to stand here all night."

He made up his mind to talk to me.

"I don't know how much you know, but it was like you said, my wife fell for Tim. That's what put me on the tramp. You can ask anybody if I wasn't a good guy before that. I was this way: what she wanted I wanted her to have. Mostly what she wanted was tough on me. But I couldn't be any other way. We'd have been a damned sight better off if I could. So I let her move out and put in divorce papers, so she could marry him, thinking he meant to.

"Pretty soon I begin to hear he's chasing this Myrtle Jennison. I couldn't go that. I'd given him his chance with Helen, fair and square. Now he was giving her the air for this Myrtle. I wasn't going to stand for that. Helen wasn't no hanky-panky. It was accidental, though, running into him at the Lake that night. When I saw him go down to them summer houses I went after him. That looked like a good quiet place to have it out.

"I guess we'd both had a little something to drink. Anyway, we had it hot and heavy. When it got too hot for him, he pulled the gun. He was yellow. I grabbed it, and in the tussle it went off. I swear to God I didn't shoot him except like that. It went off while the both of us had our hands on it. I beat it back in some bushes. But when I got in the bushes I could hear him moaning and talking. There was people coming—a girl running down from the hotel, that Myrtle Jennison.

"I wanted to go back and hear what Tim was saying, so I'd know where I stood, but I was leery of being the first one there. So I had to wait till the girl got to him, listening all the time to his squawking, but too far away to make it out. When she got to him, I ran over and got there just as he died trying to say my name.

"I didn't think about that being Whisper's name till she propositioned me with the suicide letter, the two hundred, and the rock. I'd just been stalling around, pretending to get the job lined up—being on the force then—and trying to find out where I stood. Then she makes the play and I know I'm sitting pretty. And that's the way it went till you started digging it up again."

He slopped his feet up and down in the mud and added:

"Next week my wife got killed—an accident. Uh-huh, an accident. She drove the Ford square in front of No. 6[55] where it comes down the long grade from Tanner and stopped it there."

"Is Mock Lake in this county?" I asked.

"No, Boulder County."[56]

"That's out of Noonan's territory. Suppose I take you over there and hand you to the sheriff?"

"No. He's Senator Keefer's son-in-law—Tom Cook. I might as well be here. Noonan could get to me through Keefer."

"If it happened the way you say, you've got at least an even chance of beating the rap in court."

55 This must refer to a train, No. 6, perhaps on the Butte, Anaconda & Pacific, the route of which (from Butte to Anaconda) crossed the old Yellowstone Trail, one of the first transcontinental highways. There is no historical place named "Tanner" in Montana.

56 A fictional county in Montana. Boulder is actually in Jefferson County, more than 30 miles from Butte, which is in Silver Bow County.

"They won't give me a chance. I'd have stood it if there'd been a chance in the world of getting an even break—but not with them."

"We're going back to the Hall," I said. "Keep your mouth shut."

∞

Noonan was waddling up and down the floor, cursing the half a dozen bulls who stood around wishing they were somewhere else.

"Here's something I found roaming around," I said, pushing MacSwain forward.

Noonan knocked the ex-detective down, kicked him, and told one of the coppers to take him away.

Somebody called Noonan on the phone. I slipped out without saying, "Good-night," and walked back to the hotel.

Off to the north some guns popped.

A group of three men passed me, shifty-eyed, walking pigeon-toed.

A little farther along, another man moved all the way over to the curb to give me plenty of room to pass. I didn't know him and didn't suppose he knew me.

A lone shot sounded not far away.

As I reached the hotel, a battered black touring car went down the street, hitting fifty at least, crammed to the curtains with men.

I grinned after it. Poisonville was beginning to boil out under the lid, and I felt so much like a native that even the memory of my very un-nice part in the boiling didn't keep me from getting twelve solid end-to-end hours of sleep.

A luxurious model of 1921 Birmingham Motors touring car.

CHAPTER XV

Cedar Hill Inn

Mickey Linehan used the telephone to wake me a little after noon.

"We're here," he told me. "Where's the reception committee?"

"Probably stopped to get a rope. Check your bags and come up to the hotel. Room 537. Don't advertise your visit."

I was dressed when they arrived.

Mickey Linehan was a big slob with sagging shoulders and a shapeless body that seemed to be coming apart at all its joints. His ears stood out like red wings, and his round red face usually wore the meaningless smirk of a half-wit. He looked like a comedian and was.

Dick Foley was a boy-sized Canadian with a sharp irritable face. He wore high heels to increase his height, perfumed his handkerchiefs and saved all the words he could.

They were both good operatives.

"What did the Old Man tell you about the job?" I asked when we had settled into seats. The Old Man was the manager of the Continental's San Francisco branch. He was also known as Pontius Pilate, because he smiled pleasantly when he sent us out to be crucified on suicidal jobs. He was a gentle, polite, elderly person with no more warmth in him than a hangman's rope. The Agency wits said he could spit icicles in July.

"He didn't seem to know much what it was all about," Mickey said, "except that you had wired for help. He said he hadn't got any reports from you for a couple of days."

"The chances are he'll wait a couple more. Know anything about this Personville?"

Dick shook his head. Mickey said:

"Only that I've heard parties call it Poisonville like they meant it."

I told them what I knew and what I had done. The telephone bell interrupted my tale in the last quarter.

Dinah Brand's lazy voice:

"Hello! How's the wrist?"

"Only a burn. What do you think of the crush-out?"

"It's not my fault," she said. "I did my part. If Noonan couldn't hold him, that's just too bad. I'm coming downtown to buy a hat this afternoon. I thought I'd drop in and see you for a couple of minutes if you're going to be there."

"What time?"

"Oh, around three."

"Right, I'll expect you, and I'll have that two hundred and a dime I owe you."

"Do," she said. "That's what I'm coming in for. Ta-ta."

I went back to my seat and my story.

When I had finished, Mickey Linehan whistled and said:

"No wonder you're scared to send in any reports. The Old Man wouldn't do much if he knew what you've been up to, would he?"

"If it works out the way I want it to, I won't have to report all the distressing details," I said. "It's right enough for the Agency to have rules and regulations, but when you're out on a job you've got to do it the best way you can. And anybody that brings any ethics to Poisonville is going to get them all rusty. A report is no place for the dirty details, anyway, and I don't want you birds to send any writing back to San Francisco without letting me see it first."

"What kind of crimes have you got for us to pull?" Mickey asked.

"I want you to take Pete the Finn. Dick will take Lew Yard. You'll have to play it the way I've been playing—do what you can when you can. I've an idea that the pair of them will try to make

Noonan let Whisper alone. I don't know what he'll do. He's shifty as hell and he does want to even up his brother's killing."

"After I take this Finnish gent," Mickey said, "what do I do with him? I don't want to brag about how dumb I am, but this job is plain as astronomy to me. I understand everything about it except what you have done and why, and what you're trying to do and how."

"You can start off by shadowing him. I've got to have a wedge that can be put between Pete and Yard, Yard and Noonan, Pete and Noonan, Pete and Thaler, or Yard and Thaler. If we can smash things up enough—break the combination—they'll have their knives in each other's backs, doing our work for us. The break between Thaler and Noonan is a starter. But it'll sag on us if we don't help it along.

"I could buy more dope on the whole lot from Dinah Brand. But there's no use taking anybody into court, no matter what you've got on them. They own the courts, and, besides, the courts are too slow for us now. I've got myself tangled up in something and as soon as the Old Man smells it—and San Francisco isn't far enough away to fool his nose—he's going to be sitting on the wire, asking for explanations. I've got to have results to hide the details under. So evidence won't do. What we've got to have is dynamite."

"What about our respected client, Mr. Elihu Willsson?" Mickey asked. "What are you planning to do with or to him?"

"Maybe ruin him, maybe club him into backing us up. I don't care which. You'd better stay at the Hotel Person, Mickey, and Dick can go to the National. Keep apart, and, if you want to keep me from being fired, burn the job up before the Old Man tumbles. Better write these down."

I gave them names, descriptions, and addresses when I had them, of Elihu Willsson; Stanley Lewis, his secretary; Dinah Brand; Dan Rolff; Noonan; Max Thaler, alias Whisper; his right-hand man, the chinless Jerry; Mrs. Donald Willsson; Lewis' daughter, who had been Donald Willsson's secretary; and Bill Quint, Dinah's radical ex-boy-friend.

"Now hop to it," I said. "And don't kid yourselves that there's any law in Poisonville except what you make for yourself."

Mickey said I'd be surprised how many laws he could get along without. Dick said: "So long," and they departed.

After breakfast I went over to the City Hall.

Noonan's greenish eyes were bleary, as if they hadn't been sleeping, and his face had lost some of its color. He pumped my hand up and down as enthusiastically as ever, and the customary amount of cordiality was in his voice and manner.

"Any line on Whisper?" I asked when we had finished the glad-handing.

"I think I've got something." He looked at the clock on the wall and then at his phone. "I'm expecting word any minute. Sit down."

"Who else got away?"

"Jerry Hooper and Tony Agosti are the only other ones still out. We picked up the rest. Jerry is Whisper's man-Friday, and the wop's one of his mob. He's the bozo that put the knife in Ike Bush the night of the fight."

"Any more of Whisper's mob in?"

"No. We just had the three of them, except Buck Wallace, the fellow you potted. He's in the hospital."

The chief looked at the wall clock again, and at his watch. It was exactly two o'clock. He turned to the phone. It rang. He grabbed it, said:

"Noonan talking. . . . Yes. . . . Yes. . . . Yes. . . . Right."

He pushed the phone aside and played a tune on the row of pearl buttons on his desk. The office filled up with coppers.

"Cedar Hill Inn," he said. "You follow me out with your detail, Bates. Terry, shoot out Broadway and hit the dump from behind. Pick up the boys on traffic duty as you go along. It's likely we'll need everybody we can get. Duffy, take yours out Union Street and around by the old mine road. McGraw will hold headquarters down. Get hold of everybody you can and send them after us. Jump!"

He grabbed his hat and went after them, calling over his thick shoulder to me:

"Come on, man, this is the kill."

I followed him down to the department garage, where the engines of half a dozen cars were roaring. The chief sat beside his driver. I sat in back with four detectives.

Men scrambled into the other cars. Machineguns were unwrapped. Arm-loads of rifles and riot-guns were distributed, and packages of ammunition.

The chief's car got away first, off with a jump that hammered our teeth together. We missed the garage door by half an inch, chased a couple of pedestrians diagonally across the sidewalk, bounced off the curb into the roadway, missed a truck as narrowly as we had missed the door, and dashed out King Street with our siren wide open.

Panicky automobiles darted right and left, regardless of traffic rules, to let us through. It was a lot of fun.

I looked back, saw another police car following us, a third turning into Broadway. Noonan chewed a cold cigar and told the driver:

"Give her a bit more, Pat."

Pat twisted us around a frightened woman's coupé, put us through a slot between street car and laundry wagon—a narrow slot that we couldn't have slipped through if our car hadn't been so smoothly enameled—and said:

"All right, but the brakes ain't no good."

"That's nice," the gray-mustached sleuth on my left said. He didn't sound sincere.

Out of the center of the city there wasn't much traffic to bother us, but the paving was rougher. It was a nice half-hour's ride, with everybody getting a chance to sit in everybody else's lap. The last ten minutes of it was over an uneven road that had hills enough to keep us from forgetting what Pat had said about the brakes.

We wound up at a gate topped by a shabby electric sign that had said *Cedar Hill Inn* before it lost its globes. The roadhouse, twenty feet behind the gate, was a squat wooden building painted a moldy green and chiefly surrounded by rubbish. Front door and windows were closed, blank.

We followed Noonan out of the car. The machine that had been trailing us came into sight around a bend in the road, slid to rest beside ours, and unloaded its cargo of men and weapons.

Noonan ordered this and that.

A trio of coppers went around each side of the building. Three others, including a machine-gunner, remained by the gate. The rest of us walked through tin cans, bottles, and ancient newspaper to the front of the house.

The gray-mustached detective who had sat beside me in the car carried a red ax. We stepped up on the porch.

Noise and fire came out under a window sill.

The gray-mustached detective fell down, hiding the ax under his corpse.

The rest of us ran away.

I ran with Noonan. We hid in the ditch on the Inn side of the road. It was deep enough, and banked high enough, to let us stand almost erect without being targets.

The chief was excited.

"What luck!" he said happily. "He's here, by God, he's here!"

"That shot came from under the sill," I said. "Not a bad trick."

"We'll spoil it, though," he said cheerfully. "We'll sieve the dump. Duffy ought to be pulling up on the other road by now, and Terry Shane won't be many minutes behind him. Hey, Donner!" he called to a man who was peeping around a boulder. "Swing around back and tell Duffy and Shane to start closing in as soon as they come, letting fly with all they got. Where's Kimble?"

The peeper jerked a thumb toward a tree beyond him. We could see only the upper part of it from our ditch.

"Tell him to set up his mill and start grinding," Noonan ordered. "Low, across the front, ought to do it like cutting cheese."

The peeper disappeared.

Noonan went up and down the ditch, risking his noodle over the top now and then for a look around, once in a while calling or gesturing to his men.

He came back, sat on his heels beside me, gave me a cigar, and lit one for himself.

"It'll do," he said complacently. "Whisper won't have a chance. He's done."

The machine-gun by the tree fired, haltingly, experimentally, eight or ten shots. Noonan grinned and let a smoke ring float out of his mouth. The machine-gun settled down to business, grinding out metal like the busy little death factory it was. Noonan blew another smoke ring and said:

"That's exactly what'll do it."

I agreed that it ought to. We leaned against the clay bank and smoked while, farther away, another machine-gun got going, and then a third. Irregularly, rifles, pistols, shotguns joined in. Noonan nodded approvingly and said:

"Five minutes of that will let him know there's a hell."

When the five minutes were up I suggested a look at the remains. I gave him a boost up the bank and scrambled up after him.

The roadhouse was as bleak and emptylooking as before, but more battered. No shots came from it. Plenty were going into it.

"What do you think?" Noonan asked.

"If there's a cellar there might be a mouse alive in it."

"Well, we could finish him afterwards."

He took a whistle out of his pocket and made a lot of noise. He waved his fat arms, and the gun-fire began dwindling. We had to wait for the word to go all the way around.

Then we crashed the door.

The first floor was ankle-deep with booze that was still gurgling from bullet holes in the stacked-up cases and barrels that filled most of the house.

Dizzy with the fumes of spilled hooch, we waded around until we had found four dead bodies and no live ones. The four were swarthy foreign-looking men in laborers' clothes. Two of them were practically shot to pieces.

Noonan said:

"Leave them here and get out."

His voice was cheerful, but in a flashlight's glow his eyes showed white-ringed with fear.

We went out gladly, though I did hesitate long enough to pocket an unbroken bottle labeled *Dewar.*[57]

A khaki-dressed copper was tumbling off a motorcycle at the gate. He yelled at us:

"The First National's been stuck up."

Noonan cursed savagely, bawled:

"He's foxed us, damn him! Back to town, everybody."

Everybody except us who had ridden with the chief beat it for the machines. Two of them took the dead detective with them.

57   Dewar's White Label was and is a popular brand of Scotch whiskey.

Noonan looked at me out of his eyecorners and said: "This is a tough one, no fooling."

I said, "Well," shrugged, and sauntered over to his car, where the driver was sitting at the wheel. I stood with my back to the house, talking to Pat. I don't remember what we talked about. Presently Noonan and the other sleuths joined us.

Only a little flame showed through the open roadhouse door before we passed out of sight around the bend in the road.

A Triumph Model H motorcycle, built for WWI.

CHAPTER XVI

Exit Jerry

There was a mob around the First National Bank. We pushed through it to the door, where we found sour-faced McGraw.

"Was six of them, masked," he reported to the chief as we went inside. "They hit it about two-thirty. Five of them got away clean with the jack. The watchman here dropped one of them, Jerry Hooper. He's over on the bench, cold. We got the roads blocked, and I wired around, if it ain't too late. Last seen of them was when they made the turn into King Street, in a black Lincoln."

We went over to look at the dead Jerry, lying on one of the lobby benches with a brown robe over him. The bullet had gone in under his left shoulder blade.

The bank watchman, a harmless looking old duffer, pushed up his chest and told us about it:

"There wasn't no chance to do nothing at first. They were in 'fore anybody knew anything. And maybe they didn't work fast. Right down the line, scooping it up. No chance to do anything then. But I says to myself, 'All righty, young fellows, you've got it all your own way now, but wait till you try to leave.'

"And I was as good as my word, you bet you. I runs right to the door after them and cut loose with the old firearm. I got that fellow just as he was stepping into the car. I bet you I'd of got more of them if I'd of had more cartridges, because it's kind of hard shooting down like that, standing in the—"

Clearly a bootlegger's warehouse—
therefore, presumably the province of Pete
the Finn.

Noonan stopped the monologue by patting the old duffer's
back till his lungs were empty, telling him, "That certainly is fine.
That certainly is fine."

McGraw pulled the robe up over the dead man again and
growled:

"Nobody can identify anybody. But with Jerry on it, it's a cinch
it was Whisper's caper."

The chief nodded happily and said:

"I'll leave it in your hands, Mac. Going to poke around here,
or going back to the Hall with me?" he asked me.

"Neither. I've got a date, and I want to get into dry shoes."

❦

Dinah Brand's little Marmon was standing in front of the hotel. I
didn't see her. I went up to my room, leaving the door unlocked.
I had got my hat and coat off when she came in without knocking.

"My God, you keep a boozy smelling room," she said.

"It's my shoes. Noonan took me wading in rum."

She crossed to the window, opened it, sat on the sill, and asked:

"What was that for?"

"He thought he was going to find your Max out in a dump
called Cedar Hill Inn. So we went out there, shot the joint silly,
murdered some dagoes, spilled gallons of liquor, and left the
place burning."

"Cedar Hill Inn? I thought it had been closed up for a year
or more."

"It looked it, but it was somebody's warehouse."[58]

"But you didn't find Max there?" she asked.

"While we were there he seems to have been knocking over
Elihu's First National Bank."

"I saw that," she said. "I had just come out of Bengren's, the
store two doors away. I had just got in my car when I saw a big
boy backing out of the bank, carrying a sack and a gun, with a
black handkerchief over his face."

"Was Max with them?"

"No, he wouldn't be. He'd send Jerry and the boys. That's what
he has them for. Jerry was there. I knew him as soon as he got out
of the car, in spite of the black handkerchief. They all had black
ones. Four of them came out of the bank, running down to the

car at the curb. Jerry and another fellow were in the car. When the four came across the sidewalk, Jerry jumped out and went to meet them. That's when the shooting started and Jerry dropped. The others jumped in the bus and lit out. How about that dough you owe me?"

I counted out ten twenty-dollar bills and a dime. She left the window to come for them.

"That's for pulling Dan off, so you could cop Max," she said when she had stowed the money away in her bag. "Now how about what I was to get for showing you where you could turn up the dope on his killing Tim Noonan?"

"You'll have to wait till he's indicted. How do I know the dope's any good?"

She frowned and asked:

"What do you do with all the money you don't spend?" Her face brightened. "You know where Max is now?"

"No."

"What's it worth to know?"

"Nothing."

"I'll tell you for a hundred bucks."

"I wouldn't want to take advantage of you that way."

"I'll tell you for fifty bucks."

I shook my head.

"Twenty-five."

"I don't want him," I said. "I don't care where he is. Why don't you peddle the news to Noonan?"

"Yes, and try to collect. Do you only perfume yourself with booze, or is there any for drinking purposes?"

"Here's a bottle of so-called Dewar that I picked up at Cedar Hill this afternoon. There's a bottle of King George in my bag. What's your choice?"

She voted for King George. We had a drink apiece, straight, and I said:

"Sit down and play with it while I change clothes."

When I came out of the bathroom twenty-five minutes later she was sitting at the secretary, smoking a cigarette and studying a memoranda book that had been in a side pocket of my gladstone bag.

"I guess these are the expenses you've charged up on other cases," she said without looking up. "I'm damned if I can see why

When a pickpocket first touches his or her victim, the thief is said to be "fanning" the victim. (*New Partridge Dictionary of Slang*)

you can't be more liberal with me. Look, here's a six-hundred-dollar item marked *Inf.* That's information you bought from somebody, isn't it? And here's a hundred and fifty below it—*Top*—whatever that is. And here's another day when you spent nearly a thousand dollars."

"They must be telephone numbers," I said, taking the book from her. "Where were you raised? Fanning[59] my baggage!"

"I was raised in a convent," she told me. "I won the good behavior prize every year I was there. I thought little girls who put extra spoons of sugar in their chocolate went to hell for gluttony. I didn't even know there was such a thing as profanity until I was eighteen. The first time I heard any I damned near fainted." She spit on the rug in front of her, tilted her chair back, put her crossed feet on my bed, and asked: "What do you think of that?"

I pushed her feet off the bed and said:

"I was raised in a water-front saloon. Keep your saliva off my floor or I'll toss you out on your neck."

"Let's have another drink first. Listen, what'll you give me for the inside story of how the boys didn't lose anything building the City Hall—the story that was in the papers I sold Donald Willsson?"

"That doesn't click with me. Try another."

"How about why the first Mrs. Lew Yard was sent to the insane asylum?"

"No."

"King, our sheriff, eight thousand dollars in debt four years ago, now the owner of as nice a collection of downtown business blocks as you'd want to see. I can't give you all of it, but I can show you where to get it."

"Keep trying," I encouraged her.

"No. You don't want to buy anything. You're just hoping you'll pick up something for nothing. This isn't bad Scotch. Where'd you get it?"

"Brought it from San Francisco with me."

"What's the idea of not wanting any of this information I'm offering? Think you can get it cheaper?"

"Information of that kind's not much good to me now. I've got to move quick. I need dynamite—something to blow them apart."

She laughed and jumped up, her big eyes sparkling.

"I've got one of Lew Yard's cards. Suppose we sent the bottle of Dewar you copped to Pete with the card. Wouldn't he take it as a declaration of war? If Cedar Hill was a liquor cache, it was Pete's. Wouldn't the bottle and Lew's card make him think Noonan had knocked the place over under orders?"

I considered it and said:

"Too crude. It wouldn't fool him. Besides, I'd just as leave have Pete and Lew both against the chief at this stage."

She pouted and said:

"You think you know everything. You're just hard to get along with. Take me out tonight? I've got a new outfit that'll knock them cockeyed."

"Yeah."

"Come up for me around eight."

She patted my cheek with a warm hand, said, "Ta-ta," and went out as the telephone bell began jingling.

꩜

"My chinch[60] and Dick's are together at your client's joint," Mickey Linehan reported over the wire. "Mine's been generally busier than a hustler with two bunks, though I don't know what the score is yet. Anything new?"

I said there wasn't and went into conference with myself across the bed, trying to guess what would come of Noonan's attack on Cedar Hill Inn and Whisper's on the First National Bank. I would have given something for ability to hear what was being said up at old Elihu's house by him, Pete the Finn, and Lew Yard. But I hadn't that ability, and I was never much good at guessing, so after half an hour I stopped tormenting my brain and took a nap.

It was nearly seven o'clock when I came out of the nap. I washed, dressed, loaded my pockets with a gun and a pint flask of Scotch, and went up to Dinah's.

60   "Chinch" is slang for a bedbug, a pest. Mickey is shadowing Pete the Finn.

CHAPTER XVII

Reno

She took me into her living room, backed away from me, revolved, and asked me how I liked the new dress. I said I liked it. She explained that the color was rose beige and that the dinguses on the side were something or other, winding up:

"And you really think I look good in it?"

"You always look good," I said. "Lew Yard and Pete the Finn went calling on old Elihu this afternoon."

She made a face at me and said:

"You don't give a damn about my dress. What did they do there?"

"A pow-wow, I suppose."

She looked at me through her lashes and asked:

"Don't you really know where Max is?"

Then I did. There was no use admitting I hadn't known all along. I said:

"At Willsson's, probably, but I haven't been interested enough to make sure."

"That's goofy of you. He's got reasons for not liking you and me. Take mama's advice and nail him quick, if you like living and like having mama live too."

I laughed and said:

"You don't know the worst of it. Max didn't kill Noonan's brother. Tim didn't say *Max*. He tried to say *MacSwain*, and died before he could finish."

She grabbed my shoulders and tried to shake my hundred and ninety pounds. She was almost strong enough to do it.

"God damn you!" Her breath was hot in my face. Her face was white as her teeth. Rouge stood out sharply like red labels pasted on her mouth and cheeks. "If you've framed him and made me frame him, you've got to kill him—now."

I don't like being manhandled, even by young women who look like something out of mythology when they're steamed up. I took her hands off my shoulders, and said:

"Stop bellyaching. You're still alive."

"Yes, still. But I know Max better than you do. I know how much chance anybody that frames him has got of staying alive long. It would be bad enough if we had got him right, but—"

"Don't make so much fuss over it. I've framed my millions and nothing's happened to me. Get your hat and coat and we'll feed. You'll feel better then."

"You're crazy if you think I'm going out. Not with that—"

"Stop it, sister. If he's that dangerous he's just as likely to get you here as anywhere. So what difference does it make?"

"It makes a— You know what you're going to do? You're going to stay here until Max is put out of the way. It's your fault and you've got to look out for me. I haven't even got Dan. He's in the hospital."

"I can't," I said. "I've got work to do. You're all burnt up over nothing. Max has probably forgotten all about you by now. Get your hat and coat. I'm starving."

She put her face close to mine again, and her eyes looked as if they had found something horrible in mine.

"Oh, you're rotten!" she said. "You don't give a damn what happens to me. You're using me as you use the others—that dynamite you wanted. I trusted you."[61]

"You're dynamite, all right, but the rest of it's kind of foolish. You look a lot better when you're happy. Your features are heavy. Anger makes them downright brutal. I'm starving, sister."

"You'll eat here," she said. "You're not going to get me out after dark."

She meant it. She swapped the rose beige dress for an apron, and took inventory of the ice box. There were potatoes, lettuce, canned soup and half a fruit cake. I went out and got a couple of steaks, rolls, asparagus, and tomatoes.

61 The Op is without sentiment, observes Dinah Brand—a marked contrast, for example, with the character of Race Williams, the first "hard-boiled detective." Williams, in Carroll John Daly's *The White Circle* (1926), may claim to feel "the satisfaction of one who has completed a good day's work" after he kills a man, but only a few pages earlier, he informs the reader, "If there's one thing I always feel I've got time for, that is to look at a little child—especially a sleeping one." (The comparison is made by Sinda Gregory in *Private Investigations: The Novels of Dashiell Hammett*, p. 46)

When I came back she was mixing gin, vermouth and orange bitters in a quart shaker, not leaving a lot of space for them to move around in.

"Did you see anything?" she asked.

I sneered at her in a friendly way. We carried the cocktails into the dining room and played bottoms-up while the meal cooked. The drinks cheered her a lot. By the time we sat down to the food she had almost forgotten her fright. She wasn't a very good cook, but we ate as if she were.

We put a couple of gin-gingerales in on top the dinner.

She decided she wanted to go places and do things. No lousy little runt could keep her cooped up, because she had been as square with him as anybody could be until he got nasty over nothing, and if he didn't like what she did he could go climb trees or jump in lakes, and we'd go out to the Silver Arrow where she had meant to take me, because she had promised Reno she'd show up at his party, and by God she would, and anybody who thought she wouldn't was crazy as a pet cuckoo, and what did I think of that?

"Who's Reno?" I asked while she tied herself tighter in the apron by pulling the strings the wrong way.

"Reno Starkey. You'll like him. He's a right guy. I promised him I'd show at his celebration and that's just what I'll do."

"What's he celebrating?"

"What the hell's the matter with this lousy apron? He was sprung this afternoon."

"Turn around and I'll unwind you. What was he in for? Stand still."

"Blowing a safe six or seven months ago—Turlock's, the jeweler. Reno, Put Collings, Blackie Whalen, Hank O'Marra, and a little lame guy called Step-and-a-Half. They had plenty of cover—Lew Yard—but the jewelers' association dicks tied the job to them last week. So Noonan had to go through the motions. It doesn't mean anything. They got out on bail at five o'clock this afternoon, and that's the last anybody will ever hear about it. Reno's used to it. He was already out on bail for three other capers. Suppose you mix another little drink while I'm inserting myself in the dress."

✺

The Silver Arrow was half-way between Personville and Mock Lake.

"It's not a bad dump," Dinah told me as her little Marmon carried us toward it. "Polly De Voto is a good scout and anything she sells you is good, except maybe the Bourbon. That always tastes a little bit like it had been drained off a corpse. You'll like her. You can get away with anything out here so long as you don't get noisy. She won't stand for noise. There it is. See the red and blue lights through the trees?"

We rode out of the woods into full view of the roadhouse, a very electric-lighted imitation castle set close to the road.

"What do you mean she won't stand for noise?" I asked, listening to the chorus of pistols singing *Bang-bang-bang*.

"Something up," the girl muttered, stopping the car.

Two men dragging a woman between them ran out of the roadhouse's front door, ran away into the darkness. A man sprinted out a side door, away. The guns sang on. I didn't see any flashes.

Another man broke out and vanished around the back.

A man leaned far out a front second-story window, a black gun in his hand.

Dinah blew her breath out sharply.

From a hedge by the road, a flash of orange pointed briefly up at the man in the window. His gun flashed downward. He leaned farther out. No second flash came from the hedge.

The man in the window put a leg over the sill, bent, hung by his hands, dropped.

Our car jerked forward. Dinah's lower lip was between her teeth.

The man who had dropped from the window was gathering himself up on hands and knees.

Dinah put her face in front of mine and screamed:

"Reno!"

The man jumped up, his face to us. He made the road in three leaps, as we got to him.

Dinah had the little Marmon wide open before Reno's feet were on the running board beside me. I wrapped my arms around him, and damned near dislocated them holding him on. He made it as tough as he could for me by leaning out to try for a shot at the guns that were tossing lead all around us.

Then it was all over. We were out of range, sight and sound of the Silver Arrow, speeding away from Personville.

Reno turned around and did his own holding on. I took my arms in and found that all the joints still worked. Dinah was busy with the car.

Reno said:

"Thanks, kid. I needed pulling out."

"That's all right," she told him. "So that's the kind of parties you throw?"

"We had guests that wasn't invited. You know the Tanner Road?"

"Yes."

"Take it. It'll put us over to Mountain Boulevard, and we can get back to town that-a-way."

The girl nodded, slowed up a little, and asked:

"Who were the uninvited guests?"

"Some plugs that don't know enough to leave me alone."

"Do I know them?" she asked, too casually, as she turned the car into a narrower and rougher road.

"Let it alone, kid," Reno said. "Better get as much out of the heap as it's got."

She prodded another fifteen miles an hour out of the Marmon. She had plenty to do now holding the car to the road, and Reno had plenty holding himself to the car. Neither of them made any more conversation until the road brought us into one that had more and better paving.

Then he asked:

"So you paid Whisper off?"

"Um-hmm."

"They're saying you turned rat on him."

"They would. What do you think?"

"Ditching him was all right. But throwing in with a dick and cracking the works to him is kind of sour. Damned sour, if you ask me."

He looked at me while he said it. He was a man of thirty-four or -five, fairly tall, broad and heavy without fat. His eyes were large, brown, dull, and set far apart in a long, slightly sallow horse face. It was a humorless face, stolid, but somehow not unpleasant. I looked at him and said nothing.

The girl said: "If that's the way you feel about it, you can—"

"Look out," Reno grunted.

We had swung around a curve. A long black car was straight across the road ahead of us—a barricade.

Bullets flew around us. Reno and I threw bullets around while the girl made a polo pony of the little Marmon.

She shoved it over to the left of the road, let the left wheels ride the bank high, crossed the road again with Reno's and my weight on the inside, got the right bank under the left wheels just as our side of the car began to lift in spite of our weight, slid us down in the road with our backs to the enemy, and took us out of the neighborhood by the time we had emptied our guns.

A lot of people had done a lot of shooting, but so far as we could tell nobody's bullets had hurt anybody.

Reno, holding to the door with his elbows while he pushed another clip into his automatic, said:

"Nice work, kid. You handle the bus like you meant it."

Dinah asked: "Where now?"

"Far away first. Just follow the road. We'll have to figure it out. Looks like they got the burg closed up on us. Keep your dog on it."[62]

We put ten or twelve more miles between Personville and us. We passed a few cars, saw nothing to show we were being chased. A short bridge rumbled under us. Reno said:

"Take the right turn at the top of the hill."

We took it, into a dirt road that wound between trees down the side of a rock-ridged hill. Ten miles an hour was fast going here. After five minutes of creeping along Reno ordered a halt. We heard nothing, saw nothing, during the half-hour we sat in darkness. Then Reno said:

"There's an empty shack a mile down the way. We'll camp there, huh? There's no sense trying to crash the city line again tonight."

Dinah said she would prefer anything to being shot at again. I said it was all right with me, though I would rather have tried to find some path back to the city.

We followed the dirt track cautiously until our headlights settled on a small clapboard building that badly needed the paint it had never got.

"Is this it?" Dinah asked Reno.

"Uh-huh. Stay here till I look it over."

62   Reno means, "Keep your foot on the gas pedal."

He left us, appearing soon in the beam of our lights at the shack door. He fumbled with keys at the padlock, got it off, opened the door, and went in. Presently he came to the door and called:

"All right. Come in and make yourselves to home."

Dinah cut off the engine and got out of the car.

"Is there a flashlight in the car?" I asked.

She said, "Yes," gave it to me, yawned, "My God, I'm tired. I hope there's something to drink in the hole."

I told her I had a flask of Scotch. The news cheered her up.

The shack was a one-room affair that held an army cot covered with brown blankets, a deal table with a deck of cards and some gummy poker chips on it, a brown iron stove, four chairs, an oil lamp, dishes, pots, pans and buckets, three shelves with canned food on them, a pile of firewood and a wheelbarrow.

Reno was lighting the lamp when we came in. He said:

"Not so tough. I'll hide the heap and then we'll be all set till daylight."

Dinah went over to the cot, turned back the covers, and reported:

"Maybe there's things in it, but anyway it's not alive with them. Now let's have that drink."

I unscrewed the flask and passed it to her while Reno went out to hide the car. When she had finished, I took a shot.

The purr of the Marmon's engine got fainter. I opened the door and looked out. Downhill, through trees and bushes, I could see broken chunks of white light going away. When I lost them for good I returned indoors and asked the girl:

"Have you ever had to walk home before?"

"What?"

"Reno's gone with the car."

"The lousy tramp! Thank God he left us where there's a bed, anyway."

"That'll get you nothing."

"No?"

"No. Reno had a key to this dump. Ten to one the birds after him know about it. That's why he ditched us here. We're supposed to argue with them, hold them off his trail a while."

She got up wearily from the cot, cursed Reno, me, all men from Adam on, and said disagreeably:

"You know everything. What do we do next?"

"We find a comfortable spot in the great open spaces, not too far away, and wait to see what happens."

"I'm going to take the blankets."

"Maybe one won't be missed, but you'll tip our mitts if you take more than that."

"Damn your mitts," she grumbled, but she took only one blanket.

I blew out the lamp, padlocked the door behind us, and with the help of the flashlight picked a way through the undergrowth.

On the hillside above we found a little hollow from which road and shack could be not too dimly seen through foliage thick enough to hide us unless we showed a light.

I spread the blanket there and we settled down.

The girl leaned against me and complained that the ground was damp, that she was cold in spite of her fur coat, that she had a cramp in her leg, and that she wanted a cigarette.

I gave her another drink from the flask. That bought me ten minutes of peace.

Then she said:

"I'm catching cold. By the time anybody comes, if they ever do, I'll be sneezing and coughing loud enough to be heard in the city."

"Just once," I told her. "Then you'll be all strangled."

"There's a mouse or something crawling under the blanket."

"Probably only a snake."

"Are you married?"

"Don't start that."

"Then you are?"

"No."

"I'll bet your wife's glad of it."

I was trying to find a suitable come-back to that wise-crack when a distant light gleamed up the road. It disappeared as I sh-sh'd the girl.

"What is it?" she asked.

"A light. It's gone now. Our visitors have left their car and are finishing the trip afoot."

A lot of time went by. The girl shivered with her cheek warm against mine. We heard footsteps, saw dark figures moving on the road and around the shack, without being sure whether we did or didn't.

A flashlight ended our doubt by putting a bright circle on the shack's door. A heavy voice said:

"We'll let the broad come out."

There was a half-minute of silence while they waited for a reply from indoors. Then the same heavy voice asked: "Coming?" Then more silence.

Gunfire, a familiar sound tonight, broke the silence. Something hammered boards.

"Come on," I whispered to the girl. "We'll have a try at their car while they're making a racket."

"Let them alone," she said, pulling my arm down as I started up. "I've had enough of it for one night. We're all right here."

"Come on," I insisted.

She said, "I won't," and she wouldn't, and presently, while we argued, it was too late. The boys below had kicked in the door, found the hut empty, and were bellowing for their car.

It came, took eight men aboard, and followed Reno's track downhill.

"We might as well move in again," I said. "It's not likely they'll be back this way tonight."

"I hope to God there's some Scotch left in that flask," she said as I helped her stand up.

CHAPTER XVIII

Painter Street

The shack's supply of canned goods didn't include anything that tempted us for breakfast. We made the meal of coffee cooked in very stale water from a galvanized pail.

A mile of walking brought us to a farmhouse where there was a boy who didn't mind earning a few dollars by driving us to town in the family Ford. He had a lot of questions, to which we gave him phoney answers or none. He set us down in front of a little restaurant in upper King Street, where we ate quantities of buckwheat cakes and bacon.

A taxi put us at Dinah's door a little before nine o'clock. I searched the place for her, from roof to cellar, and found no signs of visitors.

"When will you be back?" she asked as she followed me to the door.

"I'll try to pop in between now and midnight, if only for a few minutes. Where does Lew Yard live?"

"1622 Painter Street. Painter's three blocks over. 1622's four blocks up. What are you going to do there?" Before I could answer, she put her hands on my arm and begged: "Get Max, will you? I'm afraid of him."

"Maybe I'll sic Noonan on him a little later. It depends on how things work out."

She called me a damned double-crossing something or other who didn't care what happened to her as long as his dirty work got done.

I went over to Painter Street. 1622 was a red brick house with a garage under the front porch.

A block up the street I found Dick Foley in a hired drive-yourself Buick. I got in beside him, asking:

"What's doing?"

"Spot two. Out three-thirty, office to Willsson's. Mickey. Five. Home. Busy. Kept plant. Off three, seven. Nothing yet."

That was supposed to inform me that he had picked up Lew Yard at two the previous afternoon; had shadowed him to Willsson's at three-thirty, where Mickey had tailed Pete; had followed Yard away at five, to his residence; had seen people going in and out of the house, but had not shadowed any of them; had watched the house until three this morning, and had returned to the job at seven; and since then had seen nobody go in or out.

"You'll have to drop this and take a plant on Willsson's," I said. "I hear Whisper Thaler's holingup there, and I'd like an eye kept on him till I make up my mind whether to turn him up for Noonan or not."

Dick nodded and started the engine grinding. I got out and returned to the hotel.

There was a telegram from the Old Man:

SEND BY FIRST MAIL FULL EXPLANATION OF PRESENT
OPERATION AND CIRCUMSTANCES UNDER WHICH YOU
ACCEPTED IT WITH DAILY REPORTS TO DATE

I put the telegram in my pocket and hoped things would keep on breaking fast. To have sent him the dope he wanted at that time would have been the same as sending in my resignation.

I bent a fresh collar around my neck and trotted over to the City Hall.

"Hello," Noonan greeted me. "I was hoping you'd show up. Tried to get you at your hotel but they told me you hadn't been in."

He wasn't looking well this morning, but under his glad-handing he seemed, for a change, genuinely glad to see me.

As I sat down one of his phones rang. He put the receiver to his ear, said, "Yes?" listened for a moment, said, "You better go out there yourself, Mac," and had to make two attempts to get the receiver back on its prong before he succeeded. His face had gone a little doughy, but his voice was almost normal as he told me:

"Lew Yard's been knocked off—shot coming down his front steps just now."

"Any details?" I asked while I cursed myself for having pulled Dick Foley away from Painter Street an hour too soon. That was a tough break.

Noonan shook his head, staring at his lap.

"Shall we go out and look at the remains?" I suggested, getting up.

He neither got up nor looked up.

"No," he said wearily to his lap. "To tell the truth, I don't want to. I don't know as I could stand it just now. I'm getting sick of this killing. It's getting to me—on my nerves, I mean."

I sat down again, considered his low spirits, and asked:

"Who do you guess killed him?"

"God knows," he mumbled. "Everybody's killing everybody. Where's it going to end?"

"Think Reno did it?"

Noonan winced, started to look up at me, changed his mind, and repeated:

"God knows."

I went at him from another angle:

"Anybody knocked off in the battle at the Silver Arrow last night?"

"Only three."

"Who were they?"

"A pair of Johnson-brothers named Blackie Whalen and Put Collings that only got out on bail around five yesterday, and Dutch Jake Wahl, a guerrilla."

"What was it all about?"

"Just a roughhouse, I guess. It seems that Put and Blackie and the others that got out with them were celebrating with a lot of friends, and it wound up in smoke."

"All of them Lew Yard's men?"

"I don't know anything about that," he said.

I got up, said, "Oh, all right," and started for the door.

"Wait," he called. "Don't run off like that. I guess they were."

I came back to my chair. Noonan watched the top of his desk. His face was gray, flabby, damp, like fresh putty.

"Whisper's staying at Willsson's," I told him.

He jerked his head up. His eyes darkened. Then his mouth twitched, and he let his head sag again. His eyes faded.

"I can't go through with it," he mumbled. "I'm sick of this butchering. I can't stand any more of it."

"Sick enough to give up the idea of evening the score for Tim's killing, if it'll make peace?" I asked.

"I am."

"That's what started it," I reminded him. "If you're willing to call it off, it ought to be possible to stop it."

He raised his face and looked at me with eyes that were like a dog's looking at a bone.

"The others ought to be as sick of it as you are," I went on. "Tell them how you feel about it. Have a gettogether and make peace."

"They'd think I was up to some kind of a trick," he objected miserably.

"Have the meeting at Willsson's. Whisper's camping there. You'd be the one risking tricks going there. Are you afraid of that?"

He frowned and asked:

"Will you go with me?"

"If you want me."

"Thanks," he said. "I—I'll try it."

CHAPTER XIX

The Peace Conference

All the other delegates to the peace conference were on hand when Noonan and I arrived at Willsson's home at the appointed time, nine o'clock that night. Everybody nodded to us, but the greetings didn't go any further than that.

Pete the Finn was the only one I hadn't met before. The bootlegger was a bigboned man of fifty with a completely bald head. His forehead was small, his jaws enormous—wide, heavy, bulging with muscle.

We sat around Willsson's library table.

Old Elihu sat at the head. The short-clipped hair on his round pink skull was like silver in the light. His round blue eyes were hard, domineering, under their bushy white brows. His mouth and chin were horizontal lines.

On his right Pete the Finn sat watching everybody with tiny black eyes that never moved. Reno Starkey sat next to the bootlegger. Reno's sallow horse face was as stolidly dull as his eyes.

Max Thaler was tilted back in a chair on Willsson's left. The little gambler's carefully pressed pants legs were carelessly crossed. A cigarette hung from one corner of his tightlipped mouth.

I sat next to Thaler. Noonan sat on my other side.

Elihu Willsson opened the meeting.

He said things couldn't go on the way they were going. We were all sensible men, reasonable men, grown men who had seen enough of the world to know that a man couldn't have everything his own way, no matter who he was. Compromises were things everybody had to make sometimes. To get what he wanted, a man had to give other people what they wanted. He said he was sure that what we all most wanted now was to stop this insane killing. He said he was sure that everything could be frankly discussed and settled in an hour without turning Personville into a slaughter-house.

It wasn't a bad oration.

When it was over there was a moment of silence. Thaler looked past me, at Noonan, as if he expected something of him. The rest of us followed his example, looking at the chief of police.

Noonan's face turned red and he spoke huskily:

"Whisper, I'll forget you killed Tim." He stood up and held out a beefy paw. "Here's my hand on it."

Thaler's thin mouth curved into a vicious smile.

"Your bastard of a brother needed killing, but I didn't kill him," he whispered coldly.

Red became purple in the chief's face.

I said loudly:

"Wait, Noonan. We're going at this wrong. We won't get anywhere unless everybody comes clean. Otherwise we'll all be worse off than before. MacSwain killed Tim, and you know it."

He started at me with dumbfounded eyes. He gaped. He couldn't understand what I had done to him.

I looked at the others, tried to look virtuous as hell, asked:

"That's settled, isn't it? Let's get the rest of the kicks squared." I addressed Pete the Finn: "How do you feel about yesterday's accident to your warehouse and the four men?"

"One hell of an accident," he rumbled.

I explained:

"Noonan didn't know you were using the joint. He went there thinking it empty, just to clear the way for a job in town. Your men shot first, and then he really thought he had stumbled into Thaler's hideout. When he found he'd been stepping in your puddle he lost his head and touched the place off."

Thaler was watching me with a hard small smile in eyes and mouth. Reno was all dull stolidity. Elihu Willsson was leaning toward me, his old eyes sharp and wary. I don't know what Noonan was doing. I couldn't afford to look at him. I was in a good spot if I played my hand right, and in a terrible one if I didn't.

"The men, they get paid for taking chances," Pete the Finn said. "For the other, twenty-five grand will make it right."

Noonan spoke quickly, eagerly:

"All right, Pete, all right, I'll give it to you."

I pushed my lips together to keep from laughing at the panic in his voice.

I could look at him safely now. He was licked, broken, willing to do anything to save his fat neck, or to try to. I looked at him.

He wouldn't look at me. He sat down and looked at nobody. He was busy trying to look as if he didn't expect to be carved apart before he got away from these wolves to whom I had handed him.

I went on with the work, turning to Elihu Willsson:

"Do you want to squawk about your bank being knocked over, or do you like it?"

Max Thaler touched my arm and suggested:

"We could tell better maybe who's entitled to beef if you'd give us what you've got first."

I was glad to.

"Noonan wanted to nail you," I told him, "but he either got word, or expected to get word, from Yard and Willsson here to let you alone. So he thought if he had the bank looted and framed you for it, your backers would ditch you, and let him go after you right. Yard, I understand, was supposed to put his O. K. on all the capers in town. You'd be cutting into his territory, and gyping Willsson. That's how it would look. And that was supposed to make them hot enough that they'd help Noonan cop you. He didn't know you were here.

"Reno and his mob were in the can. Reno was Yard's pup, but he didn't mind crossing up his head-man. He already had the idea that he was about ready to take the burg away from Lew." I turned to Reno and asked: "Isn't that it?"

He looked at me woodenly and said:

"You're telling it."

I continued telling it:

"Noonan fakes a tip that you're at Cedar Hill, and takes all the coppers he can't trust out there with him, even cleaning the traffic detail out of Broadway, so Reno would have a clear road. McGraw and the bulls that are in on the play let Reno and his mob sneak out of the hoosegow, pull the job, and duck back in. Nice thing in alibis. Then they got sprung on bail a couple of hours later.

63   In the card games euchre and 500, the highest card (the jack) in the trump suit is called "the right bower," which is therefore the most powerful card in the deck.

"It looks as if Lew Yard tumbled. He sent Dutch Jake Wahl and some other boys out to the Silver Arrow last night to teach Reno and his pals not to take things in their own hands like that. But Reno got away, and got back to the city. It was either him or Lew then. He made sure which it would be by being in front of Lew's house with a gun when Lew came out this morning. Reno seems to have had the right dope, because I notice that right now he's holding down a chair that would have been Lew Yard's if Lew hadn't been put on ice."

Everybody was sitting very still, as if to call attention to how still they were sitting. Nobody could count on having any friends among those present. It was no time for careless motions on anybody's part.

If what I had said meant anything one way or the other to Reno he didn't show it.

Thaler whispered softly:

"Didn't you skip some of it?"

"You mean the part about Jerry?" I kept on being the life of the party: "I was coming back to that. I don't know whether he got away from the can when you crushed out, and was caught later, or whether he didn't get away, or why. And I don't know how willingly he went along on the bank caper. But he did go along, and he was dropped and left in front of the bank because he was your right bower,[63] and his being killed there would pin the trick to you. He was kept in the car till the getaway was on. Then he was pushed out, and was shot in the back. He was facing the bank, with his back to the car, when he got his."

Thaler looked at Reno and whispered:

"Well?"

Reno looked with dull eyes at Thaler and asked calmly:

"What of it?"

Thaler stood up, said, "Deal me out," and walked to the door.

Pete the Finn stood up, leaning on the table with big bony hands, speaking from deep in his chest:

"Whisper." And when Thaler had stopped and turned to face him: "I'm telling you this. You, Whisper, and all of you. That damn gunwork is out. All of you understand it. You've got no brains to know what is best for yourselves. So I'll tell you. This busting the town open is no good for business. I won't have it any more. You be nice boys or I'll make you.

"I got one army of young fellows that know what to do on any end of a gun. I got to have them in my racket. If I got to use them on you I'll use them on you. You want to play with gunpowder and dynamite? I'll show you what playing is. You like to fight? I'll give you fighting. Mind what I tell you. That's all."

Pete the Finn sat down.

Thaler looked thoughtful for a moment, and went away without saying or showing what he had thought.

His going made the others impatient. None wanted to remain until anybody else had time to accumulate a few guns in the neighborhood.

In a very few minutes Elihu Willsson and I had the library to ourselves.

We sat and looked at one another.

Presently he said:

"How would you like to be chief of police?"

"No. I'm a rotten errand boy."

"I don't mean with this bunch. After we've got rid of them."

"And got another just like them."

"Damn you," he said, "it wouldn't hurt to take a nicer tone to a man old enough to be your father."

"Who curses me and hides behind his age."

Anger brought a vein out blue in his forehead. Then he laughed.

"You're a nasty talking lad," he said, "but I can't say you haven't done what I paid you to do."

"A swell lot of help I've got from you."

"Did you need wet-nursing? I gave you the money and a free hand. That's what you asked for. What more did you want?"

"You old pirate," I said, "I blackmailed you into it, and you played against me all the way till now, when even you can see that they're hell-bent on gobbling each other up. Now you talk about what you did for me."

"Old pirate," he repeated. "Son, if I hadn't been a pirate I'd still be working for the Anaconda[64] for wages, and there'd be no Personville Mining Corporation. You're a damned little woolly lamb yourself, I suppose. I was had, son, where the hair was short. There were things I didn't like—worse things that I didn't know about until tonight—but I was caught and had to bide my time. Why since that Whisper Thaler has been here I've been a prisoner in my own home, a damned hostage!"

"Tough. Where do you stand now?" I demanded. "Are you behind me?"

"If you win."

I got up and said:

"I hope to Christ you get caught with them."

He said:

"I reckon you do, but I won't." He squinted his eyes merrily at me. "I'm financing you. That shows I mean well, don't it? Don't be too hard on me, son, I'm kind of—"

I said, "Go to hell," and walked out.

CHAPTER XX

Laudanum

Dick Foley in his hired car was at the next corner. I had him drive me over to within a block of Dinah Brand's house, and walked the rest of the way.

"You look tired," she said when I had followed her into the living room. "Been working?"

"Attending a peace conference out of which at least a dozen killings ought to grow."

The telephone rang. She answered it and called me.

Reno Starkey's voice:

"I thought maybe you'd like to hear about Noonan being shot to hell and gone when he got out of his heap in front of his house. You never saw anybody that was deader. Must have had thirty pills pumped in him."

"Thanks."

Dinah's big blue eyes asked questions.

"First fruits of the peace conference, plucked by Whisper Thaler," I told her. "Where's the gin?"

"Reno talking, wasn't it?"

"Yeah. He thought I'd like to hear about Poisonville being all out of police chiefs."

"You mean—?"

"Noonan went down tonight, according to Reno. Haven't you got any gin? Or do you like making me ask for it?"

"You know where it is. Been up to some of your cute tricks?"

I went back into the kitchen, opened the top of the refrigerator, and attacked the ice with an ice pick that had a six-inch awl-sharp blade set in a round blue and white handle. The girl stood in the doorway and asked questions. I didn't answer them while I put ice, gin, lemon juice and seltzer together in two glasses.

"What have you been doing?" she demanded as we carried our drinks into the dining room. "You look ghastly."

I put my glass on the table, sat down facing it, and complained:

"This damned burg's getting me. If I don't get away soon I'll be going blood-simple like the natives. There's been what? A dozen and a half murders since I've been here. Donald Willsson; Ike Bush; the four wops and the dick at Cedar Hill; Jerry; Lew Yard; Dutch Jake, Blackie Whalen and Put Collings at the Silver Arrow; Big Nick, the copper I potted; the blond kid Whisper dropped here; Yakima Shorty, old Elihu's prowler; and now Noonan. That's sixteen of them in less than a week, and more coming up."

She frowned at me and said sharply:

"Don't look like that."

I laughed and went on:

"I've arranged a killing or two in my time, when they were necessary. But this is the first time I've ever got the fever. It's this damned burg. You can't go straight here. I got myself tangled at the beginning. When old Elihu ran out on me there was nothing I could do but try to set the boys against each other. I had to swing the job the best way I could. How could I help it if the best way was bound to lead to a lot of killing? The job couldn't be handled any other way without Elihu's backing."

"Well, if you couldn't help it, what's the use of making a lot of fuss over it? Drink your drink."

I drank half of it and felt the urge to talk some more.

"Play with murder enough and it gets you one of two ways. It makes you sick, or you get to like it. It got Noonan the first way. He was green around the gills after Yard was knocked off, all the stomach gone out of him, willing to do anything to make peace. I took him in, suggested that he and the other survivors get together and patch up their differences.

"We had the meeting at Willsson's tonight. It was a nice party. Pretending I was trying to clear away everybody's misunderstandings by coming clean all around, I stripped Noonan naked and threw him to them—him and Reno. That broke up the meeting. Whisper declared himself out. Pete told everybody where they stood. He said battling was bad for his bootlegging racket, and anybody who started anything from then on could expect to have his booze guards turned loose on them. Whisper didn't look impressed. Neither did Reno."

"They wouldn't be," the girl said. "What did you do to Noonan? I mean how did you strip him and Reno?"

"I told the others that he had known all along that MacSwain killed Tim. That was the only lie I told them. Then I told them about the bank stickup being turned by Reno and the chief, with Jerry taken along and dropped on the premises to tie the job to Whisper. I knew that's the way it was if what you told me was right, about Jerry getting out of the car, starting toward the bank and being shot. The hole was in his back. Fitting in with that, McGraw said the last seen of the stickup car was when it turned into King Street. The boys would be returning to the City Hall, to their jail alibi."

"But didn't the bank watchman say he shot Jerry? That's the way it was in the papers."

"He said so, but he'd say anything and believe it. He probably emptied his gun with his eyes shut, and anything that fell was his. Didn't you see Jerry drop?"

"Yes, I did, and he was facing the bank, but it was all too confused for me to see who shot him. There were a lot of men shooting, and—"

"Yeah. They'd see to that. I also advertised the fact—at least, it looks like a fact to me—that Reno plugged Lew Yard. This Reno is a tough egg, isn't he? Noonan went watery, but all they got out of Reno was a 'What of it?' It was all nice and gentlemanly. They were evenly divided—Pete and Whisper against Noonan and Reno. But none of them could count on his partner backing him up if he made a play, and by the time the meeting was over the pairs had been split. Noonan was out of the count, and Reno and Whisper, against each other, had Pete against them. So everybody sat around and behaved and watched everybody else while I juggled death and destruction.

"Whisper was the first to leave, and he seems to have had time to collect some rods in front of Noonan's house by the time the chief reached home. The chief was shot down. If Pete the

65   "Rear" here means enjoyment, a powerful lift, in the sense of "raising up." Later, Dinah offers the Op "an honest to God rear" in the form of a mixture of laudanum and gin.

Finn meant what he said—and he has the look of a man who would—he'll be out after Whisper. Reno was as much to blame for Jerry's death as Noonan, so Whisper ought to be gunning for him. Knowing it, Reno will be out to get Whisper first, and that will set Pete on his trail. Besides that, Reno will likely have his hands full standing off those of the late Lew Yard's underlings who don't fancy Reno as boss. All in all it's one swell dish."

Dinah Brand reached across the table and patted my hand. Her eyes were uneasy. She said:

"It's not your fault, darling. You said yourself that there was nothing else you could do. Finish your drink and we'll have another."

"There was plenty else I could do," I contradicted her. "Old Elihu ran out on me at first simply because these birds had too much on him for him to risk a break unless he was sure they could be wiped out. He couldn't see how I could do it, so he played with them. He's not exactly their brand of cut-throat, and, besides, he thinks the city is his personal property, and he doesn't like the way they've taken it away from him.

"I could have gone to him this afternoon and showed him that I had them ruined. He'd have listened to reason. He'd have come over to my side, have given me the support I needed to swing the play legally. I could have done that. But it's easier to have them killed off, easier and surer, and, now that I'm feeling this way, more satisfying. I don't know how I'm going to come out with the Agency. The Old Man will boil me in oil if he ever finds out what I've been doing. It's this damned town. Poisonville is right. It's poisoned me.

"Look. I sat at Willsson's table tonight and played them like you'd play trout, and got just as much fun out of it. I looked at Noonan and knew he hadn't a chance in a thousand of living another day because of what I had done to him, and I laughed, and felt warm and happy inside. That's not me. I've got hard skin all over what's left of my soul, and after twenty years of messing around with crime I can look at any sort of a murder without seeing anything in it but my bread and butter, the day's work. But this getting a rear[65] out of planning deaths is not natural to me. It's what this place has done to me."

She smiled too softly and spoke too indulgently:

"You exaggerate so, honey. They deserve all they get. I wish you wouldn't look like that. You make me feel creepy."

I grinned, picked up the glasses, and went out to the kitchen for more gin. When I came back she frowned at me over anxious dark eyes and asked:

"Now what did you bring the ice pick in for?"

"To show you how my mind's running. A couple of days ago, if I thought about it at all, it was as a good tool to pry off chunks of ice." I ran a finger down its halffoot of round steel blade to the needle point. "Not a bad thing to pin a man to his clothes with. That's the way I'm betting, on the level. I can't even see a mechanical cigar lighter without thinking of filling one with nitroglycerine for somebody you don't like. There's a piece of copper wire lying in the gutter in front of your house—thin, soft, and just long enough to go around a neck with two ends to hold on. I had one hell of a time to keep from picking it up and stuffing it in my pocket, just in case—"

"You're crazy."

"I know it. That's what I've been telling you. I'm going blood-simple."

"Well, I don't like it. Put that thing back in the kitchen and sit down and be sensible."

I obeyed two-thirds of the order.

"The trouble with you is," she scolded me, "your nerves are shot. You've been through too much excitement in the last few days. Keep it up and you're going to have the heebie-jeebies for fair, a nervous breakdown."

I held up a hand with spread fingers. It was steady enough.

She looked at it and said:

"That doesn't mean anything. It's inside you. Why don't you sneak off for a couple of days' rest? You've got things here so they'll run themselves. Let's go down to Salt Lake. It'll do you good."

"Can't, sister. Somebody's got to stay here to count the dead. Besides, the whole program is based on the present combination of people and events. Our going out of town would change that, and the chances are the whole thing would have to be gone over again."

"Nobody would have to know you were gone, and I've got nothing to do with it."

"Since when?"

She leaned forward, made her eyes small, and asked:

"Now what are you getting at?"

"Nothing. Just wondering how you got to be a disinterested bystander all of a sudden. Forgotten that Donald Willsson was killed because of you, starting the whole thing? Forgotten that it was the dope you gave me on Whisper that kept the job from petering out in the middle?"

"You know just as well as I do that none of that was my fault," she said indignantly. "And it's all past, anyway. You're just bringing it up because you're in a rotten humor and want to argue."

"It wasn't past last night, when you were scared stiff Whisper was going to kill you."

"Will you stop talking about killing!"

"Young Albury once told me Bill Quint had threatened to kill you," I said.

"Stop it."

"You seem to have a gift for stirring up murderous notions in your boy friends. There's Albury waiting trial for killing Willsson. There's Whisper who's got you shivering in corners. Even I haven't escaped your influence. Look at the way I've turned. And I've always had a private notion that Dan Rolff's going to have a try at you some day."

"Dan! You're crazy. Why, I—"

"Yeah. He was a lunger and down and out, and you took him in. You gave him a home and all the laudanum he wants. You use him for errand boy, you slap his face in front of me, and slap him around in front of others. He's in love with you. One of these mornings you're going to wake up and find he's whittled your neck away."

She shivered, got up and laughed.

"I'm glad one of us knows what you're talking about, if you do," she said as she carried our empty glasses through the kitchen door.

I lit a cigarette and wondered why I felt the way I did, wondered if I were getting psychic, wondered whether there was anything in this presentiment business or whether my nerves were just ragged.

"The next best thing for you to do if you won't go away," the girl advised me when she returned with full glasses, "is to get plastered and forget everything for a few hours. I put a double slug of gin in yours. You need it."

"It's not me," I said, wondering why I was saying it, but somehow enjoying it. "It's you. Every time I mention killing, you jump on me. You're a woman. You think if nothing's said about it, maybe none of the God only knows how many people in town who might want to will kill you. That's silly. Nothing we say or don't say is going to make Whisper, for instance—"

"Please, please stop! I am silly. I am afraid of the words. I'm afraid of him. I—Oh, why didn't you put him out of the way when I asked you?"

"Sorry," I said, meaning it.

"Do you think he—?"

"I don't know," I told her, "and I reckon you're right. There's no use talking about it. The thing to do is drink, though there doesn't seem to be much body to this gin."

"That's you, not the gin. Do you want an honest to God rear?"

"I'd drink nitroglycerine tonight."

"That's just about what you're going to get," she promised me.

She rattled bottles in the kitchen and brought me in a glass of what looked like the stuff we had been drinking. I sniffed at it and said:

"Some of Dan's laudanum, huh? He still in the hospital?"

"Yes. I think his skull is fractured. There's your kick, mister, if that's what you want."

I put the doped gin down my throat. Presently I felt more comfortable. Time went by as we drank and talked in a world that was rosy, cheerful, and full of fellowship and peace on earth.

Dinah stuck to gin. I tried that for a while too, and then had another gin and laudanum.

For a while after that I played a game, trying to hold my eyes open as if I were awake, even though I couldn't see anything out of them. When the trick wouldn't fool her any more I gave it up.

The last thing I remembered was her helping me on to the living room Chesterfield.

CHAPTER XXI

The Seventeenth Murder

I dreamed I was sitting on a bench, in Baltimore, facing the tumbling fountain in Harlem Park, beside a woman who wore a veil. I had come there with her. She was somebody I knew well. But I had suddenly forgotten who she was. I couldn't see her face because of the long black veil.

Harlem Park fountain, ca. 1900, judging by the men's clothes.

I thought that if I said something to her I would recognize her voice when she answered. But I was very embarrassed and was a long time finding anything to say. Finally I asked her if she knew a man named Carroll T. Harris.

She answered me, but the roar and swish of the tumbling fountain smothered her voice, and I could hear nothing.

Fire engines went out Edmondson Avenue. She left me to run after them. As she ran she cried, "Fire! Fire!" I recognized her voice then and knew who she was, and knew she was someone important to me. I ran after her, but it was too late. She and the fire engines were gone.

I walked streets hunting for her, half the streets in the United States, Gay Street and Mount Royal Avenue in Baltimore, Colfax Avenue in Denver, Aetna Road and St. Clair Avenue in Cleveland, McKinney Avenue in Dallas, Lemartine and Cornell and Amory Streets in Boston, Berry Boulevard in Louisville, Lexington Avenue in New York, until I came to Victoria Street in Jacksonville, where I heard her voice again, though I still could not see her.

I walked more streets, listening to her voice. She was calling a name, not mine, one strange to me, but no matter how fast I walked or in what direction, I could get no nearer her voice. It was the same distance from me in the street that runs past the Federal Building in El Paso as in Detroit's Grand Circus Park. Then the voice stopped.

Tired and discouraged, I went into the lobby of the hotel that faces the railroad station in Rocky Mount, North Carolina, to rest.[66] While I sat there a train came in. She got off it and came into the lobby, over to me, and began kissing me. I was very uncomfortable because everybody stood around looking at us and laughing.

That dream ended there.

I dreamed I was in a strange city hunting for a man I hated. I had an open knife in my pocket and meant to kill him with it when I found him. It was Sunday morning. Church bells were ringing, crowds of people were in the streets, going to and from church. I walked almost as far as in the first dream, but always in this same strange city.

Then the man I was after yelled at me, and I saw him. He was a small brown man who wore an immense sombrero. He was standing on the steps of a tall building on the far side of a wide plaza, laughing at me. Between us, the plaza was crowded with people, packed shoulder to shoulder.

Keeping one hand on the open knife in my pocket, I ran toward the little brown man, running on the heads and shoulders of the people in the plaza. The heads and shoulders were of unequal heights and not evenly spaced. I slipped and floundered over them.

66 The hotel would have been the Ricks Hotel (or New Ricks Hotel), across the street from the station. The date of the postcard showing the station is probably newer than the hotel postcard, which is from the period 1900–1920.

New Ricks Hotel, across the street from the Rocky Mount, North Carolina, train station—of which the Op dreamed.

The Rocky Mount, North Carolina, train station ca. 1920.

The little brown man stood on the steps and laughed until I had almost reached him. Then he ran into the tall building. I chased him up miles of spiral stairway, always just an inch more than a hand's reach behind him. We came to the roof. He ran straight across to the edge and jumped just as one of my hands touched him.

His shoulder slid out of my fingers. My hand knocked his sombrero off, and closed on his head. It was a smooth hard round head no larger than a large egg. My fingers went all the way around it. Squeezing his head in one hand, I tried to bring the knife out of my pocket with the other—and realized that I had gone off the edge of the roof with him. We dropped giddily down toward the millions of upturned faces in the plaza, miles down.

∞

I opened my eyes in the dull light of morning sun filtered through drawn blinds.

I was lying face down on the dining room floor, my head resting on my left forearm. My right arm was stretched straight out. My right hand held the round blue and white handle of Dinah Brand's ice pick. The pick's six-inch needle-sharp blade was buried in Dinah Brand's left breast.

She was lying on her back, dead. Her long muscular legs were stretched out toward the kitchen door. There was a run down the front of her right stocking.

Slowly, gently, as if afraid of awakening her, I let go the ice pick, drew in my arm, and got up.

My eyes burned. My throat and mouth were hot, woolly. I went into the kitchen, found a bottle of gin, tilted it to my mouth, and kept it there until I had to breathe. The kitchen clock said seven-forty-one.

With the gin in me I returned to the dining room, switched on the lights, and looked at the dead girl.

Not much blood was in sight: a spot the size of a silver dollar around the hole the ice pick made in her blue silk dress. There was a bruise on her right cheek, just under the cheek bone. Another bruise, fingermade, was on her right wrist. Her hands were empty. I moved her enough to see that nothing was under her.

I examined the room. So far as I could tell, nothing had been changed in it. I went back to the kitchen and found no recognizable changes there.

The spring lock on the back door was fastened, and had no marks to show it had been monkeyed with. I went to the front door and failed to find any marks on it. I went through the house from top to bottom, and learned nothing. The windows were all right. The girl's jewelry, on her dressing table (except the two diamond rings on her hands), and four hundred odd dollars in her handbag, on a bedroom chair, were undisturbed.

In the dining room again, I knelt beside the dead girl and used my handkerchief to wipe the ice pick handle clean of any prints my fingers had left on it. I did the same to glasses, bottles, doors, light buttons, and the pieces of furniture I had touched, or was likely to have touched.

Then I washed my hands, examined my clothes for blood, made sure I was leaving none of my property behind, and went to the front door. I opened it, wiped the inner knob, closed it behind me, wiped the outer knob, and went away.

⌘

From a drug store in upper Broadway I telephoned Dick Foley and asked him to come over to my hotel. He arrived a few minutes after I got there.

"Dinah Brand was killed in her house last night or early this morning," I told him. "Stabbed with an ice pick. The police don't know it yet. I've told you enough about her for you to know that there are any number of people who might have had reason for killing her. There are three I want looked up first—Whisper, Dan Rolff and Bill Quint, the radical fellow. You've got their descriptions. Rolff is in the hospital with a dented skull. I don't know which hospital. Try the City first. Get hold of Mickey Linehan—he's still camped on Pete the Finn's trail—and have him let Pete rest while he gives you a hand on this. Find out where those three birds were last night. And time means something."

The little Canadian op had been watching me curiously while I talked. Now he started to say something, changed his mind, grunted, "Righto," and departed.

I went out to look for Reno Starkey. After an hour of searching I located him, by telephone, in a Ronney Street rooming house.

"By yourself?" he asked when I had said I wanted to see him.

"Yeah."

He said I could come out, and told me how to get there. I took a taxi. It was a dingy two-story house near the edge of town.

A couple of men loitered in front of a grocer's on the corner above. Another pair sat on the low wooden steps of the house down at the next corner. None of the four was conspicuously refined in appearance.

When I rang the bell two men opened the door. They weren't so mild looking either.

I was taken upstairs to a front room where Reno, collarless and in shirt-sleeves and vest, sat tilted back in a chair with his feet on the window sill.

He nodded his sallow horse face and said:

"Pull a chair over."

The men who had brought me up went away, closing the door. I sat down and said:

"I want an alibi. Dinah Brand was killed last night after I left her. There's no chance of my being copped for it, but with Noonan dead I don't know how I'm hitched up with the department. I don't want to give them any openings to even try to hang anything on me. If I've got to I can prove where I was last night, but you can save me a lot of trouble if you will."

Reno looked at me with dull eyes and asked:

"Why pick on me?"

"You phoned me there last night. You're the only person who knows I was there the first part of the night. I'd have to fix it with you even if I got the alibi somewhere else, wouldn't I?"

He asked:

"You didn't croak her, did you?"

I said, "No," casually.

He stared out the window a little while before he spoke. He asked:

"What made you think I'd give you the lift? Do I owe you anything for what you done to me at Willsson's last night?"

I said:

"I didn't hurt you any. The news was half-out anyhow. Whisper knew enough to guess the rest. I only gave you a show-down. What do you care? You can take care of yourself."

"I aim to try," he agreed. "All right. You was at the Tanner House in Tanner. That's a little burg twenty-thirty miles up the hill. You went up there after you left Willsson's and stayed till morning. A guy named Ricker that hangs around Murry's with a hire heap drove you up and back. You ought to know what you was doing up there. Give me your sig and I'll have it put on the register."

"Thanks," I said as I unscrewed my fountain pen.

"Don't say them. I'm doing this because I need all the friends I can get. When the time comes that you sit in with me and Whisper and Pete, I don't expect the sour end of it."

"You won't get it," I promised. "Who's going to be chief of police?"

"McGraw's acting chief. He'll likely cinch it."

"How'll he play?"

"With the Finn. Rough stuff will hurt his shop just like it does Pete's. It'll have to be hurt some. I'd be a swell mutt to sit still while a guy like Whisper is on the loose. It's me or him. Think he croaked the broad?"

"He had reason enough," I said as I gave him the slip of paper on which I had written my name. "She double-crossed him, sold him out, plenty."

"You and her was kind of thick, wasn't you?" he asked.

I let the question alone, lighting a cigarette. Reno waited a while and then said:

"You better hunt up Ricker and let him get a look at you so's he'll know how to describe you if he's asked."

A long-legged youngster of twenty-two or so with a thin freckled face around reckless eyes opened the door and came into the room. Reno introduced him to me as Hank O'Marra. I stood up to shake his hand, and then asked Reno:

"Can I reach you here if I need to?"

"Know Peak Murry?"

"I've met him, and I know his joint."

"Anything you give him will get to me," he said. "We're getting out of here. It's not so good. That Tanner lay[67] is all set."

"Right. Thanks." I went out of the house.

67   A "lay" is a plan or scheme.

CHAPTER XXII

The Ice Pick

Downtown, I went first to police headquarters. McGraw was holding down the chief's desk. His blond-lashed eyes looked suspiciously at me, and the lines in his leathery face were even deeper and sourer than usual.

"When'd you see Dinah Brand last?" he asked without any preliminaries, not even a nod. His voice rasped disagreeably through his bony nose.

"Ten-forty last night, or thereabout," I said. "Why?"

"Where?"

"Her house."

"How long were you there?"

"Why?"

"Ten minutes, maybe fifteen."

"Why?"

"Why what?"

"Why didn't you stay any longer than that?"

"What," I asked, sitting down in the chair he hadn't offered me, "makes it any of your business?"

He glared at me while he filled his lungs so he could yell, "Murder!" in my face.

I laughed and said:

"You don't think she had anything to do with Noonan's killing?"

I wanted a cigarette, but cigarettes were too well known as first aids to the nervous for me to take a chance on one just then.

McGraw was trying to look through my eyes. I let him look, having all sorts of confidence in my belief that, like a lot of people, I looked most honest when I was lying. Presently he gave up the eye-study and asked:

"Why not?"

That was weak enough. I said, "All right, why not?" indifferently, offered him a cigarette, and took one myself. Then I added: "My guess is that Whisper did it."

"Was he there?" For once McGraw cheated his nose, snapping the words off his teeth.

"Was he where?"

"At Brand's?"

"No," I said, wrinkling my forehead. "Why should he be—if he was off killing Noonan?"

"Damn Noonan!" the acting chief exclaimed irritably. "What do you keep dragging him in for?"

I tried to look at him as if I thought him crazy.

He said:

"Dinah Brand was murdered last night."

I said: "Yeah?"

"Now will you answer my questions?"

"Of course. I was at Willsson's with Noonan and the others. After I left there, around ten-thirty, I dropped in at her house to tell her I had to go up to Tanner. I had a half-way date with her. I stayed there about ten minutes, long enough to have a drink. There was nobody else there, unless they were hiding. When was she killed? And how?"

McGraw told me he had sent a pair of his dicks—Shepp and Vanaman—to see the girl that morning, to see how much help she could and would give the department in copping Whisper for Noonan's murder. The dicks got to her house at nine-thirty. The front door was ajar. Nobody answered their ringing. They went in and found the girl lying on her back in the dining room, dead, with a stab wound in her left breast.

The doctor who examined the body said she had been killed with a slender, round, pointed blade about six inches in length, at about three o'clock in the morning. Bureaus, closets, trunks, and so on, had apparently been skilfully and thoroughly ransacked. There was no money in the girl's handbag, or elsewhere in the house. The jewel case on her dressing table was empty. Two diamond rings were on her fingers.

The police hadn't found the weapon with which she had been stabbed. The fingerprint experts hadn't turned up anything they could use. Neither doors nor windows seemed to have been forced. The kitchen showed that the girl had been drinking with a guest or guests.

"Six inches, round, slim, pointed," I repeated the weapon's description. "That sounds like her ice pick."

McGraw reached for the phone and told somebody to send Shepp and Vanaman in. Shepp was a stoop-shouldered tall man whose wide mouth had a grimly honest look that probably came from bad teeth. The other detective was short, stocky, with purplish veins in his nose and hardly any neck.

McGraw introduced us and asked them about the ice pick. They had not seen it, were positive it hadn't been there. They wouldn't have overlooked an article of its sort.

"Was it there last night?" McGraw asked me.

"I stood beside her while she chipped off pieces of ice with it."

I described it. McGraw told the dicks to search her house again, and then to try to find the pick in the vicinity of the house.

"You knew her," he said when Shepp and Vanaman had gone. "What's your slant on it?"

"Too new for me to have one," I dodged the question. "Give me an hour or two to think it over. What do you think?"

He fell back into sourness, growling, "How the hell do I know?"

But the fact that he let me go away without asking me any more questions told me he had already made up his mind that Whisper had killed the girl.

I wondered if the little gambler had done it, or if this was another of the wrong raps that Poisonville police chiefs liked to hang on him. It didn't seem to make much difference now. It was a cinch he had—personally or by deputy—put Noonan out, and they could only hang him once.

⌒∞⌒

There were a lot of men in the corridor when I left McGraw. Some of these men were quite young—just kids—quite a few were foreigners, and most of them were every bit as tough looking as any men should be.

Near the street door I met Donner, one of the coppers who had been on the Cedar Hill expedition.

"Hello," I greeted him. "What's the mob? Emptying the can to make room for more?"

"Them's our new specials," he told me, speaking as if he didn't think much of them. "We're going to have a argumented force."[68]

"Congratulations," I said and went on out.

In his pool room I found Peak Murry sitting at a desk behind the cigar counter talking to three men. I sat down on the other side of the room and watched two kids knock balls around. In a few minutes the lanky proprietor came over to me.

"If you see Reno some time," I told him, "you might let him know that Pete the Finn's having his mob sworn in as special coppers."

"I might," Murry agreed.

❧

Mickey Linehan was sitting in the lobby when I got back to my hotel. He followed me up to my room, and reported:

"Your Dan Rolff pulled a sneak from the hospital somewhere after midnight last night. The croakers[69] are kind of steamed up about it. Seems they were figuring on pulling a lot of little pieces of bone out of his brain this morning. But him and his duds were gone. We haven't got a line on Whisper yet. Dick's out now trying to place Bill Quint. What's what on this girl's carving? Dick tells me you got it before the coppers."

"It—"

The telephone bell rang.

A man's voice, carefully oratorical, spoke my name with a question mark after it.

I said: "Yeah."

The voice said:

"This is Mr. Charles Proctor Dawn speaking. I think you will find it well worth your while to appear at my offices at your earliest convenience."

68 The inarticulate Donner means an "augmented" force.

69 Doctors.

"Will I? Who are you?"

"Mr. Charles Proctor Dawn, attorney-at-law. My suite is in the Rutledge Block, 310 Green Street. I think you will find it well—"

"Mind telling me part of what it's about?" I asked.

"There are affairs best not discussed over the telephone. I think you will find—"

"All right," I interrupted him again. "I'll be around to see you this afternoon if I get a chance."

"You will find it very, very advisable," he assured me.

I hung up on that.

Mickey said:

"You were going to give me the what's what on the Brand slaughter."

I said:

"I wasn't. I started to say it oughtn't to be hard to trace Rolff—running around with a fractured skull and probably a lot of bandages. Suppose you try it. Give Hurricane Street a play first."

Mickey grinned all the way across his comedian's red face, said, "Don't tell me anything that's going on—I'm only working with you," picked up his hat, and left me.

I spread myself on the bed, smoked cigarettes end to end, and thought about last night—my frame of mind, my passing out, my dreams, and the situation into which I woke. The thinking was unpleasant enough to make me glad when it was interrupted.

Fingernails scratched the outside of my door. I opened the door.

The man who stood there was a stranger to me. He was young, thin, and gaudily dressed. He had heavy eyebrows and a small mustache that were coalblack against a very pale, nervous, but not timid, face.

"I'm Ted Wright," he said, holding out a hand as if I were glad to meet him. "I guess you've heard Whisper talk about me."

I gave him my hand, let him in, closed the door, and asked:

"You're a friend of Whisper's?"

"You bet." He held up two thin fingers pressed tightly together. "Just like that, me and him."

I didn't say anything. He looked around the room, smiled nervously, crossed to the open bathroom door, peeped in, came back to me, rubbed his lips with his tongue, and made his proposition:

"I'll knock him off for you for half a grand."

"Whisper?"

"Yep, and it's dirt cheap."

"Why do I want him killed?" I asked.

"He un-womaned you, didn't he?"

"Yeah?"

"You ain't that dumb."

A notion stirred in my noodle. To give it time to crawl around I said: "Sit down. This needs talking over."

"It don't need nothing," he said, looking at me sharply, not moving toward either chair. "You either want him knocked off or you don't."

"Then I don't."

He said something I didn't catch, down in his throat, and turned to the door. I got between him and it. He stopped, his eyes fidgeting.

I said:

"So Whisper's dead?"

He stepped back and put a hand behind him. I poked his jaw, leaning my hundred and ninety pounds on the poke.

He got his legs crossed and went down.

I pulled him up by the wrists, yanked his face close to mine, and growled:

"Come through. What's the racket?"

"I ain't done nothing to you."

"Let me catch you. Who got Whisper?"

"I don't know nothing a—"

I let go of one of his wrists, slapped his face with my open hand, caught his wrist again, and tried my luck at crunching both of them while I repeated:

"Who got Whisper?"

"Dan Rolff," he whined. "He walked up to him and stuck him with the same skewer Whisper had used on the twist. That's right."

"How do you know it was the one Whisper killed the girl with?"

"Dan said so."

An old expression for a train.

"What did Whisper say?"

"Nothing. He looked funny as hell, standing there with the butt of the sticker sticking out his side. Then he flashes the rod and puts two pills in Dan just like one, and the both of them go down together, cracking heads, Dan's all bloody through the bandages."

"And then what?"

"Then nothing. I roll them over, and they're a pair of stiffs. Every word I'm telling you is gospel."

"Who else was there?"

"Nobody else. Whisper was hiding out, with only me to go between him and the mob. He killed Noonan hisself, and he didn't want to have to trust nobody for a couple of days, till he could see what was what, excepting me."

"So you, being a smart boy, thought you could run around to his enemies and pick up a little dough for killing him after he was dead?"

"I was clean, and this won't be no place for Whisper's pals when the word gets out that he's croaked," Wright whined. "I had to raise a get-away stake."

"How'd you make out so far?"

"I got a century from Pete and a century and a half from Peak Murry—for Reno—with more promised from both when I turn the trick." The whine changed into boasting as he talked. "I bet you I could get McGraw to come across too, and I thought you'd kick in with something."

"They must be high in the air to toss dough at a woozy racket like that."

"I don't know," he said superiorly. "It ain't such a lousy one at that." He became humble again. "Give me a chance, chief. Don't gum it on me. I'll give you fifty bucks now and a split of whatever I get from McGraw if you'll keep your clam shut till I can put it over and grab a rattler."[70]

"Nobody but you knows where Whisper is?"

"Nobody else, except Dan, that's as dead as he is."

"Where are they?"

"The old Redman warehouse down on Porter Street. In the back, upstairs, Whisper had a room fixed up with a bed, stove, and some grub. Give me a chance. Fifty bucks now and a cut on the rest."

I let go of his arm and said:

"I don't want the dough, but go ahead. I'll lay off for a couple of hours. That ought to be long enough."

"Thanks, chief. Thanks, thanks," and he hurried away from me.

⌘

I put on my coat and hat, went out, found Green Street and the Rutledge Block. It was a wooden building a long while past any prime it might ever have had. Mr. Charles Proctor Dawn's establishment was on the second floor. There was no elevator. I climbed a worn and rickety flight of wooden steps.

The lawyer had two rooms, both dingy, smelly, and poorly lighted. I waited in the outer one while a clerk who went well with the rooms carried my name in to the lawyer. Half a minute later the clerk opened the door and beckoned me in.

Mr. Charles Proctor Dawn was a little fat man of fifty-something. He had prying triangular eyes of a very light color, a short fleshy nose, and a fleshier mouth whose greediness was only partly hidden between a ragged gray mustache and a ragged gray Vandyke beard. His clothes were dark and unclean looking without actually being dirty.

He didn't get up from his desk, and throughout my visit he kept his right hand on the edge of a desk drawer that was some six inches open.

He said:

"Ah, my dear sir, I am extremely gratified to find that you had the good judgment to recognize the value of my counsel."

His voice was even more oratorical than it had been over the wire.

I didn't say anything.

Nodding his whiskers as if my not saying anything was another exhibition of good judgment, he continued:

"I may say, in all justice, that you will find it the invariable part of sound judgment to follow the dictates of my counsel in all cases. I may say this, my dear sir, without false modesty, appreciating with both fitting humility and a deep sense of true and lasting values, my responsibilities as well as my prerogatives as a—and why should I stoop to conceal the fact that there are those who feel justified in preferring to substitute the definite article for the indefinite?—recognized and accepted leader of the bar in this thriving state."

He knew a lot of sentences like those, and he didn't mind using them on me. Finally he got along to:

"Thus, that conduct which in a minor practitioner might seem irregular, becomes, when he who exercises it occupies such indisputable prominence in his community—and, I might say, not merely the immediate community—as serves to place him above fear of reproach, simply that greater ethic which scorns the pettier conventionalities when confronted with an opportunity to serve mankind through one of its individual representatives. Therefore, my dear sir, I have not hesitated to brush aside scornfully all trivial considerations of accepted precedent, to summon you, to say to you frankly and candidly, my dear sir, that your interests will best be served by and through retaining me as your legal representative."

I asked:

"What'll it cost?"

"That," he said loftily, "is of but secondary importance. However, it is a detail which has its deserved place in our relationship, and must be not overlooked or neglected. We shall say, a thousand dollars now. Later, no doubt—"

He ruffled his whiskers and didn't finish the sentence.

I said I hadn't, of course, that much money on me.

"Naturally, my dear sir. Naturally. But that is of not the least importance in any degree. None whatever. Any time will do for that, any time up to ten o'clock tomorrow morning."

"At ten tomorrow," I agreed. "Now I'd like to know why I'm supposed to need legal representatives."

He made an indignant face.

"My dear sir, this is no matter for jesting, of that I assure you."

I explained that I hadn't been joking, that I really was puzzled.

He cleared his throat, frowned more or less importantly, said:

"It may well be, my dear sir, that you do not fully comprehend the peril that surrounds you, but it is indubitably preposterous that you should expect me to suppose that you are without any inkling of the difficulties—the legal difficulties, my dear sir—with which you are about to be confronted, growing, as they do, out of occurrences that took place at no more remote time than last night, my dear sir, last night. However, there is no time to go into that now.

I have a pressing appointment with Judge Leffner. On the morrow I shall be glad to go more thoroughly into each least ramification of the situation—and I assure you they are many—with you. I shall expect you at ten tomorrow morning."

I promised to be there, and went out. I spent the evening in my room, drinking unpleasant whiskey, thinking unpleasant thoughts, and waiting for reports that didn't come from Mickey and Dick. I went to sleep at midnight.

CHAPTER XXIII

Mr. Charles Proctor Dawn

I was half dressed the next morning when Dick Foley came in. He reported, in his word-saving manner, that Bill Quint had checked out of the Miners' Hotel at noon the previous day, leaving no forwarding address.

A train left Personville for Ogden at twelve-thirty-five. Dick had wired the Continental's Salt Lake branch to send a man up to Ogden to try to trace Quint.

"We can't pass up any leads," I said, "but I don't think Quint's the man we want. She gave him the air long ago. If he had meant to do anything about it he would have done it before this. My guess is that when he heard she had been killed he decided to duck, being a discarded lover who had threatened her."

Dick nodded and said:

"Gun play out the road last night. Hijacking. Four trucks of hooch nailed, burned."

That sounded like Reno Starkey's answer to the news that the big bootlegger's mob had been sworn in as special coppers.

Mickey Linehan arrived by the time I had finished dressing.

"Dan Rolff was at the house, all right," he reported. "The Greek grocer on the corner saw him come out around nine yesterday morning. He went down the street wobbling and talking to himself. The Greek thought he was drunk."

"Howcome the Greek didn't tell the police? Or did he?"

"Wasn't asked. A swell department this burg's got. What do we do: find him for them and turn him in with the job all tacked up?"

"McGraw has decided Whisper killed her," I said, "and he's not bothering himself with any leads that don't lead that way. Unless he came back later for the ice pick, Rolff didn't turn the trick. She was killed at three in the morning. Rolff wasn't there at eight-thirty, and the pick was still sticking in her. It was—"

Dick Foley came over to stand in front of me and ask:

"How do you know?"

I didn't like the way he looked or the way he spoke. I said:

"You know because I'm telling you."

Dick didn't say anything. Mickey grinned his half-wit's grin and asked:

"Where do we go from here? Let's get this thing polished off."

"I've got a date for ten," I told them. "Hang around the hotel till I get back. Whisper and Rolff are probably dead—so we won't have to hunt for them." I scowled at Dick and said: "I was told that. I didn't kill either of them."

The little Canadian nodded without lowering his eyes from mine.

I ate breakfast alone, and then set out for the lawyer's office.

Turning off King Street, I saw Hank O'Marra's freckled face in an automobile that was going up Green Street. He was sitting beside a man I didn't know. The longlegged youngster waved an arm at me and stopped the car. I went over to him.

He said:

"Reno wants to see you."

"Where will I find him?"

"Jump in."

"I can't go now," I said. "Probably not till afternoon."

"See Peak when you're ready."

I said I would. O'Marra and his companion drove on up Green Street. I walked half a block south to the Rutledge Block.

With a foot on the first of the rickety steps that led up to the lawyer's floor, I stopped to look at something.

It was barely visible back in a dim corner of the first floor. It was a shoe. It was lying in a position that empty shoes don't lie in.

I took my foot off the step and went toward the shoe. Now I could see an ankle and the cuff of a black pantsleg above the shoe-top.

That prepared me for what I found.

I found Mr. Charles Proctor Dawn huddled among two brooms, a mop and a bucket, in a little alcove formed by the back of the stairs and a corner of the wall. His Vandyke beard was red with blood from a cut that ran diagonally across his forehead. His head was twisted sidewise and backward at an angle that could only be managed with a broken neck.

I quoted Noonan's, "What's got to be done has got to be done," to myself, and, gingerly pulling one side of the dead man's coat out of the way, emptied his inside coat pocket, transferring a black book and a sheaf of papers to my own pocket. In two of his other pockets I found nothing I wanted. The rest of his pockets couldn't be got at without moving him, and I didn't care to do that.

❧

Five minutes later I was back in the hotel, going in through a side door, to avoid Dick and Mickey in the lobby, and walking up to the mezzanine to take an elevator.

In my room I sat down and examined my loot.

I took the book first, a small imitation-leather memoranda book of the sort that sells for not much money in any stationery store. It held some fragmentary notes that meant nothing to me, and thirty-some names and addresses that meant as little, with one exception:

> *Helen Albury*
> *1229A Hurricane St.*

That was interesting because, first, a young man named Robert Albury was in prison, having confessed that he shot and killed Donald Willsson in a fit of jealousy aroused by Willsson's supposed success with Dinah Brand; and, second, Dinah Brand had lived, and had been murdered, at 1232 Hurricane Street, across the street from 1229A.

I did not find my name in the book.

I put the book aside and began unfolding and reading the papers I had taken with it. Here too I had to wade through a lot that didn't mean anything to find something that did.

This find was a group of four letters held together by a rubber band.

The letters were in slitted envelopes that had postmarks dated a week apart, on the average. The latest was a little more than six months old. The letters were addressed to Dinah Brand. The first—that is, the earliest—wasn't so bad, for a love letter. The second was a bit goofier. The third and fourth were swell examples of how silly an ardent and unsuccessful wooer can be, especially if he's getting on in years. The four letters were signed by Elihu Willsson.

I had not found anything to tell me definitely why Mr. Charles Proctor Dawn had thought he could blackmail me out of a thousand dollars, but I had found plenty to think about. I encouraged my brain with two Fatimas, and then went downstairs.

"Go out and see what you can raise on a lawyer named Charles Proctor Dawn," I told Mickey. "He's got offices in Green Street. Stay away from them. Don't put in a lot of time on him. I just want a rough line quick."

I told Dick to give me a five-minute start and then follow me out to the neighborhood of 1229A Hurricane Street.

∞

1229A was the upper flat in a two-story building almost directly opposite Dinah's house. 1229 was divided into two flats, with a private entrance for each. I rang the bell at the one I wanted.

The door was opened by a thin girl of eighteen or nineteen with dark eyes set close together in a shiny yellowish face under short-cut brown hair that looked damp.

She opened the door, made a choked, frightened sound in her throat, and backed away from me, holding both hands to her open mouth.

"Miss Helen Albury?" I asked.

She shook her head violently from side to side. There was no truthfulness in it. Her eyes were crazy.

I said: "I'd like to come in and talk to you a few minutes," going in as I spoke, closing the door behind me.

She didn't say anything. She went up the steps in front of me, her head twisted around so she could watch me with her scary eyes.

We went into a scantily furnished living room. Dinah's house could be seen from its windows.

The girl stood in the center of the floor, her hands still to her mouth.

I wasted time and words trying to convince her that I was harmless. It was no good. Everything I said seemed to increase her panic. It was a damned nuisance. I quit trying, and got down to business.

"You are Robert Albury's sister?" I asked.

No reply, nothing but the senseless look of utter fear.

I said:

"After he was arrested for killing Donald Willsson you took this flat so you could watch her. What for?"

Not a word from her. I had to supply my own answer:

"Revenge. You blamed Dinah Brand for your brother's trouble. You watched for your chance. It came the night before last. You sneaked into her house, found her drunk, stabbed her with the ice pick you found there."

She didn't say anything. I hadn't succeeded in jolting the blankness out of her frightened face. I said:

"Dawn helped you, engineered it for you. He wanted Elihu Willsson's letters. Who was the man he sent to get them, the man who did the actual killing? Who was he?"

That got me nothing. No change in her expression, or lack of expression. No word. I thought I would like to spank her. I said:

"I've given you your chance to talk. I'm willing to listen to your side of the story. But suit yourself."

She suited herself by keeping quiet. I gave it up. I was afraid of her, afraid she would do something even crazier than her silence if I pressed her further. I went out of the flat not sure that she had understood a single word I had said.

At the corner I told Dick Foley:

"There's a girl in there, Helen Albury, eighteen, five six, skinny, not more than a hundred, if that, eyes close together, brown, yellow skin, brown short hair, straight, got on a gray suit now. Tail her. If she cuts up on you throw her in the can. Be careful—she's crazy as a bedbug."

⸎

I set out for Peak Murry's dump, to locate Reno and see what he wanted. Half a block from my destination I stepped into an office building doorway to look the situation over.

A police patrol wagon stood in front of Murry's. Men were being led, dragged, carried, from pool room to wagon. The leaders, draggers, and carriers did not look like regular coppers. They were, I supposed, Pete the Finn's crew, now special officers. Pete, with McGraw's help, apparently was making good his threat to give Whisper and Reno all the war they wanted.

While I watched, an ambulance arrived, was loaded, and drove away. I was too far away to recognize anybody or any bodies. When the height of the excitement seemed past I circled a couple of blocks and returned to my hotel.

Mickey Linehan was there with information about Mr. Charles Proctor Dawn.

"He's the guy that the joke was wrote about: 'Is he a criminal lawyer?' 'Yes, very.' This fellow Albury that you nailed, some of his family hired this bird Dawn to defend him. Albury wouldn't have anything to do with him when Dawn came to see him. This three-named shyster nearly went over himself last year, on a blackmail rap, something to do with a parson named Hill, but squirmed out of it. Got some property out on Libert Street, wherever that is. Want me to keep digging?"

"That'll do. We'll stick around till we hear from Dick."

Mickey yawned and said that was all right with him, never being one that had to run around a lot to keep his blood circulating, and asked if I knew we were getting nationally famous.

I asked him what he meant by that.

"I just ran into Tommy Robins," he said. "The Consolidated Press sent him here to cover the doings. He tells me some of the other press associations and a big-city paper or two are sending in special correspondents, beginning to play our troubles up."

I was making one of my favorite complaints—that newspapers were good for nothing except to hash things up so nobody could unhash them—when I heard a boy chanting my name. For a dime he told me I was wanted on the phone.

Dick Foley:

"She showed right away. To 310 Green Street. Full of coppers. Mouthpiece named Dawn killed. Police took her to the Hall."

"She still there?"

"Yes, in the chief's office."

"Stick, and get anything you pick up to me quick."

I went back to Mickey Linehan and gave him my room key and instructions:

"Camp in my room. Take anything that comes for me and pass it on. I'll be at the Shannon around the corner, registered as J. W. Clark. Tell Dick and nobody."

Mickey asked, "What the hell?" got no answer, and moved his loose-jointed bulk toward the elevators.

CHAPTER XXIV

Wanted

went around to the Shannon Hotel, registered my alias, paid my day's rent, and was taken to room 321.

An hour passed before the phone rang.

Dick Foley said he was coming up to see me.

He arrived within five minutes. His thin worried face was not friendly. Neither was his voice. He said:

"Warrants out for you. Murder. Two counts—Brand and Dawn. I phoned. Mickey said he'd stick. Told me you were here. Police got him. Grilling him now."

"Yeah, I expected that."

"So did I," he said sharply.

I said, making myself drawl the words:

"You think I killed them, don't you, Dick?"

"If you didn't, it's a good time to say so."

"Going to put the finger on me?" I asked.

He pulled his lips back over his teeth. His face changed from tan to buff.

I said:

"Go back to San Francisco, Dick. I've got enough to do without having to watch you."

He put his hat on very carefully and very carefully closed the door behind him when he went out.

At four o'clock I had some lunch, cigarettes, and an *Evening Herald* sent up to me.

Dinah Brand's murder, and the newer murder of Charles Proctor Dawn, divided the front page of the *Herald*, with Helen Albury connecting them.

Helen Albury was, I read, Robert Albury's sister, and she was, in spite of his confession, thoroughly convinced that her brother was not guilty of murder, but the victim of a plot. She had retained Charles Proctor Dawn to defend him. (I could guess that the late Charles Proctor had hunted her up, and not she him.) The brother refused to have Dawn or any other lawyer, but the girl (properly encouraged by Dawn, no doubt) had not given up the fight.

Finding a vacant flat across the street from Dinah Brand's house, Helen Albury had rented it, and had installed herself therein with a pair of field glasses and one idea—to prove that Dinah and her associates were guilty of Donald Willsson's murder.

I, it seems, was one of the "associates." The *Herald* called me "a man supposed to be a private detective from San Francisco, who has been in the city for several days, apparently on intimate terms with Max ('Whisper') Thaler, Daniel Rolff, Oliver ('Reno') Starkey, and Dinah Brand." We were the plotters who had framed Robert Albury.

The night that Dinah had been killed, Helen Albury, peeping through her window, had seen things that were, according to the *Herald*, extremely significant when considered in connection with the subsequent finding of Dinah's dead body. As soon as the girl heard of the murder, she took her important knowledge to Charles Proctor Dawn. He, the police learned from his clerks, immediately sent for me, and had been closeted with me that afternoon. He had later told his clerks that I was to return the next—this—morning at ten. This morning I had not appeared to keep my appointment. At twenty-five minutes past ten, the janitor of the Rutledge Block had found Charles Proctor Dawn's body in a corner behind the staircase, murdered. It was believed that valuable papers had been taken from the dead man's pockets.[71]

At the very moment that the janitor was finding the dead lawyer, I, it seems, was in Helen Albury's flat, having forced an entrance, and was threatening her. After she succeeded in throwing me out, she hurried to Dawn's offices, arriving while the police were there, telling them her story. Police sent to my hotel had not found me there, but in my room they had found one Michael Linehan, who also represented himself to be a San Francisco private detective. Michael Linehan was still being questioned by the police. Whisper, Reno, Rolff and I were being hunted by the police, charged with murder. Important developments were expected.

Page two held an interesting half-column. Detectives Shepp and Vanaman, the discoverers of Dinah Brand's body, had mysteriously vanished. Foul play on the part of us "associates" was feared.

There was nothing in the paper about last night's hijacking, nothing about the raid on Peak Murry's joint.

෨෧

I went out after dark. I wanted to get in touch with Reno.

From a drug store I phoned Peak Murry's pool room.

"Is Peak there?" I asked.

"This is Peak," said a voice that didn't sound anything at all like his. "Who's talking?"

I said disgustedly, "This is Lillian Gish,"[72] hung up the receiver, and removed myself from the neighborhood.

I gave up the idea of finding Reno and decided to go calling on my client, old Elihu, and try to blackjack him into good behavior with the love letters he had written Dinah Brand, and which I had stolen from Dawn's remains.

I walked, keeping to the darker side of the darkest streets. It was a fairly long walk for a man who sneers at exercise. By the time I reached Willsson's block I was in bad enough humor to be in good shape for the sort of interviews he and I usually had. But I wasn't to see him for a little while yet.

I was two pavements from my destination when somebody *S-s-s-s-s'd* at me.

I probably didn't jump twenty feet.

"'S all right," a voice whispered.

It was dark there. Peeping out under my bush—I was on my hands and knees in somebody's front yard—I could make out the form of a man crouching close to a hedge, on my side of it.

My gun was in my hand now. There was no special reason why I shouldn't take his word for it that it was all right.

72 Lillian Gish was a famous silent-film star (1893-1993), called the First Lady of American Cinema. She starred in the 1921 *Orphans of the Storm*, played Mimi in King Vidor's 1926 *La Boheme* and as Hester Prynne in the 1926 *The Scarlet Letter*.

I got up off my knees and went to him. When I got close enough I recognized him as one of the men who had let me into the Ronney Street house the day before.

I sat on my heels beside him and asked:

"Where'll I find Reno? Hank O'Marra said he wanted to see me."

"He does that. Know where Kid McLeod's place is at?"

"No."

"It's on Martin Street above King, corner the alley. Ask for the Kid. Go back that-away three blocks, and then down. You can't miss it."

I said I'd try not to, and left him crouching behind his hedge, watching my client's place, waiting, I guessed, for a shot at Pete the Finn, Whisper, or any of Reno's other unfriends who might happen to call on old Elihu.

Following directions, I came to a soft drink and rummy establishment with red and yellow paint all over it. Inside I asked for Kid McLeod. I was taken into a back room, where a fat man with a dirty collar, a lot of gold teeth, and only one ear, admitted he was McLeod.

"Reno sent for me," I said. "Where'll I find him?"

"And who does that make you?" he asked.

I told him who I was. He went out without saying anything. I waited ten minutes. He brought a boy back with him, a kid of fifteen or so with a vacant expression on a pimply red face.

"Go with Sonny," Kid McLeod told me.

I followed the boy out a side door, down two blocks of back street, across a sandy lot, through a ragged gate, and up to the back door of a frame house.

The boy knocked on the door and was asked who he was.

"Sonny, with a guy the Kid sent," he replied.

The door was opened by long-legged O'Marra. Sonny went away. I went into a kitchen where Reno Starkey and four other men sat around a table that had a lot of beer on it. I noticed that two automatic pistols hung on nails over the top of the door through which I had come. They would be handy if any of the house's occupants opened the door, found an enemy with a gun there, and were told to put up their hands.

Reno poured me a glass of beer and led me through the dining room into a front room. A man lay on his belly there, with one eye to the crack between the drawn blind and the bottom of the window, watching the street.

"Go back and get yourself some beer," Reno told him.

He got up and went away. We made ourselves comfortable in adjoining chairs.

"When I fixed up that Tanner alibi for you," Reno said, "I told you I was doing it because I needed all the friends I could get."

"You got one."

"Crack the alibi yet?" he asked.

"Not yet."

"It'll hold," he assured me, "unless they got too damned much on you. Think they have?"

I did think so. I said:

"No. McGraw's just feeling playful. That'll take care of itself. How's your end holding up?"

He emptied his glass, wiped his mouth on the back of a hand, and said:

"I'll make out. But that's what I wanted to see you about. Here's how she stacks up. Pete's throwed in with McGraw. That lines coppers and beer mob up against me and Whisper. But hell! Me and Whisper are busier trying to put the chive[73] in each other than bucking the combine. That's a sour racket. While we're tangling, them bums will eat us up."

I said I had been thinking the same thing. He went on:

"Whisper'll listen to you. Find him, will you? Put it to him. Here's the proposish: he means to get me for knocking off Jerry Hooper, and I mean to get him first. Let's forget that for a couple of days. Nobody won't have to trust nobody else. Whisper don't ever show in any of his jobs anyways. He just sends the boys. I'll do the same this time. We'll just put the mobs together to swing the caper. We run them together, rub out that damned Finn, and then we'll have plenty of time to go gunning among ourselves.

"Put it to him cold. I don't want him to get any ideas that I'm dodging a rumpus with him or any other guy. Tell him I say if we put Pete out of the way we'll have more room to do our own scrapping in. Pete's holedup down in Whiskeytown. I ain't got enough men to go down there and pull him out. Neither has Whisper. The two of us together has. Put it to him."

"Whisper," I said, "is dead."

Reno said, "Is that so?" as if he thought it wasn't.

73   Slang for a knife, related to the similar word "shiv."

"Dan Rolff killed him yesterday morning, down in the old Redman warehouse, stuck him with the ice pick Whisper had used on the girl."

Reno asked:

"You know this? You're not just running off at the head?"

"I know it."

"Damned funny none of his mob act like he was gone," he said, but he was beginning to believe me.

"They don't know it. He was hiding out, with Ted Wright the only one in on the where. Ted knew it. He cashed in on it. He told me he got a hundred or a hundred and fifty from you, through Peak Murry."

"I'd have given the big umpchay twice that for the straight dope," Reno grumbled. He rubbed his chin and said: "Well, that settles the Whisper end."

I said: "No."

"What do you mean, no?"

"If his mob don't know where he is," I suggested, "let's tell them. They blasted him out of the can when Noonan copped him. Think they'd try it again if the news got around that McGraw had picked him up on the quiet?"

"Keep talking," Reno said.

"If his friends try to crack the hoosegow again, thinking he's in it, that'll give the department, including Pete's specials, something to do. While they're doing it, you could try your luck in Whiskeytown."

"Maybe," he said slowly, "maybe we'll try just that thing."

"It ought to work," I encouraged him, standing up. "I'll see you—"

"Stick around. This is as good a spot as any while there's a reader[74] out for you. And we'll need a good guy like you on the party."

I didn't like that so much. I knew enough not to say so. I sat down again.

Reno got busy arranging the rumor. The telephone was worked over-time. The kitchen door was worked as hard, letting men in and out. More came in than went out. The house filled with men, smoke, tension.

CHAPTER XXV

Whiskeytown

At half-past one Reno turned from answering a phone call to say:

"Let's take a ride."

He went upstairs. When he came down he carried a black valise. Most of the men had gone out the kitchen door by then.

Reno gave me the black valise, saying:

"Don't wrastle it around too much."

It was heavy.

The seven of us left in the house went out the front door and got into a curtained touring car that O'Marra had just driven up to the curb. Reno sat beside O'Marra. I was squeezed in between men in the back seat, with the valise squeezed between my legs.

Another car came out of the first cross street to run ahead of us. A third followed us. Our speed hung around forty, fast enough to get us somewhere, not fast enough to get us a lot of attention.

We had nearly finished the trip before we were bothered.

The action started in a block of one-story houses of the shack type, down in the southern end of the city.

A man put his head out of a door, put his fingers in his mouth, and whistled shrilly.

Somebody in the car behind us shot him down.

At the next corner we ran through a volley of pistol bullets.

Reno turned around to tell me:

"If they pop the bag, we'll all of us hit the moon. Get it open. We got to work fast when we get there."

I had the fasteners unsnapped by the time we came to rest at the curb in front of a dark three-story brick building.

Men crawled all over me, opening the valise, helping themselves to the contents, bombs made of short sections of two-inch pipe, packed in sawdust in the bag. Bullets bit chunks out of the car's curtains.

Reno reached back for one of the bombs, hopped out to the sidewalk, paid no attention to a streak of blood that suddenly appeared in the middle of his left cheek, and heaved his piece of stuffed pipe at the brick building's door.

A sheet of flame was followed by deafening noise. Hunks of things pelted us while we tried to keep from being knocked over by the concussion. Then there was no door to keep anybody out of the red brick building.

A man ran forward, swung his arm, let a pipeful of hell go through the doorway. The shutters came off the downstairs windows, fire and glass flying behind them.

The car that had followed us was stationary up the street, trading shots with the neighborhood. The car that had gone ahead of us had turned into a side street. Pistol shots from behind the red brick building, between the explosions of our cargo, told us that our advance car was covering the back door.

O'Marra, out in the middle of the street, bent far over, tossed a bomb to the brick building's roof. It didn't explode. O'Marra put one foot high in the air, clawed at his throat, and fell solidly backward.

Another of our party went down under the slugs that were cutting at us from a wooden building next to the brick one.

Reno cursed stolidly and said:

"Burn them out, Fat."

Fat spit on a bomb, ran around the back of our car, and swung his arm.

We picked ourselves up off the sidewalk, dodged flying things, and saw that the frame house was all out of whack, with flames climbing its torn edges.

"Any left?" Reno asked as we looked around, enjoying the novelty of not being shot at.

"Here's the last one," Fat said, holding out a bomb.

Fire was dancing inside the upper windows of the brick house. Reno looked at it, took the bomb from Fat, and said:

"Back off. They'll be coming out."

We moved away from the front of the house.

A voice indoors yelled:

"Reno!"

Reno slipped into the shadow of our car before he called back:
"Well?"

"We're done," a heavy voice shouted. "We're coming out. Don't shoot."

Reno asked: "Who's we're?"

"This is Pete," the heavy voice said. "There's four left of us."

"You come first," Reno ordered, "with your mitts on the top of your head. The others come out one at a time, same way, after you. And half a minute apart is close enough. Come on."

We waited a moment, and then Pete the Finn appeared in the dynamited doorway, his hands holding the top of his bald head. In the glare from the burning next-door house we could see that his face was cut, his clothes almost all torn off.

Stepping over wreckage, the bootlegger came slowly down the steps to the sidewalk.

Reno called him a lousy fish-eater[75] and shot him four times in face and body.

Pete went down. A man behind me laughed.

Reno hurled the remaining bomb through the doorway.

We scrambled into our car. Reno took the wheel. The engine was dead. Bullets had got to it.

Reno worked the horn while the rest of us piled out.

The machine that had stopped at the corner came for us. Waiting for it, I looked up and down the street that was bright with the glow of two burning buildings. There were a few faces at windows, but whoever besides us was in the street had taken to cover. Not far away, firebells sounded.

The other machine slowed up for us to climb aboard. It was already full. We packed it in layers, with the overflow hanging on the running boards.

We bumped over dead Hank O'Marra's legs and headed for home. We covered one block of the distance with safety if not comfort. After that we had neither.

A limousine turned into the street ahead of us, came half a block toward us, put its side to us, and stopped. Out of the side, gun-fire.

75   A Catholic.

Another car came around the limousine and charged us. Out of it, gun-fire.

We did our best, but we were too damned amalgamated for good fighting. You can't shoot straight holding a man in your lap, another hanging on your shoulder, while a third does his shooting from an inch behind your ear.

Our other car—the one that had been around at the building's rear—came up and gave us a hand. But by then two more had joined the opposition. Apparently Thaler's mob's attack on the jail was over, one way or the other, and Pete's army, sent to help there, had returned in time to spoil our get-away. It was a sweet mess.

I leaned over a burning gun and yelled in Reno's ear:

"This is the bunk. Let's us extras get out and do our wrangling from the street."

He thought that a good idea, and gave orders:

"Pile out, some of you hombres, and take them from the pavements."

I was the first man out, with my eye on a dark alley entrance.

Fat followed me to it. In my shelter, I turned on him and growled:

"Don't pile up on me. Pick your own hole. There's a cellarway that looks good."

He agreeably trotted off toward it, and was shot down at his third step.

I explored my alley. It was only twenty feet long, and ended against a high board fence with a locked gate.

A garbage can helped me over the gate into a brick-paved yard. The side fence of that yard let me into another, and from that I got into another, where a fox terrier raised hell at me.

I kicked the pooch out of the way, made the opposite fence, untangled myself from a clothes line, crossed two more yards, got yelled at from a window, had a bottle thrown at me, and dropped into a cobblestoned back street.

The shooting was behind me, but not far enough. I did all I could to remedy that. I must have walked as many streets as I did in my dreams the night Dinah was killed.

My watch said it was three-thirty a. m. when I looked at it on Elihu Willsson's front steps.

CHAPTER XXVI

Blackmail

I had to push my client's doorbell a lot before I got any play on it.

Finally the door was opened by the tall sunburned chauffeur. He was dressed in undershirt and pants, and had a billiard cue in one fist.

"What do you want?" he demanded, and then, when he got another look at me: "It's you, is it? Well, what do you want?"

"I want to see Mr. Willsson."

"At four in the morning? Go on with you," and he started to close the door.

I put a foot against it. He looked from my foot to my face, hefted the billiard cue, and asked:

"You after getting your kneecap cracked?"

"I'm not playing," I insisted. "I've got to see the old man. Tell him."

"I don't have to tell him. He told me no later than this afternoon that if you come around he didn't want to see you."

"Yeah?" I took the four love letters out of my pocket, picked out the first and least idiotic of them, held it out to the chauffeur, and said: "Give him that and tell him I'm sitting on the steps with the rest of them. Tell him I'll sit here five minutes and then carry the rest of them to Tommy Robins of the Consolidated Press."

The chauffeur scowled at the letter, said, "To hell with Tommy Robins and his blind aunt!" took the letter, and closed the door.

Four minutes later he opened the door again and said:

"Inside, you."

I followed him upstairs to old Elihu's bedroom.

My client sat up in bed with his love letter crushed in one round pink fist, its envelope in the other.

His short white hair bristled. His round eyes were as much red as blue. The parallel lines of his mouth and chin almost touched. He was in a lovely humor.

As soon as he saw me he shouted:

"So after all your brave talking you had to come back to the old pirate to have your neck saved, did you?"

I said I didn't anything of the sort. I said if he was going to talk like a sap he ought to lower his voice so the people in Los Angeles wouldn't learn what a sap he was.

The old boy let his voice out another notch, bellowing:

"Because you've stolen a letter or two that don't belong to you, you needn't think you—"

I put fingers in my ears. They didn't shut out the noise, but they insulted him into cutting the bellowing short.

I took the fingers out and said:

"Send the flunkey away so we can talk. You won't need him. I'm not going to hurt you."

He said, "Get out," to the chauffeur.

The chauffeur, looking at me without fondness, left us, closing the door.

Old Elihu gave me the rush act, demanding that I surrender the rest of the letters immediately, wanting to know loudly and profanely where I had got them, what I was doing with them, threatening me with this, that, and the other, but mostly just cursing me.

I didn't surrender the letters. I said:

"I took them from the man you hired to recover them. A tough break for you that he had to kill the girl."

Enough red went out of the old man's face to leave it normally pink. He worked his lips over his teeth, screwed up his eyes at me, and said:

"Is that the way you're going to play it?"

His voice came comparatively quiet from his chest. He had settled down to fight.

I pulled a chair over beside the bed, sat down, put as much amusement as I could in a grin, and said:

"That's one way."

He watched me, working his lips, saying nothing. I said:

"You're the damndest client I ever had. What do you do? You hire me to clean town, change your mind, run out on me, work against me until I begin to look like a winner, then get on the fence, and now when you think I'm licked again, you don't even want to let me in the house. Lucky for me I happened to run across those letters."

He said: "Blackmail."

I laughed and said:

"Listen who's naming it. All right, call it that." I tapped the edge of the bed with a forefinger. "I'm not licked, old top. I've won. You came crying to me that some naughty men had taken your little city away from you. Pete the Finn, Lew Yard, Whisper Thaler, and Noonan. Where are they now?

"Yard died Tuesday morning, Noonan the same night, Whisper Wednesday morning, and the Finn a little while ago. I'm giving your city back to you whether you want it or not. If that's blackmail, O. K. Now here's what you're going to do. You're going to get hold of your mayor, I suppose the lousy village has got one, and you and he are going to phone the governor—Keep still until I get through.

"You're going to tell the governor that your city police have got out of hand, what with bootleggers sworn in as officers, and so on. You're going to ask him for help—the national guard would be best. I don't know how various ruckuses around town have come out, but I do know the big boys—the ones you were afraid of—are dead. The ones that had too much on you for you to stand up to them. There are plenty of busy young men working like hell right now, trying to get into the dead men's shoes. The more, the better. They'll make it easier for the white-collar soldiers to take hold while everything is disorganized. And none of the substitutes are likely to have enough on you to do much damage.

"You're going to have the mayor, or the governor, whichever it comes under, suspend the whole Personville police department, and let the mail-order troops handle things till you can organize another. I'm told that the mayor and the governor are both pieces of your property. They'll do what you tell them. And that's what you're going to tell them. It can be done, and it's got to be done.

"Then you'll have your city back, all nice and clean and ready to go to the dogs again. If you don't do it, I'm going to turn these love letters of yours over to the newspaper buzzards, and I don't mean your *Herald* crew—the press associations. I got the letters from Dawn. You'll have a lot of fun proving that you didn't hire him to recover them, and that he didn't kill the girl doing it. But the fun you'll have is nothing to the fun people will have reading these letters. They're hot. I haven't laughed so much over anything since the hogs ate my kid brother."

I stopped talking.

The old man was shaking, but there was no fear in his shaking. His face was purple again. He opened his mouth and roared:

"Publish them and be damned!"

I took them out of my pocket, dropped them on his bed, got up from my chair, put on my hat, and said:

"I'd give my right leg to be able to believe that the girl was killed by somebody you sent to get the letters. By God, I'd like to top off the job by sending you to the gallows!"

He didn't touch the letters. He said:

"You told me the truth about Thaler and Pete?"

"Yeah. But what difference does it make? You'll only be pushed around by somebody else."

He threw the bedclothes aside and swung his stocky pajamaed legs and pink feet over the edge of the bed.

"Have you got the guts," he barked, "to take the job I offered you once before—chief of police?"

"No. I lost my guts out fighting your fights while you were hiding in bed and thinking up new ways of disowning me. Find another wet nurse."

He glared at me. Then shrewd wrinkles came around his eyes.

He nodded his old head and said:

"You're afraid to take the job. So you did kill the girl?"

I left him as I had left him the last time, saying, "Go to hell!" and walking out.

The chauffeur, still toting his billiard cue, still regarding me without fondness, met me on the ground floor and took me to the door, looking as if he hoped I would start something. I didn't. He slammed the door after me.

The street was gray with the beginning of daylight.

Up the street a black coupé stood under some trees. I couldn't see if anyone was in it. I played safe by walking in the opposite direction. The coupé moved after me.

There is nothing in running down streets with automobiles in pursuit. I stopped, facing this one. It came on. I took my hand away from my side when I saw Mickey Linehan's red face through the windshield.

He swung the door open for me to get in.

"I thought you might come up here," he said as I sat beside him, "but I was a second or two too late. I saw you go in, but was too far away to catch you."

"How'd you make out with the police?" I asked. "Better keep driving while we talk."

"I didn't know anything, couldn't guess anything, didn't have any idea of what you were working on, just happened to hit town and meet you. Old friends—that line. They were still trying when the riot broke. They had me in one of the little offices across from the assembly room. When the circus cut loose I back-windowed them."

"How'd the circus wind up?" I asked.

"The coppers shot hell out of them. They got the tipoff half an hour ahead of time, and had the whole neighborhood packed with specials. Seems it was a juicy row while it lasted—no duck soup for the coppers at that. Whisper's mob, I hear."

"Yeah. Reno and Pete the Finn tangled tonight. Hear anything about it?"

"Only that they'd had it."

"Reno killed Pete and ran into an ambush on the getaway. I don't know what happened after that. Seen Dick?"

"I went up to his hotel and was told he'd checked out to catch the evening train."

"I sent him back home," I explained. "He seemed to think I'd killed Dinah Brand. He was getting on my nerves with it."

"Well?"

"You mean, did I kill her? I don't know, Mickey. I'm trying to find out. Want to keep riding with me, or want to follow Dick back to the Coast?"

Mickey said:

"Don't get so cocky over one lousy murder that maybe didn't happen. But what the hell? You know you didn't lift her dough and pretties."[76]

"Neither did the killer. They were still there after eight that morning, when I left. Dan Rolff was in and out between then and nine. He wouldn't have taken them. The—I've got it! The coppers that found the body—Shepp and Vanaman—got there at nine-thirty. Besides the jewelry and money, some letters old Willsson had written the girl were—must have been—taken. I found them later in Dawn's pocket. The two dicks disappeared just about then. See it?

"When Shepp and Vanaman found the girl dead they looted the joint before they turned in the alarm. Old Willsson being a millionaire, his letters looked good to them, so they took them along with the other valuables, and turned them—the letters—over to the shyster to peddle back to Elihu. But Dawn was killed before he could do anything on that end. I took the letters. Shepp and Vanaman, whether they did or didn't know that the letters were not found in the dead man's possession, got cold feet. They were afraid the letters would be traced to them. They had the money and jewelry. They lit out."

"Sounds fair enough," Mickey agreed, "but it don't seem to put any fingers on any murderers."

"It clears the way some. We'll try to clear it some more. See if you can find Porter Street and an old warehouse called Redman. The way I got it, Rolff killed Whisper there, walked up to him and stabbed him with the ice pick he had found in the girl. If he did it that way, then Whisper hadn't killed her. Or he would have been expecting something of the sort, and wouldn't have let the lunger get that close to him. I'd like to look at their remains and check up."

"Porter's over beyond King," Mickey said. "We'll try the south end first. It's nearer and more likely to have warehouses. Where do you set this Rolff guy?"

"Out. If he killed Whisper for killing the girl, that marks him off. Besides, she had bruises on her wrist and cheek, and he wasn't strong enough to rough her. My notion is that he left the hospital, spent the night God knows where, showed up at the girl's house after I left that morning, let himself in with his key, found her, decided Whisper had done the trick, took the sticker out of her, and went hunting Whisper."

"So?" Mickey said. "Now where do you get the idea that you might be the boy who put it over?"

"Stop it," I said grouchily as we turned into Porter Street. "Let's find our warehouse."

CHAPTER XXVII

Warehouses

We rode down the street, jerking our eyes around, hunting for buildings that looked like deserted warehouses. It was light enough by now to see well.

Presently I spotted a big square rusty-red building set in the center of a weedy lot. Disuse stuck out all over lot and building. It had the look of a likely candidate.

"Pull up at the next corner," I said. "That looks like the dump. You stick with the heap while I scout it."

I walked two unnecessary blocks so I could come into the lot behind the building. I crossed the lot carefully, not sneaking, but not making any noises I could avoid.

I tried the back door cautiously. It was locked, of course. I moved over to a window, tried to look in, couldn't because of gloom and dirt, tried the window, and couldn't budge it.

I went to the next window with the same luck. I rounded the corner of the building and began working my way along the north side. The first window had me beaten. The second went up slowly with my push, and didn't make much noise doing it.

Across the inside of the window frame, from top to bottom, boards were nailed. They looked solid and strong from where I stood.

I cursed them, and remembered hopefully that the window hadn't made much noise when I raised it. I climbed up on the sill, put a hand against the boards, and tried them gently.

They gave.

I put more weight behind my hand. The boards went away from the left side of the frame, showing me a row of shiny nail points.

I pushed them back farther, looked past them, saw nothing but darkness, heard nothing.

With my gun in my right fist, I stepped over the sill, down into the building. Another step to the left put me out of the window's gray light.

I switched my gun to my left hand and used my right to push the boards back over the window.

A full minute of breathless listening got me nothing. Holding my gun-arm tight to my side, I began exploring the joint. Nothing but the floor came under my feet as I inch-by-inched them forward. My groping left hand felt nothing until it touched a rough wall. I seemed to have crossed a room that was empty.

I moved along the wall, hunting for a door. Half a dozen of my under-sized steps brought me to one. I leaned an ear against it, and heard no sound.

I found the knob, turned it softly, eased the door back.

Something swished.

I did four things all together: let go the knob, jumped, pulled trigger, and had my left arm walloped with something hard and heavy as a tombstone.

The flare of my gun showed me nothing. It never does, though it's easy to think you've seen things. Not knowing what else to do, I fired again, and once more.

An old man's voice pleaded:

"Don't do that, partner. You don't have to do that."

I said: "Make a light."

A match spluttered on the floor, kindled, and put flickering yellow light on a battered face. It was an old face of the useless, characterless sort that goes well with park benches. He was sitting on the floor, his stringy legs sprawled far apart. He didn't seem hurt anywhere. A table-leg lay beside him.

"Get up and make a light," I ordered, "and keep matches burning until you've done it."

He struck another match, sheltered it carefully with his hands as he got up, crossed the room, and lit a candle on a three-legged table.

77   Canadian Club was and is another popular Scotch whiskey.

I followed him, keeping close. My left arm was numb or I would have taken hold of him for safety.

"What are you doing here?" I asked when the candle was burning.

I didn't need his answer. One end of the room was filled with wooden cases piled six high, branded *Perfection Maple Syrup*.

While the old man explained that as God was his keeper he didn't know nothing about it, that all he knew was that a man named Yates had two days ago hired him as night watchman, and if anything was wrong he was as innocent as innocent, I pulled part of the top off one case.

The bottles inside had Canadian Club labels that looked as if they had been printed with a rubber stamp.[77]

I left the cases and, driving the old man in front of me with the candle, searched the building. As I expected, I found nothing to indicate that this was the warehouse Whisper had occupied.

By the time we got back to the room that held the liquor my left arm was strong enough to lift a bottle. I put it in my pocket and gave the old man some advice:

"Better clear out. You were hired to take the place of some of the men Pete the Finn turned into special coppers. But Pete's dead now and his racket has gone blooey."

When I climbed out the window the old man was standing in front of the cases, looking at them with greedy eyes while he counted on his fingers.

⌘

"Well?" Mickey asked when I returned to him and his coupé.

I took out the bottle of anything but Canadian Club, pulled the cork, passed it to him, and then put a shot into my own system.

He asked, "Well?" again.

I said: "Let's try to find the old Redman warehouse."

He said: "You're going to ruin yourself some time telling people too much," and started the car moving.

Three blocks farther up the street we saw a faded sign, *Redman & Company*. The building under the sign was long, low, and narrow, with corrugated iron roof and few windows.

"We'll leave the boat around the corner," I said. "And you'll go with me this time. I didn't have a whole lot of fun by myself last trip."

When we climbed out of the coupé, an alley ahead promised a path to the warehouse's rear. We took it.

A few people were wandering through the streets, but it was still too early for the factories that filled most of this part of town to come to life.

At the rear of our building we found something interesting. The back door was closed. Its edge, and the edge of the frame, close to the lock, were scarred. Somebody had worked there with a jimmy.

Mickey tried the door. It was unlocked. Six inches at a time, with pauses between, he pushed it far enough back to let us squeeze in.

When we squeezed in we could hear a voice. We couldn't make out what the voice was saying. All we could hear was the faint rumble of a distant man's voice, with a suggestion of quarrelsomeness in it.

Mickey pointed a thumb at the door's scar and whispered.

"Not coppers."

I took two steps inside, keeping my weight on my rubber heels. Mickey followed, breathing down the back of my neck.

Ted Wright had told me Whisper's hiding place was in the back, upstairs. The distant rumbling voice could have been coming from there.

I twisted my face around to Mickey and asked:

"Flashlight?"

He put it in my left hand. I had my gun in my right. We crept forward.

The door, still a foot open, let in enough light to show us the way across this room to a doorless doorway. The other side of the doorway was black.

I flicked the light across the blackness, found a door, shut off the light, and went forward. The next squirt of light showed us steps leading up.

We went up the steps as if we were afraid they would break under our feet.

The rumbling voice had stopped. There was something else in the air. I didn't know what. Maybe a voice not quite loud enough to be heard, if that means anything.

I had counted nine steps when a voice spoke clearly above us. It said:

78   "Peter Collins" was an imaginary or nonexistent person to whom a newcomer was sent on a silly errand as a kind of initiation into the theatrical world ("Go ask Peter Collins for some snipe juice.") It became an underworld expression for "no one" or "nobody." Hammett adopted the pseudonym of "Peter Collinson" (the son of nobody) for some of his early *Black Mask* work.

"Sure, I killed the bitch."

A gun said something, the same thing four times, roaring like a 16-inch rifle under the iron roof.

The first voice said: "All right."

By that time Mickey and I had put the rest of the steps behind us, had shoved a door out of the way, and were trying to pull Reno Starkey's hands away from Whisper's throat.

It was a tough job and a useless one. Whisper was dead.

Reno recognized me and let his hands go limp.

His eyes were as dull, his horse face as wooden, as ever.

Mickey carried the dead gambler to the cot that stood in one end of the room, spreading him on it.

The room, apparently once an office, had two windows. In their light I could see a body stowed under the cot—Dan Rolff. A Colt's service automatic lay in the middle of the floor.

Reno bent his shoulders, swaying.

"Hurt?" I asked.

"He put all four in me," he said calmly, bending to press both forearms against his lower body.

"Get a doc," I told Mickey.

"No good," Reno said. "I got no more belly left than Peter Collins."[78]

I pulled a folding chair over and sat him down on it, so he could lean forward and hold himself together.

Mickey ran out and down the stairs.

"Did you know he wasn't croaked?" Reno asked.

"No. I gave it to you the way I got it from Ted Wright."

"Ted left too soon," he said. "I was leary of something like that, and came to make sure. He trapped me pretty, playing dead till I was under the gun." He stared dully at Whisper's corpse. "Game at that, damn him. Dead, but wouldn't lay down, bandaging hisself, laying here waiting by hisself." He smiled, the only smile I had ever seen him use. "But he's just meat and not much of it now."

His voice was thickening. A little red puddle formed under the edge of his chair. I was afraid to touch him. Only the pressure of his arms, and his bentforward position, were keeping him from falling apart.

He stared at the puddle and asked:

"How the hell did you figure you didn't croak her?"

"I had to take it out in hoping I hadn't, till just now," I said. "I had you pegged for it, but couldn't be sure. I was all hopped up that night, and had a lot of dreams, with bells ringing and voices calling, and a lot of stuff like that. I got an idea maybe it wasn't straight dreaming so much as hop-head nightmares stirred up by things that were happening around me.

"When I woke up, the lights were out. I didn't think I killed her, turned off the light, and went back to take hold of the ice pick. But it could have happened other ways. You knew I was there that night. You gave me my alibi without stalling. That got me thinking. Dawn tried blackmailing me after he heard Helen Albury's story. The police, after hearing her story, tied you, Whisper, Rolff and me together. I found Dawn dead after seeing O'Marra half a block away. It looked like the shyster had tried blackmailing you. That and the police tying us together started me thinking the police had as much on the rest of you as on me. What they had on me was that Helen Albury had seen me go in or out or both that night. It was a good guess they had the same on the rest of you. There were reasons for counting Whisper and Rolff out. That left you—and me. But why you killed her's got me puzzled."

"I bet you," he said, watching the red puddle grow on the floor. "It was her own damned fault. She calls me up, tells me Whisper's coming to see her, and says if I get there first I can bushwhack him. I'd like that. I go over there, stick around, but he don't show."

He stopped, pretending interest in the shape the red puddle was taking. I knew pain had stopped him, but I knew he would go on talking as soon as he got himself in hand. He meant to die as he had lived, inside the same tough shell. Talking could be torture, but he wouldn't stop on that account, not while anybody was there to see him. He was Reno Starkey who could take anything the world had without batting an eye, and he would play it out that way to the end.

"I got tired of waiting," he went on after a moment. "I hit her door and asked howcome. She takes me in, telling me there's nobody there. I'm doubtful, but she swears she's alone, and we go back in the kitchen. Knowing her, I'm beginning to think maybe it's me and not Whisper that's being trapped."

Mickey came in, telling us he had phoned for an ambulance.

Reno used the interruption to rest his voice, and then continued with his story:

"Later, I find that Whisper did phone her he was coming, and got there before me. You were coked. She was afraid to let him in, so he beat it. She don't tell me that, scared I'll go and leave her. You're hopped and she wants protection against Whisper coming back. I don't know none of that then. I'm leary that I've walked into something, knowing her. I think I'll take hold of her and slap the truth out of her. I try it, and she grabs the pick and screams. When she squawks, I hear a man's feet hitting the floor. The trap's sprung, I think."

He spoke slower, taking more time and pains to turn each word out calmly and deliberately, as talking became harder. His voice had become blurred, but if he knew it he pretended he didn't.

"I don't mean to be the only one that's hurt. I twist the pick out of her hand and stick it in her. You gallop out, coked to the edges, charging at the whole world with both eyes shut. She tumbles into you. You go down, roll around till your hand hits the butt of the pick. Holding on to that, you go to sleep, peaceful as she is. I see it then, what I've done. But hell! she's croaked. There's nothing to do about it. I turn off the lights and go home. When you—"

A tired looking ambulance crew—Poisonville gave them plenty of work—brought a litter into the room, ending Reno's tale. I was glad of it. I had all the information I wanted, and sitting there listening to and watching him talk himself to death wasn't pleasant.

I took Mickey over to a corner of the room and muttered in his ear:

"The job's yours from now on. I'm going to duck. I ought to be in the clear, but I know my Poisonville too well to take any chances. I'll drive your car to some way station where I can catch a train for Ogden. I'll be at the Roosevelt Hotel there,[79] registered as P. F. King. Stay with the job, and let me know when it's wise to either take my own name again or a trip to Honduras."

I spent most of my week in Ogden trying to fix up my reports so they would not read as if I had broken as many Agency rules, state laws and human bones as I had.

Mickey arrived on the sixth night.

He told me that Reno was dead, that I was no longer officially a criminal, that most of the First National Bank stick-up loot had been recovered, that MacSwain had confessed killing Tim

Noonan, and that Personville, under martial law, was developing into a sweet-smelling and thornless bed of roses.

Mickey and I went back to San Francisco.

I might just as well have saved the labor and sweat I had put into trying to make my reports harmless. They didn't fool the Old Man. He gave me merry hell.

Facsimile first-edition dust jacket for *Little Caesar*.

LITTLE CAESAR[1]

BY

W. R. BURNETT

"The first law of every being, is to preserve itself and live.
You sow hemlock, and expect to see ears of corn ripen. . . ."
—*Machiavelli*

To Marjorie

Note: The characters and events in this book are entirely imaginary.

1   First published in 1929 in New York by
Lincoln McVeagh/Dial Press.

Little Caesar (London: Transworld Publishers [Corgi Books], 1957),
illustration by Oliver Brabbins.

PART I

1

Sam Vettori sat staring down into Halsted Street.[2] He was a big man, fat as a hog, with a dark oily complexion, kinky black hair and a fat aquiline face. In repose he had an air of lethargic good-nature, due entirely to his bulk; for in reality he was sullen, bad-tempered and cunning. From time to time he dragged out a huge gold watch and looked at it with raised eyebrows and pursed lips.

Near him at a round table sat Otero, called The Greek, Tony Passa and Sam Vettori's lieutenant, Rico, playing stud for small stakes. Under the green-shaded lamp Otero's dark face looked livid and cavernous. He sat immobile and said nothing, win or lose. Tony, robust and rosy, scarcely twenty years old, watched each turn of the cards intently, shouting with joy when his luck was good, cursing when it was bad, more out of excitement than interest in the stakes. Rico sat with his hat tilted over his eyes, his pale thin face slightly drawn, his fingers tapping. Rico always played to win.

Vettori, puffing, pulled himself to his feet and began to walk up and down.

"Where you suppose he is?" he asked the ceiling. "I told him eight o'clock. It is half-past."

"Joe never knows what time it is," said Tony.

"Joe's no good," said Rico without taking his eyes off the cards, "he's soft."

"Well," said Vettori, stopping to watch the game out of boredom, "maybe so. But we can't do without him, Rico. I tell

2   Halsted Street is a major thoroughfare in Chicago, on the eastern border of the Near West Side neighborhood then known as Little Italy, now University Village, in between campuses of the University of Illinois at Chicago, near Jane Addams's Hull House in the late nineteenth century. It also is a boundary of the area known as Little Sicily.

Halsted Street in Little Italy, ca. 1920s.

3   Rudolph Valentino (1895–1926), whose real name was Rodolfo Alfonso Raffaello Pierre Filibert Guglielmi di Valentina d'Antonguella was an Italian-American actor best remembered for his leading role in *The Sheik* and other silent films. He was the original Latin lover, as the press termed him, and strikingly handsome. Valentino's early death led to public outcries by his legions of female fans.

Rudolph Valentino, 1923.

4   Chicago may be said to be a city of bridges. From its earliest development, bridges were implemented to allow the city to utilize the Chicago River—a system of rivers and canals 156 miles in length—for portages and connections to the Great Lakes. Today there are fifty-two movable bridges in Chicago, forty-three of which are operable. Halsted Street features two bridges, over the north branch and the south branch of the River.

you, Rico, he can go anywhere. A front is what he's got. Swell hotels? What does it mean to that boy? He says to the clerk, I would like please a suite. A suite! You see, Rico. We can't do without him."

Rico tapped on the table, flushing slightly.

"All right, Sam," he said, "some day he'll turn yellow. Hear what I say. He's not right. What's all this dancing? A man don't dance for money."

Sam laughed.

"Oh, Rico! You don't know Joe."

Tony stared at Rico.

"Rico," he said, "Joe's right. I know what I'm saying. All that dancing is a front. He's smart. Have they ever got him once?"

Rico slammed down his cards. He hated Joe and he knew that Tony and Vettori knew it.

"All right," he said, "hear what I say. He'll turn yellow some day. A man don't take money for dancing."

"I win," said Otero.

Rico pushed the money toward him and got to his feet.

"Well, if he don't show up in ten minutes I'll take the air," said Rico.

"You stay where you are," said Vettori, his face hardening.

Tony watched the two of them intently. Otero counted his money. One day Vettori had said to Rico, "Rico, you are getting too big for us." Tony remembered the look he had seen in Rico's eyes. Lately they had all been talking about it. Rico was getting too big for them. Scabby, the informer, said: "Tony, mark what I say. It's Rico or Sam. One or the other."

"I'll stay ten minutes," said Rico.

Vettori sat down by the window and stared into Halsted Street.

"Two-fifty," said Otero.

"I'll match you for it," said Tony.

"No," said Otero.

Joe Massara opened the door and came in.

"Well," said Vettori, "you call this eight o'clock?"

Joe got out of a big ulster. He was in evening clothes. His black hair was sleek and parted in the middle. He was vain of his resemblance to the late Mr. Rudolph Valentino.[3]

"Sorry," said Joe, "the bridge was up.[4] Well, what's the dirt?"

"Draw up a chair," said Vettori, "all of you."

They grouped themselved around the table under the green-shaded lamp. Joe put his hands on the table so they could see his well-manicured nails and the diamond ring the dancer, Olga Stassoff, had given him.

"Now," said Vettori, "I'll do the talking. I know what I got to say and you birds keep quiet till I'm through . . ."

"How long will it take?" asked Joe, smiling.

"Shut up and listen," said Rico.

"All right, all right," said Vettori, patting them both, "no bad blood. Now: ever hear of the Casa Alvarado?"

"Sure," said Joe, "it's an up and up place. One of Francis Wood's joints. I nearly got an engagement there once."

Rico spread out his hands.

"See? They know him. He won't do."

"No, they never seen me. It was all done through an agent."

"All right," said Vettori, "that's the place."

Joe looked startled. Rico smiled and taking off his hat began to comb his hair with a little ivory pocket comb.

"It'd be tough," said Joe, "what's in it?"

"Plenty," said Vettori. "They only bank once or twice a week. They're careless, get that, because they've never been tapped. It's easy."

Joe took out a gold cigarette case which he handled with ostentation.

"Well? I'm listening."

Vettori refused a cigarette and pulled out a stogie. Downstairs a jazzband began to play and a saxophone sent vibrations along the floor.

"Nine o'clock," said Otero.

Vettori lit his stogie.

"They got a safe," he said, "that a baby could crack. Too easy to talk about. But that's on the side. What we're after is the cashier. The place is lousy with jack. I got the lowdown from Scabby. Well, what do you say, Joe?"

"Yeah," Rico cut in, "take it or leave it. We ain't begging you."

Vettori's face hardened but he said nothing.

"If you say it's good," said Joe, "it's good with me."

"All right, all right," said Vettori. "Now, you Tony; we want a big car. Get that. A big, fast car. Get one when I tell you.[5] Steve's got the plates all ready. Yeah?"

"I'm on, Sam."

5   According to *The Gang: A Study of 1,313 Gangs in Chicago* (Chicago: University of Chicago Press, 1927) by Frederick N. Thrasher, "It has been estimated that 90 percent of Chicago's robberies are preceded by the theft of motor cars, most of which are abandoned after they have been used in the commission of crime," (p. 446).

Tony pulled out a cigarette and lit it with a flourish, but his hands shook a little.

"Rico and Otero," said Vettori, looking at each in turn, "will handle the rods. Yeah?"

Rico said nothing. But Otero smiled, showing his stained teeth, and said:

"That's us, eh, Rico?"

"Well," Vettori went on, "I guess we got that over. Now, Joe, I want you on the inside. Dress yourself up like you are, see, and fix it so you'll get there at midnight. All the whistles'll be tooting and everybody'll be drunk and won't know nothing. See? Now you get there at midnight and go to the cigar counter for change. At twelvefive the fun'll begin. We'll set our watches by telephone, because I don't want you here that night. All right. Rico and Otero come in quick, maybe Tony, too, if you can get a good safe place to park. That's up to Rico. He's bossing the job."

Rico looked at Joe.

"Now, they'll stick you up if everything's O.K. If not, give them the high sign and they'll beat it. We ain't taking no chances, because one night don't make much difference, only New Year's Eve's a good night, see? All right. You play like you don't know them, got it? But while they're working, you got your eyes open, see? And if something happens, you got a rod, but don't use it. We got to watch that."

Vettori shifted his stogie and shook his finger sideways at Rico.

"That's your trouble, Rico. The Big Boy can't fix murder. He can fix anything but murder. Get that. You're too quick with the lead. If that guy over at the pool room'd died we wouldn't none of us be sitting here right now. . . ."

Otero broke in vehemently, surprising them.

"But he had to! He had to! Rico does what is right."

"All right," said Vettori, "but take it easy. Now, Joe, you got your hands up, but you watch. If nothing happens nobody knows the difference. But if something does happen you pull the rod and help the boys get out. All right. Here's the dope. Get what's in the cash register first. Get that because that's easy. If things go right, tackle the safe; it'll probably be open. Another thing: no frisking in the lobby. That's too dangerous and takes too long. Let the yaps keep their money. All right."

Vettori took a map from his pocket and spread it out on the table. The men crowded round him.

"You go straight in," said Vettori, marking the route with a pencil, "on the right is the check-room; watch the girls behind the counter, Joe. On the left is the cigarcounter and the cashier's desk. At the end of the lobby is a big door; the real joint's beyond that. If things go right, nobody in the place'll know it's been stuck up, except maybe some yaps in the lobby. Get the idea? With all them horns tooting and all that damn noise, see? All right. On the right of the lobby is a door and that goes into the manager's office. The box is in there. The manager's a goddam bohunk[6] and there ain't an ounce of fight in him. See? Scabby give me the lowdown."

Vettori rolled up his map, put it in his pocket, then looked at his watch.

"Well," he said, "got it all?"

Joe turned his diamond ring round on his finger and looked at the table.

"What's the word, Joe?" said Rico.

"It's a tough one, Rico. What's the guarantee?"

"Guarantee, hell!" cried Rico. "Why, a blind guy could do your stand."

"Well, I ain't doing no time for fifty bucks," said Joe.

Vettori laughed.

"I'll give you a couple hundred now," he said.

Joe nodded.

"All right, I'm in. Never mind the couple hundred."

They all got to their feet. Below them the jazzband was still playing and the saxophone was still sending vibrations along the floor.

"What'll you have, boys," said Vettori, "want some drinks sent up?"

"Not me," said Tony, "I'm going over and see my woman."

Otero clapped his hands.

"He's got a woman."

Rico hit Otero on the back.

"The Greek's got a woman too," said Rico.

Otero with his hands cupped made a series of curves in the air. Joe was patronizing; Olga Stassoff, the dancer, was his woman.

"A beauty is she, Otero?"

"Sí, señor."

"Well," said Vettori, "want any drinks sent up?"

"Sure," said Joe, "send me up a snort. I guess Rico'll take milk."

6   A slang expression for a person of central European descent, originally only those from Bohemia, usually connoting a common laborer.

Rico didn't drink.

"All right about Rico," said Vettori in a good humor, "he's a smart boy."

Tony went out followed by Vettori.

"I think I go see my woman," said Otero.

Joe laughed. Rico said:

"Goodbye, Otero. Give Seal Skin a rub for me."

When Otero had gone, Joe said:

"Has old Seal Skin got The Greek hooked yet?"

"Well," said Rico, "he spends a lot of jack on her. She ain't much to look at and she's pretty old, but what's the difference?"

Joe never could figure Rico out. Women didn't seem to interest him.

Rico went over to the window and stood looking out at the electric sign on a level with his eyes.

CLUB

P

A

L

E

R

M

O

DANCING

Rico and Joe felt queer alone together. They were silent. Joe took out his gold cigarette case and lit a cigarette. Snow began to fall past the window.

"Look," said Rico, "it's snowing."

"Yeah," said Joe, looking up mechanically, "snowing hard."

II

Vettori was sitting in his little office on the main floor. On the other side of the wall the jazzband was playing, but he paid no attention. The noise of the jazzband was the same to him as the ticking of a clock to an ordinary person. He felt very pleasant and comfortable over his bottle of wine and his plate of spaghetti. Things were right!

He congratulated himself on his subordinates. Each man a specialist. Yes, yes! That was the way to do. None of this hit or miss stuff for Sam Vettori. Rico the best gunman in Little Italy; a swelled head, all right, but he can be handled, and there you are! Otero so crazy about Rico he "don't know nothing." Follow Rico any place; do anything Rico tells him. And handy with a rod. Well, well. Not bad for a Mexican. As a rule foreigners were not right with Sam Vettori, but in general he had an open mind, and Otero was the goods.[7] And look at Joe Massara, there was a man for you! A swell Italian who could pass anywhere. One winter in Florida, so they say, Joe passed himself off as a count and hooked a rich widow for plenty. Yes, yes ! That was Joe for you. As an inside man you couldn't beat him. And Tony! He could drive a car sixty miles an hour straight up the Tribune Tower. Only one thing, sometimes Tony was undependable. Used to be a choir boy at St. Dominick's and that stuff. But he had outgrown that, maybe; anyway he was dead scared of Rico and that would shut his mouth.

Vettori leaned back, wiped his mouth with the back of his hand and unbuttoned his vest. Spaghetti and wine, what is better!

The band stopped playing. Bat Carillo, the bouncer, put his head in the door.

"Couple of hard guys looking for trouble, boss," he said.

Vettori looked up.

"Yeah? Know them?"

"Never seen them before."

Vettori heaved himself to his feet and walked with Carillo to the swinging doors which separated the back-rooms and kitchen from the club proper. He pushed the door open about a foot and peered in. Carillo pointed.

Vettori laughed and closed the door.

"Some of them dumb Irish," he said; "let 'em alone unless they get bad and start something, then bounce 'em."

"O.K., boss," said Carillo.

Waiters passed Vettori in the corridor, sweat dropping from their faces, steam rising from the dishes on the slanted trays. Vettori rubbed his hands.

"Business is good. Well, well! We won't none of us die in the poor house."

7   In this context, the phrase means "quality."

When he got back to his office he found Scabby, the informer, waiting for him. Scabby was dark and undersized with a heavy, sullen, blotched face. Passing as a police informer, he was in reality a member of the Vettori gang. He played a dangerous game as he informed on other gangs. His life wasn't worth a cent and he was jumpy and quick with a gun.

"Well, well, Giovanni," said Vettori, "what's the news?"

"Everything's jake,"[8] said Scabby, taking off his hat and revealing a shining bald head.

Vettori called a waiter.

"Some spaghetti for this man here," he said, "and a bottle of wine."

"That's the ticket," said Scabby without smiling; he never smiled; his face was melancholy and lined, and sagged like a hound's. "The boys on?"

"All set," said Vettori. "It looks easy."

Scabby nodded.

"It ought to be. But no gunplay, get that, Sam. The Big Boy'd raise hell if he knew what was up."

Vettori's face hardened.

"I heard that once, Scabby. That's enough. This is too good to pass up."

"All right," said Scabby, "I've had my say. But things ain't what they used to be, Sam. It's getting dangerous. They've even got the Big Boy scared. It's the damn newspapers. They play that crime stuff off the boards. Big headlines, see? That's the trouble."

They sat silent. Vettori, absorbed, puffed on his stogie. Finally he said:

"Listen, Scabby, you ain't heard nothing, see? I got to keep these boys on their toes. Especially Joe. Don't spill nothing about the Big Boy."

Scabby shook his head vigorously. Vettori took out his billfold and handed Scabby a fifty.

"That part of your split, Scabby. Keep your eyes open, that's all."

Scabby pocketed the money. The waiter came in bringing the spaghetti and the wine. Carillo put his head in the door.

"Reilly, the dick's, up front."

Vettori nodded.

"He's O.K. If he sticks around, send him back in about half an hour."

"Sure," said Scabby, "I'll be out of here in less than that."

III

9   This was a premium cigar. For example, in 1926, the mass-market brand *White Owl* sold three for 20 cents.

Otero lay looking out the window at the electric sign across the street.

CLUB
P
A
L
E
R
M
O
DANCING

Snow was falling past the windows. Otero lay smoking a big twenty-five cent cigar[9] and singing softly to himself. He always sang when he was with Seal Skin.

"Some snow," said Otero.

"Yeah, some snow," said Seal Skin, who was sitting with her feet on the window sill, smoking one of Otero's cigars.

"Heavy like cotton," said Otero.

"Yeah," said Seal Skin.

"Where I used to be it never snowed."

"Didn't it?"

"No, it never snowed."

Seal Skin blew out a cloud of smoke.

"How come you ever left Mexico, Ramón?"

"Well, I don't know." Otero scratched his head. "I just left."

"Was they after you?"

"No, I just left."

Otero got up and put his arms around Seal Skin.

"Some girl," he said.

Seal Skin gave him a push.

"Wait'll I finish this."

"Sure, sure," said Otero, smiling and patting her on the shoulder.

"Look," said Seal Skin, "you're a good guy, Ramón. But dumb. How come you hang after Rico?"

"Rico is a great man."

10 Francisco "Pancho" Villa was one of the leaders of the Mexican Revolution and its best-known figure. He was assassinated in 1923. The *rurales* mentioned by Otero were the fed-erally-organized rural police of Mexico.

11 Chicago—the "Windy City"—is often made frigid in the winter by winds off Lake Michigan.

12 The song "The Rosary" was composed by Ethelbert Nevin and Robert Cameron Rogers in 1898 and frequently recorded. The Taylor Trio had a hit instrumental version in 1916.

Seal Skin laughed out loud.

"Yeah? Great, but careless. He'll never die of old age."

Otero didn't understand.

"What you say?"

"They'll fill him full of lead. He's too cocky."

Otero shook his head.

"No, they'll never get Rico."

"They get 'em all."

"No," said Otero, "they'll never get Rico. Once I say to him, 'Look, you must be careful.' But he say, 'Not me, they'll never get Rico.'"

Seal Skin opened the window and flung her cigar down into the street. A gust of cold air rushed into the overheated room.

"Listen," she said, "that's bunk. Rico's no different from any-body else. You stick with Rico long enough and you'll have a swell funeral. Why don't you get into the beer racket? That's safe."

"I go with Rico," said Otero. "What do I care? I have no people. Once I had a brother but they shot him."

"The cops?"

"No, the rurales. He was with Villa."[10]

"Who the hell's Villa?"

"Villa was a great man, like Rico."

Seal Skin got up and took a drink from a bottle on the bureau. Then she said:

"Let's hit the hay, Ramón."

"Sure, sure," said Otero.

IV

It was nearly two o'clock when Tony left his woman. A lake wind[11] was blowing hard and the snow fell heavily past the street lights. Tony muffled himself in his overcoat and pulled his cap low. He felt tired and disgusted.

At the corner near his home, he turned into Sicily Pete's res-taurant. Three Italians were playing cards at a table in the back. Up front a mechanical piano ground out The Rosary.[12]

"Hello, Tony, how's the boy?" said Pete.

"Not so good," said Tony.

"You ain't looking any too good, Tony," said Pete.

Tony ran his hands over his face and stared at his image in the mirror behind the counter. Pale; circles under his eyes.

"Well, I guess I'll live," said Tony.

Pete smacked the counter with both hands.

"Love of God! Sure you'll live. You be O.K. tomorrow morning. I know, Tony, my boy. Don't forget I was a young fellow once. I know. I know."

"Sure you know," said Tony, sarcastic.

"Sure I do. You think I don't know about that little red head. Hot stuff, Tony, my boy. Only don't be a fool. Save some for tomorrow night."

Pete laughed, shaking all over, and smacked the counter with his hands.

"What the hell's wrong with you, Pete?" cried one of the card players.

"Never you mind. All right, Tony, what'll you have?"

Tony couldn't decide. Pete went to wait on one of the card players. The mechanical piano finished The Rosary on a discord. Tony went over and put a nickel in the slot.

"I got a combination to go and two Javas," cried Pete.

The mechanical piano began to play O Sole Mio.

"I'll take a combination," said Tony, "and a cup of Java."

"O.K.," said Pete; "I got two combinations, one to go and three on the Java."

"How's business, Pete?" asked Tony.

"Oh, what you call soso. Not good, not bad. I never get rich here."

"Why don't you put in a line of bottled goods?"[13] said Tony, smiling.

Pete raised both hands over his head and brought them down hard on the counter.

"None of that for Sicily Pete. Oh no. Pete's too smart for that. If the bulls don't get you, why some of them gangsters do. I know. One say, you buy from me; the other say, no, you buy from me. All the same. No matter who you buy from, bango!"

Pete brought Tony his combination and his coffee and stood at the counter with him while he ate it.

"Tony," said Pete, putting his head on one side, "you know you look like your old man. Other day when you was in here

13 Tony means that Pete should sell boot-legged liquor.

I say to the missus, look, ain't he just like his old man? Well, well. That is good. A boy should look like his old man. That is a good sign."

"Knew the old man pretty well, didn't you Pete?" said Tony, finishing his coffee.

"Yes, pretty well. When he was a young fellow he was like you. Full of pep and always after the girls. But I don't know, your mama she got hold of him, then he wasn't like he used to be. He wasn't like the same fellow. Pretty soon he died."

Tony laughed.

"Hard on the old lady, ain't you?"

"Love of God, no," said Pete, an expression of acute misery on his face, "you don't get me, Tony. I mean he got to be a good fellow, like me. Work, work, that's all he knew. Well, work is a good thing. It keeps you out of trouble, but I don't know . . ."

Pete wiped the sweat from his forehead and meditated. Tony flipped him a fifty-cent piece. The mechanical piano stopped on a prolonged, slurred discord.

"Well, I guess I'll hit for home," said Tony, "so long, Pete."

"Good night, Tony," said Pete, with one of his blandest smiles, "come in again."

The wind struck Tony in the face as he left the restaurant. The streets were white and silent. Tony walked home slowly, tired and disgusted.

As he entered the flat he saw a dim light in the front room. He tried to sneak into his bedroom, but his mother heard him. She rose from her chair, a monstrous silhouette against the dim front room light.

"A fine time for you to come in, Antonio," she said. "Have you been out again with them good-for-nothing loafers?"

"Yes," said Tony, in a bad-temper.

"So . . ." said his mother, "you don't even lie any more. Well, well ! You are doing fine. Pretty soon you won't come home at all, you bum."

"You said a mouthful," said Tony.

"Sure, you won't listen to your mother. Some day you'll remember what I told you. You loaf with crooks and bums long enough, you'll see what will happen."

"All right," said Tony, going into his room and banging the door behind him.

His mother stood in the middle of the room for a minute, then she put out the light and sat in the dark, crying.

V

The little blonde check-girl helped Joe take off his big ulster, her hand lingering on his arm. He handed her a quarter.

"Don't go on a bat with that two-bits," he said.

"No sir," said the check-girl.

She watched him walk across the long dance-floor, pick his way among the crowded tables, bowing from time to time to one he had jostled, and disappear through the employees' door at the back. Then she put checks on his coat and hat and hung them up.

"God, what a hot-looking man," she said; "I don't see how that little hunky got him."

Olga Stassoff was just putting the finishing touches to her make-up. Joe came in softly and stood watching her. She began to sing.

"If you're singing for me," said Joe, "you can stop any time."

Olga turned around.

"Well, what are you doing here? Broke?"

"Shut up," said Joe.

Then he turned and walked out of the room. Olga jumped to her feet and ran after him. She caught him near the employees' door. He pushed her away.

"Ain't that a fine way to hello to a guy!" he said. "Why, you must think you got me roped and hog-tied."

"I was just kidding, Joe," said Olga, "honest I didn't mean it. I was just kidding."

"Well, get this," said Joe, "I'm goddam sick of that line. What do you take me for? That goes big with some of your swell boy friends who've got ugly wives and ain't any too particular, but me! I don't take that kind of talk from nobody."

Olga put her arms around him, but he pushed her away.

"Listen, Joe," she said, "I got good news for you, so get out of your fighting clothes and come to earth. Can't you take a little kidding?"

14 A variation of the basic waltz box step, in which a step in any direction is followed by a close and a step in another direction.

Joe took out his gold cigarette case and selected a cigarette. He always smoked the best, when Olga had plenty of money, and he usually carried three or four different brands. With a flourish he put away his case, then, very preoccupied, he placed the selected cigarette on the back of his left hand and, with a slight tap of his right hand, flipped it into his mouth. Olga laughed.

"Now," said Joe, "spill the good news."

DeVoss, the manager, came through the swinging doors.

"Have you told him yet, Olga?" he asked.

Joe gave the manager a most ingratiating smile.

"What's the big talk, Mr. DeVoss? Am I missing something?"

"You sure are," said DeVoss. "The Stranskys broke their contract and I'm putting you on in their place."

Joe leapt into the air and executed a twinkle.[14] Olga burst out laughing.

"Well," said Joe, "how much?"

"One hundred to start, Joe, then we'll see."

"Well," said Joe, "I can't buy no limousines with that, but I'll take it."

Joe and DeVoss shook hands.

"Now," said the manager, "there's a girl out here who's just dying to dance with you, Joe."

Joe shook his head.

"No, I don't like that stuff. They always think they got to hand you something. What the hell! I don't want no dame handing me nothing."

Olga put her hand over her mouth.

"Don't worry about that, Joe," said DeVoss, "she already asked me about that and I told her you'd be insulted so she gave me a ten." DeVoss took a crumpled bill out of his pocket and handed it to Joe. "There, now get this. She's an up and up girl and she means lots of business to this place. Her old man's got a couple of million bucks and she's the real thing. All right, Joe?"

"Sure, sure," said Joe, "always willing to oblige."

DeVoss went through the swinging doors and stood waiting for Joe on the other side. Olga took Joe by the arm.

"Listen," she said, "none of your funny business now. Just do your stuff and leave it at that. I'm on to these society women. I know what they want."

Joe leapt into the air and executed another twinkle.

"Alley up!"[15] he cried, "don't you trust me, baby?"

Olga put her hands on her hips and began to laugh. How could you be sore at a guy like that?

VI

Rico was standing in front of his mirror, combing his hair with a little ivory pocket comb. Rico was vain of his hair. It was black and lustrous, combed straight back from his low forehead and arranged in three symmetrical waves.

Rico was a simple man. He loved but three things: himself, his hair and his gun. He took excellent care of all three.

15 The only sense that can be made of this is the modern "alley-oop," an expression (from the French *allez*) made at the beginning of a lifting movement—here relating to Joe's dance-step.

PART II

I

H ear me," said Rico, his face twitching, "he's turned yellow. He's turned yellow. What the hell you expect from a choir boy!"

Otero said nothing but sat with his chair tipped back against the wall smoking a cigarette, his eyes closed. Sam Vettori stood in the middle of the room and stared at his watch.

"Keep your shirt on, Rico," said Vettori, "you're on edge."

"Sure, Rico," said Otero.

Carillo came in without knocking. Vettori put away his watch. "Well!"

"O.K., boss," said Carillo, "Tony's in the alley."

Vettori took out his watch again.

"Rico, it's eleven-thirty-five. What do you say?"

"Let's get going."

Otero got slowly to his feet, stamped out his cigarette, and, taking the riot gun[16] from the table in front of him, slipped it under his overcoat. Rico examined his big automatic.[17]

Carillo went out, softly closing the door. Otero walked over and patted Rico on the shoulder.

"O.K. now, eh, Rico?"

Rico smiled. Vettori's face was covered with sweat and he pulled out a big white silk handkerchief to mop it.

"Rico," he said, "from now on you boss the job. Only, get this: for the love of God, no gunwork. That's all. I ain't ripe for the rope."

Rico said nothing. Otero shrugged.

Vettori, still mopping his face, opened a window and a gust of cold air rushed in.

Rico took out his little ivory pocket comb and mechanically combed his hair. Then he put on his hat and tilted it over his eyes.

"Well," he said to Otero, "let's go."

Otero followed Rico out. Vettori called:

"Make it clean, Rico. Make it clean."

They went down the back stairs. Carillo was waiting at the foot of the stairs and held the alley door open for them. The alley way was dark and Otero stumbled.

"Caramba!"

"Watch that gun," said Rico.

Tony was sitting at the wheel of a big, open Cadillac. He tossed his cigarette away and said:

"Well, here we are."

Rico said nothing, but got into the front seat with Tony. Otero got into the back seat. Carillo stood looking at them for a moment, then closed the door. Tony stepped on the starter.[18]

"All right," said Rico, "let's go, but take it easy. We gots lots of time."

They took it easy. Tony drove along as leisurely as though they were going to a New Year's party. Rico leaned back and smoked, watching all the passing cars. Otero, who had removed the riot gun and had it on the seat beside him, was sitting bolt upright, his hands on his knees. He could never get used to riding in an automobile.[19] Rico turned and saw the gun.

"Put that rod on the floor," he said.

Otero obeyed.

It had got colder. The snow was no longer falling and a chilly wind was blowing up in gusts from the lake. The streets were nearly deserted. Over west a whistle began to blow, discordant and shrill.

"Well," said Tony, nodding in the direction of the whistle, "it won't be long now."

But Rico leaned over and hissed in his ear.

"Police car!"

A big Packard with a hooded machine-gun in the back seat passed them. There were two plain-clothes men in the front and two in the back.

18 Automobiles of the period required the driver to step on the starter pedal to trigger the starter motor, which would then fire the engine.

19 Being from Mexico, Otero was undoubtedly more accustomed to horseback or horse-drawn carriages.

"What'll I do?" asked Tony.

One of the men leaned out and stared back at them.

"Jesus," said Tony, "he's looking at us."

"Keep your shirt on," said Rico, putting his hand on Tony's arm.

Otero took a cigarette from his pack and rolled it between his palms.

The police car slowed up. Rico's fingers closed on Tony's arm.

"Here's an alley," said Rico, "duck!"

Tony took the turn on two wheels, just missing a parked car. Otero was thrown from one end of his seat to the other, losing his cigarette. The Cadillac's exhaust roared in the narrow alley way. There was nothing but darkness ahead of them.

"It's a blind," said Tony.

"No," said Rico. "I know this place like a book. Turn to your right at the end."

Rico leaned out and stared back. Then he laughed.

"Ain't that like the damn dummies! Nothing in sight."

They came back to Michigan Boulevard by a wide detour. Here the wind blew fiercely, raising little whirlwinds of snow. Now there were whistles blowing in all parts of town. Rico looked at his wrist-watch.

"Five of twelve. All right, Tony. Step on it."

"What time, Rico?" asked Otero.

Rico told him.

"Fine, fine," said Otero, "eh, Rico?"

Half a block down the street they saw the huge electric sign of the Casa Alvarado. The street was deserted except for the parked cars. They drove along slowly now.

Rico leaned out.

"That's a break," he said, pointing to a parking place where they couldn't be hemmed in. "Listen, Tony, this ain't going to be no cinch, so you better give us a lift."

Tony pretended to be preoccupied with parking.

"Get me?"

Tony was pale and his lips were twitching.

"That ain't my stand, Rico," he said.

Rico looked at him. Tony sat silent for a moment, then, pulling at the vizer of his cap, said:

"But you're the boss, Rico."

"O.K.," said Rico, smiling. "Now, Otero, get this. I go first. You follow me with the big rod. I stick up the cashier. Tony swings the sacks. Got it?" Rico took three small neatly-folded canvas sacks out of his pocket and handed them to Tony. "Otero, you watch the door. If you see anybody coming in, let 'em come in, then back 'em up against the wall. If things go right, I'll tap the box. Got it?"

Rico looked at his watch. It was three minutes past twelve.

"Let's go," he said.

Otero got out lazily, hiding the riot gun under his coat. Rico got out, followed by Tony.

"Got your rod, Tony?" asked Rico.

Tony nodded.

"All right, keep it in your pocket. Maybe you won't need it right away. If anybody gets funny, why, pull it."

"O.K.," said Tony, "but for God's sake, Rico, no gunwork."

Otero said:

"You leave Rico alone. He does what is right."

Whistles were blowing all over town. They walked up the carpet which was laid across the pavement under the canvas marquee. Inside there was a blaze of lights and they could hear the music. The lobby was deserted except for two check girls, one waiter, a cigar clerk, and the cashier, a pale woman with a green eyeshade, who was perched on a stool. Joe Massara, in a big ulster and a derby hat, was standing at the cigar counter, kidding the clerk. He saw them out of the corner of his eye and nodded twice.

They came in quickly, Rico in front with his big automatic at ready, Otero slightly behind him and to the left, carrying the sawed-off shotgun hip-high; Tony in the rear, his hand in his overcoat pocket.

Before Rico could say anything, Joe Massara faced them, put his back up against the counter and raised his hands.

"My God," he cried, "it's a hold-up."

One of the check girls screamed piercingly. The waiter's knees buckled and he almost fell. The others stood petrified.

"You're goddam right it's a hold-up!" shouted Rico, trying to intimidate them, "and it ain't gonna be no picnic. Get that, all of you birds. I got lead in this here rod and my finger's itching. One crack out of any of you and they'll pat you with a spade. All right, Tony."

20   A German-manufactured recoil-operated semi-automatic pistol, first patented in 1898 and used by German forces in World War I. The "semi-automatic" feature meant that the pistol did not require that the hammer be cocked or that bullets be ejected manually; rather, the exploding gases forced the bullet casing out of the chamber and a new bullet into the chamber, so that each trigger-pull fired a shot without delay. This is the "automatic" that is referred to earlier—see note 17.

Tony, white as chalk, took the sacks out of his pocket and walked over to the cashier's desk. The cashier was standing behind the register, hands raised. When Tony came up she said:

"Take anything you want, only for God's sake don't touch me."

"O.K.," said Tony, "clean out the box but don't get funny."

Tony held the sacks while the cashier scooped the money into them. Tony saw pack after pack of wrapped greenbacks drop into the sacks. He began to feel a little better.

Rico left the cashier to Tony, but looked at each of the others in turn, his eyes, under his tilted hat, intimidating them as successfully as the big Luger[20] in his hand. Otero stood behind him and a little to the left, impassive, the riot gun hip-high.

The manager opened the door of his office and with a dazed look hesitated for a moment, then, with a great sigh, put his back against the wall and raised his hands. He was a Czech with a swarthy complexion which gradually turned greenish.

Rico glared at the manager.

"Stay put, you!" he said.

"All right, all right," said the Czech.

Joe Massara said:

"Jesus, my arm's paralyzed."

"Yeah," shouted Rico, "well, don't let it drop."

"All set," cried Tony.

Otero was busy at the door with a man in a top hat who had just come in. The man couldn't believe his eyes and kept muttering:

"Good Lord! Good Lord!"

Otero backed him against the wall.

In the club proper, beyond the big arched doorways, the band was playing loudly, horns were tooting, people were shouting.

"All right," said Rico, "get out your gat, Tony. I'll tap the box inside."

"God," said Tony, "it'll take too long."

Rico looked at him. Tony, holding the sacks in one arm, pulled out his gun. Rico walked over to the manager.

"Listen," he said. "I want action. Go in and open that box and slip me the jack. One funny move and I'll blow your guts out."

"Oh, my God!" cried the Czech.

They disappeared. There was a dead silence in the lobby. One of the check girls began to cry.

"Nice little hold-up," said Joe.

Nobody said anything.

"Yeah," said Joe, nonchalant, "fine little hold-up."

He smiled at the waiter, who looked hastily away and turned agonized eyes on Tony as if to say: "Look, I can't help what that bird's saying."

Two more men came in the street door and were backed up against the wall by Otero. The seconds seemed like hours to Tony, who was slowly losing his nerve.

The manager reappeared, followed by Rico, who had his gun pressed against the manager's back. Rico's pockets bulged.

"Good Lord," hissed Tony, "let's go."

Three men and two women came out into the lobby from the club proper. They stopped, petrified.

The strain was beginning to tell on Rico, whose face was ghastly.

"Stick up your hands, you," he cried, "and don't move."

Two of the men and both of the women put up their hands, but the third man, burly and red-faced, hesitated.

"Good God," said Joe, "it's Courtney, the bull."

Joe's mask of nonchalance slipped from him instantly; he dropped his hands and reached for his gun.

"Beat it," cried Rico to Tony and Otero.

They made a break for the door. One of the women with Courtney fainted and fell hard, hitting her head.

"Don't touch her," cried Rico, "my finger's itching."

Joe followed the others, backing out with his gun in his hand.

Courtney's face was purple. He glanced at his wife, lying pale and unconscious on the floor, then, shouting "you dirty bums" reached for his gun. Rico fired. Courtney took two steps toward Rico, staring. Then he fell heavily, his arms spread.

At the door Rico collided with a drunken man, who was just entering. The man tried to hug him, but he knocked him down with a blow of his fist.

Rico jumped on the running-board and bellowed:

"Open her up, Tony. This ain't no picnic."

Tony was unnerved and tears were dripping down onto his hands. Joe and Otero sat silent in the back seat. Otero rolled a cigarette between his palms. Nobody said anything.

Tony took a corner, careening. The wind had died down a little and it had begun to snow again, a thin, cold, powdery snow. The

21   In today's coarser language, Joe would say, "It's our asses for this," with the same implication.

whistles were still blowing, but fainter now, one leaving off, then another.

"Well," said Rico, "I plugged him."

"Yeah," said Joe, "I seen him fall. Like a ton of bricks."

"Well," said Otero, "what can you do? The fool, pulling a gat!"

Tony said nothing, but sat with his eyes fixed.

"It's our hips[21] for this," said Joe.

Otero shrugged and lit a cigarette.

"Losing your guts, Joe?" asked Rico.

"Me!" said Joe.

Rico Bandello (Edward G. Robinson) tries to straighten out Joe Massara (Douglas Fairbanks, Jr.), in a scene from the 1931 film of *Little Caesar*.

Tony turned into the alley way back of The Palermo. Rico put the sacks under his coat and jumped out. Otero and Joe followed him.

"Tony," said Rico, "ditch that can, then come back for your split. Hear what I say. Ditch it good and proper. We'll wait."

"Look," said Joe, "I got to have my split now. I'm on at one-twenty. Boy, I can't miss that turn."

"O.K.," said Rico.

Tony drove off down the alley. Rico knocked at the door and Carillo let them in.

II

When they came in Vettori was standing in the middle of the room mopping his forehead with his big white silk handkerchief. Beads of sweat stood out all over his swarthy, fat face.

Rico threw the sacks on the table and began to empty his pockets.

"Well," said Vettori.

"There's the dough," said Rico; "looks like a good haul."

Joe sat down at the table under the green-shaded lamp without taking off his hat or coat. Otero took the riot gun from under his coat and locked it up in a cupboard. Vettori knew there was something the matter. His eyes narrowed.

"Well," he said again.

"Everything was O.K.," said Rico, "only I had to plug a guy."

Vettori fell down into a chair and stared out the window.

"Yeah," said Joe, trying to smile, "and the guy was Courtney."

Vettori put his head on the back of his chair and stared at the ceiling. Then he sat up suddenly and banged on the table with both fists.

"Goddam!" he cried, "what did I tell you, Rico! What did I tell you! Love of God, didn't I tell you no gunwork?"

Rico was white with rage.

"Listen, Sam, you think I'm gonna let a guy pull a gat on me. What the hell! Any more of them cracks and this is my last job."

Vettori made an elaborate, tragic gesture.

"Yeah, you bet this is your last job."

Joe took off his derby and put it beside him on the table. His face was dead white.

"You said it," said Joe, "they'll get us sure for this."

Vettori shook his big head slowly from side to side.

"They'll get us dead sure for this."

Rico began to comb his hair.

"Maybe you better go over and give yourself up," he said; then dropping his sarcastic tone, "listen, how the hell they gonna get us? Why, you're the finest bunch of yellow bastards I ever seen."

"Not me," said Otero.

Joe tried to smile.

"Wait till you see the papers."

22 Likely a typographical error for "car," although it appears consistently in later editions.

23 A slang expression (also in the form "yeggmen") for a burglar or safe-cracker. The *Oxford English Dictionary* credits the first usage in 1902. Although the exact origins of the term are murky, William Pinkerton, of the Pinkerton National Detective Agency believed the term "yegg" originated with the gypsies. In a paper delivered to the International Association of Chiefs of Police in 1904, Pinkerton explained: "When a particularly clever thief is found among a gypsy tribe, he is selected as the 'Yegg' or chief thief. . . . If a tribe or band of tramps found among their number a particularly persistent beggar or daring thief, they, using the expression of the gypsies, called him a 'Yegg.' Then came the name of 'John Yegg' and finally the word 'Yeggman.'" (Reproduced under the title "The Yeggman," *American Lawyer*, 12 (1904), 384–88.)

Rico came over and leaned on the table.

"Listen, don't they always play that stuff up in the papers? Courtney's the only guy in the place that ever seen one of us before. Come on, snap out of it. And split the dough."

But Vettori sat inert, mopping his face. Suddenly he asked: "Where's Tony?"

"He's ditching the can,"[22] said Rico.

"Suppose they pick him up?"

Rico began to open the sacks.

"That'll be just too bad," said Joe.

Rico laughed.

"A fine bunch of yeggs!"[23]

Vettori got to his feet in a fury.

"You, Rico! Shut your mouth. You think I want to hang because you get yellow and shoot somebody."

Rico, very calm, put his hand in his pocket and said:

"Sam, you get funny with me and you won't get no split at all. Only a horseshoe wreath."

"Oh, hell, Sam," said Joe, "we're all in it, ain't we? Come on, split the dough."

Vettori sat down. Otero stood a little behind him, watching.

"Since you want it, Sam," said Rico, his face pale and drawn, "you're gonna get it. Listen, you split even, that's all. Hear me! You get an even split."

Vettori said nothing. Joe sat rigid, ready to dive under the table. For months Scabby had been predicting this break; now it had come. Joe feared Vettori and Rico equally, but something told him that Rico would win.

Vettori let his hands fall on the table.

"All right, Rico," he said, "I split even. Sit down and we'll divvy."

But Rico didn't move.

"You got a gun on you, Sam?" he asked.

Vettori looked up at him.

"Sure I got a gun on me."

"Well, don't try to use it."

"No," said Otero, "don't try to use it."

Vettori's face went slack. He sat tapping on the table with his fat fingers.

"Rico," he said, finally, "I split even on the square."

Rico's victory was complete. Joe looked at him with admiration. Sam was a tough bird, but Rico was tougher.

Vettori got up, walked across the room and stood looking out the window.

III

Joe handed Rico a sheet of paper full of figures. Rico read: 9331.75.[24]

"All right," said Rico, "split it five ways and we'll make up Scabby's split between us."

Otero sat with his chair tipped back against the wall, smoking a cigarette with his eyes closed. Vettori was playing solitaire and swearing softly to himself.

Joe looked at his watch.

"Quarter till. I got to beat it. Say, Sam, call Carillo and let him get me a cab, will you?"

Sam heaved himself to his feet and called Carillo. In a moment the bouncer put his flattened face in the door.

"Three dicks downstairs, boss."

"Who are they?" asked Vettori.

"Flaherty and two guys I don't know, boss. They want to see you."

Vettori stood looking at the floor. Carillo jumped in and shut the door.

"Christ," he said, "they're coming up."

Rico leapt to his feet, ran across the room and opened a panel in the wall.

"Come on, Joe," he said, "you can slip out the back way. Stay where you are, Otero, and go right on smoking. Send Joe's cab around in the alley, Bat."

Vettori looked at Rico.

"You suppose they know something, Rico?"

"Not unless they picked Tony up. You don't know nothing, Sam, see? I'll be right here listening, and if there's any trouble, why, it'll be tough on the dicks."

Vettori scooped up the money, wrapped his coat around it, and handed it to Rico. Joe went through the panel, followed by Rico. There was a knock at the door.

24   It is always difficult to compare dollar amounts from different years, but according to Samuel H. Williamson, "Seven Ways to Compute the Relative Value of a U.S. Dollar Amount, 1774 to present," Measuring Worth (https://measuringworth.com/calculators/uscompare/), 2017, the "economic status value" in 2016 dollars would be over $630,000, the "economic power value" approximately $1.7 million. The "labor value" of $9,331, using an unskilled worker's wage level, is over $430,000 in 2016 dollars. In any case, the amount taken in the robbery was a substantial amount for these men, netting each over $80,000 in 2016 dollars—not enough to retire from criminality but an amount that would significantly improve their lives.

Illinois license plates were nondescript series of numbers.

1925 Illinois license plates.

Vettori nodded and Carillo opened the door. Two plain-clothes men stepped in and stood looking around the room. One was tall and burly in a huge ulster; the other was short and very young. They both had their right hands in their overcoat pockets.

"All right, Carillo," said Vettori, "go ahead. That's all."

"Wait a minute," said the burly one, "tell Flaherty we'll be down in a couple of minutes, for him to wait."

"Sure, sure," said Carillo.

He went out closing the door softly.

"Well," said Vettori, "you want to see me?"

"Yeah," said the burly one, who did all the talking, "we want to see you, Vettori."

"Well, here I am!"

Otero opened his eyes long enough to look at them, then closed them again and went on smoking.

"Vettori," said the detective, "we want some information."

"Well?"

Vettori sat down at the table and began to shuffle the cards.

"There's a big Cadillac draped around a pole a couple of blocks down the street and we just wondered if you knew anything about it."

Vettori began to lay out a game of solitaire.

"How should I know anything about it? Ain't it got no license plates on it?"[25]

"Sure, but they're phoney."

"Yeah?"

"Yeah. It was stolen about eight o'clock tonight on the North Side and we got a pretty good description of the guy that stole it."

"Well," said Vettori, "I got a good business. What the hell'd I be doing stealing automobiles?"

He laughed and shook his head.

"Oh, you got me wrong," said the detective with elaborate innocence. "You see, it's piled up right straight down the street from here and I thought maybe it was some of the guys from your joint, see? I mean some of the young guys that come here to dance."

"Well," said Vettori, "how would I know?"

The detective took out a cigar and began to chew on it.

"Wasn't there nobody in it?" asked Otero.

"Yeah," said the detective, "one guy. But he beat it."

"I don't know nothing about it," said Vettori.

"Well, no harm in asking," said the detective. "Come on, Mike, let's get going. I guess Vettori don't know nothing about it."

The two of them walked slowly to the door. The big one turned.

"Say, Vettori," he said, "did you hear the news?"

Vettori looked up.

"What news?"

"Why, some bastard bumped Cap Courtney off over at the Casa Alvarado."

"Yeah?" said Vettori, "some guys are sure careless with the lead. That's a tough break."

The young detective opened the door and they started out.

"Ain't it?" said the big one. "Well, so long."

As soon as the door closed, Vettori went over and shot the bolt, then peeped out through the shutter. Rico came out of his hiding place.

"Well," said Vettori, glancing at Rico, "things ain't going so good."

Rico shrugged.

"They don't know nothing. Just feeling around. Listen, Sam, where's your guts? We got to stick together on this."

"I know," said Vettori, falling back into his chair, "but I never seen things break so tough."

Rico held out a roll of bills.

"Here's your split, Sam."

Vettori took the bills and stuffed them into his pocket. Rico handed Otero his. Otero got up and put on his overcoat.

"I think I go see my woman," he said.

When he had gone Rico went over and sat down beside Vettori.

"Listen, Sam," he said, "I been taking orders too long. We're done. Get the idea? But we got to see this through. We get a break and we'll come clean. Only we got to shoot straight. See what I mean? I got a rope around my neck right now and they can only hang you once. If anybody gets yellow and squeals, my gun's gonna speak its piece."

"That's O.K. with me," said Sam.

They sat silent. Down stairs the jazzband was playing and the saxophone was sending vibrations along the floor. Vettori laid out another game of solitaire.

"Funny for Tony to crash," he said.

"He lost his nerve," said Rico.

"You suppose he'll show?"

"Not till tomorrow if he's got any sense. I'll leave his split with you."

IV

Rico went over to see Ma Magdalena, the fence. Her fruit store was still open and her son Arrigo was sitting half-asleep beside a pile of oranges.

"Hello," he said.

"Where's Ma?" asked Rico.

Arrigo pulled a cord which rang a bell in the rooms beyond the store. Ma, leaning on her stick, came out into the store. Seeing Rico, she said:

"Oh, it's you! Well, well! Come back. Come back."

"Can I come too, Ma?" said Arrigo.

"You stay and mind the store, you lazy loafer," said Ma, shaking her stick at him.

Arrigo sat down once more by the pile of oranges.

Rico followed Ma Magdalena back into her little office. She pulled up a chair for him and he sat down, then she got out a bottle.

"You talk, I drink," she said, sitting down beside him and pouring herself a drink.

Rico took out his split, peeled off a few bills and handed her the rest.

"Plant it," he said.

She took the roll, counted it, and put it down inside her dress.

"Had a big New Year's Eve, did you?"

"Yeah," said Rico, "plenty big. There'll be lots of fun tomorrow."

"Well, well," said Ma, "that's the way it goes."

She poured herself another glass of wine, then she reached over and touched Rico with her stick.

"Look, Rico, you ain't got a nice little girl who wants a big diamond ring, have you?"

"Me, buy a diamond ring for a skirt?"

Ma Magdalena made a clucking noise and shook her head.

"You are cold, Rico. Don't like wine. Don't like women. You are no good, Rico."

Rico smiled.

"Me, I like women once in a while, but I ain't putting out no diamond rings."

Leaving Ma Magdalena's Rico went in the direction of Sicily Pete's. The wind was blowing hard and Rico, turning up his overcoat collar, leaned against it. It was after three o'clock and the streets were empty. Southward the lights of the Loop made a reddish glow in the sky.

At Sicily Pete's the mechanical piano was playing. Three men, all Italians, and two girls, both Americans, were sitting at a front table. They were drunk. They played with their food, spilled their coffee, and banged on the plates with their knives. Pete stood behind the counter, scowling.

When Rico came in he said: "Hello, my friend, where have you been keeping yourself?"

"I haven't been around lately. Got some noisy birds, ain't you?"

Pete shrugged his shoulders.

"Yes, the fools. They drink gin. That is no drink for an Italian."

Rico took out his cigarettes and offered Pete one. They stood smoking. One of the girls pulled up her dress and fixed her garter. Rico smiled.

"Get an eyeful of that, Pete."

"Yes, yes," said Pete, "that's all I get, an eyeful. Every night I stand here while other people have a good time."

The girl looked up at Rico and he winked at her. She said to one of the men:

"Look at that smarty over there. He thinks he's cute."

The man looked foggily at Rico. Pete put his hand on Rico's arm.

"My friend, don't start no trouble, please. That's all we have around here, trouble. With one thing and another, I think I go back to Italy."

Rico turned his back on the girl.

"O.K.," he said.

While Pete was getting Rico a cup of coffee, a newsboy came in: "EXTRA! EXTRA! All about the big hold-up."

Rico bought a paper and glanced at the three inch headlines.

26 Italy was the birthplace of American crime organizations. The earliest was incorrectly referred to as the Black Hand. In fact, the Black Hand refers not to a gang but to the method of extortion used by New York–based Italian criminals in the early twentieth-century, involving demands adorned by images of skulls, daggers, and black warning hands. According to Mike Dash's *The First Family: Terror, Extortion and the Birth of the American Mafia*, in 1907, the legendary tenor Enrico Caruso received a Black Hand letter demanding "protection" money. Caruso paid, but when threats persisted, he worked with the police to capture the extortionists in Little Italy. The bizarre form of the demands caught the public's attention, and the extortion racket was dubbed "the Black Hand" by a reporter for the *New York Herald*. The name quickly became synonymous with the principal perpetrators of the racket—the Camorra and the Mafia.

The Camorra was an outgrowth of the Carbonari, an eighteenth-century Italian political organization. In the latter half of the eighteenth century, the Naples-based Camorra, an association that specialized in blackmail, bribery, and smuggling, was encouraged by the corrupt Bourbon regime to police the city and eliminate the opposition. A crackdown was instituted in the 1880s after the unification of Italy, and the Camorra began to decline in power; its grip on Naples was fatally loosened in 1911, after several of its members were convicted in a high-profile murder trial. Thriving in the poor sections of Naples, the organization followed the waves of Neapolitan immigrants to America; so too did its Sicilian-based cousin, the Mafia, accompany the more-numerous Sicilian immigrants to the United States. According to Arthur Train's May 1912

Rico showed Pete the paper.

"Another killing," he said.

"Yes," said Pete, "kill, kill, that's all they do. I wish to God I was back in Sicily. The Mafia, what is that?[26] That is a kindergarten."

One of the Italians bought a paper and started to read the account of the hold-up aloud. All the people round the table stopped eating to listen. Rico sipped his coffee and watched them.

V

Tony hadn't slept all night. He lay in the cold dark room, sweating. The covers felt heavy as lead and from time to time he tossed them off, only to pull them over him again as the lake wind, streaming in the window, made him shiver. At intervals he would fall into a doze. Then he would see a windy street, feel a car skidding under him, feel a sickening jolt. He would wake with a start and sit up in bed.

"They'll get us for this," he kept repeating, "they'll get us sure."

Unable to control his imagination, he saw the high forbidding walls of the State Prison, the tiny death cells with their heavily-grated windows; then in the prison yard, the gallows. He remembered what Rico had said about Red Gus, on the night of his execution: "Well, they're gonna put a necktie on Gus he won't take off!" Yeah, they sure put a necktie on Gus.

Tony smoked cigarette after cigarette. In his despair he cast about for someone to put the blame on. It was all Midge's fault. Wasn't she always after him to make more jack so she could put on the dog? Hadn't he tried to go straight and drive a taxi and make an honest living? Yeah, and hadn't Sam Vettori and Rico offered him money to quit his job and give them a lift on their stick-ups? Well, you couldn't quit a gang; once you were in, you were in!

Tony sat up in bed and looked out across the roofs outside his window. The sun was coming up and a cold, windy winter morning was dawning. Of a sudden he began to feel sick at his stomach. He lay down, but that didn't help him; then he tossed from side to side.

He heard his mother moving about in the next room. She was getting dressed to go to work. An alarm-clock in a room across the court rang, then there was some loud swearing, and a window was slammed.

Tony had to vomit. He jumped out of bed and ran for the bathroom. When he came out his mother was lighting the stove. She acted as if she didn't see him. He went back to his room but stopped in the doorway.

"Hello, mom," he said.

His mother paid no attention.

"Say," said Tony, "what's the matter?"

His mother turned and with her hands on her hips stared at him.

"Go back to bed, you loafer," she said, "I am sick of you. You are no good on earth. Just like your father."

"Aw, mom," said Tony.

"Don't try to salve me," said Tony's mother. "You go back to bed and get sober. You think I don't know nothing, don't you? Just like your father."

"I'm not drunk," said Tony, "I'm sick."

His mother turned her back and went on with her cooking. Tony went into his room, slammed the door, and got back into bed. A deadly depression settled on him. The world looked black.

He heard his mother go out, then he got up, dressed and made himself some toast and coffee. Anyway, he wanted his split.

On the way to Vettori's he met Father McConagha. The priest was a big man with a big, pale face. He walked with a rolling gait and there was something arrogant about him. Tony took off his hat.

"Good morning, Father."

"Good morning, Antonio," said Father McConagha. "Where have you been, my boy? I haven't seen you for months."

"I been working," said Tony.

"What sort of work?" asked Father McConagha, putting his hand on Tony's shoulder.

"I been driving a taxi."

The priest nodded his head slowly.

"That is good work, Antonio."

article for *McClure's* magazine, "Imported Crime: The Story of the Camorra in America," the Camorra only preyed on Italians. With the rise of gangsterism after the passage of Prohibition in 1919, however, New York and other major cities became prime territory for the Mafia and the Camorra in many fields of criminality, most profitably the liquor business, prostitution, and eventually drugs.

Tony couldn't look at Father McConagha and kept twisting his hat in his hands and staring at it. Father McConagha talked to him for a minute or two about the rewards of honesty and the happiness to be derived from doing your work faithfully, then he said:

"Antonio, one day your father asked me to look out for you. Your father was a good man, but weak. Remember this, Antonio, if you are ever in any trouble I am the one to come to."

Tony flushed and said:

"Thank you, Father."

When Father McConagha had gone, Tony began to speculate. Did he know anything? Why, on this very morning, had he said something about being in trouble? Tony respected and admired Father McConagha. He felt that he could always turn to him.

Talking with the priest had made him feel stronger, but now that the priest had gone all the hopelessness of the night before rushed back on him. He took out a cigarette and lit it with shaking hands.

"They'll get us sure for this," he said.

Then once more he began to think about Red Gus and what Rico had said about him.

VI

Seal Skin couldn't get Otero sober. She made him eat tomatoes and she gave him a cold bath, but nothing seemed to do him any good. He walked about the flat in his underclothes singing songs in bastard Spanish and bragging about what a great, brave man he was. Only one man in the world braver: Rico.

Seal Skin was dead for sleep, but she didn't shut her eyes for fear Otero would do some crazy thing like shooting out the window at the street light (he had done this one night) or going out in his underclothes.

Otero sat at the table with his automatic beside him, singing at the top of his voice.

"Look," he cried, "I am Ramón Otero, a great, brave man. I ain't afraid of nobody or nothing. I can drink any man in the world under the table and I can outshoot any man that walks on two legs. Only Rico; he is my friend. He is a great man like Pancho Villa and I love him with a great love. I would not shoot Rico if he shot me first. Rico is my friend and I love him with a great love."

Then he got up and, snapping his fingers, began to dance, stamping with his heels, wiggling his hips, till Seal Skin nearly fell out of her chair laughing.

Toward morning he went to sleep with his head on the table. Seal Skin picked him up and carried him to bed (he weighed about a hundred and fifteen pounds), then, too tired to take off her clothes, she climbed in beside him.

VII

Rico bought all the papers he could find and went up to his room to read them. He sat at his table, his hat tilted over his eyes, with a pair of scissors in his hand, cutting from the papers all the articles dealing with the hold-up and the killing of Police Captain Courtney. He arranged the clippings in a neat pile, then read them over and over.

One said:

> ". . . the thug who shot Police Captain Courtney was a small, pale foreigner, probably an Italian. He was dressed in a natty overcoat and a light felt hat."

Another:

> ". . . Courtney's murderer was described by one eyewitness as a small, unhealthy-looking foreigner."

Rico tore up this clipping.

"Where do they get that unhealthy stuff!" he said. "I never been sick a day in my life."

PART III

27   Gerald Peary, in "Rico Rising: *Little Caesar* Takes Over the Screen," suggests that the *parvenu* Big Boy is based on Al Capone (p. 287).

I

Sam Vettori's heavy, dark face looked puffy and his eyes were swollen. He hadn't been sleeping well lately and he had been drinking whiskey. As wine was his usual drink, the whiskey indicated a state of mind the reverse of calm. He sat chewing a cold stogie and from time to time pouring himself a shot from the bottle at his elbow. Rico was playing solitaire, his hat tilted over his eyes. The Big Boy sat opposite Vettori, his derby on the side of his head, and his huge fists, fists which at one time had swung a pick in a section gang, lying before him on the table.[27]

The Big Boy shook his head from side to side slowly.

"Not a chance, Sam," he said, "I can't do nothing for you. Why, you must be out of your mind. Listen, they're after me hot and heavy. I got all I can do to take care of number one, see? Things was running too good for you, Sam. That's your trouble. You thought I was God himself. But listen, I ain't no miracle man. A stick-up more or less, what's that? But when it comes to plugging a bull like Courtney, that's out! No, Sam. You're on your own now. It ain't gonna be none too healthy for none of us for a while. Just don't lose your nerve, that's the main thing. Just hang on and watch the guys that are in the know."

"You leave that to me," said Rico without looking up.

"O.K.," said the Big Boy, "I think you're the goods, Rico. But don't get nervous with that gat of yours, or they'll put a necktie on you. Get this. No more stick-ups. No more jobs. Just lay low, all of you. If you run out of jack, I'll stake you. Now I got to beat it. Don't call me up no more, Sam. Because I can't do nothing for you and it might give the bulls an idea."

The Big Boy got to his feet and stood leaning his huge hairy paws on the table.

"Why, you guys are lucky and don't know it. Wood's manager got so goddam rattled he identified one of the plain-clothes men as the guy that did the inside stand. Jesus, but it was rich! Spike Rieger was boiling. Pretty soon he pinned the manager down and the damn dummy said that the guys that did the job were Poles. So they went out and grabbed Steve Gollancz. Steve and his bunch had just tapped a bank and Steve thought they had the goods[28] on him. It was funny as hell!"

The Big Boy put his head back and brayed. Sam Vettori drummed on the table irritably.

"All right, laugh," said Sam.

"Sure, I'll laugh," said the Big Boy; "if you'd seen Steve's face when he found out what it was all about you'd split your pants laughing."

"Steve's the goods," said Rico.

"You said a mouthful," said the Big Boy, "he's got them eating out of his hand. Well, I'm gonna beat it. You guys lay low and it may blow over. If things get hot, I'll tip off Scabby and then you all better hit the rods.[29] So long."

The Big Boy went out slamming the door. They heard him go downstairs; he walked as heavily as a squad of police and banged each step with his heels.

Rico went on with his game of solitaire.

"Well," said Vettori, "something just tells me we're gonna get ours."

"Oh, hell!" said Rico, pushing the cards away from him, "I'd like to get the guy that invented that game."

Vettori swore softly to himself at Rico's indifference, then, pouring himself another drink, he said: "You think Joe's safe, Rico?"

"Yeah," said Rico, "as long as they don't nab him and put it to him. He can't stand the gaff."[30]

"How about The Greek?"

Rico laughed.

"Safe as hell. Only thing with Otero, he gets lit[31] and wants to raise hell. I had to knock him down a couple of times last night.

28   "The goods" in this context means evidence to support an arrest or conviction. Note that four paragraphs later, "the goods" is used to mean "the real deal," quality, excellence. See note 7.

29   From "roads," a slang expression meaning "hit the *roads*"—that is, move on, get out of town.

30   Slang, meaning to bear up under hardship, criticism, punishment, or in this case, interrogation.

31   Inebriated; drunk.

He gets a little money and he goes nuts. That goddam greaser never saw over five dollars all at once till I picked him up in Toledo. But he's safe."

"How about Tony?"

Rico didn't say anything for a minute but picked up his cards and began to shuffle them.

"I don't know about Tony."

Sam Vettori got up and walked back and forth, mopping his forehead at intervals with his big white silk handkerchief.

"Love of God, Rico, we can't take no chances with him."

Rico dealt out a couple of poker hands and began to play an imaginary game.

"You leave that to me, Sam," he said.

Vettori put his hand on Rico's shoulder.

"That's the talk, Rico. We get a break we may come clean."

Vettori dropped back into his chair and poured himself another drink, but Rico reached across the table and pushed the glass off on the floor.

"Slow down on that stuff, Sam. You got to keep your head clear."

Vettori looked at Rico in a fury, then he lowered his eyes.

"You got the right dope, Rico. That stuff don't do nobody no good."

Vettori took the whiskey bottle and locked it up in a cupboard.

II

About nine o'clock Carillo put his head in the door. Downstairs the jazzband had just started to play.

"Well?" demanded Vettori, getting to his feet.

"Blackie wants to see you," said Carillo.

"All right."

Carillo went out.

"What you suppose he wants?" said Vettori.

Rico, who was sitting with his chair tipped back against the wall reading a magazine, shook his head without looking up or answering. He was deep in the reading of a story about a rich society girl who fell in love with a bootlegger. Rico read everything he could find that had anything to do with society. He was fascinated by a stratum of existence which seemed so remote and unreal to him. The men of this level were "saps" and "softies" to him, but he envied them their women. He had seen them getting out of limousines at the doors of Gold Coast[32] hotels. He had seen them, magnificently dressed, insolent, inaccessible, walking up the carpets under the canvas marquees. The doormen would bow. The women would disappear. Rico hated them. They were so arrogant and selfsufficient, and they did not know that there was such a person in the world as Rico.

Blackie Avezzano, who managed Sam's garage, came in and shut the door behind him. He was small and bowlegged, and he was so dark that he had been taken for a mulatto many times.

Vettori impatiently exclaimed: "Well, what's on your mind, Blackie?'"

Rico went on reading his magazine. Blackie sat down at the table and seemed to be making an effort to collect his thoughts.

"All right, spit it out," said Vettori.

Blackie couldn't speak very good English, but as Rico didn't know a word of Italian and Vettori preferred to speak English, he did the best he could.

"Tony he took sick. Listen, I tell you, Tony he no know what. He took sick. I see him, listen, I tell you, what-you-say, he no got his guts. The Madre she send me call the doctore. Listen, he say, Tony, whatyousay, you been a drink. Now listen, you cut out a drink. That's all. Tony he no drink. What a hell! One bottle of beer he can no drink. He no got his guts, that's all."

Vettori looked at Rico, who went on reading.

"Rico," he said.

"I heard him," said Rico, "I ain't deaf."

Blackie got up and stood twisting his cap in his hand. Vettori took out his billfold and handed Blackie a ten.

"Blackie," he said, "keep your eyes open, understand?"

"All right," said Blackie, "I watch, see, I know. Tony no good. All right, I watch."

When he had gone Rico said:

"Well, that's that."

"We can't take no chances, " said Vettori.

"I'll give him till tomorrow," said Rico; "he can't go far wrong with Blackie watching him. After that if he don't settle down, there won't be no more Tony."

Lake Shore Drive, aerial view, in the 1920s.

Tony had always been of a rather easy-going nature and took things as they came. His emotions, it is true, were very unstable; with him anger was almost immediately followed by a grin, and depression lasted only long enough for him to recognize that he had felt such an emotion. No, he had never before experienced the loneliness which is the result of continued despair. Now he felt it and it was too much for him. He looked back on the past as a sort of fabulous period when he had had peace of mind.

He could enjoy nothing. The fear of arrest and hanging dogged him even at the movies, formerly his chief pleasure, and in the company of Midge, his woman, he was so preoccupied that she thought he had a new woman and treated him accordingly. Even the presence of his mother, who had begun to realize that something was wrong, did not tranquilize him. He drank, played pool, rode about in an automobile, but fear pursued him and he could find no rest.

Then he began to have attacks of acute indigestion, and it got so bad that the very sight of food was repugnant to him. He lost weight rapidly.

There was nothing he could do. He could not find one avenue of escape. But little by little the thought of Father McConagha took possession of him. Tony was too unintelligent to know that what he needed most of all was someone he could unburden himself to. But he blundered toward that solution.

Blackie's solicitude helped some. Blackie came to see him every night; and once, when Tony's indigestion had been worse than usual, he had even gone for the doctor.

Tony's mother put her hand on his shoulder.

"Antonio," she said, "I think I'll go over across the street and see Mrs. Mangia. She is having a new baby. Only think! That will be twelve."

Tony tried to smile.

"Twelve!" said Tony's mother, shaking her head slowly from side to side, "and one is too much."

"A bad egg like me is."

"You ain't a bad egg, Antonio," said his mother, "you are only lazy."

Tony said nothing.

"Listen, Antonio, I left some spaghetti on the stove. If you feel better eat some. You don't want to get all run down."

"All right," said Tony.

Tony's mother went out. As soon as the door was shut, Tony wished that she hadn't gone. He was afraid. At the sound of footsteps in the corridor, he felt his hair rise and beads of sweat stood out on his forehead. He got to his feet and began to walk up and down. A fury seized him; he cursed Rico and Vettori aloud. Then suddenly the anger left him and the fear returned.

Blackie put his head in the door.

"How you feel, Tony?" he asked.

"Hello, Blackie," said Tony, "come on in and have a smoke."

Blackie took a cigarette from the proferred pack and sat down. While he smoked he kept glancing at Tony.

"Whatsa mat, Tony?" said Blackie. "You ain't look so good."

Tony stared at Blackie for a moment, then he began to shake all over.

"Jesus, Blackie," he cried, "I can't stand it. They'll get us sure. Have you seen tonight's paper?"

Blackie shrugged.

"I can no read."

"It's all up with us," said Tony. "My God, I don't see how Rico stands it."

"Rico no scared."

"Well, he ought to be. He's the one that done it."

Blackie shrugged.

"No can help. What-you-say, Cortenni pull a gat. No can help."

Tony got very pale of a sudden. He heard an automobile stop in the street below. He ran to the window and looked down, then he turned and came back.

"I thought it was the cops," he said.

"Look," said Blackie, "you no better be sick. Listen, you no got your guts, Tony. Rico say, be a man. That is good. Be a man, Rico say. You no better be sick."

"The hell with Rico," said Tony.

Blackie shrugged.

Tony stood in the middle of the room for a minute or two looking at the floor, then, suddenly making up his mind, he went over to the hatrack and got his hat.

"Where you go?" asked Blackie.

Tony hesitated.

"I go too," said Blackie.

"No, you go home," said Tony, then looking steadily at Blackie he said: "Me, I'm going down to St. Dominick's and see Father McConagha."

"What!" cried Blackie, leaping up in alarm. "Tony, my God, you no tell him nothing."

"I got to," cried Tony vehemently.

Blackie took hold of Tony's arm.

"Tony, my boy, don't go. Listen, Tony, you no sick. Be a man. Hear what I tell you. You no live, see, you no live. Be a man."

Tony pushed him away.

"You go home, Blackie."

Tony went out. Blackie heard him walking slowly down the corridor. When he could no longer hear his footsteps, he leapt to his feet, opened a back window, went down the fire-escape, and took a short cut through the alleys. He knocked at the back door of the Palermo and Carillo let him in.

IV

Vettori stared at Rico, who said nothing.

"Crazy! Crazy!" said Blackie. "I tell him, be a man, be a man. But he say, I got to, I got to."

Rico hastily put on his overcoat.

"Well, I guess that's it," said Sam Vettori.

"Yeah," said Rico, "that's it. Now get yourself a can, Sam, and let's go. We ain't got any time to waste."

Vettori rubbed both hands over his face.

"Not me," he said.

Rico looked at him.

"Take Blackie," said Vettori.

Blackie implored them with his eyes.

"Blackie's no good," said Rico.

"No," said Blackie, "I no good."

Carillo put his head in the door.

"Reilley's downstairs, boss."

"Take Carillo," said Vettori.

Carillo stared at them suspiciously. Rico leapt across the room and grabbed him by the arm.

"Listen, Bat, can you drive a can?"

"Sure."

"Will you let her out when I office[33] you?"

"Sure."

"All right, let's go."

"Take that black roadster, Carillo," said Vettori, "but for God's sake don't smash it up."

Carillo ran out leaving the door open. Rico walked over and closed the door, then he said:

"Sam, you ain't got any more guts than Tony. Now listen, get down there and talk turkey to Reilley. Get that! By God, I guess I got to boss this job myself."

Vettori looked at Rico with hatred. But he said:

"All right, Rico, you're the boss now."

Rico went out. Blackie said:

"Goodbye Tony!"

Carillo was waiting with the black roadster in the alleyway. Rico jumped in and the roadster leapt away. Carillo took a turn on two wheels.

"It's a cinch he went the shortest cut," said Rico.

"Sure," said Carillo, "I know what I'm doing."

"All right," said Rico, "do it."

The wind had risen and it began to snow, big, heavy flakes which sailed past the street lights. In a few minutes the ground was covered.

Carillo took the shortest cut and Rico, holding his big automatic on the seat beside him, sat straining his eyes. But there was no sign of Tony.

"If we miss him I'll kick hell out of Blackie," said Rico.

"Keep your shirt on, boss," said Carillo.

The tall spires of St. Dominick's[34] rose before them at the end of the block. The street was deserted. Carillo drove slowly now, hugging the curb. In a moment he pointed:

"There's a guy."

Rico leaned forward.

"Take it easy, Bat," he said, "I think it's Tony."

Carillo throttled down to five miles an hour. The man, a dim black figure in the falling snow, stopped in front of the cathedral and looked up. When the automobile came abreast of him he turned.

"Tony," called Rico.

"Yeah?" came Tony's voice. "Who is it?"

33   "The office" is slang for a warning, a tip off, or an instruction. See Morton, James, *Gangster Speak: A Dictionary of Criminal and Sexual Slang* (London: Virgin Books Ltd., 2002).

34   St. Dominic's Catholic Church was originally built in 1905, at the corner of Locust and Sedgwick, in the area formerly known as Little Sicily or Little Hell. Little Sicily was an historically Italian-centric community on the Near North Side distinct from Little Italy, home to more than 20,000 Italians at the time of publication of *Little Caesar*. The neighborhood disappeared with the construction of the Cabrini-Green public housing projects; those too have now been largely replaced with condominiums. St. Dominic's served the Near North Side for more than seventy-five years. In 2015, the church—vacant for twenty-five years—was torn down to build a condominium tower.

Gerald Peary, in "Rico Rising: *Little Caesar* Takes Over the Screen," points out that in 1926, Hymie Weiss, "rosary around his neck," had been executed in similar circumstances by Capone's henchmen in front of the Holy Name Cathedral in Chicago (p. 290).

St. Dominic's Church in 1913.

Rico fired. A long spurt of flame shot out in the darkness. Rico emptied his gun. Tony fell without a sound.

"All right now, Bat," said Rico, "let her out."

V

Joe and Olga were sitting in a quiet corner of a Gold Coast hotel dining-room. They were waiting for their dessert. Joe, comfortably full and inclined to be amiable, sat looking at Olga. She was the goods. Of course he stepped out with other broads occasionally when Olga was busy, but that didn't count. Olga was the goods and she was his woman. Other men didn't rate with her, that's all. He studied her. There she sat with her round dark face, her high cheekbones, and her dark mascaraed eyes. Her long thin fingers covered with rings fascinated him. Her slimness, her elegance made him feel very uncouth and protective and masculine.

"Well," said Olga, "take a good look."

"Listen, baby," said Joe, "you got it. I ain't kidding. You got everything. There ain't a woman in Chicago that's got half your stuff. You make 'em all look silly."

Olga reached across the table and patted his hand.

"I don't believe it, but say it again. I like it."

"No fooling."

"What a line," said Olga.

The waiter brought their dessert.

"I'll tell you," said Olga, looking at her wrist watch, "let's go to a movie. I got time."

Joe didn't like movies very well; all that sappy love stuff! But now he wanted to please Olga.

"All right. Where'll it be?"

Olga turned to the waiter.

"Bring us a paper, please."

The waiter brought a paper and handed it to Joe. He unfolded it and started to turn to the theatrical page, but instead he read with absorption an article on the front page. Olga saw him swallow several times. When he glanced up at her there was a bewildered look in his eyes and his face had begun to get pale.

"What's wrong?" she asked.

"They got Tony," said Joe.

"Who?"

"I don't know. Rico, I guess. He must have turned yellow."

Joe ran his hand across his forehead, then he took out his gold cigarette case, but without ostentation this time, and lit a cigarette. Olga took the paper from him. She read:

ANOTHER GANG KILLING

Antonio Passalacqua, known as Tony Passa, reputed to be a member of the Vettori gang, was found dead near the steps of St. Dominick's Cathedral . . . as far as the police can ascertain no one saw him killed . . . when questioned Sam Vettori denied all knowledge of the shooting and intimated that it was the work of a rival gang . . . police say that this is likely.

"Jesus!" said Joe.

Olga turned quickly to the theatrical page.

"Joe, honey," she said, "there's a good comedy at the Oriental. What do you say?"

Joe crumpled up his cigarette and put it in the ashtray.

"Boy, Rico didn't waste no time with him."

"Joe, don't you want to see that comedy?"

"Sure," said Joe, "let's go see it."

Joe sat silent in the taxi all the way to the theatre. As they were getting out, he said:

"Boy, that Rico is sure careless with a rod."

"Forget it, honey," said Olga.

VI

When Rico came in Seal Skin was sitting in a chair by the window and Otero was lying on the bed without his shirt, singing loudly. Rico walked over and put his hand on Seal Skin's shoulder.

"Listen," he said, "I thought you told me you was gonna look after The Greek?"

"I can't do nothing with him," said Seal Skin.

Rico went over to the bed and looked at Otero.

"Señor Rico," cried Otero, "listen, I will sing for you."

Rico turned.

"Seal," he said, "that bird's gonna spill something if you don't keep him sober."

"Listen," said Seal Skin, "I ain't no nurse. A guy ought to look out for himself. What the hell can I do, anyway? I can't knock him cold."

"You never did have much sense," said Rico.

"All right, wise boy. Let's see what you can do."

Rico took off his overcoat.

"Got any ice?"

"Sure," said Seal Skin without moving.

"Well, goddam it, get on your feet and get it."

Seal Skin was afraid of Rico but she didn't want him to suspect it. She got to her feet leisurely, picked up one of Otero's big cigars, lit it, and stood puffing. Then, having demonstrated her lack of fear, she went to the kitchen for the ice.

Rico went over to the bed.

"Otero," he said, "have you got any liquor around here?"

"What do I care for liquor!" cried Otero. "I will sing for you."

Rico slapped Otero's face.

"A hell of a crew I'm mixed up with," he said.

Otero looked at him, startled.

"What is wrong with me?"

"You're a dirty yellow bum."

"I am not a yellow bum," cried Otero, trying to sit up.

Rico struck him hard this time, knocking him back on the bed. Otero put his hand to his face and looked at Rico.

"If you got any more liquor here you better tell me where it is," said Rico.

Otero reached under his pillow and pulled out a quart bottle over half full. Rico slipped it into his pocket.

Otero's face got red.

"Rico," he said, "you give me back my liquor."

He tried to sit up but Rico hit him and he fell back. Seal Skin came in with a couple of pieces of ice wrapped in a towel.

"What the hell you want to beat him up for?" she said.

"I'm gonna get him sober and keep him that way."

"Yeah? Well, you're gonna have a full time job."

Rico took the ice, a piece in each hand, and began to rub it over Otero's face and chest. He rubbed hard and it hurt Otero, who struggled.

"Rico," he said, "what have I done to you? Rico, you are my friend. Why do you treat me this way?"

"He'll be bawling next," said Seal Skin.

Of a sudden Otero got angry and struggled so fiercely that he threw Rico off and climbed out of bed. The ice clattered to the floor. Rico took one step toward him and set himself for a punch, but Seal Skin grabbed his arm.

"For God's sake let up on him," she cried, "ain't he in bad enough shape?"

Rico was furious. He slapped Seal Skin across the face with his open hand.

"A fine bunch of yellow bellies and squealers I'm mixed up with," he cried. "Listen, idiot, ain't he a meal ticket? You want the black wagon to come and haul him away?"

Otero reeled across the room. Rico leapt after him and knocked him to the floor. Otero raised his head.

"Rico," he said, "what have I done to you?"

Rico picked up the ice and kneeling down beside Otero began to rub him with it, harder than before. Otero gasped.

"Listen," said Rico, "you got to get sober. I'm your friend, Otero. I don't want to see you get us all hung. Listen, Otero, do you get what I'm saying? You got to sober up and stay that way."

Tears ran down Otero's cheeks.

"All right, Rico," he said.

In half an hour Rico had him sober. Seal Skin was sitting with her feet on the window sill, smoking one of Otero's big cigars. Otero sat pale and shaken, looking at Rico.

"Well, big boy," said Seal Skin, "I got to hand it to you. You done it,"

Rico smiled. Then he took out his billfold and handed Seal Skin a ten.

"There's a little cush[35] for you. You ain't sore at me cause I socked you, are you? I got red hot mad, that's all."

"You didn't sock me hard," said Seal Skin, "but it was ten dollars' worth."

Otero didn't have much to say. He sat looking at the floor, ashamed of himself.

35 Savings, something to fall back on—a cushion.

"How do you feel?" asked Rico.

"Me, not so good," said Otero.

"Want a little drink?"

Otero looked at Rico, not trusting him, then he nodded. Rico handed him the bottle.

"I said little drink," cautioned Rico.

Otero took a swallow and handed back the bottle.

"Now," said Rico, "get your clothes on and we'll take a look at Tony."

VII

There were many rumors in Little Italy about the passing of Sam Vettori. The full truth, of course, was only guessed at, but the simple facts were known. Sam Vettori's star was setting, Rico's was rising. Rico had always been right; there was never any question of that. Rico had always inspired fear. But now, as the probable head of a big minor gang whose activities were varied and whose yearly income was enormous, his potentialities were prodigiously increased and he was treated accordingly.

When he entered Tony's flat several members of the Vettori gang, sitting near the door, got up and offered him their chairs. He merely shook his head and walked across to where Sam Vettori was sitting. Otero, who had entered a little behind Rico, stopped to talk with Blackie Avezzano.

Carillo brought a chair for Rico and Rico sat down beside Sam Vettori.

"We're going to plant the kid right," said Vettori, "that'll look good."

Rico stared across the room at a large horseshoe wreath which bore the single word: Tony. That was his contribution.

"Sure," said Rico.

He was a little uneasy. Not that he felt any remorse. What he had done was merely an act of policy. A man in this game must be a man. If he gets yellow, why, there's only one remedy for it. No, Rico was never likely to err on the side of contrition. It was the massed flowers; their sickly and overpowering odor made him vaguely uneasy.

"They sure fix 'em up good now," said Vettori, nodding in the direction of the coffin; "he don't look dead. He looks like he was asleep."

"Yeah?" said Rico.

"It beats me how they do it," said Vettori.

Carillo came across the room and whispered to Rico and Vettori.

"Two bulls in the hallway."

"They coming in?" asked Rico.

"No, just standing there."

"All right."

There was a movement at the door. Mrs. Passalacqua came in between two of her friends. She had been at St. Dominick's for over an hour. Rico got up and offered her his chair. One of the women helped her off with her hat. She sat down. Her gray hair was parted in the middle and drawn tightly down; her face was a dead white. She was wearing a plain black dress and she sat with her hands in her lap. She looked at no one, but fastened her eyes on the coffin.

Rico walked over to look at Tony. At the head of the coffin were two big candles, one of them leaning a little and dripping tallow. Tony lay with his hands folded. Rico looked down. Somehow he had expected Tony to be changed. He was not. Here lay the same Tony who used to play poker with such fury. The same Tony, yes, only dead. Rico saw the rigidity of the face, the parchment skin. He stood there, looking.

Carillo put his hand on Rico's shoulder.

"Bulls want to see you, boss."

Rico nodded.

"They want you to come out in the hall."

"All right," said Rico, turning away from the coffin, "tell Otero."

Otero came over beside Rico and stood looking at Tony.

"Listen," said Rico, "this may be a pinch. I don't know. If it is, I'll go with them. They ain't got nothing on me. But if there's any trouble, Scabby'll keep you posted. Ma's got my jack, see?"

"All right," said Otero.

Rico started across the room and Otero followed him. Before Rico reached the door Tony's mother suddenly put her hands to her face and began to sob wildly.

"Oh, Tony, Tony!" she cried.

The women who had come in with her tried to quiet her, but she pushed them away, and, rising, walked over to the coffin and stood looking down at Tony. Then, still sobbing, she let the women lead her into the next room.

"That's a woman for you," said Rico.

"Well," said Otero, shrugging, "Tony was her son."

The hallway was lined with poor Italians who, not knowing the Passalacquas, had come out of curiosity. They stood in silent groups, trying to peep in through the open door. Women in disreputable housedresses carrying dirty children ; pregnant women; old men with crinkly gray hair and seamed brown faces; young girls trying to look up-to-date and American. When Rico came out they all stared at him.

Flaherty took hold of his arm.

"Rico," he said, "come down to the end of the hall. I want to see you a minute."

"Is this a pinch?" asked Rico.

Flaherty laughed.

"Got a bad conscience, have you? Well, you ought to have."

Rico noticed that the other detective, whom he had never seen before, kept staring at him. Rico planted his feet firmly and stared back.

"What's the big idea, Flaherty?" he asked.

"Well," said Flaherty, "just to put your mind at rest I'll tell you, this ain't a pinch. It ought to be, but it ain't. Now will you take a walk . . . ?"

"Sure," said Rico.

Otero came out into the hallway and stood watching them. Rico went down to the end of the hall with the two plainclothes men. Some of the poor Italians followed them and stood staring. But Flaherty motioned them off as if he were shooing chickens.

"Beat it," he said; "go tend to your own business."

They moved away slowly, looking back.

"All right," said Rico, "let's have it."

Flaherty took out a big cigar and began chewing on it. The other man kept staring. Rico was puzzled and wondered what the game was; then he noticed that the light at their end of the hall was good, much better than any other place in the hall. The once-over? Well, what then?

"Listen, Rico," said Flaherty, "I like you and I'm going to give you a tip. It's going to be tough on you birds from now on. The

Old Man's got his back up. Now get this. If you got anything on your mind, you better spill it." Flaherty paused to light his cigar. The other detective watched Rico intently. "Because it's going to be easy for the bird that spilled it first. But God help the rest of them."

Rico smiled slightly.

"Quit stalling," he said.

Flaherty glanced at the man with him, but the man shook his head. Flaherty said:

"Well, I'm giving you a friendly tip."

"Yeah," said Rico, "you bulls always was friendly as hell. I spent two years once just thinking how friendly you was. Listen, I ain't got nothing to spill. What the hell's wrong with you, Flaherty? Did I ever do any spilling?"

Flaherty laughed.

"Well," he said, "there's a first time for everything. All right, Rico, you can go."

The two plain-clothes men pushed their way through the crowd and went down the stairs. Rico went back into Tony's flat. Sam Vettori and Otero were waiting for him. Vettori was mopping his face with his big white silk hankerchief.

"Well?" he demanded.

Rico shrugged.

"Just stalling."

"What's the game?"

"You got me. I guess Flaherty wanted this other bird to give me the once-over."

"Things getting pretty hot, Rico."

"Don't beef, Sam. We're gonna come through."

Otero said:

"The old lady sure is taking it hard."

They could hear Tony's mother sobbing loudly in the next room.

PART IV

I

For three or four years Bat Carillo, once a third-rate light-heavyweight, had been the leader of one of Vettori's gangs of hooligans. The members of this gang specialized in strong arm stuff and intimidation; they threw bombs; they smashed up barrooms and vicejoints operated by rival gangs. They were, in other words, Vettori's shock troops. Carillo was an excellent lieutenant, as he always carried out orders to the letter and was congenitally incapable of imagining himself as chief in his own right. A good honest subordinate without ambition. Vettori trusted him.

In Carillo's attitude since the killing of Courtney, therefore, Vettori saw the most unmistakable symptom of his own passing. Carillo had attached himself to Rico and called him "boss." Carillo was not careless with the word "boss"; it was not a conventional expression; when he said "boss" he meant it. Aroused, Vettori saw similar manifestations all around him; in Blackie Avezzano, in Killer Pepi, in a dozen others.

Vettori had always disliked Rico. Now he hated him. If Carillo or Killer Pepi had remained faithful he would have had one of them kill him and damn the consequences. But there was no question of that now. He knew that he was whipped and he saw the necessity of a compromise. Hanging was just over the horizon and Rico's gun promised an even more certain death. Vettori had never split with anyone. He had always taken with both hands and given as little as possible. But it was split now or die and Vettori could not contemplate the prospect of dying with any degree of complacency. He sent for Rico.

A new Rico appeared, followed by Otero, Carillo, and Killer Pepi. Rico was wearing a big ulster like Joe's and a derby also like Joe's. He had on fawncolored spats drawn over pointed patent-leather shoes; and a diamond horseshoe pin sparkled in a red, green and white striped necktie.

The gang has a tense discussion with gang leader Sam Vettori (Stanley Fields) in a scene from the 1931 film of *Little Caesar*.

Vettori looked him over and winked at Killer Pepi, but Killer Pepi's face was stony. Carillo got a chair for Rico.

"What's on your mind, Sam?" said Rico, sitting down, throwing back his ulster and pulling up his trousers to preserve the crease.

Vettori hesitated.

"I want to see you alone," he said.

"No," said Rico, "I think I know your game, Sam, and I want the boys to get an earful. Go ahead and spill it."

Vettori began to sweat. Killer Pepi said

"Yeah, we know."

"You know a hell of a lot, don't you?" said Vettori.

"We know, all right," said Pepi.

Nobody said anything. Rico took off his hat and began to comb his hair. Vettori got out his cards and began to lay out a game of solitaire.

Pepi said:

"We know you went yellow, Sam, when Tony blew his top and started after Come-To-Jesus McConagha. We know all right."

Vettori looked up at him.

"What the hell I got you guys for anyway! Who hands out the cush?"

Rico paused in the combing of his hair.

"Don't get rough, Sam."

Killer Pepi went over and stood with his back against the door. Otero sat down opposite Vettori.

"Well," said Rico, "if you want to see me, spill it quick because I ain't got all night."

Vettori sighed profoundly, then he put down his cards and looked at the men around him. He saw four hostile faces.

"All right," said Vettori, "but why the strong arm stuff, Rico? Sit down, you guys, and I'll have some drinks sent up."

The three men looked at Rico.

"All right," he said, "go bring up some drinks, Bat."

Carillo went out. Nobody said anything. Outside, a winter dusk settled and the big electric sign on a level with the windows was switched on. They sat looking at the sign.

CLUB

P

A

L

E

R

M

O

DANCING

Carillo brought in the drinks and they all sat around the table under the green-shaded lamp. Otero, Carillo, and Killer Pepi drank whiskey; Vettori wine; Rico pop.

Vettori put down his glass.

"Well, Rico," he said, "I got a proposition to make you."

"All right," said Rico, "spring it."

"Listen," said Vettori, "I'm getting old. I'll never see forty-five again and when a guy's that old he ain't worth much."[36]

"You ain't getting old, Sam, you're losing your guts," said Rico.

Killer Pepi laughed out loud and banged his fist on the table. But Vettori swallowed this insult.

"All right, Rico," he said, "that's your story. Well, here's how it is. I need a partner. You're young, Rico, and you got the guts. All the guys like you and they'll do what you say. I got the lay-out and you're looking for a chance to be a big guy. Well, here's your chance." Vettori thought for a moment, then he said: "I'll split the works with you."

Carillo and Pepi exchanged a look. Otero began to hum to himself. But Rico said:

"I'll think it over."

Vettori began to sweat again. Was Rico going to get rid of him?

"Well," he said, putting on a front, "you can take it or leave it. I like you, Rico, and I'm doing you a favor. Who's got the money? Who's got the pull? What the hell would you guys do if you didn't have the Big Boy to pull you through?"

"I'm O.K. with the Big Boy," said Rico; "he was up to see me this morning."

"Yeah," said Pepi, "I brung him."

Vettori laid out a new game of solitaire.

"Here's the thing," said Rico: "you're trying to hang on, Sam. You must think we're dumb as hell. You want me to do the work so you can take it easy. And you call that an even split. Hear what I say! That ain't my idea of a split."

"Well, I ain't handing out charity," said Vettori, losing his temper.

Rico got to his feet and buttoned up his ulster.

"All right, Sam."

Vettori slammed down his cards.

"What do you guys think?" he demanded of Carillo, Pepi and Otero.

They just looked at him.

"Ain't that a fair split?"

"No," said Rico, "I guess we can't do no business."

Rico put on his hat and walked toward the door. The other three got up and followed him. Vettori stood up.

"Well," he said, "you gonna try to run me out, Rico?"

Vettori was panicky. Rico stood at the door and looked at him.

"I was just figuring I'd open a joint across the street," he said.

37   The Tuxedo, usually capitalized until the 1930s, was a tailless evening jacket substituted for the tailcoat long worn to formal affairs. It was popularized in England in the 1880s and then moved to America, where it was frequently worn by the younger men attending social functions. Tuxedo Park was a village in upstate New York, named from a Native American word for "crooked river," that became an enclave for the smart set, and it is likely that the name became associated with the jacket there. Mark Twain resided in Tuxedo Park for a few years around 1907.

Vettori knew what that meant. He had been through half a dozen gang wars, but that was long ago when there were at least five separate gangs in the neighborhood. Things had been comparatively quiet for over three years. Vettori regretted the past bitterly. He regretted having taken up with Rico, an unknown Youngstown wop.

"Well," he said, "Rico, you're young and you ain't got any too much sense. What the hell! With things the way they are, we wouldn't none of us last a month. Listen, Rico, what's your idea of a split?"

Rico took off his hat and scratched his head, but carefully so that his hair wouldn't be disarranged.

"I'll hand you this, Sam," said Rico, "you got the layout. The split's good that way. But you got sense enough to know that no two guys can run things. The layout split is O.K. with me, but I got to have the say, get that!"

Vettori looked at the others.

"What do you guys say?"

"We're in with Rico," said Killer Pepi.

Otero and Carillo nodded. Vettori brought his hand down on the table with a smack.

"O.K.," he said.

II

The gang gave a banquet for Rico in one of Sam Vettori's big back rooms. The table was fifteen feet long and was covered by a fine white cloth. Red, green and white streamers hung from the chandeliers and Italian and American flags were crossed at intervals along the walls. At eleven o'clock the notables began to arrive. Killer Pepi in a blue suit and a brown derby, with his woman, Blue Jay, on his arm. Joe Sansone, gunman and ex-lightweight, in a Tuxedo,[37] followed by his shadow Kid Bean, a Sicilian, dark as a negro. Then Ottavio Vettori, Sam's cousin, not yet twenty-one, already famous as a gunman and spoken of as a potential gang chief. Then Otero, Blackie Avezzano and Bat Carillo, all with their women. They stood about stiffly, a little uncomfortable in their fine clothes, and tried to make conversation. The men, like all specialists, talked shop. Ottavio Vettori declared that the police were a bunch of bums. Killer Pepi agreed that they were. Joe Sansone said that the Federal men were just as bad, only smarter and crookeder. Killer Pepi agreed that they were. Ottavio Vettori didn't agree. He said that the Federal men were dumber and harder to fix. This brought on an argument.

When Sam Vettori came in the men were all shouting.

"What the hell!" said Sam, "ain't this a fine way to act at a banquet? You act like a bunch of gashouse[38] micks. Cut the chatter."

Ottavio made a noise like a goat.

"Baa! Baa!"

Everybody laughed. Otero took out a quart bottle of whiskey, drank from it and passed it to Seal Skin; she drank and passed it to Ottavio. The bottle circled the room and returned empty.

"You sure came prepared, you birds," said Sam. "Did any of you guys bring a lunch?"

"Baa! Baa!" bellowed Ottavio.

"My God, ain't that cute!" said Killer Pepi's girl.

"Hell, that ain't nothing," said Pepi, "listen." Pepi put three fingers in his mouth and blew a blast that made their eardrums ring.

"Lord," said Ottavio, "the cops! Baa! Baa!"

Three waiters came in, each carrying two quarts of whiskey. They put the bottles on the table and went out.

"That's an appetizer," said Sam.

"Apéritif," Joe Sansone corrected.

Ottavio slapped him on the back.

"What's that, little Joe? What the hell lingo is that?"

Joe pushed him away.

"You dumb birds don't know nothing. Swell people don't say appetizer; they say apéritif."

"The hell they do! Well, I expect you know all about it. You used to be a bellboy at the Blackstone."[39]

Everybody laughed. Killer Pepi blew a blast on his fingers. His girl looked at him admiringly.

"How the hell you ever learn to do that?"

"Aw, that ain't nothing."

"Say, Sam," said Carillo, "when do we eat?"

"When the boss gets here," said Pepi.

"Well, he better step on it because I'm so hungry I could eat dynamite," said Ottavio.

38   Low-class Irish.

39   A glamorous hotel in Chicago, still in operation.

"Keep your shirt on," said Pepi.

"Haven't got an old soup sandwich in your pocket, have you?" asked Ottavio.

Everybody laughed. Ottavio was the recognized wit of the Vettori gang. All that he had to do to get a laugh was to open his mouth.

Sam Vettori took one of the quarts from the table and sent it round the room. It came back empty.

"What the hell you suppose is keeping Rico?" asked Carillo.

"Keep your shirt on," said Pepi.

"I go see," said Otero.

As he went out, the Big Boy came in. He had on a big racoon coat and his derby was on the side of his head. Sam Vettori rushed over and shook hands with him.

"What the hell you doing here?" he demanded.

"Me, I came to see the fun. Things are looking up, Sam. Things sure to God are looking up. I think we got 'em whipped."

Sam Vettori smiled broadly and poured the Big Boy a drink. Well, well! If the Courtney business blew over he was sitting pretty. All things considered, he hadn't done so bad. Time after time he had seen old gang leaders go down before younger men. But here he was hanging on, getting a 50-50 split, and taking no chances. Rico was the goods. Goddam him and all his kind, but he was the goods.

"Yeah," said the Big Boy, "you got the Old Man on the run and Flaherty's about ready to do the Dutch Act.[40] It's gonna blow over, Sam. You heard me speak. It's gonna blow over. I want to see Rico."

"He ain't showed yet," said Sam.

"Damn smart boy," said the Big Boy.

Sam smiled.

"Yeah," he said, pouring the Big Boy another drink, "damn smart kid. He's young yet, but I can show him the ropes."

The Big Boy didn't say anything. He just looked at Vettori.

Otero came running in, followed by two waiters, one of whom was carrying a big ulster and a derby; the other was carrying a woman's fur coat.

"Here he comes," cried Otero.

Kid Bean, who had collected a crowd in the middle of the room, and was walking on his hands to amuse them (he had once been an acrobat), jumped hastily to his feet and backed up against the wall. The crowd followed him. Killer Pepi said:

"All right now. Everybody yell like hell when he comes in."

Rico came in slowly, talking to Blondy Belle, the swellest woman in Little Italy. She was a handsome Italian, bold and aquiline. Her complexion and eyes were dark, but her hair, naturally black, was blondined,[41] and this gave her an incongruous and a somewhat formidable appearance.

Rico was greeted by an uproar, pierced by Killer Pepi's shrill whistle. The Big Boy went to meet Rico and shook hands with him. Sam Vettori smiled and nodded, very affable, then went out to get things started. The Big Boy said to Blondy Belle:

"Got yourself a regular man, did you?"

Blondy took hold of Rico's arm.

"Surest thing you know."

The Big Boy laughed.

"What'd you do with Little Arnie?"

Rico took out a cigar and bit off the end.

"She ditched him," he said.

The Big Boy meditated. Blondy Belle had been Little Arnie's woman for a long time. Little Arnie ran the biggest gambling joint on the North Side, but he had been slipping for a year or more. He wasn't right; nobody could trust him.

"How did Little Arnie take it?" asked the Big Boy.

"He took it standing up," said Blondy Belle.

"Well, what could he do?" said Rico.

Killer Pepi, Ottavio Vettori and Joe Sansone, as the most important men in the gang next to Sam Vettori, came over to shake hands with Rico.

"A million dollars ain't in it with you," said Pepi, looking his boss over.

Rico was wearing a loud striped suit and a purple tie. He still had on his gloves, yellow kid, of which he was very proud, and his diamond horseshoe pin had been replaced by a big ruby surrounded by little diamonds. Ottavio envied him his gloves. But Joe Sansone was not impressed; he knew better.

"Yes sir, boss, you sure are lit up," said Ottavio.

"Here's the half-pint," said Killer Pepi, pushing Joe Sansone forward.

Joe shook hands with Rico.

"Yes sir," said Ottavio, "the half-pint's a good boy, but he and Gentleman Joe're too swell for us."

Rico looked around the room.

"Joe Massara here?"

"Ain't seen him," said Pepi.

"He won't be here," said Joe Sansone; "he's busy."

Rico didn't say anything. Blondy took hold of his arm.

"I want a drink."

Rico looked at Pepi.

"Get her a drink," he said.

The Big Boy took Rico aside and said:

"I want to see you a minute, Rico."

Rico said:

"Listen, if you see Joe Massara tomorrow you tell him to look me up. I got something to say to that bird."

"I'll be seeing him maybe," said the Big Boy. "I got a date with his boss tomorrow morning. There's a square guy, Rico. DeVoss is a square guy all right. Never have to nudge him for dough."

Rico seemed in a bad humor.

"They tell me you lined up something good," said the Big Boy. Rico nodded.

"Yeah, it's gonna be a money maker. Little Arnie wised me up. I'm gonna give him a split. That's the game now. Sam never had sense enough to get in on it."

"Little Arnie, eh? That guy'd double-cross his grandmother."

"He'll only double-cross me once," said Rico.

"I believe you," said the Big Boy; then, putting his hand on Rico's shoulder, he went on: "Funny for you to split with Arnie. How about Blondy?"

"Arnie don't give a damn. He's all shot to pieces. He can't do a woman no good."

"No wonder," said the Big Boy, "with a woman like that."

Rico grinned.

"Ain't she a bearcat!" he said; then his face clouded. "Wonder what the hell Joe Massara's game is?"

The Big Boy looked at Rico for a moment.

"That little hunky dancer over at DeVoss's has got him down. They tell me he's going straight."

Rico laughed unpleasantly.

"Yeah? Well, I'll have to go over and give that bird an earful."

"Better stay out of that end of town, Rico."

"To hell with that."

Sam Vettori came in, followed by three waiters bringing the soup.

"All right," said Sam, "we're all set."

Rico took his place at the head of the table. The Big Boy sat on his right and Blondy Belle on his left. The gunmen and their women arranged themselves according to rank. Blackie Avezzano sat at the foot of the table.

III

When the meal was over the Big Boy asked Rico to make a speech. There was a prolonged clamor. Rico got up.

"All right," he said, "if you birds want me to make a speech, here you are: I want to thank you guys for this banquet. It sure is swell. The liquor is good, so they tell me, I don't drink it myself, and the food don't leave nothing to be desired. I guess we all had a swell time and it sure is good to see all you guys gathered together. Well, I guess that's about all. Only I wish you guys wouldn't get drunk and raise hell, as that's the way a lot of birds get bumped off."

Rico sat down. The applause lasted for over a minute. Then Ottavio got up with a bottle in his hand.

"Here's to Rico and Blondy and the Big Boy."

Everybody shouted and made a grab for bottles and glasses. Blackie Avezzano fell under the table and stayed there, lying on his face. After the toast was drunk, Killer Pepi and Kid Bean began to quarrel. The Kid picked up a plate and struck at Pepi, who threw a bottle at the Kid, missing him by a fraction of an inch.

Rico banged on the table.

"Cut it out, you guys. Ain't that a hell of a way to act?"

Pepi and the Kid shook hands and another toast was drunk.

A waiter came in the door and went over to Rico.

"Couple of newspaper guys, boss. They want to take a flashlight."

"What's the idea?" the Big Boy inquired.

"Send 'em up," said Rico.

"We're gonna get our mugs shot," cried Blondy Belle.

"Maybe we are," said Rico.

"What's the idea?" the Big Boy reiterated.

"We ain't got nothing to hide," said Rico.

The waiter returned, followed by two newspaper men, one of whom was carrying a big camera. Rico motioned them over.

"Who sent you?" he asked.

Sam Vettori came in and went over to Rico.

"They're O.K., Rico," he said, "they been here before."

"Sure, we're O.K.," said the photographer, a little intimidated by Rico's manner.

"Well, spill it," said Rico, "what's the idea of the flashlight?"

"Well, we got a section in the Sunday paper about how different classes of people live in Chicago. See? Last week we featured Lake Forest. Had some pictures of the swells, see, and the dumps where they lived. This Sunday we want Little Italy. We just heard about the banquet they was giving you, Mr. Rico, so we kinda thought . . ."

"O.K.," said Rico, "but make it snappy."

"I'm out of this picture," said the Big Boy, rising and walking over to the doorway. Sam Vettori took his place.

After maneuvering about for a few minutes the photographer got the correct slant. He put the powder on the little tray.

"Now!" he cried.

Rico sat with his thumbs in the arm-holes of his vest, looking very stern. There was a blinding flash. Ottavio Vettori leapt into the air and crying "My God, I'm shot" fell face down across the table. Everybody laughed.

When the newspaper men had gone the Big Boy came over and put his hand on Rico's arm.

"They may pick you up on that."

"Who the hell's gonna see it?"

"You don't know who's gonna see it. That was a bad play, Rico." Rico laughed.

"If they pick me up, I'll alibi them to death."

When the banquet was over Rico had Otero call him a cab. Blondy Belle was a little drunk and Rico had to support her as they went down the stairs. As she weighed about twenty pounds more than he did, this was not an easy job. As they were going out the side-entrance, Flaherty left his table in the club and came over to them.

He put his hand on Rico's shoulder.

"Getting up in the world ain't you, Rico?"

Rico looked at him.

"Don't you know your old pal, Jim Flaherty?"

"Sure I know you. What's the big idea?"

"Go chase yourself around the block, flat-foot," said Blondy Belle; "if I ain't getting sick of seeing bulls."

"Hello, Blondy," said Flaherty, "you and Rico hitting it off, eh? That's the old ticket. Rico's a good boy, but he's young. If they don't put him behind the bars, he'll be a man yet."

"What's the idea, Flaherty?" asked Rico.

"Why, I don't want you to forget that I'm your friend," said Flaherty. "I got my eyes on you, Rico. I like to see a young guy getting up in the world."

"Yeah?" said Rico.

The cab was waiting at the curb and one of the waiters went out and opened the door for them. Rico boosted Blondy Belle into the cab. Flaherty stood in the doorway and watched them drive off.

"The nerve of that Irish bastard," said Blondy.

But Rico had forgotten Flaherty. He sat thinking about Joe Massara. Gentleman Joe was getting too good for them, eh? He was going to turn softie.

"Well, I guess not," said Rico.

42   A player-piano, powered by pneumatic or electrical-mechanical devices. Sales peaked in the mid-1920s; the growth of radio broadcasts and the phonograph record made the device superfluous.

Inside a pianola
(*photo by Tim Walker, CCA-2.0 license*).

IV

The sound of the pianola[42] woke Rico. He sat up and looked at his wrist watch. It was 2 o'clock in the afternoon. He had slept twelve hours.

Rico lived at a tension. His nervous system was geared up to such a pitch that he was never sleepy, never felt the desire to relax, was always keenly alive. He did not average over five hours sleep a night and as soon as he opened his eyes he was awake. When he sat in a chair he never thrust out his feet and lolled, but sat rigid and alert. He walked, ate, took his pleasures in the same manner. What distinguished him from his associates was his inability to live in the present. He was like a man on a long train journey to a promised land. To him the present was but a dingy way-station; he had his eyes on the end of the journey. This is the mental attitude of a man destined for success. But the resultant tension had its drawbacks. He was subject to periodic slumps. His energy would suddenly disappear; he would lose interest in everything and for several days would sleep twelve to fifteen hours at a stretch. This was a dangerous weakness, and Rico was aware of it and feared it.

Rico leapt out of bed and hastily put on his clothes.

"Twelve hours, boy," he said to his reflection in the mirror, as he stood combing his hair, "that'll never do."

He had been seeing too much of Blondy Belle; that was the trouble. Rico had very little to do with women. He regarded them with a sort of contempt; they seemed so silly, reckless and purposeless, also mendacious and extremely undependable. Not that Rico trusted men, far from it. He was temperamentally suspicious. But in the course of his life he had discovered a few men he could trust, but no women. What he feared most in women, though, was not their treachery, that could be guarded against, but their ability to relax a man, to make him soft and slack, like Joe Massara. Rico had never been deeply involved with a woman. Incapable of tender sentiments, he had escaped the commoner kind of pitfalls. He was given to short bursts of lust, and, this lust once satisfied, he looked at women impersonally for a while, as one looks at inanimate objects. But at times this lust, usually the result of an inner need and not the outcome of exterior stimulus, would be aroused by the sight of some particular woman. This had been the case with Blondy Belle; she was big, healthy and lascivious. This exactly suited Rico's tastes; she excited him, and for that very reason he was on guard against her.

"Yeah," he said, "I got to lay off Blondy for a while."

She wanted him to come and live with her, but he refused. The offer tickled his vanity, though, for Pepi or Joe Sansone would have jumped at the chance. But not Rico. He fought shy of any kind of ties. A slight relaxing of this principle and you are tangled up before you know it. The strong travel light.

He went out into the living room. Blondy, in a cerise kimono, was pedaling the pianola and singing loudly. The room was in disorder. Stockings hung from the backs of chairs, the dress Blondy had worn the night before was suspended from the chandelier on a coat-hanger, and there was a pile of clothes in the middle of the room.

Blondy turned around and smiled at him, pedaling the piano at the same time.

"What the hell kind of a piece is that?" asked Rico.

"That's an Eyetalian piece," said Blondy. "Ain't it swell?"

"No," said Rico, "I like jazz better."

Blondy stopped the pianola and backpedaled the roll.

"I got it yesterday because I thought you'd like it," she said.

"Hell, quit kidding," said Rico.

"I sure did. It's from an Opera."

"Yeah? Say, what's wrong with you?"

Blondy looked at him. She had pretensions. Ten years ago she had been a lady's maid and she felt that she was somewhat cultured. One summer she had even made Little Arnie take her to Ravinia Park[43] to hear the Opera. The soprano impressed her by her loud singing; the tenor by his beautiful legs.

"You'd think I was a regular wop to hear you talk," said Rico; "say, I was born in Youngstown and I can't even speak the lingo."

"Well, I guess I wasn't born in the old country either," said Blondy.

She put a new roll on the pianola and Rico sat smoking while she played it. Rico had no ear for music; he couldn't even whistle, or distinguish one tune from another. But he liked rhythm. There was something straightforward and primitive about jazz rhythms that impressed him.

"That's a good one," he said, when the roll was played through.

"Want to hear some more?"

"No," said Rico, "I got to go."

He rose and went over to the closet for his overcoat, but Blondy said: "Listen, Rico. I want to see you a minute before you go."

"What about?"

"About Little Arnie."

Rico stared at her.

"What's the idea? To hell with Little Arnie. As long as he's straight with me I ain't got no interest in him at all."

"He ain't straight with nobody."

Rico just looked at her.

Little Arnie had played his hand badly. At first he hadn't minded losing Blondy Belle in the least; she cost him a good

43   Located in Highland Park, Illinois, this outdoor music festival has been in operation since 1905, when it hosted the New York Philharmonic. According to the official Ravinia website, "opera was added to the concert programs in 1912, and by the end of the decade, Ravinia earned a reputation as America's summer opera capital. During Ravinia's 'Golden Age' of opera, 1919 to 1931, Ravinia audiences heard the greatest singers in the world, including such luminaries as Edward Johnson, Giovanni Martinelli, Claudia Muzio, Rosa Raisa and Tito Schipa," https://www.ravinia.org/Page/History.

The Casino building at Ravinia, now demolished.

deal of money and she bored and irritated him. But he had been kidded unmercifully. As he had no sense of humor whatever and was very touchy in a personal matter, this eventually angered him. In revenge, he talked. He told all who would listen that Blondy Belle was a liar, a crook, and had certain unnatural appetites. Killer Pepi was one of the auditors and he immediately repeated Little Arnie's assertions to his woman, Blue Jay, who ran at once to Blondy Belle. Yes, Little Arnie, who was fifty percent fool, had played his hand badly.

Blondy lit a cigarette and lay down on the davenport.

"Come over here and sit down," she said; "I'll give you an earful."

"I ain't got no time," said Rico.

Blondy blew out a cloud of smoke.

"Arnie's double-crossing you right now!" said Blondy.

"What you got on your mind?" said Rico; "spill it."

"All right," said Blondy. "Arnie's giving you a split on the house, ain't he? What's the split?"

"Thirty percent."

"How do you know you're getting thirty?"

"I look at the books."

Blondy laughed.

"Them books is crooked."

"Straight dope?" asked Rico, his face hardening.

"Sure," said Blondy. "I wasn't gonna say nothing. It wasn't none of my business, but Arnie's been peddling a lot of loose talk about me and I don't take that."

"All right," said Rico, "now you know so damn much, how we gonna prove it?"

"It's a cinch," said Blondy; "hand Arnie's boy, Joe Peeper, some dough and he'll spill the news. Joe hates Arnie."

"Good!" said Rico, banging the table with his fist; "I'll run Arnie out of town and declare you in, Blondy. You got brains."

Blondy looked at him.

"You stick to me, boy, and we'll own the town."

"Don't get swelled up," said Rico, "just because you happened to be in the know."

That's what she liked about Rico. He was hard to impress.

"Hell of a lot of thanks I get for it," said Blondy.

"Don't worry about that," said Rico, his head buzzing with projects, "you'll get something better than thanks."

Rico went to the closet and got his coat and hat.

"Wait a minute, big boy," said Blondy, "you ain't heard it all. Listen, that joint of Arnie's is worth plenty of dough. He ain't gonna give it up without a battle."

"Hell," said Rico, "he's yellow."

"Sure he is. But he's tricky. Rico, if you can't work the Joe Peeper stunt, here's a lever. Remember Limpy John?"

"Sure," said Rico, "they bumped him off."

"Who did?"

"The cops."

Blondy laughed.

"They thought they did. Arnie bumped him off."

Rico grinned.

"I got you."

Rico put on his overcoat.

"Be round tonight?" asked Blondy.

"No, I got business."

"Monkey business."

"No, I got to go cross town. I'll give you a ring tomorrow."

Blondy lay back on the davenport.

"You'll sure be missing something," she said.

"I'll ketch up," said Rico.

When Rico had gone, Blondy played a couple of rolls on the pianola, then she drank half a pint of liquor and went back to bed.

V

Rico found the door of his apartment unlocked. Before entering he unbuttoned his overcoat and took out his automatic. Only one person had a key to his apartment except himself: Otero. If Otero wasn't in there then whoever was in there was in trouble. Rico opened the door slowly. Otero was sitting with his chair tipped back against the wall, smoking a cigarette and dozing.

"Otero!"

Otero opened his eyes.

"Hello, boss."

Rico locked the door behind him.

"Listen, don't you know better than to leave that door open?"

"I forgot, Rico."

Rico took off his overcoat and hat.

"You better keep your head working, boy," said Rico, "or you'll get your neck stretched. What you doing here, anyway?"

Otero got up from his chair and stood dangling his hat.

"I want money."

Rico looked at him.

"I'm broke, boss. I ain't got a cent."

Rico laughed. Otero seemed so helpless.

"You mean to tell me you ain't got a cent out of that Casa Alvarado split?"

Otero shrugged.

"What in hell did you do with it?"

"Well, Seal she spends money, spends money. I take it out of my pocket till I ain't got any more." Otero shrugged and rolled a fresh cigarette.

Rico took out his billfold and handed Otero a fifty.

"I'll take that out of your next split."

Otero smiled.

"That's all the same to me, boss."

He was speaking the truth. He hadn't the slightest conception of the value of money. He spent till what he had was gone, then he asked Rico for more. Rico shook his head.

"Listen, Otero, ain't you never gonna get no sense ! You got over a grand and a half out of that Casa Alvarado stand. And here you are broke. Why some guys work a whole year for less than that."

Otero shrugged.

"I have worked for two pesos a week."

Rico took some small change out of his pocket and handed it to Otero.

"Go down to the corner and get a couple of Tribunes. Get three."

"Three of the same kind?"

"Sure."

Otero went out. Rico opened the window a few inches and sat down beside it. There was a touch of Spring in the air and it made him feel restless. He wanted to be doing things. In a week or less, he'd have Little Arnie's big gambling joint. That meant dough and plenty of it. He'd turn it over to Sam Vettori and let him run it. Sam was looking for something to do. Then maybe he could muscle in on the North Side graft. That wasn't easy. Pete Montana was a wise bird and he had the North Side tied up. Well, maybe the Big Boy could help him there. Rico jumped to his feet and began to pace up and down.

Otero came in with the papers. Rico took them from him and tore one of them apart till he came to the magazine section. There it was. Big type proclaimed:

ITALIAN UNDERWORLD CHIEF

GIVEN BIG FEED

Otero, looking over Rico's shoulder, saw the flashlight picture. In his excitement he pushed Rico aside and placing his finger on a section of the picture, cried:

"There I am!"

Rico took the other two papers apart and got out the magazine sections. Then he put the three sections side by side and compared them.

"All too dark," he said. Nevertheless, having chosen the clearest one of the three, he took his scissors and cut it out.

"I want one too," said Otero.

"All right," said Rico, "help yourself."

VI

DeVoss was standing in the lobby when Rico came in. DeVoss looked him over thoroughly, positive that he was out of his element in an atmosphere as exclusive as that of The Bronze Peacock. Not that Rico looked the least bit shabby. If anything, he was dressed more carefully than usual, from his modish derby to his fawn-colored spats. The big ulster he was wearing hid the loud striped suit and a plain dark muffler hid the loud striped tie. No, sartorially Rico could pass at The Bronze Peacock. But there was something vulgar and predatory about him that did not escape DeVoss.

"That's a bad one there," he told himself.

Rico glanced about the lobby, taking everything in from habit. It was not a good plant but it could be worked. Not that he had any intention of working it, but you never know. He came up to DeVoss and said:

"Excuse me, but where'll I find the manager of this place."

DeVoss looked at him coldly.

"I'm the manager."

Rico grinned.

"Well," he said, "I guess we got a mutual friend. The Big Boy tells me you and him does business together."

DeVoss's manner changed abruptly.

"Oh, yes. You're one of his friends, are you? What can I do for you?"

"I want to see Joe Massara."

"That's easy," said DeVoss, "he's back in his dressing-room. I'll take you back."

Rico followed DeVoss and they went up a few steps at the end of the lobby and came out into the club proper. It was empty except for a couple of electricians who were working on the stage spotlights.

"So you're one of the Big Boy's friends," said DeVoss, curious.

"I'm Rico."

DeVoss looked at him, startled.

"Oh," he said, "you're Rico."

All the way up the rear corridor DeVoss kept looking sideways at Rico. One of Little Arnie's men had told him about the new Vettori gang chief. Dangerous as dynamite! He congratulated himself on his acumen. By God, he kept repeating to himself, I knew he was a bad one.

DeVoss knocked at Joe's door. Someone called "come in." DeVoss opened the door and Rico followed him into the room. Joe was sitting in his shirt sleeves, his vest off, displaying a pair of fancy suspenders. (Rico made a mental note of the suspenders. His taste ran more to fancy sleeve garters. But if men like Joe were wearing fancy suspenders, why, he'd have to get himself a pair.) Olga Stassoff, in a black, red and gold Japanese kimono, was lying on a lounge, holding a Pekingese on her chest and rubbing its face against her own. A big man in evening clothes was standing with his back to the door. When Joe saw Rico he got to his feet in a hurry and stood smiling a little uneasily. The big man turned around.

"Mr. Rico wants to see you, Joe," said DeVoss; then he put his hand on Rico's arm and said: "When you get done with Joe, why, come up to the office and we'll have a little drink."

"Sorry," said Rico, "I don't use it. But thanks just the same."

DeVoss's eyebrows rose.

"You mean you don't drink!"

"Rico drinks milk," said Joe, trying to be funny.

But Rico didn't even smile.

"Yeah," he said, "sometimes I drink milk."

"Well, drop in anyway on your way out," said DeVoss.

DeVoss closed the door. Rico noticed that the girl in the Japanese kimono was staring at him. She didn't look like much to him; too skinny; all the same he insolently ran his eyes over her. The big man said:

"I guess there's no use for us to offer you a drink."

Joe took Rico by the arm.

"Olga, I want you to meet Rico. Rico, this is Olga Stassoff."

"Pleased to meet you," said Rico.

Olga sat up and tried to smile, but it was no use. Rico was repulsive to her, principally because she was certain that he had killed Joe's friend, Tony, but also because he stared at her insolently with his small, pale eyes.

"This boy here," said Joe, taking the big man familiarly by the arm, "is Mr. Willoughby, the millionaire."

"Why bring that up?" said Willoughby.

Rico had an instinctive respect for wealth. Money was power. He smiled affably and offered his hand.

"Pleased to meet you," he said.

Willoughby shook hands strenuously, then he inquired: "Have you got some private business with Joe?"

"Yeah," said Rico, "but there ain't no hurry about it."

"That's all right," said Willoughby. "Olga and I'll go over next door. Eh, Olga? When you get through, why, give us a rap and we'll come back. Don't suppose I could persuade you to join us in a little supper before the show?"

Rico was flattered.

"Well," he said, "I might."

"Good," said Willoughby; then taking Olga by the hand he pulled her to her feet. But Olga hesitated and stood looking from Joe to Rico.

"Run along, baby," said Joe.

"Well, don't take all night about it," said Olga.

"I won't keep him long," Rico put in.

When Olga and Willoughby had gone Rico said:

"Flying pretty high, ain't you, Joe?"

"Willoughby's just one of Olga's fish. He's gonna back her in a big show."

"Yeah? Well, if that bird's got a million bucks you both better clamp onto him. Nice little Jane you got, Joe."

"Olga's O.K.," said Joe.

Rico unbuttoned his ulster to display his finery. He had on one of his striped suits. It was dead black with a narrow pink stripe. The color scheme was further complicated by a pale blue shirt and an orange and white striped tie adorned with the ruby pin.

Joe stared at him.

"All lit up, ain't you, Rico?" he said.

Rico nodded, pleased.

"Yeah, I kind of got it into my head I ought to dress up now."

"They tell me you crowded Sam out," said Joe.

Rico looked at him.

"Didn't nobody tell you the boys was giving a banquet for me?"

"Yeah, they told me," said Joe, hurriedly, "but it was on at the wrong time for me."

Rico took out a cigar and bit off the end of it.

"I ain't seen you since the big stand."

"No," said Joe, looking at the floor. "I been laying low. They had me scared."

Rico banged his fist on the arm of his chair.

"Goddam it, Joe, what you got up your sleeve?"

Joe looked startled. He sat silent and from time to time raised his eyes to glance at Rico, who was staring at him.

"Spill it, Joe," said Rico.

"Well," said Joe, "I been making pretty good money with my dancing. Olga and me has got a turn together that's going over big. They want to put us in a show. Listen, Rico, I got enough of the racket. This last stand damn near fixed me. Jesus, but we was lucky."

"We ain't out yet," said Rico, "and we don't want no softies spoiling things."

Rico and Joe stared at each other for a moment. Joe began to get pale.

"You ain't dumb, Joe," said Rico, "what the devil! You mean to tell me you're gonna quit the racket. Why, boy, you ain't seen nothing yet. In a couple of weeks I'm gonna take over Little Arnie's joint. The Big Boy even wants to be declared in. Listen, Joe, you're a smart boy and I can use you. To hell with that dancing stuff. As a front it's O.K., but no man's gonna make his living that way."

Joe slumped down in his chair.

"I got your number, Joe," Rico went on, "it's that damn skirt. She's making a softie of you, Joe."

"Lord, Rico," said Joe, "can't a guy quit? I ain't gonna spill nothing. You think I want to get my neck stretched?"

"Yeah? Look at Tony. He turned soft and they patted him with a spade. Once a guy turns soft he ain't no good in this world. Didn't Humpy get soft on Red Gus and turn State's?[44] Yeah! Who got the neck stretching? Red Gus. Humpy got fifteen years and he'll be out in half of that."

Joe slumped further down in his chair.

"Rico, you know I ain't yellow."

"All right," said Rico, "if that's the dope,[45] I can use you. Ottavio and me has been figuring on a little stand that won't be half bad. I need a good inside man, Joe. A cut will be worth two grand at least."

Someone knocked at the door. It was DeVoss. He came over to Rico and said: "Mr. Rico, there's a couple of dicks out in the lobby. When I asked them what they wanted, they said they was just looking around."

Rico said:

Two bits it's Flaherty. All right, Mr. DeVoss, thanks."

DeVoss went out. Joe got to his feet and turned agonized eyes on Rico.

"What did you have to come clear across town for, Rico? Can't you let me alone?"

Rico paid no attention to him.

"There's one Irishman," he said, "that ain't long for this world."

"Rico," said Joe, "for God's sake stay over in your own end of town. I don't want the bulls coming here."

"Listen," said Rico, his eyes glowing, "if I hear any more of this softie stuff I'll only be back once more."

Willoughby and Olga came in.

44 State's evidence—that is, a witness for the government.

45 Information—the truth.

"Didn't you rap for us?" asked Willoughby.

"No, that was DeVoss," said Rico, "but we're done. Say, Mr. Willoughby, I sure am sorry but I got to pass up that invitation of yours. I got some important business with a couple of guys."

"Sorry," said Willoughby.

"Yes, we're sorry," said Olga, trying to be affable on Joe's account.

Rico shook hands with Joe.

"I'll be seeing you."

"All right, Rico," said Joe.

When Rico emerged he saw DeVoss coming down the corridor. He looked somewhat agitated.

"They're sure enough looking for you, Mr. Rico. For Lord's sake don't cause no trouble in my place."

Rico grinned.

"There won't be no trouble unless them damn dummies out there start it."

Rico followed DeVoss back through the club. On the stage the orchestra was tuning up and a few early couples were sitting at the tables. When they got to the lobby Rico saw Flaherty and another detective. Flaherty came over to him.

"Well, Rico," he said, "kind of out of your territory, ain't you?"

"What the hell of it?"

Rico buttoned his ulster and carefully arranged his muffler.

"Oh, nothing. Don't you remember I told you I was keeping an eye on you? Sure thing. I'm interested in young guys that want to get up in the world."

"Aw, can that," said Rico.

He noticed that people were coming into the place; in the club the orchestra had begun to play. He remembered what the Big Boy had said about DeVoss.

"Let's get the hell out of here," he said, "no use causing DeVoss no trouble. You bulls got about as much regard for a guy as a couple of hyenas."

"You're long on regard yourself, ain't you, Rico?" said Flaherty, laughing.

Rico nodded to DeVoss and went out. Flaherty and the other detective followed him. Rico was standing at the curb under the canvas marquee. They came up to him. He stared at Flaherty.

"Listen, Flaherty," he said, "did you ever stop to think how you'd look with a lily in your hand?"

"I never did," said Flaherty, with a sneer. "I been at this game for twenty-five years and I've got better guys than you hung, and I never got a scratch."

Rico took out a cigar and lit it. A taxi drew up at the curb.

"Well, here's my wagon," said Rico, "want to take a ride?"

"No," said Flaherty, "when we take a ride together I'll have the cuffs on you."

"No Irish bastard'll ever put no cuffs on Rico!"

Flaherty's face got red, but he turned on his heel and was about to go when Rico said: "And another thing, Flaherty, you was always O.K. with me, see, but now you ain't. You ain't got nothing on me and you ain't got no business trailing me every place I go. Take a tip. Sam and me're getting tired of seeing you guys climb the stairs. The first floor's open to anybody, they even allow cops in there, but the upstairs is private."

"Yeah?" said Flaherty, who had succeeded in controlling his temper.

"Yeah. Some day one of you wise dicks is gonna make a one way trip up them stairs."

"Getting up in the world, ain't you, Rico?" said Flaherty, "maybe you better run for mayor."

Rico slammed the door of the cab. Flaherty turned to the man with him and said:

"I'll get that swell-headed Dago if it's the last thing I ever do."

PART V

I

There were quite a few wise boys in Little Italy who thought that Rico's sensational rise was a fluke. The matter was talked about a good deal and he was unfavorably compared with Nig Po and Monk de Angelo, former leaders,[46] and there were even those who considered him inferior to Killer Pepi, Ottavio Vettori, and Joe Sansone. This confusion arose because Rico was not understood. He had none of the outward signs of greatness. Neither the great strength and hairiness of Pepi, nor the dash and effrontery of Ottavio Vettori, nor the maniacal temper of Joe Sansone. He was small, pale and quiet. In spite of his new finery he wasn't much to look at. He did not swagger, he seldom raised his voice, he never bragged. In other words, the general run of Little Italians could find nothing in him to exaggerate; they could not make a legendary figure of him because the qualities he possessed were qualities they could not comprehend. The only thing that redeemed him in their eyes was his reputation as a killer.

Rico was brave enough, but he did not flaunt his bravery like Kid Bean. Rico was cunning enough, but cunning was not an obsession with him as it was with Sam Vettori. Rico was capable of sudden audacity, but even his audacity had a sort of precision and was entirely without the dash of Ottavio's.

Rico, while he was small and pale, was capable of great endurance, but this endurance of his was nothing compared to Killer

Pepi's inhuman vitality. Rico's great strength lay in his single-mindedness, his energy and his self-discipline. The Little Italians could not appreciate qualities so abstract.

The men that were considered his rivals were really not to be compared with him. Killer Pepi was strong and courageous, but he was very erratic and a drug-addict. Ottavio Vettori was daring enough and cool in a tight place, he could shoot straight and he feared nothing, but he was light-minded, dissipated his energies on all sorts of follies, and ran after every woman that looked at him. Joe Sansone, though brave enough and dependable when it came to a sudden action, was a periodic drunkard, and, generally speaking, nervous and unreliable. Sam Vettori, a good man once, had let his congenital lethargy and his congenital love of trickery overcome him; he had become petty and had entirely lost the initiative which, years ago, had put him at the head of the gang. Now he was not even taken seriously by the men he had once led, and but for Rico's authority, he would have sunken into obscurity.

The case of Sam Vettori was a strange one, without its parallel in gang annals. In Little Italy there is no such thing as abdication unless it is accompanied by flight. The old gang leader who is superseded has two alternatives: flight or death. Sam had escaped both. His growing inability to make decisions had lost him his power, but it had also saved his life. Rico did not consider him dangerous. But that was not all. Rico considered him useful. That saved him from flight. With the proper guidance, Sam Vettori was an asset to any gang. He was wise and he knew the ropes.

Sam was docile; not that his hatred for Rico had abated; but things were breaking good, money was rolling in, and Sam loved money above all things. The Vettori gang had never known such prosperity before. Sam was quick to see where his advantage lay. Rico could be killed. Scabby, who hated Rico for some fancied slight and who, for this reason, was faithful to Sam, would have done it. But what would have been the good of that? Sam knew that he was through as a gang leader. With Rico dead, there would be a mad scramble for leadership. Besides, Rico had the devil's own luck, and Scabby might fail. If he failed, Scabby's life and his own wouldn't be worth a plugged dime. No, Sam Vettori accepted a somewhat odd situation philosophically and prospered.

Blondy Belle lolled back in her chair and put her fat hands on the table. Rico sat opposite her with his hat tilted over his eyes.

"Well," said Blondy Belle, "I guess that's it, ain't it, Rico?"

Rico nodded.

"I told you not to give that bird a chance. He thinks you're soft."

Rico smiled and twisted his diamond ring round and round.

"He raised the split to fifty percent, and the books were straight."

"Well," said Blondy, "he couldn't stand prosperity. Listen, you're gonna let him have it, ain't you?"

Blondy hated Little Arnie so that she couldn't sleep at night. She couldn't understand Rico's lenience.

"No," said Rico.

"Hell," said Blondy, "you're getting soft."

"Aw, can that," said Rico; "you want me to get my neck stretched over a dirty double-crosser that ain't worth a good bullet? Listen, I'm gonna run that bird out of town."

Blondy was disgusted. She started to get to her feet, but Rico reached across the table and pushed her back into her chair.

"Sit down," he said, "and cut the funny stuff. If you women ain't awful! Use your head, that's what you got it for."

Blondy sulked. Across the room the orchestra started up and couples crowded out into the ropedoff dance floor.

"Don't they ever get sick of dancing?" said Blondy, in a bad-temper.

Rico got to his feet.

"Listen," he said, "get yourself a cab and beat it. Go home and take some aspirin and hit the hay.[47] If you'd lay off that bad liquor you wouldn't always be beefing."

Blondy looked at Rico for a moment, then she said:

"Aw, sit down, Rico. I'll snap out of it."

"No," said Rico, "I got business to look after and I'm getting sick of this beefing. See, I'm getting sick. Any more of this kind of stuff and I'm gonna get me another woman. Hell, I might as well talk to Flaherty as you."

Blondy got to her feet without speaking. Rico never kidded; he meant what he said. Blondy was not used to men like Rico. She often wondered why it was she couldn't seem to get any hold on him.

Silently they walked around the little, roped-off dance floor. Rico told one of the waiters to get him a cab, then, to pass the time, he started putting nickels in a slot machine. After the third nickel, the bell rang and Rico won fifty cents; on the sixth nickel he won again.

"Ain't that good!" said Rico.

He called the man behind the counter.

"Say," he said, "have you seen anybody fooling with this machine?"

The man nodded.

"Yes, sir," he said, "I seen Ottavio doing something to it."

Rico laughed.

"Can you beat that petty crook! He'll be robbing blind men next. Say, tell Sam to get all the machines overhauled. What the hell! He might as well hand out nickels over the counter."

Blondy laughed, glad of this opportunity to put on a change of front.

"Boy, you don't miss anything," she said.

"Well," said Rico, serious, "what's the use of letting somebody gyp you?"

The waiter they had sent for the cab came to tell them that it was outside.

Blondy put her hand on Rico's arm.

"Listen, wise boy," she said, "you got the right dope about that Little Arnie business. Run him out, that's O.K., but do it up brown."

"You watch," said Rico.

He put her in the cab.

"Gonna give me a ring tonight, Rico?" she asked.

"Can't say."

"Well, don't let me ketch you with any more dark hairs on your coat."

"Can that!" said Rico.

Blondy slammed the cab door. Rico stood and watched the cab till it disappeared. Blondy was just like any other woman. Now she had got to the grand rush stage. Always beefing about something. Rico stood looking down the street. It was hot and the city sweltered, but now and then you could feel a breath of lake wind. He looked up at the sky. Stars everywhere.

"It's a swell night," said Rico.

Contrary to custom, he decided to walk down to the news-stand and get a paper. Since his rise, he seldom went out unaccompanied; never at night. Otero, Killer Pepi and Bat Carillo had constituted themselves his body-guard and one of them was always within calling distance. They were jealous of this privilege and sometimes quarreled among themselves. But the night tempted Rico; the atmosphere of The Palermo was vile, and the lake breeze was fresh and cool.

He had gone scarcely half a block when a large touring-car with the curtains closed passed him. He saw the car, noticing especially the closed curtains and the fact that the driver was hugging the curb, and, fearing the worst, he looked about for a shelter, but, as the car passed him and went on, he paid no further attention to it. Stopping in front of a lighted drugstore window he took out his watch and looked at it. One o'clock! Kid Bean and the Killer ought to be back any minute now. Suddenly he looked up. The big touring-car had turned and was coming back at full speed with its exhaust roaring. Rico cursed himself for his carelessness and reached under his armpit for his gun. But the car was abreast of him now and three guns blazed. Rico felt a searing pain in his shoulder and fell to the ground. His gun was stuck in its holster and he couldn't get it out. One of the men leaned out of the car and emptied his gun at Rico, who, helpless on the ground, heard the bullets sing.

"A goddam fine shot you are!" said Rico.

The big touring-car turned a corner and disappeared. Rico got to his feet and walked into the drugstore. The screen-door banged behind him and the clerk, who had been lying down behind the counter, got unsteadily to his feet.

"My God," he stammered, "what was all the popping for?"

Then he noticed that there was a torn place on the shoulder of Rico's coat.

"Was they after you, mister?" he asked.

"Yeah," said Rico, "I got brushed. Give me a roll of bandages."

The clerk stood there with his mouth open. People began to come into the store. Some of them knew who Rico was and stood staring at him.

"They put a bullet through my window," said the clerk.

"Listen," said Rico, "go get me a package of bandages."

The clerk finally came to himself and went for the bandages. A crowd had gathered in the street and now there were so many people in the drugstore that the people on the outside couldn't get in. Rico stood with his back to the counter, watching. Blood had begun to drip from his coatsleeve. Before the clerk returned with the bandages, Jastrow, the famous Little Italy cop, pushed his way through the crowd, followed almost immediately by Joe Massara.

"Well," said Jastrow, "somebody finally put one in you, did they, Rico?"

"Yeah," said Rico.

Joe Massara came over and put his hand on Rico's arm. Joe's face was white.

"Hurt you much, boss?"

"No," said Rico; "what the hell you doing way over here?"

"I got tipped off," said Joe. "I couldn't get you on the phone and I began to get nervous. We'd've made it only my cab driver got hooked for speeding."

"Who gave you the tip?" Jastrow demanded.

"Go press the bricks," said Rico, "this ain't your funeral."

Jastrow laughed.

"Rico," he said, "don't you know that the Old Man's taken an awful interest in you?"

"Well, tell him the cops couldn't get me no other way so they hired a couple of gunmen."

Joe laughed. Jastrow laughed also and taking out his notebook began to write in it. The clerk came with the bandages. Joe took them from him and paid him. Before they could get started, Killer Pepi and Otero came shoving their way through the crowd.

"Hello, boys," said Jastrow, looking up from his little book, "your boss got nudged by a hunk of lead."

"So they tell me," said the Killer.

Rico said:

"Let's get the hell out of here."

Jastrow went in front, clearing the way, followed by Otero and Killer Pepi, who had Rico between them. Joe brought up the rear. People were lined to the car-tracks; lights blazed in all the houses along the street, and men hung from the lamp-posts. When they came out of the store, the crowd was so thick that they were unable to get any farther. Jastrow took out his nightstick and flourished it, but the sight of it was enough, the crowd made a path.

As they walked along Joe came up close to Rico and whispered:

"Little Arnie."

48   A derogatory term for Jews, traced by the *Oxford English Dictionary* back to 1824.

Rico nodded. Pepi heard Joe.

"Yeah," he said, "and I'm gonna plug him tonight."

"There won't be no plugging," said Rico.

"Aw, hell," said Pepi.

Otero was excited.

"Yes, yes, Rico," he cried.

"Shut up, you birds," said Rico; "who the hell's running this show?"

A crowd was waiting for them in front of The Palermo. Bat Carillo and Ottavio Vettori began to yell as soon as they saw that Rico was on his feet.

Jastrow turned around.

"Well, I guess I done my duty."

"Sure," said Rico, "come in and have a drink."

"Nothing doing," said Jastrow, then he shouted: "You birds quit your damn yelling and get in off the sidewalk."

Everybody laughed. They all liked Jastrow, who had the reputation of being on the square. Rico went in escorted by a mob of Little Italians. In the club people were standing on the tables; the orchestra was playing loudly; and Sam Vettori, in the middle of the deserted dance-floor, was waving his arms wildly and bellowing.

When they saw Rico there was a tumult.

"Rico! Rico! Rico!"

Killer Pepi and Otero, intoxicated by the excitement, grabbed each other and began to dance. Joe waved the bandages. Rico took off his hat and smiled.

On the way up the stairs Rico turned to Joe and said:

"Go get The Sheeny."[48]

Killer Pepi took Rico by the arm.

"He's upstairs now, boss," he said; "the Kid got plugged."

"How'd you make out?" Rico inquired.

"O.K.," said Killer Pepi; "we was making a get-away on the third stand when one of the guys plugged the Kid. He ain't hurt much. Just skinned him."

Killer Pepi and Kid Bean had robbed twenty-five filling-stations in the last two weeks.

"All right," said Rico, "you guys have been on the up and up. Split the money two ways."

"That's the talk, boss," said the Killer.

Otero knocked at the door. Joe Sansone's face appeared at the grating, then the door swung open.

The Sheeny was working on Kid Bean. The Kid was lying on the card table, smoking a cigarette. His shirt was off and there was a smear of blood on his hairy chest. When he saw Rico he said:

"They damn near hit the target, boss."

He pointed to a pierced heart tattooed on his chest. He was as proud of his tattooing as a Maori chief.

"The boss got plugged," said Pepi.

"What!" yelled the Kid, sitting up; "go fix him up, Sheeny." He gave The Sheeny a push. But Rico said: "Finish up the Kid first. I can wait."

"Only jist got to bandage him yet," said The Sheeny with his ingratiating smile.

The Sheeny was a graduate doctor, but he had been sent up for an illegal operation and his license had been revoked. He said his name was Lazarro, but nobody believed him and everybody referred to him simply as The Sheeny.

Rico took off his coat and shirt, and sat waiting. His wound had stopped bleeding.

Joe Massara came over and stood by his chair. Joe's big cut for an inside job had pulled him back to the fold. He never talked any more about quitting the racket. The Courtney affair had blown over apparently, and he had regained his confidence.

"Joe," said Rico, "how come they gave you the tip?"

"Well," said Joe, "I ain't sure, but I think it was an outsider that didn't know nobody but me. He sure had the dope all right. He said the guys were gonna park at twelve. They didn't expect you out till two or three."

"A fine bunch of gunmen Arnie picked!"

"Yeah," said Joe.

The Kid climbed off the table and stood feeling his chest.

"Boy, I thought I was plugged for sure."

"They just bounce off of you," said Pepi.

The Sheeny began to bathe Rico's wound.

"'Tain't much," he said, "but it pays to be careful."

When The Sheeny had got Rico bandaged, Rico put on his shirt and sat smoking. Bat Carillo and Ottavio Vettori, whom he had sent for, came in and sat down beside him. The Sheeny put on his hat.

"Well," he said, smiling at Rico, "I guess I'm done. If you guys have any trouble with them wounds let me know."

Rico got his billfold and gave The Sheeny a fifty.

"Thank you! Thank you!" said The Sheeny, bowing.

Joe Sansone let him out.

Rico said:

"Now, listen, you birds, tonight's the big clean-up. If these guys want trouble, why, that's just what we're looking for."

"You bet," said Killer Pepi.

"Now," Rico went on, "I got things fixed with Joe Peeper and I'm gonna to give Little Arnie the grand rush right away. I want Killer Pepi and Otero and Ottavio to go with me."

"How about me?" demanded Joe Sansone.

"You too, Joe. And you, Bat, I want you to take your gang and smash up Jew Mike's. Run everybody out and then smash the place. If Little Arnie wants trouble, why that's what we got the most of. Got it?"

"O.K.," said Bat, "how about the rods?"

"Don't use 'em," said Rico; "Jew Mike's yellow and he won't put up no fight."

"Them guys of mine sure are hard to hold on to," said Carillo, grinning.

"That's your job," said Rico. "We got to watch this plugging stuff with Flaherty on our trail."

"O.K., boss," said Carillo.

III

When the doorman saw Rico get out of the automobile he stood stunned, then, pulling himself together, he made an attempt to run. But Pepi crossed the pavement in two strides, grabbed him by the collar and pushed him ahead of him up the stairs.

"Listen, Handsome," said Pepi, "you tell the look-out we're O.K. or they'll bury you."

At the head of the stairs the doorman spoke to the look-out through the shutter.

"These birds are all right," he said.

The look-out opened the door and Pepi shoved a gun against him.

"Turn your back, Buddy," said Pepi, "and march straight ahead of me."

Rico, followed by Joe Sansone, Ottavio Vettori, and Otero, climbed the long flight of stairs and entered the lobby. The lobby was deserted except for two or three couples. Beyond it, through a big arched doorway, they could see the crowded roulette wheels. Rico caught up with Pepi and said to the doorman:

"Where's Joe Peeper?"

The doorman had an agonized look. He was sure they were going to kill him. He just stood there, unable to force himself to speak.

"Say," said Pepi, "speak up."

The doorman pointed to a door.

"He's in with the boss, is he?" said Rico.

The doorman nodded.

"Yeah," said the look-out, eager to get in good, "Joe's in there with the boss and a couple of other guys."

"All right," said Rico; "now, Pepi, if the door's locked, do your stuff."

Pepi could force the heaviest door with his shoulder.

Joe Sansone tried the door; it was locked.

"Now," said Rico, "Pepi'll force the door. You cover him, Joe, in case somebody in there gets nervous and pulls a gat. I'll follow you. Otero, you stay out here and don't let nobody in. You watch this pair of hard guys here, Ottavio." Rico jerked his thumb toward the look-out and the doorman.

"You don't have to watch us," said the doorman.

They all laughed.

"All right, Pepi," said Rico.

Pepi hunched his shoulders and flung himself against the door. It opened with a crash. They saw four startled men rise half way out of their chairs and stand staring. Joe Peeper cried:

"It's Rico!"

Pepi was on his hands and knees in the middle of the room, but Joe Sansone stepped in behind him and covered the four men with his big automatic. Rico came in, took off his hat and bowed.

"Hello, Arnie," he said; "how's business?"

Little Arnie sat with his mouth slightly open. As a rule Little Arnie was imperturbable. He hid an excess of both cunning and timidity behind a cold, repellent, sallow Jewish mask. But this cyclonic entry was too much for him. His mask had slipped, revealing a pale, terrified countenance.

"Well," he said, "what's the game?"

Joe Peeper, who was in Rico's pay, said:

"Pull up a chair, you guys."

Pepi found two chairs. Joe Sansone and Rico sat down; Pepi stood behind Rico's chair.

Little Arnie turned to the two men sitting beside him. They were strangers to Rico and they looked tough.

"I don't know what this is all about," said Arnie, "but it's a private row, so you guys better beat it."

Rico said very quietly:

"Nobody's gonna leave this room."

One of the toughs shouted:

"Think not, wop! Well, who the hell's gonna stop us?"

Before Rico could reply, Joe Sansone said:

"Me, I'm gonna stop you, see! And I ain't gentle. I'm just itching to put some lead in a couple of hard guys."

"Yeah," said Rico, smiling, "you guys are invited to this private party."

The two men looked at Arnie, who sat tapping his desk with a pencil.

"Say," said one, "you sure got a fine bunch of friends, Arnie."

"Yeah," said Arnie.

Pepi laughed and said: "Yeah, he sure has. Arnie, you ought to had better sense than to get a couple of outside yaps to bump Rico off."

Nobody said anything. Arnie took out a cigar and lit it. The two strangers sat staring at Rico. Pepi sat staring at them. Finally he asked: "Where you guys from?"

The men looked uneasily at Arnie. Little by little they were losing their nerve.

"Speak up," said Pepi, "where you guys from?"

"We're from Detroit," said one of the men.

"Where the hell's that?" Joe Sansone inquired. "I never heard of it."

"Say," said Pepi, "don't you know that tough guys like you oughtn't to be running around loose? No sir. You're liable to get arrested for firing a rod in the city limits."

"Listen," said one of the men from Detroit, "what you guys got against us? We ain't done nothing. We just got in."

They were thoroughly intimidated.

Arnie, who had recovered his poise, said:

"Well, Rico, what's the talk? Let's have it."

Pepi and Joe Sansone both started to talk at once, but Rico motioned for them to be quiet.

"Arnie," said Rico, "you're through. If you ain't out of town by tomorrow morning, you won't never leave town except in a box."

Arnie said nothing but sat staring at the smoke rising from his cigar.

"In the first place," Rico went on, "you been double-crossing me for two months. In the second place you hire these bums here to pop me. Now I guess that's about all."

Arnie laughed.

"Rico," he said, "somebody has sure been stringing you. Why, you ought to know I wouldn't double-cross you. Hell, that wouldn't help me none."

"Can that," said Rico. "Your number's up, Jew. Take it like a man."

Arnie's face got red.

"Listen, Rico, if you think you can muscle into this joint you're off your nut."

"All right, Joe," said Rico, jerking his head in Joe Peeper's direction, "spill it."

Joe Peeper looked sideways at Arnie.

"The books're crooked, Rico," said Joe Peeper; "he's been gypping you out of half your split every week."

The Detroit toughs began to shift about uneasily.

"Well, you two-timing bastard," said Arnie.

Rico laughed.

"Arnie," he said, "that's that. Here's the dope. You get your hat and beat it. Leave the burg. If I ever hear about you being in town again, why, I'm gonna turn the Killer loose on you."

"Yeah," said Pepi, "and I never did like kikes."

"I ain't any too fond of them, myself," said Joe Sansone.

Arnie meditated. Rico said:

"I been square with you, Arnie, but you couldn't stand prosperity, that's all. So take it standing up."

"What the hell else can he do?" Pepi demanded.

49 Harry Horowitz (1889-1914), also known as "Gyp-the-Blood," was a notorious gang leader in New York City. Though only 5'5" tall and weighed 140 pounds, he was enormously strong. Horowitz was executed in 1914 for his part in the murder of the gambler Herman Rosenthal.

A mugshot of Harry Horowitz, alias "Gyp-the Blood," in 1912.

"I'll tell you what I can do," said Arnie, "I can have a talk with Mr. Flaherty."

Arnie studied Rico carefully to see what effect this would have. But Rico merely smiled at him.

"Getting pretty low, Arnie," he said, "when you take the bulls in with you." Then he paused and leaned forward in his chair. "If you go to see Mr. Flaherty you better have an alibi because he might ask you about Limpy John."

Arnie dropped his cigar and sat staring into space, his hands lying palms up on the table.

"All over but the shouting," said Joe Sansone, "somebody better throw in a towel. But I don't suppose the dirty bums in Detroit ever heard of towels."

"Aw, lay off of us," said one of the Detroit toughs.

Joe Sansone stared at him.

"Say, Gyp-the-Blood,[49] I bet they think you're a pretty hard bird where you live, don't they?"

Arnie turned to Joe Peeper.

"Well, Joe," he said, "you sure put the skids under me."

"Sure I did," said Joe Peeper; "you thought you could bat me around and make me like it."

Pepi laughed.

"Arnie," he said, "you better go back to Detroit with your boy friends."

When Rico and his men left Arnie's joint Joe Peeper followed them. As soon as they reached the pavement, Joe walked up to Rico and said:

"You sore at me, Rico?"

All Rico's men stopped and stood staring at Joe, wondering what his game was.

"You guys get in the car," said Rico.

They all got in except Pepi, who stood with his back against the car, his right hand in his pocket. Pepi didn't trust anybody who had ever been mixed up with Little Arnie.

"What's on your mind, Joe?" Rico demanded.

"I thought you acted like you was sore at me," said Joe Peeper; "honest to God, Rico, I didn't know nothing about them Detroit bums. I didn't know what Arnie was up to. Lord, you know I wouldn't double-cross you after all you done for me."

"Well, who said you did?"

"Nobody," said Joe, "only it looked funny, and I thought maybe you guys had got a wrong notion. I'd be a sap to pull anything like that."

Rico laughed.

"Forget it," he said.

Rico started to get into the automobile, but Joe took hold of his arm.

"How about me, Rico?" he said. "If I stick around here they'll bump me off sure."

"Yeah?" said Rico; "say, them guys wouldn't bump nobody off now. But get in. I can use you, Joe."

Joe got in the back seat with Otero and Ottavio Vettori. He talked to them all the way back to The Palermo, trying to get in good with them, but they said nothing.

IV

The next day in the society column of one of the Chicago papers there appeared a small item, which read:

"Mr. Arnold Worch, of the North Side, has just left for Detroit where he intends to spend the summer. He was accompanied by two of his Detroit friends, who have been in Chicago for a short stay."

This was the work of Ottavio Vettori. The underworld was convulsed and thousands of extra copies of the paper were sold. The clipping was to be found pasted up in all the barrooms, gambling joints, and dance-halls. Rico and Ottavio Vettori had become famous over night.

Little Arnie wasn't the only one who left town. Several of Little Arnie's henchmen, who had been closely connected with the attempted killing, followed him into exile. Joseph Pavlovsky, the doorman, who had driven the car, went to Hammond, where, on the money Arnie had given him, he opened a speak-easy. Pippy Coke, who with the two Detroit gunmen had done the shooting, went with Pavlovsky, and they were followed by two croupiers, who had shadowed Rico.

Arnie's gang was smashed and the Little Italians took over a territory they hadn't controlled since the days of Monk De Angelo.

Arnie had come to Chicago from New York about five years ago. His reputation had got so bad in New York that no one would do business with him. He came west with a small stake and was lucky enough to arrive at just the right time. Kips Berger, also formerly of New York and once one of Arnie's pals, had gone broke and was willing to sell out his big gambling joint for practically nothing. Arnie bought it and prospered. This gambling joint was in a neutral zone, touching Little Italy on the south side and the vast territory that Pete Montana controlled on the north. Arnie was acute enough to see his advantage. He worked hard at his job and in a little while had consolidated his territory. But he was not a good gang chief: first, because he was a coward, second, because his closest associate couldn't trust him, third, because he was inclined to lose his head in an emergency. His lieutenant, Jew Mike, was a tougher and more violent replica of his chief. Between them they bossed the territory, but under them the gang never prospered and their hold was at best precarious. They held on only because there was little or no opposition. Their gangsters were a poor lot and were content to take small splits. On the south, Sam Vettori was slipping and his lethargy prevented his interfering; on the north the great Pete Montana was magnificently indifferent.

Arnie had been slipping for the last year or so, and Rico's sudden rise had accelerated his decline. Arnie, fearing the worst, committed blunder after blunder; first, he made advances to Rico, then, getting Rico's protection for a thirty percent split, things looked too easy and he began to doublecross him. Lastly, although he should have known better, he made the tactical error of trying to get Rico killed. If he had succeeded his position would not have been improved; he would have been worse off, because the Vettori gang would have made short work of him.

No one regretted the passing of Little Arnie. He had never been straight with anybody. No one could depend on him and he had none of the qualities that go to make up a good gang chief. The wonder is that he lasted as long as he did.

Arnie's fall was the signal for a series of minor tumbles. Jew Mike, whose joint Bat Carillo and his gang had demolished, fled to the South Side, where he opened a couple of vice-joints. Kid

Burg moved to Cicero, and Squint Maschke, after a short exile, offered his services to Rico, who gave him twenty-four hours to make a second disappearance. With the fall of Arnie's three lieutenants, the last vestiges of his rule vanished.

V

Otero helped Rico out of his coat, then, while Rico doused his face at the wash stand, he sat down, tipped back his chair and rolled himself a cigarette.

"You better lay down, Rico, and get some rest," said Otero; "you ain't looking so good."

"I'm O.K.," said Rico.

But this was bravado. He had slept only four hours in the last two days; his face was pale and drawn and he suffered from an intermittent fever. His wound, though a slight one, was not healing properly, and The Sheeny had warned him that he had better take it easy. Inactivity at any time was abhorrent to Rico; now it was impossible. His big chance had come. Nothing could stop him now but a hunk of lead in the right spot.

Rico, a little unsteady on his legs, stood staring at Otero.

"You're sure making yourself at home," he said.

"Well," said Otero, "I think I stay."

Rico laughed.

"Listen, I don't need no nurse. Beat it."

"No," said Otero, tossing away his cigarette and starting to roll another one, "I think I stay."

Rico walked over to the bed and stood staring at it. If he had been alone he would have flopped down and been asleep in an instant.

"Think I'll catch a little sleep," he said; "you beat it, Otero."

Otero didn't say anything. He finished rolling his cigarette, lit it, and tipped his hat down over his eyes.

"Goddam it," cried Rico, "beat it! I'm sick of you trailing me like a Chicago Avenue bull. I ain't gonna drop in my tracks."

"All right," said Otero, "you lay down. I finish my cigarette."

Rico threw himself on the bed, fully dressed except for his coat. He put his hands under his head and tried to keep awake by staring at the ceiling. But in a moment he was asleep.

Otero sat looking at his chief. All along he'd known. Rico was a great man like Pancho Villa. Even in Toledo when he and Rico were sticking up filling-stations, he knew. A little, skinny young fellow with a little mustache, sure, that's what everybody saw. But everybody didn't have the eyes of Otero.

Otero flung his second cigarette on the floor and rolled another one. Rico turned from side to side in his sleep and mumbled. His face was white and drawn. Otero got to his feet and went over to look at him. No, Rico was not well. Otero put his hand on Rico's forehead. Fever! He stood looking down at his chief, shaking his head.

"Like hell!" cried Rico; "you can't hand Rico none of that bunk. No Irish bastard'll ever put no cuffs on Rico."

Otero went back to his chair and sat dozing under his big hat, while Rico tossed from side to side and talked.

Someone knocked at the door. Otero was slow in opening his eyes, but Rico sat up, stared for a moment, then jumped out of bed and got his automatic.

"Go see who it is," he said to Otero; "don't open the door. Ask them."

Otero went over to the door and called:

"Who's there?"

There was a short silence, then a voice with a marked Italian accent said:

"A couple of right guys. We want to see Rico."

Otero turned and looked at Rico, who came over to the door.

"Listen, you right guys," said Rico, "I'll give you a one-two-three to get out of that hall and then I'm gonna start pumping lead. Got it?"

There was a pause.

"Rico," said another voice, a deeper voice with no trace of an accent, "you don't know me, but I'm Pete Montana and I want to talk turkey."

Otero and Rico exchanged a stupefied look.

"Pete," said Rico, "do you know the Big Boy?"

"Sure."

"What's his name in full?"

"James Michael O'Doul."

"All right, Otero," said Rico, "let 'em in."

Otero unbarred the door. Rico, with his gun still leveled, stood a little behind the door, watching.

Pete Montana, followed by Ritz Colonna, his lieutenant, came in. Montana, in private life Pietro Fontano, was a big, solemn, respectable-looking Italian. He was dressed very quietly, wore no jewelry, and carried a cane. Colonna, once a ham prize-fighter, was a small, bull-necked man with a battered, dark face. His clothes were shabby and he wore an old cap on the side of his head.

Montana and Rico stood measuring each other. Rico looked small and frail beside the robust Montana, but Rico wasn't impressed, for Montana looked fat and puffy, like Sam Vettori. Otero barred the door.

"Get a couple of chairs, Otero," said Rico.

Otero dragged up the only two chairs in the room and Montana and Colonna sat down. Otero squatted on his heels with his back to the wall and Rico sat on the bed.

Montana took out a monogrammed cigar-case and passed it around, then he selected one of the cigars himself and cut off the end with a little gold cutter on his watch chain.

"Mopping up, ain't you, Rico?" asked Montana, who kept his eyes lowered.

"Well," said Rico, "Arnie was double-crossing me."

"He wasn't no good," said Colonna. "I was just aching to bump that bird off."

Montana motioned for him to be quiet.

"They slung some lead, didn't they, Rico?"

"Yeah, and I stopped some of it. Nothing to shout about."

"If he'd've got you, his number was up," said Montana; "you know, I been watching you ever since you muscled in on Sam Vettori."

"Yeah?"

"Sure thing. We been taking an interest in you, ain't we, Ritz?"

Ritz grinned.

"That's the word," he said.

"Sure," said Montana, "you're on the up and up with us."

"Well," said Rico, "that's O.K. with me."

Montana looked up at Rico suddenly.

"Any guy that can muscle in on Sam Vettori and Little Arnie is on the up and up with me. The Big Boy's with me there."

Rico smoked and said nothing. But he wondered what the game was. Was Pete Montana getting soft like Sam Vettori?

Could it be possible that the great Pete Montana was turning sap? All this palaver and softie talk. Rico's head began to buzz.

"Look," said Montana, "I used to work Arnie's territory myself, but it slowed down, you know what I mean. It wasn't worth nothing when Kips Berger had it, and after Arnie got it I didn't pay no attention. I got all I can handle, ain't I, Ritz?"

"That's the word," said Ritz.

"Yeah," said Montana, "by rights that territory's mine, get the idea? I could get all the protection I wanted, but I don't muscle in on no right guy, see? Kiketown's yours, Rico."

"Much obliged," said Rico; "I ain't looking for no trouble with you, Pete."

"That's the talk," said Montana; then he turned to Ritz: "See, Ritz, you had the wrong steer."[50]

"Yeah, I had the wrong steer," said Ritz.

Montana turned back to Rico.

"Yeah," he said, "some wise guys was giving Ritz a lot of bull. Ritz said you was trying to muscle in on my territory."

Rico thought he was dreaming. So this was the great Pete Montana. A guy that couldn't turn over in bed without getting plastered all over the front page. All that softie stuff was a front. Pete Montana was scared.

"No," said Rico, "them guys don't know what they're talking about."

Montana smiled blandly.

"Maybe we can team up on a job or two, Rico. I like your work. The Big Boy's no fool and he thinks you're the goods. Yeah, maybe we can team up, but I ain't making no promises. Only this. I ain't looking for no split on Arnie's layout. She's yours."

"Don't forget the hide-out, chief," said Ritz.

Montana smiled again.

"By God, I sure enough did forget it. Yeah, Rico, some of Ritz's boys has got a hide-out a half a block from Arnie's joint. That's O.K., ain't it?"

Rico's manner changed. He lost his affability and his face became serious.

"Well," he said, "as long as there ain't no cutting in. I won't stand for no cutting in."

Montana looked at Ritz. Ritz said:

"Hell, there won't be no cutting in."

"What do you say, Pete?" asked Rico.

Montana meditated, pulling at one of his thick lips. Otero sat watching Rico. Caramba! Here was little Rico telling the big Pete Montana where to get off. Otero never took his eyes off Rico's face.

"Well," said Montana, "they're my men and I'm behind them. If there's any cutting in, why, I'll settle with you, Rico. Christ, no use for us to fight over a little thing like that. Anyway, if we get along, I'll put you in on the alcohol racket."

"All right," said Rico, "you and me can do business, Pete."

Montana got up and offered Rico his hand. They pumped arms briefly. Then Pete said: "Well, I guess we'll saunter. But let me give you a tip, Rico. You're getting too much notice, get the idea? You got the bulls watching you. I know a new guy has always got to expect that, but take it easy for a while. They'll go to sleep; they always do."

Rico admired Montana's shiftiness, but he wasn't fooled. Pete was trying to tie him up, make him leery.

"Much obliged," said Rico; "a new guy has got a lot to learn."

Montana smiled blandly, certain he had scored.

"Well," said Montana, "so long. Maybe I'll drop down to your new joint and give it the once over some night."

"All right," said Rico, "just let me know."

Otero unbarred the door. Montana started out; Ritz offered his hand to Rico, then followed his chief. Otero barred the door.

Rico stood in the middle of the room, staring into space. Otero said:

"He ain't so much."

Rico laughed out loud.

"Otero," he cried, "you said a mouthful."

PART VI

51   Thrasher reported: "Members of the [Valley] gang have boasted that they have worn silk shirts and have ridden in Rolls-Royce automobiles since the war. Their great opportunity for wealth came with prohibition and their entrance into the rum-running business. Eventually they controlled a string of breweries both in and out of Chicago, and their leaders are said to have made millions in these enterprises. One of them occupies an exclusive North Shore estate purchased for $150,000. . . . At present they dress in the height of fashion, ride in large automobiles with sleek chauffeurs, and live on the fat of the land," (pp. 433–34).

I

Rico felt small and unimportant in the Big Boy's apartment.[51] He was intensely selfcentered and as a rule surroundings made no impression on him. But he had never seen anything like this before. He sat in the big, panelled diningroom, eating cautiously, dropping his fork from nervousness, and looking furtively about him. From time to time he pulled at his high, stiff collar, and when he caught the Big Boy's eye he grinned.

Joe Sansone had dressed him so that he would look presentable. It had taken a good deal of management and tact, but Joe Sansone was a stickler for clothes and persevered with Rico, who swore at him at first and wouldn't listen.

"Look, boss," he said, "you're getting up in the world. Ain't none of us ever been asked to eat with the Big Boy at his dump. Hear what I'm telling you. Nobody's ever crashed the gates before but Pete Montana. See what I mean? You don't want the Big Boy to think you ain't got no class."

Joe had his own dress suit cleaned and pressed, and punctually at five he presented himself at Rico's door with the outfit under his arm. Rico had resisted from the beginning; first, he balked at the suspenders, then the starched shirt. Joe, laboring with the studs, the buttoned shoes, the invincible collar, cursed and sweated. Rico resisted. But Joe won.

As Joe was ten pounds heavier than Rico, the dress suit was not precisely a perfect fit, but as Joe said "men are wearing their clothes a lot looser now." To which Rico sardonically replied: "Yeah? Say, they rig you up better than this in stir."[52]

Finally Joe got Rico into his harness.[53] Rico stamped about declaring that he'd be goddamned if he'd go out looking like that. Why, the Big Boy would think he was off his nut.

"You look fine, boss," said Joe.

"Yeah," said Rico, "all I need is a napkin over my arm."

But Joe moved Rico's bureau out from its corner and tipped the mirror so Rico could get a full length view of himself. He was won over immediately. Why, honest to God, he looked like one of them rich clubmen he read about in the magazines. The enormous white shirtfront, the black silk coat lapels, the neatly-tied white tie dazzled him.

"I guess I don't look so bad," he said to Joe; "we got plenty of time, let's go down to Sam's place for a while."

Rico played with his dessert and looked about the room. The Big Boy ate with gusto, smacking his lips. The magnificence of the Big Boy's apartment crushed Rico. He stared at the big pictures of oldtime guys in their gold frames; at the silver and glass ware on the serving table; at the high, carved chairs. Lord, why, it was like a hop dream.[54]

He shook his head slowly.

"Some dump you got here," he said.

"Yeah," said the Big Boy, glancing negligently about him, "and I sure paid for it. See that picture over there?" He pointed to an imitation Valesquez. "That baby set me back one hundred and fifty berries."

Rico stared.

"Jesus, one hundred and fifty berries for a picture!"

"Yeah," said the Big Boy, "but that ain't nothing. See that bunch of junk over there?" He jerked his head in the direction of the serving table. "That stuff set me back one grand."

Rico stared.

"One grand for that stuff?"

"Sure," said the Big Boy, "that's the real thing. Only what the hell, I say! A plate's to eat off of, ain't it? What's the odds what it's made of? But I got a spell about two years ago. I had a pot full of money and I thought, well, other guys that ain't got as much dough as I got put on a front, so why shouldn't I? Sure, I could buy and sell guys that's got three homes and a couple of chugwagons.[55] So I

52   Prison.

53   Uniform, outfit—especially formal wear.

54   "Hop" is opium.

55   Automobiles.

got a guy down at a big store, you know, one of them decorators, to pick me out a swell apartment and fix it up A1. So he did. I got a library too and a lot of other stuff that ain't worth a damn. I was talking to a rich guy the other day and he said I was a damn fool to buy real books because he had a library twice as big as mine and dummy books. What the hell! If a guy's gonna have a library, why, I say do it right. So there you are. I got so damn many books it gives me a headache just to look at 'em through the glass. Shakespeare and all that stuff."

"Yeah?" said Rico, stupefied.

A servant took away their dessert and brought coffee. Then he passed a humidor full of cigars. Rico took one of the fat, black cigars, lit it, and tipped his chair back. What a way to live!

"Yeah," said the Big Boy, "I got a lot of dough tied up in this dump. I get rent free, though. Eschelman, the contractor, owns this dump and he knows how I stand in the city. Boy, he puts up what he pleases and gets away with it. See the idea, Rico? If a guy stands in with me, he owns the burg."

"Sure," said Rico, "you're a big guy."

"I get him contracts, too," said the Big Boy; "course I get mine out of it, but I made that guy. When he come here from down state he didn't have an extra pair of pants, now he's climbing. Yeah, if I had a wife and a couple of kids, why, I'd build me a big house out in some swell suburb, but as it is, I'd just as leave be here on one floor. I got everything I need and then some."

"Sure," said Rico.

"Let's go in the library," said the Big Boy, "it's more comfortable in there."

The Big Boy told the servant to take their coffee into the library. Then he got up and Rico followed him. The Big Boy put his hand on Rico's shoulder.

"Kind of lit up yourself tonight, ain't you, Rico?"

"Yeah, I thought I better put on the monkey suit."

"That's right, Rico. May as well learn now."

"Sure," said Rico.

The Big Boy motioned Rico to a chair, then sat down. Rico looked about him at the great expanse of glass guarding tier after tier of books. Lord, if a guy'd read that many books he'd sure know a lot!

"Rico," said the Big Boy, "let's talk serious."

"All right," said Rico.

The Big Boy leaned forward in his chair and stared at Rico.

"Listen," he said, "I'm gonna talk and you ain't gonna hear a word I say, see, this is inside dope and if it gets out it'll be just too bad for somebody."

"You know me," said Rico.

"All right," said the Big Boy; "get this: if I didn't think a hell of a lot of you I wouldn't be asking you to eat with me. You're on the square, Rico, and you're a comer, see. You got the nerve and you're a good, sober, steady guy. That's what we need. Trouble with most of these guys they ain't got nothing from the collar up. O.K. Now, listen. Pete Montana's through."

Rico nearly leapt out of his chair.

"Yeah?"

"Now don't get excited," said the Big Boy, "because, when it gets out, there's gonna be hell to pay. Ritz Colonna and a couple of other lowdown bums is gonna make a rush, see, and that means that somebody's gonna get hurt."

"Sure," said Rico, settling back.

"But not you," said the Big Boy; "you're gonna lay back and let them dumb eggs bump each other off, then we'll get our licks in, see? Pete's through. The Old Man's gonna have a talk with him tomorrow or the next day and Pete's gonna mosey. He's all swelled up, thinks he's king and all that stuff, but wait till the Old Man gets through with him. Why, he can hang that guy. Besides that, he can turn the Federal guys loose on him for peddling narcotics. And boy, how he peddles them! He built that big house of his on 'em. Well, see how things are? I can't spill no more."

"Well," said Rico, "I'm on."

"All right," said the Big Boy, "but listen: I'm doing a hell of a lot for you and when I get you planted I want plenty of service."

"You'll sure get it," said Rico.

Rico, with the Big Boy's cigar still between his teeth, lay back in the taxi and stared out at the tangle of traffic on Michigan Boulevard. Things were sure to God looking up! Five years ago he wasn't nobody to speak of; just a lonely yegg, sticking up chain-stores and filling-stations. Chiggi had sure given him the right dope. He remembered one night in Toledo when he was pretty low. There was a blonde he used to meet at one of the call-houses

56 A "red cent"—money.

57 A tramp's stew, made of meat, potatoes, vegetables, whatever is at hand.

58 A Spanish brand of luxury automobiles.

A 1929 model Hispano-Suiza automobile.

and she sure did satisfy him, but, boy, she had to have the coin on the nose or there wasn't nothing doing. Well, he didn't have a red.[56] He was just sitting there in Chiggi's thinking about the blonde, when Chiggi came over and said: "Listen, kid, you got big town stuff in you. What you want around here? Get somebody to stake you or hit the rods. Hell, don't be a piker." Well, Chiggi staked him, but he blew the stake on the blonde, oh, boy what a couple of days, and then he hit the rods with Otero. Little Italy sure looked good to them. They didn't have a good pair of pants between them, and a bowl of mulligan[57] tasted better than the stuff he'd ate at the Big Boy's. Well, here he was riding taxis and hobnobbing with guys like James O'Doul, who paid one grand for a bunch of crockery. Yeah, here he was!

Rico saw nothing but success in the future. With the Big Boy behind him he couldn't be stopped, and when he once got some place he knew how to stay there. Play square with the guys that are square with you; the hell with everybody else.

Rico smoked his cigar slowly (he had six more of them in his pocket), and looked absently at the jam of traffic: taxis, Hispano-Suizas,[58] Fords, huge double-decked busses, leaning as they turned corners. Rico dropped the cigar butt out the window. Lying back in the seat he observed:

"And I thought Pete Montana was such a hell of a guy!"

II

Olga was only partly dressed when Joe burst in on her. She looked at him, startled.

"My Lord," she said, "what makes you so pale, Joe?"

"Got any liquor?" demanded Joe.

Olga opened a drawer and handed him a flask. He tipped it up and took a long pull, then he stood with the flask in his hand staring at the wall.

"Joe," Olga insisted, "what's wrong with you?"

Joe came to himself, screwed the top on the flask, and handed it back to Olga.

"Boy, I got a shock," said Joe.

Olga came over and put her arm around him.

"Tell Olga all about it."

"Well," said Joe, "I was finishing up my Pierrot dance, see, and you know when it's dark and they got the spot on you you can't see nothing. Well, I was circling the outside of the floor like I do before I take that last leap when some dame at a corner table gives a yell, a hell of a yell. Sibby hears the yell and switches on all the lights and here I am, right in front of a dame that looks like she's off her nut. She was standing up and she had her hands on the table and she was staring right at me. If I didn't feel funny, boy! Well, there was a guy with her and he kept asking her what was the matter, but she wouldn't say nothing. I thought she was gonna jump right on me, she looked so funny, yeah, that dame sure looked funny."

Joe paused and meditated. Olga laughed.

"Listen," she said, "you better lay off the liquor."

"No, straight," said Joe, "you know I kind of got the idea she recognized me or something, but, hell, I never seen her before. She's an old dame, about forty, and she's got peroxide hair. There was a guy with her, a nice-looking guy, and he kept saying, 'What's the matter, Nell, what's the matter, Nell,' but he couldn't get nothing out of her."

Olga laughed again.

"Well, this ain't nothing to write home about," she said. "I thought I was gonna get a thrill. We better change bootleggers, Joe."

"Aw, lay off," said Joe. "I'm telling you, you'd've got all the kick you're looking for if you'd heard that dame yell."

"Well, what happened?" demanded Olga, who was getting impatient.

Joe got out the flask and took another pull at it before he answered her. The color had come back into his face now and he felt much better.

"Soon as the boss found out there was something wrong he came in and asked this dame if he could do anything for her. And she says, "Yes, get me a taxi.' The guy with her says, "What the devil, Nell.' And she says, 'I want to go home.' So they went out. Boy, the way that dame looked at me, like I was, God, I don't know what!"

"Say, listen," said Olga, "you been hitting the pipe."[59]

59   The opium pipe, that is—the modern expression would be "Have you been smoking dope?"

"Aw, lay off," said Joe; "that dame's got something on her mind, see. She's got something on her mind."

Someone knocked. Olga called "come in" and a waiter opened the door and bowed.

"Mr. Willoughby wants to know if we can bring the table in now, Miss Stassoff."

"Sure," said Olga, "bring it in."

"Yes, ma'am," said the waiter, then he cupped his hands and called down the corridor: "Allez!"

Joe lay down on the lounge and lit a cigarette. Olga went over to her dressing-table, made up her face, and put on her Japanese kimono.

Two waiters came in carrying a table; a third followed with a cloth and silver. When the table was set one of the waiters said:

"Mr. Willoughby wants to know if he can come back now."

"Sure," said Olga, "tell him to come right back."

"Shall we start to serve?"

"Yeah," said Olga, "right away."

When the waiters had gone, Joe said:

"I'm getting fed up with this Willoughby guy. He's a dumb egg."

"Sure he's dumb," said Olga, "but I don't hold that against him. What I like about that bird is that he don't get his hand stuck in his pocket when the boy comes around with the bill."

"He sure don't, that's a fact," said Joe, laughing.

"Well, then don't be so particular," said Olga; "guys like him are few and far between."

Willoughby tapped lightly on the door and then came in. He was freshly shaven and he looked chubby and boyish.

Joe got up and shook hands with him. Olga said:

"Was you out front?"

"Yes," said Willoughby; "by the way, Joe, what was all the commotion?"

"See?" said Joe, turning to Olga. "She thought I was making it up, Mr. Willoughby."

"No, he wasn't making it up," said Willoughby, serious. "I never heard such a scream in my life."

"Don't remind me," said Joe; "boy, my hair stood straight up."

A waiter came in carrying a wine bucket, followed by another waiter carrying the soup.

"Well," said Willoughby, "shall we monjay, as they say in France?"

"Oui, monsieur," said Olga.

"Sure," said Joe, "I'm ready for the feed-bag in any language."

They sat down. One of the waiters poured the wine. Willoughby held his glass up to the light.

"I hope you like this stuff," he said, "it's out of my own cellar."

"I'd like to sleep in that cellar," said Olga.

"Well," said Willoughby, "you have a standing invitation."

They ate in silence for a moment, then Joe said:

"Say, Mr. Willoughby, what you suppose was the matter with that dame?"

"I couldn't say."

"Oh, forget it, Joe," said Olga, "she was probably full of hop."

III

Willoughby passed the cigarettes and they all left the table. Joe went back to the lounge, Olga sat in one of the armchairs, and Willoughby pulled up an ottoman and sat facing her.

Willoughby hesitated before he said:

"Olga, when we going to take that little trip?"

"I don't know," said Olga.

"What little trip?" asked Joe, looking at Olga.

"Why, I got a cabin up in Wisconsin," said Willoughby, "and I thought before it got cold it would be nice for Olga to go up and take a rest."

"Yeah?" said Joe.

As soon as Willoughby lowered his eyes, Olga winked at Joe.

"Maybe I could pull it," said Olga.

"Sure," said Joe, "Olga works too hard, that's a fact. A little rest wouldn't hurt her none."

"That's just what I was thinking," said Willoughby. "She could sure get a rest up there. I got a couple of nice motor boats and the fishing's great."

"Fishing!" said Olga, looking at Joe.

60   According to the *Encyclopedia of Chi-cago*, "[Chicago] was [p]erhaps second only to Pittsburgh in smoke pollution at the opening of the twentieth century . . . Chicago gained a national reputation for its terrible air, but it also became a leader in regulation. In the early 1900s, a movement to force railroad electrification focused on the Illinois Central's waterfront line and kept the smoke issue in the news. Still, air quality did not significantly improve until coal use began to decline after World War II," http://www.encyclopedia.chicagohistory.org/pages/32.html. The fishing in Wisconsin would have been superior as well: A study of sewage discharge into Lake Michigan in 1924 from the industries of Chicago found the water supplies of Hammond, Whiting, and East Chicago, all of which drew from the like, "unfit" and the water supply of Gary, Indiana, "seriously contaminated," while the supplies of Chicago itself were "seriously endangered by sewer pollution." "Report of an Investigation of the Pollution of Lake Michigan in the Vicinity of South Chicago and the Calumet and Indiana Harbors. 1924–1925," by H. R. Crohurst and M. V. Veldee of the U.S. Public Health Service, summarized in the *American Journal of Public Health* (1926), pp. 1236–38.

"Well," Willoughby considered, maybe you wouldn't care for that, but there are any number of things you could do. Anyway, the air's great, nothing like this Chicago muck."[60]

"Sounds good," said Olga.

The waiters came in to take away the table, but they were immediately followed by DeVoss, who motioned them out. There was something so strange about DeVoss's actions that Joe sat up and stared at him. DeVoss said:

"Joe, there's a couple of guys looking for you."

"Yeah?" said Joe. "What kind of guys?"

"Bulls," said DeVoss, "what you been up to?"

Olga got to her feet and stood staring at De Voss. Willoughby exclaimed: "What's all this! What's all this!"

Joe took an automatic from his hip pocket and put it in Olga's dressing-table. Olga took hold of DeVoss's arm and said: "Tell them Joe ain't here. Joe, honey, beat it. I'll see if I can find out what it's all about."

Willoughby was staring stupefied at Joe. He pointed to the dressing-table.

"What do you carry that thing for?" he demanded.

Olga said:

"Oh, be quiet!"

Joe grinned at Willoughby.

"Just in case," he said.

"Listen, Olga," said DeVoss, "this is serious. I could tell the way they acted. I told them I didn't think Joe was here but they just laughed."

Joe stood undecided.

"Joe," DeVoss went on, "remember that time Mr. Rico was over here and a couple of bulls shadowed him? Well, the big one's here."

"Flaherty!" cried Joe.

Olga gave Joe a push.

"Beat it, Joe. You know them bulls. They'll frame you."

"O.K., honey," said Joe.

"Why, Joe," said Willoughby, "you mean to tell me you're in some kind of trouble?"

"Oh, be quiet," said Olga.

Joe grabbed his hat from a chair and started for the door.

"Goodbye, honey," he said to Olga, "you'll hear from me."

"Better face the music," said Willoughby.

"Go out through the kitchen," said DeVoss.

Joe opened the door but closed it immediately and said: "It's all up. Here they come."

He looked in agony at Olga. Wasn't this just his goddam luck! Penned up in a room three stories above the pavement. He made a dash for the dressing-table, but Olga grabbed his arm.

"For God's sake, Joe," said DeVoss, "don't cause no trouble in my place. I don't know what they want you for and I don't give a damn. I'll get you a lawyer and see you through, but, for God's sake, don't do no shooting in my place."

Willoughby, stunned, sat staring till his cigarette burned his fingers, then he said:

"Don't worry, Joe. I'll see you through too."

"Goddam it," cried Joe, "you think I'm gonna let 'em take me like I was a purse-snatcher on his first stand."

He pushed Olga away from him and was pulling at the dressing-table drawer, when the door opened and Flaherty came in, followed by Spike Rieger. Flaherty had his right hand in his coat pocket.

"Joe," said Flaherty, "step away from that drawer and make it snappy."

Joe knew Flaherty's reputation. That boy used his rod and argued afterwards. Joe moved away from the dressing-table and stood staring at the floor.

"What the idea, Flaherty?" he demanded.

"Well," said Flaherty, "we got a big audience here and I ain't much on embarrassing people, so you better just come along and we'll have a nice little talk."

"Aw, can that," said Joe.

Willoughby walked over to Flaherty.

"My name's Willoughby," he said, "John C. Willoughby. I suppose you've heard of me. Say, what's this all about anyway? Why, I've known Joe for nearly a year and as far as I know he's a nice young fellow."

"Yeah," said Flaherty, "Joe's a pretty smooth young fellow, but we caught up with him."

"Well," said Willoughby, "I don't know what he's done, but I'm willing to go on his bail."

Flaherty turned to Rieger.

"I don't suppose there'll be much talk about bail, do you, Spike?"

Rieger grinned and shook his head.

"No bail!" Willoughby exclaimed.

"Aw, it's just one of their wise frame-ups, Mr. Willoughby," said Joe, but his face was white.

"Well, we'll see about this," said Willoughby. "I'll have my lawyer down in half an hour."

"Listen," said Flaherty, "there ain't nobody gonna see this bird for twenty-four hours."

Olga flung herself on the lounge and began to cry.

"And let me give you an earful, Mr. Willoughby," said Flaherty; "for a guy of your class you sure ain't very careful about who you mix up with. These two birds here are taking you, see, and if I was you I'd snap out of it and forget all about getting a lawyer."

"If that ain't a bull for you," said Joe.

"Don't pay no attention to him, Jack," said Olga.

"Certainly not," said Willoughby.

"All right, Spike," said Flaherty, "I guess we wasted enough time on these birds. Put the cuffs on him."

Olga jumped up and made a grab for Rieger, but DeVoss caught her from the back and held her.

"You can't do nothing that way, Olga," he said, "you'll just make it tough for Joe."

Olga screamed with rage and kicked back at DeVoss.

"Ain't dames awful?" said Flaherty.

Willoughby went over to Olga and tried to talk to her, but she continued to struggle. Rieger took out his handcuffs and walked over to Joe.

"Wait a minute, " said Joe, "you can't put no bracelets on me. Where's your warrant?"

Rieger took the warrant out of his pocket and handed it to Joe. Joe read it slowly, then, without comment, handed it back.

"Well, Joe," said Flaherty.

Joe didn't say anything; he just held out his wrists.

"What do they want you for, Joe," cried Olga.

"Never mind," said Joe, "they ain't got no case."

Olga stopped struggling.

"You mean it, Joe?"

"Sure," said Joe, "they ain't got no case at all. I'll be out in twenty-four hours."

"Shall I get my lawyer?" asked Willoughby.

"Ain't much use," said Joe.

DeVoss came over to Flaherty and said:

"Listen, Mr. Flaherty, take him out through the kitchen, can't you? I can't have cops coming in here pinching people."

"You got a nerve," said Flaherty; "why, I ought to pull you in for complicity. Didn't you come back here and tip Joe off?"

DeVoss got pale.

"Honest to God, I didn't tip him off. I just told him a couple of guys wanted to see him."

"Pipe down," said Flaherty. "Come on, Joe, let's take a ride."

Joe's face was ghastly, but he grinned.

"O.K.," he said; "it's the first ride I ever took with any of you birds."

"Well, I hope it's the last," said Flaherty.

"Want me to come down and see you, Joe?" asked Olga.

"No," said Joe.

They put Joe between two policemen in the back seat of the police car. Rieger and Flaherty sat in front. The traffic was light as it was nearly three o'clock in the morning. Rieger drove carelessly, one hand on the wheel most of the time, and talked to Flaherty.

"Boy," said Joe, "that bird don't care how he drives."

"You ain't got far to go," said one of the policemen.

"No, but I ain't sure of getting there."

The policemen laughed.

"Say," said Joe, "can I smoke?"

One of the policemen leaned forward.

"Say, chief, can this bird smoke?"

"No," said Flaherty; "what the hell you think this is, Joe! Maybe we better pick up a couple of girls for you."

The policemen laughed.

"Funny thing," said Joe, "you know, Flaherty, a friend of mine told me the other day that he didn't think you'd live long."

"Yeah," said Flaherty, "I know that friend of yours. He ain't looking any too healthy himself."

For as late as it was there was a good deal of activity at the station. A dozen plain-clothes men were waiting in the big room, when they brought Joe in, and the Assistant County Prosecutor was standing at the desk talking to the sergeant.

"Looks like big doings," said Joe.

"Shut up," said Flaherty; "recess is over. You open your mouth again and I'll close it for you."

They took Joe up to the desk to book him.

"Well, you got him," said the prosecutor, looking Joe over.

"Yeah, we got him," said Flaherty. "Did you chase the newspaper guys?"

"Yeah," said the prosecutor, "there won't be no leaks to this."

"O.K.," said Flaherty.

The sergeant nodded to him.

"All right, chief."

Flaherty took Joe by the arm.

"All right, Joe," he said, "we're gonna give you a nice little room."

"With bath?" asked Joe.

"Listen, boy," said Flaherty, "we're gonna take all that smartness out of you."

Joe didn't say anything. He was trying to keep up his front until they locked him in his cell, but he was ready to drop. They had him; they sure to God had him.

The turnkey swung the big barred door wide. Flaherty took Joe to the door of his cell, unlocked the handcuffs, and gave him a push.

"All right, boy," he said, "I'll be back later."

"Listen, Flaherty," said Joe, "can't I even have a smoke?"

Flaherty laughed, motioned for the turnkey to lock the cell door, and disappeared down the corridor.

"Say, buddy," said Joe to the turnkey, "can't you get me a pack of cigarettes?"

"Nothing doing," said the turnkey, "not for fifty bucks. I got strict orders on you, boy."

The turnkey went away. Joe stood in the middle of his cell for a moment, then he climbed up on his bunk and looked out the window. Far away down a side street he saw a big electric sign: DANCING.

Joe flung himself down on his bunk. They had him; they sure to God did.

"If I can only stick it out!" he said.

IV

Joe awoke from a doze and turned to look out the window. Still dark. He couldn't have been asleep long. Wasn't it never going to get light! He got up and walked to the front of his cell. It wouldn't be so bad if there were some other guys to talk to; but the cells on either side of him were vacant; also the ones across the corridor.

"They sure ain't taking no chances with me," said Joe.

He began to feel very uneasy. Something seemed to be dragging at his stomach and he had a rotten taste in his mouth.

"Some of that highhat grub I et," said Joe.

The turnkey came down the corridor and stopped in front of Joe's cell.

"Say, buddy," he said, "they'll be wanting you up front pretty soon."

"Yeah?" said Joe. "Listen, can't you do me a favor and get me a pack of cigs. I got plenty of money. Ask the sergeant."

"Can't cut it," said the turnkey.

"What's doing up front?" asked Joe.

"A show-up."

"Yeah?" said Joe; then, "listen, I'll give you a couple of bucks for some cigs."

The turnkey laughed.

"Say, there's a guy in 18 that'd give me a hundred berries for some snow. Not a chance. They sure are putting the clamps on us now. It's that goddam Crime Commission business.[61] Tough on you birds."

"Ain't it!" said Joe.

The turnkey went away. Joe threw himself down on his bunk. Yeah, now it was coming. That goddam peroxide dame had sure put the skids under him. Well, there you was! Can't tell how things are going to break. If he'd've been wise he'd've sent Olga to see the Big Boy or Rico. But then there's no use letting a dame get too familiar with everything. Anyway, he had an alibi. But Flaherty was a rough agent and you could never tell what he would pull. Joe felt mechanically for his absent cigarette case.

"Hell," he said, "I lost my head! I lost my head! Rico ought to put a hunk of lead in me. As long as I been in the game and then don't know no better. God, but I was dumb."

61 The Chicago Crime Commission was an organization of businessmen formed in 1919 (and continuing today), spurred in part by a notorious burglary and by a climbing murder rate, allegedly the highest in the world. The Commission implemented a system of criminal record-keeping, reformed the parole and bail-bond procedures, and assisted in numerous individual cases. In its first published report, read before the Annual Meeting of the American Institute of Criminal Law and Criminology, held in Indianapolis on September 17, 1920, the Commission declared, "The Chicago Crime Commission . . . does not contemplate the apprehension nor the prosecution of criminals. It has no political axe to grind. It is interested solely in making Chicago a place in which to live and work with a reasonable assurance that its citizens will not be the prey of gunmen and thieves. . . . Crime today is a gigantic system organized and protected, reaching into business and politics, and while still subject to indictment and prosecution, is largely immune from punishment. It is the task of the Chicago Crime Commission to deal with this system, dispose of it, and with the assistance of every right minded man and woman bring about its defeat."

The Commission furnished the following information about crime in Chicago:

Crime	Burglary	Robbery	Murder
1919	6,108	2,912	330
1920	5,495	2,782	194
1921	4,774	2,558	190
1922	4,301	2,007	228
1923	3,019	1,402	270
1924	2,136	1,755	347
1925	1,147	1,702	394
1926 (1st seven months)	536	767	210

Thus, while the Commission appeared to have been reducing burglaries and robberies, homicides were increasing steadily, perhaps as a result of the illegal-liquor business becoming the principal criminal activity of the professional gangs.

62   Originally a term for a man of Spanish parentage commonly used in the southwestern United States, according to the *Oxford English Dictionary*. Subsequently, it was applied to include Italians. It appears in print as early as 1723. Although the term's origins are obscure, some suggest that it is a corruption of "Diego," a common Spanish name applied as a generic proper name to Spaniards.

He turned over irritably and sat up. He heard the keys clanking down the corridor. A policeman stopped in front of his door and called:

"All right, dago."[62]

Joe got up. The turnkey unlocked the door. There were two policemen and a plain-clothes man standing a little way down the corridor. When Joe came out one of the policemen said:

"There's the guy that plugged Courtney."

They stared at him. Joe felt sick at his stomach.

"Yeah," said the plain-clothes man, "they won't do much to that bird."

The turnkey took Joe by the arm.

"All right, kid," he said.

Joe walked between the turnkey and the policeman, who had called him. They took him into a big room where there were three policemen and about a dozen prisoners. Joe saw Bugs Liska, Steve Gollancz's lieutenant. They exchanged a glance.

A police sergeant got to his feet and shouted: "All right, you birds, let's go."

The turnkey pushed Joe into line. A big door was swung open and he saw a small, brilliantly lighted room with a crowd of people lining the walls. Joe looked for the peroxide blonde. There she was, pale and hardboiled, between two bulls. Joe started. God, he had her now. She was standing side of Courtney when he dropped. Joe began to sweat.

The line in single file was herded in. Bugs Liska, who was in front of Joe, whispered:

"Say, what's this all about?"

The sergeant heard him and leaping across the room grabbed him by the shoulder.

"Any more of that," said the sergeant, "and some of you bad eggs is gonna get cracked."

"Drop dead," said Liska.

Joe found himself face to face with the blonde. She stared at him. Flaherty walked along the line and examined the prisoners. When he got to Joe, Joe looked away.

"How's that bath?" asked Flaherty.

"O.K.," said Joe.

Liska said:

"Say, Irish, what's this all about?"

"Shut your dirty mouth," said Flaherty.

A man Joe had never seen before, a big husky man with curly gray hair, went over to the blonde and said:

"Is he in that bunch, Mrs. Weil?"

The blonde nodded.

"Well, Mrs. Weil, this is a very serious matter so don't make any mistakes. Now if you're sure he's in that bunch, point him out."

The blonde compressed her lips and walked over to Joe.

"There he is. There's the dirty skunk."

"Jesus," said Liska, glancing at Joe, "it's your funeral, hunh?"

The blonde stood glaring at Joe.

"I hope they hang you," she cried, "shooting a guy like Jim Courtney."

"I never shot him," said Joe.

"Shut up," said Flaherty. "All right, sergeant, march 'em out."

In the big room Liska said:

"Joe, it sure looks tough for you."

"They can't prove nothing," said Joe.

The sergeant rushed at them.

"Where do you birds think you're at!" he cried.

Stepping back, he struck Joe a hard blow with his fist. Mechanically Joe set himself and raised his hands, then, coming to himself, he dropped his hands and stood looking at the floor. Liska said:

"Say, sergeant, I guess I can go home, can't I ? My old mother'll be worried to death."

The sergeant stared at Liska, then he laughed.

"I'm gonna hang on to you just for fun," he said.

"Yeah?" said Liska. "Well not long, cause Steve's gonna spring me."

The sergeant motioned for the turnkey.

"Lock the dago up," he said; "you plant yourself over there in a chair, Bugs."

Joe lay down and tried to sleep. Over his head the barred window began to get gray. Morning sure was slow in coming.

Of a sudden he thought of Red Gus. He got to his feet and began to walk back and forth. Yeah, they sure put the rope on old Gus and there wasn't a tougher guy in the world. Yeah, he was so tough he didn't die right away and kept kicking. Cops fainted and all that stuff. Joe climbed up on his bunk and stood tiptoe to look out the window. Morning was coming. He saw a milk wagon passing the jail. How come he had to think of Red Gus?

He thought he heard a noise and turned around. There were two cops standing in front of his cell, looking at him. Joe felt uneasy.

"Want me?" he called.

They didn't say anything; they just stood there looking, then went away.

Joe got down from the window and sat on his bunk. No use trying to sleep. Down the corridor someone began to scream. The turnkey passed his cell on the run. Joe felt his hair stirring and sweat stood out on his forehead.

"Christ," he said, "it's only that dope."

In a minute the turnkey came back and stopped at Joe's door.

"Couple of guys coming back to take a look at you," he said.

"Yeah?" said Joe; "say, what was all the noise?"

"The dope blew his top again," said the turnkey; "the Doc's gonna give him a shot pretty soon."

The big man with the curly gray hair, Flaherty, and two policemen came down the corridor.

"All right," said Flaherty, "let him out."

The turnkey unlocked the door and pushed Joe into the corridor. They all stood staring at Joe; nobody said anything.

Finally the gray-haired man said:

"Well, it's too bad. Nice-looking boy."

"Yeah," said Flaherty, "but he's hell with a gun."

Joe didn't say anything. But Flaherty said:

"Joe, I never thought you was the kind of a bird that'd shoot a guy in the back."

Joe didn't say anything.

"Hanging's too good for you, Joe."

"Poor old Jim never even had a gun on him. You lousy dago!" cried one of the policemen, and took a step toward Joe.

Flaherty motioned him back.

"Just let the law take its course, Luke," he said, "they'll hang this baby sure."

"Will they?" said Joe.

The gray-haired man shook his finger at Joe.

"Yes, my boy, I'm afraid they will."

"They can't prove nothing on me," said Joe; "I wasn't even in that end of town the night Courtney was bumped off. That dame's full of hop."

One of the policemen stepped past Flaherty and knocked Joe down. Flaherty grabbed the policeman and pushed him back. Joe got to his feet and stood holding his jaw.

"I'm gonna put it to you birds for this," said Joe.

Both the policemen made a rush at Joe, but Flaherty held them back.

"Well," said Flaherty, "got an eyeful, Mr. McClure?"

Joe stared at the gray-haired man. So this was the Crime Commission guy that was kicking up all the row.[63] Joe took a good look at him so he'd know him the next time he saw him. Maybe, if things broke right, he could deliver a nice package at that bird's house some morning.

"Yes," said Mr. McClure, "lock him up, turnkey."

The turnkey took Joe by the arm and flung him into his cell. Joe fell on his hands and knees.

"Say," said Joe, "what's the idea?"

The turnkey came over and put his face against the bars.

"Orders, buddy," he said, then he went away.

Yeah, it was orders all right. They wasn't going to let up on him till he spilled something. Joe felt panicky. He flung himself face down on his bunk and began to sob.

"Won't I never get out of here?" he said.

They had been questioning Joe for over two hours. He sat under a blazing light and they sat round him in the darkness. Joe was so thirsty that he could hardly swallow. They took turns at him: first, Mr. McClure, then Flaherty, then Rieger. Flaherty sat near him and when he was slow with his answers rapped him over the knuckles with a ruler. But Joe stuck it out.

The turnkey took him back to his cell and gave him some water. Joe took a big drink, then lay down on his bunk and tried to sleep, but it was no use. He felt hot all over and his tongue was swollen.

He put his hands under his head and lay looking at the square spots of sunshine in the dark corridor.

"God," he said, "I can't stand much of this."

In five minutes the turnkey came back.

"They want you again, kid," he said.

63   Henry Barret Chamberlin was the Operating Director of the Chicago Crime Commission in 1920.

"God, I can't move," said Joe.

The turnkey unlocked the door and came into the cell.

"Get on your feet," he said, "and snap it up. The prosecutor's in there now and you're gonna ketch hell."

Joe got slowly to his feet and the turnkey led him down the corridor.

V

Sam Vettori sat half-dozing in an armchair watching a crap game. It was about eleven o'clock in the morning and most of the blinds were still down. All the wheels were covered and the chairs were piled up on the tables. The game was desultory as nobody had much money. As it wasn't a house game, but merely some of the Vettori gang amusing themselves, Sam occasionally staked one or another of the players.

Since the rise of Rico, Sam had confined his efforts to the managing of Little Arnie's old joint. He was making money hand over fist and he was content to sit all day in his armchair and superintend the work of his employees. He drank wine by the gallon and ate plate after plate of spaghetti. In a month he put on fifteen pounds. As he was fat to begin with, this added poundage made him immense. His aquiline features were puffed out nearly beyond recognition and there were rolls of fat at the base of his skull. Sam had loosed the reins and gone slack. Formerly, effort had kept him in better condition, but now, perfectly at ease, free of responsibility, the deadly lethargy which had threatened him all his life took possession of him.

Sam crossed his legs with difficulty and took out a stogie. The crap game had ended in an argument. Kid Bean loudly contended that he had been gypped.

"Shut up, you guys," said Sam, "I'm doing you a favor to let you shoot in here. Any more of this kind of stuff and you don't do it no more. If you guys'd save your money you wouldn't have to be fighting over two bits."

"Aw, rest your jaw," said Kid Bean.

Joe Peeper took the dice and flung them out the window.

"Them babies'll never bother me no more," said Joe.

"Can you beat that!" said Kid Bean.

"Well," said Sam, "since Blackie's got all the jack, the rest of you guys can pitch pennies. Listen, Kid, don't forget you owe me two bucks."

"You can take it out of my hide," said the Kid.

"Your hide ain't worth it," said Sam.

Chesty, the doorman, came out of Sam's office rubbing his eyes.

"Sam," he said, "Scabby wants to see you."

"Tell him to come out here," said Sam.

"No," said Chesty, "he wants to see you private."

"Hey, Sam," said Kid Bean, "give us a deck of cards, will you?"

"No," said Sam, "you don't even know what they're for." He pulled himself slowly to his feet and turning to Chesty went on: "Get these guys a pack of cards and lock 'em up some place. They'd bump each other off for two bits and I don't want this nice carpet spoiled."

Yawning and stretching, Sam went into his office and shut the door. Scabby was standing in the middle of the room, biting his nails.

"Want a bottle of wine or something, Scabby?" asked Sam.

"Christ, no!" cried Scabby.

Sam stared at him, then dropped into a chair.

"Well," he said, "you look like you got something on your mind, so spill it."

Scabby was so nervous that he couldn't control the muscles of his face.

"You're goddam right I got something on my mind," said Scabby. "Joe spilled the works."

Sam opened his eyes wide.

"Joe who?"

"Joe Massara," said Scabby. "They nabbed him on the Courtney business and he squawked."

Sam's jaw fell and he ran his hands over his face in a bewildered way.

"Yeah?" he said.

"It's the God's truth," said Scabby; "boy, the bulls sure played this one slick. Listen, I didn't even know nothing about it. They kept the newspaper guys out and when a couple guys who were in the know came looking for Joe they told them that they must have him at the Chicago Avenue station. And out at Chicago Avenue they sent 'em some place else. Yeah, it's all over now."

This was too much for Sam. He just sat there staring at Scabby.

"God, Sam," said Scabby, astonished, "don't you get me? It's all over. Listen, if it wasn't for you I'd be on my way right now. I don't know whether I'll be named or not, but I ain't taking no chances. Love of God, Sam, don't just sit there. You got to do something."

"Joe spilled everything?" asked Sam, taking it in slowly.

"Yeah, he stuck it out for four hours, but he didn't have a chance."

There was a flash of the old Sam Vettori. He got up and took Scabby by the arm.

"Is Rico wised up?"

"No," said Scabby.

"All right," said Sam, "you keep your mouth shut."

"You don't have to tell me," said Scabby.

Sam looked about him, bewildered.

"But, good God," he cried, "what am I gonna do?"

"Well," said Scabby, "I got a can down here and I'm hitting East. Want to go with me? I'll take a chance."

Sam looked his bewilderment. Things were moving too fast for him. Why, he hadn't been out of Chicago for twenty years. He hadn't been out of Little Italy for over five. Just pick up and beat it.

"What the hell!" said Sam, "I got a good business. . . . God, what am I gonna do?"

Scabby stared at him.

"Why, Sam," he said, "you must be losing your mind."

Sam wiped the sweat from his face and sank back into his chair.

"Joe spilled it, hunh? Rico said he'd turn yellow."

Scabby took him under the arms and tried to pull him to his feet, but Sam pushed him away.

"No use running," he said, "they'll get you sure. I ain't gonna go running all over hell and back and a bunch of bulls chasing me."

Scabby swore violently in Italian.

"No," said Sam, "no use running."

"Well," said Scabby, "this bird's gonna pull his freight. Sam, you must be full of hop."

Sam sat staring at his shoes.

"Listen," said Scabby, "I can't waste no more time. Are you gonna pull out or ain't you?"

Sam didn't say anything.

"O.K.," said Scabby; "I'm moving."

"Wait," cried Sam. "Scabby, listen to me. I been good to you, ain't I?"

"You sure have."

"I give you the money to bring your old man over here, didn't I? And I give you the money to bury him, didn't I?"

"You sure did."

"Well, listen, Scabby, if Rico gets away, pop him. Goddam him; he's busted us all. Pop him, Scabby, for old Sam."

"He won't get away," said Scabby.

"You don't know that guy," said Sam, getting shakily to his feet; "sure to God as I'm a Catholic, you don't know that guy. He's got a run of luck and it may last."

"If he gets away I'll pop him," said Scabby.

The door was flung violently open and Killer Pepi stepped in.

"I heard you bastards," he said. "The Kid told me there was something up. Double-crossing the boss, hunh?"

"Go to hell," said Sam.

Scabby raised his gun but it missed fire. The Killer shot from his hip, then ran out, slamming the door.

"Did he plug you, Scabby?" cried Sam.

"No," said Scabby, "but I heard her sing."

The window behind Scabby had a bullet hole in it.

"He'll spill it sure," said Sam, his face puckered.

"Won't do him no good," said Scabby, "'cause the bulls are on their way. Well, Sam, I'm moving."

Sam just looked at him. Scabby raised the window and climbed out on the fire-escape.

"Love of God, Sam," said Scabby, "you got to do something."

Sam took his hat from the hook.

"I'll go see the Big Boy."

"It won't do you no good, Sam."

They heard someone running down the hall, then, there was a shot, followed by a rush of feet. Chesty flung open the door.

"The bulls!" he cried.

Scabby disappeared down the fire-escape. Sam took out his automatic and put his back against the wall. Spike Rieger put his head in the door, then drew it back hastily.

"Sam," he called, "better give up."

"All right," said Sam, flinging his gun on the floor.

Spike Rieger came in followed by two policemen.

"Put the cuffs on him," said Spike.

Sam held out his hands and one of the policemen snapped on the handcuffs.

"Spike," said Sam, "did you pick the Killer up on the way in?"

"No," said Spike, "we don't want him for nothing." Turning to the policemen Spike said: "All right, put him in the wagon."

"Listen, Spike," said Sam, "did you get Rico?"

"I don't know," said Spike. "Flaherty's after him. I guess you know Gentleman Joe squawked, don't you?"

"Yeah," said Sam, indifferently, "but you ain't got no case against me."

Spike laughed.

VI

The Killer knocked at Rico's door but got no response. He knocked again and again, then, getting impatient, he put his shoulder to the door and flung it open. No Rico. The Killer stood in the hall, wondering where Rico could have gone. From the landing above him, the landlady yelled:

"Hey, what did you do to that door?"

"The hell with the door," said Pepi; "do you know where the guy that lives there is?"

"No," said the landlady, "but I seen him go out with a fellow."

"What kind of a fellow?"

"A little fellow."

Otero! Killer took the stairs at a jump but slowed his pace as he reached the main floor. There was a police car at the curb. Flaherty got out leisurely and stood talking to one of the policemen in the front seat. Pepi went over to him.

"Looking for the boss?"

"Yeah," said Flaherty, "the Big Boy sent me down. I want to have a talk with him."

"Yeah?" said Pepi. "Getting wise to yourself, hunh?"

"Rico was always O.K. with me."

"That's the talk," said Pepi. "Well, the boss is upstairs by himself."

When Flaherty and one of his men had gone into the building, the Killer grinned at the others and walked slowly away, but, as soon as he had turned the corner, he broke into a run.

There were two little Italian kids sitting on the steps of the stairway that led up to Otero's. They made way for Pepi.

"Otero upstairs?" he asked.

One of the kids said:

"That funny little guy?"

"Yeah," said Pepi.

"I think I seen him go up."

"Yeah," said the other kid, "I seen him."

Pepi took the stairs at a run and rapped at Otero's door. Seal Skin opened it a few inches but Pepi pushed her aside and walked in. Otero was sitting with his feet on the bed, smoking a big cigar.

"Where's the boss?" asked Pepi.

"At Blondy's. What's the matter?"

"Joe squawked," said Pepi, "and the bulls is looking for Rico. Get your coat on and beat it, Otero. I'll go after the boss."

Otero leapt to his feet and struggled into his coat.

"Bulls looking for me too?"

"Sure," said Pepi, "it's the Courtney business. You beat it, Otero. This ain't no picnic."

"No," said Otero, "I go with Rico."

"You damn dummy," said Seal Skin.

"Yeah," said Pepi, "you beat it, Otero. Get out of town. They don't want me for nothing. I'll see if I can't get Rico on the phone; if I can't I'll go after him. Listen, the bulls is over at Rico's right now."

"Caramba!" cried Otero, and, slipping his automatic into his coat pocket, he ran out into the hall and down the stairs.

"The damn dummy!" said Seal Skin.

Pepi stood looking at Seal Skin then he said:

"Sure he's a damn dummy, but he's right." Before Otero had gone half a block in the direction of Blondy's, he saw a police car coming toward him. He ducked into a drugstore. It was empty except for a clerk who stood staring at Otero.

"Show me the back way out, you!" said Otero.

"Say!" said the clerk.

Otero took out his gun. The clerk threw himself down behind the counter. Otero ran out through the prescription room and found the back door, which opened into an alley. One end of the alley was blind, the other came out onto a busy street. Otero ran toward the open end, praying in Spanish.

All along the curbs on both sides of the street pushcarts were drawn up and peddlers were calling their wares. A slow-moving crowd of Little Italians blocked the pavements. Otero, because of his size, disappeared into the crowd, and, although he was forced to go slowly, he was safe from observation. Half a block from Blondy's he ducked down an alley, crossed a long cement court and climbed the fire-escape.

A Chicago streetscape in the 1920s.

Blondy's bedroom window was locked. Otero beat on it with his fist. For a moment there was no response, then he saw the bedroom door open slowly and Blondy's face appeared. She ran over and unlocked the window, then she turned and called:

"Rico, it's The Greek."

Rico came into the bedroom. He had his hat on.

"Did Pepi get you?"

"No, what the hell?"

The phone rang and Blondy went to answer it.

"They got Joe and he squawked," said Otero.

Rico looked at him. Blondy came running back.

"My God, Rico," she said, "the bulls're after you. Joe squealed. You ought to plugged that softie, Rico. You ought to plugged him."

Rico stood in the middle of the room, staring. By an effort of the will, he rid himself of an attitude of mind which had been growing on him since his interviews with Montana and the Big Boy. He was nobody, nobody. Worse than nobody. The bulls wanted him now and they wanted him bad. Goodbye dollar cigars and crockery at one grand, goodbye swell food and Tuxedos and security. Rico was nobody. Just a lonely Youngstown yegg that the bulls wanted. His face was ghastly.

He swung his fist at the air.

"I ought to plugged him! I ought to plugged him!"

Otero stood staring at Rico. Blondy was putting on her hat.

"All right," said Rico, "let's go."

Blondy said:

"Take me, Rico."

Rico shook his head.

"Nothing doing, Blondy. I'm traveling fast and I can't be bothered with no dame."

"Jesus, Rico," said Blondy, unable to realize what had happened, "everything was going so nice."

"Sure," said Rico, "but it's all over now and that's that. You stay planted, Blondy, and as soon as I get a chance I'll send you a stake."

Otero crawled out the window onto the fire-escape and Rico followed him. Blondy began to scream.

"Shut your mouth," said Rico, "and if the bulls come up the front way kid 'em along. Make 'em think you got me hid, see?"

"O.K., Rico," said Blondy.

Otero and Rico went down the fire-escape.

They stopped at the foot of the fire-escape and Rico took Otero by the arm.

"Listen," he said, "here's the dope. We got to get to Ma Magdalena's. She's got most of my jack and a good hide-out. It ain't gonna be easy, because the bulls're probably scattered all around. But once we get there, we're O.K."

"All right," said Otero.

They started. Rico knew every alley in the district, and he led Otero by such a safe route that they were soon within a block and a half of Ma Magdalena's without having crossed a main thoroughfare.

"Now," said Rico, "we got to watch our step. If the bulls are cruising, they're cruising this street sure."

"All right," said Otero.

"Listen," said Rico, "don't be afraid to use your gat if the fun begins. They can only hang you once."

"I ain't afraid," said Otero.

They left the alley and were half way across the street when somebody shouted at them to halt. Without turning, they broke into a run.

"It's only one bull," said Rico.

A bullet sang over them and they heard the blast of a policeman's whistle. Otero stopped in his tracks, turned, took a steady aim and fired. The policeman staggered forward three or four steps and fell to his knees.

"Got him," said Otero.

Rico turned. The policeman was kneeling in the middle of the street, trying to steady his hand for a shot.

"Duck," cried Rico, simultaneously with the firing of the policeman's gun.

Otero twisted sideways, looked at Rico with surprise, then dropped his gun, and began to walk up the alley holding his stomach. Rico put his arm around him and, pulling him over to the side of the alley where he could keep a telephone pole between them and the policeman, guided him along. But after a few steps, Otero pulled away from Rico and cried:

"Run, Rico, run. They got me sure. I can't feel nothing."

Rico grabbed him and tried to pull him along, but he resisted.

"Goddam you, Rico," cried Otero, "run! I can't go no farther. I'm done for."

Rico heard the roar of a police car. He released Otero, who staggered away from him and then fell flat on his back.

"Run, Rico," said Otero.

Rico climbed a fence, ran up through a filthy back yard, and in at an open back door. There was a young Italian girl sweeping in the hall. At Rico's sudden appearance, she dropped her broom and flattened herself against the wall. Rico took her by the arm.

"Listen, sister," he said, "the bulls're after me. I'm going out the front way, see, but if the bulls come through here you tell 'em I hopped the fence next door and doubled back. Got it?"

"Yes sir," said the girl, then looking up at Rico, "I know you."

"Yeah?" said Rico. "Well, do your stuff then, sister."

In the alley behind the house there was a shriek of brakes and someone cried in a loud voice:

"He went in that way!"

The girl picked up her broom and went on sweeping. Rico ran out through the front hall, down the long flight of stone steps, and crossed the street leisurely.

VII

Ma Magdalena let him in at the alley door.

"Well, Rico," she said; "got yourself in a nice fix, didn't you?"

Rico grinned.

"Yeah," he said, "who told you?"

"The bulls were here and searched the place."

"Didn't find the hide-out, did they?"

Ma Magdalena laughed.

"What a chance!"

Rico followed Ma down into the basement. She led him through a short tunnel and back into the hide-out. A small, round opening just large enough to admit one person had been pierced in a heavy stone wall. In front of the wall rows of pine shelves had been built and these were filled with canned goods. The section of the shelves which hid the opening was hinged and could be swung open.

Rico followed Ma through the opening and came out into a little room with a cot in one corner, a table, and one chair. Rico took off his hat and sat down.

"They got The Greek," he said.

"Yeah?" said Ma.

Rico took out a cigar and lit it.

"Listen," he said, "I want to stay here a couple of days. Then I'm gonna pull out. Get me some magazines and keep me posted."

"All right," said Ma, "but it's gonna cost you, because I'm taking chances, see, I'm taking big chances."

"Well," said Rico, "you got my roll, help yourself."

Ma Magdalena smiled broadly.

"That's the talk, Rico. Old Ma'll sure take care of you."

"O.K.," said Rico; "now, get this: in two days I want a car."

"Arrigo's got a car. If we go hooking one, it might spoil your get-away."

"That's good," said Rico; "all right, I want a jumper suit, you know, one of them suits like a garage mechanic wears, and a razor."

"All right," said Ma Magdalena.

When she had gone, Rico took off his coat and shoes, and lay down on the cot. His nerves were jumpy and he couldn't seem to get settled. He flung his cigar away and turned his face to the wall.

"Just when I thought things was on the up and up," he said.

Rico felt resentful, but his resentment was not directed at any specific group or person; it was vague as yet. He turned from side to side on his cot, then he gave it up.

Ma Magdalena came back with a big mug of coffee and a couple of papers. Rico sat down at the table.

"They got Sam," said Ma.

"Well," said Rico, "that's hips for Sam."

Rico took the papers from her and glanced at the headlines.

GENTLEMAN JOE WILTS

GANG CHIEF NAMED AS SLAYER

Ma Magdalena went out. Rico sat reading the paper and sipping his coffee.

Gentleman Joe Massara looks more like a movie actor than a gunman. When arrested he was wearing an expensive Tuxedo and the rings that were taken from him are valued at $3000.

"To hell with that," said Rico. He read on:

Cesare Bandello, known as Rico, the Vettori gang chief, was named as the actual slayer of Courtney. . . .

"Yeah," said Rico, "and I'm the only one they ain't gonna get."

PART VII

I

64 A town in Indiana, about 23 miles south-southeast of Chicago; Blue Island, Illinois, is slightly closer, almost due south of Chicago.

It was dark when Rico reached the outskirts of Hammond.[64] He drove into a field, took the license plates off and buried them, and got out of his jumpers. Then he took some clean waste from the tool box and wiped the grease from his face.

"What a cinch," he said.

Things had gone a lot better than he had expected them to. There hadn't been a hitch of any kind. A motor cop out in Blue Island had waved to him even. Rico laughed. You never know. When you're looking for things to go right they never do. When you're looking for trouble, why, things are O.K. Yeah, funny!

Rico walked to the car line. He was wearing a plain, dark suit and an army shirt Arrigo had given him. He had shaved off his mustache and the hard, short bristles on his upper lip worried him. Rico felt very proud of his escape. It was a good idea to dress himself up like a garage mechanic and drive across town in broad daylight. Yeah, it was a good idea and if things broke right he'd write to one of the papers and tell them all about it. Only the postmark would give him away. Not so good. Well, anyway, he could tell Sansotta about it.

Rico got on a street-car.

"Well, how's things?" he said to the conductor.

"All right," said the conductor; "getting cooler, ain't it? Reckon we'll have winter before we know it."

"Yeah," said Rico.

65   The practice of keeping detailed physical descriptions of criminals on file began in France in the late nineteenth century. Before fingerprinting, there was Bertillonage, or the Bertillon system, which aimed to classify criminals through bodily measurements. The system was the creation of Alphonse Bertillon (1853–1914), who joined the Paris police force in 1879 and became its head of criminal identification. Inspired by his anthropologist father, Bertillon reasoned that while a criminal might alter his appearance by wearing a wig, or conceal his identity by using an alias, his physical dimensions were nearly impossible to change. Under the Bertillon system, officers took two pictures of each suspect, one face-forward and one side view (Bertillon is often credited with popularizing both the mug shot and the crime-scene photo) and then carefully noted on an index card the precise dimensions of the suspect's head, various limbs, and appendages; any defining body characteristics; and in particular, the shape of the ear. Eleven different measurements were taken in all. The Bertillon system was officially adopted in France in 1888, and its use quickly spread to police departments throughout the world.

A self-portrait of Alphonse Bertillon, demonstrating how "Bertillon photos" were used, ca. 1900.

II

Rico went up the alley at the side of Sansotta's place and knocked at the back door. It was a long time before somebody came and took a look at him through the shutter. A voice with a marked Italian accent said:

"Who are you?"

"Where's Sansotta?" asked Rico.

"What do you care?"

"Listen, buddy," said Rico, "don't get all het up. I'm right. Go tell Sansotta that Cesare wants him."

In a few minutes the door opened and a hand motioned for Rico to come in. The hall was dark and Rico stumbled going up the stairs. The look-out took hold of his arm.

"The boss's up in his room. I'll take you up. Where you from, buddy?"

"Youngstown," said Rico.

"Where's that?"

"Over east."

The look-out led Rico down a long, dark hallway and to a door at the end of it. Light showed over a transom. The look-out knocked three times and the door was opened. Rico went in.

"Well," said Sansotta, locking the door, "here you are."

"Yeah," said Rico.

Sansotta was a small, bowlegged Italian with a dark, scarred face. He had on a striped suit, brown and red, and a stiff collar the points of which were so high that his chin rested on them. There was a big diamond stud in his shirtfront.

"You must've got a break," said Sansotta.

Rico explained how he had got away.

"Pretty nifty," said Sansotta; "I got to hand it to you on that, Cesare."

"Yeah," said Rico, "it was a good idea."

Sansotta went over to a table, opened a drawer and took out a handbill which he gave to Rico. Rico smiled.

"Raised the ante, did they? Last I heard it was five grand."

Rico read the handbill over and over and stared at the Bertillon pictures.[65]

"Them pictures don't look like me," he said.

Sansotta pursed his lips and scrutinized them.

"Not since you got the tickler off. No, and you look thinner in them pictures. How long ago was they taken?"

"About seven years ago."

The handbill read:

> Wanted for murder : Cesare Bandello, known as Rico. Age: 29. Height: 5 ft. 5 in. Weight: 125. Complexion: pale. Hair: black and wavy. Eyes: light, gray or blue. His face is thin and he walks with one foot slightly turned in. Does not take up with strangers. Solitary type, morose and dangerous. Reward: $5000, offered by management of Casa Alvarado. $2000, offered by City of Chicago, for capture dead or alive.

"Well," said Sansotta, "where you headed for?"

"I'm gonna stick around here for a while," said Rico.

"Yeah?" said Sansotta; "pretty close to trouble, ain't it?"

"I don't know," said Rico, "they ain't got any idea which way I went. I got a big stake and I don't have to worry none."

"You sure went up fast over in the big burg," said Sansotta, looking at Rico with a sort of awe.

"Yeah," said Rico, "and the hell of it was, I was just getting started. Everything was on the up and up when one of the gang turned softie. Ain't that hell?"

Rico had been very much elated over his escape from Chicago, so elated in fact that he had forgotten all about his troubles; but, now that the excitement of the escape had passed, the thought of how much he had lost struck him full force. He felt resentful.

"Yeah," said Sansotta, "that's the way it goes. It's a tough game. They picked up two of my men last night."

"That so?" said Rico, paying no attention.

Sansotta got up.

"Well, Cesare," he said, "I got business or I'd stick around and chin with you. Want to stay here with me till things blow over?"

"Yeah," said Rico.

∞

"Bertillon pictures" (more commonly known as "mug shots") were commonplace by the 1920s. For example, according to the records of the City of New York, while only 809 subjects were photographed in 1904, producing 9,468 "Bertillon pictures," only three years later, these numbers had increased to 4,587 and 54,480, respectively.

Night after night Rico lay awake looking at the arc light outside his window. His mind was filled with resentment and he went over and over the incidents which had led to his fall. Now that it was too late, he saw the mistakes he had made. He should have plugged Gentleman Joe; that's all. When a guy begins to turn softie, why there ain't no good in him. Yeah, he had been too easy. Another thing. He should have played Scabby up; that guy was in a position to do him all kinds of favors. But Scabby was a hard guy to get along with; he always thought somebody was trying to make a fool of him and he always had a chip on his shoulder.

Sometimes Rico would fall asleep for a little while, but his sleep was full of dreams and he would toss from side to side and wake up with a start. Then he would get up and smoke one cigarette after another and think about Montana and Little Arnie and the Big Boy. Often, in these short naps, he would see The Greek lying on his back in the alley, or the little Italian girl sweeping the hall, or Ma Magdalena helping him put the grease on his face. Then he would awake in confusion and stare at the unfamiliar arc light a long time before he could realize where he was.

In the day time it wasn't so bad. He could play cards with Sansotta and some of his gang, or shoot crap on a pool table in the back room. Rico always played to win and while the game was in progress he forgot his troubles. But even this was but a partial alleviation. He was nobody. Just an unknown wop who seemed to have unlimited resources. Sansotta was the only one who knew who he was. He had taken his uncle's name, Luigi De Angelo, and around Sansotta's he was called Youngstown Louis, or usually plain Louis. No, he was nobody. When a card game got hot and one of the players thought he was getting gypped, a look from Rico did not quiet the tumult as it had done in Little Italy. A look from Rico meant nothing. He was cursed with the rest of them. Often the desire to show these two-bit wops who they were yelling at would make him writhe in his chair; and his hand would move toward his armpit, but he couldn't risk it. He had his neck to think about, and there was Sansotta, a good guy, doing what he could for him. Rico kept saying to himself, you are nobody, nobody, but it was galling.

Sometimes he would go to his room early and just sit in the dark and think. He would imagine himself in the Big Boy's wonderful apartment; he would see the big pictures of the old time guys in their gold frames, the one grand crockery, and the library full of books; or he would recall the night when Little Arnie's Detroit toughs tried to bump him off and how when he came back to The Palermo the people stood on the chairs and shouted: "Rico! Rico!" God, it was hard to take!

The stories in the magazines about swell society people that he used to read with such eagerness failed to interest him now. After a paragraph or two he would fling the magazine aside and swear.

"Yeah," he would say, "ain't that great! The damn dressed-up softies. Got everything in the world and never had to turn a hand for it."

Rico was filled with resentment and when he spoke, rarely now, it was to denounce or ridicule something. The wops around Sansotta's, though they were obtuse enough, were not long in noticing this, and Rico began to be known as Crabby Louis.

They would say: "Well, Crabby Louis, it's your shot;" or "All right, Crabby, deal the cards."

The only thing that really interested Rico was the trial of Sam Vettori. Joe Massara, who had turned State's evidence, had been sentenced to life. "Lord," said Rico, when he read Joe's sentence, "I never thought they'd give Gentleman Joe a jolt like that after he turned State's. Them boys means business." Sam's trial had been rushed because of the hubbub raised by Mr. McClure and other influential men, and the outcome was never in doubt. Sam Vettori was sentenced to be hanged.

When Rico read the verdict he lay back in his chair and looked at the wall.

"Well, old Sam had a long whack at it," he said; "never seen the inside of a prison in his life. A guy's luck's bound to turn."

Then he went over in his mind the robbery of the Casa Alvarado and all the steps which had led to his own rise and fall.

"It made me and it broke me," he said.

On New Year's Eve Rico dressed up more than usual and went down into Sansotta's cabaret. It was jammed and unable to get a seat he went into Sansotta's office and had one of the waiters bring him a meal. He sat with the door open and watched the antics on the dance-floor. There was plenty of liquor about and the crowd was pretty rough. Rico saw a big blonde dancing with a fat Italian. She gave him a look and he motioned for her to come in the office. She nodded. Rico got up and closed the door. In a few minutes the Blonde came in.

"Well, kid," she said, "what's on your mind?"

"I got a room upstairs," said Rico, "that ain't occupied."

"The hell you have," said the Blonde.

"Yeah," said Rico, "and I got a bank roll that ain't got any strings on it."

"Now you're talking," said the Blonde, putting her arm around Rico.

"Well," said Rico, "let's go."

"Listen," said the Blonde, "I'll be back after while. I got a guy out here that's plenty tough and I got to humor him."

"Aw, hell," said Rico, "I'll take that toughness out of him. Stick around."

The Blonde looked at Rico and laughed.

"Say," she said, "you ain't big enough to talk so big."

"No," said Rico, resentful, "I ain't so big."

"Listen, honey," said the Blonde, "this boy would eat you alive."

"Yeah?" said Rico.

The fat Italian opened the door and came in.

"What's the idea, Micky?" he said to the Blonde.

"Why, I just happened to bump into an old friend of mine," said the Blonde, scared.

Rico got up and stood looking at the fat Italian.

"What's it to you!" he said.

"Why, listen, kid," said the fat Italian, "you better go get your big brother 'cause if you make any more cracks I'm gonna dust off the furniture with you."

The Blonde took the fat Italian by the arm.

"Come on, Paul," she said, "let's go dance."

"Yeah," said Rico, "take that bird away before something happens to him."

The fat Italian pulled away from the Blonde and started toward Rico.

"That's one crack too many," he said.

But Rico, standing with his back against Sansotta's desk, perfectly calm, reached under his armpit and pulled his gun. The fat Italian hesitated and looked bewildered.

"Well," said Rico, "kind of lost your steam, didn't you?"

The fat Italian turned and looked at the Blonde.

"That's a nice boy friend you got," he said.

The Blonde stood there with her mouth open.

"All right, big boy," said Rico, "we can get along without you."

Sansotta opened the door and stood looking from one to the other.

"What's the matter, Paul?" he inquired.

The fat Italian pointed at Rico.

"That bird there tried to grab my girl, and when I told him about it he pulled a gat on me."

Sansotta's face darkened.

"Put that gun up, Louis," he said, staring hard at Rico; "where you think you're at? Listen, Paul, Louis's a new guy here and he don't know the ropes."

"Well," said the fat Italian, "he sure is quick with a gun."

"That's all right, Paul," said the Blonde, laughing, "he needs a handicap."

Rico, furious, put on his hat and started to go. But Sansotta said:

"Wait a minute, Louis, I want to see you." Then turning to the fat Italian: "I'm sure sorry this happened, but you know how it is when a guy don't know the ropes, he'll butt in where it ain't healthy to butt in, see? Louis's all right, but he's got a bad-temper."

"Ain't he!" said Paul. "Well, I guess we better be moving up town. I ain't any too anxious to hang around where you're liable to get bumped off."

"Aw, stick around, Paul," Sansotta implored; "you won't have no more trouble."

"No," said Paul, "I'll be moving. Come on, Micky. I seen about all of your boy friend that I want to see."

Sansotta followed them out into the cabaret, trying to persuade them to remain, but Paul went over to the checkwindow and got their wraps. Rico sat down and went on with his meal. Sansotta came in and slammed the door after him.

"Goddam you, Cesare," he cried, "why don't you be more careful? That guy is Paolo, the political boss. He can close me up tomorrow if he wants to."

"Take it easy," said Rico; "how the hell did I know? You think I'm gonna let a guy take a bust at me?"

Sansotta took out a cigar and began to chew on it.

"Cesare," he said, "you got to be moving. I can't have you hanging around here no more. It's too dangerous."

Rico dropped his fork and stared at Sansotta.

"Giving me the go-by, hunh?"

"Yeah," said Sansotta, "you got to be moving."

Rico got to his feet and stood looking at Sansotta.

"Just on account of a small town ward-heeler," he said; "why that guy couldn't boss a section gang. You're a hell of a guy, Sansotta. After all the jack I spent in this dump."

"I can't help that," said Sansotta, "you got to be moving right away."

Rico laughed.

"Don't get funny," he said.

"Don't you get funny," said Sansotta; "you ain't in no shape to get funny."

"Maybe you better call the bulls and turn me up," said Rico.

"Well," said Sansotta, "you got to be moving, that's all."

IV

Rico was acutely conscious of his position. A lonely Youngstown yegg in a hostile city without friends or influence. Yeah, funny! Just a no-account yap in a burg like Hammond and not four months ago he had been a big guy in a big burg.

He put on his ulster and went out. The wind was cold and it was snowing. He walked around for a while, keeping to the dark streets, then, chilled through, he went into a little Italian restaurant for a cup of coffee and a sandwich.

The waiter, an Italian boy with a handsome dark face, brought Rico his food. When he set it down on the table he grinned and said: "Well, happy New Year."

Rico looked up in surprise.

"Yeah," he said, "thanks."

He felt better. This anonymous friendliness cheered him up. While he was eating, he watched the Italian boy, who was wiping off the counter and singing.

"Nice kid," thought Rico.

When Rico had finished his coffee, he lit a cigarette and sat smoking. He felt comfortable. Looking around the restaurant, he saw that there was a mechanical piano up front. Like Pete's!

"Say," he called, "let's have a little music."

"Sure," said the boy.

He put a slug in the piano. It played "Farewell To Thee" in tremolo. Rico felt sad. He called the boy back and gave him a dollar.

"Keep the change, kid," he said.

The mechanical piano stopped on a discord, and Rico got to his feet. While he was putting on his coat two men came in the front door. One of them went up to the counter and ordered a cup of coffee, but the other stopped and stood staring at Rico.

Rico, noticing the man's scrutiny, put his hand inside his coat and started out, but the man touched him on the shoulder and whispered:

"Things ain't going so good, are they, Rico?"

Rico stared at the man and demanded: "Who the hell are you?"

Then he recognized him. It was Little Arnie's doorman, Joseph Pavlovsky, one of the guys he had chased.

"I'm one of Arnie's boys," said Pavlovsky; "I been in Hammond ever since you gave us the rush."

"Yeah?" said Rico.

"Straight," said Pavlovsky. "I been in the beer racket over here and I cleaned up. I'm going back to the big burg next month."

Rico envied him.

"Yeah?" said Rico.

"You sure pulled one on 'em, Rico," said Pavlovsky; "you always was a smart boy, Rico."

"Aw, can that," said Rico, and, pulling away from Pavlovsky, he went out.

The wind was blowing hard now and it had stopped snowing. Rico turned up his coat collar and started toward Sansotta's. But he hadn't gone half a block when he realized that he was being followed. He turned just in time to see two men pass under an arclight.

"It's Little Arnie's boy," he said, "looking for seven grand."

Rico took out his gun, got behind a telephone pole, and fired a warning shot. The two men ran for cover and Rico ducked down an alley, ran for two blocks, then turned up another alley and doubled back. He had lost them.

When the look-out let him in he said:

"Louis, the boss wants to see you."

Rico went up to Sansotta's room.

"Well?" he said to Sansotta.

"Cesare," said Sansotta, "a friend of mine is pulling out for Toledo tomorrow night. He'll take you for fifty bucks."

"What's his game?"

"Running dope."

"It's O.K. with me," said Rico.

Rico went up to his room, took off his overcoat, and flung himself down on the bed. He'd have to pull out now whether he wanted to or not.

V

The dope-runner dropped Rico at the edge of town. It was about five o'clock in the morning and still dark. A heavy fog had come in from Lake Erie and a damp, cold wind was blowing. Rico walked up and down to keep warm while waiting for a car. He felt pretty low.

"Yeah," said Rico, "right back where I started from."

The headlight on the street-car cut through the fog. The motorman didn't see Rico and ran past him.

"Ain't that a break?" said Rico.

There wouldn't be another car for half an hour. Rico decided to walk. He turned up his coat collar against the damp wind and lit a cigar. His mind was full of resentment. Yeah, by God, a lousy street-car wouldn't even stop for him.

Rico got a room at a bachelors' hotel[66] on the waterfront, and went to bed. It was about five o'clock in the evening when he woke up. He doused his face at the washstand, put on his overcoat, and went out.

He ate at a little Italian restaurant where he and Otero used to split a bowl of soup when things were going bad. But the place had changed. New management, new waiters, new everything. Toledo seemed small and dingy and quiet to Rico. He was a little bit puzzled.

"Didn't used to be like this," he said.

As soon as he finished his meal he walked over to Chiggi's, which was about two block away. But the place was dark and when Rico went up to the door to peer in he saw that it had been padlocked by the Federal Authorities.

"Ain't that a break?" he said.

He had no place to go.

There was a fruit store next to Chiggi's and Rico went in. A little Italian girl came to wait on him.

"Listen, sister," said Rico, "you know where Chiggi is now?"

"I get my grandfather," she said.

She went into the back of the store and returned with an old Italian who had crinkly gray hair and wore earrings.

"Listen, mister," said Rico, "could you tell me where Chiggi is now?"

The old man just looked at him. Rico felt a little uneasy.

"No speak English?" he asked.

"Yes," said the old man, "I speak good English. What do you want with Chiggi?"

"Well," said Rico, "Chiggi used to be a pal of mine, but I been away for three or four years and now I don't know where to find him."

"Chiggi has had trouble," said the old man; "he is in the prison."

"Yeah?" said Rico. "Atlanta, hunh?"[67]

"Yes," said the old man, "Chiggi is in Atlanta. It is too bad. Chiggi was good to the poor. When my wife was sick and my business was not going good, Chiggi gave me money."

"Yeah," said Rico. "Chiggi staked me too."

Rico took out a cigar and gave it to the old man.

"Listen," he went on, "do you know where any of Chiggi's old bunch is?"

"Yes," said the old man, "Chiggi's boy has got a place a couple of blocks from here."

The old man wrote down the address for Rico.

Young Chiggi was a dressed-up wop and thought he was a lot better than his father. He wouldn't even wait on a customer but sat all day in the back of his joint reading the *Police Gazette* or playing solitaire. Things were breaking good for Young Chiggi and he was thinking about selling out and going to Chicago or Detroit.

67 The Atlanta Federal Penitentiary was built in 1899 as part of the expansion of the federal prison system. Al Capone was incarcerated there before his transfer to Alcatraz in 1934; many other famous figures of organized crime were imprisoned there over its history. Today it is primarily used for in-transit prisoners.

The Atlanta Federal Penitentiary, 1911.

He had been in the beer and alcohol racket for over three years, first with his father, then by himself, and now with Bill Hackett, known as Chicago Red. He bought diamonds and automobiles and he kept his woman in a big apartment.

When Rico was shown into his office by one of his bartenders, he didn't even look up but went on with his game of solitaire. The bartender went out and Rico sat down across from Young Chiggi.

"Chiggi," said Rico, "I want to talk to you a minute."

Chiggi didn't look up.

"All right," he said.

"Listen," said Rico, "put them cards down. I want to talk business."

Chiggi looked up and stared at Rico.

"Say," he said, "where the hell do you get that stuff! I don't know you."

"Your old man was a pal of mine," said Rico.

"Well, Buddy," said Chiggi, "that don't help you none with me, 'cause me and the old man had a split-up. He thought he was so damn wise, see, but they got him behind bars and I'm running loose."

"Yeah?" said Rico, "well, that's a tough break for the old man. You see, your old man staked me once and I thought I'd look him up and get even. I'm pretty well heeled right now and I'm looking for a place to lay in."

Chiggi looked at Rico with interest.

"Looking for a place to lay in, hunh? Bulls after you?"

"Yeah," said Rico.

Chiggi put his cards away. Then he took out a couple of cigars and offered Rico one. They sat smoking.

"Well," said Chiggi, "maybe I can take care of you."

"That's the talk," said Rico; "got some rooms up above?"

"No," said Chiggi, "but a friend of mine's got a boarding house next door that's O.K. Now about that jack the old man staked you to, you can give it to me, 'cause he owes me plenty."

Rico said nothing, but took out his fold and counted out a hundred and fifty dollars. He knew he had to buy his way in.

Rico selected his room carefully. It was on the side of the house and could not be reached from the outside as there were no porches near it. It had two doors, one opening into the front hall, one into the back hall. The doors themselves were heavy and could be barred from the inside. It was a good hide-out.

Rico's plans were vague. He had plenty of money and if he went easy with it he would be able to live a year or more in comparative comfort. But Rico could not bear the thought of a year of inactivity. What would he do with himself? He had no vices. He couldn't amuse himself by getting drunk, or taking dope, or playing faro. He didn't mind losing a couple hundred dollars gambling occasionally, but you can't put in a whole year gambling. He thought if things went right that maybe he'd move on to New York, but that would be risky and one slip and he was gone. No, he didn't see much ahead of him.

Rico spent most of the day in his room, lying on the bed reading, or else going over and over in his mind the episodes leading to his rise and fall. The resentment he had been experiencing ever since he got to Hammond had grown till it had become almost an obsession. He was never in a good humor. When he was not reading or thinking about Chicago he would pace up and down his room and wait for night. He got so, finally, that he could sleep twelve hours every day and this helped some.

At night he would go down to Chiggi's and play pool or shoot crap. Sometimes there would be a big poker game and he would sit in. He was known as Youngstown Louis and nobody in the place had the slightest idea who he really was.

Everything was against Rico. The very virtues that had been responsible for his rise were liabilities in his present situation. He had no outlet for his energy; the self-discipline which had marked him out from his fellows was of no use to him here; and the tenacity of purpose that had kept him at high tension while he was the Vettori gang chief had no object to expend itself on.

"I am nobody, nobody," Rico would say.

Sometimes at night he would go to one of the call-houses on a nearby street and spend a couple of hours with one of the women. But he got very little pleasure from these infrequent debauches. He used to wonder what had happened to the blonde he had spent old Chiggi's stake on, and was positive that if he could find her it would do him a lot of good, but she had disappeared and nobody had any idea where she had gone.

Rico tried to buy his way in. Chiggi was agreeable but Chicago Red was not. Chicago Red had taken a dislike to Rico from the first and never missed an opportunity of bullying him. Chicago Red had left Chicago under a cloud. There was a rumor that he had got in bad with a South Side gang over there and had left to keep from getting bumped off. Red was over six feet tall and weighed about two hundred pounds; he had muscles like a wrestler, a bull neck, and enormous hairy hands.

Rico kept away from him as much as possible to avoid trouble. But Red seemed to take a delight in worrying Rico, probably because, despite the fact that Rico never argued with him, always let him have his way, he felt that Rico was not impressed.

One night there was a big poker game going on in Chiggi's back room. Rico was winning. About midnight Red came in and wanted to sit in, but there was no place for him.

"Louis," he said, "get the hell off that chair and let a man get in the game."

"Not a chance," said Rico.

"Listen, Dago . . ." said Red.

"Don't call me Dago," said Rico, looking hard at Red.

"Get off that chair or I'll throw you off," said Red starting toward Rico.

But Chiggi grabbed Red from behind and pulled him into the next room.

When the game broke up, Chiggi came in and said to Rico:

"When you get settled up, come in the office."

After the other players had gone Rico went into Chiggi's office. Red was sitting with his feet on the desk and Chiggi was walking up and down.

"Well, Dago," said Red, "did you clean 'em?"

"Yeah," said Rico.

"Sit down, Louis," said Chiggi; "we want to talk to you."

Rico sat down.

"Louis," said Chiggi, "I don't know whether you're wised up or not, but we been hitting the rocks. The bulls got two of our men and a big load of alcohol, and a couple of days ago another one of our carts got hijacked at Monroe. See, so we're pretty low."

"Yeah?" said Rico.

"Well," said Chiggi, "we want a stake, don't we, Red?"

"Yeah," said Red, "and we ain't any too particular where we get it."

"Well," said Rico, getting up, "you got a lot of guys around here. Ask them."

"Listen, Red," said Chiggi, "you keep your goddam lip out of this."

Red got to his feet suddenly and stood glaring at Chiggi.

"Why, you lousy small-time wop, I guess you don't know who you're talking to, do you?" He raised his arm and pointed at Rico. "You see that guy there, he thinks he's the best there is, got it? He thinks he's the biggest dago outside of Italy, and here you go honeying after him like we couldn't get a stake no place else. But I ain't begging no goddam dago to stake me."

Chiggi looked helplessly at Rico.

"Yeah," said Red, "and while we're talking, I'm getting sick of the way that bird there sits around and don't say nothing and acts like he was God-only-knows-who. Yeah, I'm getting good and sick of it, Chiggi."

"Well," said Chiggi, "when you get real sick of it, why beat it."

Red laughed.

"Gonna stick to your dago buddy, are you? Well, he's got the jack. But what're you gonna do when you need a guy that's got the guts?"

This was too much for Rico. He said:

"What do you know about guts? I guess you ain't so tough or they wouldn't've run you out of Chi."

"Will you listen to that!" said Red; "all right, buddy, you said your piece and you sure spoke out of turn. Why, Dago, where I come from you wouldn't live five minutes. Now I'm gonna show you how they treat smart dagos in Chi."

Red made a motion toward his coat pocket, but Rico beat him to it. He pulled his gun from the holster under his armpit and covered Red.

"Red," he said, "in Chicago I wouldn't let you rob filling-stations for me."

Red stood with his hands up, looking from Rico to Chiggi.

"Don't bump him off, Louis," said Chiggi.

"I wouldn't waste a bullet on him," said Rico; then glaring at Red he went on: "You been getting away with this rough stuff too long, Red. I'm Cesare Bandello!"

Red's mouth fell open and he stood staring at Rico. Chiggi took Rico by the arm.

"Are you Rico?" he cried.

Rico nodded and put up his gun. Red dropped his hands, sank into a chair and wiped the sweat from his face.

"You sit down, Chiggi," said Rico, "and I'll do the talking."

68   Machine-guns. According to Eric Partridge's *Dictionary of the Underworld* (New York: Bonanza Books, 1961), the name appears to have originated with guns used to spray insecticide (p. 620)!

Chiggi sat down.

"Lord," said Red, "so you're Rico? Steve Gollancz told me you was a big fellow."

"Steve never seen me," said Rico.

Chiggi leaned forward eagerly.

"You gonna put in with us, Louis?"

Rico said:

"I'll put in a third, but I got to boss the works or I won't put in nothing."

Chiggi looked at Red.

"That's O.K. with me," said Red.

Chiggi got to his feet and danced a few steps.

"Hurray for us," he cried.

VI

Under Rico's guidance Chiggi's gang prospered. Chicago Red, impressed by Rico's reputation, carried out his orders and never argued; Chiggi also. And Chiggi's men were influenced by the attitude of their former bosses. Rico made decisions quickly, seldom asked for advice, and was nearly always right. Chiggi and Red were used to doing things on a small scale and hated to split with the authorities, but Rico had been in the game long enough to know that to make money you've got to spend money. Through Antonio Rizzio, one of Old Chiggi's friends, now a minor politician, Rico got in touch with some of the high-ups and bought protection. Chiggi's alcohol runners were no longer picked up and in a little while Chiggi's business had doubled. But, due to this increase in business, a new difficulty had risen: hijackers. They waylaid Chiggi's men and robbed them of their cargoes. There was a well-organized gang of them around Monroe, Michigan, and they began to cut into Chiggi's profits. Rico tried rerouting his runners and this was successful for a month or two, but the Monroe gang soon got on to it, and the trouble started over again. Rico took a chance. He ordered three sho-sho guns[68] from a firm in Chicago. These small automatic rifles, as formidable as machine guns, were concealed in special cases under the seats of the trucks. Rico instructed his runners in the use of them and after a few encounters the Monroe gang decided that it would be more lucrative and also safer to confine their hijacking to smaller bootleggers who were not equipped with artillery.

Rico was pleased with his success, but hardly satisfied. This was small stuff and, as he could take no active part in it, he had a good deal of time on his hands. Of course he was a pretty big guy for Toledo and around Chiggi's he was king, but, after all, Chiggi's boys were a mighty poor lot, worse even than Little Arnie's, and their adulation wasn't worth much.

But that wasn't the worst of it. Rico knew that he had blundered badly in revealing his identity to Chiggi and Chicago Red. Neither of them was very dependable. Chiggi talked incessantly, contradicting himself, forgetting what he had said two minutes after he had said it; and all this talk was directed at one object: self-glorification. An association with Cesare Bandello, of Chicago, was something to brag about and Rico knew it. Chicago Red as a rule was not very talkative, but when he got drunk he would boast about his former connection with Steve Gollancz. Rico feared them both. Sometimes when the three of them were alone together he would caution them. There was only one thing that reassured Rico. Chiggi's prosperity depended on him, and Rico knew that both Chicago Red and Chiggi were aware of it.

At about seven o'clock one night Rico went out for supper. He ate at the little Italian restaurant where he and Otero used to split a bowl of soup when things were bad. He always sat facing the front door at a table in the back of the place. In this position he could see everyone who came in and also he could keep an eye on the people at the tables. On his right and a couple of feet ahead of him was a little window which looked out on an alley. While Rico was finishing his coffee he happened to glance at the window. When he did, a face which had been pressed against the windowpane was hastily withdrawn. Rico got up, put on his hat and paid his check.

"I'm going out the back way," he said to the counterman.

"O.K., boss."

"If anybody comes in here and asks for Louis De Angelo take a good look at him."

"All right, boss," said the counterman.

Rico went out through the kitchen door, which opened onto a little cement court where the refuse from the restaurant was dumped. The big garbage cans along the wall were in the shadow and, as Rico stepped out, a man jumped up from behind one of the cans and put a gun against him. Rico threw himself to the ground, the gun exploded harmlessly, and the man made a break for the alley, stumbling over the cans. Rico fired from a prone position and missed. Then he jumped to his feet and ran out into the alley. The man had disappeared.

"God," said Rico, "if that boy didn't almost pull one on me."

One of the cooks opened the back door and put his head out.

"What the hell!" he said.

"Damned if I know," said Rico; "a couple of guys was popping at each other out here in the alley."

"Some of them bootleggers," said the cook.

Rico took a cab back to Chiggi's. He was very much perturbed. Whoever that boy was he certainly meant business.

"Well," said Rico, "somebody has sure spilled something."

As soon as he came in Chiggi rushed up to him and grabbed him by the arm.

"Louis," he said, "Red's drunk and we can't do nothing with him."

Rico stared at Chiggi.

"Where's he been?"

"Why," said Chiggi, "he's been on a bat with some Chicago guys."

"Hell," cried Rico, "where is he?"

Chiggi led Rico back into one of the private rooms. Red was sitting at a table with a half empty quart of whiskey on the table beside him. When he saw Rico he cried:

"If it ain't old Rico himself! By God, I been drinking all day. I can hardly see but nobody can put me under the table, ain't that so, boss? Yes sir, I'd like to see the bastard that could drink Rico's buddy under the table."

Rico turned to Chiggi.

"A guy tried to pop me over at Frank's. This bird has spilled something. I got to be moving."

Chiggi's eyes got big.

"You gonna pull out, Louis?"

"I got to," said Rico; "somebody's looking for that seven grand."

"Jesus, Louis," said Chiggi, "what we gonna do without you?"

"Best you can," said Rico. "Go get me a cab, Chiggi, I'm moving right now."

Chiggi went out of the room. Rico took Red by the shoulders and shook him. Red blinked his eyes.

"Red," said Rico, "was you on a bat with some Chicago guys?"

"Was I?" cried Red; "spent a hundred bucks on them birds."

"Any of them know me?"

Red rolled his head from side to side, and sang, then he smashed his fists down on the table.

"Rico," he said, "old Red's going back to the big burg, yes sir, old Red's tired of this tank town. Old Red's got a good stake now and he's moving. They run me out once but I ain't scairt of them no more. I'm going back and show 'em who Red Hackett is. Yeah bo!"

Rico shook him.

"Listen, Red," he said, "did any of them birds know me?"

Red lolled his head, trying to focus his eyes on Rico.

"One of them guys was a personal friend of yours," said Red; "fact, he asked me if you wasn't laying up here, see, he knew all right; wasn't no harm in telling him nothing."

"Who was he?" shouted Rico.

Red thought for a moment then he said :

"I can't seem to remember. He's a wop, all right, a bald-headed wop."

"Scabby!" Rico exclaimed.

Good God, wasn't that a break! Scabby hated him and Scabby would sell his own mother out for a split on seven grand. Rico felt resentful. Just his damn luck to get mixed up with a bunch of yellow-bellies and softies.

Chiggi came in.

"Cab out in front, Louis," he said.

Rico pointed at Red.

"That guy spilled the works. For two bits I'd bump him off."

Rico was furious. He made a move toward his armpit, but one of the bartenders opened the door and yelled: "The bulls!"

"What!" cried Rico.

The bartender was trembling all over and his face was white.

"Police car out in front, boss."

Rico made a dive for the door but Chiggi grabbed him by the arm.

"Out the back, Louis."

Chiggi leapt across the room and pulled a switch and all the lights in the place went out. Then he took Rico by the arm and led him through the hall and out into a little court at the rear.

"So long, Louis," he said.

Chiggi slammed the door. Rico was in utter darkness.

"A hell of a chance I got," he said.

He stepped cautiously out into the alley back of the court and took a look around. The alley was blind to his right; to his left it came out onto a main thoroughfare and there was a bright arc light at that end. Rico took out his gun and moved slowly toward the arc light.

"You can't never tell," he said; then, in an access of rage: "They'll never put no cuffs on this baby."

When he was within fifty feet of the main thoroughfare a man appeared at the end of the alley way, a big man in a derby hat. He saw Rico and immediately blew a blast on his whistle. Rico raised his gun and pulled the trigger; it missed fire.

Rico was frantic. He wanted to live. For the first time in his life he addressed a vague power which he felt to be stronger than himself.

"Give me a break! Give me a break!" he implored.

The man in the derby hat raised his arm and Rico rushed him, pumping lead. Rico saw a long spurt of flame and then something hit him a sledge-hammer blow in the chest. He took two steps, dropped his gun, and fell flat on his face. He heard a rush of feet up the alley.

"Mother of God," he said, "is this the end of Rico?"

Is this the end of Rico (Edward G. Robinson)?
The conclusion of the 1931 film of *Little Caesar*.

Introduction[69]

by W. R. Burnett

It was 1928. Winter. A cold and gloomy Chicago afternoon, with sparse snow falling from a slate colored sky. I had less than five dollars to my name, a worn overcoat, a hand me down suit that had seen better days, and I was headed for the cheapest restaurant on the North Side, but . . . I'd never been so happy before in my life. The galley proofs of *Little Caesar*, which had arrived from New York that day, were in my overcoat pocket.

I remember vividly the look of the snow covered street and of the little restaurant with the steaming coffee urns and the tired faced counterman. As I ate, with snow falling past the befogged windows and a couple of taxi drivers talking politics in a corner, I got out the galleys and ostentatiously began to go through them. To my disappointment nobody asked me what they were.

It's strange that I'd remember such an insignificant moment and forget so many more important things, but that is the truth of the matter.

It had been a long struggle. I'd written for over six years without selling a line, working meanwhile as a statistician for the State of Ohio, in Columbus. Fed up with office routine—and I still hate the sight of an office—I had quit my job and moved on to Chicago, where my father was managing repossessed hotels for the Chicago Title and Trust.

On me, an outsider, an alien from Ohio, the impact of Chicago was terrific. It seemed overwhelmingly big, teeming, dirty,

69   The following introduction first appeared in the 1957 edition of *Little Caesar*.

70   Alphonse "Al" Gabriel Capone (1899-1947) was the head of the criminal underworld in Chicago. Capone came to rise during Prohibition, as the production and distribution of liquor became a highly profitable endeavor supported by a large segment of the population. Born in New York, he moved to Chicago in his twenties, becoming the right-hand man of mob boss Johnny Torrio. When Torrio stepped down in 1925 after being attacked, Capone became the gang's leader. His corrupt relationship with Chicago mayor William Thompson (see note 71) was an important part of the primarily-Italian mob's success. Although he cultivated popularity as a modern Robin Hood, the violent killings of gangsters roused the public's ire, and he became "Public Enemy No. 1." In 1931, the federal government successfully prosecuted him for income tax evasion, and Capone went to prison. He became increasingly crippled with syphilis and gonorrhea, and when he eventually emerged from incarceration in 1939, he was a broken and deranged man.

brawling, frantically alive. The pace was so much faster than anything I'd been used to; rudeness was the rule; people seemed to have no time to be friendly, no time to desist for one moment from whatever it was they were pursuing. Broke, jobless, a nobody, I fought hard to keep my balance in one of the most blankly indifferent, one of the toughest cities in the world.

Capone[70] was King. Corruption was rampant. Big Bill Thompson,[71] the mayor, was threatening to punch King George of England in the "snoot." Gangsters were shooting each other all over town; in fact, I "heard" one killing over the radio.[72] It happened in a cafe while a dance band broadcast was in progress. Two shots came over distinctly, the music slurred to an abrupt stop, then the air went dead. I can't remember the name of the gangster who was killed to the blaring of a jazzband, but it's a matter of record.

I spent my first night in Chicago in a cheap little hotel—of the flea bag variety—on the North Side. Just as I was falling asleep there was a terrific explosion directly across the street. Windows rattled; curtains blew wildly, and my bed gave a leap that nearly threw me to the floor. Almost at once there were two more explosions, blocks away this time, but close enough. I got up, dressed, and went down to the lobby, where a sleepy eyed night clerk explained that there was a price war going on among garage owners, things had got rough, and apparently the "boys" had decided to toss a few "pineapples."[73] The clerk did not appear to be disturbed or even very interested. The whole thing seemed natural enough to him.

Early the next morning I went across the street to where a couple of dull eyed loafers were staring apathetically at a huge ragged hole the "pineapple" had made in the solid brick wall of the garage. I talked to one of the mechanics, who shrugged and said: "Aw, you know. Just one of them things."

When I, an outsider, brought all of this up in conversation, the average citizen of Chicago would laugh at me and explain that it was just a lot of nonsense in the newspapers and that as for himself, although he'd lived in the city all of his life, he'd never so much as seen a gangster. This struck me as a peculiar and rather interesting form of ostrichism.

Vincent Starrett,[74] not at all an average citizen, knew better. He said that Chicago was as archaic, as dangerous as a city of the Middle Ages.

LITTLE CAESAR

71 William "Big Bill" Hale Thompson (1869–1944) was a Chicago politician who served as mayor from 1915 to 1923 and 1927 to 1931. He created a powerful political machine, epitomized by the slogan "vote early and vote often" (occasionally attributed to Capone and later credited to Chicago Mayor Richard J. Daley) and was openly corrupt, called by some historians the most unethical mayor in history.

"Big Bill" Thompson in 1916.

72 The *Chicago Daily News* of October 12, 1926, estimated that fifty-seven gangsters were killed in Chicago between January 1 and October 11 of that year.

73 The Mk-2 anti-personnel hand grenade used by American forces in World War I gained this nickname based on the weapon's appearance.

"Mills bombs," British grenades used during World War I (photo by Jean-Louis Dubois, used with permission).

74 Starrett (1886–1974) was a bibliophile, newspaperman, author, and poet and for many years wrote the "Books Alive!" column for the *Chicago Daily News*. He was a lifelong aficionado of Sherlock Holmes, an early member of the Baker Street Irregulars, and was named a Grand Master by the Mystery Writers of America. His Sherlockian writings were an inspiration to this editor.

75　　The book was *The Gang: A Study of 1,313 Gangs in Chicago* by Frederick N. Thrasher, note 5. Thrasher's map of Chicago gangland is reproduced below:

A map of Chicago's gangs, from
The Gangs: A Study of 1,313 Gangs in Chicago
by Frederick N. Thrasher.

76　　Thrasher's account of the Sam Cardinelli gang is reproduced in its entirety here:

"The Sam Cardinelli gang was known as one of the most vicious groups of criminals in Chicago. It was held responsible for many murders and from fifty to one hundred roberries about which evidence was obtained. The nature of its activities may be indicated by a brief summary of some of its more important crimes.

"Five members of the gang, including Nicholas Viana, the 'choir-boy,' entered a soloon and in the course of a hold-up killed the proprietor and one customer. The gang escaped in an automobile driven by Santo Orlando and found

I walked about everywhere, went every place. I tried hard to take it all in. By luck, I met a police reporter who talked to me off the record. I was appalled, then interested. A book began to take shape vaguely in my mind, a book dealing with the darker side of this archaic, dangerous city.

I began to make notes. I wrote a few paragraphs, then pages. Finally I typed out the author's hopeful legend, Chapter One, and started to work in earnest. A week or so later I threw away everything I'd written, and began to read books on crime, for a lead. By chance, I discovered a volume put out by the Chicago University Press, dealing with gangsterism in Chicago.[75] In this coldly factual survey, I came across an account of the rise and fall of the Sam Cardinelli gang.[76] This account served as the nucleus for the novel that was originally called *The Furies*, and later, by a tremendous stroke of luck, *Little Caesar*.

I started again, but stopped, dissatisfied. I still didn't have the right handle, or, as they say in Hollywood, the wienie, the gimmick. Suddenly one night it came to me. The novel should be a picture of the world as seen through the eyes of a gangster. All conventional feelings, desires, and hopes should be rigidly excluded. Further, the book should be written in a style that suited the subject matter—that is, in the illiterate jargon of the Chicago gangster. I threw overboard what had been known up to then as "literature." I declared war on adjectives. I jettisoned "description." I tried to tell the story entirely through narration and dialogue, letting the action speak for itself. I also jettisoned "psychology"—and I tried hard to suppress myself and all of my opinions.

Even so, I do not think *Little Caesar* would have come off, if I hadn't met a young man on the North Side, who seemed, on first acquaintance, merely to own and manage a barbershop. We went to the fights together, we bowled, we had lunch or dinner quite often. This plausible young fellow, an Italian American in his late twenties, was the pay off man for the biggest mob on the North Side. He was close mouthed with me for a long time, until it dawned on him that though a writer I was not a newspaper man, but just a sort of oddball, who, for some God-forsaken reason, went around making up stories and writing them down, fairy tales to him.

"Why?" he wanted to know. "What's the percentage? Why don't you get a job on the Trib?"

He was a very practical young man and in many respects reminded me of the bond salesmen and businessmen I'd known in Columbus before my escape to Chicago. They, too, were practical. They, too, could not see any sense at all in writing fiction, something that had never even "happened." Why not get a job on the *Columbus Dispatch* if you wanted to be a writer? They, like the young Chicago hoodlum—let's call him John—were "all business."

John, however, had none of their second thoughts and none of their hypocrisy, and he carried practicality to an extreme that would have appalled them. For instance, in talking about a business rival, he once said: "You give him a chance, see? A good chance. You reason with him. You say, 'look, fellow; there's room for all of us, so don't be so greedy.' If he won't listen, if he stays greedy, lousing you up . . . then . . . pow! He asked for it." In other words the rival was definitely not a "practical" man and simply got what was coming to him.

I must say that when I first started to talk with John my understanding was clouded by many old-fashioned notions. I was under the impression that murder—or, as John would have said, a rub-out—was morally wrong and that the murderer was bound to suffer pangs of conscience and remorse. I even said something like this. John stared at me in consternation, then almost choked laughing. Was I kidding? Do soldiers in a war suffer stuff like that? What was the difference if a guy rubbed out Germans or "impractical" business rivals? I must be nuts.

In short, I gradually and painfully acquired from John an entirely new and fresh way of looking at the world. It was not a pretty way; it was more than a little frightening; but it was certainly "practical" and was later taken over lock, stock, and barrel by all the tyrants—all the little Caesars—of Europe. Better yet, although only realizing it little by little, I was getting exactly what I needed to make a real book of the manuscript I was laboring over: a picture of the world as seen through the eyes of a gangster.

Later, John bragged that he had bought the first copy of *Little Caesar* sold on the North Side. He thought the book was pretty good, but there was one thing that puzzled him very much. I was a college guy, wasn't I? Then how come I wrote such lousy grammar!

When I finished *Little Caesar* I gave it to my father to read. He liked it and said: "I really think you've hit it this time, Bill." I felt later at this home. Ten days later Orlando was found in the drainage canal with several bullets in his body. The police believe that the gang, fearing the arrest of Orlando and that he might confess, murdered him in cold blood.

"Several months later four members of the gang were arrested by two police officers at Twenty-first and Indiana Avenue. While being searched Viana shot one of the policemen in the groin and the other was also wounded. The gang escaped.

"On one occasion, Errico, one of the members, planned the hold-up of a South Side poolroom. He entered the place and at his signal Nicholas Viana, Frank Campione, and Tony Sansone entered with revolvers and robbed fifteen customers, Errico among the rest. During the hold-up one of the customers put his hands in his pocket and was immediately shot through the heart by Campione. He died instantaneously. After the trio had fled, Errico remained only long enough to avert suscpicion.

"Individual shares of the loot in some of these cases were ridiculously small considering the chances taken. The reputed mastermind of the gang was Sam Cardinelli, aged thirty-nine. He did not take an active part in the more important crimes, but is said to have planned them. Most of the other members were young, Viana being eighteen, while several of the others were only nineteen.

"Cardinelli, Vaian, and Campione were hanged while Errico's sentence was commuted to life-impisonment because he turned state's evidence." (Records of the Chicago Crime Commissionp, 432.)

The similarities to plot points of *Little Caesar* are evident.

very much encouraged by this, especially as my father had a strong "practical" side himself. For several years he'd been trying to get me to give up "wasting my time" and learn the hotel business.

An earlier novel of mine had been turned down by Scribner's, but the rejection had been considerably softened by a few kind words of encouragement from a Scribner's editor, Maxwell Perkins. I, being a Midwestern country boy, did not know Maxwell Perkins from Maxwell Anderson; had no idea of his standing in New York; but I remembered him as the only editor in the country—I'd tried them all with one manuscript or another—who had ever taken the trouble to send me a personal note instead of the routine rejection slip.

I was so anxious to get the ms. of *Little Caesar* off to him that, in spite of my financial condition, I sent it airmail, special. It was back in less than three weeks. Mr. Perkins did not like it. Meanwhile I'd consulted the only literary man I knew at the time—Vincent Starrett—and had discovered that Perkins was considered to be New York's leading publishers' editor. I'm afraid I bragged about this to my father and he did not let me forget it when the manuscript came back with such speed.

We had a serious talk. He said: "Are you stupid, thick, or what? You've wasted six years of your life bending over a typewriter. You are twenty-seven years old, no longer young. Get wise. Learn the hotel business."

How could I argue with him? I threw *Little Caesar* in the trunk and took a job as night clerk in a big North Side hotel. I found it harder to stand than the Columbus statistical office. One night I said to myself: "Rather than spend my life working in a hotel—or a business office—I'll walk into Lake Michigan till my hat floats."

But it turned out that this was not necessary. After a few weeks of hotel work, I got *Little Caesar* out of the trunk, reread it, liked it better than before, sent it off to The Dial Press—and . . . well . . . the rest may not be history, but it was certainly the turning point of my life.

Little Caesar was that rare thing, an all around smash. It made me. It made Eddie Robinson. And it did very well for the Literary Guild and Warner Brothers. It was published in June, 1929, nearly thirty years ago, and it is still a live book, with a new edition just off the press in England, not to mention the new American edition, a copy of which you are now holding in your hand. It has been translated into twelve languages, including English, as a witty friend of mine says.

Edward G. Robinson in his iconic role as Rico Bandello,
the eponymous "Little Caesar," from the 1931 film of *Little Caesar*.

77   A novel by Charles-Louis Phillipe first published in 1901 (not published in English until 1932), telling the story of a young prostitute in the Paris slums.

I am sure that the title had a lot to do with the novel's success. It would be hard to find one more apt, and yet I hit on it, in a sense, by accident. As I stated above, the original title was *The Furies*—far too literary and not in keeping with the tone of the book, a slang novel, even a proletarian novel, if you like, on the order of *Bubu de Montparnasse*.[77]   Well . . . when I was half through the book I started to have qualms. Rico, the leading figure, began to take on nightmare proportions in my imagination and I couldn't help wondering if I was on the right track after all—I was afraid I was giving birth to a monster. But then a consoling thought came to me—out of the blue or the subconscious, as you prefer—my leading figure, Rico Bandello, killer and gang leader, was no monster at all, but merely a little Napoleon, a little Caesar.

—W. R. Burnett
West Los Angeles, California
October, 1957

Bibliography

————. *How to See Boston*. Macullar Parker Company (1895).

Adler, Jeffrey S. *First in Violence; Deepest in Dirt: Homicide in Chicago*. Cambridge, MA: Harvard University Press (2006).

Anderson, George Parker, and Julie B. Anderson, eds. *American Hard-Boiled Crime Writers*. Detroit, San Francisco, London, Boston, and Woodbridge, CT: Gale Group (2000). (Dictionary of Literary Biography, vol. 226)

Andrews, Lorrin. *Dictionary of Hawaiian Language*. Honolulu: Island Heritage Publications (2002).

Bell, Roger. *Last among Equals: Hawaiian Statehood and American Politics*. Honolulu : University of Hawaii Press (1984).

Bentley, Christopher, "Radical Anger: Dashiell Hammett's *Red Harvest*," *American Crime Fiction: Studies in the Genre*. Edited by Brian Docherty. New York: St. Martin's Press (1988), pp. 54-70.

Breen, Jon L., and Martin Harry Greenberg, eds. *Murder off the Rack: Critical Studies of Ten Paperback Masters*. Metuchen, NJ and London: Scarecrow Press (1989).

Brunsdale, Mitzi M. *Icons of Mystery and Crime Detection*. Santa Barbara, CA, Denver, and Oxford, United Kingdom: ABC-CLIO (2010). 2 vols.

Cassiday, Bruce. *Roots of Detection : The Art of Deduction before Sherlock Holmes*. New York: Frederick Ungar (1983).

Chandler, Frank Wadleigh. *The Literature of Roguery*. Boston and New York: Houghton, Mifflin and Company (1907). 2 vols.

Clark, Sandra. *Women and Crime in the Street Literature of Early Modern England*. New York: Palgrave Macmillan (2004).

Cline, Sally. *Dashiell Hammett: Man of Mystery*. New York: Arcade Publishing (2014).

Cohen, Daniel A. *Pillars of Salt; Monuments of Grace: New England Crime Literature and the Origins of American Popular Culture, 1674-1860*. Oxford: Oxford University Press (1992).

Craig, Patricia and Mary Cadogan. *The Lady Investigates: Women Detectives and Spies in Fiction*. New York: St. Martin's Press (1981).

Crowley, Jack, "*Red Harvest* and Dashiell Hammett's Butte," *The Montana Professor*, 18, No. 2 (Spring 2008). http://mtprof.msun.edu.

Dash, Mike. *The First Family: Terror, Extortion, Revenge, Murder, and the Birth of the American Mafia*. New York: Random House Publishing Group (2010).

Daws, Gavan. *Shoal of Time: A History of the Hawaiian Islands*. Honolulu: University of Hawaii Press (1974).

Day, Gary, "Investigating the Investigator: Hammett's Continental Op," *American Crime Fiction: Studies in the Genre*. Edited by Brian Docherty. New York: St. Martin's Press (1988), pp. 39-53.

DeAndrea, William L. *Encyclopedia Mysteriosa*: *A Comprehensive Guide to the Art of Detection in Print, Film, Radio, and Television*. New York: Prentice Hall (1994).

Edenbaum, Robert L., "The Poetics of the Private-Eye: The Novels of Dashiell Hammett," *Tough Guy Writers of the Thirties*. Edited by David Madden. Carbondale and Edwardsville: Southern Illinois University Press (1968).

Flanders, Judith. *The Invention of Murder: How the Victorians Revelled in Death and Detection and Created Modern Crime*. New York: St. Martin's Press (2013).

Geherin, David. *The American Private Eye: The Image in Fiction*. New York: Frederick Ungar Publishing Co. (1985).

Gregorich, Barbara. *Charlie Chan's Poppa: Earl Derr Biggers*. Pasadena, CA: Privately printed (2018).

Gregory, Sinda. *Private Investigations: The Novels of Dashiell Hammett*. Carbondale and Edwardsville, IL: Southern Illinois University Press (1985).

Grella, George, "The Hard-Boiled Detective Novel," *Detective Fiction: A Collection of Critical Essays*. Edited by Robin W. Winks. Woodstock, VT: The Countryman Press (1988).

Haining, Peter. *The Classic Era of Crime Fiction*. Chicago: Chicago Review Press (2002).

Halttunen, Karen. *Murder Most Foul: The Killer and the American Gothic Imagination*. Cambridge: Harvard University Press (2000).

Hammett, Dashiell. *The Big Book of the Continental Op.* Edited by Richard Richard Layman and Julie M. Rivett. New York: Vintage Crime/Black Lizard (2017).

———. *Complete Novels: Red Harvest, The Dain Curse, The Maltese Falcon, The Glass Key, The Thin Man.* Edited by Steven Marcus. New York: Library of America (1999).

———. *The Continetal Op.* Edited and with an introduction by Steven Marcus. New York: Vintage Crime/Black Lizard (1992).

———. "From the Memoirs of a Private Detective," *Smart Set* (March 1923).

Hammett, Jo. *Dashiell Hammett: A Daughter Remembers.* Edited by Richard Layman with Julie M. Rivett. New York: Carroll & Graf Publishers (2001).

Haycraft, Howard. *Murder for Pleasure: The Life and Times of the Detective Story.* London: Peter Davies (1942).

Haycraft, Howard, ed. *The Art of the Mystery Story: A Collection of Critical Essays.* New York: Simon and Schuster (1946).

Herbert, Rosemary, ed. *The Oxford Companion to Crime & Mystery Writing.* New York and Oxford: Oxford University Press (1999).

Hillerman, Tony and Rosemary Herbert, eds. *The Oxford Book of American Detective Stories.* Oxford: Oxford University Press (1996).

———. and Otto Penzler, eds. *The Best American Mystery Stories of the Century (The Best American Series).* New York: Houghton Mifflin (2001).

Himmelwright, Abraham Lincoln Artman. *The San Francisco Earthquake and Fire: A Brief History of the Disaster.* New York: Roebling Construction Co., (1906).

Horsley, Lee. *The Noir Thriller.* New York: Palgrave Macmillan (2009).

Huang, Yunte. *Charlie Chan: The Untold Story of the Honorable Detective and His Rendezvous with American History.* New York: W. W. Norton & Co. (2010).

Janik, Erika. *Pistols and Petticoats: 175 Years of Lady Detectives in Fact and Fiction.* Boston: Beacon Press (2016).

Keating, H. R. F. *The Bedside Companion to Crime.* New York, London, Tokyo: The Mysterious Press (1989).

Knight, Stephen Thomas. *Crime Fiction Since 1800: Detection, Death, Diversity.* New York: Palgrave Macmillan (2010).

———. *Towards Sherlock Holmes: A Thematic History of Crime Fiction in the 19th Century World.* Jefferson, NC, and London: McFarland & Company, Inc. (2017).

Langland, James, ed. *The Daily News Almanac and Year-Book.* Chicago: Chicago Daily News (1926).

Layman, Richard. *Shadow Man: The Life of Dashiell Hammett.* New York and London: Harcourt Brace Jovanovich (1978).

Lee, Henry, ed. *Brooklyn Daily Eagle Almanac.* New York: Brooklyn Daily Eagle (1927).

Loughery, John. *Alias S. S. Van Dine: The Man Who Created Philo Vance.* New York: Charles Scribner's Sons (1992).

Lovisi, Gary. *Bad Girls Need Love Too.* Iola, WI: Krause Publications (2010).

Mansfield-Kelley, Deane, and Lois A. Marchino, eds. *The Longman Anthology of Detective Fiction.* New York, San Francisco, Boston: Pearson/Longman (2005).

McCann, Sean, "The Hard-Boiled Novel," *The Cambridge Companion to American Crime Fiction.* Edited by Catherine Ross Nickerson. Cambridge, United Kingdom: Cambridge University Press (2010).

Mellen, Joan. *Hellman and Hammett: The Legendary Passion of Lillian Hellman and Dashiell Hammett.* New York: HarperCollins (1996)

Michaels, Walter Benn. *Our America: Nativism, Modernism, and Pluralism.* Durham, NC, and London: Duke University Press (1995).

Miller, Ron. *Mystery Classics on Film: The Adaptations of 65 Novels And Stories.* Jefferson, NC and London: McFarland & Company, Inc. (2017).

Mitchell, Charles P. *A Guide to Charlie Chan Films.* Westport, CT, and London: Greenwood Press (1999). (Bibliographies and Indexes in the Performing Arts).

Morton, James. *Gangster Speak: A Dictionary of Criminal and Sexual Slang.* London: Virgin Books (2006).

Nevins, Francis M. *Royal Bloodline: Ellery Queen, Author and Detective.* Bowling Green, OH: Bowling Green University Popular Press (1974).

———. *Ellery Queen: The Art of Detection.* Perfect Crime Books (2013).

Naremore, James, "Dashiell Hammett and the Poetics of Hard-Boiled Detection," *Art in Crime Writing: Essays on Detective Fiction.* Edited by Bernard Benstock. New York: St. Martin's Press (1983).

Nickerson, Catherine Ross. *The Web of Iniquity: Early Detective Fiction by American Women.* Durham, NC, and London: Duke University Press Books (1998).

Nolan, William F. *Dashiell Hammett: A Casebook*. Santa Barbara: McNally & Loftin (1969).

Panek, LeRoy Lad. *An Introduction to the Detective Story*. Bowling Green, OH: Bowling Green State University Popular Press (1987).

———. *The Origins of the American Detective Story*. Jefferson, NC, and London: McFarland & Company, Inc. (2006).

———. *Probable Cause: Crime Fiction in America*. Bowling Green, OH: Bowling Green State University Popular Press (1990).

———. and Mary M. Bendel-Simso, eds. *Early American Detective Stories: An Anthology*. Jefferson, NC, and London: McFarland & Company, Inc. (2008).

Peary, Gerald, "Rico Rising: Little Caesar Takes Over the Screen," *The Classic American Novel & The Movies*. Edited by Gerald Peary and Roger Shatzkin. New York: Frederick Ungar Publishing Co. (1977), pp. 286-96.

Penzler, Otto, ed. *The Best American Mystery Stories of the 19th Century*. Boston and New York: Houghton Mifflin Harcourt (2014).

———. and James Ellroy, eds. *The Best American Noir of the Century*. Boston and New York: Houghton Mifflin Harcourt (2010).

Polk-Husted Directory Co.'s *Directory of the City of Honolulu and Territory of Hawaii* (1924).

R. L. Polk & Co.'s *Trow General Directory of New York City* (1922-23).

Pronzini, Bill, Martin H. Greenberg, and Charles G. Waugh, eds. *Mystery Hall of Fame: An Anthology of Classic Mystery and Suspense Stories Selected by the Mystery Writers of America*. New York: William Morrow & Company, Inc. (1984).

Queen, Ellery. *Queen's Quorum: A History of the Detective-Crime Short Story as Revealed by the 106 Most Important Books Published in this Field since 1845*. Boston: Little; Brown & Co. (1951).

———. *The Female of the Species: The Great Women Detectives and Criminals*. Boston: Little; Brown &Co. (1943).

Rawlings, Philip. *Drunks, Whores and Idle Apprentices: Criminal Biographies of the Eighteenth Century*. London and New York: Routledge (2014).

Roth, Marty. *Foul & Fair Play: Reading Genre in Classic Detective Fiction*. Athens, GA, and London: University of Georgia Press (1995).

Rielly, Edward J., ed. *Murder 101: Essays on the Teaching of Detective Fiction*. Jefferson, NC, and London: McFarland & Company, Inc. Pub

Rzepka, Charles J. *Detective Fiction (Cultural History of Literature)*. Cambridge, United Kingdom: Polity Press (2005).

Sayers, Dorothy, ed. *The Omnibus of Crime*. New York: Payson and Clarke (1929).

Sims, Michael, ed. *The Penguin Book of Victorian Women in Crime*. New York: Penguin Classics (2011).

———. *The Penguin Book of Gaslight Crime*. New York: Penguin Books (2009).

———. *The Dead Witness: A Connoisseur's Collection of Victorian Detective Stories*. Walker & Company (2012).

Slung, Michele B., ed. *Crime on Her Mind: Fifteen Stories of Female Sleuths From The Victorian Era To The Forties*. New York: Pantheon Books (1975).

Steinbrunner, Chris and Otto Penzler, eds. *Encyclopedia of Mystery and Detection*. New York, St. Louis, and San Francisco: McGraw-Hill Book Company (1976).

———. Charles Shibuk, Otto Penzler, Marvin Lachman, and Francis M. Nevins, Jr., compilers. *Detectionary: A Biographical Dictionary of the Leading Characters in Detective and Mystery Fiction*. Lock Haven, PA: Hammermill Paper Company (1972).

Sussex, Lucy. *Women Writers and Detectives in Nineteenth-Century Crime Fiction: The Mothers of the Mystery Genre*. New York: Palgrave Macmillan (2010).

Tamura, Eileen. *Americanization, Acculturation, and Ethnic Identity: The Nisei Generation in Hawaii*. Urbana and Chicago, IL: University of Illinois Press (1994).

Thrasher, Frederic M. *The Gang: A Study of 1,313 Gangs in Chicago*. Chicago: University of Chicago Press (1927).

Tuska, Jon. *Philo Vance: The Life and Times of S. S. Van Dine*. Bowling Green, OH: Bowling Green University Popular Press (1971).

Van Dover, J. K. *Making the Detective Story American: Biggers, Van Dine and Hammett and the Turning Point of the Genre, 1925-1930*. Jefferson, NC, and London: McFarland & Company (2010).

Ward, Nathan. *The Lost Detective: Becoming Dashiell Hammett*. New York and London: Bloomsbury USA (2015).

Watson, Kate. *Women Writing Crime Fiction; 1860-1880: Fourteen American, British and Australian Authors*. Jefferson, NC, and London: McFarland & Company, Inc. (2012).

Weinman, Sarah, ed. *Women Crime Writers: Four Suspense Novels of the 1940s*. New York: Library of America (2015).

———. *Women Crime Writers: Four Suspense Novels of the 1950s*. New York: Library of America (2015).

Wolfe, Peter. *Beams Falling: The Art of Dashiell Hammett*. Bowling Green, OH: Bowling Green University Popular Press (1980).

Acknowledgments

This book, which I hope will be the first of a series, is the product of my fondness for mysteries. That fondness began with the Hardy Boys and Nancy Drew but did not really flower until I discovered the Sherlock Holmes canon, in my law school years. The impact of those stories on my life has been enormous, not only in providing a doorway into a second career as a writer but also by leading me to many, many lasting friendships among fellow Sherlockians and mystery authors and readers. Once I finished the Holmes stories, I realized that there was an entire library of books waiting for me—the works of R. Austin Freeman, Dorothy Sayers, Dashiell Hammett, Raymond Chandler, Ross Macdonald, John D. MacDonald, Ian Fleming, Donald Hamilton, Mickey Spillane, and many, many other authors whose work I would come to know and love.

"Annotating" is a joy for me. It results in the close, careful reading of a book—spending a tremendous amount of time with the text. Therefore, I choose my subjects carefully, and each and every one of the tales here is one of my favorites. It was hard to limit myself to only five books from the 1920s, and it was hard to limit myself to American writers, but choices had to be made, or else this book would have been 5,000 pages in length!

As usual, as a writer, I have depended on many. My agent Don Maass believed in this book when I thought it would never come to fruition. Claiborne Hancock said yes to publishing it in less time than it took me to write this sentence, and his vision is the bedrock of this work. The book has benefitted greatly from the care and attention of the staff at Pegasus Books, Cecilia Beard, Meredith Clark, Bowen Dunnan, Sabrina Plomitallo-González, and Victoria Wenzel, and especially the beautiful design work of Maria Fernandez. As always, my attorney Jonathan Kirsch was a wise guide. Special thanks to my friend and mentor Otto Penzler, who answered questions for me based on his immense knowledge of the genre and agreed to write an introduction for this volume. Also, many thanks to my reliable editor Janet Byrne for jumping in at the last moment. My writer-friends Laurie R. King and Neil Gaiman gave me great support, and Sherlockian pals Mike Whelan, Steve Rothman, Andy Peck, and Jerry Margolin are constant cheerleaders. My family is always understanding of my deep dives into research and writing mode. Without my wife Sharon, none of my writing would ever be done. She responds to my ideas, asks wonderful questions about matters I might not have noted, listens patiently to my weird tales of exciting research tidbits, and allows me to read every single word, comma, period, and quotation mark aloud to her to compare to the text. She has always been, and remains, "the woman."

Leslie S. Klinger
Malibu, California